The Art of Short Fiction

The Art of Short Fiction

An International Anthology

Edited by Gary Geddes

HarperCollins*PublishersLtd*

Cover illustration: Robert Pope, *Woman with Suitcase*, 1988, acrylic on paper, Collection of the Canada Council Art Bank/Collection de la Banque d'oeuvres d'art du Conseil des Arts du Canada. Photographer: Yvan Bouleri.

First Edition

Canadian Cataloguing in Publication Data

Main entry under title:

The Art of short fiction

ISBN 0-00-647424-1

1. Short stories. 2. Short stories – Translations into English.
I. Geddes, Gary, 1940-

PN6120.2.A78 1992   808.83'1   C92-095390-5

93 94 95 96 97 98 99 ❖ EB 10 9 8 7 6 5 4 3 2 1

Contents

Fiction

Afterwords
WRITINGS ON THE ART OF FICTION AND THE ACT OF CRITICAL READING.....761

A Chronological Table of Contents

Fiction

☞ Acknowledgements

I am indebted to a great many writers, publishers, colleagues, friends, and former teachers whose influence has been felt in the editing of *The Art of Short Fiction*, particularly the two former teachers to whom this volume is dedicated: John Creighton, who first sparked my interest in the study of fiction at the University of British Columbia, and Hugo McPherson, who was a personal inspiration to me not only in his role as a teacher of Conrad and Ford Madox Ford at the University of Toronto, but also in his capacity as a tireless and giving friend of writers and artists. To three of the Margarets in my life—Laurence, Atwood, and Geddes—I owe the moral support of belief. To Ron Smith, one of my dearest friends, whose role in educating me goes far beyond his recognition as an advisory editor of this volume, I owe a continuing debt. And to my wife, Jan, I am especially grateful for the time, courage, affection, and freedom of mind that allowed me to embark on this project. There are others who know their part in my eventual education and do not need formal recognition here, but have my gratitude nonetheless.

To Stan Colbert, Ed Carson, and Iris Skeoch at HarperCollins I owe the opportunity to bring this long project to the light of day. To my research assistant, Russell Taylor, I owe many of the fascinating quotations and tidbits that found their way into the notes and Afterwords. A host of generous readers and academics across the country and in the U.S., including the three other advisory editors—Mark Levene, Linda Svendsen, and Roberta Buchanan—deserve a formal and grateful acknowledgement for the time and effort they put into encouraging me to consider alternative authors and selections, to broaden the scope of the anthology, as well as helping me improve the notes on the authors: Amin Malak, Carol Margaret Davison, Wayne Templeton, P. Scott Lawrence, Harry Vandervlist, Gisela Argyle, Robert Majzels, Christina Kaulbars, Steven Scott, Terence Byrnes, Robert Allen, Laura Groening, Karen Smythe, Jenny Geddes, John Asfour, Joseph Ronsley, Gerald Noonan, Joan Dolphin, D. B. Jewison, Philip V. Allingham, Toby Forshay, Don McKay, Phyllis Perrakis, Ronald Granofsky, Mark Abley, Rachel Billigheimer, Marlene Kadar, Anne S. Staveley, E. R. Epperly, S. R. MacGillivray, Annie Beer, Deborah Bowen, Rowland Smith, Edward Parkinson, Carolyn Redl, Pat Byrne, Jim Smith, Rupert Schieder, David Mazoff, Diane Watson, and some whose names have been lost but whose advice has not. And I would be remiss if I did not acknowledge the help of my in-house editor, Laura Krakowec, whose good humour and scrupulous attention to detail pulled the pieces together.

Introduction

One of my aims in putting together the materials in this anthology has been to provide, within a single volume, a critical milieu for the enjoyment and gradual understanding of short fiction. The stories gathered together here represent a cross-section of the best of what has been written in the past century and a half in the arena of short fiction. For a variety of reasons, short fiction, more specifically the short story, came into prominence only as recently as the nineteenth century, though its roots are deep in the folk tradition and in such well-known literary models as *A Thousand and One Nights*, *The Decameron*, and *Canterbury Tales*. Industrialization, which regimented the workplace and stimulated the demand for education, also spawned both a professional and entrepreneurial middle class and the phenomenon of leisure time. The worker, previously sustained by his or her feelings of solidarity within the community and by participation in a largely oral culture, became more or less isolated—some would say alienated—and had to depend on written stories, or narratives, for information, instruction, and enter-tainment. Newspaper and magazine publications, catering to the reading demands of a new urban public, began to serialize novels and provide a venue for self-contained shorter fictions, which could be more readily consumed in the brief periods punctuating the work schedule.

The growth and development of short fiction did not occur without a battle. Its arrival threatened certain vested interests in longer fiction. In the pages of *Dial* in 1917, Herbert Ellsworth Cory launched an attack on the fledgling form, equating its success with the shallowness of contemporary life. "The short story," he said, "is the blood kinsman of the quick-lunch, the vaudeville, and the joy-ride. It is the supreme art-form of those who believe in the philosophy of quick results." Cory considered the short story not only trivial and egocentric, but also lacking in spiri-tual nourishment; he described it as "a morbidly perfected miniature," and dismissed it as "a more delicate manifestation of that universal fever that has bankrupted mankind, and from which our deepest instincts of self-preservation urge us with tremendous pressure to arouse ourselves."

I'm reluctant to link my own interest in this exciting literary form with mem-bership in the quick-fix and junk-food crowd, that ocean of lost souls addicted to shortcuts, shorthand, and short-order lunches. However, even V. S. Pritchett, himself no casual scribbler, had to confess that no longer "the poor relation of the novel," the short story is nonetheless a product of our keyed-up modern nervous system: "It is a hybrid. It owes much to the quickness, the objectivity and cutting of the cinema; it owes much to the poet on the one hand and the newspaper reporter on the other; something also to the dramatic compression of the theatre, and everything to the restlessness, the alert nerve, the scientific eye and the short breath of contemporary life . . . it answers the primitive craving for art, the wit,

1

paradox and beauty of shape, the longing to see a dramatic pattern and significance in our experience, the desire for the electric shock."

Short fiction is not only compared by many of its finest practitioners with the
rigours of poetry, particularly the lyric, but also described as a "fierce pleasure" (Raymond Carver), a "healing riddle" (Tillie Olsen), an art of "snapshots" (Alice Munro),
a "redemptive act" (Flannery O'Connor), a "joke" (Robert Stone and Leandro
Urbina), a "wonderfully evolved mandible" (Terence Byrnes), "a form of prayer"
(John Berger), "an act of rebellion" (John Hawkes), and a "musical composition"
(Katherine Mansfield). Nadine Gordimer, recipient of the Nobel Prize for Literature
in 1991, is famous for her description of the short story in her *Selected Stories* (1975) as
"the life-giving drop—sweat, tear, semen, saliva—that will spread an intensity on the
page; burn a hole in it"; however, an even more useful statement is to be found in her
essay "The Flash of Fireflies":

"Certainly the short story has always been more flexible and open to experiment than the novel. Short-story writers always have been subject at the same
time to both a stricter technical discipline and a wider freedom than the novelist.
Short-story writers have known—and solved by the nature of their choice of
form—what novelists seem to have discovered in despair only now: the strongest
convention of the novel, prolonged coherence of time, to which even the most
experimental of novels must conform unless it is to fall apart, is false to the nature
of whatever can be grasped of human reality. How shall I put it? Each of us has a
thousand lives and a novel gives a character only one. *For the sake of the form.* The
novelist may juggle about with chronology and throw narrative overboard; all the
time his characters have the reader by the hand, there is a consistency of relationship throughout the experience that cannot and does not convey the quality of
human life, where contact is more like the flash of fireflies, in and out, now here,
now there, in darkness. Short-story writers see by the light of the flash; theirs is
the art of the only thing one can be sure of—the present moment. Ideally, they
have learned to do without explanation of what went before, and what happens
beyond this point. How the characters will appear, think, behave, comprehend,
tomorrow or at any other time in their lives, is irrelevant. A discrete moment of
truth is aimed at—not *the* moment of truth, because the short story doesn't deal
in cumulatives. . . . The short story recognizes that full comprehension of a particular kind in the reader, like full apprehension of a particular kind in the writer, is
something of limited duration. The short story is a fragmented and restless form, a
matter of hit or miss, and it is perhaps for this reason that it suits modern consciousness—which seems best expressed as flashes of fearful insight alternating
with near-hypnotic states of indifference."

Seeing by the light of the flash. That requires an art of extreme delicacy and precision,
of understatement. Valerie Shaw, in *The Short Story: A Critical Introduction*, insists that
"It seems reasonable to say that a firm definition of the short story is impossible." And
yet, in those same pages, she identifies *reticence* as one of the most striking features of
the short story: "It is the degree and nature of the reticence conveyed by the short
story at its best that give the genre its own decorum, a tactfulness consisting of respect

for silences or unstated feelings, and displaying itself formally in the 'artful compromise' by which, Henry James proposed, the 'space-hunger and space-cunning' of a writer's material can be 'kept down.' The surface of a story, James explained, was made 'iridescent, even in the short piece, or what is beneath it and what probes and gleams through,' and it is this that produces 'the only compactness that has a charm . . . the only sparseness that has a force . . . the only simplicity that has a grace—those, in each order, that produce the rich effect.' In many of the stories presented in this study as attaining a 'rich effect,' silence is of paramount significance."

Truman Capote calls the short story "the most difficult and disciplining form of prose writing extant. Whatever control and technique I may have I owe entirely to my training in this medium." When asked in *The Paris Review* interview to explain what he meant by control, Capote said: "I mean maintaining a stylistic and emotional upper hand over your material. Call it precious and go to hell, but I believe a story can be wrecked by a faulty rhythm in a sentence—especially if it occurs toward the end—or a mistake in paragraphing, even punctuation. Henry James is the maestro of the semicolon. Hemingway is a first-rate paragrapher. From the point of view of ear, Virginia Woolf never wrote a bad sentence." In the same interview, he concludes: "Even Joyce, our most extreme disregarder [of rules], was a superb craftsman; he could write *Ulysses* because he could write *Dubliners*. Too many writers seem to consider the writing of short stories as a kind of finger exercise. Well, in such cases, it is certainly only their fingers they are exercising. . . ."

The range of stories included in *The Art of Short Fiction* should encompass most of the forms and "-isms" that have been associated with short fiction: naturalism, all the brands of realism (including Virginia Woolf's psychological realism and that brand of the fantastical in Latin American writing now described as magic realism), surrealism, modernism, postmodernism, and metafiction. Readers interested in form will find here, in various disguises, confession, fable, parable, myth, allegory, pastoral, the tall tale, science fiction, the detective story, and the dramatic monologue. I prefer not to label or categorize, since that is often reductive and distracting to first-time readers of a text; besides, most good short fiction defies simple pigeon-holing and demands the freedom of the field or city. A reader with a sociological bent will find stories that deal with race, politics, love, loneliness, despair, tribal breakdown, war, the battle of the sexes, and a host of contemporary maladies, from AIDS and anorexia to anomie. The formalist will be able to chart the decline, fall, and restoration of such concerns as unity of effect, plot, character, setting, texture, patterning, *progression d'effets*, and closure. The notes and statements on the art of fiction should be useful in both cases, providing the often conflicting views of writers such as Doris Lessing, John Hawkes, Katherine Mansfield, and Chinua Achebe on matters as diverse as politics, autobiography, narrative, dramatic structure, and design. Achebe sees himself as a myth-maker, a sender of messages, and doesn't care if what he is doing is regarded as applied, rather than pure, art; and John Hawkes throws a monkey wrench into the machinery of conventional criticism by stating that he began writing with the view that plot, character, and setting are the enemies of fiction.

In keeping with Chaucer's habit (as Dryden saw it) of loading every rift with ore, I have tried to stuff as much useful information as possible into the notes. My assumption has been that these snippets and quotations will stimulate debate and not interfere with either the student's first reading of the text or the teacher's Socratic probings. Where statements about the craft—what might be called a "poetics of fiction"—were too long to excerpt usefully and coherently, or seemed especially important, I have included them in their entirety in the Afterwords. As a student, a teacher, and, then, as a beginning writer, I found nothing, outside the texts themselves, quite as inspiring and provocative as authors' attempts to talk about—and, at times, *around*—the creative process. Granted, much of what authors have to say is impressionistic and usually written after the fact, so that it sometimes has the cast of yet another personal fiction. Plato gave a clear warning in the *Apology*: "Will you believe me? I am almost ashamed to confess the truth, but I must say that there is hardly a person present who would not have talked better about their poetry than did the poets." I'm sure Plato would have been equally sceptical of writers of short fiction. So, with fair warning from the ancients, from modernists who counsel against committing the "intentional fallacy"—mistaking an artist's expressed aims for what is actually achieved in the completed text—and from postmodernists such as Roland Barthes who announce the "death of the Author," I still find myself on the side of Albert Guerard, who declared himself "sufficiently 'intentionalist' to remain incorrigibly interested in the psychology of composition." I would, most often, rather read what an author has to say about his craft than a dozen so-called "interpretations" of his work.

In order to make this anthology even more useful, I have decided to include a number of excerpts and essays, some of which discuss problems unique to short fiction and to the history and definition of the short story, and others that are more general. Rather than offer a potted history of the short story, in which I would have to paraphrase or quote extensively, I have decided to include Ian Reid's pithy and epigrammatic opening chapter in *The Short Story*, called "Problems of Definition." Students who want to go deeper into genre study or see how contemporary critical modes are being applied to short fiction might well dip into back issues of the periodical *Studies in Short Fiction* and such works as *Short Story Theory at the Crossroads*, edited by Susan Lohafer and Jo Ellyn Clarey. Considerations of space have precluded the inclusion of provocative essays by Michel Foucault, Roland Barthes, Ferdinand de Saussure, and Elaine Showalter, which I hope the reader will seek out in their original sources; but I am pleased to have been able to include excerpts from Jean-Paul Sartre's "Why Write?" and the entire text of Claude Lévi-Strauss's "The Writing Lesson," which raise questions respectively about the role of the reader in literature and the ethical and political implications of written communication.

In his fascinating essay "The Writing Lesson," the cultural anthropologist Lévi-Strauss suggests that "the primary function of writing, as a means of communication, is to facilitate the enslavement of other human beings." We know something about the power and authority invested in written language from current challenges to the so-called "contracts" by which imperial nations and vested interests justified their theft of aboriginal lands; and we know even more about the power of written language by observing—with or without the records provided by Amnesty International—how writings are censored or condemned and how writers are harassed, jailed, or murdered by the State for the exercise of their peculiar magic. Story is the text, and sub-text, by which we analyze and record our passage through time and our occupation of space. We cannot survive, individually or tribally, without story any more than we can survive without hope; it is our link with the past and our gift to, and promise in, the future. To know our stories—what they say and how they are constructed—is to begin to understand the nature of that passage. In fact, it is the beginning of freedom.

This paradox—that written communication may have originated to enslave, but now has the potential to free mankind—is nowhere better expressed than in Paulo Freire's *The Pedagogy of the Oppressed* and Jean-Paul Sartre's essay "Why Write?" Freire shows how peasants in the Third World are politicized by the acquisition of literacy, especially when the vocabulary learned speaks directly to the terms of their oppression. And Sartre, a keen observer of the moral failings of capitalistic and socialistic political structures, makes a powerful case for writing as a means to individual and collective liberation: "The art of prose is bound up with the only régime in which prose has meaning, democracy. When one is threatened, the other is too. And it is not enough to defend them with the pen. A day comes when the pen is forced to stop, and the writer must take up arms. Thus, however you might have come to it, whatever opinions you might have professed, literature throws you into battle. Writing is a certain way of wanting freedom; once you have begun, you are committed, willy-nilly."

Gary Geddes
Dunvegan, Ontario
1992

The
Art
of Short
Fiction

Chinua Achebe

Chinua Achebe, one of the foremost African writers, was born in Ogidi, Nigeria, in 1930. After graduating from University College, Ibadan, he worked for a number of years as director of the Nigerian Broadcasting Corporation before pursuing his writing career full time. His publications include several volumes of poetry, one of which won the Commonwealth Poetry Prize in 1974, five novels, *Things Fall Apart* (1958), *No Longer at Ease* (1960), *Arrow of God* (1964), *A Man of the People* (1966), and *Anthills of the Savannah* (1988), two books of short stories, *The Sacrificial Egg* (1962) and *Girls at War* (1972), and a book of essays, *Morning Yet on Creation Day* (1975).

As the titles of his first two novels suggest, Achebe has been particularly conscious of the dislocation, the dis-ease, that is the legacy of colonialism in Africa. Having been raised a Christian and educated in English, he is particularly well placed to explore the cultural rift—what Roland Barthes calls the "site of a loss"—in Nigerian society, where the cost of acquiring imperial culture has too often been a loss of dignity and power for indigenous peoples. "I would be quite satisfied," Achebe writes in "The Novelist As Teacher," "if my novels (especially the ones I set in the past) did no more than teach my readers that their past—with all its imperfections—was not one long night of savagery from which the first Europeans acting on God's behalf delivered them."

In addition to reclaiming African subjects and settings, Achebe has been concerned with the issue of language. Margaret Laurence has written of Achebe that "there is one theme which runs through everything he has written—human communcation and the lack of it." He found, in a country of so many languages, that writing in English made it easier for him to address national issues. In response to the question of whether the African writer can master English, Achebe gives a resounding yes: "If on the other hand you ask: Can he ever learn to use it like a native speaker? I should say: I hope not. It is neither necessary nor desirable for him to be able to do so. . . . The African writer should aim to use English in a way that brings out his message best without altering the language to the extent that its value as a medium of international exchange is lost. He should aim at fashioning out an English which is at once universal and able to carry his experience."

In order to do this, Achebe has had to work out his own unique linguistic strategies. "Among the Ibo," he writes in *Things Fall Apart*, "the art of conversation is regarded very highly and proverbs are the palm-oil with which words are eaten." His own narratives embody the spirit and many techniques of the oral tradition—the use of proverbs, parables, and a very conversational language—while maintaining the subtlety and allusiveness of the written language, an achievement that reflects the high regard in which he holds the profession of story-teller. "Story-tellers are a threat," he writes in *Anthills of the Savannah*. "They threaten all the champions of control, they frighten usurpers of the right-to-freedom of the human spirit—in state, in church or mosque, in party congresses, in the university or wherever."

"I think writing is such a serious thing that one ought to take it fairly easily and slowly, you know, at its own pace," he said in an interview with Lewis Nkosi in 1962. "I don't like forcing a story. Some days, weeks even, I can't write anything, and I don't want to go to the table and start scribbling, you see, I feel it's—it is an important thing and ought to be taken seriously." Achebe rejects the notion of a pure, disinterested art, arguing instead for writing that is both morally and aesthetically engaged: "Perhaps what I write is applied art as distinct from pure. But who cares? Art is important but so is education of the kind I have in mind. And I don't see that the two need be mutually exclusive."

Achebe accepts the traditional role of artist as myth-maker. He quotes Claude Lévi-Strauss on the subject of ancestors as the *senders* of messages (myths) and us as *receivers* of messages about the meaning of life and the values that are worth preserving. "This, to my mind, is the great myth about language and the destiny of man. Its lesson should be clear to all. It is as though the ancestors who made language and knew from what bestiality its use rescued them are saying to us: Beware of interfering with its purpose! For when language is seriously interfered with, when it is disjoined from truth, be it from mere incompetence or worse, from malice, horrors can descend again on mankind."

The Sacrificial Egg

Julius Obi sat gazing at his typewriter. The fat Chief Clerk, his boss, was snoring at his table. Outside, the gatekeeper in his green uniform was sleeping at his post. You couldn't blame him; no customer had passed through the gate for nearly a week. There was an empty basket on the giant weighing machine. A few palm-kernels lay desolately in the dust around the machine. Only the flies remained in strength.

Julius went to the window that overlooked the great market on the bank of the River Niger. This market, though still called Nkwo, had long spilled over into Eke, Oye, and Afo with the coming of civilization and the growth of the town into a big palm-oil port. In spite of this encroachment, however, it was still busiest on its original Nkwo day, because the deity who had presided over it from antiquity still cast her spell only on her own day—let men in their greed spill over themselves. It was said that she appeared in the form of an old woman in the centre of the market just before cock-crow and waved her magic fan in the four directions of the earth—in front of her, behind her, to the right and to the left—to draw to the market men and women from distant places. And they came bringing the produce of their lands—palm-oil and kernels, kola nuts, cassava, mats, baskets and earthenware pots; and took home many-coloured cloths, smoked fish, iron pots and plates. These were the forest peoples. The other half of the world who lived by the great rivers came down also—by canoe, bringing yams and fish. Sometimes it was a big canoe with a dozen or more people in it; sometimes it was a lone fisherman and his wife in a small vessel from the swift flowing Anambara. They moored their canoe on the bank and sold their fish, after much haggling. The woman then walked up the steep banks of the river to the heart of the market to buy salt and oil and, if the sales had been very good, even a length of cloth. And for her children at home she bought bean cakes and mai-mai which the Igara women cooked. As evening approached, they took up their paddles again and paddled away, the water shimmering in the sunset and their canoe becoming smaller and smaller in the distance until it was just a dark crescent on the water's face and two dark bodies swaying forwards and backwards in it. Umuru then was the meeting place of the forest people who were called Igbo and the alien riverain folk whom the Igbo called Olu and beyond whom the world stretched in indefiniteness.

Julius Obi was not a native of Umuru. He had come like countless others from some bush village inland. Having passed his Standard Six in a mission school he had come to Umuru to work as a clerk in the offices of the all-powerful European trading company which bought palm-kernels at its own price and sold cloth and metalware, also at its own price. The offices were situated beside the famous market so that in his first two or three weeks Julius had to learn to work within its huge enveloping hum. Sometimes when the Chief Clerk was away he walked to the window and looked down on the vast anthill activity. Most of these people were not there yesterday, he thought, and yet the market had been just as full. There must be many, many people in the world to be able to fill the market day after day like this. Of course they say not all who came to the great market were real people. Janet's mother, Ma, had said so.

"Some of the beautiful young women you see squeezing through the crowds are not people like you or me but mammy-wota who have their town in the depths of the river," she said. "You can always tell them, because they are beautiful with a beauty that is too perfect and too cold. You catch a glimpse of her with the tail of your eye, then you blink and look properly, but she has already vanished in the crowd."

Julius thought about these things as he now stood at the window looking down on the silent, empty market. Who would have believed that the great boisterous market could ever be quenched like this? But such was the strength of Kitikpa, the incarnate power of smallpox. Only he could drive away all those people and leave the market to the flies.

When Umuru was a little village, there was an age-grade who swept its market-square every Nkwo day. But progress had turned it into a busy, sprawling, crowded and dirty river port, a no-man's-land where strangers outnumbered by far the sons of the soil, who could do nothing about it except shake their heads at this gross perversion of their prayer. For indeed they had prayed—who will blame them—for their town to grow and prosper. And it had grown. But there is good growth and there is bad growth. The belly does not bulge out only with food and drink; it might be the abominable disease which would end by sending its sufferer out of the house even before he was fully dead.

The strangers who came to Umuru came for trade and money, not in search of duties to perform, for they had those in plenty back home in their village which was real home.

And as if this did not suffice, the young sons and daughters of Umuru soil, encouraged by schools and churches were behaving no better than the strangers. They neglected all their old tasks and kept only the revelries.

Such was the state of the town when Kitikpa came to see it and to demand the sacrifice the inhabitants owed the gods of the soil. He came in confident knowledge of the terror he held over the people. He was an evil deity, and boasted it. Lest he be offended those he killed were not killed but decorated, and no one dared weep for them. He put an end to the coming and going between neighbours and between villages. They said, "Kitikpa is in that village," and immediately it was cut off by its neighbours.

Julius was sad and worried because it was almost a week since he had seen Janet, the girl he was going to marry. Ma had explained to him very gently that he should no longer go to see them "until this thing is over, by the power of Jehovah." (Ma was a very devout Christian convert and one reason why she approved of Julius for her only daughter was that he sang in the choir of the CMS church.)

"You must keep to your rooms," she had said in hushed tones, for Kitikpa strictly forbade any noise or boisterousness. "You never know whom you might meet on the streets. That family has got it." She lowered her voice even more and pointed surreptitiously at the house across the road whose doorway was barred with a yellow palm-frond. "He has decorated one of them already and the rest were moved away today in a big government lorry."

Janet walked a short way with Julius and stopped; so he stopped too. They seemed to have nothing to say to each other yet they lingered on. Then she said goodnight and he said goodnight. And they shook hands, which was very odd, as though parting for the night were something new and grave.

He did not go straight home, because he wanted desperately to cling, even alone, to this strange parting. Being educated he was not afraid of whom he might meet, so he went to the bank of the river and just walked up and down it. He must have been there a long time because he was still there when the wooden gong of the night-mask sounded. He immediately set out for home, half-walking and half-running, for night-masks were not a matter of superstition; they were real. They chose the night for their revelry because like the bat's their ugliness was great.

In his hurry he stepped on something that broke with a slight liquid explosion. He stopped and peeped down at the footpath. The moon was not up yet but there was a faint light in the sky which showed that it would not be long delayed. In this half-light he saw that he had stepped on an egg offered in sacrifice. Someone oppressed by misfortune had brought the offering to the cross-road in the dusk. And he had stepped on it. There were the usual young palm-fronds around it. But Julius saw it differently as a house where the terrible artist was at work. He wiped the sole of his foot on the sandy path and hurried away, carrying another vague worry in his mind. But hurrying was no use now; the fleet-footed mask was already abroad. Perhaps it was impelled to hurry by the threatening imminence of the moon. Its voice rose high and clear in the still night air like a flaming sword. It was yet a long way away, but Julius knew that distances vanished before it. So he made straight for the cocoyam farm beside the road and threw himself on his belly, in the shelter of the broad leaves. He had hardly done this when he heard the rattling staff of the spirit and a thundering stream of esoteric speech. He shook all over. The sounds came bearing down on him almost pressing his face into the moist earth. And now he could hear the footsteps as if twenty evil men were running together. Panic sweat broke out all over him and he was nearly impelled to get up and run. Fortunately he kept a firm hold on himself . . . In no time at all the commotion in the air and on the earth—the thunder and torrential rain, the earthquake and flood—passed and disappeared in the distance on the other side of the road.

The next morning, at the office the Chief Clerk, a son of the soil spoke bitterly about last night's provocation of Kitikpa by the headstrong youngsters who had launched the noisy fleet-footed mask in defiance of their elders, who knew that Kitikpa would be enraged, and then . . .

The trouble was that the disobedient youths had never yet experienced the power of Kitikpa themselves; they had only heard of it. But soon they would learn.

As Julius stood at the window looking out on the emptied market he lived through the terror of that night again. It was barely a week ago but already it seemed like another life, separated from the present by a vast emptiness. This emptiness deepened with every passing day. On this side of it stood Julius, and on the other Ma and Janet whom the dread artist decorated.

Ryūnosuke Akutagawa

Born in Tokyo in 1892, Ryūnosuke Akutagawa became well known as an art collector, teacher, traveller, and writer and is the first Japanese writer to achieve distinction in a Western genre. He was a precocious child, writing stories at age ten and reading foreign authors in his early teens. His most famous collection, *Rashomon and Other Stories*, was published in Japan in 1916 when he was only twenty-three, but did not appear in English until 1948. He graduated from Tokyo Imperial University in 1916 with distinction in English Studies, having already translated numerous Western works, published widely in periodicals, and been active in editing and publishing a student literary magazine. Like many of his contemporaries, he was interested in socialism and this is reflected in his graduating thesis, "A Study of William Morris." Sent to China as an observer in 1921 by the Japanese newspaper that regularly published his fiction, Akutagawa suffered a severe physical and emotional debilitation that left him depressed and fearful of the mental collapse that had claimed his mother as a young woman. This condition was exacerbated by the death of his father and uncle, when he had to take financial responsibility for a sister whose house had burned down and whose husband had committed suicide, and by the loss of all his belongings, art objects, and early editions in the major Tokyo earthquake and fire of 1923. He became excessively inward-looking and dependent on drugs before taking his own life in 1927 by an overdose of barbiturates.

Although he was certainly a moralist in fiction, Akutagawa was nonetheless an exacting craftsman and an adherent to the notion that the artist must be free to find and explore his own materials. His aim seems to have been to create a fiction that was spare and starkly poetic, but capable of objectivity in rendering what Virginia Woolf calls "the dark places of psychology," and committed to a rigorous analysis of human behaviour. His belief in art as a form of religion, in which perfection is the aim and self-reliance the method, is reflected throughout his writings, particularly in "Art, etc." and the preface to his second volume of stories, *Tobacco and the Devil* (1917): "To speak of my feelings while I am at work, it seems like growing rather than making something. Every phenomenon, human and otherwise, follows its own unique course of development in that it happens in the way it must. So as I write I proceed from point to point, from moment to moment. If I miss one step, then I am stuck. I can not go even one step further. If I force myself, something is bound to go wrong. I must always be alert. No matter how alert, it often happens that I miss it. That is my trouble."

Although his pronouncements on art show Akutagawa to be a believer in organic form, he was enough of a formalist to suffer from divided loyalties, his urge for order and perfection driving him towards art, but the body and its needs always reclaiming him for the instinctual life. Had he been able to view his writing as an act of profound solidarity with, rather than a continually revised performance for, mankind, he might have triumphed over both the writer's blocks and the emotional depressions that continued to plague him until his death. However, his poetic temperament and the techniques of Western realism did enable him to create a vivid and gripping portrayal of the social and moral quagmires of ancient and contemporary life in Japan. The famous Japanese filmmaker Akira Kurosawa adapted Akutagawa's work in 1950, using both "Rashomon" and "In a Grove" as the basis for his film classic *Rashomon*.

Like Shakespeare with his Holinshed *Chronicles*, Akutagawa found some of his most congenial material in history, particularly in the Japanese classic "Tales Old and New." His short story "In a Grove," with its multiple perspectives of a single event, is said to owe something to Robert Browning's "The Ring and the Book."

In a Grove
Translated by Takashi Kojima

THE TESTIMONY OF A WOODCUTTER QUESTIONED BY A HIGH POLICE COMMISSIONER

Yes, sir. Certainly, it was I who found the body. This morning, as usual, I went to cut my daily quota of cedars, when I found the body in a grove in a hollow in the mountains. The exact location? About 150 meters off the Yamashina stage road. It's an out-of-the-way grove of bamboo and cedars.

The body was lying flat on its back dressed in a bluish silk kimono and a wrinkled head-dress of the Kyoto style. A single sword-stroke had pierced the breast. The fallen bamboo-blades around it were stained with bloody blossoms. No, the blood was no longer running. The wound had dried up, I believe. And also, a gadfly was stuck fast there, hardly noticing my footsteps.

You ask me if I saw a sword or any such thing?

No, nothing, sir. I found only a rope at the root of a cedar near by. And . . . well, in addition to a rope, I found a comb. That was all. Apparently he must have made a battle of it before he was murdered, because the grass and fallen bamboo-blades had been trampled down all around.

"A horse was near by?"

No, sir. It's hard enough for a man to enter, let alone a horse.

THE TESTIMONY OF A TRAVELING BUDDHIST PRIEST
QUESTIONED BY A HIGH POLICE COMMISSIONER

The time? Certainly, it was about noon yesterday, sir. The unfortunate man was on the road from Sekiyama to Yamashina. He was walking toward Sekiyama with a woman accompanying him on horseback, who I have since learned was his wife. A scarf hanging from her head hid her face from view. All I saw was the color of her clothes, a lilac-colored suit. Her horse was a sorrel with a fine mane. The lady's height? Oh, about four feet five inches. Since I am a Buddhist priest, I took little notice about her details. Well, the man was armed with a sword as well as a bow and arrows. And I remember that he carried some twenty odd arrows in his quiver.

Little did I expect that he would meet such a fate. Truly human life is as evanescent as the morning dew or a flash of lightning. My words are inadequate to express my sympathy for him.

THE TESTIMONY OF A POLICEMAN QUESTIONED
BY A HIGH POLICE COMMISSIONER

The man that I arrested? He is a notorious brigand called Tajomaru. When I arrested him, he had fallen off his horse. He was groaning on the bridge at Awataguchi. The time? It was in the early hours of last night. For the record, I might say that the other day I tried to arrest him, but unfortunately he escaped. He was wearing a dark blue silk kimono and a large plain sword. And, as you see, he got a bow and arrows somewhere. You say that this bow and these arrows look like the ones owned by the dead man? Then Tajomaru must be the murderer. The bow wound with leather strips, the black lacquered quiver, the seventeen arrows with hawk feathers—these were all in his possession I believe. Yes, sir, the horse was, as you say, a sorrel with a fine mane. A little beyond the stone bridge I found the horse grazing by the roadside, with his long rein dangling. Surely there is some providence in his having been thrown by the horse.

Of all the robbers prowling around Kyoto, this Tajomaru has given the most grief to the women in town. Last autumn a wife who came to the mountain back of the Pindora of the Toribe Temple, presumably to pay a visit, was murdered, along with a girl. It has been suspected that it was his doing. If this criminal murdered the man, you cannot tell what he may have done with the man's wife. May it please your honor to look into this problem as well.

THE TESTIMONY OF AN OLD WOMAN QUESTIONED BY A HIGH POLICE COMMISSIONER

Yes, sir, that corpse is the man who married my daughter. He does not come from Kyoto. He was a samurai in the town of Kokufu, in the province of Wakasa. His name was Kanazawa no Takehiko, and his age was twenty-six. He was of a gentle disposition, so I am sure he did nothing to provoke the anger of others.

My daughter? Her name is Masago, and her age is nineteen. She is a spirited, fun-loving girl, but I am sure she has never known any man except Takebiko. She has a small, oval, dark-complected face with a mole at the corner of her left eye.

Yesterday Takehiko left for Wakasa with my daughter. What bad luck it is that things should have come to such a sad end! What has become of my daughter? I am resigned to giving up my so-in-law as lost, but the fate of my daughter worries me sick. For heaven's sake leave no stone unturned to find her. I hate that robber Tajomaru, or whatever his name is. Not only my son-in-law, but my daughter . . . (Her later words were drowned in tears.)

TAJOMARU'S CONFESSION

I killed him, but not her. Where's she gone? I can't tell. Oh, wait a minute. No torture can make me confess what I don't know. Now things have come to such a head, I won't keep anything from you.

Yesterday a little past noon I met that couple. Just then a puff of wind blew, and raised her hanging scarf, so that I caught a glimpse of her face. Instantly it was again covered from my view. That may have been one reason; she looked like a Bodhisattva. At that moment I made up my mind to capture her even if I had to kill her man.

Why? To me killing isn't a matter of such great consequence as you might think. When a woman is captured, her man has to be killed anyway. In killing, I use the sword I wear at my side. Am I the only one who kills people? You, you don't use your swords. You kill people with your power, with your money. Sometimes you kill them on the pretext of working for their good. It's true they don't bleed. They are in the best of health, but all the same you've killed them. It's hard to say who is a greater sinner, you or me. (An ironical smile.)

But it would be good if I could capture a woman without killing her man. So, I made up my mind to capture her, and do my best not to kill him. But it's out of the question on the Yamashina stage road. So I managed to lure the couple into the mountains.

It was quite easy. I became their traveling companion, and I told them there was an old mound in the mountain over there, and that I had dug it open and found many mirrors and swords. I went on to tell them I'd buried the things in a grove behind the mountain, and that I'd like to sell them at a low price to anyone who would care to have them. Then . . . you see, isn't greed terrible? He was beginning to be moved by my talk before he knew it. In less than half an hour they were driving their horse toward the mountain with me.

When he came in front of the grove, I told them that the treasures were buried in it, and I asked them to come and see. The man had no objection—he was blinded by greed. The woman said she would wait on horseback. It was natural for her to say so, at the sight of a thick grove. To tell you the truth, my plan worked just as I wished, so I went into the grove with him, leaving her behind alone.

The grove is only bamboo for some distance. About fifty yards ahead there's a rather open clump of cedars. It was a convenient spot for my purpose. Pushing my way through the grove, I told him a plausible lie that the treasures were buried under the cedars. When I told him this, he pushed his laborious way toward the slender cedar visible through the grove. After a while the bamboo thinned out, and we came to where a number of cedars grew in a row. As soon as we got there, I seized him from behind. Because he was a trained, sword-bearing warrior, he was quite strong, but he was taken by surprise, so there was no help for him. I soon tied him up to the root of a cedar. Where did I get the rope? Thank heaven, being a robber, I had a rope with me, since I might have to scale a wall at any moment. Of course it was easy to stop him from calling out by gagging his mouth with fallen bamboo leaves.

When I disposed of him, I went to his woman and asked her to come and see him, because he seemed to have been suddenly taken sick. It's needless to say that this plan also worked well. The woman, her sedge hat off, came into the depths of the grove, where I led her by the hand. The instant she caught sight of her husband, she drew a small sword. I've never seen a woman of such violent temper. If I'd been off guard, I'd have got a thrust in my side. I dodged, but she kept on slashing at me. She might have wounded me deeply or killed me. But I'm Tajomaru. I managed to strike down her small sword without drawing my own. The most spirited woman is defenseless without a weapon. At least I could satisfy my desire for her without taking her husband's life.

Yes, . . . without taking his life. I had no wish to kill him. I was about to run away from the grove, leaving the woman behind in tears, when she frantically clung to my arm. In broken fragments of words, she asked that either her husband or I die. She said it was more trying than death to have her shame known to two men. She gasped out that she wanted to be the wife of whichever survived. Then a furious desire to kill him seized me. (Gloomy excitement.)

Telling you in this way, no doubt I seem a crueler man than you. But that's because you didn't see her face. Especially her burning eyes at that moment. As I saw her eye to eye, I wanted to make her my wife even if I were to be struck by lightning; I wanted to make her my wife . . . this single desire filled my mind. This was not only lust, as you might think. At that time if I'd had no other desire than lust, I'd surely not have minded knocking her down and running away. Then I wouldn't have stained my sword with his blood. But the moment I gazed at her face in the dark grove, I decided not to leave there without killing him.

But I didn't like to resort to unfair means to kill him. I untied him and told him to cross swords with me. (The rope that was found at the root of the cedar is the rope I dropped at the time.) Furious with anger, he drew his thick sword. And quick as thought, he sprang at me ferociously, without speaking a word. I needn't tell you how our fight turned out. The twenty-third stroke . . . please remember this. I'm impressed with this fact still. Nobody under the sun has ever clashed swords with me twenty strokes. (A cheerful smile.)

When he fell, I turned toward her, lowering my bloodstained sword. But to my great astonishment she was gone. I wondered to where she had run away. I looked for her in the clump of cedars. I listened, but heard only a groaning sound from the throat of the dying man.

As soon as we started to cross swords, she may have run away through the grove to call for help. When I thought of that, I decided it was a matter of life and death to me. So, robbing him of his sword, and bow and arrows, I ran out to the mountain road. There I found her horse still grazing quietly. It would be a mere waste of words to tell you the later details, but before I entered town I had already parted with the sword. That's all my confession. I know that my head will be hung in chains anyway, so put me down for the maximum penalty. (A defiant attitude.)

THE CONFESSION OF A WOMAN WHO HAS COME TO THE *SHIMIZU* TEMPLE

That man in the blue silk kimono, after forcing me to yield to him, laughed mockingly as he looked at my bound husband. How horrified my husband must have been! But no matter how hard he struggled in agony, the rope cut into him all the more tightly. In spite of myself I ran stumblingly toward his side. Or rather I tried to run toward him, but the man instantly knocked me down. Just at that moment I saw an indescribable light in my husband's eyes. Something beyond expression . . . his eyes make me shudder even now. That instantaneous look of my husband, who couldn't speak a word, told me all his heart. The flash in his eyes was neither anger nor sorrow . . . only a cold light, a look of loathing. More struck by the look in his eyes than by the blow of the thief, I called out in spite of myself and fell unconscious.

In the course of time I came to, and found that the man in blue silk was gone. I saw only my husband still bound to the root of the cedar. I raised myself from the bamboo-blades with difficulty, and looked into his face; but the expression in his eyes was just the same as before.

Beneath the cold contempt in his eyes, there was hatred. Shame, grief, and anger . . . I don't know how to express my heart at that time. Reeling to my feet, I went up to my husband.

"Takejiro," I said to him, "since things have come to this pass I cannot live with you. I'm determined to die, . . . but you must die, too. You saw my shame. I can't leave you alive as you are."

This was all I could say. Still he went on gazing at me with loathing and contempt. My heart breaking, I looked for his sword. It must have been taken by the robber. Neither his sword nor his bow and arrows were to be seen in the grove. But fortunately my small sword was lying at my feet. Raising it over head, once more I said, "Now give me your life. I'll follow you right away."

When he heard these words, he moved his lips with difficulty. Since his mouth was stuffed with leaves, of course his voice could not be heard at all. But at a glance I understood his words. Despising me, his look said only, "Kill me." Neither conscious nor unconscious, I stabbed the small sword through the lilac-colored kimono into his breast.

Again at this time I must have fainted. By the time I managed to look up, he had already breathed his last—still in bonds. A streak of sinking sunlight streamed through the clump of cedars and bamboos, and shone on his pale face. Gulping down my sobs, I untied the rope from his dead body. And . . . and what has become of me since I have no more strength to tell you. Anyway I hadn't the strength to die. I stabbed my own throat with the small sword, I threw myself into a pond at the foot of the mountain, and I tried to kill myself in many ways. Unable to end my life, I am still living in dishonor. (A lonely smile.) Worthless as I am, I must have been forsaken even by the most merciful Kwannon. I killed my own husband. I was violated by the robber. Whatever can I do? Whatever can I . . . I . . . (Gradually, violent sobbing.)

THE STORY OF THE MURDERED MAN, AS TOLD THROUGH A MEDIUM

After violating my wife, the robber, sitting there, began to speak comforting words to her. Of course I couldn't speak. My whole body was tied fast to the root of a cedar. But meanwhile I winked at her many times, as much as to say "Don't believe the robber." I wanted to convey some such meaning to her. But my wife, sitting dejectedly on the bamboo leaves, was looking hard at her lap. To all appearances, she was listening to his words. I was agonized by jealousy. In the meantime the robber went on with his clever talk, from one subject to another. The robber finally made his bold, brazen proposal. "Once your virtue is stained, you won't get along well with your husband, so won't you be my wife instead? It's my love for you that made me be violent toward you."

While the criminal talked, my wife raised her face as if in a trance. She had never looked so beautiful as at that moment. What did my beautiful wife say in answer to him while I was sitting bound there? I am lost in space, but I never thought of her answer without burning with anger and jealousy. Truly she said, . . . "Then take me away wherever you go."

This is not the whole of her sin. If that were all, I would not be tormented so much in the dark. When she was going out of the grove as if in a dream, her hand in the robber's, she suddenly turned pale, and pointed at me tied to the root of the cedar, and said, "Kill him! I cannot marry you as long as he lives." "Kill him!" she cried many times, as if she had gone crazy. Even now these words threaten to blow me headlong into the bottomless abyss of darkness. Has such a hateful thing come out of a human mouth ever before? Have such cursed words ever struck a human ear, even once? Even once such a . . . (A sudden cry of scorn.) At these words the robber himself turned pale. "Kill him," she cried, clinging to his arms. Looking hard at her, he answered neither yes nor no . . . but hardly had I thought about his answer before she had been knocked down into the bamboo leaves. (Again a cry of scorn.) Quietly folding his arms, he looked at me and said, "What will you do with her? Kill her or save her? You have only to nod. Kill her?" For these words alone I would like to pardon his crime.

While I hesitated, she shrieked and ran into the depths of the grove. The robber instantly snatched at her, but he failed even to grasp her sleeve.

After she ran away, he took up my sword, and my bow and arrows. With a single stroke he cut one of my bonds. I remember his mumbling, "My fate is next." Then he disappeared from the grove. All was silent after that. No, I heard someone crying. Untying the rest of my bonds, I listened carefully, and I noticed that it was my own crying. (Long silence.)

I raised my exhausted body from the root of the cedar. In front of me there was shining the small sword which my wife had dropped. I took it up and stabbed it into my breast. A bloody lump rose to my mouth, but I didn't feel any pain. When my breast grew cold, everything was as silent as the dead in their graves. What profound silence! Not a single bird-note was heard in the sky over this grave in the hollow of the mountains. Only a lonely light lingered on the cedars and mountains. By and by the light gradually grew fainter, till the cedars and bamboo were lost to view. Lying there, I was enveloped in deep silence.

Then someone crept up to me. I tried to see who it was. But darkness had already been gathering around me. Someone . . . that someone drew the small sword softly out of my breast in its invisible hand. At the same time once more blood flowed into my mouth. And once and for all I sank down into the darkness of space.

Margaret Atwood

Margaret Atwood was born in Ottawa in 1939, but spent most of her early years in the bush country of northern Ontario and Quebec, where her father was engaged in research as an entomologist. She did not spend a full year in school until Grade 8, but had already begun to write poems and stories and plays at age five. She completed her B.A. at Victoria College, University of Toronto, and her M.A. at Radcliffe College, then won a Woodrow Wilson Fellowship to Harvard, where she studied Victorian Literature. She spent the next ten years alternating between teaching and writing until she could afford to write full time. She lives with her companion, the writer Graeme Gibson, and their daughter in Toronto. Her first book of poems, *The Circle Game* (1964) won the Governor General's Award and was followed by a prodigious output of more than a dozen books of poetry; three collections of short stories, *Dancing Girls* (1977), *Bluebeard's Egg* (1983), and *Wilderness Tips* (1991); and the following novels, *The Edible Woman* (1969), *Surfacing* (1972), *Lady Oracle* (1976), *Life before Man* (1979), *Bodily Harm* (1980), and *The Handmaid's Tale* (1985), which won the Governor General's Award and was made into a film, and *Cat's Eye* (1988). Atwood is also the author of a collection of essays, *Second Words* (1982) and a controversial study of Canadian literature, *Survival* (1972).

Although she considers interviews with authors as suspect fictions, many of Atwood's most engaging comments on the nature and aims of fiction are to be found in her playful, often acerbic, replies to questions posed by interviewers. She argues, in an interview with Geoff Hancock (*Canadian Writers at Work*), that fiction should surprise, satisfy the reader's nosiness or curiosity; should evoke emotion from the reader rather than settle for self-expression; and should also "expand the possibilities of the language." In a sympathetic review (in *Second Words*) of Audrey Thomas's short fiction, Atwood praises qualities that might well be singled out in her own work: "enormous verbal skills: a passion for words—words as games, words as magic or refrain, words as puzzle or multi-levelled pun—a wonderful ear for dialogue and dialect, a flexible style."

Her comments about the genesis of stories—"As I do in the novels, I start with a scene of some kind. Or an image. Or a voice. I don't work much from an idea"—stress the importance of observation; so, too,

does her discussion of character underline the centrality of plot, or action, in her stories. "People ask me, why do your characters have these problems? If the characters have no problems, what's the book going to be about? The problem has to be an internal one, or a problem with another character, or an external problem like the Great White Shark, or the end of the world, or the people from Mars, or vampires. Something has to be there to disturb the stasis. Think of a play in which the characters do nothing at all, ever, throughout the play."

When asked about rules, or prescriptive criteria for story-writing, Atwood recalled writing *The Edible Woman* in four months in University of B.C. exam booklets, thinking that each book would contain a chapter; but the process proved unrepeatable: "Nothing works, necessarily, dependably, infallibly. No regime, no scheme, no incantation. If we knew what worked, we could sell it as an unbeatable program for writing masterpieces. Writing is very improvisational. It's like trying to fix a broken sewing machine with safety pins and rubber bands. A lot of tinkering."

When asked about hope, and the idea of art as capable of affirmation, Atwood replied: "When I finish a book I really like, no matter what the subject matter, or see a play or film, like Kurosawa's *Ran*, which is swimming in blood and totally pessimistic, but so well done, I feel very good. I *do* feel hope. Its the *well-doneness* that has that effect on me. Not the conclusion—not what is said, *per se*. . . .

"If you are tone deaf, you are not going to get much out of Beethoven. If you are colour blind, you won't get much out of Monet. But if you have those capabilities, and you see something done very, very well, something that is true to itself, you can feel for two or three minutes that the clouds have parted and you've had a vision, of something of what music or art or writing can do, at its best. A revelation of the full range of our human response to the world—this is what it means to be human, on earth. That seems to be what 'hope' is about in relation to art. Nothing so simple as 'happy endings.' "

In an article entitled "On Being a Woman Writer," Atwood declares that "the proper path for a woman writer is not an all-out manning (or womaning) of the barricades, however much she may agree with the aims of the Movement. The proper path is to become better as a writer." Much of her creative life has been devoted to working with Amnesty International,

P.E.N., and various writers' organizations, speaking out and writing against totalitarianism at the domestic or institutional level. Atwood is a radical, a feminist, and a nationalist, in the best sense of all three strategies; the operative phrase for her is *power politics*, which encompasses the domination of women, races, and other targets of tyranny, such as writers, the poor, progressives, and, of course, the environment. While she claims that, in fiction, "engagement is unavoidable," Atwood advises putting writing first. "Writers, as writers, are not propagandists or examples of social trends or preachers or politicians. They are makers of books, and unless they can make books well they will be bad writers, no matter what the social validity of their views."

Hairball

On the thirteenth of November, day of unluck, month of the dead, Kat went into the Toronto General Hospital for an operation. It was for an ovarian cyst, a large one.

Many women had them, the doctor told her. Nobody knew why. There wasn't any way of finding out whether the thing was malignant, whether it contained, already, the spores of death. Not before they went in. He spoke of "going in" the way she'd heard old veterans in TV documentaries speak of assaults on enemy territory. There was the same tensing of the jaw, the same fierce gritting of the teeth, the same grim enjoyment. Except that what he would be going into was her body. Counting down, waiting for the anaesthetic, Kat too gritted her teeth fiercely. She was terrified, but also she was curious. Curiosity has got her through a lot.

She'd made the doctor promise to save the thing for her, whatever it was, so she could have a look. She was intensely interested in her own body, in anything it might choose to do or produce; although when flaky Dania, who did layout at the magazine, told her this growth was a message to her from her body and she ought to sleep with an amethyst under her pillow to calm her vibrations, Kat told her to stuff it.

The cyst turned out to be a benign tumour. Kat liked that use of *benign*, as if the thing had a soul and wished her well. It was big as a grapefruit, the doctor said. "Big as a coconut," said Kat. Other people had grapefruits. "Coconut" was better. It conveyed the hardness of it, and the hairiness, too.

The hair in it was red—long strands of it wound round and round inside, like a ball of wet wool gone berserk or like the guck you pulled out of a clogged bathroom-sink drain. There were little bones in it too, or fragments of bone; bird bones, the bones of a sparrow crushed by a car. There was a scattering of nails, toe or finger. There were five perfectly formed teeth.

"Is this abnormal?" Kat asked the doctor, who smiled. Now that he had gone in and come out again, unscathed, he was less clenched.

"Abnormal? No," he said carefully, as if breaking the news to a mother about a freakish accident to her newborn. "Let's just say it's fairly common." Kat was a little disappointed. She would have preferred uniqueness.

She asked for a bottle of formaldehyde, and put the cut-open tumour into it. It was hers, it was benign, it did not deserve to be thrown away. She took it back to her apartment and stuck it on the mantelpiece. She named it Hairball. It isn't that different from having a stuffed bear's head or a preserved ex-pet or anything else with fur and teeth looming over your fireplace; or she pretends it isn't. Anyway, it certainly makes an impression.

Ger doesn't like it. Despite his supposed yen for the new and outré, he is a squeamish man. The first time he comes around (sneaks around, creeps around) after the operation, he tells Kat to throw Hairball out. He calls it "disgusting." Kat refuses point-blank, and says she'd rather have Hairball in a bottle on her mantelpiece than the soppy dead flowers he's brought her, which will anyway rot a lot sooner than Hairball will. As a mantelpiece ornament, Hairball is far superior. Ger says Kat has a tendency to push things to extremes, to go over the edge, merely from a juvenile desire to shock, which is hardly a substitute for wit. One of these days, he says, she will go way too far. Too far for him, is what he means.

"That's why you hired me, isn't it?" she says. "Because I go way too far." But he's in one of his analyzing moods. He can see these tendencies of hers reflected in her work on the magazine, he says. All that leather and those grotesque and tortured-looking poses are heading down a track he and others are not at all sure they should continue to follow. Does she see what he means, does she take his point? It's a point that's been made before. She shakes her head slightly, says nothing. She knows how that translates: there have been complaints from the advertisers. *Too bizarre, too kinky.* Tough.

"Want to see my scar?" she says. "Don't make me laugh, though, you'll crack it open." Stuff like that makes him dizzy: anything with a hint of blood, anything gynecological. He almost threw up in the delivery room when his wife had a baby two years ago. He'd told her that with pride. Kat thinks about sticking a cigarette into the side of her mouth, as in a black-and-white movie of the forties. She thinks about blowing the smoke into his face.

Her insolence used to excite him, during their arguments. Then there would be a grab of her upper arms, a smouldering, violent kiss. He kisses her as if he thinks someone else is watching him, judging the image they make together. Kissing the latest thing, hard and shiny, purple-mouthed, crop-headed; kissing a girl, a woman, a girl, in a little crotch-hugger skirt and skin-tight leggings. He likes mirrors.

But he isn't excited now. And she can't decoy him into bed; she isn't ready for that yet, she isn't healed. He has a drink, which he doesn't finish, holds her hand as an afterthought, gives her a couple of avuncular pats on the off-white outsized alpaca shoulder, leaves too quickly.

"Goodbye, Gerald," she says. She pronounces the name with mockery. It's a negation of him, an abolishment of him, like ripping a medal off his chest. It's a warning.

He'd been Gerald when they first met. It was she who transformed him, first to Gerry, then to Ger. (Rhymed with *flair*, rhymed with *dare*.) She made him get rid of those sucky pursed-mouth ties, told him what shoes to wear, got him to buy a loose-cut Italian suit, redid his hair. A lot of his current tastes—in food, in drink, in recreational drugs, in women's entertainment underwear—were once hers. In his new phase, with his new, hard, stripped-down name ending on the sharpened note of *r*, he is her creation.

As she is her own. During her childhood she was a romanticized Katherine, dressed by her misty-eyed, fussy mother in dresses that looked like ruffled pillow-cases. By high school she'd shed the frills and emerged as a bouncy, round-faced Kathy, with gleaming freshly washed hair and enviable teeth, eager to please and no more interesting than a health-food ad. At university she was Kath, blunt and no-bullshit in her Take-Back-the-Night jeans and checked shirt and her brick-layer-style striped-denim peaked hat. When she ran away to England, she sliced herself down to Kat. It was economical, street-feline, and pointed as a nail. It was also unusual. In England you had to do something to get their attention, especially if you weren't English. Safe in this incarnation, she Ramboed through the eighties.

It was the name, she still thinks, that got her the interview and then the job. The job with an avant-garde magazine, the kind that was printed on matte stock in black and white, with overexposed close-ups of women with hair blowing over their eyes, one nostril prominent: *the razor's edge*, it was called. Haircuts as art, some real art, film reviews, a little stardust, wardrobes of ideas that were clothes and of clothes that were ideas—the metaphysical shoulder pad. She learned her trade well, hands-on. She learned what worked.

She made her way up the ladder, from layout to design, then to the supervision of whole spreads, and then whole issues. It wasn't easy, but it was worth it. She had become a creator; she created total looks. After a while she could walk down the street in Soho or stand in the lobby at openings and witness her handiwork incarnate, strolling around in outfits she'd put together, spouting her warmed-over pronouncements. It was like being God, only God had never got around to off-the-rack lines.

By that time her face had lost its roundness, though the teeth of course remained: there was something to be said for North American dentistry. She'd shaved off most of her hair, worked on the drop-dead stare, perfected a certain turn of the neck that conveyed an aloof inner authority. What you had to make them believe was that you knew something they didn't know yet. What you also had to make them believe was that they too could know this thing, this thing that would give them eminence and power and sexual allure, that would attract envy to them but for a price. The price of the magazine. What they could never get through their heads was that it was done entirely with cameras. Frozen light, frozen time. Given the angle, she could make any woman look ugly. Any man as well. She could make anyone look beautiful, or at least interesting. It was all pho-tography, it was all iconography. It was all in the choosing eye. This was the thing that could never be bought, no matter how much of your pitiful monthly wage you blew on snakeskin.

Despite the status, *the razor's edge* was fairly low-paying. Kat herself could not afford many of the things she contextualized so well. The grottiness and expense of London began to get to her; she got tired of gorging on the canapés at literary launches in order to scrimp on groceries, tired of the fuggy smell of cigarettes ground into the red-and-maroon carpeting of pubs, tired of the pipes bursting every time it froze in winter, and of the Clarissas and Melissas and Penelopes at the magazine rabbiting on about how they had been literally, absolutely, totally freezing all night, and how it literally, absolutely, totally, usually never got that cold. It always got that cold. The pipes always burst. Nobody thought of putting in real pipes, ones that would not burst next time. Burst pipes were an English tradition, like so many others.

Like, for instance, English men. Charm the knickers off you with their mellow vowels and frivolous verbiage, and then, once they'd got them off, panic and run. Or else stay and whinge. The English called it *whinging* instead of whining. It was better, really. Like a creaking hinge. It was a traditional compliment to be whinged at by an Englishman. It was his way of saying he trusted you, he was conferring upon you the privilege of getting to know the real him. The inner, whinging him. That was how they thought of women, secretly: whinge receptacles. Kat could play it, but that didn't mean she liked it.

She had an advantage over the English women, though: she was of no class. She had no class. She was in a class of her own. She could roll around among the English men, all different kinds of them, secure in the knowledge that she was not being measured against the class yardsticks and accent-detectors they carried around in their back pockets, was not subject to the petty snobberies and resentments that lent such richness to their inner lives. The flip side of this freedom was that she was beyond the pale. She was a colonial—how fresh, how vital, how anonymous, how finally of no consequence. Like a hole in the wall, she could be told all secrets and then be abandoned with no guilt.

She was too smart, of course. The English men were very competitive; they liked to win. Several times it hurt. Twice she had abortions, because the men in question were not up for the alternative. She learned to say that she didn't want children anyway, that if she longed for a rug-rat she would buy a gerbil. Her life began to seem long. Her adrenalin was running out. Soon she would be thirty, and all she could see ahead was more of the same.

This was how things were when Gerald turned up. "You're terrific," he said, and she was ready to hear it, even from him, even though *terrific* was a word that had probably gone out with fifties crew-cuts. She was ready for his voice by that time too: the flat, metallic nasal tone of the Great Lakes, with its clear hard r's and its absence of theatricality. Dull normal. The speech of her people. It came to her suddenly that she was an exile.

Gerald was scouting, Gerald was recruiting. He'd heard about her, looked at her work, sought her out. One of the big companies back in Toronto was launching a new fashion-oriented magazine, he said: upmarket, international in its coverage, of course, but with some Canadian fashion in it too, and with lists of stores where the items portrayed could actually be bought. In that respect they felt they'd have it all over the competition, those American magazines that assumed you could only get Gucci in New York or Los Angeles. Heck, times had changed, you could get it in Edmonton! You could get it in Winnipeg!

Kat had been away too long. There was Canadian fashion now? The English quip would be to say that "Canadian fashion" was an oxymoron. She refrained from making it, lit a cigarette with her cyanide-green Covent Garden–boutique leather-covered lighter (as featured in the May issue of *the razor's edge*), looked Gerald in the eye. "London is a lot to give up," she said levelly. She glanced around the see-me-here Mayfair restaurant where they were finishing lunch, a restaurant she'd chosen because she'd known he was paying. She'd never spend that kind of money on food otherwise. "Where would I eat?"

Gerald assured her that Toronto was now the restaurant capital of Canada. He himself would be happy to be her guide. There was a great Chinatown, there was world-class Italian. Then he paused, took a breath. "I've been meaning to ask you," he said. "About the name. Is that Kat as in Krazy?" He thought this was suggestive. She'd heard it before.

"No," she said. "It's Kat as in KitKat. That's a chocolate bar. Melts in your mouth." She gave him her stare, quirked her mouth, just a twitch.

Gerald became flustered, but he pushed on. They wanted her, they needed her, they loved her, he said in essence. Someone with her fresh, innovative approach and her experience would be worth a lot of money to them, relatively speaking. But there were rewards other than the money. She would be in on the initial concept, she would have a formative influence, she would have a free hand. He named a sum that made her gasp, inaudibly of course. By now she knew better than to betray desire.

So she made the journey back, did her three months of culture shock, tried the world-class Italian and the great Chinese, and seduced Gerald at the first opportunity, right in his junior vice-presidential office. It was the first time Gerald had been seduced in such a location, or perhaps ever. Even though it was after hours, the danger frenzied him. It was the idea of it. The daring. The image of Kat kneeling on the broadloom, in a legendary bra that until now he'd seen only in the lingerie ads of the Sunday *New York Times*, unzipping him in full view of the silver-framed engagement portrait of his wife that complemented the impossible ball-point pen set on his desk. At that time he was so straight he felt compelled to take off his wedding ring and place it carefully in the ashtray first. The next day he brought her a box of David Wood Food Shop chocolate truffles. They were the best, he told her, anxious that she should recognize their quality. She found the gesture banal, but also sweet. The banality, the sweetness, the hunger to impress: that was Gerald.

Gerald was the kind of man she wouldn't have bothered with in London. He was not funny, he was not knowledgeable, he had little verbal charm. But he was eager, he was tractable, he was blank paper. Although he was eight years older than she was, he seemed much younger. She took pleasure from his furtive, boyish delight in his own wickedness. And he was so grateful. "I can hardly believe this is happening," he said, more frequently than was necessary and usually in bed.

His wife, whom Kat encountered (and still encounters) at many tedious company events, helped to explain his gratitude. The wife was a priss. Her name was Cheryl. Her hair looked as if she still used big rollers and embalm-your-hairdo spray; her mind was room-by-room Laura Ashley wallpaper: tiny, unopened pastel buds arranged in straight rows. She probably put on rubber gloves to make love, and checked it off on a list afterwards. One more messy household chore. She looked at Kat as if she'd like to spritz her with air deodorizer. Kat revenged herself by picturing Cheryl's bathrooms: hand towels embroidered with lilies, fuzzy covers on the toilet seats.

The magazine itself got off to a rocky start. Although Kat had lots of lovely money to play with, and although it was a challenge to be working in colour, she did not have the free hand Gerald had promised her. She had to contend with the company board of directors, who were all men, who were all accountants or indistinguishable from them, who were cautious and slow as moles.

"It's simple," Kat told them. "You bombard them with images of what they ought to be, and you make them feel grotty for being the way they are. You're working with the gap between reality and perception. That's why you have to hit them with something new, something they've never seen before, something they aren't. Nothing sells like anxiety."

The board, on the other hand, felt that the readership should simply be offered more of what they already had. More fur, more sumptuous leather, more cashmere. More established names. The board had no sense of improvisation, no wish to take risks; no sporting instincts, no desire to put one over on the readers just for the hell of it. "Fashion is like hunting," Kat told them, hoping to appeal to their male hormones, if any. "It's playful, it's intense, it's predatory. It's blood and guts. It's erotic." But to them it was about good taste. They wanted Dress-for-Success. Kat wanted scattergun ambush.

Everything became a compromise. Kat had wanted to call the magazine *All the Rage*, but the board was put off by the vibrations of anger in the word "rage." They thought it was too feminist, of all things. "It's a *forties* sound," Kat said. "Forties is *back*. Don't you get it?" But they didn't. They wanted to call it *Or*. French for *gold*, and blatant enough in its values, but without any base note, as Kat told them. They sawed off at *Felice*, which had qualities each side wanted. It was vaguely French-sounding, it meant "happy" (so much less threatening than rage), and, although you couldn't expect the others to notice, for Kat it had a feline bouquet which counteracted the laciness. She had it done in hot-pink lipstick-scrawl, which helped some. She could live with it, but it had not been her first love.

This battle has been fought and refought over every innovation in design, every new angle Kat has tried to bring in, every innocuous bit of semi-kink. There was a big row over a spread that did lingerie, half pulled off and with broken glass perfume bottles strewn on the floor. There was an uproar over the two nouveau-stockinged legs, one tied to a chair with a third, different-coloured stocking. They had not understood the man's three-hundred-dollar leather gloves positioned ambiguously around a neck.

And so it has gone on, for five years.

After Gerald has left, Kat paces her living room. Pace, pace. Her stitches pull. She's not looking forward to her solitary dinner of microwaved leftovers. She's not sure now why she came back here, to this flat burg beside the polluted inland sea. Was it Ger? Ludicrous thought but no longer out of the question. Is he the reason she stays, despite her growing impatience with him?

He's no longer fully rewarding. They've learned each other too well, they take short-cuts now; their time together has shrunk from whole stolen rolling and sensuous afternoons to a few hours snatched between work and dinner-time. She no longer knows what she wants from him. She tells herself she's worth more, she should branch out; but she doesn't see other men, she can't, somehow. She's tried once or twice but it didn't work. Sometimes she goes out to dinner or a flick with one of the gay designers. She likes the gossip.

Maybe she misses London. She feels caged, in this country, in this city, in this room. She could start with the room, she could open a window. It's too stuffy in here. There's an undertone of formaldehyde, from Hairball's bottle. The flowers she got for the operation are mostly wilted, all except Gerald's from today. Come to think of it, why didn't he send her any at the hospital? Did he forget, or was it a message?

"Hairball," she says, "I wish you could talk. I could have a more intelligent conversation with you than with most of the losers in this turkey farm." Hairball's baby teeth glint in the light; it looks as if it's about to speak.

Kat feels her own forehead. She wonders if she's running a temperature. Something ominous is going on, behind her back. There haven't been enough phone calls from the magazine; they've been able to muddle on without her, which is bad news. Reigning queens should never go on vacation, or have operations either. Uneasy lies the head. She has a sixth sense about these things, she's been involved in enough palace coups to know the signs, she has sensitive antennae for the footfalls of impending treachery.

The next morning she pulls herself together, downs an espresso from her mini-machine, picks out an aggressive touch-me-if-you-dare suede outfit in armour grey, and drags herself to the office, though she isn't due in till next week. Surprise, surprise. Whispering knots break up in the corridors, greet her with false welcome as she limps past. She settles herself at her minimalist desk, checks her mail. Her head is pounding, her stitches hurt. Ger gets wind of her arrival; he wants to see her a.s.a.p., and not for lunch.

He awaits her in his newly done wheat-on-white office, with the eighteenth-century desk they chose together, the Victorian inkstand, the framed blow-ups from the magazine, the hands in maroon leather, wrists manacled with pearls, the Hermès scarf twisted into a blindfold, the model's mouth blossoming lusciously beneath it. Some of her best stuff. He's beautifully done up, in a lick-my-neck silk shirt open at the throat, an eat-your-heart-out Italian silk-and-wool loose-knit sweater. Oh, cool insouciance. Oh, eyebrow language. He's a money man who lusted after art, and now he's got some, now he is some. Body art. Her art. She's done her job well; he's finally sexy.

He's smooth as lacquer. "I didn't want to break this to you until next week," he says. He breaks it to her. It's the board of directors. They think she's too bizarre, they think she goes way too far. Nothing he could do about it, although naturally he tried.

Naturally. Betrayal. The monster has turned on its own mad scientist. "I gave you life!" she wants to scream at him.

She isn't in good shape. She can hardly stand. She stands, despite his offer of a chair. She sees now what she's wanted, what she's been missing. Gerald is what she's been missing—the stable, unfashionable, previous, tight-assed Gerald. Not Ger, not the one she's made in her own image. The other one, before he got ruined. The Gerald with a house and a small child and a picture of his wife in a silver frame on his desk. She wants to be in that silver frame. She wants the child. She's been robbed.

"And who is my lucky replacement?" she says. She needs a cigarette, but does not want to reveal her shaking hands.

"Actually, it's me," he says, trying for modesty.

This is too absurd. Gerald couldn't edit a phone book. "You?" she says faintly. She has the good sense not to laugh.

"I've always wanted to get out of the money end of things here," he says, "into the creative area. I knew you'd understand, since it can't be you at any rate. I knew you'd prefer someone who could, well, sort of build on your foundations." Pompous asshole. She looks at his neck. She longs for him, hates herself for it, and is powerless.

The room wavers. He slides towards her across the wheat-coloured broadloom, takes her by the grey suede upper arms. "I'll write you a good reference," he says. "Don't worry about that. Of course, we can still see one another. I'd miss our afternoons."

"Of course," she says. He kisses her, a voluptuous kiss, or it would look like one to a third party, and she lets him. *In a pig's ear.*

She makes it home in a taxi. The driver is rude to her and gets away with it; she doesn't have the energy. In her mailbox is an engraved invitation: Ger and Cheryl are having a drinks party, tomorrow evening. Postmarked five days ago. Cheryl is behind the times.

Kat undresses, runs a shallow bath. There's not much to drink around here, there's nothing to sniff or smoke. What an oversight; she's stuck with herself. There are other jobs. There are other men, or that's the theory. Still, something's been ripped out of her. How could this have happened, to her? When knives were slated for backs, she'd always done the stabbing. Any headed her way she's seen coming in time, and thwarted. Maybe she's losing her edge.

She stares into the bathroom mirror, assesses her face in the misted glass. A face of the eighties, a mask face, a bottom-line face; push the weak to the wall and grab what you can. But now it's the nineties. Is she out of style, so soon? She's only thirty-five, and she's already losing track of what people ten years younger are thinking. That could be fatal. As time goes by she'll have to race faster and faster to keep up, and for what? Part of the life she should have had is just a gap, it isn't there, it's nothing. What can be salvaged from it, what can be redone, what can be done at all?

When she climbs out of the tub after her sponge bath, she almost falls. She has a fever, no doubt about it. Inside her something is leaking, or else festering; she can hear it, like a dripping tap. A running sore, a sore from running so hard. She should go to the Emergency ward at some hospital, get herself shot up with antibiotics. Instead she lurches into the living room, takes Hairball down from the mantelpiece in its bottle, places it on the coffee table. She sits cross-legged, listens. Filaments wave. She can hear a kind of buzz, like bees at work.

She'd asked the doctor if it could have started as a child, a fertilized egg that escaped somehow and got into the wrong place. No, said the doctor. Some people thought this kind of tumour was present in seedling form from birth, or before it. It might be the woman's undeveloped twin. What they really were was unknown. They had many kinds of tissue, though. Even brain tissue. Though of course all of these tissues lack structure.

Still, sitting here on the rug looking in at it, she pictures it as a child. It has come out of her, after all. It is flesh of her flesh. Her child with Gerald, her thwarted child, not allowed to grow normally. Her warped child, taking its revenge.

"Hairball," she says. "You're so ugly. Only a mother could love you." She feels sorry for it. She feels loss. Tears run down her face. Crying is not something she does, not normally, not lately.

Hairball speaks to her, without words. It is irreducible, it has the texture of reality, it is not an image. What it tells her is everything she's never wanted to hear about herself. This is new knowledge, dark and precious and necessary. It cuts.

She shakes her head. What are you doing, sitting on the floor and talking to a hairball? You are sick, she tells herself. Take a Tylenol and go to bed.

The next day she feels a little better. Dania from layout calls her and makes dovelike, sympathetic coos at her, and wants to drop by during lunch hour to take a look at her aura. Kat tells her to come off it. Dania gets huffy, and says that Kat's losing her job is a price for immoral behaviour in a previous life. Kat tells her to stuff it; anyway, she's done enough immoral behaviour in this life to account for the whole thing. "Why are you so full of hate?" asks Dania. She doesn't say it like a point she's making, she sounds truly baffled.

"I don't know," says Kat. It's a straight answer.

After she hangs up she paces the floor. She's crackling inside, like hot fat under the broiler. What she's thinking about is Cheryl, bustling about her cosy house, preparing for the party. Cheryl fiddles with her freeze-framed hair, positions an overloaded vase of flowers, fusses about the caterers. Gerald comes in, kisses her lightly on the cheek. A connubial scene. His conscience is nicely washed. The witch is dead, his foot is on the body, the trophy; he's had his dirty fling, he's ready now for the rest of his life.

Kat takes a taxi to the David Wood Food Shop and buys two dozen chocolate truffles. She has them put into an oversized box, then into an oversized bag with the store logo on it. Then she goes home and takes Hairball out of its bottle. She drains it in the kitchen strainer and pats it damp-dry, tenderly, with paper towels. She sprinkles it with powdered cocoa, which forms a brown pasty crust. It still smells like formaldehyde, so she wraps it in Saran Wrap and then in tinfoil, and then in pink tissue paper, which she ties with a mauve bow. She places it in the David Wood box in a bed of shredded tissue, with the truffles nestled around. She closes the box, tapes it, puts it into the bag, stuffs several sheets of pink paper on top. It's her gift, valuable and dangerous. It's her messenger, but the message it will deliver is its own. It will tell the truth, to whoever asks. It's right that Gerald should have it; after all, it's his child too.

She prints on the card, "Gerald, Sorry I couldn't be with you. This is all the rage. Love, K."

When evening has fallen and the party must be in full swing, she calls a delivery taxi. Cheryl will not distrust anything that arrives in such an expensive bag. She will open it in public, in front of everyone. There will be distress, there will be questions. Secrets will be unearthed. There will be pain. After that, everything will go way too far.

She is not well; her heart is pounding, space is wavering once more. But outside the window it's snowing, the soft, damp, windless flakes of her childhood. She puts on her coat and goes out, foolishly. She intends to walk just to the corner, but when she reaches the corner she goes on. The snow melts against her face like small fingers touching. She has done an outrageous thing, but she doesn't feel guilty. She feels light and peaceful and filled with charity, and temporarily without a name.

John Barth

John Barth was born in 1930 on the Eastern Shore of Chesapeake Bay in Cambridge, Maryland. In a whimsical essay in *The Friday Book* called "Some Reasons Why I Tell the Stories I Tell the Way I Tell Them Rather Than Some Other Stories Some Other Way," Barth attributes his literary preoccupations with being a twin (twins communicate nonverbally, so "language is for relating to the Others"), to his training as a musician ("At heart I'm an arranger still, whose chiefest literary pleasure is to take a received melody—an old narrative poem, a classical myth, a shopworn literary convention, a shard of my experience . . . and improvising like a jazzman within its constraints, reorchestrate it to present purpose"), and to his work as a filing clerk in the stacks of the classical library at Johns Hopkins University, where he completed his M.A. in 1952. His publications include several novels, *The Floating Opera* (1956), *The End of the Road* (1958), *The Sot-Weed Factor* (1960), *Giles Goat-Boy* (1966), *LETTERS* (1979), and *Sabbatical: A Romance* (1982), a collection of short stories, *Lost in the Funhouse* (1968), and three novellas collected in *Chimera* (1972). He taught at Pennsylvania State and State University of New York at Buffalo before returning to his alma mater, Johns Hopkins.

"I don't think it's a good idea, as a rule, for artists to explain their art, even if they can," Barth has written. "Jorge Luis Borges puts it arrogantly: God shouldn't stoop to theology." And yet *The Friday Book* is full of insights on the craft of fiction. "The storyteller's trade," Barth says, "is the manufacture of universes." He sees himself as a transformer, creator of meaningful alternative worlds—thus his fascination with the Arabian classic *A Thousand and One Nights*: "If anything makes a writer out of me, it will be the digestion of that enormous slightly repetitive feast of narrative . . . ," Scheherazade "yarning tirelessly through the dark hours to save her neck." He lists Kafka, Calvino, Borges, Barthelme, and Hawkes among his favourite writers: "Like all fine fantasists, Calvino grounds his flights in local, palpable detail: Along with the nebulae and the black holes and the lyricism, there is a nourishing supply of pasta, bambina, and good-looking women sharply glimpsed and gone forever. A true postmodernist, Calvino keeps one foot in the narrative past. . . ."

Asked what literature is *about*, Barth says unequivocally: art is as much about itself, its shapes, forms, organizing principles as it is about any ostensible subject, such as childhood, politics, or birds. He does not reject history or fact or particular subjects, but does make these controversial assertions: "(1) Fiction about history almost never becomes part of the history of fiction; (2) The literature that finally matters in any culture is almost never principally about that culture; (3) Whatever else it is about, great literature is almost always about itself. On rare occasions it may even be mainly about itself, though it is almost never exclusively about itself, even when it seems to be."

Barth endorses McLuhan's proposition that the medium really is the message, that the process of narration becomes, in writers such as Calvino and Borges, the content of the narrative: ". . . most of them exploit, one way or another, ambiguities of language and narrative viewpoint—especially narrative viewpoint—to make their particular sense. Neither of these is a new idea. . . . One objective of these stories—the most important to me—is to try whether different kinds of artistical felt ultimacies and cul-de-sacs can be employed against themselves to do valid new work: whether disabling contradictions, for example, can be escalated or exacerbated into enabling paradoxes. This objective represents to me in its little way a general task of civilized people nowadays."

The foregrounding of language and narrative techniques, according to Bertolt Brecht and others, may be necessary to forge a new relationship between writer and reader. What Brecht called alienating devices, which break or challenge the old sympathetic contract, the suspension of disbelief, may, in the end, heighten and deepen our understanding of art and its necessary work. The artist may well be seen as a trickster figure, but his task, in Barth's view, is not mere trickery: "If I believed my writing were no more than the formal fun-and-games that *Time* magazine makes it out to be, I'd take up some other line of work. The subject of literature, says Aristotle, is 'human life, its happiness and its misery.' I agree with Aristotle."

Barth considers other elements more important than experimentalism in art: "Passion and virtuosity are what matter; where they are, they will shine through any aesthetics." In his talk "Tales within Tales within Tales," Barth returns to his favourite text to bolster his argument: "We tell stories and listen to them because we live stories and live in them. Narrative equals language equals life. To cease to narrate, as the capital example of Scheherazade reminds us, is to die—literally for her, figuratively for the rest of us. One might add that if this is true, then not only is all fiction fiction about fiction, but all fiction about fiction is in fact fiction about life. Some of us understood that all along."

Life-Story

1

Without discarding what he'd already written he began his story afresh in a somewhat different manner. Whereas his earlier version had opened in a straightforward documentary fashion and then degenerated or at least modulated
intentionally into irrealism and dissonance he decided this time to tell his tale
from start to finish in a conservative, "realistic," unself-conscious way. He being
by vocation an author of novels and stories it was perhaps inevitable that one
afternoon the possibility would occur to the writer of these lines that his own life
might be a fiction, in which he was the leading or an accessory character. He happened at the time[1] to be in his study attempting to draft the opening pages of a
new short story; its general idea had preoccupied him for some months along with
other general ideas, but certain elements of the conceit, without which he could
scarcely proceed, remained unclear. More specifically: narrative plots may be
imagined as consisting of a "ground-situation" (Scheherazade desires not to die)
focused and dramatized by a "vehicle-situation" (Scheherazade beguiles the King
with endless stories), the several incidents of which have their final value in
terms of their bearing upon the "ground-situation." In our author's case it was the
"vehicle" that had vouchsafed itself, first as a germinal proposition in his commonplace book—D comes to suspect that the world is a novel, himself a fictional
personage—subsequently as an articulated conceit explored over several pages of
the workbook in which he elaborated more systematically his casual inspirations:
since D is writing a fictional account of this conviction he has indisputably a fictional existence in his account, replicating what he suspects to be his own situation. Moreover E, hero of D's account, is said to be writing a similar account, and
so the replication is in both ontological directions, et cetera. But the "ground-situation"—some state of affairs on D's part which would give dramatic resonance to
his attempts to prove himself factual, assuming he made such attempts—obstinately withheld itself from his imagination. As is commonly the case the question
reduced to one of stakes: what were to be the consequences of D's—and finally
E's—disproving or verifying his suspicion, and why should a reader be interested?

What a dreary way to begin a story he said to himself upon reviewing his long
introduction. Not only is there no "ground-situation," but the prose style is heavy
and somewhat old-fashioned, like an English translation of Thomas Mann, and
the so-called "vehicle" itself is at least questionable: self-conscious, vertiginously
arch, fashionably solipsistic, unoriginal—in fact a convention of twentieth-century literature. Another story about a writer writing a story! Another regressus in
infinitum! Who doesn't prefer art that at least overtly imitates something other
than its own processes? That doesn't continually proclaim "Don't forget I'm an
artifice!"? That takes for granted its mimetic nature instead of asserting it in order
(not so slyly after all) to deny it, or vice-versa? Though his critics sympathetic and
otherwise described his own work as avant-garde, in his heart of hearts he disliked

literature of an experimental, self-despising, or overtly metaphysical character, like Samuel Beckett's, Marian Cutler's. Jorge Borges's. The logical fantasies of Lewis Carroll pleased him less than straightforward tales of adventure, subtly sentimental romances, even densely circumstantial realisms like Tolstoy's. His favorite contemporary authors were John Updike, Georges Simenon, Nicole Riboud. He had no use for the theater of absurdity, for "black humor," for allegory in any form, for apocalyptic preachments meretriciously tricked out in dramatic garb.

Neither had his wife and adolescent daughters, who for that matter preferred life to literature and read fiction when at all for entertainment. Their kind of story (his too, finally) would begin if not once upon a time at least with arresting circumstance, bold character, trenchant action. C flung away the whining manuscript and pushed impatiently through the french doors leading to the terrace from his oak-wainscoted study. Pausing at the stone balustrade to light his briar he remarked through a lavender cascade of wisteria that lithe-limbed Gloria, Gloria of timorous eye and militant breast, had once again chosen his boat-wharf as her basking-place.

By Jove he exclaimed to himself. It's particularly disquieting to suspect not only that one is a fictional character but that the fiction one's in—the fiction one is—is quite the sort one least prefers. His wife entered the study with coffee and an apple-pastry, set them at his elbow on his work table, returned to the living room. Ed' pelut' kondo nedode; nyoing nyang. One manifestation of schizophrenia as everyone knows is the movement from reality toward fantasy, a progress which not infrequently takes the form of distorted and fragmented representation, abstract formalism, an increasing preoccupation, even obsession, with pattern and design for their own sakes—especially patterns of a baroque, enormously detailed character—to the (virtual) exclusion of representative "content." There are other manifestations. Ironically, in the case of graphic and plastic artists for example the work produced in the advanced stages of their affliction may be more powerful and interesting than the realistic productions of their earlier "sanity." Whether the artists themselves are gratified by this possibility is not reported.

B called upon a literary acquaintance, B———, summering with Mrs. B and children on the Eastern Shore of Maryland. "You say you lack a ground-situation. Has it occurred to you that that circumstance may be your ground-situation? What occurs to me is that if it is it isn't. And conversely. The case being thus, what's really wanting after all is a well-articulated vehicle, a foreground or upstage situation to dramatize the narrator's or author's grundlage. His what. To write merely C comes to suspect that the world is a novel, himself a fictional personage is but to introduce the vehicle; the next step must be to initiate its uphill motion by establishing and complicating some conflict. I would advise in addition the eschewal of overt and self-conscious discussion of the narrative process. The via negativa and its positive counterpart are it is to be remembered poles after all of the same cell. Returning to his study.

If I'm going to be a fictional character G declared to himself I want to be in a rousing good yarn as they say, not some piece of avant-garde preciousness. I want passion and bravura action in my plot, heroes I can admire, heroines I can love, memorable speeches, colorful accessory characters, poetical language. It doesn't matter to me how naively linear the anecdote is; never mind modernity! How reactionary J appears to be. How will such nonsense sound thirty-six years from now?[2] As if. If he can only get K through his story I reflected grimly; if he can only retain his self-possession to the end of this sentence; not go mad; not destroy himself and/or others. Then what I wondered grimly. Another sentence fast, another story. Scheherazade my only love! All those nights you kept your secret from the King my rival, that after your defloration he was unnecessary, you'd have killed yourself in any case when your invention failed.

Why could he not begin his story afresh X wondered, for example with the words why could he not begin his story afresh et cetera? Y's wife came into the study as he was about to throw out the baby with the bathwater. "Not for an instant to throw out the baby while every instant discarding the bathwater is perhaps a chief task of civilized people at this hour of the world."[3] I used to tell B—— that without success. What makes you so sure it's not a film he's in or a theater-piece?

Because U responded while he certainly felt rather often that he was merely acting his own role or roles he had no idea who the actor was, whereas even the most Stanislavsky-methodist would presumably if questioned closely recollect his offstage identity even onstage in mid-act. Moreover a great pair of T's "drama," most of his life in fact, was non-visual, consisting entirely in introspection, which the visual dramatic media couldn't manage easily. He had for example mentioned to no one his growing conviction that he was a fictional character, and since he was not given to audible soliloquizing a "spectator" would take him for a cheerful, conventional fellow, little suspecting that et cetera. It was of course imaginable that much goes on in the mind of King Oedipus in addition to his spoken sentiments; any number of interior dramas might be being played out in the actors' or characters' minds, dramas of which the audience is as unaware as are V's wife and friends of his growing conviction that he's a fictional character. But everything suggested that the medium of his life was prose fiction—moreover a fiction narrated from either the first-person or the third-person-omniscient point of view.

Why is it L wondered with mild disgust that both K and M for example choose to write such stuff when life is so sweet and painful and full of such a variety of people, places, situations, and activities other than self-conscious and after all rather blank introspection? Why is it N wondered et cetera that both M and O et cetera when the world is in such parlous explosive case? Why et cetera et cetera et cetera when the word, which was in the beginning, is now evidently nearing the end of its road? Am I being strung out in this ad libitum fashion I wondered merely to keep my author from the pistol? What sort of story is it whose drama lies always in the next frame out? If Sinbad sinks it's Scheherazade who drowns; whose neck one wonders is on her line?

2

Discarding what he'd already written as he could wish to discard the mumbling pages of his life he began his story afresh, resolved this time to eschew overt and self-conscious discussion of his narrative process and to recount instead in the straight-forwardest manner possible the several complications of his character's conviction that he was a character in a work of fiction, arranging them into dramatically ascending stages if he could for his readers' sake and leading them (the stages) to an exciting climax and dénouement if he could.

He rather suspected that the medium and genre in which he worked—the only ones for which he felt any vocation—were moribund if not already dead. The idea pleased him. One of the successfullest men he knew was a blacksmith of the old school who et cetera. He meditated upon the grandest sailing-vessel ever built, the *France II*, constructed in Bordeaux in 1911 not only when but because the age of sail had passed. Other phenomena that consoled and inspired him were the great flying-boat *Hercules*, the zeppelin *Hindenburg*, the *Tsar Pushka* cannon, the then-record Dow-Jones industrial average of 381.17 attained on September 3, 1929.

He rather suspected that the society in which he persisted—the only one with which he felt any degree of identification—was moribund if not et cetera. He knew beyond any doubt that the body which he inhabited—the only one et cetera—was et cetera. The idea et cetera. He had for thirty-years lacking a few hours been one of our dust mote's three billion tenants give or take five hundred million, and happening to be as well a white male citizen of the United States of America he had thirty-six years plus a few hours more to cope with one way or another unless the actuarial tables were mistaken, not bloody likely, or his term was unexpectedly reduced.

Had he written for his readers' sake? The phrase implied a hitherto-unappreciated metaphysical dimension. Suspense. If his life was a fictional narrative it consisted of three terms—teller, tale, told—each dependent on the other two but not in the same ways. His author could as well tell some other character's tale or some other tale of the same character as the one being told as he himself could in his own character as author; his "reader" could as easily read some other story, would be well advised to; but his own "life" depended absolutely on a particular author's original persistence, thereafter upon some reader's. From this consideration any number of things followed, some less tiresome than others. No use appealing to his author, of whom he'd come to dislike even to think. The idea of his playing with his characters' and his own self-consciousness! He himself tended in that direction and despised the tendency. The idea of his or her smiling smugly to himself as the "words" flowed from his "pen" in which his the protagonist's unhappy inner life was exposed! Ah he had mistaken the nature of his narrative; he had thought it very long, longer than Proust's, longer than any German's, longer than *The Thousand Nights and a Night* in ten quarto volumes. Moreover he'd thought it the most prolix and pedestrian *tranche-de-vie* realism, unredeemed by even the limited virtues of colorful squalor, solid specification, an engaging variety of scenes and characters—in a word a bore, of the sort he himself not only would not write but would not read either. Now he understood that his author might as probably resemble himself and the protagonist of his own story-in-progress. Like himself, like his character aforementioned, his author not impossibly deplored the obsolescence of humanism, the passing of *savoir-vivre*, et cetera; admired the outmoded values of fidelity, courage, tact, restraint, amiability, self-discipline, et cetera; preferred fictions in which were to be found stirring actions, characters to love as well as ditto to despise, speeches and deeds to affect us strongly, et cetera. He too might wish to make some final effort to put by his fictional character and achieve factuality or at least to figure in if not be hero of a more attractive fiction, but be caught like the writer of these lines in some more or less desperate tour de force. For him to attempt to come to an understanding with such an author were as futile as for one of his own creations to et cetera.

But the reader! Even if his author were his only reader as was he himself of his work-in-progress as of the sentence-in-progress and his protagonist of his, et cetera, his character as reader was not the same as his character as author, a fact which might be turned to account. What suspense.

As he prepared to explore this possibility one of his mistresses whereof he had none entered his brown study unannounced. "The passion of love," she announced, "which I regard as no less essential to a satisfying life than those values itemized above and which I infer from my presence here that you too esteem highly, does not in fact play in your life a role of sufficient importance to sustain my presence here. It plays in fact little role at all outside your imaginative and/or ary life. I tell you this not in a criticizing spirit, for I judge you to be as capable of the sentiment aforementioned as any other imagin[ative], deep-feeling man in good physical health more or less precisely in the middle of the road of our life. What hampers, even cripples you in this regard is your final preference, which I refrain from analyzing, for the sedater, more responsible pleasures of monogamous fidelity and the serener affections of domesticity, notwithstanding the fact that your enjoyment of these is correspondingly inhibited though not altogether spoiled by an essentially romantical, unstable, irresponsible, death-wishing fancy. V. S. Pritchett, English critic and author, will put the matter succinctly in a soon-to-be-written essay on Flaubert, whose work he'll say depicts the course of ardent longings and violent desires that rise from the horrible, the sensual, and the sadistic. They turn into the virginal and mystical, only to become numb by satiety. At this point pathological boredom leads to a final desire for death and nothingness—the Romantic syndrome. If, not to be unfair, we qualify somewhat the terms horrible and sadistic and understand satiety to include a large measure of vicariousness, this description undeniably applies to one aspect of yourself and your work; and while your ditto has other, even contrary aspects, the net fact is that you have elected familial responsibilities and rewards—indeed, straight-laced middle-classness in general—over the higher expenses of spirit and wastes of shame attendant upon a less regular, more glamorous style of life. So to elect is surely admirable for the layman, even essential if the social fabric, without which there can be no culture, is to be preserved. For the artist, however, and in particular the writer, whose traditional material has been the passions of men and women, the choice is fatal. You having made it I bid you goodnight probably forever."

Even as she left he reached for the sleeping pills cached conveniently in his writing desk and was restrained from their administration only by his being in the process of completing a sentence, which he cravenly strung out at some sacrifice of rhetorical effect upon realizing that he was et cetera. Moreover he added hastily he had not described the intruder for his readers' vicarious satiety: a lovely woman she was, whom he did not after all describe for his readers' et cetera inasmuch as her appearance and character were inconstant. Her interruption of his work inspired a few sentences about the extent to which his fiction inevitably made public his private life, though the trespasses in this particular were as nothing beside those of most of his profession. That is to say, while he did not draw his characters and situations directly from life nor permit his author-protagonist to do so, any moderately attentive reader of his oeuvre, his what, could infer for example that its author feared for example schizophrenia, impotence creative and sexual, suicide—in short living and dying. His fictions were preoccupied with these fears among their other, more serious preoccupations. Hot dog. As of the sentence-in-progress he was not in fact unmanageably schizophrenic, impotent in either respect, or dead by his own hand, but there was always the next sentence to worry about. But there was always the next sentence to worry about. In sum he concluded hastily such limited self-exposure did not constitute a misdemeanor, representing or mis as it did so small an aspect of his total self, negligible a portion of his total life—even which totalities were they made in public would be found remarkable only for their being so unremarkable. Well shall he continue.

Bearing in mind that he had not developed what he'd mentioned earlier about turning to advantage his situation vis-à-vis his "reader" (in fact he deliberately now postponed his return to that subject, sensing that it might well constitute the climax of his story) he elaborated one or two ancillary questions, perfectly aware that he was trying, even exhausting, whatever patience might remain to whatever readers might remain to whoever elaborated yet another ancillary question. Was the novel of his life for example a *roman à clef*. ? Of that genre he was as contemptuous as of the others aforementioned; but while in the introductory adverbial clause it seemed obvious to him that he didn't "stand for" anyone else, any more than he was an actor playing the role of himself, by the time he reached the main clause he had to admit that the question was unanswerable, since the "real" man to whom he'd correspond in a *roman à clef* would not be also in the *roman à clef* and the characters in such works were not themselves aware of their irritating correspondences.

Similarly unanswerable were such questions as when "his" story (so he regarded it for convenience and consolement though for all he knew he might be not the central character; it might be his wife's story, one of his daughters', his imaginary mistress's, the man-who-once-cleaned-his-chimney's) began. Not impossibly at his birth or even generations earlier: a *Bildungsroman*, an *Erziehungsroman*, a *roman fleuve!* More likely at the moment he became convinced of his fictional nature: that's where he'd have begun it, as he'd begun the piece currently under his pen. If so it followed that the years of his childhood and younger manhood weren't "real," he'd suspected as much, in the first-order sense, but a mere "background" consisting of a few well-placed expository insinuations, perhaps misleading, or inferences, perhaps unwarranted, from strategic hints in his present reflections. God so to speak spare his readers from heavy-footed forced expositions of the sort that begin in the countryside near ____ in May of the year ____ It occurred to the novelist ____ that his own life might be a ____, in which he was the leading or an accessory character. He happened at the time to be in the oak-wainscoted study of the old family summer residence; through a lavender cascade of hysteria he observed that his wife had once again chosen to be the subject of this clause, itself the direct object of his observation. A lovely woman she was, whom he did not describe in keeping with his policy against drawing characters from life as who should draw a condemnee to the gallows. Begging his pardon. Flinging his tiresome tale away he pushed impatiently through the french windows leading from his study to a sheer drop from the then-record high into a nearly fatal depression.

He clung onto his narrative depressed by the disproportion of its ratiocination to its dramatization, reflection to action. One had heard *Hamlet* criticized as a collection of soliloquies for which the implausible plot was a mere excuse; witnessed Italian operas whose dramatic portions were no more than interstitial relief and arbitrary continuity between the arias. If it was true that he didn't take his "real" life seriously enough even when it had him by the throat, the fact didn't lead him to consider whether the fact was a cause or a consequence of his tale's tedium or both.

Concluding these reflections he concluded these reflections: that there was at this advanced page still apparently no ground-situation suggested that his story was dramatically meaningless. If one regarded the absence of a ground-situation, more accurately the protagonist's anguish at that absence and his vain endeavors to supply the defect, as itself a sort of ground-situation, did his life-story thereby take on a kind of meaning? A "dramatic" sort he supposed, though of so sophistical a character as more likely to annoy than to engage

3

The reader! You, dogged, uninsultable, print-oriented bastard, it's you I'm addressing, who else, from inside this monstrous fiction. You've read me this far then? Even this far? For what discreditable motive? How is it you don't go to a movie, watch TV, stare at a wall, play tennis with a friend, make amorous advances to the person who comes to your mind when I speak of amorous advances? Can nothing surfeit, saturate you, turn you off? Where's your shame?

Having let go this barrage of rhetorical or at least unanswered questions and observing himself nevertheless in midst of yet another sentence he concluded and caused the "hero" of his story to conclude that one or more of three things must be true: 1) his author was his sole and indefatigable reader; 2) he was in a sense his own author, telling his story to himself, in which case in which case; and/or 3) his reader was not only tireless and shameless but sadistic, masochistic if he was himself.

For why do you suppose—you! you!—he's gone on so, so relentlessly refusing to entertain you as he might have at a less desperate than this hour of the world[4] with felicitous language, exciting situation, unforgettable character and image? Why has he as it were ruthlessly set about not to win you over but to turn you away? Because your own author bless and damn you his life is in your hands! He writes and reads himself; don't you think he knows who gives his creatures their lives and deaths? Do they exist except as he or others read their words? Age except we turn their pages? And can he die until you have no more of him? Time was obviously when his author could have turned the trick; his pen had once to left-to-right it through these words as does your kindless eye and might have ceased at any one. This. This. And did not as you see but went on like an Oriental torturemaster to the end.

But you needn't! He exclaimed to you. In vain. Had he petitioned you instead to read slowly in the happy parts, what happy parts, swiftly in the painful no doubt you'd have done the contrary or cut him off entirely. But as he longs to die and can't without your help you force him on, force him on. Will you deny you've read this sentence? This? To get away with murder doesn't appeal to you, is that it? As if your hands weren't inky with other dyings! As if he'd know you'd killed him! Come on. He dares you.

In vain. You haven't: the burden of his knowledge. That he continues means that he continues, a fortiori you too. Suicide's impossible: he can't kill himself without your help. Those petitions aforementioned, even his silly plea for death—don't you think he understands their sophistry, having authored their like for the wretches he's authored? Read him fast or slow, intermittently, continuously, repeatedly, backward, not at all, he won't know it; he only guesses someone's reading or composing his sentences, such as this one, because he's reading or composing sentences such as this one; the net effect is that there's a net effect, of continuity and an apparently consistent flow of time, though his pages do seem to pass more swiftly as they near his end.

To what conclusion will he come? He'd been about to append to his own tale inasmuch as the old analogy between Author and God, novel and world, can no longer be employed unless deliberately as a false analogy, certain things follow: 1) fiction must acknowledge its fictitiousness and metaphoric invalidity or 2) choose to ignore the question or deny its relevance or 3) establish some other, acceptable relation between itself, its author, its reader. Just as he finished doing so however his real wife and imaginary mistresses entered his study; "It's a little past midnight" she announced with a smile; "do you know what that means?"

Though she'd come into his story unannounced at a critical moment he did not describe her, for even as he recollected that he'd seen his first light just thirty-six years before the night incumbent he saw his last: that he could not after all be a character in a work of fiction inasmuch as such a fiction would be of an entirely different character from what he thought of as fiction. Fiction consisted of such monuments of the imagination as Cutler's Morganfield, Riboud's *Tales Within Tales*, his own creations; fact of such as for example read those fictions. More, he could demonstrate by syllogism that the story of his life was a work of fact: though assaults upon the boundary between life and art, reality and dream, were undeniably a staple of his own and his century's literature as they'd been of Shakespeare's and Cervantes's, yet it was a fact that in the corpus of fiction as far as he knew no fictional character had become convinced as had he that he was a character in a work of fiction. This being the case and he having in fact become thus convinced it followed that his conviction was false. "Happy birthday," said his wife et cetera, kissing him et cetera to obstruct his view of the end of the sentence he was nearing the end of, playfully reusing to be nay-said so that in fact he did at last as did his fictional character end his ending story endless by interruption, cap his pen.

1. 9:00 A.M., Monday, June 20, 1966.
2. 10:00 A.M., Monday, June 20, 1966.
3. 11:00 A.M., Monday, June 20, 1966.
4. 11:00 P.M., Monday, June 20, 1966.

Donald Barthelme

Donald Barthelme was born 1931 in Philadelphia, but grew up in Houston, Texas, where his father was an avant-garde architect. They lived in a house built by his father, which was so unusual for its time that people would park their cars on the street and stare. "We had a routine, the family, on Sundays," Barthelme says. "We used to get up from Sunday dinner, if enough cars had parked, and run out in front of the house in a sort of chorus line, doing high kicks." While a student at the University of Houston, he founded a literary magazine and worked as a reporter for a local newspaper. He served in the army briefly, then returned to Houston, where he worked in public relations and was director of a contemporary arts museum. He moved to New York in the early sixties, publishing ten stories in the *The New Yorker* in a period of two years. His collections of short stories include *Come Back, Dr. Caligari* (1964), *Unspeakable Practices, Unnatural Acts* (1968), *City Life* (1970), *Sadness* (1972), *Guilty Pleasures* (1976), *Sixty Stories* (1981), *Overnight in Many Distant Cities* (1983), and *Forty Stories* (1986). He also published several longer works of fiction, including the novels, *Snow White* (1967), *The Dead Father* (1975), and *Paradise* (1986).

Barthelme's work is highly attuned to changes in society, both physical and attitudinal. As he explains in an interview with Jo Brans in *Listen to the Voices*, "Well, I think there are two devices that have clearly had an enormous impact on language. One is television. I don't wish to blame television for all the faults of the world, but it has had a vulgarizing effect. The other is the telephone, because we don't write letters anymore. I don't write letters—I don't even write business letters. I call on the telephone. When people don't write letters, language deteriorates."

Although he admires traditional forms of fiction, particularly the work of writers such as John Cheever, Barthelme chooses to do something different. "I was trying to make art, and I didn't want to do it as Cheever does it, although I admire very much what Cheever does. . . . I was trying to do something else. I suppose I was trying—in the crudest statement—I was trying to make fiction that was like certain kinds of modern painting. You know, tending toward the abstract. But it's really very dicey in fiction, because if you get too abstract it just looks like fog, for example. . . . The project is next to impossible, which is what makes it interesting. There's nothing so beautiful as having a very

difficult problem. It gives purpose to life. And to work. I'm still worrying with it."

While he would like to think that art makes a difference in society, Barthelme admits, as a writer, to a feeling of powerlessness to bring about change. He also rejects the notion that the morality of art lies in its content. Like Joseph Conrad and Ezra Pound, he asserts that the morality of art lies in style, or technique: "I do believe that my every sentence trembles with morality. It's full of morality. But it's the morality of an attempt. It's not the morality of giving you precepts. To decide as [John] Gardner would that my enterprise is immoral because it doesn't preach to you or elevate you in some dubious way—*On Moral Fiction* was clearly an attempt at a Saint Valentine's Day Massacre. That's what's so funny about it. It's so overt."

If the making of art, as Barthelme insists, is itself a highly moral act, then the writer who labours over form, rather than merely wearing hand-me-downs from tradition, may well be functioning at the greatest moral intensity. Barthelme's own struggles with form might prompt readers to conclude that he is not writing realistic fiction, but he insists that he is a realist: "Everybody's a realist. Every writer is offering a true account of the activities of the mind. . . . I think the distinction between who's a realist and who's a surrealist and who's a superrealist is slightly specious. By definition, one can only offer the activity of the individual mind, however it's notated. It's all realism."

Barthelme has always been alert to the possibility of alternative structures for fiction, whether derived from mathematics, physics, chemistry, or the other arts, particularly music. Asked by interviewer Jerome Klinkowitz (*The New Fiction*, ed. Joe David Bellamy) about the centrality of the principle of collage in twentieth-century media, Barthelme said: "New York is or can be regarded as a collage, as opposed to, say, a tribal village in which all of the huts (or yurts, or whatever) are the same hut, duplicated. The point of collage is that unlike things are stuck together to make, in the best case, a new reality. This new reality, in the best case, may be or imply a comment on the other reality from which it came, and may be also much else. It's an itself, if it's successful: Harold Rosenberg's 'anxious object,' which does not know whether it's a work of art or a pile of junk. (Maybe I should have said that anxiety is the central principle of all art. . . .)"

Sentence

Or a long sentence moving at a certain pace down the page aiming for the bottom—
if not the bottom of this page then of some other page—where it can rest, or stop for
a moment to think about the questions raised by its own (temporary) existence,
which ends when the page is turned, or the sentence falls out of the mind that holds
it (temporarily) in some kind of an embrace, not necessarily an ardent one, but more
perhaps the kind of embrace enjoyed (or endured) by a wife who has just waked up
and is on her way to the bathroom in the morning to wash her hair, and is bumped
into by her husband, who has been lounging at the breakfast table reading the newspaper, and didn't see her coming out of the bedroom, but, when he bumps into her,
or is bumped into by her, raises his hands to embrace her lightly, transiently, because
he knows that if he gives her a real embrace so early in the morning, before she has
properly shaken the dreams out of her head, and got her duds on, she won't respond,
and may even become slightly angry, and say something wounding, and so the husband invests in this embrace not so much physical or emotional pressure as he might,
because he doesn't want to waste anything—with this sort of feeling, then, the sentence passes through the mind more or less, and there is another way of describing
the situation too, which is to say that the sentence crawls through the mind like
something someone says to you while you're listening very hard to the FM radio,
some rock group there, with its thrilling sound, and so, with your attention or the
major part of it at least already awarded, there is not much mind room you can give
to the remark, especially considering that you have probably just quarreled with that
person, the maker of the remark, over the radio being too loud, or something like
that, and the view you take, of the remark, is that you'd really rather not hear it, but
if you have to hear it, you want to listen to it for the smallest possible length of time,
and during a commercial, because immediately after the commercial they're going to
play a new rock song by your favorite group, a cut that has never been aired before,
and you want to hear it and respond to it in a new way, a way that accords with
whatever you're feeling at the moment, or might feel, if the threat of new experience
could be (temporarily) overbalanced by the promise of possible positive benefits, or
what the mind construes as such, remembering that these are often, really, disguised
defeats (not that such defeats are not, at times, good for your character, teaching you
that it is not by success alone that one surmounts life, but that setbacks, too, contribute to that roughening of the personality that, by providing a textured surface to
place against that of life, enables you to leave slight traces, or smudges, on the face of
human history—your mark) and after all, benefit-seeking always has something of
the smell of raw vanity about it, as if you wished to decorate your own brow with
laurel, or wear your medals to a cookout, when the invitation had said nothing about
them, and although the ego is always hungry (we are told) it is well to remember that
ongoing success is nearly as meaningless as ongoing lack of success, which can make
you sick, and that it is good to leave a few crumbs on the table for the rest of your
brethren, not to sweep it all into the little beaded purse of your soul but to allow
others, too, part of the gratification, and if you share in this way you will find the

clouds smiling on you, and the postman bringing you letters, and bicycles available when you want to rent them, and many other signs, however guarded and limited, of the community's (temporary) approval of you, or at least of its willingness to let you believe (temporarily) that it finds you not so lacking in commendable virtues as it had previously allowed you to think, from its scorn of your merits, as it might be put, or anyway its consistent refusal to recognize your basic humanness and its secret blackball of the project of your remaining alive, made in executive session by its ruling bodies, which, as everyone knows, carry out concealed programs of reward and punishment, under the rose, causing faint alterations of the status quo, behind your back, at various points along the periphery of community life, together with other enterprises not dissimilar in tone, such as producing films that have special qualities, or attributes, such as a film where the second half of it is a holy mystery, and girls and women are not permitted to see it, or writing novels in which the final chapter is a plastic bag filled with water, which you can touch, but not drink: in this way, or ways, the underground mental life of the collectivity is botched, or denied, or turned into something else never imagined by the planners, who, returning from the latest seminar in crisis management and being asked what they have learned, say they have learned how to throw up their hands; the sentence meanwhile, although not insensible of these considerations, has a festering conscience of its own, which persuades it to follow its star, and to move with all deliberate speed from one place to another, without losing any of the "riders" it may have picked up just being there, on the page, and turning this way and that, to see what is over there, under that oddly-shaped tree, or over there, reflected in the rain barrel of the imagination, even though it is true that in our young manhood we were taught that short, punchy sentences were best (but what did he mean? doesn't "punchy" mean punch-drunk? I think he probably intended to say "short, *punching* sentences," meaning sentences that lashed out at you, bloodying your brain if possible, and looking up the word just now I came across the nearby "punkah," which is a large fan suspended from the ceiling in India, operated by an attendant pulling a rope—that is what I want for my sentence, to keep it cool!) we are mature enough now to stand the shock of learning that much of what we were taught in our youth was wrong, or improperly understood by those who were teaching it, or perhaps shaded a bit, the shading resulting from the personal needs of the teachers, who as human beings had a tendency to introduce some of their heart's blood into their work, and sometimes this may not have been of the first water, this heart's blood, and even if they thought they were moving the "knowledge" out, as the Board of Education had mandated, they could have noticed that their sentences weren't having the knockdown power of the new weapons whose bullets tumble end-over-end (but it is true that we didn't have these weapons at that time) and they might have taken into account the fundamental dubiousness of their project (but all the intelligently conceived projects have been eaten up already, like the moon and the stars) leaving us, in our best clothes, with only things to do like conducting vigorous wars of attrition against our wives, who have now thoroughly come awake, and slipped into their striped bells, and pulled sweaters over their torsi, and adamantly refused to wear any bras under the sweaters, carefully explaining the political significance of this refusal to anyone who will listen, or look, but not touch, because that has nothing to do with it, so they say; leaving us, as it were, with only things to do like floating sheets of Reynolds Wrap around the room, trying to find out how many we can keep in the air at the same time, which at least gives us a sense of participation, as though we were the Buddha, looking down at the mystery of your smile, which needs to be investigated, and I think I'll do that right now, while there's still enough light, if you'll sit down over there, in the best chair, and take off all your clothes, and put your feet in that electric toe caddy (which prevents pneumonia) and slip into this permanent press white hospital gown, to cover your nakedness—why, if you do all that, we'll be ready to begin! after I wash my hands, because you pick up an amazing amount of exuviae in this city, just by walking around in the open air, and nodding to acquaintances, and speaking to friends, and copulating with lovers, in the ordinary course (and death to our enemies! by the by)—but I'm getting a little uptight, just about washing my hands, because I can't find the soap, which somebody has used and not put back in the soap dish, all of which is extremely irritating, if you have a beautiful patient sitting in the examining room, naked inside her gown, and peering at her moles in the mirror, with her immense brown eyes following your every movement (when they are not watching the moles, expecting them, as in a Disney nature film, to exfoliate) and her immense brown head wondering what you're going to do to her, the pierced places in the head letting that question leak out, while the therapist decides just to wash his hands in plain water, and hang the soap! and does so, and then looks around for a towel, but all the towels have been collected by the towel service, and are not there, so he wipes his hands on his pants, in the back (so as to avoid suspicious stains on the front) thinking: what must she think of me? and, all this is very unprofessional and at-sea looking! trying to visualize the contretemps from her point of view, if she has one (but how can she? she is not in the washroom) and then stopping, because it is finally his own point of view that he cares about and not hers, and with this firmly in mind, and a light, confident step, such as you might find in the works of Bulwer-Lytton, he enters the space she occupies so prettily and, taking her by the hand, proceeds to tear off the stiff white hospital gown (but no, we cannot have that kind of pornographic *merde* in this majestic and high-minded sentence, which will probably end up in the Library of Congress) (that was just something that took place inside his consciousness, as he looked at her, and since we know that consciousness is always consciousness *of* something, she is not entirely without responsibility in the matter) so, then, taking her by the hand, he falls into the stupendous white purée of her abyss, no, I mean rather that he asks her how long it has been since her last visit, and she says a fortnight, and he shudders, and tells her that with a condition like hers (she is an immensely popular soldier, and her troops win all their battles by pretending to be forests, the enemy discovering, at the last moment, that those trees they have eaten their lunch under have eyes and swords) (which reminds me of the performance, in 1845, of Robert-Houdin, called *The Fantastic Orange Tree*, wherein Robert-Houdin borrowed a lady's handkerchief, rubbed it between his hands and passed it into the center of an egg, after which he passed the egg into the center of a lemon, after which he passed the lemon into the center of an orange, then pressed the orange between his hands, making it smaller and smaller, until only a powder remained, whereupon he asked for a small potted orange tree and sprinkled the powder thereupon, upon which the tree burst into blossom, the blossoms turning into oranges, the oranges turning into butterflies, and the butterflies turning into beautiful young ladies, who then married members of the audience), a condition so damaging to real-time social intercourse of any kind, the best thing she can do is give up, and lay down her arms, and he will lie down in them, and together they will permit themselves a bit of the old slap and tickle, she wearing only her Mr. Christopher medal, on its silver chain, and he (for such is the latitude granted the professional classes) worrying about the sentence, about its thin wires of dramatic tension, which have been omitted, about whether we should write down some natural events occurring in the sky (birds, lightning bolts), and about a possible coup d'état within the sentence, whereby its chief verb would be—but at this moment a messenger rushes into the sentence, bleeding from a hat of thorns he's wearing, and cries out: "You don't know what you're doing! Stop making this sentence, and begin instead to make Moholy-Nagy cocktails, for those are what we really need, on the frontiers of bad behavior!" and then he falls to the floor, and a trap door opens under him, and he falls through that, into a damp pit where a blue narwhal waits, its horn poised (but maybe the weight of the messenger, falling from such a height, will break off the horn)—thus, considering everything carefully, in the sweet light of the ceremonial axes, in the run-mad skimble-skamble of information sickness, we must make a decision as to whether we should proceed, or go back, in the latter case enjoying the pathos of eradication, in the former case reading an erotic advertisement which begins, *How to Make Your Mouth a Blowtorch of Excitement* (but wouldn't that overtax our mouthwashes?) attempting, during the pause, while our burned mouths are being smeared with fat, to imagine a better sentence, worthier, more meaningful, like those in the Declaration of Independence, or a bank statement showing that you have seven thousand kroner more than you thought you had—a statement summing up the unreasonable demands that you make on life, and one that also asks the question, if you can imagine these demands, why are they not routinely met, tall fool? but of course it is not that query that this infected sentence has set out to answer (and hello! to our girl friend, Rosetta Stone, who has stuck by us through thin and thin) but some other query that we shall some day discover the nature of, and here comes Ludwig, the expert on sentence construction we have borrowed from the Bauhaus, who will—"Guten Tag, Ludwig!"—probably find a way to cure the sentence's sprawl, by using the improved ways of thinking developed in Weimar—"I am sorry to inform you that the Bauhaus no longer exists, that all of the great masters who formerly thought there are either dead or retired, and that I myself have been reduced to constructing books on how to pass the examination for police sergeant"—and Ludwig falls through the Tugendhat House into the history of man-made objects; a disappointment, to be sure, but it reminds us that the sentence itself is a man-made object, not the one we wanted of course, but still a construction of man, a structure to be treasured for its weakness, as opposed to the strength of stones

John Berger

John Berger was born in London, England, in 1926 and now resides in a small farming community in France, the locale of *Pig Earth* (1979), *Once in Europa* (1983), and *Lilac and Flag* (1990), the trilogy that documents the breakdown of the agrarian way of life. As he says in his essay "The Story-teller" (in *The Sense of Sight: Writings by John Berger*, 1985), "A village's portrait of itself is constructed, not out of stone, but out of words, spoken and remembered: out of opinions, stories, eye-witness reports, legends, comments and hearsay. And it is a continuous portrait; work on it never stops." Berger has worked as a screenwriter, a novelist (best known for the experimental work, G), a documentary writer, and is one of Britian's most influential art critics, whose critical works include *The Success and Failure of Picasso, Art and Revolution, The Look of Things: Selected Essays and Articles,* and *Ways of Seeing.*

Berger is as profoundly interested in story-telling, that wonderful art of shaping and constructing memory, as he is in ways of seeing. He describes the story-teller as the "historian of our time . . . who sees how events fit together." While he claims to have thought of writing not as a profession, but as "a solitary independent activity in which practice can never bestow seniority," he still sees writing as somehow communal, an act of solidarity: "Writing, as I know it, has no territory of its own. The act of writing is nothing except the act of approaching the experience written about; just as, hopefully, the act of reading the written text is a comparable act of approach.

"To approach experience, however, is not like approaching a house. Experience is indivisible and continuous, at least within a single lifetime and perhaps over many lifetimes. I never have the impression that my experience is entirely my own, and it often seems to me that it preceded me. In any case experience folds upon itself, refers backwards and forwards to itself through the referents of hope and fear; and, by the use of metaphor which is at the origin of language, it is continually comparing like with unlike, what is small with what is large, what is near with what is distant. And so the act of approaching a given moment of experience involves both scrutiny (closeness) and the capacity to connect (distance). The movement of writing resembles that of a shuttlecock: repeatedly it approaches and withdraws, closes in and takes its distance. Unlike a shuttlecock, however, it is not fixed to a static frame. As the movement of writing repeats itself, its nearness to, its intimacy with the experience increases. Finally, if one is fortunate, meaning is the fruit of this intimacy."

In this same essay, Berger identifies two forms of realism: "Professional and traditional. Professional realism, as a method chosen by an artist or writer like myself, is always consciously political; it aims to shatter an opaque part of the ruling ideology, whereby, normally, some aspect of reality is consistently distorted or denied. Traditional realism, always popular in its origins, is in a sense more scientific than political. Assuming a fund of empirical knowledge and experience, it poses the riddle of the unknown. How is it that . . . ? Unlike science it can live without an answer. But its experience is too great to allow it to ignore the question."

In another essay from *The Sense of Sight* called "The White Bird," Berger outlines the fundamentals of his aesthetic by discussing the relation of our response to art with that of our response to nature. In examining an intricately carved wooden bird, he describes our response as "at least a momentary sense of being before a mystery. One is looking at a piece of wood that has become a bird. One is looking at something that has been worked with a mysterious skill and a kind of love." The love Berger identifies exists in both creator and viewer, in writer and reader, in what we have come to call the experience of art. The essay concludes with a statement that goes some way towards explaining, albeit indirectly, what he is trying to do in is own fiction.

"Years ago, when considering the historical face of art, I wrote that I judged a work according to whether or not it helped men in the modern world claim their social rights. I hold to that. Art's other, transcendental face raises the questions of man's ontological right. . . . The notion that art is the mirror of nature is one that appeals only in periods of skepticism. Art does not imitate nature, it imitates a creation, sometimes to propose an alternative world, sometimes simply to amplify, to confirm, to make social the brief hope offered by nature. Art is an organized response to what nature allows us to glimpse occasionally. Art sets out to transform the potential recognition into an unceasing one. It proclaims man in the hope of receiving a surer reply . . . the transcendental face of art is always a form of prayer."

Play Me Something

What is it that men have and women don't and which is hard and long?

On your left is the city of Verona, announced the bus driver over the loud-speaker. Verona was conquered by the Ostrogoths, later by the Barbarians, and still later by the Austrians. In the fourteenth century Verona was the setting of the love story between Romeo and Juliet.

What is it that men have and women don't which is hard and long?

Tell us! demanded the boys.

Military service!

The flatness of the surrounding countryside was unfamiliar, making it difficult to judge distances. The coach was traveling fast, yet it seemed that time passed and nothing changed.

You see their maize? They're two months ahead of us.

Finally the coach crossed the motor causeway to the Queen of Cities. In the vaporetto the men stood up very straight, as if on parade. This was because they were reminded of the first time they had left the village as conscripts in the army. The women lounged on the deck seats, and the younger ones pulled up their skirts to bare their legs to the sun. The vaporetto swayed first to one side and then to the other, like a woman pedaling very slowly on a bicycle.

How would you like a white suit like the ship's captain?

Look at those insects!

Where?

There!

She's been drinking!

He must change it every day.

Look! Along the water line.

Good God, yes, thousands of them.

They come up for the sun.

They're crabs.

I've never seen crabs that size.

You don't know what to look at.

I tell you, it looks like a flood.

You couldn't make cheese here!

They disembarked at the Piazza San Marco and climbed the circular staircase of the Campanile. Afterwards the men were thirsty and insisted upon having a drink in one of the cafés on the piazza, which Napoleon called the largest ball-room in Europe.

It costs more to piss here than to drink a whole case at home!

Inside the café he noticed a poster announcing a festival organized by *L'Unità*, the Communist daily newspaper. Why not?

They crossed the Bridge of Sighs and stopped beneath a statue of Eve in the courtyard of the Doge's Palace.

It's a wife like that you need!

Later the men climbed onto the terrace of the Cathedral of San Marco to look at the horses.

The festival was to be held on the island of Giudecca. From the Doge's Palace he could see the coloured lights decorating the buildings across the water and from time to time he heard a strain of music.

If you're not at the bus station by two, we'll know they drowned you.

He's more adventurous than the rest of you men!

He sat in the stern of the vaporetto with his instrument case on his knees.

You're not from here.

These words were addressed to him by a young woman with magenta lipstick and white sandals.

How is that?

You look too quiet.

You know what I have in this box?

She shook her head. She had glasses and her black hair was drawn back in a chignon.

A trombone.

It's not true, she cried. Play it! Please, play something.

Not here on the boat, he said. Are you going to the festival? If you brought it with you, you must have had the idea of playing it.

We came from the mountains. I didn't want to leave it in the bus.

Around her neck was a white necklace.

You, do you live down here?

In Mestri, across the bay, where the oil tanks are. And you—I'd say you work on a farm.

How do you know?

I can smell the cows.

If she had been a man, he would have hit her.

What do you think I smell of?

Scent.

Correct. I work in a chemist's shop.

One look at your hands told me you didn't work with them. Do you know what my father calls that?

No.

Infantile proletarianism.

He said nothing. Perhaps it was a Venetian expression.

The vaporetto was approaching the island. Hung from the first-storey windows on the far side of the piazza were banderolas with slogans printed on them. He could make out the hammer and sickle. As he stepped ashore, he held his instrument case tightly under his arm. The festival, he reminded himself, was organized by the Communist Party, but this did not mean there were no thieves there. He could spot them already.

Do you like dancing? she asked.

I can't dance carrying this. Give it to me. She disappeared with his instrument case into one of the nearby buildings. And if it's stolen? he said, when she came back empty-handed.

Comrade, she replied, this is a workers' festival, and workers do not steal from one another.

Peasants do! he said.

What is your name?

Bruno. And yours?

Marietta.

He held up his arm for her to take his hand. He did not dance like a man from here, she thought. He was more single-minded, as if, when dancing, he put everything else out of his mind.

What is it like on your mountain? There are rhodos and wild goats.

Rhodos?

Little bushes of flowers.

Pink?

Blood-red. How do they vote in your village?

For the right.

And you?

I vote for anyone who promises to raise the price of milk.

That isn't good for the workers.

Milk is all we have to sell.

They were dancing round a plane tree in a corner of the piazza. In the tree was a loudspeaker, perched like an owl on one of the branches.

You came here alone? she asked.

With the whole band.

A band of friends?

The brass band of the village.

The next time the owl fell silent he proposed that they should have a drink. She guided him to a table beneath a gigantic portrait, drawn on a sheet and hung from the top windows of a house. The painted face was so large that even the flanks of the nose had been drawn with a six-inch house-painter's brush. They looked up at it together.

Do you live alone? she asked.

Yes, I've lived alone for eight years. A fifth of my life.

She liked the way he hesitated before speaking, it was very deliberate, as if each time he answered one of her questions, he came to the door of a house, opened it to a visitor, and then spoke.

How many mirrors do you have at home? She asked this as if it were a schoolgirl's riddle.

He paused to count.

One over the sink, one over the drinking trough outside.

She laughed. He poured out more white wine.

That's Karl Marx, isn't it? He nodded up at the sheet.

Marx was a great prophet. What do you see in the future? she asked.

The rich getting richer.

I mean your future.

Mine? Everything depends upon my health.

You don't look sick to me.

If you're sent to hospital when you are sick, your dog doesn't look after your cows. I live alone.

She raised her glass to his. I think I could find you work in Mestri.

He was looking at her small feet, thinking: everything between a man and a woman is a question of how much you give up of one thing to have another—an exchange.

You are bound to be influenced by the property relations of which you are a part. Her voice was tender, as if she were explaining something intimate. The Kulaks sided with the bourgeoisie, and the little peasants with the petit bourgeoisie. You are wrong to think only about the price of milk.

She comes, he told himself, from this place of water and islands where there is no earth at all.

The fact is peasants will disappear, she continued, the future lies elsewhere.

I'd like to have children, he said.

You have to find a wife.

He poured out more wine.

You'd find a wife if you moved here.

I'd cut off my right hand rather than work in a factory.

All the men dancing there, she said, they're nearly all factory workers.

He had never seen so many men in white shirts. They wore their shirts tied round their waists to show off their stomachs. They were as cunning as weasels. Their cuffs were rolled back only halfway up their forearms, as if they had just got out of bed.

Do they caress well? he asked.

Who?

The weasels over there.

Caress?

What a man should do to a woman.

Let's dance, she said.

The owl was hooting a tango.

Who's milking the cows tonight? she whispered.

Who am I dancing with?

Marietta is dancing with Bruno, she said, as he pulled her hand up and looked along their arms—as if taking aim with a gun.

As the tempo increased they advanced and turned more and more quickly. People began to watch them. His shirt and his heavy shoes announced he was from the country. But he danced well, they made a couple. Some of the bystanders began to clap in time with the music. It was like watching a duel—a duel between the paving stones and their four feet. How long would they keep it up?

Now they were walking down a narrow street, with old men on wicker chairs, and grandmothers playing with balloons to amuse their grandchildren. At the end of the street was suspended another gigantic portrait: a great domed head, like a beehive of thought, wearing glasses.

That's Gramsci.

He put his arm round her shoulders so that she could lean her head against his damp flannel shirt.

Antonio Gramsci, she said. He taught us all.

You wouldn't mistake him for a horse dealer! he said.

Past the portrait, they came to a cobbled quayside overlooking the lagoon toward Murano. In places grass had grown over the cobbles. He stared across the black water and she, carrying her sandals, wandered over to an abandoned gondola, moored by the corner of the Rio di Santa Eufemia. She sat down on the platform by the stern near the wooden oarlock. Sun and water had stripped the gondola of its paint, which was now wood grey. It must once have belonged to a wine merchant, for several demijohns lay on their sides in the prow.

Do you think they are empty? she asked him.

Instead of answering, he jumped into the gondola, which rocked violently. Making his way forward to the prow, he did his best to correct every lurch by leaning in the opposite direction, like someone dancing in a conga line.

Sit down, for God's sake, sit down! she shouted.

She was crouching in the bottom of the boat. Its sides were smacking the water and splashing the air.

He picked up a demijohn and held it against the sky with one hand as if wringing the neck of a goose.

Empty! he boomed.

Sit! she shrieked. Sit!

This is how they found themselves lying on the rush mat in the bottom of the gondola. After a while the smacking of the water ceased and a quiet lapping took its place. Yet the calm did not last long. Soon the gondola was again lurching from side to side with water dripping from its gunwales and its staves thumping the lagoon.

If we capsize, can you swim? she whispered.

No.

Yes, Bruno, yes, yes, yes . . .

Afterwards they lay on their backs, panting.

Look at the stars. Don't they make you feel small? she said.

The stars look down at us, she continued, and sometimes I think everything, everything except killing, everything takes so long because they are so far away.

His other hand was trailing in the water. Her teeth bit his ear.

The world changes so slowly.

His hand from the water grasped her breast.

One day there'll be no more classes. I believe that, don't you? she murmured and pulled his head down to her other breast.

There's always been good and bad, he said.

We're making progress, don't you believe that?

All our ancestors asked the same thing, he said, you and I will never know in this life why it was made the way it is.

He entered her again. The gondola smacked the water and splashed the air.

When they crossed the narrow island to the pierhead, where the last vaporetto would stop, the music was over. Only a few drunks, immobile as statues, remained in the piazza. Marietta went to fetch his instrument case. He gazed across the lagoon. He could see the bell-tower they had climbed. The guide said it had toppled over at the beginning of the century. No roots. He remembered the date: 14th July 1902, the year of his father's birth. To the right there were still lights in the Doge's Palace. According to the guide, the palace had been destroyed or partly destroyed by fire seven times. There had never been peace in that building. Too much power and no roots. One day it would be robbed and pillaged and after that it would be used as a hen house.

Marietta handed him his instrument case.

Play for me. Play me something.

He put the case down on the quayside. Out of his pocket he took a small mouth organ, and turning toward the Doge's Palace, began to play. The music was speaking to him.

Before it is light—

She was staring at his back, relaxed and downcast like the back of a man peeing, except that his hands were to his mouth.

—Before it is light . . . when you've dressed and gone into the stable—

With her fingers she was touching the nape of his neck.

—the animals are lying there—

She was pressing her hand between his shoulder blades and could feel his lungs and the music in the roof of his mouth.

—lying there on beech leaves, and your tiredness like a child you have dragged from its sleep—

Her hand felt under the belt of his trousers.

—and through the window you see the span of the stars—

She noticed that one of his bootlaces was undone. She knelt down to tie it for him.

—the spin of the stars into whose well we are thrown at birth like salt into water—

Neither of them noticed the vaporetto approaching the pierhead.

Come to Mestri, she sighed, come to Mestri. I'll find you work.

The bus left at 3 A.M. Most of the band wanted to sleep. Some husbands put their heads on their wives' shoulders, in other cases the wife leaned her head against her man. The lights were switched out one by one as the coach took the road for Verona. The young drummer sitting beside Bruno tried one last joke.

Do you know what hell is?

Do you?

Hell is where bottles have two holes and women have none.

Ambrose Bierce

Known as the author of *The Devil's Dictionary* (1906), which abounds in witty epigrams and scathing denunciations of all kinds of pretention, Ambrose Bierce is also the author of two collections of short stories, *In the Midst of Life*, which was privately published as *Tales of Soldiers and Civilians* in 1891, and *Can Such Things Be?* (1893). He loved the short story form for its precision and economy, contrasting it with the novel, which he describes as "a diluted story—a story cumbered with trivialities and nonessentials." He adhered to Poe's notion that the best work might be "read at a single sitting" and have "unity, totality of effect." "The first three essentials of the literary art," he wrote, "are imagination, imagination, imagination."

In denigrating the novel—"a species of composition bearing the same relation to literature that panorama bears to art"—Bierce holds up for approval the model of the romance, which he claims "knows no law but that of its own artistic development"; it is vital, essential, and free to invent. Rejecting local colour and the excesses of realistic writing, Bierce seems a precursor of such European writers as Conrad, Joyce, and Virginia Woolf. He eschews not only novels, but also short stories written for the magazine market, a talent that, he says, "can not be acquired," but must be born into: "The torch must be passed down the line by the thumbless hands of an illustrious line of prognathous ancestors unacquainted with fire." Against such third-rate journalism, what he calls the Reporter School, stories laden down with sentiment and excessive documentation, in the interests of *vraisemblance* ("Are we given dialogue? It is not enough to report what was said, but the record must be authenticated by enumeration of the inanimate objects—commonly articles of furniture—which were privileged to be present at the conversation"), Bierce reasserts the cliché that "nothing is so probable as what is true": "Fiction has nothing to do with probability; the capable writer gives it not a moment's attention, except to make what is related *seem* probable in the reading—*seem* true."

Bierce's comments on William Dean Howells, in an essay called "The Short Story," constitute one of the finest satirical attacks ever written and reveal yet another example of his abilities as a stylist: "I want to be fair: Mr. Howells has considerable abilities. He is insufferable only in fiction and when, in criticism, he is making fiction's laws with one eye upon his paper and the other upon a catalogue of his own novels. When not carrying that heavy load, himself, he has a manly enough stride. He is not upon very intimate terms with the English language, but on many subjects, and when you least expect it of him, he thinks with such precision as momentarily to subdue a disobedient vocabulary and keep out the wrong word. Now and then he catches an accidental glimpse of his subject in a sidelight and tells with capital vivacity what it is not. The one thing that he never sees is the question that he has raised by inadvertence, deciding it by implication against his convictions. If Mr. Howells had never written fiction his criticism of novels would entertain, but the imagination which can conceive him as writing a good story under any circumstances would be a precious literary possession, enabling its owner to write a better one."

The humour and wonderfully biting satire of his critical writings might not prepare a reader for the dark intensity of Bierce's fictional vision. He was born in poverty in a log cabin in Horse Cave Creek, Ohio (his date of birth, though uncertain, may have been 1842), the youngest of nine children. He had almost no formal education, except for a year at the Kentucky Military Institute. He joined the 9th Indiana Infantry as a drummer, fought throughout the Civil War, was wounded, and had the rank of major when he was discharged. Bierce found nothing glorious in war and described his career as that of a "hired assassin." He began his newspaper career in San Francisco, lived briefly in London, then settled down to write stories and columns in California until his wife left him and his two sons died tragically. Personal grief and professional neglect led him to an uncertain fate in Mexico in 1914, but not before he had supervised the publication of his twelve-volume *Collected Works*.

An Occurrence at Owl Creek Bridge

A man stood upon a railroad bridge in Northern Alabama, looking down into the swift waters twenty feet below. The man's hands were behind his back, the wrists bound with a cord. A rope loosely encircled his neck. It was attached to a stout cross-timber above his head, and the slack fell to the level of his knees. Some loose boards laid upon the sleepers supporting the metals of the railway supplied a footing for him and his executioners—two private soldiers of the Federal army, directed by a sergeant, who in civil life may have been a deputy sheriff. At a short remove upon the same temporary platform was an officer in the uniform of his rank, armed. He was captain. A sentinel at each end of the bridge stood with his rifle in the position known as "support," that is to say, vertical in front of the left shoulder, the hammer resting on the forearm thrown straight across the chest—a formal and unnatural position, enforcing an erect carriage of the body. It did not appear to be the duty of these two men to know what was occurring at the center of the bridge; they merely blockaded the two ends of the foot plank which traversed it.

Beyond one of the sentinels nobody was in sight; the railroad was lost to view. Doubtless there was an outpost further along. The other bank of the stream was open ground—a gentle acclivity crowned with a stockade of vertical tree trunks, loop-holed for rifles, with a single embrasure through which protruded the muzzle of a brass cannon commanding the bridge. Midway of the slope between bridge and fort were the spectators—a single company of infantry in line, at "parade rest," the butts of the rifles on the ground, the barrels inclining slightly backward against the right shoulder, the hands crossed upon the stock. A lieutenant stood at the right of the line, the point of his sword upon the ground, his left hand resting upon his right. Excepting the group of four at the center of the bridge not a man moved. The company faced the bridge staring stonily, motionless. The sentinels, facing the banks of the stream, might have been statues to adorn the bridge. The captain stood with folded arms, silent, observing the work of his subordinates but making no sign. Death is a dignitary who, when he comes announced, is to be received with formal manifestations of respect, even by those most familiar with him. In the code of military etiquette silence and fixity are forms of deference.

The man who was engaged in being hanged was apparently about thirty-five years of age. He was a civilian, if one might judge from his dress, which was that of a planter. His features were good—a straight nose, firm mouth, broad forehead, from which his long, dark hair was combed straight back, falling behind his ears to the collar of his well-fitting frock coat. He wore a mustache and pointed beard, but no whiskers; his eyes were large and dark grey and had a kindly expression which one would hardly have expected in one whose neck was in the hemp. Evidently this was no vulgar assassin. The liberal military code makes provision for hanging many kinds of people, and gentlemen are not excluded.

The preparations being complete, the two private soldiers stepped aside and each drew away the plank upon which he had been standing. The sergeant turned to the captain, saluted and placed himself immediately behind that officer who in turn moved apart one pace. These movements left the condemned man and the sergeant standing on the two ends of the same plank, which spanned three of the cross-ties of the bridge. The end upon which the civilian stood almost, but not quite, reached a fourth. This plank had been held in place by the weight of the captain; it was now held by that of the sergeant. At a signal from the former, the latter would step aside, the plank would tilt and the condemned man go down between two ties. The arrangement commended itself to his judgment as simple and effective. His face had not been covered nor his eyes bandaged. He looked a moment at his "unsteadfast footing," then let his gaze wander to the swirling water of the stream racing madly beneath his feet. A piece of dancing driftwood caught his attention and his eyes followed it down the current. How slowly it appeared to move! What a sluggish stream!

He closed his eyes in order to fix his last thoughts upon his wife and children. The water, touched to gold by the early sun, the brooding mists under the banks at some distance down the stream, the fort, the soldiers, the piece of drift—all had distracted him. And now he became conscious of a new disturbance. Striking through the thought of his dear ones was a sound which he could neither ignore nor understand, a sharp distinct metallic percussion like the stroke of blacksmith's hammer upon the anvil; it had the same ringing quality. He wondered what it was, and whether immeasurably distant or near by—it seemed both. Its recurrence was regular, but as slow as the tolling of a death knell. He awaited each stroke with impatience and—he knew not why—apprehension. The intervals of silence grew progressively longer; the delays became maddening. With their greater infrequency the sounds increased in strength and sharpness. They hurt his ear like the thrust of a knife; he feared he would shriek. What he heard was the ticking of his watch.

He unclosed his eyes and saw again the water below him. "If I could free my hands," he thought, "I might throw off the noose and spring into the stream. By diving I could evade the bullets, and, swimming vigorously, reach the bank, take to the woods, and get away home. My home, thank God, is as yet outside their lines; my wife and little ones are still beyond the invader's farthest advance."

As these thoughts, which have here to be set down in words, were flashed into the doomed man's brain rather than evolved from it, the captain nodded to the sergeant. The sergeant stepped aside.

II

Peyton Farquhar was a well-to-do planter, of an old and highly respected Alabama family. Being a slave owner, and, like other slave owners, a politician, he was naturally an original secessionist and ardently devoted to the Southern cause. Circumstances of an imperious nature which it is unnecessary to relate here, had prevented him from taking service with the gallant army which had fought the disastrous campaigns ending with the fall of Corinth, and he chafed under the inglorious restraint, longing for the release of his energies, the larger life of the soldier, the opportunity for distinction. That opportunity, he felt, would come, as it comes to all in war time. Meanwhile he did what he could. No service was too humble for him to perform in aid of the South, no adventure too perilous for him to undertake if consistent with the character of a civilian who was at heart a soldier, and who in good faith and without too much qualification assented to at least a part of the frankly villainous dictum that all is fair in love and war.

One evening while Farquhar and his wife were sitting on a rustic bench near the entrance to his grounds, a grey-clad soldier rode up to the gate and asked for a drink of water. Mrs. Farquhar was only too happy to serve him with her own white hands. While she was gone to fetch the water, her husband approached the dusty horseman and inquired eagerly for news from the front.

"The Yanks are repairing the railroads," said the man, "and are getting ready for another advance. They have reached the Owl Creek bridge, put it in order, and built a stockade on the other bank. The commandant has issued an order, which is posted everywhere, declaring that any civilian caught interfering with the railroad, its bridges, tunnels, or trains, will be summarily hanged. I saw the order."

"How far is it to the Owl Creek bridge?" Farquhar asked.

"About thirty miles."

"Is there no force on this side the creek?"

"Only a picket post half a mile out, on the railroad, and a single sentinel at this end of the bridge."

"Suppose a man—a civilian and student of hanging—should elude the picket post and perhaps get the better of the sentinel," said Farquhar, smiling, "what could he accomplish?"

The soldier reflected. "I was there a month ago," he replied. "I observed that the flood of last winter had lodged a great quantity of driftwood against the wooden pier at this end of the bridge. It is now dry and would burn like tow."

The lady had now brought the water, which the soldier drank. He thanked her ceremoniously, bowed to her husband, and rode away. An hour later, after night-fall, he repassed the plantation, going northward in the direction from which he had come. He was a Federal scout.

III

As Peyton Farquhar fell straight downward through the bridge, he lost consciousness and was as one already dead. From this state he was awakened—ages later, it seemed to him—by the pain of a sharp pressure upon his throat, followed by a sense of suffo-cation. Keen, poignant agonies seemed to shoot from his neck downward through every fiber of his body and limbs. These pains appeared to flash along well defined lines of ramification, and to beat with an inconceivably rapid periodicity. They seemed like streams of pulsating fire heating him to an intolerable temperature. As to his head, he was conscious of nothing but a feeling of fullness—of congestion. These sensations were unaccompanied by thought. The intellectual part of his nature was already effaced; he had power only to feel, and feeling was torment. He was con-scious of motion. Encompassed in a luminous cloud, of which he was now merely the fiery heart, without material substance, he swung through unthinkable arcs of oscilla-tion, like a vast pendulum. Then all at once, with terrible suddenness, the light about him shot upward with the noise of a loud splash; a frightful roaring was in his ears, and all was cold and dark. The power of thought was restored; he knew that the rope had broken and he had fallen into the stream. There was no additional strangu-lation; the noose about his neck was already suffocating him, and kept the water from his lungs. To die of hanging at the bottom of a river!—the idea seemed to him ludicrous. He opened his eyes in the blackness and saw above him a gleam of light, but how distant, how inaccessible! He was still sinking, for the light became fainter and fainter until it was a mere glimmer. Then it began to grow and brighten, and he knew that he was rising toward the surface—knew it with reluctance, for he was now very comfortable. "To be hanged and drowned," he thought, "that is not so bad; but I do not wish to be shot. No; I will not be shot; that is not fair."

He was not conscious of an effort, but a sharp pain in his wrist apprised him that he was trying to free his hands. He gave the struggle his attention, as an idler might observe the feat of a juggler, without interest in the outcome. What splendid effort!—what magnificent, what superhuman strength! Ah, that was a fine endeavor! Bravo! The cord fell away; his arms parted and floated upward, the hands dimly seen on each side in the growing light. He watched them with a new interest as first one and then the other pounced upon the noose at his neck. They tore it away and thrust it fiercely aside, its undulations resembling those of a water-snake. "Put it back, put it back!" He thought he shouted these words to his hands, for the undoing of the noose had been succeeded by the direst pang which he had yet experienced. His neck ached horribly; his brain was on fire; his heart, which had been fluttering faintly, gave a great leap, trying to force itself out at his mouth. His whole body was racked and wrenched with an insupportable anguish! But his disobedient hands gave no heed to the command. They beat the water vigorously with quick, downward strokes, forcing him to the surface. He felt his head emerge; his eyes were blinded by the sunlight; his chest expanded convulsively, and with supreme and crowning agony his lungs engulfed a great draught of air, which instantly he expelled in a shriek!

He was now in full possession of his physical senses. They were, indeed, preternaturally keen and alert. Something in the awful disturbance of his organic system had so exalted and refined them that they made record of things never before perceived. He felt the ripples upon his face and heard their separate sounds as they struck. He looked at the forest on the bank of the stream, saw the individual trees, the leaves and the veining of each leaf—saw the very insects upon them, the locusts, the brilliant-bodied flies, the grey spiders stretching their webs from twig to twig. He noted the prismatic colors in all the dewdrops upon a million blades of grass. The humming of the gnats that danced above the eddies of the stream, the beating of the dragon flies' wings, the strokes of the water spiders' legs, like oars which had lifted their boat—all these made audible music. A fish slid along beneath his eyes and he heard the rush of its body parting the water.

He had come to the surface facing down the stream; in a moment the visible world seemed to wheel slowly round, himself the pivotal point, and he saw the bridge, the fort, the soldiers upon the bridge, the captain, the sergeant, the two privates, his executioners. They were a silhouette against the blue sky. They shouted and gesticulated, pointing at him; the captain had drawn his pistol, but did not fire; the others were unarmed. Their movements were grotesque and horrible, their forms gigantic.

Suddenly he heard a sharp report and something struck the water smartly within a few inches of his head, spattering his face with spray. He heard a second report, and saw one of the sentinels with his rifle at his shoulder, a light cloud of blue smoke rising from the muzzle. The man in the water saw the eye of the man on the bridge gazing into his own through the sights of the rifle. He observed that it was a grey eye, and remembered having read that grey eyes were keenest and that all famous marksmen had them. Nevertheless, this one had missed.

A counter swirl had caught Farquhar and turned him half round; he was again looking into the forest on the bank opposite the fort. The sound of a clear, high voice in a monotonous singsong now rang out behind him and came across the water with a distinctness that pierced and subdued all other sounds, even the beating of the ripples in his ears. Although no soldier, he had frequented camps enough to know the dread significance of that deliberate, drawling, aspirated chant; the lieutenant on shore was taking a part in the morning's work. How coldly and pitilessly—with what an even, calm intonation, presaging and enforcing tranquillity in the men—with what accurately-measured intervals fell those cruel words:

"Attention, company. . . . Shoulder arms. . . . Ready. . . . Aim . . . Fire."

Farquhar dived—dived as deeply as he could. The water roared in his ears like the voice of Niagara, yet he heard the dulled thunder of the volley, and rising again toward the surface, met shining bits of metal, singularly flattened, oscillating slowly downward. Some of them touched him on the face and hands, then fell away, continuing their descent. One lodged between his collar and neck; it was uncomfortably warm, and he snatched it out.

As he rose to the surface, gasping for breath, he saw that he had been a long time under water; he was perceptibly farther down stream—nearer to safety. The soldiers had almost finished reloading; the metal ramrods flashed all at once in the sunshine as they were drawn from the barrels, turned in the air; and thrust into their sockets. The two sentinels fired again, independently and ineffectually.

The hunted man saw all this over his shoulder; he was now swimming vigorously with the current. His brain was as energetic as his arms and legs; he thought with the rapidity of lightning.

"The officer," he reasoned, "will not make that martinet's error a second time. It is as easy to dodge a volley as a single shot. He has probably already given the command to fire at will. God help me, I cannot dodge them all!"

An appalling plash within two yards of him, followed by a loud rushing sound, diminuendo, which seemed to travel back through the air to the fort and died in an explosion which stirred the very river to its deeps! A rising sheet of water, which curved over him, fell down upon him, blinded him, strangled him! The cannon had taken a hand in the game. As he shook his head free from the commotion of the smitten water, he heard the deflected shot humming through the air ahead, and in an instant it was cracking and smashing the branches in the forest beyond.

"They will not do that again; "the next time they will use a charge of grape. I must keep my eye upon the gun; the smoke will apprise me—the report arrives too late; it lags behind the missile. It is a good gun."

Suddenly he felt himself whirled round and round—spinning like a top. The water, the banks, the forest, the now distant bridge, fort and men—all were commingled and blurred. Objects were represented by their colors only; circular horizontal streaks of color—that was all he saw. He had been caught in a vortex and was being whirled on with a velocity of advance and gyration which made him giddy and sick. In a few moments he was flung upon the gravel at the foot of the left bank of the stream—the southern bank—and behind a projecting point which concealed him from his enemies. The sudden arrest of his motion, the abrasion of one of his hands on the gravel, restored him and he wept with delight. He dug his fingers into the sand, threw it over himself in handfuls and audibly blessed it. It looked like gold, like diamonds, rubies, emeralds; he could think of nothing beautiful which it did not resemble. The trees upon the bank were giant garden plants; he noted a definite order in their arrangement, inhaled the fragrance of their blooms. A strange, roseate light shone through the spaces among their trunks, and the wind made in their branches the music of aeolian harps. He had no wish to perfect his escape, was content to remain in that enchanting spot until retaken.

A whizz and rattle of grapeshot among the branches high above his head roused him from his dream. The baffled cannoneer had fired him a random farewell. He sprang to his feet, rushed up the sloping bank, and plunged into the forest.

All that day he travelled, laying his course by the rounding sun. The forest seemed interminable; nowhere did he discover a break in it, not even a woodman's road. He had not known that he lived in so wild a region. There was something uncanny in the revelation.

By nightfall he was fatigued, footsore, famishing. The thought of his wife and children urged him on. At last he found a road which led him in what he knew to be the right direction. It was as wide and straight as a city street, yet it seemed untravelled. No fields bordered it, no dwelling anywhere. Not so much as the barking of a dog suggested human habitation. The black bodies of the great trees formed a straight wall on both sides, terminating on the horizon in a point, like a diagram in a lesson in perspective. Overhead, as he looked up through this rift in the wood, shone great golden stars looking unfamiliar and grouped in strange constellations. He was sure they were arranged in some order which had a secret and malign significance. The wood on either side was full of singular noises, among which—once, twice, and again—he distinctly heard whispers in an unknown tongue.

His neck was in pain, and, lifting his hand to it, he found it horribly swollen. He knew that it had a circle of black where the rope had bruised it. His eyes felt congested; he could no longer close them. His tongue was swollen with thirst; he relieved its fever by thrusting it forward from between his teeth into the cool air. How softly the turf had carpeted the untravelled avenue! He could no longer feel the roadway beneath his feet!

Doubtless, despite his suffering, he fell asleep while walking, for now he sees another scene—perhaps he has merely recovered from a delirium. He stands at the gate of his own home. All is as he left it, and all bright and beautiful in the morning sunshine. He must have travelled the entire night. As he pushes open the gate and passes up the wide white walk, he sees a flutter of female garments; his wife, looking fresh and cool and sweet, steps down from the verandah to meet him. At the bottom of the steps she stands waiting, with a smile of ineffable joy, an attitude of matchless grace and dignity. Ah, how beautiful she is! He springs forward with extended arms. As he is about to clasp her, he feels a stunning blow upon the back of the neck; a blinding white light blazes all about him, with a sound like the shock of a cannon—then all is darkness and silence!

Peyton Farquhar was dead; his body, with a broken neck, swung gently from side to side beneath the timbers of the Owl Creek bridge.

Sandra Birdsell

Sandra Birdsell was born in Morris, Manitoba, in 1943 to a French-Canadian Catholic father (who she only belatedly realized was Métis) and a Russian Mennonite mother. She left school at fifteen and married at seventeen. When her three children were less dependent, she took a creative writing course from Robert Kroetsch at the University of Manitoba and has since gone on to write fulltime. Her stories have appeared in *Grain*, *NeWest Review*, and *The Capilano Review*. Two collections of short stories, *Night Travellers* (1982) and *Ladies of the House* (1984), resulted in her being judged in 1986 as one of the ten best young fiction writers in Canada. Her first novel, *The Missing Child*, appeared in 1989. She has won a National Magazine Award for fiction, co-authored a play called *A Prairie Boy's Winter*, based on a book by the artist William Kurelek, and written two film scripts that have been produced by the National Film Board. Her most recent novel is *The Chrome Suite* (1992).

Birdsell, in addressing the matter of literary appropriation (using materials and adopting the point of view of other groups, particularly minorities), dismisses it as a "limp issue." "Writers can and must write whatever they choose to write. Publishers can decline to publish it. Readers to read it. In fact, this writer would tend to want to write the very thing she was told she must not write. To say that certain points of view are off limits is to agree to censorship. . . . The typical guilt-ridden, hand-wringing response expected from the clean, white, washed, bleeding-heart middle-class Canadian writer. One need not fear putting words into the mouths of Native people. I believe that their articulate, calm, and sane public response to the Meech Lake fiasco should put an end to that fear. They do not need our patronage. What we might correctly or incorrectly portray while writing from their point of view or any other point of view that differs from our own will not make a shred of difference. We flatter ourselves if we think so. There will always be those among us who will go for the quick fix—the stereotype—and those of us who will search deeply for what we don't understand."

This is a telling comment, not only for what it says about freedom of the imagination (consider Faulkner's material and point of view in "Pantaloon in Black"), but also what it says about Birdsell's integrity as a writer. In an interview with Nancy Russell in *Books in Canada* (May 1986), she explains that her initial interest in writing was therapeutic, but that after the death of her father she had a compulsion to record personal and collective stories that might otherwise be lost. She chose the short story form because it enabled her to juggle her responsibilities as a mother and part-time employee with her need to write. Not surprisingly, she has some important things to say about women caught in marriages that do not work and from which they cannot escape. "That was what always bothered me about the very first works I read by women. Often they would just leap over the process. One day the woman would be here, and the next moment she was there. Whether she was in a family or left the family to realize her potential and become who she wanted to become—the process of becoming was missing. And I always felt cheated. I always wanted to know, was there any struggle, was there any ambivalence, was there any going back and forth for a time? How did she make a living? Those sorts of things were missing."

In response to a question about the lack of self-confidence among women, Birdsell says: "I don't know if it's particularly in writing, or if it's in anything where a woman tries to excel. I think that women don't have that same kind of confidence, or maybe we just don't put up the same façade. Maybe the lack of self-confidence isn't as buried, as hidden as in men. I think lack of self-confidence is very strong in my life as a writer. I haven't travelled around the world in a sailing ship. I have stayed home. What a dull and boring view. It's when you lack confidence that your vision or your experiences don't seem the least bit interesting to anybody else. But it's reading other women writers that makes you think, well of course it's interesting."

While her work has often been compared to that of Alice Munro, Birdsell insists that the only thing they have in common is that they are both writing rural stories and writing about women. "I think my way of telling a story is different from hers. My stories—maybe because I'm such a new writer—the form and shape are visible at times. You look at hers, and they just run off the page. You can't find the structure or the shape of it, but the story's there, and it just keeps coming back and back and back to you as you think about it." Birdsell also resists the regional label: "I don't think my writing has any Western flavour to it. . . . Wherever a writer grows up influences her writing. I just happened to grow up on the prairies. I love the prairies very much. Sometimes there's not very much to see until you get down close to it and then you see the pebble in the pool or you see the little harebells. Little tiny pretty things. Whereas in B.C., it hits you in the face all the time, and you can't appreciate it."

In a short essay called "While in the Process of Discovering" (*Event*, Vol. 20, No. 1, Spring 1991), Birdsell discusses the sense of absence that pervades our lives and that may be the source of both religion and creativity. "How to structure the world outside my window onto the page, how to give shape to emptiness and longing? (Perhaps this is work for a poet and not a story teller.) How does one write about absence except to write around it? In giving definition to the world surrounding the state of absence its shape becomes visible. Its structure is built somewhat like the spatter paintings I created at school, a bit of wire mesh, a tooth brush and spatters of poster paint defining the shape of the desired object on the blank page. I can only say that the paint is language which conveys the essence of longing and emptiness. This essence is present in the tone, voice, geographical and inner landscape of the people and place of the story. How a writer puts it there is even more vague. Perhaps it's the writer's energy or the mood he's in when he rubs the brush against the wire mesh. But I suspect that before we can give definition to absence we dream it first, carry it inside for a long time and then while engaged in the act of telling a story, we unconsciously breathe or perspire it onto the page. Now, having said this, I have to say that I can't determine whether this process has occurred in my work yet or whether it will happen. I can only hope."

Night Travellers

"When a woman has intercourse, Mika told herself, she thinks of what might happen." She climbed in the night the hill that led away from the river and James. She travelled in a black and white landscape because it was void of details that would have demanded her attention. And the night was also a cover. Above, the starlit summer sky served only to make God seem more remote, withdrawn. As she walked, she took comfort in the sound of the frogs in the moist ditches on either side of the road, the call of an owl hunting in the park below.

Men, she was certain, thinking of both James and Maurice, didn't think of such things as a seed piercing another seed and a baby growing instantly, latching itself fast to the sides of her life. Men were inside themselves when they shot their juices. It was just another trick that God played, to keep the babies coming. Replenish the earth. Well—she was doing her job.

She reached the top of the hill and then she stooped slightly, giving in to the weight of a stone which she cradled close to her breasts. If Maurice should ever think to ask, she would be able to say, "I was out gathering rocks for my rock garden. It's the only time I can go, when the children are sleeping." And she would still be telling the truth.

She stopped to catch her breath and turned to look back at the park beside the river. Lot's wife looking back with longing towards a forbidden city. But unlike Lot's wife, she did not become a pillar of salt. From among the trees in the park, light shone out from the tiny window in James's bunkhouse. He had turned on the lantern. Pride made her wish that he would have stood for a few decent moments and watched while she climbed the hill. For this reason she'd kept her back straight until she was certain he couldn't see her anymore. But already, he was stretched out, lost in one of the many books he kept on the floor beside the cot. What did she expect? That had been their agreement, not to look for anything from each other. She had Maurice and the children. He had his dream of voyages in a sailboat.

At the top of the hill, the road stretched broad and straight, one half mile to the centre of town. She could see lights as cars on Main Street headed in and swiftly out of town. She passed by the grove of fruit trees that surrounded her parents' garden. The scent of ripe fruit carried across the road and she thought of the apples her mother had given to her, baskets of them, in the bottom of the cupboard. Her parents' white cottage stood beyond the garden in the darkness. I'm sorry, she said. I forgot about the apples. But with the children my hands are already full. She thought of the children, round-cheeked and flushed with their dreams and her step quickened.

Beyond the ditch, there was a sudden rustling sound, like an animal rising up quickly. Mika, startled, stood still and listened. A dark figure stepped from the cover of the fruit trees on to the path that joined the cottage to the road.

"Who's there?" She heard movement, fabric rubbing against fabric. A dry cough. "Papa, is that you?"

Her father came forward in the darkness. Relief made her knees weak.

"Liebe, Mika. I was hoping, but I knew in my heart it was you."

Knew it was me, what? What did he know? "What are you doing up so late?" she asked instead. "The night air isn't good for your lungs."

"When one of my children is in trouble, I don't worry about such things."

"What's this, trouble?" she asked. She felt her heart jump against the stone she clutched tightly to her breast. As he turned towards her, he was illuminated by the moon and she saw that he'd pulled his pants on over his night clothes. His shirt lay open, exposing the onion-like skin on his chest to the cool breeze. She saw concern for her in the deep lines in his face. If only he would use anger, it would be easier to oppose him.

"Nah, you know of what I speak. I've seen your coming and going. I've seen him. I'm ashamed for you."

"What you've seen is me gathering rocks for a rock garden." She held up the stone. I gather them from beneath the bridge."

"Mika." There was sorrow in his voice.

It was the same tone of voice he'd used on her all her life. It made her change her course of action because she didn't want to be responsible for his sorrow. It was the same thing with Maurice. Peace at all costs. Maurice had forced himself on her and she'd forgiven him because of an offer to build a new window in the kitchen. She hated that about herself.

"So, you've seen my coming and going and you're ashamed for me. I'm not."

He blocked her path. "Come to the house. We should talk and—"

She pushed around him and began to walk away. Talk? Talk about Maurice and his black night moods? About another baby coming in a house full of babies? No, we will talk about my responsibilities instead.

"Have you travelled that far then," she heard him call after her, "that you can now make excuses for your behaviour? What am I to tell the elders at church?"

Before her, silhouetted against the sky, the flutter of wedge-shaped wings, two bats feeding on insects. They would become entangled in her hair. She heard his light step on the road and then he walked beside her. "Why should you tell them anything?" she asked. "It's none of their concern. What I do is my own business."

"We're a community," he said. "People united by our belief, like a family. When one member hurts, the whole family suffers."

"A family. I'm not part of that family," Mika said. "I don't belong anywhere."

"How can you say that? The women welcome you into their homes. They pray for you."

"Oh, they welcome me, all right. I'm to be pitied, prayed for. It gives them something to do."

They walked for a few moments without speaking. He pulled at his thick white moustache, the way he did when he was deep in thought. She stopped, turned to him. "Look. Papa. You know they don't accept Maurice. Even if he wanted to go, they don't invite him into their homes. They don't really accept me, either. So, if you feel it's important to tell the elders, tell them. I don't care."

The bats—their flight was a dance, a sudden dipping, a flutter, a smooth glide and they swerved back in among the trees. Gone. She walked faster. "The children are alone," she said.

"Oh, so you think of the children at least?" he said.

"Of course I think of them. I need something for myself too."

He put his large cool hand on her arm and drew her to the side of the road. His sun-tinged complexion had paled and there was fear in his eyes. "But not this," he said. "Not this. What are you saying? You need to ask God to forgive you. The wages of sin is death."

Always, Bible verses, given in love but becoming brick walls, erected swiftly in her path. The hair on her arms and neck prickled. "Papa," she said. "It's my sin and it's my death. Leave me be." She lifted the stone up and away from her breast and slammed it into the ground. She turned from him quickly and ran with her hands pressed against her stomach.

She undressed quickly, her heart still pounding, and listened to their sounds, the children, breathing all through the house. She'd stood first in one doorway listening for them, then in another, and finally she'd bent over the baby in the crib at the foot of her bed. She'd felt for him in the dark, found a moist lump beneath the blankets. She'd changed his diaper without awaking him. Maurice was not home. He was still at the hotel. She waited for her heart to be still so that she could sleep. She rubbed her stomach gently. What would it be, she wondered, this one that she carried with her to James? Would it be touched or bent in any way by her anger? Below, a door opened. She stiffened, then rolled over and faced the wall as Maurice came up the stairs.

"What are you thinking?" James asked.

Mika swung her legs over the side of the cot and sat up. Her feet rested in a trapezoid of moonlight which shone through the small window of the bunkhouse. She'd been half-listening to James telling her about some one person he knew who had never let him down. His voice rose and fell in its strange British accent and she was able to think above it. Through the other small window at the end of the bunkhouse, she could see her parents' cottage, a white sentinel on a hill. It was in darkness once again, but she was certain her father's white face looked out from behind the lace curtains.

"Oh, I'm not thinking about any one thing in particular." But all day she'd been wondering, how could you be forgiven by God for something you'd done if you weren't sorry you'd done it?

He rose up on his elbow and ran his hand along her arm. The smell of the bunkhouse was his smell, faintly like nutmeg, the warmth of sun trapped in weathered grey planks and it was also the smell of the other men who had slept there; the men who had come to town as James had after the flood to help clean and rebuild it. She put her hand overtop his.

"God, you're beautiful," he said.

"Don't say that."

"What, not say you're beautiful?" He laughed and sat up beside her. He reached for his cigarettes on the window-sill. "You're a strange one."

He was tired of listening to himself talk and had drawn her in by saying, "You're beautiful." In the beginning, he'd pranced around her, so obviously delighted that he'd charmed her into coming away from the riverbank with him, through the park to this bunkhouse. He'd followed her about, picking up the clothing she'd shed, hanging it over a chair so she wouldn't look rumpled when she left. He was a meticulous love-maker. He began by kissing the bottoms of her feet, the backs of her knees, her belly, causing the swing of the pendulum inside her to pause for several seconds at midpoint, so that she was neither being repelled nor attracted but suspended and still.

"Why don't you want me to tell you that you're beautiful?" James asked.

Because she didn't think she was beautiful. There was nothing beautiful about a person who would come home swollen and moist from love-making into the bed of another man. But what Maurice had done was not beautiful either. Two wrongs don't make a right, she'd instruct her own children.

"No, what I meant was, don't say God. Don't bring God into this."

Their thighs touched as they sat on the edge of the cot and she was amazed at how quickly she had become accustomed to the touch and smell of another man. The flare of his match revealed his exquisitely ugly nose. It was a fleshy hook pitted with blackheads. His chin and the skin around his mouth were deeply scarred by acne. You're so ugly, she'd once told him. She'd watched for evidence of injury, a faltering of his tremendous self-confidence. He'd laughed at her attempt, saw through it. She saw him daily as he walked past the house and he was always in a hurry, loose-jointed and thin, moving towards some vision he had of himself and his future.

He held the lit cigarette up to his watch. "Shouldn't you think about heading back? It's almost twelve."

"I've still got time."

He got up from the cot and his tanned chest moved into the trapezoid of light and then his buttocks, pinched together, muscular as he walked to the table beneath the window. He gathered up her hairpins and dropped them into her lap. He never forgot. He made certain each time that she left exactly as she'd come. She scooped the pins up and put them into the pocket of her dress.

"Don't you think you should fix your hair?"

"It's all right. Maurice is never home before I am."

He leaned over her, kissed her forehead. He slipped his hand inside her unbuttoned dress and fondled her. "I love your breasts. I think that's what I'll miss the most about Canada, your beautiful sexy breasts."

She put her arms about his neck and drew him down on top of her. "Once I'm gone," he said into her neck, "if we ever meet again, it will be chance. You know that, don't you?"

"Yes." In another month he wouldn't want her anyway. Already she could feel the baby between them. She listened to the sound of his heart pushing against her chest. The wind had fallen and the silence in the park was complete, the river still. The moment passed. She fingered the hairpins in her pocket. She pulled them loose and scattered them into the folds of his blanket. He'd find them tomorrow. When he was making his bed, tight corners, planning his day, his mind leaping forward to the next event, he'd find her pins and he'd think of her for one second. She knew he wouldn't think of her longer than that, or wonder what she might be doing at that moment or try and recall her features as she did his; she even longed for the sight of his lanky body, his brown trousers flapping loosely about his ankles, the funny way he walked, arms swinging, leading with his ugly nose. I thought of you today, he'd said once, and I got this enormous stiff prick. I think of you too. She couldn't say, I love you.

"You'd better go," he said. "Before I change my mind and keep you here with me all night."

She pushed him from her, sat up and buttoned her dress. She used his comb and began combing her hair which was tangled and damp with sweat. The comb seemed to contain some residue of his energy, a reminder of the range of feelings she'd experienced only thirty minutes before. James got up, walked to the door and she followed him. He stood naked on the step. She gave him the comb. He plucked her dark hairs from its teeth and let the breeze catch them away. Above them, the stars were brilliant and clear. "Will you come tomorrow?" he asked.

"I don't know. If I can, I will."

"Try." He took her hand in his. He pressed the hairpins into her hand. "You've forgotten these."

Mika walked up the hill away from the park, the river, James. She heard nothing of the sounds of the night, the singing of insects, the owl hunting, nor did she see the phosphorus glow of fireflies among the tall grasses in the ditch. She was listening to the sound of her feet on the road, her heart beating, her breath labouring slightly as she climbed the hill and her thoughts. How could she be forgiven by God and brought to a state of serenity and continue to see James at the same time?

When she reached the top of the hill, her father waited on the path, pacing back and forth, swishing mosquitoes from his arms with a switch of leaves. Mika walked faster so that he would know she had no intention of stopping. He ceased pacing. She lifted her head and strode by him. She felt the sting of leaves on her legs. She stopped suddenly, her breath caught in her throat, and fought back anger. He threw the switch aside.

"Where is the stone you've been searching for tonight?" he asked.

"I have nothing to say. You can't make me argue with you. If you want to argue, then do it with yourself." Her voice did not betray her anger. She still felt the biting edge of the leaves on her skin. She walked away swiftly, and then faster until she was running from him. Her breath became tight and then a spot of fire burned in her centre. But she wouldn't stop running until she was home, safe, behind the door.

She sat at the kitchen table and pressed her face against the cool arborite. To be alone for once, just to be left alone. She listened to a fly buzzing against a window. The wind in the kitchen curtain swept against the potted plant. Water dripped into the sink. Something sticky against her arms—she sat up and frowned as her hand met toast crumbs and smears of jam left behind by one of the children. Her legs felt weak as she went over to the sink to stop the dripping of water and to get a cloth to wash the table. She reached to turn the light on above the sink and saw through the window her father entering the yard. She stood with her hands pressed to her face and waited. She wouldn't answer the door and he might think that she was upstairs, sleeping.

His light touch on the door, a gentle knock and—silence. Above her, the sound of electricity in the clock. He coughed twice. She could see him fumbling for his pocket, to spit his blood-flecked mucus into a handkerchief.

"Mika, I know you're there. Mika, open the door."

It wasn't locked, but she knew he wouldn't come in unless she opened it.

"You're causing much sorrow," he said. "Your mother has been crying most of the day."

Crying over children is a waste of time, Mika thought. In the end, they do what they want.

"She says for me to tell you, think of eternity."

The anger erupted. She stepped towards the closed door. "Eternity? Eternity? Papa. I've spent all my life preparing for eternity. No one tells me how to live each day. Right here, where I am."

She heard him sigh. "But when you think of it, we're here for such a little time when you consider all of eternity," he said.

"Yes, and it's my little time. Mine. Not yours."

He didn't speak for a few moments. She held her breath. She waited for him to leave. She sensed his wretched disappointment in her, his fading spirit. I can't help that, she told herself.

"Mika, one thing," he said. His voice was barely more than a whisper. "There's something wrong with your thinking. If we could just talk. I'm not well. I need to know before I—" He broke off and began to cough.

Before I die. She finished the sentence for him. She turned her back to the door and pressed her knuckles into her teeth and bit into them. Anger rose and grew until her fists were free and raised up. That he would try to use his illness against her. It's my life, she told herself. It's my life.

"Go away," she cried. She faced the door once again and stamped her foot. "Go away." She would tear the curtains from the windows, upset chairs, bring all the children running to stare at her anger. She would let them see what had been done to her, she would tell them, it's my life. She would—she gasped. A sharp kick in her belly, then a fluttering of a limb against her walls. Another movement, a sliding downward, a memory drawing her inside instantly like a flick of a knuckle against her temple. The baby. Like all the others asleep in the rooms upstairs, it travelled with her.

"Mika, please. I care for you."

She opened the door and stood before him, head bent and arms hanging by her sides. They faced each other. His shoulders sagged beneath his thin shirt. "Come in," she said. "I'll lend you one of Maurice's sweaters." She began to cry.

He stepped inside quickly and put his hand on her shoulder. "Yes, yes," he said. "That's it. You must cry over what you've done. It's the beginning of healing. God loves a meek and contrite heart."

She leaned into him, felt the sharpness of his rib cage beneath her arms. I cry because I can't have what I want. He's going away soon. I am meek and contrite because he doesn't want anything more than just a fleeting small part of what I am. I am filled with sorrow because I know myself too well. If I could have him, I wouldn't want him.

"It's over," he said. "You won't go and see that man again."

She heard the rasping sound of fluids in his chest. She loved him.

"No, I won't see him anymore."

She turned her face against his chest and stared into the night beyond him. She felt empty, barren, but at peace. In the garden, a bright glow flared suddenly and she thought, it's a cigarette. But the glow rose and fell among the vegetation and then became bead-shaped, blue, brighter, her desire riding the night up and up in a wide arc, soaring across the garden into the branches of thick trees. A firefly, Mika thought. And she watched it until it vanished.

Neil Bissoondath

Neil Bissoondath was born in Trinidad in 1955, to a family that had come from India as indentured labourers. His grandfather had been a scholar in India; his mother was a schoolteacher in Sangre Grande; and his uncle is the celebrated writer V. S. Naipaul. As a teenager, he read two of his uncle's books and thought "My God, this is what my uncle does for a living. Those books were remarkable to me—they were icons of possibility." Bissoondath went to school in Port of Spain, then followed his uncle's example and advice and chose exile to pursue his professional interests. He enrolled in the study of French Language and Literature at age eighteen at York University in Toronto. According to the profile by Robert Fulford in *Toronto Life* (Vol. 3, No. 9, Dec. 1988), after graduating he taught English and French to corporate executives, foreign students, and Quebeckers living in Toronto. Much of the material from this period found its way into his first book of stories, *Digging Up the Mountain* (1985). He lives with one of his former students, Quebec lawyer Anne Marcoux, in Montreal, where he writes and from where he has commuted to serve as writer-in-residence at the University of Ottawa. His other works of fiction include the novels *A Casual Brutality* (1988) and *The Innocence of Age* (1992) and a second collection of stories, *On the Eve of Uncertain Tomorrows* (1990). Although his literary reputation has grown rapidly, Bissoondath seems undistracted: "It never occurred to me to feel competitive. Writing is not a horse race. A writer is in competition with himself—and no one else." Among his favourite writers, he lists Timothy Findley, Paul Theroux, Aleksandr Solzhenitsyn, and two South African writers, Nadine Gordimer and André Brink.

In an interview with Andrew Garrod (*Speaking for Myself: Canadian Writers in Interview*, 1986), Bissoondath speaks of a story writing itself. "There comes a moment when a story will simply, as I put it, sit up inside of my head and say, 'Here I am; please write me.'" He goes on to say that angle of vision is very important, that a story cannot be written until he has found the right perspective, the right voice. His training in languages and his close attention to the nuances of speech are clearly central to the success of Bissoondath's stories; so, too, are his minute observations of character and situation. In another interview, this time with Aja Norgaard in *Aurora: Leading Thinkers and Authors* (Vol. 13, No. 2., Fall 1989), he says: "Part of writing a story, of course, is finding the correct voice. . . . When I find myself beginning to manipulate things or wondering would this character say this or that, I pull back because it means that I'm not following the instincts of the character. You can manipulate things a little too much, and that, more often than not, leads to a tone of falseness in writing."

In addition to finding the correct voice, he says, another of the short story writer's problems is "learning how your brain works and learning to trust your imagination to eventually come forth with what you need. But it can come at the strangest of times. It seems to happen so often when you're wet, when you're taking a shower or washing dishes. Your place can be really clean when you write." The barely submerged humour and irony in these remarks are characteristic of Bissoondath's discussions of the craft of fiction, which tend to shy away from questions of technique or meaning. He avoided the academic study of English because he felt the "autopsy" approach he had encountered in high school killed all enthusiasm for literature. He also remains sceptical about the value of teaching or studying creative writing, suggesting that informal study of the world at large might be more valuable, "being interested in and finding out about the great civilizations. Finding out about different countries, the way people live, architecture, music, literature, and understanding as much as you possibly can. And then, of course, the thing beyond that is simply to write."

Although he rejects popular images of the literary life, choosing the difficult task of writing, rather than *being a writer*, and although he has doubts about the efficacy of literature to bring about social change, Bissoondath's comment about his uncle's novels as "icons of possibility" may be taken in at least two ways: first, the act of writing is a way for the writer to lift himself out of the cage of place or culture or race in which he finds himself locked; and second, fiction is a way to make sense of and, hence, possibly transcend those conditions—imperialism and greed, for starters—that constrain and brutalize us all. What liberates the author might, equally, liberate the engaged and attentive reader.

The Arctic Landscape High above the Equator

He remembers an endless field of shadow-dappled cloud. An arctic landscape high above the equator. It should have told him something.

Her breathing, light and regular, soothes the darkness of the room. She lies languid on the disarrayed bed, her long legs striped zebra-like by the light coming in through the venetian blind.

Rance fingers an unfiltered cigarette from the stiff pack, lights it. Flecks of tobacco and the rush of hot smoke mingle with the aftertaste of the wine they've been drinking, a bitter local red given to him by one of his informants. *Un regalo*, the man said apologetically. *Un regalo*: the man had nothing else to give him. He paid anyway.

The night is quiet, as is every night here, as befits a capital in ruins in a country at war. Only the occasional police patrol animates the street outside, the silence unnatural, the stillness a mark of the discontent he has helped create. Public utilities are no longer reliable: streetlamps are burnt out, water supplies unpredictable. It is as if he and those with whom and for whom he works have the power to change the very personality of a people.

Rance knows he should take satisfaction from this influence: it is, in the end, the ultimate goal of consular activities. But he never anticipated that the achievement would be of darkness, a retreat of the light to a small, hard circle. Disruption of lives is not what he set out to create.

Rance sucks at the cigarette. He keeps these thoughts to himself. They are, he is aware, a sign of conscience ill-directed; are, in bureaucratic eyes, threat; in ideological eyes, treason.

Her breath catches in her throat, rattles, settles down. Rance shivers at how fragile the drawing of breath seems in the darkness.

Somewhere out there, dominating the ruined city, the embassy sits pulsing in its spotlights, as secure as knowledge unchallenged in its authority.

She stirs in the bed, his name, sighed, a question. Sits up, drawing in her legs and hugging them with her slim arms. Her feet, shapely and cared for, nestled together in a strip of light. There is a tension to them—in the ankles, in the slope towards the painted toes—that captivates him, once more stirs his desire.

The room is hot, the air exhausted. The air conditioner hangs burnt out in the far wall.

She asks, her voice a whisper, tender with a lover's concern, if he is all right.

He is touched, hungry now for her. Squashes the cigarette in an ashtray, pads softly over to the foot of the bed. He hesitates, lost for a moment in the surge of his desire. Then he kneels, reaches for her left foot, cups her heel in the palm of his hand. He lowers his head, sucks gently, one by one, on her toes. They taste lightly of perspiration, the skin rough and dry. She giggles, laughs her throaty laugh. But when next she whispers his name, it is in a voice gritty with quiet passion.

The entire hill belonged to them, purchased decades before for five hundred rifles, a thousand pairs of combat boots, and a couple of "advisers".

They had carved what they needed from its heavy forest, surrounding the perimeter of cleared land with double fences of chainlink and razor wire, illuminating the security strips between and beyond with spotlights. The cameras, hooded eyes mounted on poles, came only later, with the growth in urban insurgency.

The buildings went up, imposing and whitewashed, dwarfing even the presidential palace. Word spread in mysterious whispers that the remaining forest was heavily mined. A few years later, a bored Marine spotted a dog sniffing around at the edge of the vegetation. He tossed a grenade, the blast bringing the curious to the gates of the compound. They were given a tour. A cheap goodwill gesture. Were shown the destroyed vegetation, the smatterings of bloody flesh.

Rance, rolling through the microfilm, had seen indignant reports of the incident in the local newspaper: "An explosion was heard. . . . The dog was no more. . . . The ambassador would neither confirm nor deny the rumours of minefields. . . . Citizens should be wary. . . ." Rumour was lent credence. The journalist, a man named Grimaldi, had survived through the years, had gone on to become publisher of *Cuaderno*.

From down there, in the destroyed city, the compound glowed in a splendid, spotlit isolation, what the last ambassador—recently recalled and unlikely to be replaced—liked to call in his rare public speeches a shining beacon, but he never explained for whom. For State, probably, for Langley, the glow lovingly viewed from D.C.—but Rance didn't like the lights, never had. They made him feel targeted. Living in the Bull's Eye, he called it.

His office, on the third floor at the rear of the building, looked out onto the extensive back lawn, treeless, shrubless, a manicured field of fire. In his increasingly lengthy hours of idleness, Rance would find himself fantasizing gunmen lying on the lawn, assault rifles trained on the building, the fences behind them sliced open. From his window, he picked them off with a cool, unhurried calculation.

It was the evening of his second day in the new post. A reception in the main ballroom. She walked in on Grimaldi's arm, tall and slim, young enough to be his daughter; mistresses, Rance thought, are getting younger and younger. But she was simply dressed, a silver bracelet her only adornment—the other mistresses in the room proclaimed their status in excess—and she carried herself with an assuredness that he liked. Her self-possession declared itself all hers; it had nothing to do with the man she accompanied.

Rance made his way through the crowd, introduced himself to Grimaldi.

"Ahh," Grimaldi said, extending a plump hand. "The new spook."

"My field is culture, *señor*."

Grimaldi gazed amused at him, his eyes ironic beneath bushy eyebrows. "Yes, well . . . there's culture and there's culture, isn't there?" Then, without a blink, he introduced Rance to Isabel. "His field is culture," he said with a gentle bite.

"Yes," she said. "I heard." Her grip surprised him with its strength, the other mistresses having offered only a brief flirtation with the fingertips, and she gazed frankly at him, a hint of haughtiness making her appear for a moment taller than he was.

It was probably this—the unexpected sting of her gaze—that caused Rance to turn back to Grimaldi and say, "You have exquisite taste in women, Señor Grimaldi."

"Grimaldi was silent for a moment, one fleshy lip pursed against the other. "Señor Rance," he said finally, almost whispering, "you must beware stereotypes."

"Señor?"

"Let me introduce you again, Senor Rance." He gestured at Isabel. "May I present Isabel Grimaldi, my daughter."

Rance's control faltered, blood surged to his face. "I—" He couldn't suppress a smile he knew to be idiotic. "Señorita Grimaldi—"

Her expression changed little, and Rance thought of the word unforgiving. His mind raced to the byline—I. Grimaldi—he'd seen in the microfilm rolls of *Cuaderno*. It wasn't the old man—he was Antonio—and he knew Grimaldi had no son. A cousin or a nephew then, he'd assumed. The reporting was tough, fearlessly opinionated. And he remembered the picture he'd formed of the writer: a man slightly manic in a political way, unhappy with everyone, every program. The kind of man who, working on the basis of an unstated political agenda, made enemies everywhere.

"—so you're I. Grimaldi."

"I see you've done your homework."

"I had no idea—" Hers was not an immediately arresting face; yet the imperfections—the ripple in the middle of her nose, the glittery narrow-set eyes—created an unusual attractiveness against the field of her thin face. Her cheekbones, starting high and sloping downwards to the edges of her lips, suggested the soft features of an antelope.

"I always escort my father to public functions."

"Yes, I know." Her mother, Grimaldi's wife, had been bedridden for years.

"You know? You think you know everything, don't you, Señor Rance?"

"Not everything, Señorita Grimaldi—" They each took a glass of wine from the platter of a passing waiter. "—but maybe more than you think." He noticed her hands: fingers long and slim, with well-filed, unpainted nails. Serious, sensuous fingers.

"Or maybe not." She smiled, her look softening, losing its combativeness.

"Or maybe not."

"Truce?"

"Truce."

She raised her glass to his. "*Salud,* then."

It had seemed, eighteen months ago, like a plum posting, enough going on overtly and covertly to assure the rewarding of initiative. But a little unravelling had occurred not long after his arrival, enthusiasm leading to carelessness to revelation to stalemate.

The government, of men and women dressed in combat fatigues, proclaimed another revolutionary victory, organized spontaneous demonstrations, ordered out—in prudent enthusiasm—a few lower-level members of the embassy staff.

At home, there were newspaper revelations, internal investigations, public hearings.

Funds froze, careers stalled.

The ambassador and his senior people departed, normal rotations ended, and those remaining behind had only the flag left to tend.

It was a small country, much of it inaccessible. Coffee plantations, banana plantations, stretches of jungle impenetrable except to the obsessed. The roads away from the capital were bad, unpaved and rutted, narrowing at times to overgrown lanes. He had nevertheless managed, in a series of daylong car trips before travel restrictions were imposed, to see much of it.

The coasts, untouched, were a surprise; he had somehow failed to anticipate beauty in what he understood to be a land of dangers. And the interior, except for the frequent army roadblocks—fuzz-faced teenagers casual with AK-47s—and rifle-toting peasants, was almost somnolent. It was hardly a country seething with military activity, hardly a hotbed of revolutionary enthusiasm. There were crates of military equipment mildewing on the docks, and the embassy was wild about the number of weapons openly displayed—anyone strong enough to carry a gun seemed to have one—but Rance suspected that if his own country found itself under siege and all the weapons in private hands were brought out, the sight would be not much different. Only there would be less discipline, a greater threat to the public peace. He stopped in at collective farms, housing projects, literacy classes. And the more he saw of the smaller picture, the harder it became to entertain the larger one.

Driving back to the capital late one night after an evening with the priests and lay workers at a Catholic mission, Rance couldn't help thinking of his father, a wiry man with silvered hair, physically tough, prickly with the pride of the immigrant who had made good. In the suburban house comfortably crowded with department store furniture his father read news-magazines, listened to the radio, watched television. And fears fostered in the larger picture fashioned nightmares in the smaller. Through his father's head and night-time disquisitions trekked "the marching millions", hordes of Spanish-speaking communists tramping north (the only time his father saw Latin Americans as anything but lazy and shiftless was when he saw them as hell-bent for invasion), Chinese-speaking communists plunging from the sky, Russian-speaking communists swooping up the beaches.

His father was a good man. A touch jealous of his own possessions, a bit rigid in his judgements, but a good man, nevertheless. He prided himself on what Rance recognized as acute immigrant obsessions: success, provision, a gentle invisibility. Like his neighbours, he belonged to various service clubs, owned a couple of hunting rifles, took in the occasional baseball or football game. There were summer barbecues, New Year's Eve dances, summer car trips to distant points. He mowed the lawn, paid the bills, played poker. In fact, his father differed from other fathers in only one appreciable way: he awoke every morning at five for an hour-long workout, various calisthenics followed by barbells, ending with a twenty-minute jog around the neighbourhood. His breakfast never varied: a grapefruit, bacon and eggs, a vile-smelling protein drink concocted in a blender with various powders and milk, a series of vitamin and mineral pills. His father was always in good humour in the morning, his mood darkening only at night when, after dinner, he'd worked his way through the newspaper. He watched television news, he said, only for its entertainment value.

His mother was the starkest reminder that they, his parents, had once had a different life. She was to Rance a mother like any other: she cooked, she cleaned, she tended his wounds. But there was a part of her that was inaccessible, the part that retreated every weekday afternoon to her bedroom and her books, obscure novels in her native German or, often, in translation from Swedish, Romanian, Bulgarian, or some similarly remote language. The part that glittered in her watery brown eyes when she listened with only nods and the occasional hum, to his father's excited political dissections. While upheaval and displacement—their story, his mother always said, wasn't so special that he couldn't find the grand lines of it in the history books—had simplified much for his father, his mother's manner suggested that she had come to different conclusions. It was one of the many things Rance planned to ask his mother about, some day.

It said a lot to Rance that, while his mother had retained the German edge to her accent, his father had long ago lost his in the wilful acquisition of a new identity. Rance remembered the curious sight, when he was six or seven, of his father standing before the bathroom mirror, his lips twisting into funny shapes, quietly working on his pronunciation of *with*—"vis, vis, vit, vith, ou-iss, ou-ith"—repeating it over and over again until the sounds came out to his satisfaction. Rance had long suspected that his father was secretly a little ashamed of his mother, and this prompted in him a certain shyness towards her in public. She carried with her an old-world mustiness, while his father had fully committed himself to the new. Yet his mother suggested complexities, satisfying to her, he suspected, where his father offered the reassurance of simplicities. It was what tinged his mother with an understated fragility, what made his father seem so solid.

But it was this apparent solidity that explained his father's fears. He was a man who had lost and gained—and had no intention of losing again. His fear of the marching millions was merely a sign of his insecurities, legitimate or not, a sign of his laying of a minefield. It was what made him proud of Rance and the work he did; yet his work, Rance felt, also prompted the disappointment he thought he sometimes detected in his mother's watery eyes. He would, one day, have to ask her about that, too.

Tweedledum and Tweedledee remained outside, failing to look casual on the other side of the street. Rance supposed that the lack of subtlety in their shadowing of him—of anyone who left the embassy—was part of the game, a kind of attempted intimidation. But he had—they all had—grown accustomed to them, the four two-man teams assigned to keep watch on the embassy. Tweedledum and Tweedledee, especially, had grown on him; they were a chunky pair who spent their idle time outside the gates arguing over card games. He would worry if, one day, they suddenly weren't there.

The supermarket barely justified its name. A little place, shabby on the out-side, webby on the inside. After the burning sunlight, it was several seconds before his eyes—most of the fluorescent tubes were burnt out—accustomed them-selves to the gloom.

A group of neighbourhood women sat in a corner muttering among them-selves, gossiping, perhaps, or exchanging complaints about the state of things. Several children, half-naked and brown-skinned, played beside them on the grimy floor. Two or three of the women cast suspicious glances at Rance: Cuban? Russian? American? One of the foreign "volunteers"—Swedes, Danes, Aus-tralians, Canadians—who'd flooded into the country to help build the revolu-tion? It didn't really matter: none of them was of the country, all of them were suspect. The women's conversation subsided to sighs and an uneasy patting at hair, a straightening of ragged clothes.

It was a new suspiciousness, and one Rance was not used to. The eyes, the whispers, the willed reticence: they made him feel conspicuous. He turned his gaze from them and walked with uneasy confidence farther into the gloom. The wooden shelves were mostly bare, merchandise scarce in the economic blockade, food a subtle and unacknowledged weapon. A few cans of sardines, a couple of bags of mouldy potatoes, Cuban sugar, local coffee, beer, odds and ends. Some local fruit—bananas, oranges, grapefruit—but even that was becoming difficult to obtain, the lack of Eastern-bloc tractor parts and Western fertilizer playing havoc with agriculture. This was what Rance, with nothing else to do, had come to check: the blatant effectiveness of policy. Success was bare shelves. Success was photos of breadlines, footage of public discontent.

He picked up a hand of bruised bananas, a couple of hard oranges, took them to the counter at the front.

The shopkeeper, a middle-aged man of grave demeanour leaning tired against the wall, yawned into his clenched fist.

Rance nodded at him.

The man, red eyes watering, made no move, scratched absently at his neck.

"Bueno?" Rance said, peeling a bill from his wallet. The man yawned again, scratched his crotch. "Yanqui?" he said.

It was not a question of friendly curiosity, was said with an unmistakable edge of distaste. "No," Rance said, the word too quick, too defensive to his own ears.

The man snorted, clearly disbelieving. "Pues, tu pais, tu nacionalidad—"

"Canadiense," Rance said.

"Ah, si!" The man's face grew animated. "Toronto! Montreal!"

How often had Rance seen this, not here but, younger, in Europe. He hadn't, like so many, sewn a maple leaf flag to his backpack—he avoided overt displays of nationality—but he had, at times judged opportune, claimed Canadian citizen-ship. This assumption of a mask, this denial of self, led invariably to a lowering of suspicion. And it led to what he came eventually to do with his life; led to a desire to set things right to alter the image.

". . . . un hermano en Toronto, dos primos en. . . ."

But life, he had since discovered, was a great deal more complex. The balancing of right and wrong, of the desirable and the undesirable, required compromise and a recognition of uncertainties, his role—of pursuing specific interests—demanded an acceptance of unchallenged certainties. Rance understood eventually that he could not devote his life to ideological truths, could not deny his distrust of successes. Seeking to avoid one discomfort, he had come upon another—and he still judged it prudent, at times, to disguise himself.

He paid for the fruit, turned—and found himself facing Isabel. She was standing there, just a few feet behind him, and the grin she was suppressing by biting at her lower lip told him she'd been there long enough to overhear his subterfuge. "Hola," he said automatically. "Qué tal?"

"Señor Rance." She stepped past him, paid for her soft drink.

He waited for her at the door.

"Canadian now, eh?" she said in English as they stepped out into the sunshine.

"Es un mundo—"

"Let's speak English. I don't get enough chance to practise."

"I was going to say—"

"You don't have to explain."

They walked in silence, the sunlight digging under the skin into the flesh. Isabel sipped from the bottle. Tweedledum and Tweedledee followed at an indiscreet distance.

"Where'd you learn English?" Rance asked after a few minutes.

"In your country."

"Miami?"

She chuckled. "Toronto." Offered a sip of her soft drink. It was a local cola, sugary, without fizz.

A stray dog paused in its foraging to growl at them; then, as if drained by the effort, slunk away in search of shade.

Isabel gestured behind them with her thumb. "They go with you everywhere?"

"They're harmless."

"Your activities must be more difficult?"

Rance thought of saying, I have my ways; said instead, "Not really. Besides, there aren't too many cultural festivals around these days."

"You were not just buying fruit in the supermarket."

"Checking on general conditions. I still have to file reports."

"Cultural intelligence?"

"Everything helps."

"You're going to send the fruit in the diplomatic bag?"

Rance chuckled. "That's an idea."

She did not even smile. "You're different," she said after a minute. "Not your typical spy."

"I'm not a spy."

"Information officer, then."

"That's closer to what I do."

She finished the cola, put the empty can into her purse. "You know, Señor Rance—"

"Just Rance."

"—Rance. I believe you."

He didn't know why, but her admission was a relief to him. All he could think to say was, "Thank you."

The moment she stepped into his office, he tagged her a revolution groupie. She had the face, thin and unadorned, chalky white even with a tan, with scraggly blonde hair. And she dressed the part, in sombre, baggy clothing, with earth-mother sandals—clumps of scuffed suede famous for comfort, unsurpassed for ugliness—encasing her feet. There was a frailty to her that suggested to Rance an overweening vegetarianism.

She said, sitting on the edge of the chair in front of his desk, that she had lost her passport.

Lost or sold, he wondered, but it wasn't worth asking.

She watched, wordless and nervous, as he took out the requisite forms, selected a pen from a desk drawer. He was not accustomed to performing pedestrian embassy services, but the shrunken staff had parcelled out duties. Besides, it was a way of filling the time.

He asked for details—when, where, how—and spent several quiet minutes taking down the information, her occasional sighs punctuating the scratching of pen on paper. He lit a cigarette, never taking his eyes off the forms, ignored her theatrical snort of displeasure.

People like this—people who claimed patriotism from a different angle—unsettled him. Sitting there with an ineffable air of self-righteousness, she was the antithesis of his professional personality, the magnified refraction of his private one. She, and those like her, had elevated to a way of life the unease he felt at his successes; they had embraced that unease, formed a philosophy of it, taken it to areas of the world where they saw wrongs to be righted. It was as if, by their presence and their efforts, they were apologizing for their country, and for the actions of Rance and people like him. They were not dangerous people, he knew. They lacked deceit, lived by a naive honesty. Were, as a result, powerless in a grand sense. They were not taken seriously, were simply looked down on with a kind of irritated amusement. Rance thought them rather foolish people, yet he envied them, too; they claimed a freedom for themselves which seemed truer than the service to which he had dedicated himself. In the end, unable to dismiss them, he feared them—for what they were and for what he was not.

He lit another cigarette, the first still burning in the ashtray.

Isabel held knife and fork as if they were made of air, her movements liquid.

"They won't give it up, Isabel, that's the problem."

"Of course you are right, Rance. But they were many years fighting in the mountains—"

"—and they like the comforts of the presidential palace—"

"You think this is news to us? We have eyes, we have ears."

"Then you understand our—"

"But what gives you people the right to impose—"

"—encourage—"

"—and that is why *Cuaderno* opposes them all—"

"You supported the rebels—"

"And now that they're the government—"

"You oppose them—"

"Yes! Yes! Why not? We oppose all tyranny, the right, the left, the *norteameri*—"

"Sometimes the centre is the most dangerous place—"

"But the only sensible—"

"Not if you don't survive."

"We get no support from you people—"

"What d'you—"

"You gave the generals guns, you trained their—"

"Security considerations—"

"—and you co-operated when the rebels won, at first. Economic aid—"

"But then we saw the tyranny growing—"

"Yes, but because they wouldn't play your game—"

"You don't like them any more than we do—"

"No, they jailed my father, too, just like the generals—"

"Even though you supported them—"

"You're repeating yourself—"

"—and they confiscated your newsprint—"

"—and they shut us down for weeks at a time. Yes, yes, I know!"

"So—"

"But that's our problem, Rance, *no entiendes?* Maybe we had a chance with them, but then you— Cómo se dice? Apretar los tornillos—"

"Put the screws on."

"Sí, you put the screws on them —"

"They decided on their own to turn to Fidel—"

"—but they didn't turn on you—"

"I don't believe you're defending them—"

"Not defending! Never!"

"This stuff you write, who cares—"

"The people read us—"

"The people?"

"They keep us going."

"Pawns—"

"That's the trouble, no? The people—everybody's pawns."

"Well—"

"Well what?"

"—that's reality. Political reality."

"No, Rance. That is not reality. That is games, that is greed—"

"So what's reality, then?"

"Reality? Reality is simple. Food, drink. Love and laughter. And politics is just about getting there."

"Or not."

"Or not."

Rance filled their wine glasses. He knew he was falling in love with her.

He left the movie halfway through. The off-duty Marine guards, passing a bottle of tequila from hand to hand, kept up a steady commentary on the film, conversed with the actors, answered their questions, improvised dialogue. Normally he enjoyed the spontaneity of their humour, but this evening their young voices grated on him, their laughter was intrusive.

He took the elevator up to his office from the basement, sat at his desk to try to compose his weekly report. There was little new and he found himself repeating phrases, entire sentences, from his last several cables. The bared shelves, the collapsing agriculture, the growing fiction of restaurant menus. Discontent, and creeping weariness with the war. All reasons for joy, but he knew that, for the men in the windowless offices, it would be like getting into bed with their wives. All was as it should be, but there was no edge of excitement.

He knew he should tell them about Isabel. A new contact, a new source to be courted. Possibilities of future usefulness. Part of his job this, what he had been trained to do: traders in secrets kept no secrets. But he didn't want to. He told himself he didn't yet know whether Isabel could be turned into an asset, and to mention her would be premature. True enough, but not good enough. What would he tell them, anyway?

He poured the last of the gin into a glass, tossed in a couple of ice cubes, added a dash of flat tonic water, shrugged off the lack of lemon. He had developed a taste for gin and tonic during his stint at the Madrid embassy—his tennis partner from the British embassy ended every game with a couple of tall ones—and he had come to think of it as the perfect warm weather drink, refreshing, with a bit of a buzz. Curious, though, the way many of his compatriots reacted to the drink. They preferred bourbon, scotch, vodka, tequila, spirits they understood. The gin and tonics lent him, in their eyes, a certain eccentricity. Rance wondered at the pauses, the puzzlement, the brief frowns. The first time he ordered one here, the Marine guard tending bar remarked in surprise that the gin was reserved for foreign visitors. The ambassador, chewing at the olive from his martini, chuckled and said it was all right, they'd get some more in. Rance was amused by his own unease—dare he tell anyone that he also enjoyed the occasional Ricard?—but learned soon enough to enjoy the game. To fix an exotic drink, or to order one, was to indulge in a scintilla of defiance.

He took the drink to the window, let his gaze roam over the spotlit back lawn. He was on an island looking out beyond the edges to the darkness that swallowed horizons. He felt his isolation, felt Isabel's isolation, knew it was this that attracted him to her.

Isabel had a quality rare in this country. She refused to deny complexity. She rejected the simplification of vision that formed hard and irrevocable around power, around the having of it and the wanting of it. Ideology, of the right or of the left, was here veneer, a thing to cloak yourself in depending on your aims and on who was prepared to support your struggle. You hung it around your shoulders, and soon it trapped you in its clasp. But the truth was that, in the harsh world of black and white politics, beliefs were like bullets: they were, in flight, indistinguishable, and they respected no flesh. It was, to Rance, an almost paralysing realization. Money was funnelled, arms procured, troops trained—but it all had very little to do with the country involved. It all had to do, instead, with his father, his fears and his obsessions. It had to do with anxieties dressed up as policies and plated in ideology: a pretending at higher purpose. It was where religion and politics met, the fear of Hell leading to the contemplation of Heaven. Protect your money the way you protect your soul: camouflage the essential in a scaffolding of philosophical intricacies. It was why Rance didn't like his informers. They were not men who believed in liberties; they were men who believed in power. And cash spoke to them in wondrous tongues.

All this, Isabel understood.

He went back to the desk, wrote her name. Looked at it there on the yellow notepad and felt, after a moment, like a teenager surreptitiously scribbling the name of a secret crush just to see what it looked like, to see if in the letters he could divine marvels and promises for the future. The pen moved as of its own accord, his hand its appendage, decorating the letters, shadowing them, adding curls and flourishes. Then, feeling foolish, he scratched the name out, rendered it illegible. Isabel was a contact he wanted to keep from them; she was a contact he wanted to keep all for himself.

"What is this place, Rance?"

"A safe house."

She walked carefully around the darkened room, drew a finger along a table, examined it closely. "A dirty house, too."

Rance regretted he hadn't had a chance to come by before to clean up a bit. The place hadn't been used in a long time. Many people had been through here, but it had never felt peopled before.

"So how many other women have you brought here?" Her tone was teasing, but underlaid with tension.

"You're the first."

"I must believe that?"

"It's the truth." It was, and he cared deeply that she know it. "You do believe me, don't you?"

But she didn't reply, just continued her wandering through the dark, almost sensing her way, her hands touching, feeling, making an elemental contact. It was as if she were seeking the spirits of the place.

Rance went over to the window, gingerly raised the blinds part-way so that the movement would be imperceptible from the street. The dull light of the streetlamp showed deserted sidewalks, and he thought almost with a touch of nostalgia of Tweedledum and Tweedledee sitting contentedly outside the embassy gates, secure in its illuminated inanimation.

"Do you believe in reincarnation?" she called from the bedroom.

He gently closed the blinds. "The great assembly-line of life?" He'd wanted to keep it light, but he'd spoken too quickly, failed to blunt the edge of his sarcasm.

She was silent for a moment. Then, with a light chuckle, said, "I knew you were going to say that."

He was flattered.

The bedroom light sluiced on. Rance hurried in, panic subsiding only when he saw that the blinds were down. Isabel was already stripping the bed. "Sheets?" she said, and it sounded like shits. Smiling, he pointed to the closet.

She stayed beside the bed, the dirty sheets bundled in her arms. "Well?"

"How domestic," he said, but didn't move.

Her face went serious, and she flung the sheets to the floor. "No soy tu criada, mierda!"

His hand reached up, flicked off the light. "No," he said. "Of course you're not my maid." He padded by instinct over to her, slipped his arms around her waist, pulled her close. Her body was firm and warm against him, her breath hot on his neck. Her hair smelled of the heavily perfumed local soap. He kissed her eyes, her nose, tasted inexplicable tears on her cheeks. One of her hands grasped his shoulder, the other rose to the back of his neck, pressing, urging his lips to hers. Grasping him, holding him there, claiming its rights with a tender insistence.

An eternity of telescoping time. The mind converging on sensation, wet and urgent.

Forever later, the ticking of the mattress rough on their bare skin.

The phone was heavy in his hand, hot against his ear. The sunlight through his office window burned white.

"What do you expect me to tell you, Señor Grimaldi?"

"Confirm the rumour for me, Señor Rance: yes or no?"

"I don't know anything about this."

"A list, Señor Rance. You have seen no list?"

"I've seen lots of lists, but none of the kind—"

"Come on, Señor Rance—"

"I shouldn't even be talking to you."

"Are your phones tapped? You have the technology—"

"That's not the problem. I have nothing to tell you."

"According to my information, a list has been drawn up—"

"Who by?"

"—of prominent people marked for assassination."

"I said, who by?"

"You tell me, Señor Rance."

"I resent the implication, Señor Grimaldi."

"What implication, Señor Rance?"

"We have nothing to do with assassinations."

"I didn't say you did. I'm just looking for confirmation—"

"How can I confirm the existence of something we—"

"It's your business to know things, Señor Rance."

"Yours too, if I'm not mistaken."

"A little co-operation—"

"We know nothing about assassination—"

"Let's be frank, Señor Rance. That's only because you're not very good at it—"

"I'm not about to dis—"

"—but your various proxies—"

"We have no proxies."

"—there are no controls—"

"Señor Grimaldi, you said you had a question. You asked it, I—"

"The mayor of Altamira was shot last night, and the mayor of—"

"Ask the government."

"My information is that it's the other side, your people."

"We have no people."

"It is your money that pays for—"

"Señor Grimaldi, *por favor*—"

"Señor Rance—"

"This conversation is over, Señor Grimaldi."

Rance hung up, briefly, never removing his hand from the receiver. Dialled, waited impatiently through the clicks and buzzes of the ancient phone system, and when a male voice answered said simply, "Luna."

Isabel had once been married. Still was, as far as she knew. She hadn't heard from her husband in years, and they'd never discussed divorce. "So I am," she said with a glimmer of mischievousness, "semi-detached."

He was a Canadian, someone she met while studying English in Toronto. She was young at the time—"Another life," she sighed, but not with regret, "another Isabel"—but her parents had not been displeased. It was a particularly dangerous time in her country, the war intensifying, the killings becoming more blatant, less discriminating. Her father, at her mother's behest, took to moving around with armed bodyguards, his car never left untended.

The husband's name was Philip, but she called him Felipe, after the character in the *Mafalda* comic strip. He was, she said, what the comic-book Felipe would grow up to be—thin, earnest, with a naive social idealism and a greater intellectual urge than his capacities could accommodate. He was not particularly good-looking, she said, his face too long, teeth too prominent; but his animated spirit coupled with his physical frailty to create a certain allure.

"Many times I have thought that if I write the story of my marriage—and I will one day, when we can contemplate such things in peace, when it will not be immoral to spend our days obsessed by the personal—but if I write this story, I will call it 'No Effort Required'. It tells all. We were not rich, Felipe and me, but we lacked nothing. A movie a week, a restaurant a week, dancing from time to time.

"He taught two courses of poetry at the university and he wrote science fiction in his spare time. I worked part-time for a temporary agency, office work, filing, typing. I left my brain at home every morning. This, or go crazy.

"I volunteered at an immigrant women's centre, spent a few hours a week counselling Spanish-speaking women, helping them through the bureaucracy, listening to their stories. Sad stories, frightening stories. It was good work, important work, but it was like working with glue, Rance. It stuck to you, it went home with you. You slept with it, ate with it, made love with it. After a month Felipe asked me to give it up. Not for me, but for him. He couldn't support it any more, the stories I brought home, the 'long face' I showed. So I quit, for him, for us. He got me a dog to occupy my time. I named him Ananás, because his face reminded me of Noriega. It was around then that my mother had her stroke. She lost the use of a leg, an arm. She could only mumble. My father told me not to come.

"One afternoon not long after, I was out walking Ananás when he suddenly pulled the cord from my hand and ran into the street. A car was coming, too fast. I dashed after him without thinking. The car missed me, but by very little. I fell at the edge of the sidewalk, not hurt, just frightened. The driver stopped long enough to swear at me. Ananás was on the sidewalk looking at me with his tongue hanging out. People came out from a house, tied Ananás to the fence, took me inside, gave me some water. I heard someone calling the police. But I didn't want that, there was no point. And just the word 'police' makes me shiver. Yes, I know it's stupid, it makes no sense, the Toronto police are not the police of my country. But still, some fears you don't lose. So I got up—just like that—got up and walked out of the house.

"And I walked past Ananás to a little park just a bit down the road. I sat there on a bench, partly hidden by a tree trunk. Waiting for the police to come. Watched the policeman examine Ananás, while the people from the house looked around. Looking for me, I knew, so I hid behind the tree. Watched the policeman go into the house with the people, come back out again a few minutes later, speak into his car radio, put Ananás in the back seat of his car, and drive off.

"I went home, packed a suitcase, and was on a plane home that night. I didn't forget Felipe. I left a note. He knew I was safe.

"Irresponsible? Yes, it was. But, I've told you, that was another Isabel.

"Cruel? How dare you talk to me about cruel. Happy *norteamericanos!* You people will never understand. Maybe what I did to Felipe was cruel in your context, Rance, but not in mine. But you will never understand that, you will always be too much of a *yanqui*.

"Yes, of course, that was Felipe's context too, and yes, it was cruel for him in his context. But he solved all that. He's found someone else, I hear, has a child, is even an assistant professor. But the cruelties of my context—the one that makes me everything I am—those are still with us, worse than ever.

"Abandoning Ananás, leaving Felipe: I know when I talk about it, it all sounds easy. But you're a fool if you think it was. Sure, I wish now I had done the right thing, the logical thing, the kind thing. But sometimes our need is stronger than our logic. Don't you see, Rance, I just don't have the luxury of being able to wallow in it. Felipe's context allowed him a happy ending. In my context, people are still dying."

They never exchanged pleasantries, rarely watched each other.

Rance handed over the money, rolled tight in a rubber band. Luna—it was how Rance had trained himself to think of him, only by the name assigned to the file—swiftly pocketed the roll, as if wishing to thrust from sight the tangible acknowledgement of his betrayals. The surreptitiousness of the movement always reminded Rance of his predecessor's wry comment that Luna first came to him through patriotism, continued coming to him through greed.

Luna, as usual, remained close to the door. A nervous silhouette, slender in clothes baggy and shapeless.

Rance said, "Tell me about the list."

"What list?"

"Starts with the mayors of Altamira and—"

"What about it?"

"Who drew it up?"

"Don't know."

"Don't bullshit me, Luna."

"I don't know, I tell you."

"You've seen it?"

"No."

"So how do you know it exists?"

"Talk."

"Talk means nothing."

"Talk from the right person means everything."

"Who?"

"You don't know him."

"What's his name?"

"His name will mean nothing to you."

"His name, Luna."

"Lope de Vega."

"You're bullshitting me again."

"It's the name he goes by."

"What's he do?"

"Courier. Always back and forth. Stinks of the jungle."

"Why'd he tell you—"

"News, *hombre*. Just news."

"They're not exactly keeping it quiet—"

"Part of the game, no?"

"Part of the game. Right." The game, Rance thought, the endless fucking merry-go-round of lies and deception and intimidation.

"So who is on it?"

"Many names. Many, many names."

"You sound sad."

"I should dance about this?"

"So who?"

"Fernandez, Lacruz, Tarradellas—"

"The poet?"

"The same."

"Why a poet?"

"Why not? His pen is his weapon."

"We don't take poets that seriously where I come from—"

"That's because your poets can afford to sit around playing with themselves—"

"Who else?"

"Catedrales—"

"Which one?"

"Agosto—"

"But he's just—"

"I know, a singer—"

"—and not particularly good, either—"

"—but he appears in public with the wrong people, sometimes. Waving and smiling—"

"He has a following, you'll alienate—"

"Young girls, middle-aged women. We don't need their sexless romance."

"Who else?"

"You don't need the names, you'll find—"

"The names, damn you!"

"I'm go—"

"Wait, Luna, I'm sorry. I didn't mean—"

"*Bueno, bueno.* But the time. It is getting late—"

"Who else?"

"Who else? I don't know. Ruiz-Mateos, Carrillo, Grimaldi—"

"Grimaldi? Which Grimaldi?"

"The newspaper Grimaldi—"

"There are two—"

"I don't know which—"

"Man or woman?"

"Man."

"*Cierto?*"

"*Cierto.* Lope said no women this time—"

"Absolutely certain—"

"No doubt, I tell you—"

"When?"

"Don't know."

"Find out. I need to know."

"Who knows? When the chance comes—"

"Find out, Luna."

"You must not interfere—"

"I never interfere, you know that. Just let me know when."

"If I hear—"

"Just let me know, Luna."

"Okay, okay. If I know, you'll know."

"Good. Enough, Luna, enough. Go now."

Luna didn't have to be pushed. He turned the doorknob and was gone, like a shadow slipping between two pages of a book.

Rance took out a cigarette, lit it. We are, he thought, like firemen. We put out fires when we can, create firebreaks and conduct controlled burns when we can't. But sometimes the names get away from us, they burn where they want to, and there isn't a damned thing we can do about it.

He was truly beginning to hate his job.

"You have a funny accent when you speak Spanish."

"What's funny about it?"

"It's the Spanish equivalent of an English lord—"

"You mean—"

"—*onthay, dothay, trethay*—"

"I learned Spanish in Madrid—"

"And did you visit *Barthaylona* many times?"

"You've got to admit it's got one advantage—"

"And whath's thath?"

"You're impossible."

"Grathiath—"

"That's 'grathias'—"

"—but you're not the first to dithcover thath."

"Spelling. You people can't differentiate between z, c s—"

"And how do you differenthiathe between z and c?"

"It's—"

"Admit it, Ranth, I goth you."

"Come here. Here, like this. Now—you've got to admit, I goth you, too."

"Mmmm?"

"Like thith."

"Mmmm."

"And thith."

"Mmmm."

"And thith—"

"Ahh, Ranth!"

Rance liked Grimaldi despite their mutual suspicion. He was a short, tub-like man, his ready jolliness a camouflage for the gravity of a deeper intelligence. He seemed to be always perspiring, his forehead slicked and beaded in any light. His body, internally battered by intermittent bouts of prison, contained a combative spirit.

As a young reporter, Grimaldi had indulged in a lively, engaged journalism, with no pretence at objectivity. It was a virtue, he once said to Rance, that he could not afford, evenhandedness found not in balanced articles—"The left-wing death squads said, the right-wing death squads said"—but in equal reporting of their atrocities. He showed Rance death threats he had received, neatly typed letters remarkably similar in language and spirit, differing only in ideological perspective. "This is our tragedy," Grimaldi said. "It has not changed through the decades."

And nothing else had, either. Insurgencies had come and gone and come again; governments had risen and fallen and risen again, all with casual regularity. But this remained a land of implication. Nothing could be confirmed because everything was deception; no sooner was it there than it was gone, there but not there. Even the rumours of minefields: nobody knew for sure, not State, not Langley, whether mines had been planted. It was the best kind of rumour, indistinguishable from truth and therefore, for all intents and purposes, truth itself.

All was truth, all was falsehood, all reality, all fantasy. This was the key, Rance felt, to the country, and perhaps to the entire continent; the key to the failures of policy developed in more settled northern air. And it was in the midst of these shifting spectres that Grimaldi fought, a man thrashing around at fact and fiction.

Rance wrote a report, dispatched it. God alone knew what they would make of it up there.

So far away.

He lights another cigarette, blows the smoke towards the ceiling.

Her face lies hot against his chest, her skin moist and clinging as if melting into his. He smells her hair, tastes her still in his mouth, hears still the gasps and babble of her yearning.

"Don't you ever worry about your father?"

"What do *you* think, Rance?"

"These days—"

"You mean the mayors?"

"Yes."

"Is he in any more danger now than he's ever been in? For people like my father danger is a given—"

"He's learned to live with it?"

"Don't be stupid. He's learned to live despite it."

"I don't want to go back," Rance suddenly blurts out.

"So don't."

"What do I do? Just disappear?"

"Cómo no?" She snapped her fingers. "Presto!"

"I'm serious."

"It's easier than you think, Rance."

"Come with me."

"You know this is not possible."

"How do I know that?"

"My mother—"

"And your work?"

"That too."

"You could be a journalist elsewhere. Maybe even TV—"

"Yes, and file stories for dinnertime viewing."

"Upset a few people."

"Spoil their dinners, so click, click, look, baseball!"

He knows she is right, knows he has to be blunt. "I'm asking you to be selfish. For me."

Her body stiffens, creates a psychic distance between their pressing skin. "But you don't understand, Rance. I am already selfish. For me."

"You're right, I don't understand."

"I do what I do because I have to satisfy myself."

"Don't you ever dream of a normal life? House, kids, cats and dogs?"

"That is what you dream of?"

"I never did before."

"I think about it sometimes. But there are other dreams too, *entiendes?*"

"Si," he says after a moment. "Entiendo." And he tongues a curl of her hair into his mouth.

He has been sitting at his desk since Luna's call. The time. The place. Adiós, Grimaldi.

Twice he has dialled Isabel's number, and twice he has hung up. He has not been tempted to call Grimaldi himself; he is too well trained for that.

He has sat here as the darkness encrusted itself around the compound, patched itself around his office. Sits now in light of a different quality, less diffuse than daylight, its reach ending just beyond the sill, giving the office window a glow as from a television.

He waits, sitting at his desk, calmer, he thinks, than he has any right to be. Two cigarettes burn in the ashtray. His throat is dry, and he wishes he had a full bottle of gin. The beer he has settled for is forgotten hot and half-empty on his desk. Its aftertaste, a sour coating on the flesh of his mouth, will not go away.

Eventually it comes, the dull and distant thump of an exploding bomb. Hardly a lethal sound. Like a wall of wood hitting the ground.

The sound of goodbye: how can he face Isabel now?

He waits the few minutes until the sirens reach him, their thin wail more alarming than the explosion itself. Then he stands, slings his travel bag onto his shoulder, and takes the stairs down to the basement. Pads softly past the rec room where the Marines are improvising dialogue, to the steel door that leads to the tunnel, long and dim, walls spectacularly cracked by seeping water. The ceiling is high enough for him to walk erect but instinct causes him to hunch over.

Emerges from the tunnel to the nighttime effacement of blackened forest. Senses arrested: where is up? Where is down?

He is blind, he is spinning. The ground?

The building anchors him. Through the fences, past the security strip, it sits there glowing, boasting of its invincibility. He has never before looked at it from here, never paused to examine it through the rip in the foliage, his vision intent, determinedly narrow. There is his office window, an opaque rectangle. He imagines for a moment that he sees himself peering through it: an uneasy ghost fading into the glass.

It is a life he is leaving behind, abandoning choices and possibilities by making the only one he can. His functions—this self that has been fashioned by training—are too deeply ingrained. He cannot turn his back on them, and is appalled that his betrayal of Isabel comes more easily.

He cannot imagine a future, doesn't want to remember the past. Thinks with a tremor of the revolution groupies.

Isabel. He will carry her face with him, always, her face as he imagines it now: tear-stained, crumpled in grief, warped by the horror of the inevitable he has watched evolve. There are some things, he thinks, that even love cannot conquer.

He switches on his flashlight, searches the ground for the pieces of tile imbedded in the earth that lead the long way out. There are, on this continent, villages, towns, countries where a man can easily disappear.

He firmly grasps the strap of his bag and, flashlight in hand, walks into the forest.

In the darkness, he feels the arctic landscape high above pressing down on him. Startling. Imposing.

He feels himself beginning to shatter.

Marie-Claire Blais

Marie-Claire Blais was born in Quebec City in 1939. She dropped out of school at age fifteen and worked in a shoe factory, later taking courses in French literature at Université Laval. "I began by reading the Brontë sisters when I was fifteen or sixteen years old," she says in an interview with David Homel (*Books in Canada*, Vol. 20, No. 7, Oct. 1991). "I read their novels and decided to do one too. I imitated them. The same for Dostoevsky: I wanted to write like he did. At that age, of course, the results are less brilliant. I certainly didn't come from a writing background or one where books were present. I wonder how I ever got my hands on the Brontë sisters in the first place. Back then, in that milieu, you had to hide in order to read. I don't know if it's any better now." Her first novel, *La belle bête* (1959, translated in 1960 as *Mad Shadows*) was published when she was only twenty; this was followed by *Tête blanche* (1960) and a Guggenheim Fellowship in 1962, which enabled her to spend a year in France to write *Une saison dans la vie d'Emmanuel* (1965, translated in 1966), which won the Prix France-Canada and the Prix Médicis of France. Other works include *Les manuscrits de Pauline Archange* (1968, translated in 1969), which won the Governor General's Award, *Une liaison parisienne* (1975, translated as *A Literary Affair*), and *Un joualonais sa joualonie* (1973, translated as *St. Lawrence Blues*). Blais is candid about her early struggles as a writer in Quebec in the 1950s: "I knew it would be my life. It was a need. I couldn't do anything else. I had no other essential expression than that. It wasn't easy; the milieu wasn't very open-minded. And back then, when a young writer arrived on the scene, he or she wasn't exactly welcomed with open arms. In 1959, it was a real battle. Especially if you didn't have any university credentials. I only made it through because of the unconsciousness of youth."

Of her reputation for living her characters' lives, Blais says: "That's what makes writing a book take so long. After you choose your subjects and characters, you have to live with them, walk with them, spend the night with them, you have to relive their lives. Sometimes you feel as though you're wasting your time." She also identifies with the current of feminism, and its writers: "Very much so. They're bold, they take chances. Villemaire, Marchessault, Brossard, Théoret—they're hard-working, and I don't think they've locked themselves up in a prison that could be called feminist writing." Blais admires those artists who speak out against isolation and solitude. "I've always had women alone as characters in my books, even if they have a husband or a lover, they're still alone, always alone, in perilous circumstances. The solitude of women is something unique, even if men's solitude does exist. It's completely different when a woman is alone in the world."

Blais is equally forthcoming on a variety of issues, including AIDS. "It's essential to talk about AIDS in our society. I've done it in my own humble way. The worst part is the cruelty in society. People lack pity; that's what we have to denounce. We have to feel compassion." Blais's compassion gives her a slightly different perspective from many of her contemporaries on the matter of nationalism: "I talked about nationalism in *St. Lawrence Blues*, but in a very satirical way. Wherever I go, when I see nationalism, it worries me. It means less tolerance for others, for ethnic groups, and usually out-and-out nationalism doesn't bring with it a period of creativity. It brings closed-mindedness. We're living in a closed atmosphere here as it is; nationalism will only close us in more. Maybe, for them, sovereignty is different from nationalism. . . . Maybe, if there's independence, there'll be a new generosity, but it's not guaranteed. Perhaps our artists will be able to avoid the pitfalls of blinkered nationalism. After all, this is North America; everywhere walls are falling, there's no sense going the opposite way here."

In response to the charge that she is a dark, sombre writer, Blais says: "Readers often think writers are there to entertain them. We're their court jesters. People who think I'm sombre don't see the humour in my work. My humour isn't as broad as [Réjean] Ducharme's, but it's still there, in the form of reflection. . . . I think I give my readers hope. You can't continue to write in an atmosphere of cruel despair." In response to Homel's comment about her impact on younger writers in Quebec, Blais replies: "Maybe you see it more than I do. I still consider myself a rare bird, an uprooted person. There's some good young talents coming up, but they suffer from their imprisoned state. When I come back from abroad—and I'm nearly always coming back from some foreign place—I suffer immediately from feelings of imprisonment. Think of how it must be for those who stay here all the time! That's how I see the writer: possessor of total independence and autonomy, mobile, curious, always on the run, never stopping. That's what I admire about Thomas Sanchez, my neighbour in Key West. If I didn't learn from writers like that, I'd be nothing."

An Intimate Death

Translated by Ray Ellenwood

His books are still there, untouched, just as he arranged them on the shelves of his study, the books he read, the books he wrote, his papers, his notes are still spread over his worktable, because surely he still has lots of time to finish a novel, an essay, the pictures, the drawings he loved, are also untouched on the orange wall he'd just painted, one of those pictures that remind you of Gauguin, with brown bodies in the sun, is an allegory of the sensual, paradisaical life a person can lead on an island where it's always sunny and hot, he'd hung the picture on the orange wall above the table at which he reads and writes all day, but when evening comes and his work is done you can hear him laughing with his friends, although it's a sober laugh even when he smokes the euphoriant cigarettes he offers to everyone in that hot, nocturnal, intoxicating air, because there's barely enough wind at night, a breath of cool on the back of the neck, there's nothing but intoxication on this terrace, in this garden and at night we can hear him wandering lazily through the streets of the town, yes him, the intellectual who used to be so reserved, so discreet he seemed almost haughty, letting himself go in the blissful listlessness of the island, gradually he succumbs to his voluptuous temptations because surely he still has lots of time ahead of him, later, when he doesn't have to teach at that hidebound university back there, he'll come and live here among his books and his friends, and suddenly, how did it happen, one April morning they made up a hospital bed in his room, under the towering trees that cover the roof of the tropical house with their branches, their tangled leaves, and he's thinking under this nest of lianas and stifling vegetation, lying on his hospital bed of intense pain while air comes to him in a mask and nourishment percolates drop by drop through tubes attached to his weakened flesh, he is thinking, those trees should have been cut long ago, they're so bushy, huge, they block the light, and their laughter can be heard from the garden, or the terrace, Vic and Frank and now they're here in this room leaning over him, washing him, changing him, turning him in his bed, for a few weeks already they've been here at his bedside, at first they offered him a hash cigarette, slipping it between his lips, then he refused, didn't he once tell them discreetly during a meal that he'd lost his taste for spicy food, those flavours that used to burn his throat, from now on, in the evening air, it's time for that indispensable morphine, and isn't it true they had to get rid of the young male nurse who was stealing the drugs prescribed for terminal patients at the hospital, and what would become of that kid from the black ghetto? His papers are spread over the table, the writing on them having become illegible, with hunched, tortured letters, and now he sees the misty silhouettes of Vic and Frank who are folding him in their arms because they have to change him, wash him like a baby, yesterday, indescribable consolation, they put some toys in his bed, then they took them away from him again because any object could hurt him, even a plush teddy bear, weren't his arms and legs covered with bruises, things have changed since the time they could still give him refreshing baths, now they have to turn him in his bed, he hardly weighs anything, and always those hunched, tortured letters among the notes on the worktable, under the picture that was hung on the wall painted orange last year, he's strong enough to say in a tone of deprived, repressed rage, he wants them to listen this time when he says, yes, his voice rattling, in a kind of incoherent sigh, when will it all be over, anyway, when will it all be over? Because there's other proof that his time has come, he thinks, and that is the hibiscus Peter brought yesterday, the one with the yellow flowers just blooming, which stopped suddenly, the buds glossy in the light wouldn't open, there's the sign, he thinks vaguely, the sign of departure, the trees are too high, too bushy, no ray of sun can get through any more, it's a yellow, tepid light at this hour of the morning, what did he say, Frank and Vic could barely hear him, a little water, yes, for the past few hours the water couldn't get past his burning lips any more, they'd sat him up with great tenderness, helped him support his head against the pillow, but it was no use, the cool water no longer soothed him, all he could do was repeat, when will it all be over, my friends, when will it all be over? He loved parties so much, too bad he's not here this evening with his friends, his colleagues, a few distant relatives as well, celebrating in this sumptuous historical house where Frank and Vic have organized a banquet in his honour, the man who loved parties so much is somewhere else, there in the Gulf of Mexico where his ashes are cooling, they rented a boat, says David, and the green waves rocked them, never saw so many ashes, says David, and the boat skimmed over the green water, carrying all of them along with the man who wouldn't return from the voyage, yes, but that night during the banquet the hibiscus began to bloom once more even though the air was glacial for this warm season, the hibiscus was blooming again spreading its wide, yellow corollas, and it was Peter, wasn't it, standing near the plant in shy silence, who noticed it first, the hibiscus is blooming and the man who couldn't drink or eat any more, never mind do what they asked and roll on to his side to relieve the pain a little, he too had seen that vigorous plant, the hibiscus Peter had brought him and at that moment he'd felt the breathing grow slow in his chest, Peter and the plant were the incarnation of that living beauty he would never attain again, even by stretching out his hand, that emaciated hand opening in the void, lots of time ahead of him, later on he'd come to rest and write in his island house, he'll write still more books, be an editor and poet by turns, he'll discover authors and make them known in foreign lands, and suddenly, one morning in March a male nurse pushes his wheelchair through the Miami airport and indeed it's him, the sportsman, the athlete who only yesterday was diving in the ocean waves, it is indeed him, so feeble today he can't walk any more, it is indeed him they're pushing in the wheelchair from one airport to another, under the pitying and fearful eyes of a crowd full of latent hostility, because this man passing has a contagious disease, and the contagion is formidable, it's a contagion of fear that nourishes prejudice, racism, hate he thinks while the crowd parts to let him through and he shivers with cold in this oppressive heat, touching his face and feeling the premature wrinkles under his trembling fingers, the sky is blue and hot, Vic and Frank are waiting for him there, feebly listless he'd let himself be dressed that morning in his blue sweater and grey corduroy slacks, fully aware that the young black male nurse was gradually stripping him of the morphine he'd need later on, who knows, maybe in a few days, but feebly listless, he'd let himself be dressed for the journey, but what did those people in the crowd see, under his sweater, his slacks, the sores, the black stigmata, because no part of his body had been spared, he was suffering as much inside as out, his breath was short and constricted, his pink colouring had faded in a few weeks, and when would it all be over, anyway, when would it all be over, that secret fire that wind of putrefaction blowing over him? And in this historical house on the island they were celebrating glass in hand, celebrating the man who used to be strong and beautiful, vigorous and tender, the lover of life when life was no longer there, they were celebrating the man who would never come back from the Gulf of Mexico and in the plane that was taking him back to the island the male nurse had raised him in his seat so he could see the ocean and there was a glint of joy in his blue eyes and the glint quickly disappeared as his gaze with its stricken intelligence became fixed on the green water, he saw the island lost amid thick vegetation, his island, and that evening Frank and Peter admitted they'd hardly recognized him when they saw him at the airport with the male nurse pushing the wheelchair, and in Frank's car they'd toured the island, saw once more its houses, the gardens he'd never see again and he'd said, I feel better already, they'd toured the alleys and the streets of this town full of odours surrounded by ocean, and they remembered how he'd spoken then about his eyes, yes, his eyes were still good, his sight wasn't affected, he could still read and work, and his books, his papers with the illegible, hunched, tortured letters were still there in the house under the trees, and they held a banquet in his honour but he wasn't there any more, among his relatives, his friends, he couldn't feel the night wind pass over the back of his neck, couldn't see the starry sky, at the end, said David, he wasn't aware of much, fortunately, he no longer knew what was happening to him, like a baby being changed and swabbed, such a proud man but he wasn't aware and we've got to be thankful for that small mercy, he was sinking all alone into a shadowy despair, laughing and crying, and yet he said, my God, when will it all be over, anyway, and his blue, intelligent gaze wandered all around him, around his abandoned and damaged body, the glint in his eyes suddenly paralysed in the dawn light, and they each had a copy of that recent photo of him where the dazzling glint of his blue eyes had blazed for the last time in the faded pallor of his face, on that day too he was wearing the grey corduroy slacks, the blue wool sweater and looked as if he were resting nonchalantly in a red canvas chair, holding his head in his left hand, he must have felt good that day, they said to themselves while contemplating the shy grace of his smile, and the sick man's head, so very frail, bending towards the left hand which supported the frail head as if it were about to fall, yes, that's right, said David, and they all stared at this farewell snapshot, discovering in it the premature wrinkles on his forehead, the melancholy of his smile, wasn't there a kind of laziness in his pose that day, David was saying, a sweet nonchalance like in the good old days when he used to smoke his intoxicating cigarettes beside his friends, remember that night back when he used to go bar hopping after dark and he met Lee, Lee, the Japanese boy in the striped pullover roller-skating past the sidewalk bars that night with a luminous green band around his close-cropped head glowing like a dragonfly in the night, others said, there's a kind of abandon in his smile and in that movement of the hand, and such grace too, such extreme nonchalance, he used to work a lot, but taking it easy, he also really liked doing nothing, just dreaming through the sensual sluggishness of those apparently endless summer days. . . . Behind him in the photograph there's the landscape of water and sand that belonged to him so many times, behind the man nonchalantly seated, relaxed, ready to laugh his sober laugh in the red canvas chair, he used to welcome his friends while resting in that chair in the garden, writers who'd come from every corner of the world and then they set up the hospital bed in the bedroom and he'd noticed how the trees were so high and bushy against the sky, no, the air couldn't get in any more and the sunlight, and the hibiscus Peter had placed near his bed, the hibiscus with its yellow flowers had suddenly stopped blooming as if it had been draped in a shroud of frost or deprived of the sun's glare, overwhelmed by the same contemptible, servile suffering he'd felt, even that night when he'd told his friends he didn't like spicy food any more, the lightness of his smile had faded, the cool water would no longer pass his burning lips, because a putrid fire consumed his heart, his bowels, and that devastated body was barely visible under the trembling damp sheets, even if Vic changed the sheets constantly weren't they always humid, oh! when will it all be over, anyway, when will it all be over? And then at last that glint of fierce anxiety became fixed at dawn in his eyes, the hibiscus stopped blooming finally, and it was all over, and the boats went on gliding over the green water and when the wind became too strong, the young people on their sailboards were cast out by the waves, a cold wind passed furtively over the green water and the hibiscus stopped blooming for two days when the cold wind came and you could feel it cut through you like a knife, and that was the hour a young man died, still overflowing with vitality, his books and his writings still untouched in his study on the worktable where bills in sealed envelopes were also piling up, and they were celebrating him that night, but he wasn't there any more among his relatives, his friends, to feel the breath of wind on the back of his neck and Lee no longer appeared at night on roller skates with a luminous green band around his close-cropped head, they raised their glasses but the man they celebrated wasn't there any more, the man who'd loved parties so much.

Clark Blaise

Clark Blaise was born in 1940 in Fargo, North Dakota, to an English-Canadian mother and a French-Canadian father. Growing up in both Canada and the U.S., particularly in Florida and Pittsburgh, and the Canadian prairies, Blaise describes himself as sociologically an American, having as a child processed so much data about the U.S.; psychologically a Canadian, in the way he uses and interprets that data—the irony, the self-doubt, the sense of human limits; and emotionally, a Québécois. He has been a peripatetic teacher of Creative Writing, at Concordia University in Montreal, Saratoga Springs, Columbia, and the University of Iowa, where he received his M.F.A. and where he now directs the International Writers' Program. His publications include *A North American Education* (1973), *Tribal Justice* (1974), *Lunar Attractions* (1979), *Lusts* (1983), and *Resident Alien* (1986). He has collaborated on two non-fiction works with his wife, the fiction writer Bharati Mukherjee: *Days and Nights in Calcutta* (1977) and a book about the Air India disaster called *The Sorrow and the Terror* (1989).

Clark Blaise's thoughts on the craft of fiction can be found in several essays written for anthologies edited by John Metcalf and in an interview conducted with Geoff Hancock published in *Canadian Fiction Magazine*, (No. 34/35, 1980). He is perpetually interested in matters of form. He describes the writing of stories as "line-by-line creation"; and revision, as an exhausting process: "I don't have the construction engineer's sense of 'knock this out, knock that out' and it'll work. I am a bricklayer in that sense, I have to go from brick to brick." The short story, he says "is a delicate, fluted casting; what the writer is out to capture is the rough, shaggy and broken-open mold that surrounded it, at least in his imagination." His stories, which are often low-key, originate in memories and visual impressions: "Most of the deep emotional situations that hit me or that hit people I know are too hot for me to handle. I'm in possession of a great number of stories of vast interest. But they're thoroughly useless to me; I'd make pulp of them. If they'd give me a detail instead, then I could invent the situation."

Blaise claims that the centre of his stories is not in character, but elsewhere: ". . . I do not set out to create characters. I do not set out to write a psychological case study. I am really trying to talk about, as I understand it, the world, the nature of the world, the nature of event, happenstance, accident, beauty, permanence, change, violence. I'm trying to talk about things like that. You

have to have in our humanist culture, in our humanist Western tradition, you have to have a human focus for those things or else you are writing allegory, or fable. And psychology has told us so much about probability that the character is bound to be fairly recognizable. I'm committed to representational fiction; otherwise you're doing stained-glass windows. . . .

"Yes, or sociology. So that the agreed-upon way of registering shock waves is through a perceiving consciousness and so I do that. . . . Things that really interest me are more aesthetic than psychological, so I'm willing to accept a fairly stable psychological receiver. I don't explore a great range of characterization, and I'm willing to accept that so long as I do have intensity and texture. To me that's where the interest lies, not in the characters."

The preoccupation with detail and with aesthetic questions is nowhere more evident than in Blaise's attitude to style. "Oh, I'm always very much aware of style. The style is the situation. If I want to be true to how something strikes me, I have to be as stylish or as style-conscious as that very thing that I found so gripping. I'm talking about very small things: a hedgerow, say. To do real justice to a hedgerow would require the work of a great lyric poet or Monet or (in prose) Proust—the only author I know who gives every element of nature and of character its proper space. To do real justice to anything is a matter of generosity, and character and style and you can't use the language of the butcher shop or the language of the newspaper or the textbook to do that hedgerow justice. That's the great challenge: to find language that fits the things that do not yield to language. We have no agreed-upon formula for that. We do have visual formulas in the arts, in painting and film and in music, but not in prose."

In terms of structure or design in fiction, Blaise places considerable emphasis on plot, but defines the word idiosyncratically. "For me and for me alone, plot is not planned but plot is the revelation of inevitability, the slow disclosure of something beautifully obvious, though hidden. . . . I feel sometimes that you hurtle through the vastness of time—those two billion seconds that we all have allotted to us—towards some point that was always there, something that you feared and hoped to avoid, but it was always there. And you embrace it finally and that's a plot, but until that moment, you've had (seemingly) an infinite number of choices, and ways to avoid it." He believes form is organic, not inherited, that it emerges from the material and does not necessarily follow the conventional lines of conflict, crisis, and resolution.

Blaise's response to Hancock's question about shaping strategies suggests a fascinating link between art and life in his own work. "Who knows? It's deeply related to one's own psychology obviously; introspective people write inward-looking stories. The stories, in my own mind, tend towards a kind of confirmation and towards the discovery of that which you wanted to keep hidden, and to a kind of confirmation of what you hoped was not there. . . . I hope to imply that the world was not created when the story started and it does not end when the story's over, but rather there is a continuum and the story is a plucked thread, one of possible thousands, from a sweater that remains indifferent to the process. We tease the story into a visible loop and we stare at this loop and it bothers us and it disrupts the harmony of the weave but it also goes back into the weave and disappears. End of story. For a while, it snagged at our eye. We even felt sorry for the owner of the sweater. But we also noticed that, snagged thread and all, it remains a handsome sweater. It doesn't destroy the sweater, it doesn't destroy the overall design, and there are millions more threads running in every which way which will eventually get snagged and which will become exposed and embarrassing. And that's my sense of the story. We are not talking about a whole sweater. We're talking about one out of several thousand intricately patterned, interwoven, anonymous threads and if we had the time and patience in our life we could look at every single strand, at every single moment of human life, and make of it a densely observed story. But no one has that. The sweater, however, is the shaggy old mold I was talking of earlier."

A Class of New Canadians

Norman Dyer hurried down Sherbrooke Street, collar turned against the snow. 'Superb!' he muttered, passing a basement gallery next to a French bookstore. Bleached and tanned women in furs dashed from hotel lobbies into waiting cabs. Even the neon clutter of the side streets and the honks of slithering taxis seemed remote tonight through the peaceful snow. *Superb*, he thought again, waiting for a light and backing from a slushy curb: a word reserved for wines, cigars, and delicate sauces; he was feeling superb this evening. After eighteen months in Montreal, he still found himself freshly impressed by everything he saw. He was proud of himself for having steered his life north, even for jobs that were menial by standards he could have demanded. Great just being here no matter what they paid, looking at these buildings, these faces, and hearing all the languages. He was learning to be insulted by simple bad taste, wherever he encountered it.

Since leaving graduate school and coming to Montreal, he had sampled every ethnic restaurant downtown and in the old city, plus a few Levantine places out in Outremont. He had worked on conversational French and mastered much of the local dialect, done reviews for local papers, translated French-Canadian poets for Toronto quarterlies, and tweaked his colleagues for not sympathizing enough with Quebec separatism. He attended French performances of plays he had ignored in English, and kept a small but elegant apartment near a colony of *émigré* Russians just off Park Avenue. Since coming to Montreal he'd witnessed a hold-up, watched a murder, and seen several riots. When stopped on the street for directions, he would answer in French or accented English. To live this well and travel each long academic summer, he held two jobs. He had no intention of returning to the States. In fact, he had begun to think of himself as a semi-permanent, semi-political exile.

Now, stopped again a few blocks farther, he studied the window of Holt-Renfrew's exclusive men's shop. Incredible, he thought, the authority of simple good taste. Double-breasted chalk-striped suits he would never dare to buy. Knitted sweaters, and fifty-dollar shoes. One tanned mannequin was decked out in a brash checkered sportscoat with a burgundy vest and dashing ascot. Not a price tag under three hundred dollars. Unlike food, drink, cinema, and literature, clothing had never really involved him. Someday, he now realized, it would. Dyer's clothes, thus far, had all been bought in a chain department store. He was a walking violation of American law, clad shoes to scarf in Egyptian cottons, Polish leathers, and woolens from the People's Republic of China.

He had no time for dinner tonight; this was Wednesday, a day of lectures at one university, and then an evening course in English as a Foreign Language at McGill, beginning at six. He would eat afterwards.

Besides the money, he had kept this second job because it flattered him. There was to Dyer something fiercely elemental, almost existential, about teaching both his language and his literature in a foreign country—like Joyce in Trieste, Isherwood and Nabokov in Berlin, Beckett in Paris. Also it was necessary for his students. It was the first time in his life that he had done something socially useful. What difference did it make that the job was beneath him, a recent Ph.D., while most of his colleagues in the evening school at McGill were idle housewives and bachelor civil servants? It didn't matter, even, that this job was a perversion of all the sentiments he held as a progressive young teacher. He was a god two evenings a week, sometimes suffering and fatigued, but nevertheless an omniscient, benevolent god. His students were silent, ignorant, and dedicated to learning English. No discussions, no demonstrations, no dialogue.

I love them, he thought. They need me.

He entered the room, pocketed his cap and ear muffs, and dropped his briefcase on the podium. Two girls smiled good evening.

They love me, he thought, taking off his boots and hanging up his coat; I'm not like their English-speaking bosses.

I love myself, he thought with amazement even while conducting a drill on word order. I love myself for tramping down Sherbrooke Street in zero weather just to help them with noun clauses. I love myself standing behind this podium and showing Gilles Carrier and Claude Veilleux the difference between the past continuous and the simple past; or the sultry Armenian girl with the bewitching half-glasses that 'put on' is not the same as 'take on'; or telling the dashing Mr Miguel Mayor, late of Madrid, that simple futurity can be expressed in four different ways, at least.

This is what mastery is like, he thought. Being superb in one's chosen field, not merely in one's mother tongue. A respected performer in the lecture halls of the major universities, equipped by twenty years' research in the remotest libraries, and slowly giving it back to those who must have it. Dishing it out suavely, even wittily. Being a legend. Being loved and a little feared.

'Yes, Mrs David?'

A *sabra*: freckled, reddish hair, looking like a British model, speaks with a nifty British accent, and loves me.

'No,' he smiled, 'I *were* is not correct except in the present subjunctive, which you haven't studied yet.'

The first hour's bell rang. The students closed their books for the intermission. Dyer put his away, then noticed a page of his Faulkner lecture from the afternoon class. *Absalom, Absalom!* his favourite.

'Can anyone here tell me what the *impregnable citadel of his passive rectitude* means?'

'What, sir?' asked Mr Vassilopoulos, ready to copy.

'What about the *presbyterian and lugubrious effluvium of his passive vindictiveness?*' A few girls giggled. 'O.K.,' said Dyer, 'take your break .'

In the halls of McGill they broke into the usual groups. French Canadians and South Americans into two large circles, then the Greeks, Germans, Spanish, and French into smaller groups. The patterns interested Dyer. Madrid Spaniards and Parisian French always spoke English with their New World co-linguals. The Middle Europeans spoke German together, not Russian, preferring one occupier to the other. Two Israeli men went off alone. Dyer decided to join them for the break.

Not *sabras*, Dyer concluded, not like Mrs David. The shorter one, dark and wavy-haired, held his cigarette like a violin bow. The other, Mr Weinrot, was tall and pot-bellied, with a ruddy face and thick stubby fingers. Something about him suggested truck-driving, perhaps of beer, maybe in Germany. Neither one, he decided, could supply the name of a good Israeli restaurant.

'This is really hard, you know?' said Weinrot.

'Why?'

'I think it's because I'm not speaking much of English at my job.'

'French?' asked Dyer.

'French? Pah! All the time Hebrew, sometimes German, sometimes little Polish. Crazy thing, eh? How long you think they let me speak Hebrew if I'm working in America?'

'Depends on where you're working,' he said.

'Hell, I'm working for the Canadian government, what you think? Plant I work in—I'm engineer, see—makes boilers for the turbines going up North. Look. When I'm leaving Israel I go first to Italy. Right away-bamm I'm working in Italy I'm speaking Italian like a native. Passing for a native.'

'A native Jew,' said his dark-haired friend.

'Listen to him. So in Rome they think I'm from Tyrol—that's still native, eh? So I speak Russian and German and Italian like a Jew. My Hebrew is bad, I admit it, but it's a lousy language anyway. Nobody likes it. French I understand but English I'm talking like a bum. Arabic I know five dialects. Danish fluent. So what's the matter I can't learn English?'

'It'll come, don't worry,' Dyer smiled. *Don't worry, my son;* he wanted to pat him on the arm. 'Anyway, that's what makes Canada so appealing. Here they don't force you.'

'What's this *appealing*? Means nice? Look, my friend, keep it, eh? Two years in a country I don't learn the language means it isn't a country.'

'Come on,' said Dyer. 'Neither does forcing you.'

'Let me tell you a story why I come to Canada. Then you tell me if I was wrong, O.K.?'

'Certainly,' said Dyer, flattered.

In Italy, Weinrot told him, he had lost his job to a Communist union. He left Italy for Denmark and opened up an Israeli restaurant with five other friends. Then the six Israelis decided to rent a bigger apartment downtown near the restaurant. They found a perfect nine-room place for two thousand kroner a month, not bad shared six ways. Next day the landlord told them the deal was off. 'You tell me why,' Weinrot demanded.

No Jews? Dyer wondered. 'He wanted more rent,' he finally said.

'More—you kidding? More we expected. *Less* we didn't expect. A couple with eight kids is showing up after we're gone and the law in Denmark says a man has a right to a room for each kid plus a hundred kroner knocked off the rent for each kid. What you think of that? So a guy who comes in *after* us gets a nine-room place for a thousand kroner *less*. Law says no way a bachelor can get a place ahead of a family, and bachelors pay twice as much.'

Dyer waited, then asked, 'So?'

'So, I make up my mind the world is full of communismus, just like Israel. So I take out applications next day for Australia, South Africa, U.S.A., and Canada. Canada says come right away, so I go. Should have waited for South Africa.'

'How could you?' Dyer cried. 'What's wrong with you anyway? South Africa is fascist. Australia is racist.'

The bell rang, and the Israelis, with Dyer, began walking to the room.

'What I was wondering, then,' said Mr Weinrot, ignoring Dyer's outburst, 'was if my English is good enough to be working in the United States. You're American, aren't you?'

It was a question Dyer had often avoided in Europe, but had rarely been asked in Montreal. 'Yes,' he admitted, 'your English is probably good enough for the States or South Africa, whichever one wants you first.'

He hurried ahead to the room, feeling that he had let Montreal down. He wanted to turn and shout to Weinrot and to all the others that Montreal was the greatest city on the continent, if only they knew it as well as he did. If they'd just break out of their little ghettos.

At the door, the Armenian girl with the half-glasses caught his arm. She was standing with Mrs David and Miss Parizeau, a jolly French-Canadian girl that Dyer had been thinking of asking out.

'Please, sir,' she said, looking at him over the tops of her tiny glasses, 'what I was asking earlier—*put on*—I heard on the television. A man said *You are putting me on* and everybody laughed. I think it was supposed to be funny but *put on* we learned means get dressed, no?'

'Ah—don't put me on,' Dyer laughed.

'I yaven't erd it neither,' said Miss Parizeau.

'To put some*body* on means to make a fool of him. To put some*thing* on is to wear it. O.K.?' He gave examples.

'Ah, now I know,' said Miss Parizeau. 'Like bullshitting somebody. Is it the same?'

'Ah, yes,' he said, smiling. French-Canadians were like children learning the language. 'Your example isn't considered polite. "Put on" is very common now in the States.'

'Then maybe,' said Miss Parizeau, 'we'll ave it ere in twenty years.' The Armenian giggled.

'No—I've heard it here just as often,' Dyer protested, but the girls had already entered the room.

He began the second hour with a smile which slowly soured as he thought of the Israelis. America's anti-communism was bad enough, but it was worse hearing it echoed by immigrants, by Jews, here in Montreal. Wasn't there a psychological type who chose Canada over South Africa? Or was it just a matter of visas and slow adjustment? Did Johannesburg lose its Greeks, and Melbourne its Italians, the way Dyer's students were always leaving Montreal?

And after class when Dyer was again feeling content and thinking of approaching one of the Israelis for a restaurant tip, there came the flood of small requests: should Mrs Papadopoulos go into a more advanced course; could Mr Perez miss a week for an interview in Toronto; could Mr Giguère, who spoke English perfectly, have a harder book; Mr Coté an easier one?

Then as he packed his briefcase in the empty room, Miguel Mayor, the vain and impeccable Spaniard, came forward from the hallway.

'Sir,' he began, walking stiffly, ready to bow or salute. He wore a loud grey checkered sportscoat this evening, blue shirt, and matching ascot-handkerchief, slightly mauve. He must have shaved just before class, Dyer noticed, for two fresh daubs of antiseptic cream stood out on his jaw, just under his earlobe.

'I have been wanting to ask you something, as a matter of fact,' said Dyer. 'Do you know any good Spanish restaurants I might try tonight?'

'There are not any good Spanish restaurants in Montreal,' he said. He stepped closer. 'Sir?'

'What's on your mind, then?'

'Please—have you the time to look on a letter for me?'

He laid the letter on the podium.

'Look *over* a letter,' said Dyer. 'What is it for?'

'I have applied,' he began, stopping to emphasize the present perfect construction, 'for a job in Cleveland, Ohio, and I want to know if my letter will be good. Will an American, I mean—'

'Why are you going there?'

'It is a good job.'

'But Cleveland—'

'They have a blackman mayor, I have read. But the job is not in Cleveland.'

'Let me see it.'

Most honourable Sir: I humbly beg consideration for a position in your grand company . . .

'Who are you writing this to?'

'The president,' said Miguel Mayor.

I am once a student of Dr Ramiro Gutierrez of the Hydraulic Institute of Sevilla Spain . . .

'Does the president know this Ramiro Gutierrez?'

'Oh, everybody is knowing him,' Miguel Mayor assured, 'he is the most famous expert in all Spain.'

'Did he recommend this company to you?'

'No—I have said in my letter, if you look—'

An ancient student of Dr Gutierrez, Salvador del Este is actually a boiler expert who is being employed like supervisor is formerly a friend of mine . . .

'Is he still your friend?'

Whenever you say come to my city Miguel Mayor for talking I will be coming. I am working in Montreal since two years and am now wanting more money than I am getting here now . . .

'Well . . .' Dyer sighed.

'Sir—what I want from you is knowing in good English how to interview me by this man. The letters in Spanish are not the same to English ones, you know?'

I remain humbly at your orders . . .

'Why do you want to leave Montreal?'

'It's time for a change.'

'Have you ever been to Cleveland?'

'I am one summer in California. Very beautiful there and hot like my country. Montreal is big port like Barcelona. Everybody mixed together and having no money. It is just a place to land, no?'

'Montreal? Don't be silly.'

'I thought I come here and learn good English but where I work I get by in Spanish and French. It's hard, you know?' he smiled. Then he took a few steps back and gave his cuffs a gentle tug, exposing a set of jade cufflinks.

Dyer looked at the letter again and calculated how long he would be correcting it, then up at his student. How old is he? My age? Thirty? Is he married? Where do the Spanish live in Montreal? He looks so prosperous, so confident, like a male model off a page of *Playboy*. For an instant Dyer felt that his student was mocking him, somehow pitting his astounding confidence and wardrobe, sharp chin and matador's bearing against Dyer's command of English and mastery of the side streets, bistros, and ethnic restaurants. Mayor's letter was painful, yet he remained somehow competent. He would pass his interview, if he got one. What would he care about America, and the odiousness he'd soon be supporting? It was as though a superstructure of exploitation had been revealed, and Dyer felt himself abused by the very people he wanted so much to help. It had to end someplace.

He scratched out the second 'humbly' from the letter, then folded the sheet of foolscap. 'Get it typed right away,' he said. 'Good luck.'

'Thank you, sir,' said his student, with a bow. Dyer watched the letter disappear in the inner pocket of the checkered sportscoat. Then the folding of the cashmere scarf, the draping of the camel's hair coat about the shoulders, the easing of the fur hat down to the rims of his ears. The meticulous filling of the pigskin gloves. Mayor's patent leather galoshes glistened.

'Good evening, sir,' he said.

'*Buenas noches*,' Dyer replied.

He hurried now, back down Sherbrooke Street to his daytime office where he could deposit his books. Montreal on a winter night was still mysterious, still magical. Snow blurred the arc lights. The wind was dying. Every second car was now a taxi, crowned with an orange crescent. Slushy curbs had hardened. The window of Holt-Renfrew's was still attractive. The legless dummies invited a final stare. He stood longer than he had earlier, in front of the sporty mannequin with a burgundy waistcoat, the mauve and blue ensemble, the jade cufflinks.

Good evening, sir, he could almost hear. The ascot, the shirt, the complete outfit, had leaped off the back of Miguel Mayor. He pictured how he must have entered the store with three hundred dollars and a prepared speech, and walked out again with everything off the torso's back.

I want that.

What, sir?

That.

The coat, sir?

Yes.

Very well, sir.

And *that*.

Which, sir?

All that.

'Absurd man!' Dyer whispered. There had been a moment of fear, as though the naked body would leap from the window, and legless, chase him down Sherbrooke Street. But the moment was passing. Dyer realized now that it was comic, even touching. Miguel Mayor had simply tried too hard, too fast, and it would be good for him to stay in Montreal until he deserved those clothes, that touching vanity and confidence. With one last look at the window, he turned sharply, before the clothes could speak again.

Jorge Luis Borges

Born in 1899 in Buenos Aires, where his father was a lawyer and teacher of psychology, Borges was a precocious child, who was writing in Spanish and English at age six and had published a translation before he was ten. He spent the war years at school in Geneva, studying in French, but also learning Latin, German, and Italian. On his return to Argentina from Spain in 1921, he founded the literary magazine *Sur* and embarked on his long career as a writer, writing mainly poetry and flirting with literary movements such as "Ultraism," a form of Spanish Expressionism. He was best known as an editor and essayist until the publication of *Ficciones* in 1945, a playful book of anti-realist fictions. This was followed by *Labyrinths* (1962), *The Aleph and Other Stories* (1970), and *Doctor Brodie's Report* (1973). Although he was not a politically engaged writer, Borges nonetheless ran afoul of dictator Juan Perón, who demoted him from librarian to chicken inspector. He was Charles Eliot Norton Professor of Poetry at Harvard in 1967–1968 and received various honours, including the Prix Internationale des Editeurs (Prix Formentor), which he shared with Samuel Beckett. Borges taught English and American Literature for many years at the University of Buenos Aires, until blindness forced him to retire. In his essay "Blindness," he speaks ironically, but not bitterly, of being reinstated as director of the Argentine National Library the year he became too blind to read books and of how he celebrated both events by taking up the study of Old English. Because of his remarkable memory and determination, Borges's range of literary reference was remarkable and he could recall enormous amounts of material for his lectures, conversations, and literary purposes. His ideas on the craft are gathered together in *Borges on Writing* (1973) and some of his lectures are available in *Seven Nights* (1984). He died in 1986.

Although he is a great stylist, Borges felt that style was not something to be consciously cultivated, but, rather, must grow out of a writer's convictions and long devotion to the craft. "If a writer disbelieves what he is writing, then he can hardly expect his readers to believe it. In this country, though, there is a tendency to regard any kind of writing—especially the writing of poetry—as a game of style. I have known many poets here who have written well—very fine stuff—with delicate moods and so on—but if you talk with them, the only thing they tell you is smutty stories or speak of politics in the way that everybody does, so that really

their writing turns out to be a kind of sideshow. They had learned writing in the way that a man might learn to play chess or to play bridge. They were not really poets or writers at all. It was a trick they had learned, and they had learned it thoroughly. They had the whole thing at their finger ends."

His work is dominated by ideas, yet Borges insisted that a writer not be judged by the importance of his ideas, but rather by "the enjoyment he gives and by the emotion one gets" from his work. When asked in *The Paris Review* interview, conducted by Ronald Christ, about his interest in the fantastic, Borges quoted two of his favourite writers: "Conrad thought that when one wrote, even in a realistic way, about the world, one was writing a fantastic story because the world itself is fantastic and unfathomable and mysterious. . . . I found that he was right. I talked to Bioy Cesares, who also writes fantastic stories—very, very fine stories—and he said, 'I think Conrad is right. Really, nobody knows whether the world is realistic or fantastic, that is to say, whether the world is a natural process or whether it is a kind of dream, a dream that we may or may not share with others.'"

His writing is highly allusive, but Borges argues for a plain style, unadorned, with no big dictionary words and nothing from the streets that will quickly go out of fashion. In terms of organizing principles in fiction, he says: ". . . generally speaking, what I think is most important in a short story is the plot or situation, while in a novel what's important are the characters." When asked if social or political issues should be dealt with in fiction, Borges, who has elsewhere declared himself an antagonist of *engaged writing*, plays down any links in his fiction with contemporary politics and tries to suggest that "perhaps it's about the politics of any time or any place." "Oscar Wilde said that modernity of treatment and subject should be carefully avoided by the modern artist. Of course, he was being witty, but what he was saying was based on an obvious truth. Homer, for example, wrote several centuries after the Trojan War. The idea that a writer should be contemporaneous is itself modern, but I should say it belongs more to journalism than to literature. No real writer ever tried to be contemporary."

In an essay called "The Writer's Apprenticeship," Borges quotes Chesterton's famous remark about writing: "Only one thing is needful—everything." Addressing himself to the question of what a great university, or education, should give the young writer, he includes "conversation, discussion, the art of agree-ing, and, what is perhaps most important, the art of disagreeing." He echoes Camus's dictum that creating is living doubly and urges the beginning writer to remember that "Literature is not a mere juggling of words; what matters is what is left unsaid, or what may be read between the lines. Were it not for this deep inner feeling, literature would be no more than a game, and we all know that it can be much more than that."

The Book of Sand

Translated by Norman Thomas di Giovanni

Thy rope of sands . . . .
                    –George Herbert

The line is made up of an infinite number of points; the plane of an infinite number of lines; the volume of an infinite number of planes; the hypervolume of an infinite number of volumes. . . . No, unquestionably this is not—*more geomet-rico*—the best way of beginning my story. To claim that it is true is nowadays the convention of every made-up story. Mine, however, *is* true.

I live alone in a fourth-floor apartment on Belgrano Street, in Buenos Aires. Late one evening, a few months back, I heard a knock at my door. I opened it and a stranger stood there. He was a tall man, with nondescript features—or perhaps it was my myopia that made them seem that way. Dressed in gray and carrying a gray suitcase in his hand, he had an unassuming look about him. I saw at once that he was a foreigner. At first, he struck me as old; only later did I realize that I had been misled by his thin blond hair, which was, in a Scandinavian sort of way, almost white. During the course of our conversation, which was not to last an hour, I found out that he came from the Orkneys.

I invited him in, pointing to a chair. He paused awhile before speaking. A kind of gloom emanated from him—as it does now from me.

"I sell Bibles," he said.

Somewhat pedantically, I replied, "In this house are several English Bibles, including the first—John Wiclif's. I also have Cipriano de Valera's, Luther's—which, from a literary viewpoint, is the worst—and a Latin copy of the Vulgate. As you see, it's not exactly Bibles I stand in need of."

After a few moments of silence, he said, "I don't only sell Bibles. I can show you a holy book I came across on the outskirts of Bikaner. It may interest you."

He opened the suitcase and laid the book on a table. It was an octavo volume, bound in cloth. There was no doubt that it had passed through many hands. Examining it, I was surprised by its unusual weight. On the spine were the words "Holy Writ" and, below them, "Bombay."

"Nineteenth century, probably," I remarked.

"I don't know," he said. "I've never found out."

I opened the book at random. The script was strange to me. The pages, which were worn and typographically poor, were laid out in double columns, as in a Bible. The text was closely printed, and it was ordered in versicles. In the upper corners of the pages were Arabic numbers. I noticed that one left-hand page bore the number (let us say) 40,514 and the facing right-hand page 999. I turned the leaf; it was numbered with eight digits. It also bore a small illustration, like the kind used in dictionaries—an anchor drawn with pen and ink, as if by a school-boy's clumsy hand.

It was at this point that the stranger said, "Look at the illustration closely. You'll never see it again."

I noted my place and closed the book. At once, I reopened it. Page by page, in vain, I looked for the illustration of the anchor. "It seems to be a version of Scriptures in some Indian language, is it not?" I said to hide my dismay.

"No," he replied. Then, as if confiding a secret, he lowered his voice. "I acquired the book in a town out on the plain in exchange for a handful of rupees and a Bible. Its owner did not know how to read. I suspect that he saw the Book of Books as a talisman. He was of the lowest caste; nobody but other untouchables could tread his shadow without contamination. He told me his book was called the Book of Sand, because neither the book nor the sand has any beginning or end."

The stranger asked me to find the first page.

I laid my left hand on the cover and, trying to put my thumb on the flyleaf, I opened the book. It was useless. Every time I tried, a number of pages came between the cover and my thumb. It was as if they kept growing from the book.

"Now find the last page."

Again I failed. In a voice that was not mine, I barely managed to stammer, "This can't be."

Still speaking in a low voice, the stranger said, "It can't be, but it *is*. The number of pages in this book is no more or less than infinite. None is the first page, none the last. I don't know why they're numbered in this arbitrary way. Perhaps to suggest that the terms of an infinite series admit any number."

Then, as if he were thinking aloud, he said, "If space is infinite, we may be at any point in space. If time is infinite, we may be at any point in time."

His speculations irritated me. "You are religious, no doubt?" I asked him.

"Yes, I'm a Presbyterian. My conscience is clear. I am reasonably sure of not having cheated the native when I gave him the Word of God in exchange for his devilish book."

I assured him that he had nothing to reproach himself for, and I asked if he were just passing through this part of the world. He replied that he planned to return to his country in a few days. It was then that I learned that he was a Scot from the Orkney Islands. I told him I had a great personal affection for Scotland, through my love of Stevenson and Hume.

"You mean Stevenson and Robbie Burns," he corrected.

While we spoke, I kept exploring the infinite book. With feigned indifference, I asked, "Do you intend to offer this curiosity to the British Museum?"

"No. I'm offering it to you," he said, and he stipulated a rather high sum for the book.

I answered, in all truthfulness, that such a sum was out of my reach, and I began thinking. After a minute or two, I came up with a scheme.

"I propose a swap," I said. "You got this book for a handful of rupees and a copy of the Bible. I'll offer you the amount of my pension check, which I've just collected, and my black-letter Wiclif Bible. I inherited it from my ancestors."

"A black-letter Wiclif!" he murmured.

I went to my bedroom and brought him the money and the book. He turned the leaves and studied the title page with all the fervor of a true bibliophile.

"It's a deal," he said.

It amazed me that he did not haggle. Only later was I to realize that he had entered my house with his mind made up to sell the book. Without counting the money, he put it away.

We talked about India, about Orkney, and about the Norwegian jarls who once ruled it. It was night when the man left. I have not seen him again, nor do I know his name.

I thought of keeping the Book of Sand in the space left on the shelf by the Wiclif, but in the end I decided to hide it behind the volumes of a broken set of The Thousand and One Nights. I went to bed and did not sleep. At three or four in the morning, I turned on the light. I got down the impossible book and leafed through its pages. On one of them I saw engraved a mask. The upper corner of the page carried a number, which I no longer recall, elevated to the ninth power.

I showed no one my treasure. To the luck of owning it was added the fear of having it stolen, and then the misgiving that it might not truly be infinite. These twin preoccupations intensified my old misanthropy. I had only a few friends left; I now stopped seeing even them. A prisoner of the book, I almost never went out anymore. After studying its frayed spine and covers with a magnifying glass, I rejected the possibility of contrivance of any sort. The small illustrations, I verified, came two thousand pages apart. I set about listing them alphabetically in a notebook, which I was not long in filling up. Never once was an illustration repeated. At night, in the meager intervals my insomnia granted, I dreamed of the book.

Summer came and went, and I realized that the book was monstrous. What good did it do me to think that I, who looked upon the volume with my eyes, who held it in my hands, was any less monstrous? I felt that the book was a nightmarish object, an obscene thing that affronted and tainted reality itself.

I thought of fire, but I feared that the burning of an infinite book might likewise prove infinite and suffocate the planet with smoke. Somewhere I recalled reading that the best place to hide a leaf is in a forest. Before retirement, I worked on Mexico Street, at the Argentine National Library, which contains nine hundred thousand volumes. I knew that to the right of the entrance a curved staircase leads down into the basement, where books and maps and periodicals are kept. One day I went there and, slipping past a member of the staff and trying not to notice at what height or distance from the door, I lost the Book of Sand on one of the basement's musty shelves.

Tadeusz Borowski

Born in 1922 in Zytomierz, Poland, to a dissident father who was subsequently interned in a labour camp in the Arctic and a mother who was sent to Siberia, Tadeusz Borowski not surprisingly later ran afoul of the authorities during the German occupation. His literary career and studies at underground universities were interrupted when he was arrrested for his activist associations. He was incarcerated in Auschwitz, then in Dachau, where he witnessed and participated in the Nazi torture and killing of countless thousands. After the war, he published two volumes of poems, *Imiona nurtu* (1945) and *Poszukiwania* (1945), and three collections of stories, including *This Way for the Gas, Ladies and Gentlemen* (1976), which Jan Kott describes as "one of the cruellest testimonies to what men did to men, and a pitiless verdict that anything can be done to a human being." He worked, for a time, as a propagandist for a new socialist order in Poland, but his searing memories proved too great a burden. He committed suicide by asphyxiation in 1951.

Instead of cherishing an undying hope, which was the credo of that other great Polish writer Joseph Conrad, Borowski's narrator in "Auschwitz, Our Home," attacks the "hope that makes people go without a murmur to the gas chambers, keeps them from risking revolt . . . compels man to hold on to one more day of life." As an intimate participant in these horrific events, Borowski refused to sentimentalize the victims or demonize the criminals. Critic Andrzej Wirth suggests that Borowski's narrative focus on the Kapos, the go-betweens, provides a morally ambivalent point of view that forces the reader to internalize the evil and allows both reader and author to direct their rage against the system that is responsible for creating these conditions. And, of course, the buck does not stop with the Nazis, but with the whole of Western civilization, which laid the groundwork for so colossal a slaughter.

Borowski's work raises important questions about both the nature and function of art. After the war, many German writers chose silence, rather than use a language that was in complicity with the Nazi regime; others felt that language itself was inadequate to convey the true horror of events. Some few Europeans, among them Borowski, had no option but to try to give imaginative expression to what they had experienced, creating what has been called a "literature of atrocity." While the landscape of his fiction seems devoid of values—one of his characters says that "in this war morality, justice, and human dignity had all slid off man like a rotten rag. . . . There is no crime a man will not commit to save himself"— Borowski's task is a painfully moral one, to draw us inescapably into a world where there seem to be no heroes and no simple moral choices.

More searing even than Hubert Selby's *Last Exit to Brooklyn*, Borowski's work is, nonetheless, an affirmation of the need to bear witness and calls to mind Albert Camus's remarks in *The Rebel* that even if literature "describes nostalgia, despair, frustration, it still creates a form of salvation. To talk of despair is to conquer it. Despairing literature is a contradiction in terms."

This Way for the Gas, Ladies and Gentlemen
Translated by Barbara Vedder

All of us walk around naked. The delousing is finally over, and our striped suits are back from the tanks of Cyclone B solution, an efficient killer of lice in clothing and of men in gas chambers. Only the inmates in the blocks cut off from ours by the 'Spanish goats'[1] still have nothing to wear. But all the same, all of us walk around naked: the heat is unbearable. The camp has been sealed off tight. Not a single prisoner, not one solitary louse, can sneak through the gate. The labour Kommandos have stopped working. All day, thousands of naked men shuffle up and down the roads, cluster around the squares, or lie against the walls and on top of the roofs. We have been sleeping on plain boards, since our mattresses and blankets are still being disinfected. From the rear blockhouses we have a view of the F.K.L.—*Frauen Konzentration Lager*; there too the delousing is in full swing.

Twenty-eight thousand women have been stripped naked and driven out of the barracks. Now they swarm around the large yard between the blockhouses.

The heat rises, the hours are endless. We are without even our usual diversion: the wide roads leading to the crematoria are empty. For several days now, no new transports have come in. Part of 'Canada'[2] has been liquidated and detailed to a labour Kommando—one of the very toughest—at Harmenz. For there exists in the camp a special brand of justice based on envy: when the rich and mighty fall, their friends see to it that they fall to the very bottom. And Canada, our Canada, which smells not of maple forests but of French perfume, has amassed great fortunes in diamonds and currency from all over Europe.

Several of us sit on the top bunk, our legs dangling over the edge. We slice the neat loaves of crisp, crunchy bread. It is a bit coarse to the taste, the kind that stays fresh for days. Sent all the way from Warsaw—only a week ago my mother held this white loaf in her hands . . . dear Lord, dear Lord . . .

We unwrap the bacon, the onion, we open a can of evaporated milk. Henri, the fat Frenchman, dreams aloud of the French wine brought by the transports from Strasbourg, Paris, Marseille . . . Sweat streams down his body.

'Listen, *mon ami*, next time we go up on the loading ramp, I'll bring you real champagne. You haven't tried it before, eh?'

'No. But you'll never be able to smuggle it through the gate, so stop teasing. Why not try and "organize" some shoes for me instead—you know, the perforated kind, with a double sole, and what about that shirt you promised me long ago?'

'*Patience, patience.* When the new transports come, I'll bring all you want. We'll be going on the ramp again!'

'And what if there aren't any more "cremo" transports?' I say spitefully. 'Can't you see how much easier life is becoming around here: no limit on packages, no more beatings? You even write letters home . . . One hears all kind of talk, and, dammit, they'll run out of people!'

'Stop talking nonsense.' Henri's serious fat face moves rhythmically, his mouth is full of sardines. We have been friends for a long time, but I do not even know his last name. 'Stop talking nonsense,' he repeats, swallowing with effort. 'They can't run out of people, or we'll starve to death in this blasted camp. All of us live on what they bring.'

'All? We have our packages . . .'

'Sure, you and your friend, and ten other friends of yours. Some of you Poles get packages. But what about us, and the Jews, and the Russkis? And what if we had no food, no "organization" from the transports, do you think you'd be eating those packages of yours in peace? We wouldn't let you!'

'You would, you'd starve to death like the Greeks. Around here, whoever has grub, has power.'

'Anyway, you have enough, we have enough, so why argue?'

Right, why argue? They have enough, I have enough, we eat together and we sleep on the same bunks. Henri slices the bread, he makes a tomato salad. It tastes good with the commissary mustard.

Below us, naked, sweat-drenched men crowd the narrow barracks aisles or lie packed in eights and tens in the lower bunks. Their nude, withered bodies stink of sweat and excrement; their cheeks are hollow. Directly beneath me, in the bottom bunk, lies a rabbi. He has covered his head with a piece of rag torn off a blanket and reads from a Hebrew prayer book (there is no shortage of this type of literature at the camp), wailing loudly, monotonously.

'Can't somebody shut him up? He's been raving as if he'd caught God himself by the feet.'

'I don't feel like moving. Let him rave. They'll take him to the oven that much sooner.'

'Religion is the opium of the people,' Henri, who is a Communist and a *rentier*, says sententiously. 'If they didn't believe in God and eternal life, they'd have smashed the crematoria long ago.'

'Why haven't you done it then?'

The question is rhetorical; the Frenchman ignores it.

'Idiot,' he says simply, and stuffs a tomato in his mouth.

Just as we finish our snack, there is a sudden commotion at the door. The Muslims[3] scurry in fright to the safety of their bunks, a messenger runs into the Block Elder's shack. The Elder, his face solemn, steps out at once.

'Canada! *Antreten!* But fast! There's a transport coming!'

'Great God!' yells Henri, jumping off the bunk. He swallows the rest of his tomato, snatches his coat, screams '*Raus*' at the men below, and in a flash is at the door. We can hear a scramble in the other bunks. Canada is leaving for the ramp.

'Henri, the shoes!' I call after him.

'*Keine Angst!*' he shouts back, already outside.

I proceed to put away the food. I tie a piece of rope around the suitcase where the onions and the tomatoes from my father's garden in Warsaw mingle with Portuguese sardines, bacon from Lublin (that's from my brother), and authentic sweetmeats from Salonica. I tie it all up, pull on my trousers, and slide off the bunk.

'*Platz!*' I yell, pushing my way through the Greeks. They step aside. At the door I bump into Henri.

'*Was ist los?*'

'Want to come with us on the ramp?'

'Sure, why not?'

'Come along then, grab your coat! We're short of a few men. I've already told the Kapo,' and he shoves me out of the barracks door.

We line up. Someone has marked down our numbers, someone up ahead yells, 'March, march,' and now we are running towards the gate, accompanied by the shouts of a multilingual throng that is already being pushed back to the barracks. Not everybody is lucky enough to be going on the ramp . . . We have almost reached the gate. *Links, zwei, drei, vier! Mützen ab!* Erect, arms stretched stiffly along our hips, we march past the gate briskly, smartly, almost gracefully A sleepy S.S. man with a large pad in his hand checks us off, waving us ahead in groups of five.

'*Hundert!*' he calls after we have all passed.

'*Stimmt!*' comes a hoarse answer from out front.

We march fast, almost at a run. There are guards all around, young men with automatics. We pass camp II B, then some deserted barracks and a clump of unfamiliar green—apple and pear trees. We cross the circle of watchtowers and, running, burst on to the highway. We have arrived. Just a few more yards. There, surrounded by trees, is the ramp.

A cheerful little station, very much like any other provincial railway stop: a small square framed by tall chestnuts and paved with yellow gravel. Not far off, beside the road, squats a tiny wooden shed, uglier and more flimsy than the ugliest and flimsiest railway shack; farther along lie stacks of old rails, heaps of wooden beams, barracks parts, bricks, paving stones. This is where they load freight for Birkenau: supplies for the construction of the camp, and people for the gas chambers. Trucks drive around, load up lumber, cement, people—a regular daily routine.

And now the guards are being posted along the rails, across the beams, in the green shade of the Silesian chestnuts, to form a tight circle around the ramp. They wipe the sweat from their faces and sip out of their canteens. It is unbearably hot; the sun stands motionless at its zenith.

'Fall out!'

We sit down in the narrow streaks of shade along the stacked rails. The hungry Greeks (several of them managed to come along, God only knows how) rummage underneath the rails. One of them finds some pieces of mildewed bread, another a few half-rotten sardines. They eat.

'*Schweinedreck,*' spits a young, tall guard with corn-coloured hair and dreamy blue eyes. 'For God's sake, any minute you'll have so much food to stuff down your guts, you'll bust!' He adjusts his gun, wipes his face with a handkerchief.

'Hey you, fatso! His boot lightly touches Henri's shoulder. '*Pass mal auf,* want a drink?'

'Sure, but I haven't got any marks,' replies the Frenchman with a professional air.

'*Schade,* too bad.'

'Come, come, Herr Posten, isn't my word good enough any more? Haven't we done business before? How much?'

'One hundred. *Gemacht?*'

'*Gemacht.*'

We drink the water, lukewarm and tasteless. It will be paid for by the people who have not yet arrived.

'Now you be careful,' says Henri, turning to me. He tosses away the empty bottle. It strikes the rails and bursts into tiny fragments. 'Don't take any money, they might be checking. Anyway, who the hell needs money? You've got enough to eat. Don't take suits, either, or they'll think you're planning to escape. Just get a shirt, silk only, with a collar. And a vest. And if you find something to drink, don't bother calling me. I know how to shift for myself, but you watch your step or they'll let you have it.'

'Do they beat you up here?'

'Naturally. You've got to have eyes in your ass. *Arschaugen.*'

Around us sit the Greeks, their jaws working greedily, like huge human insects. They munch on stale lumps of bread. They are restless, wondering what will happen next. The sight of the large beams and the stacks of rails has them worried. They dislike carrying heavy loads.

'*Was wir arbeiten?*' they ask.

'*Niks. Transport kommen, alles Krematorium, compris?*'

'*Alles verstehen,*' they answer in crematorium Esperanto. All is well—they will not have to move the heavy rails or carry the beams.

In the meantime, the ramp has become increasingly alive with activity, increasingly noisy. The crews are being divided into those who will open and unload the arriving cattle cars and those who will be posted by the wooden steps. They receive instructions on how to proceed most efficiently. Motor cycles drive up, delivering S.S. officers, bemedalled, glittering with brass, beefy men with highly polished boots and shiny, brutal faces. Some have brought their briefcases, others hold thin, flexible whips. This gives them an air of military readiness and agility. They walk in and out of the commissary—for the miserable little shack by the road serves as their commissary, where in the summertime they drink mineral water, *Studentenquelle*, and where in winter they can warm up with a glass of hot wine. They greet each other in the state-approved way, raising an arm Roman fashion, then shake hands cordially, exchange warm smiles, discuss mail from home, their children, their families. Some stroll majestically on the ramp. The silver squares on their collars glitter, the gravel crunches under their boots, their bamboo whips snap impatiently.

We lie against the rails in the narrow streaks of shade, breathe unevenly, occasionally exchange a few words in our various tongues, and gaze listlessly at the majestic men in green uniforms, at the green trees, and at the church steeple of a distant village.

'The transport is coming,' somebody says. We spring to our feet, all eyes turn in one direction. Around the bend, one after another, the cattle cars begin rolling in. The train backs into the station, a conductor leans out, waves his hand, blows a whistle. The locomotive whistles back with a shrieking noise, puffs, the train rolls slowly alongside the ramp. In the tiny barred windows appear pale, wilted, exhausted human faces, terror-stricken women with tangled hair, unshaven men. They gaze at the station in silence. And then, suddenly, there is a stir inside the cars and a pounding against the wooden boards.

'Water! Air!'—weary, desperate cries.

Heads push through the windows, mouths gasp frantically for air. They draw a few breaths, then disappear; others come in their place, then also disappear. The cries and moans grow louder.

A man in a green uniform covered with more glitter than any of the others jerks his head impatiently, his lips twist in annoyance. He inhales deeply, then with a rapid gesture throws his cigarette away and signals to the guard. The guard removes the automatic from his shoulder, aims, sends a series of shots along the train. All is quiet now. Meanwhile, the trucks have arrived, steps are being drawn up, and the Canada men stand ready at their posts by the train doors. The S.S. officer with the briefcase raises his hand.

'Whoever takes gold, or anything at all besides food, will be shot for stealing Reich property. Understand? *Verstanden?*'

'*Jawohl!*' we answer eagerly.

'*Also los!* Begin!'

The bolts crack, the doors fall open. A wave of fresh air rushes inside the train. People . . . inhumanly crammed, buried under incredible heaps of luggage, suitcases, trunks, packages, crates, bundles of every description (everything that had been their past and was to start their future). Monstrously squeezed together, they have fainted from heat, suffocated, crushed one another. Now they push towards the opened doors, breathing like fish cast out on the sand.

'Attention! Out, and take your luggage with you! Take out everything. Pile all your stuff near the exits. Yes, your coats too. It is summer. March to the left. Understand?'

'Sir, what's going to happen to us?' They jump from the train on to the gravel, anxious, worn-out.

'Where are you people from?'

'Sosnowiec-Będzin. Sir, what's going to happen to us?' They repeat the question stubbornly, gazing into our tired eyes.

'I don't know, I don't understand Polish.'

It is the camp law: people going to their death must be deceived to the very end. This is the only permissible form of charity. The heat is tremendous. The sun hangs directly over our heads, the white, hot sky quivers, the air vibrates, an occasional breeze feels like a sizzling blast from a furnace. Our lips are parched, the mouth fills with the salty taste of blood, the body is weak and heavy from lying in the sun. Water!

A huge, multicoloured wave of people loaded down with luggage pours from the train like a blind, mad river trying to find a new bed. But before they have a chance to recover, before they can draw a breath of fresh air and look at the sky, bundles are snatched from their hands, coats ripped off their backs, their purses and umbrellas taken away.

'But please, sir, it's for the sun, I cannot. . .'

'*Verboten!*' one of us barks through clenched teeth. There is an S.S. man standing behind your back, calm, efficient, watchful.

'*Meine Herrschaften*, this way, ladies and gentlemen, try not to throw your things around, please. Show some goodwill,' he says courteously, his restless hands playing with the slender whip.

'Of course, of course,' they answer as they pass, and now they walk alongside the train somewhat more cheerfully. A woman reaches down quickly to pick up her handbag. The whip flies, the woman screams, stumbles, and falls under the feet of the surging crowd. Behind her, a child cries in a thin little voice 'Mamele!'—a very small girl with tangled black curls.

The heaps grow. Suitcases, bundles, blankets, coats, handbags that open as they fall, spilling coins, gold, watches; mountains of bread pile up at the exits, heaps of marmalade, jams, masses of meat, sausages; sugar spills on the gravel. Trucks, loaded with people, start up with a deafening roar and drive off amidst the wailing and screaming of the women separated from their children, and the stupefied silence of the men left behind. They are the ones who had been ordered to step to the right—the healthy and the young who will go to the camp. In the end, they too will not escape death, but first they must work.

Trucks leave and return, without interruption, as on a monstrous conveyor belt. A Red Cross van drives back and forth, back and forth, incessantly: it transports the gas that will kill these people. The enormous cross on the hood, red as blood, seems to dissolve in the sun.

The Canada men at the trucks cannot stop for a single moment, even to catch their breath. They shove the people up the steps, pack them in tightly, sixty per truck, more or less. Near by stands a young, clean-shaven 'gentleman', an S.S. officer with a notebook in his hand. For each departing truck he enters a mark; sixteen gone means one thousand people, more or less. The gentleman is calm, precise. No truck can leave without a signal from him, or a mark in his notebook: *Ordnung muss sein.* The marks swell into thousands, the thousands into whole transports, which afterwards we shall simply call 'from Salonica', 'from Strasbourg', 'from Rotterdam'. This one will be called 'Sosnowiec-Będzin'. The new prisoners from Sosnowiec-Będzin will receive serial numbers 131-2-thousand, of course, though afterwards we shall simply say 131-2, for short.

The transports swell into weeks, months, years. When the war is over, they will count up the marks in their notebooks—all four and a half million of them. The bloodiest battle of the war, the greatest victory of the strong, united Germany. *Ein Reich, ein Volk, ein Führer*—and four crematoria.

The train has been emptied. A thin, pock-marked S.S. man peers inside, shakes his head in disgust and motions to our group, pointing his finger at the door.

'*Rein.* Clean it up!'

We climb inside. In the corners amid human excrement and abandoned wristwatches lie squashed, trampled infants, naked little monsters with enormous heads and bloated bellies. We carry them out like chickens, holding several in each hand.

'Don't take them to the trucks, pass them on to the women,' says the S.S. man, lighting a cigarette. His cigarette lighter is not working properly; he examines it carefully.

'Take them, for God's sake!' I explode as the women run from me in horror, covering their eyes.

The name of God sounds strangely pointless, since the women and the infants will go on the trucks, every one of them, without exception. We all know what this means, and we look at each other with hate and horror.

'What, you don't want to take them?' asks the pock-marked S.S. man with a note of surprise and reproach in his voice, and reaches for his revolver.

'You mustn't shoot, I'll carry them.' A tall, grey-haired woman takes the little corpses out of my hands and for an instant gazes straight into my eyes.

'My poor boy,' she whispers and smiles at me. Then she walks away, staggering along the path. I lean against the side of the train. I am terribly tired. Someone pulls at my sleeve.

'*En avant*, to the rails, come on!'

I look up, but the face swims before my eyes, dissolves, huge and transparent, melts into the motionless trees and the sea of people . . . I blink rapidly: Henri.

'Listen, Henri, are we good people?'

'That's stupid. Why do you ask?'

'You see, my friend, you see, I don't know why, but I am furious, simply furious with these people—furious because I must be here because of them. I feel no pity. I am not sorry they're going to the gas chamber. Damn them all! I could throw myself at them, beat them with my fists. It must be pathological, I just can't understand . . .'

'Ah, on the contrary, it is natural, predictable, calculated. The ramp exhausts you, you rebel—and the easiest way to relieve your hate is to turn against someone weaker. Why, I'd even call it healthy. It's simple logic, *compris?*' He props himself up comfortably against the heap of rails. 'Look at the Greeks, they know how to make the best of it! They stuff their bellies with anything they find. One of them has just devoured a full jar of marmalade.'

'Pigs! Tomorrow half of them will die of the shits.'

'Pigs? You've been hungry.'

'Pigs!' I repeat furiously. I close my eyes. The air is filled with ghastly cries, the earth trembles beneath me, I can feel sticky moisture on my eyelids. My throat is completely dry.

The morbid procession streams on and on—trucks growl like mad dogs. I shut my eyes tight, but I can still see corpses dragged from the train, trampled infants, cripples piled on top of the dead, wave after wave . . . freight cars roll in, the heaps of clothing, suitcases and bundles grow, people climb out, look at the sun, take a few breaths, beg for water, get into the trucks, drive away. And again freight cars roll in, again people . . . The scenes become confused in my mind—I am not sure if all of this is actually happening, or if I am dreaming. There is a humming inside my head; I feel that I must vomit.

Henri tugs at my arm.

'Don't sleep, we're off to load up the loot.'

All the people are gone. In the distance, the last few trucks roll along the road in clouds of dust, the train has left, several S.S. officers promenade up and down the ramp. The silver glitters on their collars. Their boots shine, their red, beefy faces shine. Among them there is a woman—only now I realize she has been here all along—withered, flat-chested, bony, her thin, colourless hair pulled back and tied in a 'Nordic' knot; her hands are in the pockets of her wide skirt. With a rat-like, resolute smile glued on her thin lips she sniffs around the corners of the ramp. She detests feminine beauty with the hatred of a woman who is herself repulsive, and knows it. Yes, I have seen her many times before and I know her well: she is the commandant of the F.K.L. She has come to look over the new crop of women, for some of them, instead of going on the trucks, will go on foot—to the concentration camp. There our boys, the barbers from the Zauna, will shave their heads and will have a good laugh at their 'outside world' modesty.

We proceed to load the loot. We lift huge trunks, heave them on to the trucks. There they are arranged in stacks, packed tightly. Occasionally somebody slashes one open with a knife, for pleasure or in search of vodka and perfume. One of the crates falls open; suits, shirts, books drop out on the ground . . . I pick up a small, heavy package. I unwrap it—gold, about two handfuls, bracelets, rings, brooches, diamonds . . .

'*Gib hier*,' an S.S. man says calmly, holding up his briefcase already full of gold and colourful foreign currency. He locks the case, hands it to an officer, takes another, an empty one, and stands by the next truck, waiting. The gold will go to the Reich.

It is hot, terribly hot. Our throats are dry, each word hurts. Anything for a sip of water! Faster, faster, so that it is over, so that we may rest. At last we are done, all the trucks have gone. Now we swiftly clean up the remaining dirt: there must be 'no trace left of the *Schweinerei*'. But just as the last truck disappears behind the trees and we walk, finally, to rest in the shade, a shrill whistle sounds around the bend. Slowly, terribly slowly, a train rolls in, the engine whistles back with a deafening shriek. Again weary, pale faces at the windows, flat as though cut out of paper, with huge, feverishly burning eyes. Already trucks are pulling up, already the composed gentleman with the notebook is at his post, and the S.S. men emerge from the commissary carrying briefcases for the gold and money. We unseal the train doors.

It is impossible to control oneself any longer. Brutally we tear suitcases from their hands, impatiently pull off their coats. Go on, go on, vanish! They go, they vanish. Men, women, children. Some of them know.

Here is a woman—she walks quickly, but tries to appear calm. A small child with a pink cherub's face runs after her and, unable to keep up, stretches out his little arms and cries: 'Mama! Mama!'

'Pick up your child, woman!'

'It's not mine, sir, not mine!' she shouts hysterically and runs on, covering her face with her hands. She wants to hide, she wants to reach those who will not ride the trucks, those who will go on foot, those who will stay alive. She is young, healthy, good-looking, she wants to live.

But the child runs after her, wailing loudly: 'Mama, mama, don't leave me!'

'It's not mine, not mine, no!'

Andrei, a sailor from Sevastopol, grabs hold of her. His eyes are glassy from vodka and the heat. With one powerful blow he knocks her off her feet, then, as she falls, takes her by the hair and pulls her up again. His face twitches with rage.

'Ah, you bloody Jewess! So you're running from your own child! I'll show you, you whore!' His huge hand chokes her, he lifts her in the air and heaves her on to the truck like a heavy sack of grain.

'Here! And take this with you, bitch!' and he throws the child at her feet.

'*Gut gemacht*, good work. That's the way to deal with degenerate mothers,' says the S.S. man standing at the foot of the truck. '*Gut, gut, Russki*.'

'Shut your mouth,' growls Andrei through clenched teeth, and walks away. From under a pile of rags he pulls out a canteen, unscrews the cork, takes a few deep swallows, passes it to me. The strong vodka burns the throat. My head swims, my legs are shaky, again I feel like throwing up.

And suddenly, above the teeming crowd pushing forward like a river driven by an unseen power, a girl appears. She descends lightly from the train, hops on to the gravel, looks around inquiringly, as if somewhat surprised. Her soft, blonde hair has fallen on her shoulders in a torrent, she throws it back impatiently. With a natural gesture she runs her hands down her blouse, casually straightens her skirt. She stands like this for an instant, gazing at the crowd, then turns and with a gliding look examines our faces, as though searching for someone. Unknowingly, I continue to stare at her, until our eyes meet.

'Listen, tell me, where are they taking us?'

I look at her without saying a word. Here, standing before me, is a girl, a girl with enchanting blonde hair, with beautiful breasts, wearing a little cotton blouse, a girl with a wise, mature look in her eyes. Here she stands, gazing straight into my face, waiting. And over there is the gas chamber: communal death, disgusting and ugly. And over in the other direction is the concentration camp: the shaved head, the heavy Soviet trousers in sweltering heat, the sickening, stale odour of dirty, damp female bodies, the animal hunger, the inhuman labour, and later the same gas chamber, only an even more hideous, more terrible death . . .

Why did she bring it? I think to myself, noticing a lovely gold watch on her delicate wrist. They'll take it away from her anyway.

'Listen, tell me,' she repeats.

I remain silent. Her lips tighten.

'I know,' she says with a shade of proud contempt in her voice, tossing her head. She walks off resolutely in the direction of the trucks. Someone tries to stop her; she boldly pushes him aside and runs up the steps. In the distance I can only catch a glimpse of her blonde hair flying in the breeze.

I go back inside the train; I carry out dead infants; I unload luggage. I touch corpses, but I cannot overcome the mounting, uncontrollable terror. I try to escape from the corpses, but they are everywhere: lined up on the gravel, on the cement edge of the ramp, inside the cattle cars. Babies, hideous naked women, men twisted by convulsions. I run off as far as I can go, but immediately a whip slashes across my back. Out of the corner of my eye I see an S.S. man, swearing profusely. I stagger forward and run, lose myself in the Canada group. Now, at last, I can once more rest against the stack of rails. The sun has leaned low over the horizon and illuminates the ramp with a reddish glow; the shadows of the trees have become elongated, ghostlike. In the silence that settles over nature at this time of day, the human cries seem to rise all the way to the sky.

Only from this distance does one have a full view of the inferno on the teeming ramp. I see a pair of human beings who have fallen to the ground locked in a last desperate embrace. The man has dug his fingers into the woman's flesh and has caught her clothing with his teeth. She screams hysterically, swears, cries, until at last a large boot comes down over her throat and she is silent. They are pulled apart and dragged like cattle to the truck. I see four Canada men lugging a corpse: a huge, swollen female corpse. Cursing, dripping wet from the strain, they kick out of their way some stray children who have been running all over the ramp, howling like dogs. The men pick them up by the collars, heads, arms, and toss them inside the trucks, on top of the heaps. The four men have trouble lifting the fat corpse on to the car, they call others for help, and all together they hoist up the mound of meat. Big, swollen, puffed-up corpses are being collected from all over the ramp; on top of them are piled the invalids, the smothered, the sick, the unconscious. The heap seethes, howls, groans. The driver starts the motor, the truck begins rolling.

'Halt! Halt!' an S.S. man yells after them. 'Stop, damn you!'

They are dragging to the truck an old man wearing tails and a band around his arm. His head knocks against the gravel and pavement; he moans and wails in an uninterrupted monotone: '*Ich will mit dem Herrn Kommandanten sprechen*—I wish to speak with the commandant . . .' With senile stubbornness he keeps repeating these words all the way. Thrown on the truck, trampled by others, choked, he still wails: '*Ich will mit dem . . .*'

'Look here, old man!' a young S.S. man calls, laughing jovially. 'In half an hour you'll be talking with the top commandant! Only don't forget to greet him with a *Heil Hitler!*'

Several other men are carrying a small girl with only one leg. They hold her by the arms and the one leg. Tears are running down her face and she whispers faintly: 'Sir, it hurts, it hurts . . .' They throw her on the truck on top of the corpses. She will burn alive along with them.

The evening has come, cool and clear. The stars are out. We lie against the rails. It is incredibly quiet. Anaemic bulbs hang from the top of the high lampposts; beyond the circle of light stretches an impenetrable darkness. Just one step, and a man could vanish for ever. But the guards are watching, their automatics ready.

'Did you get the shoes?' asks Henri.

'No.'

'Why?'

'My God, man, I am finished, absolutely finished!'

'So soon? After only two transports? Just look at me, I . . . since Christmas, at least a million people have passed through my hands. The worst of all are the transports from around Paris—one is always bumping into friends.'

'And what do you say to them?'

'That first they will have a bath, and later we'll meet at the camp. What would you say?'

I do not answer. We drink coffee with vodka; somebody opens a tin of cocoa and mixes it with sugar. We scoop it up by the handful, the cocoa sticks to the lips. Again coffee, again vodka.

'Henri, what are we waiting for?'

'There'll be another transport.'

'I'm not going to unload it! I can't take any more.'

'So, it's got you down? Canada is nice, eh?' Henri grins indulgently and disappears into the darkness. In a moment he is back again.

'All right. Just sit here quietly and don't let an S.S. man see you. I'll try to find you your shoes.'

'Just leave me alone. Never mind the shoes.' I want to sleep. It is very late.

Another whistle, another transport. Freight cars emerge out of the darkness, pass under the lamp-posts, and again vanish in the night. The ramp is small, but the circle of lights is smaller. The unloading will have to be done gradually. Somewhere the trucks are growling. They back up against the steps, black, ghostlike, their searchlights flash across the trees. *Wasser! Luft!* The same all over again, like a late showing of the same film: a volley of shots, the train falls silent. Only this time a little girl pushes herself halfway through the small window and, losing her balance, falls out on to the gravel. Stunned, she lies still for a moment, then stands up and begins walking around in a circle, faster and faster, waving her rigid arms in the air, breathing loudly and spasmodically, whining in a faint voice. Her mind has given way in the inferno inside the train. The whining is hard on the nerves: an S.S. man approaches calmly, his heavy boot strikes between her shoulders. She falls. Holding her down with his foot, he draws his revolver, fires once, then again. She remains face down, kicking the gravel with her feet, until she stiffens. They proceed to unseal the train.

I am back on the ramp, standing by the doors. A warm, sickening smell gushes from inside. The mountain of people filling the car almost halfway up to the ceiling is motionless, horribly tangled, but still steaming.

'*Ausladen!*' comes the command. An S.S. man steps out from the darkness. Across his chest hangs a portable searchlight. He throws a stream of light inside.

'Why are you standing about like sheep? Start unloading!' His whip flies and falls across our backs. I seize a corpse by the hand; the fingers close tightly around mine. I pull back with a shriek and stagger away. My heart pounds, jumps up to my throat. I can no longer control the nausea. Hunched under the train I begin to vomit. Then, like a drunk, I weave over to the stack of rails.

I lie against the cool, kind metal and dream about returning to the camp, about my bunk, on which there is no mattress, about sleep among comrades who are not going to the gas tonight. Suddenly I see the camp as a haven of peace. It is true, others may be dying, but one is somehow still alive, one has enough food, enough strength to work . . .

The lights on the ramp flicker with a spectral glow, the wave of people—feverish, agitated, stupefied people—flows on and on, endlessly. They think that now they will have to face a new life in the camp, and they prepare themselves emotionally for the hard struggle ahead. They do not know that in just a few moments they will die, that the gold, money, and diamonds which they have so prudently hidden in their clothing and on their bodies are now useless to them. Experienced professionals will probe into every recess of their flesh, will pull the gold from under the tongue and the diamonds from the uterus and the colon. They will rip out gold teeth. In tightly sealed crates they will ship them to Berlin.

The S.S. men's black figures move about, dignified, businesslike. The gentleman with the notebook puts down his final marks, rounds out the figures: fifteen thousand.

Many, very many, trucks have been driven to the crematoria today.

It is almost over. The dead are being cleared off the ramp and piled into the last truck. The Canada men, weighed down under a load of bread, marmalade and sugar, and smelling of perfume and fresh linen, line up to go. For several days the entire camp will live off this transport. For several days the entire camp will talk about 'Sosnowiec-Będzin'. 'Sosnowiec-Będzin' was a good, rich transport.

The stars are already beginning to pale as we walk back to the camp. The sky grows translucent and opens high above our heads—it is getting light.

Great columns of smoke rise from the crematoria and merge up above into a huge black river which very slowly floats across the sky over Birkenau and disappears beyond the forests in the direction of Trzebinia. The 'Sosnowiec-Będzin' transport is already burning.

We pass a heavily armed S.S. detachment on its way to change guard. The men march briskly, in step, shoulder to shoulder, one mass, one will.

'*Und morgen die ganze Welt. . .*' they sing at the top of their lungs.

'*Rechts ran!* To the right march!' snaps a command from up front. We move out of their way.

1. Crossed wooden beams wrapped in barbed wire.

2. 'Canada' refers to the labour gang who helped to unload the incoming transports of people destined for gas chambers. The term also designated a state of well-being and plenty.

3. 'Muslim' was the name used in camp to describe prisoners who had lost all will to survive, physical and emotional zombies whose days were numbered.

Paul Bowles

Paul Bowles, born in 1910 in New York City, was groomed by his parents for a life in the arts. He spent a year at the University of Virginia, then studied music in New York, Berlin, and Paris, first with Aaron Copeland and then with Virgil Thomson. Bowles has written operas, *The Wind Remains* and *Yerma*, and composed music for movies and for the plays of Tennessee Williams. He founded the literary magazine *Antaeus*. He speaks French, Spanish, and Maghrebi and has translated not only Federico García Lorca and Jean-Paul Sartre, but also many tales from the Maghrebi. He has written poetry, travel essays, various collections of short stories, a number of highly acclaimed novels, including *The Sheltering Sky* (1949), which was adapted for film, and an autobiography. *Collected Stories 1939–1976* appeared in 1979. He has lived in North Africa, mostly in Tangier, since the thirties, for many years with Jane Sydney Auer, who published fiction under the name Jane Bowles (she died in Malaga in 1973).

In the preface to *The Spider's House* (1982), a novel about the dissolution of the medieval way of life in the Moroccan city of Fez, which accompanied the end of French rule, Bowles describes how he had held the conviction that "fiction should always stay clear of political considerations. Even when I saw that the book that I had begun was taking a direction which would inevitably lead it into a region where politics could not be avoided, I still imagined that with sufficient dexterity I should be able to avert contact with the subject. But in situations where everyone is under great emotional stress, indifference is unthinkable; at such times all opinions are construed as political ones. To be apolitical is tantamount to having assumed a political stance, but one which pleases no one." His work tends to be intensely political at a deeper, non-partisan, level, with its concern for losses which emerge from the collision of cultures.

In his autobiography, *Without Stopping* (1972), Bowles relates how he first came to be published, after Dial Press had first turned down his book of stories and referred him to Helen Strauss, a literary agent: "A week or ten days after she and I had had lunch together, at which point I had given her my stories, she called me to say that Doubleday had offered an advance on a novel. Once I had signed the contract I began to make plans for my trip to Tangier. North Africa had long since acquired a legendary aura for me; the fact that I now had decided to go back there made the place more actual and revived hundreds of small

forgotten scenes which welled up into my consciousness of their own accord. I got on a Fifth Avenue bus one day to go uptown. By the time we had arrived at Madison Square I knew what would be in the novel and what I would call it. Before the First World War there had been a popular song called 'Down Among the Sheltering Palms'; a record of it was at the Boat House in Glenora, and upon my arrival there each summer from the age of four onward, I had sought it out and played it before any of the others. It was not the banal melody which fascinated me, but the strange word 'sheltering.' What did the palm trees shelter people from, and how sure could they be sure of such protection? 'Oh, Honey, wait for me / Out where the sun goes down about eight. . . .'

"The book was going to take place in the Sahara, where there was only the sky, and so it would be *The Sheltering Sky*. This time at least I did not have to lie awake nights searching for the right title. In essence the tale would be similar to 'A Distant Episode,' the short story I had just published in *Partisan Review*, and it would write itself, I felt certain, once I had established the characters and spilled them out onto the North African scene."

This account is interesting for the link it makes between the novel and "A Distant Episode," but also for drawing attention to the power of language—of specific words—in shaping the youthful imagination. Bowles claims to have started this short story as an antidote to an approaching dental extraction. In a taped interview with Lawrence D. Stewart (*Paul Bowles: The Illumination of North Africa*), Bowles explains that the shock element in his work is not there for its own sake, but for therapeutic purposes, for himself and for the reader: "Shock is a *sine qua non* to the story. You don't teach a thing like that unless you are able, in some way, to make the reader understand what the situation would be like to *him*. And that involves shock." When accused by a critic of being decadent, Bowles replied: "I should think in art and literature nothing is decadent but incompetence and commercialism. If I stress various facets of unhappiness, it is because I believe unhappiness should be studied very carefully; this is certainly no time for anyone to pretend to be happy, or to put his unhappiness away in the dark. (And anyone who is not unhappy now must be a monster, a saint or an idiot.) You must watch your universe as it cracks above your head."

Bowles considered the demand for character analysis and social realism in fiction to be arbitrary. "If it were possible I should write without using people at all. This is an important point. Insofar as it is practicable, I try to dispense with 'characters' entirely because they obstruct the view, and the reason they get in my way is that they don't interest me." "Character *as character*," he says, "is not important. The character is acting out a situational drama in a given setting, and the whole thing is one thing—that is, the character, the setting, the mood, the action, the situation. The character's not apart from his situation (in that sense it's existentialist—I suppose that's what they mean). The character does not exist in my writing apart from where he is and in what situation he is and what is happening to him. He is not a person outside of that. It's a closed circuit."

A Distant Episode

The September sunsets were at their reddest the week the Professor decided to visit Aïn Tadouirt, which is in the warm country. He came down out of the high, flat region in the evening by bus, with two small overnight bags full of maps, sun lotions and medicines. Ten years ago he had been in the village for three days; long enough, however, to establish a fairly firm friendship with a café-keeper, who had written him several times during the first year after his visit, if never since. "Hassan Ramani," the Professor said over and over, as the bus bumped downward through ever warmer layers of air. Now facing the flaming sky in the west, and now facing the sharp mountains, the car followed the dusty trail down the canyons into air which began to smell of other things besides the endless ozone of the heights: orange blossoms, pepper, sun-baked excrement, burning olive oil, rotten fruit. He closed his eyes happily and lived for an instant in a purely olfactory world. The distant past returned—what part of it, he could not decide.

The chauffeur, whose seat the Professor shared, spoke to him without taking his eyes from the road. "*Vous êtes géologue?*"

"A geologist? Ah, no! I'm a linguist."

"There are no languages here. Only dialects."

"Exactly. I'm making a survey of variations on Moghrebi."

The chauffeur was scornful. "Keep on going south," he said. "You'll find some languages you never heard of before."

As they drove through the town gate, the usual swarm of urchins rose up out of the dust and ran screaming beside the bus. The Professor folded his dark glasses, put them in his pocket; and as soon as the vehicle had come to a standstill he jumped out, pushing his way through the indignant boys who clutched at his luggage in vain, and walked quickly into the Grand Hotel Saharien. Out of its eight rooms there were two available—one facing the market and the other, a smaller and cheaper one, giving onto a tiny yard full of refuse and barrels, where two gazelles wandered about. He took the smaller room, and pouring the entire pitcher of water into the tin basin, began to wash the grit from his face and ears. The afterglow was nearly gone from the sky, and the pinkness in objects was disappearing, almost as he watched. He lit the carbide lamp and winced at its odor. After dinner the Professor walked slowly through the streets to Hassan Ramani's café, whose back room hung hazardously out above the river. The entrance was very low, and he had to bend down slightly to get in. A man was tending the fire. There was one guest sipping tea. The *qaouaji* tried to make him take a seat at the other table in the front room, but the Professor walked airily ahead into the back room and sat down. The moon was shining through the reed latticework and there was not a sound outside but the occasional distant bark of a dog. He changed tables so he could see the river. It was dry, but there was a pool here and there that reflected the bright night sky. The *qaouaji* came in and wiped off the table.

"Does this café still belong to Hassan Ramani?" he asked him in the Moghrebi he had taken four years to learn.

The man replied in bad French: "He is deceased."

"Deceased?" repeated the Professor, without noticing the absurdity of the word. "Really? When?"

"I don't know," said the *qaouaji*. "One tea?"

"Yes. But I don't understand . . ."

The man was already out of the room, fanning the fire. The Professor sat still, feeling lonely, and arguing with himself that to do so was ridiculous. Soon the *qaouaji* returned with the tea. He paid him and gave him an enormous tip, for which he received a grave bow.

"Tell me," he said, as the other started away. "Can one still get those little boxes made from camel udders?"

The man looked angry. "Sometimes the Reguibat bring in those things. We do not buy them here." Then insolently, in Arabic: "And why a camel-udder box?"

"Because I like them," retorted the Professor. And then because he was feeling a little exalted, he added, "I like them so much I want to make a collection of them, and I will pay you ten francs for every one you can get me."

"*Khamstache*," said the *qaouaji*, opening his left hand rapidly three times in succession.

"Never. Ten."

"Not possible. But wait until later and come with me. You can give me what you like. And you will get camel-udder boxes if there are any."

He went out into the front room, leaving the Professor to drink his tea and listen to the growing chorus of dogs that barked and howled as the moon rose higher into the sky. A group of customers came into the front room and sat talking for an hour or so. When they had left, the *qaouaji* put out the fire and stood in the doorway putting on his burnous. "Come," he said.

Outside in the street there was very little movement. The booths were all closed and the only light came from the moon. An occasional pedestrian passed, and grunted a brief greeting to the *qaouaji*.

"Everyone knows you," said the Professor, to cut the silence between them. "Yes."

"I wish everyone knew me," said the Professor, before he realized how infantile such a remark must sound.

"No one knows you," said his companion gruffly.

They had come to the other side of the town, on the promontory above the desert, and through a great rift in the wall the Professor saw the white endlessness, broken in the foreground by dark spots of oasis. They walked through the opening and followed a winding road between rocks, downward toward the nearest small forest of palms. The Professor thought: "He may cut my throat. But his café—he would surely be found out."

"Is it far?" he asked, casually.

"Are you tired?" countered the *qaouaji*. "They are expecting me back at the Hotel Saharien," he lied.

"You can't be there and here," said the *qaouaji*.

The Professor laughed. He wondered if it sounded uneasy to the other. "Have you owned Ramani's café long?"

"I work there for a friend." The reply made the Professor more unhappy than he had imagined it would.

"Oh. Will you work tomorrow?"

"That is impossible to say."

The Professor stumbled on a stone, and fell, scraping his hand. The *qaouaji* said: "Be careful."

The sweet black odor of rotten meat hung in the air suddenly.

"Agh!" said the Professor, choking. "What is it?"

The *qaouaji* had covered his face with his burnous and did not answer. Soon the stench had been left behind. They were on flat ground. Ahead the path was bordered on each side by a high mud wall. There was no breeze and the palms were quite still, but behind the walls was the sound of running water. Also, the odor of human excrement was almost constant as they walked between the walls.

The Professor waited until he thought it seemed logical for him to ask with a certain degree of annoyance: "But where are we going?"

"Soon," said the guide, pausing to gather some stones in the ditch.

"Pick up some stones," he advised. "Here are bad dogs."

"Where?" asked the Professor, but he stooped and got three large ones with pointed edges.

They continued very quietly. The walls came to an end and the bright desert lay ahead. Nearby was a ruined marabout, with its tiny dome only half standing and the front wall entirely destroyed. Behind it were clumps of stunted, useless palms. A dog came running crazily toward them on three legs. Not until it got quite close did the Professor hear its steady low growl. The *qaouaji* let fly a large stone at it, striking it square in the muzzle. There was a strange snapping of jaws and the dog ran sideways in another direction, falling blindly against rocks and scrambling haphazardly about like an injured insect.

Turning off the road, they walked across the earth strewn with sharp stones, past the little ruin, through the trees, until they came to a place where the ground dropped abruptly away in front of them.

"It looks like a quarry," said the Professor, resorting to French for the word "quarry," whose Arabic equivalent he could not call to mind at the moment. The *qaouaji* did not answer. Instead he stood still and turned his head, as if listening. And indeed, from somewhere down below, but very far below, came the faint sound of a low flute. The *qaouaji* nodded his head slowly several times. Then he said: "The path begins here. You can see it well all the way. The rock is white and the moon is strong. So you can see well. I am going back now and sleep. It is late. You can give me what you like."

Standing there at the edge of the abyss which at each moment looked deeper, with the dark face of the *qaouaji* framed in its moonlit burnous close to his own face, the Professor asked himself exactly what he felt. Indignation, curiosity, fear, perhaps, but most of all relief and the hope that this was not a trick, the hope that the *qaouaji* would really leave him alone and turn back without him.

He stepped back a little from the edge, and fumbled in his pocket for a loose note, because he did not want to show his wallet. Fortunately there was a fifty-franc bill there, which he took out and handed to the man. He knew the *qaouaji* was pleased, and so he paid no attention when he heard him saying: "It is not enough. I have to walk a long way home and there are dogs. . . ."

"Thank you and good night," said the Professor, sitting down with his legs drawn up under him, and lighting a cigarette. He felt almost happy.

"Give me only one cigarette," pleaded the man.

"Of course," he said, a bit curtly, and he held up the pack.

The *qaouaji* squatted close beside him. His face was not pleasant to see. "What is it?" thought the Professor, terrified again, as he held out his lighted cigarette toward him.

The man's eyes were almost closed. It was the most obvious registering of concentrated scheming the Professor had ever seen. When the second cigarette was burning, he ventured to say to the still-squatting Arab: "What are you thinking about?"

The other drew on his cigarette deliberately, and seemed about to speak. Then his expression changed to one of satisfaction, but he did not speak. A cool wind had risen in the air, and the Professor shivered. The sound of the flute came up from the depths below at intervals, sometimes mingled with the scraping of nearby palm fronds one against the other. "These people are not primitives," the Professor found himself saying in his mind.

"Good," said the *qaouaji*, rising slowly. "Keep your money. Fifty francs is enough. It is an honor." Then he went back into French: "*Ti n'as qu'à discendre, to' droit.*" He spat, chuckled (or was the Professor hysterical?), and strode away quickly.

The Professor was in a state of nerves. He lit another cigarette, and found his lips moving automatically. They were saying: "Is this a situation or a predicament? This is ridiculous." He sat very still for several minutes, waiting for a sense of reality to come to him. He stretched out on the hard, cold ground and looked up at the moon. It was almost like looking straight at the sun. If he shifted his gaze a little at a time, he could make a string of weaker moons across the sky. "Incredible," he whispered. Then he sat up quickly and looked about. There was no guarantee that the *qaouaji* really had gone back to town. He got to his feet and looked over the edge of the precipice. In the moonlight the bottom seemed miles away. And there was nothing to give it scale; not a tree, not a house, not a person. . . . He listened for the flute, and heard only the wind going by his ears. A sudden violent desire to run

back to the road seized him, and he turned and looked in the direction the *qaouaji* had taken. At the same time he felt softly of his wallet in his breast pocket. Then he spat over the edge of the cliff. Then he made water over it, and listened intently, like a child. This gave him the impetus to start down the path into the abyss. Curiously enough, he was not dizzy. But prudently he kept from peering to his right, over the edge. It was a steady and steep downward climb. The monotony of it put him into a frame of mind not unlike that which had been induced by the bus ride. He was murmuring "Hassan Ramani" again, repeatedly and in rhythm. He stopped, furious with himself for the sinister overtones the name now suggested to him. He decided he was exhausted from the trip. "And the walk," he added.

He was now well down the gigantic cliff, but the moon, being directly overhead, gave as much light as ever. Only the wind was left behind, above, to wander among the trees, to blow through the dusty streets of Aïn in Tadouirt, into the hall of the Grand Hotel Saharien, and under the door of his little room.

It occurred to him that he ought to ask himself why he was doing this irrational thing, but he was intelligent enough to know that since he was doing it, it was not so important to probe for explanations at that moment.

Suddenly the earth was flat beneath his feet. He had reached the bottom sooner than he had expected. He stepped ahead distrustfully still, as if he expected another treacherous drop. It was so hard to know in this uniform, dim brightness. Before he knew what had happened the dog was upon him, a heavy mass of fur trying to push him backwards, a sharp nail rubbing down his chest, a straining of muscles against him to get the teeth into his neck. The Professor thought: "I refuse to die this way." The dog fell back; it looked like an Eskimo dog. As it sprang again, he called out, very loud: "Ay!" It fell against him, there was a confusion of sensations and a pain somewhere. There was also the sound of voices very near to him, and he could not understand what they were saying. Something cold and metallic was pushed brutally against his spine as the dog still hung for a second by his teeth from a mass of clothing and perhaps flesh. The Professor knew it was a gun, and he raised his hands, shouting in Moghrebi: "Take away the dog!" But the gun merely pushed him forward, and since the dog, once it was back on the ground, did not leap again, he took a step ahead. The gun kept pushing; he kept taking steps. Again he heard voices, but the person directly behind him said nothing. People seemed to be running about; it sounded that way, at least. For his eyes, he discovered, were still shut tight against the dog's attack. He opened them. A group of men was advancing toward him. They were dressed in the black clothes of the Reguibat. "The Reguiba is a cloud across the face of the sun." "When the Reguiba appears the righteous man turns away." In how many shops and market-places had heard these maxims uttered banteringly among friends. Never to a Reguiba, to be sure, for these men do not frequent towns. They send a representative in disguise, to arrange with shady elements there for the disposal of captured goods. "An opportunity," he thought quickly, "of testing the accuracy of such statements." He did not doubt for a moment that the adventure would prove to be a kind of warning against such foolishness on his part—a warning which in retrospect would be half sinister, half farcical.

Two snarling dogs came running from behind the oncoming men and threw themselves at his legs. He was scandalized to note that no one paid any attention to this breach of etiquette. The gun pushed him harder as he tried to sidestep the animals' noisy assault. Again he cried: "The dogs! Take them away!" The gun shoved him forward with great force and he fell, almost at the feet of the crowd of men facing him. The dogs were wrenching at his hands and arms. A boot kicked them aside, yelping, and then with increased vigor it kicked the Professor in the hip. Then came a chorus of kicks from different sides, and he was rolled violently about on the earth for a while. During this time he was conscious of hands reaching into his pockets and removing everything from them. He tried to say: "You have all my money; stop kicking me!" But his bruised facial muscles would not work; he felt himself pouting, and that was all. Someone dealt him a terrific blow on the head, and he thought: "Now at least I shall lose consciousness, thank Heaven." Still he went on being aware of the guttural voices he could not understand, and of being bound tightly about the ankles and chest. Then there was black silence that opened like a wound from time to time, to let in the soft, deep notes of the flute playing the same succession of notes again and again. Suddenly he felt excruciating pain everywhere—pain and cold. "So I have been unconscious, after all," he thought. In spite of that, the present seemed only like a direct continuation of what had gone before.

It was growing faintly light. There were camels near where he was lying; he could hear their gurgling and their heavy breathing. He could not bring himself to attempt opening his eyes, just in case it should turn out to be impossible. However, when he heard someone approaching, he found that he had no difficulty in seeing.

The man looked at him dispassionately in the gray morning light. With one hand he pinched together the Professor's nostrils. When the Professor opened his mouth to breathe, the man swiftly seized his tongue and pulled on it with all his might. The Professor was gagging and catching his breath; he did not see what was happening. He could not distinguish the pain of the brutal yanking from that of the sharp knife. Then there was an endless choking and spitting that went on automatically, as though he were scarcely a part of it. The word "operation" kept going through his mind; it calmed his terror somewhat as he sank back into darkness.

The caravan left sometime toward midmorning. The Professor, not unconscious, but in a state of utter stupor, still gagging and drooling blood, was dumped doubled-up into a sack and tied at one side of a camel. The lower end of the enormous amphitheater contained a natural gate in the rocks. The camels, swift *mehara*, were lightly laden on this trip. They passed through single file, and slowly mounted the gentle slope that led up into the beginning of the desert. That night, at a stop behind some low hills, the men took him out, still in a state which permitted no thought, and over the dusty rags that remained of his clothing they fastened a series of curious belts made of the bottoms of tin cans strung together. One after another of these bright girdles was wired about his torso, his arms and legs, even across his face, until he was entirely within a suit of armor that covered him with its circular metal scales. There was a good deal of merriment during this

decking-out of the Professor. One man brought out a flute and a younger one did a not ungraceful caricature of an Ouled Naïl executing a cane dance. The Professor was no longer conscious; to be exact, he existed in the middle of the movements made by these other men. When they had finished dressing him the way they wished him to look, they stuffed some food under the tin bangles hanging over his face. Even though he chewed mechanically, most of it eventually fell out onto the ground. They put him back into the sack and left him there.

Two days later they arrived at one of their own encampments. There were women and children here in the tents, and the men had to drive away the snarling dogs they had left there to guard them. When they emptied the Professor out of his sack, there were screams of fright, and it took several hours to convince the last woman that he was harmless, although there had been no doubt from the start that he was a valuable possession. After a few days they began to move on again, taking everything with them, and traveling only at night as the terrain grew warmer.

Even when all his wounds had healed and he felt no more pain, the Professor did not begin to think again; he ate and defecated, and he danced when he was bidden, a senseless hopping up and down that delighted the children, principally because of the wonderful jangling racket it made. And he generally slept through the heat of the day, in among the camels.

Wending its way southeast, the caravan avoided all stationary civilization. In a few weeks they reached a new plateau, wholly wild and with a sparse vegetation. Here they pitched camp and remained, while the *mehara* were turned loose to graze. Everyone was happy here; the weather was cooler and there was a well only a few hours away on a seldom-frequented trail. It was here they conceived the idea of taking the Professor to Fogara and selling him to the Touareg.

It was a full year before they carried out this project. By this time the Professor was much better trained. He could do a handspring, make a series of fearful growling noises which had, nevertheless, a certain element of humor; and when the Reguibat removed the tin from his face they discovered he could grimace admirably while he danced. They also taught him a few basic obscene gestures which never failed to elicit delighted shrieks from the women. He was now brought forth only after especially abundant meals, when there was music and festivity. He easily fell in with their sense of ritual, and evolved an elementary sort of "program" to present when he was called for: dancing, rolling on the ground, imitating certain animals, and finally rushing toward the group in feigned anger, to see the resultant confusion and hilarity.

When three of the men set out for Fogara with him, they took four *mehara* with them, and he rode astride his quite naturally. No precautions were taken to guard him, save that he was kept among them, one man always staying at the rear of the party. They came within sight of the walls at dawn, and they waited among the rocks all day. At dusk the youngest started out, and in three hours he returned with a friend who carried a stout cane. They tried to put the Professor through his routine then and there, but the man from Fogara was in a hurry to get back to town, so they all set out on the *mehara*.

In the town they went directly to the villager's home, where they had coffee in the courtyard sitting among the camels. Here the Professor went into his act again, and this time there was prolonged merriment and much rubbing together of hands. An agreement was reached, a sum of money paid, and the Reguibat withdrew, leaving the Professor in the house of the man with the cane, who did not delay in locking him into a tiny enclosure off the courtyard.

The next day was an important one in the Professor's life, for it was then that pain began to stir again in his being. A group of men came to the house, among whom was a venerable gentleman, better clothed than those others who spent their time flattering him, setting fervent kisses upon his hands and the edges of his garments. This person made a point of going into classical Arabic from time to time, to impress the others, who had not learned a word of the Koran. Thus his conversation would run more or less as follows: "Perhaps at In Salah. The French there are stupid. Celestial vengeance is approaching. Let us not hasten it. Praise the highest and cast thine anathema against idols. With paint on his face. In case the police wish to look close." The others listened and agreed, nodding their heads slowly and solemnly. And the Professor in his stall beside them listened, too. That is, he was *conscious* of the sound of the old man's Arabic. The words penetrated for the first time in many months. Noises, then: "Celestial vengeance is approaching." Then: "It is an honor. Fifty francs is enough. Keep your money. Good." And the *qaouaji* squatting near him at the edge of the precipice. Then "anathema against idols" and more gibberish. He turned over panting on the sand and forgot about it. But the pain had begun. It operated in a kind of delirium, because he had begun to enter into consciousness again. When the man opened the door and prodded him with his cane, he cried out in a rage, and everyone laughed.

They got him onto his feet, but he would not dance. He stood before them, staring at the ground, stubbornly refusing to move. The owner was furious, and so annoyed by the laughter of the others that he felt obliged to send them away, saying that he would await a more propitious time for exhibiting his property, because he dared not show his anger before the elder. However, when they had left he dealt the Professor a violent blow on the shoulder with his cane, called him various obscene things, and went out into the street, slamming the gate behind him. He walked straight to the street of the Ouled Naïl, because he was sure of finding the Reguibat there among the girls, spending the money. And there in a tent he found one of them still abed, while an Ouled Naïl washed the tea glasses. He walked in and almost decapitated the man before the latter had even attempted to sit up. Then he threw his razor on the bed and ran out.

The Ouled Naïl saw the blood, screamed, ran out of her tent into the next, and soon emerged from that with four girls who rushed together into the coffee house and told the *qaouaji* who had killed the Reguiba. It was only a matter of an hour before the French military police had caught him at a friend's house, and dragged him off to the barracks. That night the Professor had nothing to eat, and the next afternoon, in the slow sharpening of his consciousness caused by increasing hunger, he walked aimlessly about the courtyard and the rooms that gave onto it. There was no one. In one room a calendar hung on the wall. The Professor watched nervously, like a dog watching a fly in front of its nose. On the white paper were black objects that made sounds in his head. He heard them: "*Grande Epicerie du Sahel. Juin. Lundi, Mardi, Mercredi. . . .*"

The tiny inkmarks of which a symphony consists may have been made long ago, but when they are fulfilled in sound they become imminent and mighty. So a kind of music of feeling began to play in the Professor's head, increasing in volume as he looked at the mud wall, and he had the feeling that he was performing what had been written for him long ago. He felt like weeping; he felt like roaring through the little house, upsetting and smashing the few breakable objects. His emotion got no further than this one overwhelming desire. So, bellowing as loud as he could, he attacked the house and its belongings. Then he attacked the door into the street, which resisted for a while and finally broke. He climbed through the opening made by the boards he had ripped apart, and still bellowing and shaking his arms in the air to make as loud a jangling as possible, he began to gallop along the quiet street toward the gateway of the town. A few people looked at him with great curiosity. As he passed the garage, the last building before the high mud archway that framed the desert beyond, a French soldier saw him. "*Tiens*," he said to himself, "a holy maniac."

Again it was sunset time. The Professor ran beneath the arched gate, turned his face toward the red sky, and began to trot along the Piste d'In Salah, straight into the setting sun. Behind him, from the garage, the soldier took a pot shot at him for good luck. The bullet whistled dangerously near the Professor's head, and his yelling rose into an indignant lament as he waved his arms more wildly, and hopped high into the air at every few steps, in an access of terror.

The soldier watched a while, smiling, as the cavorting figure grew smaller in the oncoming evening darkness, and the rattling of the tin became a part of the great silence out there beyond the gate. The wall of the garage as he leaned against it still gave forth heat, left there by the sun, but even then the lunar chill was growing in the air.

Terence Byrnes

Terence Byrnes was born in Toronto in 1949, but, like Clark Blaise, spent a good portion of his youth in the U.S. He has lived and worked all over North America, settling for a few years in Ohio, where he mixed free-lance journalism with designing and building electronic equipment for biological research. In 1975, he returned to Canada to attend the Creative Writing programme at Concordia University in Montreal, where he now teaches full time. His stories and articles have appeared in a wide range of magazines, from *Science* to *Rolling Stone*. Byrnes is also a photographer and has worked as a feature journalist for *The Gazette* in Montreal. His first collection of stories, *Wintering Over*, appeared to great acclaim in 1980. He is at work on a novel and a second collection of stories and is the editor of an anthology of short fiction called *Matinees Daily*.

Byrnes acknowledges that stories can be read as signs of something else, as cultural indicators, ideological statements, and biographical assertions. "However," he says, "one thing that disturbs me about much criticism is that the wonderfully evolved mandible, the text itself, is neglected in favour of a discussion of what it represents. For a writer working on a story, that inchoate text—the story he or she is trying to tell, the voice in which it's told—is necessarily individual and not part of a the-matic or sociological collectivity. It is not yet represen-tative of anything, its form and voice waiting to be discovered, its function or place in the wider literary world uncertain. I wish that the act of reading a story could be closer to the act of composing a story, a time when one is aware of the terrifying number of choices to be made and the always qualified nature of success."

Represents is a key word in Byrnes's discussions of the short story, since he insists that "short stories live by their own strict, highly artificial rules, not by the caprice of reality." "Because a short story is short and reasonably self-contained, it doesn't always invite comparison with the non-fictional—that is, real—world in the same way the novel does. And if we bring too much information from the outside world to bear on a story, the story itself can become lost in the other narratives we might use to interpret it, narratives such as history, sociology, psychiatry, or even the narrative of our own lives. Oddly, we sometimes have to ignore our personal experience to read a story properly."

Byrnes accepts certain limitations of the short story—duration, number of characters, and narrative complex-ity—and describes it as "unforgiving of bad or false starts" or ideological assertiveness. The brevity of the story, he says, "gives it qualities of artificiality, compres-sion, and lyricism that demand considerable skill of the writer—skill of a sort quite different from that needed to write a form as open as the novel. At the same time, these qualities make it worthwhile and productive to look at stories in terms of the way they deal with, and sometimes try to escape, the coercion of their form."

If the short story is a coercive form, driven by its need to create and test a fictional world, it is also characterized, according to Byrnes, by a high degree of expectation, "a zone of unhappiness [that others have called conflict or tension] which gives the narrative its forward movement." "Expectation is an inescapable part of our relation to language, and resides in individ-ual words and syntax," so that what *comes* next in the text is more significant than what *happens* next; in fact, words and phrases *are* what happens next. In this regard, the short story is the most pretentious and complex—and, inevitably, the most interesting—of the short narrative forms. "In a few pages, the short story must establish a world, disrupt that world, and show or intimate a consequence of that disruption."

Although he is concerned with the formal charac-teristics of the short story—its architecture and artifi-ciality—Byrnes does not dismiss the pressures of reality that drive and inform fiction. "Despite the heavy dose of ambiguity that's part of language and narrative, I think that most writers would rebel at the notion that language is incapable of transmitting meaning or that the writer's intention is unavoidably disconnected from the audience's response. If a writer did believe that, without serious reservation—believed that his or her intent were unimportant or would necessarily be misunderstood or had a meaning that signified nothing more nor less than that which is signified by the ingre-dients on the side of a corn flakes box—I can't imagine how that person could continue to write. Writing is, after all, intentional, even if the most careful use of language can't control all those intentions."

Food People

One weekend evening after a reception, the Thompsons found themselves alone with Lorraine Bellefeuille and they discovered they had something in common. "You're food people too," Lorraine delightedly exclaimed.

Ray Thompson had never thought of himself as a *food person*, then decided that everyone who ate anything had to be a food person, and then admitted to the special cachet that Lorraine obviously meant her expression to have. Looking at it that way, he didn't know if he were a food person or not, though he wasn't naïve enough to imagine that he wasn't several other kinds of person.

He loved antiques, an acquired taste. His and Mary's furniture, which they had bought third-hand what seemed a lifetime ago, was one of their claims to fame as a couple. In a decade it had crossed the line from junk to antiquity. And because other people had expressed so much envy of their furniture, he had come to love it himself. And by extension he had come to love antiques in general.

He played golf, poorly, while wearing a black pullover like Gary Player's, and dreamed about competing in the Bob Hope Classic at Long Beach. He was faithful to his wife. He had abandoned marijuana in 1965 because he didn't want to be thought of as *that* kind of person, but now knew many people who, when they could afford it, unaffectedly used cocaine. He was troubled by the future because of a secret fear that in his old age he would be poor and alone and abandoned in a government nursing home for year after lonely year. He often felt guilty because his parents had been (and were) more successful than he was.

In fact, Ray had come to accept that he would probably never have success or money. He was a painter (and felt no shame about entering the word painter on the line where the tax form asked for his profession) who had for years been exhibiting at the galleries which were never noticed in the papers and which usually folded when the landlord had a lien put on all the paintings for back rent. He had years ago gotten over the need to think of himself as an artist manqué, recognizing the bogus aura of romantic failure in that term, and now worked persistently, but without real hope. He taught part-time, which paid for his painting, and Mary uncomplainingly paid for everything else.

I'm *that kind* of person, he told himself.

"We *do* like Indian food, with all those spices," Mary told Lorraine Bellefeuille, catching him unprepared. She was a supply teacher, a brilliant manager of their money and a steady friend. He was sure that she didn't think of herself as any particular kind of person at all.

"I don't care for the south, myself," Lorraine confided. "In fact, you won't catch me setting foot outside of Delhi."

During the next several suppers at Lorraine's, they faced Mexican *moles*, groundnut stew, lobster, Bombay Duck, whitefish, buffalo, white, brown, *basmati* and wild rice. They ate at a long, plain wooden table rescued from an abandoned rectory, from Bavarian china which Lorraine's mother had given her. They liked Lorraine's other friends, who all seemed to live in wealthy municipalities on those poor little sticks of streets that hang inconspicuously from wealthier avenues. Each of her friends spoke about attending parties and dinners at the homes of the great, the successful, or the popular, and they were all well-educated and traveled, yet none were over forty. It was as though they had all put on their backpacks when they were twenty to walk across the Indian subcontinent or vacation in Goa, and they had never quite managed to take their backpacks off. Ray noticed that many of them often looked just a few dollars short of poor, as if the flannel shirts which they wore would, in middle age, smell of poverty and failure, but his own fears prevented him from ever saying this to Mary.

Without exception, Lorraine's friends had projects and plans. There was a book on early television advertising, a new and unperformed choreography, a memoir, a basement photo gallery, an unmarketed invention, cookbooks, and a story forever waiting unread on some editor's desk. As they sat around the dinner table they traded and bartered recipes—a Tagalog specialty of fish and *bullo* peppers going for someone's English grandmother's damson plum jam. And once a week they went to a restaurant, sweeping first through all the Mediterranean second-story walk-ups, then through Austria, the Caribbean, Costa del Sol, and then darting into the most economical places they could find on the edge of Alsace.

Ray and Mary were flattered by the company. It seemed that such a friendly, knowledgeable and talented group of people was bound to be discovered by some-one and that they would all benefit from it.

Then one Saturday morning Ray sat down to coffee and, plowing through the morning paper, was surprised to read his own name. It was a review which he read all the way through before returning to the first few lines to make sure the name was his. "A lucid and insistent questioning of space," he read, and lost the ability to focus his eyes clearly. "Work which is light years past the need for the pictorial, even pulling the rug out from under photo-realism."

Thompson Sleepers Languish in Predictable Academia. That was the headline. He turned cautiously to the front page to check the date, the spelling of the newspaper's name, and the reporting of other events that he had heard on the radio news, convinced that it was a fake. He read the review again, sure that one of his students must have somehow placed it with the paper, but instead recognized the name of a local critic who was syndicated nationally. "Ignore everything in the program and walk straight past all the derivative university-work until you are stopped by Thompson's weightless gouaches, undeservedly kept in a lightless corner. Here is work that is fully matured, open and full of humour. He deserves to be rescued from this place."

Ray lowered the newspaper to the kitchen table and then closed it before Mary could see the headline. He felt naked. He had not even attended the opening of the show that was being reviewed, having given the university gallery some nudes he liked, but had sketched and painted in his Life Studies class to make a point to his students. He knew that the department would hang his work where it would look buried, giving the full-time faculty and perhaps even a few graduate students the best lighting and the best locations. He had given them the work a month ago and forgotten about it, spending the evening of the show's opening at Lorraine's.

His first thought, his first hope, was that no one would bother to read the review, much less say anything about it. By the time breakfast was ready he had almost succeeded in forgetting about it himself and, because it was a cold winter morning, asked Mary to heat up a crumpet and cook some pea meal bacon after he had finished her generous omelette. Then at lunch she surprised him with an airy quiche. He had put the Reviews section of the newspaper into a bag with the rest of the week's papers and hoped that Mary wouldn't ask for it. She was little interested in most things the newspaper had to say and studied only the Home and Family section.

In the afternoon, he received a call. Mary, forgetting that it was Saturday, leapt to the phone because she had just applied for a job proofreading magazine copy and was anxiously waiting for an answer. Ray heard her formal voice tense with an unasked question. "It's for you," she called to him, her palm discreetly cupping the receiver. "It's a man."

The caller was a gallery owner, a friend of the critic who had praised Ray's work. He said he had been to the university gallery in the morning and he agreed with the review and he wondered if Ray would be interested in having the show continue at his gallery (which Ray knew would never face a lien on its contents) and perhaps expand it to have some other pieces included as well. And would Ray have coffee with him on Monday so they could discuss it further?

The call finished, Ray placed the receiver back in its cradle and told Mary that it had been someone who was interested in exhibiting his work, but he didn't tell her the name of the gallery or its owner. Mary, who had no plans for any sort of book or show, was, all the same, used to hearing everyone else's stories of near-publication, stolen ideas, unsigned contracts, kill fees, narrowly missed academic appointments and publishers' failures. "He sounded polite," was all she could think of to say. "But he should have known better than to bother you on Saturday." By supper, Ray had begun to change his mind about being noticed and retrieved the Reviews section of the newspaper from the bag beside the garbage can to show her what had been said about him. She kept on glancing up from the page to look at Ray as if she wanted to make sure that it really was him. The telephone rang a few more times with messages from people who had seen the review.

Before bed they took a shower together and made love. The telephone calls, the sparkling fall of water in the shower and Mary's approval gave a special quality to their lovemaking, and Ray felt as if he were experiencing some entirely new relation to the world.

They were late for the dinner party at a new friend of Lorraine's because their aged Valiant refused to start and they had to wait for the truck from the auto club. Ray had promised to warm the car up during the day but had been caught over another lunch with the gallery owner who, in view of the additional work Ray had given him, decided to instal the show in the larger of his two rooms. By the end of their coffee the man had called Ray a genius and offered to be his exclusive agent for sales. Ray had never considered that there might be more to what had been happening than just one big show he could invite all his friends to.

The flat they were searching for turned out to be above a Greek shoe repair store and they had to drive for fifteen minutes around long one-way streets before they found a parking place. In the building's minuscule lobby, the intercom buttons above the mailboxes were all lifeless, their springs having broken or rusted away. The curved staircase had an old bit of elegance about it but the air in the stairwell held such a sharp reminder of cat that Ray felt uneasy about even touching the sticky handrail. The back wall at the top of each landing was finished in a pinkish tile. The cats, the tile, and the smell of shoe leather from the shop on the ground floor gave the building the aura of a public urinal and Ray was grateful when the door they knocked on was opened immediately and they were admitted to the company of their friends.

The party, if not the dinner, had already begun. They deposited the red wine they had brought with Lorraine, who introduced them to their hostess ("A real food person," she said), who had a portfolio of drawings languishing in the offices of a children's book publisher, and returned to the kitchen to continue grating Parmesan by hand. Ray followed her there and watched with embarrassed pleasure while Mary, in this strange kitchen, poked in the refrigerator, lifted the lid from a pot and squatted to peer into the stained window in the door of the gas oven. Yet, their hostess seemed not to notice the inspection while she opened the bottles of wine and set them aside to breathe.

Ray, despite himself, felt that someone should have mentioned something about his review or his work. Surely they must all have seen it, or heard about it, and would he happy for him. Instead, they were peering into jars and pans in the kitchen. If they hadn't heard anything, he considered, it might be bad taste for him to mention it himself. The day before, the gallery had taken out a three-column wide ad in the newspaper to announce their spring shows and his name was fitted comfortably between names of unquestionable quality and success. Even his colleagues at the university had wryly congratulated him. He decided he would introduce the subject by inviting Lorraine to his *vernissage*.

"Peach chutney," Lorraine said, pausing in her grating while her bust, a moment out of synch, continued to quiver.

"And the strawberry cobbler. I can't tell you."

"Chokecherries."

"Use the Finnish cloudberries that come from Newfoundland."

"Ahhhh."

"It was just *too* much."

"But you have to come from one of those cultures that doesn't get all queasy at eating fish raw."

"A Scandinavian or a Jew or something."

"It was just so . . ."

"It was just too much. I can't even begin to tell you, there's just no word to talk about it."

Finding no way to enter the conversation, Ray fled the kitchen for the living room, where someone was complaining because Fortnum and Mason's had closed and that when they were staying in London, that exclusive food store was always the first stop they made after visiting American Express. The more he listened to them, the more he felt bursting with wanting to say that someone had *noticed* him, that there was hope for them all.

"Did you see I got lucky in the papers last week?" he finally said to a man who wrote reviews for an advertising weekly. "Someone's finally picked up on some of my work."

"*Your* work," the reviewer said, and told Ray that he'd been sending tear sheets to the magazines and dailies for months and that they liked to keep him on a string without ever using him.

Supper was laid out along a narrow oak table with half a dozen card table chairs on one side and an equal number of chrome and vinyl kitchen chairs on the other. The table was an entire geography, beginning at one end with a crinkly stack of papadums and crossing a dozen serving bowls and plates to tortillas at the other. It was plain right away that their hostess knew every ethnic grocery in the city and that she had made a coup because her guests hesitated for a moment before sitting and stood back to point and discuss the table. She asked them to sit down and start eating, with undisguised satisfaction. "*Glabjaman* and *flan* for dessert," she said, raising the flag over her victory.

Ray's plate seemed to fill itself up. There were so many serving dishes that he felt like he was on the receiving end of a bucket brigade. Mary sat diagonally down the long table from him and attacked something with a fork. She speared it, clamped her teeth around the tines and dragged it out between them with a high-pitched, dental kind of sound that he could even hear above the noise of other people eating. And those who were not already eating were cutting up their food and pushing it around on their plates as though they were examining sheep's entrails for a sign.

When Ray looked at his own plate, he couldn't remember having taken any of the food on it. He put what looked like a thin piece of prosciutto into his mouth and bit down. It released a slightly bitter and dusty sensation which he detected on the edges of his tongue. He swallowed the piece without chewing it and it felt like dry leaves going down his throat.

The vegetables on his plate looked like bright little decorations that people without much taste or pretension could show off in their living room in lieu of one of those paintings of a wide-eyed street urchin and his equally wide-eyed cat. Ray knew he should have felt hungry but he felt instead as if all his guts had just disappeared. He could find no reason to eat.

When he felt Mary's, Lorraine's and their hostess' eyes on him, he continued putting pieces of food that were small enough to swallow whole into his mouth. And whenever a plate of food was passed his way he touched the serving fork or spoon and sometimes faked taking another serving, then passed the plate on. By the time his own plate was empty, he felt neither hungry nor satisfied and only wanted to brush his teeth.

"It was almost perfect tonight, wasn't it?" Mary said on the way home. She was very happy. She told him that she had learned how to grow her own bean sprouts and that they were full of vitamins.

The next day, Ray skipped breakfast, pleading that he had put on weight, and promised to eat a healthy lunch at the university. Mary told him that to lose weight he should eat the things that would switch his metabolism from a fat-producing to a fat-burning kind of chemistry and made a complex analogy with setting a furnace thermostat in a way that would conserve the most fuel. She had been hired for the copy proofreading lob and it was her first day. She sat at the kitchen table wearing a slip and trying to decide between two dresses, one of which had a seam that was threatening to part and the other, the hem cut high to conform with an earlier style, too short. Her stomach made a small round bulge in the shiny slip like a Chinese gong and there was a little dimple in the material over her navel. Ray nodded his head at her explanation of his body chemistry and, watching her, decided she was so lovely it was impossible to imagine her old.

Ray skipped lunch entirely, surprised at how much extra time it left him, and used the hour to stretch a large canvas over a frame. At supper, Mary was bleary with fatigue and when she put the food on the table, he took a little of everything and sat through most of the meal with his unused fork poised above his plate. "When you don't eat, your stomach shrinks and then it starts to digest itself and you get ulcers," Mary warned. She had been surprised to find on her desk at work among the usual stories in women's and general interest magazines, a thick sheaf of manuscripts about people who included dogs, mild torture, warlike clothing made from rubber and leather, and fantastic machines in their sexual pleasures.

"The things people have an appetite for," she told him. Though she was tired, her eyes glowed with the pleasure of feeling successful and useful. She brought a shot glass full of a dozen clear and lozenge-shaped vitamin pills to the table and put it down in front of Ray. The pills themselves, their hard shells listening, went down without any trouble and left only a slight aftertaste of gelatin.

The next day, Mary was up and out of the house before he woke up. He didn't even think of having breakfast or lunch. By the late afternoon he began to feel a little tired, but very light, and remembered how as a young boy he could jump from a bed or table and somehow savour the moment of freefall so well that he imagined he was flying. When Mary came home they made love. It seemed to Ray that she could sense how sharply, newly sweet it was for him because she drew away from him for just an instant and looked at him as if to reassure herself that he really was who he appeared to be. He refused to eat supper, telling her that he had a large lunch late in the afternoon. All the same she set a place at the table for him and he guiltily occupied his chair and watched her eat. When he showered that evening he could smell on his clothes and from his skin something dark and oily and unhealthy as if all the poisons were leaving his body. And under the splashing water all his thoughts had such a pellucid clarity that it seemed he should be able to project them on the wall for everyone to see.

Days passed. Mary became frightened because he had stopped eating and she refused to believe his stories that he had been eating away from home. She took this as a sign that he was being unfaithful to her. Ray wanted to explain to her but somehow found himself unable to. How could he say that everything he saw had become so lucid and that he felt free of doubt? He had even stopped worrying about his old age and spent only three or four dreamless hours in bed at night, rising before dawn to read or sit silently sketching at the kitchen table. His weakness seemed unimportant. Where once he had taken the stairs to his classroom studio because the elevator was so cranky and slow, now he became grateful for its gentle acceleration, imagining that he would get the bends if it rose any faster. In class, his explanations, his drawings, had never been clearer or sharper, though he spoke very slowly. His students even seemed to move around him with careful gravity as though they sensed his frailness. Yet, Ray felt strong and decisive. He could see in the bathroom mirror his skin drawing back around his bony eye sockets, and when he glanced at a student in class he could see them flinch from the force of his gaze.

Lorraine invited them for supper and Mary told him that she refused to go alone. Though she still thought he was being unfaithful to her, she said nothing to him about it, as though mentioning her greatest fear would make it come true. And worse, she imagined him doing the things she had read about at work. "You don't look well," she said. "You've lost far too much weight on this diet. All those poisons are stored in your fat and if it's burned up to quickly you'll poison yourself. And your head's starting to look like a skull. And you should have a decent meal tonight because Lorraine's been shopping for it all week and all her meat's kosher so it's almost as good as if it were grown organically."

She said this all in one breath and her voice sounded as if she would begin to cry if she spoke any slower. Ray felt sorry for her, ashamed that he hadn't been eating her suppers and ashamed that he hadn't been able to make love to her when she wanted him that evening. He still couldn't find the way to tell her how clear his thoughts were and how untroubled his mind.

"I don't think you love me anymore," Mary told him as she drove them to Lorraine's. Ray felt too unsteady to drive on the snow and since the Valiant lacked power steering, had asked her. "I don't think you love me anymore," Mary repeated, and the car, as if to emphasize the point, suddenly slid sideways off the shoulder and banged flat into an eight-foot wall of snow with a soft crunch.

"Damn you!" Mary cried. "Damn you!" The motor died but when she tried it again, it caught. The old snow tires bit and they drove on in silence.

Lorraine's English sheep dog had whelped during supper when they were last at her house and now there were puppies under everyone's feet. Every once in a while someone stepped on a puppy's paw and the dog burst out with a sad and astonished cry of pain. Lorraine picked up a hurt puppy and loudly consoled the dog by telling it that it was lucky it wasn't him in Hong Kong, or they might be eating *it* for supper tonight. It was an old joke, like the one about stray cats that wander too close to the kitchen doors of Chinese restaurants, but everybody laughed anyway.

Ray held a warm drink in his hand and stood apart from his friends on the pretext of playing with a puppy. Mary had demanded that he eat or that he make up an excuse and return home before the meal was served. He told himself that, for Mary, he might try some food so she wouldn't be humiliated. She had gone to the kitchen to stare at the Cuisinart, lift the lids from pots, and look as though she might open the oven door. When supper was called, Lorraine led everyone to her rectory table heavy with food and a stack of thick paper plates. Ray saw Mary come from the kitchen and he ostentatiously picked up a plate and, without noticing what he chose, piled food on it till it was dangerously full. When he blew Mary a kiss she returned a bleak smile that made him feel the warmth of the food through the paper plate on the palm of his hand. The food itself looked runny and foreign; none of it had a recognizable shape. And despite the thickness of his plate he could feel dampness beginning to reach his palm.

Ray watched his friends crowding around the buffet for second helpings. "You're not eating," he heard Lorraine say and felt himself warm to the kindness in her voice. Had Mary been talking to her? He could see her studying his face and, dimly, Mary watching both of them from a corner of the room. It occurred to him that Lorraine might be the best person possible to tell about how he felt.

"I haven't eaten for a while now," Ray said, suddenly anxious to confess. "I don't do that anymore."

He had said it so seriously that Lorraine looked away in nervous disbelief. She turned back to hist a grimace of fear. "You have to eat," she said. "I worked hard all day to make it good."

To make it good? When he had finally told her about the show he was having, Lorraine had acted like she didn't want to hear, as if anyone's real success frightened her. He thought that she looked utterly sad and utterly lonely and wanted to ask her why she didn't have any children, why she had never finished anything, whether she ever worried that when she died there would be nothing left of her having been on earth except the remains of what a hundred friends at a thousand parties had eaten. And they were all the same. Is that what food people were? he wondered. Those whom life simply passed through?

He noticed hat Lorraine's nervous smile had disappeared and that her face wore a look of narrow-eyed distaste and alarm. When he looked past her he saw that everyone had stopped eating. There was not a sound in the room, not even the tinkling of cutlery. Had he spoken out loud or were his thoughts so clear and bright that everyone had understood them without his saying a word?

"I *am* a success at something," Lorraine hissed. She turned her back on him and walked away. When he saw her elbow crook defiantly as she raised a fork or a spoon from the plate to her mouth, he threw his loaded, sopping plate at her back as hard as he could.

At home, Mary brought him gilt-rimmed glasses of bright, plastic-surfaced vitamin pills three times a day. She helped him dress, steadied him on his way to the
bathroom, made excuses for him at school and then used her new salary to pay for
a replacement when it was clear that he would miss more that a few days of
classes. When she told him that the gallery owner had phoned saying that he
would have to delay Ray's show because he'd just acquired some new European
works and that it was absolutely necessary they be displayed right away, Ray
barely paid any attention. He touched the crown of his head and felt where a
small furry patch of hair had fallen out.

"You have anorexia," Mary said, brandishing a book which matched kitchen
remedies with afflictions and reading him recipes which called for camphor, aqua
vitae, sulphur and arsenic. Once she served him his vitamins on the one
unchipped Bavarian plate which her mother had willed her, silverware carefully
folded in a linen napkin beside his plate. Then she brought over friends, who
were overly gay and forgiving. Then she brought him home advice from a doctor
that if he didn't start eating he would be committed and would be fed intra-
venously. She sat beside his bed and cried. She tried to make him recall the feast
times of his youth, all the family holidays and all the happy gluttony. She tried
guilt. Had she been a different kind of person, she would have tried infidelity. Ray
walked quietly around the house in his bedroom slippers, making short trips to
the sink, the bathroom, the bookcase.

One day she brought him a dish bristling with tiny green sprouts. "I grew these,"
she said, "and I think that you should eat them. I *demand* that you eat them."

Ray looked dully at the dish of greens.

"If you still love me, you will eat these," she said.

Ray raised himself on his elbows. "Show them off to your friends," he said.

Mary had always been a little clumsy and when she struck him, her fist was
only half-closed, as if she had wanted to push him away and punch him at the
same time. His eyes snapped open in surprise. Mary was transformed with horror
when she saw the cut she had made across the bridge of his nose and down his
cheek and she rushed to the bathroom for a cloth to wipe away the drops of blood
that had started to run down his face. When she returned, Ray was touching his
face gingerly with the tips of his fingers and when he saw the blood on his hand,
he touched it to his lips and tasted it.

A month before Ray gave up eating, his Life Studies class inherited a model
because she had a contract for the year and no one else wanted to use her. She
was herself a kind of leftover. She was the skinniest woman he had ever seen and
he described her to Mary as one of those squatting Bangladesh scarecrows who are
all knees and elbows. During one year, the model had told him, she lost four hundred pounds and her heart stopped beating three times from the strain. He didn't
know if she had been jolly as a fat woman, but skinny she had a deflated kind of
sadness about her. It was as if she had lost three complete women with her four
hundred pounds, and her pouchy, flaccid skin was lonely for them. Thinking of

the way Mary's flesh just coddled her bones, he knew that she didn't have any-thing extra to lose. But with the fat woman, what he saw and drew so well was the incredible transubstantiation of flesh into air, and imagined a sisterly trio escaping in unhindered flight.

Italo Calvino

Italo Calvino was born in Cuba in 1923, where his father and mother were doing scientific work in the area of agriculture and soil management. The family returned to San Remo in Italy, where Calvino went to school and learned from his parents a great deal about plants and animals and liberal ideas. He enrolled in agricultural school at the University of Torino in 1941. Instead of answering his draft call to join the fascist Italian army, he became a member of the Communist Party and fought alongside the partisans in northwest Italy, an experience that informs his realistic novel *The Path of the Nest of Spiders* (1947). After the war, he completed his university degree with a thesis on Joseph Conrad and gradually wrote the experimental works for which he is best known: *Cosmicomics* (1965), *t zero* (1967), *If on a Winter's Night a Traveller* (1981), and *Invisible Cities* (1974).

Calvino has expressed his disinterest in the usual concerns of fiction, particularly the preoccupation with character and psychological analysis, and has stated a preference for social patterning and the structures of human interrelatedness. In "Two Interviews on Science and Literature," he locates himself critically in the Italian tradition, which accepts the "notion of the literary work as a map of the world, and of the knowable." "What interests me is the whole mosaic in which man is set, the interplay of relationships, the design that emerges from the squiggles on the carpet. Anyway, I know that there is no way that I can escape from what is human, even if I do not strain myself to sweat humanity from every pore. The stories I write come into being within a human brain, by means of a combination of signs worked out by the human cultures that have gone before me. And so, in the recent stories with which I end the volume *t zero*, I have tried to make narrative out of a mere process of deductive reasoning and perhaps—in this case, yes—I have departed from anthropomorphism. Or, rather, from a certain kind of anthropomorphism, since these human presences defined only by a system of relationships, by a function, are the very ones that populate the world around us in our everyday lives, good or bad as this situation might appear to us."

His brilliant short novel, *Invisible Cities*, is cast, more or less, as a series of conversations between Marco Polo and Kublai Khan, concerning the relationship between habitation and desire, or between memory and dream. Marco constructs for the amusement and edification of the emperor versions of cities he has visited or heard about, much as Scheherazade constructs adventures in *A Thousand and One Nights*. The Great Khan is no slouch as an audience; he sees Polo's stories as "a journey through memory" and accuses him of returning from his voyages "with a cargo of regrets." He pins the foreign story-teller against the wall and demands: "This is what I wanted to hear from you: confess what you are smuggling: moods, states of grace, elegies." Calvino's fictions are unconventional, shifting from the poetic to the encyclopaedic, from mood piece to tale to dialogue to essay. The cities, "stories," may be said to emerge from the exhaustion of conventional forms and values, so that the author, like the emperor of the Mongols, uses them as a means of coming to terms with both the finiteness and the interconnectedness of all things:

"It is the desperate moment when we discover that this empire, which had seemed to us the sum of all wonders, is an endless, formless ruin, that corruption's gangrene has spread too far to be healed by our sceptre, that the triumph over enemy sovereigns has made us the heirs of their long undoing. Only in Marco Polo's accounts was Kublai Khan able to discern, through the walls and towers destined to crumble, the tracery of a pattern so subtle it could escape the termites' gnawing."

Calvino's quest for new forms has taken him even to the comic strip and animated cartoon, which he says "has a lot to teach the writer, above all how to define characters and objects with a few strokes. It is a metaphorical and metonymic art at one and the same time; it is the art of metamorphosis (the great theme of novels ever since Apuleius, and one that cinema is so bad at) and of anthropomorphism. . . ." However, in his collection of essays, *The Uses of Literature* (1986), he has a good deal to say about the nature and origins of story-telling and its role in myth-making. "Myth," he says, "is the hidden part of every story, the buried part, the region that is still unexplored because there are as yet no words to enable us to get there. The narrator's voice in the daily tribal assemblies is not enough to relate the myth; one needs special times and places, exclusive meetings. The words alone are not enough; we need a whole series of signs with many meanings, which is to say a rite. Myth is nourished by silence as well as words. A silent myth makes itself felt in secular narrative and everyday words; it is a language vacuum that draws words up into its vortex and bestows a form on fable."

Having been a partisan during the war, Calvino has no doubt about the political nature of writing. Ideology and political preference cannot be hidden. However, he believes that a work is politically significant, not as a result of content or authorial design, but from the uses to which it is put by its readers. "For a start," he says, "literature has to realize how modest is its impact on politics. The struggle is decided on the basis of general strategic and tactical lines and relative strengths; in this context, a book is a grain of sand, especially a literary book." Whether the writer's politics are explicit or implicit, Calvino says, "he must bear in mind the general context in which work is situated, he must be aware that the front line also passes through the middle of his work, and that it is a front in constant movement, forever shifting the banners we thought had been raised in place for good. There are no safe territories. The work itself is and has to be a battleground."

Meiosis
Translated by William Weaver

Narrating things as they are means narrating them from the beginning, and even if I start the story at a point where the characters are multicellular organisms, for example the story of my relationship with Priscilla, I have first to define clearly what I mean when I say me and what I mean when I say Priscilla, then I can go on to establish what this relationship was. So I'll begin by saying that Priscilla is an individual of my same species and of the sex opposite mine, multicellular as I now find myself, too; but having said this I still haven't said anything, because I must specify that by multicellular individual is meant a complex of about fifty trillion cells very different among themselves but marked by certain chains of identical acids in the chromosomes of each cell of each individual, acids that determine various processes in the proteins of the cells themselves.

So narrating the story of me and Priscilla means first of all defining the relations established between my proteins and Priscilla's proteins, commanded, both mine and hers, by chains of nucleic acids arranged in identical series in each of her cells and in each of mine. Then narrating this story becomes still more complicated than when it was a question of single cell, not only because the description of the relationship must take into account so many things that happen at the same time but above all because it's necessary to establish who is having relations with whom, before specifying what sort of relations they are. Actually, when you come right down to it, defining the sort of relations isn't after all as important as it seems, because saying we have mental relations, for example, or else, for example, physical relations doesn't change much, since a mental relationship involves several billion special cells called neurons which, however, function by receiving stimuli from such a great number of other cells that we might just as well consider all the trillions of cells of the organism at once as we do when we talk about a physical relationship.

In saying how difficult it is to establish who's having relations with whom we must first clear the decks of a subject that often crops up in conversation: namely, the fact that from one moment to the next I am no longer the same I nor is Priscilla any longer the same Priscilla, because of the continuous renewal of the protein molecules in our cells through, for example, digestion or also respiration which fixes the oxygen in the bloodstream. This kind of argument takes us completely off our course because while it's true that the cells are renewed, in renewing themselves they go on following the program established by those that were there before and so in this sense you could reasonably insist that I continue to be I and Priscilla,

Priscilla. This in other words is not the problem, but perhaps it was of some use to raise it because it helps us realize that things aren't as simple as they seem and so we slowly approach the point where we will realize how complicated they are.

Well then, when I say I, or when I say Priscilla, what do I mean? I mean that special configuration which my cells and her cells assume through a special relationship between the environment and a special genetic heritage which from the beginning seemed invented on purpose to cause my cells to be mine and Priscilla's cells to be Priscilla's. As we proceed we'll see that nothing is made on purpose, that nobody has invented anything, that the way I am and Priscilla is really doesn't matter in the least to anyone: all a genetic heritage has to do is to transmit what was transmitted to it for transmitting, not giving a damn about how it's received. But for the moment let's limit ourselves to answering the question if I, in quotes, and Priscilla, in quotes, are our genetic heritage, in quotes, or our form, in quotes. And when I say form I mean both what is seen and what isn't seen, namely, all her way of being Priscilla, the fact that fuchsia or orange is becoming to her, the scent emanating from her skin not only because she was born with a glandular constitution suited to giving off that scent but also because of everything she has eaten in her life and the brands of soap she has used, in other words because of what is called, in quotes, culture, and also her way of walking and of sitting down which comes to her from the way she has moved among those who move in the cities and houses and streets where she's lived, all this but also the things she has in her memory, after having seen them perhaps just once and perhaps at the movies, and also the forgotten things which still remain recorded somewhere in the back of the neurons like all the psychic trauma a person has to swallow from infancy on.

Now, both in the form you see and don't see and in our genetic heritage, Priscilla and I have absolutely identical elements—common to the two of us, or to the environment, or to the species—and also elements which establish a difference. Then the problem begins to arise whether the relationship between me and Priscilla is the relationship only between the differential elements, because the common ones can be overlooked in both—that is, whether by "Priscilla" we must understand "what is peculiar to Priscilla as far as the other members of the species are concerned"—or whether the relationship is between the common elements, and then we must decide if it's the ones common to the species or to the environment or to the two of us as distinct from the rest of the species and perhaps more beautiful than the others.

On closer examination, if individuals of opposite sex enter into a particular relationship it clearly isn't we who decide but the species, or rather not so much the species as the animal condition, or the vegetable-animal condition of the animal-vegetives distinguished into distinct sexes. Now, in the choice I make of Priscilla to have with her relations whose nature I don't yet know—and in the choice that Priscilla makes of me, assuming that she does choose me and doesn't change her mind at the last moment—no one knows what order of priority comes first into play, therefore no one knows how many I's precede the I that I think I am, and how many Priscillas precede the Priscilla toward whom I believe I am running.

In short, the more you simplify the terms of the question the more they become complicated: once we've established that what I call "I" consists of a certain number of amino acids which line up in a certain way, it's logical that inside these molecules all possible relations are foreseen, and from outside we have nothing but the exclusion of some of the possible relations in the form of certain enzymes which block certain processes. Therefore you can say that it's as if everything possible had already happened to me, including the possibility of its not happening: once I am I the cards are all dealt, I dispose of a finite number of possibilities and no more, what happens outside counts for me only if it's translated into operations already foreseen by my nucleic acids, I'm walled up within myself chained to my molecular program: outside of me I don't have and won't have relations with anything or with anybody. And neither will Priscilla; I mean the *real* Priscilla, poor thing. If around me and around her there's some stuff that seems to have relations with other stuff, these are facts that don't concern us: in reality for me and for her nothing substantial can happen.

Hardly a cheerful situation, therefore: and not because I was expecting to have a more complex individuality than the one given me, beginning with a special arrangement of an acid and of four basic substances which in their turn command the disposition of about twenty amino acids in the forty-six chromosomes of each cell I have; but because this individuality repeated in each of my cells is mine only after a manner of speaking, since out of forty-six chromosomes twenty-three come to me from my father and twenty-three from my mother, that is, I continue carrying my parents with me in all my cells, and I'll never be able to free myself of this burden.

What my parents programmed me to be in the beginning is what I am: that and nothing else. And in my parents' instructions are contained the instructions of my parents' parents handed down in turn from parent to parent in an endless chain of obedience. The story I wanted to narrate therefore is not only impossible to narrate but first of all impossible to live, because it's all there already, contained in a past that can't be narrated since, in turn, it's included in Its own past, in the many individual pasts—so many that we can't really be sure they aren't the past of the species and of what existed before the species, a general past to which all individual pasts refer but which no matter how far you go back doesn't exist except In the form of individual cases, such as Priscilla and I might be, between which, however, nothing happens, individual or general.

What each of us really is and has is the past; all we are and have is the catalogue of the possibilities that didn't fail, of the experiences that are ready to be repeated. A present doesn't exist, we proceed blindly toward the outside and the afterward, carrying out an established program with materials we fabricate ourselves, always the same. We don't tend toward any future, there's nothing awaiting us, we're shut within the system of a memory which foresees no task but remembering itself. What now leads me and Priscilla to seek each other isn't an impulse toward the afterward: it's the final action of the past that is fulfilled through us. Good-by, Priscilla, our encounter, our embrace are useless, we remain distant, or finally near, in other words forever apart.

Separation, the impossibility of meeting, has been in us from the very beginning. We were born not from a fusion but from a juxtaposition of distinct bodies.
Two cells grazed each other: one is lazy and all pulp, the other is only a head and a
darting tail. They are egg and seed: they experience a certain timidity; then they
rush—at their different speeds—and hurry toward each other. The seed plunges
headlong into the egg; the tail is left outside; the head—all full of nucleus—is
shot at the nucleus of the egg; the two nuclei are shattered: you might expect
heaven knows what fusion or mingling or exchange of selves; instead, what was
written in one nucleus and in the other, those spaced lines, fall in and arrange
themselves, on each side, in the new nucleus, very closely printed; the words of
both nuclei fit in, whole and clearly separate. In short, nobody was lost in the
other, nobody has given in or has given himself; the two cells now one are pack-
aged together but just as they were before: the first thing they feel is a slight disappointment. Meanwhile the double nucleus has begun its sequence of duplications,
printing the combined messages of father and mother in each of the offspring
cells, perpetuating not so much the union as the unbridgeable distance that separates in each couple the two companions, the failure, the void that remains in the
midst of even the most successful couple.

Of course, on every disputed issue our cells can follow the instructions of a
single parent and thus feel free of the other's command, but we know what we
claim to be in our exterior form counts for little compared to the secret program
we carry printed in each cell, where the contradictory orders of father and mother
continue arguing. What really counts is this incompatible quarrel of father and
mother that each of us drags after him, with the rancor of every point where one
partner has had to give way to the other, who then raises his voice still louder in
his victory as dominant mate. So the characteristics that determine my interior
and exterior form, when they are not the sum or the average of the orders
received from father and mother together, are orders denied in the depth of cells,
counterbalanced by different orders which have remained latent, sapped by the
suspicion that perhaps the other orders were better. So at times I'm seized with
uncertainty as to whether I am really the sum of the dominant characteristics of
the past, the result of a series of operations that produced always a number bigger
than zero, or whether instead my true essence isn't rather what descends from the
succession of defeated characteristics, the total of the terms with the minus sign,
of everything that in the tree of derivations has remained excluded, stifled, interrupted: the weight of what hasn't been weighs on me, no less crushing than what
has been and couldn't not be.

Void, separation and waiting, that's what we are. And such we remain even on
the day when the past inside us rediscovers its original forms, clustering into
swarms of seed-cells or concentrated ripening of the egg-cells, and finally the
words written in the nuclei are no longer the same as before but are no longer part
of us either, they're a message beyond us, which already belongs to us no more. In
a hidden point in ourselves the double series of orders from the past is divided in
two and the new cells find themselves with a simple past, no longer double, which

gives them lightness and the illusion of being really new, of having a new past that almost seems a future.

Now, I've said it hastily like this but it's a complicated process, there in the darkness of the nucleus, in the depth of the sex organs, a succession of phases some a bit jumbled with others, but from which there's no turning back. At first the pairs of maternal and paternal messages which thus far had remained separate seem to remember they're couples and they join together two by two, so many fine little threads that become interwoven and confused; the desire to copulate outside myself now leads me to copulate within myself, at the depths of the extreme roots of the matter I'm made of, to couple the memory of the ancient pair I carry within me, the first couple, that is both the one that comes immediately before me, mother and father, and absolute first one, the couple at the animal-vegetal origins of the first coupling on Earth, and so the forty-six filaments that an obscure and secret cell bears in the nucleus are knotted two by two, still not giving up their old disagreement, since in fact they immediately try to disentangle themselves but remain stuck at some point in the knot, so when in the end they do succeed, with a wrench, in separating—because meanwhile the mechanism of separation has taken possession of the whole cell, stretching out its pulp—each chromosome discovers it's changed, made of segments that first belonged some to one and some to the other, and it moves from the other, now changed too, marked by the alternate exchanges of the segments, and already two cells are being detached each with twenty-three chromosomes, one cell's different from the other's, and different from those that were in the previous cell, and at the next doubling there will be four cells all different, each with twenty-three chromosomes, in which what was the father's and the mother's, or rather the fathers' and the mothers', is mingled.

So finally the encounter of the pasts which can never take place in the present of those who believe they are meeting does take place in the form of the past of him who comes afterward and who cannot live that encounter in his own present. We believe we're going toward our marriage, but it is still the marriage of the fathers and the mothers which is celebrated through our expectation and our desire. What seems to us our happiness is perhaps only the happiness of the others' story which ends just where we thought ours began.

And it's pointless for us to run, Priscilla, to meet each other and follow each other: the past disposes of us with blind indifference, and once it has moved those fragments of itself and of us, it doesn't bother afterward how we spend them. We were only the preparation, the envelope, for the encounter of pasts which happens through us but which is already part of another story, the story of the afterward: the encounters always take place before and after us, and in them the elements of the new, forbidden to us, are active: chance, risk, improbability.

This is how we live, not free, surrounded by freedom, driven, acted on by this constant wave which is the combination of the possible cases and which passes through those points of space and of time in which the rose of the pasts is joined to the rose of the futures. The primordial sea was a soup of beringed molecules traversed at intervals by the messages of the similarity and of the difference that surrounded us and imposed new combinations. So the ancient tide rises at intervals in me and in Priscilla following the course of the Moon; so the sexed species respond to the old conditioning which prescribes ages and seasons of loves and also grants extensions and postponements to the ages and the seasons and at times becomes involved in obstinacies and coercions and vices.

In other words, Priscilla and I are only meeting places for messages from the past: not only for messages among themselves, but for messages meeting answers to messages. And as the different elements and molecules answer messages in different ways—imperceptibly or boundlessly different—so the messages vary according to the world that receives them and interprets them, or else, to remain the same, they are forced to change. You might say, then, that the messages are not messages at all, that a past to transmit doesn't exist, and only so many futures exist which correct the course of the past, which give it form, which invent it.

The story I wanted to tell is the encounter of two individuals who don't exist, since they are definable only with regard to a past or a future, past and future whose reality is reciprocally doubted. Or else it's a story that cannot be separated from the story of all the rest of what exists, and, therefore from the story of what doesn't exist and not existing, causes what does exist to exist. All we can say is that in certain points and moments that interval of void which is our individual presence is grazed by the wave which continues to renew the combinations of molecules and to complicate them or erase them, and this is enough to give us the certitude that somebody is "I" and somebody is "Priscilla" in the temporal and spatial distribution of the living cells, and that something happens or has happened or will happen which involves us directly and—I would dare say—happily and totally. This is in itself enough, Priscilla, to cheer me, when I bend my outstretched neck over yours and I give you a little nip on your yellow fur and you dilate your nostrils, bare your teeth, and kneel on the sand, lowering your hump to the level of my breast so that I can lean on it and press you from behind, bearing down on my rear legs, oh how sweet those sunsets in the oasis you remember when they loosen the burden from the packsaddle and the caravan scatters and we camels feel suddenly light and you break into a run and I trot after you, overtaking you in the grove of palm trees.

Raymond Carver

Raymond Carver, whose father was a sawmill worker and mother a waitress, was born in Clatskanie, Oregon, in 1939 and raised in Yakima. He married his childhood sweetheart and had two children before the age of twenty, working at odd jobs, including the sawmill. He moved to California and enrolled at Chico State College in 1958, where he studied creative writing with the influential critic and writer John Gardner. Years of casual labour to support his family, and an endless struggle to write—spending hours with a note-pad in his car in the parking lot, to have the necessary privacy and quiet—brought him publication and some critical attention but almost no financial returns. His dreams crumbled, his marriage collapsed, and Carver succumbed to alcoholism. As he says in *The Paris Review* interview with Mona Simpson: "You never start out in life with the intention of becoming bankrupt or an alcoholic or a cheat or a thief. Or a liar."

Carver survived. While the publication of *Will You Please Be Quiet, Please* (1976) had not been enough to prevent his collapse, his second collection, *What We Talk about When We Talk about Love* (1981), proved both a critical and a commercial success; and *Cathedral* (1983) brought him a nomination for a National Book Circle Critics Award and a prestigious award and grant from the American Academy and Institute of Arts and Letters, which allowed him to leave his teaching job in Syracuse and take up part-time residence in Port Angeles, Washington, with his second wife, the poet and fiction writer Tess Gallagher. Before his death from lung cancer in 1988, Carver published *Fires* (1983) and *Where I'm Calling From* (1986), two collections of poetry, *Where Water Comes Together with Other Water* (1985) and *Ultramarine* (1986), and completed a third, *A New Path to the Waterfall*.

"The fiction I'm most interested in," Carver says, "has lines of reference to the real world. None of my stories *happened*, of course. But there's always something, some element, something said to me or that I witnessed, that may be the starting place." He mentions his affinity for the work of Chekhov, Richard Ford, Hemingway, Isaac Babel, Cheever, Anne Beattie, Anne Tyler, and Clark Blaise, particularly to its autobiographical flavour. "Stories long or short don't just come out of thin air. . . . But everything we write is, in some way, autobiographical. . . . Of course, you have to know what you're doing when you turn your life's stories into fiction. You have to be immensely daring, very skilled and imaginative and willing to tell everything on yourself. You're told time and again when you're young to write about what you know, and what do you know better than your own secrets? But unless you're a special kind of writer, and a very talented one, it's dangerous to try and write volume after volume on the Story of My Life. A great danger, or at least a great temptation, for many writers is to become too autobiographical in their approach to their fiction. A little autobiography and a lot of imagination are best."

In response to a question about the dilemmas confronting his characters, Carver said: "I think they are trying [to do what matters]. But trying and succeeding are two different matters. In some lives, people always succeed; and I think it's grand when that happens. In other lives, people don't succeed at what they try to do, at the things they want most to do, the large or small things that support the life. These lives are, of course, valid to write about, the lives of the people who don't succeed. Most of my own experience, direct or indirect, has to do with the latter situation. I think most of my characters would like their actions to count for something. But at the same time they've reached the point—as so many people do—that they know it isn't so. It doesn't add up any longer. The things you once thought important or even worth dying for aren't worth a nickel now. It's their lives they've become uncomfortable with, lives they see breaking down. They'd like to set things right, but they can't. And usually they do know it, I think, and after that they just do the best they can."

Carver claims to have problems with many postmodernist writers, because their fiction seems vague and "divorced from reality in every way, shape, and form. I'm much more interested in stories and poems that have some bearing on how we live and how we conduct ourselves and how we work out the consequences of our actions. Most of my stories start pretty near the end of the arc of the dramatic conflict. I don't give a lot of detail about what went on before; I just start it fairly near the end of the swing of the action."

Although he wrote his first drafts quickly, Carver loved to revise, doing no fewer than ten or twelve drafts of his poems and stories. "I like to mess around with my stories. I'd rather tinker with a story after writing it, and then tinker some more, changing this, changing that, than have to write the story in the first place. That initial writing just seems to me the hard place I have to get to in order to go on and have fun with the story. Rewriting for me is not a chore—it's something I like to do. I think by nature I'm more deliberate and careful than I am spontaneous, and maybe that explains something. Maybe not. . . . Maybe I revise because it gradually takes me into the heart of what the story is *about*. I have to keep trying to see if I can find that out. It's a process more than a fixed position." Carver dislikes the term "minimalist," which critics have applied to his fiction, because it suggests a lack of generosity, a smallness of vision; however, he clearly values economy and has said that if you can say something in twenty words rather than thirty, it's better to use twenty.

When asked about the aims of art, Carver described it as a "superior amusement," but one that was unlikely to bring about major psychological or political change; he described good fiction as "partly a bringing of the news from one world to another. That end is good in and of itself, I think. . . . It doesn't have to do anything. It just has to be there for the fierce pleasure we take in doing it, and the different kind of pleasure that's taken in reading something that's durable and made to last, as well as beautiful in and of itself. Something that throws off these sparks—a persistent and steady glow, however dim."

What We Talk about When We Talk about Love

My friend Mel McGinnis was talking. Mel McGinnis is a cardiologist, and sometimes that gives him the right.

The four of us were sitting around his kitchen table drinking gin. Sunlight filled the kitchen from the big window behind the sink. There were Mel and me and his second wife, Teresa—Terri, we called her—and my wife, Laura. We lived in Albuquerque then. But we were all from somewhere else.

There was an ice bucket on the table. The gin and the tonic water kept going around, and we somehow got on the subject of love. Mel thought real love was nothing less than spiritual love. He said he'd spent five years in a seminary before quitting to go to medical school. He said he still looked back on those years in the seminary as the most important years in his life.

Terri said the man she lived with before she lived with Mel loved her so much he tried to kill her. Then Terri said, "He beat me up one night. He dragged me around the living room by my ankles. He kept saying, 'I love you, I love you, you bitch.' He went on dragging me around the living room. My head kept knocking on things." Terri looked around the table. "What do you do with love like that?"

She was a bone-thin woman with a pretty face, dark eyes, and brown hair that hung down her back. She liked necklaces made of turquoise, and long pendant earrings.

"My God, don't be silly. That's not love, and you know it," Mel said. "I don't know what you'd call it, but I sure know you wouldn't call it love."

"Say what you want to, but I know it was," Terri said. "It may sound crazy to you, but it's true just the same. People are different, Mel. Sure, sometimes he may have acted crazy. Okay. But he loved me. In his own way maybe, but he loved me. There was love there, Mel. Don't say there wasn't."

Mel let out his breath. He held his glass and turned to Laura and me. "The man threatened to kill me," Mel said. He finished his drink and reached for the gin bottle. "Terri's a romantic. Terri's of the kick-me-so-I'll-know-you-love-me school. Terri, hon, don't look that way." Mel reached across the table and touched Terri's cheek with his fingers. He grinned at her.

"Now he wants to make up," Terri said.

"Make up what?" Mel said. "What is there to make up? I know what I know. That's all."

"How'd we get started on this subject, anyway?" Terri said. She raised her glass and drank from it. "Mel always has love on his mind," she said. "Don't you, honey?" She smiled. And I thought that was the last of it.

"I just wouldn't call Ed's behavior love. That's all I'm saying, honey," Mel said. "What about you guys?" Mel said to Laura and me. "Does that sound like love to you?"

"I'm the wrong person to ask," I said. "I didn't even know the man. I've only heard his name mentioned in passing. I wouldn't know. You'd have to know the particulars. But I think what you're saying is that love is an absolute."

Mel said, "The kind of love I'm talking about is. The kind of love I'm talking about, you don't try to kill people."

Laura said, "I don't know anything about Ed, or anything about the situation. But who can judge anyone else's situation?"

I touched the back of Laura's hand. She gave me a quick smile. I picked up Laura's hand. It was warm, the nails polished, perfectly manicured. I encircle the broad wrist with my fingers, and I held her.

"When I left, he drank rat poison," Terri said. She clasped her arms with her hands. "They took him to the hospital in Santa Fe. That's where we lived then, about ten miles out. They saved his life. But his gums went crazy from it. I mean they pulled away from his teeth. After that, his teeth stood out like fangs. My God," Terri said. She waited a minute then let go of her arms and picked up her glass.

"What people won't do!" Laura said.

"He's out of the action now," Mel said. "He's dead."

Mel handed me the saucer of limes. I took a section, squeezed it over my drink and stirred the ice cubes with my finger.

"It gets worse," Terri said. "He shot himself in the mouth. But he bungled that too. Poor Ed," she said. Terri shook her head.

"Poor Ed nothing," Mel said. "He was dangerous."

Mel was forty-five years old. He was tall and rangy with curly soft hair. His face and arms were brown from the tennis he played. When he was sober, his gestures, all his movements, were precise, very careful.

"He did love me though, Mel. Grant me that," Terri said. "That's all I'm asking. He didn't love me the way you love me. I'm not saying that. But he loved me. You can grant me that, can't you?"

"What do you mean, he bungled it?" I said.

Laura leaned forward with her glass. She put her elbows on the table and held her glass in both hands. She glanced from Mel to Terri and waited with a look of bewilderment on her open face, as if amazed that such things happened to people you were friendly with.

"How'd he bungle it when he killed himself?" I said.

"I'll tell you what happened," Mel said. "He took this twenty-two pistol he'd bought to threaten Terri and me with. Oh, I'm serious. The man was always threatening. You should have seen the way we lived in those days. Like fugitives. I even bought a gun myself. Can you believe it? A guy like me? But I did. I bought one for self-defense and carried it in the glove compartment. Sometimes I'd have to leave the apartment in the middle of the night. To go to the hospital, you know? Terri and I weren't married then, and my first wife had the house and kids, the dog, everything, and Terri and I were living in this apartment here. Sometimes, as I say, I'd get a call in the middle of the night and have to go in to the hospital at two or three in the morning. It'd be dark out there in the parking lot, and I'd break into a sweat before I could even get to my car. I never knew if he was going to come up out of the shrubbery or from behind a car and start shooting. I mean, the man was crazy. He was capable of wiring a bomb, anything. He used to call my service at all hours and say he needed to talk to the doctor, and when I'd return the call, he'd say, 'Son of a bitch, your days are numbered.' Little things like that. It was scary, I'm telling you."

"I still feel sorry for him," Terri said.

"It sounds like a nightmare," Laura said. "But what exactly happened after he shot himself?"

Laura is a legal secretary. We'd met in a professional capacity. Before we knew it, it was a courtship. She's thirty-five, three years younger than I am. In addition to being in love, we like each other and enjoy one another's company. She's easy to be with.

"What happened?" Laura said.

Mel said, "He shot himself in the mouth in his room. Someone heard the shot and told the manager. They came in with a passkey, saw what had happened, and called an ambulance. I happened to be there when they brought him in, alive but past recall. The man lived for three days. His head swelled up to twice the size of a normal head. I'd never seen anything like it, and I hope I never do again. Terri wanted to go in and sit with him when she found out about it. We had a fight over it. I didn't think she should see him like that. I didn't think she should see him, and I still don't."

"Who won the fight?" Laura said.

"I was in the room with him when he died," Terri said. "He never came up out of it. But I sat with him. He didn't have anyone else."

"He was dangerous," Mel said. "If you call that love, you can have it."

"It was love," Terri said. "Sure, it's abnormal in most people's eyes. But he was willing to die for it. He did die for it."

"I sure as hell wouldn't call it love," Mel said. "I mean, no one knows what he did it for. I've seen a lot of suicides, and I couldn't say anyone ever knew what they did it for."

Mel put his hands behind his neck and tilted his chair back. "I'm not interested in that kind of love," he said. "If that's love, you can have it."

Terri said, "We were afraid. Mel even made a will out and wrote to his brother in California who used to be a Green Beret. Mel told him who to look for if something happened to him."

Terri drank from her glass. She said, "But Mel's right—we lived like fugitives. We were afraid. Mel was, weren't you, honey? I even called the police at one point, but they were no help. They said they couldn't do anything until Ed actually did something. Isn't that a laugh?" Terri said.

She poured the last of the gin into her glass and waggled the bottle. Mel got up from the table and went to the cupboard. He took down another bottle.

"Well, Nick and I know what love is," Laura said. "For us, I mean," Laura said. She bumped my knee with her knee. "You're supposed to say something now," Laura said, and turned her smile on me.

For an answer, I took Laura's hand and raised it to my lips. I made a big production out of kissing her hand. Everyone was amused.

"We're lucky," I said.

"You guys," Terri said. "Stop that now. You're making me sick. You're still on the honeymoon, for God's sake. You're still gaga, for crying out loud. Just wait. How long have you been together now? How long has it been? A year? Longer than a year?"

"Going on a year and a half," Laura said, flushed and smiling.

"Oh, now," Terri said. "Wait awhile."

She held her drink and gazed at Laura.

"I'm only kidding," Terri said.

Mel opened the gin and went around the table with the bottle.

"Here, you guys," he said. "Let's have a toast. I want to propose a toast. A toast to love. To true love," Mel said.

We touched glasses.

"To love," we said.

Outside, in the backyard, one of the dogs began to bark. The leaves of the aspen that leaned past the window ticked against the glass. The afternoon sun was like a presence in this room, the spacious light of ease and generosity. We could have been anywhere, somewhere enchanted. We raised our glasses again and grinned at each other like children who had agreed on something forbidden.

"I'll tell you what real love is," Mel said. "I mean, I'll give you a good example. And then you can draw your own conclusions." He poured more gin into his glass. He added an ice cube and a sliver of lime. We waited and sipped our drinks. Laura and I touched knees again. I put a hand on her warm thigh and left it there.

"What do any of us really know about love?" Mel said. "It seems to me we're just beginners at love. We say we love each other and we do, I don't doubt it. I love Terri and Terri loves me, and you guys love each other too. You know the kind of love I'm talking about now. Physical love, that impulse that drives you to someone special, as well as love of the other person's being, his or her essence, as it were. Carnal love and, well, call it sentimental love, the day-to-day caring about the other person. But sometimes I have a hard time accounting for the fact that I must have loved my first wife too. But I did, I know I did. So I suppose I am like Terri in that regard. Terri and Ed." He thought about it and then he went on.

"There was a time when I thought I loved my first wife more than life itself. But now I hate her guts. I do. How do you explain that? What happened to that love? What happened to it, is what I'd like to know. I wish someone could tell me. Then there's Ed. Okay, we're back to Ed. He loves Terri so much he tries to kill her and he winds up killing himself." Mel stopped talking and swallowed from his glass. "You guys have been together eighteen months and you love each other. It shows all over you. You glow with it. But you both loved other people before you met each other. You've both been married before, just like us. And you probably loved other people before that too, even. Terri and I have been together five years, been married for four. And the terrible thing, the terrible thing is, but the good thing too, the saving grace, you might say, is that if something happened to one of us—excuse me for saying this—but if something happened to one of us tomorrow, I think the other one, the other person, would grieve for a while, you know, but then the surviving party would go out and love again, have someone else soon enough. All this, all of this love we talking about, it would just be a memory. Maybe not even a memory. Am I wrong? Am I way off base? Because I want you to set me straight if you think I'm wrong. I want to know. I mean, I don't know anything, and I'm the first one to admit it."

"Mel, for God's sake," Terri said. She reached out and took hold of his wrist. "Are you getting drunk? Honey? Are you drunk?"

"Honey, I'm just talking," Mel said. "All right? I don't have to be drunk to say what I think. I mean, we're all just talking, right?" Mel said. He fixed his eyes on her.

"Sweetie, I'm not criticizing," Terri said.

She picked up her glass.

"I'm not on call today," Mel said. "Let me remind you of that. I am not on call," he said.

"Mel, we love you," Laura said.

Mel looked at Laura. He looked at her as if he could not place her, as if she was not the woman she was.

"Love you too, Laura," Mel said. "And you, Nick, love you too. You know something?" Mel said. "You guys are our pals," Mel said.

He picked up his glass.

Mel said, "I was going to tell you about something. I mean, I was going to prove a point. You see, this happened a few months ago, but it's still going on right now, and it ought to make us feel ashamed when we talk like we know what we're talking about when we talk about love."

"Come on now," Terri said. "Don't talk like you're drunk if you're not drunk."

"Just shut up for once in your life," Mel said very quietly. "Will you do me a favor and do that for a minute? So as I was saying, there's this old couple who had this car wreck out on the interstate. A kid hit them and they were all torn to shit and nobody was giving them much chance to pull through."

Terri looked at us and then back at Mel. She seemed anxious, or maybe that's too strong a word.

Mel was handing the bottle around the table.

"I was on call that night," Mel said. "It was May or maybe it was June. Terri and I had just sat down to dinner when the hospital called. There been this thing out on the interstate. Drunk kid, teenager, plowed his dad's pickup into this camper with this old couple in it. They were up in their mid-seventies, that couple. The kid—eighteen, nineteen, something—he was DOA. Taken the steering wheel through his sternum. The old couple, they were alive, you understand. I mean, just barely. But they had everything. Multiple fractures, internal injuries, hemorrhaging, contusions, lacerations, the works, and each of them had themselves concussions. They were in a bad way, believe me. And, of course, their age was two strikes against them. I'd say she was worse off than he was. Ruptured spleen along with everything else. Both kneecaps broken. But they'd been wearing their seatbelts and, God knows, that's what saved them for the time being."

"Folks, this is an advertisement for the National Safety Council," Terri said. "This is your spokesman, Dr. Melvin R. McGinnis, talking." Terri laughed. "Mel," she said, "sometimes you're just too much. But I love you, hon," she said.

"Honey, I love you," Mel said.

He leaned across the table. Terri met him halfway. They kissed.

"Terri's right," Mel said as he settled himself again. "Get those seatbelts on. But seriously, they were in some shape, those oldsters. By the time I got down there, the kid was dead, as I said. He was off in a corner, laid out on a gurney. I took one look at the old couple and told the ER nurse to get me a neurologist and an orthopedic man and a couple of surgeons down there right away."

He drank from his glass. "I'll try to keep this short," he said. "So we took the two of them up to the OR and worked like fuck on them most of the night. They had these incredible reserves, those two. You see that once in a while. So we did everything that could be done, and toward morning we're giving them a fifty-fifty chance, maybe less than that for her. So here they are, still alive the next morning. So, okay, we move them into the ICU, which is where they both kept plugging away at it for two weeks, hitting it better and better on all the scopes. So we transfer them out to their own room."

Mel stopped talking. "Here," he said, "let's drink this cheapo gin the hell up. Then we're going to dinner, right? Terri and I know a new place. That's where we'll go, to this new place we know about. But we're not going until we finish up this cut-rate, lousy gin."

Terri said, "We haven't actually eaten there yet. But it looks good. From the outside, you know."

"I like food," Mel said. "If I had it to do all over again, I'd be a chef, you know? Right, Terri?" Mel said.

He laughed. He fingered the ice in his glass.

"Terri knows," he said. "Terri can tell you. But Let me say this. If I could come back again in a different life, a different time and all, you know what? I'd like to come back as a knight. You were pretty safe wearing all that armor. It was all right being a knight until gunpowder and muskets and pistols came along."

"Mel would like to ride a horse and carry a lance," Terri said.

"Carry a woman's scarf with you everywhere," Laura said.

"Or just a woman," Mel said.

"Shame on you," Laura said.

Terri said, "Suppose you came back as a serf. The serfs didn't have it so good in those days," Terri said.

"The serfs never had it good," Mel said. "But I guess even the knights were vessels to someone. Isn't that the way it worked? But then everyone is always a vessel to someone. Isn't that right? Terri? But what I liked about knights, besides their ladies, was that they had that suit of armor, you know, and they couldn't get hurt very easy. No cars in those days, you know? No drunk teenagers to tear into your ass."

"Vassals," Terri said.

"What?" Mel said.

"Vassals," Terri said. "They were called vassals, not vessels."

"Vassals, vessels," Mel said, "what the fuck's the difference? You knew what I meant anyway. All right," Mel said. "So I'm not educated. I learned my stuff. I'm a heart surgeon, sure, but I'm just a mechanic. I go in and I fuck around and I fix things. Shit," Mel said.

"Modesty doesn't become you," Terri said.

"He's just a humble sawbones," I said. "But sometimes they suffocated in all that armor, Mel. They'd even have heart attacks if it got too hot and they were too tired and worn out. I read somewhere that they'd fall off their horses and not be able to get up because they were too tired to stand with all that armor on them. They got trampled by their own horses sometimes."

"That's terrible," Mel said. "That's a terrible thing, Nicky. I guess they'd just lay there and wait until somebody came along and made a shish kebab out of them."

"Some other vessel," Terri said.

"That's right," Mel said. "Some vassal would come along and spear the bastard in the name of love. Or whatever the fuck it was they fought over in those days."

"Same things we fight over these days," Terri said.

Laura said, "Nothing's changed."

The color was still high in Laura's checks. Her eyes were bright. She brought her glass to her lips.

Mel poured himself another drink. He looked at the label closely as if studying a long row of numbers. Then he slowly put the bottle down on the table and slowly reached for the tonic water.

"What about the old couple?" Laura said. "You didn't finish that story you started."

Laura was having a hard time lighting her cigarette. Her matches kept going out.

The sunshine inside the room was different now, changing, getting thinner. But the leaves outside the window were still shimmering, and I stared at the pattern they made on the panes and on the Formica counter. They weren't the same patterns, of course.

"What about the old couple?" I said.

"Older but wiser," Terri said.

Mel stared at her.

Terri said, "Go on with your story, hon. I was only kidding. Then what happened?"

"Terri, sometimes," Mel said.

"Please, Mel," Terri said. "Don't always be so serious, sweetie. Can't you take a joke?"

"Where's the joke?" Mel said.

He held his glass and gazed steadily at his wife.

"What happened?" Laura said.

Mel fastened his eyes on Laura. He said, "Laura, if I didn't have Terri and if I didn't love her so much, and if Nick wasn't my best friend, I'd fall in love with you. I'd carry you off, honey," he said.

"Tell your story," Terri said. "Then we'll go to that new place, okay?"

"Okay," Mel said. "Where was I?" he said. He stared at the table and then he began again.

"I dropped in to see each of them every day, sometimes twice a day if I was up doing other calls anyway. Casts and bandages, head to foot, the both of them. You know, you've seen it in the movies. That's just the way they looked, just like in the movies. Little eye-holes and nose-holes and mouth-holes. And she had to have her legs slung up on top of it. Well, the husband was very depressed for the longest while. Even after he found out that his wife was going to pull through, he was still very depressed. Not about the accident, though. I mean, the accident was one thing, but it wasn't everything. I'd get up to his mouth-hole, you know, and he'd say no, it wasn't the accident exactly but it was because he couldn't see her through his eye-holes. He said that was what was making him feel so bad. Can you imagine? I'm telling you, the man's heart was breaking because he couldn't turn his goddamn head and see his goddamn wife."

Mel looked around the table and shook his head at what he was going to say.

"I mean, it was killing the old fart just because he couldn't *look* at the fucking woman."

We all looked at Mel.

"Do you see what I'm saying?" he said.

Maybe we were a little drunk by then. I know it was hard keeping things in focus. The light was draining out of the room, going back through the window where it had come from. Yet nobody made a move to get up from the table to turn on the overhead light.

"Listen," Mel said. "Let's finish this fucking gin. There's about enough left here for one shooter all around. Then let's go eat. Let's go to the new place."

"He's depressed," Terri said. "Mel, why don't you take a pill?"

Mel shook his head. "I've taken everything there is."

"We all need a pill now and then," I said.

"Some people are born needing them," Terri said.

She was using her finger to rub at something on the table. Then she stopped rubbing.

"I think I want to call my kids," Mel said. "Is that all right with everybody? I'll call my kids," he said.

Terri said, "What if Marjorie answers the phone? You guys, you've heard us on the subject of Marjorie? Honey, you know you don't want to talk to Marjorie. It'll make you feel even worse."

"I don't want to talk to Marjorie," Mel said. "But I want to talk to my kids."

"There isn't a day goes by that Mel doesn't say he wishes she'd get married again. Or else die," Terri said. "For one thing," Terri said, "she's bankrupting us. Mel says it's just to spite him that she won't get married again. She has a boyfriend who lives with her and the kids, so Mel is supporting the boyfriend too."

"She's allergic to bees," Mel said. "If I'm not praying she'll get married again, I'm praying she'll get herself stung to death by a swarm of fucking bees."

"Shame on you," Laura said.

"Bzzzzzzz," Mel said, turning his fingers into bees and buzzing them at Terri's throat. Then he let his hands drop all the way to his sides.

"She's vicious," Mel said. "Sometimes I think I'll go up there dressed like a bee-keeper. You know, that hat that's like a helmet with the plate that comes down over your face, the big gloves, and the padded coat? I'll knock on the door and let loose a hive of bees in the house. But first I'd make sure the kids were out, of course."

He crossed one leg over the other. It seemed to take him a lot of time to do it. Then he put both feet on the floor and leaned forward, elbows on the table, his chin cupped in his hands.

"Maybe I won't call the kids, after all. Maybe it isn't such a hot idea. Maybe we'll just go eat. How does that sound?"

"Sounds fine to me," I said. "Eat or not eat. Or keep drinking. I could head right on out into the sunset."

"What does that mean, honey?" Laura said.

"It just means what I said," I said. "It means I could just keep going. That's all it means."

"I could eat something myself," Laura said. "I don't think I've ever been so hungry in my life. Is there something to nibble on?"

"I'll put out some cheese and crackers," Terri said.

But Terri just sat there. She did not get up to get anything.

Mel turned his glass over. He spilled it out on the table.

"Gin's gone," Mel said.

Terri said, "Now what?"

I could hear my heart beating. I could hear everyone's heart. I could hear the human noise we sat there making, not one of us moving, not even when the room went dark.

Anton Chekhov

Anton Chekhov was born in 1860 in Taganrog, south-western Russia, where his grandfather had been an indentured peasant and his father was a grocer. He studied medicine at the University of Moscow, publishing sketches in newspapers and magazines to support himself and help the family. "I have two professions and not one," he wrote. "Medicine is my lawful wife and literature is my mistress. When I get tired of one, I spend the night with the other." After practising in a provincial setting, he eventually, with the success of *Particoloured Stories* (1886) and a second volume in 1887, was able to write full time, purchasing a small estate outside Moscow, where, in addition to his abundant writing and correspondence, he gave free medical advice to peasants. The Pushkin Prize and the success he achieved in his own lifetime were the result not only of a prodigious talent, but also of amazing productivity: "I am leading the life of a privileged vegetable which is constantly poisoned by the thought that it must write, eternally write." To a young writer, he said: "But can you have written only fifteen stories?—at this rate you won't learn to write till you are fifty. Write another twenty stories and send them. . . . Practice is essential for you." During the last decade of his life, Chekhov became involved with the Moscow Art Theatre, under the direction of Konstantin Stanislavsky, and wrote *The Seagull* (1896), *Uncle Vanya* (1898), *The Three Sisters* (1901), and *The Cherry Orchard* (1904). He married the actress Olga Knipper in 1901, but died of tuberculosis three years later.

Chekhov's abundant letters reveal him to be a dedicated craftsman and a painstakingly generous critic of the work of other writers. He praised Maxim Gorky highly, but criticized his floridity and lack of restraint; to others, he argued for more "art," "polish," compression, and objectivity; concern for the story's "architecture," which often meant trimming the beginning and end and beefing up the middle; and developing an eye for the total picture rather than "a mere summary, a dry inventory of impressions." He advised the young writer to "seize upon the little particulars" that will create a picture, that "it is better to say not enough than to say too much": "To make a face from marble means to remove everything that is not the face."

Although he has been described as a minimalist in fiction (William Trevor calls it "the art of the glimpse"), who needs the slightest detail to create a sense of character and only a hint of conflict to give momentum to his own stories, Chekhov did not underplay the importance of action in the works of others: "Your story is a good, charming, clever thing. But the action is, as always, slow, and therefore the story seems in some places to drag. Imagine a great pond out of which flows a slender current of water; imagine on the surface of the pond a number of things:—chips of wood, boards, empty barrels, leaves,—all of them, because of the slow flowing of the water, seeming to be stationary and heaped up at the mouth of the stream. This is what occurs in your story,—no movement, and a multitude of details that pile up into a great heap."

A constant concern expressed in his letters was the freedom of the writer to say what must be said. He took a number of humorous swipes at the academy of "lop-eared critics," insisting that "one cannot escape this abuse, because in our age of telegraphy, and hypercritical journalism, and telephones, abuse is the sister of advertising." However, he was a vigorous opponent of censorship of any kind, as is evident in a letter to M. V. Kiselev (1887): "But to think that the task of literature is to gather the pure grain from the muck heap, is to reject literature itself. Artistic literature is called so just because it depicts life as it really is. Its aim is truth,—unconditional and honest." The writer, he insists, is not a cosmetician, but a reporter, an analyst, for whom nothing, not even the dung heap, is unclean or unfit for attention.

Two years later, he wrote to A. N. Pleshcheyev: "I am not a liberal, not a conservative, not a believer in gradual progress, not a monk, not an indifferentist. I should like to be a free artist and nothing more, and I regret that God has not given me the power to be one. I hate lying and violence in all their forms, and am equally repelled by the secretaries of consistories and by Notovich and Gradovksy. Pharisaism, stupidity, and despotism reign not in merchants' houses and prisons alone. I see them in science, in literature, in the younger generation. . . . That is why I have no preference either for gendarmes, or for butchers, or for scientists, or for writers, or for the younger generation. I regard trademarks and labels as a superstition. My holy of holies is the human body, health, intelligence, talent, inspiration, love, and the most absolute freedom—freedom from violence and lying, whatever forms they take. This is the program I would follow if I were a great artist."

If he demanded absolute freedom from rules in content and form, Chekhov was nonetheless increasingly concerned with economy and precision in his writing.

Of "The Lady with the Pet Dog," Vladimir Nabokov has written: "All the traditional rules of story telling have been broken in his wonderful story of twenty pages or so. There is no problem, no regular climax, no point at the end. And it is one of the greatest stories ever written."

The Lady with the Pet Dog
Translated by Avrahm Yarmolinsky

I

A new person, it was said, had appeared on the esplanade: a lady with a pet dog. Dmitry Dmitrich Gurov, who had spent a fortnight at Yalta and had got used to the place, had also begun to take an interest in new arrivals. As he sat in Vernet's confectionery shop, he saw, walking on the esplanade, a fair-haired young woman of medium height, wearing a beret; a white Pomeranian was trotting behind her.

And afterwards he met her in the public garden and in the square several times a day. She walked alone, always wearing the same beret and always with the white dog; no one knew who she was and everyone called her simply "the lady with the pet dog."

"If she is here alone without husband or friends," Gurov reflected, "it wouldn't be a bad thing to make her acquaintance."

He was under forty, but he already had a daughter twelve years old, and two sons at school. They had found a wife for him when he was very young, a student in his second year, and by now she seemed half as old again as he. She was a tall, erect woman with dark eyebrows, stately and dignified and, as she said of herself, intellectual. She read a great deal, used simplified spelling in her letters, called her husband, not Dmitry, but Dimitry, while he privately considered her of limited intelligence, narrow-minded, dowdy, was afraid of her, and did not like to be at home. He had begun being unfaithful to her long ago—had been unfaithful to her often and, probably for that reason, almost always spoke ill of women, and when they were talked of in his presence used to call them "the inferior race."

It seemed to him that he had been sufficiently tutored by bitter experience to call what he pleased, and yet he could not have lived without "the inferior race" for two days together. In the company of men he was bored and ill at ease, he was chilly and uncommunicative with them; but when he was among women he felt free, and knew what to speak to them about and how to comport himself; and even to be silent with them was no strain on him. In his appearance, in his character, in his whole make-up there was something attractive and elusive that disposed women in his favor and allured them. He knew that, and some force seemed to draw him to them, too.

Oft-repeated and really bitter experience had taught him long ago that with decent people—particularly Moscow people—who are irresolute and slow to move, every affair which at first seems a light and charming adventure inevitably grows into a whole problem of extreme complexity, and in the end a painful situation is created. But at every new meeting with an interesting woman this lesson of experience seemed to slip from his memory, and he was eager for life, and every-thing seemed so simple and diverting.

One evening while he was dining in the public garden the lady in the beret walked up without haste to take the next table. Her expression, her gait, her dress, and the way she did her hair told him that she belonged to the upper class, that she was married, that she was in Yalta for the first time and alone, and that she was bored there. The stories told of the immorality in Yalta are to a great extent untrue; he despised them, and knew that such stories were made up for the most part by persons who would have been glad to sin themselves if they had had the chance; but when the lady sat down at the next table three paces from him, he recalled these stories of easy conquests, of trips to the mountains, and the tempting thought of a swift, fleeting liaison, a romance with an unknown woman of whose very name he was ignorant suddenly took hold of him.

He beckoned invitingly to the Pomeranian, and when the dog approached him, shook his finger at it. The Pomeranian growled; Gurov threatened it again.

The lady glanced at him and at once dropped her eyes.

"He doesn't bite," she said and blushed.

"May I give him a bone?" he asked; and when she nodded he inquired affably, "Have you been in Yalta long?"

"About five days."

"And I am dragging out the second week here."

There was a short silence.

"Time passes quickly, and yet it is so dull here!" she said, not looking at him.

"It's only the fashion to say it's dull here. A provincial will live in Belyov or Zhizdra and not be bored, but when he comes here it's 'Oh, the dullness! Oh, the dust!' One would think he came from Granada."

She laughed. Then both continued eating in silence, like strangers, but after dinner they walked together and there sprang up between them the light banter of people who are free and contented, to whom it does not matter where they go or what they talk about. They walked and talked of the strange light on the sea: the water was a soft, warm, lilac color, and there was a golden band of moonlight upon it. They talked of how sultry it was after a hot day. Gurov told her that he was a native of Moscow, that he had studied languages and literature at the uni-versity, but had a post in a bank; that at one time he had trained to become an opera singer but had given it up, that he owned two houses in Moscow. And he learned from her that she had grown up in Petersburg, but had lived in S——— since her marriage two years previously, that she was going to stay in Yalta for about another month, and that her husband, who needed a rest, too, might per-haps come to fetch her. She was not certain whether her husband was a member of a Government Board or served on a Zemstvo Council, and this amused her. And Gurov learned too that her name was Anna Sergeyevna.

Afterwards in his room at the hotel he thought about her—and was certain that he would meet her the next day. It was bound to happen. Getting into bed he recalled that she had been a schoolgirl only recently, doing lessons like his own daughter; he thought how much timidity and angularity there was still in her laugh and her manner of talking with a stranger. It must have been the first time in her life that she was alone in a setting in which she was followed, looked at, and spoken to for one secret purpose alone, which she could hardly fail to guess. He thought of her slim, delicate throat, her lovely gray eyes.

"There's something pathetic about her, though," he thought, and dropped off.

II

A week had passed since they had struck up an acquaintance. It was a holiday. It was close indoors, while in the street the wind whirled the dust about and blew people's hats off. One was thirsty all day, and Gurov often went into the restaurant and offered Anna Sergeyevna a soft drink or ice cream. One did not know what to do with oneself.

In the evening when the wind had abated they went out on the pier to watch the steamer come in. There were a great many people walking about the dock; they had come to welcome someone and they were carrying bunches of flowers. And two peculiarities of a festive Yalta crowd stood out: the elderly ladies were dressed like young ones and there were many generals.

Owing to the choppy sea, the steamer arrived late, after sunset, and it was a long time tacking about before it put in at the pier. Anna Sergeyevna peered at the steamer and the passengers through her lorgnette as though looking for acquaintances, and whenever she turned to Gurov her eyes were shining. She talked a great deal and asked questions jerkily, forgetting the next moment what she had asked; then she lost her lorgnette in the crush.

The festive crowd began to disperse; it was now too dark to see people's faces; there was no wind any more, but Gurov and Anna Sergeyevna still stood as though waiting to see someone else come off the steamer. Anna Sergeyevna was silent now, and sniffed her flowers without looking at Gurov.

"The weather has improved this evening," he said. "Where shall we go now? Shall we drive somewhere?"

She did not reply.

Then he looked at her intently, and suddenly embraced her and kissed her on the lips, and the moist fragrance of her flowers enveloped him; and at once he looked round him anxiously, wondering if anyone had seen them.

"Let us go to your place," he said softly. And they walked off together rapidly.

The air in her room was close and there was the smell of the perfume she had bought at the Japanese shop. Looking at her, Gurov thought: "What encounters life offers!" From the past he preserved the memory of carefree, good-natured women whom love made gay and who were grateful to him for the happiness he gave them, however brief it might be; and of women like his wife who loved without sincerity, with too many words, affectedly, hysterically, with an expression that it was not love or passion that engaged them but something more significant; and of two or three others, very beautiful, frigid women, across whose faces would suddenly flit a rapacious expression—an obstinate desire to take from life more than it could give, and these were women no longer young, capricious, unreflecting, domineering, unintelligent, and when Gurov grew cold to them their beauty aroused his hatred, and the lace on their lingerie seemed to him to resemble scales.

But here there was the timidity, the angularity of inexperienced youth, a feeling of awkwardness; and there was a sense of embarrassment, as though someone had suddenly knocked at the door. Anna Sergeyevna, "the lady with the pet dog," treated what had happened in a peculiar way, very seriously, as though it were her fall—so it seemed, and this was odd and inappropriate. Her features drooped and faded, and her long hair hung down sadly on either side of her face; she grew pensive and her dejected pose was that of a Magdalene in a picture by an old master.

"It's not right," she said. "You don't respect me now, you first of all."

There was a watermelon on the table. Gurov cut himself a slice and began eating it without haste. They were silent for at least half an hour.

There was something touching about Anna Sergeyevna; she had the purity of a well-bred, naive woman who has seen little of life. The single candle burning on the table barely illuminated her face, yet it was clear that she was unhappy.

"Why should I stop respecting you, darling?" asked Gurov. "You don't know what you're saying."

"God forgive me," she said, and her eyes filled with tears. "It's terrible."

"It's as though you were trying to exonerate yourself."

"How can I exonerate myself? No. I am a bad, low woman; I despise myself and I have no thought of exonerating myself. It's not my husband but myself I have deceived. And not only just now; I have been deceiving myself for a long time. My husband may be a good, honest man, but he is a flunkey! I don't know what he does, what his work is, but I know he is a flunkey! I was twenty when I married him. I was tormented by curiosity; I wanted something better. 'There must be a different sort of life,' I said to myself. I wanted to live! To live, to live! Curiosity kept eating at me—you don't understand it, but I swear to God I could no longer control myself; something was going on in me; I could not be held back. I told my husband I was ill, and came here. And here I have been walking about as though in a daze, as though I were mad; and now I have become a vulgar, vile woman whom anyone may despise."

Gurov was already bored with her; he was irritated by her naive tone, by her repentance, so unexpected and so out of place, but for the tears in her eyes he might have thought she was joking or play-acting.

"I don't understand, my dear," he said softly. "What do you want?"

She hid her face on his breast and pressed close to him.

"Believe me, believe me, I beg you," she said, "I love honesty and purity, and sin is loathsome to me; I don't know what I'm doing. Simple people say, 'The Evil One has led me astray.' And I may say of myself now that the Evil One has led me astray."

"Quiet, quiet," he murmured.

He looked into her fixed, frightened eyes, kissed her, spoke to her softly and affectionately, and by degrees she calmed down, and her gaiety returned; both began laughing.

Afterwards when they went out there was not a soul on the esplanade. The town with its cypresses looked quite dead, but the sea was still sounding as it broke upon the beach; a single launch was rocking on the waves and on it a lantern was blinking sleepily.

They found a cab and drove to Oreanda.

"I found out your surname in the hall just now: it was written on the board—von Dideritz," said Gurov. "Is your husband German?"

"No; I believe his grandfather was German, but he is Greek Orthodox himself."

At Oreanda they sat on a bench not far from the church, looked down at the sea, and were silent. Yalta was barely visible through the morning mist; white clouds rested motionlessly on the mountaintops. The leaves did not stir on the trees, cicadas twanged, and the monotonous muffled sound of the sea that rose from below spoke of the peace, the eternal sleep awaiting us. So it rumbled below when there was no Yalta, no Oreanda here; so it rumbles now, and it will rumble as indifferently and as hollowly when we are no more. And in this constancy, in this complete indifference to the life and death of each of us, there lies, perhaps, a pledge of our eternal salvation, of the unceasing advance of life upon earth, of unceasing movement towards perfection. Sitting beside a young woman who in the dawn seemed so lovely, Gurov, soothed and spellbound by these magical surroundings—the sea, the mountains, the clouds, the wide sky—thought how everything is really beautiful in this world when one reflects: everything except what we think or do ourselves when we forget the higher aims of life and our own human dignity.

A man strolled up to them—probably a guard—looked at them and walked away. And this detail, too, seemed so mysterious and beautiful. They saw a steamer arrive from Feodosia, its lights extinguished in the glow of dawn.

"There is dew on the grass," said Anna Sergeyevna, after a silence.

"Yes, it's time to go home."

They returned to the city.

Then they met every day at twelve o'clock on the esplanade, lunched and dined together, took walks, admired the sea. She complained that she slept badly, that she had palpitations, asked the same questions, troubled now by jealousy and now by the fear that he did not respect her sufficiently. And often in the square or the public garden, when there was no one near them, he suddenly drew her to him and kissed her passionately. Complete idleness, these kisses in broad daylight exchanged furtively in dread of someone's seeing them, the heat, the smell of the sea, and the continual flitting before his eyes of idle, well-dressed, well-fed people, worked a complete change in him; he kept telling Anna Sergeyevna how beautiful she was, how seductive, was urgently passionate; he would not move a step away from her, while she was often pensive and continually pressed him to confess that he did not respect her, did not love her in the least, and saw in her nothing but a common woman. Almost every evening rather late they drove somewhere out of town, to Oreanda or to the waterfall; and the excursion was always a success, the scenery invariably impressed them as beautiful and magnificent.

They were expecting her husband, but a letter came from him saying that he had eye-trouble, and begging his wife to return home as soon as possible. Anna Sergeyevna made haste to go.

"It's a good thing I am leaving," she said to Gurov. "It's the hand of Fate!"

She took a carriage to the railway station, and he went with her. They were driving the whole day. When she had taken her place in the express, and when the second bell had rung, she said, "Let me look at you once more—let me look at you again. Like this."

She was not crying but was so sad that she seemed ill and her face was quivering.

"I shall be thinking of you—remembering you," she said. "God bless you; be happy. Don't remember evil against me. We are parting forever—it has to be, for we ought never to have met. Well, God bless you."

The train moved off rapidly, its lights soon vanished, and a minute later there was no sound of it, as though everything had conspired to end as quickly as possible that sweet trance, that madness. Left alone on the platform, and gazing into the dark distance, Gurov listened to the twang of the grasshoppers and the hum of the telegraph wires, feeling as though he had just waked up. And he reflected, musing, that there had now been another episode or adventure in his life, and it, too, was at an end, and nothing was left of it but a memory. He was moved, sad, and slightly remorseful: this young woman whom he would never meet again had not been happy with him; he had been warm and affectionate with her, but yet in his manner, his tone, and his caresses there had been a shade of light irony, the slightly coarse arrogance of a happy male who was, besides, almost twice her age. She had constantly called him kind, exceptional, high-minded; obviously he had seemed to her different from what he really was, so he had involuntarily deceived her.

Here at the station there was already a scent of autumn in the air; it was a chilly evening.

"It is time for me to go north, too," thought Gurov as he left the platform. "High time!"

III

At home in Moscow the winter routine was already established; the stoves were heated, and in the morning it was still dark when the children were having break-fast and getting ready for school, and the nurse would light the lamp for a short time. There were frosts already. When the first snow falls, on the first day the sleighs are out, it is pleasant to see the white earth, the white roofs; one draws easy, delicious breaths, and the season brings back the days of one's youth. The old limes and birches, white with hoar-frost, have a good-natured look; they are closer to one's heart than cypresses and palms, and near them one no longer wants to think of mountains and the sea.

Gurov, a native of Moscow, arrived there on a fine frosty day, and when he put on his fur coat and warm gloves and took a walk along Petrovka, and when on Saturday night he heard the bells ringing, his recent trip and the places he had visited lost all charm for him. Little by little he became immersed in Moscow life, greedily read three newspapers a day, and declared that he did not read the Moscow papers on principle. He already felt a longing for restaurants, clubs, formal dinners, anniversary celebrations, and it flattered him to entertain distinguished lawyers and actors, and to play cards with a professor at the physicians' club. He could eat a whole portion of meat stewed with pickled cabbage and served in a pan, Moscow style.

A month or so would pass and the image of Anna Sergeyevna, it seemed to him, would become misty in his memory, and only from time to time he would dream of her with her touching smile as he dreamed of others. But more than a month went by, winter came into its own, and everything was still clear in his memory as though he had parted from Anna Sergeyevna only yesterday. And his memories glowed more and more vividly. When in the evening stillness the voices of his children preparing their lessons reached his study, or when he listened to a song or to an organ playing in a restaurant, or when the storm howled in the chimney, suddenly everything would rise up in his memory; what had happened on the pier and the early morning with the mist on the mountains, and the steamer coming from Feodosia, and the kisses. He would pace about his room a long time, remembering and smiling; then his memories passed into reveries, and in his imagination the past would mingle with what was to come. He did not dream of Anna Sergeyevna, but she followed him about everywhere and watched him. When he shut his eyes he saw her before him as though she were there in the flesh, and she seemed to him lovelier, younger, tenderer than she had been, and he imagined himself a finer man than he had been in Yalta. Of evenings she peered out at him from the bookcase, from the fireplace, from the corner—he heard her breathing, the caressing rustle of her clothes. In the street he followed the women with his eyes, looking for someone who resembled her.

Already he was tormented by a strong desire to share his memories with someone. But in his home it was impossible to talk of his love, and he had no one to talk to outside; certainly he could not confide in his tenants or in anyone at the bank. And what was there to talk about? He hadn't loved her then, had he? Had there been anything beautiful, poetical, edifying, or simply interesting in his relations with Anna Sergeyevna? And he was forced to talk vaguely of love, of women, and no one guessed what he meant; only his wife would twitch her black eyebrows and say, "The part of a philanderer does not suit you at all, Dimitry."

One evening, coming out of the physicians' club with an official with whom he had been playing cards, he could not resist saying:

"If you only knew what a fascinating woman I became acquainted with at Yalta!"

The official got into his sledge and was driving away, but turned suddenly and shouted:

"Dmitry Dmitrich!"

"What is it?"

"You were right this evening: the sturgeon was a bit high."

These words, so commonplace, for some reason moved Gurov to indignation, and struck him as degrading and unclean. What savage manners, what mugs!

What stupid nights, what dull, humdrum days! Frenzied gambling, gluttony, drunkenness, continual talk always about the same thing! Futile pursuits and conversations always about the same topics take up the better part of one's time, the better part of one's strength, and in the end there is left a life clipped and wingless, an absurd mess, and there is no escaping or getting away from it—just as though one were in a madhouse or a prison.

Gurov, boiling with indignation, did not sleep all night. And he had a headache all the next day. And the following nights too he slept badly; he sat up in bed, thinking, or paced up and down his room. He was fed up with his children, fed up with the bank; he had no desire to go anywhere or to think of anything.

In December during the holidays he prepared to take a trip and told his wife he was going to Petersburg to do what he could for a young friend—and he set off for S——. What for? He did not know, himself. He wanted to see Anna Sergeyevna and talk with her, to arrange a rendezvous if possible.

He arrived at S—— in the morning, and at the hotel took the best room, in which the floor was covered with gray army cloth, and on the table there was an inkstand, gray with dust and topped by a figure on horseback, its hat in its raised hand and its head broken off. The porter gave him the necessary information: von Dideritz lived in a house of his own on Staro-Goncharnaya Street, not far from the hotel: he was rich and lived well and kept his own horses; everyone in the town knew him. The porter pronounced the name: "Dridiritz."

Without haste Gurov made his way to Staro-Goncharnaya Street and found the house. Directly opposite the house stretched a long gray fence studded with nails.

"A fence like that would make one run away," thought Gurov, looking now at the fence, now at the windows of the house.

He reflected: this was a holiday, and the husband was apt to be at home. And in any case, it would be tactless to go into the house and disturb her. If he were to send her a note, it might fall into her husband's hands, and that might spoil everything. The best thing was to rely on chance. And he kept walking up and down the street and along the fence, waiting for the chance. He saw a beggar go in at the gate and heard the dogs attack him; then an hour later he heard a piano, and the sound came to him faintly and indistinctly. Probably it was Anna Sergeyevna playing. The front door opened suddenly, and an old woman came out, followed by the familiar white Pomeranian. Gurov was on the point of calling to the dog, but his heart began beating violently, and in his excitement he could not remember the Pomeranian's name.

He kept walking up and down, and hated the gray fence more and more, and by now he thought irritably that Anna Sergeyevna had forgotten him, and was perhaps already diverting herself with another man, and that that was very natural in a young woman who from morning till night had to look at that damn fence. He went back to his hotel room and sat on the couch for a long while, not knowing what to do, then he had dinner and a long nap.

"How stupid and annoying all this is!" he thought when he woke and looked at the dark windows: it was already evening. "Here I've had a good sleep for some reason. What am I going to do at night?"

He sat on the bed, which was covered with a cheap gray blanket of the kind seen in hospitals, and he twitted himself in his vexation:

"So there's your lady with the pet dog. There's your adventure. A nice place to cool your heels in."

That morning at the station a playbill in large letters had caught his eye. *The Geisha* was to be given for the first time. He thought of this and drove to the theater.

"It's quite possible that she goes to first nights," he thought.

The theater was full. As in all provincial theaters, there was a haze above the chandelier, the gallery was noisy and restless; in the front row, before the beginning of the performance the local dandies were standing with their hands clasped behind their backs; in the Governor's box the Governor's daughter, wearing a boa, occupied the front seat, while the Governor himself hid modestly behind the portiere and only his hands were visible; the curtain swayed; the orchestra was a long time tuning up. While the audience was coming in and taking their seats, Gurov scanned the faces eagerly.

Anna Sergeyevna, too, came in. She sat down in the third row, and when Gurov looked at her his heart contracted, and he understood clearly that in the whole world there was no human being so near, so precious, and so important to him; she, this little, undistinguished woman, lost in a provincial crowd, with a vulgar lorgnette in her hand, filled his whole life now, was his sorrow and his joy, the only happiness that he now desired for himself, and to the sounds of the bad orchestra, of the miserable local violins, he thought how lovely she was. He thought and dreamed.

A young man with small side-whiskers, very tall and stooped, came in with Anna Sergeyevna and sat down beside her; he nodded his head at every step and seemed to be bowing continually. Probably this was the husband whom at Yalta, in an excess of bitter feeling, she had called a flunkey. And there really was in his lanky figure, his side-whiskers, his small bald patch, something of a flunkey's retiring manner; his smile was mawkish, and in his buttonhole there was an academic badge like a waiter's number.

During the first intermission the husband went out to have a smoke; she remained in her seat. Gurov, who was also sitting in the orchestra, went up to her and said in a shaky voice, with a forced smile:

"Good evening!"

She glanced at him and turned pale, then looked at him again in horror, unable to believe her eyes, and gripped the fan and the lorgnette tightly together in her hands, evidently trying to keep herself from fainting. Both were silent. She was sitting, he was standing, frightened by her distress and not daring to take a seat beside her. The violins and the flute that were being tuned up sang out. He suddenly felt frightened: it seemed as if all the people in the boxes were looking at them. She got up and went hurriedly to the exit; he followed her, and both of them walked blindly along the corridors and up and down stairs, and figures in the uniforms prescribed for magistrates, teachers, and officials of the Department of Crown Lands, all wearing badges, flitted before their eyes, as did also ladies, and fur coats on hangers; they were conscious of drafts and the smell of stale tobacco. And Gurov, whose heart was beating violently, thought:

"Oh, Lord! Why are these people here and this orchestra!"

And at that instant he suddenly recalled how when he had seen Anna Sergeyevna off at the station he had said to himself that all was over between them and that they would never meet again. But how distant the end still was!

On the narrow, gloomy staircase over which it said "To the Amphitheater," she stopped.

"How you frightened me!" she said, breathing hard, still pale and stunned. "Oh, how you frightened me! I am barely alive. Why did you come? Why?"

"But do understand, Anna, do understand—" he said hurriedly, under his breath. "I implore you, do understand—"

She looked at him with fear, with entreaty, with love; she looked at him intently, to keep his features more distinctly in her memory.

"I suffer so," she went on, not listening to him. "All this time I have been thinking of nothing but you; I live only by the thought of you. And I wanted to forget, to forget; but why, oh, why have you come?"

On the landing above them two high school boys were looking down and smoking, but it was all the same to Gurov; he drew Anna Sergeyevna to him and began kissing her face and hands.

"What are you doing, what are you doing!" she was saying in horror, pushing him away. "We have lost our senses. Go away today; go away at once—I conjure you by all that is sacred, I implore you—People are coming this way!"

Someone was walking up the stairs.

"You must leave," Anna Sergeyevna went on in a whisper. "Do you hear, Dmitry Dmitrich? I will come and see you in Moscow. I have never been happy; I am unhappy now, and I never, never shall be happy, never! So don't make me suffer still more! I swear I'll come to Moscow. But now let us part. My dear, good, precious one, let us part!"

She pressed his hand and walked rapidly downstairs, turning to look round at him, and from her eyes he could see that she really was unhappy. Gurov stood for a while, listening, then when all grew quiet, he found his coat and left the theater.

IV

And Anna Sergeyevna began coming to see him in Moscow. Once every two or three months she left S—— telling her husband that she was going to consult a doctor about a woman's ailment from which she was suffering—and her husband did and did not believe her. When she arrived in Moscow she would stop at the Slavyansky Bazar Hotel, and at once send a man in a red cap to Gurov. Gurov came to see her, and no one in Moscow knew of it.

Once he was going to see her in this way on a winter morning (the messenger had come the evening before and not found him in). With him walked his daughter, whom he wanted to take to school; it was on the way. Snow was coming down in big wet flakes.

"It's three degrees above zero, and yet it's snowing," Gurov was saying to his daughter. "But this temperature prevails only on the surface of the earth; in the upper layers of the atmosphere there is quite a different temperature."

"And why doesn't it thunder in winter, papa?"

He explained that, too. He talked, thinking all the while that he was on his way to a rendezvous, and no living soul knew of it, and probably no one would ever know. He had two lives, an open one, seen and known by all who needed to know it, full of conventional truth and conventional falsehood, exactly like the lives of his friends and acquaintances; and another life that went on in secret. And through some strange, perhaps accidental, combination of circumstances, everything that was of interest and importance to him, everything that was essential to him, everything about which he felt sincerely and did not deceive himself, everything that constituted the core of his life, was going on concealed from others; while all that was false, the shell in which he hid to cover the truth—his work at the bank, for instance, his discussions at the club, his references to the "inferior race," his appearances at anniversary celebrations with his wife—all that went on in the open. Judging others by himself, he did not believe what he saw, and always fancied that every man led his real, most interesting life under cover of secrecy as under cover of night. The personal life of every individual is based on secrecy, and perhaps it is partly for that reason that civilized man is so nervously anxious that personal privacy should be respected.

Having taken his daughter to school, Gurov went on to the Slavyansky Bazar Hotel. He took off his fur coat in the lobby, went upstairs, and knocked gently at the door. Anna Sergeyevna, wearing his favorite gray dress, exhausted by the journey and by waiting, had been expecting him since the previous evening. She was pale, and looked at him without a smile, and he had hardly entered when she flung herself on his breast. That kiss was a long, lingering one, as though they had not seen one another for two years.

"Well, darling, how are you getting on there?" he asked. "What news?"

"Wait; I'll tell you in a moment—I can't speak."

She could not speak; she was crying. She turned away from him, and pressed her handkerchief to her eyes.

"Let her have her cry; meanwhile I'll sit down," he thought, and he seated himself in an armchair.

Then he rang and ordered tea, and while he was having his tea she remained standing at the window with her back to him. She was crying out of sheer agitation, in the sorrowful consciousness that their life was so sad; that they could only see each other in secret and had to hide from people like thieves! Was it not a broken life?

"Come, stop now, dear!" he said.

It was plain to him that this love of theirs would not be over soon, that the end of it not in sight. Anna Sergeyevna was growing more and more attached to him. She adored him, and it was unthinkable to tell her that their love was bound to come to an end some day; besides, she would not have believed it!

He went up to her and took her by the shoulders, to fondle her and say something diverting, and at that moment he caught sight of himself in the mirror.

His hair was already beginning to turn gray. And it seemed odd to him that he had grown so much older in the last few years, and lost his looks. The shoulders on which his hands rested were warm and heaving. He felt compassion for this life, still so warm and lovely, but probably already about to begin to fade and wither like his own. Why did she love him so much? He always seemed to women different from what he was, and they loved in him not himself, but the man whom their imagination created and whom they had been eagerly seeking all their lives; and afterwards, when they saw their mistake, they loved him nevertheless. And not one of them had been happy with him. In the past he had met women, come together with them, parted from them, but he had never once loved; it was anything you please, but not love. And only now when his head was gray he had fallen in love, really, truly—for the first time in his life.

Anna Sergeyevna and he loved each other as people do who are very close and intimate, like man and wife, like tender friends; it seemed to them that Fate itself had meant them for one another, and they could not understand why he had a wife and she a husband; and it was as though they were a pair of migratory birds, male and female, caught and forced to live in different cages. They forgave each other what they were ashamed of in their past, they forgave everything in the present, and felt that this love of theirs had altered them both.

Formerly in moments of sadness he had soothed himself with whatever logical arguments came into his head, but now he no longer cared for logic, he felt profound compassion, he wanted to be sincere and tender.

"Give it up now, my darling," he said. "You've had your cry; that's enough. Let us have a talk now, we'll think up something."

Then they spent a long time taking counsel together, they talked of how to avoid the necessity for secrecy, for deception, for living in different cities, and not seeing one another for long stretches of time. How could they free themselves from these intolerable fetters?

"How? How?" he asked, clutching his head. "How?"

And it seemed as though in a little while the solution would be found, and then a new and glorious life would begin; and it was clear to both of them that the end was still far off, and that what was to be most complicated and difficult for them was only just beginning.

Joseph Conrad

Jozef Teodor Konrad Nalecz Korzeniowski was born near Kiev in 1857, at a time when much of Poland was under the heel of Czarist Russia. His father, a poet, translator of Shakespeare, and a strong advocate of Polish independence, was exiled to Russia; his mother died three years later in exile, leaving Conrad in the care of his wealthy uncle, Tadeusz Bobrowski. At the age of seventeen, Conrad left for Marseilles, where he lived beyond his means and became enamoured of personalities associated with the cause of restoring the Carlist monarchy to Spain. He described himself at that stage as "an incorrigible Don Quixote." His extravagant affairs and dangerous skirmishes as a gun-runner for the Carlists brought on what appears to have been a nervous breakdown and attempted suicide. The long apprenticeship with the sea in the French and British merchant service that followed gave Conrad the stability, not to mention the varied experiences, that would serve him so well in his career as a writer. He published his first novel, *Almayer's Folly*, in 1895 and shortly after settled to write in England, whose language he had adopted. He is best known for *Heart of Darkness* (1895), *The Nigger of the "Narcissus"* (1897), *Lord Jim* (1902), *Nostromo* (1904), *The Secret Agent* (1907), and *Victory* (1915), though he also produced a fascinating body of short fiction, including stories and novellas. "An Outpost of Progress," which he describes as a turning-point in his career— "I found there a different moral attitude. I seemed able to capture new reactions, new suggestions, and even new rhythms for my paragraphs"—Conrad called "the lightest part of the loot I carried off from Central Africa, the main portion being of course the Heart of Darkness."

Conrad's romantic temperament and his sceptical cast of mind produced in him an existential awareness that, in his early years, often found extreme expression, as in this letter to R. B. Cunninghame Graham: "'Put out the tongue,' why not? One ought to really and the machine will run all the same. The question is whether the fatigue of the muscular exertion is worth the transient pleasure of indulgent scorn. On the other hand one may ask whether scorn, love or hate are justified in the face of such shadowy illusions. The machine is thinner than air and as evanescent as a flash of lightning. The attitude of cold unconcern is the only reasonable one. Of course reason is hateful,—but why? Because it demonstrates

(to those who have the courage) that we, living, are out of life,—utterly out of it. The mysteries of a universe made up of drops of fire and clods of mud do not concern us in the least. The fate of a humanity condemned ultimately to perish from cold is not worth troubling about. If you take it to heart it becomes an undendurable tragedy. . . . Life knows us not and we do not know life,—we don't even know our own thoughts. Half the words we use have no meaning whatever and of the other half each man understands each word after the fashion of his own folly and conceit. Faith is a myth and beliefs shift like mists on the shore: thoughts vanish: words, once pronounced, die: and the memory of yesterday is as shadowy as the hope of tomorrow— only the string of my platitudes seems to have no end. As our peasants say: 'Pray, brother, forgive me for the love of God.' And we don't know what forgiveness is, nor what love is, nor where God is. *Assez!*"

The bleakness of this vision is modified somewhat in the later writings. As he says in his essay "Books," "To be hopeful in an artistic sense it is not necessary to think that the world is good. It is enough to believe that there is no impossibility of its being made so." Work, particularly the work of writing, was for Conrad a great moral comfort, though he had few illusions about its potential for finding political cures. As he says in "Autocracy and War," "The true peace of the world will be a place of refuge much less like a beleaguered fortress and more, let us hope, in the nature of an Inviolable Temple. It will be built on less perishable foundations than those of material interests. But it must be confessed that the architectural aspect of the universal city remains as yet inconceivable—that the very ground for its erection has not been cleared of the jungle."

Conrad's aesthetic may be gleaned from the fiction, of course, but also by a careful reading of his letters, essays, prefaces, and *A Personal Record*. Writing to Arnold Bennett, he said: "Now realism in art will never approach reality. And your art, your gift, should be put to the service of a larger and freer faith." Instead, he advised the writer to "cultivate his poetic faculty," to aim for plasticity, suggestiveness, and "an unremitting never-discouraged care for the shape and ring of sentences." Conrad's imagery here—*faith, temple, hope, forgiveness*—is significant, for it reflects his view of art as a sacred trust, a religious commitment. In a letter to Arthur Symons, he says: "One thing I am certain of is that I have approached the object of my task, things human, in a spirit of piety. The earth is a temple where there is going on a mystery play, childish and poignant, ridiculous and awful enough, in all conscience. Once in I've tried to behave decently. I have not degraded any quasi-religious sentiment by tears and groans; and if I have been amused or indignant, I've neither grinned nor gnashed my teeth. In other words, I've tried to write with dignity, not out of a regard for myself, but for the sake of the spectacle, the play with an obscure beginning and an unfathomable dénouement. I don't think this has been noticed. It is your penitent beating the floor with his forehead and the ecstatic worshipper at the rails that are obvious to the public's eye. The man standing quietly in the shadow of the pillar, if noticed at all, runs the risk of being suspected of sinister designs. Thus I've been called a heartless wretch, a man without ideals and a poseur of brutality. But I will confess to you under seal of secrecy that I *don't believe* I am such as I appear to mediocre minds."

An Outpost of Progress

There were two white men in charge of the trading station. Kayerts, the chief, was short and fat; Carlier, the assistant, was tall, with a large head and a very broad trunk perched upon a long pair of thin legs. The third man on the staff was a Sierra Leone nigger, who maintained that his name was Henry Price. However, for some reason or other, the natives down the river had given him the name of Makola, and it stuck to him through all his wanderings about the country. He spoke English and French with a warbling accent, wrote a beautiful hand, understood bookkeeping, and cherished in his innermost heart the worship of evil spirits. His wife was a negress from Loanda, very large and very noisy. Three children rolled about in sunshine before the door of his low, shed-like dwelling. Makola, taciturn and impenetrable, despised the two white men. He had charge of a small clay storehouse with a dried-grass roof, and pretended to keep a correct account of beads, cotton cloth, red kerchiefs, brass wire, and other trade goods it contained. Besides the storehouse and Makola's hut, there was only one large building in the cleared ground of the station. It was built neatly of reeds, with a verandah on all the four sides. There were three rooms in it. The one in the middle was the living-room, and had two rough tables and a few stools in it. The other two were the bedrooms for the white men. Each had a bedstead and a mosquito net for all furniture. The plank floor was littered with the belongings of the white men; open half-empty boxes, town wearing apparel, old boots; all the things dirty, and all the things broken, that accumulate mysteriously round untidy men. There was also another dwelling-place some distance away from the buildings. In it, under a tall cross much out of the perpendicular, slept the man who had seen the beginning of all this; who had planned and had watched the construction of this outpost of progress. He had been, at home, an unsuccessful painter who, weary of pursuing fame on an empty stomach, had gone out there through high protections. He had been the first chief of that station. Makola had watched the energetic artist die of fever in the just finished house with his usual kind of "I told you so" indifference. Then, for a time, he dwelt alone with his family, his account books, and the Evil Spirit that rules the lands under the equator. He got on very well with his god. Perhaps he had propitiated him by a promise of more white men to play with, by and by. At any rate the director of the Great Trading Company, coming up in a steamer that resembled an enormous sardine box with a flat-roofed shed erected on it, found the station in good order, and Makola as usual quietly diligent. The director had the cross put up over the first agent's grave, and appointed Kayerts to the post. Carlier was told off as second in charge. The director was a man ruthless and efficient, who at times, but very imperceptibly, indulged in grim humour. He made a speech to Kayerts and Carlier, pointing out to them the promising aspect of their station. The nearest trading-post was about three hundred miles away. It was an exceptional opportunity for them to distinguish themselves and to earn percentages on the trade. This appointment was a favour done to beginners. Kayerts was moved almost to tears by his director's kindness. He would, he said, by doing his best, try to justify the flattering confidence, &c., &c. Kayerts had been in the Administration of the Telegraphs, and knew how to express himself correctly. Carlier, an ex-non-commissioned officer of cavalry in an army guaranteed from harm by several European Powers, was less impressed. If there were commissions to get, so much the better; and, trailing a sulky glance over the river, the forests, the impenetrable bush that seemed to cut off the station from the rest of the world, he muttered between his teeth, "We shall see, very soon."

Next day, some bales of cotton goods and a few cases of provisions having been thrown on shore, the sardine-box steamer went off, not to return for another six months. On the deck the director touched his cap to the two agents, who stood on the bank waving their hats, and turning to an old servant of the Company on his passage to headquarters, said, "Look at those two imbeciles. They must be mad at home to send me such specimens. I told those fellows to plant a vegetable garden, build new storehouses and fences, and construct a landing-stage. I bet nothing will be done! They won't know how to begin. I always thought the station on this river useless, and they just fit the station!"

"They will form themselves there," said the old stager with a quiet smile.

"At any rate, I am rid of them for six months," retorted the director.

The two men watched the steamer round the bend, then, ascending arm in arm the slope of the bank, returned to the station. They had been in this vast and dark country only a very short time, and as yet always in the midst of other white men, under the eye and guidance of their superiors. And now, dull as they were to the subtle influences of surroundings, they felt themselves very much alone, when suddenly left unassisted to face the wilderness; a wilderness rendered more strange, more incomprehensible by the mysterious glimpses of the vigorous life it contained. They were two perfectly insignificant and incapable individuals, whose existence is only rendered possible through the high organization of civilized crowds. Few men realize that their life, the very essence of their character, their capabilities and their audacities, are only the expression of their belief in the safety of their surroundings. The courage, the composure, the confidence; the emotions and principles; every great and every insignificant thought belongs not to the individual but to the crowd: to the crowd that believes blindly in the irresistible force of its institutions and of its morals, in the power of its police and of its opinion. But the contact with pure unmitigated savagery, with primitive nature and primitive man, brings sudden and profound trouble into the heart. To the sentiment of being alone of one's kind, to the clear perception of the loneliness of one's thoughts, of one's sensations—to the negation of the habitual, which is safe, there is added the affirmation of the unusual, which is dangerous; a suggestion of things vague, uncontrollable, and repulsive, whose discomposing intrusion excites the imagination and tries the civilized nerves of the foolish and the wise alike.

Kayerts and Carlier walked arm in arm, drawing close to one another as children do in the dark; and they had the same, not altogether unpleasant, sense of danger which one half suspects to be imaginary. They chatted persistently in familiar tones. "Our station is prettily situated," said one. The other assented with enthusiasm, enlarging volubly on the beauties of the situation. Then they passed near the grave. "Poor devil!" said Kayerts. "He died of fever, didn't he?" muttered Carlier, stopping short. "Why," retorted Kayerts, with indignation, "I've been told that the fellow exposed himself recklessly to the sun. The climate here, everybody says, is not at all worse than at home, as long as you keep out of the sun. Do you hear that, Carlier? I am chief here, and my orders are that you should not expose yourself to the sun!" He assumed his superiority jocularly, but his meaning was serious. The idea that he would, perhaps, have to bury Carlier and remain alone, gave him an inward shiver. He felt suddenly that this Carlier was more precious to him here, in the centre of Africa, than a brother could be anywhere else. Carlier, entering into the spirit of the thing, made a military salute and answered in a brisk tone, "Your orders shall be attended to, chief!" Then he burst out laughing, slapped Kayerts on the back and shouted, "We shall let life run easily here! Just sit still and gather in the ivory those savages will bring. This country has its good points, after all!" They both laughed loudly while Carlier thought: That poor Kayerts; he is so fat and unhealthy. It would be awful if I had to bury him here. He is a man I respect. . . . Before they reached the verandah of their house they called one another "my dear fellow."

The first day they were very active, pottering about with hammers and nails and red calico, to put up curtains, make their house habitable and pretty; resolved to settle down comfortably to their new life. For them an impossible task. To grapple effectually with even purely material problems requires more serenity of mind and more lofty courage than people generally imagine. No two beings could have been more unfitted for such a struggle. Society, not from any tenderness, but because of its strange needs, had taken care of those two men, forbidding them all independent thought, all initiative, all departure from routine; and forbidding it under pain of death. They could only live on condition of being machines. And now, released from the fostering care of men with pens behind the ears, or of men with gold lace on the sleeves, they were like those lifelong prisoners who, liberated after many years, do not know what use to make of their freedom. They did not know what use to make of their faculties, being both, through want of practice, incapable of independent thought.

At the end of two months Kayerts often would say, "If it was not for my Melie, you wouldn't catch me here." Melie was his daughter. He had thrown up his post in the Administration of the Telegraphs, though he had been for seventeen years perfectly happy there, to earn a dowry for his girl. His wife was dead, and the child was being brought up by his sisters. He regretted the streets, the pavements, the cafés, his friends of many years; all the things he used to see, day after day; all the thoughts suggested by familiar things—the thoughts effortless, monotonous, and soothing of a Government clerk; he regretted all the gossip, the small enmities, the mild venom, and the little jokes of Government offices. "If I had had a decent brother-in-law," Carlier would remark, "a fellow with a heart, I would not be here." He had left the army and had made himself so obnoxious to his family by his laziness and impudence, that an exasperated brother-in-law had made superhuman efforts to procure him an appointment in the Company as a second-class agent. Having not a penny in the world he was compelled to accept this means of livelihood as soon as it became quite clear to him that there was nothing more to squeeze out of his relations. He, like Kayerts, regretted his old life. He regretted the clink of sabre and spurs on a fine afternoon, the barrack-room witticisms, the girls of garrison towns; but, besides, he had also a sense of grievance. He was evidently a much ill-used man. This made him moody, at times. But the two men got on well together in the fellowship of their stupidity and laziness. Together they did nothing, absolutely nothing, and enjoyed the sense of idleness for which they were paid. And in time they came to feel something resembling affection for one another.

They lived like blind men in a large room, aware only of what came in contact with them (and of that only imperfectly), but unable to see the general aspect of things. The river, the forest, all the great land throbbing with life, were like a great emptiness. Even the brilliant sunshine disclosed nothing intelligible. Things appeared and disappeared before their eyes in an unconnected and aimless kind of way. The river seemed to come from nowhere and flow nowhither. It flowed through a void. Out of that void, at times, came canoes, and men with spears in their hands would suddenly crowd the yard of the station. They were naked, glossy black, ornamented with snowy shells and glistening brass wire, perfect of limb. They made an uncouth babbling noise when they spoke, moved in a stately manner, and sent quick, wild glances out of their startled, never-resting eyes. Those warriors would squat in long rows, four or more deep, before the verandah, while their chiefs bargained for hours with Makola over an elephant tusk. Kayerts sat on his chair and looked down on the proceedings, understanding nothing. He stared at them with his round blue eyes, called out to Carlier, "Here, look! look at that fellow there—and that other one, to the left. Did you ever see such a face? Oh, the funny brute!"

Carlier, smoking native tobacco in a short wooden pipe, would swagger up twirling his moustaches, and surveying the warriors with haughty indulgence, would say—

"Fine animals. Brought any bone? Yes? It's not any too soon. Look at the muscles of that fellow—third from the end. I wouldn't care to get a punch on the nose from him. Fine arms, but legs no good below the knee. Couldn't make cavalry men of them." And after glancing down complacently at his own shanks, he always concluded: "Pah! Don't they stink! You, Makola! Take that herd over to the fetish" (the storehouse was in every station called the fetish, perhaps because of the spirit of civilization it contained) "and give them up some of the rubbish you keep there. I'd rather see it full of bone than full of rags."

Kayerts approved.

"Yes, yes! Go and finish that palaver over there, Mr. Makola. I will come round when you are ready, to weigh the tusk. We must be careful." Then turning to his companion: "This is the tribe that lives down the river; they are rather aromatic. I remember, they had been once before here. D'ye hear that row? What a fellow has got to put up with in this dog of a country! My head is split."

Such profitable visits were rare. For days the two pioneers of trade and progress would look on their empty courtyard in the vibrating brilliance of vertical sunshine. Below the high bank, the silent river flowed on glittering and steady. On the sands in the middle of the stream, hippos and alligators sunned themselves side by side. And stretching away in all directions, surrounding the insignificant cleared spot of the trading post, immense forests, hiding fateful complications of fantastic life, lay in the eloquent silence of mute greatness. The two men understood nothing, cared for nothing but for the passage of days that separated them from the steamer's return. Their predecessor had left some torn books. They took up these wrecks of novels, and, as they had never read anything of the kind before, they were surprised and amused. Then during long days there were interminable and silly discussions about plots and personages. In the centre of Africa they made acquaintance of Richelieu and of d'Artagnan, of Hawk's Eye and of Father Goriot, and of many other people. All these imaginary personages became subjects for gossip as if they had been living friends. They discounted their virtues, suspected their motives, decried their successes; were scandalized at their duplicity or were doubtful about their courage. The accounts of crimes filled them with indignation, while tender or pathetic passages moved them deeply. Carlier cleared his throat and said in a soldierly voice, "What nonsense!" Kayerts, his round eyes suffused with tears, his fat cheeks quivering, rubbed his bald head, and declared, "This is a splendid book. I had no idea there were such clever fellows in the world." They also found some old copies of a home paper. That print discussed what it was pleased to call "Our Colonial Expansion" in high-flown language. It spoke much of the rights and duties of civilization, of the sacredness of the civilizing work, and extolled the merits of those who went about bringing light, and faith and commerce to the dark places of the earth. Carlier and Kayerts read, wondered, and began to think better of themselves. Carlier said one evening, waving his hand about, "In a hundred years, there will be perhaps a town here. Quays, and warehouses, and barracks, and—and—billiard-rooms. Civilization, my boy, and virtue—and all. And then, chaps will read that two good fellows, Kayerts and Carlier, were the first civilized men to live in this very spot!" Kayerts nodded, "Yes, it is a consolation to think of that." They seemed to forget their dead predecessor; but, early one day, Carlier went out and replanted the cross firmly. "It used to make me squint whenever I walked that way," he explained to Kayerts over the morning coffee. "It made me squint, leaning over so much. So I just planted it upright. And solid, I promise you! I suspended myself with both hands to the cross-piece. Not a move. Oh, I did that properly."

At times Gobila came to see them. Gobila was the chief of the neighbouring villages. He was a gray-headed savage, thin and black, with a white cloth round his loins and a mangy panther skin hanging over his back. He came up with long strides of his skeleton legs, swinging a staff as tall as himself, and, entering the common room of the station, would squat on his heels to the left of the door. There he sat, watching Kayerts, and now and then making a speech which the other did not understand. Kayerts, without interrupting his occupation, would from time to time say in a friendly manner: "How goes it, you old image?" and they would smile at one another. The two whites had a liking for that old and incomprehensible creature, and called him Father Gobila. Gobila's manner was paternal, and he seemed really to love all white men. They all appeared to him very young, indistinguishably alike (except for stature), and he knew that they were all brothers, and also immortal. The death of the artist, who was the first white man whom he knew intimately, did not disturb this belief, because he was firmly convinced that the white stranger had pretended to die and got himself buried for some mysterious purpose of his own, into which it was useless to inquire. Perhaps it was his way of going home to his own country? At any rate, these were his brothers, and he transferred his absurd affection to them. They returned it in a way. Carlier slapped him on the back, and recklessly struck off matches for his amusement. Kayerts was always ready to let him have a sniff at the ammonia bottle. In short, they behaved just like that other white creature that had hidden itself in a hole in the ground. Gobila considered them attentively. Perhaps they were the same being with the other—or one of them was. He couldn't decide—clear up that mystery; but he remained always very friendly. In consequence of that friendship the women of Gobila's village walked in single file through the reedy grass, bringing every morning to the station, fowls, and sweet potatoes, and palm wine, and sometimes a goat. The Company never provisions the stations fully, and the agents required those local supplies to live. They had them through the good-will of Gobila, and lived well. Now and then one of them had a bout of fever, and the other nursed him with gentle devotion. They did not think much of it. It left them weaker, and their appearance changed for the worse. Carlier was hollow-eyed and irritable. Kayerts showed a drawn, flabby face above the rotundity of his stomach, which gave him a weird aspect. But being constantly together, they did not notice the change that took place gradually in their appearance, and also in their dispositions. Five months passed in that way.

Then, one morning, as Kayerts and Carlier, lounging in their chairs under the verandah, talked about the approaching visit of the steamer, a knot of armed men came out of the forest and advanced towards the station. They were strangers to that part of the country. They were tall, slight, draped classically from neck to heel in blue fringed cloths, and carried percussion muskets over their bare right shoulders. Makola showed signs of excitement, and ran out of the storehouse (where he spent all his days) to meet these visitors. They came into the courtyard and looked about them with steady, scornful glances. Their leader, a powerful and determined-looking negro with bloodshot eyes, stood in front of the verandah and made a long speech. He gesticulated much, and ceased very suddenly.

There was something in his intonation, in the sounds of the long sentences he used, that startled the two whites. It was like a reminiscence of something not exactly familiar, and yet resembling the speech of civilized men. It sounded like one of those impossible languages which sometimes we hear in our dreams.

"What lingo is that?" said the amazed Carlier. "In the first moment I fancied the fellow was going to speak French. Anyway, it is a different kind of gibberish to what we ever heard."

"Yes," replied Kayerts. "Hey, Makola, what does he say? Where do they come from? Who are they?"

But Makola, who seemed to be standing on hot bricks, answered hurriedly, "I don't know. They come from very far. Perhaps Mrs. Price will understand. They are perhaps bad men."

The leader, after waiting for a while, said something sharply to Makola, who shook his head. Then the man, after looking round, noticed Makola's hut and walked over there. The next moment Mrs. Makola was heard speaking with great volubility. The other strangers—they were six in all—strolled about with an air of ease, put their heads through the door of the storeroom, congregated round the grave, pointed understandingly at the cross, and generally made themselves at home.

"I don't like those chaps—and, I say, Kayerts, they must be from the coast; they've got firearms," observed the sagacious Carlier.

Kayerts also did not like those chaps. They both, for the first time, became aware that they lived in conditions where the unusual may be dangerous, and that there was no power on earth outside of themselves to stand between them and the unusual. They became uneasy, went in and loaded their revolvers. Kayerts said, "We must order Makola to tell them to go away before dark."

The strangers left in the afternoon, after eating a meal prepared for them by Mrs. Makola. The immense woman was excited, and talked much with the visitors. She rattled away shrilly, pointing here and there at the forests and at the river. Makola sat apart and watched. At times he got up and whispered to his wife. He accompanied the strangers across the ravine at the back of the station-ground, and returned slowly looking very thoughtful. When questioned by the white men he was very strange, seemed not to understand, seemed to have forgotten French—seemed to have forgotten how to speak altogether. Kayerts and Carlier agreed that the nigger had had too much palm wine.

There was some talk about keeping a watch in turn, but in the evening everything seemed so quiet and peaceful that they retired as usual. All night they were disturbed by a lot of drumming in the villages. A deep, rapid roll near by would be followed by another far off—then all ceased. Soon short appeals would rattle out here and there, then all mingle together, increase, become vigorous and sustained, would spread out over the forest, roll through the night, unbroken and ceaseless, near and far, as if the whole land had been one immense drum booming out steadily an appeal to heaven. And through the deep and tremendous noise sudden yells that resembled snatches of songs from a madhouse darted shrill and high in discordant jets of sound which seemed to rush far above the earth and drive all peace from under the stars.

Carlier and Kayerts slept badly. They both thought they had heard shots fired during the night—but they could not agree as to the direction. In the morning Makola was gone somewhere. He returned about noon with one of yesterday's strangers, and eluded all Kayerts' attempts to close with him: had become deaf apparently. Kayerts wondered. Carlier, who had been fishing off the bank, came back and remarked while he showed his catch, "The niggers seem to be in a deuce of a stir; I wonder what's up. I saw about fifteen canoes cross the river during the two hours I was there fishing." Kayerts, worried, said, "Isn't this Makola very queer to-day?" Carlier advised, "Keep all our men together in case of some trouble."

II

There were ten station men who had been left by the Director. Those fellows, having engaged themselves to the Company for six months (without having any idea of a month in particular and only a very faint notion of time in general), had been serving the cause of progress for upwards of two years. Belonging to a tribe from a very distant part of the land of darkness and sorrow, they did not run away, naturally supposing that as wandering strangers they would be killed by the inhabitants of the country; in which they were right. They lived in straw huts on the slope of a ravine overgrown with reedy grass, just behind the station build-ings. They were not happy, regretting the festive incantations, the sorceries, the human sacrifices of their own land; where they also had parents, brothers, sisters, admired chiefs, respected magicians, loved friends, and other ties supposed gen-erally to be human. Besides, the rice rations served out by the Company did not agree with them, being a food unknown to their land, and to which they could not get used. Consequently they were unhealthy and miserable. Had they been of any other tribe they would have made up their minds to die—for nothing is easier to certain savages than suicide—and so have escaped from the puzzling difficulties of existence. But belonging, as they did, to a warlike tribe with filed teeth, they had more grit, and went on stupidly living through disease and sorrow. They did very little work, and had lost their splendid physique. Carlier and Kayerts doctored them assiduously without being able to bring them back into condition again. They were mustered every morning and told off to differ-ent tasks—grass-cutting, fence-building, tree-felling, &c., &c., which no power on earth could induce them to execute efficiently. The two whites had practi-cally very little control over them.

In the afternoon Makola came over to the big house and found Kayerts watch-ing three heavy columns of smoke rising above the forests. "What is that?" asked Kayerts. "Some villages burn," answered Makola, who seemed to have regained his wits. Then he said abruptly: "We have got very little ivory—bad six months' trading. Do you like get a little more ivory?"

"Yes," said Kayerts, eagerly. He thought of percentages which were low.

"Those men who came yesterday are traders from Loanda who have got more ivory than they can carry home. Shall I buy? I know their camp."

"Certainly," said Kayerts. "What are those traders?"

"Bad fellows," said Makola, indifferently. "They fight with people, and catch women and children. They are bad men, and got guns. There is a great disturbance in the country. Do you want ivory?"

"Yes," said Kayerts. Makola said nothing for a while. Then: "Those workmen of ours are no good at all," he muttered, looking round. "Station in very bad order, sir. Director will growl. Better get a fine lot of ivory, then he say nothing."

"I can't help it; the men won't work," said Kayerts. "When will you get that ivory?"

"Very soon," said Makola. "Perhaps to-night. You leave it to me, and keep indoors, sir. I think you had better give some palm wine to our men to make a dance this evening. Enjoy themselves. Work better tomorrow. There's plenty palm wine—gone a little sour."

Kayerts said yes, and Makola, with his own hands, carried big calabashes to the door of his hut. They stood there till the evening, and Mrs. Makola looked into every one. The men got them at sunset. When Kayerts and Carlier retired, a big bonfire was flaring before the men's huts. They could hear their shouts and drumming. Some men from Gobila's village had joined the station hands, and the entertainment was a great success.

In the middle of the night, Carlier waking suddenly, heard a man shout loudly; then a shot was fired. Only one. Carlier ran out and met Kayerts on the verandah. They were both startled. As they went across the yard to call Makola, they saw shadows moving in the night. One of them cried, "Don't shoot! It's me, Price." Then Makola appeared close to them. "Go back, go back, please," he urged, "you spoil all." "There are strange men about," said Carlier. "Never mind; I know," said Makola. Then he whispered, "All right. Bring ivory. Say nothing! I know my business." The two white men reluctantly went back to the house, but did not sleep. They heard footsteps, whispers, some groans. It seemed as if a lot of men came in, dumped heavy things on the ground, squabbled a long time, then went away. They lay on their hard beds and thought: "This Makola is invaluable." In the morning Carlier came out, very sleepy, and pulled at the cord of the big bell. The station hands mustered every morning to the sound of the bell. That morning nobody came. Kayerts turned out also, yawning. Across the yard they saw Makola come out of his hut, a tin basin of soapy water in his hand. Makola, civilized nigger, was very neat in his person! He threw the soapsuds skillfully over a wretched little yellow cur he had, then turning his face to the agent's house, he shouted from the distance, "All the men gone last night!"

They heard him plainly, but in their surprise they both yelled out together: "What!" Then they stared at one another. "We are in a proper fix now," growled Carlier. "It's incredible!" muttered Kayerts. "I will go to the huts and see," said Carlier, striding off. Makola coming up found Kayerts standing alone.

"I can hardly believe it," said Kayerts, tearfully. "We took care of them as if they had been our children."

"They went with the coast people," said Makola after a moment of hesitation.

"What do I care with whom they went—the ungrateful brutes!" exclaimed the other. Then with sudden suspicion, and looking hard at Makola, he added: "What do you know about it?"

Makola moved his shoulders, looking down on the ground. "What do I know? I think only. Will you come and look at the ivory I've got there? It is a fine lot. You never saw such."

He moved towards the store. Kayerts followed him mechanically, thinking about the incredible desertion of the men. On the ground before the door of the fetish lay six splendid tusks.

"What did you give for it?" asked Kayerts, after surveying the lot with satisfaction.

"No regular trade," said Makola. "They brought the ivory and gave it to me. I told them to take what they most wanted in the station. It is a beautiful lot. No station can show such tusks. Those traders wanted carriers badly, and our men were no good here. No trade, no entry in books; all correct."

Kayerts nearly burst with indignation. "Why!" he shouted, "I believe you have sold our men for these tusks!" Makola stood impassive and silent. "I—I—will I," stuttered Kayerts. "You fiend!" he yelled out.

"I did the best for you and the Company," said Makola, imperturbably. "Why you shout so much? Look at this tusk."

"I dismiss you! I will report you—I won't look at the tusk. I forbid you to touch them. I order you to throw them into the river. You—you!"

"You very red, Mr. Kayerts. If you are so irritable in the sun, you will get fever and die like the first chief!" pronounced Makola impressively.

They stood still, contemplating one another with intense eyes, as if they had been looking with effort across immense distances. Kayerts shivered. Makola had meant no more than he said, but his words seemed to Kayerts full of ominous menace! He turned sharply and went away to the house. Makola retired into the bosom of his family; and the tusks, left lying before the store, looked very large and valuable in the sunshine.

Carlier came back on the verandah. "They're all gone, hey?" asked Kayerts from the far end of the common room in a muffled voice. "You did not find anybody?"

"Oh, yes," said Carlier, "I found one of Gobila's people lying dead before the huts—shot through the body. We heard that shot last night."

Kayerts came out quickly. He found his companion staring grimly over the yard at the tusks, away by the store. They both sat in silence for a while. Then Kayerts related his conversation with Makola. Carlier said nothing. At the midday meal they ate very little. They hardly exchanged a word that day. A great silence seemed to lie heavily over the station and press on their lips. Makola did not open the store; he spent the day playing with his children. He lay full-length on a mat outside his door, and the youngsters sat on his chest and clambered all over him. It was a touching picture. Mrs. Makola was busy cooking all day as usual. The white men made a somewhat better meal in the evening. Afterwards, Carlier smoking his pipe strolled over to the store; he stood for a long time over the tusks, touched one or two with his foot, even tried to lift the largest one by its small end. He came back to his chief, who had not stirred from the verandah, threw himself in the chair and said—

"I can see it! They were pounced upon while they slept heavily after drinking all that palm wine you've allowed Makola to give them. A put-up job! See? The worst is, some of Gobila's people were there, and got carried off too, no doubt. The least drunk woke up, and got shot for his sobriety. This is a funny country. What will you do now?"

"We can't touch it, of course," said Kayerts.

"Of course not," assented Carlier.

"Slavery is an awful thing," stammered out Kayerts in an unsteady voice.

"Frightful—the sufferings," grunted Carlier with conviction.

They believed their words. Everybody shows a respectful deference to certain sounds that he and his fellows can make. But about feelings people really know nothing. We talk with indignation or enthusiasm; we talk about oppression, cruelty, crime, devotion, self-sacrifice, virtue, and we know nothing real beyond the words. Nobody knows what suffering or sacrifice mean—except, perhaps the victims of the mysterious purpose of these illusions.

Next morning they saw Makola very busy setting up in the yard the big scales used for weighing ivory. By and by Carlier said: "What's that filthy scoundrel up to?" and lounged out into the yard. Kayerts followed. They stood watching. Makola took no notice. When the balance was swung true, he tried to lift a tusk into the scale. It was too heavy. He looked up helplessly without a word, and for a minute they stood round that balance as mute and still as three statues. Suddenly Carlier said: "Catch hold of the other end, Makola—you beast!" and together they swung the tusk up. Kayerts trembled in every limb. He muttered, "I say! O! I say!" and putting his hand in his pocket found there a dirty bit of paper and the stump of a pencil. He turned his back on the others, as if about to do something tricky, and noted stealthily the weights which Carlier shouted out to him with unnecessary loudness. When all was over Makola whispered to himself: "The sun's very strong here for the tusks." Carlier said to Kayerts in a careless tone: "I say, chief, I might just as well give him a lift with this lot into the store."

As they were going back to the house Kayerts observed with a sigh: "It had to be done." And Carlier said: "It's deplorable, but, the men being Company's men the ivory is Company's ivory. We must look after it." "I will report to the Director, of course," said Kayerts. "Of course; let him decide," approved Carlier.

At midday they had a hearty meal. Kayerts sighed from time to time. Whenever they mentioned Makola's name they always added to it an opprobrious epithet. It eased their conscience. Makola gave himself a half-holiday, and bathed his children in the river. No one from Gobila's villages came near the station that day. No one came the next day, and the next, nor for a whole week. Gobila's people might have been dead and buried for any sign of life they gave. But they were only mourning for those they had lost by the witchcraft of white men, who had brought wicked people into their country. The wicked people were gone, but fear remained. Fear always remains. A man may destroy everything within himself, love and hate and belief, and even doubt; but as long as he clings to life he cannot destroy fear: the fear, subtle, indestructible, and terrible, that pervades his being; that tinges his thoughts; that lurks in his heart; that watches on his lips the struggle of his last breath. In his fear, the mild old Gobila offered extra human sacrifices to all the Evil Spirits that had taken possession of his white friends. His heart was heavy. Some warriors spoke about burning and killing, but the cautious old savage dissuaded them. Who could foresee the woe those mysterious creatures, if irritated, might bring? They should be left alone. Perhaps in time they would disappear into the earth as the first one had disappeared. His people must keep away from them, and hope for the best.

Kayerts and Carlier did not disappear, but remained above on this earth, that, somehow, they fancied had become bigger and very empty. It was not the absolute and dumb solitude of the post that impressed them so much as an inarticulate feeling that something from within them was gone, something that worked for their safety, and had kept the wilderness from interfering with their hearts. The images of home; the memory of people like them, of men that thought and felt as they used to think and feel, receded into distances made indistinct by the glare of unclouded sunshine. And out of the great silence of the surrounding wilderness, its very hopelessness and savagery seemed to approach them nearer, to draw them gently, to look upon them, to envelop them with a solicitude irresistible, familiar, and disgusting.

Days lengthened into weeks, then into months. Gobila's people drummed and yelled to every new moon, as of yore, but kept away from the station. Makola and Carlier tried once in a canoe to open communications, but were received with a shower of arrows, and had to fly back to the station for dear life. That attempt set the country up and down the river into an uproar that could be very distinctly heard for days. The steamer was late. At first they spoke of delay jauntily, then anxiously, then gloomily. The matter was becoming serious. Stores were running short. Carlier cast his lines off the bank, but the river was low, and the fish kept out in the stream. They dared not stroll far away from the station to shoot. Moreover, there was no game in the impenetrable forest. Once Carlier shot a hippo in the river. They had no boat to secure it, and it sank. When it floated up it drifted away, and Gobila's people secured the carcase. It was the occasion for a national holiday, but Carlier had a fit of rage over it and talked about the necessity of exterminating all the niggers before the country could be made habitable. Kayerts mooned about silently; spent hours looking at the portrait of his Melie. It represented a little girl with long bleached tresses and a rather sour face. His legs were much swollen, and he could hardly walk. Carlier, undermined by fever, could not swagger any more, but kept tottering about, still with a devil-may-care air, as became a man who remembered his crack regiment. He had become hoarse, sarcastic, and inclined to say unpleasant things. He called it "being frank with you." They had long ago reckoned their percentages on trade, including in them that last deal of "this infamous Makola." They had also concluded not to say anything about it. Kayerts hesitated at first—was afraid of the Director.

"He has seen worse things done on the quiet," maintained Carlier, with a hoarse laugh. "Trust him! He won't thank you if you blab. He is no better than you or me. Who will talk if we hold our tongues? There is nobody here."

That was the root of the trouble! There was nobody there; and being left there alone with their weakness, they became daily more like a pair of accomplices than like a couple of devoted friends. They had heard nothing from home for eight months. Every evening they said, "To-morrow we shall see the steamer." But one of the Company's steamers had been wrecked, and the Director was busy with the other, relieving very distant and important stations on the main river. He thought that the useless station, and the useless men, could wait. Meantime Kayerts and Carlier lived on rice boiled without salt, and cursed the Company, all Africa, and the day they were born. One must have lived on such diet to discover what ghastly trouble the necessity of swallowing one's food may become. There was literally nothing else in the station but rice and coffee; they drank the coffee without sugar. The last fifteen lumps Kayerts had solemnly locked away in his box, together with a half-bottle of Cognac, "in case of sickness," he explained. Carlier approved. "When one is sick," he said, "any little extra like that is cheering."

They waited. Rank grass began to sprout over the courtyard. The bell never rang now. Days passed, silent, exasperating, and slow. When the two men spoke, they snarled; and their silences were bitter, as if tinged by the bitterness of their thoughts.

One day after a lunch of boiled rice, Carlier put down his cup untasted, and said: "Hang it all! Let's have a decent cup of coffee for once. Bring out that sugar, Kayerts!"

"For the sick," muttered Kayerts, without looking up.

"For the sick," mocked Carlier. "Bosh! . . . Well! I am sick."

"You are no more sick than I am, and I go without," said Kayerts in a peaceful tone.

"Come! out with that sugar, you stingy old slave-dealer."

Kayerts looked up quickly. Carlier was smiling with marked insolence. And suddenly it seemed to Kayerts that he had never seen that man before. Who was he? He knew nothing about him. What was he capable of? There was a surprising flash of violent emotion within him, as if in the presence of something undreamt-of, dangerous, and final. But he managed to pronounce with composure—

"That joke is in very bad taste. Don't repeat it."

"Joke!" said Carlier, hitching himself forward on his seat. "I am hungry—I am sick—I don't joke! I hate hypocrites. You are a hypocrite. You are a slave-dealer. I am a slave-dealer. There's nothing but slave-dealers in this cursed country. I mean to have sugar in my coffee to-day, anyhow!"

"I forbid you to speak to me in that way," said Kayerts with a fair show of resolution.

"You!—What?" shouted Carlier, jumping up.

Kayerts stood up also. "I am your chief," he began, trying to master the shakiness of his voice.

"What?" yelled the other. "Who's chief? There's no chief here. There's nothing here: there's nothing but you and I. Fetch the sugar—you pot-bellied ass."

"Hold your tongue. Go out of this room," screamed Kayerts. "I dismiss you—you scoundrel!"

Carlier swung a stool. All at once he looked dangerously in earnest. "You flabby, good-for-nothing civilian—take that!" he howled.

Kayerts dropped under the table, and the stool struck the grass inner wall of the room. Then, as Carlier was trying to upset the table, Kayerts in desperation made a blind rush, head low, like a cornered pig would do, and over-turning his friend, bolted along the verandah, and into his room. He locked the door, snatched his revolver, and stood panting. In less than a minute Carlier was kicking at the door furiously, howling, "If you don't bring out that sugar, I will shoot you at sight, like a dog. Now then—one—two—three or won't? I will show you who's the master."

Kayerts thought the door would fall in, and scrambled through the square hole that served for a window in his room. There was then the whole breadth of the house between them. But the other was apparently not strong enough to break in the door, and Kayerts heard him running round. Then he also began to run laboriously on his swollen legs. He ran as quickly as he could, grasping the revolver, and unable yet to understand what was happening to him. He saw in succession Makola's house, the store, the river, the ravine, and the low bushes; and he saw all those things again as he ran for the second time round the house. Then again they flashed past him. That morning he could not have walked a yard without a groan.

And now he ran. He ran fast enough to keep out of sight of the other man.

Then as, weak and desperate, he thought, "Before I finish the next round I shall die," he heard the other man stumble heavily, then stop. He stopped also. He had the back and Carlier the front of the house, as before. He heard him drop into a chair cursing, and suddenly his own legs gave way, and he slid down into a sitting posture with his back to the wall. His mouth was as dry as a cinder, and his face was wet with perspiration—and tears. What was it all about? He thought it must be a horrible illusion; he thought he was dreaming; he thought he was going mad! After a while he collected his senses. What did they quarrel about? That sugar! How absurd! He would give it to him—didn't want it himself. And he began scrambling to his feet with a sudden feeling of security. But before he had fairly stood upright, a common-sense reflection occurred to him and drove him back into despair. He thought: If I give way now to that brute of a soldier, he will begin this horror again to-morrow—and the day after—every day—raise other pretensions, trample on me, torture me, make me his slave and I will be lost! Lost! The steamer may not come for days—may never come. He shook so that he had to sit down on the floor again. He shivered forlornly. He felt he could not, would not move any more. He was completely distracted by the sudden perception that the position was without issue—that death and life had in a moment become equally difficult and terrible.

All at once he heard the other push his chair back; and he leaped to his feet with extreme facility. He listened and got confused. Must run again! Right or left? He heard footsteps. He darted to the left, grasping his revolver, and at the very same instant, as it seemed to him, they came into violent collision. Both shouted with surprise. A loud explosion took place between them; a roar of red fire, thick smoke; and Kayerts, deafened and blinded, rushed back thinking: I am hit—it's all over. He expected the other to come round—to gloat over his agony. He caught hold of an upright of the roof—"All over!" Then he heard a crashing fall on the other side of the house, as if somebody had tumbled headlong over a chair—then silence. Nothing more happened. He did not die. Only his shoulder felt as it it had been badly wrenched, and he had lost his revolver. He was disarmed and helpless! He waited for his fate. The other man made no sound. It was a stratagem. He was stalking him now! Along what side? Perhaps he was taking aim this very minute!

After a few moments of an agony frightful and absurd, he decided to go and meet his doom. He was prepared for every surrender. He turned the corner, steadying himself with one hand on the wall; made a few paces, and nearly swooned. He had seen on the floor, protruding past the other corner, a pair of turned-up feet. A pair of white naked feet in red slippers. He felt deadly sick, and stood for a time in profound darkness. Then Makola appeared before him, saying quietly: "Come along, Mr. Kayerts. He is dead." He burst into tears of gratitude; a loud, sobbing fit of crying. After a time he found himself sitting in a chair and looking at Carlier, who lay stretched on his back. Makola was kneeling over the body.

"Is this your revolver?" asked Makola, getting up.

"Yes," said Kayerts; then he added very quickly, "He ran after me to shoot me—you saw!"

"Yes, I saw," said Makola. "There is only one revolver; where's his?"

"Don't know," whispered Kayerts in a voice that had become suddenly very faint.

"I will go and look for it," said the other, gently. He made the round along the verandah, while Kayerts sat still and looked at the corpse. Makola came back empty-handed, stood in deep thought, then stepped quietly into the dead man's room, and came out directly with a revolver, which he held up before Kayerts. Kayerts shut his eyes. Everything was going round. He found life more terrible and difficult than death. He had shot an unarmed man.

After meditating for a while, Makola said softly, pointing at the dead man who lay there with his right eye blown out—

"He died of fever." Kayerts looked at him with a stony stare. "Yes," repeated Makola, thoughtfully, stepping over the corpse, "I think he died of fever. Bury him tomorrow."

And he went away slowly to his expectant wife, leaving the two white men alone on the verandah.

Night came, and Kayerts sat unmoving on his chair. He sat quiet as if he had taken a dose of opium. The violence of the emotions he had passed through produced a feeling of exhausted serenity. He had plumbed in one short afternoon the depths of horror and despair, and now found repose in the conviction that life held no more secrets for him: neither had death! He sat by the corpse thinking; thinking very actively, thinking very new thoughts. He seemed to have broken loose from himself altogether. His old thoughts, convictions, likes and dislikes, things he respected and things he abhorred, appeared in their true light at last! Appeared contemptible and childish, false and ridiculous. He revelled in his new wisdom while he sat by the man he had killed. He argued with himself about all things under heaven with that kind of wrong-headed lucidity which may be observed in some lunatics. Incidentally he reflected that the fellow dead there had been a noxious beast anyway; that men died every day in thousands; perhaps in hundreds of thousands—who could tell?—and that in the number, that one death could not possibly make any difference; couldn't have any importance, at least to a thinking creature. He, Kayerts, was a thinking creature. He had been all his life, till that moment, a believer in a lot of nonsense like the rest of mankind—who are fools; but now he thought! He knew! He was at peace; he was familiar with the highest wisdom! Then he tried to imagine himself dead, and Carlier sitting in his chair watching him; and his attempt met with such unexpected success, that in a very few moments he became not at all sure who was dead and who was alive. This extraordinary achievement of his fancy startled him, however, and by a clever and timely effort of mind he saved himself just in time from becoming Carlier. His heart thumped, and he felt hot all over at the thought of that danger. Carlier! What a beastly thing! To compose his now disturbed nerves—and no wonder!— he tried to whistle a little. Then, suddenly, he fell asleep, or thought he had slept; but at any rate there was a fog, and somebody had whistled in the fog.

He stood up. The day had come, and a heavy mist had descended upon the land: the mist penetrating, enveloping, and silent; the morning mist of tropical lands; the mist that clings and kills; the mist white and deadly, immaculate and poisonous. He stood up, saw the body, and threw his arms above his head with a cry like that of a man who, waking from a trance finds himself immured forever in a tomb. *"Help. . . . My God!"*

A shriek inhuman, vibrating and sudden, pierced like a sharp dart the white shroud of that land of sorrow. Three short, impatient screeches followed, and then, for a time, the fog-wreaths rolled on, undisturbed, through a formidable silence. Then many more shrieks, rapid and piercing, like the yells of some exasperated and ruthless creature, rent the air. Progress was calling to Kayerts from the river. Progress and civilization and all the virtues. Society was calling to its accomplished child to come, to be taken care of, to be instructed, to be judged, to be condemned; it exiled him to return to that rubbish heap from which he had wandered away, so that justice could be done.

Kayerts heard and understood. He stumbled out of the verandah, leaving the other man quite alone for the first time since they had been thrown there together. He groped his way through the fog, calling in his ignorance upon the invisible heaven to undo its work. Makola flitted by in the mist, shouting as he ran—

"Steamer! Steamer! They can't see. They whistle for the station. I go ring the bell. Go down to the landing, sir. I ring."

He disappeared. Kayerts stood still. He looked upwards; the fog rolled low over his head. He looked round like a man who has lost his way; and he saw a dark smudge, a cross-shaped stain, upon the shifting purity of the mist. As he began to stumble towards it, the station bell rang in a tumultuous peal its answer to the impatient clamour of the steamer.

The Managing Director of the Great Civilizing Company since we know that civilization follows trade) landed first, and incontinently lost sight of the steamer. The fog down by the river was exceedingly dense; above, at the station, the bell rang unceasing and brazen.

The Director shouted loudly to the steamer:

"There is nobody down to meet us; there may be something wrong, though they are ringing. You had better come, too!"

And he began to toil up the steep bank. The captain and the engine-driver of the boat followed behind. As they scrambled up the fog thinned, and they could see their Director a good way ahead. Suddenly they saw him start forward, calling to them over his shoulder:—"Run! Run to the house! I've found one of them. Run, look for the other!"

He had found one of them! And even he, the man of varied and startling experience, was somewhat discomposed by the manner of this finding. He stood and fumbled in his pockets (for a knife) while he faced Kayerts, who was hanging by a leather strap from the cross. He had evidently climbed the grave, which was high and narrow, and after tying the end of the strap to the arm, had swung himself off. His toes were only a couple of inches above the ground; his arms hung stiffly down; he seemed to be standing rigidly at attention, but with one purple cheek playfully posed on the shoulder. And, irreverently, he was putting out a swollen tongue at his Managing Director.

Robert Coover

Robert Coover was born in Charles City, Iowa, in 1932. He graduated from Indiana University in 1953 and, after service in the U.S. Navy in Europe, did graduate work at the University of Chicago. His fiction, which includes three novels, *The Origin of the Brunists* (1966), and *The Universal Baseball Association, J. Henry Waugh, Prop.* (1968), and *The Public Burning* (1977), and a collection of stories, *Pricksongs & Descants* (1969), has won him the William Faulkner Award, the Brandeis Citation, and a Rockefeller Foundation grant. He worked for ten years in England before returning the U.S., where he has taught at Princeton, Iowa, and Brown Universities. Although his work is situated somewhere between black comedy and absurdist drama, Coover is still very much a moralist in fiction: "I've always been contentious with my writing," he says in an interview with Frank Gado; "I've never turned away from unpleasantness in order to provide escapism. The world itself being a construct of fictions, I believe the fiction maker's function is to furnish better fictions with which we can re-form our notions of things."

In the same interview (*First Person Singular: Conversations on Writers and Writing*, 1973), Coover describes himself as standing at the end of a tradition, a way of viewing the world, as part of "a radical shift in sensibilities. We are no longer convinced of the *nature* of things, of design as justification. Everything seems itself random. . . . Under these conditions of arbitrariness, the artistic impulse is directed toward putting the random parts together in any order which provides a pattern for living." He describes the impact Karl Jaspers's writings had on his own struggle with religious belief: "For Jaspers, the argument was obvious: if you throw the rest out, you've got to throw the Resurrection out too. But, why throw any of it out? Why not accept it all as story; not as literal truth but simply as a story that tells us something, metaphorically, about ourselves and the world? Jaspers concluded that the only way to struggle against myth is on myth's own terms."

Although he insists that "mere design is not that appealing. . . . *What matters is that it be generative and exciting for me while I'm creating,*" Coover is clearly committed to technical experiment. Thus his affection for Mark Twain—"he was playful with the technical aspects of story telling. I could see him incarnated as Kurt Vonnegut"—and his use of numbers, musical analogues, and other structural devices in his stories. "Even though structure is not profoundly meaningful in itself, I love to use it. This has been the case ever since the earliest things I wrote when I made an arbitrary commitment to design. The reason is not that I have some notion of an underlying order which fiction imitates, but a delight with the rich ironic possibilities that the use of structure affords. Any idea, even one which on the surface doesn't seem very interesting, fitted with a perfect structure, can blossom into something that even I did not suspect was there originally. Engaging in that process of discovery is the excitement of making fiction."

Coover explains the title *Pricksongs & Descants* in this way: "They are musical terms. In a way, the title is redundant because a pricksong is a descant. There is a shade of difference, however. 'Pricksong' derives from the physical manner in which the song was printed— the notes were literally pricked out; 'descant' refers to the form of the music in which there is a *cantus firmus*, a basic line, and variations that the other voices play against it. The early descants, being improvisations, were unwritten; when they began writing them, the idea of counterpoint, of a full, beautiful harmony emerged.

"Of course, there is also the obvious sexual suggestion. In this connection, I thought of the descants as feminine decorations around the pricking of the basic line. Thus: the masculine thrust of narrative and the lyrical play around it."

He claims to be fascinated with the myth of transformation that informs Ovid's writing and with the formal possibilities of myth. "Perhaps 'form' is not precisely the word, but certainly the force of myth and mythopoeic thought is with us for all time. The crucial beliefs of people are mystic in nature; whether at the level of the Cinderella story or of the Resurrection, the language is mythopoeic rather than rational. To try to apply reason to such beliefs is like trying to solve a physics problem by psychoanalysis.

"There's no sense in decrying this fact; on the contrary, it is a useful—even necessary—means of navigating through life. In part because individual human existence is so brief, in part because each single instant of the world is so impossibly complex, we cannot accumulate all the data needed for a complete, objective statement. To hope to behave as though this were possible is to invite paralysis through crushing despair. And so we fabricate; we invent constellations that permit an illusion of order to enable us to get from here to there. And we devise short cuts— ways of thinking without thinking through: code words that are in themselves a form of mythopoeia.

"Thus, in a sense, we are all creating fictions all the time, out of necessity. We constantly test them against the experience of life. Some continue to be functional; we are content to let them be rather than try to analyze them and, in the process, forget something else that is even more important. Others outlive their usefulness. They disturb life in some unnecessary way, and so it becomes necessary to break them up and perhaps change their force."

The Babysitter

She arrives at 7:40, ten minutes late, but the children, Jimmy and Bitsy, are still eating supper, and their parents are not ready to go yet. From other rooms come the sounds of a baby screaming, water running, a television musical (no words: probably a dance number—patterns of gliding figures come to mind). Mrs. Tucker sweeps into the kitchen, fussing with her hair, and snatches a baby bottle full of milk out of a pan of warm water, rushes out again. "Harry!" she calls. "The babysitter's here already!"

That's My Desire? I'll Be Around? He smiles toothily, beckons faintly with his head, rubs his fast balding pate. Bewitched, maybe? Or, What's the Reason ? He pulls on his shorts, gives his hips a slap. The baby goes silent in mid-scream. Isn't this the one who used their tub last time ? Who's Sorry Now, that's it.

Jack is wandering around town, not knowing what to do. His girlfriend is babysitting at the Tuckers', and later, when she's got the kids in bed, maybe he'll drop over there. Sometimes he watches TV with her when she's babysitting, it's about the only chance he gets to make out a little since he doesn't own wheels, but they have to be careful because most people don't like their sitters to have boyfriends over. Just kissing her makes her nervous. She won't close her eyes because she has to be watching the door all the time. Married people really have it good, he thinks.

"Hi," the babysitter says to the children, and puts her books on top of the refrigerator. "What's for supper?" The little girl, Bitsy, only stares at her obliquely. She joins them at the end of the kitchen table. "I don't have to go to bed until nine," the boy announces flatly, and stuffs his mouth full of potato chips. The babysitter catches a glimpse of Mr. Tucker hurrying out of the bathroom in his underwear.

Her tummy. Under her arms. And her feet. Those are the best places. She'll spank him, she says sometimes. Let her.

That sweet odor that girls have. The softness of her blouse. He catches a glimpse of the gentle shadows amid her thighs, as she curls her legs up under her. He stares hard at her. He has a lot of meaning packed into that stare, but she's not even looking. She's popping her gum and watching television. She's sitting right there, inches away, soft, fragrant, and ready: but what's his next move? He notices his buddy Mark in the drugstore, playing the pinball machine, and joins him. "Hey, this mama's cold, Jack baby! She needs your touch!"

❖ ❖ ❖

Mrs. Tucker appears at the kitchen doorway, holding a rolled-up diaper. "Now, don't just eat potato chips, Jimmy! See that he eats his hamburger, dear." She hurries away to the bathroom. The boy glares sullenly at the babysitter, silently daring her to carry out the order. "How about a little of that good hamburger now, Jimmy?" she says perfunctorily. He lets half of it drop to the floor. The baby is silent and a man is singing a love song on the TV. The children crunch chips.

❖ ❖ ❖

He loves her. She loves him. They whirl airily, stirring a light breeze, through a magical landscape of rose and emerald and deep blue. Her light brown hair coils and wisps softly in the breeze, and the soft folds of her white gown tug at her body and then float away. He smiles in a pulsing crescendo of sincerity and song.

❖ ❖ ❖

"You mean she's alone?" Mark asks. "Well, there's two or three kids," Jack says. He slides the coin in. There's a rumble of steel balls tumbling, lining up. He pushes a plunger with his thumb, and one ball pops up in place, hard and glittering with promise. His stare? to say he loves her. That he cares for her and would protect her, would shield her, if need be, with his own body. Grinning, he bends over the ball to take careful aim: he and Mark have studied this machine and have it figured out, but still it's not that easy to beat.

❖ ❖ ❖

On the drive to the party, his mind is partly on the girl, partly on his own high-school days, long past. Sitting at the end of the kitchen table there with his children, she had seemed to be self-consciously arching her back, jutting her pert breasts, twitching her thighs: and for whom if not for him? So she'd seen him coming out of there, after all. He smiles. Yet what could he ever do about it? Those good times are gone, old man. He glances over at his wife, who, readjusting a garter, asks: "What do you think of our babysitter?"

❖ ❖ ❖

He loves her. She loves him. And then the babies come. And dirty diapers and one goddamn meal after another. Dishes. Noise. Clutter. And fat. Not just tight, her girdle actually hurts. Somewhere recently she's read about women getting heart attacks or cancer or something from too-tight girdles. Dolly pulls the car door shut with a grunt, strangely irritated, not knowing why. Party mood. Why is her husband humming, "Who's Sorry Now?" Pulling out of the drive, she glances back at the lighted kitchen window. "What do you think of our babysitter?" she asks. While her husband stumbles all over himself trying to answer, she pulls a stocking tight, biting deeper with the garters.

❖ ❖ ❖

"Stop it!" she laughs. Bitsy is pulling on her skirt and he is tickling her in the ribs. "Jimmy! Don't!" But she is laughing too much to stop him. He leaps on her, wrapping his legs around her waist, and they all fall to the carpet in front of the TV, where just now a man in a tuxedo and a little girl in a flouncy white dress are doing a tapdance together. The babysitter's blouse is pulling out of her skirt, showing a patch of bare tummy: the target. "I'll spank!"

❖ ❖ ❖

Jack pushes the plunger, thrusting up a steel ball, and bends studiously over the machine. "You getting any off her?" Mark asks, and clears his throat, flicks ash from his cigarette. "Well, not exactly, not yet," Jack says, grinning awkwardly, but trying to suggest more than he admits to, and fires. He heaves his weight gently against the machine as the ball bounds off a rubber bumper. He can feel her warming up under his hands, the flippers suddenly coming alive, delicate rapid-fire patterns emerging in the flashing of the lights. 1000 WHEN LIT: *now!* "Got my hand on it, that's about all." Mark glances up from the machine, cigarette dangling from his lip. "Maybe you need some help," he suggests with a wry one-sided grin. "Like maybe together, man, we could do it."

❖ ❖ ❖

She likes the big tub. She uses the Tuckers' bath salts, and loves to sink into the hot fragrant suds. She can stretch out, submerged, up to her chin. It gives her a good sleepy tingly feeling.

❖ ❖ ❖

"What do you think of our babysitter?" Dolly asks, adjusting a garter. "Oh, I hardly noticed," he says. "Cute girl. She seems to get along fine with the kids. Why?" "I don't know." His wife tugs her skirt down, glances at a lighted window they are passing, adding: "I'm not sure I trust her completely, that's all. With the baby, I mean. She seems a little careless. And the other time, I'm almost sure she had a boyfriend over." He grins, claps one hand on his wife's broad gartered thigh. "What's wrong with that?" he asks. Still in anklets, too. Bare thighs, no girdles, nothing up there but a flimsy pair of panties and soft adolescent flesh. He's flooded with vague remembrances of football rallies and movie balconies.

❖ ❖ ❖

How tiny and rubbery it is! she thinks, soaping between the boy's legs, giving him his bath. Just a funny jiggly little thing that looks like it shouldn't even be there at all. Is that what all the songs are about?

❖ ❖ ❖

Jack watches Mark lunge and twist against the machine. Got her running now, racking them up. He's not too excited about the idea of Mark fooling around with his girlfriend, but Mark's a cooler operator than he is, and maybe, doing it together this once, he'd get over his own timidity. And if she didn't like it, there were other girls around. If Mark went too far, he could cut him off, too. He feels his shoulders tense: enough's enough, man . . . but sees the flesh, too. "Maybe I'll call her later," he says.

❖ ❖ ❖

"Hey, Harry! Dolly! Glad you could make it!" "I hope we're not late." "No, no, you're one of the first, come on in! By golly, Dolly, you're looking younger every day! How do you do it? Give my wife your secret, will you?" He pats her on her girdled bottom behind Mr. Tucker's back, leads them in for drinks.

❖ ❖ ❖

8:00. The babysitter runs water in the tub, combs her hair in front of the bathroom mirror. There's a western on television, so she lets Jimmy watch it while she gives Bitsy her bath. But Bitsy doesn't want a bath. She's angry and crying because she has to be first. The babysitter tells her if she'll take her bath quickly, she'll let her watch television while Jimmy takes his bath, but it does no good. The little girl fights to get out of the bathroom, and the babysitter has to squat with her back against the door and forcibly undress the child. There are better places to babysit. Both children mind badly, and then, sooner or later, the baby is sure to wake up for a diaper change and more bottle. The Tuckers do have a good color TV, though, and she hopes things will be settled down enough to catch the 8:30 program.

She thrusts the child into the tub, but she's still screaming and thrashing around. "Stop it now, Bitsy, or you'll wake the baby!" "I have to go potty!" the child wails, switching tactics. The babysitter sighs, lifts the girl out of the tub and onto the toilet, getting her skirt and blouse all wet in the process. She glances at herself in the mirror. Before she knows it, the girl is off the seat and out of the bathroom. "Bitsy! Come back here!"

❖ ❖ ❖

"Okay, that's enough!" Her skirt is ripped and she's flushed and crying. "Who says?" "I do, man!" The bastard goes for her, but he tackles him. They roll and tumble. Tables tip, lights topple, the TV crashes to the floor. He slams a hard right to the guy's gut, clips his chin with a rolling left.

❖ ❖ ❖

"We hope it's a girl." That's hardly surprising, since they already have four boys. Dolly congratulates the woman like everybody else, but she doesn't envy her, not a bit. That's all she needs about now. She stares across the room at Harry, who is slapping backs and getting loud, as usual. He's spreading out through the middle, so why the hell does he have to complain about her all the time? "Dolly, you're looking younger every day!" was the nice greeting she got tonight. "What's your secret?" And Harry: "It's all those calories. She's getting back her baby fat." "Haw haw! Harry, have a heart!"

❖ ❖ ❖

"Get her feet!" he hollers at Bitsy, his fingers in her ribs, running over her naked tummy, tangling in the underbrush of straps and strange clothing. "Get her shoes off!" He holds her pinned by pressing his head against her soft chest. "No! No, Jimmy! Bitsy, stop!" But though she kicks and twists and rolls around, she doesn't get up, she can't get up, she's laughing too hard, and the shoes come off, and he grabs a stockinged foot and scratches the sole ruthlessly, and she raises up her legs, trying to pitch him off, she's wild, boy, but he hangs on, and she's laughing, and on the screen there's a rattle of hooves, and he and Bitsy are rolling around and around on the floor in a crazy rodeo of long bucking legs.

❖ ❖ ❖

He slips the coin in. There's a metallic fall and a sharp click as the dial tone begins. "I hope the Tuckers have gone," he says. "Don't worry, they're at our place," Mark says. "They're always the first ones to come and the last ones to go home. My old man's always bitching about them." Jack laughs nervously and dials the number. "Tell her we're coming over to protect her from getting raped," Mark suggests, and lights a cigarette. Jack grins, leaning casually against the door jamb of the phonebooth, chewing gum, one hand in his pocket. He's really pretty uneasy, though. He has the feeling he's somehow messing up a good thing.

❖ ❖ ❖

Bitsy runs naked into the livingroom, keeping a hassock between herself and the babysitter. "Bitsy . . . !" the babysitter threatens. Artificial reds and greens and purples flicker over the child's wet body, as hooves clatter, guns crackle, and stage-coach wheels thunder over rutted terrain. "Get outa the way, Bitsy!" the boy complains. "I can't see!" Bitsy streaks past and the babysitter chases, cornering the girl in the back bedroom. Bitsy throws something that hits her softly in the face: a pair of men's undershorts. She grabs the girl scampering by, carries her struggling to the bathroom, and with a smart crack on her glistening bottom, pops her back into the tub. In spite, Bitsy peepees in the bathwater.

❖ ❖ ❖

Mr. Tucker stirs a little water into his bourbon and kids with his host and another man, just arrived, about their golf games. They set up a match for the weekend, a threesome looking for a fourth. Holding his drink in his right hand, Mr. Tucker swings his left through the motion of a tee-shot. "You'll have to give me a stroke a hole," he says. "I'll give you a stroke!" says his host: "Bend over!" Laughing, the other man asks: "Where's your boy Mark tonight?" "I don't know," replies the host, gathering up a trayful of drinks. Then he adds in a low growl: "Out chasing tail probably." They chuckle loosely at that, then shrug in commiseration and return to the livingroom to join their women.

❖ ❖ ❖

Shades pulled. Door locked. Watching the TV. Under a blanket maybe. Yes, that's right, under a blanket. Her eyes close when he kisses her. Her breasts, under both their hands, are soft and yielding.

❖ ❖ ❖

A hard blow to the belly. The face. The dark beardy one staggers. The lean-jawed sheriff moves in, but gets a spurred boot in his face. The dark one hurls himself forward, drives his shoulder into the sheriff's hard midriff, her own tummy tightens, withstands, as the sheriff smashes the dark man's nose, slams him up against a wall, slugs him again! and again! The dark man grunts rhythmically, backs off, then plunges suicidally forward—her own knees draw up protectively—the sheriff staggers! caught low! but instead of following through, the other man steps back—a pistol! the dark one has a pistol! the sheriff draws! shoots from the hip! explosions! she clutches her hands between her thighs—no! the sheriff spins! wounded! the dark man hesitates, aims, her legs stiffen toward the set, the sheriff rolls desperately in the straw, fires: dead! the dark man is dead! groans, crumples, his pistol drooping in his collapsing hand, dropping, he drops. The sheriff, spent, nicked, watches weakly from the floor where he lies. Oh, to be whole! to be good and strong and right! to embrace and be embraced by harmony and wholeness! The sheriff, drawing himself painfully up on one elbow, rubs his bruised mouth with the back of his other hand.

❖ ❖ ❖

"Well, we just sorta thought we'd drop over," he says, and winks broadly at Mark. "Who's we?" "Oh, me and Mark here." "Tell her, good thing like her, gotta pass it around," whispers Mark, dragging on his smoke, then flicking the butt over under the pinball machine. "What's that?" she asks. "Oh, Mark and I were just saying, like two's company, three's an orgy," Jack says, and winks again. She giggles. "Oh, Jack!" Behind her, he can hear shouts and gunfire. "Well, okay, for just a little while, if you'll both be good." Way to go, man.

❖ ❖ ❖

Probably some damn kid over there right now. Wrestling around on the couch in front of his TV. Maybe he should drop back to the house. Just to check. None of that stuff, she was there to do a job! Park the car a couple doors down, slip in the front door before she knows it. He sees the disarray of clothing, the young thighs exposed to the flickering television light, hears his baby crying. "Hey, what's going on here! Get outa here, son, before I call the police!" Of course, they haven't really been doing anything. They probably don't even know how. He stares benignly down upon the girl, her skirt rumpled loosely around her thighs. Flushed, frightened, yet excited, she stares back at him. He smiles. His finger touches a knee, approaches the hem. Another couple arrives. Filling up here with people. He wouldn't be missed. Just slip out, stop back casually to pick up something or other he forgot, never mind what. He remembers that the other time they had this babysitter, she took a bath in their house. She had a date afterwards, and she'd just come from cheerleading practice or something. Aspirin maybe. Just drop quietly and casually into the bathroom to pick up some aspirin. "Oh, excuse me, dear! I only . . .!" She gazes back at him, astonished, yet strangely moved. Her soft wet breasts rise and fall in the water, and her tummy looks pale and ripply. He recalls that her pubic hairs, left in the tub, were brown. Light brown.

❖ ❖ ❖

She's no more than stepped into the tub for a quick bath, when Jimmy announces from outside the door that he has to go to the bathroom. She sighs: just an excuse, she knows. "You'll have to wait." The little nuisance. "I can't wait." "Okay, then come ahead, but I'm taking a bath." She supposes that will stop him, but it doesn't. In he comes. She slides down into the suds until she's eye-level with the edge of the tub. He hesitates. "Go ahead, if you have to," she says, a little awkwardly, "but I'm not getting out." "Don't look," he says. She: "I will if I want to."

❖ ❖ ❖

She's crying. Mark is rubbing his jaw where he's just slugged him. A lamp lies shattered. "Enough's enough, Mark! Now get outa here!" Her skirt is ripped to the waist, her bare hip bruised. Her panties lie on the floor like a broken balloon. Later, he'll wash her wounds, help her dress, he'll take care of her. Pity washes through him, giving him a sudden hard-on. Mark laughs at it, pointing. Jack crouches, waiting, ready for anything.

❖ ❖ ❖

Laughing, they roll and tumble. Their little hands are all over her, digging and pinching. She struggles to her hands and knees, but Bitsy leaps astride her neck, bowing her head to the carpet. "Spank her, Jimmy!" His swats sting: is her skirt up? The phone rings. "The cavalry to the rescue!" she laughs, and throws them off to go answer.

❖ ❖ ❖

Kissing Mark, her eyes closed, her hips nudge toward Jack. He stares at the TV screen, unsure of himself, one hand slipping cautiously under her skirt. Her hand touches his arm as though to resist, then brushes on by to rub his leg. This blanket they're under was a good idea. "Hi! This is Jack!"

❖ ❖ ❖

Bitsy's out and the water's running. "Come on, Jimmy, your turn!" Last time, he told her he took his own baths, but she came in anyway. "I'm not gonna take a bath," he announces, eyes glued on the set. He readies for the struggle. "But I've already run your water. Come on, Jimmy, please!" He shakes his head. She can't make him, he's sure he's as strong as she is. She sighs. "Well, it's up to you. I'll use the water myself then," she says. He waits until he's pretty sure she's not going to change her mind, then sneaks in and peeks through the keyhole in the bathroom door: just in time to see her big bottom as she bends over to stir in the bubblebath. Then she disappears. Trying to see as far down as the keyhole will allow, he bumps his head on the knob. "Jimmy, is that you?" "I—I have to go to the bathroom!" he stammers.

❖ ❖ ❖

Not actually in the tub, just getting in. One foot on the mat, the other in the water. Bent over slightly, buttocks flexed, teats swaying, holding on to the edge of the tub. "Oh, excuse me! I only wanted . . . !" He passes over her astonishment, the awkward excuses, moves quickly to the part where he reaches out to—"What on earth are you doing, Harry?" his wife asks, staring at his hand. His host, passing, laughs. "He's prac- tising his swing for Sunday, Dolly, but it's not going to do him a damn bit of good!" Mr. Tucker laughs, sweeps his right hand on through the air as though lifting a seven-iron shot onto the green. He makes a *dok*! sound with his tongue. "In there!"

❖ ❖ ❖

"No, Jack, I don't think you'd better." "Well, we just called, we just, uh, thought we'd, you know, stop by for a minute, watch television for thirty minutes, or, or something." "Who's we?" "Well, Mark's here, I'm with him, and he said he'd like to, you know, like if it's all right, just—" "Well, it's *not* all right. The Tuckers said no." "Yeah, but if we only—" "And they seemed awfully suspicious about last time." "Why? We didn't—I mean, I just thought—" "No, Jack, and that's period." She hangs up. She returns to the TV, but the commercial is on. Anyway, she's missed most of the show. She decides maybe she'll take a quick bath. Jack might come by anyway, it'd make her mad, that'd be the end as far as he was concerned, but if he should, she doesn't want to be all sweaty. And besides, she likes the big tub the Tuckers have.

❖ ❖ ❖

He is self-conscious and stands with his back to her, his little neck flushed. It takes him forever to get started, and when it finally does come, it's just a tiny trickle. "See, it was just an excuse," she scolds, but she's giggling inwardly at the boy's embarrassment. "You're just a nuisance, Jimmy." At the door, his hand on the knob, he hesitates, staring timidly down on his shoes. "Jimmy?" She peeks at him over the edge of the tub, trying to keep a straight face, as he sneaks a nervous glance back over his shoulder. "As long as you bothered me," she says, "you might as well soap my back."

❖ ❖ ❖

"The aspirin . . ." They embrace. She huddles in his arms like a child. Lovingly, paternally, knowledgeably, he wraps her nakedness. How compact, how tight and small her body is! Kissing her ear, he stares down past her rump at the still clear water. "I'll join you," he whispers hoarsely.

❖ ❖ ❖

She picks up the shorts Bitsy threw at her. Men's underwear. She holds them in front of her, looks at herself in the bedroom mirror. About twenty sizes too big for her, of course. She runs her hand inside the opening in front, pulls out her thumb. How funny it must feel!

❖ ❖ ❖

"Well, man, I say we just go rape her," Mark says flatly, and swings his weight against the pinball machine. "Uff! Ahh! Get in there, you mother! Look at that! Hah! Man, I'm gonna turn this baby over!" Jack is embarrassed about the phone conversation. Mark just snorted in disgust when he hung up. He cracks down hard on his gum, angry that he's such a chicken. "Well, I'm game if you are," he says coldly.

❖ ❖ ❖

8:30. "Okay, come on, Jimmy, it's time." He ignores her. The western gives way to a spy show. Bitsy, in pyjamas, pads into the livingroom. "No, Bitsy, it's time to go to bed." "You said I could watch!" the girl whines, and starts to throw another tantrum. "But you were too slow and it's late. Jimmy, you get in that bathroom, and right now!" Jimmy stares sullenly at the set, unmoving. The babysitter tries to catch the opening scene of the television program so she can follow it later, since Jimmy gives himself his own baths. When the commercial interrupts, she turns off the sound, stands in front of the screen. "Okay, into the tub, Jimmy Tucker, or I'll take you in there and give you your bath myself!" "Just try it," he says, "and see what happens."

❖ ❖ ❖

They stand outside, in the dark, crouched in the bushes, peeking in. She's on the floor, playing with the kids. Too early. They seem to be tickling her. She gets to her hands and knees, but the little girl leaps on her head, pressing her face to the floor. There's an obvious target, and the little boy proceeds to beat on it. "Hey, look at that kid go!" whispers Mark, laughing and snapping his fingers softly. Jack feels uneasy out here. Too many neighbors, too many cars going by, too many people in the world. That little boy in there is one up on him, though: he's never thought about tickling her as a starter.

❖ ❖ ❖

His little hand, clutching the bar of soap, lathers shyly a narrow space between her shoulderblades. She is doubled forward against her knees, buried in rich suds, peeking at him over the edge of her shoulder. The soap slithers out of his grip and plunks into the water. "I . . . I dropped the soap," he whispers. She: "Find it."

❖ ❖ ❖

"I dream of Jeannie with the light brown pubic hair!" "Harry! Stop that! You're drunk!" But they're laughing, they're all laughing, damn! he's feeling pretty goddamn good at that, and now he just knows he needs that aspirin. Watching her there, her thighs spread for him, on the couch, in the tub, hell, on the kitchen table for that matter, he tees off on Number Nine, and—*whap!*—swats his host's wife on the bottom. "Hole in one!" he shouts. "Harry!" Why can't his goddamn wife Dolly ever get happy-drunk instead of sour-drunk all the time? "Gonna be tough Sunday, old buddy!" "You're pretty tough right now, Harry," says his host.

❖ ❖ ❖

The babysitter lunges forward, grabs the boy by the arms and hauls him off the couch, pulling two cushions with him, and drags him toward the bathroom. He lashes out, knocking over an end table full of magazines and ashtrays. "You leave my brother alone!" Bitsy cries and grabs the sitter around the waist. Jimmy jumps on her and down they all go. On the silent screen, there's a fade-in to a dark passageway in an old apartment building in some foreign country. She kicks out and somebody falls between her legs. Somebody else is sitting on her face. "Jimmy! Stop that!" the babysitter laughs, her voice muffled.

❖ ❖ ❖

She's watching television. All alone. It seems like a good time to go in. Just remember: really, no matter what she says, she wants it. They're standing in the bushes, trying to get up the nerve. "We'll tell her to be good," Mark whispers, "and if she's not good, we'll spank her." Jack giggles softly, but his knees are weak. She stands. They freeze. She looks right at them. "She can't see us," Mark whispers tensely. "Is she coming out?" "No," says Mark, "she's going into—that must be the bathroom!" Jack takes a deep breath, his heart pounding. "Hey, is there a window back there?" Mark asks.

❖ ❖ ❖

The phone rings. She leaves the tub, wrapped in a towel. Bitsy gives a tug on the towel. "Hey, Jimmy, get the towel!" she squeals. "Now stop that, Bitsy!" the babysitter hisses, but too late: with one hand on the phone, the other isn't enough to hang on to the towel. Her sudden nakedness awes them and it takes them a moment to remember about tickling her. By then, she's in the towel again. "I hope you got a good look," she says angrily. She feels chilled and oddly a little frightened. "Hello?" No answer. She glances at the window—is somebody out there? Something, she saw something, and a rustling—footsteps?

❖ ❖ ❖

"Okay, I don't care, Jimmy, don't take a bath," she says irritably. Her blouse is pulled out and wrinkled, her hair is all mussed, and she feels sweaty. There's about a million things she'd rather be doing than babysitting with these two. Three: at least the baby's sleeping. She knocks on the overturned end table for luck, rights it, replaces the magazines and ashtrays. The one thing that really makes her sick is a dirty diaper. "Just go on to bed." "I don't have to go to bed until nine," he reminds her. Really, she couldn't care less. She turns up the volume on the TV, settles down on the couch, poking her blouse back into her skirt, pushing her hair out of her eyes. Jimmy and Bitsy watch from the floor. Maybe, once they're in bed, she'll take a quick bath. She wishes Jack would come by. The man, no doubt the spy, is following a woman, but she doesn't know why. The woman passes another man. Something seems to happen, but it's not clear what. She's probably already missed too much. The phone rings.

❖ ❖ ❖

Mark is kissing her. Jack is under the blanket, easing her panties down over her squirming hips. Her hand is in his pants, pulling it out, pulling it toward her, pulling it hard. She knew just where it was! Mark is stripping, too. God, it's really happening! he thinks with a kind of pious joy, and notices the open door. "Hey! What's going on here?"

❖ ❖ ❖

He soaps her back, smooth and slippery under his hand. She is doubled over, against her knees, between his legs. Her light brown hair, reaching to her gleaming shoulders, is wet at the edges. The soap slips, falls between his legs. He fishes for it, finds it, slips it behind him. "Help me find it," he whispers in her ear. "Sure Harry," says his host, going around behind him. "What'd you lose?"

❖ ❖ ❖

Soon be nine, time to pack the kids off to bed. She clears the table, dumps paper plates and leftover hamburgers into the garbage, puts glasses and silverware into the sink, and the mayonnaise, mustard, and ketchup in the refrigerator. Neither child has eaten much supper finally, mostly potato chips and ice cream, but it's really not her problem. She glances at the books on the refrigerator. Not much chance she'll get to them, she's already pretty worn out. Maybe she'd feel better if she had a quick bath. She runs water into the tub, tosses in bubblebath salts, undresses. Before pushing down her panties, she stares for a moment at the smooth silken panel across her tummy, fingers the place where the opening would be if there were one. Then she steps quickly out of them, feeling somehow ashamed, unhooks her brassiere. She weighs her breasts in the palms of her hands, watching herself in the bathroom mirror, where, in the open window behind her, she sees a face. She screams.

❖ ❖ ❖

She screams: "Jimmy! Give me that!" "What's the matter?" asks Jack on the other end. "Jimmy! Give me my towel! Right now!" "Hello? Hey, are you still there?" "I'm sorry, Jack," she says, panting. "You caught me in the tub. I'm just wrapped in a towel and these silly kids grabbed it away!" "Gee, I wish I'd been there!" "Jack—!" "To protect you, I mean." "Oh, sure," she says, giggling. "Well, what do you think, can I come over and watch TV with you?" "Well, not right this minute," she says. He laughs lightly. He feels very cool. "Jack?" "Yeah?" "Jack, I . . . I think there's somebody outside the window!"

❖ ❖ ❖

She carries him, fighting all the way, to the tub, Bitsy pummeling her in the back and kicking her ankles. She can't hang on to him and undress him at the same time. "I'll throw you in, clothes and all, Jimmy Tucker!" she gasps. "You better not!" he cries. She sits on the toilet seat, locks her legs around him, whips his shirt up over his head before he knows what's happening. The pants are easier. Like all little boys his age, he has almost no hips at all. He hangs on desperately to his underpants, but when she succeeds in snapping these down out of his grip, too, he gives up, starts to bawl, and beats her wildly in the face with his fists. She ducks her head, laughing hysterically, oddly entranced by the spectacle of that pale little thing down there, bobbing and bouncing rubberily about with the boy's helpless fury and anguish.

❖ ❖ ❖

"Aspirin? Whaddaya want aspirin for, Harry? I'm sure they got aspirin here, if you—" "Did I say aspirin? I meant, uh, my glasses. And, you know, I thought, well, I'd sorta check to see if everything was okay at home." Why the hell is it his mouth feels like it's got about six sets of teeth packed in there, and a tongue the size of that liverwurst his host's wife is passing around? "Whaddaya want your glasses for, Harry? I don't understand you at all!" "Aw, well, honey, I was feeling kind of dizzy or something, and I thought—" "Dizzy is right. If you want to check on the kids, why don't you just call on the phone?"

❖ ❖ ❖

They can tell she's naked and about to get into the tub, but the bathroom window is frosted glass, and they can't see anything clearly. "I got an idea," Mark whispers. "One of us goes and calls her on the phone, and the other watches when she comes out." "Okay, but who calls?" "Both of us, we'll do it twice. Or more."

❖ ❖ ❖

Down forbidden alleys. Into secret passageways. Unlocking the world's terrible secrets. Sudden shocks: a trapdoor! a fall! or the stunning report of a rifle shot, the *whaaii-ii-ing!* of the bullet biting concrete by your ear! Careful! Then edge forward once more, avoiding the light, inch at a time, now a quick dash for an open doorway—look out! there's a knife! a struggle! no! the long blade glistens! jerks!

thrusts! *stabbed!* No, no, it missed! The assailant's down, yes! the spy's on top, pinning him, a terrific thrashing about, the spy rips off the assailant's mask: *a woman!*

❖ ❖ ❖

Fumbling behind her, she finds it, wraps her hand around it, tugs. "Oh!" she gasps, pulling her hand back quickly, her ears turning crimson. "I . . . I thought it was the soap!" He squeezes her close between his thighs, pulls her back toward him, one hand sliding down her tummy between her legs. I Dream of Jeannie—"I have to go to the bathroom!" says someone outside the door.

❖ ❖ ❖

She's combing her hair in the bathroom when the phone rings. She hurries to answer it before it wakes the baby. "Hello, Tuckers." There's no answer. "Hello?" A soft click. Strange. She feels suddenly alone in the big house, and goes in to watch TV with the children.

❖ ❖ ❖

"Stop it!" she screams. "Please, stop!" She's on her hands and knees, trying to get up, but they're too strong for her. Mark holds her head down. "Now, baby, we're gonna teach you how to be a nice girl," he says coldly, and nods at Jack. When she's doubled over like that, her skirt rides up her thighs to the leg bands of her panties. "C'mon, man, go! This baby's cold! She needs your touch!"

❖ ❖ ❖

Parks the car a couple blocks away. Slips up to the house, glances in his window. Just like he's expected. Her blouse is out and the kid's shirt is unbuttoned. He watches, while slowly, clumsily, childishly, they fumble with each other's clothes. My God, it takes them forever. "Some party!" "You said it!" When they're more or less naked, he walks in. "Hey! What's going on here?" They go white as bleu cheese. Haw haw! "What's the little thing you got sticking out there, boy?" "Harry, behave yourself!" No, he doesn't let the kid get dressed, he sends him home bareassed. "Bareassed!" He drinks to that. "Promises, promises," says his host's wife. "I'll mail you your clothes, son!" He gazes down on the naked little girl on his couch. "Looks like you and me, we got a little secret to keep, honey," he says coolly. "Less you wanna go home the same way your boyfriend did!" He chuckles at his easy wit, leans down over her, and unbuckles his belt. "Might as well make it two secrets, right?" "What in God's name are you talking about, Harry?" He staggers out of there, drink in hand, and goes to look for his car.

❖ ❖ ❖

"Hey! What's going on here?" They huddle half-naked under the blanket, caught utterly unawares. On television: the clickety-click of frightened running feet on foreign pavements. Jack is fumbling for his shorts, tangled somehow around his ankles. The blanket is snatched away. "On your feet there!" Mr. Tucker, Mrs.

Tucker, Mark's mom and dad, the police, the neighbors, everybody comes crowding in. Hopelessly, he has a terrific erection. So hard it hurts. Everybody stares down at it.

❖ ❖ ❖

Bitsy's sleeping on the floor. The babysitter is taking a bath. For more than an hour now, he's had to use the bathroom. He doesn't know how much longer he can wait. Finally, he goes to knock on the bathroom door. "I have to use the bathroom." "Well, come ahead, if you have to." "Not while you're in there." She sighs loudly. "Okay, okay, just a minute," she says, "but you're a real nuisance, Jimmy!" He's holding on, pinching it as tight as he can. "*Hurry!*" He holds his breath, squeezing shut his eyes. No. Too late. At last, she opens the door. "Jimmy!" "I *told* you to hurry!" he sobs. She drags him into the bathroom and pulls his pants down.

❖ ❖ ❖

He arrives just in time to see her emerge from the bathroom, wrapped in a towel, to answer the phone. His two kids sneak up behind her and pull the towel away. She's trying to hang onto the phone and get the towel back at the same time. It's quite a picture. She's got a sweet ass. Standing there in the bushes, pawing himself with one hand, he lifts his glass with the other and toasts her sweet ass, which his son now swats. Haw haw, maybe that boy's gonna shape up, after all.

❖ ❖ ❖

They're in the bushes, arguing about their next move, when she comes out of the bathroom, wrapped in a towel. They can hear the baby crying. Then it stops. They see her running, naked, back to the bathroom like she's scared or something. "I'm going in after her, man, whether you're with me or not!" Mark whispers, and he starts out of the bushes. But just then, a light comes sweeping up through the yard, as a car swings in the drive. They hit the dirt, hearts pounding. "Is it the cops?" "I don't know!" "Do you think they saw us?" "Sshh!" A man comes staggering up the walk from the drive, a drink in his hand, stumbles on in the kitchen door and then straight into the bathroom. "It's Mr. Tucker!" Mark whispers. A scream. "Let's get outa here, man!"

❖ ❖ ❖

9:00. Having missed most of the spy show anyway and having little else to do, the babysitter has washed the dishes and cleaned the kitchen up a little. The books on the refrigerator remind her of her better intentions, but she decides that first she'll see what's next on TV. In the livingroom, she finds little Bitsy sound asleep on the floor. She lifts her gently, carries her into her bed, and tucks her in. "Okay, Jimmy, it's nine o'clock, I've let you stay up, now be a good boy." Sullenly, his sleepy eyes glued still to the set, the boy backs out of the room toward his bedroom. A drama comes on. She switches channels. A ballgame and a murder mystery. She switches back to the drama. It's a love story of some kind. A man married to an aging invalid wife, but in love with a younger girl. "Use the bathroom and brush your teeth before going to bed, Jimmy!" she calls, but as quickly regrets it, for she hears the baby stir in its crib.

❖ ❖ ❖

She pulls them on, over her own, standing in front of the bedroom mirror, holding her skirt bundled up around the waist. About twenty sizes too big for her, of course. She pulls them tight from behind, runs her hand inside the opening in front, pulls out her thumb. "And what a good boy am I!" She giggles: how funny it must feel! Then, in the mirror, she sees him: in the doorway behind her, sullenly watching. "Jimmy! You're supposed to be in bed!" "Those are my daddy's!" the boy says. "I'm gonna tell!"

❖ ❖ ❖

"Jimmy!" She drags him into the bathroom and pulls his pants down. "Even your shoes are wet! Get them off!" She soaps up a warm washcloth she's had with her in the bathtub, scrubs him from the waist down with it. Bitsy stands in the doorway, staring. "Get out! Get out!" the boy screams at his sister. "Go back to bed, Bitsy. It's just an accident." "Get out!" The baby wakes and starts to howl.

❖ ❖ ❖

The young lover feels sorry for her rival, the invalid wife; she believes the man has a duty toward the poor woman and insists she is willing to wait. But the man argues that he also has a duty toward himself: his life, too, is short, and he could not love his wife now even were she well. He embraces the young girl feverishly; she twists away in anguish. The door opens. They stand there grinning, looking devilish, but pretty silly at the same time. "Jack! I thought told you not to come!" She's angry, but she's also glad in a way: she was beginning to feel a little too alone in the big house, with the children all sleeping. She should have taken that bath, after all. "We just came by to see if you were being a good girl," Jack says and blushes. The boys glance at each other nervously.

❖ ❖ ❖

She's just sunk down into the tubful of warm fragrant suds, ready for a nice long soaking, when the phone rings. Wrapping a towel around her, she goes to answer: no one there. But now the baby's awake and bawling. She wonders if that's Jack bothering her all the time. If it is, brother, that's the end. Maybe it's the end anyway. She tries to calm the baby with the half-empty bottle, not wanting to change it until she's finished her bath. The bathroom's where the dirty diapers go, and they make it stink to high heaven. "Shush, shush!" she whispers, rocking the crib. The towel slips away, leaving an airy empty tingle up and down her backside. Even before she stoops for the towel, even before she turns around, she knows there's somebody behind her.

❖ ❖ ❖

"We just came by to see if you were being a good girl," Jack says, grinning down at her. She's flushed and silent, her mouth half open. "Lean over," says Mark amiably. "We'll soap your back, as long as we're here." But she just huddles there, down in the suds, staring up at them with big eyes.

❖ ❖ ❖

"Hey! What's going on here?" It's Mr. Tucker, stumbling through the door with a drink in his hand. She looks up from the TV. "What's the matter, Mr. Tucker?" "Oh, uh, I'm sorry, I got lost—no, I mean, I had to get some aspirin. Excuse me!" And he rushes past her into the bathroom, caroming off the livingroom door jamb on the way. The baby wakes.

❖ ❖ ❖

"Okay, get off her, Mr. Tucker!" "Jack!" she cries, "what are *you* doing here?" He stares hard at them a moment: so that's where it goes. Then, as Mr. Tucker swings heavily off, he leans into the bastard with a hard right to the belly. Next thing he knows, though, he's got a face full of an old man's fist. He's not sure, as the lights go out, if that's his girlfriend screaming or the baby . . .

❖ ❖ ❖

Her host pushes down on her fat fanny and tugs with all his might on her girdle, while she bawls on his shoulder: "I don't *wanna* go to a rest home!" "Now, now, take it easy, Dolly, nobody's gonna make you—" "Ouch! Hey, you're hurting!" "You should buy a bigger girdle, Dolly." "You're telling me?" Some other guy pokes his head in. "Whatsamatter? Dolly fall in?" "No, she fell out. Give me a hand."

❖ ❖ ❖

By the time she's chased Jack and Mark out of there, she's lost track of the program she's been watching on television. There's another woman in the story now for some reason. That guy lives a very complicated life. Impatiently, she switches channels. She hates ballgames, so she settles for the murder mystery. She switches just in time, too: there's a dead man sprawled out on the floor of what looks like an office or a study or something. A heavy-set detective gazes up from his crouch over the body: "He's been strangled." Maybe she'll take that bath, after all.

❖ ❖ ❖

She drags him into the bathroom and pulls his pants down. She soaps up a warm washcloth she's had in the tub with her, but just as she reaches between his legs, it starts to spurt, spraying her arms and hands. "Oh, Jimmy! I thought you were done!" she cries, pulling him toward the toilet and aiming it into the bowl. How moist and rubbery it is! And you can turn it every which way. How funny it must feel!

❖ ❖ ❖

"Stop it!" she screams. "Please stop!" She's on her hands and knees and Jack is holding her head down. "Now we're gonna teach you how to be a nice girl," Mark says and lifts her skirt. "Well, I'll be damned!" "What's the matter?" asks Jack, his heart pounding. "Look at this big pair of men's underpants she's got on!" "Those are my daddy's!" says Jimmy, watching them from the doorway. "I'm gonna tell!"

❖ ❖ ❖

People are shooting at each other in the murder mystery, but she's so mixed up, she doesn't know which ones are the good guys. She switches back to the love story. Something seems to have happened, because now the man is kissing his invalid wife tenderly. Maybe she's finally dying. The baby wakes, begins to scream. Let it. She turns up the volume on the TV.

❖ ❖ ❖

Leaning down over her, unbuckling his belt. It's all happening just like he's known it would. Beautiful! The kid is gone, though his pants, poor lad, remain. "Looks like you and me, we got a secret to keep, child!" But he's cramped on the couch and everything is too slippery and small. "Lift your legs up, honey. Put them around my back." But instead, she screams. He rolls off, crashing to the floor. There they all come, through the front door. On television, somebody is saying: "Am I a burden to you, darling?" "Dolly! My God! Dolly, I can explain . . . !"

❖ ❖ ❖

The game of the night is Get Dolly Tucker Back in Her Girdle Again. They've got her down on her belly in the livingroom and the whole damn crowd is working on her. Several of them are stretching the girdle, while others try to jam the fat inside. "I think we made a couple inches on this side! Roll her over!" Harry?

❖ ❖ ❖

She's just stepped into the tub, when the phone rings, waking the baby. She sinks down in the suds, trying not to hear. But that baby doesn't cry, it screams. Angrily, she wraps a towel around herself, stamps peevishly into the baby's room, just letting the phone jangle. She tosses the baby down on its back, unpins its diapers hastily, and gets yellowish baby stool all over her hands. Her towel drops away. She turns to find Jimmy staring at her like a little idiot. She slaps him in the face with her dirty hand, while the baby screams, the phone rings, and nagging voices argue on the TV. There are better things she might be doing.

❖ ❖ ❖

What's happening? Now there's a young guy in it. Is he after the young girl or the old invalid? To tell the truth, it looks like he's after the same man the women are. In disgust, she switches channels. "The strangler again," growls the fat detective, hands on hips, staring down at the body of a half-naked girl. She's considering either switching back to the love story or taking a quick bath, when a hand suddenly clutches her mouth.

❖ ❖ ❖

"You're both chicken," she says, staring up at them. "But what if Mr. Tucker comes home?" Mark asks nervously.

❖ ❖ ❖

How did he get here? He's standing pissing in his own goddamn bathroom, his wife is still back at the party, the three of them are, like good kids, sitting in there in the livingroom watching TV. One of them is his host's boy Mark. "It's a good murder mystery, Mr. Tucker," Mark said, when he came staggering in on them a minute ago. "Sit still!" he shouted, "I'm just home for a moment!" Then whump thump on into the bathroom. Long hike for a weewee, Mister. But something keeps bothering him. Then it hits him: the girl's panties, hanging like a broken balloon from the rabbit-ear antennae on the TV! He barges back in there, giving his shoulder a helluva crack on the livingroom door jamb on the way—but they're not hanging there any more. Maybe he's only imagined it. "Hey, Mr. Tucker," Mark says flatly. "Your fly's open."

❖ ❖ ❖

The baby's dirty. Stinks to high heaven. She hurries back to the livingroom, hearing sirens and gunshots. The detective is crouched outside a house, peering in. Already, she's completely lost. The baby screams at the top of its lungs. She turns up the volume. But it's all confused. She hurries back in there, claps an angry hand to the baby's mouth. "Shut up!" she cries. She throws the baby down on its back, starts to unpin the diaper, as the baby tunes up again. The phone rings. She answers it, one eye on the TV. "*What?*" The baby cries so hard it starts to choke. Let it. "I said, hi, this is Jack!" Then it hits her: oh no! the diaper pin!

❖ ❖ ❖

"The aspirin . . ." But she's already in the tub. Way down in the tub. Staring at him through the water. Her tummy looks pale and ripply. He hears sirens, people on the porch.

❖ ❖ ❖

Jimmy gets up to go to the bathroom and gets his face slapped and smeared with baby poop. Then she hauls him off to the bathroom, yanks off his pyjamas, and throws him into the tub. That's okay, but next she gets naked and acts like she's gonna get in the tub, too. The baby's screaming and the phone's ringing like crazy and in walks his dad. Saved! he thinks, but, no, his dad grabs him right back out of the tub and whales the dickens out of him, no questions asked, while she watches, then sends him—*whack!*—back to bed. So he's lying there, wet and dirty and naked and sore, and he still has to go to the bathroom, and outside his window he hears two older guys talking. "Listen, you know where to do it if we get her pinned?" "No! Don't you?"

❖ ❖ ❖

"Yo ho heave ho! *Ugh!*" Dolly's on her back and they're working on the belly side. Somebody got the great idea of buttering her down first. Not to lose the ground they've gained, they've shot it inside with a basting syringe. But now suddenly there's this big tug-of-war under way between those who want to stuff her in and those who want to let her out. Something rips, but she feels better. The odor of hot butter makes her think of movie theaters and popcorn. "Hey, has anybody seen Harry?" she asks. "Where's Harry?"

❖ ❖ ❖

Somebody's getting chased. She switches back to the love story, and now the man's back kissing the young lover again. What's going on? She gives it up, decides to take a quick bath. She's just stepping into the tub, one foot in, one foot out, when Mr. Tucker walks in. "Oh, excuse me! I only wanted some aspirin . . ." She grabs for a towel, but he yanks it away. "Now, that's not how it's supposed to happen, child," he scolds. "Please! Mr. Tucker . . . !" He embraces her savagely, his calloused old hands clutching roughly at her backside. "Mr. Tucker!" she cries, squirming. "Your wife called—!" He's pushing something between her legs, hurting her. She slips, they both slip—something cold and hard slams her in the back, cracks her skull, she seems to be sinking into a sea . . .

❖ ❖ ❖

They've got her over the hassock, skirt up and pants down. "Give her a little lesson there, Jack baby!" The television lights flicker and flash over her glossy flesh. 1000 WHEN LIT. Whack! Slap! Bumper to bumper! He leans into her, feeling her come alive.

❖ ❖ ❖

The phone rings, waking the baby. "Jack, is that you? Now, you listen to me—!" "No, dear, this is Mrs. Tucker. Isn't the TV awfully loud?" "Oh, I'm sorry, Mrs. Tucker! I've been getting—" "I tried to call you before, but I couldn't hang on. To the phone, I mean. I'm sorry, dear." "Just a minute, Mrs. Tucker, the baby's—" "Honey, listen! Is Harry there? Is Mr. Tucker there, dear?"

❖ ❖ ❖

"Stop it!" she screams and claps a hand over the baby's mouth. "Stop it! Stop it! *Stop it!*" Her other hand is full of baby stool and she's afraid she's going to be sick. The phone rings. "No!" she cries. She's hanging on to the baby, leaning woozily away, listening to the phone ring. "Okay, okay," she sighs, getting ahold of herself. But when she lets go of the baby, it isn't screaming any more. She shakes it. Oh no . . .

❖ ❖ ❖

"Hello?" No answer. Strange. She hangs up and, wrapped only in a towel, stares out the window at the cold face staring in—she screams!

❖ ❖ ❖

She screams, scaring the hell out of him. He leaps out of the tub, glances up at the window she's gaping at just in time to see two faces duck away, then slips on the bathroom tiles, and crashes to his ass, whacking his head on the sink on the way down. She stares down at him, trembling, a towel over her narrow shoulders. "Mr. Tucker! Mr. Tucker, are you all right . . . ?" Who's Sorry Now? Yessir, whose back is breaking with each . . . He stares up at the little tufted locus of all his woes, and passes out, dreaming of Jeannie . . .

❖ ❖ ❖

The phone rings. "Dolly! It's for you!" "Hello?" "Hello, Mrs. Tucker?" "Yes, speaking." "Mrs. Tucker, this is the police calling . . ."

❖ ❖ ❖

It's cramped and awkward and slippery, but he's pretty sure he got it in her, once anyway. When he gets the suds out of his eyes, he sees her staring up at them. Through the water. "Hey, Mark! Let her up!"

❖ ❖ ❖

Down in the suds. Feeling sleepy. The phone rings, startling her. Wrapped in a towel, she goes to answer. "No, he's not here, Mrs. Tucker." Strange. Married people act pretty funny sometimes. The baby is awake and screaming. Dirty, a real mess. Oh boy, there's a lot of things she'd rather be doing than babysitting in this madhouse. She decides to wash the baby off in her own bathwater. She removes her towel, unplugs the tub, lowers the water level so the baby can sit. Glancing back over her shoulder, she sees Jimmy staring at her. "Go back to bed, Jimmy." "I have to go to the bathroom." "Good grief, Jimmy! It looks like you already have!" The phone rings. She doesn't bother with the towel—what can Jimmy see he hasn't already seen?—and goes to answer. "No, Jack, and that's final." Sirens, on the TV, as the police move in. But wasn't that the channel with the love story? Ambulance maybe. Get this over with so she can at least catch the news. "Get those wet pyjamas off, Jimmy, and I'll find clean ones. Maybe you better get in the tub, too." "I think something's wrong with the baby," he says. "It's down in the water and it's not swimming or anything."

❖ ❖ ❖

She's staring up at them from the rug. They slap her. Nothing happens. "You just tilted her, man!" Mark says softly. "We gotta get outa here!" Two little kids are standing wide-eyed in the doorway. Mark looks hard at Jack. "No, Mark, they're just little kids . . . !" "We gotta, man, or we're dead."

❖ ❖ ❖

"Dolly! My God! Dolly, I can explain!" She glowers down at them, her ripped girdle around her ankles. "What the four of you are doing in the bathtub with *my* babysitter?" she says sourly. "I can hardly wait!"

❖ ❖ ❖

Police sirens wail, lights flash. "I heard the scream!" somebody shouts. "There were two boys!" "I saw a man!" "She was running with the baby!" "My God!" somebody screams, "they're *all* dead!" Crowds come running. Spotlights probe the bushes.

❖ ❖ ❖

"Harry, where the hell you been?" his wife whines, glaring blearily up at him from the carpet. "I can explain," he says. "Hey, whatsamatter, Harry?" his host asks, smeared with butter for some goddamn reason. "You look like you just seen a ghost!" Where did he leave his drink? Everybody's laughing, everybody except Dolly, whose cheeks are streaked with tears. "Hey, Harry, you won't let them take me to a rest home, will you, Harry?"

❖ ❖ ❖

10:00 The dishes done, children to bed, her books read, she watches the news on television. Sleepy. The man's voice is gentle, soothing. She dozes—awakes with a start: a babysitter? Did the announcer say something about a babysitter?

❖ ❖ ❖

"Just want to catch the weather," the host says, switching on the TV. Most of the guests are leaving, but the Tuckers stay to watch the news. As it comes on, the announcer is saying something about a babysitter. The host switches channels. "They got a better weatherman on four," he explains. "Wait!" says Mrs. Tucker. "There was something about a babysitter . . . !" The host switches back. "Details have not yet been released by the police," the announcer says. "Harry, maybe we'd better go . . ."

❖ ❖ ❖

They stroll casually out of the drugstore, run into a buddy of theirs. "Hey! Did you hear about the babysitter?" the guy asks. Mark grunts, glances at Jack. "Got a smoke?" he asks the guy.

❖ ❖ ❖

"I think I hear the baby screaming!" Mrs. Tucker cries, running across the lawn from the drive.

❖ ❖ ❖

She wakes, startled, to find Mr. Tucker hovering over her. "I must have dozed off!" she exclaims. "Did you hear the news about the babysitter?" Mrs. Tucker asks.

"Part of it," she says, rising. "Too bad wasn't it?" Mr. Tucker is watching the report of the ball scores and golf tournaments. "I'll drive you home in just a minute, dear," he says. "Why, how nice!" Mrs. Tucker exclaims from the kitchen. "The dishes are all done!"

❖ ❖ ❖

"What can I say, Dolly?" the host says with a sigh, twisting the buttered strands of her ripped girdle between his fingers. "Your children are murdered, your husband gone, a corpse in your bathtub, and your house is wrecked. I'm sorry. But what can I say?" On the TV, the news is over, and they're selling aspirin. "Hell, *I* don't know," she says. "Let's see what's on the late late movie."

Julio Cortázar

Julio Cortázar was born in Brussels in 1914, where his father was an Argentinian diplomat. Though he was educated in Buenos Aires and supported himself through teaching and translating, he eventually returned to France in 1952, where he held dual citizenship and remained until his death in 1984. Cortázar, a genuine man of letters who produced poems, short stories, novels, and essays, was also an amateur jazz musician and a member of the editorial board of the Cuban literary journal *Casa de las Americas*. Towards the end of his life, he became more and more committed to socialism as the only means of rescuing Latin America from extremes of poverty and social injustice and concerned with the role of the intellectual in post-revolutionary society. He was a frequent visitor to Cuba and championed the cause of the Sandinistas in Nicaragua.

In a letter (translated by Jo Anne Englebert) to Robert Fernández Retamar, editor of *Casa de las Americas*, Cortázar tries to articulate his position vis-à-vis the writer and social justice: "I am completely ignorant of political philosophy; I have not come to feel myself a writer of the left as a result of an intellectual process but as a result of the same mechanism that makes me write the way I write or live the way I live—a state in which intuition, some magical sharing of the rhythm of men and things, charts my course without giving or asking explanations." Although he rejects the claims of regionalism and nationalism, and has no truck with the idea of a sentimental return to roots, Cortázar tries to make clear in his letter that his problem is a metaphysical one: "a continual struggle between the monstrous error of being what we are as individuals and as people of this century, and the possibility of an idea: a future in which society will finally culminate in that archetype of which socialism provides a practical vision and poetry provides a spiritual one. . . . If, once upon a time, a man could be a great writer without feeling like a participant in the immediate history of mankind, this is no longer true. No one can write today without this participation: it is a responsibility and an obligation. Works that assume this obligation, even though they are imaginative works displaying the entire gamut of games writers can invent, are the only ones that can approach greatness. Even though they never allude directly to that participation, in some ineffable way they will contain that tremor, that presence, that atmosphere that makes them recognizable and enduring and awakens in the reader a sense of contact and closeness." He makes an eloquent response to a UPI cable in which Robert McNamara, once U.S. Secretary of Defense, speaks matter-of-factly about the possibility of exploding fifty nuclear bombs on Chinese cities, destroying half that country's industrial capability and fifty million people.

"I quote this paragraph because I think that after reading it, no writer worthy of the name would be able to return to his books as if nothing had happened. I cannot keep writing with the comfortable feeling that a writer's mission is accomplished in the mere exercise of a vocation as novelist, poet or dramatist. When I read such a paragraph, I know which of the two elements of my nature has won the battle. Incapable of political action, I do not renounce my solitary cultural vocation, my obstinate ontological search, the games of the imagination in their most dizzying planes. But all this does not merely revolve about itself; it no longer even resembles the comfortable humanism of the Mandarins of the West. In the most gratuitous thing I might write there will always appear a will to make contact with the historical present of man, to share in his long march toward excellence as a collectivity and as humanity. I am convinced that only the work of those intellectuals who respond to that impulse and that rebellion will become part of the consciousness of peoples and so justify this profession of writing for which we were born."

Cortázar's work has been at the forefront of technical experiment in fiction. He rejected what he called the naive forms of realism for a fiction that subverted conventional narrative devices and juxtaposed the fantastic and the quotidien. The resulting forms, which have been described as *magical realism*, or the *marvellous real*, are intended to activate our subconscious reservoirs of feeling and image. This is most evident in a story like "Blow-Up," which was made into a feature film starring Vanessa Redgrave and David Hemmings, where a seemingly innocent scene observed in a park setting begins, under the close scrutiny of photographic blow-ups, to reveal its sinister implications. His experiments do not stop with narrative devices, but go on, as this quotation from "Bestiary" suggests, to challenge the very foundations of the sentence: "She felt afraid, delighted, smell of the willow trees and the *u* in Funes was getting mixed in with the rice pudding, so late to be still up, and get up to bed, right now."

Cortázar's publications include the story collections, *End of the Game and Other Stories* (1967), *Blow-Up and Other Stories* (1968), *All Fires the Fire*

(1973), *A Change of Light* (1980), and *We Love Glenda So Much* (1983), the novels *Hopscotch* (1966), which has been compared with Joyce's *Ulysses*, and *A Model Kit* (1972), and various collections of poetry and essays.

Bestiary

Translated by Paul Blackburn

Between the last spoonful of rice pudding with milk (very little cinnamon, a shame) and the goodnight kisses before going up to bed, there was a tinkling in the telephone room and Isabel hung around until Inés came from answering it and said something into their mother's ear. They looked at one another, then both of them looked at Isabel who was thinking about the broken birdcage and the long division problems and briefly of old lady Lucera being angry because she'd pushed her doorbell on the way back from school. She wasn't all that worried, Inés and her mother were looking as if they were gazing past her somewhere, almost taking her as an excuse; but they were looking at her.

"I don't like the idea of her going, believe you me," Inés said. "Not so much because of the tiger, after all they're very careful in that respect. But it's such a depressing house and only that boy to play with her . . . "

"I don't like the idea either," her mother said, and Isabel knew, as if she were on a toboggan, that they were going to send her to the Funes' for the summer. She flung herself into the news, into the great green wave, the Funes', the Funes', sure they were going to send her. They didn't like it, but it was convenient. Delicate lungs, Mar del Plata so very expensive, difficult to manage such a spoiled child, stupid, the way she always acted up with that wonderful Miss Tania, a restless sleeper, toys underfoot everyplace, questions, buttons to be sewn back on, filthy knees. She felt afraid, delighted, smell of the willow trees and the *u* in Funes was getting mixed in with the rice pudding, so late to be still up, and get up to bed, right now.

Lying there, the light out, covered with kisses and rueful glances from Inés and their mother, not fully decided but already decided in spite of everything to send her. She was enjoying beforehand the drive up in the phaeton, the first breakfast, the happiness of Nino, hunter of cockroaches, Nino the toad, Nino the fish (a memory of three years before, Nino showing her some small cutouts he'd glued in an album and telling her gravely, "This-is-a-toad, and THIS is-a-fish"). Now Nino in the park waiting for her with the butterfly net, and also Rema's soft hands—she saw them coming out of the darkness, she had her eyes open and instead of Nino's face—zap!—Rema's hands, the Funes' younger daughter. "Aunt Rema loves me a lot," and Nino's eyes got large and wet, she saw Nino again disjointedly floating in the dim light of the bedroom, looking at her contentedly. Nino the fish. Falling asleep wanting the week to be over that same night, and the goodbyes, the train, the last half-mile in the phaeton, the gate, the eucalyptus trees along the road leading up to the house. Just before falling asleep, she had a moment of terror when she imagined that she was maybe dreaming. Stretching out all at once, her feet hit the brass bars at the foot of the bed, they hurt through the covers, and she heard her mother and Inés talking in the big dining room, baggage, see the doctor about those pimples, cod-liver oil and concentrate of witch hazel. It wasn't a dream, it wasn't a dream.

It wasn't a dream. They took her down to Constitution Station one windy morning, small flags blowing from the pushcarts in the plaza, a piece of pie in the railroad station restaurant, and the enormous entrance to platform 14. Between Inés and her mother they kissed her so much that her face felt like it'd been walked on, soft and smelly, rouge and Coty powder, wet around the mouth, a squeamish feeling of filth that the wind eradicated with one large smack. She wasn't afraid to travel alone because she was a big girl, with nothing less than twenty pesos in her pocketbook, Sansinena Co., Frozen Meats a sweetish stink seeping in the window, the railroad trestle over the yellow brook and Isabel already back to normal from having had to have that crying spell at the station, happy, dead with fear, active, using fully the seat by the window, almost the only traveler in that portion of the coach from which one could examine all the different places and see oneself in the small mirrors. She thought once or twice of her mother, of Inés—they'd already be on the 97 car, leaving Constitution—she read no smoking, spitting is forbidden by law, seating capacity 42 passengers, they were passing through Banfield at top speed, vavooom! country more country more country intermingled with the taste of Milky Way and the menthol drops. Inés had reminded her that she would be working on the green wool in such a way that Isabel packed the knitting into the most inaccessible part of the suitcase, poor Inés, and what a stupid idea.

At the station she was a little bit worried because if the phaeton . . . But there it was, with don Nicanor very red and respectful, yes miss, this miss, that miss, was the trip fine, was her mother as well as ever, of course it had rained—Oh the swinging motion of the phaeton to get her back into the whole aquarium of her previous visit to Los Horneros. Everything smaller, more crystalline and pink, without the tiger then, don Nicanor with fewer white hairs, barely three years ago, Nino a toad, Nino a fish, and Rema's hands which made you want to cry and feel them on your head forever, a caress like death almost and pastries with vanilla cream, the two best things on earth.

They gave her a room upstairs all to herself, the loveliest room. A grownup's room (Nino's idea, all black curls and eyes, handsome in his blue overalls; in the afternoon, of course, Luis made him dress up, his slate-grey suit and a red tie) and inside, another tiny room with an enormous wild cardinal. The bathroom was two doors away (but inside doors through the rooms so that you could go without checking beforehand where the tiger was), full of spigots and metal things, though they did not fool Isabel easily, you could tell it was a country bathroom, things were not as perfect as in a city bath. And it smelled old, the second morning she found a waterbug taking a walk in the washbasin. She barely touched it, it rolled itself into a timid ball and disappeared down the gurgling drain.

Dear mama, I'm writing to—They were eating in the dining room with the chandelier because it was cooler. The Kid was complaining every minute about the heat, Luis said nothing, but every once in a while you could see the sweat break out on his forehead or his chin. Only Rema was restful, she passed the plates slowly and always as if the meal were a birthday party, a little solemnly and impressively. (Isabel was secretly studying her way of carving and of ordering the servants.) For the most part, Luis was always reading, fist to brow, and the book leaning against a siphon. Rema touched his arm before passing him a plate, and the Kid would interrupt him once in a while to call him philosopher. It hurt Isabel that Luis might be a philosopher, not because of that, but because of the Kid, that he had an excuse then to joke and call him that.

They ate like this: Luis at the head of the table, Rema and Nino on one side, the Kid and Isabel on the other, so that there was an adult at the end and a child and a grownup at either side. When Nino wanted to tell her something serious, he'd give her a kick on the shin with his shoe. Once Isabel yelled and the Kid got angry and said she was badly brought up. Rema looked at her continuously until Isabel was comforted by the gaze and the potato soup.

Mama, before you go in to eat it's like all the rest of the time, you have to look and see if—Almost always it was Rema who went to see if they could go into the dining room with the crystal chandelier. The second day she came to the big living room and said they would have to wait. It was a long time before a farm-hand came to tell them that the tiger was in the clover garden, then Rema took the children's hands and everyone went in to eat. The fried potatoes were pretty dry that morning, though only Nino and the Kid complained.

You told me I was not supposed to go around making—Because Rema seemed to hold off all questions with her terse sweetness. The setup worked so well that it was unnecessary to worry about the business of the rooms. It was an absolutely enormous house, and at worst, there was only one room they couldn't go into; never more than one, so it didn't matter. Isabel was as used to it as Nino, after a couple of days. From morning until evening they played in the grove of willows, and if they couldn't play in the willow grove, there was always the clover garden, the park with its hammocks, and the edge of the brook. It was the same in the house, they had their bedrooms, the hall down the center, the library downstairs (except one Thursday when they couldn't go into the library) and the dining room with the chandelier. They couldn't go into Luis' study because Luis was reading all the time, once in a while he would call to his son and give him picture books; but Nino always took them out, they went to the living room or to the front garden to look at them. They never went into the Kid's study because they were afraid he would throw a tantrum. Rema told them that it was better that way, she said it as though she were warning them; they'd already learned how to read her silences.

After all's said, it was a sad life. Isabel wondered one night why the Funes' had invited her for the summer. She wasn't old enough to understand that it was for Nino not for her, a summer plaything to keep Nino happy. She only managed to see the sadness of the house, that Rema seemed always tired, that it hardly ever rained and that, nonetheless, things had that air of being damp and abandoned. After a few days she got used to the rules of the house and the not difficult discipline of that summer at Los Horneros. Nino was beginning to learn to use the microscope Luis had given him; they spent a magnificent week growing insects in a trough with stagnant water and lily pads, putting drops on the glass slide to look at the microbes. "They're mosquito larvae, you're not going to see microbes with that microscope," Luis told them, his smile somewhat pained and distant. They could never believe that that wriggling horror was not a microbe. Rema brought them a kaleidoscope which she kept in her wardrobe, but they still preferred detecting microbes and counting their legs. Isabel carried a notebook and kept notations of their experiments, she combined biology with chemistry and putting together a medicine chest. They made the medicine chest in Nino's room after ransacking the whole house to get things for it. Isabel told Luis, "We want some of everything: things." Luis gave them Andreu lozenges, pink cotton, a test tube. The Kid came across with a rubber bag and a bottle of green pills with the label worn off. Rema came to see the medicine chest, read the inventory in the notebook, and told them that they were learning a lot of useful things. It occurred to her or to Nino (who always got excited and wanted to show off in front of Rema) to assemble an herbarium. As it was possible that morning to go down to the clover garden, they went about collecting samples and by nightfall they had both their bedroom floors filled with leaves and flowers on bits of paper, there was hardly room to step. Before going to bed, Isabel noted: "Leaf #74: green, heart-shaped, with brown spots." It annoyed her a little that almost all the leaves were green, nearly all smooth, and nearly all lanceolate.

The day they went out ant-hunting she saw the farmhands. She knew the foreman and the head groom because they brought reports to the house. But these other younger hands stood there against the side of the sheds with an air of siesta, yawning once in a while and watching the kids play. One of them asked Nino, "Why'ya collectin' all them bugs?" and tapped him on top of his head with all the curls, using two fingers. Isabel would have liked Nino to lose his temper, to show that he was the boss's son. They already had the bottle crawling with ants and on the bank of the brook they ran across a bug with an enormous hard shell and stuck him in the bottle too, to see what would happen. The idea of an ant-farm they'd gotten out of *The Treasure of Youth*, and Luis loaned them a big, deep glass tank. As they left, both of them carrying it off, Isabel heard him say to Rema, "Better this way, they'll be quiet in the house." Also it seemed to her that Rema sighed. Before dropping off to sleep, when faces appear in the darkness, she remembered again the Kid going out onto the porch for a smoke, thin, humming to himself, saw Rema who was bringing him out coffee and he made a mistake taking the cup so clumsily that he caught Rema's fingers while trying to get the cup, Isabel had seen from the dining room Rema pulling her hand back and the Kid was barely able to keep the cup from falling and laughed at the tangle. Black ants better than the red ones: bigger, more ferocious. Afterward let loose a pile of red ones, watch the war from outside the glass, all very safe. Except they didn't fight. Made two anthills, one in each corner of the glass tank. They consoled one another by studying the distinctive habits, a special notebook for each kind of ant. But almost sure they would fight, look through the glass at war without quarter, and just one notebook.

Rema didn't like to spy on them, she passed by the bedrooms sometimes and would see them with the ant-farm beside the window, impassioned and important. Nino was particularly good at pointing out immediately any new galleries, and Isabel enlarged the diagram traced in ink on double pages. On Luis' advice they collected black ants only, and the ant-farm was already enormous, the ants appeared to be furious and worked until nightfall, excavating and moving earth with a thousand methods and maneuvers, the careful rubbing of feelers and feet, abrupt fits of fury or vehemence, concentrations and dispersals for no apparent reason. Isabel no longer knew what to take notes on, little by little she put the notebook aside and hours would pass in studying and forgetting what had been discovered. Nino began to want to go back to the garden, he mentioned the hammocks and the colts. Isabel was somewhat contemptuous of him for that. The ant-farm was worth the whole of Los Horneros, and it gave her immense pleasure to think that the ants came and went without fear of any tiger, sometimes she tried to imagine a tiny little tiger like an eraser, roaming the galleries of the ant-farm; maybe that was why the dispersals and concentrations. And now she liked to rehearse the real world in the one of glass, now that she felt a little like a prisoner, now that she was forbidden to go down to the dining room until Rema said so.

She pushed her nose against one of the glass sides, promptly all attention because she liked for them to look at her; she heard Rema stop in the doorway, just silent, looking at her. She heard those things with such a sharp brightness when it was Rema.

"You're alone here? Why?"

"Nino went off to the hammocks. This big one must be a queen, she's huge."

Rema's apron was reflected in the glass. Isabel saw one of her hands slightly raised, with ... it looked as if it were inside the ant-farm; suddenly she ... and offering a cup of coffee to the Kid, but now there ... er fingers, ants instead of the cup and the Kid's hand

..." ...a," she asked.

... ction was scaring the ants."

... ng room now, you can go down."

... Rema?"

... lass like a bird through a window. It looked to

Isa ... eally scared this time, that they ran from the
refl ... ng now, Rema had left, she went down the hall
as if ... Isabel felt afraid of the question herself, a dull
fear, ... t the question but seeing Rema run off that
way, ... glass where the galleries emptied out and
twisted ... e soil.

It was si ... n, handball against the wall which overlooked th ... atching shots that looked impossible and

climbing up to the roof on a vine to get the ball loose where it was caught between two tiles. A son of one of the farmhands came out from beside the willows and played with them, but he was slow and clumsy and shots got away from him. Isabel could smell the terebinth leaves and at one moment, returning with a backhand an insidious low shot of Nino's, she felt the summer's happiness very deep inside her. For the first time she understood her being at Los Horneros, the vacation, Nino. She thought of the ant-farm up there and it was an oozy dead thing, a horror of legs trying to get out, false air, poisonous. She hit the ball angrily, happily, she bit off a piece of a terebinth leaf with her teeth, bitter, she spit it out in disgust, happy for the first time really, and at last, under the sun in the country.

The window glass fell like hail. It was in the Kid's study. They saw him rise in his shirtsleeves and the broad black eyeglasses.

"Filthy pains-in-the-ass!"

The little peon fled. Nino set himself alongside Isabel, she felt him shaking with the same wind as the willows.

"We didn't mean to do it, uncle."

"Honest, Kid, we didn't mean to do it."

He wasn't there any longer.

She had asked Rema to take away the ant-farm and Rema promised her. After, chatting while she helped her hang up her clothes and get into her pajamas, they forgot. When Rema put out the light, Isabel felt the presence of the ants, Rema went down the hall to say goodnight to Nino who was still crying and repentant, but she didn't have the nerve to call her back again. Rema would have thought that she was just a baby. She decided to go to sleep immediately and was wider awake than ever. When the moment came when there were faces in the darkness, she saw her mother and Inés looking at one another and smiling like accomplices and pulling on gloves of phosphorescent yellow. She saw Nino weeping, her mother and Inés with the gloves on that now were violet hairdos that twirled and twirled round their heads, Nino with enormous vacant eyes—maybe from having cried too much—and thought that now she would see Rema and Luis, she wanted to see them, she didn't want to see the Kid, but she saw the Kid without his glasses with the same tight face that he'd had when he began hitting Nino and Nino fell backwards until he was against the wall and looked at him as though expecting that would finish it, and the Kid continued to whack back and forth across his face with a loose soft slap that sounded moist, until Rema intruded herself in front of Nino and the Kid laughed, his face almost touching Rema's, and then they heard Luis returning and saying from a distance that now they could go into the dining room. Everything had happened so fast because Nino had been there and Rema had come to tell them not to leave the living room until Luis found out what room the tiger was in and she stayed there with them watching the game of checkers. Nino won and Rema praised him, then Nino was so happy that he put his arms around her waist and wanted to kiss her. Rema had bent down, laughing, and Nino kissed her on the nose and eyes, the two of them laughing and Isabel also, they were so happy playing. They didn't see the Kid coming, when he got up to them he grabbed Nino, jerked at him, said something about the ball breaking the window in his room and started to hit him, he looked at Rema while he hit him, he seemed furious with Rema and she defied him with her eyes for a moment. Terrified, Isabel saw her face up to him, then she stepped in between to protect Nino. The whole evening meal was a deceit, a lie, Luis thought that Nino was crying from having taken a tumble, the Kid looked at Rema as if to order her to shut up, Isabel saw him now with his hard, handsome mouth, very red lips; in the dimness they were even more scarlet, she could see his teeth, barely revealed, glittering. A puffed cloud emerged from his teeth, a green triangle, Isabel blinked her eyes to wipe out the images and Inés and her mother appeared again with their yellow gloves; she gazed at them for a moment, then thought of the ant-farm: that was there and you couldn't see it; the yellow gloves were not there and she saw them instead as if in bright sunlight. It seemed almost curious to her, she couldn't make the ant-farm come out, instead she felt it as a kind of weight there, a chunk of thick, live space. She felt it so strongly that she reached about for the matches, the night-lamp. The ant-farm leaped from the nothingness, wrapped in shifting shadow. Isabel lifted the lamp and came closer. Poor ants, they were going to think that the sun was up. When she could see one of the sides, she was frightened; the ants had been working in all that blackness. She watched them swarm up and down, in silence, so visible, palpable. They were working away inside there as though they had not yet lost their hope of getting out.

It was almost always the foreman who kept them advised of the tiger's movements; Luis had the greatest confidence in him, and since he passed almost the whole day working in his study, he neither emerged nor let those who came down from the next floor move about until don Roberto sent in his report. But they had to rely on one another also. Busy with the household chores inside, Rema knew exactly what was happening upstairs and down. At other times, it was the children who brought the news to the Kid or to Luis. Not that they'd seen anything, just that don Roberto had run into them outside, indicated the tiger's whereabouts to them, and they came back in to pass it on. They believed Nino without question, Isabel less, she was new and might make a mistake. Later, though, since she always went about with Nino stuck to her skirt, they finally believed both of them equally. That was in the morning and afternoon; at night it was the Kid who went out to check and see that the dogs were tied up or that no live coals had been left close to the houses. Isabel noticed that he carried the revolver and sometimes a stick with a silver handle.

She hadn't wanted to ask Rema about it because Rema clearly found it something so obvious and necessary; to pester her would have meant looking stupid, and she treasured her pride before another woman. Nino was easy, he talked straight. Everything clear and obvious when he explained it. Only at night, if she wanted to reconstruct that clarity and obviousness, Isabel noticed that the important reasons were still missing. She learned quickly what was really important: if you wanted to leave the house, or go down to the dining room, to Luis' study, or to the library, find out first. "You have to trust don Roberto," Rema had said. Her and Nino as well. She hardly ever asked Luis because he hardly ever knew. The Kid, who always knew, she never asked. And so it was always easy, the life organized itself for Isabel with a few more obligations as far as her movements went, and a few less when it came to clothes, meals, the time to go to bed. A real summer, the way it should be all year round.

. . . see you soon. They're all fine. I have an ant-farm with Nino and we play and are making a very large herbarium. Rema sends her kisses, she is fine. I think she's sad, the same as Luis who is very nice. I think that Luis has some trouble although he studies all the time. Rema gave me some lovely colored handkerchiefs, Inés is going to like them. Mama, it's nice here and I'm enjoying myself with Nino and don Roberto, he's the foreman and tells us when we can go out and where, one afternoon he was almost wrong and sent us to the edge of the brook, when a farmhand came to tell us no, you should have seen how awful don Roberto felt and then Rema, she picked Nino up and was kissing him, and she squeezed me so hard. Luis was going about saying that the house was not for children, and Nino asked him who the children were, and everybody laughed even the Kid laughed. Don Roberto is the foreman.

If you come to get me you could stay a few days and be with Rema and cheer her up. I think that she . . .

But to tell her mother that Rema cried at night, that she'd heard her crying going down the hall, staggering a little, stop at Nino's door, continue, go downstairs (she must have been drying her eyes) and Luis' voice in the distance: "What's the matter, Rema? Aren't you well?", a silence, the whole house like an enormous ear, then a murmur and Luis' voice again: "He's a bastard, a miserable bastard . . ." almost as though he were coldly confirming a fact, making a connection, a fate.

. . . is a little ill, it would do her good if you came and kept her company. I have to show you the herbarium and some stones from the brook the farmhands brought me. Tell Inés. . .

It was the kind of night she liked, insects, damp, reheated bread, and custard with Greek raisins. The dogs barked constantly from the edge of the brook, and an enormous praying mantis flew in and landed on the mantelpiece and Nino went to fetch the magnifying glass; they trapped it with a wide-mouthed glass and poked at it to make it show the color of its wings.

"Throw that bug away," Rema pleaded. "They make me so squeamish."

"It's a good specimen," Luis admitted. "Look how he follows my hand with his eyes. The only insect that can turn its head."

"What a goddamned night," the Kid said from behind his newspaper.

Isabel would have liked to cut the mantis' head off, a good snip with the scissors, and see what would happen.

"Leave it in the glass," she asked Nino. "Tomorrow we can put it in the ant farm and study it."

It got hotter, by ten-thirty you couldn't breathe. The children stayed with Rema in the inside dining room, the men were in their studies. Nino was the first to say that he was getting sleepy.

"Go on up by yourself, I'll come see you later. Everything is all right upstairs."

And Rema took him about the waist with that expression he liked so well.

"Tell us a story, Aunt Rema?"

"Another night."

They were down there alone, with the mantis which looked at them. Luis came to say his goodnights to them, muttering something about the hour that children ought to go to bed, Rema smiled at him when she kissed him.

"Growly bear," she said, and Isabel, bent over the mantis' glass, thought that she'd never seen Rema kissing the Kid or a praying mantis that was so so green. She moved the glass a little and the mantis grew frantic. Rema came over to tell her to go to bed.

"Throw that bug away, it's horrible."

"Rema, tomorrow."

She asked her to come up and say goodnight to her. The Kid had the door of his study left partly open and was pacing up and down in his shirtsleeves, the collar open. He whistled to her as she passed.

"I'm going to bed, Kid."

"Listen to me: tell Rema to make me a nice cold lemonade and bring it to me here. Then you go right up to your room."

Of course she was going to go up to her room, she didn't see why he had to tell her to. She went back to the dining room to tell Rema, she saw her hesitate.

"Don't go upstairs yet. I'm going to make the lemonade and you take it down yourself."

"He said for you . . ."

"Please."

Isabel sat down at the side of the table. Please. There were clouds of insects whirling under the carbide lamp, she would have stayed there for hours looking at nothing, repeating: Please, please. Rema, Rema. How she loved her, and that unhappy voice, bottomless, without any possible reason, the voice of sadness itself. Please. Rema, Rema . . . A feverish heat reached her face, a wish to throw herself at Rema's feet, to let Rema pick her up in her arms, a wish to die looking at her and Rema be sorry for her, pass her cool, delicate fingers through her hair, over the eyelids . . .

Now she was holding out a green tumbler full of ice and sliced lemons.

"Take it to him."

"Rema . . ."

Rema seemed to tremble, she turned her back on the table so that she shouldn't see her eyes.

"I'll throw the mantis out right now, Rema."

One sleeps poorly in the viscous heat and all that buzzing of mosquitoes. Twice she was on the point of getting up, to go out into the hall or to go to the bathroom to put cold water on her face and wrists. But she could hear someone walking, downstairs, someone was going from one side of the dining room to the other, came to the bottom of the stairway, turned around . . . They weren't the confused, long steps of Luis' walk, nor was it Rema's. How warm the Kid had felt that night, how he'd drunk the lemonade in great gulps. Isabel saw him drinking the tumblerful, his hands holding the green tumbler, the yellow discs wheeling in the water under the lamp; but at the same time she was sure the Kid had never drunk the lemonade, that he was still staring at the glass she had brought him, over to the table, like someone looking at some kind of infinite naughtiness. She didn't want to think about the Kid's smile, his going to the door as though he were about to go into the dining room for a look, his slow turning back.

"She was supposed to bring it to me. You, I told you to go up to your room."

And the only thing that came to her mind was a very idiot answer:

"It's good and cold, Kid."

And the tumbler, green as the praying mantis.

Nino was the first one up, it was his idea that they go down to the brook to look for snails. Isabel had hardly slept at all, she remembered rooms full of flowers, tinkling bells, hospital corridors, sisters of charity, thermometers in jars of bichlorate, scenes from her first communion, Inés, the broken bicycle, the restaurant in the railroad station, the gypsy costume when she had been eight. Among all this, like a delicate breeze between the pages of an album, she found herself wide awake, thinking of things that were not flowers, bells, hospital corridors. She got out of bed grudgingly, washed her face hard, especially the ears. Nino said that it was ten o'clock and that the tiger was in the music room, so that they could go down to the brook right away. They went downstairs together, hardly saying good morning to Luis and the Kid who were both reading with their doors open. You could find the snails mostly on the bank nearest the wheat fields. Nino moved along blaming Isabel for her distraction, said she was no kind of friend at all and wasn't helping form the collection. She saw him suddenly as so childish, such a little boy with his snails and his leaves.

She came back first, when they raised the flag at the house for lunch. Don Roberto came from his inspection and Isabel asked him the same question as always. Then Nino was coming up slowly, carrying the box of snails and the rakes; Isabel helped him put the rakes away on the porch and they went in together. Rema was standing there, white and silent. Nino put a blue snail into her hand.

"The nicest one, for you."

The Kid was eating already, the newspaper beside him, there was hardly enough room for Isabel to rest her arm. Luis was the last to come from his room, contented as he always was at noon. They ate, Nino was talking about the snails, the snail eggs in the reeds, the collection itself, the sizes and the colors. He was going to kill them by himself, it hurt Isabel to do it, they'd put them to dry on a zinc sheet. After the coffee came and Luis looked at them with the usual question, Isabel got up first to look for don Roberto, even though don Roberto had already told her before. She made the round of the porch and when she came in again, Rema and Luis had their heads together over the snail box, it was like a family photograph, only Luis looked up at her and she said, "It's in the Kid's study," and stayed watching how the Kid shrugged his shoulders, annoyed, and Rema who touched a snail with a fingertip, so delicately that her finger even seemed part snail. Afterwards, Rema got up to go look for more sugar, and Isabel tailed along behind her babbling until they came back in laughing from a joke they'd shared in the pantry. When Luis said he had no tobacco and ordered Nino to look in his study, Isabel challenged him that she'd find the cigarettes first and they went out together. Nino won, they came back in running and pushing, they almost bumped into the Kid going to the library to read his newspaper, complaining because he couldn't use his study. Isabel came over to look at the snails, and Luis waiting for her to light his cigarette as always saw that she was lost, studying the snails which were beginning to ooze out slowly and move about, looking at Rema suddenly, but dropping her like a flash, captivated by the snails, so much so that she didn't move at the Kid's first scream, they were all running and she was still standing over the snails as if she did not hear the Kid's new choked cry, Luis beating against the library door, don Roberto coming in with the dogs, the Kid's moans amid the furious barking of the dogs, and Luis saying over and over again, "But if it was in his study! She said it was in his own study!", bent over the snails willowy as fingers, like Rema's fingers maybe, or it was Rema's hand on her shoulder, made her raise her head to look at her, to stand looking at her for an eternity, broken by her ferocious sob into Rema's skirt, her unsettled happiness, and Rema running her hand over her hair, quieting her with a soft squeeze of her fingers and a murmuring against her ear, a stuttering as of gratitude, as of an unnameable acquiescence.

Stephen Crane

Stephen Crane was born in 1871 in Newark, New Jersey, and died of tuberculosis in Germany in 1900. After the early death of his father, who was a Methodist minister, Crane and his thirteen siblings were supported by their mother, who wrote articles for the religious and secular press. He attended Lafayette College and Syracuse University, but seems to have been an indifferent student, more interested in baseball and boxing and journalism. When he was only twenty-two, he wrote *Maggie: A Girl of the Streets*, which he had to publish at his own expense in 1893 because of its graphic portrayal of slum life and its sexual frankness, followed two years later by *The Red Badge of Courage*, his masterful novel of the American Civil War. This established his reputation and enabled him to find work as a war correspondent. During this period, he covered the Greco-Turkish War and the Spanish-American War in Cuba. The experience that was to form the basis for "The Open Boat" took place on New Year's Day, 1897, when the steamship *Commodore* on which he was a passenger was wrecked en route to Florida.

When he was not playing baseball and skipping classes, Crane was wandering through New York, particularly the Bowery, absorbing its shapes and texture. He describes his apprenticeship in this way: "When I was sixteen I began to write for the New York newspapers, doing correspondence from Ashbury Park and other places. Then I began to write special articles and short stories for the Sunday papers and one of the literary syndicates, reading a great deal in the meantime and gradually acquiring a style. I decided that the nearer a writer gets to life the greater he becomes as an artist, and most of my prose writings have been toward the goal partially described by that misunderstood and abused word, realism. Tolstoi is the writer I admire most of all. I've been a free lance during most of the time I have been doing literary work, writing stories and articles about anything under heaven that seemed to possess interest, and selling them wherever I could. It was hopeless work. Of all human lots for a person of sensibility that of an obscure free lance in literature and journalism is, I think, the most discouraging."

Stephen Crane seems to have been consumed by a desire to transcend the stylistic limitations imposed by his formal education and his career as a journalist. As he explains in a letter to John Northern Hilliard: "As far as myself and my own meagre success are concerned, I began the battle of life with no talent, no equipment, but with an ardent admiration and desire. I did little work at school, but confined my abilities such as they were, to the diamond. Not that I disliked books, but the cut-and-dried curriculum of the college did not appeal to me. Humanity was a much more interesting study. When I ought to have been at recitations I was studying faces on the streets, and when I ought to have been studying my next day's lessons I was watching the trains roll in and out of the Central Station. So, you see, I had, first of all, to recover from college. I had to build up, so to speak. And my chiefest desire was to write plainly and unmistakably, so that all men (and some women) might read and understand. That to my mind is good writing. There is a great deal of hard labour connected with literature. I think that is the hardest thing about it. There is nothing to respect in art save one's own opinion of it. . . ."

Although he admired Tolstoy's vivid scenes and moral vision, Crane found *War and Peace* overwritten: "He could have done the whole business in one third the time and made it just as wonderful. It goes on and on like Texas." He aimed for a plainer, more spare style that anticipates a writer such as Hemingway, also trained as a journalist. "The true artist," Crane said, "is the man who leaves pictures of his own time as they appear to him." Like Conrad, he believed that art is not a matter of prescription, but of temperament: "A man is born into the world with his own pair of eyes, and he is not responsible for his vision—he is merely responsible for his quality of personal honesty."

Crane expands on this credo in a letter to Lily Brandon Munroe: "My career has been more of a battle than a journey. You know, when I left you, I renounced the clever school in literature. It seemed to me that there must be something more in life than to sit and cudgel one's brains for clever and witty expedients. So I developed all alone a little creed of art which I thought was a good one. Later I discovered that my creed was identical with the one of Howells and Garland and in this way I became involved in the beautiful war between those who say that art is man's substitute for nature and we are the most successful in art when we approach nearest to nature and truth, and those who say—well, I don't know what they say. They don't, they can't say much but they fight villainously and keep Garland and I out of the big magazines." In addition to his concern for economy and accuracy, he felt that good writing should not be doctrinaire: "I have been very careful not to let any theories or pet ideas of my own be seen in my writing.

Preaching is fatal to literature. I try to give to readers a slice out of life and if there is any moral or lesson in it I do not point it out. I let the reader find it for himself. As Emerson said, 'There should be a long logic beneath the story, but it should be kept carefully out of sight.' "

There is no finer appreciation of Stephen Crane than the brief note about him and his work that appears in Joseph Conrad's *Notes on Life and Letters*. Conrad understood Crane's gifts and the tragic nature of his life, which involved extreme financial hardships, lack of critical sympathy, and, eventually, frail health. He speaks of Crane as "a wonderful artist in words"

whose "impressionism of phrase went really deeper than the surface." He describes their last meeting at Dover, when Crane, gravely ill, was being taken by his common-law wife, Cora Stewart, to a spa in Germany: "When I stopped at the door for another look I saw that he had turned his head on the pillow and was staring wistfully out of the window at the sails of a cutter yacht that glided slowly across the frame, like a dim shadow against the grey sky. . . . his passage on this earth was like that of a horseman riding swiftly in the dawn of a day fated to be short and without sunshine."

The Open Boat

A TALE INTENDED TO BE AFTER THE FACT BEING THE EXPERIENCE OF FOUR MEN FROM THE SUNK STEAMER COMMODORE

I

None of them knew the color of the sky. Their eyes glanced level, and were fastened upon the waves that swept toward them. These waves were of the hue of slate, save for the tops, which were of foaming white, and all of the men knew the colors of the sea. The horizon narrowed and widened, and dipped and rose, and at all times its edge was jagged with waves that seemed thrust up in points like rocks.

Many a man ought to have a bath-tub larger than the boat which here rode upon the sea. These waves were most wrongfully and barbarously abrupt and tall, and each froth-top was a problem in small boat navigation.

The cook squatted in the bottom and looked with both eyes at the six inches of gunwale which separated him from the ocean. His sleeves were rolled over his fat forearms, and the two flaps of his unbuttoned vest dangled as he bent to bail out the boat. Often he said: "Gawd! That was a narrow clip." As he remarked it he invariably gazed eastward over the broken sea.

The oiler, steering with one of the two oars in the boat, sometimes raised himself suddenly to keep clear of water that swirled in over the stern. It was a thin little oar and it seemed often ready to snap.

The correspondent, pulling at the other oar, watched the waves and wondered why he was there.

The injured captain, lying in the bow, was at this time buried in that profound dejection and indifference which comes, temporarily at least, to even the bravest and most enduring when, willy nilly, the firm fails, the army loses, the ship goes down. The mind of the master of a vessel is rooted deep in the timbers of her, though he command for a day or a decade, and this captain had on him the stern impression of a scene in the grays of dawn of seven turned faces, and later a stump of a top-mast with a white ball on it that slashed to and fro at the waves, went low and lower, and down. Thereafter there was something strange in his voice. Although steady, it was deep with mourning, and of a quality beyond oration or tears.

"Keep 'er a little more south, Billie," said he.

"'A little more south,' sir," said the oiler in the stern.

A seat in this boat was not unlike a seat upon a bucking bronco, and, by the same token, a bronco is not much smaller. The craft pranced and reared, and plunged like an animal. As each wave came, and she rose for it, she seemed like a horse making at a fence outrageously high. The manner of her scramble over these walls of water is a mystic thing, and, moreover, at the top of them were ordinarily these problems in white water, the foam racing down from the summit of each wave, requiring a new leap, and a leap from the air. Then, after scornfully bumping a crest, she would slide, and race, and splash down a long incline and arrive bobbing and nodding in front of the next menace.

A singular disadvantage of the sea lies in the fact that after successfully surmounting one wave you discover that there is another behind it just as important and just as nervously anxious to do something effective in the way of swamping boats. In a ten-foot dingey one can get an idea of the resources of the sea in the line of waves that is not probable to the average experience, which is never at sea in a dingey. As each slaty wall of water approached, it shut all else from the view of the men in the boat, and it was not difficult to imagine that this particular wave was the final outburst of the ocean, the last effort of the grim water. There was a terrible grace in the move of the waves, and they came in silence, save for the snarling of the crests.

In the wan light, the faces of the men must have been gray. Their eyes must have glinted in strange ways as they gazed steadily astern. Viewed from a balcony, the whole thing would doubtlessly have been weirdly picturesque. But the men in the boat had no time to see it, and if they had had leisure there were other things to occupy their minds. The sun swung steadily up the sky, and they knew it was broad day because the color of the sea changed from slate to emerald-green, streaked with amber lights, and the foam was like tumbling snow. The process of the breaking day was unknown to them. They were aware only of this effect upon the color of the waves that rolled toward them.

In disjointed sentences the cook and the correspondent argued as to the difference between a life-saving station and a house of refuge. The cook had said: "There's a house of refuge just north of the Mosquito Inlet Light, and as soon as they see us, they'll come off in their boat and pick us up."

"As soon as who see us?" said the correspondent.

"The crew," said the cook.

"Houses of refuge don't have crews," said the correspondent. "As I understand them, they are only places where clothes and grub are stored for the benefit of shipwrecked people. They don't carry crews."

"Oh, yes, they do," said the cook.

"No, they don't," said the correspondent.

"Well, we're not there yet, anyhow," said the oiler, in the stern.

"Well," said the cook, "perhaps it's not a house of refuge that I'm thinking of as being near Mosquito Inlet Light. Perhaps it's a life-saving station."

"We're not there yet," said the oiler, in the stern.

II

As the boat bounced from the top of each wave, the wind tore through the hair of the hatless men, and as the craft plopped her stern down again the spray slashed past them. The crest of each of these waves was a hill, from the top of which the men surveyed, for a moment, a broad tumultuous expanse, shining and wind-riven. It was probably splendid. It was probably glorious, this play of the free sea, wild with lights of emerald and white and amber.

"Bully good thing it's an on-shore wind," said the cook. "If not where would we be? Wouldn't have a show."

"That's right," said the correspondent.

The busy oiler nodded his assent.

Then the captain, in the bow, chuckled in a way that expressed humor, contempt, tragedy, all in one. "Do you think we've got a show, now, boys?" said he.

Whereupon the three went silent, save for a trifle of hemming and hawing. To express any particular optimism at this time they felt to be childish and stupid, but they all doubtless possessed this sense of the situation in their mind. A young man thinks doggedly at such times. On the other hand, the ethics of their condition was decidedly against any open suggestion of hopelessness. So they were silent.

"Oh, well," said the captain, soothing his children, "we'll get ashore all right."

But there was that in his tone which made them think, so the oiler quoth: "Yes! If this wind holds!"

The cook was bailing. "Yes! If we don't catch hell in the surf."

Canton flannel gulls flew near and far. Sometimes they sat down on the sea, near patches of brown sea-weed that rolled over the waves with a movement like carpets on a line in a gale. The birds sat comfortably in groups, and they were envied by some in the dingey, for the wrath of the sea was no more to them than it was to a covey of prairie chickens a thousand miles inland. Often they came very close and stared at the men with black bead-like eyes. At these times they were uncanny and sinister in their unblinking scrutiny, and the men hooted angrily at them, telling them to be gone. One came, and evidently decided to alight on the top of the captain's head. The bird flew parallel to the boat and did not circle, but made short side-long jumps in the air in chicken-fashion. His black eyes were wistfully fixed upon the captain's head. "Ugly brute," said the oiler to the bird. "You look as if you were made with a jack-knife." The cook and the correspondent swore darkly at the creature. The captain naturally wished to knock it away with the end of the heavy painter, but he did not dare do it, because anything resembling an emphatic gesture would have capsized this freighted boat, and so with his open hand, the captain gently and carefully waved the gull away. After it had been discouraged from the pursuit the captain breathed easier on account of his hair, and others breathed easier because the bird struck their minds at this time as being somehow gruesome and ominous.

In the meantime the oiler and the correspondent rowed. And also they rowed.

They sat together in the same seat, and each rowed an oar. Then the oiler took both oars; then the correspondent took both oars; then the oiler; then the correspondent. They rowed and they rowed. The very ticklish part of the business was when the time came for the reclining one in the stern to take his turn at the oars. By the very last star of truth, it is easier to steal eggs from under a hen than it was to change seats in the dingey. First the man in the stern slid his hand along the thwart and moved with care, as if he were of Sèvres. Then the man in the rowing seat slid his hand along the other thwart. It was all done with the most extraordinary care. As the two sidled past each other, the whole party kept watchful eyes on the coming wave, and the captain cried: "Look out now! Steady there!"

The brown mats of sea-weed that appeared from time to time were like islands, bits of earth. They were travelling, apparently, neither one way nor the other. They were, to all intents, stationary. They informed the men in the boat that it was making progress slowly toward the land.

The captain, rearing cautiously in the bow, after the dingey soared on a great swell, said that he had seen the light-house at Mosquito Inlet. Presently the cook remarked that he had seen it. The correspondent was at the oars, then, and for some reason he too wished to look at the light-house, but his back was toward the far shore and the waves were important, and for some time he could not seize an opportunity to turn his head. But at last there came a wave more gentle than the others, and when at the crest of it he swiftly scoured the western horizon.

"See it?" said the captain.

"No," said the correspondent, slowly, "I didn't see anything."

"Look again," said the captain. He pointed. "It's exactly in that direction."

At the top of another wave, the correspondent did as he was bid, and this time his eyes chanced on a small still thing on the edge of the swaying horizon. It was precisely like the point of a pin. It took an anxious eye to find a light-house so tiny.

"Think we'll make it, Captain?"

"If this wind holds and the boat don't swamp, we can't do much else," said the captain.

The little boat, lifted by each towering sea, and splashed viciously by the crests, made progress that in the absence of sea-weed was not apparent to those in her. She seemed just a wee thing wallowing, miraculously, top-up, at the mercy of five oceans. Occasionally, a great spread of water, like white flames, swarmed into her.

"Bail her, cook," said the captain, serenely.

"All right, Captain," said the cheerful cook.

III

It would be difficult to describe the subtle brotherhood of men that was here established on the seas. No one said that it was so. No one mentioned it. But it dwelt in the boat, and each man felt it warm him. They were a captain, an oiler, a cook, and a correspondent, and they were friends, friends in a more curiously iron-bound degree than may be common. The hurt captain, lying against the water-jar in the bow, spoke always in a low voice and calmly, but he could never command a more ready and swiftly obedient crew than the motley three of the dingey. It was more than a mere recognition of what was best for the common safety. There was surely in it a quality that was personal and heartfelt. And after this devotion to the commander of the boat there was this comradeship that the correspondent, for instance, who had been taught to be cynical of men, knew even at the time was the best experience of his life. But no one said that it was so. No one mentioned it.

"I wish we had a sail," remarked the captain. "We might try my overcoat on the end of an oar and give you two boys a chance to rest." So the cook and the correspondent held the mast and spread wide the overcoat. The oiler steered, and the little boat made good way with her new rig. Sometimes the oiler had to scull sharply to keep a sea from breaking into the boat, but otherwise sailing was a success.

Meanwhile the light-house had been growing slowly larger. It had now almost assumed color, and appeared like a little gray shadow on the sky. The man at the oars could not be prevented from turning his head rather often to try for a glimpse of this little gray shadow.

At last, from the top of each wave the men in the tossing boat could see land. Even as the light-house was an upright shadow on the sky, this land seemed but a long black shadow on the sea. It certainly was thinner than paper. "We must be about opposite New Smyrna," said the cook, who had coasted this shore often in schooners. "Captain, by the way, I believe they abandoned that life-saving station there about a year ago."

"Did they?" said the captain.

The wind slowly died away. The cook and the correspondent were not now obliged to slave in order to hold high the oar. But the waves continued their old impetuous swooping at the dingey, and the little craft, no longer under way, struggled woundily over them. The oiler or the correspondent took the oars again.

Shipwrecks are *apropos* of nothing. If men could only train for them and have them occur when the men had reached pink condition, there would be less drowning at sea. Of the four in the dingey none had slept any time worth mentioning for two days and two nights previous to embarking in the dingey, and in the excitement of clambering about the deck of a foundering ship they had also forgotten to eat heartily.

For these reasons, and for others, neither the oiler nor the correspondent was fond of rowing at this time. The correspondent wondered ingenuously how in the name of all that was sane could there be people who thought it amusing to row a boat. It was not an amusement, it was a diabolical punishment, and even a genius of mental aberrations could never conclude that it was anything but a horror to the muscles and a crime against the back. He mentioned to the boat in general how the amusement of rowing struck him, and the weary-faced oiler smiled in full sympathy. Previously to the foundering, by the way, the oiler had worked double-watch in the engine-room of the ship.

"Take her easy, now, boys," said the captain. "Don't spend yourselves. If we have to run a surf you'll need all your strength, because we'll sure have to swim for it. Take your time."

Slowly the land arose from the sea. From a black line it became a line of black and a line of white—trees and sand. Finally, the captain said that he could make out a house on the shore. "That's the house of refuge, sure," said the cook. "They'll see us before long, and come out after us."

The distant light-house reared high. "The keeper ought to be able to make us out now, if he's looking through a glass," said the captain. "He'll notify the life-saving people."

"None of those other boats could have got ashore to give word of the wreck," said the oiler, in a low voice. "Else the life-boat would be out hunting us."

Slowly and beautifully the land loomed out of the sea. The wind came again. It had veered from the northeast to the southeast. Finally, a new sound struck the ears of the men in the boat. It was the low thunder of the surf on the shore. "We'll never be able to make the light-house now," said the captain. "Swing her head a little more north, Billie."

"'A little more north,' sir," said the oiler.

Whereupon the little boat turned her nose once more down the wind, and all but the oarsman watched the shore grow. Under the influence of this expansion doubt and direful apprehension were leaving the minds of the men. The management of the boat was still most absorbing, but it could not prevent a quiet cheerfulness. In an hour, perhaps, they would be ashore.

Their back-bones had become thoroughly used to balancing in the boat and they now rode this wild colt of a dingey like circus men. The correspondent thought that he had been drenched to the skin, but happening to feel in the top pocket of his coat, he found therein eight cigars. Four of them were soaked with sea-water; four were perfectly scatheless. After a search, somebody produced three dry matches, and thereupon the four waifs rode impudently in their little boat, and with an assurance of an impending rescue shining in their eyes, puffed at the big cigars and judged well and ill of all men. Everybody took a drink of water.

IV

"Cook," remarked the captain, "there don't seem to be any signs of life about your house of refuge."

"No," replied the cook. "Funny they don't see us!"

A broad stretch of lowly coast lay before the eyes of the men. It was of dunes topped with dark vegetation. The roar of the surf was plain, and sometimes they could see the white lip of a wave as it spun up the beach. A tiny house was blocked out black upon the sky. Southward, the slim light-house lifted its little gray length.

Tide, wind, and waves were swinging the dingey northward. "Funny they don't see us," said the men.

The surf's roar was here dulled, but its tone was, nevertheless, thunderous and mighty. As the boat swam over the great rollers, the men sat listening to this roar. "We'll swamp sure," said everybody.

It is fair to say here that there was not a life-saving station within twenty miles in either direction, but the men did not know this fact and in consequence they made dark and opprobrious remarks concerning the eyesight of the nation's life-savers. Four scowling men sat in the dingey and surpassed records in the invention of epithets.

"Funny they don't see us."

The light-heartedness of a former time had completely faded. To their sharpened minds it was easy to conjure pictures of all kinds of incompetency and blindness and, indeed, cowardice. There was the shore of the populous land, and it was bitter and bitter to them that from it came no sign.

"Well," said the captain, ultimately, "I suppose we'll have to make a try for ourselves. If we stay out here too long, we'll none of us have strength left to swim after the boat swamps."

And so the oiler, who was at the oars, turned the boat straight for the shore. There was a sudden tightening of muscles. There was some thinking.

"If we don't all get ashore—" said the captain. "If we don't all get ashore, I suppose you fellows know where to send news of my finish?"

They then briefly exchanged some addresses and admonitions. As for the reflections of the men, there was a great deal of rage in them. Perchance they might be formulated thus: "If I am going to be drowned—if I am going to be drowned—if I am going to be drowned, why, in the name of the seven mad gods who rule the sea, was I allowed to come thus far and contemplate sand and trees? Was I brought here merely to have my nose dragged away as I was about to nibble the sacred cheese of life? It is preposterous. If this old ninny-woman, Fate, cannot do better than this, she should be deprived of the management of men's fortunes. She is an old hen who knows not her intention. If she has decided to drown me, why did she not do it in the beginning and save me all this trouble. The whole affair is absurd. . . . But, no, she cannot mean to drown me. She dare not drown me. She cannot drown me. Not after all this work." Afterward the man might have had an impulse to shake his fist at the clouds. "Just you drown me, now, and then hear what I call you!"

The billows that came at this time were more formidable. They seemed always just about to break and roll over the little boat in a turmoil of foam. There was a preparatory and long growl in the speech of them. No mind unused to the sea would have concluded that the dingey could ascend these sheer heights in time. The shore was still afar. The oiler was a wily surfman. "Boys," he said, swiftly, "she won't live three minutes more and we're too far out to swim. Shall I take her to sea again, Captain?"

"Yes! Go ahead!" said the captain.

This oiler, by a series of quick miracles, and fast and steady oarsmanship, turned the boat in the middle of the surf and took her safely to sea again.

There was a considerable silence as the boat bumped over the furrowed sea to deeper water. Then somebody in gloom spoke. "Well, anyhow, they must have seen us from the shore by now."

The gulls went in slanting flight up the wind toward the gray desolate east. A squall, marked by dingy clouds, and clouds brick-red, like smoke from a burning building, appeared from the southeast.

"What do you think of those life-saving people? Ain't they peaches?"

"Funny they haven't seen us."

"Maybe they think we're out here for sport! Maybe they think we're fishin'. Maybe they think we're damned fools."

It was a long afternoon. A changed tide tried to force them southward, but wind and wave said northward. Far ahead, where coast-line, sea, and sky formed their mighty angle, there were little dots which seemed to indicate a city on the shore.

"St. Augustine?"

The captain shook his head. "Too near Mosquito Inlet."

And the oiler rowed, and then the correspondent rowed. Then the oiler rowed. It was a weary business. The human back can become the seat of more aches and pains than are registered in books for the composite anatomy of a regiment. It is a limited area, but it can become the theatre of innumerable muscular conflicts, tangles, wrenches, knots, and other comforts.

"Did you ever like to row, Billie?" asked the correspondent.

"No," said the oiler. "Hang it."

When one exchanged the rowing-seat for a place in the bottom of the boat, he suffered a bodily depression that caused him to be careless of everything save an obligation to wiggle one finger. There was cold sea-water swashing to and fro in the boat, and he lay in it. His head, pillowed on a thwart, was within an inch of the swirl of a wave crest, and sometimes a particularly obstreperous sea came inboard and drenched him once more. But these matters did not annoy him. It is almost certain that if the boat had capsized he would have tumbled comfortably out upon the ocean as if he felt sure that it was a great soft mattress.

"Look! There's a man on the shore!"

"Where?"

"There! See 'im? See 'im?"

"Yes, sure! He's walking along."

"Now he's stopped. Look! He's facing us!"

"He's waving at us!"

"So he is! By thunder!"

"Ah, now, we're all right! There'll be a boat out here for us in half an hour."

"He's going on. He's running. He's going up to that house there."

The remote beach seemed lower than the sea, and it required a searching glance to discern the little black figure. The captain saw a floating stick and they rowed to it. A bath-towel was by some weird chance in the boat, and, tying this on the stick, the captain waved it. The oarsman did not dare turn his head, so he was obliged to ask questions.

"What's he doing now?"

"He's standing still again. He's looking, I think. . . . There he goes again. Toward the house. . . . Now he stopped again."

"Is he waving at us?"

"No, not now! He was, though."

"Look! There comes another man!"

"He's running."

"Look at him go, would you."

"Why, he's on a bicycle. Now he's met the other man. They're both waving at us. Look!"

"There comes something up the beach."

"What the devil is that thing?"

"Why, it looks like a boat."

"Why, certainly it's a boat."

"No, it's on wheels."

"Yes, so it is. Well, that must be the life-boat. They drag them along shore on a wagon."

"That's the life-boat, sure."

"No, by, it's—it's an omnibus."

"I tell you it's a life-boat."

"It is not! It's an omnibus. I can see it plain. See? One of those big hotel omnibuses."

"By thunder, you're right. It's an omnibus, sure as fate. What do you suppose they are doing with an omnibus? Maybe they are going around collecting the life-crew, hey?"

"That's it, likely. Look! There's a fellow waving a little black flag. He's standing on the steps of the omnibus. There come those other two fellows. Now they're all talking together. Look at the fellow with the flag. Maybe he ain't waving it!"

"That ain't a flag, is it? That's his coat. Why, certainly, that's his coat."

"So it is. It's his coat. He's taken it off and is waving it around his head. But would you look at him swing it!"

"Oh, say, there isn't any life-saving station there. That's just a winter resort hotel omnibus that has brought over some of the boarders to see us drown."

"What's that idiot with the coat mean? What's he signaling, anyhow?"

"It looks as if he were trying to tell us to go north. There must be a life-saving station up there."

"No! He thinks we're fishing. Just giving us a merry hand. See? Ah, there, Willie."

"Well, I wish I could make something out of those signals. What do you suppose he means?"

"He don't mean anything. He's just playing."

"Well, if he'd just signal us to try the surf again, or to go to sea and wait, or go north, or go south, or go to hell—there would be some reason in it. But look at him. He just stands there and keeps his coat revolving like a wheel. The ass!"

"There come more people."

"Now there's quite a mob. Look! Isn't that a boat?"

"Where? Oh, I see where you mean. No, that's no boat."

"That fellow is still waving his coat."

"He must think we like to see him do that. Why don't he quit it. It don't mean anything."

"I don't know. I think he is trying to make us go north. It must be that there's a life-saving station there somewhere."

"Say, he ain't tired yet. Look at 'im wave."

"Wonder how long he can keep that up. He's been revolving his coat ever since he caught sight of us. He's an idiot. Why aren't they getting men to bring a boat out. A fishing boat—one of those big yawls—could come out here all right. Why don't he do something?"

"Oh, it's all right, now."

"They'll have a boat out here for us in less than no time, now that they've seen us."

A faint yellow tone came into the sky over the low land. The shadows on the sea slowly deepened. The wind bore coldness with it, and the men began to shiver.

"Holy smoke!" said one, allowing his voice to express his impious mood, "if we keep on monkeying out here! If we've got to flounder out here all night!"

"Oh, we'll never have to stay here all night! Don't you worry. They've seen us now, and it won't be long before they'll come chasing out after us."

The shore grew dusky. The man waving a coat blended gradually into this gloom, and it swallowed in the same manner the omnibus and the group of people. The spray, when it dashed uproariously over the side, made the voyagers shrink and swear like men who were being branded.

"I'd like to catch the chump who waved the coat. I feel like soaking him one, just for luck."

"Why? What did he do?"

"Oh, nothing, but then he seemed so damned cheerful."

In the meantime the oiler rowed, and then the correspondent rowed, and then the oiler rowed. Gray-faced and bowed forward, they mechanically, turn by turn, plied the leaden oars. The form of the light-house had vanished from the southern horizon, but finally a pale star appeared, just lifting from the sea. The streaked saffron in the west passed before the merging darkness, and the sea to the east was black. The land had vanished, and was expressed only by the low and drear thunder of the surf.

"If I am going to be drowned—if I am going to be drowned—if I am going to be drowned, why, in the name of the seven mad gods who rule the sea, was I allowed to come thus far and contemplate sand and trees? Was I brought here merely to have my nose dragged away as I was about to nibble the sacred cheese of life?"

The patient captain, drooped over the water-jar, was sometimes obliged to speak to the oarsman.

"Keep her head up! Keep her head up!"

" 'Keep her head up,' sir." The voices were weary and low.

This was surely a quiet evening. All save the oarsman lay heavily and listlessly in the boat's bottom. As for him, his eyes were just capable of noting the tall black waves that swept forward in a most sinister silence, save for an occasional subdued growl of a crest.

The cook's head was on a thwart, and he looked without interest at the water under his nose. He was deep in other scenes. Finally he spoke. "Billie," he murmured, dreamfully, "what kind of pie do you like best?"

V

"Pie," said the oiler and the correspondent, agitatedly. "Don't talk about those things, blast you!"

"Well," said the cook, "I was just thinking about ham sandwiches, and—"

A night on the sea in an open boat is a long night. As darkness settled finally, the shine of the light, lifting from the sea in the south, changed to full gold. On the northern horizon a new light appeared, a small bluish gleam on the edge of the waters. These two lights were the furniture of the world. Otherwise there was nothing but waves.

Two men huddled in the stern, and distances were so magnificent in the dingey that the rower was enabled to keep his feet partly warmed by thrusting them under his companions. Their legs indeed extended far under the rowing-seat until they touched the feet of the captain forward. Sometimes, despite the efforts of the tired oarsman, a wave came piling into the boat, an icy wave of the night, and the chilling water soaked them anew. They would twist their bodies for a moment and groan, and sleep the dead sleep once more, while the water in the boat gurgled about them as the craft rocked.

The plan of the oiler and the correspondent was for one to row until he lost the ability, and then arouse the other from his sea-water couch in the bottom of the boat.

The oiler plied the oars until his head drooped forward, and the overpowering sleep blinded him. And he rowed yet afterward. Then he touched a man in the bottom of the boat, and called his name. "Will you spell me for a little while?" he said, meekly.

"Sure, Billie," said the correspondent, awakening and dragging himself to a sitting position. They exchanged places carefully, and the oiler, cuddling down in the sea-water at the cook's side, seemed to go to sleep instantly.

The particular violence of the sea had ceased. The waves came without snarling. The obligation of the man at the oars was to keep the boat headed so that the tilt of the rollers would not capsize her, and to preserve her from filling when the crests rushed past. The black waves were silent and hard to be seen in the darkness. Often one was almost upon the boat before the oarsman was aware.

In a low voice the correspondent addressed the captain. He was not sure that the captain was awake, although this iron man seemed to be always awake. "Captain, shall I keep her making for that light north, sir?"

The same steady voice answered him. "Yes. Keep it about two points off the port bow."

The cook had tied a life-belt around himself in order to get even the warmth which this clumsy cork contrivance could donate, and he seemed almost stove-like when a rower, whose teeth invariably chattered wildly as soon as he ceased his labor, dropped down to sleep.

The correspondent, as he rowed, looked down at the two men sleeping under foot. The cook's arm was around the oiler's shoulders, and, with their fragmentary clothing and haggard faces, they were the babes of the sea, a grotesque rendering of the old babes in the wood.

Later he must have grown stupid at his work, for suddenly there was a growling of water, and a crest came with a roar and a swash into the boat, and it was a wonder that it did not set the cook afloat in his life-belt. The cook continued to sleep, but the oiler sat up, blinking his eyes and shaking with the new cold.

"Oh, I'm awful sorry, Billie," said the correspondent, contritely.

"That's all right, old boy," said the oiler, and lay down again and was asleep.

Presently it seemed that even the captain dozed, and the correspondent thought that he was the one man afloat on all the oceans. The wind had a voice as it came over the waves, and it was sadder than the end.

There was a long, loud swishing astern of the boat, and a gleaming trail of phosphorescence, like blue flame, was furrowed on the black waters. It might have been made by a monstrous knife.

Then there came a stillness, while the correspondent breathed with the open mouth and looked at the sea.

Suddenly there was another swish and another long flash of bluish light, and this time it was alongside the boat, and might almost have been reached with an oar. The correspondent saw an enormous fin speed like a shadow through the water, hurling the crystalline spray and leaving the long glowing trail.

The correspondent looked over his shoulder at the captain. His face was hidden, and he seemed to be asleep. He looked at the babes of the sea. They certainly were asleep. So, being bereft of sympathy, he leaned a little way to one side and swore softly into the sea.

But the thing did not then leave the vicinity of the boat. Ahead or astern, on one side or the other, at intervals long or short, fled the long sparkling streak, and there was to be heard the whirroo of the dark fin. The speed and power of the thing were greatly to be admired. It cut the water like a gigantic and keen projectile.

The presence of this biding thing did not affect the man with the same horror that it would if he had been a picnicker. He simply looked at the sea dully and swore in an undertone.

Nevertheless, it is true that he did not wish to be alone with the thing. He wished one of his companions to awaken by chance and keep him company with it. But the captain hung motionless over the water-jar and the oiler and the cook in the bottom of the boat were plunged in slumber.

VI

"If I am going to be drowned—if I am going to be drowned—if I am going to be drowned, why, in the name of the seven mad gods who rule the sea, was I allowed to come thus far and contemplate sand and trees?"

During this dismal night, it may be remarked that a man would conclude that it was really the intention of the seven mad gods to drown him, despite the abominable injustice of it. For it was certainly an abominable injustice to drown a man who had worked so hard, so hard. The man felt it would be a crime most unnatural. Other people had drowned at sea since galleys swarmed with painted sails, but still—

When it occurs to a man that nature does not regard him as important, and that she feels she would not maim the universe by disposing of him, he at first wishes to throw bricks at the temple, and he hates deeply the fact that there are no bricks and no temples. Any visible expression of nature would surely be pelleted with his jeers.

Then, if there be no tangible thing to hoot he feels, perhaps, the desire to confront a personification and indulge in pleas, bowed to one knee, and with hands supplicant, saying: "Yes, but I love myself."

A high cold star on a winter's night is the word he feels that she says to him. Thereafter he knows the pathos of his situation.

The men in the dingey had not discussed these matters, but each had, no doubt, reflected upon them in silence and according to his mind. There was seldom any expression upon their faces save the general one of complete weariness. Speech was devoted to the business of the boat.

To chime the notes of his emotion, a verse mysteriously entered the correspondent's head. He had even forgotten that he had forgotten this verse, but it suddenly was in his mind.

> A soldier of the Legion lay dying in Algiers,
> There was lack of woman's nursing, there was dearth of woman's tears;
> But a comrade stood beside him, and he took that comrade's hand
> And he said: "I never more shall see my own, my native land."

In his childhood, the correspondent had been made acquainted with the fact that a soldier of the Legion lay dying in Algiers, but he had never regarded it as important. Myriads of his school-fellows had informed him of the soldier's plight, but the dinning had naturally ended by making him perfectly indifferent. He had never considered it his affair that a soldier of the Legion lay dying in Algiers, nor had it appeared to him as a matter for sorrow. It was less to him than the breaking of a pencil's point.

Now, however, it quaintly came to him as a human, living thing. It was no longer merely a picture of a few throes in the breast of a poet, meanwhile drinking tea and warming his feet at the grate; it was an actuality—stern, mournful, and fine.

The correspondent plainly saw the soldier. He lay on the sand with his feet out straight and still. While his pale left hand was upon his chest in an attempt to thwart the going of his life, the blood came between his fingers. In the far Algerian distance, a city of low square forms was set against a sky that was faint with the last sunset hues. The correspondent, plying the oars and dreaming of the slow and slower movements of the lips of the soldier, was moved by a profound and perfectly impersonal comprehension. He was sorry for the soldier of the Legion who lay dying in Algiers.

The thing which had followed the boat and waited had evidently grown bored at the delay. There was no longer to be heard the slash of the cut-water, and there was no longer the flame of the long trail. The light in the north still glimmered, but it was apparently no nearer to the boat. Sometimes the boom of the surf rang in the correspondent's ears, and he turned the craft seaward then and rowed harder. Southward, some one had evidently built a watch-fire on the beach. It was too low and too far to be seen, but it made a shimmering, roseate reflection upon the bluff back of it, and this could be discerned from the boat. The wind came stronger, and sometimes a wave suddenly raged out like a mountain-cat and there was to be seen the sheen and sparkle of a broken crest.

The captain, in the bow, moved on his water-jar and sat erect. "Pretty long night," he observed to the correspondent. He looked at the shore. "Those life-saving people take their time."

"Did you see that shark playing around?"

"Yes, I saw him. He was a big fellow, all right."

"Wish I had known you were awake."

Later the correspondent spoke into the bottom of the boat.

"Billie!" There was a slow and gradual disentanglement. "Billie, will you spell me?"

"Sure," said the oiler.

As soon as the correspondent touched the cold comfortable sea-water in the bottom of the boat, and had huddled close to the cook's life-belt he was deep in sleep, despite the fact that his teeth played all the popular airs. This sleep was so good to him that it was but a moment before he heard a voice call his name in a tone that demonstrated the last stages of exhaustion. "Will you spell me?"

"Sure, Billie."

The light in the north had mysteriously vanished, but the correspondent took his course from the wide-awake captain.

Later in the night they took the boat farther out to sea, and the captain directed the cook to take one oar at the stern and keep the boat facing the seas. He was to call out if he should hear the thunder of the surf. This plan enabled the oiler and the correspondent to get respite together. "We'll give those boys a chance to get into shape again," said the captain. They curled down and, after a few preliminary chatterings and trembles, slept once more the dead sleep. Neither knew they had bequeathed to the cook the company of another shark, or perhaps the same shark.

As the boat caroused on the waves, spray occasionally bumped over the side and gave them a fresh soaking, but this had no power to break their repose. The ominous slash of the wind and the water affected them as it would have affected mummies.

"Boys," said the cook, with the notes of every reluctance in his voice, "she's drifted in pretty close. I guess one of you had better take her to sea again." The correspondent, aroused, heard the crash of the toppled crests.

As he was rowing, the captain gave him some whiskey and water, and this steadied the chills out of him. "If I ever get ashore and anybody shows me even a photograph of an oar—"

At last there was a short conversation.

"Billie. . . . Billie, will you spell me?"

"Sure," said the oiler.

VII

When the correspondent again opened his eyes, the sea and the sky were each of the gray hue of the dawning. Later, carmine and gold was painted upon the waters. The morning appeared finally, in its splendor, with a sky of pure blue, and the sunlight flamed on the tips of the waves.

On the distant dunes were set many little black cottages, and a tall white wind-mill reared above them. No man, nor dog, nor bicycle appeared on the beach. The cottages might have formed a deserted village.

The voyagers scanned the shore. A conference was held in the boat. "Well," said the captain, "if no help is coming, we might better try a run through the surf right away. If we stay out here much longer we will be too weak to do anything for ourselves at all." The others silently acquiesced in this reasoning. The boat was headed for the beach. The correspondent wondered if none ever ascended the tall wind-tower, and if then they never looked seaward. This tower was a giant, standing with its back to the plight of the ants. It represented in a degree, to the correspondent, the serenity of nature amid the struggles of the individual—nature in the wind, and nature in the vision of men. She did not seem cruel to him then, nor beneficent, nor treacherous, nor wise. But she was indifferent, flatly indifferent. It is, perhaps, plausible that a man in this situation, impressed with the unconcern of the universe, should see the innumerable flaws of his life and have them taste wickedly in his mind and wish for another chance. A distinction between right and wrong seems absurdly clear to him, then, in this new ignorance of the grave-edge, and he understands that if he were given another opportunity he would mend his conduct and his words, and be better and brighter during an introduction, or at a tea.

"Now, boys," said the captain, "she is going to swamp sure. All we can do is to work her in as far as possible, and then when she swamps, pile out and scramble for the beach. Keep cool now, and don't jump until she swamps sure."

The oiler took the oars. Over his shoulders he scanned the surf. "Captain," he said, "I think I'd better bring her about, and keep her head-on to the seas and back her in."

"All right, Billie," said the captain. "Back her in." The oiler swung the boat then and, seated in the stern, the cook and the correspondent were obliged to look over their shoulders to contemplate the lonely and indifferent shore.

The monstrous inshore rollers heaved the boat high until the men were again enabled to see the white sheets of water scudding up the slanted beach. "We won't get in very close," said the captain. Each time a man could wrest his attention from the rollers, he turned his glance toward the shore, and in the expression of the eyes during this contemplation there was a singular quality. The correspondent, observing the others, knew that they were not afraid, but the full meaning of their glances was shrouded.

As for himself, he was too tired to grapple fundamentally with the fact. He tried to coerce his mind into thinking of it, but the mind was dominated at this time by the muscles, and the muscles said they did not care. It merely occurred to him that if he should drown it would be a shame.

There were no hurried words, no pallor, no plain agitation. The men simply looked at the shore. "Now, remember to get well clear of the boat when you jump," said the captain.

Seaward the crest of a roller suddenly fell with a thunderous crash, and the long white comber came roaring down upon the boat.

"Steady now," said the captain. The men were silent. They turned their eyes from the shore to the comber and waited. The boat slid up the incline, leaped at the furious top, bounced over it, and swung down the long back of the wave. Some water had been shipped and the cook bailed it out.

But the next crest crashed also. The tumbling boiling flood of white water caught the boat and whirled it almost perpendicular. Water swarmed in from all sides. The correspondent had his hands on the gunwale at this time, and when the water entered at that place he swiftly withdrew his fingers, as if he objected to wetting them.

The little boat, drunken with this weight of water, reeled and snuggled deeper into the sea.

"Bail her out, cook! Bail her out," said the captain.

"All right, Captain," said the cook.

"Now boys, the next one will do for us, sure," said the oiler. "Mind to jump clear of the boat."

The third wave moved forward, huge, furious, implacable. It fairly swallowed the dingey, and almost simultaneously the men tumbled into the sea. A piece of life-belt had lain in the bottom of the boat, and as the correspondent went overboard he held this to his chest with his left hand.

The January water was icy, and he reflected immediately that it was colder than he had expected to find it off the coast of Florida. This appeared to his dazed mind as a fact important enough to be noted at the time. The coldness of the water was sad; it was tragic. This fact was somehow so mixed and confused with his opinion of his own situation that it seemed almost a proper reason for tears. The water was cold.

When he came to the surface he was conscious of little but the noisy water. Afterward he saw his companions in the sea. The oiler was ahead in the race. He was swimming strongly and rapidly. Off to the correspondent's left, the cook's great white and corked back bulged out of the water, and in the rear the captain was hanging with his one good hand to the keel of the overturned dingey.

There is a certain immovable quality to a shore, and the correspondent wondered at it amid the confusion of the sea.

It seemed also very attractive, but the correspondent knew that it was a long journey, and he paddled leisurely. The piece of life-preserver lay under him, and sometimes he whirled down the incline of a wave as if he were on a hand-sled.

But finally he arrived at a place in the sea where travel was beset with difficulty. He did not pause swimming to inquire what manner of current had caught him, but there his progress ceased. The shore was set before him like a bit of scenery on a stage, and he looked at it and understood with his eyes each detail of it.

As the cook passed, much farther to the left, the captain was calling to him, "Turn over on your back, cook! Turn over on your back and use the oar."

"All right, sir." The cook turned on his back, and, paddling with an oar, went ahead as if he were a canoe.

Presently the boat also passed to the left of the correspondent with the captain clinging with one hand to the keel. He would have appeared like a man raising himself to look over a board fence, if it were not for the extraordinary gymnastics of the boat. The correspondent marvelled that the captain could still hold to it.

They passed on, nearer to shore—the oiler, the cook, the captain—and following them went the water-jar, bouncing gayly over the seas.

The correspondent remained in the grip of this strange new enemy—a current. The shore, with its white slope of sand and its green bluff, topped with little silent cottages, was spread like a picture before him. It was very near to him then, but he was impressed as one who in a gallery looks at a scene from Brittany or Holland.

He thought: "I am going to drown? Can it be possible? Can it be possible? Can it be possible?" Perhaps an individual must consider his own death to be the final phenomenon of nature.

But later a wave perhaps whirled him out of his small deadly current, for he found suddenly that he could again make progress toward the shore. Later still, he was aware that the captain, clinging with one hand to the keel of the dingey, had his face turned away from the shore and toward him, and was calling his name. "Come to the boat! Come to the boat!"

In his struggle to reach the captain and the boat, he reflected that when one gets properly wearied, drowning must really be a comfortable arrangement, a cessation of hostilities accompanied by a large degree of relief, and he was glad of it, for the main thing in his mind for some moments had been the horror of the temporary agony. He did not wish to be hurt.

Presently he saw a man running along the shore. He was undressing with most remarkable speed. Coat, trousers, shirt, everything flew magically off him.

"Come to the boat," called the captain.

"All right, Captain." As the correspondent paddled, he saw the captain let himself down to bottom and leave the boat. Then the correspondent performed his one little marvel of the voyage. A large wave caught him and flung him with ease and supreme speed completely over the boat and far beyond it. It struck him even then as an event in gymnastics, and a true miracle of the sea. An overturned boat in the surf is not a plaything to a swimming man.

The correspondent arrived in water that reached only to his waist, but his condition did not enable him to stand for more than a moment. Each wave knocked him into a heap, and the under-tow pulled at him.

Then he saw the man who had been running and undressing, and undressing and running, come bounding into the water. He dragged ashore the cook, and then waded toward the captain, but the captain waved him away, and sent him to the correspondent. He was naked, naked as a tree in winter, but a halo was about his head, and he shone like a saint. He gave a strong pull, and a long drag, and a bully heave at the correspondent's hand. The correspondent, schooled in the minor formulae, said: "Thanks, old man." But suddenly the man cried: "What's that?" He pointed a swift finger. The correspondent said: "Go."

In the shallows, face downward, lay the oiler. His forehead touched sand that was periodically, between each wave, clear of the sea.

The correspondent did not know all that transpired afterward. When he achieved safe ground he fell, striking the sand with each particular part of his body. It was as if he had dropped from a roof, but the thud was grateful to him.

It seems that instantly the beach was populated with men with blankets, clothes, and flasks, and women with coffee-pots and all the remedies sacred to their minds. The welcome of the land to the men from the sea was warm and generous, but a still and dripping shape was carried slowly up the beach, and the land's welcome for it could only be the different and sinister hospitality of the grave.

When it came night, the white waves paced to and fro in the moonlight, and the wind brought the sound of the great sea's voice to the men on shore, and they felt that they could then be interpreters.

William Faulkner

William Faulkner was born in New Albany, Mississippi, in 1897 and raised in Oxford, where he spent most of his life, except for a brief stint in the Royal Canadian Air Force in World War I, six months as a rum-runner and beginning novelist in New Orleans, where he met and befriended Sherwood Anderson and wrote *Soldier's Pay* (1926), and some months as a scriptwriter in Hollywood. He worked at odd jobs, including that of a coal porter in a power plant, where he wrote *As I Lay Dying* (1930) in his spare hours during a six-week period. Faulkner attended the University of Mississippi, but never completed a degree and never pursued a public, or literary, life; he wrote sketches and stories for the New Orleans *Times-Picayune* and *The Toronto Star* early in his career, but was very reclusive and resistant to playing the role of artist; only after winning the Nobel Prize for Literature in 1950 did he consent regularly to make himself available for speeches and interviews. Faulkner's reticence may have something to do with the anti-intellectual environment from which he emerged, as this comment from his essay "On Privacy" suggests: "America has not yet found any place for him who deals only in things of the human spirit except to use his notoriety to sell soap or cigarettes or fountain pens or to advertise automobiles and cruises and resort hotels (or if he can be taught to contort fast enough to meet the standards) in radio and moving pictures where he can produce enough income tax to be worth attention."

Although he wrote nothing extensive on the art of fiction and was often deliberately vague or devious in his interviews, Faulkner did, however, offer a few clues concerning his aims and strategies in fiction. He considered language "the damndest clumsiest frailest awkwardest tool" he could have been given, yet one that might reveal something of man's soul, his divinity. His letters to publishers' editors reveal his intense interest in all matters of style, including punctuation, typography, how to telegraph the shift from an objective to a subjective mode, and so on; yet he declared style to be "unimportant": "I think that if one spends too much time bothering too much about his style, he'll finish with having nothing left but style." Faulkner considered that each new work "demands its own style"; beyond that, he felt style to be more a matter of temperament, impinged on, for Americans, by a Puritan sense of urgency and the culture of mass production. While Hemingway forged an "undeviable style," Faulkner claimed that he and Thomas Wolfe did not have that kind of instinct: "We tried to crowd and cram everything, all experience, into each paragraph, to get the whole complete nuance of the moment's experience, all of the recaptured light rays, into each paragraph. That's why it's clumsy and hard to read. . . . We just couldn't help it." More likely, he needed his long, labyrinthine sentences and shifting points of view to accommodate the range and complexity of his materials.

"A writer needs 3 things: experience, observation, imagination, any two of which, at times any one of which, can supply the lack of the others," Faulkner wrote. "With me, a story usually begins with a single idea or memory or mental picture. The writing of the story is simply a matter of working up to that moment, to explain why it happened or what it caused to follow. A writer is trying to create credible people in credible moving situations in the most moving way he can." He stressed understatement as the best means of drawing character: "Remember, all Tolstoy said about Anna Karenina was that she was beautiful and could see in the dark like a cat. That's all he ever said to describe her. . . . And it's best to take the gesture, the shadow of the branch and let the mind create the tree."

Faulkner often described himself as a failed poet, but his real aim seems to have been to draw attention to the poetic nature of both his prose and his narrative structures. Plot, for him, was "anything that moves you enough to keep working on it. A story usually makes its own plot, works itself out as you go." In other words, the action derives from the intersection of character and context, or situation. His knowledge of human nature and his close reading of his society meant that he had to invent very little: "Beginning with *Sartoris*, I discovered that my own little postage stamp of native soil was worth writing about and that I would never live long enough to exhaust it, and by sublimating the actual into the apocryphal I would have complete liberty to use whatever talent I might have to its absolute top."

By this, he did not mean that he only needed to report or record the events of his time. "Just to report facts, to report injustice sometimes, is not enough. That doesn't move people. The writer's got to add the gift of his talent; he has got to take the truth and set it on fire so that people will remember it." Music, he thought, would be an easier, more satisfying medium through which to give imaginative expression to feelings, to catch the fire; however, as a story-teller, a man of words, he had to accept that "the thunder and the music of prose take place in silence."

In many of his public statements, Faulkner appears cautious and conservative, nowhere more so than in his pronouncements on racial integration, where he was an advocate of gradualism. However, in a handful of novels, including *The Sound and the Fury* (1929), *Light in August* (1932), and *Absolom, Absolom!* (1936), and a gathering of short stories—available in *Collected Stories* (1950) and *Go Down, Moses* (1942), where our present selection first appeared, few twentieth-century writers have come closer to capturing both the fire and the thunder of our racially and morally turbulent times.

Pantaloon in Black

He stood in the worn, faded clean overalls which Mannie herself had washed only a week ago, and heard the first clod stride the pine box. Soon he had one of the shovels himself, which in his hands (he was better than six feet and weighed better than two hundred pounds) resembled the toy shovel a child plays with at the shore, its half cubic foot of flung dirt no more than the light gout of sand the child's shovel would have flung. Another member of his sawmill gang touched his arm and said, "Lemme have hit, Rider." He didn't even falter. He released one hand in midstroke and flung it backward, striking the other across the chest, jolting him back a step, and restored the hand to the moving shovel, flinging the dirt with that effortless fury so that the mound seemed to be rising of its own volition, not built up from above but thrusting visibly upward out of the earth itself, until at last the grave, save for its rawness, resembled any other marked off without order about the barren plot by shards of pottery and broken bottles and old brick and other objects insignificant to sight but actually of a profound meaning and fatal to touch, which no white man could have read. Then he straightened up and with one hand flung the shovel quivering upright in the mound like a javelin and turned and began to walk away, walking on even when an old woman came out of the meagre clump of his kin and friends and a few old people who had known him and his dead wife both since they were born, and grasped his forearm. She was his aunt. She had raised him. He could not remember his parents at all.

"Whar you gwine?" she said.

"Ah'm goan home," he said. "You dont wants ter go back dar by yoself," she said. "You needs to eat. You come on home and eat."

"Ah'm goan home," he repeated, walking out from under her hand, his forearm like iron, as if the weight on it were no more than that of a fly, the other members of the mill gang whose head he was giving way quietly to let him pass. But before he reached the fence one of them overtook him; he did not need to be told it was his aunt's messenger.

"Wait, Rider," the other said. "We gots a jug in de bushes—" Then the other said what he had not intended to say, what he had never conceived of himself saying in circumstances like these, even though everybody knew it—the dead who either will not or cannot quit the earth yet although the flesh they once lived in has been returned to it, let the preachers tell and reiterate and affirm how they left it not only without regret but with joy, mounting toward glory: "You dont wants ter go back dar. She be wawkin yit."

He didn't pause, glancing down at the other, his eyes red at the inner corners in his high, slightly backtilted head. "Lemme lone, Acey," he said. "Doan mess wid me now," and went on, stepping over the three-strand wire fence without even breaking his stride, and crossed the road and entered the woods. It was middle dusk when he emerged from them and crossed the last field, stepping over that fence too in one stride, into the lane. It was empty at this hour of Sunday evening—no family in wagon, no rider, no walkers churchward to speak to him and carefully refrain from looking after him when he had passed—the pale, powder-light, powder-dry dust of August from which the long week's marks of hoof and wheel had been blotted by the strolling and unhurried Sunday shoes, with somewhere beneath them, vanished but not gone, fixed and held in the annealing dust, the narrow, splay-toed prints of his wife's bare feet where on Saturday afternoons she would walk to the commissary to buy their next week's supplies while he took his bath; himself, his own prints, setting the period now as he strode on, moving almost as fast as a smaller man could have trotted, his body breasting the air her body had vacated, his eyes touching the objects—post and tree and field and house and hill—her eyes had lost.

The house was the last one in the lane, not his but rented from Carothers Edmonds, the local white landowner. But the rent was paid promptly in advance, and even in just six months he had refloored the porch and rebuilt and roofed the kitchen, doing the work himself on Saturday afternoon and Sunday with his wife helping him, and bought the stove. Because he made good money: sawmilling ever since he began to get his growth at fifteen and sixteen and now, at twenty-four, head of the timber gang itself because the gang he headed moved a third again as much timber between sunup and sundown as any other moved, handling himself at times out of the vanity of his own strength logs which ordinarily two men would have handled with canthooks; never without work even in the old days when he had not actually needed the money, when a lot of what he wanted, needed perhaps, didn't cost money—the women bright and dark and for all purposes nameless he didn't need to buy and it didn't matter to him what he wore and there was always food for him at any hour of day or night in the house of his aunt who didn't even want to take the two dollars he gave her each Saturday—so there had been only the Saturday and Sunday dice and whiskey that had to be paid for until that day six months ago when he saw Mannie, whom he had known all his life, for the first time and said to himself: "Ah'm thu wid all dat," and they married and he rented the cabin from Carothers Edmonds and built a fire on the hearth on their wedding night as the tale told how Uncle Lucas Beauchamp, Edmonds' oldest tenant, had done on his forty-five years ago and which had burned ever since; and he would rise and dress and eat his breakfast by lamplight to walk the four miles to the mill by sunup, and exactly one hour after sundown he would enter the house again, five days a week, until Saturday. Then the first hour would not have passed noon when he would mount the steps and knock, not on post or doorframe but on the underside of the gallery roof itself, and enter and ring the bright cascade of silver dollars onto the scrubbed table in the kitchen where his dinner simmered on the stove and the galvanised tub of hot water and the baking powder can of soft soap and the towel made of scalded flour sacks sewn together and his clean overalls and shirt waited, and Mannie would gather up the money and walk the half-mile to the commissary and buy their next week's supplies and bank the rest of the money in Edmonds' safe and return and they would eat once again without haste or hurry after five days—the sidemeat, the greens, the cornbread, the buttermilk from the well-house, the cake which she baked every Saturday now that she had a stove to bake in.

But when he put his hand on the gate it seemed to him suddenly that there was nothing beyond it. The house had never been his anyway, but now even the new planks and sills and shingles, the hearth and stove and bed, were all a part of the memory of somebody else, so that he stopped in the half-open gate and said aloud, as though he had gone to sleep in one place and then waked suddenly to find himself in another: "Whut's Ah doin hyar?" before he went on. Then he saw the dog. He had forgotten it. He remembered neither seeing nor hearing it since it began to howl just before dawn yesterday—a big dog, a hound with a strain of mastiff from somewhere (he had told Mannie a month after they married: "Ah needs a big dawg. You's de onliest least thing whut ever kep up wid me one day, leff alone fo weeks.") coming out from beneath the gallery and approaching, not running but seeming rather to drift across the dusk until it stood lightly against his leg, its head raised until the tips of his fingers just touched it, facing the house and making no sound; whereupon, as if the animal controlled it, had lain guardian before it during his absence and only this instant relinquished, the shell of planks and shingles facing him solidified, filled, and for the moment he believed that he could not possibly enter it. "But Ah needs to eat," he said. "Us bofe needs to eat," he said, moving on though the dog did not follow until he turned and cursed it. "Come on hyar!" he said. 'Whut you skeered of? She lacked you too, same as me," and they mounted the steps and crossed the porch and entered the house—the dusk-filled single room where all those six months were now crammed and crowded into one instant of time until there was no space left for air to breathe, crammed and crowded about the hearth where the fire which was to have lasted to the end of them, before which in the days before he was able to buy the stove he would enter after his four-mile walk from the mill and find her, the shape of her narrow back and haunches squatting, one narrow spread hand shielding her face from the blaze over which the other hand held the skillet, had already fallen to a dry, light soilure of dead ashes when the sun rose yesterday—and himself standing there while the last of light died about the strong and indomitable beating of his heart and the deep steady arch and collapse of his chest which walking fast over the rough going of woods and fields had not increased and standing still in the quiet and fading room had not slowed down.

Then the dog left him. The light pressure went off his flank; he heard the click and hiss of its claws on the wooden floor as it surged away and he thought at first that it was fleeing. But it stopped just outside the front door, where he could see it now, and the outline of its head as the howl began, and then he saw her too. She was standing in the kitchen door, looking at him. He didn't move. He didn't breathe nor speak until he knew his voice would be all right, his face fixed too not to alarm her. "Mannie," he said. "Hit's awright. Ah aint afraid." Then he took a step toward her, slow, not even raising his hand yet, and stopped. Then he took another step. But this time as soon as he moved she began to fade. He stopped at once, not breathing again, motionless, willing his eyes to see that she had stopped too. But she had not stopped. She was fading, going. "Wait," he said, talking as sweet as he had ever heard his voice speak to a woman: "Den lemme go wid you, honey." But she was going. She was going fast now, he could actually feel between them the insuperable barrier of that very strength which could handle alone a log which would have taken any two other men to handle, of the blood and bones and flesh too strong, invincible for life, having learned at least once with his own eyes how tough, even in sudden and violent death, not a young man's bones and flesh perhaps but the will of that bone and flesh to remain alive, actually was.

Then she was gone. He walked through the door where she had been standing, and went to the stove. He did not light the lamp. He needed no light. He had set the stove up himself and built the shelves for the dishes, from among which he took two plates by feel and from the pot sitting cold on the cold stove he ladled onto the plates the food which his aunt had brought yesterday and of which he had eaten yesterday though now he did not remember when he had eaten it nor what it was, and carried the plates to the scrubbed bare table beneath the single small fading window and drew two chairs up and sat down, waiting again until he knew his voice would be what he wanted it to be. "Come on hyar, now," he said roughly. "Come on hyar and eat yo supper. Ah aint gonter have no—" and ceased, looking down at his plate, breathing the strong, deep pants, his chest arching and collapsing until he stopped it presently and held himself motionless for perhaps a half minute, and raised a spoonful of the cold and glutinous peas to his mouth. The congealed and lifeless mass seemed to bounce on contact with his lips. Not even warmed from mouth-heat, peas and spoon spattered and rang upon the plate; his chair crashed backward and he was standing, feeling the muscles of his jaw beginning to drag his mouth open, tugging upward the top half of his head. But he stopped that too before it became sound, holding himself again while he rapidly scraped the food from his plate onto the other and took it up and left the kitchen, crossed the other room and the gallery and set the plate on the bottom step and went on toward the gate.

The dog was not there, but it overtook him within the first half mile. There was a moon then, their two shadows flitting broken and intermittent among the trees or slanted long and intact across the slope of pasture or old abandoned fields upon the hills, the man moving almost as fast as a horse could have moved over that ground, altering his course each time a lighted window came in sight, the dog trotting at heel while their shadows shortened to the moon's curve until at last they trod them and the last far lamp had vanished and the shadows began to lengthen on the other hand, keeping to heel even when a rabbit burst from almost beneath the man's foot, then lying in the gray of dawn beside the man's prone body, beside the labored heave and collapse of the chest, the loud harsh snoring which sounded not like groans of pain but like someone engaged without arms in prolonged single combat.

When he reached the mill there was nobody there but the fireman—an older man just turning from the woodpile, watching quietly as he crossed the clearing, striding as if he were going to walk not only through the boiler shed but through (or over) the boiler too, the overalls which had been clean yesterday now draggled and soiled and drenched to the knees with dew, the cloth cap flung onto the side of his head, hanging peak downward over his ear as he always wore it, the whites of his eyes rimmed with red and with something urgent and strained about them. "Whar yo bucket?" he said. But before the fireman could answer he had stepped past him and lifted the polished lard pail down from a nail in a post. "Ah just wants a biscuit," he said.

"Eat hit all," the fireman said. "Ah'll eat outen de yuthers' buckets at dinner. Den you gawn home and go to bed. You dont looks good."

"Ah aint come hyar to look," he said, sitting on the ground, his back against the post, the open pail between his knees, cramming the food into his mouth with his hands, wolfing it—peas again, also gelid and cold, a fragment of yesterday's Sunday fried chicken, a few rough chunks of this morning's fried sidemeat, a biscuit the size of a child's cap—indiscriminate, tasteless. The rest of the crew was gathering now, with voices and sounds of movement outside the boiler shed; presently the white foreman rode into the clearing on a horse. He did not look up, setting the empty pail aside, rising, looking at no one, and went to the branch and lay on his stomach and lowered his face to the water, drawing the water into himself with the same deep, strong, troubled inhalations that he had snored with, or as when he had stood in the empty house at dusk yesterday, trying to get air.

Then the trucks were rolling. The air pulsed with the rapid beating of the exhaust and the whine and clang of the saw, the trucks rolling one by one up to the skidway, he mounting the trucks in turn, to stand balanced on the load he freed, knocking the chocks out and casting loose the shackle chains and with his cant-hook squaring the sticks of cypress and gum and oak one by one to the incline and holding them until the next two men of his gang were ready to receive and guide them, until the discharge of each truck became one long rumbling roar punctuated by grunting shouts and, as the morning grew and the sweat came, chanted phrases of song tossed back and forth. He did not sing with them. He rarely ever did, and this morning might have been no different from any other—himself man-height again above the heads which carefully refrained from looking at him, stripped to the waist now, the shirt removed and the overalls knotted about his hips by the suspender straps, his upper body bare except for the handkerchief about his neck and the cap clapped and clinging somehow over his right ear, the mounting sun sweat-glinted steel-blue on the midnight-colored bunch and slip of muscles until the whistle blew for noon and he said to the two men at the head of the skidway: "Look out. Git out de way," and rode the log down the incline, balanced erect upon it in short rapid backward-running steps above the headlong thunder.

His aunt's husband was waiting for him—an old man, as tall as he was, but lean, almost frail, carrying a tin pail in one hand and a covered plate in the other; they too sat in the shade beside the branch a short distance from where the others were opening their dinner pails. The bucket contained a fruit jar of buttermilk packed in a clean damp towsack. The covered dish was a peach pie, still warm. "She baked hit fer you dis mawin," the uncle said. "She say fer you to come home." He didn't answer, bent forward a little, his elbows on his knees, holding the pie in both hands, wolfing at it, the syrupy filling smearing and trickling down his chin, blinking rapidly as he chewed, the whites of his eyes covered a little more by the creeping red. "Ah went to yo house last night, but you want dar. She sent me. She wants you to come on home. She kept de lamp burnin all last night fer you."

"Ah'm awright," he said.

"You aint awright. De Lawd guv, and He tuck away. Put yo faith and trust in Him. And she kin help you."

"Whut faith and trust?" he said. "Whut Mannie ever done ter Him? Whut He wanter come messin wid me and—"

"Hush!" the old man said. "Hush!"

Then the trucks were rolling again. Then he could stop needing to invent to himself reasons for his breathing, until after a while he began to believe he had forgot about breathing since now he could not hear it himself above the steady thunder of the rolling logs; whereupon as soon as he found himself believing he had forgotten it, he knew that he had not, so that instead of tipping the final log onto the skidway he stood up and cast his cant-hook away as if it were a burnt match and in the dying reverberation of the last log's rumbling descent he vaulted down between the two slanted tracks of the skid, facing the log which still lay on the truck. He had done it before—taken a log from the truck onto his hands, balanced, and turned with it and tossed it onto the skidway, but never with a stick of this size, so that in a complete cessation of all sound save the pulse of the exhaust and the light free-running whine of the disengaged saw since every eye there, even that of the white foreman, was upon him, he nudged the log to the edge of the truckframe and squatted and set his palms against the underside of it. For a time there was no movement at all. It was as if the unrational and inanimate wood had invested, mesmerized the man with some of its own primal inertia. Then a voice said quietly: "He got hit. Hit's off de truck," and they saw the crack and gap of air, watching the infinitesimal straightening of the braced legs until the knees locked, the movement mounting infinitesimally through the belly's insuck, the arch of the chest, the neck cords, lifting the lip from the white clench of teeth in passing, drawing the whole head backward and only the bloodshot fixity of the eyes impervious to it, moving on up the arms and the straightening elbows until the balanced log was higher than his head. "Only he aint gonter turn wid dat un," the same voice said. "And when he try to put hit back on de truck, hit gonter kill him." But none of them moved. Then—there was no gathering of supreme effort—the log seemed to leap suddenly backward over his bead of its own volition, spinning, crashing and thundering down the incline; he turned and stepped over the slanting track in one stride and walked through them as they gave way and went on across the clearing toward the woods even though the foreman called after him: "Rider!" and again: "You, Rider!"

At sundown he and the dog were in the river swamp four miles away—another clearing, itself not much larger than a room, a hut, a hovel partly of planks and partly of canvas, an unshaven white man standing in the door beside which a shotgun leaned, watching him as he approached, his hand extended with four silver dollars on the palm. "Ah wants a jug," he said.

"A jug?" the white man said. "You mean a pint. This is Monday. Aint you all running this week?"

"Ah laid off," he said. "Whar's my jug?" waiting, looking at nothing apparently, blinking his bloodshot eyes rapidly in his high, slightly back-tilted head, then turning, the jug hanging from his crooked middle finger against his leg, at which moment the white man looked suddenly and sharply at his eyes as though seeing them for the first time—the eyes which had been strained and urgent this morning and which now seemed to be without vision too and in which no white showed at all—and said,

"Here. Gimme that jug. You dont need no gallon. I'm going to give you that pint, give it to you. Then you get out of here and stay out. Dont come back until—" Then the white man reached and grasped the jug, whereupon the other swung it behind him, sweeping his other arm up and out so that it struck the white man across the chest.

"Look out, white folks," he said. "Hit's mine. Ah done paid you."

The white man cursed him. "No you aint. Here's your money. Put that jug down, nigger."

"Hit's mine," he said, his voice quiet, gentle even, his face quiet save for the rapid blinking of the red eyes. "Ah done paid for hit," turning on, turning his back on the man and the gun both, and recrossed the clearing to where the dog waited beside the path to come to heel again. They moved rapidly on between the close walls of impenetrable cane-stalks which gave a sort of blondness to the twilight and possessed something of that oppression, that lack of room to breathe in, which the walls of his house had had. But this time, instead of fleeing it, he stopped and raised the jug and drew the cob stopper from the fierce duskreek of uncured alcohol and drank, gulping the liquid solid and cold as ice water, without either taste or heat until he lowered the jug and the air got in. "Hah," he said. "Dat's right. Try me. Try me, big boy. Ah gots something hyar now dat kin whup you."

And, once free of the bottom's unbreathing blackness, there was the moon again, his long shadow and that of the lifted jug slanting away as he drank and then held the jug poised, gulping the silver air into his throat until he could breathe again, speaking to the jug: "Come on now. You always claim you's a better man den me. Come on now. Prove it." He drank again, swallowing the chill liquid tamed of taste or heat either while the swallowing lasted, feeling it flow solid and cold with fire, past then enveloping the strong steady panting of his lungs until they too ran suddenly free as his moving body ran in the silver solid wall of air he breasted. And he was all right, his striding shadow and the trotting one of the dog travelling swift as those of two clouds along the hill; the long cast of his motionless shadow and that of the lifted jug slanting across the slope as he watched the frail figure of his aunt's husband toiling up the hill.

"Dey tole me at de mill you was gone," the old man said. "Ah knowed whar to look. Come home, son. Dat ar cant help you."

"Hit done awready hope me," he said. "Ah'm awready home. Ah'm snakebit now and pizen cant hawm me."

"Den stop and see her. Leff her look at you. Dat's an she axes: just leff her look at you—" But he was already moving. "Wait!" the old man cried. "Wait!"

"You cant keep up," he said, speaking into the silver air, breasting aside the silver solid air which began to flow past him almost as fast as it would have flowed past a moving horse. The faint frail voice was already lost in the night's infinitude, his shadow and that of the dog scudding the free miles, the deep strong panting of his chest running free as air now because he was all right.

Then, drinking, he discovered suddenly that no more of the liquid was entering his mouth. Swallowing, it was no longer passing down his throat, his throat and mouth filled now with a solid and unmoving column which without reflex or revulsion sprang, columnar and intact and still retaining the mold of his gullet, outward glinting in the moonlight, splintering, vanishing into the myriad murmur of the dewed grass. He drank again. Again his throat merely filled solidly until two icy rills ran from his mouth-corners; again the intact column sprang silvering, glinting, shivering, while he panted the chill of air into his throat, the jug poised before his mouth while he spoke to it: "Awright. Ah'm ghy try you again. Soon as you makes up yo mind to stay whar I puts you, Ah'll leff you alone." He drank, filling his gullet for the third time and lowered the jug one instant ahead of the bright intact repetition, panting, indrawing the cool of air until he could breathe. He stoppered the cob carefully back into the jug and stood, panting, blinking, the long cast of his solitary shadow slanting away across the hill and beyond, across the mazy infinitude of all the night-bound earth. "Awright," he said. "Ah just misread de sign wrong. Hit's done done me all de help Ah needs. Ah'm awright now. Ah doan needs no mo of hit."

He could see the lamp in the window as he crossed the pasture, passing the black-and-silver yawn of the sandy ditch where he had played as a boy with empty snuff-tins and rusted harness-buckles and fragments of trace-chains and now and then an actual wheel, passing the garden patch where he had hoed in the spring days while his aunt stood sentry over him from the kitchen window, crossing the grassless yard in whose dust he had sprawled and crept before he learned to walk. He entered the house, the room, the light itself, and stopped in the door, his head backtilted a little as if he could not see, the jug hanging from his crooked finger, against his leg. "Unc Alec say you wanter see me," he said.

"Not just to see you," his aunt said. "To come home whar we kin help you."

"Ah'm awright," he said. "Ah doan needs no help."

"No," she said. She rose from the chair and came and grasped his arm as she had grasped it yesterday at the grave. Again, as on yesterday, the forearm was like iron under her hand. "No! When Alec come back and tole me how you had wawked off de mill and de sun not half down, Ah knowed why and whar. And dat cant help you."

"Hit done awready hope me. Ah'm awright now."

"Dont lie to me," she said. "You aint never lied to me. Dont lie to me now."

Then he said it. It was his own voice, without either grief or amazement, speaking quietly out of the tremendous panting of his chest which in a moment now would begin to strain at the walls of this room too. But he would be gone in a moment.

"Nome," he said, "Hit aint done me no good."

"And hit cant! Cant nothing help you but Him! Ax Him! Tole Him about hit! He wants to hyar you and help you!"

"Efn He God, Ah dont needs to tole Him. Efn He God, He awready know hit. Awright. Hyar Ah is. Leff Him come down hyar and do me some good."

"On yo knees!" she cried. "On yo knees and ax Him!"

But it was not his knees on the floor, it was his feet. And for a space he could hear her feet too on the planks of the hall behind him and her voice crying after him from the door: "Spoot! Spoot!"—crying after him across the moon-dappled yard the name he had gone by in his childhood and adolescence, before the men he worked with and the bright dark nameless women he had taken in course and forgotten until he saw Mannie that day and said, "Ah'm thu wid all dat," began to call him Rider.

It was just after midnight when he reached the mill. The dog was gone now. This time he could not remember when nor where. At first he seemed to remember hurling the empty jug at it. But later the jug was still in his hand and it was not empty, although each time he drank now the two icy runnels streamed from his mouth-corners, sopping his shirt and overalls until he walked constantly in the fierce chill of the liquid tamed now of flavor and heat and odor too even when the swallowing ceased. "Sides that," he said, "Ah wouldn't thow nothin at him. Ah mout kick him efn he needed hit and was close enough. But Ah wouldn't ruint no dog chunkin hit."

The jug was still in his hand when he entered the clearing and paused among the mute soaring of the moon-blond lumber-stacks. He stood in the middle now of the unimpeded shadow which he was treading again as he had trod it last night, swaying a little, blinking about at the stacked lumber, the skidway, the piled logs waiting for tomorrow, the boiler-shed all quiet and blanched in the moon. And then it was all right. He was moving again. But he was not moving, he was drinking, the liquid cold and swift and tasteless and requiring no swallowing, so that he could not tell if it were going down inside or outside. But it was all right. And now he was moving, the jug gone now and he didn't know the when or where of that either. He crossed the clearing and entered the boiler shed and went on through it, crossing the junctureless backloop of time's trepan, to the door of the tool-room, the faint glow of the lantern beyond the plank-joints, the surge and fall of living shadow, the mutter of voices, the mute click and scutter of the dice, his hand loud on the barred door, his voice loud too: "Open hit. Hit's me. Ah'm snakebit and bound to die."

Then he was through the door and inside the tool-room. They were the same faces—three members of his timber gang, three or four others of the mill crew, the white night-watchman with the heavy pistol in his hip pocket and the small heap of coins and worn bills on the floor before him, one who was called Rider and was Rider standing above the squatting circle, swaying a little, blinking, the dead muscles of his face shaped into smiling while the white man stared up at him. "Make room, gamblers," he said. "Make room. Ah'm snakebit and de pizen cant hawm me."

"You're drunk," the white man said. "Get out of here. One of you niggers open the door and get him out of here."

"Dass awright, boss-man," he said, his voice equable, his face still fixed in the faint rigid smiling beneath the blinking of the red eyes; "Ah aint drunk. Ah just cant wawk straight fer dis yar money weighin me down."

Now he was kneeling too, the other six dollars of his last week's pay on the floor before him, blinking, still smiling at the face of the white man opposite, then, still smiling, he watched the dice pass from hand to hand around the circle as the white man covered the bets, watching the soiled and palm-worn money in front of the white man gradually and steadily increase, watching the white man cast and win two doubled bets in succession then lose on for twenty-five cents, the dice coming to him at last, the cupped snug clicking of them in his fist. He spun a coin into the center.

"Shoots a dollar," he said, and cast, and watched the white man pick up the dice and flip them back to him. "Ah lets hit lay," he said. "Ah'm snakebit. Ah kin pass wid anything," and cast, and this time one of the negroes flipped the dice back. "Ah lets hit lay," he said, and cast, and moved as the white man moved, catching the white man's wrist before his hand reached the dice, the two of them squatting, facing each other above the dice and the money, his left hand grasping the white man's wrist, his face still fixed in the rigid and deadened smiling, his voice equable, almost deferential: "Ah kin pass even wid miss-outs. But dese hyar yuther boys—" until the white man's hand sprang open and the second pair of dice clattered onto the floor beside the first two and the white man wrenched free and sprang up and back land reached the hand backward toward the pocket where the pistol was.

The razor hung between his shoulder-blades from a loop of cotton string round his neck inside his shirt. The same motion of the hand which brought the razor forward over his shoulder flipped the blade open and freed it from the cord, the blade opening on until the back edge of it lay across the knuckles of his fist, his thumb pressing the handle into his closing fingers, so that in the second before the half-drawn pistol exploded he actually struck at the white man's throat not with the blade but with a sweeping blow of his fist, following through in the same motion so that not even the first jet of blood touched his hand or arm.

2

After it was over—it didn't take long; they found the prisoner on the following day, hanging from the bell-rope in a negro schoolhouse about two miles from the sawmill, and the coroner had pronounced his verdict of death at the hands of a person or persons unknown and surrendered the body to its next of kin all within five minutes—the sheriff's deputy who had been officially in charge of the business was telling his wife about it. They were in the kitchen. His wife was cooking supper. The deputy had been out of bed and in motion ever since the jail delivery shortly before midnight of yesterday and had covered considerable ground since, and he was spent now from lack of sleep and hurried food at hurried and curious hours and, sitting in a chair beside the stove, a little hysterical too.

"Them damn niggers," he said. "I swear to godfrey, it's a wonder we have as little trouble with them as we do. Because why? Because they aint human. They look like a man and they walk on their hind legs like a man, and they can talk and you can understand them and you think they are understanding you, at least now and then. But when it comes to the normal human feelings and sentiments of human beings, they might just as well be a damn herd of wild buffaloes. Now you take this one today—"

"I wish you would," his wife said harshly. She was a stout woman, handsome once, graying now and with a neck definitely too short, who looked not harried at all but composed in fact, only choleric. Also, she had attended a club rook-party that afternoon and had won the first, the fifty-cent, prize until another member had insisted on a recount of the scores and the ultimate throwing out of one entire game. "Take him out of my kitchen, anyway. You sheriffs! Sitting around that courthouse all day long, talking. It's no wonder two or three men can walk in and take prisoners out from under your very noses. They would take your chairs and desks and window sills too if you ever got your feet and backsides off of them that long."

"It's more of them Birdsongs than just two or three," the deputy said. "There's forty-two active votes in that connection. Me and Maydew taken the poll-list and counted them one day. But listen—" The wife turned from the stove, carrying a dish. The deputy snatched his feet rapidly out of the way as she passed him, passed almost over him, and went into the dining room. The deputy raised his voice a little to carry the increased distance: "His wife dies on him. All right. But does he grieve? He's the biggest and busiest man at the funeral. Grabs a shovel before they even got the box into the grave they tell me, and starts throwing dirt onto her faster than a slip scraper could have done it. But that's all right—" His wife came back. He moved his feet again and altered his voice again to the altered range: "—maybe that's how he felt about her. There aint any law against a man rushing his wife into the ground, provided he never had nothing to do with rushing her to the cemetery too. But here the next day he's the first man back at work except the fireman, getting back to the mill before the fireman had his fire going, let alone steam up; five minutes earlier and he could even have helped the fireman wake Birdsong up so Birdsong could go home and go back to bed again, or he could even have cut Birdsong's throat then and saved everybody trouble.

"So he comes to work, the first man on the job, when McAndrews and everybody else expected him to take the day off since even a nigger couldn't want no better excuse for a holiday than he had just buried his wife, when a white man would have took the day off out of pure respect no matter how he felt about his wife, when even a little child would have had sense enough to take a day off when he would still get paid for it too. But not him. The first man there, jumping from one log truck to another before the starting whistle quit blowing even, snatching up ten-foot cypress logs by himself and throwing them around like matches. And then, when everybody had finally decided that that's the way to take him, the way he wants to be took, he walks off the job in the middle of the afternoon without by-your-leave or much obliged or goodbye to McAndrews or nobody else, gets himself a whole gallon of bust-skull white-mule whisky, comes straight back to the mill and to the same crap game where Birdsong has been running crooked dice on them mill niggers for fifteen years, goes straight to the same game where he has been peace-fully losing a probably steady average ninety-nine percent of his pay ever since he got big enough to read the spots on them miss-out dice, and cuts Birdsong's throat clean to the neckbone five minutes later." The wife passed him again and went to the dining room. Again he drew his feet back and raised his voice:

"So me and Maydew go out there. Not that we expected to do any good, as he had probably passed Jackson, Tennessee, about daylight; and besides, the simplest way to find him would be just to stay close behind them Birdsong boys. Of course there wouldn't be nothing hardly worth bringing back to town after they did find him, but it would close the case. So it's just by the merest chance that we go by his house; I dont even remember why we went now, but we did; and there he is. Sitting behind the barred front door with a open razor on one knee and a loaded shotgun on the other? No. He was asleep. A big pot of field peas et clean empty on the stove, and him laying in the back yard asleep in the broad sun with just his head under the edge of the porch in the shade and a dog that looked like a cross between a bear and a Polled Angus steer yelling fire and murder from the back door. And we wake him and he sets up and says, 'Awright, white folks. Ah done it. Jest dont lock me up,' and Maydew says, 'Mr Birdsong's kinfolks aint going to lock you up neither. You'll have plenty of fresh air when they get hold of you,' and he says, 'Ah done it. Jest dont lock me up'—advising, instructing the sheriff not to lock him up; he done it all right and it's too bad but it aint convenient for him to be cut off from the fresh air at the moment. So we loaded him into the car, when here come the old woman—his ma or aunt or something—panting up the road at a dog-trot, wanting to come with us too, and Maydew trying to explain to her what would maybe happen to her too if them Birdsong kin catches us before we can get him locked up, only she is coming anyway, and like Maydew says, her being in the car too might be a good thing if the Birdsongs did happen to run into us, because after all interference with the law cant be condoned even if the Bird-song connection did carry that beat for Maydew last summer.

"So we brought her along too and got him to town and into the jail all right and turned him over to Ketcham and Ketcham taken him on up stairs and the old woman coming too, right on up to the cell, telling Ketcham, 'Ah tried to raise him right. He was a good boy. He aint never been in no trouble till now. He will suffer for what he done. But dont let the white folks get him,' until Ketcham says, 'You and him ought to thought of that before he started barbering white men without using no lather first.' So he locked them both up in the cell because he felt like Maydew did, that her being in there with him might be a good influence on the Birdsong boys if anything started if he should happen to be running for sheriff or something when Maydew's term was up. So Ketcham come on back down stairs and pretty soon the chain gang come in and went on up to the bull pen and he thought things had settled down for a while when all of a sudden he begun to hear the yelling, not howling: yelling, though there wasn't no words in it, and he grabbed his pistol and run back up stairs to the bull pen where the chain gang was and Ketcham could see into the cell where the old woman was kind of squinched down in one corner and where that nigger had done tore that iron cot clean out of the floor it was bolted to and was standing in the middle of the cell, holding the cot over his head like it was a baby's cradle, yelling, and says to the old woman, 'Ah aint goan hurt you,' and throws the cot against the wall and comes and grabs holt of that steel barred door and rips it out of the wall, bricks hinges and all, and walks out of the cell toting the door over his head like it was a gauze window-screen, hollering, 'It's awright. It's awright. Ah aint trying to git away.'

"Of course Ketcham could have shot him right there, but like he said, if it wasn't going to be the law, then them Birdsong boys ought to have the first lick at him. So Ketcham dont shoot. Instead, he jumps in behind where them chain gang niggers was kind of backed off from that steel door, hollering, 'Grab him! Throw him down!' except the niggers hung back at first too until Ketcham gets in where he can kick the ones he can reach, batting at the others with the flat of the pistol until they rush him. And Ketcham says that for a full minute that nigger would grab them as they come in and fling them clean across the room like they was rag dolls, saying, 'Ah aint tryin to git out. Ah aint tryin to git out,' until at last they pulled him down—a big mass of nigger heads and arms and legs boiling around on the floor and even then Ketcham says every now and then a nigger would come flying out and go sailing through the air across the room, spraddled out like a flying squirrel and with his eyes sticking out like car headlights, until at last they had him down and Ketcham went in and begun peeling away niggers until he could see him laying there under the pile of them, laughing, with tears big as glass marbles running across his face and down past his ears and making a kind of popping sound on the floor like somebody dropping bird eggs, laughing and laughing and saying, 'Hit look lack Ah just cant quit thinking. Look lack Ah just cant quit.' And what do you think of that?"

"I think if you eat any supper in this house you'll do it in the next five minutes," his wife said from the dining room. "I'm going to clear this table then and I'm going to the picture show."

Timothy Findley

Timothy Findley was born in Toronto in 1930. He was first trained as an actor, working in New York, London, and Stratford with Alec Guinness, Tyrone Guthrie, and Peter Brook, and this interest has continued through the writing of film, radio, and television scripts. Findley is perhaps best known for his novel *The Wars* (1977), which won the Governor General's Award and was made into a film, but this work was preceded by two novels, *The Last of the Crazy People* (1967) and *The Butterfly Plague* (1969), and followed by *Famous Last Words* (1981), *Not Wanted on the Voyage* (1984), and *The Telling of Lies* (1986). Findley's short stories are collected in *Dinner Along the Amazon* (1984) and *Stones* (1988). He lives on a farm in Cannington, Ontario.

In an interview with Donald Cameron in 1971 (*Conversations with Canadian Novelists*, I), Findley speaks of the difficulties that beset an author who is willing to confront the demands of his material, his vision. "It's vicious being a writer. Along with all the other impossible things, such as the loneliness and the lack of security—not just financial security, either—one of the worst things is the inner demand that you be professional. You have to be a professional. You have to be utterly disciplined about whatever you're doing, which is to say you have to make yourself do the thing your integrity has told you is the right thing to do, despite all the fearful and cautionary advice you get from your mind. All authors are whispered to by their characters. The characters want life, and you have to give it to them. It's a little like rape, with no recourse to abortion. They take your body, and you have to give birth. So 'professionalism' is obedience, to be obedient to the whispering inside of you, among others. That's one of the great disciplines. . . ."

In an interview with Alan Twigg in 1984 (*Strong Voices*), Findley acknowledges that his writing takes the form of exploration, not explanation. "I don't make the map before I go. . . . It's all a question of recognition on my part. Trusting the inner thing, whether it's instinct or whatever it is you're trusting." Trusting instinct does not mean dispensing with your internal editor, but, rather, being willing to set it aside in order to explore areas of thought and experience that may be painful, frightening, and fraught with various taboos. In his work, Findley has been willing to explore the violence that besets us as a society, and as individuals, all those signs of fascism that are manifested not only in our institutions, but also in our treatment of women, minorities, loved ones, the environment, and, ultimately, ourselves. The world, he suggests, is a precious ark that must be cherished; only an understanding of our mutual interdependence with all living things will save us.

Findley's work is known, not surprisingly, for its theatricality, for movement, structure, design, the sense of character. In his creative memoir, *Inside Memory: Pages from a Writer's Workbook* (1990), Findley explains how the writer's antennae are alert to the tiniest nuance in any situation: "So this is what writing is like—for me. Your eye and your ear are always poised upon the moment. So that whenever there is speech, you hear it and whenever there is gesture you see it: no matter where it occurs in the room. . . ." His interest in characters who border on madness stems from his awareness that, somehow, the "mad" person can see things—"the heart of things. Of hurt, for instance"—that we do not see, because he or she has no protective walls: "one thing about the 'mad,' you see, is they don't like lies. So this is why I seize so often upon these people as the heroes of my work. It's only because they have this straight, flung-out connection through the mind to some kind of absolute clarity. And this is what fiction is all about: achieving the clarity obscured by facts."

When asked by his companion, William Whitehead, in a mock interview, to relate his training as dancer, actor, and painter to the task of writing, Findley said: "Yes. Yes. Words. Well, now. . . . Take dance. What a dancer does is make a series of statements. And the statements are made out of gestures: gestures in a sequence. So words—words are the vocabulary of literate gesture. And the combinations of your words have to be as precise as the combinations of gestures used by a dancer to make an articulate statement in dance. And there's something else, I think, to be said about this. You know, when you learn to dance—when you learn to move—you learn to move, to make each gesture from the centre of your body: from the solar plexus—from the diaphragm. You learn that everything must originate and grow outward towards the conclusion of the gesture: the formation of the statement. And, as an actor, when you learn how to speak—you learn to speak from there: from the centre—from the diaphragm. And, oddly enough—and here we come to writing—when a sentence *hits*—or when a paragraph *hits*—that's where it hits. In the solar plexus. . . . Words in a sentence are a written gesture. And if the cadence is wrong—if the rhythm is wrong—if a single syllable is out of place—the sentence fails . . . the book fails. Why? Because you have failed to impel the reader forward with every gesture . . . right to the 'fingertips'—all the way from the solar plexus. That's where books are written. That's where readers read."

Dinner Along the Amazon

For Robin Phillips

Perhaps the house was to blame. Once, it had been Olivia's pride; her safe, good place. Everyone else—including Michael—found it charming. Prestigious. Practical. North Seton Drive was a great location. Running out of Rosedale down towards the ravine, all its back yards were set with trees and rolling lawns. Autumn and spring, Olivia could happily walk or ride her bicycle to Branksome Hall, where she had been teaching now for six years. She really had no right to complain. Number 38 was handsome enough—its glass all shining; its paint unchipped.

Recently, however, Olivia had begun to balk at the physical act of arriving there; of being on the sidewalk and turning in towards the house, admitting that she belonged on that cement and was meant to walk through that front door. There was always something lying on the grass she would not allow was hers: a torn, wet *Star* or a bit of orange peel—(*I didn't put that there!*)—something left by a neighbour's child or someone else's dog. And even, once, a sinister pair of men's blue undershorts.

Inside, the house gave off the smell of discontent; of ashes in the sink and slippers prowling through the halls at night; of schisms rusting like a set of knives. Also the odour—faintly underarm—of Michael's petulance and Olivia's silence hiding in the closets. *Boo. . . .*

Today, on the twenty-eighth of April, Olivia entered the house with her arms full of flowers at five in the afternoon. The flowers were done up in green paper cones, but still the smell of them was rampant under her chin and she stood in the middle of the hall not speaking—only listening—dizzy with the scent of freesia.

Michael was in here somewhere. Up in the sun room, probably. Drunk. Conrad's car was in the driveway, rubbing its already damaged bumper up against the garage. This could only signal they would both be drunk: not only Michael but Conrad, too. Old friends and empty bottles. Poor deadly Conrad, dragging the unwelcome past with all its frayed address books and stringy love affairs behind him, had come to 'visit for a while'—i.e. to crash until he'd pulled himself together. God damn old friends.

It could not be borne. There wasn't time for the past in their lives. Not now. Not ever. All it did was crowd you into corners and turn out the lights. Then it rattled you with guilt and regret and left you inarticulate and incapacitated. Who needs that? *I'm taking enough of a beating from the present, thank you very much,* Olivia thought. *Damn you, Conrad. Much as I love you, if you hadn't come, I could talk to Michael. Now. Tonight. I could tell him and get it over with.*

No I couldn't.

Olivia peered to her left, into the dim shuttered light of Michael's den. She tried to imagine the thing in her belly running through that doorway into those shadows to find its father. It was impossible. He would slam the door in its face. *Get out!*

She knew this was only a coward's excuse. Michael didn't hate children: he hated the future—and that was different. He hated anything he couldn't control: he hated anything he didn't know. Certainty was the only ally you could trust, in Michael's books. Certainty and literature. History—(maybe)—and a few poems written on the backs of envelopes. He *wanted* children, but he didn't want their lives to run beyond his own. He couldn't bear to inject them into the future—only into the past. Michael would like it best if his children had preceded him. Then he could say to them; 'Everything I told you was the truth. I have never lied. It is all borne out by what you have seen: the known—the safe.' The future was his enemy.

In Michael's den, there were piles and piles of notebooks and reams of paper. These were his diatribes—some of them four or six or ten years old. They were covered with marmalade fungi and peanut butter mushrooms. Olivia smiled. The rug was stained with his solipsisms. She had listened to him roaring there, amongst his books—knocking over his drinks—jabbing his fingers at her: 'Just you wait, Olivia! Every word I say is true. . . .' Then he would have to verify every word—dragging down all the pertinent books, drawing out all the pertinent pieces of paper, going crazy—ranting—when he couldn't find what he wanted. In its way, it was a sad, dead room. Echoes hiding in the curtains. The roll-top desk had pigeon holes that smelled, Olivia swore, of pigeons: all the pigeons flown away with their messages—the words that Michael couldn't find. In a bowl, he kept all his paper clips attached to rubber bands—ready to fire at the passing parade or at any rash intruder who brought the future into his presence: man, woman or child . . .

No. There could be no child.

Olivia turned towards the kitchen, leaning her ear in the direction of the stair-well, hoping to hear the sound of sober conversation. Even of laughter. But there was nothing. Only the silence between drinks. Up there, sitting in the sun room, they were probably holding their breath: Michael and Conrad, hiding from Olivia. *Don't give away our secret, Connie.* Mustn't let her know we're only ten years old, when she thinks we're twelve, at least.

Olivia took a deep breath that left her gasping for another.

It *was* the house: its airlessness; its *culs-de-sac*; its bear pits waiting for the bears. It had lost its capacity to generate dreams. All it reflected, as you moved from room to room, was the tidy horror of what was really going to happen.

As Olivia entered the kitchen, the sun room made a creaking noise above her head. She looked up, thinking; *they're walking on tiptoe. How ridiculous. Two grown men . . .*

She crossed to the sink, making sure her heels could be heard as she went. Still clothed in all her outer garments, her tweed coat; her three layers of scarves; her soft, rich sweater; her wool lined boots—she set her briefcase on one cutting board and the packets of flowers on the other. She turned on the tap for a glass of water and reached to the left for a thick, red tumbler with a crack in it. Habit. It was always there, the last of its kind. There had once been eight—a gift from Conrad. Pinned to the curtain above the sink was one of Mrs Kemp's inimitable notes:

> Mrs Penny I done the back room up for Mr Fastbinder and put a towl and a wash cloth on his burow. You run out of blue sheets so he only got one and the other ones yellow. Grennel is loss again. Hiden.

Olivia, reading, was holding the tumbler under the tap.

> I could not find no more OLD DUTCH so have put down OLD DUTCH on the list. 4 large ones please as the bathroom really eats them up. Mr Fastbinder near creamed the garge. Dont let them tell you different. I will be in tomorrow to clean up after.
>
> Lilah Kemp.

The cold water ran on Olivia's hands, comforting, numbing.

> Ps Prof Penny did not eat his sandwhich. Toona if you want one.

All the usual digs at Michael were intact. Mortal enemies—Michael Penny and Mrs Kemp. And Grendel. Grendel was Michael's beloved dog and, like his master, he always hid from Mrs Kemp and her dreaded vacuum cleaner and her dreadful tuna sandwiches, the edges of which she always left in Grendel's dish.

Olivia set aside the tumbler and took down the note, threw it into the garbage pail and replaced the pin in the folds of the curtain. As she drank her water, she wondered where the dog might be this time. Lying poisoned, perhaps, in someone's flowerbed—the victim of Mrs Kemp's 'toona'. The detritus of neglect. Poor old Grendel.

Poor old Grendel had a habit of lying dead in other people's flowerbeds, but his favourite place of all was in behind the curtain of the shower stall, where he portrayed with alarming veracity the corpses of his master and his mistress—one and then the other. Michael and Olivia, dead.

Olivia's hand went down to rest on her belly and the red tumbler, in the other hand, shook. *Michael first and then Olivia—dead.* I am not a murderer. Not. I am doing what is right. The only right thing: the only possible thing.

She began to cry—(*oh why am I crying?*)—her gaze shifting sideways, awash—(*please: it's so shaming*)—towards the flowers—(*and stupid: stop*). What had the flowers been for, she wondered, setting the tumbler aside. To get her past the front door without throwing up? Not that. No. She could tolerate the tension one more week—so what had the flowers been for? Perhaps, she decided, they were for Grendel, always 'dying'. Or for Michael, still alive. Or for the undug grave in her belly. Pick a card—any card. Now put it back in the deck. Just don't tell me which card it was. . . .

'Hallo.'

Olivia grabbed the sink and nearly fell before she turned.

Standing in the doorway was a man she had never seen before. A man—a 'boy'. He was in his early twenties.

'Yes?' she said.

His arms were full of brown paper packages.

'Who are you?' he said, with casual, inbred impertinence.

Olivia was flabbergasted. 'I'm . . . Olivia Penny,' she said. *And this is my house,* she almost added. But didn't.

'Are you Professor Penny's sister, then?' The young man barged completely into the kitchen. The brown paper packages were clinking suspiciously like future toasts, and the young man was trying not to spill them before they could be proposed.

'No, I am not Professor Penny's God damn sister. I am Professor Penny's God damn wife,' said Olivia, stepping aside to avoid being trampled. 'And who the hell are you?'

'I'm with Conrad,' the young man said. He laid his loot—eight bottles of wine, four bottles of scotch—beside and on top of the flowers and turned to smile at Olivia. 'You're a scream,' he said, and put out his hand. 'Conrad didn't tell me you were *funny*,' he added. 'I'm Rodney Farquhar.' (His grip was like the proverbial vise.) 'Or should I say I'm Conrad's God damn lover?'

'Why are you here?' said Olivia.

Rodney Farquhar's face was emptied of all expression. Perhaps he didn't know the answer to the question.

'You've just set all your things on top of my flowers,' Olivia continued. 'Would you please find some other place?'

Rodney moved in on the bottles and began to shift them, two by two, onto the kitchen table.

'Why are you here?' Olivia repeated.

'I was sent to get the booze,' he said. 'I've just come back. . . .'

'I can see that. Booze for what?'

'For the party,' said Rodney. His back was to her.

Party?

'What party?' said Olivia. Her eyes had narrowed. Her blood was rising.

'Conrad's party,' said Rodney.

'Conrad is giving a party? Where?'

'Here, of course.'

Olivia ground her teeth and was speechless for a moment. Then she said, 'Am I invited?'

Conrad was lying in the bath. The bathroom was full of steam and the steam was scented with Conrad's favourite cologne: *Chanel 19.* Michael was seated on the toilet, the lid down—its grey fur cover slightly damp beneath him. Conrad could barely be seen in the fog.

'Aren't you going to boil yourself to death in there?' Michael asked.

'Never,' said Conrad. 'The heat is wonderful. It spreads the alcohol faster through the system. Give me another. . . .'

Conrad's hand, with goblet, appeared from the steam. Michael poured more scotch and the hand withdrew and then Michael poured more scotch into his own Waterford goblet and took a great, raw mouthful; 'ahhhh . . .' He set the goblet on the floor, fingering its cut design. 'Always drink the best from the best,' he said. 'So, who have you invited?'

'Fabiana Holbach,' said Conrad.

'Yes. And who else?'

'Who cares who else? Fabiana Holbach. That's all that matters.'

'So I gather,' Michael sighed. He lighted a damp cigarette, with a damp recalcitrant match. 'Are you sure this is really a good idea? Inviting Fabiana after all these years?'

'All these years number precisely three,' said Conrad. 'Give me a cigarette.'

Michael handed over the one already lit and lighted another.

'You realize, of course,' he said, 'she's married, now.'

'People can always be convinced their current marriages don't work,' said Conrad.

Michael muttered 'yes' and 'amen' to this, but not loud enough for Conrad to hear.

'What's her name, now?' said Conrad.

'Mrs Jackman Powell.'

The bath fell silent. Not a ripple.

'You don't approve, I take it,' said Michael.

'It's neither here nor there,' said Conrad. 'Truth is, I always thought that *Jackman* had to be the most pretentious name a man could have. Isn't his brother's name plain old Tom?'

'Yes.'

'Maybe their mother's name was Jackman.'

'No. Their mother's name was Tompkins.'

Conrad laughed. Then sobered. 'Son-of-a-bitch,' he said. 'So she married Jackman Powell.'

'That's right.' Michael was watching all he could see of Conrad—the arm that lay along the rim of the tub; the shape of the neck; the thrust of the head as it bent to the glass to drink; above all, the tension in the hand that held the cigarette so hard against the tub, the cigarette broke and the lighted end of it fell to the floor. Conrad didn't even notice. All he did was mutter: 'sons-of-bitches.'

'Who?'

'All of them,' Conrad said with a kind of vehemence Michael had never heard from his friend before. 'All of the God damn Powells. God damn sons-of-bitches.' Conrad sat disconsolate, still barely visible.

What, Michael wondered, could have happened to Conrad—usually so resilient and now, apparently, defeated by the mention of a mere name. They had spent all their school days laughing. Not that a person could go on laughing forever. Michael was perfectly aware of this and of the darker things that had affected Conrad's life. But this was something new; unknown. As if the laughter had escaped and Conrad could not locate it.

'I suppose,' Conrad said, 'this means Fabiana will actually bring him with her. Jackman. I suppose this means I'll have to face him . . . stand there and actually shake his God damn hand.'

'I suppose so. Does it matter?'

'Yes. It matters.'

'Why?'

'Won't go into it. Later, maybe. After they've gone. Not now. The son-of-a-bitch. . . .'

'You've said that. Several times.'

'I know I have. Leave me alone.'

'You know I can't leave you alone, Con. . . .' (Michael was using a swishy, sibilant voice—the one he always used to tease Conrad.) 'I adore you.'

'Don't,' said Conrad. 'This isn't funny.'

'I'm sorry.' Michael lighted another cigarette and handed it through the mist to Conrad. Ever since Conrad's father had died, three years ago, there were things you couldn't talk about. Not always having to do with Fastbinder senior (whose name had been Karl). Sometimes with mysteries Michael wasn't privy to. The causes of Conrad's silence: the long sojourn abroad in Italy and Spain; his sudden reappearance; Rodney Farquhar; Fabiana Holbach Powell. . . . God knew, any or all of these things could and should be the centres of conversation. But, more often than not, they were the cause of snapping jaws and bitten tongues.

'Change the subject,' said Conrad. 'Help me understand what's wrong between you and Olivia. Give me something to laugh about.'

'You think we're going to laugh about *that*?' said Michael.

'Maybe,' said Conrad. 'Is there another woman?'

'No,' said Michael. 'I wish there was.'

'What do you mean? Is there someone you love?'

'Yes.'

'Someone you can't have?'

'Yes. I suppose you could put it that way.'

'Who?'

'Olivia.'

'Oh.' Conrad drank from his glass and took a drag from his cigarette. 'Have you ever seriously thought of falling in love with me?' he said.

'I wouldn't know how to behave in bed,' said Michael, trying to be funny: failing. 'What do you do with Rodney?'

'I admire him, dear,' said Conrad. 'He adores it. I tell him he has the most beautiful pudendum known to man or boy. A palpable lie of course. But Rodney believes it. Sometimes I pull it for him.'

'Don't be so God damn crude. That's disgusting.'

'Well—you asked.'

'It's so childish.'

'Precisely. And Rodney is a child.'

'And you? What do you get out of all this?'

'Notoriety. Open doors. Rodney's connections are quite spectacular, you know.'

'But you don't need open doors, Con. Every door is open to you.'

Conrad was silent. Then he said: '*was*.'

'You mean to tell me you've taken up with that young man just to get through a few doors? It's grotesque.'

'How the hell else am I supposed to get through? Who else would take me? I'm a forty-year-old faggot without a cent to my name.'

'That's only temporary, Con.'

'You're damn right it is. Any minute now, I'm going to be a forty-*one*-year-old faggot without a cent to my name. And stop laughing! Rodney's getting restless. The young always do. They wake up one morning and they *see* you. That's why I always insist on separate rooms. Never let your lover see you, Michael. It's death.' Conrad held out his goblet. 'If anyone turns up here tonight, it's only going to be because Rodney Farquhar asked them. I may be the attraction—but it's Rodney's circus.'

Michael said, 'That's ridiculous' and poured more scotch.

'It's not ridiculous. Alas,' said Conrad, lying back in the bath. 'I overheard him on the phone. "*Do come and see old Conrad again. He's so amusing. Tells such wonderfully funny stories. Even gets drunk and falls down . . . but never loses consciousness. I tell you, it's a scream. He once had a whole conversation with the Princess of Rheims lying flat on his back in the middle of the floor. The whole room flocked to him. People were actually introduced while he lay there. The footmen brought him drinks and got on their knees to serve him.*" I heard him, Michael. He could sell tickets. But I can't. I'm the one they all come to see, lying down on the rug. You do have a rug, I hope.'

Michael could see Conrad, now. The steam was beginning to dissipate. His skin was alarmingly pale; his arms and shoulders lacked entirely the tension of muscles; his neck was like a girl's, stretching to hold the tremulous chin in place and the large, round head with its dank, stringy hair seemed unable to contain his skull which pushed against the skin like a swollen melon about to burst. His hands were almost ridiculously fine; waxen, beautifully shaped and manicured. . . .

'Please stop staring,' said Conrad. 'Tell me about Olivia.'

Michael did not say all of this that follows. He only said the parts he could articulate. The rest—the precision and the syntax—were in his mind, but silent under a cloud of scotch and daydreams. Downstairs, he could hear Olivia setting the table in the dining room—telling Rodney she didn't have anything that matched by way of crystal and china—all because Mrs Kemp had her own definition of the word 'set': '*break eight and leave four.* . . .' Rodney could also be heard on the telephone, ordering food from Fenton's. Grendel was found in the hall closet and came up the stairs to lie outside the bathroom door.

Michael said: 'When you said you always insisted on separate rooms, I understood. Our bed—Olivia's and mine—is divided down the middle by the Grand Canyon. We might as well live in separate hotels.'

Conrad glanced at Michael, huge and majestic, just a shape in the steam: back-lit—hovering on the toilet seat—holding both the bottle and his goblet—his head turned sideways, looking for the words. Michael was six foot four and he had a club foot that no one ever talked about. It affected his walk, of course, but not outrageously and on the occasions when it pained him, he would remove the boot and rest the foot on a table or a chair. He was resting it now on the edge of the tub.

She's gone away somewhere, Con: gone without going, of course.

Conrad waved his hand in the soapy water, watching it vanish.

Now what am I? A sort of bachelor, living in her house; always on the periphery of Olivia's life. 'Goodbye, Michael.' 'Goodbye, Olivia.' 'I'm going to the other end of the sofa, now.' Gone. Like that.

I saw a movie once. One of those 'Nature of Things' on the CBC. It was a film about some tribe in Borneo. One of those primitive tribes—still living almost a prehistoric existence. Ceremonial killings. Sexual segregation. Ritual circumcision. Unbelievable savagery. The way they treated one another—slaughtered their animals—slaughtered their enemies. Three things stood out: three I will never forget. One was the pig thing.

The women with children lived in special houses—groups of women and children—until the children grew to be a certain age. And they had these pigs, you see, as pets. The women and the babies and pigs all lived together and, the way it was shown, they seemed to be quite happy. Then the men would decide it was time to have a nice feast of pork and they would come and drag away the pigs and they would kill them. The women's pets, you see. The children's pets. But it was only the men who got to eat them. Pork was supposed to induce some special kind of magic. So off they went—the men—to their bachelors' quarters where they'd roast these pigs and sit around having magic dreams.

Another thing was the women killing their babies. But only their boy babies. Only their boys. But it wasn't always . . . I mean, they didn't necessarily kill every boy.

What you have to know is, the women did all the work. The only thing they didn't do was hunt. But everything else was left up to them and they had to do it all with their babies on their backs and their children dragging along behind them. You could see it must drive them mad; all these children and all this work and, all of a sudden, there would be this moment when one of them would take off down to the river. Where she would drown her baby son. Not quite dispassionately—certainly with anger—but suddenly: coldly—methodically—without remorse. It was awful. You knew it was revenge for how the men had made them live and for what the men had done to their pigs.

And then there was this other thing—the third thing I remember.

This is about the bachelors. Even the husbands were 'bachelors'. And they moved in and out of the women's lives—mating with them—not 'making love' but truly mating, animal style. And stealing their pigs and watching the women—always from a distance. There were these huts—retreats—high up in the mountains where the bachelors went. Also, there were these compounds where the growing boys were kept. Not just kept with the men—but, really, kept apart from the women. And this was some kind of privilege. Different, you see, from the dowdy huts and the little, crowded farmyards where the women lived with all the pigs and babies. The men and boys had contests. They played games and laughed. They created a culture of male totems . . .

'Why?' said Conrad.

'Fear,' said Michael.

That was the basis of it. Fear. Partly disgust and a sort of mystical distrust of the women because of menstruation. But also a childlike fear of the power of women to give birth. And this fear was real and so tacit that, even though the men had segregated the women—even though they had succeeded in debasing them and disinheriting them, the women taunted the men. And they got away with it. They stood on the hillsides in groups and they laughed at the men in the compounds and they dared the boys to come out and have sexual intercourse. Dared them with all kinds of lewd, graphic gestures and always laughing. And, of course, the boys wouldn't go. They were afraid. They backed off. They hid. Or else, they came outside the compound in an army and they'd kill the pigs. Sometimes, too, they made war on their neighbours. Anything, rather than go to the women.

'Are you sure it was really the women they were afraid of?'

Michael did not answer this.

Conrad pulled the plug and the water began to surge toward the drain. He lay back watching it ebbing, revealing his pallid, hairless body.

'Anyhow, that's how I see myself now,' Michael said. 'A kind of ritual bachelor, living in retreat. Taunted from the hillsides. Being watched and listened to. But silently . . .'

'What about her pigs?'

Michael thought of the yelling matches and the slamming doors and the undone, promised things. He also thought of the silence with which Olivia seemed to be rebuking him. 'I guess I've killed a few,' he said. 'But I haven't had the benefit of any God damn magic dreams.'

The last of the water drew away with a great, loud sucking noise and was gone. Conrad lay there in the empty tub, with his goblet in his hand and his toes sticking up.

After a moment, he spoke and he said, 'This is how they found my father. Just exactly three years ago. The twenty-ninth of April. With his wrists slashed.'

'Today's the twenty-eighth,' said Michael.

Outside the bathroom door, Grendel threw up the remnants of Mrs Kemp's toona sandwich. It was now 6:45. The guests would arrive at eight and still no one knew—but Rodney—who they would be.

'Conrad wants an egg.'

'But we're going to eat in an hour-and-a-half.'

'I don't think he wants it to eat,' said Michael.

'He's going to throw it at someone, is that it?' Olivia was undoing the boxes from Fenton's and setting the contents in bowls and soufflé dishes. Rodney was arranging her flowers in crystal vases on the cutting board.

'All I know is, he wants an egg.'

'He wants it to lift his face with,' said Rodney. 'If you have a pastry brush, you'd better send that up, too. And a nice little dish to separate the egg in.'

'Has he been doing this long?' Michael asked.

'About a year,' said Rodney. 'And only at parties. It makes him look Chinese.'
'All we need,' said Michael. 'The Empress of China.'

They arrived in the first warm rain.

There was a girl whose name was Louellen Potts who had once been one of Michael's students. She was now out taking care of other people's children in a daycare centre, wasting her talents as a first rate critic. She had come, this evening, ostensibly as Rodney's 'date'—but she seemed to have an ulterior motive: at least, in Michael's view. She was one of those dreadful women who hound you with their beauty while they beat you with their mind. Michael cringed from the thought of what lay ahead: Louellen attempting to best him at every turn in the conversation, opening one and then two more buttons of her blouse and thrusting her breasts into the lamplight. If only she were less attractive, he could be sure of winning.

Olivia rather liked Louellen Potts. She was one of perhaps six students both she and Michael had encountered in the classroom and the lecture hall over the years. What Olivia instilled from *Heart of Darkness*, Michael destroyed with *Frankenstein*. Kurtz and the Monster, walking hand in hand: *that* was the future, according to Michael.

When Fabiana Holbach Powell arrived, she was not with her husband, but her husband's brother Tom and Tom's wife Betty. Fabiana's husband, Jackman, was enigmatically 'abroad'. The word 'abroad' was delivered by Tom, while Fabiana looked the other way.

They had drunk for half-an-hour, waiting for Conrad to come downstairs. Michael put on some passable tapes (acceptable to everyone, that is, except Louellen) and the atmosphere was actually bearable. Under the influence of Cleo Laine, things loosened up a bit. The sailing voice cut through the dreadful, early chit-chat and very soon people were asking freely for 'another scotch' or another glass of white wine. If only Louellen would stop exposing herself, life might be endurable.

Tom Powell was a cold-eyed blond who had just come back from Nassau. He had one of those infuriating tans and an even more infuriating physique. He didn't say much. The eyes said it all. They never left Fabiana, unless they were turned on Michael (perhaps '*through*' Michael would be more accurate) during the course of such questions as: 'When was the last time we saw you?' and statements, such as the patently ridiculous: 'You're looking well, Mike.'

Betty Powell just sat on the sofa and rummaged in her pocket book for something she never found.

Fabiana, on the other hand, was radiant—as always. She carried with her—just as she had as a child—that wonderful and wondrous sense of someone always on the verge of imparting the secret of life, if only she could remember the wording. Her gaze would drift away towards the answer—beautiful and oddly heartbreaking—only to return yet again with the words; 'no—that's not it . . .' implicit in the wounded, blue confusion of her eyes. She had once been kidnapped and the ransom had been a million dollars. Lucien Holbach, her father, had refused to pay it—even though he had sixty millions and his wife twenty millions more. Fabiana had escaped, unharmed.

Or had she? Michael wondered.

At any rate, she had escaped and, shortly thereafter, she had been married to Jackman Powell—who was currently 'abroad'. She claimed to have never seen her captors, having been forced to wear a blindfold the whole time. It was when, after hours of silence, she had discovered she was standing in the middle of an empty house that she made her escape. All of this had happened in Jamaica: a place to which Fabiana had never returned.

Years and years and years ago—when they were children—Conrad Fastbinder had fallen in love with Fabiana Holbach and, for a while—in later years, before the kidnap, it seemed that Fabiana might return his love. But three things had happened in rapid succession, dashing all those hopes forever: until now. Fastbinder's father had died, leaving him penniless: Fabiana had been kidnapped and Jackman Powell—('that son-of-a-bitch!')—had married her.

Tonight, through some fortuitous twist of fate, she had turned up in Michael and Olivia Penny's living room without her husband—and only her brother-in-law ('that other son-of-a-bitch!') to watch over her.

Conrad waited for Cleo to begin singing '*Traces*' before he made his entrance.

> '*A faded photograph,*
> *Covered, now, with lines and creases . . .*'

Fabiana claimed not to recognize him.

Michael, never having seen his friend in lacquer before, tended to agree with Fabiana. Conrad, decked out in summer whites and with his hair plastered back, looked like someone trying to escape from a Somerset Maugham short story. His tie was a florid pink (admittedly, in fashion, if you glanced at the right magazines) and he reeked of Chanel 19. As for the face—it was true. Conrad Fastbinder had descended from the upper reaches in a Chinese mask.

The trouble was, he couldn't speak—whether because of all the scotch he had drunk in the afternoon, or because of the strictures of his 'facelift' or, perhaps, because of both. As a consequence, he merely bowed over Fabiana's hand, and kissed it—after which, they all went in to dinner.

Michael sat at the head of the table, leaning back in his chair. He was turned to one side in order to accommodate his foot which increasingly troubled him as the evening wore on. He watched his guests—or rather, Conrad's guests, through a haze of pain and liquor.

Far off, he could just make out Olivia seated at the other end of the table. She was smiling—oh rare event—and, though the smile was somewhat fixed, it appeared to be genuine. What could she be smiling about? Michael regretted he had not begun to count as soon as the smile had turned up—just to see how long it would stay. It was rather like a visitor: another guest at the table: a stranger. He should keep a little book, like Hamlet: 'My tables—meet it is, I set it down . . . Olivia smiled today for twenty seconds.'

Why?

Michael looked around the table.

See who's here; he thought. All the bachelors. This is a bachelors' dinner. Rodney, Conrad, me. And Tom Powell—*he's* a bachelor. So's his wife. Look at them! I bet they touch each other with tongs. Or perhaps they wear gloves. Louellen Potts is a bachelor. (Damn it.) So is Fabiana.

So is Olivia.

Every damn one of us, living alone.

Here we are on the hillside—having killed the pig—and about to fall beneath the spell of the magic dream, perhaps.

Louellen Potts was sitting beside him: green eyed and green in tailored tweed. Breathtaking: youthful. Budding. Hair that falls—every hair in place and smelling of skin and flesh, no perfumes, only air and apples and sitting with one hand near his own, turned up—so innocent—or was that innocence? Maybe it was disdain. Knowing the harmless impotence of pockmarked hosts in their cups . . .

Not pockmarked. No. Do not go cruel into that good face. Be kinder. Kinder to yourself. Be kind.

Then, on the other side of the table, next to that blazered booby—Rodney Farquhar, pal and pudendum to the fallen Conrad—there was someone weeping.

Fabiana.

Was it true? Was she weeping?

Tom had told the tale at dinner—the dinner just finished, the one whose little bones were scattered under the grape seeds even now mounting on the plates as the bachelors lingered over their wine.

Tom, without saying so, had made it clear that Fabiana was waiting for a divorce. Her husband, his brother Jackman, had disappeared. He was a civil engineer—or something—and, though Fabiana's lawyers (working, of course for *him*) had told her he had 'left her' and had gone somewhere, they would not say where. Not precisely. Only 'into the Amazon region.' That was all. That was how they had put it to her: 'Jackman has gone'—into roughly speaking one million square green miles of rain forest. Now, he had been gone eight months and the lawyers had said, 'he is probably not coming back.'

So she could not get a divorce. She could only wait the mandatory seven years, after which she could declare herself a widow. Not that Jackman would be dead. He had gone there with her money. It was the money that was dead.

There was more, of course. Money. Enough for Conrad to cultivate, if he'd only take that egg off his face.

Michael watched Fabiana.

Just as Olivia's badge was neatness, Fabiana's badge was a restless wrist—her left—which she constantly massaged with her right hand, adjusting her watch and her bracelets and her bones, while the wrist turned slowly, this way and that. She also never looked at whoever was speaking, but set her eyes on those who were listening, watching perhaps for some clue as to the importance and meaning of what was being said. Now, it was Olivia who was speaking and Fabiana was watching

Betty Powell, her sister-in-law. Betty Powell was cutting up an apple with a knife and there was blood on her napkin, of which she seemed to be entirely unaware.

Olivia was still smiling.

The subject under discussion had been famous mistresses and who had performed that function best in history. Olivia had just said something startling and amusing and even Michael was laughing.

Olivia had suggested that Antinous, the beloved of the Emperor Hadrian, had been the world's greatest mistress.

'Why?' Louellen Potts had asked.

'Because,' Olivia had answered, 'he couldn't bear children.'

'Do you mean he couldn't stand them?' Betty asked. 'Or just that he couldn't have them . . .'

She was ignored.

It was then that disaster struck, as it will out of silence.

Thinking he spoke in a confidential tone, and being quite drunk, Conrad turned towards Michael and reached out his hand as if to emphasize his words. As a result of the gesture, he knocked over Betty Powell's glass. Wine and blood and an apple core.

But that was not the disaster. The disaster was in what he said.

What he said was, 'There's your answer, Michael. You and Olivia should have a baby.'

Michael said; 'Thanks for the advice and shut up.'

Conrad said; 'Oh, I see . . .' and he laughed. 'You're afraid Olivia will kill it.'

For a moment, there was only the sound of dripping wine and of someone breathing and then Louellen Potts turned down the table in Conrad's direction and said, 'Do you think that's funny, Mr Fastbinder? Do you really think that's funny?' Then she turned to Michael and she said, 'Why don't you hit him? If I were you, I'd hit him.'

'You are not me, Miss Potts,' said Michael. He was looking at Olivia, who looked away.

Now, Louellen turned to her and she said, 'Mrs Penny? Don't you want to be defended?'

Olivia didn't answer her. She was looking at her napkin.

'Really, Professor Penny,' Louellen said—still standing—'I think it is outrageous. And if you won't hit him, I will!'

'Sit down, Potts.' (Michael)

'I will not sit down! This appalling man has just said the most appalling thing about your wife and . . .'

'SIT DOWN!'

'Michael . . .' This was Olivia. 'Leave her alone.'

'I beg your pardon,' said Michael, alarmed, his voice rising. 'I beg your bloody pardon?'

'You heard her,' said Louellen—somewhat tipsy herself. 'She says you're to leave me alone.'

Michael said, 'You condescending green-eyed bitch!'

'Michael!' said Olivia.

'Don't you "Michael" me—you down there in the dark! What the hell right has she to put herself in my shoes?'

'She's only expressing her feelings, Michael. And whether or not they're valid, she has a right to express them.'

'Not at my table, she hasn't!'

'This is our table, Michael. Not your table. Ours.' Olivia did not even raise her voice.

Michael snapped. 'Well she's sitting at my end!'

And Louellen said, with great vehemence, '*Standing!*'

And suddenly, everyone was laughing. Everyone, that is, except the Powells. They did not seem to know what to do in the presence of laughter.

Louellen Potts sat down and there was then a second, but minor disaster. Her hand had fallen onto the table rather near Michael's. And now, unthinking, Michael took it—merely as a gesture of forgiveness. Except that he did not let go.

Louellen looked at the table, not quite focusing on her upturned fingers resting under Michael's hand. Her main awareness was of Olivia's eyes.

Michael felt the reverberation and he, too, became aware of Olivia's eyes. He turned his hand away slowly and withdrew it all the way back to his head, where he pushed back his hair.

'Conrad,' he said.

'Yes, sir,' said Conrad.

'Tell us about the time you got lost in that hotel and ended up in Princess Diana's bedroom.'

In the living room, Conrad was lying on the rug, smoking a cigarette and staring at the ceiling. Michael, limping as unobtrusively as possible, was going about the room and bestowing second brandies into upheld glasses, including Conrad's.

Beyond them, the dining room glowed in the flickering light of its guttering candles. The table was an ordered ruin, with its eight distinct place settings, each distinctly destroyed by a separate pair of hands; the eight plates marred with the elegant parings of apples and cheese and pears; the wine glasses emptied to an exact degree, each one a signature; and the napkins, folded or thrown down and the chairs pushed back, reflective or violent or simply dispensed with—and the low, silver bowl of freesia, the flowers drooping as if they had been assaulted—and the mirrors that reflected mirrors that reflected mirrors—each one holding its perfect image a further remove, like sign posts down a road that led into darkness.

Rodney was playing the piano.

Otherwise—silence.

Olivia returned from the hallway, having opened the front door to let in some air. Outside, there was a spring rain and the strong smell of budding. She picked up her glass—allowed Michael to fill it—touched him with her pensiveness as he passed—and leaned against the door jamb, neither here nor there.

It was warm—and Fabiana's wrist was moving.

Slowly—it was imperceptible at first—as if a butterfly had entered the room and caught their attention only by degrees—Fabiana began to talk. She began in the middle of some interior monologue that perhaps had occupied her for some time—which yet seemed pertinent to the monologue of each of the others; one long sentence describing their mutual apprehension, whether it be about the past or the present or the future; arising out of that common literature which is the mind, peopled with common characters, moving over a common landscape, like a book they had all read—from which now one of their voices began to quote aloud:

'. . . I know he went there without me in order to escape me. And yet I never bothered or pursued him. I was always standing still, it seems. I hadn't wanted him at first; but only let myself be wanted. The way a dog will let itself be wanted, not understanding why, except that out of being wanted—wanting comes. And out of being chosen—choosing. And out of being longed for—longing. Con knows. I never gave my loving. Never trusted myself to give. Never let it happen. I was always the little sister—sitting in the front seat, watching in the mirror. Until I met him—Jackman Powell. He was like a drug you take at a party, for fun. And then you wonder what it was. And then you ask for more. And then you realize you're hooked. And you never stop to think they've hooked you on purpose. You only think what a lovely feeling it is—and all you want is more. Until one day, they refuse. *There isn't any more.* Or worse, *there is—but I'm not going to let you have it.* And then they hold it up—they keep on holding it up where you can see it—and saying to you: *no; no more, Fabiana. Never any more.* And then they shoot it into the air, they waste it before your eyes. And they walk away—and they leave you with this empty syringe—and nothing to fill it with. And nothing to fill your veins with. And they haven't told you what it was—so you don't know how to ask for more. Because it was unique; it was *theirs*—they grew it, manufactured it or conjured it out of the air. And then they get on a boat and they don't even wave good-bye. And they're gone. And then you get a message—telling you they've disappeared forever.'

Nobody watched her while she finished.

Instead, they each one welcomed the anaesthetic that prevented, if only for the moment, the idea that hope itself—anticipation—had disappeared for all of them into the Amazon region along with Jackman Powell.

Michael looked with a dreadful panic at Olivia.

Louellen Potts—the briefest of his dreams—got up to leave the room.

'It's time to go,' she whispered, having lost her voice in Fabiana's recitation. 'Late,' she said. And went upstairs to collect her coat.

3:00 a.m. and Grendel made a tour of the house, making his presence known to all the mice and to all the ghosts who haunted the dark, including the dark at the edge of everyone's dreams. Finally, he settled at the foot of the stairs, intermittently waking to stare out the open door through the screen at the sidewalks sparkling with rain—and to listen to the droning in the den, which to Grendel was like a cave, inhabited by bears or perhaps by giant, cave-dwelling birds whose wings were lifted in constant repetition, casting their immense shadows across the floor towards his paws. Michael's curtains. He eyed them with a careful wariness. He never completely slept. When there was thunder, the piano would echo its dying reverberations and the cello, in its corner, would hum a low, solemn note. The crystal prisms that hung from the candlesticks also sang and the dying fire in the grate made another song and the floorboards creaked in the faraway sun room and the windows sighed all over the house.

His ears hurt—chewed in a week-old battle—and his gums were tender, having been torn. All along his back, he ached. No position was comfortable.

Everyone had gone upstairs—and he was alone. All the food—anything of real interest—was locked away. Except . . .

One bone, he remembered—put down by Michael under the kitchen table.

Grendel got up and fetched the bone and brought it back to the foot of the stairs. All through the next hour, he held it tenderly between his paws and wrecked it—very slowly—with his chipped and broken teeth.

The sound of gnawing—bone against bone—was all that could be heard. That, and the sluicing of the rain. And Olivia's voice, as she lay in the bed with her gaze on the patterns running down the walls. 'Michael . . . ?'

She was smiling.

Far in the Amazon region, a pin dropped.

Keath Fraser

Keath Fraser was born in 1944 in Vancouver, where he still lives. He has published two collections of stories, *Taking Cover* (1982) and *Foreign Affairs* (1985), which was short-listed for the Governor General's Award. Fraser is at work on a novel and has edited an anthology of writers' worst journeys, called *Bad Trips* (1991). Of his early years, he has written ("Becoming Complicit," in *Brick*), "When I was growing up I was refused the world by class, religion, and penury. Or so I believed. In what I was encouraged to think a happy childhood, I felt enjoined by loyalty, Catholicism, and debt to make the best of what I had. What I had was a not unperky time, scarred by doubt and a deep yearning to be of the world. I wanted to travel, be loved, afford new shoes. The size and diversity of my family, just as much as its tenderness for outsiders, held little significance in what to me was my narrow and dutiful place." For the young Fraser, "fiction was a way of wandering out through the gates, into forbidden territory. . ." He studied for three years in London, preparing to teach, but decided that "when the Last Day dawned he'd prefer to be judged on how he'd handled his ignorance about writing than how he'd bestowed his knowledge of literature."

Fraser describes the role of the writer as that of an impostor or voyeur who must be always peering through windows. "I think we fail to understand ourselves and what's everywhere around us if we neglect to view the local and familiar up against the foreign and exotic: hairpins, lapis lazuli, grief, exuberance, poverty, Club Med, Calcutta. . . . The net purchase is a refurbished notion of here. Writers hang around windows the way bankers do around interest rates, and pan-handlers around coins." "Writing fiction and reading it ought to feel illicit," Fraser says. "It attracts us by what is seemingly forbidden and unseemingly revealed. . . . The writer, the character, the reader become complicitous in the secret knowledge of the world."

In an essay called "Notes toward a Supreme Fiction" (*Canadian Literature*, No. 100, 1984), Fraser outlines his three criteria for excellence in fiction: it must be autobiographical, subversive, and wonderful. He dismisses the naive notion of autobiography, which is evident in the reviewer's or audience's compulsion to ask, did this really happen to you? What he proposes, instead, is the the view that all fiction is, at least, emotionally biographical. "Fiction of any quality above the level of Harlequin Romance and Potboiler must be autobiographical by its very nature. This is to say that

writing is an act inseparable from the mind that conceives it. The act of imagining is a real event. It happens. It happens to the author, and it happens to reveal his quality of mind, depth of vision, deftness of touch. . . . Potboilers and Harlequins are cynical and voiceless works because the author sets himself up (especially if he's only writing for money) as a mind apart from its product, instead of one engaged in argument with itself. No fiction worth writing has ever been undertaken, it seems to me, without the writer's doubting his ability to complete it in the way he dares hope. Every completed story or novel should be a miracle, at least to its author, if it has any chance at all of conveying the wonder of its being alive."

Fraser does not associate the subversive element in literature exclusively with form, as many writers do, but locates it at a deeper level. "Thinking of English and American fiction, say, we notice that innovation has never prospered when form was in excess of content, as form often is today in what we sometimes call 'experimental' fiction. True innovation is inseparable from content. And the content of Supreme Fiction is subversive. I am talking about fiction that overturns expectation by juxtaposition, nexus, dislocation. I am talking about fiction that aspires to an understanding of cultural anorexia; fiction that creates the complexity capable of engaging our imaginations; fiction capable of perceiving the many ways that our received culture, for all its splendours of cohesion, for all our diplomacy, is suffering from edema of the soul." The struggle for a genuinely subversive art, he says, is a fight not against "technical old-fashionedness," but against boredom. Innovation and fashion are too often mistaken for vision. "The fiction I am arguing for aspires to wide appeal and thus to cliché. It wants to be used up by familiarity, swallowed up as idiom, gobbled up and digested as proverb. This is its hope. This is its subversion: the unexpected resulting in the unforgettable, worn-out smile of the Mona Lisa, the opening bars of Beethoven's Fifth, Hamlet's To Be speech. It's the task of succeeding generations of artists to refurbish traditional ways of seeing, to reinvigorate worn-out idioms, to subvert the familiar. The novelist's hope is to make his own unfamiliarity dangerously familiar to the generation that succeeds him."

What makes fiction wonderful, Fraser says, is the writer's love of life, which is predicated on his or her awareness of death. Memory is the great vehicle for confronting death. "The subversion of the present is the inevitable consequence of possessing memory." Fiction not only celebrates the here and now as an ideal, he says, but also inhibits time. "The Other Worldness of great fiction makes everything happen, or so it seems, for the writer's mandate isn't to change the world but to show that within the imagination, capable of evoking both the sublime and darkness together, exists a metaphor for God. The fiction we value more is inclusive rather than exclusive. It offers no answers except the order and multiplicity of its vision, the nuances of its humblest details, the miraculousness of its language. It offers a sense of Earth. But it offers more than this, for it is a benevolent and finally human God, interested in understanding the relations of man and nature in the broadest sense of man and man. This God, this imagination, this fiction is Wonderful, for there is no getting through or around the authority of its vision and the intuitive logic of its means."

Roget's Thesaurus

I had begun my lists. Mother was always saying, "Peter, why not play outside like other boys?" Her patience with collectors was not prodigal; she didn't understand my obsession. I wanted to polish words like shells, before I let them in. Sometimes I tied on bits of string to watch them sway, bump maybe, like chestnuts. They were treasures these words. I could have eaten them had the idiom not existed, even then, to mean remorse. I loved the way they smelled, their inky scent of coal. Sniffing their penny notebook made me think of fire. (See FERVOUR.)

I fiddled with sounds and significations. No words could exist, even in their thousands, until I made them objects on paper: hairpins, lapis lazuli, teeth, fish hooks, dead bees . . . Later on my study became a museum for the old weapons poets had used. Mother would have died. By then, of course, she had; pleased I had grown up to become what she approved, a doctor.

My young wife died of tumours the size of apples. That I was a practitioner of healing seemed absurd. It smothered me like fog, her dying, her breath in the end so moist. When *his* wife died my uncle took a razor to his throat. (See DESPAIR, see INSANITY, see OMEGA.) He died disbelieving in the antidote of language. Oh, my wife, I have only words to play with.

When I retired it was because of deafness. My passion for travel spent, my sense of duty to the poor used up, I remembered listening for words everywhere. At the Athenaeum, among the dying in Millbank Penitentiary, after concerts, at the Royal Society, during sermons in St Pancras. I started to consolidate. At last I could describe—not prescribe. After fifty years I concluded synonyms were reductive, did not exist, were only analogous words. Unlike Dr Johnson I was no poet. My book would be a philosopher's tool, my soubriquet a thesaurus.

My contribution was to relationships. I created families out of ideas like Space and Matter and Affections. I grouped words in precisely a thousand ways: reacquainted siblings, introduced cousins, befriended black sheep, mediated between enemies. I printed place names and organized a banquet.

London had never seen anything quite like it. Recalcitrant louts, my words, they scented taxonomy and grew inebrious. Mother was well out of it.

She knew me for my polite accomplishments, my papers on optics, comparative anatomy, the poor, zoology, human ageing, mathematics, the deaf and dumb. I was a Renaissance man for I chewed what I bit off. Still, I was no more satisfied with my Bridgewater Treatise on the design of all natural history than with my report for the Water Commission on pollution in the Thames. Only less pessimistic. By the time Asiatic cholera broke out, and people were vomiting and diarrhoetic, my work had been forgotten. Not until I fathered my *Thesaurus* did I dream of prinking. Who knew, perhaps crazy poets would become Roget's trollops, when they discovered his interest in truth not eloquence.

My book appeared the same year as volumes by Dickens, Hawthorne, Melville—fabulators, all of us. (See FICTION.) I too dreamed of the unity of man's existence, and offered a tool for attacking false logic, truisms, jargon, sophism. Though any fretless voice can sing if words are as precise as notes, men in power often sound discordant. Music isn't accident, nor memory history. Language (like the violin) so long to learn.

There is no language, I used to say to Mother, like our own. Look how nations that we oppress trust it. It's the bridge we use to bring back silks and spices, tobacco leaves and cinnamon. Yet all one reviewer wrote of my work was it "made eloquence too easy for the lazy and ignorant". Eloquence I have always distrusted. Maybe this is why my *Thesaurus* has gone through twenty-eight editions.

Men are odd animals. I have never felt as at home around *them* as around their words; without these they're monkeys. (See TRUISM.) The other day I was going through my book and it struck me I have more words for Disapprobation than Approbation. Why is this?

So I spend my last days at West Malvern in my ninety-first year. I no longer walk in parks. I'm pleased I fear death, it makes me feel younger. Death is a poet's idiom to take the mind off complacency. (See SWAN SONG, see CROSSING THE BAR, see THE GREAT ADVENTURE.) I have never thought of death but that it has refurbished me.

Mavis Gallant

Mavis de Trafford Young was born in Montreal in 1922 and attended schools there and in the eastern U.S. She worked at the National Film Board and as a feature writer at the *Montreal Standard*, and was married briefly to John Gallant, before leaving for Paris in 1950. Her first publication in *The New Yorker* appeared in 1951. Apart from frequent visits to Canada and a stint as writer-in-residence at the University of Toronto in 1983, she has lived most of her adult life in Paris, which accounts for the tardiness with which Canadians have recognized her prodigious talent. Her publications include two novels, *Green Water, Green Sky* (1959) and *A Fairly Good Time* (1970), and various books of stories: *The Other Paris* (1956), *My Heart Is Broken* (1959), *The Peignitz Junction* (1973), *From the Fifteenth District* (1979), which won the Governor General's Award, *Home Truths* (1981), and *In Transit* (1988). She is also the author of *Paris Notebooks: Essays and Reviews* (1986) and two books of non-fiction, one on the Dreyfus affair and the other a study of the public response to a French schoolteacher's love affair with an adolescent student, *The Affair of Gabrielle Russier* (1971).

In the introduction to *Home Truths*, Gallant objects strongly to the notion that she or anyone else should have to "paint Canadian": to the critic who demands this, she claims a "wider allegiance," the freedom of the imagination. "He thinks there is more than meets the eye, and in a sense he is right: fiction, like painting, consists entirely of more than meets the eye; otherwise it is not worth a second's notice." Gallant rejects political fashions and tub-thumping nationalism in favour of a centre of gravity to be found in those childhood experiences that "give rise to a national consciousness": "A deeper culture is contained in memory. Memory is something that cannot be subsidized or ordained. It can, however, be destroyed; and it is inseparable from language."

Gallant has been a faithful student of both language and memory since she made the decision to write full time. "My goal was to get free and write. The only thing I don't know is why I waited so long. I never sent a story anywhere until I was twenty-seven years old. I don't know why. I had piles of stories. Then suddenly I decided this was it. Twenty-seven is, I think, a watershed age." In an interview with Alan Twigg (*Strong Voices*) conducted in 1981, she describes her typical process of creation as follows:

"I begin in pencil. It's usually a visual image in a situation. Sometimes the first image isn't even in the story at the end. I start in longhand. Then for the next few days there are bits of the story that come. It's almost as if the story already existed and I was getting scraps of it. It just comes. And I don't know where from. I don't mean I'm a mystic. I don't mean it comes from the planet Venus or anything.

"You get an accumulation of things. Written on buses, I'm not joking. Even on match-covers. Once I had a story written on a metro ticket. A little bit of dialogue. Then I type it. Then I make all the corrections. The form then is very clear. Once it's typed there's no doubt that that's the beginning and that's the end of it and the story does this. Then I correct in pencil again and it's all around the edges. Then I type it all again to get it clean. Then I think it's no good."

Gallant insists that plausibility, not experience, is what matters in fiction. "Even if a thing happened, if it's completely eccentric, there's no point writing about it. If it isn't plausible, it doesn't matter." In response to Twigg's remark that "In the Tunnel," though grossly comic, was entirely plausible, Gallant said: "That's barely caricature, believe me. I was at a dinner party of Brits in exile in the south of France. The man across from me leaned over with those light eyes. He leaned acrosss and said: 'Don't you think there are people so rotten that they have to be killed?' I remember thinking, rotten for what kind of world? Suppose I was an African, brought up with completely different legends, gods, realities, and that man with his very light eyes said this. The story began out of that."

Gallant's whimsical account of the mechanics of the creative process and her insistence upon plausibility cannot hide the fact that she is a painstaking stylist, attentive to her characters' every nuance of gesture and speech and how these might best be rendered in words on the page. She considers style to be "not a last minute addition to prose, a charming and universal slip-cover, a coat of paint used to mask the failings of a structure," but, rather, the "author's thumbprint": "Style is inseparable from structure, part of the conformation of whatever the author has to say. What he says—this is what fiction is about—is that something is taking place and that nothing lasts. Against the sustained tick of a watch, fiction takes the measure of a life, a season, a look exchanged, the turning point, desire as brief as a dream, the grief and terror that after childhood we cease to express. The life, the look, the grief are without permanence. The watch continues to tick where the story stops."

In Youth Is Pleasure

My father died, then my grandmother; my mother was left, but we did not get on. I was probably disagreeable with anyone who felt entitled to give me instructions and advice. We seldom lived under the same roof, which was just as well. She had found me civil and amusing until I was ten, at which time I was said to have become pert and obstinate. She was impulsive, generous, in some ways better than most other people, but without any feeling for cause and effect; this made her at the least unpredictable and at the most a serious element of danger. I was fascinated by her, though she worried me; then all at once I lost interest. I was fifteen when this happened. I would forget to answer her letters and even to open them. It was not rejection or anything so violent as dislike but a simple indifference I cannot account for. It was much the way I would be later with men I fell out of love with, but I was too young to know that then. As for my mother, whatever I thought, felt, said, wrote, and wore had always been a positive source of exasperation. From time to time she attempted to alter the form, the outward shape at least, of the creature she thought she was modelling, but at last she came to the conclusion there must be something wrong with the clay. Her final unexpected upsurge of attention coincided with my abrupt unconcern: one may well have been the reason for the other.

It took the form of digging into my diaries and notebooks and it yielded, among other documents, a two-year-old poem, Kiplingesque in its rhythms, entitled 'Why I Am a Socialist'. The first words of the first line were 'You ask . . .', then came a long answer. But it was not an answer to anything she'd wondered. Like all mothers—at least, all I have known—she was obsessed with the entirely private and possibly trivial matter of a daughter's virginity. Why I was a Socialist she rightly conceded to be none of her business. Still, she must have felt she had to say something, and the something was 'You had better be clever, because you will never be pretty.' My response was to take—take, not grab—the poem from her and tear it up. No voices were raised. I never mentioned the incident to anyone. That is how it was. We became, presently, mutually unconcerned. My detachment was put down to the coldness of my nature, hers to the exhaustion of trying to bring me up. It must have been a relief to her when, in the first half of Hitler's war, I slipped quietly and finally out of her life. I was now eighteen, and completely on my own. By 'on my own' I don't mean a show of independence with Papa-Mama footing the bills: I mean that I was solely responsible for my economic survival and that no living person felt any duty toward me.

On a bright morning in June I arrived in Montreal, where I'd been born, from New York, where I had been living and going to school. My luggage was a small suitcase and an Edwardian picnic hamper—a preposterous piece of baggage my father had brought from England some twenty years before; it had been with me since childhood, when his death turned my life into a helpless migration. In my purse was a birth certificate and five American dollars, my total fortune, the parting gift of a Canadian actress in New York, who had taken me to see *Mayerling* before I got on the train. She was kind and good and terribly hard up, and she had no idea that apart from some loose change I had nothing more. The birth certificate, which testified I was Linnet Muir, daughter of Angus and of Charlotte, was my right of passage. I did not own a passport and possibly never had seen one. In those days there was almost no such thing as a 'Canadian'. You were Canadian-born, and a British subject, too, and you had a third label with no consular reality, like the racial tag that on Soviet passports will make a German of someone who has never been to Germany. In Canada you were also whatever your father happened to be, which in my case was English. He was half Scot, but English by birth, by mother, by instinct. I did not feel a scrap British or English, but I was not an American either. In American schools I had refused to salute the flag. My denial of that curiously Fascist-looking celebration, with the right arm stuck straight out, and my silence when the others intoned the trusting '. . . and justice for all' had never been thought offensive, only stubborn. Americans then were accustomed to gratitude from foreigners but did not demand it; they quite innocently could not imagine any country fit to live in except their own. If I could not recognize it, too bad for me. Besides, I was not a refugee—just someone from the backwoods. 'You got schools in Canada?' I had been asked. 'You got radios?' And once, from a teacher, 'What do they major in up there? Basket-weaving?'

My travel costume was a white piqué jacket and skirt that must have been crumpled and soot-flecked, for I had sat up all night. I was reading, I think, a novel by Sylvia Townsend Warner. My hair was thick and long. I wore my grandmother's wedding ring, which was too large, and which I would lose before long. I desperately wanted to look more than my age, which I had already started to give out as twenty-one. I was travelling light; my picnic hamper contained the poems and journals I had judged fit to accompany me into my new, unfettered existence, and some books I feared I might not find again in clerical Quebec—Zinoviev and Lenin's *Against the Stream*, and a few beige pamphlets from the Little Lenin Library, purchased second hand in New York. I had a picture of Mayakovsky torn out of *Cloud in Trousers* and one of Paddy Finucane, the Irish R.A.F. fighter pilot, who was killed the following summer. I had not met either of these men, but I approved of them both very much. I had abandoned my beloved but cumbersome anthologies of American and English verse, confident that I had whatever I needed by heart. I knew every word of Stephen Vincent Benét's 'Litany for Dictatorship' and 'Notes to Be Left in a Cornerstone,' and the other one that begins:

> They shot the Socialists at half-past five
> In the name of victorious Austria. . . .

I could begin anywhere and rush on in my mind to the end. 'Notes . . .' was the New York I knew I would never have again, for there could be no journeying backward; the words 'but I walked it young' were already a gate shut on a part of my life. The suitcase held only the fewest possible summer clothes. Everything else had been deposited at the various war-relief agencies of New York. In those days I made symbols out of everything, and I must have thought that by leaving a tartan skirt somewhere I was shedding past time. I remember one of those wartime agencies well because it was full of Canadian matrons. They wore pearl earrings like the Duchess of Kent's and seemed to be practising her tiny smile.

Brooches pinned to their cashmere cardigans carried some daft message about the Empire. I heard one of them exclaiming, 'You don't expect me, a Britisher, to drink tea made with tea bags!' Good plain girls from the little German towns of Ontario, christened probably Wilma, Jean, and Irma, they had flowing eighteenth-century names like Georgiana and Arabella now. And the Americans, who came in with their arms full of every stitch they could spare, would urge them, the Canadian matrons, to stand fast on the cliffs, to fight the fight, to slug the enemy on the landing fields, to belt him one on the beaches, to keep going with whatever iron rations they could scrape up in Bronxville and Scarsdale; and the Canadians half-shut their eyes and tipped their heads back like Gertrude Lawrence and said in thrilling Benita Hume accents that they would do that—indeed they would. I recorded 'They're all trained nurses, actually. The Canadian ones have a good reputation. They managed to marry these American doctors.'

Canada had been in Hitler's war from the very beginning, but America was still uneasily at peace. Recruiting had already begun; I had seen a departure from New York for Camp Stewart in Georgia, and some of the recruits' mothers crying and even screaming and trying to run alongside the train. The recruits were going off to drill with broomsticks because there weren't enough guns; they still wore old-fashioned headgear and were paid twenty-one dollars a month. There was a song about it: 'For twenty-one dollars a day, once a month.' As my own train crossed the border to Canada I expected to sense at once an air of calm and grit and dedication, but the only changes were from prosperous to shabby, from painted to unpainted, from smiling to dour. I was entering a poorer and a curiously empty country, where the faces of the people gave nothing away. The crossing was my sea change. I silently recited the vow I had been preparing for weeks: that I would never be helpless again and that I would not let anyone make a decision on my behalf.

When I got down from the train at Windsor Station, a man sidled over to me. He had a cap on his head and a bitter Celtic face, with deep indentations along his cheeks, as if his back teeth were pulled. I thought he was asking a direction. He repeated his question, which was obscene. My arms were pinned by the weight of my hamper and suitcase. He brushed the back of his hand over my breasts, called me a name, and edged away. The murderous rage I felt and the revulsion that followed were old friends. They had for years been my reaction to what my diaries called 'their hypocrisy'. 'They' was a world of sly and mumbling people, all of them older than myself. I must have substituted 'hypocrisy' for every sort of aggression, because fright was a luxury I could not afford. What distressed me was my helplessness—I who had sworn only a few hours earlier that I'd not be vulnerable again. The man's gaunt face, his drunken breath, the flat voice which I assigned to the graduate of some Christian Brothers teaching establishment haunted me for a long time after that. 'The man at Windsor Station' would lurk in the windowless corridors of my nightmares; he would be the passenger, the only passenger, on a dark tram. The first sight of a city must be the measure for all second looks.

But it was not my first sight. I'd had ten years of it here—the first ten. After that, and before New York (in one sense, my deliverance), there had been a long spell of grief and shadow in an Ontario city, a place full of mean judgements and grudging minds, of paranoid Protestants and slovenly Catholics. To this day I cannot bear the sight of brick houses, or of a certain kind of empty treeless street on a Sunday afternoon. My memory of Montreal took shape while I was there. It was not a random jumble of rooms and summers and my mother singing 'We've Come to See Miss Jenny Jones', but the faithful record of the true survivor. I retained, I rebuilt a superior civilization. In that drowned world, Sherbrooke Street seemed to be glittering and white; the vision of a house upon that street was so painful that I was obliged to banish it from the memorial. The small hot rooms of a summer cottage became enormous and cool. If I say that Cleopatra floated down the Chateauguay River, that the Winter Palace was stormed on Sherbrooke Street, that Trafalgar was fought on Lake St Louis, I mean it naturally; they were the natural backgrounds of my exile and fidelity. I saw now at the far end of Windsor Station—more foreign, echoing, and mysterious than any American station could be—a statue of Lord Mount Stephen, the founder of the Canadian Pacific, which everyone took to be a memorial to Edward VII. Angus, Charlotte, and the smaller Linnet had truly been: this was my proof; once upon a time my instructions had been to make my way to Windsor Station should I ever be lost and to stand at the foot of Edward VII and wait for someone to find me.

I have forgotten to say that no one in Canada knew I was there. I looked up the number of the woman who had once been my nurse, but she had no telephone. I found her in a city directory, and with complete faith that 'O. Carette' was indeed Olivia and that she would recall and welcome me I took a taxi to the east end of the city—the French end, the poor end. I was so sure of her that I did not ask the driver to wait (to take me where?) but dismissed him and climbed two flights of dark-brown stairs inside a house that must have been built soon after Waterloo. That it was Olivia who came to the door, that the small grey-haired creature I recalled as dark and towering had to look up at me, that she unhesitatingly offered me shelter all seem as simple now as when I broke my fiver to settle the taxi. Believing that I was dead, having paid for years of Masses for the repose of my heretic soul, almost the first thing she said to me was '*Tu vis?*' I understood '*Tu es ici?*' We straightened it out later. She held both my hands and cried and called me *belle et grande*. *Grande* was good, for among American girls I'd seemed a shrimp. I did not see what there was to cry for; I was here. I was as naturally selfish with Olivia as if her sole reason for being was me. I stayed with her for a while and left when her affection for me made her possessive, and I think I neglected her. On her deathbed she told one of her daughters, the reliable one, to keep an eye on me forever. Olivia was the only person in the world who did not believe I could look after myself. Where she and I were concerned I remained under six.

Now, at no moment of this remarkable day did I feel anxious or worried or forlorn. The man at Windsor Station could not really affect my view of the future. I had seen some of the worst of life, but I had no way of judging it or of knowing what the worst could be. I had a sensation of loud, ruthless power, like an enormous waterfall. The past, the part I would rather not have lived, became small and remote, a dark pinpoint. My only weapons until now had been secrecy and insolence. I had stopped running away from schools and situations when I finally understood that by becoming a name in a file, by attracting attention, I would merely prolong my stay in prison—I mean, the prison of childhood itself. My rebellions then consisted only in causing people who were physically larger and legally sovereign to lose their self-control, to become bleached with anger, to shake with such temper that they broke cups and glasses and bumped into chairs. From the malleable, sunny child Olivia said she remembered, I had become, according to later chroniclers, cold, snobbish, and presumptuous. 'You need an iron hand, Linnet.' I can still hear that melancholy voice which belonged to a friend of my mother's. 'If anybody ever marries you he'd better have an iron hand.' After today I would never need to hear this, or anything approaching it, for the rest of my life.

And so that June morning and the drive through empty, sunlit, wartime streets are even now like a roll of drums in the mind. My life was my own revolution—the tyrants deposed, the constitution wrenched from unwilling hands; I was, all by myself, the liberated crowd setting the palace on fire; I was the flags, the trees, the bannered windows, the flower-decked trains. The singing and the skyrockets of the 1848 I so trustingly believed would emerge out of the war were me, no one but me; and, as in the lyrical first days of any revolution, as in the first days of any love affair there wasn't the whisper of a voice to tell me, 'You might compromise.'

   If making virtue of necessity has ever had a meaning it must be here: for I was independent *inevitably*. There were good-hearted Americans who knew a bit of my story—as much as I wanted anyone to know—and who hoped I would swim and not drown, but from the moment I embarked on my journey I went on the dark side of the moon. 'You seemed so sure of yourself,' they would tell me, still troubled, long after this. In the cool journals I kept I noted that my survival meant nothing in the capitalist system, I was one of those not considered to be worth helping, saving, or even investigating. Thinking with care, I see this was true. What could I have turned into in another place? Why, a librarian at Omsk or a file clerk at Tomsk. Well, it hadn't happened that way; I had my private revolution and I settled in with Olivia in Montreal. Sink or swim? Of course I swam. Jobs were for the having; you could pick them up off the ground. Working for a living meant just what it says—a brisk necessity. It would be the least important fragment of my life until I had what I wanted. The cheek of it, I think now: penniless, sleeping in a shed room behind the kitchen of Olivia's cold-water flat, still I pointed across the wooden balustrade in a long open office where I was being considered for employment and said, 'But I won't sit *there*.' Girls were there, penned in like sheep. I did not think men better than women—only that they did more interesting work and got more money for it. In my journals I called other girls 'coolies'. I did not know if life made them bearers or if they had been born with a natural gift for giving in. 'Coolie' must have been the secret expression of one of my deepest fears. I see now that I had an immense conceit: I thought I occupied a world other people could scarcely envision, let alone attain. It involved giddy risks and changes, stepping off the edge blindfolded, one's hand on nothing more than a birth certificate and a five-dollar bill. At this time of sitting in judgement I was earning nine dollars a week (until I was told by someone that the local minimum wage was twelve, on which I left for greener fields) and washing my white piqué skirt at night and ironing at dawn, and coming home at all hours so I could pretend to Olivia I had dined. Part of this impermeable sureness that I needn't waver or doubt came out of my having lived in New York. The first time I ever heard people laughing in a cinema was there. I can still remember the wonder and excitement and amazement I felt. I was just under fourteen and I had never heard people expressing their feelings in a public place in my life. The easy reactions, the way a poignant moment caught them, held them still—all that was new. I had come there straight from Ontario, where the reaction to a love scene was a kind of unhappy giggling, while the image of a kitten or a baby induced a long flat 'Aaaah', followed by shamed silence. You could image them blushing in the dark for having said that—just that 'Aaaah'. When I heard that open American laughter I thought I could be like these people too, but had been told not to be by everyone, beginning with Olivia: '*Pas si fort*' was something she repeated to me so often when I was small that my father had made a tease out of it, called 'passy four.' From a tease it became oppressive too: 'For the love of God, Linnet, passy four.' What were these new people? Were they soft, too easily got at? I wondered that even then. Would a dictator have a field day here? Were they, as Canadian opinion had it, vulgar? Perhaps the notion of vulgarity came out of some incapacity on the part of the refined. Whatever they were, they couldn't all be daft; if they weren't I probably wasn't either. I supposed I stood as good a chance of being miserable here as anywhere, but at least I would not have to pretend to be someone else.

Now, of course there is much to be said on the other side: people who do not display what they feel have practical advantages. They can go away to be killed as if they didn't mind; they can see their sons off to war without a blink. Their upbringing is intended for a crisis. When it comes, they behave themselves. But it is murder in everyday life—truly murder. The dead of heart and spirit litter the landscape. Still, keeping a straight face makes life tolerable under stress. It makes *public* life tolerable—that is all I am saying; because in private people still got drunk, went after each other with bottles and knives, rang the police to complain that neighbours were sending poison gas over the transom, abandoned infant children and aged parents, wrote letters to newspapers in favour of corporal punishment, with inventive suggestions. When I came back to Canada that June at least one thing had been settled: I knew that it was all right for people to laugh and cry and even to make asses of themselves. I had actually known people like that, had lived with them, and they were fine, mostly—not crazy at all. That was where a lot of my confidence came from when I began my journey into a new life and a dream past.

My father's death had been kept from me. I did not know its exact circumstances or even the date. He died when I was ten. At thirteen I was still expected to believe a fable about his being in England. I kept waiting for him to send for me, for my life was deeply wretched and I took it for granted he knew. Finally I began to suspect that death and silence can be one. How to be sure? Head-on questions got me nowhere. I had to create a situation in which some adult (not my mother, who was far too sharp) would lose all restraint and hurl the truth at me. It was easy: I was an artist at this. What I had not foreseen was the verbal violence of the scene or the effect it might have. The storm that seemed to break in my head, my need to maintain the pose of indifference ('What are you telling me that for? What makes you think I care?') were such a strain that I had physical reactions, like stigmata, which doctors would hopelessly treat on and off for years and which vanished when I became independent. The other change was that if anyone asked about my father I said, 'Oh, he died.' Now, in Montreal, I could confront the free adult world of falsehood and evasion on an equal footing; they would be forced to talk to me as they did to each other. Making appointments to meet my father's friends—Mr Archie McEwen, Mr Stephen Ross-Colby, Mr Quentin Keller—I left my adult name, 'Miss Muir.' These were the men who eight, nine, ten years ago had asked, 'Do you like your school?'—not knowing what else to say to children. I had curtsied to them and said, 'Good night.' I think what I wanted was special information about despair, but I should have known that would be taboo in a place where 'like' and 'don't like' were heavy emotional statements.

Archie McEwen, my father's best friend, or the man I mistook for that, kept me standing in his office on St James Street West, he standing too, with his hands behind his back, and he said the following—not reconstructed or approximate but recalled, like 'The religions of ancient Greece and Rome are extinct' or 'O come, let us sing unto the Lord':

'Of course, Angus was a very sick man. I saw him walking along Sherbrooke Street. He must have just come out of hospital. He couldn't walk upright. He was using a stick. Inching along. His hair had turned grey. Nobody knew where Charlotte had got to, and we'd heard you were dead. He obviously wasn't long for this world either. He had too many troubles for any one man. I crossed the street because I didn't have the heart to shake hands with him. I felt terrible.'

Savage? Reasonable? You can't tell, with those minds. Some recent threat had scared them. The Depression was too close, just at their heels. Archie McEwen did not ask where I was staying or where I had been for the last eight years; in fact, he asked only two questions. In response to the first I said, 'She is married.'

There came a gleam of interest—distant, amused: 'So she decided to marry him, did she?'

My mother was highly visible; she had no secrets except unexpected ones. My father had nothing but. When he asked, 'Would you like to spend a year in England with your Aunt Dorothy?' I had no idea what he meant and I still don't. His only brother, Thomas, who was killed in 1918, had not been married; he'd had no sisters, that anyone knew. Those English mysteries used to be common. People came out to Canada because they did not want to think about the Thomases and Dorothys anymore. Angus was a solemn man, not much of a smiler. My mother, on the other hand—I won't begin to describe her, it would never end—smiled, talked, charmed anyone she didn't happen to be related to, swam in scandal like a partisan among the people. She made herself the central figure in loud, spectacular dramas which she played with the houselights on; you could see the audience too. That was her mistake; they kept their reactions, like their lovemaking, in the dark. You can imagine what she must have been in this world where everything was hushed, muffled, disguised: she must have seemed all they had by way of excitement, give or take a few elections and wars. It sounds like a story about the old and stale, but she and my father had been quite young eight and ten years before. The dying man creeping along Sherbrooke Street was thirty-two. First it was light chatter, then darker gossip, and then it went too far (*he* was ill and he couldn't hide it; *she* had a lover and didn't try); then suddenly it became tragic, and open tragedy was disallowed. And so Mr Archie McEwen could stand in his office and without a trace of feeling on his narrow Lowland face—not unlike my father's in shape—he could say, 'I crossed the street.'

Stephen Ross-Colby, a bachelor, my father's painter chum: the smell of his studio on St Mark Street was the smell of a personal myth. I said timidly, 'Do you happen to have anything of his—a drawing or anything?' I was humble because I was on a private, personal terrain of vocation that made me shy even of the dead.

He said, 'No, nothing. You could ask around. She junked a lot of his stuff and he junked the rest when he thought he wouldn't survive. You might try . . .' He gave me a name or two. 'It was all small stuff,' said Ross-Colby. 'He didn't do anything big.' He hurried me out of the studio for a cup of coffee in a crowded place—the Honey Dew on St Catherine Street, it must have been. Perhaps in the privacy of his studio I might have heard him thinking. Years after that he would try to call me 'Lynn', which I never was, and himself 'Steve'. He'd come into his own as an artist by then, selling wash drawings of Canadian war graves, sun-splashed, wisteria-mauve, lime-green, with drifts of blossom across the name of the regiment; gained a reputation among the heartbroken women who bought these impersonations, had them framed—the only picture in the house. He painted the war memorial at Caen. ('Their name liveth forever.') His stones weren't stones but mauve bubbles— that is all I have against them. They floated off the page. My objection wasn't to 'He didn't do anything big' but to Ross-Colby's way of turning the dead into thistledown. He said, much later, of that meeting, 'I felt like a bastard, but I was broke, and I was afraid you'd put the bite on me.'

Let me distribute demerits equally and tell about my father's literary Jewish friend, Mr Quentin Keller. He was older than the others, perhaps by some twelve years. He had a whispery voice and a long pale face and a daughter older than I. 'Bossy Wendy' I used to call her when, forced by her parents as I was by mine, Bossy Wendy had to take a whole afternoon of me. She had a room full of extraordinary toys, a miniature kitchen in which everything worked, of which all I recall her saying is 'Don't touch.' Wendy Keller had left Smith after her freshman year to marry the elder son of a Danish baron. Her father said to me, 'There is only one thing you need to know and that is that your father was a gentleman.'

Jackass was what I thought. Yes, Mr Quentin Keller was a jackass. But he was a literary one, for he had once written a play called *Forbearance*, in which I'd had a role. I had bounded across the stage like a tennis ball, into the arms of a young woman dressed up like an old one, and cried my one line: 'Here I am, Granny!' Of course, he did not make his living fiddling about with amateur theatricals; thanks to our meeting I had a good look at the inside of a conservative architect's private office—that was about all it brought me.

What were they so afraid of, I wondered. I had not yet seen that I was in a false position where they were concerned; being 'Miss Muir' had not made equals of us but lent distance. I thought they had read my true passport, the invisible one we all carry, but I had neither the wealth nor the influence a provincial society requires to make a passport valid. My credentials were lopsided: the important half of the scales was still in the air. I needed enormous collateral security—fame, an alliance with a powerful family, the power of money itself. I remember how Archie McEwen, trying to place me in some sensible context, to give me a voucher so he could take me home and show me to his wife, perhaps, asked his second question: 'Who inherited the—?'

'The what, Mr McEwen?'

He had not, of course, read 'Why I Am a Socialist'. I did not believe in inherited property. 'Who inherited the—?' could not cross my mind again for another ten years, and then it would be a drawer quickly opened and shut before demons could escape. To all three men the last eight years were like minutes; to me they had been several lives. Some of my confidence left me then. It came down to 'Next time I'll know better,' but would that be enough? I had been buffeted until now by other people's moods, principles, whims, tantrums; I had survived, but perhaps I had failed to grow some outer skin it was now too late to acquire. Olivia thought that; she was the only one. Olivia knew more about the limits of nerve than I did. Her knowledge came out of the clean, swept, orderly poverty that used to be tucked away in the corners of cities. It didn't spill out then, or give anyone a bad conscience. Nobody took its picture. Anyway, Olivia would not have sat for such a portrait. The fringed green rug she put over her treadle sewing machine was part of a personal fortune. On her mantelpiece stood a copper statuette of Voltaire in an armchair. It must have come down to her from some robustly anti-clerical ancestor. 'Who is he?' she said to me. 'You've been to school in a foreign country.' 'A governor of New France,' I replied. She knew Voltaire was the name of a bad man and she'd have thrown the figurine out, and it would have made one treasure less in the house. Olivia's maiden name was Ouvrardville, which was good in Quebec, but only really good if you were one of the rich ones. Because of her maiden name she did not want anyone ever to know she had worked for a family; she impressed this on me delicately—it was like trying to understand what a dragonfly wanted to tell. In the old days she had gone home every weekend, taking me with her if my parents felt my company was going to make Sunday a very long day. Now I understood what the weekends were about: her daughters, Berthe and Marguerite, for whose sake she worked, were home from their convent schools Saturday and Sunday and had to be chaperoned. Her relatives pretended not to notice that Olivia was poor or even that she was widowed, for which she seemed grateful. The result of all this elegant sham was that Olivia did not say, 'I was afraid you'd put the bite on me,' or keep me standing. She dried her tears and asked if there was a trunk to follow. No? She made a pot of tea and spread a starched cloth on the kitchen table and we sat down to a breakfast of toast and honey. The honey tin was a ten-pounder decorated with bees the size of hornets. Lifting it for her, I remarked, '*C'est collant*,' a word out of a frozen language that started to thaw when Olivia said, '*Tu vis?*'

On the advice of her confessor, who was to be my rival from now on, Olivia refused to tell me whatever she guessed or knew, and she was far too dignified to hint. Putting together the three men's woolly stories, I arrived at something about tuberculosis of the spine and a butchery of an operation. He started back to England to die there but either changed his mind or was too ill to begin the journey; at Quebec City, where he was to have taken ship, he shot himself in a public park at five o'clock in the morning. That was one version; another was that he died at sea and the gun was found in his luggage. The revolver figured in all three accounts. It was an officer's weapon from the Kaiser's war, that had belonged to his brother. Angus kept it at the back of a small drawer in the tall chest used for men's clothes and known in Canada as a highboy. In front of the revolver was a pigskin stud box and a pile of ironed handkerchiefs. Just describing that drawer dates it. How I happen to know the revolver was loaded and how I learned never to point a gun even in play is another story. I can tell you that I never again in my life looked inside a drawer that did not belong to me.

I know a woman whose father died, she thinks, in a concentration camp. Or was he shot in a schoolyard? Or hanged and thrown in a ditch? Were the ashes that arrived from some eastern plain his or another prisoner's? She invents different deaths. Her inventions have become her conversation at dinner parties. She takes on a child's voice and says 'My father died at Buchenwald.' She chooses and rejects elements of the last act; one avoids mentioning death, shooting, capital punishment, cremation, deportation, even fathers. Her inventions are not thought neurotic or exhibitionist but something sanctioned by history. Peacetime casualties are not like that. They are lightning bolts out of a sunny sky that strike only one house. All around the ashy ruin lilacs blossom, leaves gleam. Speculation in public about the disaster would be indecent. Nothing remains but a silent, recurring puzzlement to the survivors: Why here and not there? Why this and not that? Before July was out I had settled his fate in my mind and I never varied: I thought he had died of homesickness; sickness for England was the consumption, the gun, the everything. 'Everything' had to take it all in, for people in Canada then did not speak of irrational endings to life, and newspapers did not print that kind of news: this was because of the spiritual tragedy for Catholic families, and because the act had long been considered a criminal one in British law. If Catholic feelings were spared it gave the impression no one but Protestants ever went over the edge, which was unfair; and so the possibility was eliminated, and people came to a natural end in a running car in a closed garage, hanging from a rafter in the barn, in an icy lake with a canoe left to drift empty. Once I had made up my mind, the whole story somehow became none of my business: I had looked in a drawer that did not belong to me. More, if I was to live my own life I had to let go. I wrote in my journal that 'they' had got him but would not get me, and after that there was scarcely ever a mention.

My dream past evaporated. Montreal, in memory, was a leafy citadel where I knew every tree. In reality I recognized nearly nothing and had to start from scratch. Sherbrooke Street had been the dream street, pure white. It was the avenue poor Angus descended leaning on a walking stick. It was a moat I was not allowed to cross alone; it was lined with gigantic spreading trees through which light fell like a rain of coins. One day, standing at a corner, waiting for the light to change, I understood that the Sherbrooke Street of my exile—my Mecca, my Jerusalem—was this. It had to be: there could not be two. It was *only* this. The limitless green where in a perpetual spring I had been taken to play was the campus of McGill University. A house, whose beauty had brought tears to my sleep, to which in sleep I'd returned to find it inhabited by ugly strangers, gypsies, was a narrow stone thing with a shop on the ground floor and offices above—if that was it, for there were several like it. Through the bare panes of what might have been the sitting room, with its deep private window seats, I saw neon strip-lighting along a ceiling. Reality, as always, was narrow and dull. And yet what dramatic things had taken place on this very corner: Once Satan had approached me—furry dark skin, claws, red eyes, the lot. He urged me to cross the street and I did, in front of a car that braked in time. I explained, 'The Devil told me to.' I had no idea until then that my parents did not believe what I was taught in my convent school. (Satan is not bilingual, by the way; he speaks Quebec French.) My parents had no God and therefore no Fallen Angel. I was scolded for lying, which was a thing my father detested, and which my mother regularly did but never forgave in others.

Why these two nonbelievers wanted a strong religious education for me is one of the mysteries. (Even in loss of faith they were unalike, for he was ex-Anglican and she was ex-Lutheran and that is not your same atheist—no, not at all.) 'To make you tolerant' was a lame excuse, as was 'French', for I spoke fluent French with Olivia, and I could read in two languages before I was four. Discipline might have been one reason—God knows, the nuns provided plenty of that—but according to Olivia I did not need any. It cannot have been for the quality of the teaching, which was lamentable. I suspect that it was something like sending a dog to a trainer (they were passionate in their concern for animals, especially dogs), but I am not certain it ever brought me to heel. The first of my schools, the worst, the darkest, was on Sherbrooke Street too. When I heard, years later, it had been demolished, it was like the burial of a witch. I had remembered it penitentiary size, but what I found myself looking at one day was simply a very large stone house. A crocodile of little girls emerged from the front gate and proceeded along the street—white-faced, black-clad, eyes cast down. I knew they were bored, fidgety, anxious, and probably hungry. I should have felt pity, but at eighteen all that came to me was thankfulness that I had been correct about one thing throughout my youth, which I now considered ended: time had been on my side, faithfully, and unless you died you were always bound to escape.

Nadine Gordimer

Nadine Gordimer, who won the Nobel Prize for Literature in 1991, was born in 1923 in a small mining town called Spring in Transvaal, South Africa, to an English mother and a Latvian father, who was a watchmaker and later a jeweller. She had dreamed of being a dancer, but a minor heart ailment in childhood resulted in her being withdrawn from physical activities and acquiring much of her education by way of private tutoring; as a result, her energies were diverted into reading and writing. She published her first story at age fifteen, attended Witwatersrand University briefly, and established herself early as a writer of short stories, publishing her first book in 1949 and selling fiction to *The New Yorker*. She describes her gradual awareness and breaking out of the colour bar as a second birth, which gave her writing depth and focus. Many of her books were banned in South Africa for their frank and unrelenting portrait of apartheid, but she refused to go into exile and has continued to support the idea of black majority rule. She did not travel outside South Africa until she was thirty, but has since been very much in demand for lectures and public appearances, winning numerous international awards for her more than twenty-seven books. Her first book of stories, *Face to Face*, was published in 1949; this was followed by *The Soft Voice of the Serpent* (1952), *Friday's Footprint and Other Stories* (1960), *Not for Publication and Other Stories* (1965), *Livingstone's Companions* (1971), *Selected Stories* (1976), *Crimes of Conscience: Selected Short Stories* (1991), and many novels, the best known of which are *A World of Strangers* (1958), *Occasion for Loving* (1963), *The Conservationist* (1974), *Burger's Daughter* (1979), *July's People* (1981), and *A Sport of Nature* (1987). Gordimer's novel *My Son's Story* (1990) won the Nobel Prize for Literature in 1991. Her ideas on the craft of fiction and the world of South African politics are available in *Conversations with Nadine Gordimer* (1990), edited by Nancy Topping Bazin and Marilyn Dallman Seymour. Gordimer has one daughter and one son and lives in Johannesburg with her second husband, Reinhold Cassirer, an art dealer.

Gordimer believes that "the function of the writer is to make sense of life." She describes herself as a "natural writer," who came to politics by looking clearly at her own society: "I began writing out of a sense of wonder about life, a sense of its mystery, and also out of a sense of its chaos." However, harsh reality soon invaded her life and work: "I have come to the abstractions of politics through the flesh and blood of individual behaviour. I didn't know what politics was about until I saw it all happening to people," she said to Alan Ross in 1965. Although she suggests that "character is politics in South Africa," Gordimer claims never to have written for any specific audience: "My eyes are not out there; my struggle is with the material. It's like a net that you keep putting down into these mysterious waters of life around you, and you are struggling to bring up what is there, what is there in the depths, and of course you're also struggling with yourself because you're also down there." Gordimer distinguishes between art and propaganda, insisting that "the protest can only be as good as the writing." She advises writing posthumously: "The ideal way to write is as if you were dead and will be unaffected by any repercussions."

As she said to interviewer Pat Schwartz in 1977, Gordimer considers the matter of technique "a very delicate and complex question." "For me it is a matter of finding the approach that will release the most from the subject. The form is dictated by the subject. In some people's writing you are very conscious of the writer—the writer is between you and the subject all the time. My own aim is to be invisible and to make the identification for the reader with what is being written about and with the people in the work—not to distance the reader." She regards the creation of character as a "subconscious process," which includes a blending of everything a writer knows with much that is revealed only in the process of writing: "My method is to let the general seep up through the individual, whether or not the theme can be summed up afterwards as 'Jealousy,' 'Racial Conflict' or what have you." As she says to Jill Fullerton-Smith, "Yes, I do use descriptions sparingly, because I think it's very difficult to describe people's physical characteristics. I prefer to let the reader imagine them from the way the person speaks, moves, reacts and from a few little clues if they have some outstanding physical characteristics one way or another. I think this comes from having started as a short-story writer. . . . In a short story you've got to find signficant detail. You're not going to describe a person from head to foot, so just maybe the way they sit, some little tic that they have is going to create a line from which the reader can build up the whole picture. And I don't think it should be done all at once as was done in a nineteenth-century novel. . . . I prefer to drop these little sketches or hints through the work as it goes along, so that readers can build up their own picture of what this person looks like."

In a fascinating comment to Alan Ross, Gordimer describes the conception of much of her work: "My stories often originate in what might be called the tail-tip of a situation as it is whisked out of sight. A look, a sentence hanging in mid-air (I'm a great unconscious eavesdropper, always have been, on street corners, in restaurants, planes, etc.). A train of associations begins to play out; the story begins to form about the fragment. When stories arise of out actual experiences of my own, there is usually a lapse of months or even years between the happening and the writing, a lapse during which the experience lies dormant, gathers like a magnet those characters, phrases, ideas, ancillary events, that belong with it in kind, and will transform it. Time means nothing in that part of the mind where this takes place; something that happened ten years ago on the other side of the world coexists with something observed yesterday."

In terms of structure, Gordimer prefers the musical analogy. "A story to me is like a piece of music," she said to John Barkham in 1962, "with its distinctive movements, rhythms, and cadences. Only when I have worked these out to my satisfaction do I write them down, and, once on paper, I rarely have to change anything. Every story presents its own technical problems, and I confess that I enjoy grappling with them." As recently as 1986, she reasserted her interest in formal complexity and suggested to interviewers Marchant, Kitchen, and Rubin why she sometimes feels pushed towards longer forms such as the novel: "No, it's a matter of thematic layers. Even in my stories, I'm not satisfied with one layer. It's really like peeling an onion: once you begin to invent an alternative life for others, once you begin to find out why they are as they are, you just go deeper and deeper and deeper, and sometimes it seems the story doesn't give enough space to do that."

The Ultimate Safari

'The African adventure lives on . . . You can do it! The ultimate safari or expedition with leaders who know Africa.'

—Travel advertisement, *Observer*, 27 November 1988

That night our mother went to the shop and she didn't come back. Ever. What happened? I don't know. My father also had gone away one day and never come back; but he was fighting in the war. We were in the war, too, but we were children, we were like our grandmother and grandfather, we didn't have guns. The people my father was fighting—the bandits, they are called by our government—ran all over the place and we ran away from them like chickens chased by dogs. We didn't know where to go. Our mother went to the shop because someone said you could get some oil for cooking. We were happy because we hadn't tasted oil for a long time; perhaps she got the oil and someone knocked her down in the dark and took that oil from her. Perhaps she met the bandits. If you meet them, they will kill you. Twice they came to our village and we ran and hid in the bush and when they'd gone we came back and found they had taken everything; but the third time they came back there was nothing to take, no oil, no food, so they burned the thatch and the roofs of our houses fell in. My mother found some pieces of tin and we put those up over part of the house. We were waiting there for her that night she never came back.

We were frightened to go out, even to do our business, because the bandits did come. Not into our house—without a roof it must have looked as if there was no one in it, everything gone—but all through the village. We heard people screaming and running. We were afraid even to run, without our mother to tell us where. I am the middle one, the girl, and my little brother clung against my stomach with his arms round my neck and his legs round my waist like a baby monkey to its mother. All night my first-born brother kept in his hand a broken piece of wood from one of our burnt house-poles. It was to save himself if the bandits found him.

We stayed there all day. Waiting for her. I don't know what day it was; there was no school, no church any more in our village, so you didn't know whether it was a Sunday or a Monday.

When the sun was going down, our grandmother and grandfather came. Some-one from our village had told them we children were alone, our mother had not come back. I say 'grandmother' before 'grandfather' because it's like that: our grandmother is big and strong, not yet old, and our grandfather is small, you don't know where he is, in his loose trousers, he smiles but he hasn't heard what you're saying, and his hair looks as if he's left it full of soap suds. Our grandmother took us—me, the baby, my first-born brother, our grandfather—back to her house and we were all afraid (except the baby, asleep on our grandmother's back) of meeting the bandits on the way. We waited a long time at our grandmother's place. Perhaps it was a month. We were hungry. Our mother never came. While we were waiting for her to fetch us, our grandmother had no food for us, no food for our grandfather and herself. A woman with milk in her breasts gave us some for my little brother, although at our house he used to eat porridge, same as we did. Our grandmother took us to look for wild spinach but everyone else in the village did the same and there wasn't a leaf left.

Our grandfather, walking a little behind some young men, went to look for our mother but didn't find her. Our grandmother cried with other women and I sang the hymns with them. They brought a little food—some beans—but after two days there was nothing again. Our grandfather used to have three sheep and a cow and a vegetable garden but the bandits had long ago taken the sheep and the cow, because they were hungry, too; and when planting time came our grandfa-ther had no seed to plant.

So they decided—our grandmother did; our grandfather made little noises and rocked from side to side, but she took no notice—we would go away. We children were pleased. We wanted to go away from where our mother wasn't and where we were hungry. We wanted to go where there were no bandits and there was food. We were glad to think there must be such a place; away.

Our grandmother gave her church clothes to someone in exchange for some dried mealies and she boiled them and tied them in a rag. We took them with us when we went and she thought we would get water from the rivers but we didn't come to any river and we got so thirsty we had to turn back. Not all the way to our grandparents' place but to a village where there was a pump. She opened the basket where she carried some clothes and the mealies and she sold her shoes to buy a big plastic container for water. I said, *Gogo*, how will you go to church now even without shoes, but she said we had a long journey and too much to carry. At that village we met other people who were also going away. We joined them because they seemed to know where that was better than we did.

To get there we had to go through the Kruger Park. We knew about the Kruger Park. A kind of whole country of animals—elephants, lions, jackals, hyenas, hippos, crocodiles, all kinds of animals. We had some of them in our own country, before the war (our grandfather remembers; we children weren't born yet) but the bandits kill the elephants and sell their tusks, and the bandits and our soldiers have eaten all the buck. There was a man in our village without legs—a crocodile took them off, in our river; but all the same our country is a country of people, not animals. We knew about the Kruger Park because some of our men used to leave home to work there in the places where white people came to stay and look at the animals.

So we started to go away again. There were women and other children like me who had to carry the small ones on their backs when the women got tired. A man led us into the Kruger Park: are we there yet, are we there yet, I kept asking our grandmother. Not yet, the man said, when she asked him for me. He told us we had to take a long way to get round the fence, which he explained would kill you, roast off your skin the moment you touched it, like the wires high up on poles that give electric light in our towns. I've seen that sign of a head without ears or skin or hair on an iron box at the mission hospital we used to have before it was blown up.

When I asked the next time, they said we'd been walking in the Kruger Park for an hour. But it looked just like the bush we'd been walking through all day, and we hadn't seen any animals except the monkeys and birds which live around us at home, and a tortoise that, of course, couldn't get away from us. My first-born brother and the other boys brought it to the man so it could be killed and we could cook and eat it. He let it go because he told us we could not make a fire; all the time we were in the Park we must not make a fire because the smoke would show we were there. Police, wardens, would come and send us back where we came from. He said we must move like animals among the animals, away from the roads, away from the white people's camps. And at that moment I heard—I'm sure I was the first to hear—cracking branches and the sound of something parting grasses and I almost squealed because I thought it was the police, wardens— the people he was telling us to look out for—who had found us already. And it was an elephant, and another elephant, and more elephants, big blots of dark moved wherever you looked between the trees. They were curling their trunks round the red leaves of the mopane trees and stuffing them into their mouths. The babies leaned against their mothers. The almost grown-up ones wrestled like my first-born brother with his friends—only they used trunks instead of arms. I was so interested I forgot to be afraid. The man said we should just stand still and be quiet while the elephants passed. They passed very slowly because elephants are too big to need to run from anyone.

The buck ran from us. They jumped so high they seemed to fly. The wart-hogs stopped dead, when they heard us, and swerved off the way a boy in our village used to zigzag on the bicycle his father had brought back from the mines. We followed the animals to where they drank. When they had gone, we went to their waterholes. We were never thirsty without finding water, but the animals ate, ate all the time. Whenever you saw them they were eating, grass, trees, roots. And there was nothing for us. The mealies were finished. The only food we could eat was what the baboons ate, dry little figs full of ants, that grow along the branches of the trees at the rivers. It was hard to be like the animals.

When it was very hot during the day we would find lions lying asleep. They were the colour of the grass and we didn't see them at first but the man did, and he led us back and a long way round where they slept. I wanted to lie down like the lions. My little brother was getting thin but he was very heavy. When our grandmother looked for me, to put him on my back, I tried not to see. My first-born brother stopped talking; and when we rested he had to be shaken to get up again, as if he was just like our grandfather, he couldn't hear. I saw flies crawling on our grandmother's face and she didn't brush them off; I was frightened. I picked up a palm leaf and chased them.

We walked at night as well as by day. We could see the fires where the white people were cooking in the camps and we could smell the smoke and the meat. We watched the hyenas with their backs that slope as if they're ashamed, slipping through the bush after the smell. If one turned its head, you saw it had big brown shining eyes like our own, when we looked at each other in the dark. The wind brought voices in our own language from the compounds where the people who work in the camps live. A woman among us wanted to go to them at night and ask them to help us. They can give us the food from the dustbins, she said, she started wailing and our grandmother had to grab her and put a hand over her mouth. The men who led us had told us that we must keep out of the way of our people who worked at the Kruger Park; if they helped us they would lose their work. If they saw us, all they could do was pretend we were not there; they had seen only animals.

Sometimes we stopped to sleep for a little while at night. We slept close together. I don't know which night it was—because we were walking, walking, any time, all the time—we heard the lions very near. Not groaning loudly the way they did far off. Panting, like we do when we run, but it's a different kind of panting: you can hear they're not running, they're waiting, somewhere near. We all rolled closer together, on top of each other, the ones on the edge fighting to get into the middle. I was squashed against a woman who smelled bad because she was afraid but I was glad to hold tight on to her. I prayed to God to make the lions take someone on the edge and go. I shut my eyes not to see the tree from which a lion might jump right into the middle of us, where I was. The man who led us jumped up instead, and beat on the tree with a dead branch. He had taught us never to make a sound but he shouted. He shouted at the lions like a drunk man shouting at nobody in our village. The lions went away. We heard them groaning, shouting back at him from far off.

We were tired, so tired. My first-born brother and the man had to lift our grandfather from stone to stone where we found places to cross the rivers. Our grandmother is strong but her feet were bleeding. We could not carry the basket on our heads any longer, we couldn't carry anything except my little brother. We left our things under a bush. As long as our bodies get there, our grandmother said. Then we ate some wild fruit we didn't know from home and our stomachs ran. We were in the grass called elephant grass because it is nearly as tall as an elephant, that day we had those pains, and our grandfather couldn't just get down in front of people like my little brother, he went off into the grass to be on his own. We had to keep up, the man who led us always kept telling us, we must catch up, but we asked him to wait for our grandfather.

So everyone waited for our grandfather to catch up. But he didn't. It was the middle of the day; insects were singing in our ears and we couldn't hear him moving through the grass. We couldn't see him because the grass was so high and he was so small. But he must have been somewhere there inside his loose trousers and his shirt that was torn and our grandmother couldn't sew because she had no cotton. We knew he couldn't have gone far because he was weak and slow. We all went to look for him, but in groups, so we too wouldn't be hidden from each other in that grass. It got into our eyes and noses; we called him softly but the noise of the insects must have filled the little space left for hearing in his ears. We looked and looked but we couldn't find him. We stayed in that long grass all night. In my sleep I found him curled round in a place he had tramped down for himself, like the places we'd seen where the buck hide their babies.

When I woke up he still wasn't anywhere. So we looked again, and by now there were paths we'd made by going through the grass many times, it would be easy for him to find us if we couldn't find him. All that day we just sat and waited. Everything is very quiet when the sun is on your head, inside your head, even if you lie, like the animals, under the trees. I lay on my back and saw those ugly birds with hooked beaks and plucked necks flying round and round above us. We had passed them often where they were feeding on the bones of dead animals, nothing was ever left there for us to eat. Round and round, high up and then lower down and then high again. I saw their necks poking to this side and that. Flying round and round. I saw our grandmother, who sat up all the time with my little brother on her lap, was seeing them, too.

In the afternoon the man who led us came to our grandmother and told her the other people must move on. He said, If their children don't eat soon they will die.

Our grandmother said nothing.

I'll bring you water before we go, he told her.

Our grandmother looked at us, me, my first-born brother, and my little brother on her lap. We watched the other people getting up to leave. I didn't believe the grass would be empty, all around us, where they had been. That we would be alone in this place, the Kruger Park, the police or the animals would find us. Tears came out of my eyes and nose on to my hands but our grandmother took no notice. She got up, with her feet apart the way she puts them when she is going to lift firewood, at home in our village, she swung my little brother on to her back, tied him in her cloth—the top of her dress was torn and her big breasts were showing but there was nothing in them for him. She said, Come.

So we left the place with the long grass. Left behind. We went with the others and the man who led us. We started to go away, again.

There's a very big tent, bigger than a church or a school, tied down to the ground. I didn't understand that was what it would be, when we got there, away. I saw a thing like that the time our mother took us to the town because she heard our soldiers were there and she wanted to ask them if they knew where our father was. In that tent, people were praying and singing. This one is blue and white like that one but it's not for praying and singing, we live in it with other people who've come from our country. Sister from the clinic says we're 200 without counting the babies, and we have new babies, some were born on the way through the Kruger Park.

Inside, even when the sun is bright it's dark and there's a kind of whole village in there. Instead of houses each family has a little place closed off with sacks or cardboard from boxes—whatever we can find to show the other families it's yours and they shouldn't come in even though there's no door and no windows and no thatch, so that if you're standing up and you're not a small child you can see into everybody's house. Some people have even made paint from ground rocks and drawn designs on the sacks.

Of course, there really is a roof the tent is the roof, far, high up. It's like a sky. It's like a mountain and we're inside it; through the cracks paths of dust lead down, so thick you think you could climb them. The tent keeps off the rain overhead but the water comes in at the sides and in the little streets between our places you can only move along them one person at a time—the small kids like my little brother play in the mud. You have to step over them. My little brother doesn't play. Our grandmother takes him to the clinic when the doctor comes on Mondays. Sister says there's something wrong with his head, she thinks it's because we didn't have enough food at home. Because of the war. Because our father wasn't there. And then because he was so hungry in the Kruger Park. He likes just to lie about on our grandmother all day, on her lap or against her somewhere and he looks at us and looks at us. He wants to ask something but you can see he can't. If I tickle him he may just smile. The clinic gives us special powder to make into porridge for him and perhaps one day he'll be all right.

When we arrived we were like him—my first-born brother and I. I can hardly remember. The people who lived in the village near the tent took us to the clinic, it's where you have to sign that you've come—away, through the Kruger Park. We sat on the grass and everything was muddled. One Sister was pretty with her hair straightened and beautiful high-heeled shoes and she brought us the special powder. She said we must mix it with water and drink it slowly. We tore the packets open with our teeth and licked it all up, it stuck round my mouth and I sucked it from my lips and fingers. Some other children who had walked with us vomited. But I only felt everything in my belly moving, the stuff going down and around like a snake, and hiccups hurt me. Another Sister called us to stand in line on the veranda of the clinic but we couldn't. We sat all over the place there, falling against each other: the Sisters helped each of us up by the arm and then stuck a needle in it. Other needles drew our blood into tiny bottles. This was against sickness, but I didn't understand, every time my eyes dropped closed I thought I was walking, the grass was long. I saw the elephants, I didn't know we were away.

But our grandmother was still strong, she could still stand up, she knows how to write and she signed for us. Our grandmother got us this place in the tent against one of the sides, it's the best kind of place there because although the rain comes in, we can lift the flap when the weather is good and then the sun shines on us, the smells in the tent go out. Our grandmother knows a woman here who showed her where there is good grass for sleeping mats, and our grandmother made some for us. Once every month the food truck comes to the clinic. Our grandmother takes along one of the cards she signed and when it has been punched we get a sack of mealie meal. There are wheelbarrows to take it back to the tent: my first-born brother does this for her and then he and the other boys have races, steering the empty wheelbarrows back to the clinic. Sometimes he's lucky and a man who's bought beer in the village gives him money to deliver it—though that's not allowed, you're supposed to take that wheelbarrow straight back to the Sisters. He buys a cold drink and shares it with me if I catch him. On another day, every month, the church leaves a pile of old clothes in the clinic yard. Our grandmother has another card to get punched, and then we can choose something: I have two dresses, two pants and a jersey, so I can go to school.

The people in the village have let us join their school. I was surprised to find they speak our language; our grandmother told me, That's why they allow us to stay on their land. Long ago, in the time of our fathers, there was no fence that kills you, there was no Kruger Park between them and us, we were the same people under our own king, right from our village we left to this place we've come to.

Now that we've been in the tent so long—I have turned eleven and my little brother is nearly three although he is so small, only his head is big, he's not come right in it yet—some people have dug up the bare ground around the tent and planted beans and mealies and cabbage. The old men weave branches to put up fences round their gardens. No one is allowed to look for work in the towns but some of the women have found work in the village and can buy things. Our grandmother, because she's still strong, finds work where people are building houses—in this village the people build nice houses with bricks and cement, not mud like we used to have at our home. Our grandmother carries bricks for these people and fetches baskets of stones on her head. And so she has money to buy sugar and tea and milk and soap. The store gave her a calendar she has hung up on our flap of the tent. I am clever at school and she collected advertising paper people throw away outside the store and covered my school-books with it. She makes my first-born brother and me do our homework every afternoon before it gets dark because there is no room except to lie down, close together, just as we did in the Kruger Park, in our place in the tent, and candles are expensive. Our grandmother hasn't been able to buy herself a pair of shoes for church yet, but she has bought black school shoes and polish to clean them with for my first-born brother and me. Every morning, when people are getting up in the tent, the babies are crying, people are pushing each other at the taps outside and some children are already pulling the crusts of porridge off the pots we ate from last night, my first-born brother and I clean our shoes. Our grandmother makes us sit on our mats with our legs straight out so she can look carefully at our shoes to make sure we have done it properly. No other children in the tent have real school shoes. When we three look at them it's as if we are in a real house again, with no war, no away.

Some white people came to take photographs of our people living in the tent—they said they were making a film, I've never seen what that is though I know about it. A white woman squeezed into our space and asked our grandmother questions which were told to us in our language by someone who understands the white woman's.

'How long have you been living like this?'

'She means here?' Our grandmother said. 'In this tent, two years and one month.'

'And what do you hope for the future?'

'Nothing. I'm here.'

'But for your children?'

'I want them to learn so that they can get good jobs and money.'

'Do you hope to go back to your own country?'

'I will not go back.'

'But when the war is over—you won't be allowed to stay here? Don't you want to go home?'

I didn't think our grandmother wanted to speak again. I didn't think she was going to answer the white woman. The white woman put her head on one side and smiled at us.

Our grandmother looked away from her and spoke. 'There is nothing. No home.'

Why does our grandmother say that? Why? I'll go back. I'll go back through that Kruger Park. After the war, if there are no bandits any more, our mother may be waiting for us. And maybe when we left our grandfather, he was only left behind, he found his way somehow, slowly, through the Kruger Park, and he'll be there. They'll be home, and I'll remember them.

John Hawkes

John Hawkes was born in Stamford, Connecticut, in 1925. He briefly experienced wartime Germany as a driver for the American Field Service and taught for many years at Brown University in Providence, Rhode Island. He is perhaps the most startling and original fiction writer in the U.S. since Faulkner, his work having attracted the attention of critics such as Albert Guerrard, Leslie Fielder, and Robert Scholes; but he is relatively unknown by the fiction-reading public. His disturbing allegories call to mind the work of Kafka, fantastic worlds minutely rendered with images that seem to have been dredged from the labyrinths of the subconscious mind. His works include *The Cannibal* (1949), *The Beetle Leg* (1951), *The Owl* (1954), *The Lime Twig* (1961), *Second Skin* (1964), *Lunar Landscapes* (1969), *The Blood Oranges* (1971), *Death, Sleep & the Traveller* (1974), *Travesty* (1976), and *The Passion Artist* (1979). *A John Hawkes Symposium: Design and Debris* (*Insights I*), edited by Anthony Santore and Michael Pocalyko, and *John Hawkes: An Annotated Bibliography*, edited by Carol Hryciw are also available.

In response to Robert Scholes's comment that he has "the capacity to enjoy ugliness and to take a benign interest in the horrible" (a 1971 interview printed in *The New Fiction*, edited by Joe David Bellamy), John Hawkes confesses: "Yes, I write for precisely those two purposes. But on the other hand, I should think that most serious writers have similar purposes. After all, trying to reveal the essential beauty of the ugly, trying to elicit our own potential for weakness, failure, is not so unusual. All interesting fiction attempts to extend our sympathies, to allow us to fulfill all of the characteristics which conventional society would repress and destroy. From Conrad to Shakespeare, obviously, these same impulses and motivations are true."

The exchange here is doubly interesting, for it calls to mind something that Picasso said to Gertrude Stein about the nature of genuine creation: "You see, the situation is very simple. Anybody that creates a new thing has to make it ugly. The effort of creation is so great, that trying to get away from the other things, the contemporary insistence, is so great that the effort to break it gives the appearance of ugliness. Your followers can make it pretty, so generally followers are accepted before the master. The master has the stain of ugliness. The followers who make it pretty are accepted. The people then go back to the original. They see the beauty and bring it back to the original."

"It seems to me that fiction should achieve revenge for all the indignities of our childhood," Hawkes says; "it should be an act of rebellion against all constraints of the conventional pedestrian reality around us. Surely it should destroy conventional reality. I suppose all this is to say that to me the act of writing is criminal. If the act of the revolutionary is one of supreme idealism, it's also criminal. Obviously I think that the so-called criminal act is necessary to our survival. . . . I think the acts of courage and the acts of creativity evident in the writing of fiction are similar to the qualities evident in revolutionary acts. I think clear vision, detachment, personal strength, selflessness—these are needed to change the world literally and, no doubt, are also essential to the imaginative act."

While his subjects may shock and his critical terminology challenge the way we think about art and its functions, Hawkes seems very much a moralist in the deepest sense: "I think to write fiction that portrays the nightmarish aspects of the unconscious is simply to say at the outset that the opposite is equally true and equally valid. All of my fiction is, in a sense, lyrical, even the most terrifying of it. The nightmare simply leads one toward—or the nightmare could not exist without an awareness of—purity. But even in the most paradisal of worlds I've created, the roses conceal deadly thorns." In the same interview, he refutes W. H. Auden's pessimism about the social impact of art: "It seems obvious that the great acts of imagination are intimately related to the great acts of life—that history and the inner psychic history must dance their creepy minuet together if we are to save ourselves from total oblivion. . . . The great acts of the imagination create inner climates in which psychic events occur, which in themselves are important, and also affect the other literal events in time and space through what has occured in the act of reading."

Hawkes has been a candid and enthusiastic explainer of his aims in fiction. He describes his work as "almost totally visual, and the language depends almost totally on image." While he is interested in dreams and the unconscious, he rejects the murkiness of surrealism: "I believe in coldness, detachment, ruthlessness, a lot of consciousness in the choice of narrative material, in the creation of scenes and so on. It's simply that in the process of writing my hope is to liberate the kind of energy and to uncover the kinds of material that seem desperately and beautifully essential to us as readers." Not surprisingly, in a writer of what

Robert Scholes calls extended dramatic monologues that depend on a high degree of shock and complicity, references to the reader abound in Hawkes's critical commentaries and interviews; so, too, the works themselves, Gothic in subject and transformational in intent, never lose sight for a moment of the psychological involvement of the reader. "I write what I would like to read. I think that we read for joy, for pleasure, for excitement, for challenge. It would seem pretty obvious, however, that fiction is its own province. Fiction is a made thing—a man-made thing. It has its own beauties, its own structures, its own delights. Its only good is to please us and to relate to our essential growth. I don't see how we could live without it. It may be that the art of living is no more than to exercise the act of imagination in a more irrevocable way. It may be that to read a fiction is only to explore life's possibilities in a special way. I think that fiction and living are entirely separate and that one could not exist without the other."

A Song Outside

The vulture wheeled and bumped briefly against an invisible disturbance in the air and, surveying the desert, let fall some bitter discard from its curving unsheathed beak. Down below, its shadow rode uneasily and erratically on the sand. The bird sat up in the air, glaring, pushed and pulled in the palms of the sky, black and indigent. Now it hovered and turned, as if it had a quaking one-way rudder, in guardian flight over the whole desert and over the small motionless outcropping of white adobe buildings below as well. The vulture was not high, it glided, strayed only several hundred feet above the earth; yet, peering bottomward through its pinched red eye, it saw that it had a long way to fall.

It paused with a grinding of bare bone and watched something hop out of one hole in the desert and escape down another, crossing the hot red strata in a glance. But the vulture rested where it was as if it could not bear to drop its ballast and descend. It jerked its pointed head toward the mountains, seeming to fly in the face of the far-off blue and white of the peaks. And it leaned steeply over, circling, looking over the edge of this altitude and leaning into the dry wind, trusting its ragged heavy self on high.

The vulture approached over the buildings now from the southeast, flying until hunger should come to it, and hung its head limply on its breast for a good look at the village, staring down slowly and covertly at the small white figure of a naked man who lay on one of the flat roofs in the morning sun. The vulture twisted suddenly from the grasp of the air currents and calmly returned, slightly lower, to pass again over the roof and man. Then, watching, poised as steadily as it could, having dropped one aged glassy foot, it shuddered, closed its eyes and began to float straight up, unappeased and rasping.

The vulture drifted high enough to enter a current of cold air off the ice of the mountains, the crest of the sleeping lady. It quickly stretched out a wing and beat its way down to a softer, warmer zone. The desert turned like a circle of red clay. The vulture drew around again, flapping forward through the sun until it could see the bare road which did not enter the village but curved to pass away a good distance from the buildings. Once more the vulture spiralled, venturing to manoeuvre its split wings in the wind, head hanging always forward, loathing and apprehensive, as the serrated sand running with red and brown dipped and fell away. This vulture waited over the world; then, seeing the low humps of cacti moving faster, while the air passed clearly and harmlessly by, it began to make an almost undetectable noise, a mere sullen rattle in the throat. Then it was done, and in panic, squeezing its claws, the vulture suddenly began to fall. It did not glide serenely down but dropped with its red neck burning and its pale undercarriage shriveling for the crash. Momentarily the image of the naked man rose up, then disappeared, and the vulture landed.

It hit the sand with the dust of a volcano all around it, the heat of the earth covered it in the first instance of its return; and still prostrate, still settling, before it could feel that all its ugliness was safely removed from the air, a boot struck heavily into its side, and the vulture, square and hollow and feathered, rolled over, righted, drew back and exposed its black and white poisonous parts to the laughing men. It waited, then slowly retreated, trembling and dragging of tail.

"I see it," said one of the men, "I see right through it."

"Let's give it the boot again," said the other.

"It was hovering over us," said the first, laughing.

"Talking to us," said the other. "How would you like that thing making down on your grave, man."

The two men—they had left the adobe buildings and come out upon the desert merely to await the vulture's landing—moved side by side, their hands touching now and then as they walked back across the sand toward the shadows of empty doors and roof poles. Neither wore shirts. They were dressed in black trousers and to their bare feet were strapped identical pairs of large brown Indian sandals carved with images of bulls and serpents. On their bodies lay no fat or muscle, only the suggestion of shoulders and thin, barely jointed arms, all slender and white as if they, together, had cracked their way out from some large dry shell deposited on the sand. One of them was bald and had a small hard naked skull with a suggestion of lace across the forehead. The other's head was covered with hair, black hair greased and cut so that it drew to a sharp edge from the top of his brain to the bottom of his neck. A head of feathered black cultivated hair.

"Is it a vulture?" asked the man with the black hair. "That hot bird, is it a vulture?"

"It's a taboo," answered the man with the lace drawn gently apart for his eyes. "It's a mistake." He looked away to the mountains without blinking.

"Do you see it, man? Do you see it?"

"Sure. I see it."

Then, stopping, "I want to ride on it. You look at it, man, but I want to ride on it." The other turned toward him a face wrapped perfectly around the skull to which clung two small waxen ears.

"Don't get carried away, man."

They reached the buildings and side by side went under the arch like two figures into a tangled wood. They stooped and, neither standing aside, reluctant to part even at the entrance to a narrow way, brushed aside a drapery of black netting and climbed through a low door into a patio which was walled with rock and which radiated the white sun. A dry empty pool lay sunken in the middle of the patio. The native children had told them that if an ear was pressed to the drain hole of the pool, dead ladies could be heard singing and dancing in the pits of the earth. Now the men sat cross-legged against opposite walls and stared at each other across the narrow patio. Slowly their white shoulders began to burn.

They sat in the patio and breathed heavily, soricine and white, thin and light-headed under the pulseless sun and high on the altitude of the plain. Their razor-edged knees were crossed and they watched each other, while the sun made the floor of the patio glisten, turn brown or pink, and drew some faint odor from the dry manure falling to dust in the abandoned stable just over the wall. And the sun, the adobe, the plateau of the desert—out there squatted the vulture—and the buildings, the black holes of windows like cannon ports, the cornices of white and the silence: for the men all this was the mere end of a bus ride, the space for which there was no rent.

They lived in the patio—and in a small adjoining room which was connected to the patio by a door and an iron-barred window—like tropical birds, except that they ate beans and a kind of red soup and scrubbed their plates with sand after dark. They bathed one at a time at dusk, stood each alone by the pool and tipped a leather water bottle up on its trickling end. A pair of blue suspenders and a shirt in the corner of the patio and a few cigarettes hidden beneath an orange earthen jar were the only signs they left to tell that they were, or had been, in the village.

"*Lazy River*," said one, "*Lazy River!*" He leaned forward to see the movement on the other's lips or to catch the heartbeat. He put both hands to the sides of his head, cupping the palms around the greased sweepback of the hair, and watched his companion as if he himself might be intoxicated by the message of the sound. He whispered, "*Lazy River*," and his fingers slipped from his head to his shoulders and dragged down his chest until they lay in his lap, leaving long red lines down the length of the white skin.

He was humming. His lips were set, his cheekbones were motionless, the sun shone on top of the pompadour, rounded and contoured like something to be kept in a box of green grass. There was a rhythmic jerking in one of the crossed black legs. And immobile under the sun, shielded from the desert by the close wall, hard of eye and fluttering his hands, thinking—but not of wicker baskets drying in the sun, nor of the silver peaks, nor of the women dancing with golden moons pinned to their ears—this man who had been pulled by timid donkey from where the bus had stopped to the village, merely sat and hummed.

All at once he appeared to need more air; the mouth opened, snapped shut again; and the chest, though the white ribs had not moved, was satisfied. He hummed, and without melody; planting one harmonic structure upon another, evoked a bitter terrifying image of the vulture landing and sliding head first across the sand to devour its prey.

Nathaniel Hawthorne

Nathaniel Hawthorne was born in 1804 in Salem, Massachusetts. His father, who was a sea captain, died in the East Indies when Hawthorne was four. Hawthorne was educated at Bowdoin College in Maine and was a classmate of Longfellow and Franklin Pierce, who would later become president of the United States. After graduation, he returned to Salem to write. His early efforts, which appeared in 1837 in *Twice-Told Tales*, brought him neither money nor recognition, so he worked for a time in the Boston custom house and tried living at Brook Farm, a commune established by the Transcendental Club. He married in 1842 and worked as a surveyor of customs for the port of Salem. Hawthorne did not receive significant public recognition until the publication of *The Scarlet Letter* (1850). From 1853 to 1857, he held the post of United States Consul at Liverpool, after which he moved to Italy to improve his health. From 1860 until his death four years later, he resided in the States. His other works include *Mosses from an Old Manse* (1846), *The House of the Seven Gables* (1851), *The Blithedale Romance* (1852), and *The Marble Faun* (1861).

The Preface to the 1851 edition of *Twice-Told Tales*, appears on first reading to be a painfully self-deprecating bridge into the fiction, reflecting, obviously, Hawthorne's memory of the initially cool reception of his work. He describes the stories as unduly meditative, rather than dramatic; sentimental, rather than passionate; allegorical, rather than realistic; tame, rather than robust; pale and otherworldly, rather than vibrant. Still, he claimed for these sketches accessibility and clarity of expression: "It is, in fact, the style of a man of society. Every sentence, so far as it embodies thought or sensibility, may be understood and felt by anybody who will give himself the trouble to read it, and will take up the book in a proper mood." He describes these writings, finally—and this is an important observation—as an attempt "to open an intercourse with the world."

Hawthorne's efforts to open an intercourse with the world, of course, had to be made against the prevailing literary modes and expectations of his day. His introduction to "Rapuccini's Daughter," which appeared first in the *Democratic Review*, describes subtly some of his primary concerns as a writer of fiction. Hawthorne speaks of himself, once again, in the third person: "His writings, to do them justice, are not altogether destitute of fancy and originality; they might have won him greater reputation but for an inveterate love of allegory, which is apt to invest his plots and characters with the aspect of scenery and people in the clouds, and to steal away the human warmth out of his own conceptions. His fictions are sometimes historical, sometimes of the present day, and sometimes, so far as can be discovered, have little or no reference either to time or to space. In any case, he generally contents himself with a very slight embroidery of outward manners,—the faintest possible counterfeit of real life,—and endeavors to create an interest by some less obvious peculiarity of the subject. Occasionally a breath of Nature, a raindrop of pathos and tenderness, or a gleam of humor, will find its way into the midst of his fantastic imagery, and make us feel as if, after all, we were yet within the limits of our native earth. . . ."

While these remarks might be regarded as a form of self-criticism, Hawthorne's comments are less an *apologia* than a subtle guide to readers of his fiction, encouraging a shift in expectations and a greater generosity of spirit in approaching new work. Not for nothing had he learned his diplomatic skills in the custom house and in government service in Liverpool. As he suggests in "The Custom House," where the scribbler of story-books is described as no better than a degenerate or a fiddler, writers were often regarded with suspicion, if not hostility, given the prevailing Puritanism and anti-intellectualism of the New World. Hawthorne's Puritan heritage—both his great-grandfather and grandfather had been judges, the latter presiding over the Salem witch trials—and his literary apprenticeship conspired to require of him the more allegorical mode, which he called the "tale," and the "romance," which would allow him the greatest possible imaginative freedom.

The Artist of the Beautiful

An elderly man, with his pretty daughter on his arm, was passing along the street, and emerged from the gloom of the cloudy evening into the light that fell across the pavement from the window of a small shop. It was a projecting window; and on the inside were suspended a variety of watches, pinchbeck, silver, and one or two of gold, all with their faces turned from the streets, as if churlishly disinclined to inform the wayfarers what o'clock it was. Seated within the shop, sidelong to the window, with his pale face bent earnestly over some delicate piece of mechanism on which was thrown the concentrated lustre of a shade lamp, appeared a young man.

"What can Owen Warland be about?" muttered old Peter Hovenden, himself a retired watchmaker, and the former master of this same young man whose occupation he was now wondering at. "What can the fellow be about? These six months past I have never come by his shop without seeing him just as steadily at work as now. It would be a flight beyond his usual foolery to seek for the perpetual motion; and yet I know enough of my old business to be certain that what he is now so busy with is no part of the machinery of a watch."

"Perhaps, father," said Annie, without showing much interest in the question, "Owen is inventing a new kind of timekeeper. I am sure he has ingenuity enough."

"Poh, child! He has not the sort of ingenuity to invent anything better than a Dutch toy," answered her father, who had formerly been put to much vexation by Owen Warland's irregular genius. "A plague on such ingenuity! All the effect that ever I knew of it was to spoil the accuracy of some of the best watches in my shop. He would turn the sun out of its orbit and derange the whole course of time, if, as I said before, his ingenuity could grasp anything bigger than a child's toy!"

"Hush, father! He hears you!" whispered Annie, pressing the old man's arm. "His ears are as delicate as his feelings; and you know how easily disturbed they are. Do let us move on."

So Peter Hovenden and his daughter Annie plodded on without further conversation, until in a by-street of the town they found themselves passing the open door of a blacksmith's shop. Within was seen the forge, now blazing up and illuminating the high and dusky roof, and now confining its lustre to a narrow precinct of the coal-strewn floor, according as the breath of the bellows was puffed forth or again inhaled into its vast leathern lungs. In the intervals of brightness it was easy to distinguish objects in remote corners of the shop and the horseshoes that hung upon the wall; in the momentary gloom the fire seemed to be glimmering amidst the vagueness of unenclosed space. Moving about in this red glare and alternate dusk was the figure of the blacksmith, well worthy to be viewed in so picturesque an aspect of light and shade, where the bright blaze struggled with the black night, as if each would have snatched his comely strength from the other. Anon he drew a white-hot bar of iron from the coals, laid it on the anvil, uplifted his arm of might, and was soon enveloped in the myriads of sparks which the strokes of his hammer scattered into the surrounding gloom.

"Now, that is a pleasant sight," said the old watchmaker. "I know what it is to work in gold; but give me the worker in iron after all is said and done. He spends his labor upon a reality. What say you, daughter Annie?"

"Pray don't speak so loud, father," whispered Annie, "Robert Danforth will hear you."

"And what if he should hear me?" said Peter Hovenden. "I say again, it is a good and a wholesome thing to depend upon main strength and reality, and to earn one's bread with the bare and brawny arm of a blacksmith. A watchmaker gets his brain puzzled by his wheels within a wheel, or loses his health or the nicety of his eyesight, as was my case, and finds himself at middle age, or a little after, past labor at his own trade and fit for nothing else, yet too poor to live at his ease. So I say once again, give me main strength for my money. And then, how it takes the nonsense out of a man! Did you ever hear of a blacksmith being such a fool as Owen Warland yonder?"

"Well said, uncle Hovenden!" shouted Robert Danforth from the forge, in a full, deep, merry voice, that made the roof reëcho. "And what says Miss Annie to that doctrine? She, I suppose, will think it a genteeler business to tinker up a lady's watch than to forge a horseshoe or make a gridiron."

Annie drew her father onward without giving him time for reply.

But we must return to Owen Warland's shop, and spend more meditation upon his history and character than either Peter Hovenden, or probably his daughter Annie, or Owen's old school-fellow, Robert Danforth, would have thought due to so slight a subject. From the time that his little fingers could grasp a penknife, Owen had been remarkable for a delicate ingenuity, which sometimes produced pretty shapes in wood, principally figures of flowers and birds, and sometimes seemed to aim at the hidden mysteries of mechanism. But it was always for purposes of grace, and never with any mockery of the useful. He did not, like the crowd of school-boy artisans, construct little windmills on the angle of a barn or watermills across the neighboring brook. Those who discovered such peculiarity in the boy as to think it worth their while to observe him closely, sometimes saw reason to suppose that he was attempting to imitate the beautiful movements of Nature as exemplified in the flight of birds or the activity of little animals. It seemed, in fact, a new development of the love of the beautiful, such as might have made him a poet, a painter, or a sculptor, and which was as completely refined from all utilitarian coarseness as it could have been in either of the fine arts. He looked with singular distaste at the stiff and regular processes of ordinary machinery. Being once carried to see a steam engine, in the expectation that his intuitive comprehension of mechanical principles would be gratified, he turned pale and grew sick, as if something monstrous and unnatural had been presented to him. This horror was partly owing to the size and terrible energy of the iron laborer; for the character of Owen's mind was microscopic, and tended naturally to the minute, in accordance with his diminutive frame and the marvellous smallness and delicate power of his fingers. Not that his sense of beauty was thereby diminished into a sense of prettiness. The beautiful idea has no relation to size, and may be as perfectly developed in a space too minute for any but microscopic investigation as within the ample verge that is measured by the arc of the rainbow. But, at all events, this characteristic minuteness in his objects and accomplishments made the world even more incapable than it might otherwise have been of appreciating Owen Warland's genius. The boy's relatives saw nothing better to be done—as perhaps there was not—than to bind him apprentice to a watchmaker, hoping that his strange ingenuity might thus be regulated and put to utilitarian purposes.

Peter Hovenden's opinion of his apprentice has already been expressed. He could make nothing of the lad. Owen's apprehension of the professional mysteries, it is true, was inconceivably quick; but he altogether forgot or despised the grand object of a watchmaker's business, and cared no more for the measurement of time than if it had been merged into eternity. So long, however, as he remained under his old master's care, Owen's lack of sturdiness made it possible, by strict injunctions and sharp oversight, to restrain his creative eccentricity within bounds; but when his apprenticeship was served out, and he had taken the little shop which Peter Hovenden's failing eyesight compelled him to relinquish, then did people recognize how unfit a person was Owen Warland to lead old blind Father Time along his daily course. One of his most rational projects was to connect a musical operation with the machinery of his watches, so that all the harsh dissonances of life might be rendered tuneful, and each flitting moment fall into the abyss of the past in golden drops of harmony. If a family clock was intrusted to him for repair,—one of those tall, ancient clocks that have grown nearly allied to human nature by measuring out the lifetime of many generations,—he would take upon himself to arrange a dance or funeral procession of figures across its venerable face, representing twelve mirthful or melancholy hours. Several freaks of this kind quite destroyed the young watchmaker's credit with that steady and matter-of-fact class of people who hold the opinion that time is not to be trifled with, whether considered as the medium of advancement and prosperity in this world or preparation for the next. His custom rapidly diminished—a misfortune, however, that was probably reckoned among his better accidents by Owen Warland, who was becoming more and more absorbed in a secret occupation which drew all his science and manual dexterity into itself, and likewise gave full employment to the characteristic tendencies of his genius. This pursuit had already consumed many months.

After the old watchmaker and his pretty daughter had gazed at him out of the obscurity of the street, Owen Warland was seized with a fluttering of the nerves, which made his hand tremble too violently to proceed with such delicate labor as he was now engaged upon.

"It was Annie herself!" murmured he. "I should have known it by this throbbing of my heart, before I heard her father's voice. Ah, how it throbs! I shall scarcely be able to work again on this exquisite mechanism to-night. Annie! dearest Annie! thou shouldst give firmness to my heart and hand, and not shake them thus, for if I strive to put the very spirit of beauty into form and give it motion, it is for thy sake alone. O throbbing heart, be quiet! If my labor be thus thwarted, there will come vague and unsatisfied dreams which will leave me spiritless to-morrow."

As he was endeavoring to settle himself again to his task, the shop door opened and gave admittance to no other than the stalwart figure which Peter Hovenden had paused to admire, as seen amid the light and shadow of the blacksmith's shop. Robert Danforth had brought a little anvil of his own manufacture, and peculiarly constructed, which the young artist had recently bespoken. Owen examined the article and pronounced it fashioned according to his wish.

"Why, yes," said Robert Danforth, his strong voice filling the shop as with the sound of a bass viol, "I consider myself equal to anything in the way of my own trade; though I should have made but a poor figure at yours with such a fist as this," added he, laughing, as he laid his vast hand beside the delicate one of Owen. "But what then? I put more main strength into one blow of my sledge hammer than all that you have expended since you were a 'prentice. Is not that the truth?"

"Very probably," answered the low and slender voice of Owen. "Strength is an earthly monster. I make no pretensions to it. My force, whatever there may be of it, is altogether spiritual."

"Well, but, Owen, what are you about?" asked his old school-fellow, still in such a hearty volume of tone that it made the artist shrink, especially as the question related to a subject so sacred as the absorbing dream of his imagination. "Folks do say that you are trying to discover the perpetual motion."

"The perpetual motion? Nonsense!" replied Owen with a movement of disgust; for he was full of little petulances. "It can never be discovered. It is a dream that may delude men whose brains are mystified with matter, but not me. Besides, if such a discovery were possible, it would not be worth my while to make it only to have the secret turned to such purposes as are now effected by steam and water power. I am not ambitious to be honored with the paternity of a new kind of cotton machine."

"That would be droll enough!" cried the blacksmith, breaking out into such an uproar of laughter that Owen himself and the bell glasses on his workboard quivered in unison. "No, no, Owen! No child of yours will have iron joints and sinews. Well, I won't hinder you any more. Good night, Owen, and success, and if you need any assistance, so far as a downright blow of hammer upon anvil will answer the purpose, I'm your man."

And with another laugh the man of main strength left the shop.

"How strange it is," whispered Owen Warland to himself, leaning his head upon his hand, "that all my musings, my purposes, my passion for the beautiful, my consciousness of power to create it,—a finer, more ethereal power, of which this earthly giant can have no conception,—all, all, look so vain and idle whenever my path is crossed by Robert Danforth! He would drive me mad were I to meet him often. His hard, brute force darkens and confuses the spiritual element within me; but I, too, will be strong in my own way. I will not yield to him."

He took from beneath a glass a piece of minute machinery, which he set in the condensed light of his lamp, and looking intently at it through a magnifying glass, proceeded to operate with a delicate instrument of steel. In an instant, however, he fell back in his chair and clasped his hands, with a look of horror on his face that made its small features as impressive as those of a giant would have been.

"Heaven! What have I done?" exclaimed he. "The vapor, the influence of that brute force,—it has bewildered and obscured my perception. I have made the very stroke—the fatal stroke—that I have dreaded from the first. It is all over—the toil of months, the object of my life. I am ruined!"

And there he sat, in strange despair, until his lamp flickered in the socket and left the Artist of the Beautiful in darkness.

Thus it is that ideas, which grow up within the imagination and appear so lovely to it and of a value beyond whatever men call valuable, are exposed to be shattered and annihilated by contact with the practical. It is requisite for the ideal artist to possess a force of character that seems hardly compatible with its delicacy; he must keep his faith in himself while the incredulous world assails him with its utter disbelief; he must stand up against mankind and be his own sole disciple, both as respects his genius and the objects to which it is directed.

For a time Owen Warland succumbed to this severe but inevitable test. He spent a few sluggish weeks with his head so continually resting in his hands that the towns-people had scarcely an opportunity to see his countenance. When at last it was again uplifted to the light of day, a cold, dull, nameless change was perceptible upon it. In the opinion of Peter Hovenden, however, and that order of sagacious understandings who think that life should be regulated, like clockwork, with leaden weights, the alteration was entirely for the better. Owen now, indeed, applied himself to business with dogged industry. It was marvellous to witness the obtuse gravity with which he would inspect the wheels of a great old silver watch, thereby delighting the owner, in whose fob it had been worn till he deemed it a portion of his own life and was accordingly jealous of its treatment. In consequence of the good report thus acquired, Owen Warland was invited by the proper authorities to regulate the clock in the church steeple. He succeeded so admirably in this matter of public interest that the merchants gruffly acknowledged his merits on 'Change; the nurse whispered his praises as she gave the potion in the sick-chamber; the lover blessed him at the hour of the appointed interview; and the town in general thanked Owen for the punctuality of dinner time. In a word, the heavy weight upon his spirits kept everything in order, not merely within his own system, but wheresoever the iron accents of the church clock were audible. It was a circumstance, though minute, yet characteristic of his present state, that, when employed to engrave names or initials on silver spoons, he now wrote the requisite letters in the plainest possible style, omitting a variety of fanciful flourishes that had heretofore distinguished his work in this kind.

One day, during the era of this happy transformation, old Peter Hovenden came to visit his former apprentice.

"Well, Owen," said he, "I am glad to hear such good accounts of you from all quarters, and especially from the town clock yonder, which speaks in your commendation every hour of the twenty-four. Only get rid altogether of your nonsensical trash about the beautiful, which I nor nobody else, nor yourself to boot, could ever understand,—only free yourself of that, and your success in life is as sure as daylight. Why, if you go on in this way, I should even venture to let you doctor this precious old watch of mine; though, except my daughter Annie, I have nothing else so valuable in the world."

"I should hardly dare touch it, sir," replied Owen, in a depressed tone; for he was weighed down by his old master's presence.

"In time," said the latter,—"in time, you will be capable of it."

The old watchmaker, with the freedom naturally consequent on his former authority, went on inspecting the work which Owen had in hand at the moment, together with other matters that were in progress. The artist, meanwhile, could scarcely lift his head. There was nothing so antipodal to his nature as this man's cold, unimaginative sagacity, by contact with which everything was converted into a dream except the densest matter of the physical world. Owen groaned in spirit and prayed fervently to be delivered from him.

"But what is this?" cried Peter Hovenden abruptly, taking up a dusty bell glass, beneath which appeared a mechanical something, as delicate and minute as the system of a butterfly's anatomy. "What have we here? Owen! Owen! there is witchcraft in these little chains, and wheels, and paddles. See! with one pinch of my finger and thumb I am going to deliver you from all future peril."

"For Heaven's sake," screamed Owen Warland, springing up with wonderful energy, "as you would not drive me mad, do not touch it! The slightest pressure of your finger would ruin me forever."

"Aha, young man! And is it so?" said the old watchmaker, looking at him with just enough of penetration to torture Owen's soul with the bitterness of worldly criticism. "Well, take your own course; but I warn you again that in this small piece of mechanism lives your evil sprit. Shall I exorcise him?"

"You are my evil spirit," answered Owen, much excited,—"you and the hard, coarse world! The leaden thoughts and the despondency that you fling upon me are my clogs, else I should long ago have achieved the task that I was created for."

Peter Hovenden shook his head, with the mixture of contempt and indignation which mankind, of whom he was partly a representative, deem themselves entitled to feel towards all simpletons who seek other prizes than the dusty one along the highway. He then took his leave, with an uplifted finger and a sneer upon his face that haunted the artist's dreams for many a night afterwards. At the time of his old master's visit, Owen was probably on the point of taking up the relinquished task; but, by this sinister event, he was thrown back into the state whence he had been slowly emerging.

But the innate tendency of his soul had only been accumulating fresh vigor during its apparent sluggishness. As the summer advanced he almost totally relinquished his business, and permitted Father Time, so far as the old gentleman was represented by the clocks and watches under his control, to stray at random through human life, making infinite confusion among the train of bewildered hours. He wasted the sunshine, as people said, in wandering through the woods and fields and along the banks of streams. There, like a child, he found amusement in chasing butterflies or watching the motions of water insects. There was something truly mysterious in the intentness with which he contemplated these living playthings as they sported on the breeze or examined the structure of an imperial insect whom he had imprisoned. The chase of butterflies was an apt emblem of the ideal pursuit in which he had spent so many golden hours; but would the beautiful idea ever be yielded to his hand like the butterfly that symbolized it? Sweet, doubtless, were these days, and congenial to the artist's soul. They were full of bright conceptions, which gleamed through his intellectual world as the butterflies gleamed through the outward atmosphere, and were real to him, for the instant, without the toil, and perplexity, and many disappointments of attempting to make them visible to the sensual eye. Alas that the artist, whether in poetry, or whatever other material, may not content himself with the inward enjoyment of the beautiful, but must chase the flitting mystery beyond the verge of his ethereal domain, and crush its frail being in seizing it with a material grasp. Owen Warland felt the impulse to give external reality to his ideas as irresistibly as any of the poets or painters who have arrayed the world in a dimmer and fainter beauty, imperfectly copied from the richness of their visions.

The night was now his time for the slow progress of re-creating the one idea to which all his intellectual activity referred itself. Always at the approach of dusk he stole into the town, locked himself within his shop, and wrought with patient delicacy of touch for many hours. Sometimes he was startled by the rap of the watchman, who, when all the world should be asleep, had caught the gleam of lamplight through the crevices of Owen Warland's shutters. Daylight, to the morbid sensibility of his mind, seemed to have an intrusiveness that interfered with his pursuits. On cloudy and inclement days, therefore, he sat with his head upon his hands, muffling, as it were, his sensitive brain in a mist of indefinite musings; for it was a relief to escape from the sharp distinctness with which he was compelled to shape out his thoughts during his nightly toil.

From one of these fits of torpor he was aroused by the entrance of Annie Hovenden, who came into the shop with the freedom of a customer, and also with something of the familiarity of a childish friend. She had worn a hole through her silver thimble, and wanted Owen to repair it.

"But I don't know whether you will condescend to such a task," said she, laughing, "now that you are so taken up with the notion of putting spirit into machinery."

"Where did you get that idea, Annie?" said Owen, starting in surprise.

"Oh, out of my own head," answered she, "and from something that I heard you say, long ago, when you were but a boy and I a little child. But come; will you mend this poor thimble of mine?"

"Anything for your sake, Annie," said Owen Warland,—"anything, even were it to work at Robert Danforth's forge."

"And that would be a pretty sight!" retorted Annie, glancing with imperceptible slightness at the artist's small and slender frame. "Well; here is the thimble."

"But that is a strange idea of yours," said Owen, "about the spiritualization of matter."

And then the thought stole into his mind that this young girl possessed the gift to comprehend him better than all the world besides. And what a help and strength would it be to him in his lonely toil if he could gain the sympathy of the only being whom he loved! To persons whose pursuits are insulated from the common business of life—who are either in advance of mankind or apart from it—there often comes a sensation of moral cold that makes the spirit shiver as if it had reached the frozen solitudes around the pole. What the prophet, the poet, the reformer, the criminal, or any other man with human yearnings, but separated from the multitude by a peculiar lot, might feel, poor Owen felt.

"Annie," cried he, growing pale as death at the thought, "how gladly would I tell you the secret of my pursuit! You, methinks, would estimate it rightly. You, I know, would hear it with a reverence that I must not expect from the harsh, material world."

"Would I not? to be sure I would!" replied Annie Hovenden, lightly laughing. "Come; explain to me quickly what is the meaning of this little whirligig, so delicately wrought that it might be a plaything for Queen Mab. See! I will put it in motion."

"Hold!" exclaimed Owen, "hold!"

Annie had but given the slightest possible touch, with the point of a needle, to the same minute portion of complicated machinery which has been more than once mentioned, when the artist seized her by the wrist with a force that made her scream aloud. She was affrighted at the convulsion of intense rage and anguish that writhed across his features. The next instant he let his head sink upon his hands.

"Go, Annie," murmured he; "I have deceived myself, and must suffer for it. I yearned for sympathy, and thought, and fancied, and dreamed that you might give it me; but you lack the talisman, Annie, that should admit you into my secrets. That touch has undone the toil of months and the thought of a lifetime! It was not your fault, Annie; but you have ruined me!"

Poor Owen Warland! He had indeed erred, yet pardonably; for if any human spirit could have sufficiently reverenced the processes so sacred in his eyes, it must have been a woman's. Even Annie Hovenden, possibly, might not have disappointed him had she been enlightened by the deep intelligence of love.

The artist spent the ensuing winter in a way that satisfied any persons who had hitherto retained a hopeful opinion of him that he was, in truth, irrevocably doomed to inutility as regarded the world, and to an evil destiny on his own part. The decease of a relative had put him in possession of a small inheritance. Thus freed from the necessity of toil, and having lost the steadfast influence of a great purpose,—great, at least, to him,—he abandoned himself to habits from which it might have been supposed the mere delicacy of his organization would have availed to secure him. But when the ethereal portion of a man of genius is obscured, the earthly part assumes an influence the more uncontrollable, because the character is now thrown off the balance to which Providence had so nicely adjusted it, and which, in coarser natures, is adjusted by some other method. Owen Warland made proof of whatever show of bliss may be found in riot. He looked at the world through the golden medium of wine, and contemplated the visions that bubble up so gayly around the brim of the glass, and that people the air with shapes of pleasant madness, which so soon grow ghostly and forlorn. Even when this dismal and inevitable change had taken place, the young man might still have continued to quaff the cup of enchantments, though its vapor did but shroud life in gloom and fill the gloom with spectres that mocked at him. There was a certain irksomeness of spirit, which, being real, and the deepest sensation of which the artist was now conscious, was more intolerable than any fantastic miseries and horrors that the abuse of wine could summon up. In the latter case he could remember, even out of the midst of his trouble, that all was but a delusion; in the former, the heavy anguish was his actual life.

From this perilous state he was redeemed by an incident which more than one person witnessed, but of which the shrewdest could not explain or conjecture the operation on Owen Warland's mind. It was very simple. On a warm afternoon of spring, as the artist sat among his riotous companions with a glass of wine before him, a splendid butterfly flew in at the open window and fluttered about his head.

"Ah," exclaimed Owen, who had drank freely, "are you alive again, child of the sun and playmate of the summer breeze, after your dismal winter's nap? Then it is time for me to be at work!"

And, leaving his unemptied glass upon the table, he departed and was never known to sip another drop of wine.

And now, again, he resumed his wanderings in the woods and fields. It might be fancied that the bright butterfly, which had come so spirit-like into the window as Owen sat with the rude revellers, was indeed a spirit commissioned to recall him to the pure, ideal life that had so etherealized him among men. It might be fancied that he went forth to seek this spirit in its sunny haunts; for still, as in the summer time gone by, he was seen to steal gently up wherever a butterfly had alighted, and lose himself in contemplation of it. When it took flight his eye followed the winged vision, as if its airy track would show the path to heaven. But what could be the purpose of the unseasonable toil, which was again resumed, as the watchman knew by the lines of lamplight through the crevices of Owen Warland's shutters? The towns-people had one comprehensive explanation of all these singularities. Owen Warland had gone mad! How universally efficacious—how satisfactory, too, and soothing to the injured sensibility of narrowness and dulness—is this easy method of accounting for whatever lies beyond the world's most ordinary scope! From St. Paul's days down to our poor little Artist of the Beautiful, the same talisman had been applied to the elucidation of all mysteries in the words or deeds of men who spoke or acted too wisely or too well. In Owen Warland's case the judgment of his towns-people may have been correct. Perhaps he was mad. The lack of sympathy—that contrast between himself and his neighbors which took away the restraint of example—was enough to make him so. Or possibly he had caught just so much of ethereal radiance as served to bewilder him, in an earthly sense, by its intermixture with the common daylight.

One evening, when the artist had returned from a customary ramble and had just thrown the lustre of his lamp on the delicate piece of work so often interrupted, but still taken up again, as if his fate were embodied in its mechanism, he was surprised by the entrance of old Peter Hovenden. Owen never met this man without a shrinking of the heart. Of all the world he was the most terrible, by reason of a keen understanding which saw so distinctly what it did see, and disbelieved so uncompromisingly in what it could not see. On this occasion the old watchmaker had merely a gracious word or two to say.

"Owen, my lad," said he, "we must see you at my house to-morrow night."

The artist began to mutter some excuse.

"Oh, but it must be so," quoth Peter Hovenden, "for the sake of the days when you were one of the household. What, my boy! don't you know that my daughter Annie is engaged to Robert Danforth? We are making an entertainment, in our humble way, to celebrate the event."

"Ah!" said Owen.

That little monosyllable was all he uttered; its tone seemed cold and unconcerned to an ear like Peter Hovenden's; and yet there was in it the stifled outcry of the poor artist's heart, which he compressed within him like a man holding down an evil spirit. One slight outbreak, however, imperceptible to the old watchmaker, he allowed himself. Raising the instrument with which he was about to begin his work, he let it fall upon the little system of machinery that had, anew, cost him months of thought and toil. It was shattered by the stroke!

Owen Warland's story would have been no tolerable representation of the troubled life of those who strive to create the beautiful, if, amid all other thwarting influences, love had not interposed to steal the cunning from his hand. Outwardly he had been no ardent or enterprising lover; the career of his passion had confined its tumults and vicissitudes so entirely within the artist's imagination that Annie herself had scarcely more than a woman's intuitive perception of it; but, in Owen's view, it covered the whole field of his life. Forgetful of the time when she had shown herself incapable of any deep response, he had persisted in connecting all his dreams of artistical success with Annie's image; she was the visible shape in which the spiritual power that he worshiped, and on whose altar he hoped to lay a not unworthy offering, was made manifest to him. Of course he had deceived himself; there were no such attributes in Annie Hovenden as his imagination had endowed her with. She, in the aspect which she wore to his inward vision, was as much a creature of his own as the mysterious piece of mechanism would be were it ever realized. Had he become convinced of his mistake through the medium of successful love,—had he won Annie to his bosom, and there beheld her fade from angel into ordinary woman,—the disappointment might have driven him back, with concentrated energy, upon his sole remaining object. On the other hand, had he found Annie what he fancied, his lot would have been so rich in beauty that out of its mere redundancy he might have wrought the beautiful into many a worthier type than he had toiled for; but the guise in which his sorrow came to him, the sense that the angel of his life had been snatched away and given to a rude man of earth and iron, who could neither need nor appreciate her ministrations,—this was the very perversity of fate that makes human existence appear too absurd and contradictory to be the scene of one other hope or one other fear. There was nothing left for Owen Warland but to sit down like a man that had been stunned.

He went through a fit of illness. After his recovery his small and slender frame assumed an obtuser garniture of flesh than it had ever before worn. His thin cheeks became round; his delicate little hand, so spiritually fashioned to achieve fairy task-work, grew plumper than the hand of a thriving infant. His aspect had a childishness such as might have induced a stranger to pat him on the head—pausing, however, in the act, to wonder what manner of child was here. It was as if the spirit had gone out of him, leaving the body to flourish in a sort of vegetable existence. Not that Owen Warland was idiotic. He could talk, and not irrationally. Somewhat of a babbler, indeed, did people begin to think him; for he was apt to discourse at wearisome length of marvels of mechanism that he had read about in books, but which he had learned to consider as absolutely fabulous. Among them he enumerated the Man of Brass, constructed by Albertus Magnus, and the Brazen Head of Friar Bacon; and, coming down to later times, the automata of a little coach and horses, which it was pretended had been manufactured for the Dauphin of France; together with an insect that buzzed about the ear like a living fly, and yet was but a contrivance of minute steel springs. There was a story, too, of a duck that waddled, and quacked, and ate; though, had any honest citizen purchased it for dinner, he would have found himself cheated with the mere mechanical apparition of a duck.

"But all these accounts," said Owen Warland, "I am now satisfied are mere impositions."

Then, in a mysterious way, he would confess that he once thought differently. In his idle and dreamy days he had considered it possible, in a certain sense, to spiritualize machinery, and to combine with the new species of life and motion thus produced a beauty that should attain to the ideal which Nature has proposed to herself in all her creatures, but has never taken pains to realize. He seemed, however, to retain no very distinct perception either of the process of achieving this object or of the design itself.

"I have thrown it all aside now," he would say. "It was a dream such as young men are always mystifying themselves with. Now that I have acquired a little common sense, it makes me laugh to think of it."

Poor, poor and fallen Owen Warland! These were the symptoms that he had ceased to be an inhabitant of the better sphere that lies unseen around us. He had lost his faith in the invisible, and now prided himself, as such unfortunates invariably do, in the wisdom which rejected much that even his eye could see, and trusted confidently in nothing but what his hand could touch. This is the calamity of men whose spiritual part dies out of them and leaves the grosser understanding to assimilate them more and more to the things of which alone it can take cognizance; but in Owen Warland the spirit was not dead nor passed away; it only slept.

How it awoke again is not recorded. Perhaps the torpid slumber was broken by a convulsive pain. Perhaps, as in a former instance, the butterfly came and hovered about his head and reinspired him,—as indeed this creature of the sunshine had always a mysterious mission for the artist,—reinspired him with the former purpose of his life. Whether it were pain or happiness that thrilled through his veins, his first impulse was to thank Heaven for rendering him again the being of thought, imagination, and keenest sensibility that he had long ceased to be.

"Now for my task," said he. "Never did I feel such strength for it as now."

Yet, strong as he felt himself, he was incited to toil the more diligently by an anxiety lest death should surprise him in the midst of his labors. This anxiety, perhaps, is common to all men who set their hearts upon anything so high, in their own view of it, that life becomes of importance only as conditional to its accomplishment. So long as we love life for itself, we seldom dread the losing it. When we desire life for the attainment of an object, we recognize the frailty of its texture. But, side by side with this sense of insecurity, there is a vital faith in our invulnerability to the shaft of death while engaged in any task that seems assigned by Providence as our proper thing to do, and which the world would have cause to mourn for should we leave it unaccomplished. Can the philosopher, big with the inspiration of an idea that is to reform mankind, believe that he is to be beckoned from this sensible existence at the very instant when he is mustering his breath to speak the word of light? Should he perish so, the weary ages may pass away—the world's, whose life sand may fall, drop by drop—before another intellect is prepared to develop the truth that might have been uttered then. But history affords many an example where the most precious spirit, at any particular epoch manifested in human shape, has gone hence untimely, without space allowed him, so far as mortal judgment could discern, to perform his mission on the earth. The prophet dies, and the man of torpid heart and sluggish brain lives on. The poet leaves his song half sung, or finishes it, beyond the scope of mortal ears, in a celestial choir. The painter—as Allston did—leaves half his conception on the canvas to sadden us with its imperfect beauty, and goes to picture forth the whole, if it be no irreverence to say so, in the hues of heaven. But rather such incomplete designs of this life will be perfected nowhere. This so frequent abortion of man's dearest projects must be taken as a proof that the deeds of earth, however etherealized by piety or genius, are without value, except as exercises and manifestations of the spirit. In heaven, all ordinary thought is higher and more melodious than Milton's song. Then, would he add another verse to any strain that he had left unfinished here?

But to return to Owen Warland. It was his fortune, good or ill, to achieve the purpose of his life. Pass we over a long space of intense thought, yearning effort, minute toil, and wasting anxiety, succeeded by an instant of solitary triumph: let all this be imagined; and then behold the artist, on a winter evening, seeking admittance to Robert Danforth's fireside circle. There he found the man of iron, with his massive substance thoroughly warmed and attempered by domestic influences. And there was Annie, too, now transformed into a matron, with much of her husband's plain and sturdy nature, but imbued, as Owen Warland still believed, with a finer grace, that might enable her to be the interpreter between strength and beauty. It happened, likewise, that old Peter Hovenden was a guest this evening at his daughter's fireside, and it was his well-remembered expression of keen, cold criticism that first encountered the artist's glance.

"My old friend Owen!" cried Robert Danforth, starting up, and compressing the artist's delicate fingers within a hand that was accustomed to gripe bars of iron. "This is kind and neighborly to come to us at last. I was afraid your perpetual motion had bewitched you out of the remembrance of old times."

"We are glad to see you," said Annie, while a blush reddened her matronly cheek. "It was not like a friend to stay from us so long."

"Well, Owen," inquired the old watchmaker, as his first greeting, "how comes on the beautiful? Have you created it at last?"

The artist did not immediately reply, being startled by the apparition of a young child of strength that was tumbling about on the carpet,—a little personage who had come mysteriously out of the infinite, but with something so sturdy and real in his composition that he seemed moulded out of the densest substance which earth could supply. This hopeful infant crawled towards the new-comer, and setting himself on end, as Robert Danforth expressed the posture, stared at Owen with a look of such sagacious observation that the mother could not help exchanging a proud glance with her husband. But the artist was disturbed by the child's look, as imagining a resemblance between it and Peter Hovenden's habitual expression. He could have fancied that the old watchmaker was compressed into this baby shape, and looking out of those baby eyes, and repeating, as he now did, the malicious question:—

"The beautiful, Owen! How comes on the beautiful? Have you succeeded in creating the beautiful?"

"I have succeeded," replied the artist, with a momentary light of triumph in his eyes and a smile of sunshine, yet steeped in such depth of thought that it was almost sadness. "Yes, my friends, it is the truth. I have succeeded."

"Indeed!" cried Annie, a look of maiden mirthfulness peeping out of her face again. "And is it lawful, now, to inquire what the secret is?"

"Surely; it is to disclose it that I have come," answered Owen Warland. "You shall know, and see, and touch, and possess the secret! For, Annie,—if by that name I may still address the friend of my boyish years,—Annie, it is for your bridal gift that I have wrought this spiritualized mechanism, this harmony of motion, this mystery of beauty. It comes late, indeed; but it is as we go onward in life, when objects begin to lose their freshness of hue and our souls their delicacy of perception, that the spirit of beauty is most needed. If,—forgive me, Annie,—if you know how to value this gift, it can never come too late."

He produced, as he spoke, what seemed a jewel box. It was carved richly out of ebony by his own hand, and inlaid with a fanciful tracery of pearl, representing a boy in pursuit of a butterfly, which, elsewhere, had become a winged spirit, and was flying heavenward; while the boy, or youth, had found such efficacy in his strong desire that he ascended from earth to cloud, and from cloud to celestial atmosphere, to win the beautiful. This case of ebony the artist opened, and bade Annie to place her finger on its edge. She did so, but almost screamed as a butterfly fluttered forth, and, alighting on her finger's tip, sat waving the ample magnificence of its purple and gold-speckled wings, as if in prelude to a flight. It is impossible to express by words the glory, the splendor, the delicate gorgeousness which were soft-ened into the beauty of this object. Nature's ideal butterfly was here realized in all its perfection; not in the pattern of such faded insects as flit among earthly flowers, but of those which hover across the meads of paradise for child-angels and the spir-its of departed infants to disport themselves with. The rich down was visible upon its wings; the lustre of its eyes seemed instinct with spirit. The firelight glimmered around this wonder—the candles gleamed upon it; but it glistened apparently by its own radiance, and illuminated the finger and outstretched hand on which it rested with a white gleam like that of precious stones. In its perfect beauty, the consideration of size was entirely lost. Had its wings overreached the firmament, the mind could not have been more filled or satisfied.

"Beautiful! beautiful!" exclaimed Annie. "Is it alive? Is it alive?"

"Alive? To be sure it is," answered her husband. "Do you suppose any mortal has skill enough to make a butterfly, or would put himself to the trouble of making one, when any child may catch a score of them in a summer's afternoon? Alive? Certainly! But this pretty box is undoubtedly of our friend Owen's manufacture; and really it does him credit."

At this moment the butterfly waved its wings anew, with a motion so absolutely lifelike that Annie was startled, and even awe-stricken; for, in spite of her husband's opinion, she could not satisfy herself whether it was indeed a living creature or a piece of wondrous mechanism.

"Is it alive?" she repeated, more earnestly than before.

"Judge for yourself," said Owen Warland, who stood gazing in her face with fixed attention.

The butterfly now flung itself upon the air, fluttered round Annie's head, and soared into a distant region of the parlor, still making itself perceptible to sight by the starry gleam in which the motion of its wings enveloped it. The infant on the floor followed its course with his sagacious little eyes. After flying about the room, it returned in a spiral curve and settled again on Annie's finger.

"But is it alive?" exclaimed she again; and the finger on which the gorgeous mystery had alighted was so tremulous that the butterfly was forced to balance himself with his wings. "Tell me if it be alive, or whether you created it."

"Wherefore ask who created it, so it be beautiful?" replied Owen Warland. "Alive? Yes, Annie; it may well be said to possess life, for it has absorbed my own being into itself; and in the secret of that butterfly, and in its beauty,—which is not merely outward, but deep as its whole system,—is represented the intellect, the imagination, the sensibility, the soul of an Artist of the Beautiful! Yes; I created it. But"—and here his countenance somewhat changed—"this butterfly is not now to me what it was when I beheld it afar off in the daydreams of my youth."

"Be it what it may, it is a pretty plaything," said the blacksmith, grinning with childlike delight. "I wonder whether it would condescend to alight on such a great clumsy finger as mine? Hold it hither, Annie."

By the artist's direction, Annie touched her finger's tip to that of her husband; and, after a momentary delay, the butterfly fluttered from one to the other. It preluded a second flight by a similar, yet not precisely the same, waving of wings as in the first experiment; then, ascending from the blacksmith's stalwart finger, it rose in a gradually enlarging curve to the ceiling, made one wide sweep around the room, and returned with an undulating movement to the point whence it had started.

"Well, that does beat all nature!" cried Robert Danforth, bestowing the heartiest praise that he could find expression for; and, indeed, had he paused there, a man of finer words and nicer perception could not easily have said more. "That goes beyond me, I confess. But what then? There is more real use in one downright blow of my sledge hammer than in the whole five years' labor that our friend Owen has wasted on this butterfly."

Here the child clapped his hands and made a great babble of indistinct utterance, apparently demanding that the butterfly should be given him for a plaything.

Owen Warland, meanwhile, glanced sidelong at Annie, to discover whether she sympathized in her husband's estimate of the comparative value of the beautiful and the practical. There was, amid all her kindness towards himself, amid all the wonder and admiration with which she contemplated the marvellous work of his hands and incarnation of his idea, a secret scorn—too secret, perhaps, for her own consciousness, and perceptible only to such intuitive discernment as that of the artist. But Owen, in the latter stages of his pursuit, had risen out of the region in which such a discovery might have been torture. He knew that the world, and Annie as the representative of the world, whatever praise might be bestowed, could never say the fitting word nor feel the fitting sentiment which should be the perfect recompense of an artist who, by symbolizing a lofty moral by a material trifle,—converting what was earthly to spiritual gold,—had won the beautiful into his handiwork. Not at this latest moment was he to learn that the reward of all high performance must be sought within itself, or sought in vain. There was, however, a view of the matter which Annie and her husband, and even Peter Hovenden, might fully have understood, and which would have satisfied them that the toil of years had here been worthily bestowed. Owen Warland might have told them that this butterfly, this plaything, this bridal gift of a poor watchmaker to a blacksmith's wife, was, in truth, a gem of art that a monarch would have purchased with honors and abundant wealth, and have treasured it among the jewels of his kingdom as the most unique and wondrous of them all. But the artist smiled and kept the secret to himself.

"Father," said Annie, thinking that a word of praise from the old watchmaker might gratify his former apprentice, "do come and admire this pretty butterfly."

"Let us see," said Peter Hovenden, rising from his chair, with a sneer upon his face that always made people doubt, as he himself did, in everything but a material existence. "Here is my finger for it to alight upon. I shall understand it better when once I have touched it."

But, to the increased astonishment of Annie, when the tip of her father's finger was pressed against that of her husband, on which the butterfly still rested, the insect drooped its wings and seemed on the point of falling to the floor. Even the bright spots of gold upon its wings and body, unless her eyes deceived her, grew dim, and the glowing purple took a dusky hue, and the starry lustre that gleamed around the blacksmith's hand became faint and vanished.

"It is dying! it is dying!" cried Annie, in alarm.

"It has been delicately wrought," said the artist, calmly. "As I told you, it has imbibed a spiritual essence—call it magnetism, or what you will. In an atmosphere of doubt and mockery its exquisite susceptibility suffers torture, as does the soul of him who instilled his own life into it. It has already lost its beauty; in a few moments more its mechanism would be irreparably injured."

"Take away your hand, father!" entreated Annie, turning pale. "Here is my child; let it rest on his innocent hand. There, perhaps, its life will revive and its colors grow brighter than ever."

Her father, with an acrid smile, withdrew his finger. The butterfly then appeared to recover the power of voluntary motion, while its hues assumed much of their original lustre, and the gleam of starlight, which was its most ethereal attribute, again formed a halo round about it. At first, when transferred from Robert Danforth's hand to the small finger of the child, this radiance grew so powerful that it positively threw the little fellow's shadow back against the wall. He, meanwhile, extended his plump hand as he had seen his father and mother do, and watched the waving of the insect's wings with infantine delight. Nevertheless, there was a certain odd expression of sagacity that made Owen Warland feel as if here were old Peter Hovenden, partially, and but partially, redeemed from his hard scepticism into childish faith.

"How wise the little monkey looks!" whispered Robert Danforth to his wife.

"I never saw such a look on a child's face," answered Annie, admiring her own infant, and with good reason, far more than the artistic butterfly. "The darling knows more of the mystery than we do."

As if the butterfly, like the artist, were conscious of something not entirely congenial in the child's nature, it alternately sparkled and grew dim. At length it arose from the small hand of the infant with an airy motion that seemed to bear it upward without an effort, as if the ethereal instincts with which its master's spirit had endowed it impelled this fair vision involuntarily to a higher sphere. Had there been no obstruction, it might have soared into the sky and grown immortal. But its lustre gleamed upon the ceiling; the exquisite texture of its wings brushed against that earthly medium; and a sparkle or two, as of stardust, floated downward and lay glimmering on the carpet. Then the butterfly came fluttering down, and, instead of returning to the infant, was apparently attracted towards the artist's hand.

"Not so! not so!" murmured Owen Warland, as if his handiwork could have understood him. "Thou has gone forth out of thy master's heart. There is no return for thee."

With a wavering movement, and emitting a tremulous radiance, the butterfly struggled, as it were, towards the infant, and was about to alight upon his finger; but while it still hovered in the air, the little child of strength, with his grandsire's sharp and shrewd expression in his face, made a snatch at the marvellous insect and compressed it in his hand. Annie screamed. Old Peter Hovenden burst into a cold and scornful laugh. The blacksmith, by main force, unclosed the infant's hand, and found within the palm a small heap of glittering fragments, whence the mystery of beauty had fled forever. And as for Owen Warland, he looked placidly at what seemed the ruin of his life's labor, and which was yet no ruin. He had caught a far other butterfly than this. When the artist rose high enough to achieve the beautiful, the symbol by which he made it perceptible to mortal senses became of little value in his eyes while his spirit possessed itself in the enjoyment of the reality.

Ernest Hemingway

Ernest Hemingway was born in Oak Park, Illinois, in 1899. He graduated from high school in 1917 and went to work for the *Kansas City Star*. He was an ambulance driver for the Red Cross in Italy in the later stages of World War I and was seriously wounded. He was a foreign correspondent briefly for *The Toronto Star*, before leaving for Paris where he joined the so-called Lost Generation of expatriate writers and artists. His first book of stories, *In Our Time*, was published in 1925, followed by two novels, *The Sun Also Rises* (1926) and *A Farewell to Arms* (1929). He served as a correspondent on the Loyalist side in the Spanish Civil War, from which grew *For Whom the Bell Tolls* (1940), and then as a foreign correspondent in Europe and Asia during World War II. Of his formal training, he said: "I went to war instead of college. When I came back from the war it was too late to go to college." Asked if there are any tricks to writing, he replied: "No. The hardest trade in the world to do is the writing of straight, honest prose about human beings." He lived in Cuba until the Revolution and was awarded the Nobel Prize for Literature in 1954. In poor health and unable to write, he shot himself in 1961 at his hunting lodge in Ketchum, Idaho.

"Every man should have a built-in crap detector operating inside him," Hemingway said. "It also should have a manual drill and crank handle in case the machine breaks down." In almost all of his conversations and public pronouncements about writing, the words *truth* and *honesty* are to be found. As he explains in *A Moveable Feast*, an account of his early years in Paris, when he was a guest at 27 rue de Fleurus, where Gertrude Stein held court, there was one thing he had to remind himself of when starting a new story: "'All you have to do is write one true sentence. Write the truest sentence that you know.' So finally I would write one true sentence, and then go on from there. It was easy then because there was always one true sentence that I knew or had seen or had heard someone say. If I started to write elaborately, or like someone introducing or presenting something, I found that I could cut that scrollwork or ornament out and throw it away and start with the first true simple declarative sentence I had written."

For writing, he recommended curiosity and training in recall: "When you walk into a room and you get a certain feeling or emotion, remember back until you see exactly what it was that gave you the emotion. Remember what the noises and smells were and what was said. Then write it down, making it clear so the reader will see it too and have the same feeling you had. And watch people, observe, try to put yourself in somebody else's head. If two men argue, don't just think who is right and who is wrong. Think what both their sides are. As a man, you know who is right and who is wrong; you have to judge. As a writer, you should not judge, you should understand."

"What a writer must try to do," Hemingway said, "is to write as truly as he can. For a writer of fiction has to invent out of what he knows in order to make something not photographic, or naturalistic, or realistic, which will be something entirely new and invented out of his own knowledge. . . . A writer should try . . . to make something which will be so written that it will become a part of the experience of those who read him." He claims to have struggled "to break down all my writing and get rid of all facility and try to make instead of describe." Asked how he would define his style, Hemingway told his interviewer: "In stating as fully as I could how things really were, it was often very difficult and I wrote awkwardly and the awkwardness is what they called my style."

Asked in *The Paris Review* interview what the technical problem was that made him rewrite the last page of *A Farewell to Arms* thirty-nine times, he replied, simply: "Getting the words right. . . . I always try to write on the principle of the iceberg. There is seventh-eighths of it underwater for every part that shows. Anything you know you can eliminate and it only strengthens your iceberg. It is the part that doesn't show. If a writer omits something because he does not know it then there is a hole in the story. . . . In writing you are limited by what has already been done satisfactorily [by other writers]. So I have tried to learn to do something else. First I have tried to eliminate everything unnecessary to conveying experience. . . . A writer, if he is any good, does not describe. He invents or *makes* out of knowledge personal and impersonal and sometimes he seems to have unexplained knowledge which could come from forgotten racial or family experience. Who teaches the homing pigeon to fly as he does; where does a fighting bull get his bravery, or a hunting dog his nose?"

Hills like White Elephants

The hills across the valley of the Ebro were long and white. On this side there was no shade and no trees and the station was between two lines of rails in the sun. Close against the side of the station there was the warm shadow of the building and a curtain, made of strings of bamboo beads, hung across the open door into the bar, to keep out flies. The American and the girl with him sat at a table in the shade outside the building. It was very hot and the express from Barcelona would come in forty minutes. It stopped at this junction for two minutes and went on to Madrid.

"What should we drink?" the girl asked. She had taken off her hat and put it on the table.

"It's pretty hot," the man said.

"Let's drink beer."

"Dos cervezas," the man said into the curtain.

"Big ones?" a woman asked from the doorway.

"Yes. Two big ones."

The woman brought two glasses of beer and two felt pads. She put the felt pads and the beer glasses on the table and looked at the man and the girl. The girl was looking off at the line of hills. They were white in the sun and the country was brown and dry.

"They look like white elephants," she said.

"I've never seen one," the man drank his beer.

"No, you wouldn't have."

"I might have," the man said. "Just because you say I wouldn't have doesn't prove anything."

The girl looked at the bead curtain. "They've painted something on it," she said. "What does it say?"

"Anis del Toro. It's a drink."

"Could we try it?"

The man called "Listen" through the curtain. The woman came out from the bar.

"Four reales."

"We want two Anis del Toro."

"With water?"

"Do you want it with water?"

"I don't know," the girl said. "Is it good with water?"

"It's all right."

"You want them with water?" asked the woman.

"Yes, with water."

"It tastes like licorice," the girl said and put the glass down.

"That's the way with everything."

"Yes," said the girl. "Everything tastes of licorice. Especially all the things you've waited so long for, like absinthe."

"Oh, cut it out."

"You started it," the girl said. "I was being amused. I was having a fine time."

"Well, let's try and have a fine time."

"All right. I was trying. I said the mountains looked like white elephants. Wasn't that bright?"

"That was bright."

"I wanted to try this new drink. That's all we do, isn't it—look at things and try new drinks?"

"I guess so."

The girl looked across at the hills.

"They're lovely hills," she said. "They don't really look like white elephants. I just meant the coloring of their skin through the trees."

"Should we have another drink?"

"All right."

The warm wind blew the bead curtain against the table.

"The beer's nice and cool," the man said.

"It's lovely," the girl said.

"It's really an awfully simple operation, Jig," the man said. "It's not really an operation at all."

The girl looked at the ground the table legs rested on.

"I know you wouldn't mind it, Jig. It's really not anything. It's just to let the air in."

The girl did not say anything.

"I'll go with you and I'll stay with you all the time. They just let the air in and then it's all perfectly natural."

"Then what will we do afterward?"

"We'll be fine afterward. Just like we were before."

"What makes you think so?"

"That's the only thing that bothers us. It's the only thing that's made us unhappy."

The girl looked at the bead curtain, put her hand out and took hold of two of the strings of beads.

"And you think then we'll be all right and be happy."

"I know we will. You don't have to be afraid. I've known lots of people that have done it."

"So have I," said the girl. "And afterward they were all so happy."

"Well," the man said, "if you don't want to you don't have to. I wouldn't have you do it if you didn't want to. But I know it's perfectly simple."

"And you really want to?"

"I think it's the best thing to do. But I don't want you to do it if you don't really want to."

"And if I do it you'll be happy and things will be like they were and you'll love me?"

"I love you now. You know I love you."

"I know. But if I do it, then it will be nice again if I say things are like white elephants, and you'll like it?"

"I'll love it. I love it now but I just can't think about it. You know how I get when I worry."

"If I do it you won't ever worry?"

"I won't worry about that because it's perfectly simple."

"Then I'll do it. Because I don't care about me."

"What do you mean?"

"I don't care about me."

"Well, I care about you."

"Oh, yes. But I don't care about me. And I'll do it and then everything will be fine."

"I don't want you to do it if you feel that way."

The girl stood up and walked to the end of the station. Across, on the other side, were fields of grain and trees along the banks of the Ebro. Far away, beyond the river, were mountains. The shadow of a cloud moved across the field of grain and she saw the river through the trees.

"And we could have all this," she said. "And we could have everything and every day we make it more impossible."

"What did you say?"

"I said we could have everything."

"We can have everything."

"No, we can't."

"We can have the whole world."

"No, we can't."

"We can go everywhere."

"No, we can't. It isn't ours any more."

"It's ours."

"No, it isn't. And once they take it away, you never get it back."

"But they haven't taken it away."

"We'll wait and see."

"Come on back in the shade," he said. "You mustn't feel that way."

"I don't feel any way," the girl said. "I just know things."

"I don't want you to do anything that you don't want to do—"

"Nor that isn't good for me," she said. "I know. Could we have another beer?"

"All right. But you've got to realize—"

"I realize," the girl said. "Can't we maybe stop talking?"

They sat down at the table and the girl looked across at the hills on the dry side of the valley and the man looked at her and at the table.

"You've got to realize," he said, "that I don't want you to do it if you don't want to. I'm perfectly willing to go through with it if it means anything to you."

"Doesn't it mean anything to you? We could get along."

"Of course it does. But I don't want anybody but you. I don't want any one else. And I know it's perfectly simple."

"Yes, you know it's perfectly simple."

"It's all right for you to say that, but I do know it."

"Would you do something for me now?"

"I'd do anything for you."

"Would you please please please please please please please stop talking?"

He did not say anything but looked at the bags against the wall of the station. There were labels on them from all the hotels where they had spent nights.

"But I don't want you to," he said, "I don't care anything about it."

"I'll scream," the girl said.

The woman came out through the curtains with two glasses of beer and put them down on the damp felt pads. "The train comes in five minutes," she said.

"What did she say?" asked the girl.

"That the train is coming in five minutes."

The girl smiled brightly at the woman, to thank her.

"I'd better take the bags over to the other side of the station," the man said. She smiled at him.

"All right. Then come back and we'll finish the beer."

He picked up the two heavy bags and carried them around the station to the other tracks. He looked up the tracks but could not see the train. Coming back, he walked through the barroom, where people waiting for the train were drinking. He drank an Anis at the bar and looked at the people. They were all waiting reasonably for the train. He went out through the bead curtain. She was sitting at the table and smiled at him.

"Do you feel better?" he asked.

"I feel fine," she said. "There's nothing wrong with me. I feel fine."

Amy Hempel

Amy Hempel was born in Chicago in 1951, but moved to Denver in the third grade, and to San Francisco when she was in high school. In spite of the suicide of her mother when Hempel was only eighteen, she attributes to her mother her own love of words: "About the only time we really talked and got along was when we were talking about books. I read above my level because my mother was a real, real reader. How we communicated, when we did, was to talk about the books we read. I read as a way to talk to her. She'd always use words I didn't know and she wouldn't tell me what they meant. I had to read the dictionary to look up the words. I read it the way you'd read a book, just to keep up with her." She attended Whittier College in California, studied journalism, worked as a veterinarian's assistant, as publicist at Putnam's, and as an editorial assistant at Crown Publishers; later, she participated in writing workshops at Breadloaf and Columbia University, where she studied with Gordon Lish and wrote the much-anthologized story "In the Cemetery Where Al Jolson Is Buried" as an assignment to write about personal failure. Although she has chosen to live in New York, Hempel writes almost exclusively about California, where, she says, "It's very easy to have your worst fears made tangible in the form of natural disaster. Every year, they'll have these fires. And then there are the floods and mudslides and the quakes. I've been through all that." Hempel is a contributing editor to *Vanity Fair*. Her first collection of stories, *Reasons to Live*, was published in 1985; it was followed in 1990 by *At the Gates of the Animal Kingdom*.

While she is often linked to the minimalists in fiction, Hempel rejects the designation, arguing that a story should only be as long as it needs to be. "I think that what I'm doing, because of the compression and phrasing, has more to do with poetry than with conventional short stories. . . . Someone recently asked me if I was looking forward to writing a novel or longer work, and I said that I was looking forward to writing *shorter* work." Her thoughts on editing and brevity in fiction are to be found in the first issue of *The Quarterly*, where she discusses her story "The Harvest," based on her own experience of being in a serious accident. "The trick," she says in an interview with Michael Schumacher in *Reasons to Believe: New Voices in American Fiction*, "is to find a tiny way into a huge subject. In my case, it's loss. Every story in this book [*Reasons to Live*] has to do with some kind of loss. As I was writing these stories, I discovered that the way I write was like piecing a crazy quilt. I'd have these scraps and little bits of information and phrases and so on, and I'd kind of piece them together. If I did it right, they accumulated and signified by the end of the story. This ties in with the notion I got from my editor, Gordon Lish, who was also my writing teacher: he used to say 'Do it right in the small and the large will take care of itself.'"

Pondering the choice of the writer's material, and why she does not write about sex, Hempel suggests that she prefers to avoid what everyone is writing about it, and not very well: "Then, too, one of my favorite lines in all of literature is one that's never been published. My little brother once tried to write an erotic story when he was about twelve. When I read this piece of erotica by my twelve-year-old brother, it contained the line: 'Then he unzipped her negligee.' That just stayed with me forever. If I ever write about sex, it will sound like 'and then he unzipped her negligee.' I just know it would. It's like this sign that comes up when I get toward that territory."

Although she strives in her work to touch readers, to enable them to move towards affirmation, Hempel rejects the notion of fiction as mere confession or therapy. "Looking for catharsis or a way to salve pain is a bad reason to go into fiction, but it's a good reason to keep a journal. . . . Extremity—that's what I respond to. I'm endlessly, endlessly interested in people who have *come through* something, and the more they have come through, the more interested I am in them and their stories. That's what it's all about: How do you get through?"

The Harvest

The year I began to say *vahz* instead of *vase*, a man I barely knew nearly accidentally killed me.

The man was not hurt when the other car hit ours. The man I had known for one week held me in the street in a way that meant I couldn't see my legs. I remember knowing that I shouldn't look, and knowing that I *would* look if it wasn't that I couldn't.

My blood was on the front of this man's clothes.

He said, "You'll be okay, but this sweater is ruined."

I screamed from the fear of pain. But I did not feel any pain. In the hospital, after injections, I knew there was pain in the room—I just didn't know whose pain it was.

What happened to one of my legs required four hundred stitches, which, when I told it, became five hundred stitches, because nothing is ever quite as bad as it *could* be.

The five days they didn't know if they could save my leg or not I stretched to ten.

The lawyer was the one who used the word. But I won't get around to that until a couple of paragraphs.

We were having the looks discussion—how important *are* they. Crucial is what I had said.

I think looks are crucial.

But this guy was a lawyer. He sat in an aqua vinyl chair drawn up to my bed. What he meant by looks was how much my loss of them was worth in a court of law.

I could tell that the lawyer liked to say *court of law*. He told me he had taken the bar three times before he had passed. He said that his friends had given him handsomely embossed business cards, but where these lovely cards were supposed to say *Attorney-at-Law*, his cards said *Attorney-at-Last*.

He had already covered loss of earnings, that I could not now become an air-line stewardess. That I had never considered becoming one was immaterial, he said, legally.

"There's another thing," he said. "We have to talk here about marriageability."

The tendency was to say marriage-a-*what*? although I knew what he meant the first time I heard it.

I was eighteen years old. I said, "First, don't we talk about *date*ability?"

The man of a week was already gone, the accident driving him back to his wife.

"Do you, think looks are important?" I asked the man before he left.

"Not at first," he said.

In my neighborhood there is a fellow who was a chemistry teacher until an explosion took his face and left what was left behind. The rest of him is neatly dressed in dark suits and shined shoes. He carries a briefcase to the college campus. What a comfort—his family, people said—until his wife took the kids and moved out.

In the solarium, a woman showed me a snapshot. She said, "This is what my son used to look like."

I spent my evenings in Dialysis. They didn't mind when a lounger was free. They had wide-screen color TV, better than they had in Rehab. Wednesday nights we watched a show where women in expensive clothes appeared on lavish sets and promised to ruin one another.

On one side of me was a man who spoke only in phone numbers. You would ask him how he felt, he would say, "924-3130." Or he would say, "757-1366." We guessed what these numbers might be, but nobody spent the dime.

There was sometimes, on the other side of me, a twelve-year-old boy. His lashes were thick and dark from blood-pressure medication. He was next on the transplant list, as soon as—the word they used was *harvest*—as soon as a kidney was harvested.

The boy's mother prayed for drunk drivers.

I prayed for men who were not discriminating.

Aren't we all, I thought, somebody's harvest?

The hour would end, and a floor nurse would wheel me back to my room. She would say, "Why watch that trash? Why not just ask me how my day went?"

I spent fifteen minutes before going to bed squeezing rubber grips. One of the medications was making my fingers stiffen. The doctor said he'd give it to me till I couldn't button my blouse—a figure of speech to someone in a cotton gown.

The lawyer said, "Charitable works."

He opened his shirt and showed me where an acupuncture person had dabbed at his chest with cola syrup, sunk four needles, and told him that the real cure was charitable works.

I said, "Cure for what?"

The lawyer said, "Immaterial."

As soon as I knew that I would be all right, I was sure that I was dead and didn't know it. I moved through the days like a severed head that finishes a sentence. I waited for the moment that would snap me out of my seeming life.

The accident happened at sunset, so that is when I felt this way the most. The man I had met the week before was driving me to dinner when it happened. The place was at the beach, a beach on a bay that you can look across and see the city lights, a place where you can see everything without having to listen to any of it.

A long time later I went to that beach myself. *I* drove the car. It was the first good beach day; I wore shorts.

At the edge of the sand I unwound the elastic bandage and waded into the surf. A boy in a wet suit looked at my leg. He asked me if a shark had done it; there were sightings of great whites along that part of the coast.

I said that, yes, a shark had done it.

"And you're going back in?" the boy asked.

I said, "And I'm going back in."

I leave a lot out when I tell the truth. The same when I write a story. I'm going to start now to tell you what I left out of "The Harvest," and maybe begin to wonder why I had to leave it out.

There was no other car. There was only the one car, the one that hit me when I was on the back of the man's motorcycle. But think of the awkward syllables when you have to say *motorcycle*.

The driver of the car was a newspaper reporter. He worked for a local paper. He was young, a recent graduate, and he was on his way to a labor meeting to cover a threatened strike. When I say I was then a journalism student, it is something you might not have accepted in "The Harvest."

In the years that followed, I watched for the reporter's byline. He broke the People's Temple story that resulted in Jim Jones's flight to Guyana. Then he covered Jonestown. In the city room of the San Francisco *Chronicle*, as the death toll climbed to nine hundred, the numbers were posted like donations on pledge night. Somewhere in the hundreds, a sign was fixed to the wall that said JUAN CORONA, EAT YOUR HEART OUT.

In the emergency room, what happened to one of my legs required not four hundred stitches but just over three hundred stitches. I exaggerated even before I began to exaggerate, because it's true—nothing *is* ever quite as bad as it could be.

My lawyer was no attorney-at-last. He was a partner in one of the city's oldest law firms. He would never have opened his shirt to reveal the site of acupuncture, which is something that he never would have had.

"Marriageability" was the original title of "The Harvest."

The damage to my leg was considered cosmetic although I am still, fifteen years later, unable to kneel. In an out-of-court settlement the night before the trial, I was awarded nearly $100,000. The reporter's car insurance went up $12.43 per month.

It had been suggested that I rub my leg with ice, to bring up the scars, before I hiked my skirt three years later for the court. But there was no ice in the judge's chambers, so I did not get a chance to pass or fail that moral test.

The man of a week, whose motorcycle it was, was not a married man. But when you thought he had a wife, wasn't I liable to do anything? And didn't I have it coming?

After the accident, the man got married. The girl he married was a fashion model. ("Do you think looks are important?" I asked the man before he left. "Not at first," he said.)

In addition to being a beauty, the girl was worth millions of dollars. Would you have accepted this in "The Harvest"—that the model was also an heiress?

It is true we were headed for dinner when it happened. But the place where you can see everything without having to listen to any of it was not a beach on a bay—it was the top of Mount Tamalpais. We had the dinner with us as we headed up the twisting mountain road. This is the version that has room for perfect irony, so you won't mind when I say that for the next several months, from my hospital bed, I had a dead-on spectacular view of that very mountain.

I would have written this next part into the story if anybody would have believed it. But who would have? I was there and I didn't believe it.

On the day of my third operation, there was an attempted breakout in the Maximum Security Adjustment Center, adjacent to Death Row, at San Quentin prison. "Soledad Brother" George Jackson, a twenty-nine-year-old black man, pulled out a smuggled-in .38 caliber pistol, yelled, "This is it!" and opened fire. Jackson was killed; so were three guards and two "tier-tenders," inmates who bring other prisoners their meals.

Three other guards were stabbed in the neck. The prison is a five-minute drive from Marin General, so that is where the injured guards were taken. The people who brought them were three kinds of police, including California Highway Patrol and Marin County sheriff's deputies, heavily armed.

Police were stationed on the roof of the hospital with rifles; they were posted in the hallways, waving patients and visitors back into their rooms.

When I was wheeled out of Recovery later that day, bandaged waist to ankle, three officers and an armed sheriff frisked me.

On the news that night, there was footage of the riot.

They showed my surgeon talking to reporters, indicating, with a finger to his throat, how he had saved one of the guards by sewing up a slice from ear to ear.

I watched this on television, and because it was my doctor, and because hospital patients are self-absorbed, and because I was drugged, I thought the surgeon was talking about me. I thought that he was saying, "Well, she's dead. I'm announcing it to her in her bed."

The psychiatrist I saw at the surgeon's referral said that the feeling was a common one. She said that victims of trauma who have not yet assimilated the trauma often believe they are dead and do not know it.

The great white sharks in the waters near my home attack one to seven people a year. Their primary victim is the abalone diver. With abalone steaks at thirty-five dollars a pound and going up, the Department of Fish and Game expects the shark attacks to show no slackening.

Jack Hodgins

Jack Hodgins was born on Vancouver Island in 1938 and raised on a stump ranch in the Comox Valley, where the spoken word was even more important to his training than books. He majored in English and Mathematics at the University of British Columbia, but also enrolled in Earle Birney's Creative Writing class. His first collection of stories, *Spit Delaney's Island*, appeared in 1976, while he was teaching high school in Nanaimo. Two novels, *The Invention of the World* (1978) and *The Resurrection of Joseph Bourne* (1979), were followed by the publication of *The Barclay Family Theatre* (1981), a collection of linked stories in the tradition of Sherwood Anderson's *Winesberg, Ohio* and George P. Elliott's *The Kissing Man*. Hodgins won the Governor General's Award and now teaches in the Creative Writing Department at the University of Victoria. He published *The Honorary Patron* in 1987 and *Innocent Cities* in 1990. *Over Forty in Broken Hill*, a book about his travels in the Australian outback, appeared in 1992.

Hodgins's rural roots have provided him with a rich vein for his fiction. "I couldn't help but recall the numbers of people who have said to me, 'Aren't you afraid that if you stay on Vancouver Island, you'll run out of things to write about?' As if it's a tiny village, as if one book could exhaust its possibilities. There is an immense area to be discovered. One of the things that writing is for me is discovering. Discovering place and the meaning of place. Discovering character and the mystery that's behind character." However, as he points out to interviewer Geoff Hancock (*Canadian Writers at Work*), "I am not particularly obsessed with 'getting the region right' so much as I am in getting the people right. If I can get a person in Vancouver Island just right on paper, he's not too different from someone in Montreal or New York."

About the question of how to get down to the material that he wants to write, Hodgins replies: "One way I've approached that question is to decide that I've got to write every book as though it's the only book I'll ever write. I cannot see myself partitioning myself over a lifetime and thinking I'm going to write a little bit in this book and save something for another book. When I'm writing a book I have to treat it as though it's my only chance." Of the writers who have exerted some influence on his fiction and his way of viewing reality, Hodgins lists Faulkner, Margaret Laurence, Irish writers such as Frank O'Connor and Edna O'Brien, and Latin American writers such as Gabriel García Márquez, Mario Vargas Llosa, and Miguel Asturias.

"What do they [the Latin Americans] have that I respond to? *Energy*. There's an energy coming off the pages which I see so seldom coming off the pages in North American writing. Even more important than the energy is the sense of enjoyment! I have the feeling when I'm reading them that the writer is really having a good time. Otherwise how can he expect his reader to enjoy what he's done? I have got so used to the idea that the writing and reading of the novel was a painful experience. So I appreciated that energy, that love of what you're doing. And one other thing, the same thing I had fallen in love with in William Faulkner, the *sense of community*. The whole world gets in on those Latin American novels just as the whole world got in on a William Faulkner novel. This is such a contrast to the many novels that tend to be about one's personal problems. . . ."

Hodgins has shown scant interest in writing autobiographical fiction. "I've written very little out of personal experience. I'm not all that interested in doing it. My first motivation in writing is a *nosiness* about other people. I already know more than enough about myself. I like to take somebody who's out there and pull him up close and have a good look at him. Not only that but to get inside and find out what it's like to be him. It also makes life more varied and interesting. How many people can go through life pretending to be other than themselves? Without being put in an institution?" He considers writers to be "more than mapmakers," to be engaged more in the creation of meaning than in mere *naming*.

Although he claims not to be "playing games with words" or manipulating his readers, Hodgins is, in fact, a conscious craftsman, what some critics might call a *fabulator*. He seems to be fully aware that his fictions are many-layered and often border on allegory. While he claims to be describing "reality," Hodgins also seems intent to move beyond the limits of realism: "What you and I call the ocean is to me only a metaphor. All those trees, for instance, are metaphors; the reality lies beyond them. The act of writing to me is an attempt to shine a light on that ocean and those trees so bright that we can see right through them to the reality that is constant." Similarly, he claims for himself a certain political function: "But still a writer anywhere is political in another sense, I suppose in a moral sense. A fiction writer is creating myth and societies live by myths. The myths that are important to society create the way that people in it treat each other. Like John Gardner, I feel strongly that a writer has a responsibility to be aware of the moral implications of what he's doing."

Hodgins is a complicated interviewee, stressing his simplicity and innocence of theory if the questions become too cerebral, or arguing for his own craftiness if the interviewer overemphasizes realism or regionalism. In an interview with Alan Twigg (*Strong Voices*), he says: "For myself, I often think of fiction as high class gossip. Really, what you're doing is saying listen, I've got a story I want to tell you about the guys who live down the road. This is what they did and isn't that something." What this dance indicates, primarily, is that he wishes not to be labelled or tied exclusively to any group or school of writing. In the interview with Peter O'Brien (*So to Speak*), Hodgins suggests he prefers not to talk too much about the bones or mechanics of his fiction, for fear that he—and, perhaps, his readers and critics—will too easily identify patterns that should be seen as changing and evolving from book to book.

After the Season

About fifty miles up the coast past the end of all public roads, in a little bay where the wildest tides throw logs and broken lumber far up the land like spat-out bones, Hallie Crane ran a café and a small cabaret for tourists staying at the fishing camp. Although there was a wharf built well out into the bay so fishing boats could tie up without being smashed against rocks, and down in the curve of the shore there was a small gravel beach where the bravest American tourists could run in for a quick swim and rush out again, Hallie's place and most other buildings were perched up on the rock and looked as if a good wind would fling them right out into the strait. The café was so close to the edge it had legs straight down into the water and whenever Hallie wanted to go anywhere, down the slope to Morgan's boat rental or around the bay to the well, she had to walk on a rickety boardwalk that ran right past her door and hung out over the sea. Tourists kept life jackets on their children the whole time they stayed in the camp.

Hallie liked it well enough, at least in the summer. When the last tourists left in September she squinted up her two bright green eyes at them and told them it had been fun just having them around. "Now there'll be nobody here at all for the next eight months except Morgan and me." She had a grown family down-island where the grey ribbon of highway went right under their noses when they sat in their living room, and she could have moved down to stay with them any time she wanted if she was willing to keep off the bottle, but she never did.

She never went back, hadn't seen her own daughter for eight years. They told her when she left not to bother unless she could stay sober, and though she hadn't touched a drink now for two years she still hadn't got around to packing up and catching the boat out for the winter. She could imagine herself landing in on them easily enough, tall and straight and good looking as ever, and hear their shrieks of surprise: "What? You can't be old enough to be this baby's grandmother!" But oh yes, she was, she was fifty-one years old. She was tall and straight, could walk like a youngster on her long narrow legs, could tell a joke with all the youth she knew was still inside, could snap her eyes in anger or fun as sharp and quick as she ever could. She touched up her hair now; natural blonde faded out faster than any other colour. But her face, though it had added laugh lines around the eyes and the skin was drier than it used to be, was still striking, still pretty. She could see herself going back, could imagine the fuss they'd make, but every fall when the season ended a sharp cold fear inside told her to put it off for another year.

During the summer Morgan, who owned the camp and ran it practically single-handed except for Hallie's help, lived down in his rooms behind the boat house and Hallie lived in the back of her café. They treated each other like strangers, like employer and employee, like invisible beings. When he came into the café and sat with his hairy arms folded on the counter, he ordered coffee without look-ing at her. When she walked down to his place, picked her way along the board-walk hanging on to the rail, to tell him the plumbing was plugged up or the toaster needed fixing, she walked in and out amongst the boats while she talked, touching them as if feeling whether the paint was good enough to last the season. But when the tourists had gone and Hallie had tidied up the café and the little cabaret room beside it and closed the shutters over the windows, she moved down the hill into Morgan's rooms, into Morgan's bed, and stayed there until the first lot of people arrived the next June.

Not suddenly. Not just like that as if they had been thinking about it all summer and could hardly wait. Every year she was a little surprised all over again. Morgan was only thirty-three years old and still romantic, and he insisted on courting her, luring her, as if every October were their first. If she had just packed her suitcase and carried it down the hill and moved in he would have been disappointed, might even have tossed her out, and probably would have pouted all through the winter.

Every October he arrived at her door soon after the others had gone: a grin-ning, hairy, solid little man. "Dammit," he said, "you're a good-looking woman!" He came up behind and put his arms around her and ran his hands down her breasts and stomach and thighs. "Dammit, you've got it all over them other girls!" She slapped his hands and he went away for a while. But he came back again and again. He told her he was getting so randy for you-know-what that he was scared he'd go crazy and run screaming over the hills behind. He asked her how would she like to be raped. He brought gifts: chunks of smoked fish, handfuls of shells he'd found, magazines left behind in the cabins by tourists. It was usually about a week before Hallie recognized the signals that said it was all right for her to start giving in now. She stopped slapping his hands, stopped threatening to radio out for help, stopped keeping her distance. She packed her suitcase.

This year though, when the last boat had sailed out of sight down the strait, she didn't feel like going through all that drawn-out procedure, she just didn't have the energy. "Cut it out," she said. "I can't see any point in all this fooling around. Can't I just pack up and move down?"

But he insisted. "What do you want to be?" he said. "A whore?" His breath smelled of smoked fish.

"All right, I'll pretend then. I'll pretend I won't do it but we both know I will. How can it be any fun?"

He put his hands on her and told her what a good-looking woman she still was but she slapped the side of his head hard enough to knock him against the wall. "What the hell?" he said, his blue eyes hot with tears.

"You wanted me to pretend, well I'm pretending. Now leave me alone."

He grinned at her. "You don't want me to touch you because you've put on weight."

"Go to hell."

"You're afraid if I touch you I'll find out how fat you've got," he said, leering. "I saw you gorging yourself all summer on them apple pies. Putting on pound after pound."

"I'd like to know how you noticed what I was doing when you never once tore your little piggy eyes off that blonde bitch from Seattle."

"Shoving it in when you thought no one else was looking. Putting on layer after layer of fat. Turning into a big cow."

"I haven't put on a single pound, and," skirting his outstretched hand, "you'll just have to take my word for it."

Two days later they were just getting to the stage where he would threaten to rape her when the stranger arrived and interrupted the whole business.

It was the worst October she could remember. Black cloud moved in and sat on them like a heavy lid. Rain came down steadily through night and day. A wind had whipped the sea into such a turmoil and thrown the tide so high up the land that sometimes Hallie expected to wake up in the morning and find herself floating. It was always a small surprise to discover no walls had been ripped off, no windows bashed in, no pieces of roof lifted. She kept a fire roaring in the cast-iron stove and got up several times during the night to shake the grates and add more wood. If she didn't drown, she would probably burn to death.

She was on the boardwalk tossing garbage down for the few gulls that still clung to the coast when she saw the stranger's boat. At first she thought it was nothing but a driftwood log, dipping and leaping with the waves, and when it got closer there appeared to be something alive, a large bird perhaps, perched in the middle and riding. It wasn't until it had entered the bay and came rushing in towards shore that she saw it was a small aluminum boat with a man inside holding on for dear life and not even trying to steer with the handle on the useless little outboard motor. She ran down the boardwalk and across the beach in time to see it thrown ahead onto the gravel, sucked back, then thrown ahead again far enough for the man to leap out, fall to his knees, get up again, grab the rope, and drag the boat up high enough to tie it to a log. He turned two pale runny eyes on her and said, "Thank God I got to civilization."

"You didn't," she said. "There's only me and Morgan and all these empty shacks. Even our radio set-up went on the blink a couple days ago."

He wiped a hand over his wet face, shook himself like a dog, tipped forward to let water run off the back of his neck. "It'll have to do," he said, flicking an ear. "I'm not going back out into that."

Morgan came out of the boat house, walking—as he always did—as if his body besides being solid and heavy was also hot and he had to keep both hands and arms well away in order not to get burned. He looked the little man over like an interesting log the sea had washed in, then looked at Hallie as if to say, "Now what have you done?"

"We better get you somewhere and dry you off," Hallie said.

The little man bent down again and wrung out his straight blond hair, then flung it back with a snap that could have broken his neck, and turned to look out at the water. "I wouldn't want to've spent much longer on that," he said.

"You wouldn't've," Hallie said. "You'd've been in it before long, dead as a thrown-back dogfish. Come on, let's get you over to Morgan's place, warm you up."

Morgan stood in their way and scowled at Hallie. Then, suddenly, he smiled as if the scowl had been about something else altogether, and said, "Don't you think your place would be better?"

"Nothing wrong with yours," she said. "It's good and warm."

"Too warm," Morgan said. "And too small. I bet you've got a nice fire on up there in the café, maybe even a cup of coffee."

"Look," the man said, "I don't care where you put me, just so long as I can go somewhere to dry off. I may drown right here or shore if you keep arguing." And he started walking up the slope towards the café.

When they'd stripped him down to dry out his clothes there wasn't very much to him. In his undershorts he looked like a young boy—Hallie had seen bigger bones in a turkey—but his face was the face of a man in his forties. When he handed over his clothes for her to hang up above the stove, looking so small and drenched and lost, she wanted to tickle him under the chin and say, "Cheer up, little man, you haven't fallen off the end of the world!" But there was something about his face, a long narrow pointed face with sunken cheeks and pale fast-moving eyes, that told her if she so much as touched him, treated him like a child, he would snarl and growl and maybe knock her hand away with one of those frail arms.

"Here," she said. "You can put on my robe and we'll dry out your undershorts too."

Morgan eyed him as if he expected to see him turn into a rat and start gnawing the house down. Hallie could see resentment already settling in around his mouth.

"I'm a teacher," he told them when his white jockey shorts were hanging on the line over the stove and he was wrapped up in Hallie's red chenille bath robe. He found a cigar in one of his pockets but it was too wet to light and he threw it in the fire, spitting pieces of damp tobacco off his tongue. "I taught high school geography but I quit my job in June and started exploring up and down this coast."

"You should've tried elementary," Hallie said. "The kids wouldn't've been so big and scary there."

The little man looked at Hallie as if she were the stupidest pupil he'd ever run across. Then he looked up at the bare rafters. "My name is Hamilton Grey," he said. "I have never been afraid of a person, big or small, in my life. Least of all a geography student. What scares me is not people but mankind." And he looked at her again, as if it were all her fault, as if she were the mother of the whole blessed lot. "The stupidity of mankind appals me."

Hallie looked at Morgan and Morgan rolled his eyes. "I don't know anything about smart or stupid," she said. "Nice is good enough for me. If a person's considerate of other people it don't matter how much brains he's got."

He looked up again and snorted. He and the rafters knew she'd just proved his point. "Nice people are spilling oil into the oceans," he said. "Nice people are busy inventing new biological warfare weapons."

He told them he had this theory. Whatever your instincts tell you is right is exactly wrong. He told them instincts were good enough for the individual's survival but all wrong for society. For example, he told them, everybody's instinct says pornography increases sex crimes but the opposite is true, look at Denmark. He told them everybody's instinct says if a kid is bad hit him but that is the surest way to make him worse. Look at wild land, he said, instinct says tame it, kill all the scary animals, log off the useless trees, turn it into something we can handle. And prisons too, he said. The whole idea of punishment is instinctive but does exactly the opposite to what is good for society.

"Mister Grey," she said. "Is there anything at all good about people in your opinion?"

He looked as if he'd never encountered that question before. He thought for a long time, stroking his pointed jaw. Finally, he said, "Yes, one thing. His potential. Man has one thing—mind—that makes everything possible."

"How long you plan on staying?" Morgan said.

"I didn't plan anything. My motor's conked out."

"I can fix that," Morgan said.

"And I'm not setting out again as long as this storm keeps up."

When Hallie went out into the kitchen Morgan followed her and said, "You let him have your bed and come on down to my place tonight."

She told him he'd better watch his tongue. "There's a spare bed in my back room," she said. "Besides, what would he think of us?"

"He already doesn't think much of us. It wouldn't make any difference."

"He's a school teacher," she said. "It wouldn't be right. I just couldn't do it."

Morgan sat down and tried to pull her onto his knee but she held back. "He doesn't care. It's none of his business."

"My son-in-law is a teacher," she said. "I won't do it."

"In that case," Morgan said, "we will have to get rid of him."

It wasn't easy. All the next day he worked on the little man's outboard motor. He took it apart, washed every piece in gasoline, put in new spark plugs. He replaced a part in the water pump. By evening it was running as smooth as a new motor but the storm hadn't died down.

"Looks like it's settled in for a long haul," Mr. Grey said, looking out the front windows of the café. "I'm not heading out into that." He brought all his equipment in from the boat—his tent and sleeping bag and cooking utensils and food and books—and dropped them in the middle of Hallie's floor.

"Put them up on the stage out of the way," she said.

So he set up camp on the raised alcove beside the piano that Hallie played whenever there was a crowd that wanted to dance. There was a harvest moon painted on the back wall with SWING YOUR PARTNER printed across it. He set up the tent as if he could foresee rain coming through the roof, laid out his sleeping bag inside, and opened up his camp stove.

"I'll radio for a plane," Morgan said.

"No plane would fly in this," Hallie said. "And besides, the set is broke."

And while he spent the next day trying to get the radio set to work, Hallie tried to find out more about Hamilton Grey. Because it was a long time since she'd talked to any teacher except her son-in-law, a sharp-eyed man who made her nervous, she didn't know how to go about making conversation. She scrubbed floors and cleaned windows and stacked furniture in the dance room and he listened to her questions from behind a book, sitting on the edge of the stage.

"You got somebody somewhere worrying about you right now? Somebody scared you're drowned?"

A page turned. "Mmph."

"No wife? No children, no parents?"

He lowered the book and looked at her. "If I had all that lot hanging around my neck, would I be sailing up and down the strait taking my own sweet time? There isn't a soul to care if I end up at the bottom of the ocean."

"It may not look like it," Hallie said, "but I've got a family. A grown daughter."

There was no indication that he had heard her but she continued. "She's married to a teacher too, like you, only he teaches chemistry and is a lot taller. They live in the same house my husband and I lived in for all twelve years of our marriage, right on the damn highway, only the highway's been widened since then, and every time a car goes by you'd think it was coming right through the living room. I'm surprised they don't move out and build a house of their own, but I guess all the savings they have get used up just living through the summer. They've got two kids."

He turned a page, then turned back to reread the bottom line and turned again.

"I bet you never thought I was a grandmother," Hallie said.

He looked up to see if he'd missed anything, then looked down again.

Hallie shifted chairs around noisily. "If bad manners is something they're teaching at universities now you must've got top marks but I can't say that I'm impressed."

He closed the book but kept a finger between the pages. "What I'm wondering, he said, "is why you haven't gone back to stay with your daughter. How come you're all alone up here with that Tarzan the ape-man when you could be with your family?"

"Scared I guess, she said, quickly, because if she had paused to think about it she would have told him none of his business. "I'd be back on the bottle in a week if I went down there. I'd be so useless—don't know how to talk to kids, not even my own grandchildren, without feeling like a fool—and that long beak-nosed son-in-law watching me like a hawk to see what makes me tick—I'd be throwing back the rye just to get through the day."

After supper Morgan came into her kitchen and said he hadn't been able to get anything on the radio. He sat down at her table, spread out his elbows, and slurped up a cup of coffee. He swore after every mouthful.

"Morgan," she said. "Would you say I'm getting old looking?"

"Naw."

"Well, since he came you haven't said one nice thing to me. If I'm getting old and fat just tell me."

"Hell no," he said, and pulled her down onto his lap. He dug fingers into the flesh of her thigh. "You're still a good-looking woman."

"That Mr. Grey makes me feel old and stupid."

"Oh him," Morgan said, and threw a sneer at the wall that separated the kitchen from the café and dance room. He ran one hand up the inside of her skirt but she put her hand on top of it and held it still.

"You're not doing much to get rid of him," she said. "Maybe he'll be here all winter."

He looked down at the lump his own hand made under her skirt and scowled. "I'll get rid of the bastard," he said, and pushed her off him so he could stand up. "But first I guess I better go in and tell him about the radio."

After Morgan had gone back to his boat house Mr. Grey told her the ape-man had nearly attacked him. His hair was on end, as if he had been running his fingers through it backwards, and his quick pale eyes were darting everywhere. Hallie couldn't help feeling sorry for him; after all he was a teacher and probably not used to people like Morgan, mean and free, without school rules to hold him back.

But just when she was beginning to feel warm inside with the pity she felt, he started to laugh, confusing her. He took out a handkerchief and blew his nose, one hard snort on either side. "You know what he told me?" he said.

"Don't listen to him," she said. "Morgan's liable to make all sorts of threats he won't carry out. There's not much harm in him."

"He said, 'You know what you're buttin' in on?'"

"What?"

"He said I walked in on the middle of a mating ritual, that's what he told me."

"A mating dance of two horny people," Morgan had said. "You landed in here when we'd hardly got started. Hell, every year we go at it all over again like a couple of rutting mountain sheep, only we wait until after the season." He rolled his eyes as if to say, You know what I mean. "Right through the summer while the tourists are here we don't hardly talk to each other. She lives up here in her dance hall serving meals and I live down there in my boat house. A person wouldn't even think we knew each other."

"This is none of my business," Mr. Grey had said.

But Morgan had gone on. "Then every October we look around, see, and there's nobody left here. The tourists are all gone. The loggers, they're back but they're inland a ways. So pretty soon we're sniffing around each other, see, and then we're snarling and clawing each other. Finally we land in bed like a clap of thunder and that's where we spend most of the winter."

"Like a couple of animals!"

"You bet, mister," Morgan had said. "You ever see a mountain sheep going after it? If he wants to he can run sixty miles an hour on his back legs. Think about that coming together!"

Hallie didn't wait for Mr. Grey to tell her anything more that Morgan had said or how he had got around to almost attacking him. She left the room and shut the door behind her, gently so he wouldn't think she was upset. She stood stiffly for a long time in front of the little mirror that hung over the kitchen sink, her head throbbing like an inboard motor, her hand laid out stiff and white against the vibrations of her breast. She was a good-looking woman—the mirror told her that—and not even the dyed hair could make her look cheap. She was one of those women who kept their looks, who stayed smart and slim and attractive even into old age, but that was a different thing from what Morgan had made her sound like. It wasn't a mountain sheep he made her sound like; it was a mink.

She went out onto the boardwalk and sat on a bench that leaned against her front wall. The wind had died down a little and the rain had stopped falling but the surface of the water was still slate-black and heaving. There wasn't a gull to be seen, gone inland for safety. She sat facing all of it, wouldn't have moved even if an earth tremor had sent the whole building down crazily into the bay, and felt the hot flush of shame creeping up her face. The crashing of the waves against the pilings beneath her was no stronger in her than the beating of her own heart. She wanted a drink.

Hallie Crane had felt real shame only once before in her life. She wasn't a person who did things she later regretted. Most of her actions were deliberate, considered, and consistent. Memories were usually pleasant. But once, just once, she had fallen into something she was so ashamed of that even now, eighteen years later, its memory could send her to bed for a day or more. When the phone call came telling her that her husband had died in the Vancouver hospital, she was at a community dance, nearly drunk. Her daughter had taken the message.

That wasn't me! she wanted to scream at the memory of it. That wasn't the real me, that was someone else.

And now, too, she wanted to tell that little school teacher in there that he had been given the wrong impression. She wanted to set things straight in his mind. She went back into the kitchen, checked her face in the mirror, and walked into the café where he was helping himself to a handful of sugar cubes.

"You shouldn't listen to Morgan," she said. "He's given you the wrong impression about us. Probably wanted to shock you."

He threw a sugar cube into his mouth and crunched it between his teeth. "Is there some place around here where a person can go for a walk?"

When they both had their rain clothes on, she led him up the trail that climbed in a series of switch-backs up the slope of the hill behind the buildings. "Deer made this," she said, "and elk." The wet leaves of salal and Oregon grape knocked against their legs and soaked the bottom half of their slacks. When Mr. Grey hung onto a small scrubby pine to help pull himself up a particularly steep part of the trail, its roots were so shallow in the rocky soil that he pulled it right out and fell backward a few feet and rolled over against a windfall fir.

At last they reached the top, however, and she stood aside for him to see that beyond it there was only a small swampy valley of burnt snags and another, higher hill. "From down there I thought this was the end," he said, and she told him no, that it was only the beginning. "Just the first small step. It goes up and up and finally you're above timber altogether and in year-round snow and then it drops straight down into the Pacific."

The fishing camp below was nearly obscured by the fine rain which had started and by the mist. The small handful of buildings looked as if they too, like Mr.

Grey, had been washed in by the tide and left stranded between the sea and this hill. Smoke from the little café stood up in a thin white column, then spread out level and flat as if somewhere between the roof and the top of the hill there was an invisible ceiling.

Hallie sat down on a rock. No matter how hard she looked she could not see the mainland mountains through the dense grey wall of cloud. Below, the tiny figure of Morgan left one of the cabins and walked across to the boat house. "You shouldn't pay him any attention," she said. "He'll just give you the worst impression of things."

Mr. Grey sat down on the ground beside her. "It doesn't matter to me," he said. "I don't give a damn what you two do. When I get out of here I'll probably never think of either one of you again."

She could see him going through his life, wiping out the people he met as if they were only figures on a chalkboard. Or as if he were that wall of cloud, blocking out the whole world.

"There's nothing about you that's special. There's no way that either one of you have touched me or entered me or altered my life. When I leave I'll be the same as when I arrived, my life won't be changed, and there won't be a thing about my stay here worth remembering."

Hallie gritted her teeth. He may be a smart school teacher who thought he knew everything but there was one thing she knew better than he did. "You can't touch someone else without it affecting your life in some way," she said.

"Ah, but here's the difference: you haven't touched me." He broke off a branch of salal and started chewing on its tip. "You circle around me, you and that hairy ape of yours, making faces and screeching noises at me, but it's as if I'm watching from inside a bubble of glass. You can't penetrate. You can't touch me. You never will. I'll go on watching your mating dance without being affected in any way."

Hallie shuddered. "Mating dance?" He sounded as crude as Morgan. "Is that what you really think, just because he said it. Do you really think I'm like that?"

But he didn't answer. He found the veins in a salal leaf more interesting than her. He probably thought she had never done anything educational in her whole life, never even read a book. Well listen, she had. She told him about this story she once read, an old-fashioned tale in some book somebody'd given to her when she was a little girl. This girl in the story, this Proser-something, was out running around in a place something like this, pulling a bush right out of the ground just like Mr. Grey had and up out of that hole came old Pluto, the king of the underworld, riding in a chariot, and hauled her off against her will down into his deep horrible black place.

"Proserpina," he said. "I know the story, yes." He got up and started following the trail back from the edge, towards the swamp. She hurried to catch up to him.

"Her old lady found her all right," she said, "but not before she'd half broken a promise not to eat a thing down there. So for the rest of her life, if you can believe it, she had to spend six months with her mother and six months down in the underworld with him."

"With Pluto," he tossed over his shoulder. "I didn't think anyone remembered those tales any more." They were walking on logs now; the ground was soft and damp, with a musty swamp smell. Burnt snags stood around like silent black totems.

"Anyway, that's what I feel like. Only I don't get six and six. I get three months, four if I'm lucky, of normal living with people treating me like a human being. Then along comes October and he starts in dragging me down."

"Morgan?" Mr. Grey stood on the edge of the little lake, a hundred feet of green scum in front of him, a log laid out on it like a wharf. He turned and his pale eyes crinkled, as if he was ready to disbelieve whatever she was going to say next.

Hallie stopped walking. "Pulling me down into his hell with him. Clawing at me and slobbering and pulling me down, living in slime."

Mr. Grey walked out onto the log, straight out over that floor of scum. "If I remember the story right, the girl didn't mind it so much. She got so she kind of liked old Pluto."

Hallie felt as if she might explode. "Nobody likes living in hell," she cried.

At the other end of the log he turned and faced her. "The whole world loves it," he said. He looked slightly amused, as if she were a child run up against something every adult understood. "As soon as a human being chooses to pay attention to his five senses he's electing to live in hell." He let her chew on that for a while, then bounced a little on the log to watch it disturb the thick surface of the lake. "If he pays attention to the demands of the senses, if he uses them to make judgments, if he listens to their reports of pain and disease, he's living in hell. There's nothing so special about you."

Hallie walked by herself back to the edge of the slope and sat down. After a while he came up behind her and she said, "All right, mister, you know so much. Is there a way out?"

He chuckled. "Sure there is," he said. He started down the hill. "I guess you were hoping I'd say everybody is doomed to be miserable and so you're pretty normal after all. D'you think that just because I'm soured on humanity I don't see its possibilities? Well, lady, like it or not, there are some happy people in the world."

"Who?" she demanded.

He stopped on the trail and looked up at her. "It'd be a lot easier for all of us if we didn't look around once in a while and see people who can smile."

"Who are they?" she said, running down to catch up and nearly crashing right into him.

He pushed his face so close to hers she had to step back. He spoke as if he were chipping the words out one at a time, once and for all. "Those who refuse to ride in the chariot!"

Hallie felt as if his breath had turned all of her into some cold rigid material. She looked into his eyes, pale, murky, trembling from the force of his words. A thin, barely visible red line ran from the edge of one grey disc down into the corner by the tear duct, casual as a lost thread. He was human. He was human. She lifted one hand and brushed a finger against his cheek.

Mr. Grey leapt back from her touch and tripped over a rock. He rolled over and over down the hill, slid a few feet, then rolled again until he slammed up against a tree. By the time Hallie got down that far he was on his feet again, walking with a slight limp down the deer trail to the fishing camp.

She'd handled it all wrong, she knew. She hadn't even behaved the way Hallie Crane normally would. That night in bed she thought of all the people she had known back home, the friendly nosy country people who had been her neighbours for nearly twenty years, and she tried to see herself as they would. Hallie Crane? You want to know how Hallie Crane would treat a little shit like that, spouting his nonsense? She'd throw back her head and laugh. You'd see her long white throat. You'd hear her deep harsh laugh. Hallie Crane has the sexiest laugh a man ever heard and that's exactly what she'd turn on that smart-alec school teacher. She'd laugh and ask him who the hell he thought he was.

But she hadn't done that. She didn't even have her old laugh any more. She'd kept her looks and her figure and her long slim legs, but somewhere along the way she'd lost her deep throaty laugh. Those people wouldn't recognize her without it. No wonder she's scared to come home, they'd say. Hallie Crane without her laugh isn't Hallie Crane.

And she knew that she would never go back. There was nothing strong enough to pull her back to that place; not friends, not daughter, not grandchildren. She didn't want to see her son-in-law again. She didn't want to see the house again, or the small farms that surrounded it. Some day, maybe, she would send down enough money for her daughter and the children to fly up and spend part of the summer with her. That would be nice. Her daughter could help out in the café, talk to the tourists, find out that the kind of life her old lady lived wasn't so bad after all. Maybe Morgan would take them fishing.

While Hallie was lying in bed planning her future she heard Mr. Grey get up and go outside. Just keep on walking, she thought, walk right on over the mountains and down-island until you find the road, then keep on walking still. You've stirred up here all that needs to be stirred. How nice it would be to wake up in the morning and find he had gone, that he had shoved out to sea in his boat and disappeared. She would worry perhaps, for a few minutes, that he was in danger or even drowned, but soon she would say it was his own choice and forget him.

Though Hallie believed a little in the power of thought, she never expected immediate results. The sound of lumber breaking, snapping like kindling, and a long scream right outside the café brought her up out of the bed and to her feet. Outside her front door she discovered a large section of the boardwalk railing had been broken away. There was no sound below but the slapping of the sea. "Mr. Grey?" she said, in case he was close by and watching her. But no answer came so she yelled his name into the dark. She felt for a moment as if she were alone, the only person left in the world, abandoned. She screamed for Morgan, who came up the slope eventually with a strong flashlight he aimed down into the water, splashing sloppily around the pilings, and it wasn't until morning that they found Mr. Grey's body, back under the boardwalk and nudging like a dead fish against the rock her house was built on.

"You son of a bitch," Hallie said to Morgan. "Did you do this?" Morgan came up close and looked hard at her. The rain was rolling off his flattened hair and down his face, dripping from the end of his nose.

"Do you think that?" he said.

She looked into his eyes, steady as stone. "No," she said, and turned away. She went back into the café and waited until he had fished the body out and came to bang on her door.

"We'll have to bury him," he said.

She shuddered. "We're not *that* far from civilization. It doesn't seem right."

She turned away but he stepped in and walked around to face her and wrapped his arms so tight around her she couldn't move. She could smell the smoked fish on his breath, could see the black spikes of his week-old beard. She tried to push away but his grip was too tight, his arms too strong.

"What're you going to do?" he said.

"Going home."

"Hell you are. You're home now."

"I mean down-island, back to my family. I'll fly out as soon as the weather changes. I want to get away from this goddam hole."

"You'll never go back there again and you know it."

During the following week the storm continued. Waves hit the rocks and leapt up almost as high as the boardwalk railings. The wind, coming in from the strait like a giant flat hand, bent the seaside pines and firs down almost to the ground. Morgan walked up to the café every day and tried to talk her into moving down to the boat house but she didn't talk to him at all. She rolled up Hamilton Grey's sleeping bag and folded his tent and left them piled on the stage beside the piano for the day when the RCMP would be finally contacted and come to ask questions about his death.

At the end of the week Morgan came to the door and asked if she wanted to help bury the little school teacher. She nearly laughed and said "No, but thank you for thinking of me," but instead just shook her head and shut the door in his face. Through the window of a back room she watched him drag the body out of the shed and haul it, wrapped in one of her blankets and laid out flat on a piece of canvas, up the steep slope of the hill. She ran out into the rain with Mr. Grey's books, scrambled up the hill until she caught up with Morgan, and said, "Throw these in too." She tossed the books, whose titles she hadn't even noticed, onto the canvas beside the body and hurried back down the hill before he started digging the grave.

That evening the wind was quieter, the rain silent, but Morgan still hadn't fixed the radio set. Hallie sat for a long time at the window, looking out to sea, listening to the intense beating of her own heart. Then she packed her suitcase and walked down the boardwalk, slowly, casually as if she hoped for a ship to appear from behind the point of land and sail in to pick her up by the time she got down to the gravel beach. But no ship came and Hallie Crane walked past the beach, gravel crunching under her heels, walked past Mr. Grey's little aluminum boat still tied to a driftwood log, and knocked lightly on the boat-house door.

Inside, she put down her suitcase and took a good look around. "The first thing you can do," she told Morgan, "is go up and bring down my own bed. I'm just here for the company."

"Sure you are," he said, and shut the door.

"I can't stand being alone for long."

"Sit down," he said. "I was making some coffee."

She smiled. "Did you dig a deep enough grave?"

"Deep enough so the rain won't wash him out, shallow enough for people or relatives to dig up if they want to see the body."

"He had no relatives," she said, taking off her coat. "He said he had no one." She smiled. She would like to have laughed, like the old Hallie, but she turned instead to the window and looked out for a moment across the little bay. "He told me there was no one in the world who could touch him, not even us."

Henry James

There is an essay about Henry James in *Notes on Life and Letters*, in which Joseph Conrad talks about fiction as "human history"; in that compelling essay, which ought to be read in its entirety, he describes James as "the historian of fine consciences." The phrase is apt, since, as Conrad goes on to explain, James's fiction seems concerned with "the nice discrimination of shades of conduct." Conrad is defending James against the criticism that not enough happens in his fiction, by arguing that the rendering of psychological insights, or inner moral struggles, can be every bit as dramatic as the rendering of mere physical events in a work of art. A typical narrator, which James describes as his "central intelligence," will give such a sense of intimate understanding, or misunderstanding, of the situation being rendered that conventional action seems superfluous to the sophisticated modern reader. James found no conflict between the competing demands of character and plot; instead, he linked them in a unique way: "What is character but the determination of incident? What is incident but the illustration of character?"

It's not surprising that James was interested in such intimate exploration of character. He was born in 1843 in New York City into an unusually gifted family; his father, Henry James, Sr., was wealthy and a religious philosopher, and his brother was the renowned philosopher and psychologist William James. James was educated mostly by tutors in Europe and the U.S.; he attended Harvard Law School briefly, but a private income allowed him to indulge a preference for travel, independent study, and writing. He published his first short story at age twenty-one and moved to Europe at thirty-two, settling permanently in Rye, England, in 1896. His thoughts on the "art of fiction" are to be found in an essay of that title and in his letters, essays, and prefaces, many of which discuss the "*donnée*," or germ, of his stories and novels. He was particularly intrigued by the artist's relation to society and has written numerous stories around this subject, all collected in *Stories of Artists & Writers*, edited with an introduction by F. O. Matthiessen.

James shares with some of his fictional artists a "passion for form" and a determination to "give the impression of life itself" in his work. In the preface to *The Portrait of a Lady* (1881), he asserts "the dependence of the 'moral' sense of a work of art on the amount of *felt life* concerned in producing it" (italics added). In order to produce this sense of felt life, the artist must be able to render his material—showing, not telling—objectively, perhaps indirectly, through an artistic scheme or strategy that is "like a complex figure in a Persian carpet." The artist must cultivate his "faculty of attention"; although he is "fed by life," the artist must create meaning through concern for the shape, the "architecture," of his materials. The struggle to forge a style that gives the illusion of life demands more than literary reportage, as he said in his famous exchange with H. G. Wells; art requires "plasticity," "stylization," and "passionate correct[ion]" of so-called reality, if it is to be more than "merely referential narrative." In the words of Dencombe, the writer in "The Middle Years," "We work in the dark—we do what we can—we give what we have. Our doubt is our passion and our passion is our task. The rest is the madness of art."

James's critical prefaces are collected in *The Art of the Novel* (1934), with an introduction by R. P. Blackmur. James describes these prefaces as "a sort of comprehensive manual or *vade mecum* for aspirants in our arduous profession." These prefaces include useful clues to James's technical preoccupations. Of characterization, he wrote: "A character is interesting as it comes out, and by the process and duration of that emergence; just as a procession is effective by the way it unrolls, turning to a mere mob if it all passes at once." Certain writerly words and phrases indicative of form and design recur in James's prefaces: *shapely, organic form, mosaic, proportion, a rare alchemy, the ideal of economy, a fine complicated air*. Most often he was haunted by the "ever-importunate murmur, 'Dramatise it, dramatise it!'"

James was particularly fascinated by the relation of the artist to his fictional materials and to the transformation those materials undergo in the creative process: "We can surely account for nothing in the novelist's work that hasn't passed through the crucible of his imagination, hasn't in that perpetually simmering caldron, his intellectual pot-au-feu, been reduced to savory fusion. We here figure the morsel, of course not as boiled to nothing, but as exposed, in return for the taste it gives out, to a new and richer saturation. In this state it is in due course picked out and served, and a meager esteem will await, a poor importance attend, if it doesn't speak most of its late genial medium, the good, the wonderful company it has, as I hint, aesthetically kept. It has entered, in fine, into new relations, it emerges for new ones. Its final savor has been constituted, but its prime identity destroyed—which was what was to be demonstrated. Thus it has become a different and, thanks to a rare alchemy, a better thing." The process, he explains further, is that the materials out of which fiction is shaped—events, memories, experiences, whatever—cease to be things of fact and become, instead, things of truth.

The Real Thing

I

When the porter's wife, who used to answer the house-bell, announced "A gentleman and a lady, sir," I had, as I often had in those days—the wish being father to the thought—an immediate vision of sitters. Sitters my visitors in this case proved to be; but not in the sense I should have preferred. There was nothing at first however to indicate that they mightn't have come for a portrait. The gentleman, a man of fifty, very high and very straight, with a moustache slightly grizzled and a dark grey walking-coat admirably fitted, both of which I noted professionally—I don't mean as a barber or yet as a tailor—would have struck me as a celebrity if celebrities often were striking. It was a truth of which I had for some time been conscious that a figure with a good deal of frontage was, as one might say, almost never a public institution. A glance at the lady helped to remind me of this paradoxical law: she also looked too distinguished to be a "personality." Moreover one would scarcely come across two variations together.

Neither of the pair immediately spoke—they only prolonged the preliminary gaze suggesting that each wished to give the other a chance. They were visibly shy; they stood there letting me take them in—which, as I afterwards perceived, was the most practical thing they could have done. In this way their embarrassment served their cause. I had seen people painfully reluctant to mention that they desired anything so gross as to be represented on canvas; but the scruples of my new friends appeared almost insurmountable. Yet the gentleman might have said "I should like a portrait of my wife," and the lady might have said "I should like a portrait of my husband." Perhaps they weren't husband and wife—this naturally would make the matter more delicate. Perhaps they wished to be done together—in which case they ought to have brought a third person to break the news.

"We come from Mr. Rivet," the lady finally said with a dim smile that had the effect of a moist sponge passed over a "sunk" piece of painting, as well as of a vague allusion to vanished beauty. She was as tall and straight, in her degree, as her companion, and with ten years less to carry. She looked as sad as a woman could look whose face was not charged with expression; that is her tinted oval mask showed waste as an exposed surface shows friction. The hand of time had played over her freely, but to an effect of elimination. She was slim and stiff, and so well-dressed, in dark blue cloth, with lappets and pockets and buttons, that it was clear she employed the same tailor as her husband. The couple had an indefinable air of prosperous thrift—they evidently got a good deal of luxury for their money. If I was to be one of their luxuries it would behoove me to consider my terms.

"Ah Claude Rivet recommended me?" I echoed; and I added that it was very kind of him, though I could reflect that, as he only painted landscape, this wasn't a sacrifice.

The lady looked very hard at the gentleman, and the gentleman looked round the room. Then staring at the floor a moment and stroking his moustache, he rested his pleasant eyes on me with the remark: "He said you were the right one."

"I try to be, when people want to sit."

"Yes, we should like to," said the lady anxiously.

"Do you mean together?"

My visitors exchanged a glance. "If you could do anything with *me* I suppose it would be double," the gentleman stammered.

"Oh yes, there's naturally a higher charge for two figures than for one."

"We should like to make it pay," the husband confessed.

"That's very good of you," I returned, appreciating so unwonted a sympathy— for I supposed he meant pay the artist.

A sense of strangeness seemed to dawn on the lady. "We mean for the illustrations—Mr. Rivet said you might put one in."

"Put in—an illustration?" I was equally confused.

"Sketch her off, you know," said the gentleman, coloring.

It was only then that I understood the service Claude Rivet had rendered me; he had told them how I worked in black-and-white, for magazines, for storybooks, for sketches of contemporary life, and consequently had copious employment for models. These things were true, but it was not less true—I may confess it now; whether because the aspiration was to lead to everything or to nothing I leave the reader to guess—that I couldn't get the honors, to say nothing of the emoluments, of a great painter of portraits out of my head. My "illustrations" were my pot-boilers; I looked to a different branch of art—far and away the most interesting it had always seemed to me—to perpetuate my fame. There was no shame in looking to it also to make my fortune; but that fortune was by so much further from being made from the moment my visitors wished to be "done" for nothing. I was disappointed; for in the pictorial sense I had immediately seen them. I had seized their type—I had already settled what I would do with it. Something that wouldn't absolutely have pleased them, I afterwards reflected.

"Ah you're—you're—a?" I began as soon as I had mastered my surprise. I couldn't bring out the dingy word "models": it seemed so little to fit the case.

"We haven't had much practice," said the lady.

"We've got to do something, and we've thought that an artist in your line might perhaps make something of us," her husband threw off. He further mentioned that they didn't know many artists and that they had gone first, on the off-chance—he painted views of course, but sometimes put in figures; perhaps I remembered—to Mr. Rivet, whom they had met a few years before at a place in Norfolk where he was sketching.

"We used to sketch a little ourselves," the lady hinted.

"It's very awkward, but we absolutely must do something," her husband went on.

"Of course we're not so very young," she admitted with a wan smile.

With the remark that I might as well know something more about them the husband had handed me a card extracted from a neat new pocket-book—their appurtenances were all of the freshest—and inscribed with the words "Major Monarch." Impressive as these words were they didn't carry my knowledge much further; but my visitor presently added: "I've left the army and we've had the misfortune to lose our money. In fact our means are dreadfully small."

"It's awfully trying—a regular strain," said Mrs. Monarch.

They evidently wished to be discreet—to take care not to swagger because they were gentlefolk. I felt them willing to recognize this as something of a drawback, at the same time that I guessed at an underlying sense—their consolation in adversity—that they *had* their points. They certainly had; but these advantages struck me as preponderantly social; such for instance as would help to make a drawing-room look well. However, a drawing-room was always, or ought to be, a picture.

In consequence of his wife's allusion to their age Major Monarch observed: "Naturally, it's more for the figure that we thought of going in. We can still hold ourselves up." On the instant I saw that the figure was indeed their strong point. His "naturally" didn't sound vain, but it lighted up the question. "*She* has got the best," he continued, nodding at his wife, with a pleasant after-dinner absence of circumlocution. I could only reply, as if we were in fact sitting over our wine, that this didn't prevent his own from being very good; which led him in turn to rejoin: "We thought that if you ever have to do people like us, we might be something like it. *She*, particularly—for a lady in a book, you know."

I was so amused by them that, to get more of it, I did my best to take their point of view; and though it was an embarrassment to find myself appraising physically, as if they were animals on hire or useful blacks, a pair whom I should have expected to meet only in one of the relations in which criticism is tacit, I looked at Mrs. Monarch judicially enough to be able to exclaim, after a moment, with conviction: "Oh yes, a lady in a book!" She was singularly like a bad illustration.

"We'll stand up, if you like," said the Major; and he raised himself before me with a really grand air.

I could take his measure at a glance—he was six feet two and a perfect gentleman. It would have paid any club in process of formation and in want of a stamp to engage him at a salary to stand in the principal window. What struck me immediately was that in coming to me they had rather missed their vocation; they could surely have been turned to better account for advertising purposes. I couldn't of course see the thing in detail, but I could see them make someone's fortune—I don't mean their own. There was something in them for a waistcoat-maker, an hotel-keeper, or a soap-vendor. I could imagine "We always use it" pinned on their bosoms with the greatest effect; I had a vision of the promptitude with which they would launch a table d'hôte.

Mrs. Monarch sat still, not from pride but from shyness, and presently her husband said to her: "Get up my dear and show how smart you are." She obeyed, but she had no need to get up to show it. She walked to the end of the studio, and then she came back blushing, with her fluttered eyes on her husband. I was reminded of an incident I had accidentally had a glimpse of in Paris—being with a friend there, a dramatist about to produce a play—when an actress came to him to ask to be intrusted with a part. She went through her paces before him, walked up and down as Mrs. Monarch was doing. Mrs. Monarch did it quite as well, but I abstained from applauding. It was very odd to see such people apply for such poor pay. She looked as if she had ten thousand a year. Her husband had used the word that described her: she was in the London current jargon essentially and typically "smart." Her figure was, in the same order of ideas, conspicuously and irreproachably "good." For a woman of her age her waist was surprisingly small; her elbow moreover had the orthodox crook. She held her head at the conventional angle, but why did she come to *me*? She ought to have tried on jackets at a big shop. I feared my visitors were not only destitute but "artistic"—which would be a great complication. When she sat down again I thanked her, observing that what a draughtsman most valued in his model was the faculty of keeping quiet.

"Oh *she* can keep quiet," said Major Monarch. Then he added jocosely: "I've always kept her quiet."

"I'm not a nasty fidget, am I?" It was going to wring tears from me, I felt, the way she hid her head, ostrich-like, in the other broad bosom.

The owner of this expanse addressed his answer to me. "Perhaps it isn't out of place to mention—because we ought to be quite businesslike, oughtn't we?—that when I married her she was known as the Beautiful Statue."

"Oh dear!" said Mrs. Monarch ruefully.

"Of course I should want a certain amount of expression," I rejoined.

"*Of course!*"—and I had never heard such unanimity.

"And then I suppose you know that you'll get awfully tired."

"Oh, we *never* get tired!" they eagerly cried.

"Have you had any kind of practice?"

They hesitated—they looked at each other. "We've been photographed—*immensely*," said Mrs. Monarch.

"She means the fellows have asked us themselves," added the Major.

"I see—because you're so good-looking."

"*I* don't know what they thought, but they were always after us."

"We always got our photographs for nothing," smiled Mrs. Monarch.

"We might have brought some, my dear," her husband remarked.

"I'm not sure we have any left. We've given quantities away," she explained to me.

"With our autographs and that sort of thing," said the Major.

"Are they to be got in the shops?" I enquired as a harmless pleasantry.

"Oh yes, *hers*—they used to be."

"Not now," said Mrs. Monarch, with her eyes on the floor.

II

I could fancy the "sort of thing" they put on the presentation copies of their photographs, and I was sure they wrote a beautiful hand. It was odd how quickly I was sure of everything that concerned them. If they were now so poor as to have to earn shillings and pence they could never have had much of a margin. Their good looks had been their capital, and they had good-humoredly made the most of the career that this resource marked out for them. It was in their faces, the blankness, the deep intellectual repose of the twenty years of country-house-visiting that had given them pleasant intonations. I could see the sunny drawing-rooms, sprinkled with periodicals she didn't read, in which Mrs. Monarch had continually sat; I could see the wet shrubberies in which she had walked, equipped to admiration for either exercise. I could see the rich covers the Major had helped to shoot and the wonderful garments in which, late at night, he repaired to the smoking-room to talk about them. I could imagine their leggings and waterproofs, their knowing tweeds and rugs, their rolls of sticks and cases of tackle and neat umbrellas; and I could evoke the exact appearance of their servants and the compact variety of their luggage on the platforms of country stations.

They gave small tips, but they were liked; they didn't do anything themselves, but they were welcome. They looked so well everywhere, they gratified the general relish for stature, complexion, and "form." They knew it without fatuity or vulgarity, and they respected themselves in consequence. They weren't superficial; they were thorough and kept themselves up—it had been their line. People with such a taste for activity had to have some line. I could feel how even in a dull house they could have been counted on for the joy of life. At present something had happened—it didn't matter what, their little income had grown less, it had grown least—and they had to do something for pocket-money. Their friends could like them, I made out, without liking to support them. There was something about them that represented credit—their clothes, their manners, their type; but if credit is a large empty pocket in which an occasional chink reverberates, the chink at least must be audible. What they wanted of me was to help to make it so. Fortunately they had no children—I soon divined that. They would also perhaps wish our relations to be kept secret: this was why it was "for the figure"—the reproduction of the face would betray them.

I liked them—I felt, quite as their friends must have done—they were so simple; and I had no objection to them if they would suit. But somehow with all their perfections I didn't easily believe in them. After all they were amateurs, and the ruling passion of my life was the detestation of the amateur. Combined with this was another perversity—an innate preference for the represented subject over the real one: the defect of the real one was so apt to be a lack of representation. I like things that appeared; then one was sure. Whether they *were* or not was a subordinate and almost always a profitless question. There were other considerations, the first of which was that I already had two or three recruits in use, notably a young person with big feet, in alpaca, from Kilburn, who for a couple of years had come to me regularly for my illustrations and with whom I was still—perhaps ignobly—satisfied. I frankly explained to my visitors how the case stood, but they had taken more precautions than I supposed. They had reasoned out their opportunity, for Claude Rivet had told them of the projected *édition de luxe* of one of the writers of our day—the rarest of the novelists—who, long neglected by the multitudinous vulgar and dearly prized by the attentive (need I mention Philip Vincent?), had had the happy fortune of seeing, late in life, the dawn and then the full light of a higher criticism; an estimate in which on the part of the public there was something really of expiation. The edition preparing, planned by a publisher of taste, was practically an act of high reparation; the wood-cuts with which it was to be enriched were the homage of English art to one of the most independent representatives of English letters. Major and Mrs. Monarch confessed to me they had hoped I might be able to work *them* into my branch of the enterprise. They knew I was to do the first of the books, "Rutland Ramsay," but I had to make clear to them that my participation in the rest of the affair—this first book was to be a test—must depend on the satisfaction I should give. If this should be limited my employers would drop me with scarce common forms. It was therefore a crisis for me, and naturally I was making special preparations, looking about for new people, should they be necessary, and securing the best types. I admitted however that I should like to settle down to two or three good models who would do for everything.

"Should we have often to—a—put on special clothes?" Mrs. Monarch timidly demanded.

"Dear yes—that's half the business."

"And should we be expected to supply our own costumes?"

"Oh no; I've got a lot of things. A painter's models put on—or put off—anything he likes."

"And you mean—a—the same?"

"The same?"

Mrs. Monarch looked at her husband again.

"Oh she was just wondering," he explained, "if the costumes are in *general use.*" I had to confess that they were, and I mentioned further that some of them—I had a lot of genuine greasy last-century things—had served their time, a hundred years ago, on living world-stained men and women; on figures not perhaps so far removed, in that vanished world, from their type, the Monarchs', *quoi!* of a breeched and bewigged age. "We'll put on anything that *fits,*" said the Major.

"Oh I arrange that—they fit in the pictures."

"I'm afraid I should do better for the modern books. I'd come as you like," said Mrs. Monarch.

"She has got a lot of clothes at home: they might do for contemporary life," her husband continued.

"Oh I can fancy scenes in which you'd be quite natural." And indeed I could see the slipshod rearrangements of stale properties—the stories I tried to produce pictures for without the exasperation of reading them—whose sandy tracts the good lady might help to people. But I had to return to the fact that for this sort of work—the daily mechanical grind—I was already equipped: the people I was working with were fully adequate.

"We only thought we might be more like *some* characters," said Mrs. Monarch mildly, getting up.

Her husband also rose; he stood looking at me with a dim wistfulness that was touching in so fine a man. "Wouldn't it be rather a pull sometimes to have—a—to have—?" He hung fire; he wanted me to help him by phrasing what he meant. But I couldn't—I didn't know. So he brought it out awkwardly: "The *real* thing; a gentleman, you know, or a lady." I was quite ready to give a general assent—I admitted that there was a great deal in that. This encouraged Major Monarch to say, following up his appeal with an unacted gulp: "It's awfully hard—we've tried everything." The gulp was communicative; it proved too much for his wife. Before I knew it Mrs. Monarch had dropped again upon a divan and burst into tears. Her husband sat down beside her, holding one of her hands; whereupon she quickly dried her eyes with the other, while I felt embarrassed as she looked up at me. "There isn't a confounded job I haven't applied for—waited for—prayed for. You can fancy we'd be pretty bad first. Secretaryships and that sort of thing? You might as well ask for a peerage. I'd be *anything*—I'm strong; a messenger or a coal heaver. I'd put on a gold-laced cap and open carriage-doors in front of the haberdasher's; I'd hang about a station to carry portmanteaux; I'd be a postman. But they won't *look* at you; there are thousands as good as yourself already on the ground. *Gentlemen,* poor beggars, who've drunk their wine, who've kept their hunters!"

I was as reassuring as I knew how to be, and my visitors were presently on their feet again while, for the experiment, we agreed on an hour. We were discussing it when the door opened and Miss Churm came in with a wet umbrella. Miss Churm had to take the omnibus to Maida Vale and then walk half a mile. She looked a trifle blowsy and slightly splashed. I scarcely ever saw her come in without thinking afresh how odd it was that, being so little in herself, she should yet be so much in others. She was a meagre little Miss Churm, but was such an ample heroine of romance. She was only a freckled cockney, but she could represent everything, from a fine lady to a shepherdess; she had the faculty as she might have had a fine voice or long hair. She couldn't spell and she loved beer, but she had two or three "points," and practice, and a knack, and mother-wit, and a whimsical sensibility, and a love of the theatre, and seven sisters, and not an ounce of respect, especially for the *h*. The first thing my visitors saw was that her umbrella was wet, and in their spotless perfection they visibly winced at it. The rain had come on since their arrival.

"I'm all in a soak; there was a mess of people in the 'bus. I wish you lived near a station," said Miss Churm. I requested her to get ready as quickly as possible, and she passed into the room in which she always changed her dress. But before going out she asked me what she was to get into this time.

"It's the Russian princess, don't you know?" I answered; "the one with the 'golden eyes,' in black velvet, for the long thing in the *Cheapside*."

"Golden eyes? I *say*!" cried Miss Churm, while my companions watched her with intensity as she withdrew. She always arranged herself, when she was late, before I could turn round; and I kept my visitors a little on purpose, so that they might get an idea, from seeing her, what would be expected of themselves. I mentioned that she was quite my notion of an excellent model—she was really very clever.

"Do you think she looks like a Russian princess?" Major Monarch asked with lurking alarm.

"When I make her, yes."

"Oh if you have to *make* her—!" he reasoned, not without point.

"That's the most you can ask. There are so many who are not makeable."

"Well now, *here's* a lady"—and with a persuasive smile he passed his arm into his wife's—"who's already made!"

"Oh I'm not a Russian princess," Mrs. Monarch protested a little coldly. I could see she had known some and didn't like them. There at once was a complication of a kind I never had to fear with Miss Churm.

This young lady came back in black velvet—the gown was rather rusty and very low on her lean shoulders—and with a Japanese fan in her red hands. I reminded her that in the scene I was doing she had to look over some one's head. "I forget whose it is; but it doesn't matter. Just look over a head."

"I'd rather look over a stove," said Miss Churm; and she took her station near the fire. She fell into position, settled herself into a tall attitude, gave a certain backward inclination to her head and a certain forward droop to her fan, and looked, at least to my prejudiced sense, distinguished and charming, foreign and dangerous. We left her looking so while I went downstairs with Major and Mrs. Monarch.

"I believe I could come about as near it as that," said Mrs. Monarch.

"Oh you think she's shabby, but you must allow for the alchemy of art."

However, they went off with an evident increase of comfort founded on their demonstrable advantage in being the real thing. I could fancy them shuddering over Miss Churm. She was very droll about them when I went back, for I told her what they wanted.

"Well, if *she* can sit I'll tyke to book-keeping," said my model.

"She's very ladylike," I replied as an innocent form of aggravation.

"So much the worse for you. That means she can't turn round."

"She'll do for the fashionable novels."

"Oh yes, she'll do for them!" my model humorously declared. "Ain't they bad enough without her?" I had often sociably denounced them to Miss Churm.

III

It was for the elucidation of a mystery in one of these works that I first tried Mrs. Monarch. Her husband came with her, to be useful if necessary—it was sufficiently clear that as a general thing he would prefer to come with her. At first I wondered if this were for "propriety's" sake—if he were going to be jealous and meddling. The idea was too tiresome, and if it had been confirmed it would speedily have brought our acquaintance to a close. But I soon saw there was nothing in it and that if he accompanied Mrs. Monarch it was—in addition to the chance of being wanted—simply because he had nothing else to do. When they were separate his occupation was gone and they never *had* been separate. I judged rightly that in their awkward situation their close union was their main comfort and that this union had no weak spot. It was a real marriage, an encouragement to the hesitating, a nut for pessimists to crack. Their address was humble—I remember afterwards thinking it had been the only thing about them that was really professional—and I could fancy the lamentable lodgings in which the Major would have been left alone. He could sit there more or less grimly with his wife—he couldn't sit there anyhow without her.

He had too much tact to try and make himself agreeable when he couldn't be useful; so when I was too absorbed in my work to talk he simply sat and waited. But I liked to hear him talk—it made my work, when not interrupting it, less mechanical, less special. To listen to him was to combine the excitement of going out with the economy of staying at home. There was only one hindrance—that I seemed not to know any of the people this brilliant couple had known. I think he wondered extremely, during the term of our intercourse, whom the deuce I *did* know. He hadn't a stray sixpence of an idea to fumble for, so we didn't spin it very fine; we confined ourselves to questions of leather and even of liquor—saddlers and breeches-makers and how to get excellent claret cheap—and matters like "good trains" and the habits of small game. His lore on these last subjects was astonishing—he managed to interweave the station-master with the ornithologist. When he couldn't talk about greater things he could talk cheerfully about smaller, and since I couldn't accompany him into reminiscences of the fashionable world he could lower the conversation without a visible effort to my level.

So earnest a desire to please was touching in a man who could so easily have knocked one down. He looked after the fire and had an opinion on the draught of the stove without my asking him, and I could see that he thought many of my arrangements not half knowing. I remember telling him that if I were only rich I'd offer him a salary to come and teach me how to live. Sometimes he gave a random sigh of which the essence might have been: "Give me even such a bare old barrack as *this*, and I'd do something with it!" When I wanted to use him he came alone; which was an illustration of the superior courage of women. His wife could bear her solitary second floor, and she was in general more discreet; showing by various small reserves that she was alive to the propriety of keeping our relations markedly professional—not letting them slide into sociability. She wished it to remain clear that she and the Major were employed, not cultivated, and if she approved of me as a superior, who could be kept in his place, she never thought me quite good enough for an equal.

She sat with great intensity, giving the whole of her mind to it, and was capable of remaining for an hour almost as motionless as before a photographer's lens. I could see she had been photographed often, but somehow the very habit that made her good for that purpose unfitted her for mine. At first I was extremely pleased with her ladylike air, and it was a satisfaction, on coming to follow her lines, to see how good they were and how far they could lead the pencil. But after a little skirmishing I began to find her too insurmountably stiff; do what I would with it my drawing looked like a photograph or a copy of a photograph. Her figure had no variety of expression—she herself had no sense of variety. You may say that this was my business and was only a question of placing her. Yet I placed her in every conceivable position and she managed to obliterate their differences. She was always a lady certainly, and into the bargain was always the same lady. She was the real thing, but always the same thing. There were moments when I rather writhed under the serenity of her confidence that she *was* the real thing. All her dealings with me and all her husband's were an implication that this was lucky for *me*. Meanwhile I found myself trying to invent types that approached her own, instead of making her own transform itself—in the clever way that was not impossible for instance to poor Miss Churm. Arrange as I would and take the precautions I would, she always came out, in my pictures, too tall—landing me in the dilemma of having represented a fascinating woman as seven feet high, which (out of respect perhaps to my own very much scantier inches) was far from my idea of such a personage.

The case was worse with the Major—nothing I could do would keep him down, so that he became useful only for the representation of brawny giants. I adored variety and range, I cherished human accidents, the illustrative note; I wanted to characterize closely, and the thing in the world I most hated was the danger of being ridden by a type. I had quarreled with some of my friends about it; I had parted company with them for maintaining that one had to be, and that if the type was beautiful—witness Raphael and Leonardo—the servitude was only a gain. I was neither Leonardo nor Raphael—I might only be a presumptuous young modern searcher; but I held that everything was to be sacrificed sooner than character. When they claimed that the obsessional form could easily *be* character I retorted, perhaps superficially, "Whose?" It couldn't be everybody's—it might end in being nobody's.

After I had drawn Mrs. Monarch a dozen times I felt surer even than before that the value of such a model as Miss Churm resided precisely in the fact that she had no positive stamp, combined of course with the other fact that what she did have was a curious and inexplicable talent for imitation. Her usual appearance was like a curtain which she could draw up at request for a capital performance. This performance was simply suggestive; but it was a word to the wise—it was vivid and pretty. Sometimes even I thought it, though she was plain herself, too insipidly pretty; I made it a reproach to her that the figures drawn from her were monotonously (*bêtement*, as we used to say) graceful. Nothing made her more angry; it was so much her pride to feel she could sit for characters that had nothing in common with each other. She would accuse me at such moments of taking away her "reputytion."

It suffered a certain shrinkage, this queer quantity, from the repeated visits of my new friends. Miss Churm was greatly in demand, never in want of employment, so I had no scruple in putting her off occasionally, to try them more at my ease. It was certainly amusing at first to do the real thing—it was amusing to do Major Monarch's trousers. They *were* the real thing, even if he did come out colossal. It was amusing to do his wife's back hair—it was so mathematically neat—and the particular "smart" tension of her tight stays. She lent herself especially to positions in which the face was somewhat averted or blurred; she abounded in ladylike back views and profils perdus. When she stood erect she took naturally one of the attitudes in which court painters represent queens and princesses; so that I found myself wondering whether, to draw out this accomplishment, I couldn't get the editor of the *Cheapside* to publish a really royal romance, "A Tale of Buckingham Palace." Sometimes however the real thing and the make-believe came into contact; by which I mean that Miss Churm, keeping an appointment or coming to make one on days when I had much work in hand, encountered her invidious rivals. The encounter was not on their part, for they noticed her no more than if she had been the housemaid; not from intentional loftiness, but simply because as yet, professionally, they didn't know how to fraternize, as I could imagine they would have liked—or at least that the Major would. They couldn't talk about the omnibus—they always walked; and they didn't know what else to try—she wasn't interested in good trains or cheap claret. Besides, they must have felt—in the air—that she was amused at them, secretly derisive of their ever knowing how. She wasn't a person to conceal the limits of her faith if she had had a chance to show them. On the other hand Mrs. Monarch didn't think her tidy; for why else did she take pains to say to me—it was going out of the way, for Mrs. Monarch—that she didn't like dirty women?

One day when my young lady happened to be present with my other sitters— she even dropped in, when it was convenient, for a chat—I asked her to be so good as to lend a hand in getting tea, a service with which she was familiar and which was one of a class that, living as I did in a small way with slender domestic resources, I often appealed to my models to render. They liked to lay hands on my property, to break the sitting, and sometimes the china—it made them feel Bohemian. The next time I saw Miss Churm after this incident she surprised me greatly by making a scene about it—she accused me of having wished to humiliate her. She hadn't resented the outrage at the time, but had seemed obliging and amused, enjoying the comedy of asking Mrs. Monarch, who sat vague and silent, whether she would have cream and sugar, and putting an exaggerated simper into the question. She had tried intonations—as if she too wished to pass for the real thing—till I was afraid my other visitors would take offense.

Oh they were determined not to do this, and their touching patience was the measure of their great need. They would sit by the hour, uncomplaining, till I was ready to use them; they would come back on the chance of being wanted and would walk away cheerfully if it failed. I used to go to the door with them to see in what magnificent order they retreated. I tried to find other employment for them—I introduced them to several artists.

But they didn't "take," for reasons I could appreciate, and I became rather anxiously aware that after such disappointments they fell back upon me with a heavier weight. They did me the honor to think me most *their* form. They weren't romantic enough for the painters, and in those days there were few serious workers in black-and-white. Besides, they had an eye to the great job I had mentioned to them—they had secretly set their hearts on supplying the right essence for my pictorial vindication of our fine novelist. They knew that for this undertaking I should want no costume-effects, none of the frippery of past ages—that it was a case in which everything would be contemporary and satirical and presumably genteel. If I could work them into it their future would be assured, for the labor would of course be long and the occupation steady.

One day Mrs. Monarch came without her husband—she explained his absence by his having had to go to the City. While she sat there in her usual relaxed majesty there came at the door a knock which I immediately recognized as the subdued appeal of a model out of work. It was followed by the entrance of a young man whom I at once saw to be a foreigner and who proved in fact an Italian acquainted with no English word but my name, which he uttered in a way that made it seem to include all others. I hadn't then visited his country, nor was I proficient in his tongue; but as he was not so meanly constituted—what Italian is?—as to depend only on that member for expression he conveyed to me, in familiar but graceful mimicry, that he was in search of exactly the employment in which the lady before me was engaged. I was not struck with him at first, and while I continued to draw I dropped few signs of interest or encouragement. He stood his ground however—not importunately, but with a dumb dog-like fidelity in his eyes that amounted to innocent impudence, the manner of a devoted servant—he might have been in the house for years—unjustly suspected. Suddenly it struck me that this very attitude and expression made a picture; whereupon I told him to sit down and wait till I should be free. There was another picture in the way he obeyed me, and I observed as I worked that there were others still in the way he looked wonderingly, with his head thrown back, about the high studio. He might have been crossing himself in Saint Peter's. Before I finished I said to myself "The fellow's a bankrupt orange-monger, but a treasure."

When Mrs. Monarch withdrew he passed across the room like a flash to open the door for her, standing there with the rapt pure gaze of the young Dante spellbound by the young Beatrice. As I never insisted, in such situations, on the blankness of the British domestic, I reflected that he had the making of a servant—and I needed one, but couldn't pay him to be only that—as well as of a model; in short I resolved to adopt my bright adventurer if he would agree to officiate in the double capacity. He jumped at my offer, and in the event my rashness—for I had really known nothing about him—wasn't brought home to me. He proved a sympathetic though a desultory ministrant, and had in a wonderful degree the *sentiment de la pose*. It was uncultivated, instinctive, a part of the happy instinct that had guided him to my door and helped him to spell out my name on the card nailed to it. He had had no other introduction to me than a guess, from the shape of my high north window, seen outside, that my place was a studio and that as a studio it would contain an artist. He had wandered to England in search of fortune, like other itinerants, and had embarked, with a partner and a small green hand-cart, on the sale of penny ices. The ices had melted away and the partner had dissolved in their train. My young man wore tight yellow trousers with reddish stripes and his name was Oronte. He was sallow but fair, and when I put him into some old clothes of my own he looked like an Englishman. He was as good as Miss Churm, who could look, when requested, like an Italian.

IV

I thought Mrs. Monarch's face slightly convulsed when, on her coming back with her husband, she found Oronte installed. It was strange to have to recognize in a scrap of a lazzarone a competitor to her magnificent Major. It was she who scented danger first, for the Major was anecdotically unconscious. But Oronte gave us tea, with a hundred eager confusions—he had never been concerned in so queer a process—and I think she thought better of me for having at last an "establishment." They saw a couple of drawings that I had made of the establishment, and Mrs. Monarch hinted that it never would have struck her he had sat for them. "Now the drawings you make from *us*, they look exactly like us," she reminded me, smiling in triumph; and I recognized that this was indeed just their defect. When I drew the Monarchs I couldn't anyhow get away from them—get into the character I wanted to represent; and I hadn't the least desire my model should be discoverable in my picture. Miss Churm never was, and Mrs. Monarch thought I hid her, very properly, because she was vulgar; whereas if she was lost it was only as the dead who go to heaven are lost—in the gain of an angel the more.

By this time I had got a certain start with "Rutland Ramsay," the first novel in the great projected series; that is I had produced a dozen drawings, several with the help of the Major and his wife, and I had sent them in for approval. My understanding with the publishers, as I have already hinted, had been that I was to be left to do my work, in this particular case, as I liked, with the whole book committed to me; but my connection with the rest of the series was only contingent. There were moments when, frankly, it was a comfort to have the real thing under one's hand; for there were characters in "Rutland Ramsay" that were very much like it. There were people presumably as erect as the Major and women of as good a fashion as Mrs. Monarch. There was a great deal of country-house life—treated, it is true, in a fine fanciful ironical generalized way—and there was a considerable implication of knickerbockers and kilts. There were certain things I had to settle at the outset; such things for instance as the exact appearance of the hero and the particular bloom and figure of the heroine. The author of course gave me a lead, but there was a margin for interpretation. I took the Monarchs into my confidence, I told them frankly what I was about, I mentioned my embarrassments and alternatives. "Oh take *him*!" Mrs. Monarch murmured sweetly, looking at her husband; and "What could you want better than my wife?" the Major enquired with the comfortable candor that now prevailed between us.

I wasn't obliged to answer these remarks—I was only obliged to place my sitters. I wasn't easy in mind, and I postponed a little timidly perhaps the solving of my question. The book was a large canvas, the other figures were numerous, and I worked off at first some of the episodes in which the hero and the heroine were not concerned. When once I had set them up I should have to stick to them—I couldn't make my young man seven feet high in one place and five feet nine in another. I inclined on the whole to the latter measurement, though the Major more than once reminded me that *he* looked about as young as any one. It was indeed quite possible to arrange him, for the figure, so that it would have been difficult to detect his age. After the spontaneous Oronte had been with me a month, and after I had given him to understand several times over that his native exuberance would presently constitute an insurmountable barrier to our further intercourse, I waked to a sense of his heroic capacity. He was only five feet seven, but the remaining inches were latent. I tried him almost secretly at first, for I was really rather afraid of the judgment my other models would pass on such a choice. If they regarded Miss Churm as little better than a snare what would they think of the representation by a person so little the real thing as an Italian street-vendor of a protagonist formed by a public school?

If I went a little in fear of them it wasn't because they bullied me, because they had got an oppressive foothold, but because in their really pathetic decorum and mysteriously permanent newness they counted on me so intensely. I was therefore very glad when Jack Hawley came home: he was always of such good counsel. He painted badly himself, but there was no one like him for putting his finger on the place. He had been absent from England for a year; he had been somewhere—I don't remember where—to get a fresh eye. I was in a good deal of dread of any such organ, but we were old friends; he had been away for months and a sense of emptiness was creeping into my life. I hadn't dodged a missile for a year.

He came back with a fresh eye, but with the same old black velvet blouse, and the first evening he spent in my studio we smoked cigarettes till the small hours. He had done no work himself, he had only got the eye; so the field was clear for the production of my little things. He wanted to see what I had produced for the *Cheapside*, but he was disappointed in the exhibition. That at least seemed the meaning of two or three comprehensive groans which, as he lounged on my big divan, his leg folded under him, looking at my latest drawings, issued from his lips with the smoke of the cigarette.

"What's the matter with you?" I asked.

"What's the matter with *you*?"

"Nothing save that I'm mystified."

"You are indeed. You're quite off the hinge. What's the meaning of this new fad?" And he tossed me, with visible irreverence, a drawing in which I happened to have depicted both my elegant models. I asked if he didn't think it good, and he replied that it struck him as execrable, given the sort of thing I had always represented myself to him as wishing to arrive at; but I let that pass—I was so anxious to see exactly what he meant. The two figures in the picture looked colossal, but I supposed this was *not* what he meant, inasmuch as, for aught he knew to the contrary, I might have been trying for some such effect. I maintained that I was working exactly in the same way as when he last had done me the honor to tell me I might do something some day. "Well, there's a screw loose somewhere," he answered; "wait a bit and I'll discover it." I depended upon him to do so: where else was the fresh eye? But he produced at last nothing more luminous than "I don't know—I don't like your types." This was lame for a critic who had never consented to discuss with me anything but the question of execution, the direction of strokes, and the mystery of values.

"In the drawings you've been looking at I think my types are very handsome."

"Oh they won't do!"

"I've been working with new models."

"I see you have. *They* won't do."

"Are you very sure of that?"

"Absolutely—they're stupid."

"You mean I am—for I ought to get round that."

"You *can't*—with such people. Who are they?"

I told him, so far as was necessary, and he concluded heartlessly: "*Ce sont des gens qu'il faut mettre à la porte.*"

"You've never seen them; they're awfully good"—I flew to their defense.

"Not seen them? Why all this recent work of yours drops to pieces with them. It's all I want to see of them."

"No one else has said anything against it—the *Cheapside* people are pleased."

"Every one else is an ass, and the *Cheapside* people the biggest asses of all. Come, don't pretend at this time of day to have pretty illusions about the public, especially about publishers and editors. It's not for *such* animals you work—it's for those you know, *coloro che sanno*; so keep straight for *me* if you can't keep straight for yourself. There was a certain sort of thing you used to try for—and a very good thing it was. But this twaddle isn't *in* it." When I talked with Hawley later about "Rutland Ramsay" and its possible successors he declared that I must get back into my boat again or I should go to the bottom. His voice in short was the voice of warning.

I noted the warning, but I didn't turn my friends out of doors. They bored me a good deal; but the very fact that they bored me admonished me not to sacrifice them—if there was anything to be done with them—simply to irritation. As I look back at this phase they seem to me to have pervaded my life not a little. I have a vision of them as most of the time in my studio, seated against the wall on an old velvet bench to be out of the way, and resembling the while a pair of patient courtiers in a royal ante-chamber. I'm convinced that during the coldest weeks of the winter they held their ground because it saved them fire. Their newness was losing its gloss, and it was impossible not to feel them objects of charity. Whenever Miss Churm arrived they went away, and after I was fairly launched in "Rutland Ramsay" Miss Churm arrived pretty often. They managed to express to me tacitly that they supposed I wanted her for the low life of the book, and I let them suppose it, since they had attempted to study the work—it was lying about the studio—without discovering that it dealt only with the highest circles. They had dipped into the most brilliant of our novelists without deciphering many passages. I still took an hour from them, now and again, in spite of Jack Hawley's warning: it would be time enough to dismiss them, if dismissal should be necessary, when the rigor of the season was over. Hawley had made their acquaintance—he had met them at my fireside—and thought them a ridiculous pair. Learning that he was a painter they tried to approach him, to show him too that they were the real thing; but he looked at them, across the big room, as if they were miles away: they were a compendium of everything he most objected to in the social system of his country. Such people as that, all convention and patent-leather, with ejaculations that stopped conversation, had no business in a studio. A studio was a place to learn to see, and how could you see through a pair of feather-beds?

The main inconvenience I suffered at their hands was that at first I was shy of letting it break upon them that my artful little servant had begun to sit to me for "Rutland Ramsay." They knew I had been odd enough—they were prepared by this time to allow oddity to artists—to pick a foreign vagabond out of the streets when I might have had a person with whiskers and credentials; but it was some time before they learned how high I rated his accomplishments. They found him in an attitude more than once, but they never doubted I was doing him as an organ-grinder. There were several things they never guessed, and one of them was that for a striking scene in the novel, in which a footman briefly figured, it occurred to me to make use of Major Monarch as the menial. I kept putting this off, I didn't like to ask him to don the livery—besides the difficulty of finding a livery to fit him. At last, one day late in the winter, when I was at work on the despised Oronte, who caught one's idea on the wing, and was in the glow of feeling myself go very straight, they came in, the Major and his wife, with their society laugh about nothing (there was less and less to laugh at); came in like country-callers—they always reminded me of that—who have walked across the park after church and are presently persuaded to stay to luncheon. Luncheon was over, but they could stay to tea—I knew they wanted it. The fit was on me, however, and I couldn't let my ardor cool and my work wait, with the fading daylight, while my model prepared it. So I asked Mrs. Monarch if she would mind laying it out—a request which for an instant brought all the blood to her face. Her eyes were on her husband's for a second, and some mute telegraphy passed between them. Their folly was over the next instant; his cheerful shrewdness put an end to it. So far from pitying their wounded pride, I must add, I was moved to give it as complete a lesson as I could. They bustled about together and got out the cups and saucers and made the kettle boil. I know they felt as if they were waiting on my servant, and when the tea was prepared I said: "He'll have a cup, please—he's tired." Mrs. Monarch brought him one where he stood, and he took it from her as if he had been a gentleman at a party squeezing a crush-hat with an elbow.

Then it came over me that she had made a great effort for me—made it with a kind of nobleness—and that I owed her a compensation. Each time I saw her after this I wondered what the compensation could be. I couldn't go on doing the wrong thing to oblige them. Oh it *was* the wrong thing, the stamp of the work for which they sat—Hawley was not the only person to say it now. I sent in a large number of the drawings I had made for "Rutland Ramsay," and I received a warning that was more to the point than Hawley's. The artistic adviser of the house for which I was working was of opinion that many of my illustrations were not what had been looked for. Most of these illustrations were the subjects in which the Monarchs had figured. Without going into the question of what *had* been looked for, I had to face the fact that at this rate I shouldn't get the other books to do. I hurled myself in despair on Miss Churm—I put her through all her paces. I not only adopted Oronte publicly as my hero, but one morning when the Major looked in to see if I didn't require him to finish a *Cheapside* figure for which he had begun to sit the week before, I told him I had changed my mind—I'd do the drawing from my man. At this my visitor turned pale and stood looking at me. "Is *he* your idea of an English gentleman?" he asked.

I was disappointed, I was nervous, I wanted to get on with my work so I replied with irritation: "Oh my dear Major—I can't be ruined for *you!*"

It was a horrid speech, but he stood another moment—after which, without a word, he quitted the studio. I drew a long breath, for I said to myself that I shouldn't see him again. I hadn't told him definitely that I was in danger of having my work rejected, but I was vexed at his not having felt the catastrophe in the air, read with me the moral of our fruitless collaboration, the lesson that in the deceptive atmosphere of art even the highest respectability may fail of being plastic.

I didn't owe my friends money, but I did see them again. They reappeared together three days later; and, given all the other facts, there was something tragic in that one. It was a clear proof they could find nothing else in life to do. They had threshed the matter out in a dismal conference—they had digested the bad news that they were not in for the series. If they weren't useful to me for the *Cheapside* their function seemed difficult to determine, and I could only judge at first that they had come, forgivingly, decorously, to take a last leave. This made me rejoice in secret that I had little leisure for a scene; for I had placed both my other models in position together and I was pegging away at a drawing from which I hoped to derive glory. It had been suggested by the passage in which Rutland Ramsay, drawing up a chair to Artemisia's piano-stool, says extraordinary things to her while she ostensibly fingers out a difficult piece of music. I had done Miss Churm at the piano before—it was an attitude in which she knew how to take on an absolutely poetic grace. I wished the two figures to "compose" together with intensity, and my little Italian had entered perfectly into my conception. The pair were vividly before me, the piano had been pulled out; it was a charming show of blended youth and murmured love, which I had only to catch and keep. My visitors stood and looked at it, and I was friendly to them over my shoulder.

They made no response, but I was used to silent company and went on with my work, only a little disconcerted—even though exhilarated by the sense that *this* was at least the ideal thing—at not having got rid of them after all. Presently I heard Mrs. Monarch's sweet voice beside or rather above me: "I wish her hair were a little better done." I looked up and she was staring with a strange fixedness at Miss Churm, whose back was turned to her. "Do you mind my just touching it?" she went on—a question which made me spring up for an instant as with the instinctive fear that she might do the young lady a harm. But she quieted me with a glance I shall never forget—I confess I should like to have been able to paint *that*—and went for a moment to my model. She spoke to her softly, laying a hand on her shoulder and bending over her; and as the girl, understanding, gratefully assented, she disposed her rough curls, with a few quick passes, in such a way as to make Miss Churm's head twice as charming. It was one of the most heroic personal services I've ever seen rendered. Then Mrs. Monarch turned away with a low sigh and, looking about her as if for something to do, stooped to the floor with a noble humility and picked up a dirty rag that had dropped out of my paint-box.

The Major meanwhile had also been looking for something to do, and, wandering to the other end of the studio, saw before him my breakfast things neglected, unremoved. "I say, can't I be useful *here?*" he called out to me with an irrepressible quaver. I assented with a laugh that I fear was awkward, and for the next ten minutes, while I worked, I heard the light clatter of china and the tinkle of spoons and glass. Mrs. Monarch assisted her husband—they washed up my crockery, they put it away. They wandered off into my little scullery, and I afterwards found that they had cleaned my knives and that my slender stock of plate had an unprecedented surface. When it came over me, the latent eloquence of what they were doing, I confess that my drawing was blurred for a moment—the picture swam. They had accepted their failure, but they couldn't accept their fate. They had bowed their heads in bewilderment to the perverse and cruel law in virtue of which the real thing could be so much less precious than the unreal; but they didn't want to starve. If my servants were my models, then my models might be my servants. They would reverse the parts—the others would sit for the ladies and gentlemen and *they* would do the work. They would still be in the studio—it was an intense dumb appeal to me not to turn them out. "Take us on," they wanted to say—"we'll do *anything*."

My pencil dropped from my hand; my sitting was spoiled and I got rid of my sitters, who were also evidently rather mystified and awestruck. Then, alone with the Major and his wife I had a most uncomfortable moment. He put their prayer into a single sentence: "I say, you know—just let *us* do for you, can't you?" I couldn't—it was dreadful to see them emptying my slops; but I pretended I could, to oblige them, for about a week. Then I gave them a sum of money to go away, and I never saw them again. I obtained the remaining books, but my friend Hawley repeats that Major and Mrs. Monarch did me a permanent harm, got me into false ways. If it be true I'm content to have paid the price—for the memory.

James Joyce

James Joyce was born in 1882 near Dublin, Ireland. He was educated at Conglowes Wood College from age six to nine, until his parents fell on difficult times financially. Later he was educated by the Jesuits at Bellevedere and University College, Dublin. His love affair with and self-imposed exile from Ireland, which he described as "an old sow that eats its farrow," was one of poverty and hardships, which included a ten-year struggle to find a publisher for *Dubliners* (1914) which sold less than five hundred copies. The book was savagely attacked by publishers and editors; even the plates themselves were destroyed at the printer's. A *Portrait of the Artist as a Young Man* had a more immediate success and won the approval of T. S. Eliot and Ezra Pound, both of whom helped garner support for his two major works, *Ulysses* (1922) and *Finnegans Wake* (1939). His survival in Trieste, Zurich, and Paris was, at best, precarious, with occasional teaching, commissions, and handouts from family and friends.

Joyce wrote very little about the art of fiction that was not, finally, incorporated into the fabric of his novels, particularly in the aesthetic ascribed to Stephen Dedalus in A *Portrait of the Artist as a Young Man*. However, there are in the letters a number of comments about fiction that are worthy of mention. Of *Dubliners*, he said: "My intention was to write a chapter of the moral history of my country and I chose Dublin for the scene because that city seemed to me the centre of paralysis. I have tried to present it to the indifferent public under four of its aspects: childhood, adolescence, maturity and public life. The stories are arranged in this order. I have written it for the most part in a style of scrupulous meanness and with the conviction that he is a very bold man who dares to alter in the presentment, still more to deform, whatever he has seen and heard. I cannot do any more than this. I cannot alter what I have written."

Joyce was preoccupied with attacks from editors, printers, and the public over many aspects of his work: "I have come to the conclusion that I cannot write without offending people. The printer denounces *Two Gallants* and *Counterparts*. A Dubliner would denounce *Ivy Day in the Committee-Room*. The more subtle inquisitor will denounce *An Encounter*, the enormity of which the printer cannot see because he is, as I said, a plain blunt man. The Irish priest will denounce *The Sisters*. The Irish boarding-house keeper will denounce *The Boarding-House*. Do not let the printer imagine, for goodness' sake, that he is going to have all the barking to himself."

The letters reveal him to be extremely scrupulous about the physical details of his stories, writing to friends in Dublin to ask them to check the name of a street, whether municipal elections can take place in October, and whether the police are supplied with provisions by government or private contacts. There is a wonderful letter from Joyce to Grant Richards, whose firm had contracted to publish *Dubliners*, but who had written to Joyce to say: "If I had written your stories I should certainly wish to be able to afford your attitude; but as I stand on the publisher's side, I feel most distinctly that for more than one reason you cannot afford it. . . . You won't get a publisher—a real publisher—to issue it as it stands. . . . After all, remember, *it is only words and sentences that have to be altered* [italics added]; and it seems to me that the man who cannot convey his meaning by more than one set of words and sentences has not yet realized the possibilities of the English language." Apparently, the publisher and his reader took exception to, among other things, use of the word *bloody* and the phrase *she changed the position of her legs often.*

To this Joyce responded: "The first passage I could alter. The second passage (with infinite regret) I could alter by omitting the word simply. But the third passage I absolutely could not alter. Read *The Boarding-House* yourself and tell me frankly what you think. The word, the exact expression I have used ["he'd bloody well put his teeth down his throat, so he would"], is in my opinion the one expression in the English language which can create on the reader the effect which I wish to create. Surely you can see this for yourself? And if the word appears once in the book it may as well appear three times. Is it not ridiculous that my book cannot be published because it contains this one word which is neither indecent nor blasphemous?" Joyce's reply barely veils his anger and justified contempt. "The objections raised against *Counterparts* seem to me equally trivial. Is it possible that at this age of the world in the country which the ingenuous Latins are fond of calling 'the home of liberty' an allusion to 'two establishments' cannot appear in print or that I cannot write the phrase 'she changed the position of her legs often?' To invoke the name of Areopagitica in this connection would be to render the artist as absurd as the printer.

"You say it is a small thing I am asked to do, to efface a word here and there. But do you not see clearly that in a short story above all such effacement may be fatal. You cannot say that the phrases objected to are gratuitous and impossible to print and at the same time approve of the tenor of the book. Granted this latter as legitimate I cannot see how anyone can consider these minute and necessary details illegitimate." The argument that you cannot divorce content from the form it acquires, or assumes, seems to have escaped the publisher.

Even when he managed to overcome difficulties in the way of publication, Joyce lived on the razor's edge financially, as a letter to Ezra Pound explains: "I live in a flat with eleven other people and have had great difficulty in securing time and peace enough to write those two chapters." He claimed to have no money to buy adequate clothes and to have to wear his son's shoes and castoff suit; he read newspapers and returned them for a refund, spending "the greatest part of my time sprawled across two beds surrounded by mountains of notes." His labours with *Ulysses* seem, appropriately, to have been Herculean; the book, which had begun as a short story for *Dubliners*, was abandoned and later grew to be "a kind of encyclopaedia." Among the many misconceptions people had of him, Joyce found most amusing the idea that he was lazy: "I calculate I have spent nearly 20,000 hours in writing *Ulysses*. . . . The task I set myself technically in writing a book from eighteen different points of view and in as many different styles, all apparently unknown or undiscovered by my fellow tradesmen, that and the nature of the legend chosen would be enough to upset anyone's mental balance. I want to finish the book and try to settle my entangled material affairs definitely one way or the other (somebody here said of me: 'They call him a poet. He appears to be interested chiefly in mattresses'). And in fact, I was. After that I want a good long rest in which to forget *Ulysses* completely."

Clay

The matron had given her leave to go out as soon as the women's tea was over and Maria looked forward to her evening out. The kitchen was spick and span: the cook said you could see yourself in the big copper boilers. The fire was nice and bright and on one of the side-tables were four very big barmbracks. These barmbracks seemed uncut; but if you went closer you would see that they had been cut into long thick even slices and were ready to be handed round at tea. Maria had cut them herself.

Maria was a very, very small person indeed but she had a very long nose and a very long chin. She talked a little through her nose, always soothingly: Yes, *my dear*, and No, *my dear*. She was always sent for when the women quarrelled over their tubs and always succeeded in making peace. One day the matron had said to her:

—Maria, you are a veritable peace-maker!

And the sub-matron and two of the Board ladies had heard the compliment. And Ginger Mooney was always saying what she wouldn't do to the dummy who had charge of the irons if it wasn't for Maria. Everyone was so fond of Maria.

The women would have their tea at six o'clock and she would be able to get away before seven. From Ballsbridge to the Pillar, twenty minutes; from the Pillar to Drumcondra, twenty minutes; and twenty minutes to buy the things. She would be there before eight. She took out her purse with the silver clasps and read again the words A *Present from Belfast*. She was very fond of that purse because Joe had brought it to her five years before when he and Alphy had gone to Belfast on a Whit-Monday trip. In the purse were two half-crowns and some coppers. She would have five shillings clear after paying tram fare. What a nice evening they would have, all the children singing! Only she hoped that Joe wouldn't come in drunk. He was so different when he took any drink.

Often he had wanted her to go and live with them; but she would have felt herself in the way (though Joe's wife was ever so nice with her) and she had become accustomed to the life of the laundry. Joe was a good fellow. She had nursed him and Alphy too; and Joe used often say:

—Mamma is mamma but Maria is my proper mother.

After the break-up at home the boys had got her that position in the *Dublin by Lamplight* laundry, and she liked it. She used to have such a bad opinion of Protestants but now she thought they were very nice people, a little quiet and serious, but still very nice people to live with. Then she had her plants in the conservatory and she liked looking after them. She had lovely ferns and wax-plants and, whenever anyone came to visit her, she always gave the visitor one or two slips from her conservatory. There was one thing she didn't like and that was the tracts on the walls; but the matron was such a nice person to deal with, so genteel.

When the cook told her everything was ready she went into the women's room and began to pull the big bell. In a few minutes the women began to come in by twos and threes, wiping their steaming hands in their petticoats and pulling down the sleeves of their blouses over their red steaming arms. They settled down before their huge mugs which the cook and the dummy filled up with hot tea, already mixed with milk and sugar in huge tin cans. Maria superintended the distribution of the barmbrack and saw that every woman got her four slices. There was a great deal of laughing and joking during the meal. Lizzie Fleming said Maria was sure to get the ring and, though Fleming had said that for so many Hallow Eves, Maria had to laugh and say she didn't want any ring or man either; and when she laughed her grey-green eyes sparkled with disappointed shyness and the tip of her nose nearly met the tip of her chin. Then Ginger Mooney lifted up her mug of tea and proposed Maria's health while all the other women clattered with their mugs on the table, and said she was sorry she hadn't a sup of porter to drink it in. And Maria laughed again till the tip of her nose nearly met the tip of her chin and till her minute body nearly shook itself asunder because she knew that Mooney meant well though, of course, she had the notions of a common woman.

But wasn't Maria glad when the women had finished their tea and the cook and the dummy had begun to clear away the tea-things! She went into her little bedroom and, remembering that the next morning was a mass morning, changed the hand of the alarm from seven to six. Then she took off her working skirt and her house-boots and laid her best skirt out on the bed and her tiny dress-boots beside the foot of the bed. She changed her blouse too and, as she stood before the mirror, she thought of how she used to dress for mass on Sunday morning when she was a young girl; and she looked with quaint affection at the diminutive body which she had so often adorned. In spite of its years she found it a nice tidy little body.

When she got outside the streets were shining with rain and she was glad of her old brown raincloak. The tram was full and she had to sit on the little stool at the end of the car, facing all the people, with her toes barely touching the floor. She arranged in her mind all she was going to do and thought how much better it was to be independent and to have your own money in your pocket. She hoped they would have a nice evening. She was sure they would but she could not help thinking what a pity it was Alphy and Joe were not speaking. They were always falling out now but when they were boys together they used to be the best of friends: but such was life.

She got out of her tram at the Pillar and ferreted her way quickly among the crowds. She went into Downes's cake-shop but the shop was so full of people that it was a long time before she could get herself attended to. She bought a dozen of mixed penny cakes, and at last came out of the shop laden with a big bag. Then she thought what else would she buy: she wanted to buy something really nice. They would be sure to have plenty of apples and nuts. It was hard to know what to buy and all she could think of was cake. She decided to buy some plumcake but Downes's plumcake had not enough almond icing on top of it so she went over to a shop in Henry Street. Here she was a long time in suiting herself and the stylish young lady behind the counter, who was evidently a little annoyed by her, asked her was it wedding-cake she wanted to buy. That made Maria blush and smile at the young lady; but the young lady took it all very seriously and finally cut a thick slice of plumcake, parcelled it up and said:

—Two-and-four, please.

She thought she would have to stand in the Drumcondra tram because none of the young men seemed to notice her but an elderly gentleman made room for her. He was a stout gentleman and he wore a brown hard hat; he had a square red face and a greying moustache. Maria thought he was a colonel-looking gentleman and she reflected how much more polite he was than the young men who simply stared straight before them. The gentleman began to chat with her about Hallow Eve and the rainy weather. He supposed the bag was full of good things for the little ones and said it was only right that the youngsters should enjoy themselves while they were young. Maria agreed with him and favoured him with demure nods and hems. He was very nice with her, and when she was getting out at the Canal Bridge she thanked him and bowed, and he bowed to her and raised his hat and smiled agreeably; and while she was going up along the terrace, bending her tiny head under the rain, she thought how easy it was to know a gentleman even when he has a drop taken.

Everybody said: *O, here's Maria!* when she came to Joe's house. Joe was there, having come home from business, and all the children had their Sunday dresses on. There were two big girls in from next door and games were going on. Maria gave the bag of cakes to the eldest boy, Alphy, to divide and Mrs Donnelly said it was too good of her to bring such a big bag of cakes and made all the children say:

Thanks, Maria.

But Maria said she had brought something special for papa and mamma, something they would be sure to like, and she began to look to for her plumcake. She tried in Downes's bag and then in the pockets of her raincloak and then on the hallstand but nowhere could she find it. Then she asked all the children had any of them eaten it—by mistake, of course—but the children all said no and looked as if they did not like to eat cakes if they were to be accused of stealing. Everybody had a solution for the mystery and Mrs Donnelly said it was plain that Maria had left it behind her in the tram. Maria, remembering how confused the gentleman with the greyish moustache had made her, coloured with shame and vexation and disappointment. At the thought of the failure of her little surprise and of the two and fourpence she had thrown away for nothing she nearly cried outright.

But Joe said it didn't matter and made her sit down by the fire. He was very nice with her. He told her all that went on in his office, repeating for her a smart answer which he had made to the manager. Maria did not understand why Joe laughed so much over the answer he had made but she said that the manager must have been a very overbearing person to deal with. Joe said he wasn't so bad when you knew how to take him, that he was a decent sort so long as you didn't rub him the wrong way. Mrs Donnelly played the piano for the children and they danced and sang. Then the two next-door girls handed round the nuts. Nobody could find the nutcrackers and Joe was nearly getting cross over it and asked how did they expect Maria to crack nuts without a nutcracker. But Maria said she didn't like nuts and that they weren't to bother about her. Then Joe asked would she take a bottle of stout and Mrs Donnelly said there was port wine too in the house if she would prefer that. Maria said she would rather they didn't ask her to take anything: but Joe insisted.

So Maria let him have his way and they sat by the fire talking over old times and Maria thought she would put in a good word for Alphy. But Joe cried that God might strike him stone dead if ever he spoke a word to his brother again and Maria said she was sorry she had mentioned the matter. Mrs Donnelly told her husband it was a great shame for him to speak that way of his own flesh and blood but Joe said that Alphy was no brother of his and there was nearly being a row on the head of it. But Joe said he would not lose his temper on account of the night it was and asked his wife to open some more stout. The two next-door girls had arranged some Hallow Eve games and soon everything was merry again. Maria was delighted to see the children so merry and Joe and his wife in such good spirits. The next-door girls put some saucers on the table and then led the children up to he table, blindfold. One got the prayer-book and the other three got the water; and when one of the next-door girls got the ring Mrs Donnelly shook her finger at the blushing girl as much as to say: O, *I know all about it!* They insisted then on blindfolding Maria and leading her up to the table to see what she would get; and, while they were putting on the bandage, Maria laughed and laughed again till the top of her nose nearly met the tip of her chin.

They led her up to the table amid laughing and joking and she put her hand out in the air as she was told to do. She moved her hand about here and there in the air and descended on one of the saucers. She felt a soft wet substance with her fingers and was surprised that nobody spoke or took off her bandage. There was a pause for a few seconds; and then a great deal of scuffling and whispering. Somebody said something about the garden, and at last Mrs Donnelly said something very cross to one of the next-door girls and told her to throw it out at once: that was no play. Maria understood that it was wrong that time and so she had to do it over again: and this time she got the prayer-book.

After that Mrs Donnelly played Miss McCloud's Reel for the children and Joe made Maria take a glass of wine. Soon they were all quite merry again and Mrs Donnelly said Maria would enter a convent before the year was out because she had got the prayer-book. Maria had never seen Joe so nice to her as he was that night, so full of pleasant talk and reminiscences. She said they were all very good to her.

At last the children grew tired and sleepy and Joe asked Maria would she not sing some little song before she went, one of the old songs. Mrs Donnelly said *Do, please, Maria!* and so Maria had to get up and stand beside the piano. Mrs Donnelly bade the children be quiet and listen to Maria's song. Then she played the prelude and said *Now, Maria!* and Maria, blushing very much, began to sing in a tiny quavering voice. She sang *I Dreamt that I Dwelt*, and when she came to the second verse she sang again:

> *I dreamt that I dwelt in marble halls*
> *With vassals and serfs at my side*
> *And of all who assembled within those walls*
> *That I was the hope and the pride.*
> *I had riches too great to count, could boast*
> *Of a high ancestral name,*
> *But I also dreamt, which pleased me most,*
> *That you loved me still the same.*

But no one tried to show her her mistake; and when she had ended her song Joe was very much moved. He said that there was no time like the long ago and no music for him like poor old Balfe, whatever other people might say; and his eyes filled up so much with tears that he could not find what he was looking for and in the end he had to ask his wife to tell him where the corkscrew was.

Franz Kafka

Franz Kafka was born in Prague, Czechoslovakia, in 1883 to Jewish parents, who sent him to German schools in the city. After studying at the German University in Prague, where he received a doctorate in jurisprudence, Kafka found work as a civil service lawyer with the Workers' Accident Insurance Company. His domineering father, with whom he continued to live, was successful in the wholesale clothing business and seems to have played a destructive role in Kafka's psychic development, withholding affection and approval and contributing to his stutter. Kafka was twice engaged, fathering a son he knew nothing about, but he never married. His diary jottings reveal a man sadly deprived of human intimacy, both physical and emotional. He suffered from insomnia, which perhaps enabled him to write for long stretches at night, but which could not have contributed to his health or well-being. His desperation was quietly endured, but by no means unrecorded; his works convey brilliantly the frustrations and suffering of mankind, confronting faceless bureaucracy, the anonymous state, and the depersonalization of social relations in modern life. He published in his lifetime the following volumes of stories and sketches: *Meditation* (1912), *The Stoker: A Fragment* (1913), *The Metamorphosis* (1915), *The Judgment* (1916), *In the Penal Colony* (1919), and *A Country Doctor* (1920).

According to Gustav Janouch, Kafka described art as "a mirror which—like a clock running fast—foretells the future," but he had no faith in that future; in fact, he was apologetic about his own vision: "One must be silent, if one can't give any help. No one, through his own lack of hope, should make the condition of the patient worse. For that reason, all my scribbling is to be destroyed. I am no light. I have merely lost my way among my own thorns. I'm a dead end." He was diagnosed as having tuberculosis in 1917 and died in 1924, giving instructions to his friend Max Brod to burn all his manuscripts. Fortunately, Brod preserved those materials, which included the novels *Amerika*, *The Trial*, and *The Castle*, all published posthumously. Also available are *The Diaries of Franz Kafka* (1948), a deeply moving and inspiring collection of casual writings that range from personal musings and philosophical inquiries to short fragments of fiction that are often haunting and brilliant, *Letters to Felice* (his fiancée), *Letters to Milena* (his Czech translator), and *Franz Kafka: Letters to Friends, Family, and Editors* (1977).

In a letter to Osham Pollak, written in 1902, Kafka said: "I believe we should write only books that bite and sting us. We need books which affect us like a very painful calamity, like the death of someone whom we love more than ourselves, like being cast out into forests far from all human beings, like suicide; a book must be the axe for the frozen sea within us."

John Updike describes Kafka as a man without any protective skin, having "a sensitivity acute beyond usefulness, as if the nervous system, flayed of its old hide of social usage and religious belief, must record every touch as pain." The writing of fiction seems to have been one of the few great moral comforts to Kafka and his work is anything but self-indulgent, with its immense reserves of humour and compassion. The diaries abound with comments about the writing life that confirm its importance to him personally. The eight-hour stint he spent in September 1912, for example, writing "The Judgment" is described as a major event in his life:

"This story, 'The Judgment,' I wrote at one sitting during the night of the 22nd–23rd, from ten o'clock at night to six o'clock in the morning. I was hardly able to pull my legs out from under the desk, they had got so stiff from sitting. The fearful strain and joy, how the story developed before me, as if I were advancing over water. Several times during this night I heaved my own weight on my back. How everything can be said, how for everything, for the strangest fancies, there waits a great fire in which they perish and rise up again. How it turned blue outside the window. A wagon rolled by. Two men walked across the bridge. At two I looked at the clock for the last time. As the maid walked through the ante-room for the first time I wrote the last sentence. Turning out the light and the light of day. The slight pains around my heart. The weariness that disappeared in the middle of the night. The trembling entrance into my sisters' room. Reading aloud. Before that, stretching in the presence of the maid and saying, 'I've been writing until now.' The appearance of the undisturbed bed, as though it had just been brought in. The conviction verified that with my novel-writing I am in the shameful lowlands of writing. Only *in this way* can writing be done, only with such coherence, with such a complete opening out of the body and the soul. Morning in bed. The always clear eyes. Many emotions carried along in the writing, joy, for example, that I shall have something beautiful for Max's Arkadia, thoughts about Freud, of course; in one passage, of Arnold Beer; in another, of

Wasserman; in one, of Werfel's giantess; of course, also of my 'The Urban world.' "

This story, which he uncharacteristically praised for its *Zweifellosigkeit*, or indubitableness, seems to have opened the door technically and emotionally to the writing of "The Metamorphosis" and the novels. The fact that "The Judgment" has a more than faintly autobiographical edge to it is further suggested in the long diary extract for February 11, 1913, which is included in its entirety in the Afterwords.

The Judgment

It was a Sunday morning in the very height of spring. Georg Bendemann, a young merchant, was sitting in his own room on the first floor of one of a long row of small, ramshackle houses stretching beside the river which were scarcely distinguishable from each other except in height and coloring. He had just finished a letter to an old friend of his who was now living abroad, had put it into its envelope in a slow and dreamy fashion and with his elbows propped on the writing table was gazing out of the window at the river, the bridge and the hills on the farther bank with their tender green.

He was thinking about his friend, who had actually run away to Russia some years before, being dissatisfied with his prospects at home. Now he was carrying on a business in St. Petersburg, which had flourished to begin with but had long been going downhill, as he always complained on his increasingly rare visits. So he was wearing himself out to no purpose in a foreign country, the unfamiliar full beard he wore did not quite conceal the face Georg had known so well since childhood, and his skin was growing so yellow as to indicate some latent disease. By his own account he had no regular connection with the colony of his fellow countrymen out there and almost no social intercourse with Russian families, so that he was resigning himself to becoming a permanent bachelor.

What could one write to such a man, who had obviously run off the rails, a man one could be sorry for but could not help. Should one advise him to come home, to transplant himself and take up his old friendships again—there was nothing to hinder him—and in general to rely on the help of his friends? But that was as good as telling him, and the more kindly the more offensively, that all his efforts hitherto had miscarried, that he should finally give up, come back home, and be gaped at by everyone as a returned prodigal, that only his friends knew what was what and that he himself was just a big child who should do what his successful and home-keeping friends prescribed. And was it certain, besides, that all the pain one would have to inflict on him would achieve its object? Perhaps it would not even be possible to get him to come home at all—he said himself that he was now out of touch with commerce in his native country—and then he would still be left an alien in a foreign land embittered by his friends' advice and more than ever estranged from them. But if he did follow their advice and then didn't fit in at home—not out of malice, of course, but through force of circumstances—couldn't get on with his friends or without them, felt humiliated, couldn't be said to have either friends or a country of his own any longer, wouldn't it have been better for him to stay abroad just as he was? Taking all this into account, how could one be sure that he would make a success of life at home?

For such reasons, supposing one wanted to keep up correspondence with him, one could not send him any real news such as could frankly be told to the most distant acquaintance. It was more than three years since his last visit, and for this he offered the lame excuse that the political situation in Russia was too uncertain, which apparently would not permit even the briefest absence of a small business man while it allowed hundreds of thousands of Russians to travel peacefully abroad. But during these three years Georg's own position in life had changed a lot. Two years ago his mother had died, since when he and his father had shared the household together, and his friend had of course been informed of that and had expressed his sympathy in a letter phrased so dryly that the grief caused by such an event, one had to conclude, could not be realized in a distant country. Since that time, however, Georg had applied himself with greater determination to the business as well as to everything else.

Perhaps during his mother's lifetime his father's insistence on having everything his own way in the business had hindered him from developing any real activity of his own, perhaps since her death his father had become less aggressive, although he was still active in the business, perhaps it was mostly due to an accidental run of good fortune—which was very probable indeed—but at any rate during those two years the business had developed in a most unexpected way, the staff had had to be doubled, the turnover was five times as great, no doubt about it, farther progress lay just ahead.

But Georg's friend had no inkling of this improvement. In earlier years, perhaps for the last time in that letter of condolence, he had tried to persuade Georg to emigrate to Russia and had enlarged upon the prospects of success for precisely Georg's branch of trade. The figures quoted were microscopic by comparison with the range of Georg's present operations. Yet he shrank from letting his friend know about his business success, and if he were to do it now retrospectively that certainly would look peculiar.

So Georg confined himself to giving his friend unimportant items of gossip such as rise at random in the memory when one is idly thinking things over on a quiet Sunday. All he desired was to leave undisturbed the idea of the home town which his friend must have built up to his own content during the long interval. And so it happened to Georg that three times in three fairly widely separated letters he had told his friend about the engagement of an unimportant man to an equally unimportant girl, until indeed, quite contrary to his intentions, his friend began to show some interest in this notable event.

Yet Georg preferred to write about things like these rather than to confess that he himself had got engaged a month ago to a Fräulein Frieda Brandenfeld, a girl from a well-to-do family. He often discussed this friend of his with his fiancée and the peculiar relationship that had developed between them in their correspondence. "So he won't be coming to our wedding," said she, "and yet I have a right to get to know all your friends." "I don't want to trouble him," answered Georg, "don't misunderstand me, he would probably come, at least I think so, but he would feel that his hand had been forced and he would be hurt, perhaps he would envy me and certainly he'd be discontented and without being able to do anything about his discontent he'd have to go away again alone. Alone—do you know what that means?" "Yes, but may he not hear about our wedding in some other fashion?" "I can't prevent that, of course, but it's unlikely, considering the way he lives." "Since your friends are like that, Georg, you shouldn't ever have got engaged at all." "Well, we're both to blame for that; but I wouldn't have it any other way now." And when, breathing quickly under his kisses, she still brought out: "All the same, I do feel upset," he thought it could not really involve him in trouble were he to send the news to his friend. "That's the kind of man I am and he'll just have to take me as I am," he said to himself, "I can't cut myself to another pattern that might make a more suitable friend for him."

And in fact he did inform his friend, in the long letter he had been writing that Sunday morning, about his engagement, with these words: "I have saved my best news to the end. I have got engaged to a Fräulein Frieda Brandenfeld, a girl from a well-to-do family, who only came to live here a long time after you went away, so that you're hardly likely to know her. There will be time to tell you more about her later, for today let me just say that I am very happy and as between you and me the only difference in our relationship is that instead of a quite ordinary kind of friend you will now have in me a happy friend. Besides that, you will acquire in my fiancée, who sends her warm greetings and will soon write you herself, a genuine friend of the opposite sex, which is not without importance to a bachelor. I know that there are many reasons why you can't come to see us, but would not my wedding be precisely the right occasion for giving all obstacles the go-by? Still, however that may be, do just as seems good to you without regarding any interests but your own."

With this letter in his hand Georg had been sitting a long time at the writing table, his face turned towards the window. He had barely acknowledged, with an absent smile, a greeting waved to him from the street by a passing acquaintance.

At last he put the letter in his pocket and went out of his room across a small lobby into his father's room, which he had not entered for months. There was in fact no need for him to enter it, since he saw his father daily at business and they took their midday meal together at an eating house; in the evening, it was true, each did as he pleased, yet even then, unless Georg—as mostly happened—went out with friends or, more recently, visited his fiancée, they always sat for a while, each with his newspaper, in their common sitting room.

It surprised Georg how dark his father's room was even on this sunny morning. So it was overshadowed as much as that by the high wall on the other side of the narrow courtyard. His father was sitting by the window in a corner hung with various mementoes of Georg's dead mother, reading a newspaper which he held to one side before his eyes in an attempt to overcome a defect of vision. On the table stood the remains of his breakfast, not much of which seemed to have been eaten.

"Ah, Georg," said his father, rising at once to meet him. His heavy dressing gown swung open as he walked and the skirts of it fluttered round him.—"My father is still a giant of a man," said Georg to himself.

"It's unbearably dark here," he said aloud.

"Yes, it's dark enough," answered his father.

"And you've shut the window, too?"

"I prefer it like that."

"Well, it's quite warm outside," said Georg, as if continuing his previous remark, and sat down.

His father cleared away the breakfast dishes and set them on a chest.

"I really only wanted to tell you," went on Georg, who had been vacantly following the old man's movements, "that I am now sending the news of my engagement to St. Petersburg." He drew the letter a little way from his pocket and let it drop back again.

"To St. Petersburg?" asked his father.

"To my friend there," said Georg, trying to meet his father's eye.—In business hours he's quite different, he was thinking, how solidly he sits here with his arms crossed.

"Oh yes. To your friend," said his father, with peculiar emphasis.

"Well, you know, Father, that I wanted not to tell him about my engagement at first. Out of consideration for him, that was the only reason. You know yourself he's a difficult man. I said to myself that someone else might tell him about my engagement, although he's such a solitary creature that that was hardly likely—I couldn't prevent that—but I wasn't ever going to tell him myself."

"And now you've changed your mind?" asked his father, laying his enormous newspaper on the window sill and on top of it his spectacles, which he covered with one hand.

"Yes, I've been thinking it over. If he's a good friend of mine, I said to myself, my being happily engaged should make him happy too. And so I wouldn't put off telling him any longer. But before I posted the letter I wanted to let you know."

"Georg," said his father, lengthening his toothless mouth, "listen to me! You've come to me about this business, to talk it over with me. No doubt that does you honor. But it's nothing, it's worse than nothing, if you don't tell me the whole truth. I don't want to stir up matters that shouldn't be mentioned here. Since the death of our dear mother certain things have been done that aren't right. Maybe the time will come for mentioning them, and maybe sooner than we think. There's many a thing in the business I'm not aware of, maybe it's not done behind my back—I'm not going to say that it's done behind my back—I'm not equal to things any longer, my memory's failing, I haven't an eye for so many things any longer. That's the course of nature in the first place, and in the second place the death of our dear mother hit me harder than it did you.—But since we're talking about it, about this letter, I beg you, Georg, don't deceive me. It's a trivial affair, it's hardly worth mentioning, so don't deceive me. Do you really have this friend in St. Petersburg?"

Georg rose in embarrassment. "Never mind my friends. A thousand friends wouldn't make up to me for my father. Do you know what I think? You're not taking enough care of yourself. But old age must be taken care of. I can't do without you in the business, you know that very well, but if the business is going to undermine your health, I'm ready to close it down tomorrow forever. And that won't do. We'll have to make a change in your way of living. But a radical change. You sit here in the dark, and in the sitting room you would have plenty of light. You just take a bite of breakfast instead of properly keeping up your strength. You sit by a closed window, and the air would be so good for you. No, Father! I'll get the doctor to come, and we'll follow his orders. We'll change your room, you can move into the front room and I'll move in here. You won't notice the change, all your things will be moved with you. But there's time for all that later, I'll put you to bed now for a little, I'm sure you need to rest. Come, I'll help you to take off your things, you'll see I can do it. Or if you would rather go into the front room at once, you can lie down in my bed for the present. That would be the most sensible thing."

Georg stood close beside his father, who had let his head with its unkempt white hair sink on his chest.

"Georg," said his father in a low voice, without moving.

Georg knelt down at once beside his father, in the old man's weary face he saw the pupils, over-large, fixedly looking at him from the corners of the eyes.

"You have no friend in St. Petersburg. You've always been a leg-puller and you haven't even shrunk from pulling my leg. How could you have a friend out there! I can't believe it."

"Just think back a bit, Father," said Georg, lifting his father from the chair and slipping off his dressing gown as he stood feebly enough, "it'll soon be three years since my friend came to see us last. I remember that you used not to like him very much. At least twice I kept you from seeing him, although he was actually sitting with me in my room. I could quite well understand your dislike of him, my friend has his peculiarities. But then later, you got on with him very well. I was proud because you listened to him and nodded and asked him questions. If you think back you're bound to remember. He used to tell us the most incredible stories of the Russian Revolution. For instance, when he was on a business trip to Kiev and ran into a riot, and saw a priest on a balcony who cut a broad cross in blood on the palm of his hand and held the hand up and appealed to the mob. You've told that story yourself once or twice since."

Meanwhile Georg had succeeded in lowering his father down again and carefully taking off the woollen drawers he wore over his linen underpants and his socks. The not particularly clean appearance of this underwear made him reproach himself for having been neglectful. It should have certainly been his duty to see that his father had clean changes of underwear. He had not yet explicitly discussed with his bride-to-be what arrangements should be made for his father in the future, for they had both of them silently taken it for granted that the old man would go on living alone in the old house. But now he made a quick, firm decision to take him into his own future establishment. It almost looked, on closer inspection, as if the care he meant to lavish there on his father might come too late.

He carried his father to bed in his arms. It gave him a dreadful feeling to notice that while he took the few steps towards the bed the old man on his breast was playing with his watch chain. He could not lay him down on the bed for a moment, so firmly did he hang on to the watch chain.

But as soon as he was laid in bed, all seemed well. He covered himself up and even drew the blankets farther than usual over his shoulders. He looked up at Georg with a not unfriendly eye.

"You begin to remember my friend, don't you?" asked Georg, giving him an encouraging nod.

"Am I well covered up now?" asked his father, as if he were not able to see whether his feet were properly tucked in or not.

"So you find it snug in bed already," said Georg, and tucked the blankets more closely round him.

"Am I well covered up?" asked the father once more, seeming to be strangely intent upon the answer.

"Don't worry, you're well covered up."

"No!" cried his father, cutting short the answer, threw the blankets off with a strength that sent them all flying in a moment and sprang erect in bed. Only one hand lightly touched the ceiling to steady him.

"You wanted to cover me up, I know, my young sprig, but I'm far from being covered up yet. And even if this is the last strength I have, it's enough for you, too much for you. Of course I know your friend. He would have been a son after my own heart. That's why you've been playing him false all these years. Why else? Do you think I haven't been sorry for him? And that's why you had to lock yourself up in your office—the Chief is busy, mustn't be disturbed—just so that you could write your lying little letters to Russia. But thank goodness a father doesn't need to be taught how to see through his son. And now that you thought you'd got him down, so far down that you could set your bottom on him and sit on him and he wouldn't move, then my fine son makes up his mind to get married!"

Georg stared at the bogey conjured up by his father. His friend in St. Petersburg, whom his father suddenly knew too well, touched his imagination as never before. Lost in the vastness of Russia he saw him. At the door of an empty, plundered warehouse he saw him. Among the wreckage of his showcases, the slashed remnants of his wares, the falling gas brackets, he was just standing up. Why did he have to go so far away!

"But attend to me!" cried his father, and Georg, almost distracted, ran towards the bed to take everything in, yet came to a stop halfway.

"Because she lifted up her skirts," his father began to flute, "because she lifted her skirt like this, the nasty creature," and mimicking her he lifted his shirt so high that one could see the scar on his thigh from his war wound, "because she lifted her skirts like this and this you made up to her, and in order to make free with her undisturbed you have disgraced your mother's memory, betrayed your friend and stuck your father into bed so that he can't move. But he can move, or can't he?"

And he stood up quite unsupported and kicked his legs out. His insight made him radiant.

Georg shrank into a corner, as far away from his father as possible. A long time ago he had firmly made up his mind to watch closely every least movement so that he should not be surprised by any indirect attack, a pounce from behind or above. At this moment he recalled this long-forgotten resolve and forgot it again, like a man drawing a short thread through the eye of a needle.

"But your friend hasn't been betrayed after all!" cried his father, emphasizing the point with stabs of his forefinger. "I've been representing him here on the spot."

"You comedian!" Georg could not resist the retort, realized at once the harm done and, his eyes starting in his head, bit his tongue back, only too late, till the pain made his knees give.

"Yes, of course I've been playing a comedy! A comedy! That's a good expression! What other comfort was left to a poor old widower? Tell me—and while you're answering me be you still my living son—what else was left to me, in my back room, plagued by disloyal staff, old to the marrow of my bones? And my son strutting through the world, finishing off deals that I had prepared for him, bursting with triumphant glee and stalking away from his father with the closed face of a respectable business man! Do you think I didn't love you, I, from whom you are sprung?"

Now he'll lean forward, thought Georg, what if he topples and smashes himself! These words went hissing through his mind.

His father leaned forward but did not topple. Since Georg did not come any nearer, as he had expected, he straightened himself again.

"Stay where you are, I don't need you! You think you have strength enough to come over here and that you're only hanging back of your own accord. Don't be too sure! I am still much the stronger of us two. All by myself I might have had to give way, but your mother has given me so much of her strength that I've established a fine connection with your friend and I have your customers here in my pocket!"

"He has pockets even in his shirt!" said Georg to himself, and believed that with this remark he could make him an impossible figure for all the world. Only for a moment did he think so, since he kept on forgetting everything.

"Just take your bride on your arm and try getting in my way! I'll sweep her from your very side, you don't know how!"

Georg made a grimace of disbelief. His father only nodded, confirming the truth of his words, towards Georg's corner.

"How you amused me today, coming to ask me if you should tell your friend about your engagement. He knows it already, you stupid boy, he knows it all! I've been writing to him, for you forgot to take my writing things away from me. That's why he hasn't been here for years, he knows everything a hundred times better than you do yourself, in his left hand he crumples your letters unopened while in his right hand he holds up my letters to read through!"

In his enthusiasm he waved his arm over his head. "He knows everything a thousand times better!" he cried.

"Ten thousand times!" said Georg, to make fun of his father, but in his very mouth the words turned into deadly earnest.

"For years I've been waiting for you to come with some such question! Do you think I concern myself with anything else? Do you think I read my newspapers? Look!" and he threw Georg a newspaper sheet which he had somehow taken to bed with him. An old newspaper, with a name entirely unknown to Georg.

"How long a time you've taken to grow up! Your mother had to die, she couldn't see the happy day, your friend is going to pieces in Russia, even three years ago he was yellow enough to be thrown away, and as for me, you see what condition I'm in. You have eyes in your head for that!"

"So you've been lying in wait for me!" cried Georg.

His father said pityingly, in an offhand manner: "I suppose you wanted to say that sooner. But now it doesn't matter." And in a louder voice: "So now you know what else there was in the world besides yourself, till now you've known only about yourself! An innocent child, yes, that you were, truly, but still more truly have you been a devilish human being!—And therefore take note: I sentence you now to death by drowning!"

Georg felt himself urged from the room, the crash with which his father fell on the bed behind him was still in his ears as he fled. On the staircase, which he rushed down as if its step were an inclined plane, he ran into his charwoman on her way up to do the morning cleaning of the room. "Jesus!" she cried, and covered her face with her apron, but he was already gone. Out of the front door he rushed, across the roadway, driven towards the water. Already he was grasping at the railings as a starving man clutches food. He swung himself over, like the distinguished gymnast he had once been in his youth, to his parents' pride. With weakening grip he was still holding on when he spied between the railings a motor-bus coming which would easily cover the noise of his fall, called in a low voice: "Dear parents, I have always loved you, all the same," and let himself drop.

At this moment an unending stream of traffic was just going over the bridge.

Thomas King

Thomas King is a writer of mixed Cherokee, German, and Greek descent. He was born in Roseville, California, in 1943 and, although his story "Borders" may make saying so seem rather ironic, he has dual Canadian and American citizenship. He has taught in the Native Studies Department at the University of Lethbridge and is currently teaching in the American Studies Department at the University of Minnesota. He co-edited a volume of critical essays on Native literature and has edited an issue of *Canadian Fiction Magazine* (No. 60, 1987) on Native fiction that provided the groundwork for his anthology of contemporary Canadian Native fiction, *All My Relations* (1990). His poems and short stories have appeared widely in magazines in Canada and the U.S. His first novel, *Medicine River*, was published in 1990.

In the Introduction to *All My Relations*, King stresses the centrality of the idea of family, or community—"intricate webs of kinship"—in Native culture. "'All my relations' is at first a reminder of who we are and of our relationship with both our family and our relatives. It also reminds us of the extended relationship we share with all human beings. But the relationships that Native people see go further, the web of kinship extending to the animals, to the birds, to the fish, to the plants, to all the animate and inanimate forms that can be seen or imagined. More than that, 'all my relations' is an encouragement for us to accept the responsibilities we have within this universal family by living our lives in a harmonious and moral manner (a common admonishment is to say of someone that they act as if they have no relations)." While there is, as yet, no clear definition of Native literature, King accepts the view that it is "literature produced by Natives and not by non-Natives, recognizing that being Native is a matter of race rather than something more transitory such as nationality."

In response to the question of why Native writers avoid historical settings, particularly the nineteenth century, King says: "Some of the reasons for this avoidance are obvious. The literary stereotypes and clichés for which the period is famous have been, I think, a deterrent to many of us. Feathered warriors on Pinto ponies, laconic chiefs in full regalia, dusky raven-haired maidens, demonic shamans with eagle-claw rattles and scalping knives are all picturesque and exciting images, but they are, more properly, servants of a non-Native imagination. Rather than try to unravel the complex relationship between the nineteenth-century Indian and the white mind, or to craft a new set of images that still reflects the time but

avoids the flat, static depiction of the Native and the two-dimensional quality of the culture, most of us have consciously set out literature in the present, a period that is reasonably free of literary monoliths and which allows for greater latitude in the creation of characters and situations, and, more important, allows us the opportunity to create for ourselves and our respective cultures both a present and a future."

In an interview conducted by Laura Groening, where she suggests that there is no border between past and present for Native writers, King tries to explain in greater detail the Native writer's relation to the past. "In my own fiction that's absolutely true. I don't make any designation between the past and the present. I am always very happy to bring what appears to be older materials forward and present them in a contemporary context. A lot of my coyote stories do that, they mix the past and the present, and so they're filled with what we in the 'biz' call anachronisms—things that just don't go together, because of the time period in which they exist. I feel comfortable talking about when the world was created and throwing in a couple of television sets along with everything else that gets created at that period of time. It doesn't rest too easily [with some], but to me the connections are quite easy to make."

King emphasizes the orality of Native fiction, suggesting that he and many other Native writers try to maintain in their written fictions as much of the character of oral story-telling as possible. While he admits that most of his stories "start off with a piece of oral literature or a title or a character," he occasionally starts with an idea, as in "The Border." "The philosophical stuff is just a small percentage," he says. "It's always hardest to make sure that the message doesn't get in the way of the story, that it doesn't stick its nose out from behind the curtain. If it does that, people see it and it ruins the fiction, it ruins the moment."

Regarding the current debate about the appropriation of voice, King admits that he would expect to learn more about Native experience from reading Native writers, just as he would expect to learn more about women's experience by reading women writers, though he acknowledges that there are exceptional cases where non-Natives write insightfully about Native experience and men write well about women. However, he suggests a political consideration worth noting: "I don't think that you can be successful writing about an oppressed people if you are one of the oppressors. The societal set, the mindset that you have, is very different from the person who has to suffer under that oppression."

Borders

When I was twelve, maybe thirteen, my mother announced that we were going to go to Salt Lake City to visit my sister who had left the reserve, moved across the line, and found a job. Laetitia had not left home with my mother's blessing, but over time my mother had come to be proud of the fact that Laetitia had done all of this on her own.

"She did real good," my mother would say.

Then there were the fine points to Laetitia's going. She had not, as my mother liked to tell Mrs. Manyfingers, gone floating after some man like a balloon on a string. She hadn't snuck out of the house, either, and gone to Vancouver or Edmonton or Toronto to chase rainbows down alleys. And she hadn't been pregnant.

"She did real good."

I was seven or eight when Laetitia left home. She was seventeen. Our father was from Rocky Boy on the American side.

"Dad's American," Laetitia told my mother, "so I can go and come as I please."

"Send us a postcard."

Laetitia packed her things, and we headed for the border. Just outside of Milk River, Laetitia told us to watch for the water tower.

"Over the next rise. It's the first thing you see."

"We got a water tower on the reserve," my mother said. "There's a big one in Lethbridge, too."

"You'll be able to see the tops of the flagpoles, too. That's where the border is."

When we got to Coutts, my mother stopped at the convenience store and bought her and Laetitia a cup of coffee. I got an Orange Crush.

"This is real lousy coffee."

"You're just angry because I want to see the world."

"It's the water. From here on down, they got lousy water."

"I can catch the bus from Sweetgrass. You don't have to lift a finger."

"You're going to have to buy your water in bottles if you want good coffee."

There was an old wooden building about a block away, with a tall sign in the yard that said "Museum." Most of the roof had been blown away. Mom told me to go and see when the place was open. There were boards over the windows and doors. You could tell that the place was closed, and I told Mom so, but she said to go and check anyway. Mom and Laetitia stayed by the car. Neither one of them moved. I sat down on the steps of the museum and watched them, and I don't know that they ever said anything to each other. Finally, Laetitia got her bag out of the trunk and gave Mom a hug.

I wandered back to the car. The wind had come up, and it blew Laetitia's hair across her face. Mom reached out and pulled the strands out of Laetitia's eyes, and Laetitia let her.

"You can still see the mountain from here," my mother told Laetitia in Blackfoot.

"Lots of mountains in Salt Lake," Laetitia told her in English.

"The place is closed," I said. "Just like I told you."

Laetitia tucked her hair into her jacket and dragged her bag down the road to the brick building with the American flag flapping on a pole. When she got to where the guards were waiting, she turned, put the bag down, and waved to us. We waved back. Then my mother turned the car around, and we came home.

We got postcards from Laetitia regular, and, if she wasn't spreading jelly on the truth, she was happy. She found a good job and rented an apartment with a pool.

"And she can't even swim," my mother told Mrs. Manyfingers.

Most of the postcards said we should come down and see the city, but whenever I mentioned this, my mother would stiffen up.

So I was surprised when she bought two new tires for the car and put on her blue dress with the green and yellow flowers. I had to dress up, too, for my mother did not want us crossing the border looking like Americans. We made sandwiches and put them in a big box with pop and potato chips and some apples and bananas and a big jar of water.

"But we can stop at one of those restaurants, too, right?"

"We maybe should take some blankets in case you get sleepy."

"But we can stop at one of those restaurants, too, right?"

The border was actually two towns, though neither one was big enough to amount to anything. Coutts was on the Canadian side and consisted of the convenience store and gas station, the museum that was closed and boarded up, and a motel. Sweetgrass was on the American side, but all you could see was an overpass that arched across the highway and disappeared into the prairies. Just hearing the names of these towns, you would expect that Sweetgrass, which is a nice name and sounds like it is related to other places such as Medicine Hat and Moose Jaw and Kicking Horse Pass, would be on the Canadian side, and that Coutts, which sounds abrupt and rude, would be on the American side. But this was not the case.

Between the two borders was a duty-free shop where you could buy cigarettes and liquor and flags. Stuff like that.

We left the reserve in the morning and drove until we got to Coutts.

"Last time we stopped here," my mother said, "you had an Orange Crush. You remember that?"

"Sure," I said. "That was when Laetitia took off."

"You want another Orange Crush?"

"That means we're not going to stop at a restaurant, right?"

My mother got a coffee at the convenience store, and we stood around and watched the prairies move in the sunlight. Then we climbed back in the car. My mother straightened the dress across her thighs, leaned against the wheel, and drove all the way to the border in first gear, slowly, as if she were trying to see through a bad storm or riding high on black ice.

The border guard was an old guy. As he walked to the car, he swayed from side to side, his feet set wide apart, the holster on his hip pitching up and down. He leaned into the window, looked into the back seat, and looked at my mother and me.

"Morning, ma'am."

"Good morning."

"Where you heading?"

"Salt Lake City."

"Purpose of your visit?"

"Visit my daughter."

"Citizenship?"

"Blackfoot," my mother told him.

"Ma'am?"

"Blackfoot," my mother repeated.

"Canadian?"

"Blackfoot."

It would have been easier if my mother had just said "Canadian" and been done with it, but I could see she wasn't going to do that. The guard wasn't angry or anything. He smiled and looked towards the building. Then he turned back and nodded.

"Morning, ma'am."

"Good morning."

"Any firearms or tobacco?"

"No."

"Citizenship?"

"Blackfoot."

He told us to sit in the car and wait, and we did. In about five minutes, another guard came out with the first man. They were talking as they came, both men swaying back and forth like two cowboys headed for a bar or a gunfight.

"Morning, ma'am."

"Good morning."

"Cecil tells me you and the boy are Blackfoot."

"That's right."

"Now, I know that we got Blackfeet on the American side and the Canadians got Blackfeet on their side. Just so we can keep our records straight, what side do you come from?"

I knew exactly what my mother was going to say, and I could have told them if they had asked me.

"Canadian side or American side?" asked the guard.

"Blackfoot side," she said.

It didn't take them long to lose their sense of humour, I can tell you that. The one guard stopped smiling altogether and told us to park our car at the side of the building and come in.

We sat on a wood bench for about an hour before anyone came over to talk to us. This time it was a woman. She had a gun, too.

"Hi," she said. "I'm Inspector Pratt. I understand there is a little misunderstanding."

"I'm going to visit my daughter in Salt Lake City," my mother told her. "We don't have any guns or beer."

"It's a legal technicality, that's all."

"My daughter's Blackfoot, too."

The woman opened a briefcase and took out a couple of forms and began to write on one of them. "Everyone who crosses our border has to declare their citizenship. Even Americans. It helps us keep track of the visitors we get from the various countries."

She went on like that for maybe fifteen minutes, and a lot of the stuff she told us was interesting.

"I can understand how you feel about having to tell us your citizenship, and here's what I'll do. You tell me, and I won't put it down on the form. No-one will know but you and me."

Her gun was silver. There were several chips in the wood handle and the name "Stella" was scratched into the metal butt.

We were in the border office for about four hours, and we talked to almost everyone there. One of the men bought me a Coke. My mother brought a couple of sandwiches in from the car. I offered part of mine to Stella, but she said she wasn't hungry.

I told Stella that we were Blackfoot and Canadian, but she said that that didn't count because I was a minor. In the end, she told us that if my mother didn't declare her citizenship, we would have to go back to where we came from. My mother stood up and thanked Stella for her time. Then we got back in the car and drove to he Canadian border, which was only about a hundred yards away.

I was disappointed. I hadn't seen Laetitia for a long time, and I had never been to Salt Lake City. When she was still at home, Laetitia would go on and on about Salt Lake City. She had never been here, but her boyfriend Lester Tallbull had spent a year in Salt Lake at a technical school.

"It's a great place," Lester would say. "Nothing but blondes in the whole state."

Whenever he said that, Laetitia would slug him on his shoulder hard enough to make him flinch. He had some brochures on Salt Lake and some maps, and every so often the two of them would spread them out on the table.

"That's the temple. It's right downtown. You got to have a pass to get in."

"Charlotte says anyone can go in and look around."

"When was Charlotte in Salt Lake? Just when the hell was Charlotte in Salt Lake?"

"Last year."

"This is Liberty Park. It's got a zoo. There's good skiing in the mountains."

"Got all the skiing we can use," my mother would say. "People come from all over the world to ski at Banff. Cardston's got a temple, if you like those kinds of things."

"Oh, this one is real big," Lester would say. "They got armed guards and everything."

"Not what Charlotte says."

"What does she know?"

Lester and Laetitia broke up, but I guess the idea of Salt Lake stuck in her mind.

The Canadian border guard was a young woman, and she seemed happy to see us. "Hi," she said. "You folks sure have a great day for a trip. Where are you coming from?"

"Standoff."

"Is that in Montana?"

"No."

"Where are you going?"

"Standoff."

The woman's name was Carol and I don't guess she was any older than Laetitia. "Wow, you both Canadians?"

"Blackfoot."

"Really? I have a friend I went to school with who is Blackfoot. Do you know Mike Harley?"

"No."

"He went to school in Lethbridge, but he's really from Browning."

It was a nice conversation and there were no cars behind us, so there was no rush.

"You're not bringing any liquor back, are you?"

"No."

"Any cigarettes or plants or stuff Like that?"

"No."

"Citizenship?"

"Blackfoot."

"I know," said the woman, "and I'd be proud of being Blackfoot if I were Black-foot. But you have to be American or Canadian."

When Laetitia and Lester broke up, Lester took his brochures and maps with him, so Laetitia wrote to someone in Salt Lake City, and, about a month later, she got a big envelope of stuff. We sat at the table and opened up all the brochures, and Laetitia read each one out loud.

"Salt Lake City is the gateway to some of the world's most magnificent skiing.

"Salt Lake City is the home of one of the newest professional basketball fran-chises, the Utah Jazz.

"The Great Salt Lake is one of the natural wonders of the world."

It was kind of exciting seeing all those colour brochures on the table and lis-tening to Laetitia read all about how Salt Lake City was one of the best places in the entire world.

"That Salt Lake City place sounds too good to be true," my mother told her.

"It has everything."

"We got everything right here."

"It's boring here."

"People in Salt Lake City are probably sending away for brochures of Calgary and Lethbridge and Pincher Creek right now."

In the end, my mother would say that maybe Laetitia should go to Salt Lake City, and Laetitia would say that maybe she would.

We parked the car to the side of the building and Carol led us into a small room on the second floor. I found a comfortable spot on the couch and flipped through some back issues of *Saturday Night* and *Alberta Report*.

When I woke up, my mother was just coming out of another office. She didn't say a word to me. I followed her down the stairs and out to the car. I thought we were going home, but she turned the car around and drove back towards the American border, which made me think we were going to visit Laetitia in Salt Lake City after all. Instead she pulled into the parking lot of the duty-free store and stopped.

"We going to see Laetitia?"

"No."

"We going home?"

Pride is a good thing to have, you know. Laetitia had a lot of pride, and so did my mother. I figured that someday, I'd have it, too.

"So where are we going?"

Most of that day, we wandered around the duty-free store, which wasn't very large. The manager had a name tag with a tiny American flag on one side and a tiny Canadian flag on the other. His name was Mel. Towards evening, he began suggesting that we should be on our way. I told him we had nowhere to go, that neither the Americans nor the Canadians would let us in. He laughed at that and told us that we should buy something or leave.

The car was not very comfortable, but we did have all that food and it was April, so even if it did snow as it sometimes does on the prairies, we wouldn't freeze. The next morning my mother drove to the American border.

It was a different guard this time, but the questions were the same. We didn't spend as much time in the office as we had the day before. By noon, we were back at the Canadian border. By two we were back in the duty-free shop parking lot.

The second night in the car was not as much fun as the first, but my mother seemed in good spirits, and, all in all, it was as much an adventure as an inconvenience. There wasn't much food left and that was a problem, but we had lots of water as there was a faucet at the side of the duty-free shop.

One Sunday, Laetitia and I were watching television. Mom was over at Mrs. Manyfingers's. right in the middle of the programme, Laetitia turned off the set and said she was going to Salt Lake City, that life around here was too boring. I had wanted to see the rest of the programme and really didn't care if Laetitia went to Salt Lake City or not. When Mom got home, I told her what Laetitia had said.

What surprised me was how angry Laetitia got when she found out that I had told Mom.

"You got a big mouth."

"That's what you said."

"What I said is none of your business."

"I didn't say anything."

"Well, I'm going for sure, now."

That weekend, Laetitia packed her bags, and we drove her to the border.

Mel turned out to be friendly. When he closed up for the night and found us still parked in the lot, he came over and asked us if our car was broken down or something. My mother thanked him for his concern and told him that we were fine, that things would get straightened out in the morning.

"You're kidding," said Mel. "You'd think they could handle the simple things."

"We got some apples and a banana," I said, "but we're all out of ham sandwiches."

"You know, you read about these things, but you just don't believe it."

"Hamburgers would be even better because they got more stuff for energy."

My mother slept in the back seat. I slept in the front because I was smaller and could lie under the steering wheel. Late that night, I heard my mother open the car door. I found her sitting on her blanket leaning against the bumper of the car.

"You see all those stars," she said. "When I was a little girl, my grandmother used to take me and my sisters out on the prairies and tell us stories about all the stars."

"Do you think Mel is going to bring us any hamburgers?"

"Every one of those stars has a story. You see that bunch of stars over there that look like a fish?"

"He didn't say no."

"Coyote went fishing, one day. That's how it all started." We sat out under the stars that night, and my mother told me all sorts of stories. She was serious about it, too. She'd tell them slow, repeating parts as she went, as if she expected me to remember each one.

Early the next morning, the television vans began to arrive, and guys in suits and women in dresses came trotting over to us, dragging microphones and cameras and lights behind them. One of the vans had a table set up with orange juice and sandwiches and fruit. It was for the crew, but when I told them we hadn't eaten for a while, a really skinny blonde woman told us we could eat as much as we wanted.

They mostly talked to my mother. Every so often one of the reporters would come over and ask me questions about how it felt to be an Indian without a country. I told them we had a nice house on the reserve and that my cousins had a couple of horses we rode when we went fishing. Some of the television people went over to the American border, and then they went to the Canadian border.

Around noon, a good-looking guy in a dark blue suit and an orange tie with little ducks on it drove up in a fancy car. He talked to my mother for a while, and, after they were done talking, my mother called me over, and we got into our car. Just as my mother started the engine, Mel came over and gave us a bag of peanut brittle and told us that justice was a damn hard thing to get, but that we shouldn't give up.

I would have preferred lemon drops, but it was nice of Mel anyway.

"Where are we going now?"

"Going to visit Laetitia."

The guard who came out to our car was all smiles. The television lights were so bright they hurt my eyes, and, if you tried to look through the windshield in certain directions, you couldn't see a thing.

"Morning, ma'am."

"Good morning."

"Where you heading?"

"Salt Lake City."

"Purpose of your visit?"

"Visit my daughter."

"Any tobacco, liquor, or firearms?"

"Don't smoke."

"Any plants or fruit?"

"Not any more."

"Citizenship?"

"Blackfoot."

The guard rocked back on his heels and jammed his thumbs into his gun belt. "Thank you," he said, his fingers patting the butt of the revolver. "Have a pleasant trip."

My mother rolled the car forward, and the television people had to scramble out of the way. They ran alongside the car as we pulled away from the border, and, when they couldn't run any farther, they stood in the middle of the highway and waved and waved and waved.

We got to Salt Lake City the next day. Laetitia was happy to see us, and, that first night, she took us out to a restaurant that made really good soups. The list of pies took up a whole page. I had cherry. Mom had chocolate. Laetitia said that she saw us on television the night before and, during the meal, she had us tell her the story over and over again.

Laetitia took us everywhere. We went to a fancy ski resort. We went to the temple. We got to go shopping in a couple of large malls, but they weren't as large as the one in Edmonton, and Mom said so.

After a week or so, I got bored and wasn't at all sad when my mother said we should be heading back home. Laetitia wanted us to stay longer, but Mom said no, that she had things to do back home and that next time, Laetitia should come up and visit. Laetitia said she was thinking about moving back, and Mom told her to do as she pleased, and Laetitia said that she would.

On the way home, we stopped at the duty-free shop, and my mother gave Mel a green hat that said "Salt Lake" across the front. Mel was a funny guy. He took the hat and blew his nose and told my mother that she was an inspiration to us all. He gave us some more peanut brittle and came out into the parking lot and waved at us all the way to the Canadian border.

It was almost evening when we left Coutts. I watched the border through the; rear window until all you could see were the tops of the flagpoles and the blue water tower, and then they rolled over a hill and disappeared.

Margaret Laurence

Jean Margaret Wemyss (pronounced Weems) was born in Neepawa, Manitoba, in 1926. Her mother died when she was four, her father when she was ten, and she was raised by one of her aunts. Her difficult childhood years, spent in the sphere of a dominating grandfather, are explored in a collection of stories called *A Bird in the House* (1970). Laurence attended United College and received her B.A. from the University of Winnipeg in 1947, the same year she married civil engineer Jack Laurence. She did short stints writing for the Winnipeg *Citizen* and working as a registrar at the YWCA before moving for seven years to Africa, where she spent two years in the Haud desert of Somaliland, an account of which appears in *The Prophet's Camel Bell* (1963). She edited and translated for the Somali government a collection of poems and fables called *A Tree for Poverty* (1954). Laurence lived in Vancouver from 1957 to 1962, where she completed her first novel, *This Side Jordan* (1960), while gathering the impressions for a later work, *The Fire-Dwellers* (1969). When she and her husband separated, Laurence moved to England, to Elm Cottage, High Wycombe, not far from London, where much of her best work was written: *The Stone Angel* (1964), *The Tomorrow-Tamers and Other Stories* (1964), *A Jest of God* (1966, made into a Warner Bros. film called *Rachel, Rachel*), *Long Drums and Cannons: Nigerian Dramatists and Novelists, 1952–1966* (1968), and *The Diviners* (1974). She was writer-in-residence at the University of Toronto in 1968–69 and returned to Canada in 1974, settling in Lakefield, Ontario. Her memoir, *Dance on the Earth* (1989), was published after her death in January 1987, at age sixty.

Laurence holds a special place in the imagination of Canadians for her work on behalf of her "tribe" of fellow writers. Although she was a deeply religious and moral person, she was vigorously persecuted by self-righteous religious bigots in Peterborough County who managed to have her books removed from the shelves of schools and libraries. This persecution exacted a great cost, emotionally and artistically, but it did not stop her from taking up causes such as racial equality, freedom of the press, disarmament, human rights, and Canadian independence. "It is my feeling," she says in "My Final Hour," an address to the Trent University Philosophy Society, on March 29, 1983 (published in *Canadian Literature*, 50), "that as we grow older we should become not less radical but more so." She believed in the social gospel, which puts the central premises of Christianity into practice; and, as an artist, she believed that art "is,

deeply, an honouring of the past, a perception of the present in one way or another and a looking towards the future. . . . Art, by its very nature of necessary expression, is an act of faith, an acknowledgement of the profound mystery at the core of life."

While she is a passionate advocate of human rights, Laurence rejects the use of art for partisan purposes. As she said to writer Barry Callaghan, in an interview published in *Books in Canada* (Vol. 16, No. 2, 1987), "I think very few writers, maybe none, can be novelists and political propagandists at the same time. I think they find themselves writing propaganda. It becomes propaganda rather than a novel because when a writer becomes highly political, he thinks he knows the answers and wants to make you hold the same political point of view, whereas a novel is almost always a kind of discovery. I don't think the writer herself knows entirely what's going to happen, or what's going to emerge, and she has to be prepared for the unexpected. In fact, you partly write to discover something you didn't know before."

As for experimental writing, she confesses, "Well, sometimes I see my work in terms of deep Celtic gloom, to tell you the truth. I think maybe some of those writers are too far out, and I say to myself, 'Margaret, you're too far in'—but I can't help it. The fact is, I know that my prose style is essentially a traditional one, but for me to try to change simply for the sake of changing, or for the sake of trying to be more 'with it'. . . this would be so phony, nothing would happen—except disaster. So all I can really do is to try and put down things according to my own way of seeing, and if the style changes naturally, by itself, and develops, well . . . well and good, and if it doesn't, I'm stuck with the idiom of myself. . . . The only thing, really, that concerns me is to try to put down things as I see them, because it is all you've got. You've got your own pair of eyes, that's all, and the thing I would like to be able to do more than anything else is to create characters that step off the page, because this is what really obsesses me. This is still what I look for in a novel. What I'm interested in more than anything else is character."

Laurence made no distinction between formal problems and concerns of the novel and short story, except to say that in the short story she may focus on a single theme, or dilemma, whereas, in the novel, she may be able to handle many.

Laurence is equally adamant about form and links her problems once again to the creation of character.

"Generally speaking, I believe that most writers work out their own forms and means of expression through a strong compulsion to get closer to their material, to express it more fully.... I have never thought of forms and means of expression (I refuse to use that odious word 'style') as having any meaning in themselves.... Form for its own sake is an abstraction which carries no allure for me. I do not make this as a qualitative statement—I only say that it happens to be true for myself. I am concerned mainly, I think, with finding a form which will enable a novel [or story] to reveal itself, a form through which the characters can breathe. When I try to think of form by itself, I have to put it in visual terms—I see it not like a house or a cathedral or any enclosing edifice, but rather as a forest, through which one can see outward, in which the shapes of trees do not prevent air and sun, and in which the trees themselves are growing structures, something alive. That is, of course, an ideal, not something that can ever be achieved." Laurence concludes her address, "Gadgetry or Growing: Form and Voice in the Novel," given at the University of Toronto in 1969 and reprinted in *The Journal of Canadian Fiction*, with this statement: "What I'm looking for, which—as far as form in writing is concerned—is the kind of vehicle capable of risking that peculiar voyage of exploration which constitutes a novel [or story]."

The Loons

Just below Manawaka, where the Wachakwa River ran brown and noisy over the pebbles, the scrub oak and grey-green willow and chokecherry bushes grew in a dense thicket. In a clearing at the centre of the thicket stood the Tonnerre family's shack. The basis of this dwelling was a small square cabin made of poplar poles and chinked with mud, which had been built by Jules Tonnerre some fifty years before, when he came back from Batoche with a bullet in his thigh, the year that Riel was hung and the voices of the Metis entered their long silence. Jules had only intended to stay the winter in the Wachakwa Valley, but the family was still there in the thirties, when I was a child. As the Tonnerres had increased, their settlement had been added to, until the clearing at the foot of the town hill was a chaos of lean-tos, wooden packing cases, warped lumber, discarded car tires, ramshackle chicken coops, tangled strands of barbed wire and rusty tin cans.

The Tonnerres were French half-breeds, and among themselves they spoke a *patois* that was neither Cree nor French. Their English was broken and full of obscenities. They did not belong among the Cree of the Galloping Mountain reservation, further north, and they did not belong among the Scots-Irish and Ukrainians of Manawaka, either. They were, as my Grandmother MacLeod would have put it, neither flesh, fowl, nor good salt herring. When their men were not working at odd jobs or as section hands on the C.P.R., they lived on relief. In the summers, one of the Tonnerre youngsters, with a face that seemed totally unfamiliar with laughter, would knock at the doors of the town's brick houses and offer for sale a lard-pail full of bruised wild strawberries, and if he got as much as a quarter he would grab the coin and run before the customer had time to change her mind. Sometimes old Jules, or his son Lazarus, would get mixed up in a Saturday-night brawl, and would hit out at whoever was nearest, or howl drunkenly among the offended shoppers on Main Street, and then the Mountie would put them for the night in the barred cell underneath the Court House, and the next morning they would be quiet again.

Piquette Tonnerre, the daughter of Lazarus, was in my class at school. She was older than I, but she had failed several grades, perhaps because her attendance had always been sporadic and her interest in school-work negligible. Part of the reason she had missed a lot of school was that she had had tuberculosis of the bone, and had once spent many months in hospital. I knew this because my father was the doctor who had looked after her. Her sickness was almost the only thing I knew about her, however. Otherwise, she existed for me only as a vaguely embarrassing presence, with her hoarse voice and her clumsy limping walk and her grimy cotton dresses that were always miles too long. I was neither friendly nor unfriendly towards her. She dwelt and moved somewhere within my scope of vision, but I did not actually notice her very much until that peculiar summer when I was eleven.

'I don't know what to do about that kid,' my father said at dinner one evening. 'Piquette Tonnerre, I mean. The damn bone's flared up again. I've had her in hospital for quite a while now, and it's under control all right, but I hate like the dickens to send her home again.'

'Couldn't you explain to her mother that she has to rest a lot?' my mother said.

'The mother's not there,' my father replied. 'She took off a few years back. Can't say I blame her. Piquette cooks for them, and she says Lazarus would never do anything for himself as long as she's there. Anyway, I don't think she'd take much care of herself, once she got back. She's only thirteen, after all. Beth, I was thinking—what about taking her up to Diamond Lake with us this summer? A couple of months rest would give that bone a much better chance.'

My mother looked stunned.

'But Ewen—what about Roddie and Vanessa?'

'She's not contagious,' my father said. 'And it would be company for Vanessa.'

'Oh dear,' my mother said in distress, 'I'll bet anything she has nits in her hair.'

'For Pete's sake,' my father said crossly, 'do you think Matron would let her stay in the hospital for all this time like that? Don't be silly, Beth.'

Grandmother MacLeod, her delicately featured face as rigid as a cameo, now brought her mauve-veined hands together as though she were about to begin a prayer.

'Ewen, if that half-breed youngster comes along to Diamond Lake, I'm not going,' she announced. 'I'll go to Morag's for the summer.'

I had trouble in stifling my urge to laugh, for my mother brightened visibly and quickly tried to hide it. If it came to a choice between Grandmother MacLeod and Piquette, Piquette would win hands down, nits or not.

'It might be quite nice for you, at that,' she mused. 'You haven't seen Morag for over a year, and you might enjoy being in the city for a while. Well, Ewen dear, you do what you think best. If you think it would do Piquette some good, then we'll be glad to have her, as long as she behaves herself.'

So it happened that several weeks later, when we all piled into my father's old Nash, surrounded by suitcases and boxes of provisions and toys for my ten-month-old brother, Piquette was with us and Grandmother MacLeod, miraculously, was not. My father would only be staying at the cottage for a couple of weeks, for he had to get back to his practice, but the rest of us would stay at Diamond Lake until the end of August.

Our cottage was not named, as many were, 'Dew Drop Inn' or 'Bide-a-Wee,' or 'Bonnie Doon.' The sign on the roadway bore in austere letters only our name, MacLeod. It was not a large cottage, but it was on the lakefront. You could look out the windows and see, through the filigree of the spruce trees, the water glistening greenly as the sun caught it. All around the cottage were ferns, and sharp-branched raspberry bushes, and moss that had grown over fallen tree trunks. If you looked carefully among the weeds and grass, you could find wild strawberry plants which were in white flower now and in another month would bear fruit, the fragrant globes hanging like miniature scarlet lanterns on the thin hairy stems. The two grey squirrels were still there, gossiping at us from the tall spruce beside the cottage, and by the end of the summer they would again be tame enough to take pieces of crust from my hands. The broad moose antlers that hung above the back door were a little more bleached and fissured after the winter, but otherwise everything was the same. I raced joyfully around my kingdom, greeting all the places I had not seen for a year. My brother, Roderick, who had not been born when we were here last summer, sat on the car rug in the sunshine and examined a brown spruce cone, meticulously turning it round and round in his small and curious hands. My mother and father toted the luggage from car to cottage, exclaiming over how well the place had wintered, no broken windows, thank goodness, no apparent damage from storm-felled branches or snow.

Only after I had finished looking around did I notice Piquette. She was sitting on the swing, her lame leg held stiffly out, and her other foot scuffing the ground as she swung slowly back and forth. Her long hair hung black and straight around her shoulders, and her broad coarse-featured face bore no expression—it was blank, as though she no longer dwelt within her own skull, as though she had gone elsewhere. I approached her very hesitantly.

'Want to come and play?'

Piquette looked at me with a sudden flash of scorn.

'I ain't a kid,' she said.

Wounded, I stamped angrily away, swearing I would not speak to her for the rest of the summer. In the days that followed, however, Piquette began to interest me, and I began to want to interest her. My reasons did not appear bizarre to me. Unlikely as it may seem, I had only just realized that the Tonnerre family, whom I had always heard called half-breeds, were actually Indians, or as near as made no difference. My acquaintance with Indians was not extensive. I did not remember ever having seen a real Indian, and my new awareness that Piquette sprang from the people of Big Bear and Poundmaker, of Tecumseh, of the Iroquois who had eaten Father Brebeuf's heart—all this gave her an instant attraction in my eyes. I was a devoted reader of Pauline Johnson at this age, and sometimes would orate aloud and in an exalted voice, *West Wind, blow from your prairie nest; Blow from the mountains, blow from the west*—and so on. It seemed to me that Piquette must be in some way a daughter of the forest, a kind of junior prophetess of the wilds who might impart to me, if I took the right approach, some of the secrets which she undoubtedly knew—where the whippoorwill made her nest how the coyote reared her young, or whatever it was that it said in *Hiawatha*.

I set about gaining Piquette's trust. She was not allowed to go swimming, with her bad leg, but I managed to lure her down to the beach—or rather she came because there was nothing else to do. The water was always icy, for the lake was fed by springs, but I swam like a dog, thrashing my arms and legs around at such speed and with such an output of energy that I never grew cold. Finally, when I had had enough, I came out and sat beside Piquette on the sand. When she saw me approaching, her hand squashed flat the sand castle she had been building, and she looked at me sullenly, without speaking.

'Do you like this place?' I asked, after a while, intending to lead on from there into the question of forest lore.

Piquette shrugged. 'It's okay. Good as anywhere.'

'I love it,' I said. 'We come here every summer.'

'So what?' Her voice was distant, and I glanced at her uncertainly, wondering what I could have said wrong.

'Do you want to come for a walk?' I asked her. 'We wouldn't need to go far. If you walk just around the point there, you come to a bay where great big reeds grow in the water, and all kinds of fish hang around there. Want to? Come on.'

She shook her head.

'Your dad said I ain't supposed to do no more walking than I got to.'

I tried another line.

'I bet you know a lot about the woods and all that, eh?' I began respectfully.

Piquette looked at me from her large dark unsmiling eyes.

'I don't know what in hell you're talkin' about,' she replied. 'You nuts or some-thin'? If you mean where my old man, and me, and all them live, you better shut up, by Jesus, you hear?'

I was startled and my feelings were hurt, but I had a kind of dogged persever-ance. I ignored her rebuff.

'You know something, Piquette? There's loons here, on this lake. You can see their nests just up the shore there, behind those logs. At night, you can hear them even from the cottage, but it's better to listen from the beach. My dad says we should listen and try to remember how they sound, because in a few years when more cot-tages are built at Diamond Lake and more people come in, the loons will go away.'

Piquette was picking up stones and snail shells and then dropping them again.

'Who gives a good goddamn?' she said.

It became increasingly obvious that, as an Indian, Piquette was a dead loss. That evening I went out by myself, scrambling through the bushes that overhung the steep path, my feet slipping on the fallen spruce needles that covered the ground. When I reached the shore, I walked along the firm damp sand to the small pier that my father had built, and sat down there. I heard someone else crashing through the undergrowth and the bracken, and for a moment I thought Piquette had changed her mind, but it turned out to be my father. He sat beside me on the pier and we waited, without speaking.

At night the lake was like black glass with a streak of amber which was the path of the moon. All around, the spruce trees grew tall and close-set, branches blackly sharp against the sky, which was lightened by a cold flickering of stars. Then the loons began their calling. They rose like phantom birds from the nests on the shore, and flew out onto the dark still surface of the water.

No one can ever describe that ululating sound, the crying of the loons, and no one who has heard it can ever forget it. Plaintive, and yet with a quality of chilling mockery, those voices belonged to a world separated by aeons from our neat world of summer cottages and the lighted lamps of home.

'They must have sounded just like that,' my father remarked, 'before any person ever set foot here.'

Then he laughed. 'You could say the same, of course, about sparrows, or chipmunks, but somehow it only strikes you that way with the loons.'

'I know,' I said.

Neither of us suspected that this would be the last time we would ever sit here together on the shore, listening. We stayed for perhaps half an hour, and then we went back to the cottage. My mother was reading beside the fireplace. Piquette was looking at the burning birch log, and not doing anything.

'You should have come along,' I said, although in fact I was glad she had not.

'Not me,' Piquette said. 'You wouldn' catch me walkin' way down there jus' for a bunch of squawkin' birds.'

Piquette and I remained ill at ease with one another. I felt I had somehow failed my father, but I did not know what was the matter, nor why she would not or could not respond when I suggested exploring the woods or playing house. I thought it was probably her slow and difficult walking that held her back. She stayed most of the time in the cottage with my mother, helping her with the dishes or with Roddie, but hardly ever talking. Then the Duncans arrived at their cottage, and I spent my days with Mavis, who was my best friend. I could not reach Piquette at all, and I soon lost interest in trying. But all that summer she remained as both a reproach and a mystery to me.

That winter my father died of pneumonia, after less than a week's illness. For some time I saw nothing around me, being completely immersed in my own pain and my mother's. When I looked outward once more, I scarcely noticed that Piquette Tonnerre was no longer at school. I do not remember seeing her at all until four years later, one Saturday night when Mavis and I were having Cokes in the Regal Café. The jukebox was booming like tuneful thunder, and beside it, leaning lightly on its chrome and its rainbow glass, was a girl.

Piquette must have been seventeen then, although she looked about twenty. I stared at her, astounded that anyone could have changed so much. Her face, so stolid and expressionless before, was animated now with a gaiety that was almost violent. She laughed and talked very loudly with the boys around her. Her lipstick was bright carmine, and her hair was cut short and frizzily permed. She had not been pretty as a child, and she was not pretty now, for her features were still heavy and blunt. But her dark and slightly slanted eyes were beautiful, and her skin-tight skirt and orange sweater displayed to enviable advantage a soft and slender body.

She saw me, and walked over. She teetered a little, but it was not due to her once-tubercular leg, for her limp was almost gone.

'Hi, Vanessa.' Her voice still had the same hoarseness. 'Long time no see, eh?'

'Hi,' I said. 'Where've you been keeping yourself, Piquette?'

'Oh, I been around,' she said. 'I been away almost two years now. Been all over the place—Winnipeg, Regina, Saskatoon. Jesus, what I could tell you! I come back this summer, but I ain't stayin'. You kids goin' to the dance?'

'No,' I said abruptly, for this was a sore point with me. I was fifteen, and thought I was old enough to go to the Saturday-night dances at the Flamingo. My mother, however, thought otherwise.

'Y'oughta come,' Piquette said. 'I never miss one. It's just about the on'y thing in this jerkwater town that's any fun. Boy, you couldn' catch me stayin' here. I don't give a shit about this place. It stinks.'

She sat down beside me, and I caught the harsh over-sweetness of her perfume.

'Listen, you wanna know something, Vanessa?' she confided, her voice only slightly blurred. 'Your dad was the only person in Manawaka that ever done anything good to me.'

I nodded speechlessly. I was certain she was speaking the truth. I knew a little more than I had that summer at Diamond Lake, but I could not reach her now any more than I had then. I was ashamed, ashamed of my own timidity, the frightened tendency to look the other way. Yet I felt no real warmth towards her—I only felt that I ought to, because of that distant summer and because my father had hoped she would be company for me, or perhaps that I would be for her, but it had not happened that way. At this moment, meeting her again, I had to admit that she repelled and embarrassed me, and I could not help despising the self-pity in her voice. I wished she would go away. I did not want to see her. I did not know what to say to her. It seemed that we had nothing to say to one another.

'I'll tell you something else,' Piquette went on. 'All the old bitches an' biddies in this town will sure be surprised. I'm gettin' married this fall—my boyfriend, he's an English fella, works in the stockyards in the city there, a very tall guy, got blond wavy hair. Gee, is he ever handsome. Got this real classy name. Alvin Gerald Cummings—some handle, eh? They call him Al.'

For the merest instant, then, I saw her. I really did see her, for the first and only time in all the years we had both lived in the same town. Her defiant face, momentarily, became unguarded and unmasked, and in her eyes there was a terrifying hope.

'Gee, Piquette—' I burst out awkwardly, 'that's swell. That's really wonderful. Congratulations—good luck—I hope you'll be happy—'

As I mouthed the conventional phrases, I could only guess how great her need must have been, that she had been forced to seek the very things she so bitterly rejected.

When I was eighteen, I left Manawaka and went away to college. At the end of my first year, I came back home for the summer. I spent the first few days in talking non-stop with my mother, as we exchanged all the news that somehow had not found its way into letters—what had happened in my life and what had happened here in Manawaka while I was away. My mother searched her memory for events that concerned people I knew.

'Did I ever write you about Piquette Tonnerre, Vanessa?' she asked one morning.

'No I don't think so,' I replied. 'Last I heard of her, she was going to marry some guy in the city. Is she still there?'

My mother looked perturbed, and it was a moment before she spoke, as though she did not know how to express what she had to tell and wished she did not need to try.

'She's dead,' she said at last. Then, as I stared at her, 'Oh, Vanessa, when it happened, I couldn't help thinking of her as she was that summer—so sullen and gauche and badly dressed. I couldn't help wondering if we could have done something more at that time—but what could we do? She used to be around in the cottage there with me all day, and honestly, it was all I could do to get a word out of her. She didn't even talk to your father very much, although I think she liked him, in her way.'

'What happened?' I asked.

'Either her husband left her, or she left him,' my mother said. 'I don't know which. Anyway, she came back here with two youngsters, both only babies—they must have been born very close together. She kept house, I guess, for Lazarus and her brothers, down in the valley there, in the old Tonnerre place. I used to see her on the street sometimes, but she never spoke to me. She'd put on an awful lot of weight, and she looked a mess, to tell you the truth, a real slattern, dressed any old how. She was up in court a couple of times—drunk and disorderly, of course. One Saturday night last winter, during the coldest weather, Piquette was alone in the shack with the children. The Tonnerres made home brew all the time, so I've heard, and Lazarus said later she'd been drinking most of the day when he and the boys went out that evening. They had an old woodstove there—you know the kind, with exposed pipes. The shack caught fire. Piquette didn't get out, and neither did the children.'

I did not say anything. As so often with Piquette, there did not seem to be anything to say. There was a kind of silence around the image in my mind of the fire and the snow, and I wished I could put from my memory the look that I had seen once in Piquette's eyes.

I went up to Diamond Lake for a few days that summer, with Mavis and her family. The MacLeod cottage had been sold after my father's death, and I did not even go to look at it, not wanting to witness my long-ago kingdom possessed now by strangers. But one evening I went down to the shore by myself.

The small pier which my father had built was gone, and in its place there was a large and solid pier built by the government, for Galloping Mountain was now a national park, and Diamond Lake had been re-named Lake Wapakata, for it was felt that an Indian name would have a greater appeal to tourists. The one store had become several dozen, and the settlement had all the attributes of a flourishing resort—hotels, a dance-hall, cafés with neon signs, the penetrating odours of potato chips and hot dogs.

I sat on the government pier and looked out across the water. At night the lake at least was the same as it had always been, darkly shining and bearing within its black glass the streak of amber that was the path of the moon. There was no wind that evening, and everything was quiet all around me. It seemed too quiet, and then I realized that the loons were no longer here. I listened for some time, to make sure, but never once did I hear that long-drawn call, half mocking and half plaintive, spearing through the stillness across the lake.

I did not know what had happened to the birds. Perhaps they had gone away to some far place of belonging. Perhaps they had been unable to find such a place, and had simply died out, having ceased to care any longer whether they lived or not.

I remembered how Piquette had scorned to come along, when my father and I sat there and listened to the lake birds. It seemed to me now that in some unconscious and totally unrecognized way, Piquette might have been the only one, after all, who had heard the crying of the loons.

D. H. Lawrence

David Herbert Lawrence was born in 1885 in East-wood, Nottinghamshire, England. Some of the flavour of his childhood and adolescence, as the son of a miner and an overly possessive middle-class mother, is recorded in his novel *Sons and Lovers* (1913). Lawrence obtained his teacher's certificate from Nottingham University College, but ill-health (subsequently diagnosed as tuberculosis) forced him to cut short his teaching career. He first appeared in print as a poet in the *English Review* in 1909, the same year that his first novel, *The White Peacock*, was published. Lawrence met Frieda von Richthoffen, the wife of a former professor, and they left for the Continent, but returned to England prior to the outbreak of World War I. They married, but were never comfortable in England, because of persecution and censorship, and became voluntary wanderers in Italy, Australia, New Mexico, and Mexico, seeking a dry, healthy climate and, it seems, a refuge that might offer both freedom and security. While he is best known for his novels, including *Women in Love* (1920) and *Lady Chatterley's Lover* (1928), Lawrence also published several collections of stories: *The Prussian Officer* (1914), *England, My England* (1922), *The Ladybird* (1923), *Glad Ghosts* (1926), and *The Woman Who Rode Away* (1928). He returned to Europe in 1929, a year before his death.

As a victim of censorship, Lawrence, not surprisingly, had something to say on the subject. As he says in a letter to Morris Ernst in 1928, "Myself, I believe censorship helps nobody; and hurts many. Our civilisation cannot afford to let the censor-moron loose. The censor-moron does not really hate anything but the living and growing human consciousness. It is our developing and extending consciousness that he threatens—and our consciousness in its newest, most sensitive activity, its vital growth. To arrest or circumscribe the vital consciousness is to produce morons, and nothing but a moron would wish to do it."

Lawrence, using a metaphor appropriate to his upbringing, called literature "a mine of practical truth." He was a social critic and visionary, who called into question the rules of conventional morality and sexual etiquette, as is evident in his famous statement: "The business of art is to reveal the relation between man and his circumambient universe, at the living moment. As mankind is always struggling in the toils of old relationships, art is always ahead of the 'times,' which themselves are always far in the rear of the living moment." In the same essay, called "Morality

and the Novel," Lawrence claims fiction has become immoral by being forced to dictate on ethical issues: "The novel is the highest example of subtle interrelatedness that man has discovered. Everything is true in its own time, place, circumstance, and untrue outside its own place, time, circumstance. If you try to nail anything down, in the novel, either it kills the novel, or the novel gets up and walks away with the nail." While he was reluctant to prescribe for the novel or the story, Lawrence was not averse to making pronouncements about life itself: "The great relationship, for humanity, will always be the relation between man and woman. And the relation between man and woman will change for ever, and will for ever be the new central clue to human life. It is the relation itself which is the quick and the central clue to life."

In a letter to his agent, Edward Garnet, Lawrence tried to explain his conception of character in fiction. He dismissed the "old-fashioned" approach to character, "which causes one to conceive a character in a certain moral scheme and make him consistent. The certain moral scheme is what I object to. . . . You mustn't look in my novel for the old stable ego—of the character. There is another ego, according to whose action the individual is unrecognizable, and passes through, as it were, allotropic states which it needs in a deeper sense than any we've been used to exercise, to discover are states of the same single radically unchanged element. . . . Don't look for the development of the novel to follow the lines of certain characters: the characters fall into the form of some other rhythmic form, as when one draws a fiddle-bow across a fine tray delicately sanded, the sand takes lines unknown."

Although he is speaking here of the novel, Lawrence's comments on character apply equally well to the short story, which, unless it is mere imitation, will have its own rules of construction. He was constantly struggling to refine his own techniques to enable him to explore experience more deeply, as this letter to a young writer, Kyle Crichton, suggests: "You are too journalistic, too much concerned with facts. You don't concern yourself with the human inside at all, only with the insides of steel works. It's the sort of consciousness the working man has: but at the same time he's got a passionate sub-conscious. And it's the sub-conscious which makes the story: otherwise you have journalism. Now you want to be an artist, so you've got to use the artist's faculty of making the sub-conscious conscious.

Take your Andy, a boy as blank as most American boys. . . . What was there in the mines that held the boy's feelings? The darkness, the mystery, the other-worldliness, the peculiar camaraderie, the sort of naked intimacy: men as gods in the underworld, or as elementals. Create *that* in a picture."

The Horse Dealer's Daughter

'Well, Mabel, and what are you going to do with yourself?' asked Joe, with foolish flippancy. He felt quite safe himself. Without listening for an answer, he turned aside, worked a grain of tobacco to the tip of his tongue, and spat it out. He did not care about anything, since he felt safe himself.

The three brothers and the sister sat round the desolate breakfast-table, attempting some sort of desultory consultation. The morning's post had given the final tap to the family fortunes, and all was over. The dreary dining-room itself, with its heavy mahogany furniture, looked as if it were waiting to be done away with.

But the consultation amounted to nothing. There was a strange air of ineffectuality about the three men, as they sprawled at table, smoking and reflecting vaguely on their own condition. The girl was alone, a rather short, sullen-looking young woman of twenty-seven. She did not share the same life as her brothers. She would have been good-looking, save for the impressive fixity of her face, 'bull-dog', as her brothers called it.

There was a confused tramping of horses' feet outside. The three men all sprawled round in their chairs to watch. Beyond the dark holly bushes that separated the strip of lawn from the high-road, they could see a cavalcade of shire horses swinging out of their own yard, being taken for exercise. This was the last time. These were the last horses that would go through their hands. The young men watched with critical, callous look. They were all frightened at the collapse of their lives, and the sense of disaster in which they were involved left them no inner freedom.

Yet they were three fine, well-set fellows enough. Joe, the eldest, was a man of thirty-three, broad and handsome in a hot, flushed way. His face was red, he twisted his black moustache over a thick finger, his eyes were shallow and restless. He had a sensual way of uncovering his teeth when he laughed, and his bearing was stupid. Now he watched the horses with a glazed look of helplessness in his eyes, a certain stupor of downfall.

The great draught-horses swung past. They were tied head to tail, four of them, and they heaved along to where a lane branched off from the high-road, planting their great hoofs floutingly in the fine black mud, swinging their great rounded haunches sumptuously, and trotting a few sudden steps as they were led into the lane, round the corner. Every movement showed a massive, slumbrous strength, and a stupidity which held them in subjection. The groom at the head looked back, jerking the leading rope. And the cavalcade moved out of sight up the lane, the tail of the last horse, bobbed up tight and stuff, held out taut from the swinging great haunches as they rocked behind the hedges in a motion-like sleep.

Joe watched with glazed hopeless eyes. The horses were almost like his own body to him. He felt he was done for now. Luckily he was engaged to a woman as old as himself, and therefore her father, who was steward of a neighbouring estate, would provide him with a job. He would marry and go into harness. His life was over, he would be a subject animal now.

He turned uneasily aside, the retreating steps of the horses echoing in his ears. Then, with foolish restlessness, he reached for the scraps of bacon-rind from the plates, and making a faint whistling sound, flung them to the terrier that lay against the fender. He watched the dog swallow them, and waited till the creature looked into his eyes. Then a faint grin came on his face, and in a high, foolish voice he said:

'You won't get much more bacon, shall you, you little b—?'

The dog faintly and dismally wagged its tail, then lowered its haunches, circled round, and lay down again.

There was another helpless silence at the table. Joe sprawled uneasily in his seat, not willing to go till the family conclave was dissolved. Fred Henry, the second brother, was erect, clean-limbed, alert. He had watched the passing of the horses with more *sang-froid*. If he was an animal, like Joe, he was an animal which controls, not one which is controlled. He was master of any horse, and he carried himself with a well-tempered air of mastery. But he was not master of the situations of life. He pushed his coarse brown moustache upwards, off his lip, and glanced irritably at his sister, who sat impassive and inscrutable.

'You'll go and stop with Lucy for a bit, shan't you?' he asked. The girl did not answer.

'I don't see what else you can do,' persisted Fred Henry.

'Go as a skivvy,' Joe interpolated laconically.

The girl did not move a muscle.

'If I was her, I should go in training for a nurse,' said Malcolm, the youngest of them all. He was the baby of the family, a young man of twenty-two, with a fresh, jaunty *museau*.

But Mabel did not take any notice of him. They had talked at her and round her for so many years, that she hardly heard them at all.

The marble block on the mantelpiece softly chimed the half-hour, the dog rose uneasily from the hearth-rug and looked at the party at the breakfast-table. But still they sat on in ineffectual conclave.

'Oh, all right,' said Joe suddenly, apropos of nothing. 'I'll get a move on.'

He pushed back his chair, straddled his knees with a downward jerk, to get them free, in horsey fashion, and went to the fire. Still he did not go out of the room; he was curious to know what the others would do or say. He began to charge his pipe, looking down at the dog and saying in a high, affected voice:

'Going wi' me? Going wi' me are ter? Tha'rt goin' further than tha counts on just now, dost hear?'

The dog faintly wagged its tail, the man stuck out his jaw and covered his pipe with his hands, and puffed intently, losing himself in the tobacco, looking down all the while at the dog with an absent brown eye. The dog looked up at him in mournful distrust. Joe stood with his knees stuck out, in real horsey fashion.

'Have you had a letter from Lucy?' Fred Henry asked of his sister.

'Last week,' came the neutral reply.

'And what does she say?'

There was no answer.

'Does she *ask* you to go and stop there?' persisted Fred Henry.

'She says I can if I like.'

'Well, then, you'd better. Tell her you'll come on Monday.'

This was received in silence.

'That's what you'll do then, is it?' said Fred Henry, in some exasperation.

But she made no answer. There was a silence of futility and irritation in the room. Malcolm grinned fatuously.

'You'll have to make up your mind between now and next Wednesday,' said Joe loudly, 'or else find yourself lodgings on the kerbstone.'

The face of the young woman darkened, but she sat on immutable.

'Here's Jack Fergusson!' exclaimed Malcolm, who was looking aimlessly out of the window.

'Where?' exclaimed Joe loudly.

'Just gone past.'

'Coming in?'

Malcolm craned his neck to see the gate.

'Yes,' he said.

There was a silence. Mabel sat on like one condemned, at the head of the table. Then a whistle was heard from the kitchen. The dog got up and barked sharply. Joe opened the door and shouted:

'Come on.'

After a moment a young man entered. He was muffled up in overcoat and a purple woollen scarf, and his tweed cap, which he did not remove, was pulled down on his head. He was of medium height, his face was rather long and pale, his eyes looked tired.

'Hello, Jack! Well, Jack!' exclaimed Malcolm and Joe. Fred Henry merely said: 'Jack.'

'What's doing?' asked the newcomer, evidently addressing Fred Henry.

'Same. We've got to be out by Wednesday. Got a cold?'

'I have—got it bad, too.'

'Why don't you stop in?'

'*Me* stop in? When I can't stand on my legs, perhaps I shall have a chance.' The young man spoke huskily. He had a slight Scotch accent.

'It's a knock-out isn't it,' said Joe, boisterously, 'if a doctor goes round croaking with a cold. Looks bad for the patients, doesn't it?'

The young doctor looked at him slowly.

'Anything the matter with *you*, then?' he asked sarcastically.

'Not as I know of. Damn your eyes, I hope not. Why?'

'I thought you were very concerned about the patients, wondered if you might be one yourself.'

'Damn it, no, I've never been patient to no flaming doctor, and hope I never shall be,' returned Joe.

At this point Mabel rose from the table, and they all seemed to become aware of her existence. She began putting the dishes together. The young doctor looked at her, but did not address her. He had not greeted her. She went out of the room with the tray, her face impassive and unchanged.

'When are you off then, all of you?' asked the doctor.

'I'm catching the eleven-forty,' replied Malcolm. 'Are you goin' down wi' th' trap, Joe?'

'Yes, I've told you I'm going down wi' the' trap, haven't I?'

'We'd better be getting her in then. So long, Jack, if I don't see you before I go,' said Malcolm, shaking hands.

He went out, followed by Joe, who seemed to have his tail between his legs.

'Well, this is the devil's own,' exclaimed the doctor, when he was left alone with Fred Henry. 'Going before Wednesday, are you?'

'That's the orders,' replied the other.

'Where, to Northampton?'

'That's it.'

'The devil!' exclaimed Fergusson, with quiet chagrin.

And there was silence between the two.

'All settled up, are you?' asked Fergusson.

'About.'

There was another pause.

'Well, I shall miss yer, Freddy, boy,' said the young doctor.

'And I shall miss thee, Jack,' returned the other.

'Miss you like hell,' mused the doctor.

Fred Henry turned aside. There was nothing to say. Mabel came in again, to finish clearing the table.

'What are *you* going to do, then, Miss Pervin?' asked Fergusson. 'Going to your sister's, are you?'

Mabel looked at him with her steady, dangerous eyes, that always made him uncomfortable, unsettling his superficial ease.

'No,' she said.

'Well, what in the name of fortune *are* you going to do? Say what you mean to do,' cried Fred Henry, with futile intensity.

But she only averted her head, and continued her work. She folded the white table-cloth, and put on the chenille cloth.

'The sulkiest bitch that ever trod!' muttered her brother.

But she finished her task with perfectly impassive face, the young doctor watching her interestedly all the while. Then she went out.

Fred Henry stared after her, clenching his lips, his blue eyes fixing in sharp antagonism, as he made a grimace of sour exasperation.

'You could bray her into bits, and that's all you'd get out of her,' he said, in a small, narrowed tone.

The doctor smiled faintly.

'What's she *going* to do, then?' he asked.

'Strike me if *I* know!' returned the other.

There was a pause. Then the doctor stirred.

'I'll be seeing you to-night, shall I?' he said to his friend.

'Ay—where's it to be? Are we going over to Jessdale?'

'I don't know. I've got such a cold on me. I'll come round to the "Moon and Stars", anyway.'

'Let Lizzie and May miss their night for once, eh?'

'That's it—if I feel as I do now.'

'All's one—'

The two young men went through the passage and down to the back door together. The house was large, but it was servantless now, and desolate. At the back was a small bricked house-yard and beyond that a big square, gravelled fine and red, and having stables on two sides. Sloping, dank, winter-dark fields stretched away on the open sides.

But the stables were empty. Joseph Pervin, the father of the family, had been a man of no education, who had become a fairly large horse dealer. The stables had been full of horses, there was a great turmoil and come-and-go of horses and of dealers and grooms. Then the kitchen was full of servants. But of late things had declined. The old man had married a second time, to retrieve his fortunes. Now he was dead and everything was gone to the dogs, there was nothing but debt and threatening.

For months, Mabel had been servantless in the big house, keeping the home together in penury for her ineffectual brothers. She had kept house for ten years. But previously it was with unstinted means. Then, however brutal and coarse everything was, the sense of money had kept her proud, confident. The men might be foul-mouthed, the women in the kitchen might have bad reputations, her brothers might have illegitimate children. But so long as there was money, the girl felt herself established, and brutally proud, reserved.

No company came to the house, save dealers and coarse men. Mabel had no associates of her own sex, after her sister went away. But she did not mind. She went regularly to church, she attended to her father. And she lived in the memory of her mother, who had died when she was fourteen, and whom she had loved. She had loved her father, too, in a different way, depending upon him, and feeling secure in him, until at the age of fifty-four he married again. And then she had set hard against him. Now he had died and left them all hopelessly in debt.

She had suffered badly during the period of poverty. Nothing, however, could shake the curious, sullen, animal pride that dominated each member of the family. Now, for Mabel, the end had come. Still she would not cast about her. She would follow her own way just the same. She could always hold the keys of her own situation. Mindless and persistent, she endured from day to day. Why should she think? Why should she answer anybody? It was enough that this was the end, and there was no way out. She need not pass any more darkly along the main street of the small town, avoiding every eye. She need not demean herself any more, going into the shops and buying the cheapest food. This was at an end. She thought of nobody, not even of herself. Mindless and persistent, she seemed in a sort of ecstasy to be coming nearer to her fulfilment, her own glorification, approaching her dead mother, who was glorified.

In the afternoon she took a little bag, with shears and sponge and a small scrubbing-brush, and went out. It was a grey, wintry day, with saddened, dark green fields and an atmosphere blackened by the smoke of foundries not far off. She went quickly, darkly along the causeway, heeding nobody, through the town to the churchyard.

There she always felt secure, as if no one could see her, although as a matter of fact she was exposed to the stare of everyone who passed along under the church-yard wall. Nevertheless, once under the shadow of the great looming church, among the graves, she felt immune from the world, reserved within the thick churchyard wall as in another country.

Carefully she clipped the grass from the grave, and arranged the pinky white, small chrysanthemums in the tin cross. When this was done, she took an empty jar from a neighbouring grave, brought water, and carefully, most scrupulously sponged the marble headstone and the coping-stone.

It gave her sincere satisfaction to do this. She felt in immediate contact with the world of her mother. She took minute pains, went through the park in a state bordering on pure happiness, as if in performing this task she came into a subtle, intimate connection with her mother. For the life she followed here in the work was far less real than the world of death she inherited from her mother.

The doctor's house was just by the church. Fergusson, being a mere hired assis-tant, was slave to the country-side. As he hurried now to attend to the out-patients in the surgery, glancing across the graveyard with his quick eye, he saw the girl at her task at the grave. She seemed so intent and remote, it was like looking into another world. Some mystical element was touched in him. He slowed down as he walked, watching her as if spellbound.

She lifted her eyes, feeling him looking. Their eyes met. And each looked again at once, each feeling, in some way, found out by the other. He lifted his cap and passed on down the road. There remained distinct in his consciousness, like a vision, the memory of her face, lifted from the tombstone in the churchyard and looking at him with slow, large, portentous eyes. It *was* portentous, her face. It seemed to mesmerize him. There was a heavy power in her eyes which laid hold of his whole being, as if he had drunk some powerful drug. He had been feeling weak and done before. Now the life came back into him, he felt delivered from his own fretted, daily self.

He finished his duties at the surgery as quickly as might be, hastily filling up the bottles of the waiting people with cheap drugs. Then, in perpetual haste, he set off again to visit several cases in another part of his round, before tea-time. At all times he preferred to walk if he could, but particularly when he was not well. He fancied the motion restored him

The afternoon was falling. It was grey, deadened, and wintry, with a slow, moist, heavy coldness sinking in and deadening all the faculties. But why should he think or notice? He hastily climbed the hill and turned across the dark green fields, following the black cinder-track. In the distance, across a shallow dip in the country, the small town was clustered like smouldering ash, a tower, a spire, a heap of low, raw, extinct houses. And on the nearest fringe of the town, sloping into the dip, was Oldmeadow, the Pervins' house. He could see the stables and the outbuildings distinctly, as they lay towards him on the slope. Well, he would not go there many more times! Another resource would be lost to him, another place gone: the only company he cared for in the alien, ugly little town he was losing. Nothing but work, drudgery, constant hastening from dwelling to dwelling among the colliers and the iron-workers. It wore him out, but at the same time he had a craving for it. It was a stimulant to him to be in the homes of the working people, moving, as it were, through the innermost body of their life. His nerves were excited and gratified. He could come so near, into the very lives of the rough, inarticulate, powerfully emotional men and women. He grumbled, he said he hated the hellish hole. But as a matter of fact it excited him, the contact with the rough, strongly-feeling people was a stimulant applied direct to his nerves.

Below Oldmeadow, in the green, shallow, soddened hollow of fields, lay a square, deep pond. Roving across the landscape, the doctor's quick eye detected a figure in black passing through the gate of the field, down towards the pond. He looked again. It would be Mabel Pervin. His mind suddenly became alive and attentive.

Why was she going down there? He pulled up on the path on the slope above, and stood staring. He could just make sure of the small black figure moving in the hollow of the failing day. He seemed to see her in the midst of such obscurity, that he was like a clairvoyant, seeing rather with the mind's eye than with ordinary sight. Yet he could see her positively enough, whilst he kept his eye attentive. He felt, if he looked away from her, in the thick, ugly falling dusk, he would lose her altogether.

He followed her minutely as she moved, direct and intent, like something transmitted rather than stirring in voluntary activity, straight down the field towards the pond. There she stood on the bank for a moment. She never raised her head. Then she waded slowly into the water.

He stood motionless as the small black figure walked slowly and deliberately towards the centre of the, very slowly, gradually moving deeper into the motion-less water, and still moving forward as the water got up to her breast. Then he could see her no more in the dusk of the dead afternoon.

'There!' he exclaimed. 'Would you believe it?'

And he hastened straight down, running over the wet, soddened fields, pushing through the hedges, down into the depression of callous wintry obscurity. It took him several minutes to come to the pond. He stood on the bank, breathing heavily. He could see nothing. His eyes seemed to penetrate the dead water. Yes, perhaps that was the dark shadow of her black clothing beneath the surface of the water.

He slowly ventured into the pond. The bottom was deep, soft clay, he sank in, and the water clasped dead cold round his legs. As he stirred he could smell the cold, rotten clay that fouled up into the water. It was objectionable in his lungs. Still, repelled and yet not heeding, he moved deeper into the pond. The cold water rose over his thighs, over his loins, upon his abdomen. The lower part of his body was all sunk in the hideous cold element. And the bottom was so deeply soft and uncertain, he was afraid of pitching with his mouth underneath. He could not swim, and was afraid.

He crouched a little, spreading his hands under the water and moving them round, trying to feel for her. The dead cold pond swayed upon his chest. He moved again, a little deeper, and again, with his hands underneath, he felt all around under the water. And he touched her clothing. But it evaded his fingers. He made a desperate effort to grasp it.

And so doing he lost his balance and went under, horribly, suffocating in the foul earthy water, struggling madly for a few moments. At last, after what seemed an eternity, he got his footing, rose again into the air and looked around. He gasped, and knew he was in the world. Then he looked at the water. She had risen near him. He grasped her clothing, and drawing her nearer, turned to take his way to land again.

He went very slowly, carefully, absorbed in the slow progress. He rose higher, climbing out of the pond. The water was now only about his legs; he was thankful, full of relief to be out of the clutches of the pond. He lifted her and staggered on to the bank, out of the horror of wet, grey clay.

He laid her down on the bank. She was quite unconscious and running with water. He made the water come from her mouth, he worked to restore her. He did not have to work very long before he could feel the breathing begin again in her; she was breathing naturally, He worked a little longer. He could feel her live beneath his hands; she was coming back. He wiped her face, wrapped her in his overcoat, looked round into the dim, dark grey world, then lifted her and staggered down the bank and across the fields.

It seemed an unthinkably long way, and his burden so heavy he felt he would never get to the house. But as last he was in the stable-yard, and then in the house-yard. He opened the door and went into the house. In the kitchen he laid her down on the hearth-rug and called. The house was empty. But the fire was burning in the grate.

Then again he kneeled to attend to her. She was breathing regularly, her eyes were wide open and as if conscious, but there seemed something missing in her look. She was conscious in herself, but unconscious of her surroundings.

He ran upstairs, took blankets from a bed, and put them before the fire to warm. Then he removed her saturated, earthy-smelling clothing, rubbed her dry with a towel, and wrapped her naked in the blankets. Then he went into the dining-room, to look for spirits. There was a little whisky. He drank a gulp himself, and put some into her mouth.

The effect was instantaneous. She looked full into his face, as if she had been seeing him for some time, and yet had only just become conscious of him.

'Dr. Fergusson?' she said.

'What?' he answered.

He was divesting himself of his coat, intending to find some dry clothing upstairs. He could not bear the smell of the dead, clayey water, and he was mortally afraid for his own health.

'What did I do?' she asked.

'Walked into the pond,' he replied. He had begun to shudder like one sick, and could hardly attend to her. Her eyes remained full on him, he seemed to be going dark in his mind, looking back at her helplessly. The shuddering became quieter in him, his life came back to him, dark and unknowing, but strong again.

'Was I out of my mind?' she asked, while her eyes were fixed on him all the time.

'Maybe, for the moment,' he replied. He felt quiet, because his strength had come back. The strange fretful strain had left him.

'Am I out of my mind now?' she asked.

'Are you?' he reflected a moment. 'No,' he answered truthfully. 'I don't see that you are.' He turned his face aside. He was afraid now, because he felt dazed, and felt dimly that her power was stronger than his, in this issue. And she continued to look at him fixedly all the time. 'Can you tell me where I shall find some dry things to put on?' he asked.

'Did you dive into the pond for me?' she asked.

'No,' he answered. 'I walked in. But I went in overhead as well.'

There was silence for a moment. He hesitated. He very much wanted to go upstairs to get into dry clothing. But there was another desire in him. And she seemed to hold him. His will seemed to have gone to sleep, and left him, standing there slack before her. But he felt warm inside himself. He did not shudder at all, though his clothes were sodden on him.

'Why did you?' she asked.

'Because I didn't want you to do such a foolish thing,' he said.

'It wasn't foolish,' she said, still gazing at him as she lay on the floor, with a sofa cushion under her head. 'It was the right thing to do. *I* knew best, then.'

'I'll go and shift these wet things,' he said. But still he had not the power to move out of her presence, until she sent him. It was as if she had the life of his body in her hands, and he could not extricate himself. Or perhaps he did not want to.

Suddenly she sat up. Then she became aware of her own immediate condition. She felt the blankets about her, she knew her own limbs. For a moment it seemed as if her reason were going. She looked round, with wild eye, as if seeking something. He stood still with fear. She saw her clothing lying scattered.

'Who undressed me?' she asked, her eyes resting full and inevitable on his face.

'I did,' he replied, 'to bring you round.'

For some moments she sat and gazed at him awfully, her lips parted.

'Do you love me, then?' she asked.

He only stood and stared at her, fascinated. His soul seemed to melt.

She shuffled forward on her knees, and put her arms round him, round his legs, as he stood there, pressing her breasts against his knees and thighs, clutching him with strange, convulsive certainty, pressing his thighs against her, drawing him to her face, her throat, as she looked up at him with flaring, humble eyes of transfiguration, triumphant in first possession.

'You love me,' she murmured, in strange transport, yearning and triumphant and confident. 'You love me. I know you love me, I know.'

And she was passionately kissing his knees, through the wet clothing, passionately and indiscriminately kissing his knees, his legs, as if unaware of everything.

He looked down at the tangled wet hair, the wild, bare, animal shoulders. He was amazed, bewildered, and afraid. He had never thought of loving her. He had never wanted to love her. When he rescued her and restored her, he was a doctor, and she was a patient. He had had no single personal thought of her. Nay, this introduction of the personal element was very distasteful to him, a violation of his professional honour. It was horrible to have her there embracing his knees. It was horrible. He revolted from it, violently. And yet—and yet—he had not the power to break away.

She looked at him again, with the same supplication of powerful love, and that same transcendent, frightening light of triumph. In view of the delicate flame which seemed to come from her face like a light, he was powerless. And yet he had never intended to love her. He had never intended. And something stubborn in him could not give way.

'You love me,' she repeated, in a murmur of deep, rhapsodic assurance. 'You love me.'

Her hands were drawing him, drawing him down to her. He was afraid, even a little horrified. For he had, really, no intention of loving her. Yet her hands were drawing him towards her. He put out his hand quickly to steady himself and grasped her bare shoulder. A flame seemed to burn the hand that grasped her soft shoulder. He had no intention of loving her: his whole will was against his yielding. It was horrible. And yet wonderful was the touch of her shoulders, beautiful the shining of her face. Was she perhaps mad? He had a horror of yielding to her. Yet something in him ached also.

He had been staring away at the door, away from her. But his hand remained on her shoulder. She had gone suddenly very still. He looked down at her. Her eyes were now wide with fear, with doubt, the light was dying from her face, a shadow of terrible greyness was returning. He could not bear the touch of her eyes' question upon him, and the look of death behind the question.

With an inward groan he gave way and let his heart yield towards her. A sudden gentle smile came on his face. And her eyes, which never left his face, slowly, slowly filled with tears. He watched the strange water rise in her eyes, like some slow fountain coming up. And his heart seemed to burn and melt away in his breast.

He could not bear to look at her any more. He dropped on his knees and caught her head with his arms and pressed her face against his throat. She was very still. His heart, which seemed to have broken, was burning with a kind of agony in his breast. And he felt her slow, hot tears wetting his throat. But he could not move.

He felt the hot tears wet his neck and the hollows of his neck, and he remained motionless, suspended through one of man's eternities. Only now it had become indispensable to him to have her face pressed close to him; he could never let her go again. He could never let her head go away from the close clutch of his arm. He wanted to remain like that for ever, with his heart hurting him in a pain that was also life to him. Without knowing, he was looking down on her damp, soft brown hair.

Then, as it were suddenly, he smelt the horrid stagnant smell of that water. And at the same moment she drew away from him and looked at him. Her eyes were wistful and unfathomable. He was afraid of them, and he fell to kissing her, not knowing what he was doing. He wanted her eyes not to have that terrible, wistful, unfathomable look.

When she turned her face to him again, a faint delicate flush was glowing, and there was again dawning that terrible shining of joy in her eyes, which really terrified him, and yet which he now wanted to see, because he feared the look of doubt still more.

'You love me?' she said, rather faltering.

'Yes.' The word cost him a painful effort. Not because it wasn't true. But because it was too newly true, the *saying* seemed to tear open again his newly-torn heart. And he hardly wanted it to be true, even now.

She lifted her face to him, and he bent forward and kissed her on the mouth, gently, with the one kiss that is an eternal pledge. And as he kissed her his heart strained again in his breast. He never intended to love her. But now it was over. He had crossed over the gulf to her, and all that he had left behind had shrivelled and become void.

After the kiss, her eyes again slowly filled with tears. She sat still, away from him, with her face drooped aside, and her hands folded in her lap. The tears fell very slowly. There was complete silence. He too sat there motionless and silent on the hearth-rug. The strange pain of his heart that was broken seemed to consume him. That he should love her? That this was love! That he should be ripped open in this way! Him, a doctor! How they would all jeer if they knew! It was agony to him to think they might know.

In the curious naked pain of the thought he looked again to her. She was sitting there drooped into a muse. He saw a tear fall, and his heart flared hot. He saw for the first time that one of her shoulders was quite uncovered, one arm bare, he could see one of her small breasts; dimly, because it had become almost dark in the room.

'Why are you crying?' he asked, in an altered voice.

She looked up at him, and behind her tears the consciousness of her situation for the first time brought a dark look of shame to her eyes.

'I'm not crying, really,' she said, watching him, half frightened.

He reached his hand, and softly closed it on her bare arm.

'I love you! I love you!' he said in a soft, low vibrating voice, unlike himself.

She shrank, and dropped her head. The soft, penetrating grip of his hand on her arm distressed her. She looked up at him.

'I want to go,' she said. 'I want to go and get you some dry things.'

'Why?' he said. 'I'm all right.'

'But I want to go,' she said. 'And I want you to change your things.'

He released her arm, and she wrapped herself in the blanket, looking at him rather frightened. And still she did not rise.

'Kiss me,' she said wistfully.

He kissed her, but briefly, half in anger.

Then, after a second, she rose nervously, all mixed up in the blanket. He watched her in her confusion as she tried to extricate herself and wrap herself up so that she could walk. He watched her relentlessly, as she knew. And as she went, the blanket trailing, and as he saw a glimpse of her feet and her white leg, he tried to remember her as she was when he had wrapped her in the blanket. But then he didn't want to remember, because she had been nothing to him then, and his nature revolted from remembering her as she was when she was nothing to him.

A tumbling, muffled noise from within the dark house startled him. Then he heard her voice: 'There are clothes.' He rose and went to the foot of the stairs, and gathered up the garments she had thrown down. Then he came back to the fire, to rub himself down and dress. He grinned at his own appearance when he had finished.

The fire was sinking, so he put on coal. The house was now quite dark, save for the light of a street-lamp that shone in faintly from beyond the holly trees. He lit the gas with matches he found on the mantelpiece. Then he emptied the pockets of his own clothes, and threw all his wet things in a heap into the scullery. After which he gathered up her sodden clothes, gently, and put them in a separate heap on the copper-top in the scullery.

It was six o'clock on the clock. His own watch had stopped. He ought to go back to the surgery. He waited, and still she did not come down. So he went to the foot of the stairs and called:

'I shall have to go.'

Almost immediately he heard her coming down. She had on her best dress of black voile, and her hair was tidy, but still damp. She looked at him—and in spite of herself, smiled.

'I don't like you in those clothes,' she said.

'Do I look a sight?' he answered.

They were shy of one another.

'I'll make you some tea,' she said.

'No, I must go.'

'Must you?' And she looked at him again with the wide, strained, doubtful eyes. And again, from the pain of his breast, he knew how he loved her. He went and bent to kiss her, gently, passionately, with his heart's painful kiss.

'And my hair smells so horrible,' she murmured in distraction. 'And I'm so awful, I'm so awful. Oh, no, I'm too awful.' And she broke into bitter, heart-broken sobbing. 'You can't want to love me, I'm horrible.'

'Don't be silly, don't be silly,' he said, trying to comfort her, kissing her, holding her in his arms. 'I want you, I want to marry you, we're going to be married, quickly, quickly—tomorrow if I can.'

But she only sobbed terribly, and cried:

'I feel awful, I feel awful. I feel I'm horrible to you.'

'No, I want you, I want you,' was all he answered, blindly, with that terrible intonation which frightened her almost more than her horror lest he should *not* want her.

Ursula K. Le Guin

Ursula Kroeber was born in California in 1929, to a mother who was a writer and a father who was a professor of Anthropology at Berkeley. She attended Radcliffe College and then studied Medieval Romance Literature at Columbia University. Although she began writing as a young girl, she did not publish her first story until she was thirty-two. This was followed by several novels, including *Rocanon's World* (1966) and *The Left Hand of Darkness* (1969), and a series of interconnected works that includes *The Planet of Exile* (1966), *City of Illusions* (1967), *The Dispossessed* (1974), *The Word for World Is Forest* (1976), and *The Wind's Twelve Quarters* (1976). Le Guin is one of the most accessible science fiction writers and her works have a broad non-specialist readership. Her writings on fiction and science fiction are to be found in *The Language of Night: Essays on Fantasy and Science Fiction* (1979) and *Dancing at the Edge of the World* (1989). She married historian Charles Le Guin in 1953.

Le Guin speaks of fiction as "world-making" and asserts the primacy of imagination: "what artists do is make a particularly skillful selection of fragments of cosmos, unusually useful and entertaining bits chosen and arranged to give an illusion of coherence and duration amidst the uncontrollable streaming of events. An artist makes the world her world. An artist makes her world the world. For a little while. For as long as it takes to look at or listen to or watch or read the work of art. Like a crystal, the work of art seems to contain the whole, and to imply eternity. And yet all it is is an explorer's sketch-map. A chart of shorelines on a foggy coast."

In "Where Do You Get Your Ideas From?" Le Guin identifies five principal elements at work in the writing process: the patterns of language; patterns of syntax and grammar; patterns of images; patterns of ideas; and patterns of feelings. Of these five, she regards imagery as the central one: "Verbal imagery (such as a simile or a description of a place or an event) is more physical, more bodily, than thinking or feeling, but less physical, more internal, than the actual sounds of the words. Imagery takes place in 'the imagination,' which I take to be the meeting place of the thinking mind with the sensing body. What is imagined isn't physically real, but it *feels as if it were*: the reader sees or hears or feels what goes on in the story, is drawn into it, exists in it, among its images, in the imagination (the reader's? the writer's?) while reading."

In response to the Le Guin issue of *Science Fiction Studies*, No. 7, she complains about the undue atten-

tion given to ideas, at the expense of craft, in discussions of science fiction: "But at times ideas alone are discussed as if the books existed through and for their ideas; and this involves a process of translation with which I am a bit uncomfortable. Somehow the point has been lost in translation. It's as if one should discuss the ideas expressed by St. Paul's cathedral without ever observing what the walls are built of or how the dome is supported. But it wasn't Wren's ideas that kept that dome standing through the bombings of 1940. It was the way he used the stones he built with. This is the artist's, the artisan's view; it is a meaner, humbler view than the philosopher's or ideologue's. But all the same, what makes a novel a novel is something non-intellectual, though not simple; something visceral, not cerebral (sorry, Dr. Plank, there's that stomach again); something that rises from touch, not thought, from sounds, rests, rhythms. . . . It involves ideas, of course, and ideas issue from it, the splendid affirmation of the dome rises above the terror and the rubble and the smoke . . . but all the thinking in the world won't hold that dome up. Theory is not enough. There must be stones."

In the essay "Some Thoughts on Narrative," Le Guin speaks of narrative as "a stratagem of mortality. It is a means, a way of living. It does not seek immortality: it does not seek to triumph over or escape from time (as lyric poetry does). It asserts, affirms, participates in directional time, time experienced, time as meaningful. If the human mind had a temporal spectrum, the nirvana of the physicist or the mystic would be way over in the ultraviolet, and at the opposite end, in the infrared, would be *Wuthering Heights*." To make her point, she puts the matter in slightly different terms: "Narrative is a central function of language. Not, in origin, an artifact of culture, an art, but a fundamental operation of the normal functioning mind in society. To learn to speak is to learn to tell a story."

She sees narrative as our means of making sense of experience, by organizing it, giving it shape and meaning, not unlike the process of interpreting dreams: "Dreamwork is *rationalization*, therefore it is *falsification*: a cover-up. The mind is an endless Watergate. Some primitive 'reality' or 'truth' is forever being distorted, lied about, tidied up." "Dream narrative differs from conscious narrative in using sensory symbol more than language. In dream the sense of the directionality of time is often replaced by spatial metaphor, or may be lowered, or reversed, or vanish. The connections dream makes between events are most often unsatisfactory to the rational intellect and the aesthetic mind. Dreams tend to flout Aristotle's rules of plausibility and muddle up his instructions concerning plot. Yet they are undeniably narrative: they connect events, fit things together in an order or a pattern that makes, to some portion of our mind, sense."

Le Guin quotes George Steiner's statement that "language is the main instrument of man's refusal to accept the world as it is," and then proceeds to identify the subjunctive mood as central to her own work and vision: "In recent centuries we speakers of this lovely language have reduced the English verb almost entirely to the indicative mood. But beneath that specious and arrogant assumption of certainty all the ancient, cloudy, moody powers and options of the subjunctive remain in force. The indicative points its bony finger at primary experiences, at the Things; but it is the subjunctive that joins them, with the bonds of analogy, possibility, probability, contingency, contiguity, memory, desire, fear, and hope: the narrative connection. As J. T. Fraser puts it, moral choice, which is to say human freedom, is made possible 'by language, which permits us to give accounts of possible and impossible worlds in the past, in the future, or in a faraway land.'"

Buffalo Gals, Won't You Come Out Tonight

"You fell out of the sky," the coyote said.

Still curled up tight, lying on her side, her back pressed against the overhanging rock the child watched the coyote with one eye. Over the other eye she kept her hand cupped, its back on the dirt.

"There was a burned place in the sky, up there alongside the rimrock and then you fell out of it," the coyote repeated, patiently, as if the news was getting a bit stale. "Are you hurt?"

She was all right. She was in the plane with Mr. Michaels, and the motor was so loud she couldn't understand what he said even when he shouted, and the way the wind rocked the wings was making her feel sick but it was all right. They were flying to Canyonville. In the plane.

She looked. The coyote was still sitting there. It yawned. It was a big one, in good condition, its coat silvery and thick. The dark tear-line from its long yellow eye was as clearly marked as a tabby cat's.

She sat up, slowly, still holding her right hand pressed to her right eye.

"Did you lose an eye?" the coyote asked, interested.

"I don't know," the child said. She caught her breath and shivered. "I'm cold."

"I'll help you look for it," the coyote said. "Come on! If you move around you won't have to shiver. The sun's up."

Cold lonely brightness lay across the falling land, a hundred miles of sagebrush. The coyote was trotting busily around, nosing under clumps of rabbit-brush and cheat-grass, pawing at a rock. "Aren't you going to look?" it said, suddenly sitting down on its haunches and abandoning the search. "I knew a trick once where I could throw my eyes way up into a tree and see everything from up there, and then whistle, and they'd come back into my head. But that goddam bluejay stole them, and when I whistled nothing came. I had to stick lumps of pine pitch into my head so I could see anything. You could try that. But you've got one eye that's OK, what do you need two for? Are you coming, or are you dying there?"

The child crouched, shivering.

"Well, come if you want to," said the coyote, yawned again, snapped at a flea, stood up, turned, and trotted away among the sparse clumps of rabbit-brush and sage, along the long slope that stretched on down and down into the plain streaked across by long shadows of sagebrush. The slender, grey-yellow animal was hard to keep in sight, vanishing as the child watched.

She struggled to her feet, and without a word, though she kept saying in her mind, "Wait, please wait," she hobbled after the coyote. She could not see it. She kept her hand pressed over the right eyesocket. Seeing with one eye there was no depth; it was like a huge, flat picture. The coyote suddenly sat in the middle of the picture, looking back at her, its mouth open, its eyes narrowed, grinning. Her legs began to steady and her head did not pound so hard, though the deep, black ache was always there. She had nearly caught up to the coyote when it trotted off again. This time she spoke. "Please wait!" she said.

"OK," said the coyote, but it trotted right on. She followed, walking downhill into the flat picture that at each step was deep.

Each step was different underfoot; each sage bush was different, and all the same. Following the coyote she came out from the shadow of the rimrock cliffs, and the sun at eyelevel dazzled her left eye. Its bright warmth soaked into her muscles and bones at once. The air, that all night had been so hard to breathe, came sweet and easy.

The sage bushes were pulling in their shadows and the sun was hot on the child's back when she followed the coyote along the rim of a gully. After a while the coyote slanted down the undercut slope and the child scrambled after, through scrub willows to the thin creek in its wide sandbed. Both drank.

The coyote crossed the creek, not with a careless charge and splashing like a dog, but singlefoot and quiet like a cat; always it carried its tail low. The child hesitated, knowing that wet shoes make blistered feet, and then waded across in as few steps as possible. Her right arm ached with the effort of holding her hand up over her eye. "I need a bandage," she said to the coyote. It cocked its head and said nothing. It stretched out its forelegs and lay watching the water, resting but alert. The child sat down nearby on the hot sand and tried to move her right hand. It was glued to the skin around her eye by dried blood. At the little tearing-away pain, she whimpered; though it was a small pain it frightened her. The coyote came over close and poked its long snout into her face. Its strong, sharp smell was in her nostrils. It began to lick the awful, aching blindness, cleaning and cleaning with its curled, precise, strong, wet tongue, until the child was able to cry a little with relief, being comforted. Her head was bent close to the grey-yellow ribs, and she saw the hard nipples, the whitish belly-fur. She put her arm around the she-coyote, stroking the harsh coat over back and ribs.

"OK," the coyote said, "let's go!" And set off without a backward glance. The child scrambled to her feet and followed. "Where are we going?" she said, and the coyote, trotting on down along the creek answered, "On down along the creek . . ."

There must have been a while she was asleep while she walked, because she felt like she was waking up, but she was walking along, only in a different place. She didn't know how she knew it was different. They were still following the creek though the gully was flattened out to nothing much, and there was still sagebrush range as far as the eye could see. The eye—the good one—felt rested. The other one still ached, but not so sharply, and there was no use thinking about it. But where was the coyote?

She stopped. The pit of cold into which the plane had fallen re-opened and she fell. She stood falling, a thin whimper making itself in her throat.

"Over here!"

The child turned. She saw a coyote gnawing at the half-dried-up carcass of a crow, black feathers sticking to the black lips and narrow jaw.

She saw a tawny-skinned woman kneeling by a campfire, sprinkling something into a conical pot. She heard the water boiling in the pot, though it was propped between rocks, off the fire. The woman's hair was yellow and grey, bound back with a string. Her feet were bare. The upturned soles looked as dark and hard as shoe soles, but the arch of the foot was high, and the toes made two neat curving rows. She wore bluejeans and an old white shirt. She looked over at the girl. "Come on, eat crow!" she said. The child slowly came toward the woman and the fire, and squatted down. She had stopped falling and felt very light and empty; and her tongue was like a piece of wood stuck in her mouth.

Coyote was now blowing into the pot or basket or whatever it was. She reached into it with two fingers, and pulled her hand away shaking it and shouting, "Ow! Shit! Why don't I ever have any spoons?" She broke off a dead twig of sagebrush, dipped it into the pot, and licked it. "Oh, boy," she said. "Come on!"

The child moved a little closer, broke off a twig, dipped. Lumpy pinkish mush clung to the twig. She licked. The taste was rich and delicate.

"What is it?" she asked after a long time of dipping and licking.

"Food. Dried salmon mush," Coyote said. "It's cooling down." She stuck two fingers into the mush again, this time getting a good load, which she ate very neatly. The child, when she tried, got mush all over her chin. It was like chopsticks, it took practice. She practiced. They ate turn and turn until nothing was left in the pot but three rocks. The child did not ask why there were rocks in the mushpot. They licked the rocks clean. Coyote licked out the inside of the pot-basket, rinsed it once in the creek and put it onto her head. It fit nicely, making a conical hat. She pulled off her bluejeans. "Piss on the fire!" she cried, and did so, standing straddling it. "Ah, steam between the legs!" she said. The child, embarrassed, thought she was supposed to do the same thing, but did not want to, and did not. Bare-assed, Coyote danced around the dampened fire, kicking her long thin legs out and singing,

"Buffalo gals, won't you come out tonight,
Come out tonight, come out tonight,
Buffalo gals, won't you come out tonight,
And dance by the light of the moon?"

She pulled her jeans back on. The child was burying the remains of the fire in creek-sand, heaping it over, seriously, wanting to do right. Coyote watched her.

"Is that you?" she said. "A Buffalo Gal? What happened to the rest of you?"

"The rest of me?" The child looked at herself, alarmed.

"All your people."

"Oh. Well, Mom took Bobbie, he's my little brother, away with Uncle Norm. He isn't really my uncle, or anything. So Mr. Michaels was going there anyway so he was going to fly me over to my real father, in Canyonville. Linda, my step-mother, you know, she said it was OK for the summer anyhow if I was there, and then we could see. But the plane."

In the silence the girl's face became dark red, then greyish white. Coyote watched, fascinated. "Oh," the girl said, "Oh—Oh—Mr. Michaels—he must be— Did the—"

"Come on!" said Coyote, and set off walking.

The child cried, "I ought to go back—"

"What for?" said Coyote. She stopped to look round at the child, then went on faster. "Come on, Gal!" She said it as a name; maybe it was the child's name, Myra, as spoken by Coyote. The child, confused and despairing, protested again, but followed her. "Where are we going? Where *are* we?"

"This is my country," Coyote answered, with dignity, making a long, slow ges-ture all round the vast horizon. "I made it. Every goddam sage bush."

And they went on. Coyote's gait was easy, even a little shambling, but she covered the ground; the child struggled not to drop behind. Shadows were begin-ning to pull themselves out again from under the rocks and shrubs. Leaving the creek, they went up a long, low, uneven slope that ended away off against the sky in rimrock. Dark trees stood one here, another way over there; what people called a juniper forest, a desert forest, one with a lot more between the trees than trees. Each juniper they passed smelled sharply, cat-pee smell the kids at school called it, but the child liked it; it seemed to go into her mind and wake her up. She picked off a juniper berry and held it in her mouth, but after a while spat it out. The aching was coming back in huge black waves, and she kept stumbling. She found that she was sitting down on the ground. When she tried to get up her legs shook and would not go under her. She felt foolish and frightened, and began to cry.

"We're home!" Coyote called from way on up the hill.

The child looked with her one weeping eye, and saw sagebrush, juniper, cheat-grass, rimrock. She heard a coyote yip far off in the dry twilight.

She saw a little town up under the rimrock board houses, shacks, all unpainted. She heard Coyote call again, "Come on, pup! Come on, Gal, we're home!" She could not get up, so she tried to go on all fours, the long way up the slope to the houses under the rimrock. Long before she got there, several people came to meet her. They were all children, she thought at first, and then began to understand that most of them were grown people, but all were very short; they were broad-bodied, fat, with fine, delicate hands and feet. Their eyes were bright. Some of the women helped her stand up and walk, coaxing her, "It isn't much farther, you're doing fine." In the late dusk lights shone yellow-bright through doorways and through unchinked cracks between boards. Woodsmoke hung sweet in the quiet air. The

short people talked and laughed all the time, softly. "Where's she going to stay?"—
"Put her in with Robin, they're all asleep already!"—"Oh, she can stay with us."

The child asked hoarsely, "Where's Coyote?"

"Out hunting," the short people said.

A deeper voice spoke: "Somebody new has come into town?"

"Yes, a new person," one of the short men answered.

Among these people the deep-voiced man bulked impressive; he was broad
and tall, with powerful hands, a big head, a short neck. They made way for him
respectfully. He moved very quietly, respectful of them also. His eyes when he
stared down at the child were amazing. When he blinked, it was like the passing
of a hand before a candle-flame.

"It's only an owlet," he said. "What have you let happen to your eye, new person?"

"I was—We were flying—"

"You're too young to fly," the big man said in his deep, soft voice. "Who
brought you here?"

"Coyote."

And one of the short people confirmed: "She came here with Coyote, Young
Owl."

"Then maybe she should stay in Coyote's house tonight," the big man said.

"It's all bones and lonely in there," said a short woman with fat cheeks and a
striped shirt. "She can come with us."

That seemed to decide it. The fat-cheeked woman patted the child's arm and
took her past several shacks and shanties to a low, windowless house. The doorway was so low even the child had to duck down to enter. There were a lot of
people inside, some already there and some crowding in after the fat-cheeked
woman. Several babies were fast asleep in cradle-boxes in corners. There was a
good fire, and a good smell, like toasted sesame seeds. The child was given food,
and ate a little, but her head swam and the blackness in her right eye kept coming
across her left eye so she could not see at all for a while. Nobody asked her name
or told her what to call them. She heard the children call the fat-cheeked woman
Chipmunk. She got up courage finally to say, "Is there somewhere I can go to
sleep, Mrs. Chipmunk?"

"Sure, come on," one of the daughters said, "in here," and took the child into a
back room, not completely partitioned off from the crowded front room, but dark
and uncrowded. Big shelves with mattresses and blankets lined the walls. "Crawl
in!" said Chipmunk's daughter, patting the child's arm in the comforting way they
had. The child climbed onto a shelf, under a blanket. She laid down her head.
She thought, "I didn't brush my teeth."

II

She woke; she slept again. In Chipmunk's sleeping room it was always stuffy,
warm, and half-dark day and night. People came in and slept and got up and left,
night and day. She dozed and slept, got down to drink from the bucket and dipper
in the front room, and went back to sleep and doze.

She was sitting up on the shelf, her feet dangling, not feeling bad any more, but dreamy, weak. She felt in her jeans pockets. In the left front one was a pocket comb and a bubblegum wrapper, in the right front, two dollar bills and a quarter and a dime.

Chipmunk and another woman, a very pretty dark-eyed plump one, came in. "So you woke up for your dance!" Chipmunk greeted her, laughing, and sat down by her with an arm around her.

"Jay's giving you a dance," the dark woman said. "He's going to make you all right. Let's get you all ready!"

There was a spring up under the rimrock that flattened out into a pool with slimy, reedy shores. A flock of noisy children splashing in it ran off and left the child and the two women to bathe. The water was warm on the surface, cold down on the feet and legs. All naked, the two soft-voiced laughing women, their round bellies and breasts, broad hips and buttocks gleaming warm in the late afternoon light, sluiced the child down, washed and stroked her limbs and hands and hair, cleaned around the cheekbone and eyebrow of her right eye with infinite softness, admired her, sudsed her, rinsed her, splashed her out of the water, dried her off, dried each other off, got dressed, dressed her, braided her hair, braided each other's hair, tied feathers on the braid-ends, admired her and each other again, and brought her back down into the little straggling town and to a kind of playing field or dirt parking lot in among the houses. There were no streets, just paths and dirt, no lawns and gardens, just sagebrush and dirt. Quite a few people were gathering or wandering around the open place, looking dressed up, wearing colorful shirts, print dresses, strings of beads, earrings. "Hey there, Chipmunk, Whitefoot!" they greeted the women.

A man in new jeans, with a bright blue velveteen vest over a clean, faded blue work shirt, came forward to meet them, very handsome, tense, and important. "All right, Gal!" he said in a harsh, loud voice, which startled among all these soft-speaking people. "We're going to get that eye fixed right up tonight! You just sit down here and don't worry about a thing." He took her wrist, gently despite his bossy, brassy manner, and led her to a woven mat that lay on the dirt near the middle of the open place. There, feeling very foolish, she had to sit down, and was told to stay still. She soon got over feeling that everybody was looking at her, since nobody paid her more attention than a checking glance or, from Chipmunk or Whitefoot and their families, a reassuring wink. Every now and then Jay rushed over to her and said something like, "Going to be as good as new!" and went off again to organize people, waving his long blue arms and shouting.

Coming up the hill to the open place, a lean, loose, tawny figure—and the child started to jump up, remembered she was to sit still, and sat still, calling out softly, "Coyote! Coyote!"

Coyote came lounging by. She grinned. She stood looking down at the child. "Don't let that Bluejay fuck you up, Gal," she said, and lounged on.

The child's gaze followed her, yearning.

People were sitting down now over on one side of the open place, making an uneven half-circle that kept getting added to at the ends until there was nearly a circle of people sitting on the dirt around the child, ten or fifteen paces from her. All the people wore the kind of clothes the child was used to, jeans and jeans-jackets, shirts, vests, cotton dresses, but they were all barefoot; and she thought they were more beautiful than the people she knew, each in a different way, as if each one had invented beauty. Yet some of them were also very strange: thin black shining people with whispery voices, a long-legged woman with eyes like jewels. The big man called Young Owl was there, sleepy-looking and dignified, like Judge McCown who owned a sixty-thousand acre ranch; and beside him was a woman the child thought might be his sister, for like him she had a hook nose and big, strong hands; but she was lean and dark and there was a crazy look in her fierce eyes. Yellow eyes, but round, not long and slanted like Coyote's. There was Coyote sitting yawning, scratching her armpit, bored. Now somebody was entering the circle: a man, wearing only a kind of kilt and a cloak painted or beaded with diamond shapes, dancing to the rhythm of the rattle he carried and shook with a buzzing fast beat. His limbs and body were thick yet supple, his movements smooth and pouring. The child kept her gaze on him as he danced past her, around her, past again. The rattle in his hand shook almost too fast to see, in the other hand was something thin and sharp. People were singing around the circle now, a few notes repeated in time to the rattle, soft and tuneless. It was exciting and boring, strange and familiar. The Rattler wove his dancing closer and closer to her, darting at her. The first time she flinched away, frightened by the lunging movement and by his flat, cold face with narrow eyes, but after that she sat still, knowing her part. The dancing went on, the singing went on, till they carried her past boredom into a floating that could go on forever.

Jay had come strutting into the circle, and was standing beside her. He couldn't sing, but he called out, "Hey! Hey! Hey! Hey!" in his big, harsh voice, and everybody answered from all round, and the echo came down from the rim-rock on the second beat. Jay was holding up a stick with a ball on it in one hand, and something like a marble in the other. The stick was a pipe: he got smoke into his mouth from it and blew it in four directions and up and down and then over the marble, a puff each time. Then the rattle stopped suddenly, and everything was silent for several breaths. Jay squatted down and looked intently into the child's face, his head cocked to one side. He reached forward, muttering something in time to the rattle and the singing that had started up again louder than before; he touched the child's right eye in the black center of the pain. She flinched and endured. His touch was not gentle. She saw the marble, a dull yellow ball like beeswax, in his hand; then she shut her seeing eye and set her teeth.

"There!" Jay shouted. "Open up. Come on! Let's see!"

Her jaw clenched like a vise, she opened both eyes. The lid of the right one stuck and dragged with such a searing white pain that she nearly threw up as she sat there in the middle of everybody watching.

"Hey, can you see? How's it work? It looks great!" Jay was shaking her arm, railing at her. "How's it feel? Is it working?"

What she saw was confused, hazy, yellowish. She began to discover, as everybody came crowding around peering at her, smiling, stroking and patting her arms and shoulders, that if she shut the hurting eye and looked with the other, everything was clear and flat; if she used them both, things were blurry and yellowish, but deep.

There, right close, was Coyote's long nose and narrow eyes and grin. "What is it, Jay?" she was asking, peering at the new eye. "One of mine you stole that time?"

"It's pine pitch," Jay shouted furiously. "You think I'd use some stupid second-hand coyote eye? I'm a doctor!"

"Ooooh, ooooh, a doctor," Coyote said. "Boy, that is one ugly eye. Why didn't you ask Rabbit for a rabbit-dropping? That eye looks like shit." She put her lean face yet closer, till the child thought she was going to kiss her; instead, the thin, firm tongue once more licked accurate across the pain, cooling, clearing. When the child opened both eyes again the world looked pretty good.

"It works fine," she said.

"Hey!" Jay yelled. "She says it works fine! It works fine, she says so! I told you! What'd I tell you?" He went off waving his arms and yelling. Coyote had disappeared. Everybody was wandering off.

The child stood up, stiff from long sitting. It was nearly dark; only the long west held a great depth of pale radiance. Eastward the plains ran down into night.

Lights were on in some of the shanties. Off at the edge of town somebody was playing a creaky fiddle, a lonesome chirping tune.

A person came beside her and spoke quietly: "Where will you stay?"

"I don't know," the child said. She was feeling extremely hungry. "Can I stay with Coyote?"

"She isn't home much," the soft-voiced woman said. "You were staying with Chipmunk, weren't you? Or there's Rabbit, or Jackrabbit, they have families . . ."

"Do you have a family?" the girl asked, looking at the delicate, soft-eyed woman.

"Two fawns," the woman answered, smiling. "But I just came into town for the dance."

"I'd really like to stay with Coyote," the child said after a little pause, timid, but obstinate.

"OK, that's fine. Her house is over here." Doe walked along beside the child to a ramshackle cabin on the high edge of town. No light shone from inside. A lot of junk was scattered around the front. There was no step up to the half-open door. Over the door a battered pine board, nailed up crooked, said BIDE-A-WEE.

"Hey, Coyote? Visitors," Doe said. Nothing happened.

Doe pushed the door farther open and peered in. "She's out hunting, I guess. I better be getting back to the fawns. You going to be OK? Anybody else here will give you something to eat—you know . . . OK?"

"Yeah. I'm fine. Thank you," the child said.

She watched Doe walk away through the clear twilight, a severely elegant walk, small steps; like a woman in high heels, quick precise, very light.

Inside Bide-A-Wee it was too dark to see anything and so cluttered that she fell over something at every step. She could not figure out where or how to light a fire. There was something that felt like a bed, but when she lay down on it, it felt more like a dirty-clothes pile, and smelt like one. Things bit her legs, arms, neck, and back. She was terribly hungry. By smell she found her way to what had to be a dead fish hanging from the ceiling in one corner. By feel she broke off a greasy flake and tasted it. It was smoked dried salmon. She ate one succulent piece after another until she was satisfied, and licked her fingers clean. Near the open door starlight shone on water in a pot of some kind; the child smelled it cautiously, tasted it cautiously, and drank just enough to quench her thirst, for it tasted of mud and was warm and stale. Then she went back to the bed of dirty clothes and fleas, and lay down. She could have gone to Chipmunk's house, or other friendly households; she thought of that as she lay forlorn in Coyote's dirty bed. But she did not go. She slapped at fleas until she fell asleep.

Along in the deep night somebody said, "Move over, pup," and was warm beside her.

❖ ❖ ❖

Breakfast, eaten sitting in the sun in the doorway, was dried-salmon-powder mush. Coyote hunted, mornings and evenings, but what they ate was not fresh game but salmon, and dried stuff, and any berries in season. The child did not ask about this. It made sense to her. She was going to ask Coyote why she slept at night and waked in the day like humans, instead of the other way round like coyotes, but when she framed the question in her mind she saw at once that night is when you sleep and day when you're awake; that made sense too. But one question she did ask one hot day when they were lying around slapping fleas.

"I don't understand why you all look like people," she said.

"We are people."

"I mean, people like me, humans."

"Resemblance is in the eye," Coyote said. "How is that lousy eye, by the way?"

"It's fine. But—like you wear clothes—and live in houses—with fires and stuff—"

"That's what you think . . . If that loudmouth Jay hadn't horned in, I could have done a really good job."

The child was quite used to Coyote's disinclination to stick to any one subject, and to her boasting. Coyote was like a lot of kids she knew, in some respects. Not in others.

"You mean what I'm seeing isn't true? Isn't real—like on TV, or something?"

"No," Coyote said. "Hey, that's a tick on your collar." She reached over, flicked the tick off, picked it up on one finger, bit it, and spat out the bits.

"Yecch!" the child said. "So?"

"So, to me you're basically greyish yellow and run on four legs. To that lot"— she waved disdainfully at the warren of little houses next down the hill—"you hop around twitching your nose all the time. To Hawk, you're an egg or maybe getting pinfeathers. See? It just depends on how you look at things. There are only two kinds of people."

"Humans and animals?"

"No. The kind of people who say, 'There are two kinds of people' and the kind of people who don't." Coyote cracked up, pounding her thigh and yelling with delight at her joke. The child didn't get it, and waited.

"OK," Coyote said. "There's the first people, and then the others. That's the two kinds."

"The first people are—?"

"Us, the animals . . . and things. All the old ones. You know. And you pups, kids, fledglings. All first people."

"And the—others?"

"Them," Coyote said. "You know. The others. The new people. The ones who came." Her fine, hard face had gone serious, rather formidable. She glanced directly, as she seldom did, at the child, a brief gold sharpness. "We were here," she said. "We were always here. We are always here. Where we are is here. But it's their country now. They're running it . . . Shit, even I did better!"

The child pondered and offered a word she had used to hear a good deal: "They're illegal immigrants."

"Illegal!" Coyote said, mocking, sneering. "Illegal is a sick bird. What the fuck's illegal mean? You want a code of justice from a coyote? Grow up, kid!"

"I don't want to."

"You don't want to grow up?"

"I'll be the other kind if I do."

"Yeah. So," Coyote said, and shrugged. "That's life." She got up and went around the house, and the child heard her pissing in the back yard.

A lot of things were hard to take about Coyote as a mother. When her boyfriends came to visit, the child learned to go stay with Chipmunk or the Rabbits for the night, because Coyote and her friend wouldn't even wait to get on the bed but would start doing that right on the floor or even out in the yard. A couple of times Coyote came back late from hunting with a friend, and the child had to lie up against the wall in the same bed and hear and feel them doing that right next to her. It was something like fighting and something like dancing, with a beat to it, and she didn't mind too much except that it made it hard to stay asleep.

Once she woke up and one of Coyote's friends was stroking her stomach in a creepy way. She didn't know what to do, but Coyote woke and realized what he was doing, bit him hard, and kicked him out of bed. He spent the night on the floor, and apologized next morning—"Aw, hell, Ki, I forgot the kid was there, I thought it was you—"

Coyote, unappeased, yelled, "You think I don't got any standards? You think I'd let some coyote rape a kid in my bed?" She kicked him out of the house, and grumbled about him all day. But a while later he spent the night again, and he and Coyote did that three or four times.

Another thing that was embarrassing was the way Coyote peed anywhere, taking her pants down in public. But most people here didn't seem to care. The thing that worried the child most, maybe, was when Coyote did number two anywhere and then turned around and talked to it. That seemed so awful. As if Coyote was—the way she often seemed, but really wasn't—crazy.

The child gathered up all the old dry turds from around the house one day while Coyote was having a nap, and buried them in a sandy place near where she and Bobcat and some of the other people generally went and did and buried their number twos.

Coyote woke up, came lounging out of Bide-A-Wee, rubbing her hands through her thick fair, greyish hair and yawning, looked an around once with those narrow eyes, and said, "Hey! Where are they?" Then she shouted, "Where are you? Where are you?"

And a faint, muffled chorus came from over in the sandy draw, "Mommy! Mommy! We're here!"

Coyote trotted over, squatted down, raked out every turd, and talked with them for a long time. When she came back she said nothing, but the child, red-faced and heart pounding, said, "I'm sorry I did that."

"It's just easier when they're all around close by," Coyote said, washing her hands (despite the filth of her house, she kept herself quite clean, in her own fashion.)

"I kept stepping on them," the child said, trying to justify her deed.

"Poor little shits," said Coyote, practicing dance-steps.

Coyote, the child said timidly. "Did you ever have any children? I mean real pups?"

"Did I? Did I have children? Litters! That one that tried feeling you up, you know? that was my son. Pick of the litter . . . Listen, Gal. Have daughters. When you have anything have daughters. At least they clear out."

III

The child thought of herself as Gal, but also sometimes as Myra. So far as she knew, she was the only person in town who had two names. She had to think about that, and about what Coyote had said about the two kinds of people; she had to think about where she belonged. Some persons in town made it clear that as far as they were concerned she didn't and never would belong there. Hawk's furious stare burned through her; the Skunk children made audible remarks about what she smelled like. And though Whitefoot and Chipmunk and their families were kind, it was the generosity of big families, where one more or less simply doesn't count. If one of them, or Cottontail, or Jackrabbit, had come upon her in the desert lying lost and half-blind, would they have stayed with her, like Coyote? That was Coyote's craziness, what they called her craziness. She wasn't afraid. She went between the two kinds of people, she crossed over. Buck and Doe and their beautiful children weren't really afraid, because they lived so constantly in danger. The Rattler wasn't afraid, because he was so dangerous. And yet maybe he was afraid of her, for he never spoke, and never came close to her. None of them treated her the way Coyote did. Even among the children, her only constant play-mate was one younger than herself, a preposterous and fearless little boy called Horned Toad Child. They dug and built together, out among the sagebrush, and played at hunting and gathering and keeping house and holding dances, all the great games. A pale, squatty child with fringed eyebrows, he was a self-contained but loyal friend; and he knew a good deal for his age.

"There isn't anybody else like me here," she said, as they sat by the pool in the morning sunlight.

"There isn't anybody much like me anywhere," said Horned Toad Child.

"Well, you know what I mean."

"Yeah . . . There used to be people like you around, I guess."

"What were they called?"

"Oh—people. Like everybody . . . "

"But where do my people live? They have towns. I used to live in one. I don't know where they are, is all. I ought to find out. I don't know where my mother is now, but my daddy's in Canyonville. I was going there when."

"Ask Horse," said Horned Toad Child, sagaciously. He had moved away from the water, which he did not like and never drank and was plaiting rushes.

"I don't know Horse."

"He hangs around the butte down there a lot of the time. He's waiting till his uncle gets old and he can kick him out and be the big honcho. The old man and the women don't want him around till then. Horses are weird. Anyway, he's the one to ask. He gets around a lot. And his people came here with the new people, that's what they say, anyhow."

Illegal immigrants, the girl thought. She took Horned Toad's advice, and one long day when Coyote was gone on one of her unannounced and unexplained trips, she took a pouchful of dried salmon and salmonberries and went off alone to the flat-topped butte miles away in the southwest.

There was a beautiful spring at the foot of the butte, and a trail to it with a lot of footprints on it. She waited there under willows by the clear pool, and after a while Horse came running, splendid, with copper-red skin and long, strong legs, deep chest, dark eyes, his black hair whipping his back as he ran. He stopped, not at all winded, and gave a snort as he looked at her. "Who are you?"

Nobody in town asked that—ever. She saw it was true: Horse had come here with her people, people who had to ask each other who they were.

"I live with Coyote," she said, cautiously.

"Oh, sure, I heard about you," Horse said. He knelt to drink from the pool, long deep drafts, his hands plunged in the cool water. When he had drunk he wiped his mouth, sat back on his heels, and announced, "I'm going to be king."

"King of the Horses?"

"Right! Pretty soon now. I could lick the old man already, but I can wait. Let him have his day," said Horse, vainglorious, magnanimous. The child gazed at him, in love already, forever.

"I can comb your hair, if you like," she said.

"Great!" said Horse, and sat still while she stood behind him, tugging her pocket comb through his coarse, black shining yard-long hair. It took a long time to get it smooth. She tied it in a massive ponytail with willowbark when she was done. Horse bent over the pool to admire himself. "That's great," he said. "That's really beautiful!"

"Do you ever go . . . where the other people are?" she asked in a low voice.

He did not reply for long enough that she thought he wasn't going to; then he said, "You mean the metal places, the glass places? The holes? I go around them. There are all the walls now. There didn't used to be so many. Grandmother said there didn't used to be any walls. Do you know Grandmother?" he asked naively, looking at her with his great, dark eyes.

"Your grandmother?"

"Well, yes—Grandmother—You know. Who makes the web. Well, anyhow. I know there's some of my people, horses, there. I've seen them across the walls. They act really crazy. You know, we brought the new people here. They couldn't have got here without us, they only have two legs, and they have those metal shells. I can tell you that whole story. The King has to know the stories."

"I like stories a lot."

"It takes three nights to tell it. What do you want to know about them?"

"I was thinking that maybe I ought to go there. Where they are."

"It's dangerous. Really dangerous. You can't go through—they'd catch you."

"I'd just like to know the way."

"I know the way," Horse said, sounding for the first time entirely adult and reliable; she knew he did know the way. "It's a long run for a colt." He looked at her again. I've got a cousin with different-color eyes, he said, looking from her right to her left eye. "One brown and one blue. But she's an Appaloosa."

"Bluejay made the yellow one," the child explained. "I lost my own one. In the . . . when . . . You don't think I could get to those places?"

"Why do you want to?"

"I sort of feel like I have to."

Horse nodded. He got up. She stood still.

"I could take you, I guess," he said.

"Could you? When?"

"Oh, now, I guess. Once I'm King I won't be able to leave, you know. Have to protect the women. And I sure wouldn't let my people get anywhere near those places!" A shudder ran right down his magnificent body, yet he said, with a toss of his head, "They couldn't catch me, of course, but the others can't run like I do . . ."

"How long would it take us?"

Horse thought a while. "Well, the nearest place like that is over by the red rocks. If we left now we'd be back here around tomorrow noon. It's just a little hole."

She did not know what he meant by "a hole," but did not ask.

"You want to go?" Horse said, flipping back his ponytail.

"OK," the girl said, feeling the ground go out from under her.

"Can you run?"

She shook her head. "I walked here, though."

Horse laughed, a large, cheerful laugh. "Come on," he said, and knelt and held his hands back-turned like stirrups for her to mount to his shoulders. "What do they call you?" he teased, rising easily, setting right off at a jogtrot. "Gnat? Fly? Flea?"

"Tick, because I stick!" the child cried, gripping the willowbark tie of the black mane, laughing with delight at being suddenly eight feet tall and travelling across the desert without even trying, like the tumbleweed, as fast as the wind.

❖   ❖   ❖

Moon, a night past full, rose to light the plains for them. Horse jogged easily on and on. Somewhere deep in the night they stopped at a Pygmy Owl camp, ate a little, and rested. Most of the owls were out hunting, but an old lady entertained them at her campfire, telling them tales about the ghost of a cricket, about the great invisible people, tales that the child heard interwoven with her own dreams as she dozed and half-woke and dozed again. Then Horse put her up on his shoulders and on they went at a tireless slow lope. Moon went down behind them, and before them the sky paled into rose and gold. The soft nightwind was gone; the air was sharp, cold, still. On it, in it, there was a faint, sour smell of burning. The child felt Horse's gait change, grow tighter, uneasy.

"Hey, Prince!"

A small, slightly scolding voice: the child knew it, and placed it as soon as she saw the person sitting by a juniper tree, neatly dressed, wearing an old black cap.

"Hey, Chickadee!" Horse said, coming round and stopping. The child had observed, back in Coyote's town, that everybody treated Chickadee with respect. She didn't see why. Chickadee seemed an ordinary person, busy and talkative like most of the small birds, nothing like so endearing as Quail or so impressive as Hawk or Great Owl.

"You're going on that way?" Chickadee asked Horse.

"The little one wants to see if her people are living there," Horse said, surprising the child. Was that what she wanted?

Chickadee looked disapproving, as she often did. She whistled a few notes thoughtfully, another of her habits, and then got up. "I'll come along."

"That's great," Horse said, thankfully.

"I'll scout," Chickadee said, and off she went, surprisingly fast, ahead of them, while Horse took up his steady long lope.

The sour smell was stronger in the air.

Chickadee halted, way ahead of them on a slight rise, and stood still. Horse dropped to a walk and then stopped.

"There," he said in a low voice.

The child stared. In the strange light and slight mist before sunrise she could not see clearly, and when she strained and peered she felt as if her left eye were not seeing at all. "What is it?" she whispered.

"One of the holes. Across the wall—see?"

It did seem there was a line, a straight, jerky line drawn across the sagebrush plain, and on the far side of it—nothing? Was it mist? Something moved there— "It's cattle!" she said. Horse stood silent, uneasy. Chickadee was coming back towards them.

"It's a ranch," the child said. "That's a fence. There's a lot of Herefords." The words tasted like iron, like salt in her mouth. The things she named wavered in her sight and faded, leaving nothing—a hole in the world, a burned place like a cigarette burn. "Go closer!" she urged Horse. "I want to see."

And as if he owed her obedience, he went forward, tense but unquestioning.

Chickadee came up to them. "Nobody around," she said in her small, dry voice, "but there's one of those fast turtle things coming."

Horse nodded, but kept going forward.

Gripping his broad shoulders, the child stared into the blank and as if Chickadees words had focused her eyes, she saw again: the scattered whitefaces, a few of them looking up with bluish, rolling eyes—the fences—over the rise a chimneyed house-roof and a high barn—and then in the distance something moving fast, too fast, burning across the ground straight at them at terrible speed. "Run!" she yelled to Horse, "run away! Run!" As if released from bonds he wheeled and ran, flat out, in great reaching strides, away from sunrise, the fiery burning chariot, the smell of acid, iron, death. And Chickadee flew before them like a cinder on the air of dawn.

IV

"Horse?" Coyote said. "That prick? Catfood!"

Coyote had been there when the child got home to Bide-A-Wee, but she clearly hadn't been worrying about where Gal was, and maybe hadn't even noticed she was gone. She was in a vile mood, and took it all wrong when the child tried to tell her where she had been.

"If you're going to do damn fool things, next time do 'em with me, at least I'm an expert," she said, morose, and slouched out the door. The child saw her squatting down, poking an old, white turd with a stick trying to get it to answer some question she kept asking it. The turd lay obstinately silent. Later in the day the child saw two coyote men, a young one and a mangy-looking older one, loitering around near the spring, looking over at Bide-A-Wee. She decided it would be a good night to spend somewhere else.

The thought of the crowded rooms of Chipmunk's house was not attractive. It was going to be a warm night again tonight, and moonlit. Maybe she would sleep outside. If she could feel sure some people wouldn't come around, like the Rattler . . . She was standing indecisive halfway through town when a dry voice said, "Hey, Gal."

"Hey, Chickadee."

The trim, black-capped woman was standing on her doorstep shaking out a rug. She kept her house neat, trim like herself. Having come back across the desert with her the child now knew, though she still could not have said, why Chickadee was a respected person.

"I thought maybe I'd sleep out tonight," the child said, tentative.

"Unhealthy," said Chickadee. "What are nests for?"

"Mom's kind of busy," the child said.

"Tsk!" went Chickadee, and snapped the rug with disapproving vigor. "What about your little friend? At least they're decent people."

"Horny-toad? His parents are so shy . . ."

"Well. Come in and have something to eat, anyhow," said Chickadee.

The child helped her cook dinner. She knew now why there were rocks in the mush-pot.

"Chickadee," she said, "I still don't understand, can I ask you? Mom said it depends who's seeing it, but still, I mean if I see you wearing clothes and everything like humans, then how come you cook this way, in baskets, you know, and there aren't any—any of the things like they have—there where we were with Horse this morning?"

"I don't know," Chickadee said. Her voice indoors was quite soft and pleasant. "I guess we do things the way they always were done. When your people and my people lived together, you know. And together with everything else here. The rocks, you know. The plants and everything." She looked at the basket of willow-bark fernroot, and pitch, at the blackened rocks that were heating in the fire. "You see how it all goes together . . . ?"

"But you have fire—That's different—"

"Ah!" said Chickadee, impatient, "you people! Do you think you invented the sun?"

She took up the wooden tongs, plopped the heated rocks into the water-filled basket with a terrific hiss and steam and loud bubblings. The child sprinkled in the pounded seeds, and stirred.

Chickadee brought out a basket of fine blackberries. They sat on the newly-shaken-out rug, and ate. The child's two-finger scoop technique with mush was now highly refined.

"Maybe I didn't cause the world," Chickadee said, "but I'm a better cook than Coyote."

The child nodded, stuffing.

"I don't know why I made Horse go there," she said, after she had stuffed. "I got just as scared as him when I saw it. But now I feel again like I have to go back there. But I want to stay here. With my, with Coyote. I don't understand."

"When we lived together it was all one place," Chickadee said in her slow, soft home-voice. "But now the others, the new people, they live apart. And their places are so heavy. They weigh down on our place, they press on it, draw it, suck it, eat it, eat holes in it, crowd it out . . . Maybe after a while longer there'll only be one place again, their place. And none of us here. I knew Bison, out over the mountains. I knew Antelope right here. I knew Grizzly and Greywolf, up west there. Gone. All gone. And the salmon you eat at Coyote's house, those are the dream salmon, those are the true food; but in the rivers, how many salmon now? The rivers that were red with them in spring? Who dances, now, when the First Salmon offers himself? Who dances by the river? Oh, you should ask Coyote about all this. She knows more than I do! But she forgets . . . She's hopeless, worse than Raven, she has to piss on every post, she's a terrible housekeeper . . ." Chickadee's voice had sharpened. She whistled a note or two, and said no more.

After a while the child asked very softly, "Who is Grandmother?"

"Grandmother," Chickadee said. She looked at the child, and ate several blackberries thoughtfully. She stroked the rug they sat on.

"If I built the fire on the rug, it would burn a hole in it," she said. "Right? So we build the fire on sand, on dirt . . . Things are woven together. So we call the weaver the Grandmother." She whistled four notes, looking up the smokehole. "After all," she added, "maybe all this place, the other places too, maybe they're all only one side of the weaving. I don't know. I can only look with one eye at a time, how can I tell how deep it goes?"

Lying that night rolled up in a blanket in Chickadee's back yard, the child heard the wind soughing and storming in the cottonwoods down in the draw, and then slept deeply, weary from the long night before. Just at sunrise she woke. The eastern mountains were a cloudy dark red as if the level light shone through them as through a hand held before the fire. In the tobacco patch—the only farming anybody in this town did was to raise a little wild tobacco—Lizard and Beetle were singing some kind of growing song or blessing song, soft and desultory, huh-huh-huh-huh, huh-huh-huh-huh, and as she lay warm-curled on the ground the song made her feel rooted in the ground, cradled on it and in it, so where her fingers ended and the dirt began she did not know, as if she were dead, but she was wholly alive, she was the earth's life. She got up dancing, left the blanket folded neatly on Chickadee's neat and already empty bed, and danced up the hill to Bide-A-Wee. At the half-open door she sang,

> "Danced with a gal with a hole in her stocking
> And her knees kept a knocking and her toes kept a rocking,
> Danced with a gal with a hole in her stocking,
> Danced by the light of the moon!"

Coyote emerged, tousled and lurching, and eyed her narrowly. "Sheeeoot," she said. She sucked her teeth and then went to splash water all over her head from the gourd by the door. She shook her head and the water-drops flew. "Let's get out of here," she said. "I have had it. I don't know what got into me. If I'm pregnant again, at my age, oh, shit. Let's get out of town. I need a change of air."

In the foggy dark of the house, the child could see at least two coyote men sprawled snoring away on the bed and floor. Coyote walked over to the old white turd and kicked it. "Why didn't you stop me?" she shouted.

"I *told* you," the turd muttered sulkily.

"Dumb shit," Coyote said. "Come on, Gal. Let's go. Where to?" She didn't wait for an answer. "I know. Come on!"

And she set off through town at that lazy-looking rangy walk that was so hard to keep up with. But the child was full of pep, and came dancing, so that Coyote began dancing too, skipping and pirouetting and fooling around all the way down the long slope to the level plains. There she slanted their way off north-eastward. Horse Butte was at their backs, getting smaller in the distance.

Along near noon the child said, "I didn't bring anything to eat."

"Something will turn up," Coyote said, "sure to." And pretty soon she turned aside, going straight to a tiny grey shack hidden by a couple of half-dead junipers and a stand of rabbit-brush. The place smelled terrible. A sign on the door said: FOX. PRIVATE. NO TRESPASSING!—but Coyote pushed it open, and trotted right back out with half a small smoked salmon. "Nobody home but us chickens," she said, grinning sweetly.

"Isn't that stealing?" the child asked, worried.

"Yes," Coyote answered, trotting on.

They ate the fox-scented salmon by a dried-up creek, slept a while, and went on.

Before long the child smelled the sour burning smell, and stopped. It was as if a huge, heavy hand had begun pushing her chest, pushing her away, and yet at the same time as if she had stepped into a strong current that drew her forward, helpless.

"Hey, getting close!" Coyote said, and stopped to piss by a juniper stump.

"Close to what?"

"Their town. See?" She pointed to a pair of sage-spotted hills. Between them was an area of greyish blank.

"I don't want to go there."

"We won't go all the way in. No way! We'll just get a little closer and look. It's fun," Coyote said, putting her head on one side, coaxing. "They do all these weird things in the air."

The child hung back.

Coyote became business-like, responsible. "We're going to be very careful," she announced. "And look out for big dogs, OK? Little dogs I can handle. Make a good lunch. Big dogs, it goes the other way. Right? Let's go, then."

Seemingly as casual and lounging as ever, but with a tense alertness in the carriage of her head and the yellow glance of her eyes, Coyote led off again, not looking back; and the child followed.

All around them the pressures increased. It was if the air itself was pressing on them, as if time was going too fast, too hard, not flowing but pounding, pounding, pounding, faster and harder till it buzzed like Rattler's rattle. Hurry, you have to hurry! everything said, there isn't time! everything said. Things rushed past screaming and shuddering. Things turned, flashed, roared, stank, vanished. There was a boy—he came into focus all at once, but not on the ground: he was going along a couple of inches above the ground, moving very fast, bending his legs from side to side in a kind of frenzied swaying dance, and was gone. Twenty children sat in rows in the air all singing shrilly and then the walls closed over them. A basket no a pot no a can, a garbage can, full of salmon smelling wonderful, no full of stinking deer-hides and rotten cabbage stalks, keep out of it, Coyote! Where was she?

"Mom!" the child called. "Mother!"—standing a moment at the end of an ordinary small-town street near the gas station, and the next moment in a terror of blanknesses, invisible walls, terrible smells and pressures and the overwhelming rush of Time straight forward rolling her helpless as a twig in the race above a waterfall. She clung, held on trying not to fall—"Mother!"

Coyote was over by the big basket of salmon, approaching it, wary, but out in the open, in the full sunlight, in the full current. And a boy and a man borne by the same current were coming down the long, sage-spotted hill behind the gas station, each with a gun, red hats, hunters, it was killing season. "Hell, will you look at that damn coyote in broad daylight big as my wife's ass," the man said, and cocked aimed shot all as Myra screamed and ran against the enormous drowning torrent. Coyote fled past her yelling, "Get out of here!" She turned and was borne away.

Far out of sight of that place, in a little draw among low hills, they sat and breathed air in searing gasps until after a long time it came easy again.

"Mom, that was *stupid*," the child said furiously.

"Sure was," Coyote said. "But did you see all that food!"

"I'm not hungry," the child said sullenly. "Not till we get all the way away from here."

"But they're your folks," Coyote said. "All yours. Your kith and kin and cousins and kind. Bang! Pow! There's Coyote! Bang! There's my wife's ass! Pow! There's anything—BOOOOM! Blow it away, man! BOOOOOOOM!"

"I want to go home," the child said.

"Not yet," said Coyote. "I got to take a shit." She did so, then turned to the fresh turd, leaning over it. "It says I have to stay," she reported, smiling.

"It didn't say anything! I was listening!"

"You know how to understand? You hear everything Miss Big Ears? Hears all— Sees all with her crummy gummy eye—"

"You have pine-pitch eyes too! You told me so!"

"That's a story," Coyote snarled. "You don't even know a story when you hear one! Look, do what you like, it's a free country. I'm hanging around here tonight. I like the action." She sat down and began patting her hands on the dirt in a soft four-four rhythm and singing under her breath, one of the endless tuneless songs that kept time from running too fast, that wove the roots of trees and bushes and ferns and grass in the web that held the stream in the streambed and the rock in the rock's place and the earth together. And the child lay listening.

"I love you," she said.

Coyote went on singing.

Sun went down the last slope of the west and left a pale green clarity over the desert hills.

Coyote had stopped singing. She sniffed. "Hey," she said. "Dinner." She got up and moseyed along the little draw. "Yeah," she called back softly. "Come on!"

Stiffly, for the fear-crystals had not yet melted out of her joints, the child got up and went to Coyote. Off to one side along the hill was one of the lines, a fence. She didn't look at it. It was OK. They were outside it.

"Look at that!"

A smoked salmon, a whole chinook, lay on a little cedar-bark mat. "An offering! Well, I'll be damned!" Coyote was so impressed she didn't even swear. "I haven't seen one of these for years! I thought they'd forgotten!"

"Offering to who?"

"Me! Who else? Boy, *look* at that!"

The child looked dubiously at the salmon.

"It smells funny."

"How funny?"

"Like burned."

"It's smoked, stupid! Come on."

"I'm not hungry."

"OK. It's not your salmon anyhow. It's mine. My offering, for me. Hey, you people! You people over there! Coyote thanks you! Keep it up like this and maybe I'll do some good things for you too!"

"Don't, don't yell, Mom! They're not that far away—"

"They're all my people," said Coyote with a great gesture, and then sat down cross-legged, broke off a big piece of salmon, and ate.

Evening Star burned like a deep, bright pool of water in the clear sky. Down over the twin hills was a dim suffusion of light, like a fog. The child looked away from it, back at the star.

"Oh," Coyote said. "Oh, shit."

"What's wrong?"

"That wasn't so smart, eating that," Coyote said, and then held herself and began to shiver, to scream, to choke—her eyes rolled up, her long arms and legs flew out jerking and dancing, foam spurted out between her clenched teeth. Her body arched tremendously backwards, and the child, trying to hold her, was thrown violently off by the spasms of her limbs. The child scrambled back and held the body as it spasmed again, twitched, quivered, went still.

By moonrise Coyote was cold. Till then there had been so much warmth under the tawny coat that the child kept thinking maybe she was alive, maybe if she just kept holding her, keeping her warm, she would recover, she would be all right. She held her close, not looking at the black lips drawn back from the teeth, the white balls of the eyes. But when the cold came through the fur as the presence of death, the child let the slight, stiff corpse lie down on the dirt.

She went nearby and dug a hole in the stony sand of the draw, a shallow pit. Coyote's people did not bury their dead, she knew that. But her people did. She carried the small corpse to the pit, laid it down, and covered it with her blue and white bandanna. It was not large enough; the four stiff paws stuck out. The child heaped the body over with sand and rocks and a scurf of sagebrush and tumbleweed held down with more rocks. She also went to where the salmon had lain on the cedar mat, and finding the carcass of a lamb heaped dirt and rocks over the poisoned thing. Then she stood up and walked away without looking back.

At the top of the hill she stood and looked across the draw toward the misty glow of the lights of the town lying in the pass between the twin hills.

"I hope you all die in pain," she said aloud. She turned away and walked down into the desert.

V

It was Chickadee who met her, on the second evening, north of Horse Butte.

"I didn't cry," the child said.

"None of us do," said Chickadee. "Come with me this way now. Come into Grandmother's house."

It was underground, but very large, dark and large, and the Grandmother was there at the center, at her loom. She was making a rug or blanket of the hills and the black rain and the white rain, weaving in the lightning. As they spoke she wove.

"Hello, Chickadee. Hello, New Person."

"Grandmother," Chickadee greeted her.

The child said, "I'm not one of them."

Grandmother's eyes were small and dim. She smiled and wove. The shuttle thrummed through the warp.

"Old Person, then," said Grandmother. "You'd better go back there now, Granddaughter. That's where you live."

"I lived with Coyote. She's dead. They killed her."

"Oh, don't worry about Coyote!" Grandmother said, with a little huff of laughter. "She gets killed all the time."

The child stood still. She saw the endless weaving.

"Then I—Could I go back home—to her house—?"

"I don't think it would work," Grandmother said. "Do you, Chickadee?"

Chickadee shook her head once, silent.

"It would be dark there now, and empty, and fleas . . . You got outside your people's time, into our place; but I think that Coyote was taking you back, see. Her way. If you go back now, you can still live with them. Isn't your father there?"

The child nodded.

"They've been looking for you."

"They have?"

"Oh, yes, ever since you fell out of the sky. The man was dead, but you weren't there—they kept looking."

"Serves him right. Serves them all right," the child said. She put her hands up over her face and began to cry terribly, without tears.

"Go on, little one, Granddaughter," Spider said. "Don't be afraid. You can live well there. I'll be there too, you know. In your dreams, in your ideas, in dark corners in the basement. Don't kill me, or I'll make it rain . . ."

"I'll come around," Chickadee said. "Make gardens for me."

The child held her breath and clenched her hands until her sobs stopped and let her speak.

"Will I ever see Coyote?"

"I don't know," the Grandmother replied.

The child accepted this. She said, after another silence, "Can I keep my eye?"

"Yes. You can keep your eye."

"Thank you, Grandmother," the child said. She turned away then and started up the night slope towards the next day. Ahead of her in the air of dawn for a long way a little bird flew, black-capped, light-winged.

Doris Lessing

Doris Taylor was born in 1919 in Kermanshah, Persia (Iran), and taken by her parents to Southern Rhodesia (Zimbabwe) in 1924. She attended a convent school and Girls' High School, then set out at age fourteen for Salisbury, where she worked as a nursemaid and secretary, writing and eventually participating in the political and intellectual life of the city. In her late twenties, she left Southern Rhodesia with a novel and collection of stories and took up permanent residence in London. Lessing was married twice, but claimed: "I don't think marriage is one of my talents." Her passion for social justice engaged her, inevitably, in the great social issues of our time—economic inequality, women's rights, and race relations—and determined, to some extent, the directions of her fiction, particularly the five-volume sequence of novels, *Children of Violence*, of which *The Golden Notebook* (1962) is the most famous.

Although she left Southern Rhodesia, where "you spend all your time in a torment of conscientiousness," Lessing's love for the country and its people is evident in her collected African stories and in her commitment to the old tradition of story-telling. The "real history of Africa is still in the custody of black historians, medicine men," she says in the Preface to *The Golden Notebook*, "it is a verbal history, still kept safe from the white man and his predations. Everywhere, if you keep your mind open, you will find the truth in words *not* written down. So never let the printed page be your master." Mostly self-educated, Lessing has been a fierce opponent of authority, attacking institutions, such as education, marriage, religion, and the literary establishment that teach us to distrust our own judgement and to close the shutters against new information and experience.

Lessing's iconoclasm—"I feel as if the Bomb has gone off inside myself, and in people around me. That's what I mean by cracking up. It's as if the structure of the mind is being battered from inside"—often manifests itself aesthetically in terms of formal experiment, such as breaking with narrative conventions or branching out into science fiction. "Dreams have always been important to me," she says in an interview with Jonah Raskin. "The hidden domain of our mind communicates with us through dreams. . . . The unconscious artist who resides in our depths is a very economical individual. With a few symbols a dream can define the whole of one's life, and warn us of the future, too." Related to her interest in dreams is Lessing's fascination with mental illness: "For the last twenty years I have been closely associated with psychiatrists and mentally ill people. I did not make a deliberate choice in the matter, but I started a process which is now common. Twenty years ago it was considered unsual to have a psychiatrist. Now, almost everyone I know has had a breakdown, is in psychoanalysis, or pops in and out of mental hospitals. Mental illness is part of the mainstream. People who are classified as sick are becoming more and more important in England, the U.S.A., and in socialist countries too. People who are called mentally ill are often those who say to the society, 'I'm not going to live according to your rules. I'm not going to conform.' Madness can be a form of rebellion."

One of Lessing's struggles as a writer has been to find a balance between the claims of extreme subjectivity in art and the confinements of social realism. "The way to deal with the problem of 'subjectivity,' that shocking business of being preoccupied with the tiny individual who is at the same time caught up in such an explosion of terrible and marvellous possibilities, is to see him as a microcosm and in this way to break through the personal, the subjective, making the personal general, as indeed life always does, transforming a private experience—or so you think of it when still a child, 'I am falling in love,' 'I am feeling this or that emotion, or thinking that or the other thought,'—into something much larger: growing up is after all only the understanding that one's unique and incredible experience is what everyone shares."

Although her work pushes against the boundaries of conventional fiction and is constantly questing after new ideas, Lessing remains committed to the realist tradition, which continues to explore both society, with its systems and patterns of behaviour, and the labyrinths of the human mind. "I define realism as an art which springs so vigorously and naturally from a strongly held, though not necessarily intellectually defined, view of life that it absorbs symbolism. I hold the view that the realist novel, the realist story, is the highest form of prose writing."

Lessing's collections of stories include *This Was the Old Chief's Country* (1950), *Five* (1953), which won the Somerset Maugham Award, and *The Habit of Loving* (1957). Of "To Room 19," she has said: "Every writer feels when he, she, hits a different level. A certain kind of writing or emotion comes from it. But you don't know who it is who lives there. It is very frightening to write a story . . . soaked in emotions that you don't remember as your own."

To Room 19

This is a story, I suppose, about a failure in intelligence: the Rawlings' marriage was grounded in intelligence.

They were older when they married than most of their married friends: in their well-seasoned late twenties. Both had had a number of affairs, sweet rather than bitter; and when they fell in love—for they did fall in love—had known each other for some time. They joked that they had saved each other "for the real thing." That they had waited so long (but not too long) for this real thing was to them a proof of their sensible discrimination. A good many of their friends had married young, and now (they felt) probably regretted lost opportunities; while others, still unmarried, seemed to them arid, self-doubting, and likely to make desperate or romantic marriages.

Not only they, but others, felt they were well-matched: their friends' delight was an additional proof of their happiness. They had played the same roles, male and female, in this group or set, if such a wide, loosely connected, constantly changing constellation of people could be called a set. They had both become, by virtue of their moderation, their humour, and their abstinence from painful experience, people to whom others came for advice. They could be, and were, relied on. It was one of those cases of a man and a woman linking themselves whom no one else had ever thought of linking, probably because of their similarities. But then everyone exclaimed: Of course! How right! How was it we never thought of it before!

And so they married amid general rejoicing, and because of their foresight and their sense for what was probable, nothing was a surprise to them.

Both had well-paid jobs. Matthew was subeditor on a large London newspaper, and Susan worked in an advertising firm. He was not the stuff of which editors or publicised journalists are made, but he was much more than "a subeditor," being one of the essential background people who in fact steady, inspire, and make possible the people in the limelight. He was content with this position. Susan had a talent for commercial drawing. She was humorous about the advertisements she was responsible for, but she didn't feel strongly about them one way or the other.

Both, before they married, had had pleasant flats, but they felt it unwise to base a marriage on either flat, because it might seem like a submission of personality on the part of the one whose flat it was not. They moved into a new flat in South Kensington on the clear understanding that when their marriage had settled down (a process they knew would not take long, and was in fact more a humorous concession to popular wisdom than what was due to themselves) they would buy a house and start a family.

And this is what happened. They lived in their charming flat for two years, giving parties and going to them, being a popular young married couple, and then Susan became pregnant, she gave up her job, and they bought a house in Richmond. It was typical of this couple that they had a son first, then a daughter, then twins, son and daughter. Everything right, appropriate, and what everyone would wish for, if they could choose. But people did feel these two had chosen;

this balanced and sensible family was no more than what was due to them because of their infallible sense for *choosing* right.

And so they lived with their four children in their gardened house in Richmond and were happy. They had everything they had wanted and had planned for.

And yet. . . .

Well, even this was expected, that there must be a certain flatness. . . .

Yes, yes, of course, it was natural they sometimes felt like this. Like what?

Their life seemed to be like a snake biting its tail. Matthew's job for the sake of Susan, children, house, and garden—which caravanserai needed a well-paid job to maintain it. And Susan's practical intelligence for the sake of Matthew, the children, the house, and the garden—which unit would have collapsed in a week without her.

But there was no point about which either could say: "For the sake of *this* is all at rest." Children? But children can't be a centre of life and a reason for being. They can be a thousand things that are delightful, interesting, satisfying, but they can't be a wellspring to live from. Or they shouldn't be. Susan and Matthew knew that well enough.

Matthew's job? Ridiculous. It was an interesting job, but scarcely a reason for living. Matthew took pride in doing it well, but he could hardly be expected to be proud of the newspaper; his newspaper he read, *his* newspaper, was not the one he worked for.

Their love for each other? Well, that was nearest it. If this wasn't a centre, what was? Yes, it was around this point, their love, that the whole extraordinary structure revolved. For extraordinary it certainly was. Both Susan and Matthew had moments of thinking so, of looking in secret disbelief at this thing they had created: marriage, four children, big house, garden, charwomen, friends, cars . . . and this *thing*, this entity, all of it had come into existence, been blown into being out of nowhere, because Susan loved Matthew and Matthew loved Susan. Extraordinary. So that was the central point, the wellspring.

And if one felt that it simply was not strong enough, important enough, to support it all, well whose fault was that? Certainly neither Susan's nor Matthew's. It was in the nature of things. And they sensibly blamed neither themselves nor each other.

On the contrary, they used their intelligence to preserve what they both created from a painful and explosive world: they looked around them, and took lessons. All around them, marriages collapsing, or breaking, or rubbing along (even worse, they felt). They must not make the same mistakes, they must not.

They had avoided the pitfall so many of their friends had fallen into—of buying a house in the country for the sake of the children, so that the husband became a weekend husband, a weekend father, and the always careful not to ask what went on in the town flat which they called (in joke) a bachelor flat. No, Matthew was a full-time husband, a full-time father, and at night, in the big married bed in the big married bedroom (which had an attractive view of the river), they lay beside each other talking and he told her about his day, and what he had done, and whom he had met, and she told him about her day (not as interesting, but that was not her fault), for both knew of the hidden resentments and deprivations of that woman who has lived her own life—and above all, has earned her own living and is now dependent on a husband for outside interests and money.

Nor did Susan make the mistake of taking a job for the sake of her independence, which she might very well have done, since her old firm, missing her qualities of humour, balance, and sense, invited her often to go back. Children needed their mother to a certain age, that both parents knew and agreed on; and when these four healthy wisely brought up children were of the right age, Susan would work again, because she knew, and so did he, what happened to women of fifty at the height of their energy and ability, with grownup children who no longer needed their full devotion.

So here was this couple, testing their marriage, looking after it, treating it like a small boat full of helpless people in a very stormy sea. Well, of course, so it was. . . . The storms of the world were bad, but not too close—which is not to say they were selfishly felt: Susan and Matthew were both well-informed and responsible people. And the inner storms and quicksands were understood and charted. So everything was all right. Everything was in order. Yes, things were under control.

So what did it matter if they felt dry, flat? People like themselves, fed on a hundred books (psychological, anthropological, sociological), could scarcely be unprepared for the dry, controlled wistfulness which is the distinguishing mark of the intelligent marriage. Two people, endowed with education with discrimination, with judgement, linked together voluntarily from their will to be happy together and to be of use to others—one sees them everywhere, one knows them, one even is that thing oneself: sadness because so much is after all so little. These two, unsurprised, turned towards each other with even more courtesy and gentle love: this was life, that two people, no matter how carefully chosen, could not be everything to each other. In fact, even to say so, to think in such a way, was banal; they were ashamed to do it.

It was banal, too, when one night Matthew came home late and confessed he had been to a party, taken a girl home, and slept with her. Susan forgave him, of course. Except that forgiveness is hardly the word. Understanding, yes. But if you understand something, you don't forgive it, you are the thing itself: forgiveness is for what you *don't* understand. Nor had he confessed—what sort of word is that?

The whole thing was not important. After all, years ago they had joked: Of course I'm not going to be faithful to you, no one can be faithful to one other person for a whole lifetime. (And there was the word "faithful"—stupid, all these words, stupid, belonging to a savage old world.) But the incident left both of them irritable. Strange, but they were both bad-tempered, annoyed. There was something unassimilable about it.

Making love splendidly after he had come home that night, both had felt that the idea that Myra Jenkins, a pretty girl met at a party, could be seen relevant was ridiculous. They had loved each other for over a decade, would love each other for years more. Who, then, was Myra Jenkins?

Except, thought Susan, unaccountably bad-tempered, she was (is?) the first. In ten years. So either the ten years' fidelity was not important, or she isn't. (No, no, there is something wrong with this way of thinking, there must be.) But if she isn't important, presumably it wasn't important either when Matthew and I first went to bed with each other that afternoon whose delight even now (like a very long shadow at sundown) lays a long, wandlike finger over us. (Why did I say sundown?) Well, if what we felt that afternoon was not important, nothing is important, because if it hadn't been for what we felt, we wouldn't be Mr. and Mrs. Rawlings with four children, et cetera, et cetera. The whole thing is *absurd*—for him to have come home and told me was absurd. For him not to have told me was absurd. For me to care or, for that matter, not to care, is absurd . . . and who is Myra Jenkins? Why, no one at all.

There was only one thing to do, and of course these sensible people did it; they put the thing behind them, and consciously, knowing what the were doing, moved forward into a different phase of their marriage, giving thanks for the past good fortune as they did so.

For it was inevitable that the handsome, blond, attractive, manly man, Matthew Rawlings, should be at times tempted (oh, what a word!) by the attractive girls at parties she could not attend because of the four children; and that sometimes he would succumb (a word even more repulsive, if possible) and that she, a goodlooking woman in the big well-tended garden at Richmond, would sometimes be pierced as by an arrow from the sky with bitterness. Except that bitterness was not in order, it was out of court. Did the casual girls touch the marriage? They did not. Rather it was they who knew defeat because of the handsome Matthew Rawlings' marriage body and soul to Susan Rawlings.

In that case why did Susan feel (though luckily not for longer than a few seconds at a time) as if life had become a desert, and that nothing mattered, and that her children were not her own?

Meanwhile her intelligence continued to assert that all was well. What if her Matthew did have an occasional sweet afternoon, the odd affair? For she knew quite well, except in her moments of aridity, that they were very happy, that the affairs were not important.

Perhaps that was the trouble? It was in the nature of things that the adventures and delights could no longer be hers, because of the four children and the big house that needed so much attention. But perhaps she was secretly wishing, and even knowing that she did, that the wildness and the beauty could be his. But he was married to her. She was married to him. They were married inextricably. And therefore the gods could not strike him with the real magic, not really. Well, was it Susan's fault that after he came home from an adventure he looked harassed rather than fulfilled? (In fact, that was how she knew he had been *unfaithful*, because of his sullen air, and his glances at her, similar to hers at him: What is it that I share with this person that shields all delight from me?) But none of it by anybody's fault. (But what did they feel ought to be somebody's fault?) Nobody's fault, nothing to be at fault, no one to blame, no one to offer or to take it . . . and nothing wrong, either, except that Matthew never was really struck, as he wanted to be, by joy; and that Susan was more and more often threatened by emptiness. (It was usually in the garden that she was invaded by this feeling: she was coming to avoid the garden, unless the children or Matthew were with her.) There was no need to use the dramatic words "unfaithful," "forgive," and the rest: intelligence forbade them. Intelligence barred, too, quarrelling, sulking, anger, silences of withdrawal, accusations, and tears. Above all, intelligence forbids tears.

A high price has to be paid for the happy marriage with the four healthy children in the large white gardened house.

And they were paying it, willingly, knowing what they were doing. When they lay side by side or breast to breast in the big civilised bedroom overlooking the wild sullied river, they laughed, often, for no particular reason; but they knew it was really because of these two small people, Susan and Matthew, supporting such an edifice on their intelligent love. The laugh comforted them; it saved them both, though from what, they did not know.

They were now both fortyish. The older children, boy and girl, were ten and eight, at school. The twins, six, were still at home. Susan did not have nurses or girls to help her: childhood is short; and she did not regret the hard work. Often enough she was bored, since small children can be boring; she was often very tired; but she regretted nothing. In another decade, she would turn herself back into being a woman with a life of her own.

Soon the twins would go to school, and they would be away from home from nine until four. These hours, so Susan saw it, would be the preparation for her own slow emancipation away from the role of hub-of-the-family into woman-with-her-own-life. She was already planning for the hours of freedom when all the children would be "off her hands." That was the phrase used by Matthew and by Susan and by their friends, for the moment when the youngest child went off to school. "They'll be off your hands, darling Susan, and you'll have time to yourself." So said Matthew, the intelligent husband, who had often enough commended and consoled Susan, standing by her in spirit during the years when her soul was not her own, as she said, but her children's.

What it amounted to was that Susan saw herself as she had been at twenty-eight, unmarried; and then again somewhere about fifty, blossoming from the root of what she had been twenty years before. As if the essential Susan were in abeyance, as if she were in cold storage. Matthew said something like this to Susan one night: and she agreed that it was true—she did feel something like that. What, then, was this essential Susan? She did not know. Put like that it sounded ridiculous, and she did not really feel it. Anyway, they had a long discussion about the whole thing before going off to sleep in each other's arms.

So the twins went off to their school, two bright affectionate children who had no problems about it, since their older brother and sister had trodden this path so successfully before them. And now Susan was going to be alone in the big house, every day of the school term, except for the daily woman who came in to clean.

It was now, for the first time in this marriage, that something happened which neither of them had foreseen.

This is what happened. She returned, at nine-thirty, from taking the twins to the school by car, looking forward to seven blissful hours of freedom. On the first morning she was simply restless, worrying about the twins "naturally enough" since this was their first day away at school. She was hardly able to contain herself until they came back. Which they did happily, excited by the world of school, looking forward to the next day. And the next day Susan took them, dropped them, came back, and found herself reluctant to enter her big and beautiful home because it was as if something was waiting for her there that she did not wish to confront. Sensibly, however, she parked the car in the garage, entered the house, spoke to Mrs. Parkes, the daily woman, about her duties, and went up to her bedroom. She was possessed by a fever which drove her out again, downstairs, into the kitchen, where Mrs. Parkes was making cake and did not need her, and into the garden. There she sat on a bench and tried to calm herself looking at trees, at a brown glimpse of the river. But she was filled with tension, like a panic: as if an enemy was in the garden with her. She spoke to herself severely, thus: All this is quite natural. First, I spent twelve years of my adult life working, *living my own life.* Then I married, and from the moment I became pregnant for the first time I signed myself over, so to speak, to other people. To the children. Not for one moment in twelve years have I been alone, had time to myself. So now I have to learn to be myself again. That's all.

And she went indoors to help Mrs. Parkes cook and clean, and found some sewing to do for the children. She kept herself occupied every day. At the end of the first term she understood she felt two contrary emotions. First: secret astonishment and dismay that during those weeks when the house was empty of children she had in fact been more occupied (had been careful to keep herself occupied) than ever she had been when the children were around her needing her continual attention. Second: that now she knew the house would be full of them, and for five weeks, she resented the fact she would never be alone. She was already looking back at those hours of sewing, cooking (but by herself) as at a lost freedom which would not be hers for five long weeks. And the two months of term which would succeed the five weeks stretched alluringly open to her—*freedom.* But what freedom—when in fact she had been so careful *not* to be free of small duties during the last weeks? She looked at herself, Susan Rawlings, sitting in a big chair by the window in the bedroom, sewing shirts or dresses, which she might just as well have bought. She saw herself making cakes for hours at a time in the big family kitchen: yet usually she bought cakes. What she saw was a woman alone, that was true, but she had not felt alone. For instance, Mrs. Parkes was always somewhere in the house. And she did not like being in the garden at all, because of the closeness there of the enemy—irritation, restlessness, emptiness, whatever it was—which keeping her hands occupied made less dangerous for some reason.

Susan did not tell Matthew of these thoughts. They were not sensible. She did not recognise herself in them. What should she say to her dear friend and husband, Matthew? "When I go into the garden, that is, if the children are not there, I feel as if there is an enemy there waiting to invade me." "What enemy, Susan darling?" "Well I don't know, really. . . ." "Perhaps you should see a doctor?"

No, clearly this conversation should not take place. The holiday began and Susan welcomed them. Four children, lively, energetic, intelligent, demanding:

she was never, not for a moment of her day, alone. If she was in a room, they would be in the next room, or waiting for her to do something for them; or it would soon be time for lunch or tea, or to take one of them to the dentist. Something to do: five weeks of it, thank goodness.

On the fourth day of these so welcome holidays, she found she was storming with anger at the twins; two shrinking beautiful children who (and this is what checked her) stood hand in hand looking at her with sheer dismayed disbelief. This was their calm mother, shouting at them. And for what? They had come to her with some game, some bit of nonsense. They looked at each other, moved closer for support, and went off hand in hand, leaving Susan holding on to the windowsill of the livingroom, breathing deep, feeling sick. She went to lie down, telling the older children she had a headache. She heard the boy Harry telling the little ones: "It's all right, Mother's got a headache." She heard that *It's all right* with pain.

That night she said to her husband: "Today I shouted at the twins, quite unfairly." She sounded miserable, and he said gently: "Well, what of it?"

"It's more of an adjustment than I thought, their going to school."

"But Susie, Susie darling. . . . " For she was crouched weeping on the bed. He comforted her: "Susan, what is all this about? You shouted at them? What of it? If you shouted at them fifty times a day it wouldn't be more than the little devils deserve." But she wouldn't laugh. She wept. Soon he comforted her with his body. She became calm. Calm, she wondered what was wrong with her, and why she should mind so much that she might, just once, have behaved unjustly with the children. What did it matter? They had forgotten it all long ago: Mother had a headache and everything was all right.

It was a long time later that Susan understood that that night, when she had wept and Matthew had driven the misery out of her with his big solid body, was the last time, ever in their married life, that they had been—to use their mutual language—with each other. And even that as a lie, because she had not told him of her real fears at all.

The five weeks passed, and Susan was in control of herself, and good and kind, and she looked forward to the holidays with a mixture of fear and longing. She did not know what to expect. She took the twins off to school (the elder children took themselves to school) and she returned to the house determined to face the enemy wherever he was, in the house, or the garden or—where?

She was again restless, she was possessed by restlessness. She cooked and sewed and worked as before, day after day, while Mrs. Parkes remonstrated: "Mrs. Rawlings, what's the need for it? I can do that, it's what you pay me for."

And it was so irrational that she checked herself. She would put the car in the garage, go up to her bedroom, and sit, hands in her lap, forcing herself to be quiet. She listened to Mrs. Parkes moving around the house. She looked out into the garden and saw the branches shake the trees. She sat defeating the enemy, restlessness. Emptiness. She ought to be thinking about her life, about herself. But she did not. Or perhaps she could not. As soon as she forced her mind to think about Susan (for what else did she want to be alone for?), it skipped off to thoughts of butter or school clothes. Or it thought of Mrs. Parkes. She realised that she sat listening for the movements of the cleaning woman, following her every turn, bend, thought. She followed her in her mind from kitchen to bathroom, from table to oven, and it was as if the duster, the cleaning cloth, the saucepan, were in her own hand. She would hear herself saying: No, not like that, don't put that there. . . . Yet she did not give a damn what Mrs. Parkes did, or if she did it at all. Yet she could not prevent herself from being conscious of her, every minute. Yes, this was what was wrong with her: she needed, when she was alone, to be really alone, with no one near. She could not endure the knowledge that in ten minutes or in half an hour Mrs. Parkes would call up the stairs: "Mrs. Rawlings, there's no silver polish. Madam, we're out of flour."

So she left the house and went to sit in the garden where she was screened from the house by trees. She waited for the demon to appear and claim her, but he did not.

She was keeping him off, because she had not, after all, come to an end of arranging herself.

She was planning how to be somewhere where Mrs. Parkes would not come after her with a cup of tea, or a demand to be allowed to telephone (always irritating, since Susan did not care who she telephoned or how often), or just a nice talk about something. Yes, she needed a place, or state of affairs, where it would not be necessary to keep reminding herself: In ten minutes I must telephone Matthew about . . . and at half past three I must leave early for the children because the car needs cleaning. And at ten o'clock tomorrow I must remember. . . . She was possessed with resentment that the seven hours of freedom in every day (during weekdays in the school term) were not free, that never, not for one second, ever, was she free from the pressure of time, from having to remember this or that. She could never forget herself; never really let herself go into forgetfulness.

Resentment. It was poisoning her. (She looked at this emotion and thought it was absurd. Yet she felt it.) She was a prisoner. (She looked at this thought too, and it was no good telling herself it was a ridiculous one.) She must tell Matthew—but what? She was filled with emotions that were utterly ridiculous, that she despised, yet that nevertheless she was feeling so strongly she could not shake them off.

The school holidays came round, and this time they were for nearly two months, and she behaved with a conscious controlled decency that nearly drove her crazy. She would lock herself in the bathroom, and sit on the edge of the bath, breathing deep, trying to let go into some kind of calm. Or she went up into the spare room, usually empty, where no one would expect her to be. She heard the children calling "Mother, Mother," and kept silent, feeling guilty. Or she went to the very end of the garden, by herself, and looked at the slow-moving brown river; she looked at the river and closed her eyes and breathed slow and deep, taking it into her being, into her veins.

Then she returned to the family, wife and mother, smiling and responsible, feeling as if the pressure of these people—four lively children and her husband—were a painful pressure on the surface of her skin, a hand pressing on her brain. She did not once break down into irritation during these holidays, but it was like living out a prison sentence, and when the children went back to school, she sat on a white stone near the flowing river, and she thought: It is not even a year since the twins went to school, since *they were off my hands* (What on earth did I think I meant when I used that stupid phrase?), and yet I'm a different person. I'm simply not myself. I don't understand it.

Yet she had to understand it. For she knew that this structure—big white house, on which the mortgage still cost four hundred a year, a husband, so good and kind and insightful; four children, all doing so nicely; and the garden where she sat; and Mrs. Parkes, the cleaning woman—all this depended on her, and yet she could not understand why, or even what it was she contributed to it.

She said to Matthew in their bedroom: "I think there must be something wrong with me."

And he said: "Surely not, Susan? You look marvellous—you're as lovely as ever."

She looked at the handsome blond man, with his clear, intelligent, blue-eyed face, and thought: Why is it I can't tell him? Why not? And she said: "I need to be alone more than I am."

At which he swung his slow blue gaze at her, and she saw what she had been dreading: Incredulity. Disbelief. And fear. An incredulous blue stare from a stranger who was her husband, as close to her as her own breath.

He said: "But the children are at school and off your hands."

She said to herself: I've got to force myself to say: Yes, but do you realize that I never feel free? There's never a moment I can say to myself: There's nothing I have to remind myself about, nothing I have to do in half an hour, or an hour, or two hours. . . .

But she said: "I don't feel well."

He said: "Perhaps you need a holiday."

She said, appalled: "But not without you, surely?" For she could not imagine herself going off without him. Yet that was what he meant. Seeing her face, he laughed, and opened his arms, and she went into them, thinking: Yes, yes, but why can't I say it? And what is it I have to say?

She tried to tell him, about never being free. And he listened and said: "But Susan, what sort of freedom can you possibly want—short of being dead! And I ever free? I go to the office, and I have to be there at ten—all right, half past ten, sometimes. And I have to do this or that, don't I? Then I've got to come home at a certain time—I don't mean it, you know I don't—but if I'm not going to be back home at six I telephone you. When can I ever say to myself: I have nothing to be responsible for in the next six hours?"

Susan, hearing this, was remorseful. Because it was true. The good marriage, the house, the children, depended just as much on his voluntary bondage as it did on hers. But why did he not feel bound? Why didn't he chafe and become restless? No, there was something really wrong with her and this proved it.

And that word "bondage"—why had she used it? She had never felt marriage, or the children, as bondage. Neither had he, or surely they wouldn't be together lying in each other's arms content after twelve years of marriage.

No, her state (whatever it was) was irrelevant, nothing to do with her real good life with her family. She had to accept the fact that, after all, she was an irrational person and to live with it. Some people had to live with crippled arms, or stammers, or being deaf. She would have to live know she was subject to a state of mind she could not own.

Nevertheless, as a result of this conversation with her husband, there was a new regime next holidays.

The spare room at the top of the house now had a cardboard sign saying: PRIVATE! DO NOT DISTURB! on it. (This sign had been drawn in a coloured chalks by the children, after a discussion between the parents in which it was decided this was psychologically the right thing.) The family and Mrs. Parkes knew this was "Mother's Room" and that she was entitled to her privacy. Many serious conversations took place between Matthew and the children about not taking Mother for granted. Susan overheard the first, between father and Harry, the older boy, and was surprised at her irritation over it. Surely she could have a room somewhere in that big house and retire into it without such a fuss being made? Without it being so solemnly discussed? Why couldn't she simply have announced: "I'm going to fit out the little top room for myself, and when I'm in it I'm not to be disturbed for anything short of fire"? Just that, and finished; instead of long earnest discussions. When she heard Harry and Matthew explaining it to the twins with Mrs. Parkes coming in—"Yes, well, a family sometimes gets on top of a woman"—she had to go right away to the bottom of the garden until the devils of exasperation had finished their dance in her blood.

But now there was a room, and she could go there when she liked, she used it seldom: she felt even more caged there than in her bedroom. One day she had gone up there after a lunch for ten children she had cooked and served because Mrs. Parkes was not there, and had sat alone for a while looking into the garden. She saw the children stream out from the kitchen and stand looking up at the window where she sat behind the curtains. They were all—her children and their friends—discussing Mother's Room. A few minutes later, the chase of children in some game came pounding up the stairs, but ended as abruptly as if they had fallen over a ravine, so sudden was the silence. They had remembered she was there, and had gone silent in a great gale of "Hush! Shhhhhh! Quiet, you'll disturb her. . . ." And they went tiptoeing downstairs like criminal conspirators. When she came down to make tea for them, they all apologised. The twins put their arms around her, from front and back, making a human cage of loving limbs, and promised it would never occur again. "We forgot, Mummy, we forgot all about it!"

What it amounted to was that Mother's Room, and her need for privacy, had become a valuable lesson in respect for other people's rights. Quite soon Susan was going up to the room only because it was a lesson it was a pity to drop. Then she took sewing up there, and the children and Mrs. Parkes came in and out: it had become another family room.

She sighed, and smiled, and resigned herself—she made jokes at her own expense with Matthew over the room. That is, she did from the self she liked, she respected. But at the same time, something inside her howled with impatience, with rage. . . . And she was frightened. One day she found herself kneeling by her bed and praying: "Dear God, keep it away from me, keep him away from me." She meant the devil, for she now thought of it, not caring if she was irrational, as some sort of demon. She imagined him, or it, as a youngish man, or perhaps a middleaged man pretending to be young. Or a man young-looking from immaturity? At any rate, she saw the young-looking face which, when she drew closer, had dry lines about mouth and eyes. He was thinnish, meagre in build. And he had a reddish complexion, and ginger hair. That was he—a gingery, energetic man, and he wore a reddish hairy jacket, unpleasant to the touch.

Well, one day she saw him. She was standing at the bottom of the garden, watching the river ebb past, when she raised her eyes and saw this person, or being, sitting on the white stone bench. He was looking at her, and grinning. In his hand was a long crooked stick, which he had picked off the ground, or broken off the tree above him. He was absent-mindedly, out of an absent-minded or freakish impulse of spite, using the stick to stir round in the coils of a blindworm or a grass snake (or some kind of snake-like creature: it was whitish and unhealthy to look at, unpleasant). The snake was twisting about, flinging its coils from side to side in a kind of dance of protest against the teasing prodding stick.

Susan looked at him, thinking: Who is the stranger? What is he doing into our garden? Then she recognized the man around whom her terrors had crystallised. As she did so, he vanished. She made herself walk over to the bench. A shadow from a branch lay across thin emerald grass, moving jerkily its roughness, and she could see why she had taken it for a snake, lashing and twisting. She went back to the house thinking: Right, then, so I've seen him with my own eyes, so I'm not crazy after all—there *is* a danger because I've seen him. He is lurking in the garden and sometimes even in the house, and he wants to *get into me and to take me over.*

She dreamed of having a room or a place, anywhere, where she could go and sit, by herself, no one knowing where she was.

Once, near Victoria, she found herself outside a news agent that had Rooms to Let advertised. She decided to rent a room, telling no one. Sometimes she could take the train into Richmond and sit alone in it for an hour or two. Yet how could she? A room would cost three or four pounds a week, and she earned no money, and how could she explain to Matthew that she needed such a sum? What for? It did not occur to her that she was taking it for granted she wasn't going to tell him about the room.

Well, it was out of the question, having a room; yet she knew she must.

One day, when a school term was well established, and none of the children had measles or other ailments, and everything seemed in order, she did the shopping early, explained to Mrs. Parkes she was meeting an old school friend, took the train to Victoria, searched until she found a small quiet hotel, and asked for a room for the day. They did not let rooms by the day, the manageress said, looking doubtful, since Susan so obviously was not the kind of woman who needed a room for unrespectable reasons. Susan made a long explanation about not being well, being unable to shop without frequent rests for lying down. At last she was allowed to rent the room provided she paid a full night's price for it. She was taken up by the manageress and a maid, both concerned over the state of her health ... which must be pretty bad if, living at Richmond (she had signed her name and address in the register), she needed a shelter at Victoria.

The room was ordinary and anonymous, and was just what Susan needed. She put a shilling in the gas fire, and sat, eyes shut, in a dingy armchair with her back to a dingy window. She was alone. She was alone. She was alone. She could feel pressures lifting off her. First the sounds of traffic came very loud; then they seemed to vanish; she might even have slept a little. A knock on the door: it was Miss Townsend, the manageress, bringing her a cup of tea with her own hands, so concerned was she over Susan's long silence and possible illness.

Miss Townsend was a lonely woman of fifty, running this hotel with all the rectitude expected of her, and she sensed in Susan the possibility of understanding companionship. She stayed to talk. Susan found herself in the middle of a fantastic story about her illness, which got more and more impossible as she tried to make it tally with the large house at Richmond, well-off husband, and four children. Suppose she said instead: Miss Townsend, I'm here in your hotel because I need to be alone for a few hours, above all *alone and with no one knowing where I am.* She said it mentally, and saw, mentally, the look that would inevitably come on Miss Townsend's elderly maiden's face. "Miss Townsend, my four children and my husband are driving me insane, do you understand that? Yes, I can see from the gleam of hysteria in your eyes that comes from loneliness controlled but only just contained that I've got everything in the world you've ever longed for. Well, Miss Townsend, I don't want any of it. You can have it, Miss Townsend. I wish I was absolutely alone in the world, like you. Miss Townsend, I'm besieged by seven devils, Miss Townsend, Miss Townsend, let me stay here in your hotel where the devils can't get me. ... " Instead of saying all this, she described her anaemia, agreed to try Miss Townsend's remedy for it, which was raw liver, minced, between whole-meal bread, and said yes, perhaps it would be better if she stayed at home and let a friend do shopping for her. She paid her bill and left the hotel, defeated.

At home Mrs. Parkes said she didn't really like it, no, not really, when Mrs. Rawlings was away from nine in the morning until five. The teacher had telephoned from school to say Joan's teeth were paining her, and she hadn't known what to say; and what was she to make for the children's tea, Mrs. Rawlings hadn't said.

All this was nonsense, of course. Mrs. Parkes's complaint was that Susan had withdrawn herself spiritually, leaving the burden of the big house on her.

Susan looked back at her day of "freedom" which had resulted in her becoming a friend of the lonely Miss Townsend, and in Mrs. Parkes's remonstrances. Yet she remembered the short blissful hour of being alone, really alone. She was determined to arrange her life, no matter what it cost, so that she could have that solitude more often. An absolute solitude, where no one knew her or cared about her.

But how? She thought of saying to her old employer: I want you to back me up in a story with Matthew that I am doing part-time work for you. The truth is that. . . . But she would have to tell him a lie too, and which lie? She could not say: I want to sit by myself three or four times a week in a rented room. And besides, he knew Matthew, and she could not really ask him to tell lies on her behalf, apart from being bound to think it meant a lover.

Suppose she really took a part-time job, which she could get through fast and efficiently, leaving time for herself. What job? Addressing envelopes? Canvassing?

And there was Mrs. Parkes, working widow, who knew exactly what she was prepared to give to the house, who knew by instinct when her mistress withdrew in spirit from her responsibilities. Mrs. Parkes was one of the servers of this world, but she needed someone to serve. She had to have Mrs. Rawlings, her madam, at the top of the house or in the garden, so that she could come and get support from her: "Yes, the bread's not what it was when I was a girl. . . . Yes, Harry's got a wonderful appetite, I wonder where be puts it all. . . . Yes, it's lucky the twins are so much of a size, they can car each other's shoes, that's a saving in these hard times. . . . Yes, the cherry jam from Switzerland is not a patch on the jam from Poland, and three times the price. . . . " And so on. That sort of talk Mrs. Parkes must have, every day, or she would leave, not knowing herself why she left.

Susan Rawlings, thinking these thoughts, found that she was prowling through the great thicketed garden like a wild cat: she was walking up the stairs, down the stairs, through the rooms into the garden, along the brown running river, back, up through the house, down again. . . . It was a wonder Mrs. Parkes did not think it strange. But, on the contrary, Mrs. Rawlings could do what she liked, she could stand on her head if she wanted, provided she was *there*. Susan Rawlings prowled and muttered through her house, hating Mrs. Parkes, hating poor Miss Townsend, dreaming of her hour of solitude in the dingy respectability of Miss Townsend's hotel bedroom, and she knew quite well she was mad. Yes, she was mad.

She said to Matthew that she must have a holiday. Matthew agreed with her. This was not as things had been once—how they had talked in each other's arms in the marriage bed. He had, she knew, diagnosed her finally as *unreasonable*. She had become someone outside himself that he had to manage. They were living side by side in this house like two tolerably friendly strangers.

Having told Mrs. Parkes—or rather, asked for her permission—she went off on a walking holiday in Wales. She chose the remotest place she knew of. Every morning the children telephoned her before they went off to school, to encourage and support her, just as they had over Mother's Room. Every evening she telephoned them, spoke to each child in turn, and then to Matthew. Mrs. Parkes, given permission to telephone for instructions or advice, did so every day at lunchtime. When, as happened three times, Mrs. Rawlings was out on the mountainside, Mrs. Parkes asked that she should ring back at such-and-such a time, for she would not be happy in what she was doing without Mrs. Rawlings' blessing.

Susan prowled over wild country with the telephone wire holding her to her duty like a leash. The next time she must telephone, or wait to be telephoned, nailed her to her cross. The mountains themselves seemed trammelled by her unfreedom. Everywhere on the mountains, where she met no one at all, from breakfast time to dusk, excepting sheep, or a shepherd, she came face to face with her own craziness, which might attack her in the broadest valleys, so that they seemed too small, or on a mountain top from which she could see a hundred other mountains and valleys, so that they seemed too low, too small, with the sky pressing down too close. She would stand gazing at a hillside brilliant with ferns and bracken, jewelled with running water, and see nothing but her devil, who lifted inhuman eyes at her from where he leaned negligently on a rock, switching at his ugly yellow boots with a leafy twig.

She returned to her home and family, with the Welsh emptiness at the back of her mind like a promise of freedom.

She told her husband she wanted to have an *au pair* girl.

They were in their bedroom, it was late at night, the children slept. He sat, shirted and slippered, in a chair by the window, looking out. She sat brushing her hair and watching him in the mirror. A time-hallowed scene in the connubial bedroom. He said nothing, while she heard the arguments coming into his mind, only to be rejected because every one was *reasonable*.

"It seems strange to get one now; after all, the children are in school most of the day. Surely the time for you to have help was when you were stuck with them day and night. Why don't you ask Mrs. Parkes to cook for you? She's even offered to—I can understand if you are tired of cooking for six people. But you know that an *au pair* girl means all kinds of problems; it's not like having an ordinary char in during the day. . . ."

Finally he said carefully: "Are you thinking of going back to work?"

"No," she said, "no, not really." She made herself sound vague, rather stupid. She went on brushing her black hair and peering at herself so as to be oblivious of the short uneasy glances her Matthew kept giving her. "Do you think we can't afford it?" she went on vaguely, not at all the old efficient Susan who knew exactly what they could afford.

"It's not that," he said, looking out of the window at dark trees, so as not to look at her. Meanwhile she examined a round, candid, pleasant face with clear dark brows and clear grey eyes. A sensible face. She brushed thick healthy black hair and thought: Yet that's the reflection of a madwoman. How very strange! Much more to the point if what looked back at me was the gingery green-eyed demon with his dry meagre smile. . . . Why wasn't Matthew agreeing? After all, what else could he do? She was breaking her part of the bargain and there was no way of forcing her to keep it: that her spirit, her soul, should live in this house, so that the people in it could grow like plants in water, and Mrs. Parkes remain content in their service. In return for this, he would be a good loving husband, and responsible towards the children. Well, nothing like this had been true of either of them for a long time. He did his duty, perfunctorily; she did not even pretend to do hers. And he had become like other husbands, with his real life in his work and the people he met there, and very likely a serious affair. All this was her fault.

At last he drew heavy curtains, blotting out the trees, and turned to force her attention: "Susan, are you really sure we need a girl?" But she would not meet his appeal at all. She was running the brush over her hair again and again, lifting fine black clouds in a small hiss of electricity. She was peering in and smiling as if she were amused at the clinging hissing hair that followed the brush.

"Yes, I think it would be a good idea, on the whole," she said, with the cunning of a madwoman evading the real point.

In the mirror she could see her Matthew lying on his back, his hands behind his head, staring upwards, his face sad and hard. She felt her heart (the old heart of Susan Rawlings) soften and call out to him. But she set it to be indifferent.

He said: "Susan, the children?" It was an appeal that *almost* reached her. He opened his arms, lifting them palms up, empty. She had only to run across and fling herself into them, onto his hard, warm chest, and melt into herself, into Susan. But she could not. She would not see his lifted arms. She said vaguely: "Well, surely it'll be even better for them? We'll get a French or a German girl and they'll learn the language."

In the dark she lay beside him, feeling frozen, a stranger. She felt as if Susan had been spirited away. She disliked very much this woman who lay here, cold and indifferent beside a suffering man, but she could not change her.

Next morning she set about getting a girl, and very soon came Sophie Traub from Hamburg, a girl of twenty, laughing, healthy, blue-eyed, intending to learn English. Indeed, she already spoke a good deal. In return for a room—"Mother's Room"—and her food, she undertook to do some light cooking, and to be with the children when Mrs. Rawlings asked. She was an intelligent girl and understood perfectly what was needed. Susan said: "I go off sometimes, for the morning or for the day—well, sometimes the children run home from school, or they ring up, or a teacher rings up. I should be here, really. And there's the daily woman. . . ." And Sophie laughed her deep fruity *Fräulein's* laugh, showed her fine white teeth and her dimples, and said: "You want some person to play mistress of the house sometimes, not so?"

"Yes, that is just so," said Susan, a bit dry, despite herself, thinking in secret fear how easy it was, how much nearer to the end she was than she thought. Healthy Fraulein Traub's instant understanding of their position proved this to be true.

The *au pair* girl, because of her own commonsense, or (as Susan said to herself, with her new inward shudder) because she had been *chosen* so well by Susan, was a success with everyone, the children liking her, Mrs. Parkes forgetting almost at once that she was German, and Matthew finding her "nice to have around the house." For he was now taking things as they came, from the surface of life, withdrawn both as a husband and a father from the household.

One day Susan saw how Sophie and Mrs. Parkes were talking and laughing in the kitchen, and she announced that she would be away until tea time. She knew exactly where to go and what she must look for. She took the District Line to South Kensington, changed to the Circle, got off at Paddington, and walked around looking at the smaller hotels until she was satisfied with one which had

FRED'S HOTEL painted on windowpanes that needed cleaning. The facade was a faded shiny yellow, like unhealthy skin. A door at the end of a passage said she must knock; she did, and Fred appeared. He was not at all attractive, not in any way, being fattish, and run-down, and wearing a tasteless striped suit. He had small sharp eyes in a white creased face, and was quite prepared to let Mrs. Jones (she chose the farcical name deliberately, staring him out) have a room three days a week from ten until six. Provided of course that she paid in advance each time she came? Susan produced fifteen shillings (no price had been set by him) and held it out, still fixing him with a bold unblinking challenge she had not known until then she could use at will. Looking at her still, he took up a ten-shilling note from her palm between thumb and forefinger, fingered it, then shuffled up two half-crowns, held out his own palm with these bits of money displayed thereon, and let his gaze lower broodingly at them. They were standing in the passage, a red-shaded light above, bare boards beneath, and a strong smell of floor polish rising about them. He shot his gaze up at her over the still-extended palm, and smiled as if to say: What do you take me for? "I shan't," said Susan, "be using this room for the purposes of making money." He still waited. She added another five shillings, at which he nodded and said: "You pay, and I ask no questions." "Good," said Susan. He now went past her to the stairs, and there waited a moment: the light from the street door being in her eyes, she lost sight of him momentarily. Then she saw a sober-suited, white-faced, white-balding little man trotting up the stairs like a waiter, and she went after him. They proceeded in utter silence up the stairs of this house where no questions were asked—Fred's Hotel, which could afford the freedom for its visitors that poor Miss Townsend's hotel could not. The room was hideous. It had a single window, with thin green brocade curtains, a three-quarter bed that had a cheap green satin bedspread on it, a fireplace with a gas fire and a shilling meter by it, a chest of drawers, and a green wicker armchair.

"Thank you," said Susan, knowing that Fred (if this was Fred, and not George, or Herbert, or Charlie) was looking at her, not so much with curiosity, an emotion he would not own to, for professional reasons, but with a philosophical sense of what was appropriate. Having taken her money and shown her up and agreed to everything, he was clearly disapproving of her for coming here. She did not belong here at all, so his look said. (But she knew, already, how very much she did belong: the room had been waiting for her to join it.) "Would you have me called at five o'clock, please?" and he nodded and went downstairs.

It was twelve in the morning. She was free. She sat in the armchair, she simply sat, she closed her eyes and sat and let herself be alone. She was alone and no one knew where she was. When a knock came on the door she was annoyed, and prepared to show it: but it was Fred himself; it was five o'clock and he was calling her as ordered. He flicked his sharp little eyes over the room—bed, first. It was undisturbed. She might never have been in the room at all. She thanked him, said she would be returning the day after tomorrow, and left. She was back home in time to cook supper, to put the children to bed, to cook a second supper for her husband and herself later. And to welcome Sophie back from the pictures where she had gone with a friend. All these things she did cheerfully, willingly. But she was thinking all the time of the hotel room; she was longing for it with her whole being.

Three times a week. She arrived promptly at ten, looked Fred in the eyes, gave him twenty shillings, followed him up the stairs, went into the room and shut the door on him with gentle firmness. For Fred, disapproving of her being here at all, was quite ready to let friendship, or at least acquaintanceship, follow his disapproval, if only she would let him. But he was content to go off on her dismissing nod, with the twenty shillings in his hand.

She sat in the armchair and shut her eyes.

What did she *do* in the room? Why, nothing at all. From the chair, when it had rested her, she went to the window, stretching her arms, smiling, treasuring her anonymity, to look out. She was no longer Susan Rawlings, mother of four, wife of Matthew, employer of Mrs. Parkes and of Sophie Traub, with these and those relations with friends, school-teachers, tradesmen. She no longer was mistress of the big white house and garden, owning clothes suitable for this and that activity or occasion. She was Mrs. Jones, and she was alone, and she had no past and no future. Here I am, she thought, after all these years of being married and having children and playing those roles of responsibility—and I'm just the same. Yet there have been times I thought that nothing existed of me except the roles that went with being Mrs. Matthew Rawlings. Yes, here I am, and if I never saw any of my family again, here I would still be . . . how very strange that is! And she leaned on the sill, and looked into the street, loving the men and women who passed, because she did not know them. She looked at the down-trodden buildings over the street, and at the sky, wet and dingy, or sometimes blue, and she felt she had never seen buildings or sky before. And then she went back to the chair, empty, her mind a blank. Sometimes she talked aloud, saying nothing—an exclamation, meaningless, followed by a comment about the floral pattern on the thin rug, or a stain on the green satin coverlet. For the most part, she wool-gathered—what word is there for it?—brooded, wandered, simply went dark, feeling emptiness run deliciously through her veins like the movement of her blood.

This room had become more her own than the house she lived in. One morning she found Fred taking her a flight higher than usual. She stopped, refusing to go up, and demanded her usual room, Number 19. "Well, you'll have to wait half an hour, then," he said. Willingly she descended to the dark disinfectant-smelling hall, and sat waiting until the two, man and woman, came down the stairs, giving her swift indifferent glances before they hurried out into the street, separating at the door. She went up to the room, *her* room, which they had just vacated. It was no less hers, though the windows were set wide open, and a maid was straightening the bed as she came in.

After these days of solitude, it was both easy to play her part as mother and wife, and difficult—because it was so easy: she felt an imposter. She felt as if her shell moved here, with her family, answering to Mummy, Mother, Susan, Mrs. Rawlings. She was surprised no one saw through her, that she wasn't turned out of doors, as a fake. On the contrary, it seemed the children loved her more; Matthew and she "got on" pleasantly, and Mrs. Parkes was happy in her work under (for the most part, it must be confessed) Sophie Traub. At night she lay beside her husband, and they made love again, apparently just as they used to, when they were really married. But she, Susan, or the being who answered so readily and improbably to the name of Susan, was not there: she was in Fred's Hotel, in Paddington, waiting for the easing hours of solitude to begin.

Soon she made a new arrangement with Fred and with Sophie. It was for five days a week. As for the money, five pounds, she simply asked Matthew for it. She saw that she was not even frightened he might ask what for: he would give it to her, she knew that, and yet it was terrifying it could be so, for this close couple, these partners, had once known the destination of every shilling they must spend. He agreed to give her five pounds a week. She asked for just so much, not a penny more. He sounded indifferent about it. It was as if he were paying her, she thought: *paying her off*—yes, that was it. Terror came back for a moment when she understood this, but she stilled it: things had gone too far for that. Now, every week, on Sunday nights, he gave her five pounds, turning away from her before their eyes could meet on the transaction. As for Sophie Traub, she was to be somewhere in or near the house until six at night, after which she was free. She was not to cook, or to clean; she was simply to be there. So she gardened or sewed, and asked friends in, being a person who was bound to have a lot of friends. If the children were sick, she nursed them. If teachers telephoned, she answered them sensibly. For the five daytimes in the school week, she was altogether the mistress of the house.

One night in the bedroom, Matthew asked: "Susan, I don't want to interfere— don't think that, please—but are you sure you are well?"

She was brushing her hair at the mirror. She made two more strokes on either side of her head, before she replied: "Yes, dear, I am sure I am well."

He was again lying on his back, his blond head on his hands, his elbows angled up and part-concealing his face. He said: "Then Susan, I have to ask you this question, though you must understand, I'm not putting any sort of pressure on you." (Susan heard the word "pressure" with dismay, because this was inevitable; of course she could not go on like this.) "Are things going to go on like this?"

"Well," she said, going vague and bright and idiotic again, so as to escape: "Well, I don't see why not."

He was jerking his elbows up and down, in annoyance or in pain, and, looking at him, she saw he had got thin, even gaunt; and restless angry movements were not what she remembered of him. He said: "Do you want a divorce, is that it?"

At this, Susan only with the greatest difficulty stopped herself from laughing: she could hear the bright bubbling laughter she *would* have emitted, had she let herself. He could only mean one thing: she had a lover, and that was why she spent her days in London, as lost to him as if she had vanished to another continent.

Then the small panic set in again: she understood that he hoped she did have a lover, he was begging her to say so, because otherwise it would be too terrifying.

She thought this out as she brushed her hair, watching the fine black stuff fly up to make its little clouds of electricity, hiss, hiss, hiss. Behind her head, across the room, was a blue wall. She realised she was absorbed in watching the black hair making shapes against the blue. She should be answering him. "Do *you* want a divorce, Matthew?"

He said: "That surely isn't the point, is it?"

"You brought it up, I didn't," she said, brightly, suppressing meaningless tinkling laughter.

Next day she asked Fred: "Have enquiries been made for me?"

He hesitated, and she said: "I've been coming here a year now. I've made no trouble, and you've been paid every day. I have a right to be told."

"As a matter of fact, Mrs. Jones, a man did come asking."

"A man from a detective agency?"

"Well, he could have been, couldn't he?"

"I was asking you. . . . Well, what did you tell him?"

"I told him a Mrs. Jones came every weekday from ten until five or six and stayed in Number 19 by herself."

"Describing me?"

"Well, Mrs. Jones, I had no alternative. Put yourself in my place."

"By rights I should deduct what that man gave you for the information."

He raised shocked eyes: she was not the sort of person to make jokes like this! Then he chose to laugh: a pinkish wet slit appeared across his white crinkled face; his eyes positively begged her to laugh, otherwise he might lose some money. She remained grave, looking at him.

He stopped laughing and said: "You want to go up now?"—returning to the familiarity, the comradeship, of the country where no questions are asked, on which (and he knew it) she depended completely.

She went up to sit in her wicker chair. But it was not the same. Her husband had searched her out. (The world had searched her out.) The pressures were on her. She was here with his connivance. He might walk in at any moment, here, into Room 19. She imagined the report from the detective agency: "A woman calling herself Mrs. Jones, fitting the description of your wife (et cetera, et cetera, et cetera), stays alone all day in Room No. 19. She insists on this room, waits for it if it is engaged. As far as the proprietor knows, she receives no visitors there, male or female." A report something on these lines Matthew must have received.

Well, of course he was right: things couldn't go on like this. He had put an end to it all simply by sending a detective after her.

She tried to shrink herself back into the shelter of the room, a snail pecked out of its shell and trying to squirm back. But the peace of the room had gone. She was trying consciously to revive it, trying to let go into the dark creative trance (or whatever it was) that she had found there. It was no use, yet she craved for it, she was as ill as a suddenly deprived addict.

Several times she returned to the room, to look for herself there, but instead she found the unnamed spirit of restlessness, a pricking fevered hunger for movement, an irritable self-consciousness that made her brain feel as if it had coloured lights going on and off inside it. Instead of the soft dark that had been the room's air, were now waiting for her demons that made her dash blindly about, muttering words of hate; she was impelling herself from point to point like a moth dashing itself against a windowpane, sliding to the bottom, fluttering off on broken wings, then crashing into the invisible barrier again. And again and again. Soon she was exhausted, and she told Fred that for a while she would not be needing the room, she was going on a holiday. Home she went, to the big white house by the river. The middle of a weekday, and she felt guilty at returning to her own home when not expected. She stood unseen, looking in at the kitchen window. Mrs. Parkes, wearing a discarded floral overall of Susan's, was stooping to slide something into the oven. Sophie, arms folded, was leaning her back against a clipboard and laughing at some joke made by a girl not seen before by Susan—a dark foreign girl, Sophie's visitor. In an armchair Molly, one of the twins, lay curled, sucking her thumb and watching the grownups. She must have some sickness, to be kept from school. The child's listless face, the dark circles under her eyes, hurt Susan: Molly was looking at the three grownups working and talking in exactly the same way Susan looked at the four through the kitchen window: she was remote, shut off from them.

But then, just as Susan imagined herself going in, picking up the little girl, and sitting in an armchair with her, stroking her probably heated forehead, Sophie did just that: she had been standing on one leg, the other knee flexed, its foot set against the wall. Now she let her foot in its ribbon-tied red shoe slide down the wall, stood solid on two feet, clapping her hands before and behind her, and sang a couple of lines in German, so that the child lifted her heavy eyes at her and began to smile. Then she walked, or rather skipped, over to the child, swung her up, and let her fall into her lap at the same moment she sat herself. She said "Hopla! Hopla! Molly . . ." and began stroking the dark untidy young head that Molly laid on her shoulder for comfort.

Well. . . . Susan blinked the tears of farewell out of her eyes, and went quietly up through the house to her bedroom. There she sat looking at the river through the trees. She felt at peace, but in a way that was new to her. She had no desire to move, to talk, to do anything at all. The devils that had haunted the house, the garden, were not there; but she knew it was because her soul was in Room 19 in Fred's Hotel; she was not really here at all. It was a sensation that should have been frightening: to sit at her own bedroom window, listening to Sophie's rich young voice sing German nursery songs to her child, listening to Mrs. Parkes clatter and move below, and to know that all this had nothing to do with her: she was already out of it.

Later, she made herself go down and say she was home: it was unfair to be here unannounced. She took lunch with Mrs. Parkes, Sophie, Sophie's Italian friend Maria, and her daughter Molly, and felt like a visitor.

A few days later, at bedtime, Matthew said: "Here's your five pounds," and pushed them over at her. Yet he must have known she had not been leaving the house at all.

She shook her head, gave it back to him, and said, in explanation, not in accusation: "As soon as you knew where I was, there was no point."

He nodded, not looking at her. He was turned away from her: thinking, she knew, how best to handle this wife who terrified him.

He said: "I wasn't trying to. . . . It's just that I was worried."

"Yes, I know."

"I must confess that I was beginning to wonder. . . ."

"You thought I had a lover?"

"Yes, I am afraid I did."

She knew that he wished she had. She sat wondering how to say: "For a year now I've been spending all my days in a very sordid hotel room. It's the place where I'm happy. In fact, without it I don't exist." She heard herself saying this, and understood how terrified he was that she might. So instead she said: "Well, perhaps you're not far wrong."

Probably Matthew would think the hotel proprietor lied: he would want to think so.

"Well," he said, and she could hear his voice spring up, so to speak, with relief, "in that case I must confess I've got a bit of an affair on myself."

She said, detached and interested: "Really? Who is she?" and saw Matthew's startled look because of this reaction.

"It's Phil. Phil Hunt."

She had known Phil Hunt well in the old unmarried days. She was thinking: No, she won't do, she's too neurotic and difficult. She's never been happy yet. Sophie's much better. Well, Matthew will see that himself, as sensible as he is.

This line of thought went on in silence, while she said aloud: "It's no point telling you about mine, because you don't know him."

Quick, quick, invent, she thought. Remember how you invented all that nonsense for Miss Townsend.

She began slowly, careful not to contradict herself: "His name is Michael" (*Michael What?*)—"Michael Plant." (What a silly name!) "He's rather like you—in looks, I mean." And indeed, she could imagine herself being touched by no one but Matthew himself. "He's a publisher." (Really? Why?) "He's got a wife already and two children."

She brought out this fantasy, proud of herself.

Matthew said: "Are you two thinking of marrying?"

She said, before she could stop herself: "Good God, *no!*"

She realized, if Matthew wanted to marry Phil Hunt, that this was too emphatic, but apparently it was all right, for his voice sounded relieved as he said: "It is a bit impossible to imagine oneself married to anyone else, isn't it?" With which he pulled her to him, so that her head lay on his shoulder. She turned her face into the dark of his flesh, and listened to the blood pounding through her ears saying: I am alone, I am alone, I am alone.

In the morning Susan lay in bed while he dressed.

He had been thinking things out in the night, because now he said: "Susan, why don't we make a foursome?"

Of course, she said to herself, of course he would be bound to say that. If one is sensible, if one is reasonable, if one never allows oneself a base thought or an envious emotion, naturally one says: Let's make a foursome.

"Why not?" she said.

"We could all meet for lunch. I mean, it's ridiculous, you sneaking off to filthy hotels, and me staying late at the office, and all the lies everyone has to tell."

What on earth did I say his name was?—she panicked, then said: "I think it's a good idea, but Michael is away at the moment. When he comes back, though— and I'm sure you two would like each other."

"He's away, is he? So that's why you've been. . . ." Her husband put his hand to the knot of his tie in a gesture of male coquetry she would not before have associated with him; and he bent to kiss her cheek with the expression that goes with the words: Oh you naughty little puss! And she felt its answering look, naughty and coy, come onto her face.

Inside she was dissolving in horror at them both, at how far they had both sunk from honesty of emotion.

So now she was saddled with a lover, and he had a mistress! How ordinary, how reassuring, how jolly! And now they would make a foursome of it, and go about to theatres and restaurants. After all, the Rawlings could well afford that sort of thing, and presumably the publisher Michael Plant could afford to do himself and his mistress quite well. No, there was nothing to stop the four of them developing the most intricate relationship of civilised tolerance, all enveloped in a charming afterglow of autumnal passion. Perhaps they would all go off on holidays together? She had known people who did. Or perhaps Matthew would draw the line there? Why should he, though, if he was capable of talking about "foursomes" at all?

She lay in the empty bedroom, listening to the car drive off with Matthew in it, off to work. Then she heard the children clattering off to school to the accompaniment of Sophie's cheerfully ringing voice. She slid down into the hollow of the bed, for shelter against her own irrelevance. And she stretched out her hand to the hollow where her husband's body had lain, but found no comfort there: he was not her husband. She curled herself up in a small tight ball under the clothes: she could stay here all day, all week, indeed, all her life.

But in a few days she must produce Michael Plant, and—but how? She must presumably find some agreeable man prepared to impersonate a publisher called Michael Plant. And in return for which she would—what? Well, for one thing they would make love. The idea made her want to cry with sheer exhaustion. Oh no, she had finished with all that—the proof of it was that the words "make love," or even imagining it, trying hard to revive no more than the pleasures of sensuality, let alone affection, or love, made her want to run away and hide from the sheer effort of the thing. . . . Good Lord, why make love at all? Why make love with anyone? If you are going to make love, what does it matter who with? Why shouldn't she simply walk into the street, pick up a man, and have a roaring sexual affair with him? Why not? Or even with Fred? What difference did it make?

But she had let herself in for it—an interminable stretch of time with a lover, called Michael, as part of a gallant civilised foursome. Well, she could not, and she would not.

She got up, dressed, went down to find Mrs. Parkes, and asked her the loan of a pound, since Matthew, she said, had forgotten to leave her money. She exchanged with Mrs. Parkes variations on the theme that husbands are all the same, they don't think, and without saying a word to Sophie, whose voice could be heard upstairs from the telephone, walked to the underground, travelled to South Kensington, changed to the Inner Circle, got out at Paddington, and walked to Fred's Hotel. There she told Fred that she wasn't going on holiday after all, she needed the room. She would have to wait an hour, Fred said. She went to a busy tearoom-cum-restaurant around the corner, and sat watching the people flow in and out the door that kept swinging open and shut, watched them mingle and merge, and separate, felt her being flow into them, into their movement. When the hour was up, she left a half-crown for her pot of tea, and left the place without looking back at it, just as she had left her house, the big, beautiful white house, without another look, but silently dedicating it to Sophie. She returned to Fred, received the key of Number 19, now free, and ascended the grimy stairs slowly, letting floor after floor fall away below her, keeping her eyes lifted, so that floor after floor descended jerkily to her level of vision, and fell away out of sight.

Number 19 was the same. She saw everything with an acute, narrow, checking glance: the cheap shine of the satin spread, which had been placed carelessly after the two bodies had finished their convulsions under it; a trace of powder on the glass that topped the chest of drawers; an intense green shade in a fold of the curtain. She stood at the window, looking down, watching people pass and pass and pass until her mind went dark from the constant movement. Then she sat in the wicker chair, letting herself go slack. But she had to be careful, because she did not want, today, to be surprised by Fred's knock at five o'clock.

The demons were not here. They had gone forever, because she was buying her freedom from them. She was slipping already into the dark fructifying dream that seemed to caress her inwardly, like the movement of her blood . . . but she had to think about Matthew first. Should she write a letter for the coroner? But what should she say? She would like to leave him with the look on his face she had seen this morning—banal, admittedly, but at least confidently healthy. Well, that was impossible, one did not look like that with a wife dead from suicide. But how to leave him believing she was dying because of a man—because of the fascinating publisher Michael Plant? Oh, how ridiculous! How absurd! How humiliating! But she decided not to trouble about it, simply not to think about the living. If he wanted to believe she had a lover, he would believe it. And he *did* want to believe it. Even when he had found out that there was no publisher in London called Michael Plant, he would think: Oh poor Susan, she was afraid to give me his real name.

And what did it matter whether he married Phil Hunt or Sophie? Though it ought to be Sophie, who was already the mother of those children . . . and what hypocrisy to sit here worrying about the children, when she was going to leave them because she had not got the energy to stay.

She had about four hours. She spent them delightfully, darkly, sweetly, letting herself slide gently, gently, to the edge of the river. Then, with hardly a break in her consciousness, she got up, pushed the thin rug against the door, made sure the windows were tight shut, put two shillings in the meter, and turned on the gas. For the first time since she had been in the room she lay on the hard bed that smelled stale, that smelled of sweat and sex.

She lay on her back on the green satin cover, but her legs were chilly. She got up, found a blanket folded in the bottom of the chest of drawers, and carefully covered her legs with it. She was quite content lying there, listening to the faint soft hiss of the gas that poured into the room, into her lungs, into her brain, as she drifted off into the dark river.

Alistair MacLeod

Alistair MacLeod was born in 1936 in North Battleford, Saskatchewan, to Cape Breton parents. He was raised in Alberta and Inverness, Nova Scotia, and educated at Nova Scotia Teachers' College, St. Francis Xavier University, and Notre Dame University. He has worked as a labourer, milkman, miner, public relations man, and teacher, from a one-room school to the Universities of New Brunswick, Indiana, and Windsor, where, since 1969, he has taught English and Creative Writing. MacLeod is not a prolific writer, but has had considerable recognition for his painstaking craftsmanship, his work having been included in *Best American Stories* and numerous anthologies. His books include *The Lost Salt Gift of Blood* (1976) and *As Birds Bring Forth the Sun and Other Stories* (1986).

MacLeod writes primarily about the families of miners and fishermen in Cape Breton, their confrontation with the land and with changing conditions in the world around them. There is a stark, almost mythic quality to his writing, as if the characters have stepped outside of contemporary history, or conventional reality as we know it, and are seen moving against the backdrop of eternity. As he says in an interview with Mark Fortier (*Books in Canada*, Aug./Sept. 1986), "I like to think of myself as basically a kind of realistic writer, not steeped in pessimism. I like to think of myself as telling the truth as I see it. What else can I do? In an urbanized world there is more of a chance to escape death, because you don't have to see it. But if you grow up in a rural world, where the animals are always being killed, that is part of your reality. I don't think that's pessimistic."

Writing in the tradition of Faulkner and Flannery O'Connor, MacLeod is a regional writer whose work has a universal appeal. He quotes T. S. Eliot's comment in *The Four Quartets* that home is where we start from; and yet, he does not deny the power of ancient, tribal memory at work in his characters. "Well, the world that we live in is not necessarily all that we have. And the world that we comprehend intellectually is not all that we have either. A lot of these characters are not instant North Americans. They go back a long way, and, whether this is any good or not, they have no choice. You cannot not know what you do know."

MacLeod is committed, imaginatively, to his small piece of turf, but would not wish to be described as "the voice of Cape Breton." He prefers to think of himself, this time quoting Elizabeth Spencer, as inscribing a "landscape of the heart." "I write about

what I want to write about, which I think is a good way to write. I think of that material almost as you think of someone you love. If I were free to spend all my time with someone, who would I spend it with? That material is who—or what—I want to spend my time with. What's happened over the years is that I've come to think of it as being more worthwhile—this is as good a way to spend your life as any other. Why not do it? Alice Munro has said about her own work, 'Everything I do is an offering, and people can take from it what they wish.' That's all I can do, is put it out as well as I possibly can. That's all you can do."

In a brief statement entitled "A Voice from Rural Canada" (*Transitions II*, 1978), MacLeod tries to articulate his sense of the depth of experience that lies in often remote rural communities: "In the older, more isolated communities the patterns are more firmly established. There is a weight of history behind the traditions and the occupations associated with them. Such 'narrowness' as it might be called is often a 'deepness' as well; what is lost in breadth is compensated for in depth. For many people this results in a fierce intensity that has to do with where they stand in place and time and how they spend their alloted years. What they have learned and what they possess to pass on is often personal and almost physical. You cannot learn to be a good trapper or a good fisherman by going to university, and The Flying Wallendas do not run ads in Help Wanted columns."

In an interview with Andrew Garrod (*Speaking for Myself: Canadian Writers in Interview*, 1986), MacLeod justifies his sometimes long descriptive passages on the grounds that "my description is the whereness against which events take place." He also links his commitment to the short story to its potential for intensity: "I like to write in a kind of intense manner, and you can only be intense for so long." This process, which may resemble the hundred-yard dash but which is by no means quick and easy, involves rigorous rewriting, reading the work aloud to see if it works orally, and attention to linguistic devices such as repetition, which "obviously gives you emphasis, and if it's not overdone, I think it has a sort of oral appeal. I write for sound as well as for sense. This is why in medieval literature or ballad literature or whatever, refrain is very important. This is ritual."

MacLeod is interested in the "great prices paid" by the isolated protagonists in his stories for whatever they accept or reject in their lives. He has, as a writer, paid a price, in popularity and immediate recognition, for his decision to limit his focus and to carve his stories so carefully and lovingly. However, as he suggests in the Afterwords included in this anthology, the great writer must keep his eye on eternity, not on the stock market or the best-seller list. As a teacher of writing and as fiction editor of the *University of Windsor Review*, he insists that "I'm looking for whether I care about what happens, whether I care about the people. I also look to see if the language is beautiful, whether what is described is done so with beauty. I don't care what the subjects are. The office is full of manuscripts from everywhere. I read them and see whether they make my heart beat faster or something like that."

As Birds Bring Forth the Sun

Once there was a family with a Highland name who lived beside the sea. And the man had a dog of which he was very fond. She was large and grey, a sort of staghound from another time. And if she jumped up to lick his face, which she loved to do, her paws would jolt against his shoulders with such force that she would come close to knocking him down and he would be forced to take two or three backward steps before he could regain his balance. And he himself was not a small man, being slightly over six feet and perhaps one hundred and eighty pounds.

She had been left, when a puppy, at the family's gate in a small handmade box and no one knew where she had come from or that she would eventually grow to such a size. Once, while still a small pup, she had been run over by the steel wheel of a horse-drawn cart which was hauling kelp from the shore to be used as fertilizer. It was in October and the rain had been falling for some weeks and the ground was soft. When the wheel of the cart passed over her, it sunk her body into the wet earth as well as crushing some of her ribs; and apparently the silhouette of her small crushed body was visible in the earth after the man lifted her to his chest while she yelped and screamed. He ran his fingers along her broken bones, ignoring the blood and urine which fell upon his shirt, trying to soothe her bulging eyes and her scrabbling front paws and her desperately licking tongue.

The more practical members of his family, who had seen run-over dogs before, suggested that her neck be broken by his strong hands or that he grasp her by the hind legs and swing her head against a rock, thus putting an end to her misery. But he would not do it.

Instead, he fashioned a small box and lined it with woollen remnants from a sheep's fleece and one of his old and frayed shirts. He placed her within the box and placed the box behind the stove and then he warmed some milk in a small saucepan and sweetened it with sugar. And he held open her small and trembling jaws with his left hand while spooning in the sweetened milk with his right, ignoring the needle-like sharpness of her small teeth. She lay in the box most of the remaining fall and into the early winter, watching everything with her large brown eyes.

Although some members of the family complained about her presence and the odour from the box and the waste of time she involved, they gradually adjusted to her: and as the weeks passed by, it became evident that her ribs were knitting together in some form or other and that she was recovering with the resilience of the young. It also became evident that she would grow to a tremendous size, as she outgrew one box and then another and the grey hair began to feather from her huge front paws. In the spring she was outside almost all of the time and followed the man everywhere; and when she came inside during the following months, she had grown so large that she would no longer fit into her accustomed place behind the stove and was forced to lie beside it. She was never given a name but was referred to in Gaelic as *cù mòr glas*, the big grey dog.

By the time she came into her first heat, she had grown to a tremendous height, and although her signs and her odour attracted many panting and highly aroused suitors, none was big enough to mount her and the frenzy of their disappointment and the longing of her unfulfillment were more than the man could stand. He went, so the story goes, to a place where he knew there was a big dog. A dog not as big as she was, but still a big dog, and he brought him home with him. And at the proper time he took the *cù mòr glas* and the big dog down to the sea where he knew there was a hollow in the rock which appeared only at low tide. He took some sacking to provide footing for the male dog and he placed the *cù mòr glas* in the hollow of the rock and knelt beside her and steadied her with his left arm under her throat and helped position the male dog above her and guided his blood-engorged penis. He was a man used to working with the breeding of animals, with the guiding of rams and bulls and stallions and often with the funky smell of animal semen heavy on his large and gentle hands.

The winter that followed was a cold one and ice formed on the sea and frequent squalls and blizzards obliterated the offshore islands and caused the people to stay near their fires much of the time, mending clothes and nets and harness and waiting for the change in season. The *cù mòr glas* grew heavier and even more huge until there was hardly room for her around the stove or even under the table. And then one morning, when it seemed that spring was about to break, she was gone.

The man and even his family, who had become more involved than they cared to admit, waited for her but she did not come. And as the frenzy of spring wore on, they busied themselves with readying their land and their fishing gear and all of the things that so desperately required their attention. And then they were into summer and fall and winter and another spring which saw the birth of the man and his wife's twelfth child. And then it was summer again.

That summer the man and two of his teenaged sons were pulling their herring nets about two miles offshore when the wind began to blow off the land and the water began to roughen. They became afraid that they could not make it safely back to shore, so they pulled in behind one of the offshore islands, knowing that they would be sheltered there and planning to outwait the storm. As the prow of their boat approached the gravelly shore, they heard a sound above them, and looking up they saw the *cù mòr glas* silhouetted on the brow of the hill which was the small island's highest point.

"M'eudal *cù mòr glas*" shouted the man in his happiness—*m'eudal* meaning something like dear or darling; and as he shouted, he jumped over the side of his boat into the waist-deep water, struggling for footing on the rolling gravel as he waded eagerly and awkwardly towards her and the shore. At the same time, the *cù mòr glas* came hurtling down towards him in a shower of small rocks dislodged by her feet; and just as he was emerging from the water, she met him as she used to, rearing up on her hind legs and placing her huge front paws on his shoulders while extending her eager tongue.

The weight and speed of her momentum met him as he tried to hold his balance on the sloping angle and the water rolling gravel beneath his feet, and he staggered backwards and lost his footing and fell beneath her force. And in that instant again, as the story goes, there appeared over the brow of the hill six more huge grey dogs hurtling down towards the graveled strand. They had never seen him before; and seeing him stretched prone beneath their mother, they misunderstood, like so many armies, the intention of their leader.

They fell upon him in a fury, slashing his face and tearing aside his lower jaw and ripping out his throat, crazed with blood-lust or duty or perhaps starvation. The *cù mòr glas* turned on them in her own savagery, slashing and snarling and, it seemed, crazed by their mistake; driving them bloodied and yelping before her, back over the brow of the hill where they vanished from sight but could still be heard screaming in the distance. It all took perhaps little more than a minute.

The man's two sons, who were still in the boat and had witnessed it all, ran sobbing through the salt water to where their mauled and mangled father lay; but there was little they could do other than hold his warm and bloodied hands for a few brief moments. Although his eyes "lived" for a small fraction of time, he could not speak to them because his face and throat had been torn away, and of course there was nothing they could do except to hold and be held tightly until that too slipped away and his eyes glazed over and they could no longer feel his hands holding theirs. The storm increased and they could not get home and so they were forced to spend the night huddled beside their father's body. They were afraid to try to carry the body to the rocking boat because he was so heavy and they were afraid that they might lose even what little of him remained and they were afraid also, huddled on the rocks, that the dogs might return. But they did not return at all and there was no sound from them, no sound at all, only the moaning of the wind and the washing of the water on the rocks.

In the morning they debated whether they should try to take his body with them or whether they should leave it and return in the company of older and wiser men. But they were afraid to leave it unattended and felt that the time needed to cover it with protective rocks would be better spent in trying to get across to their home shore. For a while they debated as to whether one should go in the boat and the other remain on the island, but each was afraid to be alone and so in the end they managed to drag and carry and almost float him towards the bobbing boat. They laid him face down and covered him with what clothes there were and set off across the still-rolling sea. Those who waited on the shore missed the large presence of the man within the boat and some of them waded into the water and others rowed out in skiffs, attempting to hear the tearful messages called out across the rolling waves.

The *cù mòr glas* and her six young dogs were never seen again, or perhaps I should say they were never seen again in the same way. After some weeks, a group of men circled the island tentatively in their boats but they saw no sign. They went again and then again but found nothing. A year later, and grown much braver, they beached their boats and walked the island carefully, looking into the small sea caves and the hollows at the base of the wind-ripped trees, thinking perhaps that if they did not find the dogs, they might at least discover their whitened bones; but again they discovered nothing.

The *cù mòr glas*, though, was supposed to be sighted here and there for a number of years. Seen on a hill in one region or silhouetted on a ridge in another or loping across the valleys or glens in the early morning or the shadowy evening. Always in the area of the half perceived. For a while she became rather like the Loch Ness monster or the Sasquatch on a smaller scale. Seen but not recorded. Seen when there were no cameras. Seen but never taken.

The mystery of where she went became entangled with the mystery of whence she came. There was increased speculation about the handmade box in which she had been found and much theorizing as to the individual or individuals who might have left it. People went to look for the box but could not find it. It was felt she might have been part of a *buidseachd* or evil spell cast on the man by some mysterious enemy. But no one could go much further than that. All of his caring for her was recounted over and over again and nobody missed any of the ironies.

What seemed literally known was that she had crossed the winter ice to have her pups and had been unable to get back. No one could remember ever seeing her swim; and in the early months at least, she could not have taken her young pups with her.

The large and gentle man with the smell of animal semen often heavy on his hands was my great-great-great-grandfather, and it may be argued that he died because he was too good at breeding animals or that he cared too much about their fulfillment and well-being. He was no longer there for his own child of the spring who, in turn, became my great-great-grandfather, and he was perhaps too much there in the memory of his older sons who saw him fall beneath the ambiguous force of the *cù mòr glas*. The youngest boy in the boat was haunted and tormented by the awfulness of what he had seen. He would wake at night screaming that he had seen the *cù mòr glas a′ bhàis*, the big grey dog of death, and his screams filled the house and the ears and minds of the listeners, bringing home again and again the consequences of their loss. One morning, after a night in which he saw the *cù mòr glas a′ bhàis* so vividly that his sheets were drenched with sweat, he walked to the high cliff which faced the island and there he cut his throat with a fish knife and fell into the sea.

The other brother lived to be forty, but, again so the story goes, he found himself in a Glasgow pub one night, perhaps looking for answers, deep and sodden with the whisky which had become his anaesthetic. In the half darkness he saw a large, grey-haired man sitting by himself against the wall and mumbled something to him. Some say he saw the *cù mòr glas a′ bhàis* or uttered the name. And perhaps the man heard the phrase through ears equally affected by drink and felt he was being called a dog or a son of a bitch or something of that nature. They rose to meet one another and struggled outside into the cobblestoned passageway behind the pub where, most improbably, there were supposed to be six other large, grey-haired men who beat him to death on the cobblestones, smashing his bloodied head into the stone again and again before vanishing and leaving him to die with his face turned to the sky. The *cù mòr glas a' bhàis* had come again, said his family, as they tried to piece the tale together.

This is how the *cù mòr glas a' bhàis* came into our lives, and it is obvious that all of this happened a long, long time ago. Yet with succeeding generations it seemed the spectre had somehow come to stay and that it had become *ours*—not in the manner of an unwanted skeleton in the closet from a family's ancient past but more in the manner of something close to a genetic possibility. In the deaths of each generation, the grey dog was seen by some—by women who were to die in childbirth; by soldiers who went forth to the many wars but did not return; by those who went forth to feuds or dangerous love affairs; by those who answered mysterious midnight messages; by those who swerved on the highway to avoid the real or imagined grey dog and ended in masses of crumpled steel. And by one professional athlete who, in addition to his ritualized athletics superstitions, carried another fear or belief as well. Many of the man's descendants moved like careful hemophiliacs, fearing that they carried unwanted possibilities deep within them. And others, while they laughed, were like members of families in which there is a recurrence over the generations of repeated cancer or the diabetes which comes to those beyond middle age. The feeling of those who may say little to others but who may say often and quietly to themselves, "It has not happened to me," while adding always the cautionary "*yet*".

I am thinking all of this now as the October rain falls on the city of Toronto and the pleasant, white-clad nurses pad confidently in and out of my father's room. He lies quietly amidst the whiteness, his head and shoulders elevated so that he is in that hospital position of being neither quite prone nor yet sitting. His hair is white upon his pillow and he breathes softly and sometimes unevenly, although it is difficult ever to be sure.

My five grey-haired brothers and I take turns beside his bedside, holding his heavy hands in ours and feeling their response, hoping ambiguously that he will speak to us, although we know that it may tire him. And trying to read his life and ours into his eyes when they are open. He has been with us a long time, well into our middle age. Unlike those boys in that boat of so long ago, we did not see him taken from us in our youth. And unlike their youngest brother who, in turn, became our great-great-grandfather, we did not grow into a world in which there was no father's touch. We have been lucky to have this large and gentle man so deep into our lives.

No one in this hospital has mentioned the *cù mòr glas a' bhàis*. Yet as my mother said ten years ago, before slipping into her own death as quietly as a grown-up child who leaves or enters her parents' house in the early hours, "It is hard to *not* know what you do know."

Even those who are most sceptical, like my oldest brother who has driven here from Montreal, betray themselves by their nervous actions. "I avoided the

Greyhound bus stations in both Montreal and Toronto," he smiled upon his arrival, and then added, "Just in case."

He did not realize how ill our father was and has smiled little since then. I watch him turning the diamond ring upon his finger, knowing that he hopes he will not hear the Gaelic phrase he knows too well. Not having the luxury, as he once said, of some who live in Montreal and are able to pretend they do not understand the "other" language. You cannot *not* know what you do know.

Sitting here, taking turns holding the hands of the man who gave us his life, we are afraid for him and for ourselves. We are afraid of what he may see and we are afraid to hear the phrase born of the vision. We are aware that it may become confused with what the doctors call "the will to live" and we are aware that some beliefs are what others would dismiss as "garbage". We are aware that there are men who believe the earth is flat and that the birds bring forth the sun.

Bound here in our own peculiar mortality, we do not wish to see or see others see that which signifies life's demise. We do not want to hear the voice of our father, as did those other sons, calling down his own particular death upon him.

We would shut our eyes and plug our ears, even as we know such actions to be of no avail. Open still and fearful to the grey hair rising on our necks if and when we hear the scrabble of the paws and the scratching at the door.

☙ David Malouf

David Malouf was born in Brisbane, Australia, in 1934, to a mother whose family was from London and a father whose family had come from Lebanon to Australia in the 1880s. He was educated at the Brisbane Grammar School and the University of Queensland. He spent ten years abroad, travelling in Europe and teaching in England. When he returned to Australia in 1968, he taught for a while at Sydney University. He now divides his time between Australia and Italy. Malouf is a poet, fiction writer, and librettist. His fiction works, including *Johnno* (1975), *An Imaginary Life* (1978), *Child's Play* (1982), *Fly Away Peter* (1982), *Harland's Half Acre* (1984), *Antipodes* (1985), and *Great World* (1990) have received numerous awards, most recently the Booker Prize. He is also the author of several books of poetry and a work of autobiography and non-fiction, *12 Edmonstone Street* (1986). James Tulip has edited *David Malouf: Johnno, Short Stories, Poems, and Interviews* (1990).

In an interview conducted in 1986 by Richard Kelly Tipping (*Southerly*, Vol. 49, No. 3, Sept. 1989), Malouf outlines his conception of the writer. "I think the writer learns very early on—not as a writer, but as a little experiencing person—the best ways of getting to see what is going on in the world and making sense of it. He has to act like a spy, like a voyeur, like an eavesdropper, sometimes like a burglar—I mean a burglar of other people's memories, other people's experiences, as well as of facts or objects. What I mean by that is, a person who intrudes, who gets his experience by putting himself in somebody else's position; but that is really to *steal* their position, to steal their experience, make it his own."

In the same interview, Malouf has a good deal to say about the idea of place in fiction. Initially, he suggests that, personally, he is somewhat indifferent to place: "But when it comes to actually living in a place, I mostly live in an imaginary place anyway; it's in my head, a combination of non-existent, never-was Brisbane and places I create on the page." However, he claims to have moved to the inner-city core from his Cremorne Point dwelling in well-to-do Sydney because it was too manicured: "Whenever you look out you see beautiful harbour and beautiful sails and it really is like living inside a cigarette advertisement. I just found, in the end, that I hated it." He speaks at length about *mapping* his fiction, creating the impression of his characters moving through real places, whether rooms, the interior of houses, or imaginary cities: "That seems to

me as important, in my way of constructing a book, as the actual plot. The plot was partly created out of those moves. . . . The geography of that place is absolutely integral to what happens in the book, to the plot, to the characters, to the inner lives of the characters as they're worked out. In the way you can relate geography or the particular architecture, domestic architecture, of the place, to people's inner lives." Malouf then draws attention to the first piece in his book *12 Edmonstone Street*, which is intended "as an exploration of that question of place and in those terms: how a child's view of the world, how his sense of space—of the relation between inner and outer, of up and down—may be determined by the particular domestic space he first grows up in . . . a speculative piece about how we go about building up our picture of the world, what paradigms we have that come from early architecture, early space, and how different we might be as Australians according to the different parts of the continent we've grown up in. . . ."

Malouf describes himself as a "lyric novelist" whose fictions "are constructed like poems rather than in a series of dramatic scenes in which characters come into conflict with one another." In an interview with Paul Kavanagh (*Southerly*, Vol. 46, No. 3, Sept. 1986), Malouf endeavours to define the link between poetry and fiction in his own work. "If one wanted to make the simplest distinction between the language of prose and the language of poetry, one would say the language of poetry is always more intense, and dense. But to some extent over the last sixty years, prose has moved in that direction. Think of Joyce. I can't imagine a use of language more dense or aware of words as such, and of objects as words, than in *Ulysses*. At the same time, a lot of poetry has developed a lightweight language, a throwaway attitude to subject and situation, which is going in the opposite direction. You feel that more difficult things are being done in prose, with a denser language, than are being done in most of the poetry being written. I think that strange crossover does put people who are working in both forms in a strange position. For me, the opposite of the anecdotal or situational thing in poetry was music. I think it is an honourable thing to try to revive the pure lyric, which is the great line of our poetry but may be very difficult to do in our time."

Malouf claims that his works "are constructed in terms of correspondences, analogies, metaphors, rather than plot. That is an attempt to render the way

I see the world, or at least the way I want to *read* the world: that things make sense in terms of those correspondences." He is interested in art as a means of naming, of reconciling the gap between words and the objects they represent: "Every time you offer a description in a novel or write a poem, what you are trying to do is present that landscape or that object, make it present, as if it were absolutely freshly made, for you and for the reader. But made is what it is. Words are being used in some way magically. . . . Writing, it seems to me is one of those ways in which the healing takes place. When we read, or when we write, the word and the object are absolutely one, as if there never was any question of mind and object being separate, or word and object being separate. In that way, all my writing is an attempt to make that true, against the whole of our cultural history."

Southern Skies

From the beginning he was a stumbling-block, the Professor. I had always thought of him as an old man as one thinks of one's parents as old, but he can't in those days have been more than fifty. Squat, powerful, with a good deal of black hair on his wrists, he was what was called a 'ladies man'—though that must have been far in the past and in another country. What he practised now was a formal courtliness, a clicking of heels and kissing of plump fingers that was the extreme form of a set of manners that our parents clung to because it belonged, along with much else, to the Old Country, and which we young people, for the same reason, found it imperative to reject. The Professor had a 'position'—he taught mathematics to apprentices on day-release. He was proof that a breakthrough into the new world was not only possible, it was a fact. Our parents, having come to a place where their qualifications in medicine or law were unacceptable, had been forced to take work as labourers or factory-hands or to keep dingy shops; but we, their clever sons and daughters, would find our way back to the safe professional classes. For our parents there was deep sorrow in all this, and the Professor offered hope. We were invited to see in him both the embodiment of a noble past and a glimpse of what, with hard work and a little luck or grace, we might claim from the future.

He was always the special guest.

'Here, pass the Professor this slice of Torte,' my mother would say, choosing the largest piece and piling it with cream, or 'Here, take the Professor a nice cold Pils, and see you hand it to him proper now and don't spill none on the way': this on one of those community outings we used to go to in the early years, when half a dozen families would gather at Suttons Beach with a crate of beer bottles in straw jackets and a spread of homemade sausage and cabbage rolls. Aged six or seven, in my knitted bathing-briefs, and watching out in my bare feet for bindy-eye, I would set out over the grass to where the great man and my father, easy now in shirtsleeves and braces, would be pursuing one of their interminable arguments. My father had been a lawyer in the Old Country but worked now at the Vulcan Can Factory. He was passionately interested in philosophy, and the Professor was his only companion on those breathless flights that were, along with the music of Beethoven and Mahler, his sole consolation on the raw and desolate shore where he was marooned. Seeing me come wobbling towards them with the Pils—which I had slopped a little—held breast-high before me, all golden in the sun, he would look startled, as if I were a spirit of the place he had failed to allow for. It was the

Professor who recognized the nature of my errand. 'Ah, how kind,' he would say. 'Thank you, my dear. And thank the good mama too. Anton, you are a lucky man.' And my father, reconciled to the earth again, would smile and lay his hand very gently on the nape of my neck while I blushed and squirmed.

The Professor had no family—or not in Australia. He lived alone in a house he had built to his own design. It was of pinewood, as in the Old Country, and in defiance of local custom was surrounded by trees—natives. There was also a swimming pool where he exercised twice a day. I went there occasionally with my father, to collect him for an outing, and had sometimes peered at it through a glass door; but we were never formally invited. The bachelor did not entertain. He was always the guest, and what his visits meant to me, as to the children of a dozen other families, was that I must be especially careful of my manners, see that my shoes were properly polished, my nails clean, my hair combed, my tie straight, my socks pulled up, and that when questioned about school or about the games I played I should give my answers clearly, precisely, and without making faces.

So there he was all through my childhood, an intimidating presence, and a heavy reminder of that previous world; where his family owned a castle, and where he had been, my mother insisted, a real scholar.

Time passed and as the few close-knit families of our community moved to distant suburbs and lost contact with one another, we children were released from restriction. It was easy for our parents to give in to new ways now that others were not watching. Younger brothers failed to inherit our confirmation suits with their stiff white collars and cuffs. We no longer went to examinations weighed down with holy medals, or silently invoked, before putting pen to paper, the good of offices of the Infant of Prague—whose influence, I decided, did not extend to Brisbane, Queensland. Only the Professor remained as a last link.

'I wish, when the Professor comes,' my mother would complain, 'that you try to speak better. The vowels! For my sake, darling, but also for your father, because we want to be proud of you,' and she would try to detain me as, barefoot, in khaki shorts and an old T-shirt, already thirteen, I wriggled from her embrace. 'And put shoes on, or sandals at least, and a nice clean shirt. I don't want that the Professor think we got an Arab for a son. And your Scout belt! And comb your hair a little, my darling—please!'

She kissed me before I could pull away. She was shocked, now that she saw me through the Professor's eyes, at how far I had grown from the little gentleman I might have been, all neatly suited and shod and brushed and polished, if they had never left the Old Country, or if she and my father had been stricter with me in this new one.

The fact is, I had succeeded, almost beyond my own expectations, in making myself indistinguishable from the roughest of my mates at school. My mother must have wondered at times if I could ever be smoothed out and civilized again, with my broad accent, my slang, my feet toughened and splayed from going barefoot. I was spoiled and wilful and ashamed of my parents. My mother knew it, and now, in front of the Professor, it was her turn to be ashamed. To assert my independence, or to show them that I did not care, I was never so loutish, I never slouched or mumbled or scowled so darkly as when the Professor appeared. Even my father, who was too dreamily involved with his own thoughts to notice me on most occasions, was aware of it and shocked. He complained to my mother, who shook her head and cried. I felt magnificently justified, and the next time the Professor made his appearance I swaggered even more outrageously and gave every indication of being an incorrigible tough.

The result was not at all what I had had in mind. Far from being repelled by my roughness the Professor seemed charmed. The more I showed off and embarrassed my parents, the more he encouraged me. My excesses delighted him. He was entranced.

He really was, as we younger people had always thought, a caricature of a man. You could barely look at him without laughing, and we had all become expert, even the girls, at imitating his hunched stance, his accent (which was at once terribly foreign and terribly English) and the way he held his stubby fingers when, at the end of a meal, he dipped sweet biscuits into wine and popped them whole into his mouth. My own imitations were designed to torment my mother.

'Oh you shouldn't!' she would whine, suppressing another explosion of giggles. 'You mustn't! Oh stop it now, your father will see—he would be offended. The Professor is a fine man. May you have such a head on your shoulders one day, and such a position.'

'Such a head on my shoulders,' I mimicked, hunching my back like a stork so that I had no neck, and she would try to cuff me, and miss as I ducked away.

I was fifteen and beginning to spring up out of pudgy childhood into clean-limbed, tumultuous adolescence. By staring for long hours into mirrors behind locked doors, by taking stock of myself in shop windows, and from the looks of some of the girls at school, I had discovered that I wasn't at all bad-looking, might even be good-looking, and was already tall and well-made. I had chestnut hair like my mother and my skin didn't freckle in the sun but turned heavy gold. There was a whole year between fifteen and sixteen when I was fascinated by the image of myself I could get back from people simply by playing up to them—it scarcely mattered whom: teachers, girls, visitors to the house like the Professor, passers-by in the street. I was obsessed with myself, and lost no opportunity of putting my powers to the test.

Once or twice in earlier days, when I was playing football on Saturday afternoon, my father and the Professor had appeared on the sidelines, looking in after a walk. Now, as if by accident, the Professor came alone. When I came trotting in to collect my bike, dishevelled, still spattered and streaked from the game, he would be waiting. He just happened, yet again, to be passing, and had a book for me to take home, or a message: he would be calling for my father at eight and could I please remind him, or yes, he would be coming next night to play Solo. He was very formal on these occasions, but I felt his interest; and sometimes, without thinking of anything more than the warm sense of myself it gave me to command his attention, I would walk part of the way home with him, wheeling my bike and chatting about nothing very important: the game, or what I had done with my holiday, or since he was a dedicated star-gazer, the new comet that had appeared. As these meetings increased I got to be more familiar with him. Sometimes, when two or three of the others were there (they had come to recognize him and teased me a little, making faces and jerking their heads as he made his way, hunched and short-sighted, to where we were towelling ourselves at the tap) I would for their benefit show off a little, without at first realizing, in my reckless passion to be admired, that I was exceeding all bounds and that they now included me as well as the Professor in their humorous contempt. I was mortified. To ease myself back into their good opinion I passed him off as a family nuisance, whose attentions I knew were comic but whom I was leading on for my own amusement. This was acceptable enough and I was soon restored to popularity, but felt doubly treacherous. He was, after all, my father's closest friend, and there was as well that larger question of the Old Country. I burned with shame, but was too cowardly to do more than brazen things out.

For all my crudeness and arrogance I had a great desire to act nobly, and in this business of the Professor I had miserably failed. I decided to cut my losses. As soon as he appeared now, and had announced his message, I would mount my bike, sling my football boots over my shoulder and pedal away. My one fear was that he might enquire what the trouble was, but of course he did not. Instead he broke off his visits altogether or passed the field without stopping, and I found myself regretting something I had come to depend on—his familiar figure hunched like a bird on the sidelines, our talks, some fuller sense of my own presence to add at the end of the game to the immediacy of my limbs after violent exercise.

Looking back on those days I see myself as a kind of centaur, half-boy, half-bike, forever wheeling down suburban streets under the poincianas, on my way to football practice or the library or to a meeting of the little group of us, boys and girls, that came together on someone's verandah in the evenings after tea.

I might come across the Professor then on his after-dinner stroll, and as often as not he would be accompanied by my father, who would stop me and demand (partly, I thought, to impress the Professor) where I was off to or where I had been; insisting, with more than his usual force, that I come home right away, with no argument.

On other occasions, pedalling past his house among the trees, I would catch a glimpse of him with his telescope on the roof. He might raise a hand and wave if he recognized me; and sprinting away, crouched low over the handlebars, I would feel, or imagine I felt, that the telescope had been lowered and was following me to the end of the street, losing me for a time, then picking me up again two streets further on as I flashed away under the bunchy leaves.

I spent long hours cycling back and forth between our house and my girlfriend Helen's or to Ross McDowell or Jimmy Larwood's, my friends from school, and the Professor's house was always on the route.

I think of those days now as being all alike, and the nights also: the days warmish, still, endlessly without event, and the nights quivering with expectancy but also uneventful, heavy with the scent of jasmine and honeysuckle and lighted by enormous stars. But what I am describing, of course, is neither a time nor a place but the mood of my own bored, expectant, uneventful adolescence. I was always abroad and waiting for something significant to occur, for life somehow to declare itself and catch me up. I rode my bike in slow circles or figures-of-eight, took it for sprints across the gravel of the park, or simply hung motionless in the saddle, balanced and waiting.

Nothing ever happened. In the dark of front verandahs we lounged and swapped stories, heard gossip, told jokes, or played show-poker and smoked. One night each week I went to Helen's and we sat a little scared of one other in her garden-swing, touching in the dark. Helen liked me better, I thought, than I liked her—I had that power over her—and it was this more than anything else that attracted me, though I found it scary as well. For fear of losing me she might have gone to any one of the numbers that in those days marked the stages of sexual progress and could be boasted about, in a way that seemed shameful afterwards, in locker-rooms or round the edge of the pool. I could have taken us both to 6, 8, 10, but what then? The numbers were not infinite.

I rode around watching my shadow flare off gravel; sprinted, hung motionless, took the rush of warm air into my shirt; afraid that when the declaration came, it too, like the numbers, might be less than infinite. I didn't want to discover the limits of the world. Restlessly impelled towards some future that would at last offer me my real self, I nevertheless drew back, happy for the moment, even in my unhappiness, to be half-boy, half-bike, half aimless energy and half a machine that could hurtle off at a moment's notice in any one of a hundred directions. Away from things—but away, most of all, from my self. My own presence had begun to be a source of deep dissatisfaction to me, my vanity, my charm, my false-ness, my preoccupation with sex. I was sick of myself and longed for the world to free me by making its own rigorous demands and declaring at last what I must be.

One night, in our warm late winter, I was riding home past the Professor's house when I saw him hunched as usual beside his telescope, but too absorbed on this occasion to be aware of me.

I paused at the end of the drive, wondering what it was that he saw on clear nights like this, that was invisible to me when I leaned my head back and filled my gaze with the sky.

The stars seemed palpably close. In the high September blueness it was as if the odour of jasmine blossoms had gathered there in a single shower of white. You might have been able to catch the essence of it floating down, as sailors, they say, can smell new land whole days before they first catch sight of it.

What I was catching, in fact, was the first breath of change—a change of season. From the heights I fell suddenly into deep depression, one of those sweet-sad glooms of adolescence that are like a bodiless drifting out of yourself into the immensity of things, when you are aware as never again—or never so poignantly—that time is moving swiftly on, that a school year is very nearly over and childhood finished, that you will have to move up a grade at football into a tougher class—shifts that against the vastness of space are minute, insignificant, but at that age solemnly felt.

I was standing astride the bike, staring upwards, when I became aware that my name was being called, and for the second or third time. I turned my bike into the drive with its border of big-leafed saxifrage and came to where the Professor, his hand on the telescope, was leaning out over the roof.

'I have some books for your father,' he called. 'Just come to the gate and I will get them for you.'

The gate was wooden, and the fence, which made me think of a stockade, was of raw slabs eight feet high, stained reddish-brown. He leaned over the low parapet and dropped a set of keys.

'It's the thin one,' he told me. 'You can leave your bike in the yard.' He meant the paved courtyard inside, where I rested it easily against the wall. Beyond, and to the left of the pine-framed house, which was stained the same colour as the fence, was a garden taken up almost entirely by the pool. It was overgrown with dark tropical plants, monstera, hibiscus, banana-palms with their big purplish flowers, glossily pendulous on stalks, and fixed to the paling-fence like trophies in wads of bark, elk-horn, tree-orchids, showers of delicate maidenhair. It was too cold for swimming, but the pool was filled and covered with a shifting scum of jacaranda leaves that had blown in from the street, where the big trees were stripping to bloom.

I went round the edge of the pool and a light came on, reddish, in one of the inner rooms. A moment later the Professor himself appeared, tapping for attention at a glass door.

'I have the books right here,' he said briskly; but when I stood hesitating in the dark beyond the threshold, he shifted his feet and added: 'But maybe you would like to come in a moment and have a drink. Coffee. I could make some. Or beer. Or a Coke if you prefer it. I have Coke.'

I had never been here alone, and never, even with my father, to this side of the house. When we came to collect the Professor for an outing we had always waited in the tiled hallway while he rushed about with one arm in the sleeve of his overcoat laying out saucers for cats, and it was to the front door, in later years, that I had delivered bowls of gingerbread fish that my mother had made specially because she knew he liked it, or cabbage rolls or herring. I had never been much interested in what lay beyond the hallway, with its fierce New Guinea masks, all tufted hair and boar's tusks, and the Old Country chest that was just like our own. Now, with the books already in my hands, I hesitated and looked past him into the room.

'All right. If it's no trouble.'

'No, no, no trouble at all!' He grinned, showing his teeth with their extravagant caps. 'I am delighted. Really! Just leave the books there. You see they are tied with string, quite easy for you I'm sure, even on the bike. Sit where you like. Anywhere. I'll get the drink.'

'Beer then,' I said boldly, and my voice cracked, destroying what I had hoped might be the setting of our relationship on a clear, man-to-man basis that would wipe out the follies of the previous year. I coughed, cleared my throat, and said again 'Beer, thanks,' and sat abruptly on a sofa that was too low and left me prone and sprawling.

He stopped a moment and considered, as if I had surprised him by crossing a second threshold.

'Well then, if it's to be beer, I shall join you. Maybe you are also hungry. I could make a sandwich.'

'No, no thank you, they're expecting me. Just the beer.'

He went out, his slippers shushing over the tiles, and I shifted immediately to a straight-backed chair opposite and took the opportunity to look around.

There were rugs on the floor, old threadbare Persians, and low down, all round the walls, stacks of the heavy seventy-eights I carried home when my father borrowed them: sonatas by Beethoven, symphonies by Sibelius and Mahler. Made easy by the Professor's absence, I got up and wandered round. On every open surface, the glass table-top, the sideboard, the long mantel of the fireplace, were odd bits and pieces that he must have collected in his travels: lumps of coloured quartz, a desert rose, slabs of clay with fern or fish fossils in them, glass paperweights, snuff-boxes, meerschaum pipes of fantastic shape—one a Saracen's head, another the torso of a woman like a ship's figurehead with full breasts and golden nipples—bits of Baltic amber, decorated shards of pottery, black on terracotta, and one unbroken object, a little earthenware lamp that when I examined it more closely turned out to be a phallic grotesque. I had just discovered what it actually was when the Professor stepped into the room. Turning swiftly to a framed photograph on the wall above, I found myself peering into a stretch of the Old Country, a foggy, sepia world that I recognized immediately from similar photographs at home.

'Ah,' he said, setting the tray down on an empty chair, 'you have discovered my weakness.' He switched on another lamp. 'I have tried, but I am too sentimental. I cannot part with them.'

The photograph, I now observed, was one of three. They were all discoloured with foxing on the passe-partout mounts, and the glass of one was shattered, but so neatly that not a single splinter had shifted in the frame.

The one I was staring at was of half a dozen young men in military uniform. It might have been from the last century, but there was a date in copperplate: 1921. Splendidly booted and sashed and frogged, and hieratically stiff, with casque helmets under their arms, swords tilted at the thigh, white gloves tucked into braided epaulettes, they were a chorus line from a Ruritanian operetta. They were also, as I knew, the heroes of a lost but unforgotten war.

'You recognize me?' the Professor asked.

I looked again. It was difficult. All the young men strained upright with the same martial hauteur, wore the same little clipped moustaches, had the same flat hair parted in the middle and combed in wings over their ears. Figures from the past can be as foreign, as difficult to identify individually, as the members of another race. I took the plunge, set my forefinger against the frame, and turned to the Professor for confirmation. He came to my side and peered.

'No,' he said sorrowfully. 'But the mistake is entirely understandable. He was my great friend, almost a brother. I am here. This is me. On the left.'

He considered himself, the slim assured figure, chin slightly tilted, eyes fixed ahead, looking squarely out of a class whose privileges—inherent in every point of the stance, the uniform, the polished accoutrements—were not to be questioned, and from the ranks of an army that was invincible. The proud caste no longer existed. Neither did the army nor the country it was meant to defend, except in the memory of people like the Professor and my parents and, in a ghostly way, half a century off in another hemisphere, my own.

He shook his head and made a clucking sound. 'Well,' he said firmly, 'it's a long time ago. It is foolish of me to keep such things. We should live for the present. Or like you younger people', bringing the conversation back to me, 'for the future.'

I found it easier to pass to the other photographs.

In one, the unsmiling officer appeared as an even younger man, caught in an informal, carefully posed moment with a group of ladies. He was clean-shaven and lounging on the grass in a striped blazer; beside him a discarded boater—very English. The ladies, more decorously disposed, wore long dresses with hats and ribbons. Neat little slippers peeped out under their skirts.

'Yes, yes,' he muttered, almost impatient now, 'that too. Summer holidays— who can remember where? And the other a walking trip.'

I looked deep into a high meadow, with broken cloud-drift in the dip below. Three young men in shorts, maybe schoolboys, were climbing on the far side of the wars. There were flowers in the foreground, glowingly out of focus, and it was this picture whose glass was shattered; it was like looking through a brilliant spider's web into a picture-book landscape that was utterly familiar, though I could never have been there. *That is the place,* I thought. *That is the land my parents mean when they say 'the Old Country': the country of childhood and first love that they go back to in their sleep and which I have no memory of, though I was born there. Those flowers are the ones, precisely those, that blossom in the songs they sing.* And immediately I was back in my mood of just a few minutes ago, when I had stood out there gazing up at the stars. *What is it,* I asked myself, *that I will remember and want to preserve, when in years to come I think of the Past? What will be important enough?* For what the photographs had led me back to, once again, was myself. It was always the same. No matter how hard I tried to think my way out into other people's lives, into the world beyond me, the feelings I discovered were my own.

'Come. Sit,' the Professor said, 'and drink your beer. And do eat one of these sandwiches. It's very good rye bread, from the only shop. I go all the way to South Brisbane for it. And Gürken. I seem to remember you like them.'

'What do you do up on the roof?' I asked, my mouth full of bread and beer, feeling uneasy again now that we were sitting with nothing to fix on.

'I make observations, you know. The sky, which looks so still, is always in motion, full of drama if you understand how to read it. Like looking into a pond. Hundreds of events happening right under your eyes, except that most of what we see is already finished by the time we see it—ages ago—but important just the same. Such large events. Huge! Bigger even than we can imagine. And beautiful, since they unfold, you know, to a kind of music, to numbers of infinite dimension like the ones you deal with in equations at school, but more complex, and entirely visible.'

He was moved as he spoke by an emotion that I could not identify, touched by occasions a million light-years off and still unfolding towards him, in no way personal. The room for a moment lost its tension. I no longer felt myself to be the focus of his interest, or even of my own. I felt liberated, and for the first time the Professor was interesting in his own right, quite apart from the attention he paid me or the importance my parents attached to him.

'Maybe I could come again,' I found myself saying. 'I'd like to see.'

'But of course,' he said, 'any time. Tonight is not good—there is a little haze, but tomorrow if you like. Or any time.'

I nodded. But the moment of easiness had passed. My suggestion, which might have seemed like another move in a game, had brought me back into focus for him and his look was quizzical, defensive. I felt it and was embarrassed, and at the same time saddened. Some truer vision of myself had been in the room for a moment. I had almost grasped it. Now I felt it slipping away as I moved back into my purely physical self.

I put the glass down, not quite empty.

'No thanks, really,' I told him when he indicated the half finished bottle on the tray. 'I should have been home nearly an hour ago. My mother, you know.'

'Ah yes, of course. Well, just call whenever you wish, no need to be formal. Most nights I am observing. It is a very interesting time. Here—let me open the door for you. The books, I see, are a little awkward, but you are so expert on the bicycle I am sure it will be OK.'

I followed him round the side of the pool into the courtyard and there was my bike at its easy angle to the wall, my other familiar and streamlined self. I wheeled it out while he held the gate.

Among my parents' oldest friends were a couple who had recently moved to a new house on the other side of the park, and at the end of winter, in the year I turned seventeen, I sometimes rode over on Sundays to help John clear the big overgrown garden. All afternoon we grubbed out citrus trees that had gone wild, hacked down morning-glory that had grown all over the lower part of the yard and cut the knee-high grass with a sickle to prepare it for mowing. I enjoyed the work. Stripped down to shorts in the strong sunlight, I slashed and tore at the weeds till my hands blistered, and in a trancelike preoccupation with tough green things that clung to the earth with a fierce tenacity, forgot for a time my own turmoil and lack of roots. It was something to *do*.

John, who worked up ahead, was a dentist. He paid me ten shillings a day for the work, and this, along with my pocket-money, would take Helen and me to the pictures on Saturday night, or to a flash meal at one of the city hotels. We worked all afternoon, while the children, who were four and seven, watched and got in the way. Then about five-thirty Mary would call us for tea.

Mary had been at school with my mother and was the same age, though I could never quite believe it; she had children a whole ten years younger than I was, and I had always called her Mary. She wore bright bangles on her arm, liked to dance at parties, never gave me presents like handkerchiefs or socks, and had always treated me, I thought, as a grownup. When she called us for tea I went to the garden tap, washed my feet, splashed water over my back that was streaked with soil and sweat and stuck all over with little grass clippings, and was about to buckle on my loose sandals when she said from the doorway where she had been watching: 'Don't bother to get dressed. John hasn't.' She stood there smiling, and I turned away aware suddenly of how little I had on; and had to use my V-necked sweater to cover an excitement that might otherwise have been immediately apparent in the khaki shorts I was wearing without under-pants because of the heat.

As I came up the steps towards her she stood back to let me pass, and her hand, very lightly, brushed the skin between my shoulder-blades.

'You're still wet,' she said.

It seemed odd somehow to be sitting at the table in their elegant dining-room without a shirt; though John was doing it, and was already engaged like the chil-dren in demolishing a pile of neat little sandwiches.

I sat at the head of the table with the children noisily grabbing at my left and John on my right drinking tea and slurping it a little, while Mary plied me with raisin-bread and Old Country cookies. I felt red, swollen, confused every time she turned to me, and for some reason it was the children's presence rather than John's that embarrassed me, especially the boy's.

Almost immediately we were finished John got up.

'I'll just go,' he said, 'and do another twenty minutes before it's dark.' It was dark already, but light enough perhaps to go on raking the grass we had cut and were carting to the incinerator. I made to follow. 'It's all right,' he told me. 'I'll finish off. You've earned your money for today.'

'Come and see our animals!' the children yelled, dragging me down the hall to their bedroom, and for ten minutes or so I sat on the floor with them, setting out farm animals and making fences, till Mary, who had been clearing the table, appeared in the doorway.

'Come on now, that's enough, it's bathtime, you kids. Off you go!'

They ran off, already half-stripped, leaving her to pick up their clothes and fold them while I continued to sit cross-legged among the toys, and her white legs, in their green sandals, moved back and forth at eye-level. When she went out I too got up, and stood watching at the bathroom door.

She was sitting on the edge of the bath, soaping the little boy's back, as I remembered my mother doing, while the children splashed and shouted. Then she dried her hands on a towel, very carefully and I followed her into the unlighted lounge. Beyond the glass wall in the depths of the garden, John was stooping to gather armfuls of the grass we had cut, and staggering with it to the incinerator.

She sat and patted the place beside her. I followed as in a dream. The children's voices at the end of the hallway were complaining quarrelling, shrilling. I was sure John could see us through the glass as he came back for another load.

Nothing was said. Her hand moved over my shoulder, down my spine, brushed very lightly, without lingering, over the place where my shorts tented; then rested easily on my thigh. When John came in he seemed unsurprised to find us sitting close in the dark. He went right past us to the drinks cabinet, which suddenly lighted up. I felt exposed and certain now that he must see where her hand was and say something.

All he said was: 'Something to drink, darling?' Without hurry she got up to help him and they passed back and forth in front of the blazing cabinet, with its mirrors and its rows of bottles and cut-crystal glasses. I was sweating worse than when I had worked in the garden, and began, self-consciously, to haul on the sweater.

I pedalled furiously away, glad to have the cooling air pour over me and to feel free again.

Back there I had been scared—but of what? Of a game in which I might, for once, be the victim—not passive, but with no power to control the moves. I slowed down and considered that, and was, without realizing it, at the edge of something. I rode on in the softening dark. It was good to have the wheels of the bike roll away under me as I rose on the pedals, to feel on my cheeks the warm scent of jasmine that was invisible all round. It was a brilliant night verging on spring. I didn't want it to be over; I wanted to slow things down. I dismounted and walked a little, leading my bike along the grassy edge in the shadow of trees, and without precisely intending it, came on foot to the entrance to the Professor's drive, and paused, looking up beyond the treetops to where he might be installed with his telescope—observing what? What events up there in the infinite sky?

I leaned far back to see. A frozen waterfall it might have been, falling slowly towards me, sending out blown spray that would take centuries, light-years, to break in thunder over my head. Time. What did one moment, one night, a lifespan mean in relation to all that?

'Hullo there!'

It was the Professor. I could see him now, in the moonlight beside the telescope, which he leaned on and which pointed not upward to the heavens but down to where I was standing. It occurred to me, as on previous occasions, that in the few moments of my standing there with my head flung back to the stars, what he might have been observing was *me*. I hesitated, made no decision. Then, out of a state of passive expectancy, willing nothing but waiting poised for my own life to occur; out of a state of being open to the spring night and to the emptiness of the hours between seven and ten when I was expected to be in, or thirteen (was it?) and whatever age I would be when manhood finally came to me; out of my simply being there with my hand on the saddle of the machine, bare-legged, loose-sandalled, going nowhere, I turned into the drive, led my bike up to the stockade gate and waited for him to throw down the keys.

'You know which one it is,' he said, letting them fall. 'Just use the other to come in by the poolside.'

I unlocked the gate, rested my bike against the wall of the courtyard and went round along the edge of the pool. It was clean now but heavy with shadows. I turned the key in the glass door, found my way (though this part of the house was new to me) to the stairs, and climbed to where another door opened straight on to the roof.

'Ah,' he said, smiling. 'So at last! You are here.'

The roof was unwalled but set so deep among trees that it was as if I had stepped out of the city altogether into some earlier, more darkly-wooded era. Only lighted windows, hanging detached in the dark, showed where houses, where neighbours were.

He fixed the telescope for me and I moved into position. 'There,' he said, 'what you can see now is Jupiter with its four moons—you see?—all in line, and with the bands across its face.'

I saw. Later it was Saturn with its rings and the lower of the two pointers to the cross, Alpha Centauri, which was not one star but two. It was miraculous. From that moment below when I had looked up at a cascade of light that was still ages off, I might have been catapulted twenty thousand years into the nearer past, or into my own future. Solid spheres hovered above me, tiny balls of matter moving in concert like the atoms we drew in chemistry, held together by invisible lines of force; and I thought oddly that if I were to lower the telescope now to where I had been standing at the entrance to the drive I would see my own puzzled, upturned face, but as a self I had already outgrown and abandoned, not minutes but aeons back. He shifted the telescope and I caught my breath. One after another, constellations I had known since childhood as points of light to be joined up in the mind (like those picture-puzzles children make, pencilling in the scattered dots till Snow White and the Seven Dwarfs appear, or an old jalopy), came together now, not as an imaginary panhandle or bull's head or belt and sword, but at some depth of vision I hadn't known I possessed, as blossoming abstractions, equations luminously exploding out of their own depths, brilliantly solving themselves and playing the results in my head as a real and visible music. I felt a power in myself that might actually burst out at my ears, and at the same time saw myself, from *out there*, as just a figure with his eye to a lens. I had a clear sense of being one more hard little point in the immensity—but part of it, a source of light like all those others—and was aware for the first time of the grainy reality of my own life, and then, a fact of no large significance, of the certainty of my death; but in some dimension where those terms were too vague to be relevant. It was at the point where my self ended and the rest of it began that Time, or Space, showed its richness to me. I was overwhelmed.

Slowly, from so far out, I drew back, re-entered the present and was aware again of the close suburban dark—of its moving now in the shape of a hand. I must have known all along that it was there, working from the small of my back to my belly, up the inside of my thigh, but it was of no importance, I was too far off. Too many larger events were unfolding for me to break away and ask, as I might have, 'What are you doing?'

I must have come immediately. But when the stars blurred in my eyes it was with tears, and it was the welling of this deeper salt, filling my eyes and rolling down my cheeks, that was the real overflow of the occasion. I raised my hand to brush them away and it was only then that I was aware, once again, of the Professor. I looked at him as from a distance. He was getting to his feet, and his babble of concern, alarm, self-pity, sentimental recrimination, was incomprehensible to me. I couldn't see what he meant.

'No no, it's nothing,' I assured him, turning aside to button my shorts. 'It was nothing. Honestly.' I was unwilling to say more in case he misunderstood what I did not understand myself.

We stood on opposite sides of the occasion. Nothing of what he had done could make the slightest difference to me, I was untouched: youth is too physical to accord very much to that side of things. But what I had *seen*—what he had led me to see—my bursting into the life of things—I would look back on that as the real beginning of my existence, as the entry into a vocation, and nothing could diminish the gratitude I felt for it. I wanted, in the immense seriousness and humility of this moment, to tell him so, but I lacked the words, and silence was fraught with all the wrong ones.

'I have to go now,' was what I said.

'Very well. Of course.'

He looked hopeless. He might have been waiting for me to strike him a blow— not a physical one. He stood quietly at the gateway while I wheeled out the bike.

I turned then and faced him, and without speaking, offered him, very formally, my hand. He took it and we shook—as if, in the magnanimity of my youth, I had agreed to overlook his misdemeanour or forgive him. That misapprehension too was a weight I would have to bear.

Carrying it with me, a heavy counterpoise to the extraordinary lightness that was my whole life, I bounced unsteadily over the dark tufts of the driveway and out onto the road.

Katherine Mansfield

Born in Wellington, New Zealand, in 1888, Kathleen Mansfield Beauchamp was educated in the village school in Karori and a private school for girls before completing four years at Queen's College, London. At the age of nineteen, she persuaded her merchant father to permit her to return to London, on a continuing allowance to pursue a career as a writer. She became pregnant that first year in London, married a man who was not the father of the child, had a miscarriage, and lived briefly in Germany. This restless period was followed by a number of happy years married to critic and journalist John Middleton Murry, marred only by the death of her younger brother in World War I and her gradually failing health. She was influenced by the work of Chekhov, diminishing the importance of plot and letting small, seemingly insignificant details carry the emotional weight of her stories: "an overheard word can bring down the empire of the self." Her first book of stories, *In a German Pension*, was published in 1911; *Bliss and Other Stories* appeared in 1920; and *The Garden Party and Other Stories* in 1922. She died of tuberculosis in 1923 at the age of thirty-four, while in pursuit of physical and spiritual relief at the Gurdjieff Institute in France.

Mansfield seems to have considered character to be less central to the short story than other matters: "The short story, by reason of its aesthetics, is not, and is not intended to be, the medium either for the exploration or long-term development of character. Character cannot be more than *shown—it is there for use, the use is dramatic. Foreshortening is not only unavoidable, it is right.*" Colour, tone, verbal texture seem more important to her. In a letter to S. S. Koteliansky, she writes about how she even dreams of the "smallest details": "Do you, too feel an infinite delight and value in *detail*—not for the sake of detail but for the life *in* the life of it. I never can express myself (and you can laugh as much as you please). But do you ever feel as though the Lord threw you into eternity—into the very exact centre of eternity, and even as you plunged you felt every ripple that flowed out from your plunging— every single ripple floating away and touching and drawing into its circle every slightest thing it touched."

In a letter to Richard Murry, she writes: "It's a very queer thing how *craft* comes into writing. I mean down to details. Par exemple. In Miss Brill I chose not only the length of every sentence, but even the sound of every sentence—I chose the rise and fall of every paragraph to fit her—and to fit her on that day at that very moment. After I'd written it I read it aloud— numbers of times—just as one would *play over* a musical composition, trying to get it nearer and nearer to the expression of Miss Brill—until it fitted her. . . . I often wonder whether other writers do the same. If a thing has really come off it seems to me there mustn't be one single word out of place or one word that could be taken out. That's how I AIM at writing. It will take some time to get anywhere near there."

Mansfield kept journals—she called them "minute notebooks"—which are chockfull of poems, story ideas, plans, personal pep talks. She claimed to be "always trembling on the brink of poetry," yet, strangely, often unable to write: "I pose myself, yet once more, my Eternal Question. What is it that makes the moment of delivery so difficult for me? If I were to sit down—now—and just to write out, plain, some of the stories—all written, all ready, in my mind 'twould take me days. There are so many of them. I sit and *think* them out, and if I overcome my lassitude and *do* take the pen they ought (they are so word perfect) to write themselves. But it's the activity. I haven't a place to write in or on—the chair isn't comfortable—yet even as I complain *this* seems the place and *this* the chair. And don't I want to write them? Lord! Lord! it's my only desire—my one *happy issue*."

In words that recall the letters of Flaubert and Conrad, she addresses the issue of writing as work, as a religious vocation: "Work. Shall I be able to express, one day, my love of work—my desire to be a better writer—my longing to take greater pains. And the passion I feel. It takes the place of religion—it *is* my religion—of people—I create my people: of 'life'—it *is* Life. The temptation is to kneel before it, to adore, to prostrate myself, to stay too long in a state of ecstasy before the *idea* of it. I must be more busy about my master's business."

Mansfield's struggles are fascinating, the ecstasy and the hard labour of creation, the difficult mixture of self-congratulation and self-doubt, the fear of literary pride that "interferes very much with work. One can't be calm, clear, good as one must be, while it goes on. I look at the mountains, I try to pray and I think of something *clever*. It's a kind of excitement within one, which shouldn't be there. Calm yourself. Clear yourself. And anything that I write in this mood will be no good; it will be full of *sediment*. If I were well, I would go off by myself somewhere and sit under a tree. One must learn, one must practise, to *forget* oneself. I can't tell the truth about Aunt Anne unless I am free to enter into her life without selfconsciousness. Oh God! I am divided still, I am bad. I fail in my personal life. I lapse into impatience, temper, vanity, and so I fail as thy priest. Perhaps poetry will help."

A Dill Pickle

And then, after six years, she saw him again. He was seated at one of those little bamboo tables decorated with a Japanese vase of paper daffodils. There was a tall plate of fruit in front of him, and very carefully, in a way she recognized immediately as his 'special' way, he was peeling an orange.

He must have felt that shock of recognition in her for he looked up and met her eyes. Incredible! He didn't know her! She smiled; he frowned. She came towards him. He closed his eyes an instant, but opening them his face lit up as though he had struck a match in a dark room. He laid down the orange and pushed back his chair, and she took her little warm hand out of her muff and gave it to him.

'Vera!' he exclaimed. 'How strange. Really, for a moment I didn't know you. Won't you sit down? You've had lunch? Won't you have some coffee?'

She hesitated, but of course she meant to.

'Yes, I'd like some coffee.' And she sat down opposite him.

'You've changed. You've changed very much,' he said, staring at her with that eager, lighted look. 'You look so well. I've never seen you look so well before.'

'Really?' She raised her veil and unbuttoned her high fur collar. 'I don't feel very well. I can't bear this weather, you know.'

'Ah, no. You hate the cold. . . .'

'Loathe it.' She shuddered. 'And the worst of it is that the older one grows . . .'

He interrupted her. 'Excuse me,' and tapped on the table for the waitress. 'Please bring some coffee and cream.' To her: 'You are sure you won't eat anything? Some fruit, perhaps. The fruit here is very good.'

'No, thanks. Nothing.'

'Then that's settled.' And smiling just a hint too broadly he took up the orange again. 'You were saying—the older one grows—'

'The colder,' she laughed. But she was thinking how well she remembered that trick of his—the trick of interrupting her—and of how it used to exasperate her six years ago. She used to feel then as though he, quite suddenly, in the middle of what she was saying, put his hand over her lips, turned from her, attended to something different, and then took his hand away, and with just the same slightly too broad smile, gave her his attention again. . . . Now we are ready. That is settled.

'The colder!' He echoed her words, laughing too. 'Ah, ah. You still say the same things. And there is another thing about you that is not changed at all—your beautiful voice your beautiful way of speaking.' Now he was very grave; he leaned towards her, and she smelled the warm, stinging scent of the orange peel. 'You have only to say one word and I would know your voice among all other voices. I don't know what it is—I've often wondered—that makes your voice such a—haunting memory. . . . Do you remember that first afternoon we spent together at Kew Gardens? You were so surprised because I did not know the names of any flowers. I am still just as ignorant for all your telling me. But whenever it is very fine and warm, and I see some bright colours—it's awfully strange—I hear your voice saying: "Geranium, marigold, and verbena." And I feel those three words are all I recall of some forgotten, heavenly language. . . . You remember that afternoon?'

'Oh, yes, very well.' She drew a long, soft breath, as though the paper daffodils between them were almost too sweet to bear. Yet, what had remained in her mind of that particular afternoon was an absurd scene over the tea table. A great many people taking tea in a Chinese pagoda, and he behaving like a maniac about the wasps—waving them away, flapping at them with his straw hat, serious and infuriated out of all proportion to the occasion. How delighted the sniggering tea drinkers had been. And how she had suffered.

But now, as he spoke, that memory faded. His was the truer. Yes, it had been a wonderful afternoon, full of geranium and marigold and verbena, and—warm sunshine. Her thoughts lingered over the last two words as though she sang them.

In the warmth, as it were, another memory unfolded. She saw herself sitting on a lawn. He lay beside her, and suddenly, after a long silence, he rolled over and put his head in her lap.

'I wish,' he said, in a low, troubled voice, 'I wish that I had taken poison and were about to die—here now!'

At that moment a little girl in a white dress, holding a long, dripping water lily, dodged from behind a bush, stared at them, and dodged back again. But he did not see. She leaned over him.

'Ah, why do you say that? I could not say that.'

But he gave a kind of soft moan, and taking her hand he held it to his cheek.

'Because I know I am going to love you too much—far too much. And I shall suffer so terribly, Vera, because you never, never will love me.'

He was certainly far better looking now than he had been then. He had lost all that dreamy vagueness and indecision. Now he had the air of a man who has found his place in life, and fills it with a confidence and an assurance which was, to say the least, impressive. He must have made money, too. His clothes were admirable, and at that moment he pulled a Russian cigarette case out of his pocket.

'Won't you smoke?'

'Yes, I will.' She hovered over them. 'They look very good.'

'I think they are. I get them made for me by a little man in St James's Street. I don't smoke very much. I'm not like you—but when I do, they must be delicious, very fresh cigarettes. Smoking isn't a habit with me; it's a luxury—like perfume. Are you still so fond of perfumes? Ah, when I was in Russia . . .'

She broke in: 'You've really been to Russia?'

'Oh, yes. I was there for over a year. Have you forgotten how we used to talk of going there?'

'No, I've not forgotten.'

He gave a strange half laugh and leaned back in his chair. 'Isn't it curious. I have really carried out all those journeys that we planned. Yes, I have been to all those places that we talked of, and stayed in them long enough to—as you used to

say, "air oneself" in them. In fact, I have spent the last three years of my life travelling all the time. Spain, Corsica, Siberia, Russia, Egypt. The only country left is
China, and I mean to go there, too, when the war is over.'

As he spoke, so lightly, tapping the end of his cigarette against the ash-tray, she
felt the strange beast that had slumbered so long within her bosom stir, stretch
itself, yawn, prick up its ears, and suddenly bound to its feet, and fix its longing,
hungry stare upon those far away places. But all she said was, smiling gently: 'How
I envy you.'

He accepted that. 'It has been,' he said, 'very wonderful—especially Russia.
Russia was all that we had imagined, and far, far more. I even spent some days
on a river boat on the Volga. Do you remember that boatman's song that you
used to play?'

'Yes.' It began to play in her mind as she spoke.

'Do you ever play it now?'

'No, I've no piano.'

He was amazed at that. 'But what has become of your beautiful piano?'

She made a little grimace. 'Sold. Ages ago.'

'But you were so fond of music,' he wondered.

'I've no time for it now,' said she.

He let it go at that. 'That river life,' he went on, 'is something quite special.
After a day or two you cannot realize that you have ever known another. And it is
not necessary to know the language—the life of the boat creates a bond between
you and the people that's more than sufficient. You eat with them, pass the day
with them, and in the evening there is that endless singing.'

She shivered, hearing the boatman's song break out again loud and tragic, and
seeing the boat floating on the darkening river with melancholy trees on either
side. . . . 'Yes, I should like that,' said she, stroking her muff.

'You'd like almost everything about Russian life,' he said warmly. 'It's so informal,
so impulsive, so free without question. And then the peasants are so splendid. They
are such human beings—yes, that is it. Even the man who drives your carriage
has—has some real part in what is happening. I remember the evening a party of us,
two friends of mine and the wife of one of them, went for a picnic by the Black Sea.
We took supper and champagne and ate and drank on the grass. And while we were
eating the coachman came up. "Have a dill pickle," he said. He wanted to share
with us. That seemed to me so right, so—you know what I mean?'

And she seemed at that moment to be sitting on the grass beside the mysteriously Black Sea, black as velvet, and rippling against the banks in silent, velvet
waves. She saw the carriage drawn up to one side of the road, and the little group
on the grass, their faces and hands white in the moonlight. She saw the pale dress
of the woman outspread and her folded parasol, lying on the grass like a huge pearl
crochet hook. Apart from them, with his supper in a cloth on his knees, sat the
coachman. 'Have a dill pickle,' said he, and although she was not certain what a
dill pickle was, she saw the greenish glass jar with a red chili like a parrot's beak
glimmering through. She sucked in her cheeks; the dill pickle was terribly sour. . . .

'Yes, I know perfectly what you mean,' she said.

In the pause that followed they looked at each other. In the past when they had looked at each other like that they had felt such a boundless understanding between them that their souls had, as it were, put their arms round each other and dropped into the same sea, content to be drowned, like mournful lovers. But now, the surprising thing was that it was he who held back. He who said:

'What a marvelous listener you are. When you look at me with those wild eyes I feel that I could tell you things that I would never breathe to another human being.'

Was there just a hint of mockery in his voice or was it her fancy? She could not be sure.

'Before I met you,' he said, 'I had never spoken of myself to anybody. How well I remember one night, the night that I brought you the little Christmas tree, telling you all about my childhood. And of how I was so miserable that I ran away and lived under a cart in our yard for two days without being discovered. And you listened, and your eyes shone, and I felt that you had even made the little Christmas tree listen too, as in a fairy story.'

But of that evening she had remembered a little pot of caviare. It had cost seven and sixpence. He could not get over it. Think of it—a tiny jar like that costing seven and sixpence. While she ate it he watched her, delighted and shocked.

'No, really, that is eating money. You could not get seven shillings into a little pot that size. Only think of the profit they must make. . . . 'And he had begun some immensely complicated calculations. . . . But now good-bye to the caviare. The Christmas tree was on the table, and the little boy lay under the cart with his head pillowed on the yard dog.

'The dog was called Bosun,' she cried delightedly.

But he did not follow. 'Which dog? Had you a dog? I don't remember a dog at all.'

'No, no. I meant the yard dog when you were a little boy.' He laughed and snapped the cigarette case to.

'Was he? Do you know I had forgotten that. It seems such ages ago. I cannot believe that it is only six years. After I had recognized you today—I had to take such a leap—I had to take a leap over my whole life to get back to that time. I was such a kid then.' He drummed on the table. 'I've often thought how I must have bored you. And now I understand so perfectly why you wrote to me as you did—although at the time that letter nearly finished my life. I found it again the other day, and I couldn't help laughing as I read it. It was so clever—such a true picture of me.' He glanced up. 'You're not going?'

She had buttoned her collar again and drawn down her veil.

'Yes, I am afraid I must,' she said, and managed a smile. Now she knew that he had been mocking.

'Ah, no, please,' he pleaded. 'Don't go just for a moment,' and he caught up one of her gloves from the table and clutched at it as if that would hold her. 'I see so few people to talk to nowadays, that I have turned into a sort of barbarian,' he said. 'Have I said something to hurt you?'

'Not a bit,' she lied. But as she watched him draw her glove through his fingers, gently, gently, her anger really did die down, and besides, at the moment he looked more like himself of six years ago. . . .

'What I really wanted then,' he said softly, 'was to be a sort of carpet—to make myself into a sort of carpet for you to walk on so that you need not be hurt by the sharp stones and the mud that you hated so. It was nothing more positive than that—nothing more selfish. Only I did desire, eventually, to turn into a magic carpet and carry you away to all those lands you longed to see.'

As he spoke she lifted her head as though she drank something; the strange beast in her bosom began to purr. . . .

'I felt that you were more lonely than anybody else in the world,' he went on, 'and yet, perhaps, that you were the only person in the world who was really, truly alive. Born out of your time,' he murmured, stroking the glove, 'fated.'

Ah, God! What had she done! How had she dared to throw away her happiness like this. This was the only man who had ever understood her. Was it too late? Could it be too late? *She* was that glove that he held in his fingers. . . .

'And then the fact that you had no friends and never had made friends with people. How I understood that, for neither had I. Is it just the same now?'

'Yes,' she breathed. 'Just the same. I am as alone as ever.'

'So am I,' he laughed gently, 'just the same.'

Suddenly with a quick gesture he handed her back the glove and scraped his chair on the floor. 'But what seemed to me so mysterious then is perfectly plain to me now. And to you, too, of course. . . . It simply was that we were such egoists, so self-engrossed, so wrapped up in ourselves that we hadn't a corner in our hearts for anybody else. Do you know,' he cried, naïve and hearty, and dreadfully like another side of that old self again, 'I began studying a Mind System when I was in Russia, and I found that we were not peculiar at all. It's quite a well known form of . . .'

She had gone. He sat there, thunder-struck, astounded beyond words. . . . And then he asked the waitress for his bill.

'But the cream has not been touched,' he said. 'Please do not charge me for it.'

Gabriel García Márquez

Gabriel García Márquez was born in 1928 in Aracataca, a small town in Colombia surrounded by banana plantations. He has lived in Mexico since 1961, supporting himself by journalism until fiction brought him fame. He has published numerous novels, including *No One Writes to the Colonel* (1961), *Evil Hour* (1962), and *The Autumn of the Patriach* (1975), but it is *One Hundred Years of Solitude* (1967) that brought his work international recognition. He has written several volumes of short stories, including *No One Writes to the Colonel and Other Stories* (1968), *Leaf Storm and Other Stories* (1972), *Innocente Eréndira and Other Stories* (1978), and *Collected Stories* (1984). He received the Nobel Prize for Literature in 1982.

García Márquez says, in *The Paris Review* interview with Peter H. Stone, that he started his creative activities as a child by drawing cartoons. Although he had a reputation in school as a writer, he said he did not actually do anything serious until reading Kafka's story "The Metamorphosis": "When I read the line ['As Gregor Samsa awoke that morning from uneasy dreams, he found himself transformed in his bed into a gigantic insect. . . .'] I thought to myself that I didn't know anyone was allowed to write things like that. If I had known, I would have started writing a long time ago. So I immediately started writing stories." He claims to have learned the technique of interior monologue from reading Joyce's *Ulysses*. What allowed him to progress beyond the writing of stories that were intellectual exercises to work that had a deeper "relationship with life" were three things: reading writers of the American Lost Generation, such as Hemingway and Fitzgerald; experiencing the riots of April 9, 1948, when the political leader Gaitan was shot and the people of Bogotá went on a rampage in the streets; and returning with his mother to sell the childhood home in Aracataca: "When I got there it was at first quite shocking because I was now twenty-two and hadn't been there since the age of eight. Nothing had really changed, but I felt that I wasn't really looking at the village, but I was *experiencing* it as if I were reading it. It was as if everything I saw had already been written, and all I had to do was to sit down and copy what was already there and what I was just reading. For all practical purposes everything had evolved into literature: the houses, the people, and the memories." It was after this experience that he wrote his first short novel, *Leaf Storm* (1953).

"It always amuses me," García Márquez says, "that the biggest praise for my work comes for the imagination, while the truth is that there's not a single line in all my work that does not have a basis in reality. The problem is that Caribbean reality resembles the wildest imagination." In terms of audience, he claims that "in the end all books are written for your friends." The evolution of his literary style was influenced by his journalism, his nostalgia, and the struggle to work out the relationship between literature and politics; still, he felt something was missing: "I was not sure what it was until one day I discovered the right tone—the tone that I eventually used in *One Hundred Years of Solitude*. It was based on the way my grandmother used to tell her stories. She told things that sounded supernatural and fantastic, but she told them with complete naturalness. When I finally discovered the tone I had to use, I sat down for eighteen months and worked every day."

When asked to elaborate on how he was able to give his fantastical material such a sense of reality, García Márquez says: "That's a journalistic trick which you can also apply to literature. For example, if you say that there are elephants flying in the sky, people are not going to believe you. But if you say that there are four hundred and twenty-five elephants in the sky, people will probably believe you. . . . The problem for every writer is credibility. Anybody can write anything so long as it's believed."

García Márquez makes the point that a writer must be disciplined, not only in terms of keeping to a schedule, but also in terms of the specifics of the craft: "One of the most difficult things is the first paragraph. I have spent many months on a first paragraph, and once I get it, the rest just comes out very easily. In the first paragraph you solve most of the problems with your book. The theme is defined, the style, the tone. At least in my case, the first paragraph is·a kind of sample of what the rest of the book is going to be. That's why writing a book of short stories is much more difficult than writing a novel. Every time you write a short story, you have to begin all over again."

"Ultimately, literature is nothing but carpentry," García Márquez says. "Both are very hard work. Writing something is almost as hard as making a table. With both you are working with reality, a material just as hard as wood. Both are full of tricks and techniques. Basically very little magic and a lot of hard work are involved. And as Proust, I think, said, it takes ten percent inspiration and ninety percent perspiration. I never have done any carpentry but it's the job I admire most, especially because you can never find anyone to do it for you."

In response to a question about the solitude of the writer, García Márquez says: "It has a lot to do with the solitude of power. The writer's very attempt to portray reality often leads him to a distorted view of it. In trying to transpose reality he can end up losing contact with it, in an ivory tower, as they say. Journalism is a very good guard against that. That's why I have always tried to keep on doing journalism, because it keeps me in contact with the real world, particularly political journalism and politics."

Asked if he feels there are things the novel or fiction can do that journalism can't, García Márquez says:

"Nothing. I don't think there is any difference. The sources are the same, the material is the same, the resources and the language are the same. *The Journal of the Plague Year* by Daniel Defoe is a great novel and *Hiroshima* [by John Hersey] is a great work of journalism. . . . In journalism just one fact that is false prejudices the entire work. In contrast, in fiction one single fact that is true gives legitimacy to the entire work. That's the only difference, and it lies in the commitment of the writer. A novelist can do anything he wants so long as he makes people believe in it."

One of These Days

Monday dawned warm and rainless. Aurelio Escovar, a dentist without a degree, and a very early riser, opened his office at six. He took some false teeth, still mounted in their plaster mould, out of the glass case and put on the table a fistful of instruments which he arranged in size order, as if they were on display. He wore a collarless striped shirt, closed at the neck with a golden stud, and pants held up by suspenders. He was erect and skinny, with a look that rarely corresponded to the situation, the way deaf people have of looking.

When he had things arranged on the table, he pulled the drill toward the dental chair and sat down to polish the false teeth. He seemed not to be thinking about what he was doing, but worked steadily, pumping the drill with his feet, even when he didn't need it.

After eight he stopped for a while to look at the sky through the window, and he saw two pensive buzzards who were drying themselves in the sun on the ridgepole of the house next door. He went on working with the idea that before lunch it would rain again. The shrill voice of his eleven-year-old son interrupted his concentration.

"Papá."

"What?"

"The Mayor wants to know if you'll pull his tooth."

"Tell him I'm not here."

He was polishing a gold tooth. He held it at arm's length, and examined it with his eyes half closed. His son shouted again from the little waiting room.

"He says you are, too, because he can hear you."

The dentist kept examining the tooth. Only when he had put it on the table with the finished work did he say:

"So much the better."

He operated the drill again. He took several pieces of a bridge out of a cardboard box where he kept the things he still had to do and began to polish the gold.

"Papá."

"What?"

He still hadn't changed his expression.

"He says if you don't take out his tooth, he'll shoot you."

Without hurrying, with an extremely tranquil movement, he stopped pedaling the drill, pushed it away from the chair, and pulled the lower drawer of the table all the way out. There was a revolver. "O.K.," he said. "Tell him to come and shoot me."

He rolled the chair over opposite the door, his hand resting on the edge of the drawer. The Mayor appeared at the door. He had shaved the left side of his face, but the other side, swollen and in pain, had a five-day-old beard. The dentist saw many nights of desperation in his dull eyes. He closed the drawer with his fingertips and said softly:

"Sit down."

"Good morning," said the Mayor.

"Morning," said the dentist.

While the instruments were boiling, the Mayor leaned his skull on the headrest of the chair and felt better. His breath was icy. It was a poor office: an old wooden chair, the pedal drill, a glass case with ceramic bottles. Opposite the chair was a window with a shoulder-high cloth curtain. When he felt the dentist approach, the Mayor braced his heels and opened his mouth.

Aurelio Escovar turned his head toward the light. After inspecting the infected tooth, he closed the Mayor's jaw with a cautious pressure of his fingers.

"It has to be without anesthesia," he said.

"Why?"

"Because you have an abscess."

The Mayor looked him in the eye. "All right," he said, and tried to smile. The dentist did not return the smile. He brought the basin of sterilized instruments to the worktable and took them out of the water with a pair of cold tweezers, still without hurrying. Then he pushed the spittoon with the tip of his shoe, and went to wash his hands in the washbasin. He did all this without looking at the Mayor. But the Mayor didn't take his eyes off him.

It was a lower wisdom tooth. The dentist spread his feet and grasped the tooth with the hot forceps. The Mayor seized the arms of the chair, braced his feet with all his strength, and felt an icy void in his kidneys, but didn't make a sound. The dentist moved only his wrist. Without rancor, rather with a bitter tenderness, he said:

"Now you'll pay for our twenty dead men."

The Mayor felt the crunch of bones in his jaw, and his eyes filled with tears. But he didn't breathe until he felt the tooth come out. Theu he saw it through his tears. It seemed so foreign to his pain that he failed to understand his torture of the five previous nights.

Bent over the spittoon, sweating, panting, he unbuttoned his tunic and reached for the handkerchief in his pants pocket. The dentist gave him a clean cloth.

"Dry your tears," he said.

The Mayor did. He was trembling. While the dentist washed his hands, he saw the crumbling ceiling and a dusty spider web with spider's eggs and dead insects. The dentist returned, drying his hands. "Go to bed," he said, "and gargle with salt water." The Mayor stood up, said goodbye with a casual military salute, and walked toward the door, stretching his legs, without buttoning up his tunic.

"Send the bill," he said.

"To you or the town?"

The Mayor didn't look at him. He closed the door and said through the screen: "It's the same damn thing."

Bobbie Ann Mason

Bobbie Ann Mason was born in 1940 and raised on a farm near Mayfield, Kentucky, the setting for much of her fiction. Her stories appear frequently in *The New Yorker*, *The Atlantic Monthly*, *Redbook*, and other literary magazines. She is the author of two collections of short stories, *Shiloh and Other Stories* (1982) and *Love Life* (1989), and a novel, *In Country* (1985), which have been greeted with considerable fanfare. She studied journalism at the University of Kentucky, writing articles in New York City about pop culture, then completed a Ph.D. at the University of Connecticut with a thesis on Vladimir Nabokov, later published as *Nabokov's Garden*. She also published *The Girl Sleuth: A Feminist Guide to the Bobbsey Twins, Nancy Drew, and Their Sisters*.

Mason, who now lives in Philadelphia, lists as her main influences Hemingway, Fitzgerald, Salinger, and the New Journalists. However, her work is most often compared with that of Raymond Carver, particularly for its depiction of the domestic dramas of very ordinary people. While her fiction is often praised for its laconic prose style, its surface detail, and its use of brand names, the stories have been criticized for lack of resolution, or closure, and a certain absence of "emotional gravity." Open-endedness, of course, is a regular feature of contemporary fiction, as if to say that life, too, is open-ended and that its secrets—*disclosures* might be the appropriate word in this context—are most likely to be revealed in texts that are not twisted or mangled to fit the familiar structural curves of comedy, tragedy, and the conventional well-made tale. Certainly her work has a consistency of tone and a unity of place and focus that are characteristic of the traditional short story; similarly, the stories derive much of their power from an intimate focus on the telling rhythms and particulars that bring a character so palpably before us.

Mason has been described as a sort of literary ventriloquist for her ability to create authentic voices. Certainly, a writer cannot throw out plot, setting, or any other convention of the genre without doubly satisfying a reader's need for a wedge or slice of intense characterization. Her truck drivers, cashiers, and "shopping mall generation" are palpably there when they open their mouths, or when we are allowed to witness their bizarre thought processes. Many of Mason's stories deal with relationships between men and women that are dysfunctional, or near breakdown. "I'm interested in that tension between longing to stay and longing to go. And

I think that world sets up a lot of frustrations and there are a lot of limits set for people."

In an interview with Lila Havens (in the literary magazine *Crazy Horse*, 1985), Mason laughs at the terms other writers have applied to her stories and fictional material: "John Barth calls them 'blue-collar minimalist hyper-realist!' An editor in England calls it 'dirty realism.' I love those terms!" Mason believes that art has traditionally played to the upper classes, to so-called high culture, and that what she is doing fictionally may represent a threat to some readers and arbiters of taste: "There are certain themes that come through, like the idea of residents and transients, the title of one of my stories. Some people stay home and others are born to run. But my larger concerns are tending, I think, toward a strong curiosity about and sympathy for the lower classes. I don't mean to sound political and I have no political statement to make, but I'm constantly preoccupied with the class struggle and I'm exploring various kinds of culture shock— people moving from one class to another, people being intimidated by the class above them, people being status conscious, people being threatened by other people's ways and values—and those attitudes come into play with each other, especially when people do leave home or when the outside world comes prancing in via the television."

Mason expresses amazement at how the creative process works. "When I was studying literature, I was studying it in terms of its meanings and learning how to analyze image patterns and symbols and themes; and I had the notion that the authors must have had all that in mind from the beginning. It wasn't until I started writing that I discovered how different that could be. First of all, I had to learn how to write from scratch: no amount of studying literature prepared me for knowing how a story is coaxed out of the imagination. I knew how to analyze and read the finished product but not how to create it. So I started out, really at an elementary level, and began to discover something as simple as the principle of unity at the creative level. And then what was even more astounding was the discovery of how much order can come out of the unconscious. Often I would come up with elements that fit together but quite without my knowing it. It's still one of the greatest pleasures in writing, to find those things out, especially when readers discover things in stories that I didn't know were there."

Shiloh

Leroy Moffitt's wife, Norma Jean, is working on her pectorals. She lifts three-pound dumbbells to warm up, then progresses to a twenty-pound barbell. Standing with her legs apart, she reminds Leroy of Wonder Woman.

"I'd give anything if I could just get these muscles to where they're real hard," says Norma Jean. "Feel this arm. It's not as hard as the other one."

"That's 'cause you're right-handed," says Leroy, dodging as she swings the barbell in an arc.

"Do you think so?"

"Sure."

Leroy is a truckdriver. He injured his leg in a highway accident four months ago, and his physical therapy, which involves weights and a pulley, prompted Norma Jean to try building herself up. Now she is attending a body-building class. Leroy has been collecting temporary disability since his tractor-trailer jackknifed in Missouri, badly twisting his left leg in its socket. He has a steel pin in his hip. He will probably not be able to drive his rig again. It sits in the backyard, like a gigantic bird that has flown home to roost. Leroy has been home in Kentucky for three months, and his leg is almost healed, but the accident frightened him and he does not want to drive any more long hauls. He is not sure what to do next. In the meantime, he makes things from craft kits. He started by building a miniature log cabin from notched Popsicle sticks. He varnished it and placed it on the TV set, where it remains. It reminds him of a rustic Nativity scene. Then he tried string art (sailing ships on black velvet), a macramé owl kit, a snap-together B-17 Flying Fortress, and a lamp made out of a model truck, with a light fixture screwed in the top of the cab. At first the kits were diversions, something to kill time, but now he is thinking about building a full-scale log house from a kit. It would be considerably cheaper than building a regular house, and besides, Leroy has grown to appreciate how things are put together. He has begun to realize that in all the years he was on the road he never took time to examine anything. He was always flying past scenery.

"They won't let you build a log cabin in any of the new subdivisions," Norma Jean tells him.

"They will if I tell them it's for you," he says, teasing her. Ever since they were married, he has promised Norma Jean he would build her a new home one day. They have always rented, and the house they live in is small and nondescript. It does not even feel like a home, Leroy realizes now.

Norma Jean works at the Rexall drugstore, and she has acquired an amazing amount of information about cosmetics. When she explains to Leroy the three stages of complexion care, involving creams, toners, and moisturizers, he thinks happily of other petroleum products—axle grease, diesel fuel. This is a connection between him and Norma Jean. Since he has been home, he has felt unusually tender about his wife and guilty over his long absences. But he can't tell what she feels about him. Norma Jean has never complained about his travelling; she has never made hurt remarks, like calling his truck a "widow-maker." He is reasonably certain she has been faithful to him, but he wishes she would celebrate his permanent homecoming more happily. Norma Jean is often startled to find Leroy at home, and he thinks she seems a little disappointed about it. Perhaps he reminds her too much of the early days of their marriage, before he went on the road. They had a child who died as an infant, years ago. They never speak about their memories of Randy, which have almost faded, but now that Leroy is home all the time, they sometimes feel awkward around each other, and Leroy wonders if one of them should mention the child. He has the feeling that they are waking up out of a dream together—that they must create a new marriage, start afresh. They are lucky they are still married. Leroy has read that for most people losing a child destroys the marriage—or else he heard this on *Donahue*. He can't always remember where he learns things anymore.

At Christmas, Leroy bought an electric organ for Norma Jean. She used to play the piano when she was in high school. "It don't leave you," she told him once. "It's like riding a bicycle."

The new instrument had so many keys and buttons that she was bewildered by it at first. She touched the keys tentatively, pushed some buttons, then pecked out "Chopsticks." It came out in an amplified fox-trot rhythm, with marimba sounds.

"It's an orchestra!" she cried.

The organ had a pecan-look finish and eighteen preset chords, with optional flute, violin, trumpet, clarinet, and banjo accompaniments. Norma Jean mastered the organ almost immediately. At first she played Christmas songs. Then she bought *The Sixties Songbook* and learned every tune in it, adding variations to each with the rows of brightly colored buttons.

"I didn't like these old songs back then," she said. "But I have this crazy feeling I missed something."

"You didn't miss a thing," said Leroy.

Leroy likes to lie on the couch and smoke a joint and listen to Norma Jean play "Can't Take My Eyes Off You" and "I'll Be Back." He is back again. After fifteen years on the road, he is finally settling down with the woman he loves. She is still pretty. Her skin is flawless. Her frosted curls resemble pencil trimmings.

Now that Leroy has come home to stay, he notices how much the town has changed. Subdivisions are spreading across western Kentucky like an oil slick. The sign at the edge of town says "Pop: 11,500"—only seven hundred more than it said twenty years before. Leroy can't figure out who is living in all the new houses. The farmers who used to gather around the courthouse square on Saturday afternoons to play checkers and spit tobacco juice have gone. It has been years since Leroy has thought about the farmers, and they have disappeared without his noticing.

Leroy meets a kid named Stevie Hamilton in the parking lot at the new shopping center. While they pretend to be strangers meeting over a stalled car, Stevie tosses an ounce of marijuana under the front seat of Leroy's car. Stevie is wearing orange jogging shoes and a T-shirt that says CHATTAHOOCHEE SUPER-RAT. His father is a prominent doctor who lives in one of the expensive subdivisions in a new white-columned brick house that looks like a funeral parlor. In the phone book under his name there is a separate number, with the listing "Teenagers."

"Where do you get this stuff?" asks Leroy. "From your pappy?"

"That's for me to know and you to find out," Stevie says. He is slit-eyed and skinny.

"What else you got?"

"What you interested in?"

"Nothing special. Just wondered."

Leroy used to take speed on the road. Now he has to go slowly. He needs to be mellow. He leans back against the car and says, "I'm aiming to build me a log house, soon as I get time. My wife, though, I don't think she likes the idea."

"Well, let me know when you want me again," Stevie says. He has a cigarette in his cupped palm, as though sheltering it from the wind. He takes a long drag, then stomps it on the asphalt and slouches away.

Stevie's father was two years ahead of Leroy in high school. Leroy is thirty-four. He married Norma Jean when they were both eighteen, and their child Randy was born a few months later, but he died at the age of four months and three days. He would be about Stevie's age now. Norma Jean and Leroy were at the drive-in, watching a double feature (*Dr. Strangelove* and *Lover Come Back*), and the baby was sleeping in the back seat. When the first movie ended, the baby was dead. It was the sudden infant death syndrome. Leroy remembers handing Randy to a nurse at the emergency room, as though he were offering her a large doll as a present. A dead baby feels like a sack of flour. "It just happens sometimes," said the doctor, in what Leroy always recalls as a nonchalant tone. Leroy can hardly remember the child anymore, but he still sees vividly a scene from *Dr. Strangelove* in which the President of the United States was talking in a folksy voice on the hot line to the Soviet premier about the bomber accidentally headed toward Russia. He was in the War Room, and the world map was lit up. Leroy remembers Norma Jean standing catatonically beside him in the hospital and himself thinking: Who is this strange girl? He had forgotten who she was. Now scientists are saying that crib death is caused by a virus. Nobody knows anything, Leroy thinks. The answers are always changing.

When Leroy gets home from the shopping center, Norma Jean's mother, Mabel Beasley, is there. Until this year, Leroy has not realized how much time she spends with Norma Jean. When she visits, she inspects the closets and then the plants, informing Norma Jean when a plant is droopy or yellow. Mabel calls the plants "flowers," although there are never any blooms. She always notices if Norma Jean's laundry is piling up. Mabel is a short, overweight woman whose tight, brown-dyed curls look more like a wig than the actual wig she sometimes wears. Today she has brought Norma Jean an off-white dust ruffle she made for the bed; Mabel works in a custom-upholstery shop.

"This is the tenth one I made this year," Mabel says. "I got started and couldn't stop."

"It's real pretty," says Norma Jean.

"Now we can hide things under the bed," says Leroy, who gets along with his mother-in-law primarily by joking with her. Mabel has never really forgiven him for disgracing her by getting Norma Jean pregnant. When the baby died, she said that fate was mocking her.

"What's that thing?" Mabel says to Leroy in a loud voice, pointing to a tangle of yarn on a piece of canvas.

Leroy holds it up for Mabel to see. "It's my needlepoint," he explains. "This is a *Star Trek* pillow cover."

"That's what a woman would do," says Mabel. "Great day in the morning!"

"All the big football players on TV do it," he says.

"Why, Leroy, you're always trying to fool me. I don't believe you for one minute. You don't know what to do with yourself—that's the whole trouble. Sewing!"

"I'm aiming to build us a log house," says Leroy. "Soon as my plans come."

"Like *heck* you are," says Norma Jean. She takes Leroy's needlepoint and shoves it into a drawer. "You have to find a job first. Nobody can afford to build now anyway."

Mabel straightens her girdle and says, "I still think before you get tied down y'all ought to take a little run to Shiloh."

"One of these days, Mama," Norma Jean says impatiently.

Mabel is talking about Shiloh, Tennessee. For the past few years, she has been urging Leroy and Norma Jean to visit the Civil War battleground there. Mabel went there on her honeymoon—the only real trip she ever took. Her husband died of a perforated ulcer when Norma Jean was ten, but Mabel, who was accepted into the United Daughters of the Confederacy in 1975, is still preoccupied with going back to Shiloh.

"I've been to kingdom come and back in that truck out yonder," Leroy says to Mabel, "but we never yet set foot in that battleground. Ain't that something? How did I miss it?"

"It's not even that far," Mabel says.

After Mabel leaves, Norma Jean reads to Leroy from a list she has made. "Things you could do," she announces. "You could get a job as a guard at Union Carbide, where they'd let you set on a stool. You could get on at the lumberyard. You could do a little carpenter work, if you want to build so bad. You could—"

"I can't do something where I'd have to stand up all day."

"You ought to try standing up all day behind a cosmetics counter. It's amazing that I have strong feet, coming from two parents that never had strong feet at all." At the moment Norma Jean is holding on to the kitchen counter, raising her knees one at a time as she talks. She is wearing two-pound ankle weights.

"Don't worry," says Leroy. "I'll do something."

"You could truck calves to slaughter for somebody. You wouldn't have to drive any big old truck for that."

"I'm going to build you this house," says Leroy. "I want to make you a real home."

"I don't want to live in any log cabin."

"It's not a cabin. It's a house."

"I don't care. It looks like a cabin."

"You and me together could lift those logs. It's just like lifting weights."

Norma Jean doesn't answer. Under her breath, she is counting. Now she is marching through the kitchen. She is doing goose steps.

Before his accident, when Leroy came home he used to stay in the house with Norma Jean, watching TV in bed and playing cards. She would cook fried chicken, picnic ham, chocolate pie—all his favorites. Now he is home alone much of the time. In the mornings, Norma Jean disappears, leaving a cooling place in the bed. She eats a cereal called Body Buddies, and she leaves the bowl on the table, with the soggy tan balls floating in a milk puddle. He sees things about Norma Jean that he never realized before. When she chops onions, she stares off into a corner, as if she can't bear to look. She puts on her house slippers almost precisely at nine o'clock every evening and nudges her jogging shoes under the couch. She saves bread heels for the birds. Leroy watches the birds at the feeder. He notices the peculiar way goldfinches fly past the window. They close their wings, then fall, then spread their wings to catch and lift themselves. He wonders if they close their eyes when they fall. Norma Jean closes her eyes when they are in bed. She wants the lights turned out. Even then, he is sure she closes her eyes.

He goes for long drives around town. He tends to drive a car rather carelessly. Power steering and an automatic shift make a car feel so small and inconsequential that his body is hardly involved in the driving process. His injured leg stretches out comfortably. Once or twice he has almost hit something, but even the prospect of an accident seems minor in a car. He cruises the new subdivisions, feeling like a criminal rehearsing for a robbery. Norma Jean is probably right about a log house being inappropriate here in the new subdivisions. All the houses look grand and complicated. They depress him.

One day when Leroy comes home from a drive he finds Norma Jean in tears. She is in the kitchen making a potato and mushroom-soup casserole, with grated-cheese topping. She is crying because her mother caught her smoking.

"I didn't hear her coming. I was standing here puffing away pretty as you please," Norma Jean says, wiping her eyes.

"I knew it would happen sooner or later," says Leroy, putting his arm around her.

"She don't know the meaning of the word 'knock,'" says Norma Jean. "It's a wonder she hadn't caught me years ago."

"Think of it this way," Leroy says. "What if she caught me with a joint?"

"You better not let her!" Norma Jean shrieks. "I'm warning you, Leroy Moffitt!"

"I'm just kidding. Here, play me a tune. That'll help you relax."

Norma Jean puts the casserole in the oven and sets the timer. Then she plays a ragtime tune, with horns and banjo, as Leroy lights up a joint and lies on the couch, laughing to himself about Mabel's catching him at it. He thinks of Stevie Hamilton—a doctor's son pushing grass. Everything is funny. The whole town seems crazy and small. He is reminded of Virgil Mathis, a boastful policeman Leroy used to shoot pool with. Virgil recently led a drug bust in a back room at a bowling alley, where he seized ten thousand dollars' worth of marijuana. The newspaper had a picture of him holding up the bags of grass and grinning widely. Right now, Leroy can imagine Virgil breaking down the door and arresting him with a lungful of smoke. Virgil would probably have been alerted to the scene because of all the racket Norma Jean is making. Now she sounds like a hard-rock band. Norma Jean is terrific. When she switches to a Latin-rhythm version of "Sunshine Superman," Leroy hums along. Norma Jean's foot goes up and down, up and down.

"Well, what do you think?" Leroy says, when Norma Jean pauses to search through her music.

"What do I think about what?"

His mind has gone blank. Then he says, "I'll sell my rig and build us a house." That wasn't what he wanted to say. He wanted to know what she thought—what she *really* thought—about them.

"Don't start in on that again," says Norma Jean. She begins playing "Who'll Be the Next in Line?"

Leroy used to tell hitchhikers his whole life story—about his travels, his hometown, the baby. He would end with a question: "Well, what do you think?" It was just a rhetorical question. In time, he had the feeling that he'd been telling the same story over and over to the same hitchhikers. He quit talking to hitchhikers when he realized how his voice sounded—whining and self-pitying, like some teenage-tragedy song. Now Leroy has the sudden impulse to tell Norma Jean about himself, as if he had just met her. They have known each other so long they have forgotten a lot about each other. They could become reacquainted. But when the oven timer goes off and she runs to the kitchen, he forgets why he wants to do this.

The next day, Mabel drops by. It is Saturday and Norma Jean is cleaning. Leroy is studying the plans of his log house, which have finally come in the mail. He has them spread out on the table—big sheets of stiff blue paper, with diagrams and numbers printed in white. While Norma Jean runs the vacuum, Mabel drinks coffee. She sets her coffee cup on a blueprint.

"I'm just waiting for time to pass," she says to Leroy, drumming her fingers on the table.

As soon as Norma Jean switches off the vacuum, Mabel says in a loud voice, "Did you hear about the datsun dog that killed the baby?"

Norma Jean says, "The word is 'dachshund.'"

"They put the dog on trial. It chewed the baby's legs off. The mother was in the next room all the time." She raises her voice. "They thought it was neglect."

Norma Jean is holding her ears. Leroy manages to open the refrigerator and get some Diet Pepsi to offer Mabel. Mabel still has some coffee and she waves away the Pepsi.

"Datsuns are like that," Mabel says. "They're jealous dogs. They'll tear a place to pieces if you don't keep an eye on them."

"You better watch out what you're saying, Mabel," says Leroy.

"Well, facts is facts."

Leroy looks out the window at his rig. It is like a huge piece of furniture gathering dust in the backyard. Pretty soon it will be an antique. He hears the vacuum cleaner. Norma Jean seems to be cleaning the living room rug again.

Later, she says to Leroy, "She just said that about the baby because she caught me smoking. She's trying to pay me back."

"What are you talking about?" Leroy says, nervously shuffling blueprints.

"You know good and well," Norma Jean says. She is sitting in a kitchen chair with her feet up and her arms wrapped around her knees. She looks small and helpless. She says, "The very idea, her bringing up a subject like that. Saying it was neglect."

"She didn't mean that," Leroy says.

"She might not have *thought* she meant it. She always says things like that. You don't know how she goes on."

"But she didn't really mean it. She was just talking."

Leroy opens a king-sized bottle of beer and pours it into two glasses, dividing it carefully. He hands a glass to Norma Jean and she takes it from him mechanically. For a long time, they sit by the kitchen window watching the birds at the feeder.

Something is happening. Norma Jean is going to night school. She has graduated from her six-week body-building course and now she is taking an adult-education course in composition at Paducah Community College. She spends her evenings outlining paragraphs.

"First you have a topic sentence," she explains to Leroy. "Then you divide it up. Your secondary topic has to be connected to your primary topic."

To Leroy, this sounds intimidating. "I never was any good in English," he says.

"It makes a lot of sense."

"What are you doing this for, anyhow?"

She shrugs. "It's something to do." She stands up and lifts her dumbbells a few times.

"Driving a rig, nobody cared about my English."

"I'm not criticizing your English."

Norma Jean used to say, "If I lose ten minutes' sleep, I just drag all day." Now she stays up late, writing compositions. She got a B on her first paper—a how-to theme on soup-based casseroles. Recently Norma Jean has been cooking unusual foods— tacos, lasagna, Bombay chicken. She doesn't play the organ anymore, though her second paper was called "Why Music Is Important to Me." She sits at the kitchen table, concentrating on her outlines, while Leroy plays with his log house plans, practicing with a set of Lincoln Logs. The thought of getting a truckload of notched, numbered logs scares him, and he wants to be prepared. As he and Norma Jean work together at the kitchen table, Leroy has the hopeful thought that they are sharing something, but he knows he is a fool to think this. Norma Jean is miles away. He knows he is going to lose her. Like Mabel, he is just waiting for time to pass.

One day, Mabel is there before Norma Jean gets home from work, and Leroy finds himself confiding in her. Mabel, he realizes, must know Norma Jean better than he does.

"I don't know what's got into that girl," Mabel says. "She used to go to bed with the chickens. Now you say she's up all hours. Plus her a-smoking. I like to died."

"I want to make her this beautiful home," Leroy says, indicating the Lincoln Logs. "I don't think she even wants it. Maybe she was happier with me gone."

"She don't know what to make of you, coming home like this."

"Is that it?"

Mabel takes the roof off his Lincoln Log cabin. "You couldn't get me in a log cabin," she says. "I was raised in one. It's no picnic, let me tell you."

"They're different now," says Leroy.

"I tell you what," Mabel says, smiling oddly at Leroy.

"What?"

"Take her on down to Shiloh. Y'all need to get out together, stir a little. Her brain's all balled up over them books."

Leroy can see traces of Norma Jean's features in her mother's face. Mabel's worn face has the texture of crinkled cotton, but suddenly she looks pretty. It occurs to Leroy that Mabel has been hinting all along that she wants them to take her with them to Shiloh.

"Let's all go to Shiloh," he says. "You and me and her. Come Sunday."

Mabel throws up her hands in protest. "Oh, no, not me. Young folks want to be by theirselves."

When Norma Jean comes in with groceries, Leroy says excitedly, "Your mama here's been dying to go to Shiloh for thirty-five years. It's about time we went, don't you think?"

"I'm not going to butt in on anybody's second honeymoon," Mabel says.

"Who's going on a honeymoon, for Christ's sake?" Norma Jean says loudly.

"I never raised no daughter of mine to talk that-a-way," Mabel says.

"You ain't seen nothing yet," says Norma Jean. She starts putting away boxes and cans, slamming cabinet doors.

"There's a log cabin at Shiloh," Mabel says. "It was there during the battle. There's bullet holes in it."

"When are you going to *shut up* about Shiloh, Mama?" asks Norma Jean.

"I always thought Shiloh was the prettiest place, so full of history," Mabel goes on. "I just hoped y'all could see it once before I die, so you could tell me about it." Later, she whispers to Leroy, "You do what I said. A little change is what she needs."

"Your name means 'the king,'" Norma Jean says to Leroy that evening. He is trying to get her to go to Shiloh, and she is reading a book about another century.

"Well, I reckon I ought to be right proud."

"I guess so."

"Am I still king around here?"

Norma Jean flexes her biceps and feels them for hardness. "I'm not fooling around with anybody, if that's what you mean," she says.

"Would you tell me if you were?"

"I don't know."

"What does *your* name mean?"

"It was Marilyn Monroe's real name."

"No kidding!"

"Norma comes from the Normans. They were invaders," she says. She closes her book and looks hard at Leroy. "I'll go to Shiloh with you if you'll stop staring at me."

On Sunday, Norma Jean packs a picnic and they go to Shiloh. To Leroy's relief, Mabel says she does not want to come with them. Norma Jean drives, and Leroy, sitting beside her, feels like some boring hitchhiker she has picked up. He tries some conversation, but she answers him in monosyllables. At Shiloh, she drives aimlessly through the park, past bluffs and trails and steep ravines. Shiloh is an immense place, and Leroy cannot see it as a battleground. It is not what he expected. He thought it would look like a golf course. Monuments are everywhere, showing through the thick clusters of trees. Norma Jean passes the log cabin Mabel mentioned. It is surrounded by tourists looking for bullet holes.

"That's not the kind of log house I've got in mind," says Leroy apologetically.

"I know *that*."

"This is a pretty place. Your mama was right."

"It's O.K.," says Norma Jean. "Well, we've seen it. I hope she's satisfied."

They burst out laughing together.

At the park museum, a movie on Shiloh is shown every half hour, but they decide that they don't want to see it. They buy a souvenir Confederate flag for Mabel, and then they find a picnic spot near the cemetery. Norma Jean has brought a picnic cooler, with pimiento sandwiches, soft drinks, and Yodels. Leroy eats a sandwich and then smokes a joint, hiding it behind the picnic cooler. Norma Jean has quit smoking altogether. She is picking cake crumbs from the cellophane wrapper, like a fussy bird.

Leroy says, "So the boys in gray ended up in Corinth. The Union soldiers zapped 'em finally. April 7, 1862."

They both know that he doesn't know any history. He is just talking about some of the historical plaques they have read. He feels awkward, like a boy on a date with an older girl. They are still just making conversation.

"Corinth is where Mama eloped to," says Norma Jean.

They sit in silence and stare at the cemetery for the Union dead and, beyond, at a tall cluster of trees. Campers are parked nearby, bumper to bumper, and small children in bright clothing are cavorting and squealing. Norma Jean wads up the cake wrapper and squeezes it tightly in her hand. Without looking at Leroy, she says, "I want to leave you."

Leroy takes a bottle of Coke out of the cooler and flips off the cap. He holds the bottle poised near his mouth but cannot remember to take a drink. Finally he says, "No, you don't."

"Yes, I do."

"I won't let you."

"You can't stop me."

"Don't do me that way."

Leroy knows Norma Jean will have her own way. "Didn't I promise to be home from now on?" he says.

"In some ways, a woman prefers a man who wanders," says Norma Jean. "That sounds crazy, I know."

"You're not crazy."

Leroy remembers to drink from his Coke. Then he says, "Yes, you *are* crazy. You and me could start all over again. Right back at the beginning."

"We *have* started all over again," says Norma Jean. "And this is how it turned out."

"What did I do wrong?"

"Nothing."

"Is this one of those women's lib things?" Leroy asks.

"Don't be funny."

The cemetery, a green slope dotted with white markers, looks like a subdivision site. Leroy is trying to comprehend that his marriage is breaking up, but for some reason he is wondering about white slabs in a graveyard.

"Everything was fine till Mama caught me smoking," says Norma Jean, standing up. "That set something off."

"What are you talking about?"

"She won't leave me alone—*you* won't leave me alone." Norma Jean seems to be crying, but she is looking away from him. "I feel eighteen again. I can't face that all over again." She starts walking away. "No, it *wasn't* fine. I don't know what I'm saying. Forget it."

Leroy takes a lungful of smoke and closes his eyes as Norma Jean's words sink in. He tries to focus on the fact that thirty-five hundred soldiers died on the grounds around him. He can only think of that war as a board game with plastic soldiers. Leroy almost smiles, as he compares the Confederates' daring attack on the Union camps and Virgil Mathis's raid on the bowling alley. General Grant, drunk and furious, shoved the Southerners back to Corinth, where Mabel and Jet Beasley were married years later, when Mabel was still thin and good-looking. The next day, Mabel and Jet visited the battleground, and then Norma Jean was born, and then she married Leroy and they had a baby, which they lost, and now Leroy and Norma Jean are here at the same battleground. Leroy knows he is leaving out a lot. He is leaving out the insides of history. History was always just names and dates to him. It occurs to him that building a house out of logs is similarly empty—too simple. And the real inner workings of a marriage, like most of history, have escaped him. Now he sees that building a log house is the dumbest idea he could have had. It was clumsy of him to think Norma Jean would want a log house. It was a crazy idea. He'll have to think of something else, quickly. He will wad the blueprints into tight balls and fling them into the lake. Then he'll get moving again. He opens his eyes. Norma Jean has moved away and is walking through the cemetery, following a serpentine brick path.

Leroy gets up to follow his wife, but his good leg is asleep and his bad leg still hurts him. Norma Jean is far away, walking rapidly toward the bluff by the river, and he tries to hobble toward her. Some children run past him, screaming noisily. Norma Jean has reached the bluff, and she is looking out over the Tennessee River. Now she turns toward Leroy and waves her arms. Is she beckoning to him? She seems to be doing an exercise for her chest muscles. The sky is unusually pale—the color of the dust ruffle Mabel made for their bed.

Bharati Mukherjee

Bharati Mukherjee was born in 1940 into a wealthy family in Calcutta, but received most of her early education in boarding schools in England and Switzerland. She completed her B.A. at the University of Calcutta and her M.A. at the University of Boroda in 1961. However, she left India and her privileged lifestyle behind when she registered in the University of Iowa Writers' Workshop. There, she discovered twentieth-century literature, was encouraged to take writing seriously, revelled in new-found freedom and privacy, and completed an M.F.A. and Ph.D. There, too, she met and married Canadian writer Clark Blaise, with whom she has collaborated on two non-fiction books, *Days and Nights in Calcutta* and *The Sorrow and the Terror*, an account of the Air India bombing. She lived in Canada from 1966 to 1980, teaching English at McGill University and writing her first two books of fiction, *The Tiger's Daughter* (1971) and *Wife* (1975). Unfortunately, although she became a Canadian citizen, Mukherjee felt uncomfortable in Canada, a literary outsider writing expatriate novels and a victim of racism in a society that boasted of tolerance and a multicultural perspective. "In Canada I was frequently taken for a prostitute or shoplifter, frequently assumed to be a domestic," as she explains in the angry introduction to *Darkness* (1985). "The society itself, or important elements in that society, routinely made crippling assumptions about me and my 'kind.'" Her dissatisfaction took the family back to the States, where she became a commuter wife and mother and a peripatetic part-time teacher, but where she found she was able to feel at home and pursue her writing with renewed vigour. In addition to *Darkness*, she completed *The Middleman and Other Stories* (1988), which won the National Book Critics Circle Award and a novel, *Jasmine* (1989). She is in demand on U.S. radio and television and has written for *The New York Times*, most recently an article entitled "Immigrant Writing: Give Us Your Maximalists." As she explains to Joel Yanofsky (*Books in Canada*, Jan./Feb. 1990), she is now an American citizen and loves it: "After all ... I am the melting-pot lady."

In an interview with Geoff Hancock (*Canadian Fiction Magazine*, No. 59), Mukherjee talks about her editing of a special issue of *The Literary Review* (1986), called "Writers of the Indian Commonwealth," which represents Indian literature less as a geographical phenomenon than as a "habit of mind." She sees Indian literature as belonging to a dispersed people—including India-based writers and those of the Caribbean, Fiji, Africa, Europe and North America—but claims for herself a much broader literary heritage: "If you are asking me, do I see myself as another V. S. Naipaul, the answer is: no. The generational gap between us manifests itself more dramatically than the generational gap between, let's say, me and Mavis Gallant. Naipaul seems to have made himself the spokesman for the permanent and, one's tempted to say, the professional expatriate from the Third World. His characters savour their marginality. I write about new Americans and new Canadians, about belated homesteaders from non-traditional countries. My characters grow and change with the change in citizenships."

Speaking of literary technique, Mukherjee expresses her concern not only for larger narrative strategies, such as controlling metaphors, but also for precision of language. "Short stories don't always occur to me as being about a character. Sometimes a line or a possible title will set me going. 'The Lady from Lucknow,' for instance, began with the title. In stories, the hard thing is to find the right 'voice.' I don't seem to need to revise drastically. When I wrote novels, I found myself doing three drafts—the first to find out what the novel was really about; the second to sharpen the narrative; the third to catch any infelicities. But nowadays the short stories usually come to me at one sitting. I believe in revision, though. Or rather, I believe that good writing consists of decisions and calculations. One must know why one chooses this word instead of that. I share Isaac Babel's belief that the well-placed comma can stab the heart. I try to make my writing students sensitive to how a word looks and sounds."

Although she avoids academic debates on the relative merits of "moral" and "experimental" fiction, Mukherjee admits that her own writing "always locates a moral centre. The characters themselves may be immoral or amoral, but they operate in a deeply moral world. Some readers have written to tell me that they find my stories scary or unsettling because of this 'moral centre.'" When asked if she writes about alienation and victimization, she replies: "I don't think about my fiction as being about alienation. On the contrary, I mean for it to be about assimilation. My stories centre on a new breed and generation of North American pioneers. I am fascinated by people who have enough gumption, energy, ambition, to pull up their roots. My stories are irreverent, and, I like to think, funny. My stories are about conquests, and not about loss." She also insists that while trying to subvert Anglo literary conventions, she is engaged in more than mere mimicry: "Parody and subversion have energy; mimicry doesn't."

When asked about texture in her fiction, Mukherjee makes the point that texture is never added: "To me a character is who she is because of the language she thinks and feels in. My characters are often in the process of forgetting one language and inventing another." Many of her comments about writing are focussed on process rather than product, suggesting that she has left behind "the mordant and self-protective irony" of the expatriate writer for the celebratory stance of the fully integrated. As she says in *Darkness*, "That energy interests me now. For a writer, energy is aggression; urgency colliding with confidence. Suddenly, everything is possible. Excluded worlds are opened, secretive characters reveal themselves. The writing-self is somehow united with the universe."

The Management of Grief

A woman I don't know is boiling tea the Indian way in my kitchen. There are a lot of women I don't know in my kitchen, whispering, and moving tactfully. They open doors, rummage through the pantry, and try not to ask me where things are kept. They remind me of when my sons were small, on Mother's Day or when Vikram and I were tired, and they would make big, sloppy omelettes. I would lie in bed pretending I didn't hear them.

Dr Sharma, the treasurer of the Indo-Canada Society, pulls me into the hallway. He wants to know if I am worried about money. His wife, who has just come up from the basement with a tray of empty cups and glasses, scolds him. "Don't bother Mrs Bhave with mundane details." She looks so monstrously pregnant her baby must be days overdue. I tell her she shouldn't be carrying heavy things. "Shaila," she says, smiling, "this is the fifth." Then she grabs a teenager by his shirt-tails. He slips his Walkman off his head. He has to be one of her four children, they have the same domed and dented foreheads. "What's the official word now?" she demands. The boy slips the headphones back on. "They're acting evasive, Ma. They're saying it could be an accident or a terrorist bomb."

All morning, the boys have been muttering, Sikh Bomb, Sikh Bomb. The men, not using the word, bow their heads in agreement. Mrs Sharma touches her forehead at such a word. At least they've stopped talking about space debris and Russian lasers.

Two radios are going in the dining room. They are tuned to different stations. Someone must have brought the radios down from my boys' bedrooms. I haven't gone into their rooms since Kusum came running across the front lawn in her bathrobe. She looked so funny, I was laughing when I opened the door.

The big TV in the den is being whizzed through American networks and cable channels.

"Damn!" some man swears bitterly. "How can these preachers carry on like nothing's happened?" I want to tell him we're not that important. You look at the audience, and at the preacher in his blue robe with his beautiful white hair, the potted palm trees under a blue sky, and you know they care about nothing.

The phone rings and rings. Dr Sharma's taken charge. "We're with her," he keeps saying. "Yes, yes, the doctor has given calming pills. Yes, yes, pills are having necessary effect." I wonder if pills alone explain this calm. Not peace, just a deadening quiet. I was always controlled, but never repressed. Sound can reach me, but my body is tensed, ready to scream. I hear their voices all around me. I hear my boys and Vikram cry, "Mommy, Shaila!" and their screams insulate me, like headphones.

The woman boiling water tells her story again and again. "I got the news first. My cousin called from Halifax before 6 a.m., can you imagine? He'd gotten up for prayers and his son was studying for medical exams and he heard on a rock channel that something had happened to a plane. They said first it had disappeared from the radar, like a giant eraser just reached out. His father called me, so I said to him, what do you mean 'something bad'? You mean a hijacking? And he said, *bebn*, there is no confirmation of anything yet, but check with your neighbours because a lot of them must be on that plane. So I called poor Kusum straightaway. I knew Kusum's husband and daughter were booked to go yesterday."

Kusum lives across the street from me. She and Satish had moved in less than a month ago. They said they needed a bigger place. All these people, the Sharmas and friends from the Indo-Canada Society, had been there for the housewarming. Satish and Kusum made homemade tandoori on their big gas grill and even the white neighbours piled their plates high with that luridly red, charred, juicy chicken. Their younger daughter had danced, and even our boys had broken away from the Stanley Cup telecast to put in a reluctant appearance. Everyone took pictures for their albums and for the community newspapers—another of our families had made it big in Toronto—and now I wonder how many of those happy faces are gone. "Why does God give us so much if all along He intends to take it away?" Kusum asks me.

I nod. We sit on carpeted stairs, holding hands like children. "I never once told him that I loved him," I say. I was too much the well brought up woman. I was so well brought up I never felt comfortable calling my husband by his first name.

"It's all right," Kusum says. "He knew. My husband knew. They felt it. Modern young girls have to say it because what they feel is fake."

Kusum's daughter, Pam, runs in with an overnight case. Pam's in her McDonald's uniform. "Mummy! You have to get dressed!" Panic makes her cranky. "A reporter's on his way here."

"Why?"

"You want to talk to him in your bathrobe?" She starts to brush her mother's long hair. She's the daughter who's always in trouble. She dates Canadian boys and hangs out in the mall, shopping for tight sweaters. The younger one, the goody-goody one according to Pam, the one with a voice so sweet that when she sang *bhajans* for Ethiopian relief even a frugal man like my husband wrote out a hundred-dollar cheque, *she* was on that plane. *She* was going to spend July and August with grandparents because Pam wouldn't go. Pam said she'd rather waitress at McDonald's. "If it's a choice between Bombay and Wonderland, I'm picking Wonderland," she'd said.

"Leave me alone," Kusum yells. "You know what I want to do? If I didn't have to look after you now, I'd hang myself."

Pam's young face goes blotchy with pain. "Thanks," she says, "don't let me stop you."

"Hush," pregnant Mrs Sharma scolds Pam. "Leave your mother alone. Mr Sharma will tackle the reporters and fill out the forms. He'll say what has to be said."

Pam stands her ground. "You think I don't know what Mummy's thinking? *Why her?* that's what. That's sick! Mummy wishes my little sister were alive and I were dead."

Kusum's hand in mine is trembly hot. We continue to sit on the stairs.

She calls before she arrives, wondering if there's anything I need. Her name is Judith Templeton and she's an appointee of the provincial government. "Multiculturalism?" I ask, and she says, "Partially," but her mandate is bigger. "I've been told you knew many people on the flight," she says. "Perhaps if you'd agree to help us reach the others . . . ?"

She gives me time at least to put on tea water and pick up the mess in the front room. I have a few *samosas* from Kusum's housewarming that I could fry up, but then I think, Why prolong this visit?

Judith Templeton is much younger than she sounded. She wears a blue suit with a white blouse and a polka dot tie. Her blond hair is cut short, her only jewelry is pearl drop earrings. Her briefcase is new and expensive looking, a gleaming cordovan leather. She sits with it across her lap. When she looks out the front windows on to the street, her contact lenses seem to float in front of her light blue eyes.

"What sort of help do you want from me?" I ask. She has refused the tea, out of politeness, but I insist, along with some slightly stale biscuits.

"I have no experience," she admits. "That is, I have an MSW and I've worked in liaison with accident victims, but I mean I have no experience with a tragedy of this scale—"

"Who could?" I ask.

"—and with the complications of culture, language, and customs. Someone mentioned that Mrs Bhave is a pillar—because you've taken it more calmly."

At this, perhaps, I frown, for she reaches forward, almost to take my hand. "I hope you understand my meaning, Mrs Bhave. There are hundreds of people in Metro directly affected, like you, and some of them speak no English. There are some widows who've never handled money or gone on a bus, and there are old parents who still haven't eaten or gone outside their bedrooms. Some houses and apartments have been looted. Some wives are still hysterical. Some husbands are in shock and profound depression. We want to help, but our hands are tied in so many ways. We have to distribute money to some people, and there are legal documents—these things can be done. We have interpreters, but we don't always have the human touch, or maybe the right human touch. We don't want to make mistakes, Mrs Bhave, and that's why we'd like to ask you to help us."

"More mistakes, you mean," I say.

"Police matters are not in my hands," she answers.

"Nothing I can do will make any difference," I say. "We must all grieve in our own way."

"But you are coping very well. All the people said, Mrs Bhave is the strongest person of all. Perhaps if the others could see you, talk with you, it would help them."

"By the standards of the people you call hysterical, I am behaving very oddly and very badly, Miss Templeton." I want to say to her, *I wish I could scream, starve, walk into Lake Ontario, jump from a bridge.* "They would not see me as a model. I do not see myself as a model."

I am a freak. No one who has ever known me would think of me reacting this way. This terrible calm will not go away.

She asks me if she may call again, after I get back from a long trip that we all must make. "Of course," I say. "Feel free to call, anytime."

Four days later, I find Kusum squatting on a rock overlooking a bay in Ireland. It isn't a big rock, but it juts sharply out over water. This is as close as we'll ever get to them. June breezes balloon out her sari and unpin her knee-length hair. She has the bewildered look of a sea creature whom the tides have stranded.

It's been one hundred hours since Kusum came stumbling and screaming across my lawn. Waiting around the hospital, we've heard many stories. The police, the diplomats, they tell us things thinking we're strong, that knowledge is helpful to the grieving, and maybe it is. Some, I know, prefer ignorance, or their own versions. The plane broke in two, they say. Unconsciousness was instantaneous. No one suffered. My boys must have just finished their breakfasts. They loved eating on planes, they loved the smallness of plates, knives, and forks. Last year they saved the airline salt and pepper shakers. Half an hour more and they would have made it to Heathrow.

Kusum says that we can't escape our fate. She says that all those people—our husbands, my boys, her girl with the nightingale voice, all those Hindus, Christians, Sikhs, Muslims, Parsis, and atheists on that plane—were fated to die together off this beautiful bay. She learned this from a swami in Toronto.

I have my Valium.

Six of us "relatives"—two widows and four widowers—choose to spend the day today by the waters instead of sitting in a hospital room and scanning photographs of the dead. That's what they call us now: relatives. I've looked through twenty-seven photos in two days. They're very kind to us, the Irish are very understanding. Sometimes understanding means freeing a tourist bus for this trip to the bay, so we can pretend to spy our loved ones through the glassiness of waves or in sun-speckled cloud shapes.

I could die here, too, and be content.

"What is that, out there?" She's standing and flapping her hands and for a moment I see a head shape bobbing in the waves. She's standing in the water, I on the boulder. The tide is low, and a round, black, head-sized rock has just risen from the waves. She returns, her sari end dripping and ruined and her face is a twisted remnant of hope, the way mine was a hundred hours ago, still laughing but inwardly knowing that nothing but the ultimate tragedy could bring two women together at six o'clock on a Sunday morning. I watch her face sag into blankness.

"That water felt warm, Shaila," she says at length.

"You can't," I say. "We have to wait for our turn to come."

I haven't eaten in four days, haven't brushed my teeth.

"I know," she says. "I tell myself I have no right to grieve. They are in a better place than we are. My swami says I should be thrilled for them. My swami says depression is a sign of our selfishness."

Maybe I'm selfish. Selfishly I break away from Kusum and run, sandals slapping against stones, to the water's edge. What if my boys aren't lying pinned under the debris? What if they aren't stuck a mile below that innocent blue chop? What if, given the strong currents . . .

Now I've ruined my sari, one of my best. Kusum has joined me, knee-deep in water that feels to me like a swimming pool. I could settle in the water, and my husband would take my hand and the boys would slap water in my face just to see me scream.

"Do you remember what good swimmers my boys were, Kusum?"

"I saw the medals," she says.

One of the widowers, Dr Ranganathan from Montreal, walks out to us, carrying his shoes in one hand. He's an electrical engineer. Someone at the hotel mentioned his work is famous around the world, something about the place where physics and electricity come together. He has lost a huge family, something indescribable. "With some luck," Dr Ranganathan suggests to me, "a good swimmer could make it safely to some island. It is quite possible that there may be many many microscopic islets scattered around."

"You're not just saying that?" I tell Dr Ranganathan about Vinod, my elder son. Last year he took diving as well.

"It's a parent's duty to hope," he says. "It is foolish to rule out possibilities that have not been tested. I myself have not surrendered hope."

Kusum is sobbing once again. "Dear lady," he says, laying his free hand on her arm, and she calms down.

"Vinod is how old?" he asks me. He's very careful, as we all are. *Is*, not was.

"Fourteen. Yesterday he was fourteen. His father and uncle were going to take him down to the Taj and give him a big birthday party. I couldn't go with them because I couldn't get two weeks off from my stupid job in June." I process bills for a travel agent. June is a big travel month.

Dr Ranganathan whips the pockets of his suit jacket inside out. Squashed roses, in darkening shades of pink, float on the water. He tore the roses off creepers in somebody's garden. He didn't ask anyone if he could pluck the roses, but now there's been an article about it in the local papers. When you see an Indian person, it says, please give him or her flowers.

"A strong youth of fourteen," he says, "can very likely pull to safety a younger one."

My sons, though four years apart, were very close. Vinod wouldn't let Mithun drown. *Electrical engineering*, I think, foolishly perhaps: this man knows important secrets of the universe, things closed to me. Relief spins me lightheaded. No wonder my boys' photographs haven't turned up in the gallery of photos of the recovered dead. "Such pretty roses," I say.

"My wife loved pink roses. Every Friday I had to bring a bunch home. I used to say, Why? After twenty odd years of marriage you're still needing proof positive of my love?" He has identified his wife and three of his children. Then others from Montreal, the lucky ones, intact families with no survivors. He chuckles as he wades back to shore. Then he swings around to ask me a question. "Mrs. Bhave, you are wanting to throw in some roses for your loved ones? I have two big ones left."

But I have other things to float: Vinod's pocket calculator; a half-painted model B-52 for my Mithun. They'd want them on their island. And for my husband? For him I let fall into the calm, glassy waters a poem I wrote in the hospital yesterday. Finally he'll know my feelings for him.

"Don't tumble, the rocks are slippery," Dr Ranganathan cautions. He holds out a hand for me to grab.

Then it's time to get back on the bus, time to rush back to our waiting posts on hospital benches.

Kusum is one of the lucky ones. The lucky ones flew here, identified in multiplicate their loved ones, then will fly to India with the bodies for proper ceremonies. Satish is one of the few males who surfaced. The photos of faces we saw on the walls in an office at Heathrow and here in the hospital are mostly of women. Women have more body fat, a nun said to me matter-of-factly. They float better.

Today I was stopped by a young sailor on the street. He had loaded bodies, he'd gone into the water when—he checks my face for signs of strength—when the sharks were first spotted. I don't blush, and he breaks down. "It's all right," I say. "Thank you." I had heard about the sharks from Dr Ranganathan. In his orderly mind, science brings understanding, it holds no terror. It is the shark's duty. For every deer there is a hunter, for every fish a fisherman.

The Irish are not shy; they rush to me and give me hugs and some are crying. I cannot imagine reactions like that on the streets of Toronto. Just strangers, and I am touched. Some carry flowers with them and give them to any Indian they see.

After lunch, a policeman I have gotten to know quite well catches hold of me. He says he thinks he has a match for Vinod. I explain what a good swimmer Vinod is.

"You want me with you when you look at photos?" Dr Ranganathan walks ahead of me into the picture gallery. In these matters, he is a scientist, and I am grateful. It is a new perspective. "They have performed miracles," he says. "We are indebted to them."

The first day or two the policemen showed us relatives only one picture at a time; now they're in a hurry, they're eager to lay out the possibles, and even the probables.

The face on the photo is of a boy much like Vinod; the same intelligent eyes, the same thick brows dipping into a V. But this boy's features, even his cheeks, are puffier, wider, mushier.

"No." My gaze is pulled by the other pictures. There are five other boys who look like Vinod.

The nun assigned to console me rubs the first picture with a fingertip. "When they've been in the water for a while, love, they look a little heavier." The bones under the skin are broken, they said on the first day—try to adjust your memories. It's important.

"It's not him. I'm his mother. I'd know."

"I know this one!" Dr Ranganathan cries out suddenly from the back of the gallery. "And this one!" I think he senses that I don't want to find my boys. "They are the Kutty brothers. They were also from Montreal." I don't mean to be crying. On the contrary, I am ecstatic. My suitcase in the hotel is packed heavy with dry clothes for my boys.

The policeman starts to cry. "I am so sorry, I am so sorry, ma'am. I really thought we had a match."

With the nun ahead of us and the policeman behind, we, the unlucky ones without our children's bodies, file out of the makeshift gallery.

From Ireland most of us go on to India. Kusum and I take the same direct flight to Bombay, so I can help her clear customs quickly. But we have to argue with a man in uniform. He has large boils on his face. The boils swell and glow with sweat as we argue with him. He wants Kusum to wait in line and he refuses to take authority because his boss is on a tea break. But Kusum won't let her coffins out of sight, and I shan't desert her though I know that my parents, elderly and diabetic, must be waiting in a stuffy car in a scorching lot.

"You bastard!" I scream at the man with the popping boils. Other passengers press closer. "You think we're smuggling contraband in those coffins!"

Once upon a time we were well brought up women; we were dutiful wives who kept our heads veiled, our voices shy and sweet.

In India, I become, once again, an only child of rich, ailing parents. Old friends of the family come to pay their respects. Some are Sikh, and inwardly, involuntarily, I cringe. My parents are progressive people; they do not blame communities for a few individuals.

In Canada it is a different story now.

"Stay longer," my mother pleads. "Canada is a cold place. Why would you want to be all by yourself?" I stay.

Three months pass. Then another.

"Vikram wouldn't have wanted you to give up things!" they protest. They call my husband by the name he was born with. In Toronto he'd changed to Vik so the men he worked with at his office would find his name as easy as Rod or Chris. "You know, the dead aren't cut off from us!"

My grandmother, the spoiled daughter of a rich *zamindar*, shaved her head with rusty razor blades when she was widowed at sixteen. My grandfather died of childhood diabetes when he was nineteen, and she saw herself as the harbinger of bad luck. My mother grew up without parents, raised indifferently by an uncle, while her true mother slept in a hut behind the main estate house and took her food with the servants. She grew up a rationalist. My parents abhor mindless mortification.

The zamindar's daughter kept stubborn faith in Vedic rituals; my parents rebelled. I am trapped between two modes of knowledge. At thirty-six, I am too old to start over and too young to give up. Like my husband's spirit, I flutter between worlds.

Courting aphasia, we travel. We travel with our phalanx of servants and poor relatives. To hill stations and to beach resorts. We play contract bridge in dusty gymkhana clubs. We ride stubby ponies up crumbly mountain trails. At tea dances, we let ourselves be twirled twice around the ballroom. We hit the holy spots we hadn't made time for before. In Varanasi, Kalighat, Rishikesh, Hardwar, astrologers and palmists seek me out and for a fee offer me cosmic consolations.

Already the widowers among us are being shown new bride candidates. They cannot resist the call of custom, the authority of their parents and older brothers. They must marry; it is the duty of a man to look after a wife. The new wives will be young widows with children, destitute but of good family. They will make loving wives, but the men will shun them. I've had calls from the men over crackling Indian telephone lines. "Save me," they say, these substantial, educated, successful men of forty. "My parents are arranging a marriage for me." In a month they will have buried one family and returned to Canada with a new bride and partial family.

I am comparatively lucky. No one here thinks of arranging a husband for an unlucky widow.

Then, on the third day of the sixth month into this odyssey, in an abandoned temple in a tiny Himalayan village, as I make my offering of flowers and sweetmeats to the god of a tribe of animists, my husband descends to me. He is squatting next to a scrawny *sadhu* in moth-eaten robes. Vikram wears the vanilla suit he wore the last time I hugged him. The *sadhu* tosses petals on a butter-fed flame, reciting Sanskrit mantras and sweeps his face of flies. My husband takes my hands in his.

You're beautiful, he starts. Then, *What are you doing here?*

Shall I stay? I ask. He only smiles, but already the image is fading. *You must finish alone what we started together.* No seaweed wreathes his mouth. He speaks too fast just as he used to when we were an envied family in our pink split-level. He is gone.

In the windowless altar room, smoky with joss sticks and clarified butter lamps, a sweaty hand gropes for my blouse. I do not shriek. The *sadhu* arranges his robe. The lamps hiss and sputter out.

When we come out of the temple, my mother says, "Did you feel something weird in there?"

My mother has no patience with ghosts, prophetic dreams, holy men, and cults. "No," I lie. "Nothing."

But she knows that she's lost me. She knows that in days I shall be leaving.

Kusum's put her house up for sale. She wants to live in an ashram in Hardwar. Moving to Hardwar was her swami's idea. Her swami runs two ashrams, the one in Hardwar and another here in Toronto.

"Don't run away," I tell her.

"I'm not running away," she says. "I'm pursuing inner peace. You think you or that Ranganathan fellow are better off?"

Pam's left for California. She wants to do some modelling, she says. She says when she comes into her share of the insurance money she'll open a yoga-cum-aerobics studio in Hollywood. She sends me postcards so naughty I daren't leave them on the coffee table. Her mother has withdrawn from her and the world.

The rest of us don't lose touch, that's the point. Talk is all we have, says Dr Ranganathan, who has also resisted his relatives and returned to Montreal and to his job, alone. He says, whom better to talk with than other relatives? We've been melted down and recast as a new tribe.

He calls me twice a week from Montreal. Every Wednesday night and every Saturday afternoon. He is changing jobs, going to Ottawa. But Ottawa is over a hundred miles away, and he is forced to drive two hundred and twenty miles a day. He can't bring himself to sell his house. The house is a temple, he says; the king-sized bed in the master bedroom is a shrine. He sleeps on a folding cot. A devotee.

There are still some hysterical relatives. Judith Templeton's list of those needing help and those who've "accepted" is in nearly perfect balance. Acceptance means you speak of your family in the past tense and you make active plans for moving ahead with your life. There are courses at Seneca and Ryerson we could be taking. Her gleaming leather briefcase is full of college catalogues and lists of cultural societies that need our help. She has done impressive work, I tell her.

"In the textbooks on grief management," she replies—I am her confidante, I realize, one of the few whose grief has not sprung bizarre obsessions—"there are stages to pass through: rejection, depression, acceptance, reconstruction." She has compiled a chart and finds that six months after the tragedy, none of us still reject reality, but only a handful are reconstructing. "Depressed Acceptance" is the plateau we've reached. Remarriage is a major step in reconstruction (though she's a little surprised, even shocked, over *how* quickly some of the men have taken on new families). Selling one's house and changing jobs and cities is healthy.

How do I tell Judith Templeton that my family surrounds me, and that like creatures in epics, they've changed shapes? She sees me as calm and accepting but worries that I have no job, no career. My closest friends are worse off than I. I cannot tell her my days, even my nights, are thrilling.

She asks me to help with families she can't reach at all. An elderly couple in Agincourt whose sons were killed just weeks after they had brought their parents over from a village in Punjab. From their names, I know they are Sikh. Judith Templeton and a translator have visited them twice with offers of money for air fare to Ireland, with bank forms, power-of-attorney forms, but they have refused to sign, or to leave their tiny apartment. Their sons' money is frozen in the bank. Their sons' investment apartments have been trashed by tenants, the furnishings sold off. The parents fear that anything they sign or any money they receive will end the company's or the country's obligations to them. They fear they are selling their sons for two airline tickets to a place they've never seen.

The high-rise apartment is a tower of Indians and West Indians with a sprinkling of Orientals. The nearest bus stop kiosk is lined with women in saris. Boys practise cricket in the parking lot. Inside the building, even I wince a bit from the ferocity of onion fumes, the distinctive and immediate Indianness of frying *ghee*, but Judith Templeton maintains a steady flow of information. These poor old people are in imminent danger of losing their place and all their services.

I say to her, "They are Sikh. They will not open up to a Hindu woman." And what I want to add is, as much as I try not to, I stiffen now at the sight of beards and turbans. I remember a time when we all trusted each other in this new country, it was only the new country we worried about.

The two rooms are dark and stuffy. The lights are off, and an oil lamp sputters on the coffee table. The bent old lady has let us in, and her husband is wrapping a white turban over his oiled, hip-length hair. She immediately goes to the kitchen, and I hear the most familiar sound of an Indian home, tap water hitting and filling a teapot.

They have not paid their utility bills, out of fear and the inability to write a cheque. The telephone is gone; electricity and gas and water are soon to follow. They have told Judith their sons will provide. They are good boys, and they have always earned and looked after their parents.

We converse a bit in Hindi. They do not ask about the crash and I wonder if I should bring it up. If they think I am here merely as a translator, then they may feel insulted. There are thousands of Punjabi-speakers, Sikhs, in Toronto to do a better job. And so I say to the old lady, "I too have lost my sons, and my husband, in the crash."

Her eyes immediately fill with tears. The man mutters a few words which sound like a blessing. "God provides and God takes away," he says.

I want to say, But only men destroy and give back nothing. "My boys and my husband are not coming back," I say. "We have to understand that."

Now the old woman responds. "But who is to say? Man alone does not decide these things." To this her husband adds his agreement.

Judith asks about the bank papers, the release forms. With a stroke of a pen, they will have a provincial trustee to pay their bills, invest their money, send them a monthly pension.

"Do you know this woman?" I ask them.

The man raises his hand from the table, turns it over and seems to regard each finger separately before he answers. "This young lady is always coming here, we make tea for her and she leaves papers for us to sign." His eyes scan a pile of papers in the corner of the room. "Soon we will be out of tea, then will she go away?"

The old lady adds, "I have asked my neighbours and no one else gets *angrezi* visitors. What have we done?"

"It's her job," I try to explain. "The government is worried. Soon you will have no place to stay, no lights, no gas, no water."

"Government will get its money. Tell her not to worry, we are honourable people."

I try to explain the government wishes to give money, not take. He raises his hand. "Let them take," he says. "We are accustomed to that. That is no problem."

"We are strong people," says the wife. "Tell her that."

"Who needs all this machinery?" demands the husband. "It is unhealthy, the bright lights, the cold air on a hot day, the cold food, the four gas rings. God will provide, not government."

"When our boys return," the mother says. Her husband sucks his teeth. "Enough talk," he says.

Judith breaks in. "Have you convinced them?" The snaps on her cordovan briefcase go off like firecrackers in that quiet apartment. She lays the sheaf of legal papers on the coffee table. "If they can't write their names, an X will do—I've told them that."

Now the old lady has shuffled to the kitchen and soon emerges with a pot of tea and two cups. "I think my bladder will go first on a job like this," Judith says to me, smiling. "If only there was some way of reaching them. Please thank her for the tea. Tell her she's very kind."

I nod in Judith's direction and tell them in Hindi, "She thanks you for the tea. She thinks you are being very hospitable but she doesn't have the slightest idea what it means."

I want to say, Humour her. I want to say, My boys and my husband are with me too, more than ever. I look in the old man's eyes and I can read his stubborn, peasant's message: *I have protected this woman as best I can. She is the only person I have left. Give to me or take from me what you will, but I will not sign for it. I will not pretend that I accept.*

In the car, Judith says, "You see what I'm up against? I'm sure they're lovely people, but their stubbornness and ignorance are driving me crazy. They think signing a paper is signing their sons' death warrants, don't they?"

I am looking out the window. I want to say, *In our culture, it is a parent's duty to hope.*

"Now Shaila, this next woman is a real mess. She cries all day and night, and she refuses all medical help. We may have to—"

"—Let me out at the subway," I say.

"I beg your pardon?" I can feel those blue eyes staring at me.

It would not be like her to disobey. She merely disapproves, and slows at a corner to let me out. Her voice is plaintive. "Is there anything I said? Anything I did?"

I could answer her suddenly in a dozen ways, but I choose not to. "Shaila? Let's talk about it," I hear, then slam the door.

A wife and mother begins her new life in a new country, and that life is cut short. Yet her husband tells her: Complete what we have started. We who stayed out of politics and came half-way around the world to avoid religious and political feuding have been the first in the New World to die from it. I no longer know what we started, nor how to complete it. I write letters to the editors of local papers and to members of Parliament. Now at least they admit it was a bomb. One MP answers back, with sympathy, but with a challenge. You want to make a difference? Work on a campaign. Work on mine. Politicize the Indian voter.

My husband's old lawyer helps me set up a trust. Vikram was a saver and a careful investor. He had saved the boys' boarding school and college fees. I sell the pink house at four times what we paid for it and take a small apartment downtown. I am looking for a charity to support.

We are deep in the Toronto winter, grey skies, icy pavements. I stay indoors, watching television. I have tried to assess my situation, how best to live my life, to complete what we began so many years ago. Kusum has written me from Hardwar that her life is now serene. She has seen Satish and has heard her daughter sing again. Kusum was on a pilgrimage, passing through a village when she heard a young girl's voice, singing one of her daughter's favorite *bhajans*. She followed the music through the squalor of a Himalayan village, to a hut where a young girl, an exact replica of her daughter, was fanning coals under the kitchen fire. When she appeared, the girl cried out, "Ma!" and ran away. What did I think of that?

I think I can only envy her.

Pam didn't make it to California, but writes me from Vancouver. She works in a department store, giving make-up hints to Indian and Oriental girls. Dr Ranganathan has given up his commute, given up his house and job, and accepted an academic position in Texas where no one knows his story and he has vowed not to tell it. He calls me now once a week.

I wait, I listen, and I pray, but Vikram has not returned to me. The voices and the shapes and the nights filled with visions ended abruptly several weeks ago.

I take it as a sign.

One rare, beautiful, sunny day last week, returning from a small errand on Yonge Street, I was walking through the park from the subway to my apartment. I live equidistant from the Ontario Houses of Parliament and the University of Toronto. The day was not cold, but something in the bare trees caught my attention. I looked up from the gravel, into the branches and the clear blue sky beyond. I thought I heard the rustling of larger forms, and I waited a moment for voices. Nothing.

"What?" I asked.

Then as I stood in the path looking north to Queen's Park and west to the university, I heard the voices of my family one last time. *Your time has come*, they said. *Go, be brave.*

I do not know where this voyage I have begun will end. I do not know which direction I will take. I dropped the package on a park bench and started walking.

Alice Munro

Alice Munro was born in Wingham, Ontario, in 1931 and grew up in a Huron County farming community, where her father raised silver foxes. After two years at the University of Western Ontario, she married and moved to Vancouver and then Victoria, where raising children and working in a bookstore left little time for writing. In 1968, at the age of thirty-seven, she published *Dance of the Happy Shades*, which won the Governor General's Award for fiction. This was followed by a collection of interlocking short stories called *Lives of Girls and Women* (1971), *Something I've Been Meaning to Tell You* (1974), *Who Do You Think You Are?* (1978), *The Moons of Jupiter* (1982), *The Progress of Love* (1986), and *Friend of My Youth* (1990). Her stories, which have won numerous awards, share certain affinities with the work of such Southern writers as Eudora Welty and Flannery O'Connor: "It was nothing . . . definite," Munro says. "It was more like a way you could see ordinary life. A way of seeing perhaps grotesque things, comic things. It wasn't anything technical, though I imitate techniques without thinking about it. . . ."

There is a paragraph at the end of "Who Do You Think You Are?" that seems to embody a central concern in Munro's fiction—the relation of verisimilitude to moral sympathy. The central figure, Rose, feels a certain shame for her acting talents, a shame that, perhaps, she has, in her devotion to surface and gesture—to appearances—missed the essence of a character: "The thing she was ashamed of, in acting, was that she might be paying attention to the wrong things, reporting antics, when there was always something further, a tone, a depth, a light, that she couldn't get and wouldn't get." Rose's dilemma is also the dilemma of her creator, whose concern for both accuracy and depth keeps her on the trail of a character or story or situation when most authors would lay down their pens, satisfied with a minor victory or revelation. That urgency to know all—not necessarily to tell all, of course—informs all her work.

In an interview with Geoff Hancock, published in *Canadian Fiction Magazine*, Munro dismisses both plot and setting as essential ingredients in fiction. "What happens as event doesn't really matter much. When the event becomes the thing that matters, the story isn't working too well." Feeling, she says, must predominate over both plot and setting. "I don't think the setting matters at all. A lot of people think I'm a regional writer. And I use the region where I grew up a lot. But I don't have any idea of writing to show the kind of things that happen in a certain place. These things happen and the place is part of it. But, in a way, it's incidental."

In order to create a feeling, or climate, in a story, Munro depends on her eye for texture and detail. "I know I get excited by ordinary things," Munro says. "Even totally commonplace things like a shopping centre and a supermarket and things like that are just sort of endlessly interesting in their physical reality. I find them that way. That they seem to mean something beyond themselves. But I can't explain much more than that." She differentiates between the person she is, who would lament the destruction of woodland to put up a service station, and the writer in her, who would find the comings and goings at that station endlessly fascinating.

On the genesis and gestation of stories, Munro's observations are fascinating. "I have this picture. It generates some other images and attracts them like a magnet." She describes herself as a juggler, trying to keep these images and anecdotes in the air; then, as an architect without a blueprint, striving to discover the structure or form that will house the feeling, the "soul of the story," that has been building up in her. "A story must be made in the same way our dreams are made, truth in them being cast, with what seems to us often a rather high-handed frivolity, in any kind of plausible, implausible, giddy, strange, humdrum terms at all. This is the given story . . . and from that I work, getting no more help, doing the hard repetitive work of putting it in words that are hardly any good at all, then a little better, then quite a bit better, at times satisfactory."

"I love doing things right. All that accuracy," Munro says, even if doing things right involves making the story deliberately grainy or awkward. In an interview with Alan Twigg in *Strong Voices*, Munro admits her lack of sympathy for literary expressionism, the free-fall and let-it-all-hang-out school of writing: "It's as if I must take great care of everything. Instead of splashing the colours off and trusting that they will all come together." Her concern for accuracy extends not only to language and form, but also to the desire for psychological realism that drives her writing. As she explains to Hancock: "I like to look at people's lives over a number of years, without continuity. Like catching them in snapshots. And I like the way people relate, or don't relate, to the people they were earlier. This is the sense of life that interests me a lot. . . . I think this is why I'm not drawn to writing novels. Because I don't see that people develop and arrive somewhere. I just see people living in flashes."

Lives of Girls and Women

The snow banks along the main street got to be so high that an archway was cut in one of them, between the street and the sidewalk, in front of the post office. A picture was taken of this and published in the Jubilee *Herald-Advance*, so that people could cut it out and send it to relatives and acquaintances living in less heroic climates, in England or Australia or Toronto. The red-brick clocktower of the post office was sticking up above the snow and two women were standing in the archway, to show it was no trick. Both these women worked in the post office, had put their coats on without buttoning them. One was Fern Dogherty, my mother's boarder.

My mother cut this picture out, because it had Fern in it, and because she said I should keep it, to show to my children.

"They will never see a thing like that," she said. "By then the snow will all be collected in machines and—dissipated. Or people will be living under transparent domes, with a controlled temperature. There will be no such thing as seasons anymore."

How did she collect all her unsettling information about the future? She looked forward to a time when towns like Jubilee would be replaced by domes and mushrooms of concrete, with moving skyways to carry you from one to the other, when the countryside would be bound and tamed forever under broad sweeping ribbons of pavement. Nothing would be the same as we knew it today, no frying pans or bobby pins or printed pages or fountain pens would remain. My mother would not miss a thing.

Her speaking of children amazed me too, for I never meant to have any. It was glory I was after, walking the streets of Jubilee like an exile or a spy, not sure from which direction fame would strike, or when, only convinced from my bones out that it had to. In this conviction my mother had shared, she had been my ally, but now I would no longer discuss it with her; she was indiscreet, and her expectations took too blatant a form.

Fern Dogherty. There she was in the paper, both hands coquettishly holding up the full collar of her good winter coat, which through pure luck she had worn to work that day. "I look the size of a watermelon," she said. "In that coat."

Mr. Chamberlain, looking with her, pinched her arm above the bracelet wrinkle of the wrist.

"Tough rind, tough old watermelon."

"Don't get vicious," said Fern. "I mean it." Her voice was small for such a big woman, plaintive, put-upon, but in the end good-humored, yielding. All those qualities my mother had developed for her assault on life—sharpness, smartness, determination, selectiveness—seemed to have their opposites in Fern, with her diffuse complaints, lazy movements, indifferent agreeableness. She had a dark skin, not olive but dusty looking, dim, with brown-pigmented spots as large as coins; it was like the dappled ground under a tree on a sunny day. Her teeth were square, white, slightly protruding, with little spaces between them. These two characteristics, neither of which sounds particularly attractive in itself, did give her a roguish, sensual look.

She had a ruby-colored satin dressing gown, a gorgeous garment, fruitily molding, when she sat down, the bulges of her stomach and thighs. She wore it Sunday mornings, when she sat in our dining room smoking, drinking tea, until it was time to get ready for church. It parted at the knees to show some pale clinging rayon—a nightgown. Nightgowns were garments I could not bear, because of the way they twisted around and worked up on you while you slept and also because they left you uncovered between the legs. Naomi and I when we were younger used to draw pictures of men and women with startling gross genitals, the women's fat, bristling with needly hair, like a porcupine's back. Wearing a nightgown one could not help being aware of this vile bundle, which pajamas could decently shroud and contain. My mother at the same Sunday breakfast table wore large striped pajamas, a faded rust-colored kimono with a tasseled tie, the sort of slippers that are woolly socks, with a sole sewn in.

Fern Dogherty and my mother were friends in spite of differences. My mother valued in people experience of the world, contact with any life of learning or culture, and finally any suggestion of being dubiously received in Jubilee. And Fern had not always worked for the post office. No; at one time she had studied singing, she had studied at the Royal Conservatory of Music. Now she sang in the United Church choir, sang "I Know that My Redeemer Liveth" on Easter Sunday, and at weddings she sang "Because" and "O Promise Me" and "The Voice That Breathed O'er Eden." On Saturday afternoons, the post office being closed, she and my mother would listen to the broadcasts of the Metropolitan Opera. My mother had a book of operas. She would get it out and follow the story, identifying the arias, for which translations were provided. She had questions for Fern, but Fern did not know as much about operas as you would think she might; she would even get mixed up about which one it was they were listening to. But sometimes she would lean forward with her elbows on the table, not now relaxed, but alertly supported, and sing, scorning the foreign words. "*Do*—daa—do, da, *do*, da do-do—" The force, the seriousness of her singing voice always came as a surprise. It didn't embarrass her, letting loose those grand, inflated emotions she paid no attention to in life.

"Did you plan to be an opera singer?" I asked.

"No. I just planned to be the lady working in the post office. Well, I did and I didn't. The work, the *training*. I just didn't have the ambition for it, I guess that was my trouble. I always preferred having a good time." She wore slacks on Saturday afternoons, and sandals that showed her pudgy, painted toes. She was dropping ashes on her stomach, which, ungirdled, popped out in a pregnant curve. "Smoking is ruining my voice," she said meditatively.

Fern's style of singing, though admired, was regarded in Jubilee as being just a hair's breadth from showing off, and sometimes children did screech or warble after her, in the street. My mother could take this for persecution. She would construct such cases out of the flimsiest evidence, seeking out the Jewish couple who ran the Army Surplus store, or the shrunken silent Chinese in the laundry, with bewildering compassion, loud slow-spoken overtures of friendship. They did not know what to make of her. Fern was not persecuted, that I could see. Though my old aunts, my father's aunts, would say her name in a peculiar way, as if it had a stone in it, that they would have to suck, and spit out. And Naomi did tell me, "That Fern Dogherty had a baby."

"She never did," I said, automatically defensive.

"She did so. She had it when she was nineteen years old. That's why she got kicked out of the Conservatory."

"How do you know?"

"My mother knows."

Naomi's mother had spies everywhere, old childbed cases, deathbed companions, keeping her informed. In her nursing job, going from one house to another, she was able to operate like an underwater vacuum tube, sucking up what nobody else could get at. I felt I had to argue with Naomi about it because Fern was our boarder, and Naomi was always saying things about people in our house. ("Your mother's an atheist," she would say with black relish, and I would say, "No she isn't, she's an agnostic," and all through my reasoned hopeful explanation Naomi would chant *same difference, same difference*.) I was not able to retaliate, either out of delicacy or cowardice, though Naomi's own father belonged to some odd and discredited religious sect, and wandered all over town talking prophecies without putting his false teeth in.

I took to noticing pictures of babies in the paper, or in magazines, when Fern was around, saying, "Aw, isn't it *cute?*" and then watching her closely for a flicker of remorse, maternal longing, as if someday she might actually be persuaded to burst into tears, fling out her empty arms, struck to the heart by an ad for talcum powder or strained meat.

Furthermore, Naomi said Fern did everything with Mr. Chamberlain, just the same as if they were married.

It was Mr. Chamberlain who got Fern boarding with us in the first place. We rented the house from his mother, now in her third year, blind and bedridden, in the Wawanash County Hospital. Fern's mother was in the same place; it was there, in fact, on a visiting day, that they had met. She was working in the Blue River Post Office at that time. Mr. Chamberlain worked at the Jubilee radio station and lived in a small apartment in the same building, not wanting the trouble of a house. My mother spoke of him as "Fern's friend," in a clarifying tone of voice, as if to insist that the word friend in this case meant no more than it was supposed to mean.

"They enjoy each other's company," she said. "They don't bother about any nonsense."

Nonsense meant romance; it meant vulgarity; it meant sex.

I tried out on my mother what Naomi said.

"Fern and Mr. Chamberlain might just as well be married."

"What? What do you mean? Who said that?"

"Everybody knows it."

"I don't. Everybody does not. Nobody ever said such a thing in my hearing. It's that Naomi said it, isn't it?"

Naomi was not popular in my house, nor I in hers. Each of us was suspected of carrying the seeds of contamination—in my case, of atheism, in Naomi's, of sexual preoccupation.

"It's dirty mindedness that is just rampant in this town, and will never let people alone."

"If Fern Dogherty was not a good woman," my mother concluded, with a spacious air of logic, "do you think I would have her living in my house?"

This year, our first year in high school, Naomi and I held almost daily discussions on the subject of sex, but took one tone, so that there were degrees of candor we could never reach. This tone was ribald, scornful, fanatically curious. A year ago we had liked to imagine ourselves victims of passion; now we were established as onlookers, or at most cold and gleeful experimenters. We had a book Naomi had found in her mother's old hope chest, under the moth-balled best blankets.

Care should be taken during the initial connection, we read aloud, *particularly if the male organ is of an unusual size. Vaseline may prove a helpful lubricant.*

"I prefer butter myself. Tastier."

Intercourse between the thighs is often resorted to in the final stages of pregnancy.

"You mean they still do it *then?*"

The rear-entry position is sometimes indicated in cases where the female is considerably obese.

"Fern," Naomi said. "That how he does it to Fern. She's considerably obese."

"Aggh. This book makes me sick."

The male sexual organ in erection, we read, had been known to reach a length of fourteen inches. Naomi spat out her chewing gum and rolled it between her palms, stretching it longer and longer, then picked it up by one end and dangled it in the air.

"Mr. Chamberlain, the record breaker!"

Thereafter whenever she came to my place, and Mr. Chamberlain was there, one of us, or both, if we were chewing gum, would take it out and roll it this way and dangle it innocently, till even the adults noticed and Mr. Chamberlain said, "That's quite a game you got there," and my mother said, "Stop that, it's filthy." (She meant the gum.) We watched Mr. Chamberlain and Fern for signs of passion, wantonness, lustful looks, or hands up the skirt. We were not rewarded, my defense of them turning out to be truer than I wished it to be. For I as much as Naomi liked to entertain myself with thoughts of their grunting indecencies, their wallowing in jingly beds (in tourist cabins, Naomi said, every time they drove to Tupperton to have a look at the lake). Disgust did not rule out enjoyment, in my thoughts; indeed they were inseparable.

Mr. Chamberlain, Art Chamberlain, read the news on the Jubilee radio. He also did all the more serious and careful announcing. He had a fine professional voice, welcome as dark chocolate flowing in and out of the organ music on the Sunday afternoon program *In Memoriam*, sponsored by a local funeral parlor. He sometimes got Fern singing on this program, sacred songs—"I Wonder as I

Wander"—and nonsacred but mournful songs—"The End of a Perfect Day." It was not hard to get on the Jubilee radio; I myself had recited a comic poem, on the *Saturday Morning Young Folks Party*, and Naomi had played "The Bells of St. Mary's" on the piano. Every time you turned it on there was a good chance of hearing someone you knew, or at least of hearing the names of people you knew mentioned in the dedications. ("We are going to play this piece also for Mr. and Mrs. Carl Otis on the occasion of their twenty-eighth wedding anniversary, requested by their son George and wife Etta, and their three grandchildren, Lorraine, Mark, and Lois, also by Mr. Otis' sister Mrs. Bill Townley of the Porterfield Road.") I had phoned up myself and dedicated a song to Uncle Benny on his fortieth birthday; my mother would not have her name mentioned. She preferred listening to the Toronto station, which brought us the Metropolitan Opera, and news with no commercials, and a quiz program in which she competed with four gentlemen who, to judge from their voices, would all have little, pointed beards.

Mr. Chamberlain had to read commercials, too, and he did it with ripe concern, recommending Vick's Nose Drops from Cross' Drugstore, and Sunday dinner at the Brunswick Hotel, and Lee Wickert and Sons for dead-livestock removal. "How's the dead livestock, soldier?" Fern would greet him, and he might slap her lightly on the rump. "I'll tell them you need their services!" "Looks to me more like you do," said Fern without much malice, and he would drop into a chair and smile at my mother for pouring him tea. His light blue-green eyes had no expression, just that color, so pretty you would want to make a dress out of it. He was always tired.

Mr. Chamberlain's white hands, his nails cut straight across, his graying, thinning, nicely-combed hair, his body that did not in any way disturb his clothes but seemed to be made of the same material as they were, so that he might have been shirt and tie and suit all the way through, were strange to me in a man. Even Uncle Benny, so skinny and narrow-chested, with his damaged bronchial tubes, had some look or way of moving that predicted chance or intended violence, something that would make disorder; my father had this too, though he was so moderate in his ways. Yet it was Mr. Chamberlain, tapping his ready-made cigarette in the ashtray, Mr. Chamberlain who had been in the war, he had been in the Tank Corps. If my father was there when he came to see us—to see Fern, really, but he did not quickly make that apparent—my father would ask him questions about the war. But it was clear that they saw the war in different ways. My father saw it as an overall design, marked off in campaigns, which had a purpose, which failed or succeeded. Mr. Chamberlain saw it as a conglomeration of stories, leading nowhere in particular. He made his stories to be laughed at.

For instance he told us about the first time he went into action, what confusion there was. Some tanks had gone into a wood, got turned around, were coming out the wrong way, where they expected the Germans to come from. So the first shots they fired were at one of their own tanks.

"Blew it up!" said Mr. Chamberlain blithely, unapologetically.

"Were there soldiers in that tank?"

He looked at me in mocking surprise as he always did when I said anything: you would think I had just stood on my head for him. "Well, I wouldn't be too surprised if there were!"

"Were they—killed, then?"

"Something happened to them. I certainly never saw them around again. Poof!"

"Shot by their own side, what a terrible thing," said my mother, scandalized but less than ordinarily sure of herself.

"Things like that happen in a war," said my father quietly but with some severity, as if to object to any of this showed a certain female naiveté. Mr. Chamberlain just laughed. He went on to tell about what they did on the last day of the war. They blew up the cookhouse, turned all the guns on it in the last jolly blaze they would get.

"Sounds like a bunch of kids," said Fern. "Sounds like you weren't grown-up enough to fight a *war*. It just sounds like you had one big, idiotic, good time."

"What I always try to have, isn't it? A good time."

Once it came out that he had been in Florence, which was not surprising, since he had fought the war in Italy. But my mother sat up, she jumped a little in her chair, she quivered with attention.

"Were *you* in Florence?"

"Yes, ma'am," said Mr. Chamberlain without enthusiasm.

"In Florence, you were in Florence," repeated my mother, confused and joyful. I had an inkling of what she felt, but hoped she would not reveal too much. "I never thought," she said. "Well, of course I knew it was Italy but it seems so strange—" She meant that this Italy we had been talking about, where the war was fought, was the same place history happened, in the very place, where the old Popes were, and the Medici, and Leonardo. The Cenci. The cypresses. Dante Alighieri.

Rather oddly, in view of her enthusiasm for the future, she was excited by the past. She hurried into the front room and came back with the art-and-architecture supplement to the encyclopedia, full of statues, paintings, buildings, mostly photographed in a cloudy, cool, museum-gray light.

"There!" she opened it up on the table in front of him.

"There's your Florence. Michelangelo's statue of David. Did you see that?"

A naked man. His marble thing hanging on him for everybody to look at; like a drooping lily petal. Who but my mother in her staunch and dreadful innocence would show a man, would show us all, a picture like that? Fern's mouth was swollen, with the effort to contain her smile.

"I never got to see it, no. The place is full of statues. Famous this and famous that. You can't turn around for them."

I could see he was not a person to talk to, about things like this. But my mother kept on.

"Well surely you saw the bronze doors? The magnificent bronze doors? It took the artist his whole life to do them. Look at them, they're here. What was his name—Ghiberti. Ghiberti. His whole life."

Some things Mr. Chamberlain admitted he had seen, some he had not. He looked at the book with a reasonable amount of patience, then said he had not cared for Italy.

"Well, Italy, maybe that was all right. It was the Italians."

"Did you think they were decadent?" said my mother regretfully.

"Decadent, I don't know. I don't know what they were. They don't care. On the streets in Italy I've had a man come up to me and offer to sell me his own daughter. It happened all the time."

"What would they want to sell a girl for?" I said, adopting as I easily could my bold and simple façade of innocence. "For a slave?"

"In a manner of speaking," said my mother, and she shut the book, relinquishing Michelangelo and the bronze doors.

"No older than Del here," said Mr. Chamberlain, with a disgust that in him seemed faintly fraudulent. "Not so old, some of them."

"They mature earlier," Fern said. "Those hot climates."

"Del. You take this book, put it away." Alarm in my mother's voice was like the flap of rising wings.

Well, I had heard. I did not come back to the dining room but went upstairs and undressed. I put on my mother's black rayon dressing gown, splattered with bunches of pink and white flowers. Impractical gift she never wore. In her room I stared, goose-pimpled and challenging, into the three-way mirror. I pulled the material off my shoulders and bunched it over my breasts, which were just about big enough to fit those wide, shallow cones of paper laid in sundae dishes. I had turned on the light beside the dressing table; it came meekly, warmly through a bracket of butterscotch glass, and laid a kind of glow on my skin. I looked at my high round forehead, pink freckled skin, my face as innocent as an egg, and my eyes managed to alter what was there, to make me sly and creamy, to change my hair, which was light brown, fine as a crackling bush, into rich waves more gold than muddy. Mr. Chamberlain's voice in my mind, saying *no older than Del here*, acted on me like the touch of rayon silk on my skin, surrounded me, made me feel endangered and desired. I thought of girls in Florence, girls in Rome, girls my age that a man could buy. Black Italian hair under their arms. Black down at the corners of their mouths. *They mature earlier in those hot climates.* Roman Catholics. A man paid you to let him do it. What did he say? Did he take your clothes off or did he expect you to do that yourself? Did he take down his pants or did he simply unzip himself and point his thing at you? It was the stage of transition, bridge between what was possible, known and normal behavior, and the magical, bestial act, that I could not imagine. Nothing about that was in Naomi's mother's book.

There was a house in Jubilee with three prostitutes in it. That is, three if you counted Mrs. McQuade who ran it; she was at least sixty years old. The house was at the north end of the main street, in a yard all run to hollyhocks and dandelions, beside the B.A. service station. On sunny days the two younger women would sometimes come out and sit in canvas chairs. Naomi and I had made several trips past and had once seen them. They wore print dresses and slippers; their white legs were bare. One of them was reading the *Star Weekly*. Naomi said that this one's name was Peggy, and that one night in the men's toilet at the Gay-la dance hall she had been persuaded to serve a line-up, standing up. Was such a thing possible? (I heard this story another time, only now it was Mrs. McQuade herself who performed or endured this feat, and it was not at the Gay-la dance hall but against the back wall of the Blue Owl Cafe.) I wished I had seen more of this Peggy than the soft, mouse-brown nest of curls above the paper; I wished I had seen her face. I did expect something—a foul shimmer of corruption, some emanation, like marsh gas. I was surprised, in a way, that she would read a paper, that the words in it would mean the same things to her, presumably, as they did to the rest of us, that she ate and drank, was human still. I thought of her as having gone right beyond human functioning into a condition of perfect depravity, at the opposite pole from sainthood but similarly isolated, unknowable. What appeared to be ordinariness here—the *Star Weekly*, dotted curtains looped back, geraniums growing hopefully out of tin cans in the whorehouse window, seemed to me deliberate and tantalizing deception—the skin of everyday appearances stretched over such shamelessness, such consuming explosions of lust.

I rubbed my hipbones through the cool rayon. If I had been born in Italy my flesh would already be used, bruised, knowing. It would not be my fault. The thought of whoredom, not my fault, bore me outward for a moment; a restful, alluring thought, because it was so final, and did away with ambition and anxiety.

After this I constructed in several halting imperfect installments a daydream. I imagined that Mr. Chamberlain saw me in my mother's black flowered dressing gown, pulled down off the shoulders, as I had seen myself in the mirror. Then I proposed to have the dressing gown come off, let him see me with nothing on at all. How could it happen? Other people who would ordinarily be in the house with us would have to be got rid of. My mother I sent out to sell encyclopedias; my brother I banished to the farm. It would have to be in the summer holidays, when I was home from school. Fern would not yet be home from the post office. I would come downstairs in the heat of the late afternoon, a sulphurous still day, wearing only this dressing gown. I would get a drink of water at the sink, not seeing Mr. Chamberlain sitting quietly in the room, and then—what? A strange dog, introduced into our house for this occasion only, might jump on me, pulling the dressing gown off. I might turn and somehow catch the material on the nail of a chair, and the whole thing would just slither to my feet. The thing was that it had to be an accident; no effort on my part, and certainly none on Mr. Chamberlain's. Beyond the moment of revelation my dream did not go. In fact it often did not get that far, but lingered among the preliminary details, solidifying them. The moment of being seen naked could not be solidified, it was a stab of light. I never pictured Mr. Chamberlain's reaction, I never very clearly pictured him. His presence was essential but blurred; in the corner of my daydream he was featureless but powerful, humming away electrically like a blue fluorescent light.

Naomi's father caught us, as we raced past his door on our way downstairs. "You young ladies come in and visit me a minute, make yourselves comfortable."

It was spring by this time, windy yellow evening. Nevertheless he was burning garbage in a round tin stove in his room, it was hot and smelly. He had washed his socks and underwear and hung them on strings along the wall. Naomi and her mother treated him unceremoniously. When her mother was away, as now, Naomi would open a can of spaghetti and dump it on a plate, for his dinner. I would say, "Aren't you going to heat it?" and she would say, "Why bother? He wouldn't know the difference anyway."

In his room, on the floor, he had stacks of newsprint pamphlets which I supposed had to do with the religion he believed in. Naomi sometimes had to bring them from the post office. Taking her cue from her mother, she had great contempt for his beliefs. "It's all prophecies and prophecies," she said. "They have prophesied the end of the world three times now."

We sat on the edge of the bed, which had no spread on it, only a rough, rather dirty blanket, and he sat in his rocker opposite us. He was an old man. Naomi's mother had nursed him before she married him. Between his words there were usually large gaps, during which he would not forget about you, however, but fix his pale eyes on your forehead as if he expected to find the rest of his thought written out there.

"Reading from the Bible," he said genially and unnecessarily, and rather in the manner of one who chooses not to see objections he knows are there. He opened a large-print Bible with the place already marked and began to read in a piercing elderly voice, with some odd stops, and difficulties of phrasing.

> Then shall the kingdom of heaven be likened unto ten virgins, which took their lamps, and went forth to meet the bridegroom.
> And five of them were wise, and five were foolish.
> They that were foolish took their lamps, and took no oil with them:
> But the wise took oil in their vessels with their lamps.
> While the bridegroom tarried, they all slumbered and slept.
> And at midnight there was a cry made, Behold, the bridegroom cometh; go ye out to meet him.
> Then all those virgins arose, and trimmed their lamps.
> And the foolish said unto the wise, Give us of your oil; for our lamps are gone out.

Then it turned out of course—now I remembered hearing all this before—that the wise virgins would not give up any of their oil for fear they would not have enough, and the foolish virgins had to go out and buy some, and so missed the bridegroom coming and were shut out. I had always supposed this parable, which I did not like, had to do with prudence, preparedness, something like that. But I could see that Naomi's father believed it to be about sex. I looked sideways at Naomi to catch that slight sucking in of the corners of the mouth, the facial drollery with which she always recognized this subject, but she was looking obstinate and miserable, disgusted by the very thing that was my secret pleasure—the poetic flow of words, archaic expressions. *Said unto; tarried; Behold the bridegroom cometh.* She was so offended by all this that she could not even enjoy the word *virgins*.

His toothless mouth shut. Sly and proper as a baby's.

"No more for now. Think about it when the time comes. There's a lesson for young girls."

"Stupid old bugger," said Naomi, on the stairs.

"I feel—sorry for him."

She jabbed me in the kidney.

"Hurry up, let's get out of here. He's liable to find something else. Reads the Bible till his eyes fall out. Serve him right."

We ran outside, up Mason Street. These long light evenings we visited every part of town. We loitered past the Lyceum Theatre, the Blue Owl Cafe, the poolroom. We sat on the benches by the cenotaph, and if any car honked at us we waved. Dismayed by our greenness, our leggy foolishness, they drove on by; they laughed out their windows. We went into the ladies' toilet in the Town Hall—wet floor, sweating cement walls, harsh ammoniac smell—and there on the toilet door where only bad brainless girls wrote up their names, we wrote the names of the two reigning queens of our class—Marjory Coutts, Gwen Mundy. We wrote in lipstick and drew tiny obscene figures underneath. Why did we do this? Did we hate those girls, to whom we were unfailingly obsequiously pleasant? No. Yes. We hated their immunity, well-bred lack of curiosity, whatever kept them floating, charitable and pleased, on the surface of life in Jubilee, and would float them on to sororities, engagements, marriages to doctors or lawyers in more prosperous places far away. We hated them just because they could never be imagined entering the Town Hall toilets.

Having done this, we ran away, not sure whether or not we had committed a criminal act.

We dared each other. Walking under street lights still as pale as flowers cut out of tissue paper, walking past unlighted windows from which we hoped the world watched, we did dares.

"Be like you have cerebral palsy. *Dare.*"

At once I came unjointed, lolled my head, rolled my eyes, began to talk incomprehensively, in a cross insistent babble.

"Do it for a block. Never mind who we meet. Don't stop. Dare."

We met old Dr. Comber, spindly and stately, beautifully dressed. He stopped, and tapped his stick, and objected.

"What is this performance?"

"A fit, sir," said Naomi plaintively. "She's always having these fits."

Making fun of poor, helpless, afflicted people. The bad taste, the heartlessness, the joy of it.

We went to the park, which was neglected, deserted, a triangle of land made too gloomy by its big cedar trees, for children's play, and not attracting people who went for walks. Why should anybody in Jubilee walk to see more grass and dirt and trees, the same thing that pushed in on the town from every side? They would walk downtown, to look at stores, meet on the sidewalks, feel the hope of activity. Naomi and I all by ourselves climbed the big cedar trees, scraped our knees on the bark, screamed as we never needed to when we were younger, seeing the branches part, revealing the tilted earth. We hung from the branches by our locked hands, by our ankles; we pretended to be baboons, prattling and gibbering. We felt the whole town lying beneath us, gaping, ready to be astounded.

There were noises peculiar to the season. Children on the sidewalks, skipping and singing in their clear, devout voices.

> On the mountain stands a lady
> Who she is I do not know.
> All she wears is gold and silver.
> All she needs is a new pair of shoes!

And the peacocks crying. We dropped from the trees and set off to look at them, down past the park, down a poor unnamed street running to the river. The peacocks belonged to a man named Pork Childs who drove the town garbage truck. The street had no sidewalks. We walked around puddles gleaming in the soft mud. Pork Childs had a barn behind his house for his fowl. Neither barn nor house was painted.

There were peacocks, walking around under the bare oak trees. How could we forget them, from one spring to the next?

The hens were easily forgotten, the sullen colors of their yard. But the males were never disappointing. Their astonishing, essential color, blue of breasts and throats and necks, darker feathers showing there like ink blots, or soft vegetation under tropical water. One had his tail spread, to show the blind eyes, painted satin. The little kingly, idiotic heads. Glory in the cold spring, a wonder of Jubilee.

The noise beginning again did not come from any of them. It pulled eyes up to what it was hard to believe we had not seen immediately—the one white peacock up in a tree, his tail full out, falling down through the branches like water over rock. Pure white, pure blessing. And hidden up above, his head gave out these frantic and upbraiding and disorderly cries.

"It's sex makes them scream," said Naomi.

"Cats scream," I said, remembering something from the farm. "They will scream like anything when a tomcat is doing it to them."

"Wouldn't you?" said Naomi.

Then we had to go, because Pork Childs appeared among his peacocks, walking quickly, rocking forward. All his toes had been amputated, we knew, after being frozen when he lay in a ditch long ago, too drunk to get home, before he joined the Baptist Church. "Good evening, boys!" he hollered at us, his old greeting, his old joke. *Hello, boys! Hello, girls!* yelled from the cab of the garbage truck, yelled down all streets bleak or summery, never getting any answer. We ran.

Mr. Chamberlain's car was parked in front of our house.

"Let's go in," said Naomi. "I want to see what he's doing to old Fern."

Nothing. In the dining room Fern was trying on the flowered chiffon dress my mother was helping her to make for Donna Carling's wedding, at which she would be the soloist. My mother was sitting sideways on the chair in front of the sewing machine, while Fern revolved, like a big half-opened parasol, in front of her.

Mr. Chamberlain was drinking a real drink, whisky and water. He drove to Porterfield to buy his whisky, Jubilee being dry. I was both proud and ashamed to have Naomi see the bottle on the sideboard, a thing that would never appear in her house. My mother excused his drinking, because he had been through the war.

"Here come these two lovely young ladies," said Mr. Chamberlain with great insincerity. "Full of springtime and grace. All fresh from the out-of-doors."

"Give us a drink," I said, showing off in front of Naomi. But he laughed and put a hand over his glass.

"Not until you tell us where you've been."

"We went down to Pork Childs' to look at the peacocks."

"Down to see the pea-cocks. To see the pretty pea-cocks," sang Mr. Chamberlain.

"Give us a drink."

"Del, behave yourself," said my mother with a mouth full of pins.

"All I want is to find out what it tastes like."

"Well I can't give you a drink for nothing. I don't see you doing any tricks for me. I don't see you sitting up and begging like a good doggie."

"I can be a seal. Do you want to see me be a seal?"

This was one thing I loved to do. I never felt worried that it might not be perfect, that I might not be able to manage it; I was never afraid that anybody would think me a fool. I had even done it at school, for the Junior Red Cross amateur hour, and everyone laughed; this marveling laughter was so comforting, so absolving that I could have gone on being a seal forever.

I went down on my knees and held my elbows at my sides and worked my hands like flippers, meanwhile barking, my wonderful braying bark. I had copied it from an old Mary Martin movie where Mary Martin sings a song beside a turquoise pool and the seals bark in chorus.

Mr. Chamberlain gradually lowered his glass and brought it close to my lips, withdrawing it, however, every time I stopped barking. I was kneeling by his chair. Fern had her back to me, her arms raised; my mother's head was hidden, as she pinned the material at Fern's waist. Naomi who had seen the seal often enough before and had an interest in dressmaking was looking at Fern and my mother. Mr. Chamberlain at last allowed my lips to touch the rim of the glass which he held in one hand. Then with the other hand he did something nobody could see. He rubbed against the damp underarm of my blouse and then inside the loose armhole of the jumper I was wearing. He rubbed quick, hard against the bottom over my breast. So hard he pushed the yielding flesh up, flattened it. And at once withdrew. It was like a slap, to leave me stung.

"Well, what does it taste like?" Naomi asked me afterwards.

"Like piss."

"You never tasted piss." She gave me a shrewd baffled look; she could always sense secrets.

I meant to tell her, but I did not, I held it back. If I told her, it would have to be re-enacted.

"How? How did he have his hand when he started? How did he get it under your jumper? Did he rub or squeeze, or both? With his fingers or his palm? Like this?"

There was a dentist in town, Dr. Phippen, brother of the deaf librarian, who was supposed to have put his hand up a girl's leg while looking at her back teeth. Naomi and I passing under his window would say loudly, "Don't you wish you had an appointment with Dr. Phippen? Dr. Feely Phippen. He's a thorough man!" It would be like that with Mr. Chamberlain; we would turn it into a joke, and hope for scandal, and make up schemes to entrap him, and that was not what I wanted.

"It was beautiful," said Naomi, sounding tired.

"What?"

"That peacock. In the tree."

I was surprised, and a little annoyed, to hear her use the word *beautiful*, about something like that, and to have her remember it, because I was used to have her act in a certain way, be aware of certain things, nothing else. I had already thought, running home, that I would write a poem about the peacock. To have her thinking about it too was almost like trespassing; I never let her or anyone in that part of my mind.

I did start writing my poem when I went upstairs to bed.

> What in the trees is crying these veiled
> nights?
> The peacocks crying or the winter's ghost?

That was the best part of it.

I also thought about Mr. Chamberlain, his hand which was different from anything he had previously shown about himself, in his eyes, his voice, his laugh, his stories. It was like a signal, given where it will be understood. Impertinent violation, so perfectly sure of itself, so authoritative, clean of sentiment.

Next time he came I made it easy for him to do something again, standing near him while he was getting his rubbers on in the dark hall. Every time, then, I waited for the signal, and got it. He did not bother with a pinch on the arm or a pat on the arm or a hug around the shoulders, fatherly or comradely. He went straight for the breasts, the buttocks, the upper thighs, brutal as lightning. And this was what I expected sexual communication to be—a flash of insanity, a dreamlike, ruthless, contemptuous breakthrough in a world of decent appearances. I had discarded those ideas of love, consolation, and tenderness, nourished by my feelings for Frank Wales; all that now seemed pale and extraordinarily childish. In the secret violence of sex would be recognition, going away beyond kindness, beyond good will or persons.

Not that I was planning on sex. One stroke of lightning does not have to lead anywhere, but to the next stroke of lightning.

Nevertheless my knees weakened, when Mr. Chamberlain honked the horn at me. He was waiting half a block from the school. Naomi was not with me; she had tonsillitis.

"Where's your girl friend?"

"She's sick."

"That's a shame. Want a lift home?"

In the car I trembled. My tongue was dry, my whole mouth was dry so I could hardly speak. Was this what desire was? Wish to know, fear to know, amounting to anguish? Being alone with him, no protection of people or circumstances, made a difference. What could he want to do here, in broad daylight, on the seat of his car?

He did not make a move towards me. But he did not head for River Street; he drove sedately along various side streets, avoiding winter-made potholes.

"You think you're the girl to do me a favor, if I asked you?"

"All right."

"What do you think it might be?"

"I don't know."

He parked the car behind the creamery, under the chestnut tree with the leaves just out, bitter yellowy green. Here?

"You get into Fern's room? You could get into her room when everybody was out of the house?"

I brought my mind back, slowly, from expectations of rape.

"You could get in her room and do a little investigation for me on what she's got there. Something that might interest me. What do you think it would be, eh? What do you think interests me?"

"What?"

"Letters," said Mr. Chamberlain with a sudden drop in tone, becoming matter-of-fact, depressed by some reality he could look into and I couldn't. "See if she has got any old letters. They might be in her drawers. Might be in her closet. Probably keeps them in an old box of some kind. Tied up in bundles, that's what women do."

"Letters from who?"

"From me. What do you think? You don't need to read them, just look at the signature. Written some time ago, the paper might be showing age. I don't know. Written in pen I recall so they're probably still legible. Here. I'll give you a sample of my handwriting, that'll help you out." He took an envelope out of the glove compartment and wrote on it: *Del is a bad girl.*

I put it in my Latin book.

"Don't let Fern see that, she'd recognize the writing. And not your Mama. She might wonder about what I wrote. Be a surprise to her, wouldn't it?"

He drove me home. I wanted to get out at the corner of River Street, but he said no. "That just looks as if we've got something to hide. Now, how are you going to let me know? How about Sunday night, when I come around for supper, I'll ask you whether you've got your homework done! If you've found them, you'll say yes. If you've looked and you haven't found them, you'll say no. If for some reason you never got a chance to take a look, you say you forget whether you had any."

He made me repeat, "Yes means found them, no means didn't find them, forget means didn't get a chance to look." This drill insulted me; I was famous for my memory.

"All right. Cheers." Below the level that anybody could see, looking at the car, he bounced his fist off my leg, hard enough to hurt. I hauled myself and my books out, and once I was alone, my thigh still tingling, I took out the envelope and read what he had written. *Del is a bad girl.* Mr. Chamberlain assumed without any trouble at all that there was treachery in me, as well as criminal sensuality, waiting to be used. He had known I would not cry out when he flattened my breast, he had known I would not mention it to my mother; he knew now I would not report this conversation to Fern, but would spy on her as he had asked. Could he have hit upon my true self? It was true that in the dullness of school I had worked with my protractor and compass, I had written out Latin sentences [*having pitched camp and slaughtered the horses of the enemy by means of stealth, Vercingetorix prepared to give battle on the following day*] and all the time been conscious of my depravity vigorous as spring wheat, my body flowering with invisible bruises in those places where it had been touched. Wearing blue rompers, washing with soap that would nearly take your skin off, after a volleyball game, I had looked in the mirror of the girls' washroom and smiled secretly at my ruddy face, to think what lewdness I had been invited to, what deceits I was capable of.

I got into Fern's room on Saturday morning, when my mother had gone out to do some cleaning at the farm. I looked around at leisure, at the koala bear sitting on her pillow, powder spilled on the dresser, jars with a little bit of dried-up deodorant, salve, night cream, old lipstick, and nail polish with the top stuck on. A picture of a lady in a dress of many dripping layers, like an arrangement of scarves, probably Fern's mother, holding a fat woollied baby, probably Fern. Fern for sure in soft focus with butterfly sleeves, holding a sheaf of roses, curls laid in layers on her head. And snapshots stuck around the mirror, their edges curling. Mr. Chamberlain in a sharp straw hat, white pants, looking at the camera as if he knew more than it did. Fern not so plump as now, but plump, wearing shorts, sitting on a log in some vacation time woods. Mr. Chamberlain and Fern dressed up—she with a corsage—snapped by a street photographer in a strange city, walking under the marquee of a movie house where *Anchors Aweigh!* was showing. The post office employees' picnic in the park at Tupperton, a cloudy day, and Fern, jolly in slacks, holding a baseball bat.

I did not find any letters. I looked through her drawers, on her closet shelves, under her bed, even inside her suitcases. I did find three separate saved bundles of paper, with elastic bands around them.

One bundle contained a chain letter and a great many copies of the same verse, in pencil or ink, different handwritings, some typewritten or mimeographed.

> This prayer has already been around the world six times. It was originated in the Isle of Wight by a clairvoyant seer who saw it in a dream. Copy this letter out six times and mail it to six friends, then copy the attached prayer out and mail it to six names at the top of the attached list. Six days from the time you receive this letter you will begin to get copies of this prayer from all corners of the earth and they will bring you blessings and good luck IF YOU DO NOT BREAK THE CHAIN. If you break the chain you may expect something sad and unpleasant to happen to you six months to the day from the day when you receive this letter. DO NOT BREAK THE CHAIN. DO NOT OMIT THE SECRET WORD AT THE END. BY MEANS OF THIS PRAYER HAPPINESS AND GOOD LUCK ARE BEING SPREAD THROUGH-OUT THE WORLD.

> Peace and love, O Lord I pray
> Shower on this friend today.
> Heal his (her) troubles, bless his (her) heart,
> From the source of strength and love may
> he (she) never have to part.

                                                    KARKAHMD

Another bundle was made up of several sheets of smudgy printing broken by blurred gray illustrations of what I thought at first were enema bags with tangled tubes, but which on reading the text I discovered to be cross sections of the male and female anatomy, with such things as pessaries, tampons, condoms (these proper terms were all new to me) being inserted or fitted on. I could not look at these illustrations without feeling alarm and a strong local discomfort, so I started reading. I read about a poor farmer's wife in North Carolina throwing herself under a wagon when she discovered she was going to have her ninth child, about women dying in tenements from complications of pregnancy or childbirth or terrible failed abortions which they performed with hatpins, knitting needles, bubbles of air. I read, or skipped, statistics about the increase in population, laws which had been passed in various countries for and against birth control, women who had gone to jail for advocating it. Then there were the instructions on using different devices. Naomi's mother's book had had a chapter about this too, but we never got around to reading it, being bogged down in "Case Histories and Varieties of Intercourse." All I read now about foam and jelly, even the use of the word "vagina," made the whole business seem laborious and domesticated, somehow connected with ointments and bandages and hospitals, and it gave me the same feeling of disgusted, ridiculous helplessness I had when it was necessary to undress at the doctor's.

In the third bundle were typewritten verses. Some had titles. "Homemade Lemon Squeeze." "The Lament of the Truck Driver's Wife."

> Husband, dear husband, what am I to do?
> I'm wanting some hard satisfaction from you.
> You're never at home or you're never awake.
> (A big cock in my pussy is all it would take!)

I was surprised that any adult would know, or still remember, these words. The greedy progression of verses, the short chunky words set in shameless type, fired up lust at a great rate, like squirts of kerosene on bonfires. But they were repetitive, elaborate; after awhile the mechanical effort needed to contrive them began to be felt, and made them heavy going; they grew bewilderingly dull. But the words themselves still gave off flashes of power, particularly *fuck*, which I had never been able to really look at on fences or sidewalks. I had never been able to contemplate before its thrust of brutality, hypnotic swagger.

I said no to Mr. Chamberlain, when he asked me if I had got my homework done. He did not touch me all evening. But when I came out of school on Monday, he was there.

"Girl friend still sick? That's too bad. Nice though. Isn't it nice?"

"What?"

"Birds are nice. Trees are nice. Nice you can come for a drive with me, do my little investigations for me." He said this in an infantile voice. Evil would never be grand, with him. His voice suggested that it would be possible to do anything, anything at all, and pass it off as a joke, a joke on all the solemn and guilty, all the moral and emotional people in the world, the people who "took themselves seriously." That was what he could not stand in people. His little smile was repulsive; self-satisfaction stretched over quite an abyss of irresponsibility, or worse. This did not give me second thoughts about going with him, and doing whatever it was he had in mind to do. His moral character was of no importance to me there; perhaps it was even necessary that it should be black.

Excitement owing something to Fern's dirty verses had got the upper hand of me, entirely.

"Did you get a good look?" he said in a normal voice.

"Yes."

"Didn't find a thing? Did you look in all her drawers? I mean her *dresser* drawers. Hatboxes, suitcases? Went through her closet?"

"I looked and looked everywhere," I said demurely.

"She must have got rid of them."

"I guess she isn't sentimental."

"Sennamenal? I don't know what dose big words mean, little dirl."

We were driving out of town. We drove south on the No. 4 Highway and turned down the first side road. "Beautiful morning," said Mr. Chamberlain. "Pardon me—beautiful afternoon, beautiful day." I looked out the window; the countryside I knew was altered by his presence, his voice, overpowering foreknowledge of the errand we were going on together. For a year or two I had been looking at trees, fields, landscape with a secret, strong exaltation. In some moods, some days, I could feel for a clump of grass, a rail fence, a stone pile, such pure unbounded emotion as I used to hope for, and have inklings of, in connection with God. I could not do it when I was with anybody, of course, and now with Mr. Chamberlain I saw that the whole nature became debased, maddeningly erotic. It was just now the richest, greenest time of year; ditches sprouted coarse daisies, toadflax, buttercups, hollows were full of nameless faintly golden bushes and the gleam of high creeks. I saw all this as a vast arrangement of hiding places, ploughed fields beyond rearing up like shameless mattresses. Little paths, opening in the bushes, crushed places in the grass, where no doubt a cow had lain, seemed to me specifically, urgently inviting as certain words or pressures.

"Hope we don't meet your mama, driving along here."

I did not think it possible. My mother inhabited a different layer of reality from the one I had got into now.

Mr. Chamberlain drove off the road, following a track that ended soon, in a field half gone to brush. The stopping of the car, cessation of that warm flow of sound and motion in which I had been suspended, jarred me a little. Events were becoming real.

"Let's take a little walk down to the creek."

He got out on his side, I got out on mine. I followed him, down a slope between some hawthorn trees, in bloom, yeasty smelling. This was a traveled route, with cigarette packages, a beer bottle, a Chiclet box lying on the grass. Little trees, bushes closed around us.

"Why don't we call a halt here?" said Mr. Chamberlain in a practical way. "It gets soggy down by the water."

Here in the half-shade above the creek I was cold, and so violently anxious to know what would be done to me that all the heat and dancing itch between my legs had gone dead, numb as if a piece of ice had been laid to it. Mr. Chamberlain opened his jacket and loosened his belt, then unzipped himself. He reached in to part some inner curtains, and "Boo!" he said.

Not at all like marble David's, it was sticking straight out in front of him, which I knew from my reading was what they did. It had a sort of head on it, like a mushroom, and its color was reddish purple. It looked blunt and stupid, compared, say, to fingers and toes with their intelligent expressiveness, or even to an elbow or a knee. It did not seem frightening to me, though I thought this might have been what Mr. Chamberlain intended, standing there with his tightly watching look, his hands holding his pants apart to display it. Raw and blunt, ugly-colored as a wound, it looked to me vulnerable, playful and naive, like some strong-snouted animal whose grotesque simple looks are some sort of guarantee of good will. (The opposite of what beauty usually is.) It did not bring back any of my excitement, though. It did not seem to have anything to do with me.

Still watching me, and smiling, Mr. Chamberlain placed his hand around this thing and began to pump up and down, not too hard, in a controlled efficient rhythm. His face softened; his eyes, still fixed on me, grew glassy. Gradually, almost experimentally, he increased the speed of his hand; the rhythm became less smooth. He crouched over, his smile opened out and drew the lips back from his teeth and his eyes rolled slightly upward. His breathing became loud and shaky, now he worked furiously with his hand, moaned, almost doubled over in spasmodic agony. The face he thrust out at me, from his crouch, was blind and wobbling like a mask on a stick, and those sounds coming out of his mouth, involuntary, last-ditch human noises, were at the same time theatrical, unlikely. In fact the whole performance, surrounded by calm flowering branches, seemed imposed, fantastically and predictably exaggerated, like an Indian dance. I had read about the body being in extremities of pleasure, possessed, but these expressions did not seem equal to the terrible benighted effort, deliberate frenzy, of what was going on here. If he did not soon get to where he wanted to be, I thought he would die. But then he let out a new kind of moan, the most desperate and the loudest yet; it quavered as if somebody was hitting him on the voice box. This died, miraculously, into a peaceful grateful whimper, as stuff shot out of him, the real whitish stuff, the seed, and caught the hem of my skirt. He straightened up, shaky, out of breath, and tucked himself quickly back inside his trousers. He got out a handkerchief and wiped first his hands then my skirt.

"Lucky for you? Eh?" He laughed at me, though he still had not altogether got his breath back.

After such a convulsion, such a revelation, how could a man just put his hand-kerchief in his pocket, check his fly, and start walking back—still somewhat flushed and bloodshot—the way we had come?

The only thing he said was in the car, when he sat for a moment composing himself before he turned the key.

"Quite a sight, eh?" was what he said.

The landscape was postcoital, distant and meaningless. Mr. Chamberlain may have felt some gloom too, or apprehension, for he made me get down on the floor of the car as we re-entered town, and then he drove around and let me out in a lonely place, where the road dipped down near the CNR station. He felt enough like himself, however, to tap me in the crotch with his fist, as if testing a coconut for soundness.

That was a valedictory appearance for Mr. Chamberlain, as I ought to have guessed it might be. I came home at noon to find Fern sitting at the dining-room table, which was set for dinner, listening to my mother calling from the kitchen over the noise of the potato masher.

"Doesn't matter what anybody says. You weren't married. You weren't engaged. It's nobody's business. Your life is your own."

"Want to see my little love letter?" said Fern, and fluttered it under my nose.

> Dear Fern, Owing to circumstances beyond my control, I am taking off this evening in my trusty Pontiac and heading for points west. There is a lot of the world I haven't see yet and no sense getting fenced in. I may send you a postcard from California or Alaska, who knows? Be a good girl as you always were and keep licking those stamps and steaming open the mail, you may find a hundred-dollar-bill yet. When Mama dies I will probably come home, but not for long. Cheers, Art.

The same hand that had written: *Del is a bad girl.*

"Tampering with the mails is a Federal offense," said my mother, coming in. "I don't think that is very witty, what he says."

She distributed canned carrots, mashed potatoes, meat loaf. No matter what the season, we ate a heavy meal in the middle of the day.

"Looks like it hasn't put me off my food, anyway," said Fern, sighing. She poured ketchup. "I could have had him. Long ago, if I'd wanted. He even wrote me letters mentioning marriage. I should have kept them, I could have breach-of-promised him."

"A good thing you didn't," said my mother spiritedly, "or where would you be today?"

"Didn't what? Breach-of-promise him or married him?"

"Married him. Breach-of-promise is a degradation to women."

"Oh, I wasn't in danger of marriage."

"You had your singing. You had your interest in life."

"I was just usually having too good a time. I knew enough about marriage to know that's when your good times stop."

When Fern talked about having a good time she meant going to dances at the Lakeshore Pavilion, going to the Regency Hotel in Tupperton for drinks and dinner,

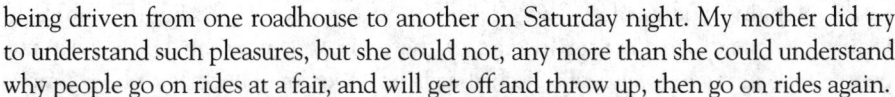

being driven from one roadhouse to another on Saturday night. My mother did try to understand such pleasures, but she could not, any more than she could understand why people go on rides at a fair, and will get off and throw up, then go on rides again.

Fern was not one to grieve, in spite of her acquaintance with opera. Her expressed feeling was that men always went, and better they did before you got sick of them. But she grew very talkative; she was never silent.

"As bad as Art was," she said to Owen, eating supper, "he wouldn't touch any yellow vegetable. His mother should have taken the paddle to him when he was little. That's what I used to tell him."

"You're built the opposite from Art," she told my father. "The trouble with getting his suits fitted was he was so long in the body, short in the leg. Ransom's in Tupperton was the only place that could fit him.

"Only one time I saw him lose his temper. At the Pavilion when we went to a dance there, and a fellow asked me to dance, and I got up with him because what can you do, and he put his face down, right away down on my neck. Guzzling me up like I was chocolate icing! Art said to him, if you have to slobber don't do it on my girlfriend, I might want her myself! And he yanked him off. He did so!"

I would come into a room where she was talking to my mother and there would be an unnatural, waiting silence. My mother would be listening with a trapped, determinedly compassionate, miserable face. What could she do? Fern was her good, perhaps her only, friend. But there were things she never thought she would have to hear. She may have missed Mr. Chamberlain.

"He treated you shabbily," she said to Fern, against Fern's shrugs and ambiguous laugh. "He did. He did. My estimation of a person has never gone down so fast. But nevertheless I miss him when I hear them trying to read the radio news."

For the Jubilee station had not found anybody else who could read the news the way it was now, full of Russian names, without panicking, and they had let somebody call Bach *Batch* on *In Memoriam*, when they played "Jesu Joy of Man's Desiring." It made my mother wild.

I had meant to tell Naomi all about Mr. Chamberlain, now it was over. But Naomi came out of her illness fifteen pounds lighter, with a whole new outlook on life. Her forthrightness was gone with her chunky figure. Her language was purified. Her daring had collapsed. She had a new delicate regard for herself. She sat under a tree with her skirt spread around her, watching the rest of us play volleyball, and kept feeling her forehead to see if she was feverish. She was not even interested in the fact that Mr. Chamberlain had gone, so preoccupied was she with herself and her illness. Her temperature had risen to over a hundred and five degrees. All the grosser aspects of sex had disappeared from her mind although she talked a good deal about Dr. Wallis, and how he had sponged her legs himself, and she had been quite helplessly exposed to him, when she was sick.

So I had not the relief of making what Mr. Chamberlain had done into a funny, though horrifying, story. I did not know what to do with it. I could not get him back to his old role, I could not make him play the single-minded, simple-minded, vigorous, obliging lecher of my daydreams. My faith in simple depravity had weakened. Perhaps nowhere but in daydreams did the trap door open so sweetly and easily, plunging bodies altogether free of thought, free of personality, into self-indulgence, mad bad license. Instead of that, Mr. Chamberlain had shown me, people take along a good deal—flesh that is not overcome but has to be thumped into ecstasy, all the stubborn puzzle and dark turns of themselves.

In June there was the annual strawberry supper on the lawns behind the United Church. Fern went down to sing at it, wearing the flowered chiffon dress my mother had helped her make. It was not very tight at the waist. Since Mr. Chamberlain had gone Fern had put on weight, so that she was not now soft and bulgy but really fat, swollen up like a boiled pudding, her splotched skin not shady any more but stretched and shiny.

She patted herself around the midriff. "Anyway they won't be able to say I'm pining, will they? It'll be a scandal if I split the seams."

We heard her high heels going down the sidewalk. On leafy, cloudy, quiet evenings under the trees, sounds carried a long way. Sociable noise of the United Church affair washed as far as our steps. Did my mother wish she had a hat and a summer sheer dress on, and was going? Her agnosticism and sociability were often in conflict in Jubilee, where social and religious life were apt to be one and the same. Fern had told her to come ahead. "You're a member. Didn't you tell me you joined when you got married?"

"My ideas weren't formed then. Now I'd be a hypocrite. I'm not a believer."

"Think all of them are?"

I was on the veranda reading *Arch of Triumph*, a book I had got out of the library. The library had been left some money and had bought a supply of new books, mostly on the recommendation of Mrs. Wallis, the doctor's wife, who had a college degree but not perhaps the tastes the Council had been counting on. There had been complaints, people had said it should have been left up to Bella Phippen, but only one book—*The Hucksters*—had actually been removed from the shelves. I had read it first. My mother had picked it up and read a few pages and been saddened.

"I never expected to see such a use made of the printed word."

"It's about the advertising business, how corrupt it is."

"That's not the only thing is corrupt, I'm afraid. Next day they will be telling about how they go to the toilet, why do they leave that out? There isn't any of that in *Silas Marner*. There isn't in the classic writers. They were good writers, they didn't need it."

I had turned away from my old favorites, *Kristin Lavransdatter*, historical novels. I read modern books now. Somerset Maugham, Nancy Mitford. I read about rich and titled people who despised the very sort of people who in Jubilee were at the top of society—druggists, dentists, storekeepers. I learned names like Balenciaga, Schiaparelli. I knew about drinks. Whisky and soda. Gin and tonic. Cinzano, Benedictine, Grand Marnier. I knew the names of hotels, streets, restaurants, in London, Paris, Singapore. In these books people did go to bed together, they did it all the time, but the descriptions of what they were up to there were not thorough, in spite of what my mother thought. One book compared having sexual intercourse to going through a train tunnel (presumably if you were the whole train) and blasting out into a mountain meadow so high, so blest and beautiful, you felt as if you were in the sky. Books always compared it to something else, never told about it by itself.

"You can't read there," my mother said. "You can't read in that light. Come down on the steps."

So I came, but she did not want me to read at all. She wanted company.

"See, the lilacs are turning. Soon we'll be going out to the farm."

Along the front of our yard, by the sidewalk, were purple lilacs gone pale as soft, delicate scrub rags, rusty specked. Beyond them the road, already dusty, and banks of wild blackberry bushes growing in front of the boarded-up factory, on which we could still read the big, faded, vainglorious letters: MUNDY PIANOS.

"I'm sorry for Fern," my mother said. "I'm sorry for her life."

Her sad confidential tone warned me off.

"Maybe she'll find a new boy friend tonight."

"What do you mean? She's not after a new boy friend. She's had enough of all that. She's going to sing 'Where'er You Walk.' She's got a lovely voice, still."

"She's getting fat."

My mother spoke to me in her grave, hopeful, lecturing voice.

"There is a change coming I think in the lives of girls and women. Yes. But it is up to us to make it come. All women have had up till now has been their connection with men. All we have had. No more lives of our own, really, than domestic animals. *He shall hold thee, when his passion shall have spent its novel force, a little closer than his dog, a little dearer than his horse.* Tennyson wrote that. It's true. *Was* true. You will want to have children, though."

That was how much she knew me.

"But I hope you will—use your brains. Use your brains. Don't be distracted. Once you make that mistake, of being—distracted, over a man, your life will never be your own. You will get the burden, a woman always does."

"There is birth control nowadays," I reminded her, and she looked at me startled, though it was she herself who had publicly embarrassed our family, writing to the Jubilee *Herald-Advance* that "prophylactic devices should be distributed to all women on public relief in Wawanash County, to help them prevent any further increase in their families." Boys at school had yelled at me, "Hey, when is your momma giving out the proplastic devices?"

"That is not enough, though of course it is a great boon and religion is the enemy of it as it is of everything that might ease the pangs of life on earth. It is self-respect I am really speaking of. Self-respect."

I did not quite get the point of this, or if I did get the point I was set up to resist it. I would have had to resist anything she told me with such earnestness, such stubborn hopefulness. Her concern about my life, which I needed and took for granted, I could not bear to have expressed. Also I felt that it was not so different from all the other advice handed out to women, to girls, advice that assumed being female made you damageable, that a certain amount of carefulness and solemn fuss and self-protection were called for, whereas men were supposed to be able to go out and take on all kinds of experiences and shuck off what they didn't want and come back proud. Without even thinking about it, I had decided to do the same.

Joyce Carol Oates

Joyce Carol Oates was born in Lockport, New York, in 1938. She attended Syracuse University in 1956 and began publishing stories in *Cosmopolitan*, *The Literary Review*, and *Prairie Schooner*. She completed her M.A. at the University of Wisconsin, followed shortly by the publication of her first book of stories, *By the North Gate* (1963). Her stories have won a number of O. Henry Awards and the National Book Award, been published in *The Best American Short Stories*, and been translated into many languages. She has published many novels, including *Do with Me What You Will* (1973), *The Assassins* (1975), *Unholy Loves* (1979), and *Bellefleur* (1980), and numerous collections of stories, including *Upon the Sweeping Flood* (1966), *The Wheel of Love and Other Stories* (1970), *Marriages and Infidelities* (1972), *Night Side* (1977), *Last Days* (1985), and *Raven's Wing* (1986). She taught at the University of Detroit from 1962 to 1967, then taught for eleven years at the University of Windsor, where she was a contributing editor to *The Ontario Review*. In 1978, she returned to the U.S. to teach at Princeton.

While she considers writing a means of moral discovery and of bearing witness to her times, Oates does not consider fiction a primarily didactic mode, as she suggests in an interview conducted by Leif Sjöberg (*Interviews with Contemporary Writers*, Second Series): "First I must state my position about all forms of creativity, including my own: these acts are gratuitous offerings and bring something—a vision, an argument, an illumination of a certain corner of the world, a style, a music, an aspect of personality—into the world which did not previously exist. The creative act is an *acte gratuite*. It withdraws nothing from the world—not the intellectual world, not the material world. At its base it is a spontaneous birth, usually presented to the world as an offering or gift. Consequently the creative act and its product are an end in themselves, complete. Like a bird's song—on a much higher structural level. The artist is forever being called upon in the United States to justify himself or herself: and in a way that for instance the manufacturer of toothpaste, automobiles, cigarettes, every sort of material goods is not." Asked about the political significance of literature, or art, Oates recalls Abraham Lincoln's remark about nineteenth-century writer Harriet Beecher Stowe (author of *Uncle Tom's Cabin*) that "here was the person who brought about the Civil War, hence the freeing of the slaves." She sees writing as having a healing, restorative power for the

individual and for the society at large. What she admires in Flaubert is that his works are "devastating in their power to arouse sympathy in others."

In responding to Sanford Pinsker's question about whether there is anything new to say about the American short story ("Speaking About Short Fiction: An Interview with Joyce Carol Oates," in *Studies in Short Fiction*, Vol. 18, No. 3, 1981), Oates writes: "Poe's remarks are inappropriate to our time, and in fact to the marvelous modern tradition of the story that begins with Chekhov, Joyce, Conrad, and James. Speculation about short fiction should probably remain minimal since 'speculation' about most works of art is usually a waste of time. Those of us who love the practice of an art often hate theorizing because it is always theorizing based upon past models: as such, it must inevitably incline toward the conservative, the reactionary, the exhortative, the school of *should* and *should not*. Genuine artists create their own models of art and nothing interests them except the free play of the imagination. Poe's and Hawthorne's impulses in fiction were bound up with the allegorical, the static, and the highly romantic (which is to say, the impersonal). How can one draw a reasonably sober line between Hawthorne, James, Stephen Crane, Faulkner, and Hubert Selby, Jr. . . . ? Where would Beckett or Flannery O'Connor or Saul Bellow fit in? It isn't even true that short stories are necessarily short."

Oates claims that nothing is inappropriate to the short story: "The 'short story' is a highly elastic term, after all. A brief enigmatic dream-tale by Kafka . . . a dense, meditative, slow-moving story by Henry James . . . a spare exchange of dialogue by Hemingway: all can be considered 'stories' yet each differs radically from the others." She claims never to have been interested in experimentation for its own sake, unless a story's protagonist "is 'postmodernist' in sensibility." "As time passes and I become more and more comfortable with telling a linear story and populating it with characters, I inevitably become more and more interested in the structures into which fiction can be put, and the kinds of language used to evoke them. . . . I admit to a current fascination with the phenomenon of time—I seem to want to tell a story as if it were sheer lyric, all its components present simultaneously."

In *The Paris Review* interview of 1976 with Robert Phillips, Oates makes a distinction between poetry, which she calls image-centred, and fiction, which is narrative-centred: "Poetry focusses upon the image, the particular thing, or emotion, or feeling, while prose fiction focusses upon motion through time and space. The one impulse is toward stasis, the other toward movement." In much of her work, including the novel *Childwold* (1976), she plays upon the tension between these two impulses, producing what might be described as fiction with a more lyrical structure. "The short story is the form in which I have worked most with experimentation. Virtually each story is an attempt to do something different—consequently it is extremely difficult for me to speak of my short stories in general terms. They proceed from a basis of psychological realism; however, often they take place in an individual's mind."

When asked to write about herself for *The New York Times Book Review* in a series called "The Making of the Writer," Oates professes how impossible is the task of making complete sense of her writing life and creative impulses. What she does say is that the act of writing satisfies many desires, one of which is to hear stories told by telling them yourself; another is the desire to create something beautiful, something that will have extraordinary powers, that will, like a talisman, ward off evil. Most of all, she loves the process itself: "A work of prose may be many things to many people, but to the author it is a monument to a certain chunk of time: so many pulsebeats, so much effort." But time spent thus is not a monumental loss: "Life is energy, and energy is creativity. And even when we as individuals pass on, the energy is retained in the work or art, locked in it and awaiting release if only someone will take the time and care to unlock it."

The Molesters

I am six years old. There, at the end of the porch, is the old lilac tree. Everything is blurred with light, because there was a fog the night before and it is lifting slowly. I am sitting on the porch step playing with something—a doll. It has no clothes and is scuffed. It is neither a boy nor a girl; its hair was pulled off; its body is smooth and its eyes staring as if they saw something that frightened them. In the lilac tree some blackbirds are arguing. Not too far away is the cherry orchard; the birds fly over from the cherry trees and in a minute will fly back again. My father has put tin foil up in the trees to scare the birds away, but it doesn't work. If I lean forward I can see the brilliant tin foil gleaming high up in the trees—it moves with the rocking of the limbs, in the wind. My father has gone to work and does not come home until supper. The odor of supper and the harsh sound of my father's car turning into the cinder drive go together; everything goes together.

I climb up into the lilac tree. The first branch is hard to hold. The birds fly away. The doll is back there, by the steps. My grandmother gave me that doll, and the funny thing about it is this: I never remember it or think about it until I see it lying somewhere, then I pick it up and hug it. There little chair in the lilac tree made by three branches that come together. I like to sit here and hide. Once I fell down and cried and Mommy ran out onto the porch, but that was a long time ago when I was little. I am much bigger now. My legs dangle beneath me, scuffed like the doll's skin. My knees are marred with old scratches that are about to flake off and one milky white scar that will never go away.

My mother comes outside. The chickens run toward her even though they know it isn't time to be fed; they come anyway. My mother puts something up on the clothesline. The clothesline is always up, running from tree to tree.

"What are you doing?" Mommy says. I thought she couldn't see me but she can.

"Can I go down to the crick?" I ask her.

There, in the grass, her feet are almost hidden. The grass is jagged and seems like waves of water. "Tommy isn't home," she says, without looking around. She finishes hanging the towels up—she has clothespins in her pocket and they make her stomach look funny. "Why do you always want to play there?" she says. "Can't you play up here?"

"Tommy can go down anytime—"

"Tommy's bigger, Tommy doesn't fall down." She looks past me. There is something soft about her face—nothing bad stays in it. When I was little I kept going back into the kitchen to make sure she was there and she was always there. The big kids teased me and said she was gone, but she was always there. She would pick me up with a laugh.

I take the path through the field to the creek. There is more than one path: a path from our house and the Sullivans' house, and a path for fishermen who come from the road. Our path runs along flat but curves around, and there are prickly bushes that scratch you. By the creek the path dips downhill and goes to the bank. The fishermen's path comes down from the road, alongside the bridge. Fishermen leave their cars up on the road and come down the path, slipping and sliding because it is so steep. When fishermen come we have to leave. Mommy says we have to leave. One of the big boys threw stones in the creek once, to scare the fish away and the fisherman ran up to the Sullivans' house and was mad. He was from the city.

The creek has a smell I like. I always forget it until I come back to it; there it is. There are big flat white rocks by the shore, covered with dried-up moss that is green in the water but white outside. This is what smells. It smells dry and strange; there is something dead about it. There are dead things by the creek. Little fish and yellow birds and toads; once a garter snake. The fishermen throw little fish down on the stones and let them rot. When the fishermen are from around here we can stay and watch—they're like my father, they talk like him. When they're from the city they talk different.

Everybody has their rocks. Tommy's rock is the biggest one and nobody can sit on it but him. I have a rock too. I sit on it and my feet get in the water by mistake. That's bad. My mother will holler. I try not to let them slip in but my rock is too little, I can't sit on it right. I let my feet go back in the water. I like the way the water feels.

I have a dam made out of stones, between two rocks. When I look around I see the fisherman behind me.

He has a strange dark face; I saw someone like him in a movie once. He has a fishing pole and a paper bag and some things in his pockets. His hat looks dusty. "Do you live up there?" he says. He has a nice voice.

That makes me think of my mother. I don't know how to talk to grownups. They talk too loud to you, and something is always wrong. I don't say anything to him. There are two crabs behind the dam, little ones. Their bodies are soft to touch but they'd bite you if they could; their pincers are too little. Tommy and the boys use them for fishing, instead of worms.

"Do you live close by here?"

The fisherman is squatting on the bank now. His hat is off and next to him. He has dark hair. I tell him yes. My face is prickly, because of him looking at it. There is something funny about him.

"How old are you?" he says.

They always ask that. I don't answer but let a stone fall in the water to show I'm not afraid of him.

"Are you fishing?"

"No."

"What are you doing?"

He is squatting on the bank and calling over to me. A grownup would just walk out and see what I had, or he would walk away; he wouldn't care. This man is squatting and watching me. The bank is bare from people always standing on it. We play here all the time. When I was little I could look down from higher up and see the boys down here, playing. Mommy wouldn't let me come down then. Now I can come down by myself, alone. I am getting big. The bank tilts down toward the creek, and there are a whole lot of stones and rocks where the creek is dried up, then the water begins but is shallow, like where I am, but then farther out it is deep and only the big rocks stick up. The boys can wade out there but not me. There are holes somewhere too; it is dangerous to walk out there. Then, across the creek, is a big tangle of bushes and trees. Somebody owns that land. On this side nobody owns it, but that side has a fence. Farther down where the bushes are gone, cows come down to the creek sometimes. The boys throw stones at them. When I throw a stone it goes up in the air and comes down right away.

"What have you got there?"

"A dam."

He smiles and puts his hand to his ear. "A what?"

I don't answer him, but pretend to be fixing something.

"Can I come look?" he says.

I tell him yes. Up there, nobody cares about what I do, except if I break or spill something; then they holler. This man is different. He is like my father but not like him because he talks to me. My father says things to me but doesn't talk to me, he doesn't look at me for long because there are too many other things going on. He is always driving back and forth in the car. This man looks right at me. His eyes are dark, like Daddy's. He left his hat back on the bank. His hair is funny. He must have been out in the sun because his skin is dark. He is darker than Tommy with his suntan.

"A little dam," he says. "Well, that's real nice."

The crabs are inside yet. He doesn't see them.

"I got two crabs," I say.

The man bends down right away to look. I can smell something by him, something sweet. It makes me think of the store down the road. "Hey, look at that—I see them crabs. They'd like to bite a nice little girl like you."

I pick up one of the crabs to show him I'm not afraid. I am never afraid of crabs but only of fish that they catch and tear off the hook and let lay around to die.

They flop around on the grass, bleeding, and their eyes look right at you. I'm afraid of them but not of crabs.

"Hey, don't let him bite you!" The man laughs.

"He can't bite."

The crab gets away and falls back into the water. It swims backward in quick little jerks and gets under a rock. It is the rock the man has his foot on. He has big black shoes like my father's, but caked with mud and cracked. He stands with one foot on a rock and the other in a little bit of water. He can do that if he wants to, nobody can holler at him.

"Do you like to play down here?"

"Yes."

"Do you go to school?"

"I'm going next year."

The sun comes out and is bright. When I look up at him my eyes have to squint. He is bending over me. "I went to school too," he says. He smiles at me. "Hey, you got yourself dirty," he says.

I look down and there is mud on me, on my knees and legs and arms. It makes me giggle.

"Will your mommy be mad?" he says. Now, slowly, he squats down. He is leaning over me the way some of them in town do, my mother's people. You can smell smoke or something in their breaths and it isn't nice, it makes me not like them. This man smells of something like candy.

"Little girls shouldn't get dirty," he says. "Don't you want to be nice and clean and pretty?"

I splash in the water again because I know it's all right. He won't holler.

"Little boys like to be dirty but little girls like to be clean," he says. He talks slow. Like he was doing something dangerous—walking from rock to rock, or trying to keep his balance on a fence.

"You've got some stuff in your hair," he says. He touches my hair. I stop what I'm doing and am quiet, like when Mommy takes burrs out. He rubs the top of my head and my neck. "Your hair is real nice," he says.

"It's got snarls underneath. She has to cut them out."

"It's real pretty hair," he says. "Hey, you know in the city little girls have two daddies. One goes to work and the other stays home to play. Do you know that?"

Something makes me giggle. His hand is on my shoulder. He has dark, staring eyes with tight lines around them. He looks like he is staring into a lamp.

"Would you like another daddy?" he says.

"I got a daddy."

He touches my arm. He looks at me as if he was really seeing me. He is not thinking about anybody else; in a minute he won't stand up and yell out to somebody else, like my mother does. He is really with me. He puts his finger to his mouth to get it wet and then he rubs at the dirt on my arm. "I wouldn't never spank no little girl of mine either," he says. He shifts forward. His legs must ache, bent so tight like that. "You think they'd spank you at home for being dirty?"

"I can wash it off." I put my arm in the water. When you knock over a stone in the water a little puff of mud comes and hides the crabs that jump out—that saves them. When you can see again they're all hid.

"Maybe you better get washed up down here. I sure wouldn't want you to get spanked again," the man says. His voice is soft, like music. His hands are warm and heavy but I don't mind them. He is holding my arm; with his thumb he is rubbing it. I look but can't see any dirt where he is rubbing it.

"Hey, don't touch your hair. You'll get mud in it," he says. He pulls my hand away. "You can wash right here in the crick. They won't never know you were dirty then. Okay? We can keep it a secret."

"Tommy has some secrets."

"It can be a secret, and we'll be friends. Okay? Don't you tell anybody about it."

"Okay."

"I'll get you all nice and clean and then we'll be friends. And you won't tell them about it. I can come back here to visit sometimes." He looks back at the bank for something. "I got some real nice licorice in there. You like that, huh?"

I tell him yes.

"When you get cleaned up you can have some then. I bet you like it."

He smiles when I say yes. Now I know what the smell is about him—licorice. It reminds me of the store down the road where the licorice sticks are standing up in a plastic thing and when you touch them they're soft. They stick to your teeth.

"Little girls don't know how to wash themselves," he says. He pats water on my arm and washes it. I sit there and don't move. There is nothing that hurts, like there is sometimes with a washcloth and hot water. He washes me slow and careful. His face is serious; he isn't in a hurry. He looks like somebody that is listening to the radio but you can't hear what he hears.

He washes my legs. "You're a real pretty little girl," he says. "They shouldn't spank you. Shouldn't nobody spank you. I'd kill them if I saw it." He looks like he might cry. Something draws his face all in, and his eyes seem to be going in, looking somewhere inside him.

"But I'll get you clean, nice and clean," he says. "Then you can have some licorice."

"Is it from the store?"

He moves his hand on my back, slow, like you pet a cat. The cat makes his back go stiff and I do the same thing. I understand what it is like to be a cat.

"Do you want to walk in the water a little?"

"I can't do that."

"Just here. By these rocks."

"They don't let me do it."

I look at him, waiting for permission. My shoes are already soaked. But if I play out in the sun afterward then they will get dry.

"Sure. They ain't nowhere around here. *I* say you can do it," he whispers. He leans back and watches me. Because he is so close I am safe and it's all right to wade in the water. Nobody else ever sat and watched me so close. Nobody else ever wanted me to walk in the water and would sit there to catch me if I tripped.

"Is it nice? Does the water feel nice?"

The water comes up to my knees in the deepest place. I can t go out any farther than this. I was swimming somewhere, but not here; we go to a lake. There they have sand and people lying on blankets, but here there isn't anything except stones. The stones are sharp sometimes.

After a while the man stands up. His face is squinting in the sun. He walks alongside me, watching me; his feet will get wet. Something makes me yawn. I feel tired. I look down and see that I am making clouds of mud underwater.

"You better come out now," he says.

When I step out on the stones my shoes make a squishy noise. It makes me laugh to see the water running out. Inside my shoes my toes are cold.

He takes my hand and walks with me back to the bank. His hand is very warm. "You had a real nice time out there, didn't you?" he says. "Little girls like to play in the water and get clean."

He wets his finger and rubs something on my face. I close my eyes until it's clean.

The licorice stick isn't as good as the ones at the store. I want to take it back home but the man says no, I have to eat it down here. I keep yawning and want to go to bed. When I play in the water I get tired, the sun makes my eyes tired.

The man washes my hands with creek water, his own hands wet and rubbing with mine like he was washing his own.

"This is our own secret and don't never tell anybody," he says.

He wipes our hands on his shirt. He is squatting down all the time to be just as tall as I am. He has a black comb he combs my hair with, but there are snarls underneath and he has to stop. He pulls the hairs out of the comb.

"Now you have another daddy, and don't never tell them," he says.

When I turn around to look at him from higher up on the t path, he is bending to get his fishing pole. I forgot about looking at the pole and want to run back to see it, if it's a glass pole like some of them, but now he looks like somebody I don't know. With his back to me he is like some fisherman from the city that I don't know and am afraid of.

II

I am six years old. At this time we are still living in the country; in a few years we will move to the city, in with my grandmother. But now my father is still well enough to work. My brother and his friends have gone on a bike trip. They have mustard sandwiches wrapped in wax paper and emptied pop bottles with water in them. I went out to the road and watched them ride away. Nobody cared about me; the boys call me baby if they are nice and push me away and tease me if they're bad. I hate my brother because he pushes me with his hand, like people do in the movies when they want to knock somebody out of the way. "Move it, kid," he says and pushes me. If I run to Mommy it won't do any good. He is four years older than me and so I can never catch up to him.

The day is hot. It's August, in the morning. The high grass in the orchard is dried up; the birds are always fighting in the trees—the leaves churn to show their sleek black wings. Tommy has a BB gun and shoots the birds sometimes, but when they hear the noise they fly away; birds are smart. The cat ate one of the dead birds and then threw up the feathers and stuff, right on the kitchen floor.

I am playing with my doll. Inside, Mommy is still canning cherries. On Sundays Daddy sits out front under the tree and tries to sell baskets of cherries to people that drive by. You can't go out by him and talk because he is always mad. The kitchen is ugly and hot. There are steamed jars everywhere, and bowls of cherries. Once I liked cherries, but the last time they made me sick. I saw a little worm in a cherry, by the pit. Twenty-five years from now I will drive by cherry orchards and the nausea will rise up in me; a tiny white worm. My mind will always be pushed back to this farm, and there is nothing I can do about it. I will never be able to get away.

Today is a weekday. Later on I will learn the number of it, from hearing so much about it. But now I know nothing except there are two or three days until Sunday, when Daddy stays home and sits out in front and waits for cars to stop.

My mother comes outside to see where I am. She wears an old dress with cherry stains on it. The stains make me look at them, they remind me of something. Of blood. She has her hair pushed back. Her hair is streaked up in front, by the sun, but brown everywhere else. There is a picture of her when she had long hair; she isn't my mother but somebody else. Around the house she is barefoot. Her legs look strong; she could probably run fast if she wanted to but she never wants to. Everything is slow around her. The chickens are nervous, picking in the dirt and watching her for food. They jerk their heads from side to side. If she raises her hand they will flutter their wings, waiting to be fed.

My mother comes over to me where I am sitting on the branches. She brushes my hair out of my eyes. "Can't you wait for Tommy to come back, to go down there?" she says.

"I want to play with my dam," I tell her. I lean back so she can't touch my hair. When she works in the kitchen her pale hands are stained from cherries. I don't like them to touch me then. When she gives me my bath they're like that too. I don't always like her. I can like her if I want to, but I don't have to. I like Daddy better, on purpose, even though Mommy is nicer to me. She never knows what I am thinking.

"I can take you down in a while, myself," she says. "Okay?"

I stare down at nothing. My face gets hard.

"What the hell is so good about playing in that dirty water?" she says.

This makes my heart beat hard, with hating her.

Her eyebrows are thin and always look surprised. I see her pluck at them sometimes. That must hurt. She stands with her hands thrust in her pockets, and her shoulders slump. I always know before she does what she is going to say.

"All right, then, go on down. But don't get wet."

I run around back of our orchard and through the next-door neighbor's field. Nothing is planted there. Then a path begins that goes down the big hill to the creek. In August the creek is shallow and there is filth in little patches in it, from sewers up creek. Fishermen fish anywhere along the creek, but there are some spots they like more than others. We always play by the rocks. There are also pieces of iron lying around, from when the new bridge was built. I can't remember any other bridge, but there was one.

I have my own little rock, that Tommy lets me have. It is shaped like a funny loaf of bread and has little dents in it. It looks like birds chipped at it, but they couldn't do that. When I come down and run through the bushes, some yellow birds fly up in surprise. Then everything is quiet. I walk in the water right away, to get my shoes wet. I hate my mother. Yesterday she was sitting on Daddy's lap; she was barefoot and her feet were dirty. They told me to come by them but I wouldn't. I ran outside by myself. Down at the creek I am happier by myself, but something makes me shiver. It is too quiet. If I was to fall in the water and drown nobody would know about it or care.

A man drowned in this creek, a few miles away. It was out back of a tavern. I heard my father talk about it.

When I look around there is a man standing on the bank. His car is parked up on the road but I didn't see it before. The man waves at me and grins. I can see his teeth way out here.

"Real nice day to play in the water," he says.

I narrow my eyes and watch him. Something touches the back of my neck, trying to tell me something. I start to shiver but stop. He reminds me of the man that drowned. Maybe his body wasn't taken out of the creek but lost. This man is too tall. His arms hang down. He has a fishing pole in one hand that is long and gawky like he is. There is something about the way he is standing—with his legs apart, as if he thought somebody might run and knock him down that makes my eyes get narrow.

"You live around here?" he says.

He takes off his hat and tosses it down as if he was tired of it. Now I know what he is: a colored man. I know what a colored man is like. But this one isn't black like the one my grandmother pointed out when we were driving. This one has a light brown skin. When Tommy gets real brown he's almost that dark.

"How old are you?" he says.

I should run past him and up the hill and go home. I know this. Mommy told me so. But something makes me stay where I am. To make Mommy sorry, I will stay here, right where I am. I think of her watching me, standing up on top of the hill and watching and feeling sorry for me.

"I'm six," I tell the man. With my head lowered I can still see him through my lashes. My eyes are half closed.

Everything is prickly and strange. Like when you are going to be sick but don't know it yet and are just waiting for something to happen. Something is going to happen. Or like when there is a spider on the ceiling, in just the second before you turn your head to see it. You know it's there but don't know why. There is something between us like a wet soft cobweb that keeps us watching each other, the colored man and me. I can tell he is afraid too.

"What are you doing?" he says. He squats down on the bank. He puts the fishing pole and the bag behind him. He looks like a dog waiting for his dish; he knows he can't come until it's ready. I could throw a stone at him, and he could reach out and catch it with a laugh.

"Can I come look?" he says.

He gets up slowly. His legs are long and he walks like he isn't used to walking. He comes right out to where I am and looks at what I have: a little dam made with stones between my rock and another rock. The water is running slowly through it. Nothing can stop that water. There is scum on it, greasy spots, and I touch them with my finger even though I hate them.

"I got two crabs in here," I tell the man.

I can hear him breathing when he bends down to look. A smell of licorice by him—and this makes me know I should run away. Men smell like smoke or something. They smell like beer, or the outside, or sweat. He is different from them.

"A crab would like to bite a nice little girl like you," he says. Right in the middle of talking he makes a swallowing sound. I keep playing in the water just like I was alone. I seem to see my mother coming out on the porch, frowning and making that sharp line like a cut between her eyebrows. She looks down and sees my doll on the steps, by itself. If she would come down to get me I would be all right. But she won't. She will just go back in the house and forget about me.

Now the colored man squats besides me. He is still taller than I am. I am sitting with my feet in the water, and it makes me think of how the water might stop me, pulling at my feet, if I wanted to run. The water is quiet. If an airplane would fly past we could look up at it, but nothing happens. After a while the man starts to talk to me.

He says I have mud on me. Yes, this is right. It is like in a dream; maybe he puts the mud on me somehow when I wasn't watching. I'm afraid to look at him, but his voice is soft and nice. He talks about little boys and little girls. I know he is not a daddy from the way he talks.

"Your hair is real nice," he says.

As soon as he touches me I am not afraid. He takes something out of my hair and shows me—a dried-up leaf. We both laugh.

He is bending toward me. His eyes are funny. The eyelid is sleepy and would push down to close the eyes, except the eyeball bulges too much. It can't see enough. We are so close together that I can see tiny little threads of blood in his eyes. He smells nice. Dark skin like that is funny to me, I never saw it so close. I would like to touch it but I don't dare. The man's mouth keeps moving. Sometimes it is a smile, then it gets bigger, then it changes back to nothing. It is as if he doesn't know what it's doing. His teeth are yellowish. The top ones are big, and when he smiles I can see his gums—a bright pink color, like a dog's. When he breathes his nostrils get small and then larger. I can almost see the warm air coming out of him, mixed with the smell of licorice and the dark smell of his skin.

He touches my shoulders and arms. He is saying something. He talks about my father and says he knows him, and he would like to be my father too. But he is not like any of the fathers because he talks in a whisper and nobody does that. He would not hit me or get mad. His eyelids come down over his big eyes and he must see me like you see something in a fog. His neck has a cord in it or something that moves; my grandmother has that too. It is the only ugly thing about him.

Now he is washing me. His breath is fast and warm against my skin. "They'll spank you if you're not clean. You got to be clean. All clean," he says. When he pulls my shirt off over my head the collar gets stuck by my nose and hurts me, I but I know it is too late to run away. The water keeps coming and making a noise. "Now this. Hold on here," he says, with his voice muffled as if it was pushed in a pillow, and he pulls my shorts down and takes them off.

I can't stop shivering now. He stares at me. His hand is big and dark by my arm. I say I want to go home, and my voice is a surprise, because it is ready to cry. "Now you just be nice," he says. He moves his hand on my back so that I am pressed up by him. I wait for something to hurt me but nothing hurts me. He would never hurt me like they would. His breath is fast and he could be drowning, and then he pushes me back a little. "Why don't you walk in the water a little?"

His forehead is wrinkled, and in the wrinkles there are drops of sweat that won't run down. I wouldn't want to touch his hair. He stares at me while I wade in the water. Everywhere he touched me I feel strange, and where he looks at me I feel strange. I know how he is watching. I can feel how he likes me. He would never hurt me. Something that makes me want to laugh comes up into my throat and almost scares me.

The sun is hot and makes me tired.

He takes my clothes and dresses me on the bank. He is very quiet. He drops my shirt and picks it up again, right away. Then with his long forefinger he rubs my arm down to the wrist, as if he doesn't understand what it is. His hands are real funny inside—a pink color, not like the rest of him. His fingernails are light too but ridged with dirt.

"Don't leave yet," he says. "Please. Sit and eat this with me."

When we eat the licorice he seems to forget about it, even when it's in his mouth. He forgets to chew it. I can see something coming into his eyes that makes him forget about me; he is listening to something.

We have a secret together that I won't ever tell.

When I come home Mommy is still in the kitchen. But everything looks different. It is the same but different. The air is wet. The way Mommy looks at me when I come in is different. She is smoking a cigarette.

"For Christ's sake, look at your shoes!"

She might be going to hit me, and I jerk back. But she just bends down and starts to unlace my shoe. "Just lucky for you these are the old ones," she says. The top of her head is damp. I can see her white scalp in places right through her hair. "Come on, put your foot up," she says, tugging at my shoe.

When the shoes are off she straightens up, and her face shows that she feels something hurt her.

"What the hell is that?" she says.

My heart starts to pound. "What?"

"On your teeth."

She stares at me. I can see the little lines on her face that will get to be like Grandma's.

"I said what is that? What have you been eating?"

I try to pull away from her. "Nothing."

"What have you been eating? Licorice? Who gave it to you?"

Her face gets hard. She leans down to me and sniffs, like a cat. I think of how I hate her because she can know every secret.

"Who gave it to you?"

"Nobody."

"I said who gave it to you!"

She slaps me. Her hand moves so fast both of us are afraid of it. She makes me cry.

"Who gave it to you? Who was it? Was it somebody down at the creek?"

"A man . . . a man had it—"

"What man?"

"A man down there."

"A fisherman?"

"Yes."

Her head is moving a little, rocking back and forth as if her heart began to pound too hard.

"Why did he give it to you? Were you alone?"

"He liked me."

"Why did he give it to you?"

Her eyes are like the cat's eyes. They are too big for her face. What I see in them is terrible.

"Did he . . . did he do anything to you?" she says. Her voice is getting higher. "What did he do? What did he do?"

"Nothing."

She pulls me in from the door, like she doesn't know what she is doing. "God," she says. She doesn't know I can hear it. "My God. My God."

I try to push against her legs. I would like to run back out the door and away from her and back down to the creek.

"What did he do?" she says.

I am crying now. "Nothing. I like him. I like him better than you!"

She pulls me to the kitchen chair and knocks me against it, as if she was trying to make me sit on it but forgot how. The chair hurts my back. "Tell me what he did!" she screams.

She knocks me against the chair again. She is trying to hurt me, to kill me. Her face is terrible. It is somebody else's. She is like somebody from the city come to get me. It seems to me that the colored man is hiding behind me, afraid of her eyes and her screaming, that awful voice I never heard before. She is trying to get both of us.

"What did he do? Oh, my God, my God!" Her words all run together. She is touching me everywhere, my arms, my legs. Her fingers want to pinch me but she won't let them. "He took your clothes off, didn't he?" she says. "He took them off. He took them off—this is on backwards, this is . . ."

She begins to scream. Her arms swing around and one of the jars is knocked off the table and breaks on the floor. I try to get away from her. I kick her leg. She is going to kill me, her face is red and everything is different, her voice is going higher and higher and nothing can stop it. I know from the way her eyes stare at me that something terrible happened and that everything is changed.

III

I am six years old. Down at the creek, I am trying to sit on a rock but my feet keep sliding off. Am I too big for the rock now? How big am I? Am I six years old or some other age? My toes curl inside my shoes but I can't take hold of the rock.

The colored man leans toward me and touches my hair. "I'm going to be your new daddy," he says.

The colored man leans toward me and touches my shoulders. His hand is warm and heavy.

The colored man leans toward me and put his big hand around the back of my neck. He touches me with his mouth, and then I can feel his teeth and his tongue all soft and wet on my shoulder. "I love you," he says. The words come back inside my head over and over, so that I am saying that to him: "I love you."

Then I am in the water and it touches me everywhere. I start to scream. My mouth tries to make noises but I can't hear them until somebody saves me.

"Honey, wake up. Wake up."

My mother is by the bed. She pulls me awake.

"What's wrong, honey?" she says. "What did you dream about?"

In the light from the lamp her face is lined and not pretty.

I can hear myself crying. My throat is sore. When I see her face it makes me cry harder. What if they all come in behind her, all those people again, to look at me? The doctor had something cold that touched me. I hated them all. I wanted them to die.

But only my father comes in. He stumbles against the bureau. "Another one of them dreams, huh?" he says in a voice like a doctor's. He is walking fast but then he slows down. The first night he was in here before my mother, to help me.

My mother presses me against her. Her hands rub my back and remind me of something . . . the creek again, and the dead dry smell and the rush of terror like ice that came up in me, from way down in my stomach. Now it comes again and I can't stop crying.

"Hey, little girl, come on now," my father says. He bends over me with his two hands on his thighs, frowning. He stares at me and then at my mother. He is wondering who we are.

"We better drive her back to the doctor tomorrow," he says.

"Leave her alone, she's all right," my mother says.

"What the hell do you know about it?"

"She wasn't hurt, it's all in her head. It's in her head," my mother says sharply. She leans back and looks at me as if she is trying to look inside my head. "I can take care of her."

"Look, I can't take this much longer. It's been a year now—"

"It has not been a year!" my mother says.

My crying runs down. It always stops. Then they go out and I hear them walk in the kitchen. Alone in bed, I lie with my legs stiff and my arms stiff; something bad will happen if I move. I have to stay just the way I am when they snap off my light, or something will happen to me. I have to stay like this until morning.

They are out in the kitchen. At first they talk too low for me to hear, then louder. If they argue it will get louder. One night they talked about the nigger and I could hear them. Tommy could hear them too; I know he was awake. The nigger was caught and a state trooper that Daddy knows real well kicked him in the face—he was kicked in the face. I can't remember that face now. Yes, I can remember it. I can remember some face. He did something terrible, and what was terrible came onto me, like black tar you can't wash off, and they are sitting out there talking about it. They are trying to remember what that nigger did to me. They weren't there and so they can't remember it. They will sit there until morning and then I will smell coffee. They are talking about what to do, what to do with me, and they keep trying to remember what that nigger did to me.

My mother's voice lifts sleepily. "Oh, you bastard!" she says. Something made of glass touches something else of glass.

The rooster out back has been crowing for hours.

"Look," says my father, and then his voice drops and I can't hear it. I lie still with my legs and arms stiff like they were made of ice or stone, trying to hear him. I can never hear him.

". . . time is it?" says my mother.

The room is starting to get light and so I know everything is safe again.

Flannery O'Connor

Flannery O'Connor was born in 1925 in Savannah, Georgia, but her father's affliction with disseminated lupus forced the family to move back to the security of Milledgeville, where her ancestors had lived since prior to the Civil War. Her rigorous Catholic upbringing did not prevent her from pursuing her literary interests in high school and then at Georgia State College for Women. A literary fellowship took her to the Writers' Workshop at the University of Iowa, where she earned her M.F.A. in 1946 and sold her first story. She attended the Yaddo writers' colony in Saratoga Springs, New York, where she made various contacts that helped her towards the publication of her work. In 1950, she became ill with the same disease that had killed her father, so she moved from New York back to the family dairy farm in Milledgeville, where she wrote and raised peacocks and from whence, while her health permitted, she made frequent sallies to teach, lecture, and serve as writer-in-residence. Before her death in 1964, she had published two novels, *Wise Blood* (1952) and *The Violent Bear It Away* (1960), and written thirty-one short stories, collected in *A Good Man Is Hard to Find* (1955) and in the posthumous volume, *Everything That Rises Must Converge* (1965). Her *Complete Stories* won the National Book Award for fiction in 1972.

Readers are fortunate to have not only O'Connor's fiction, but also her remarkable observations on the creative process in *Mystery and Manners* (1969), particularly on the relation between craft and vision. She once said, "The only way, I think, to learn to write stories is to write them and then try to discover what you have done," but she had some very practical statements to make as well. She had no use for thematic criticism and used to bristle at the mention of the word *theme*; her own work was a struggle for what she called *meaning*, but she felt that meaning was inseparable from the words themselves. "A story isn't any good unless it successfully resists paraphrase, unless it hangs on and expands in the mind." She felt that a good story was likely to be regional, literal, and rooted in the senses. "A good story is literal in the same sense that a child's drawing is literal. When a child draws, he doesn't intend to distort what he sees, and as his gaze is direct, he sees the lines that create motion. Now the lines of motion that interest the writer are usually invisible. They are the lines of spiritual motion."

By regional writing, she meant not parochialism or local colour, but "reading a small history in a universal light." "It is the knowledge that the writer finds in his community. When he ceases to find it there, he will cease to write, or at least he will cease to write anything enduring. The writer operates at a peculiar crossroads where time and place and eternity somehow meet. His problem is to find that location." Like the work of Faulkner and Margaret Laurence and Alice Munro, her so-called regional stories are universal precisely because they put down a taproot that reaches to the well-springs of human emotion.

Although she is a Christian writer, O'Connor never uses religious dogma or ideas as props in her fiction. Her primary concern in terms of craft, which she shares with Conrad, is to reach the reader through sensory images: "Fiction begins where human knowledge begins—with the senses—and every fiction writer is bound by this fundamental aspect of his medium." "He appeals through the senses, and you cannot appeal to the senses through abstractions." She aims for a gradual accumulation of detail, slower in the novel than in the story. "It's always necessary to remember that the fiction writer is much less immediately concerned with grand ideas and bristling emotions than he is with putting list slippers on clerks."

The accretions of detail that interest her are most often the dress, habits, and patterns of speech of her characters. "If you start with a real personality, a real character, then something is bound to happen; and you don't know what before you begin. In fact, it may be better if you don't know what before you begin. You ought to be able to discover something from your stories. If you don't, probably nobody else will." There are two qualities, she says, that make good fiction: "One is the sense of mystery and the other is the sense of manners. You get the manners from the texture of existence that surrounds you."

And where do you get the mystery? Probably not from teachers: "the teacher's work is largely negative . . . largely a matter of saying 'This doesn't work because . . .' or 'This does work because.' The *because* is very important . . . So many people can now write competent stories that the short story is in danger of dying of competence. We want competence, but competence by itself is deadly. What is needed is the vision to go with it, and you do not get this from a writing class." In the end, craft alone is not enough. "The peculiar problem of the short story writer is how to make the action he describes reveal as much of the mystery of existence as possible."

For O'Connor art is a form of revelation, but one that mirrors the revelation of fallen man raised again by Christ's redemptive act. So the stories themselves are not so much realistic portraits of life seen, as parables of life experienced, by the visionary artist or prophet: "The prophet is a *realist of distances*, and it is this kind of realism that you find in the best modern instances of the grotesque" (italics added).

Good Country People

Besides the neutral expression that she wore when she was alone, Mrs. Freeman had two others, forward and reverse, that she used for all her human dealings. Her forward expression was steady and driving like the advance of a heavy truck. Her eyes never swerved to left or right but turned as the story turned as if they followed a yellow line down the center of it. She seldom used the other expression because it was not often necessary for her to retract a statement, but when she did, her face came to a complete stop, there was an almost imperceptible movement of her black eyes, during which they seemed to be receding, and then the observer would see that Mrs. Freeman, though she might stand there as real as several grain sacks thrown on top of each other, was no longer there in spirit. As for getting anything across to him when this was the case, Mrs. Hopewell had given it up. She might talk her head off. Mrs. Freeman could never be brought to admit herself wrong on any point. She would stand there and if she could be brought to say anything, it was something like, "Well, I wouldn't of said it was and I wouldn't of said it wasn't," or letting her gaze range over the top kitchen shelf where there was an assortment of dusty bottles, she might remark, "I see you ain't ate many of them figs you put up last summer."

They carried on their most important business in the kitchen at breakfast. Every morning Mrs. Hopewell got up at seven o'clock and lit her gas heater and Joy's. Joy was her daughter, a large blonde girl who had an artificial leg. Mrs. Hopewell thought of her as a child though she was thirty-two years old and highly educated. Joy would get up while her mother was eating and lumber into the bathroom and slam the door, and before long, Mrs. Freeman would arrive at the back door. Joy would hear her mother call, "Come on in," and then they would talk for a while in low voices that were indistinguishable in the bathroom. By the time Joy came in, they had usually finished the weather report and were on one or the other of Mrs. Freeman's daughters, Glynese or Carramae. Joy called them Glycerin and Caramel. Glynese, a redhead, was eighteen and had many admirers; Carramae, a blonde, was only fifteen but already married and pregnant. She could not keep anything on her stomach. Every morning Mrs. Freeman told Mrs. Hopewell how many times she had vomited since the last report.

Mrs. Hopewell liked to tell people that Glynese and Carramae were two of the finest girls she knew and that Mrs. Freeman was a *lady* and that she was never ashamed to take her anywhere or introduce her to anybody they might meet. Then she would tell how she had happened to hire the Freemans in the first place and how they were a godsend to her and how she had had them four years. The reason for her keeping them so long was that they were not trash. They were good country people. She had telephoned the man whose name they had given as a reference and he had told her that Mr. Freeman was a good farmer but that his wife was the nosiest woman ever to walk the earth. "She's got to be into everything," the man said. "If she don't get there before the dust settles, you can bet she's dead, that's all. She'll want to know all your business. I can stand him real good," he had said, "but me nor my wife neither could have stood that woman one more minute on this place." That had put Mrs. Hopewell off for a few days.

She had hired them in the end because there were no other applicants but she had made up her mind beforehand exactly how she would handle the woman. Since she was the type who had to be into everything, then, Mrs. Hopewell had decided, she would not only let her be into everything, she would *see to it* that she was into everything—she would give her the responsibility of everything, she would put her in charge. Mrs. Hopewell had no bad qualities of her own but she was able to use other people's in such a constructive way that she never felt the lack. She had hired the Freemans and she had kept them four years.

Nothing is perfect. This was one of Mrs. Hopewell's favorite sayings. Another was: that is life! And still another, the most important, was: well, other people have their opinions too. She would make these statements, usually at the table, in a tone of gentle insistence as if no one held them but her, and the large hulking Joy, whose constant outrage had obliterated every expression from her face, would stare just a little to the side of her, her eyes icy blue, with the look of someone who had achieved blindness by an act of will and means to keep it.

When Mrs. Hopewell said to Mrs. Freeman that life was like that, Mrs. Freeman would say, "I always said so myself." Nothing had been arrived at by anyone that had not first been arrived at by her. She was quicker than Mr. Freeman. When Mrs. Hopewell said to her after they had been on the place a while, "You know, you're the wheel behind the wheel," and winked, Mrs. Freeman had said, "I know it, I've always been quick. It's some that are quicker than others."

"Everybody is different," Mrs. Hopewell said.

"Yes, most people is," Mrs. Freeman said.

"It takes all kinds to make the world."

"I always said it did myself."

The girl was used to this kind of dialogue for breakfast and more of it for dinner; sometimes they had it for supper too. When they had no guest they ate in the kitchen because that was easier. Mrs. Freeman always managed to arrive at some point during the meal and to watch them finish it. She would stand in the doorway if it were summer but in the winter she would stand with one elbow on top of the refrigerator and look down on them, or she would stand by the gas heater, lifting the back of her skirt slightly. Occasionally she would stand against the wall and roll her head from side to side. At no time was she in any hurry to leave. All this was very trying on Mrs. Hopewell but she was a woman af great patience. She realized that nothing is perfect and that in the Freemans she had good country people and that if, in this day and age, you get good country people, you had better hang onto them.

She had had plenty of experience with trash. Before the Freemans she had averaged one tenant family a year. The wives of these farmers were not the kind you would want to be around you for very long. Mrs. Hopewell, who had divorced her husband long ago, needed someone to walk over the fields with her; and when Joy had to be impressed for these services, her remarks were usually so ugly and her face so glum that Mrs. Hopewell would say, "If you can't come pleasantly, I don't want you at all," to which the girl, standing square and rigid-shouldered with her neck thrust slightly forward, would reply, "If you want me, here I am—LIKE I AM."

Mrs. Hopewell excused this attitude because of the leg (which had been shot off in a hunting accident when Joy was ten). It was hard for Mrs. Hopewell to realize that her child was thirty-two now and that for more than twenty years she had had only one leg. She thought of her still as a child because it tore her heart to think instead of the poor stout girl in her thirties who had never danced a step or had any *normal* good times. Her name was really Joy but as soon as she was twenty-one and away from home, she had had it legally changed. Mrs. Hopewell was certain that she had thought and thought until she had hit upon the ugliest name in any language. Then she had gone and had the beautiful name, Joy, changed without telling her mother until after she had done it. Her legal name was Hulga.

When Mrs. Hopewell thought the name, Hulga, she thought of the broad blank hull of a battleship. She would not use it. She continued to call her Joy to which the girl responded but in a purely mechanical way.

Hulga had learned to tolerate Mrs. Freeman who saved her from taking walks with her mother. Even Glynese and Carramae were useful when they occupied attention that might otherwise have been directed at her. At first she had thought she could not stand Mrs. Freeman for she had found that it was not possible to be rude to her. Mrs. Freeman would take on strange resentments and for days together she would be sullen but the source of her displeasure was always obscure; a direct attack, a positive leer, blatant ugliness to her face—these never touched her. And without warning one day, she began calling her Hulga.

She did not call her that in front of Mrs. Hopewell who would have been incensed but when she and the girl happened to be out of the house together, she would say something and add the name Hulga to the end of it, and the big spectacled Joy-Hulga would scowl and redden as if her privacy had been intruded upon. She considered the name her personal affair. She had arrived at it first purely on the basis of its ugly sound and then the full genius of its fitness had struck her. She had a vision of the name working like the ugly sweating Vulcan who stayed in the furnace and to whom, presumably, the goddess had to come when called. She saw it as the name of her highest creative act. One of her major triumphs was that her mother had not been able to turn her dust into Joy, but the greater one was that she had been able to turn it herself into Hulga. However, Mrs. Freeman's relish for using the name only irritated her. It was as if Mrs. Freeman's beady steel-pointed eyes had penetrated far enough behind her face to reach some secret fact. Something about her seemed to fascinate Mrs. Freeman and then one day Hulga realized that it was the artificial leg. Mrs. Freeman had a special fondness for the details of secret infections, hidden deformities, assaults upon children. Of diseases, she preferred the lingering or incurable. Hulga had heard Mrs. Hopewell give her the details of the hunting accident, how the leg had been literally blasted off, how she had never lost consciousness. Mrs. Freeman could listen to it any time as if it had happened an hour ago.

When Hulga stumped into the kitchen in the morning (she could walk without making the awful noise but she made it—Mrs. Hopewell was certain—because it was ugly-sounding), she glanced at them and did not speak. Mrs. Hopewell would be in her red kimono with her hair tied around her head in rags. She would be sitting at the table, finishing her breakfast and Mrs. Freeman would be hanging by her elbow outward from the refrigerator, looking down at the table. Hulga always put her eggs on the stove to boil and then stood over them with her arms folded, and Mrs. Hopewell would look at her—a kind of indirect gaze divided between her and Mrs. Freeman—and would think that if she would only keep herself up a little, she wouldn't be so bad looking. There was nothing wrong with her face that a pleasant expression wouldn't help. Mrs. Hopewell said that people who looked on the bright side of things would be beautiful even if they were not.

Whenever she looked at Joy this way, she could not help but feel that it would have been better if the child had not taken the Ph.D. It had certainly not brought her out any and now that she had it, there was no more excuse for her to go to school again. Mrs. Hopewell thought it was nice for girls to go to school to have a good time but Joy had "gone through." Anyhow, she would not have been strong enough to go again. The doctors had told Mrs. Hopewell that with the best of care, Joy might see forty-five. She had a weak heart. Joy had made it plain that if it had not been for this condition, she would be far from these red hills and good country people. She would be in a university lecturing to people who knew what she was talking about. And Mrs. Hopewell could very well picture her there, looking like a scarecrow and lecturing to more of the same. Here she went about all day in a six-year-old skirt and a yellow sweat shirt with a faded cowboy on a horse embossed on it. She thought this was funny; Mrs. Hopewell thought it was idiotic and showed simply that she was still a child. She was brilliant but she didn't have a grain of sense. It seemed to Mrs. Hopewell that every year she grew less like other people and more like herself—bloated, rude, and squint-eyed. And she said such strange things! To her own mother she had said—without warning, without excuse, standing up in the middle of a meal with her face purple and her mouth half full—"Woman! do you ever look inside? Do you ever look inside and see what you are *not*? God!" she had cried sinking down again and staring at her plate, "Malebranche was right: we are not our own light. We are not our own light!" Mrs. Hopewell had no idea to this day what brought that on. She had only made the remark, hoping Joy would take it in, that a smile never hurt anyone.

The girl had taken the Ph.D. in philosophy and this left Mrs. Hopewell at a complete loss. You could say, "My daughter is a nurse," or "My daughter is a school teacher," or even, "My daughter is a chemical engineer." You could not say, "My daughter is a philosopher." That was something that had ended with the Greeks and Romans. All day Joy sat on her neck in a deep chair, reading. Sometimes she went for walks but she didn't like dogs or cats or birds or flowers or nature or nice young men. She looked at nice young men as if she could smell their stupidity.

One day Mrs. Hopewell had picked up one of the books the girl had just put down and opening it at random, she read, "Science, on the other hand, has to assert its soberness and seriousness afresh and declare that it is concerned solely with what-is. Nothing—how can it be for science anything but a horror and a phantasm? If science is right, then one thing stands firm: science wishes to know nothing of nothing. Such is after all the strictly scientific approach to Nothing. We know it by wishing to know nothing of Nothing." These words had been underlined with a blue pencil and they worked on Mrs. Hopewell like some evil incantation in gibberish. She shut the book quickly and went out of the room as if she were having a chill.

This morning when the girl came in, Mrs. Freeman was on Carramae. "She thrown up four times after supper," she said, "and was up twice in the night after three o'clock. Yesterday she didn't do nothing but ramble in the bureau drawer. All she did. Stand up there and see what she could run up on."

"She's got to eat," Mrs. Hopewell muttered, sipping her coffee, while she watched Joy's back at the stove. She was wondering what the child had said to the Bible salesman. She could not imagine what kind of a conversation she could possibly have had with him.

He was a tall gaunt hatless youth who had called yesterday to sell them a Bible. He had appeared at the door, carrying a large black suitcase that weighted him so heavily on one side that he had to brace himself against the door facing. He seemed on the point of collapse but he said in a cheerful voice, "Good morning, Mrs. Cedars!" and set the suitcase down on the mat. He was not a bad-looking young man though he had on a bright blue suit and yellow socks that were not pulled up far enough. He had prominent face bones and a streak of sticky-looking brown hair falling across his forehead.

"I'm Mrs. Hopewell," she said.

"Oh!" he said, pretending to look puzzled but with his eyes sparkling, "I saw it said 'The Cedars,' on the mailbox so I thought you was Mrs. Cedars!" and he burst out in a pleasant laugh. He picked up the satchel and under cover of a pant, he fell forward into her hall. It was rather as if the suitcase had moved first, jerking him after it. "Mrs. Hopewell!" he said and grabbed her hand. "I hope you are well!" and he laughed again and then all at once his face sobered completely. He paused and gave her a straight earnest look and said, "Lady, I've come to speak of serious things."

"Well, come in," she muttered, none too pleased because her dinner was almost ready. He came into the parlor and sat down on the edge of a straight chair and put the suitcase between his feet and glanced around the room as if he were sizing her up by it. Her silver gleamed on the two sideboards; she decided he had never been in a room as elegant as this.

"Mrs. Hopewell," he began, using her name in a way that sounded almost intimate, "I know you believe in Chrustian service."

"Well, yes," she murmured.

"I know," he said and paused, looking very wise with his head cocked on one side, "that you're a good woman. Friends have told me."

Mrs. Hopewell never liked to be taken for a fool. "What are you selling?" she asked.

"Bibles," the young man said and his eye raced around the room before he added, "I see you have no family Bible in your parlor, I see that is the one lack you got!"

Mrs. Hopewell could not say, "My daughter is an atheist and won't let me keep the Bible in the parlor." She said, stiffening slightly, "I keep my Bible by my bed-side." This was not the truth. It was in the attic somewhere.

"Lady," he said, "the word of God ought to be in the parlor."

"Well, I think that's a matter of taste," she began. "I think . . ."

"Lady," he said, "for a Chrustian, the word of God ought to be in every room in the house besides in his heart. I know you're a Chrustian because I can see it in every line of your face."

She stood up and said, "Well, young man, I don't want to buy a Bible and I smell my dinner burning."

He didn't get up. He began to twist his hands and looking down at them, he said softly, "Well lady, I'll tell you the truth—not many people want to buy one nowadays and besides, I know I'm real simple. I don't know how to say a thing but to say it. I'm just a country boy." He glanced up into her unfriendly face. "People like you don't like to fool with country people like me!"

"Why!" she cried, "good country people are the salt of the earth! Besides, we all have different ways of doing, it takes all kinds to make the world go 'round. That's life!"

"You said a mouthful," he said.

"Why, I think there aren't enough good country people in the world!" she said, stirred. "I think that's what's wrong with it!"

His face had brightened. "I didn't inraduce myself," he said. "I'm Manley Pointer from out in the country around Willohobie, not even from a place, just from near a place."

"You wait a minute," she said. "I have to see about my dinner." She went out to the kitchen and found Joy standing near the door where she had been listening.

"Get rid of the salt of the earth," she said, "and let's eat."

Mrs. Hopewell gave her a pained look and turned the heat down under the vegetables. "I can't be rude to anybody," she murmured and went back into the parlor.

He had opened the suitcase and was sitting with a Bible on each knee.

"You might as well put those up," she told him. "I don't want one."

"I appreciate your honesty," he said. "You don't see any more real honest people unless you go way out in the country."

"I know," she said, "real genuine folks!" Through the crack in the door she heard a groan.

"I guess a lot of boys come telling you they're working their way through college," he said, "but I'm not going to tell you that. Somehow," he said, "I don't want to go to college. I want to devote my life to Chrustian service. See," he said, lowering his voice, "I got this heart condition. I may not live long. When you know it's something wrong with you and you may not live long, well then, lady . . ." He paused, with his mouth open, and stared at her.

He and Joy had the same condition! She knew that her eyes were filling with tears but she collected herself quickly and murmured, "Won't you stay for dinner? We'd love to have you!" and was sorry the instant she heard herself say it.

"Yes mam," he said in an abashed voice, "I would sher love to do that!"

Joy had given him one look on being introduced to him and then throughout the meal had not glanced at him again. He had addressed several remarks to her, which she had pretended not to hear. Mrs. Hopewell could not understand deliberate rudeness, although she lived with it, and she felt she had always to overflow with hospitality to make up for Joy's lack of courtesy. She urged him to talk about himself and he did. He said he was the seventh child of twelve and that his father had been crushed under a tree when he himself was eight year old. He had been crushed very badly, in fact, almost cut in two and was practically not recognizable. His mother had got along the best she could by hard working and she had always seen that her children went to Sunday School and that they read the Bible every evening. He was now nineteen year old and he had been selling Bibles for four months. In that time he had sold seventy-seven Bibles and had the promise of two more sales. He wanted to become a missionary because he thought that was the way you could do most for people. "He who losest his life shall find it," he said simply and he was so sincere, so genuine and earnest that Mrs. Hopewell would not for the world have smiled. He prevented his peas from sliding onto the table by blocking them with a piece of bread which he later cleaned his plate with. She could see Joy observing sidewise how he handled his knife and fork and she saw too that every few minutes, the boy would dart a keen appraising glance at the girl as if he were trying to attract her attention.

After dinner Joy cleared the dishes off the table and disappeared and Mrs. Hopewell was left to talk with him. He told her again about his childhood and his father's accident and about various things that had happened to him. Every five minutes or so she would stifle a yawn. He sat for two hours until finally she told him she must go because she had an appointment in town. He packed his Bibles and thanked her and prepared to leave, but in the doorway he stopped and wrung her hand and said that not on any of his trips had he met a lady as nice as her and he asked if he could come again. She had said she would always be happy to see him.

Joy had been standing in the road, apparently looking at something in the distance, when he came down the steps toward her, bent to the side with his heavy valise. He stopped where she was standing and confronted her directly. Mrs. Hopewell could not hear what he said but she trembled to think what Joy would say to him. She could see that after a minute Joy said something and that then the boy began to speak again, making an excited gesture with his free hand. After a minute Joy said something else at which the boy began to speak once more. Then to her amazement, Mrs. Hopewell saw the two of them walk off together, toward the gate. Joy had walked all the way to the gate with him and Mrs. Hopewell could not imagine what they had said to each other, and she had not yet dared to ask.

Mrs. Freeman was insisting upon her attention. She had moved from the refrigerator to the heater so that Mrs. Hopewell had to turn and face her in order to seem to be listening. "Glynese gone out with Harvey Hill again last night," she said. "She had this sty."

"Hill," Mrs. Hopewell said absently, "is that the one who works in the garage?"

"Nome, he's the one that goes to chiropracter school," Mrs. Freeman said. "She had this sty. Been had it two days. So she says when he brought her in the other night he says, 'Lemme get rid of that sty for you,' and she says, 'How?' and he says, 'You just lay yourself down across the seat of that car and I'll show you.' So she done it and he popped her neck. Kept on a-popping it several times until she made him quit. This morning," Mrs. Freeman said, "she ain't got no sty. She ain't got no traces of a sty."

"I never heard of that before," Mrs. Hopewell said.

"He ast her to marry him before the Ordinary," Mrs. Freeman went on, "and she told him she wasn't going to be married in no *office*."

"Well, Glynese is a fine girl," Mrs. Hopewell said. "Glynese and Carramae are both fine girls."

"Carramae said when her and Lyman was married Lyman said it sure felt sacred to him. She said he said he wouldn't take five hundred dollars for being married by a preacher."

"How much would he take?" the girl asked from the stove.

"He said he wouldn't take five hundred dollars," Mrs. Freeman repeated.

"Well we all have work to do," Mrs. Hopewell said.

"Lyman said it just felt more sacred to him," Mrs. Freeman. said. "The doctor wants Carramae to eat prunes. Says instead of medicine. Says them cramps is coming from pressure. You know where I think it is?"

"She'll be better in a few weeks," Mrs. Hopewell said.

"In the tube," Mrs. Freeman said. "Else she wouldn't be as sick as she is."

Hulga had cracked her two eggs into a saucer and was bringing them to the table along with a cup of coffee that she had filled too full. She sat down carefully and began to eat, meaning to keep Mrs. Freeman there by questions if for any reason she showed an inclination to leave. She could perceive her mother's eye on her. The first roundabout question would be about the Bible salesman and she did not wish to bring it on. "How did he pop her neck?" she asked.

Mrs. Freeman went into a description of how he had popped her neck. She said he owned a '55 Mercury but that Glynese said she would rather marry a man with only a '36 Plymouth who would be married by a preacher. The girl asked what if he had a '32 Plymouth and Mrs. Freeman said what Glynese had said was a '36 Plymouth.

Mrs. Hopewell said there were not many girls with Glynese's common sense. She said what she admired in those girls was their common sense. She said that reminded her that they had had a nice visitor yesterday, a young man selling Bibles. "Lord," she said, "he bored me to death but he was so sincere and genuine I couldn't be rude to him. He was just good country people, you know," she said, "—just the salt of the earth."

"I seen him walk up," Mrs. Freeman said, "and then later—I seen him walk off," and Hulga could feel the slight shift in her voice, the slight insinuation, that he had not walked off alone, had he? Her face remained expressionless but the color rose into her neck and she seemed to swallow it down with the next spoonful of egg. Mrs. Freeman was looking at her as if they had a secret together.

"Well, it takes all kinds of people to make the world go 'round," Mrs. Hopewell said. "It's very good we aren't all alike."

"Some people are more alike than others," Mrs. Freeman said.

Hulga got up and stumped, with about twice the noise that was necessary, into her room and locked the door. She was to meet the Bible salesman at ten o'clock at the gate. She had thought about it half the night. She had started thinking of it as a great joke and then she had begun to see profound implications in it. She had lain in bed imagining dialogues for them that were insane on the surface but that reached below to depths that no Bible salesman would be aware of. Their conversation yesterday had been of this kind.

He had stopped in front of her and had simply stood there. His face was bony and sweaty and bright, with a little pointed nose in the center of it, and his look was different from what it had been at the dinner table. He was gazing at her with open curiosity, with fascination, like a child watching a new fantastic animal at the zoo, and he was breathing as if he had run a great distance to reach her. His gaze seemed somehow familiar but she could not think where she had been regarded with it before. For almost a minute he didn't say anything. Then on what seemed an insuck of breath, he whispered "You ever ate a chicken that was two days old?"

The girl looked at him stonily. He might have just put this question up for consideration at the meeting of a philosophical association. "Yes," she presently replied as if she had considered it from all angles.

"It must have been mighty small!" he said triumphantly and shook all over with little nervous giggles, getting very red in the face, and subsiding finally into his gaze of complete admiration, while the girl's expression remained exactly the same.

"How old are you?" he asked softly.

She waited some time before she answered. Then in a flat voice she said, "Seventeen."

His smiles came in succession like waves breaking on the surface of a little lake. "I see you got a wooden leg," he said. "I think you're real brave. I think you're real sweet."

The girl stood blank and solid and silent.

"Walk to the gate with me," he said. "You're a brave sweet little thing and I liked you the minute I seen you walk in the door."

Hulga began to move forward.

"What's your name?" he asked, smiling down on the top of her head.

"Hulga," she said.

"Hulga," he murmured, "Hulga. Hulga. I never heard of anybody name Hulga before. You're shy, aren't you, Hulga?" he asked.

She nodded, watching his large red hand on the handle of the giant valise.

"I like girls that wear glasses," he said. "I think a lot. I'm not like these people that a serious thought don't ever enter their heads. It's because I may die."

"I may die too," she said suddenly and looked up at him. His eyes were very small and brown, glittering feverishly.

"Listen," he said, "don't you think some people was meant to meet on account of what all they got in common and all? Like they both think serious thoughts and all?" He shifted the valise to his other hand so that the hand nearest her was free. He caught hold of her elbow and shook it a little. "I don't work on Saturday," he said. "I like to walk in the woods and see what Mother Nature is wearing. O'er the hills and far away. Pic-nics and things. Couldn't we go on a pic-nic tomorrow? Say yes, Hulga," he said and gave her a dying look as if he felt his insides about to drop out of him. He had even seemed to sway slightly toward her.

During the night she had imagined that she seduced him. She imagined that the two of them walked on the place until they came to the storage barn beyond the two back fields and there, she imagined, that things came to such a pass that she very easily seduced him and that then, of course, she had to reckon with his remorse. True genius can get an idea across even to an inferior mind. She imagined that she took his remorse in hand and changed it into a deeper understanding of life. She took all his shame away and turned it into something useful.

She set off for the gate at exactly ten o'clock, escaping without drawing Mrs. Hopewell's attention. She didn't take anything to eat, forgetting that food is usually taken on a picnic. She wore a pair of slacks and a dirty white shirt, and as an afterthought, she had put some Vapex on the collar of it since she did not own any perfume. When she reached the gate no one was there.

She looked up and down the empty highway and had the furious feeling that she had been tricked, that he had only meant to make her walk to the gate after the idea of him. Then suddenly he stood up, very tall, from behind a bush on the opposite embankment. Smiling, he lifted his hat which was new and wide-brimmed. He had not worn it yesterday and she wondered if he had bought it for the occasion. It was toast-colored with a red and white band around it and was slightly too large for him. He stepped from behind the bush still carrying the black valise. He had on the same suit and the same yellow socks sucked down in his shoes from walking. He crossed the highway and said, "I knew you'd come!"

The girl wondered acidly how he had known this. She pointed to the valise and asked, "Why did you bring your Bibles?"

He took her elbow, smiling down on her as if he could not stop. "You can never tell when you'll need the word of God, Hulga," he said. She had a moment in which she doubted that this was actually happening and then they began to climb the embankment. They went down into the pasture toward the woods. The boy walked lightly by her side, bouncing on his toes. The valise did not seem to be heavy today; he even swung it. They crossed half the pasture without saying any-thing and then, putting his hand easily on the small of her back, he asked softly, "Where does your wooden leg join on?"

She turned an ugly red and glared at him and for an instant the boy looked abashed. "I didn't mean you no harm," he said. "I only meant you're so brave and all. I guess God takes care of you."

"No," she said, looking forward and walking fast, "I don't even believe in God."

At this he stopped and whistled. "No!" he exclaimed as if he were too aston-ished to say anything else.

She walked on and in a second he was bouncing at her side, fanning with his hat. "That's very unusual for a girl," he remarked, watching her out of the corner of his eye. When they reached the edge of the wood, he put his hand on her back again and drew her against him without a word and kissed her heavily.

The kiss, which had more pressure than feeling behind it, produced that extra surge of adrenalin in the girl that enables one to carry a packed trunk out of a burning house, but in her, the power went at once to the brain. Even before he released her, her mind, clear and detached and ironic anyway, was regarding him from a great dis-tance, with amusement but with pity. She had never been kissed before and she was pleased to discover that it was an unexceptional experience and all a matter of the mind's control. Some people might enjoy drain water if they were told it was vodka. When the boy, looking expectant but uncertain, pushed her gently away, she turned and walked on, saying nothing as if such business, for her, were common enough.

He came along panting at her side, trying to help her when he saw a root that she might trip over. He caught and held back the long swaying blades of thorn vine until she had passed beyond them. She led the way and he came breathing heavily behind her. Then they came out on a sunlit hillside, sloping softly into another one a little smaller. Beyond, the could see the rusted top of the old barn where the extra hay was stored.

The hill was sprinkled with small pink weeds. "Then you ain't saved?" he asked suddenly, stopping.

The girl smiled. It was the first time she had smiled at him at all. "In my economy," she said, "I'm saved and you are damned but I told you I didn't believe in God."

Nothing seemed to destroy the boy's look of admiration. He gazed at her now as if the fantastic animal at the zoo had put its paw through the bars and given him a loving poke. She thought he looked as if he wanted to kiss her again and she walked on before he had the chance.

"Ain't there somewheres we can sit down sometime?" he murmured, his voice softening toward the end of the sentence.

"In that barn," she said.

They made for it rapidly as if it might slide away like a train. It was a large two-story barn, cool and dark inside. The boy pointed up the ladder that led into the loft and said, "It's too bad we can't go up there."

"Why can't we?" she asked.

"Yer leg," he said reverently.

The girl gave him a contemptuous look and putting both hands on the ladder, she climbed it while he stood below apparently awestruck. She pulled herself expertly through the opening and then looked down at him and said, "Well, come on if you're coming," and he began to climb the ladder, awkwardly bringing the suitcase with him.

"We won't need the Bible," she observed.

"You never can tell," he said, panting. After he had got into the loft, he was a few seconds catching his breath. She had sat down in a pile of straw. A wide sheath of sunlight, filled with dust particles, slanted over her. She lay back against a bale, her face turned away, looking out the front opening of the barn where hay was thrown from a wagon into the loft. The two pink-speckled hillsides lay back against a dark ridge of woods. The sky was cloudless and cold blue. The boy dropped down by her side and put one arm under her and the other over her and began methodically kissing her face, making little noises like a fish. He did not remove his hat but it was pushed far enough back not to interfere. When her glasses got in his way, he took them off of her and slipped them into his pocket.

The girl at first did not return any of the kisses but presently she began to and after she had put several on his cheek, she reached his lips and remained there, kissing him again and again as if she were trying to draw all the breath out of him. His breath was clear and sweet like a child's and the kisses were sticky like a child's. He mumbled about loving her and about knowing when he first seen her that he loved her, but the mumbling was like the sleepy fretting of a child being put to sleep by his mother. Her mind, throughout this, never stopped or lost itself for a second to her feelings. "You ain't said you loved me none," he whispered finally, pulling back from her. "You got to say that."

She looked away from him off into the hollow sky and then down at a black ridge and then down farther into what appeared to be two green swelling lakes. She didn't realize he had taken her glasses but this landscape could not seem exceptional to her for she seldom paid any close attention to her surroundings.

"You got to say it," he repeated. "You got to say you love me."

She was always careful how she committed herself. "In a sense," she began, "if you use the word loosely, you might say that. But it's not a word I use. I don't have illusions. I'm one of those people who see *through* to nothing."

The boy was frowning. "You got to say it. I said it and you got to say it," he said.

The girl looked at him almost tenderly. "You poor baby," she murmured. "It's just as well you don't understand," and she pulled him by the neck, face-down, against her. "We are all damned," she said, "but some of us have taken off our blindfolds and see that there's nothing to see. It's a kind of salvation."

The boy's astonished eyes looked blankly through the ends of her hair. "Okay," he almost whined, "but do you love me or don'tcher?"

"Yes," she said and added, "in a sense. But I must tell you something. There mustn't be anything dishonest between us." She lifted his head and looked him in the eye. "I am thirty years old," she said. "I have a number of degrees."

The boy's look was irritated but dogged. "I don't care," he said. "I don't care a thing about what all you done. I just want to know if you love me or don'tcher?" and he caught her to him and wildly planted her face with kisses until she said, "Yes, yes."

"Okay then," he said, letting her go. "Prove it."

She smiled, looking dreamily out on the shifty landscape. She had seduced him without even making up her mind to try. "How?" she asked, feeling that he should be delayed a little.

He leaned over and put his lips to her ear. "Show me where your wooden leg joins on," he whispered.

The girl uttered a sharp little cry and her face instantly drained of color. The obscenity of the suggestion was not what shocked her. As a child she had sometimes been subject to feelings of shame but education had removed the last traces of that as a good surgeon scrapes for cancer; she would no more have felt it over what he was asking than she would have believed in his Bible. But she was as sensitive about the artificial leg as a peacock about his tail. No one ever touched it but her. She took care of it as someone else would his soul in private and almost with her own eyes turned away. "No," she said.

"I known it," he muttered, sitting up. "You're just playing me for a sucker."

"Oh no no!" she cried. "It joins on at the knee. Only at the knee. Why do you want to see it?"

The boy gave her a long penetrating look. "Because," he said, "it's what makes you different. You ain't like anybody else."

She sat staring at him. There was nothing about her face or her round freezing-blue eyes to indicate that this had moved her; but she felt as if her heart had stopped and left her mind to pump her blood. She decided that for the first time in her life she was face to face with real innocence. This boy, with an instinct that came from beyond wisdom, had touched the truth about her. When after a minute, she said in a hoarse high voice, "All right," it was like surrendering to him completely. It was like losing her own life and finding it again, miraculously, in his.

Very gently he began to roll the slack leg up. The artificial limb, in a white sock and brown flat shoe, was bound in a heavy material like canvas and ended in an ugly jointure where it was attached to the stump. The boy's face and his voice were entirely reverent as he uncovered it and said, "Now show me how to take it off and on."

She took it off for him and put it back on again and then he took it off himself, handling it as tenderly as if it were a real one. "See!" he said with a delighted child's face. "Now I can do it myself!"

"Put it back on," she said. She was thinking that she would run away with him and that every night he would take the leg off and every morning put it back on again. "Put it back on," she said.

"Not yet," he murmured, setting it on its foot out of her reach. "Leave it off for a while. You got me instead."

She gave a little cry of alarm but he pushed her down and began to kiss her again. Without the leg she felt entirely dependent on him. Her brain seemed to have stopped thinking altogether and to be about some other function that it was not very good at. Different expressions raced back and forth over her face. Every now and then the boy, his eyes like two steel spikes, would glance behind him where the leg stood. Finally she pushed him off and said, "Put it back on me now."

"Wait," he said. He leaned the other way and pulled the valise toward him and opened it. It had a pale blue spotted lining and there were only two Bibles in it. He took one of these out and opened the cover of it. It was hollow and contained a pocket flask of whiskey, a pack of cards, and a small blue box with printing on it. He laid these out in front of her one at a time in an evenly-spaced row, like one presenting offerings at the shrine of a goddess. He put the blue box in her hand. THIS PRODUCT TO BE USED ONLY FOR THE PREVENTION OF DISEASE, she read, and dropped it. The boy was unscrewing the top of the flask. He stopped and pointed, with a smile, to the deck of cards. It was not an ordinary deck but one with an obscene picture on the back of each card. "Take a swig," he said, offering her the bottle first. He held it in front of her, but like one mesmerized, she did not move.

Her voice when she spoke had an almost pleading sound. "Aren't you," she murmured, "aren't you just good country people?"

The boy cocked his head. He looked as if he were just beginning to understand that she might be trying to insult him. "Yeah," he said, curling his lip slightly, "but it ain't held me back none. I'm as good as you any day in the week."

"Give me my leg," she said.

He pushed it farther away with his foot. "Come on now, let's begin to have us a good time," he said coaxingly. "We ain't got to know one another good yet."

"Give me my leg!" she screamed and tried to lunge for it but he pushed her down easily.

"What's the matter with you all of a sudden?" he asked, frowning as he screwed the top on the flask and put it quickly back inside the Bible. "You just a while ago said you didn't believe in nothing. I thought you was some girl!"

Her face was almost purple. "You're a Christian!" she hissed. "You're a fine Christian! You're just like them all—say one thing and do another. You're a perfect Christian, you're . . ."

The boy's mouth was set angrily. "I hope you don't think," he said in a lofty indignant tone, "that I believe in that crap! I may sell Bibles but I know which end is up and I wasn't born yesterday and I know where I'm going!"

"Give me my leg!" she screeched. He jumped up so quickly that she barely saw him sweep the cards and the blue box back into the Bible and throw the Bible into the valise. She saw him grab the leg and then she saw it for an instant slanted forlornly across the inside of the suitcase with a Bible at either side of its opposite ends. He slammed the lid shut and snatched up the valise and swung it down the hole and then stepped through himself.

When all of him had passed but his head, he turned and regarded her with a look that no longer had any admiration in it. "I've gotten a lot of interesting things," he said. "One time I got a woman's glass eye this way. And you needn't to think you'll catch me because Pointer ain't really my name. I use a different name at every house I call at and don't stay nowhere long. And I'll tell you another thing, Hulga," he said, using the name as if he didn't think much of it, "you ain't so smart. I been believing in nothing ever since I was born!" and then the toast-colored hat disappeared down the hole and the girl was left, sitting on the straw in the dusty sunlight. When she turned her churning face toward the opening, she saw his blue figure struggling successfully over the green speckled lake.

Mrs. Hopewell and Mrs. Freeman, who were in the back pasture, digging up onions, emerge a little later from the woods and head across the meadow toward the highway. "Why, that looks like that nice dull young man that tried to sell me a Bible yesterday," Mrs. Hopewell said, squinting. "He must have been selling them to the Negroes back in there. He was so simple," she said, "but I guess the world would be better off if we were all that simple."

Mrs. Freeman's gaze drove forward and just touched him before he disappeared under the hill. Then she returned her attention to the evil-smelling onion shoot she was lifting from the ground. "Some can't be that simple," she said. "I know I never could."

Frank O'Connor

Frank O'Connor was born Michael Francis O'Donovan in Cork, Ireland, in 1903 in conditions of extreme poverty, which enabled him to go no further than Grade 4 in the Christian Brothers School. During the struggles for independence, he joined the Irish Republican Army while still a teenager, for which he spent eighteen months in prison. He had an equal interest in painting and writing, but chose the latter for reasons of economy. He worked in Cork and Dublin as a librarian and wrote under the pseudonym Frank O'Connor to protect his position. He was also an itinerant teacher of Gaelic and manager of the Abbey Theatre in Dublin. He published *Guests of the Nation* in 1931, the title story of which appeared in *The Atlantic Monthly*. His chief influences appear to have been Maupassant, Chekhov, Gogol, Turgenev, and Isaac Babel. He published many books of fiction up to 1952, when he moved to the United States to teach at Harvard and Northwestern University. His distinguished career included fourteen volumes of short fiction, collected in *Frank O'Connor: Collected Stories* (1981) and two volumes of criticism: *The Mirror in the Roadway* (1956), essays on the modern novel, and *The Lonely Voice* (1962), a study of the short story and some of its famous practitioners. He died in 1966.

In the introduction to *The Lonely Voice*, O'Connor makes a number of claims for the short story, including the assertion that it is a "modern art form" and "represents, better than poetry or drama, our own attitude to life." When he says "our *own* attitude," O'Connor is suggesting that the short story is a more intimate, less public, form than the novel. "It began, and continues to function, as a private art, intended to satisfy the standards of the individual, solitary, critical reader." He claims that the short story has "never had a hero" and, referring to the work of Gogol, Chekhov, and James Joyce, that it is the birthplace of the "Little Man" of modern consciousness. To some degree, he says, the short story exists to celebrate "submerged population groups . . . outlawed figures wandering about the fringes of society." As such, the short story is a kind of hymn to loneliness: "The short story remains by its very nature remote from the community—romantic, individualistic, and intransigent."

O'Connor dismisses the notion of "essential form" in the short story. "Because his frame of reference can never be the totality of a human life, [the short story writer] must be forever selecting the point at which he can approach it, and each selection he makes contains

the possibility of a new form as well as the possibility of a complete fiasco." If the form of the short story is organic, determined by the germ, or *donnée*, which gives it rise, then there can be no prescription as to required length, and no formula for balancing the three elements O'Connor sees as necessary in a story: exposition, development, and drama. He denies that the short story is a miniaturist art and insists that the term *short story* is a misnomer. "Basically, the difference between the short story and the novel is not one of length. It is a difference between pure and applied storytelling, and in case someone has still failed to get the point, I am not trying to decry applied storytelling. Pure storytelling is more artistic, that is all, and in storytelling I am not sure how much art is preferable to nature."

Aside from the formal considerations that abound in his criticism, especially his careful attention to the minute particulars of prose style, what O'Connor most values is evidence of an author's imaginative sympathy. He praises Chekhov's sympathy for even the most despicable of his characters; he also draws attention to the Russian writer's propensity to focus, not on large-scale moral questions, but on the "venial sins," those small moments of cruelty, meanness, and selfishness that are the truest tests of character. He also acknowledges that a short story should arise out of a feeling of necessity, of the need to impart something that ought to be public knowledge, so that the writer has the feeling he must take someone by the lapels and say, "Listen, you ought to know this." In this regard, he says, the writer is more of an informer than an observer.

Indeed, O'Connor's comments on other writers are equally important for what they say about his own view of the short story. Although he has a high regard for the best work of Hemingway, O'Connor says: "In a Hemingway story, drama, because it is stylized in the same way as the narrative, tends to lose its full impact. Dialogue, the autonomous element of drama, begins to blur, and the conversation becomes more like the conversation of alcoholics, drug addicts, or experts in Basic English." What he finds lacking in Hemingway's work is a genuine sense of place and related social and historical conditions. While admitting that the short story endeavours to situate iself at "a point outside time from which past and future can be viewed simultaneously," and acknowledging Hemingway's debt to Gertrude Stein and the German Expressionists, O'Connor nonetheless has reservations about fictional efforts to generalize experience. "It is all too abstract.

Nobody in Hemingway ever seems to have a job or a home unless the job or the home fits into the German scheme of capital letters. Everybody seems to be permanently on holiday or getting a divorce, or as *Die Frau* in 'Hills like White Elephants' puts it, 'That's all we do, isn't it—look at things and try new drinks?'"

A more detailed statement of O'Connor's view of the short story and its affinities with poetry is to be found in *The Paris Review* interview of 1957, reprinted in *Writers at Work* (First Series) and excerpted for inclusion in this anthology.

Guests of the Nation

At dusk the big Englishman, Belcher, would shift his long legs out of the ashes and say "Well, chums, what about it?" and Noble or me would say "All right, chum" (for we had picked up some of their curious expressions), and the little Englishman, Hawkins, would light the lamp and bring out the cards. Sometimes Jeremiah Donovan would come up and supervise the game and get excited over Hawkins's cards, which he always played badly, and shout at him as if he was one of our own "Ah, you divil, you, why didn't you play the tray?"

But ordinarily Jeremiah was a sober and contented poor devil like the big Englishman, Belcher, and was looked up to only because he was a fair hand at documents, though he was slow enough even with them. He wore a small cloth hat and big gaiters over his long pants, and you seldom saw him with his hands out of his pockets. He reddened when you talked to him, tilting from toe to heel and back, and looking down all the time at his big farmer's feet. Noble and me used to make fun of his broad accent, because we were from the town.

I couldn't at the time see the point of me and Noble guarding Belcher and Hawkins at all, for it was my belief that you could have planted that pair down anywhere from this to Claregalway and they'd have taken root there like a native weed. I never in my short experience seen two men to take to the country as they did.

They were handed on to us by the Second Battalion when the search for them became too hot, and Noble and myself, being young, took over with a natural feeling of responsibility, but Hawkins made us look like fools when he showed that he knew the country better than we did.

"You're the bloke they calls Bonaparte," he says to me. "Mary Brigid O'Connell told me to ask you what you done with the pair of her brother's socks you borrowed."

For it seemed, as they explained it, that the Second used to have little evenings, and some of the girls of the neighbourhood turned in, and, seeing they were such decent chaps, our fellows couldn't leave the two Englishmen out of them. Hawkins learned to dance "The Walls of Limerick," "The Siege of Ennis," and "The Waves of Tory" as well as any of them, though, naturally, he couldn't return the compliment, because our lads at that time did not dance foreign dances on principle.

So whatever privileges Belcher and Hawkins had with the Second they just naturally took with us, and after the first day or two we gave up all pretense of keeping a close eye on them. Not that they could have got far, for they had accents you could cut with a knife and wore khaki tunics and overcoats with civilian pants and boots. But it's my belief that they never had any idea of escaping and were quite content to be where they were.

It was a treat to see how Belcher got off with the old woman of the house where we were staying. She was a great warrant to scold, and cranky even with us, but before ever she had a chance of giving our guests, as I may call them, a lick of her tongue, Belcher had made her his friend for life. She was breaking sticks, and Belcher, who hadn't been more than ten minutes in the house, jumped up from his seat and went over to her.

"Allow me, madam," he says, smiling his queer little smile, "please allow me"; and he takes the bloody hatchet. She was struck too paralytic to speak, and after that, Belcher would be at her heels, carrying a bucket, a basket, or a load of turf, as the case might be. As Noble said, he got into looking before she leapt, and hot water, or any little thing she wanted, Belcher would have it ready for her. For such a huge man (and though I am five foot ten myself I had to look up at him) he had an uncommon shortness—or should I say lack?—of speech. It took us some time to get used to him, walking in and out, like a ghost, without a word. Especially because Hawkins talked enough for a platoon, it was strange to hear big Belcher with his toes in the ashes come out with a solitary "Excuse me, chum," or "That's right, chum." His one and only passion was cards, and I will say for him that he was a good card-player. He could have fleeced myself and Noble, but whatever we lost to him Hawkins lost to us, and Hawkins played with the money Belcher gave him.

Hawkins lost to us because he had too much old gab, and we probably lost to Belcher for the same reason. Hawkins and Noble would spit at one another about religion into the early hours of the morning, and Hawkins worried the soul out of Noble, whose brother was a priest, with a string of questions that would puzzle a cardinal. To make it worse even in treating of holy subjects, Hawkins had a deplorable tongue. I never in all my career met a man who could mix such a variety of cursing and bad language into an argument. He was a terrible man, and a fright to argue. He never did stroke of work, and when he had no one else to talk to, he got stuck in the old woman.

He met his match in her, for one day when he tried to get her to complain profanely of the drought, she gave him a great come-down by blaming it entirely on Jupiter Pluvius (a deity neither Hawkins nor I have ever heard of, though Noble said that among the pagans it was believed that he had something to do with the rain). Another day he was swearing at the capitalists for starting the German war when the old lady laid down her iron, puckered up her little crab's mouth, and said: "Mr. Hawkins, you can say what you like about the war, and think you'll deceive me because I'm only a simple poor countrywoman, but I know what started the war. It was the Italian Count that stole the heathen divinity out of the temple in Japan. Believe me, Mr. Hawkins, nothing but sorrow and want can follow the people that disturb the hidden powers."

A queer old girl, all right.

II

We had our tea one evening, and Hawkins lit the lamp and we all sat into cards. Jeremiah Donovan came in too, and sat down and watched us for a while, and it suddenly struck me that he had no great love for the two Englishmen. It came as a great surprise to me, because I hadn't noticed anything about him before.

Late in the evening a really terrible argument blew up between Hawkins and Noble, about capitalists and priests and love of your country.

"The capitalists," says Hawkins with an angry gulp, "pays the priests to tell you about the next world so as you won't notice what the bastards are up to in this."

"Nonsense, man!" says Noble, losing his temper. "Before ever a capitalist was thought of, people believed in the next world."

Hawkins stood up as though he was preaching a sermon.

"Oh, they did, did they?" he says with a sneer. "They believed all the things you believe, isn't that what you mean? And you believe that God created Adam, and Adam created Shem, and Shem created Jehoshophat. You believe all that silly old fairytale about Eve and Eden and the apple. Well, listen to me, chum. If you're entitled to hold a silly belief like that, I'm entitled to hold my silly belief— which is that the first thing your God created was a bleeding capitalist, with morality and Rolls-Royce complete. Am I right, chum?" he says to Belcher.

"You're right, chum," says Belcher with his amused smile, and got up from the table to stretch his long legs into the fire and stroke his moustache. So, seeing that Jeremiah Donovan was going, and that there was no knowing when the argument about religion would be over, I went out with him. We strolled down to the village together, and then he stopped and started blushing and mumbling and saying I ought to be behind, keeping guard on the prisoners. I didn't like the tone he took with me, and anyway I was bored with life in the cottage, so I replied by asking him what the hell we wanted guarding them at all for. I told him I'd talked it over with Noble, and that we'd both rather be out with a fighting column.

"What use are those fellows to us?" says I.

He looked at me in surprise and said: "I thought you knew we were keeping them as hostages."

"Hostages?" I said.

"The enemy have prisoners belonging to us," he says, "and now they're talking of shooting them. If they shoot our prisoners, we'll shoot theirs."

"Shoot them?" I said.

"What else did you think we were keeping them for?" he says.

"Wasn't it very unforeseen of you not to warn Noble and myself of that in the beginning?" I said.

"How was it?" says he. "You might have known it."

"We couldn't know it, Jeremiah Donovan," says I. "How could we when they were on our hands so long?"

"The enemy have our prisoners as long and longer," says he.

"That's not the same thing at all," says I.

"What difference is there?" says he.

I couldn't tell him, because I knew he wouldn't understand. If it was only an old dog that was going to the vet's, you'd try and not get too fond of him, but Jeremiah Donovan wasn't a man that would ever be in danger of that.

"And when is this thing going to be decided?" says I.

"We might hear tonight," he says. "Or tomorrow or the next day at latest. So if it's only hanging round here that's a trouble to you, you'll be free soon enough."

It wasn't the hanging round that was a trouble to me at all by this time. I had worse things to worry about. When I got back to the cottage the argument was still on. Hawkins was holding forth in his best style, maintaining that there was no next world, and Noble was maintaining that there was; but I could see that Hawkins had had the best of it.

"Do you know what, chum?" he was saying with a saucy smile. "I think you're just as big a bleeding unbeliever as I am. You say you believe in the next world, and you know just as much about the next world as I do which is sweet damn-all. What's heaven? You don't know. Where's heaven? You don't know. You know sweet damn-all! I ask you again, do they wear wings?"

"Very well, then," says Noble, "they do. Is that enough for you? They do wear wings."

"Where do they get them, then? Who makes them? Have they a factory for wings? Have they a sort of store where you hands in your chit and takes your bleeding wings?"

"You're an impossible man to argue with," says Noble. "Now, listen to me—" And they were off again.

It was long after midnight when we locked up and went to bed. As I blew out the candle I told Noble what Jeremiah Donovan was after telling me. Noble took it very quietly. When we'd been in bed about an hour he asked me did I think we ought to tell the Englishmen. I didn't think we should, because it was more than likely that the English wouldn't shoot our men, and even if they did, the brigade officers, who were always up and down with the Second Battalion and knew the Englishmen well, wouldn't be likely to want them plugged. "I think so too," says Noble. "It would be great cruelty to put the wind up them now."

"It was very unforeseen of Jeremiah Donovan anyhow," says I.

It was next morning that we found it so hard to face Belcher and Hawkins. We went about the house all day scarcely saying a word. Belcher didn't seem to notice; he was stretched into the ashes as usual, with his usual look of waiting in quietness for something unforeseen to happen, but Hawkins noticed and put it down to Noble's being beaten in the argument of the night before.

"Why can't you take a discussion in the proper spirit?" he says severely. "You and your Adam and Eve! I'm a Communist, that's what I am. Communist or anarchist, it all comes to much the same thing." And for hours he went round the house, muttering when the fit took him. "Adam and Eve! Adam and Eve! Nothing better to do with their time than picking bleeding apples!"

III

I don't know how we got through that day, but I was very glad when it was over, the tea things were cleared away, and Belcher said in his peaceable way: "Well, chums, what about it?" We sat round the table and Hawkins took out the cards, and just then I heard Jeremiah Donovan's footstep on the path and a dark presentiment crossed my mind. I rose from the table and caught him before he reached the door.

"What do you want?" I asked.

"I want those two soldier friends of yours," he says, getting red.

"Is that the way, Jeremiah Donovan?" I asked.

"That's the way. There were four of our lads shot this morning, one of them a boy of sixteen."

"That's bad," I said.

At that moment Noble followed me out, and the three of us walked down the path together, talking in whispers. Feeney, the local intelligence officer, was standing by the gate.

"What are you going to do about it?" I asked Jeremiah Donovan.

"I want you and Noble to get them out; tell them they're being shifted again; that'll be the quietest way."

"Leave me out of that," says Noble under his breath.

Jeremiah Donovan looks at him hard.

"All right," he says. "You and Feeney get a few tools from the shed and dig a hole by the far end of the bog. Bonaparte and myself will be after you. Don't let anyone see you with the tools. I wouldn't like it to go beyond ourselves."

We saw Feeney and Noble go round to the shed and went in ourselves. I left Jeremiah Donovan to do the explanations. He told them that he had orders to send them back to the Second Battalion. Hawkins let out a mouthful of curses, and you could see that though Belcher didn't say anything, he was a bit upset too. The old woman was for having them stay in spite of us, and she didn't stop advising them until Jeremiah Donovan lost his temper and turned on her. He had a nasty temper, I noticed. It was pitch-dark in the cottage by this time, but no one thought of lighting the lamp, and in the darkness the two Englishmen fetched their topcoats and said good-bye to the old woman.

"Just as a man makes a home of a bleeding place, some bastard at headquarters thinks you're too cushy and shunts you off," says Hawkins, shaking her hand.

"A thousand thanks, madam," says Belcher. "A thousand thanks for everything"—as though he'd made it up.

We went round to the back of the house and down towards the bog. It was only then that Jeremiah Donovan told them. He was shaking with excitement.

"There were four of our fellows shot in Cork this morning and now you're to be shot as a reprisal."

"What are you talking about?" snaps Hawkins. "It's bad enough being mucked about as we are without having to put up with your funny jokes."

"It isn't a joke," says Donovan. "I'm sorry, Hawkins, but it's true," and begins on the usual rigmarole about duty and how unpleasant it is.

I never noticed that people who talk a lot about duty find it much of a trouble to them.

"Oh, cut it out!" says Hawkins.

"Ask Bonaparte," says Donovan, seeing that Hawkins isn't taking him seriously. "Isn't it true, Bonaparte?"

"It is," I say, and Hawkins stops.

"Ah, for Christ's sake, chum!"

"I mean it, chum," I say.

"You don't sound as if you mean it."

"If he doesn't mean it, I do," says Donovan, working himself up.

"What have you against me, Jeremiah Donovan?"

"I never said I had anything against you. But why did your people tale out four of our prisoners and shoot them in cold blood?"

He took Hawkins by the arm and dragged him on, but it was impossible to make him understand that we were in earnest. I had the Smith and Wesson in my pocket and I kept fingering it and wondering what I'd do if they put up a fight for it or ran, and wishing to God they'd do one or the other. I knew if they did run for it, that I'd never fire on them. Hawkins wanted to know was Noble in it, and when we said yes, he asked us why Noble wanted to plug him. Why did any of us want to plug him? What had he done to us? Weren't we all chums? Didn't we understand him and didn't he understand us? Did we imagine for an instant that he'd shoot us for all the so-and-so officers in the so-and-so British Army?

By this time we'd reached the bog, and I was so sick I couldn't even answer him. We walked along the edge of it in the darkness, and every now and then Hawkins would call a halt and begin all over again, as if he was wound up, about our being chums, and I knew that nothing but the sight of the grave would convince him that we had to do it. And all the time I was hoping that something would happen; that they'd run for it or that Noble would take over the responsibility from me. I had the feeling that it was worse on Noble than on me.

IV

At last we saw the lantern in the distance and made towards it. Noble was carrying it, and Feeney was standing somewhere in the darkness behind him, and the picture of them so still and silent in the bogland brought it home to me that we were in earnest, and banished the last bit of hope I had.

Belcher, on recognizing Noble, said: "Hallo, chum," in his quiet way, but Hawkins flew at him at once, and the argument began all over again, only this time Noble had nothing to say for himself and stood with his head down, holding the lantern between his legs.

It was Jeremiah Donovan who did the answering. For the twentieth time, as though it was haunting his mind, Hawkins asked if anybody thought he'd shoot Noble.

"Yes, you would," says Jeremiah Donovan.

"No, I wouldn't, damn you!"

"You would, because you'd know you'd be shot for not doing it."

"I wouldn't, not if I was to be shot twenty times over. I wouldn't shoot a pal. And Belcher wouldn't—isn't that right, Belcher?"

"That's right, chum," Belcher said, but more by way of answering the question than of joining in the argument. Belcher sounded as though whatever unforeseen thing he'd always been waiting for had come at last.

"Anyway, who says Noble would be shot if I wasn't? What do you think I'd do if I was in his place, out in the middle of a blasted bog?"

"What would you do?" asks Donovan.

"I'd go with him wherever he was going, of course. Share my last bob with him and stick by him through thick and thin. No one can ever say of me that I let down a pal."

"We had enough of this," says Jeremiah Donovan, cocking his revolver. "Is there any message you want to send?"

"No, there isn't."

"Do you want to say your prayers?"

Hawkins came out with a cold-blooded remark that even shocked me and turned on Noble again.

"Listen to me, Noble," he says. "You and me are chums. You can't come over to my side, so I'll come over to your side. That show you I mean what I say? Give me a rifle and I'll go along with you and the other lads."

Nobody answered him. We knew that was no way out.

"Hear what I'm saying?" he says. "I'm through with it. I'm a deserter or anything else you like. I don't believe in your stuff, but it's no worse than mine. That satisfy you?"

Noble raised his head, but Donovan began to speak and he lowered it again without replying.

"For the last time, have you any messages to send?" says Donovan in a cool, excited sort of voice.

"Shut up, Donovan! You don't understand me, but these lads do. They're not the sort to make a pal and kill a pal. They're not the tools of any capitalist."

I alone of the crowd saw Donovan raise his Webley to the back of Hawkins's neck, and as he did so I shut my eyes and tried to pray. Hawkins had begun to say something else when Donovan fired, and as I opened my eyes at the bang, I saw Hawkins stagger at the knees and lie out flat at Noble's feet, slowly and as quiet as a kid falling asleep, with the lantern-light on his lean legs and bright farmer's boots. We all stood very still, watching him settle out in the last agony.

Then Belcher took out a handkerchief and began to tie it about his own eyes (in our excitement we'd forgotten to do the same for Hawkins), and, seeing it wasn't big enough, turned and asked for the loan of mine. I gave it to him and he knotted the two together and pointed with his foot at Hawkins.

"He's not quite dead," he says. "Better give him another."

Sure enough, Hawkins's left knee is beginning to rise. I bend down and put my gun to his head; then, recollecting myself, I get up again. Belcher understands what's in my mind.

"Give him his first," he says. "I don't mind. Poor bastard, we don't know what's happening to him now."

I knelt and fired. By this time I didn't seem to know what I was doing. Belcher, who was fumbling a bit awkwardly with the handkerchiefs, came out with a laugh as he heard the shot. It was the first time I heard him laugh and it sent a shudder down my back; it sounded so unnatural.

"Poor bugger!" he said quietly. "And last night he was so curious about it all. It's very queer, chums, I always think. Now he knows as much about it as they'll ever let him know, and last night he was all in the dark."

Donovan helped him to tie the handkerchiefs about his eyes. "Thanks chum," he said. Donovan asked if there were any messages he wanted sent.

"No, chum," he says. "Not for me. If any of you would like to write to Hawkins's mother, you'll find a letter from her in his pocket. He and his mother were great chums. But my missus left me eight years ago. Went away with another fellow and took the kid with her. I like the feeling of a home, as you may have noticed, but I couldn't start again after that."

It was an extraordinary thing, but in those few minutes Belcher said more than in all the weeks before. It was just as if the sound of the shot had started a flood of talk in him and he could go on the whole night like that, quite happily, talking about himself. We stood round like fools now that he couldn't see us any longer. Donovan looked at Noble, and Noble shook his head. Then Donovan raised his Webley, and at that moment Belcher gives his queer laugh again. He may have thought we were talking about him, or perhaps he noticed the same thing I'd noticed and couldn't understand it.

"Excuse me, chums," he says. "I feel I'm talking the hell of a lot, and so silly, about my being so handy about a house and things like that. But this thing came on me suddenly. You'll forgive me, I'm sure."

"You don't want to say a prayer?" asks Donovan.

"No, chum," he says. "I don't think it would help. I'm ready, and you boys want to get it over."

"You understand that we're only doing our duty?" says Donovan.

Belcher's head was raised like a blind man's, so that you could only see his chin and the tip of his nose in the lantern-light.

"I never could make out what duty was myself," he said. "I think you're all good lads, if that's what you mean. I'm not complaining."

Noble, just as if he couldn't bear any more of it, raised his fist at Donovan, and in a flash Donovan raised his gun and fired. The big man went over like a sack of meal, and this time there was no need of a second shot.

I don't remember much about the burying, but that it was worse than all the rest because we had to carry them to the grave. It was all mad lonely with nothing but a patch of lantern-light between ourselves and the dark, and birds hooting and screeching all round, disturbed by the guns. Noble went through Hawkins's belongings to find the letter from his mother, and then joined his hands together. He did the same with Belcher. Then, when we'd filled the grave, we separated from Jeremiah Donovan and Feeney and took our tools back to the shed. All the way we didn't speak a word. The kitchen was dark and cold as we'd left it, and the old woman was sitting over the hearth, saying her beads. We walked past her into the room, and Noble struck a match to light the lamp. She rose quietly and came to the doorway with all her cantankerousness gone.

"What did ye do with them?" she asked in a whisper, and Noble started so that the match went out in his hand.

"What's that?" he asked without turning round.

"I heard ye," she said.

"What did you hear?" asked Noble.

"I heard ye. Do ye think I didn't hear ye, putting the spade back in the houseen?"

Noble struck another match and this time the lamp lit for him.

"Was that what ye did to them?" she asked.

Then, by God, in the very doorway, she fell on her knees and began praying, and after looking at her for a minute or two Noble did the same by the fireplace. I pushed my way out past her and left them at it. I stood at the door, watching the stars and listening to the shrieking of the birds dying out over the bogs. It is so strange what you feel at times like that you can't describe it. Noble says he saw everything ten times the size, as though there were nothing in the whole world but that little patch of bog with the two Englishmen stiffening into it, but with me it was as if the patch of bog where the Englishmen were was a million miles away, and even Noble and the old woman, mumbling behind me, and the birds and the bloody stars were all far away, and I was somehow very small and very lost and lonely like a child astray in the snow. And anything that happened to me afterwards, I never felt the same about again.

Tillie Olsen

Born in Omaha, Nebraska, in 1913, Tillie Olsen has become a touchstone in feminist literary circles, not only for her determination to write, but also for her painful articulation of the difficulties women face when they try to combine art, motherhood, and full-time paid employment. The daughter of Russian refugees from Czarist repression, Olsen was a high school drop-out by age fifteen. She lived through the Depression of the thirties, working in factories and offices, trying to raise her children properly and keep alive the creative spark that had started her writing a novel at age nineteen. She and her child were abandoned by her first husband. She was a member of the Young Communist League and had been jailed briefly for her activities on behalf of the packing-house workers in Kansas City, so it is not surprising that she later married Jack Olsen, a political activist. Three more children, a job, and pressing political causes left her no time to write. Although she had published a chapter of her unfinished novel in *Partisan Review* in 1934, her first book, a collection of four stories called *Tell Me a Riddle*, was not published until 1961, after she had enrolled in a fiction writing class at San Francisco State College and been awarded a Stanford University writing fellowship in the mid-fifties. In 1974, she published *Yonnondio*, from what she had been able to reconstruct of the novel started forty-three years earlier. *Silences*, a collection of essays, appeared in 1978.

In *Silences*, her moving account of the obstacles women face in trying to create, Tillie Olsen takes up the theme Virginia Woolf first addressed in *A Room of One's Own*. She speaks of Balzac's claim that there is something about the creative process that recalls motherhood: "Yes, in intelligent passionate motherhood there are similarities, and in more than the toil and patience. The calling upon total capacities; the reliving and new using of the past; the comprehensions; the fascination, absorption, intensity. All almost certain death to creation—(so far).

"Not because the capacities to create no longer exist, or the need (though for a while, as in any fullness of life, the need may be obscured), but because the circumstances for sustained creation have been almost impossible. The need cannot be first. It can have, at best, only part self, part time. (Unless someone else does the nurturing. Read Dorothy Fisher's 'Babushka Farnham' in *Fables for Parents*.) More than in any other human relationship, overwhelmingly more, motherhood means being instantly interruptable, responsive, responsible. Children need one *now* (and remember, in our society, the family must often try to be the centre for love and health the outside world is not). The very fact that these are real needs, that one feels them as one's own (love, not duty); *that there is no one else responsible for these needs*, gives them primacy. It is distraction, not meditation, that becomes habitual; interruption, not continuity; spasmodic, not constant toil. The rest has been said here. Work interrupted, deferred, relinquished, makes blockage—at best, less accomplishment. Unused capacities atrophy, cease to be."

This discussion, which is continued in a larger extract from *Silences* in the Afterwords section, helps to suggest why Olsen's work has been the subject of such keen interest—Margaret Atwood uses the term *reverence*—and why it has been translated into many languages. Her exploration of the riddles and enigmas of existence, her unique fictionalizing of autobiographical materials, and her use of stream-of-consciousness techniques give her stories a timeless, deceptively simple, resonance and appeal.

I Stand Here Ironing

I stand here ironing, and what you asked me moves tormented back and forth with the iron.

"I wish you would manage the time to come in and talk with me about your daughter. I'm sure you can help me understand her. She's a youngster who needs help and whom I'm deeply interested in helping."

"Who needs help." . . . Even if I came, what good would it do? You think because I am her mother I have a key, or that in some way you could use me as a key? She has lived for nineteen years. There is all that life that has happened outside of me, beyond me.

And when there is time to remember, to sift, to weigh, to estimate, to total? I will start and there will be an interruption and I will have to gather together again. Or I will become engulfed with all I did or did not do, with what should have been and what cannot be helped.

She was a beautiful baby. The first and only one of our five that was beautiful at birth. You do not guess how new and uneasy her tenancy in her now-loveliness. You did not know her all those years she was thought homely, or see her poring over her baby pictures, making me tell her over and over how beautiful she had been—and would be, I would tell her—and was now, to the seeing eye. But the seeing eyes were few or nonexistent. Including mine.

I nursed her. They feel that's important nowadays. I nursed all the children, but with her, with all the fierce rigidity of first motherhood, I did like books then said. Though her cries battered me to trembling and my breasts ached with swollenness, I waited till the clock decreed.

Why do I put that first? I do not even know if it matters, or if it explains anything.

She was a beautiful baby. She blew shining bubbles of sound. She loved motion, loved light, loved color and music and textures. She would lie on the floor in her blue overalls patting the surface so hard in ecstasy her hands and feet would blur. She was a miracle to me, but when she was eight months old I had to leave her daytimes with the woman downstairs to whom she was no miracle at all, for I worked or looked for work and for Emily's father, who "could no longer endure" (he wrote in his good-bye note) "sharing want with us."

I was nineteen. It was the pre-relief, pre-WPA world of the depression. I would start running as soon as I got off the streetcar, running up the stairs, the place smelling sour, and awake or asleep to startle awake, when she saw me she would break into a clogged weeping that could not be comforted, a weeping I can hear yet.

After a while I found a job hashing at night so I could be with her days, and it was better. But it came to where I had to bring her to his family and leave her.

It took a long time to raise the money for her fare back. Then she got chicken pox and I had to wait longer. When she finally came, I hardly knew her, walking quick and nervous like her father, looking like her father, thin, and dressed in a shoddy red that yellowed her skin and glared at the pockmarks. All the baby loveliness gone.

She was two. Old enough for nursery school they said, and I did not know then what I know now—the fatigue of the long day, and the lacerations of group life in the kinds of nurseries that are only parking places for children.

Except that it would have made no difference if I had known. It was the only place there was. It was the only way we could be together, the only way I could hold a job.

And even without knowing, I knew. I knew the teacher that was evil because all these years it has curdled into my memory, the little boy hunched in the corner, her rasp, "why aren't you outside, because Alvin hits you? that's no reason, go out, scaredy." I knew Emily hated it even if she did not clutch and implore "don't go Mommy" like the other children, mornings.

She always had a reason why we should stay home. Momma, you look sick. Momma, I feel sick. Momma, the teachers aren't there today, they're sick. Momma, we can't go, there was a fire last night. Momma, it's a holiday today, no school, they told me.

But never a direct protest, never rebellion. I think of our others in their three-, four-year-oldness—the explosions, the tempers, the denunciations, the demands—and I feel suddenly ill. I put the iron down. What in me demanded that goodness in her? And what was the cost, the cost to her of such goodness?

The old man living in the back once said in his gentle way: "You should smile at Emily more when you look at her." What *was* in my face when I looked at her? I loved her. There were all the acts of love.

It was only with the others I remembered what he said, and it was the face of joy, and not of care or tightness or worry I turned to them—too late for Emily. She does not smile easily, let alone almost always as her brothers and sisters do. Her face is closed and sombre, but when she wants, how fluid. You must have seen it in her pantomimes, you spoke of her rare gift for comedy on the stage that rouses laughter out of the audience so dear they applaud and applaud and do not want to let her go.

Where does it come from, that comedy? There was none of it in her when she came back to me that second time, after I had to send her away again. She had a new daddy now to learn to love, and I think perhaps it was a better time.

Except when we left her alone nights, telling ourselves she was old enough.

"Can't you go some other time, Mommy, like tomorrow?" she would ask. "Will it be just a little while you'll be gone? Do you promise?"

The time we came back, the front door open, the clock on the floor in the hall. She rigid awake. "It wasn't just a little while. I didn't cry. Three times I called you, just three times, and then I ran downstairs to open the door so you could come faster. The clock talked loud. I threw it away, it scared me what it talked."

She said the clock talked loud again that night I went to the hospital to have Susan. She was delirious with the fever that comes before red measles, but she was fully conscious all the week I was gone and the week after we were home when she could not come near the new baby or me.

She did not get well. She stayed skeleton thin, not wanting to eat, and right after night she had nightmares. She would call for me, and I would rouse from exhaustion to sleepily call back: "You're all right, darling, go to sleep, it's just a dream," and if she still called, in a sterner voice, "now go to sleep, Emily, there's nothing to hurt you." Twice, only twice, when I had to get up for Susan anyhow, I went in to sit with her.

Now when it is too late (as if she would let me hold her and comfort her like I do the others) I get up and go to her at once at her moan or restless stirring. "Are you awake, Emily? Can I get you something?" And the answer is always the same: "No, I'm all right, go back to sleep, Mother."

They persuaded me at the clinic to send her away to a convalescent home in the country where "she can have the kind of food and care you can't manage for her, and you'll be free to concentrate on the new baby." They still send children to that place. I see pictures on the society page of sleek young women planning affairs to raise money for it, or dancing at the affairs, or decorating Easter eggs or filling Christmas stockings for the children.

They never have a picture of the children so I do not know if the girls still wear those gigantic red bows and the ravaged looks on the every other Sunday when parents can come to visit "unless otherwise notified"—as we were notified the first six weeks.

Oh it is a handsome place, green lawns and tall trees and fluted flower beds. High up on the balconies of each cottage the children stand, the girls in their red bows and white dresses, the boys in white suits and giant red ties. The parents stand below shrieking up to be heard and the children shriek down to be heard, and between them the invisible wall "Not to Be Contaminated by Parental Germs or Physical Affection."

There was a tiny girl who always stood hand in hand with Emily. Her parents never came. One visit she was gone. "They moved her to Rose Cottage" Emily shouted in explanation. "They don't like you to love anybody here."

She wrote once a week, the labored writing of a seven-year-old. "I am fine. How is the baby. If I write my leter nicly I will have a star. Love." There never was a star. We wrote every other day, letters she could never hold or keep but only hear read—once. "We simply do not have room for children to keep any personal possessions," they patiently explained when we pieced one Sunday's shrieking together to plead how much it would mean to Emily, who loved so to keep things, to be allowed to keep her letters and cards.

Each visit she looked frailer. "She isn't eating," they told us.

(They had runny eggs for breakfast or mush with lumps, Emily said later, I'd hold it in my mouth and not swallow. Nothing ever tasted good, just when they had chicken.)

It took us eight months to get her released home, and only the fact that she gained back so little of her seven lost pounds convinced the social worker.

I used to try to hold and love her after she came back, but her body would stay stiff, and after a while she'd push away. She ate little. Food sickened her, and I think much of life too. Oh she had physical lightness and brightness, twinkling by on skates, bouncing like a ball up and down up and down over the jump rope, skimming over the hill; but these were momentary.

She fretted about her appearance, thin and dark and foreign-looking at a time when every little girl was supposed to look or thought she should look a chubby blonde replica of Shirley Temple. The doorbell sometimes rang for her, but no one seemed to come and play in the house or to be a best friend. Maybe because we moved so much.

There was a boy she loved painfully through two school semesters. Months later she told me how she had taken pennies from my purse to buy him candy. "Licorice was his favorite and I brought him some every day but he still liked Jennifer better'n me. Why, Mommy?" The kind of question for which there is no answer.

School was a worry for her. She was not glib or quick in a world where glibness and quickness were easily confused with ability to learn. To her overworked and exasperated teachers she was an overconscientious "slow learner" who kept trying to catch up and was absent entirely too often.

I let her be absent, though sometimes the illness was imaginary. How different from my now-strictness about attendance with the others. I wasn't working. We had a new baby. I was home anyhow. Sometimes, after Susan grew old enough, I would keep her home from school, too, to have them together.

Mostly Emily had asthma, and her breathing, harsh and labored, would fill the house with a curiously tranquil sound. I would bring the two old dresser mirrors and her boxes of collections to her bed. She would select beads and single ear-rings, bottle tops and shells, dried flowers and pebbles, old postcards and scraps, all sorts of oddments; then she and Susan would play Kingdom, setting up land-scapes and furniture, peopling them with action.

Those were the only times of peaceful companionship between her and Susan. I have edged away from it, that poisonous feeling between them, that terrible bal-ancing of hurts and needs I had to do between the two, and did so badly, those earlier years.

Oh there were conflicts between the others too, each one human, needing, demanding, hurting, taking—but only between Emily and Susan, no, Emily toward Susan that corroding resentment. It seems so obvious on the surface, yet it is not obvious. Susan, the second child, Susan, golden- and curly-haired and chubby, quick and articulate and assured, everything in appearance and manner Emily was not; Susan, not able to resist Emily's precious things, losing or sometimes clumsily breaking them; Susan telling jokes and riddles to company for applause while Emily sat silent (to say to me later: that was *my* riddle, Mother, I told it to Susan); Susan, who for all the five years' difference in age was just a year behind Emily in developing physically.

I am glad for that slow physical development that widened the difference between her and her contemporaries, though she suffered over it. She as too vul-nerable for that terrible world of youthful competition, of preening and parading, of constant measuring of yourself against every other, of envy, "If I had that copper hair," "If I had that skin. . . ." She tormented herself enough about not looking like the others, there was enough of unsureness, the having to be con-scious of words before you speak, the constant caring—what are they thinking of me? without having it all magnified by the merciless physical drives.

Ronnie is calling. He is wet and I change him. It is rare there is such a cry now. That time of motherhood is almost behind me when the ear is not one's own but must always be racked and listening for the child cry, the child call. We sit for a while and I hold him, looking out over the city spread in charcoal with its soft aisles of light. "Shoogily," he breathes and curls closer. I carry him back to bed, asleep. *Shoogily.* A funny word, a family word, inherited from Emily, invented by her to say: *comfort.*

In this and other ways she leaves her seal, I say aloud. And startle at my saying it. What do I mean? What did I start to gather together, to try and make coherent? I was at the terrible, growing years. War years. I do not remember them well. I was working, there were four smaller ones now, there was not time for her. She had to help be a mother, and housekeeper, and shopper. She had to get her seal. Mornings of crisis and near hysteria trying to get lunches packed, hair combed, coats and shoes found, everyone to school or Child Care on time, the baby ready for transportation. And always the paper scribbled on by a smaller one, the book looked at by Susan then mislaid, the homework not done. Running out to that huge school where she was one, she was lost, she was a drop; suffering over the unpreparedness, stammering and unsure in her classes.

There was so little time left at night after the kids were bedded down. She would struggle over books, always eating (it was in those years she developed her enormous appetite that is legendary in our family) and I would be ironing, or preparing food for the next day, or writing V-mail to Bill, or tending the baby. Sometimes, to make me laugh, or out of her despair, she would imitate happenings or types at school.

I think I said once: "Why don't you do something like this in the school amateur show?" One morning she phoned me at work, hardly understandable through the weeping: "Mother, I did it. I won, I won; they gave me first prize; they clapped and clapped and wouldn't let me go."

Now suddenly she was Somebody, and as imprisoned in her difference as she had been in anonymity.

She began to be asked to perform at other high schools, even in colleges, then at city and statewide affairs. The first one we went to, I only recognized her that first moment when thin, shy, she almost drowned herself into the curtains. Then: Was this Emily? The control, the command, the convulsing and deadly clowning, the spell, then the roaring, stamping audience, unwilling to let this rare and precious laughter out of their lives.

Afterwards: You ought to do something about her with a gift like that—but without money or knowing how, what does one do? We have left it all to her, and the gift has so often eddied inside, clogged and clotted, as been used and growing.

She is coming. She runs up the stairs two at a time with her light graceful step, and I know she is happy tonight. Whatever it was that occasioned your call did not happen today.

"Aren't you ever going to finish the ironing, Mother? Whistler painted his mother in a rocker. I'd have to paint mine standing over an ironing board." This is one of her communicative nights and she tells me everything and nothing as she fixes herself a plate of food out of the icebox.

She is so lovely. Why did you want me to come in at all? Why were you concerned? She will find her way.

She starts up the stairs to bed. "Don't get me up with the rest in the morning." "But I thought you were having midterms." "Oh, those," she comes back in, kisses me, and says quite lightly, "in a couple of years when we'll all be atom-dead they won't matter a bit."

She has said it before. She *believes* it. But because I have been denying the past, and all that compounds a human being is so heavy and meaningful in me, I cannot endure it tonight.

I will never total it all. I will never come in to say: She was a child seldom smiled at. Her father left me before she was a year old. I had to work her first six years when there was work, or I sent her home and to his relatives. There were years she had care she hated. She was dark and thin and foreign-looking in a world where the prestige went to blondeness and curly hair and dimples, she was slow where glibness was prized. She was a child of anxious, not proud, love. We were poor and could not afford for her the soil of easy growth. I was a young mother, I was a distracted mother. There were other children pushing up, demanding. Her younger sister seemed all that she was not. There were years she did not want me to touch her. She kept too much in herself, her life was such she had to keep too much in herself. My wisdom came too late. She has much to her and probably little will come of it. She is a child of her age, of depression, of war, of fear.

Let her be. So all that is in her will not bloom—but in how many does it? There is still enough left to live by. Only help her to know—help make it so there is cause for her to know—that she is more than this dress on the ironing board, helpless before the iron.

Jayne Anne Phillips

Jayne Anne Phillips was born in Buckhannon, West Virginia, in 1952. She supported herself through the University of West Virginia by working in the home improvement business, then travelled across the U.S. working as a waitress. At age twenty-four, she was accepted into the University of Iowa writing program for the M.F.A. on the strength of poems and two short stories. She published her first book of short prose pieces, *Sweethearts*, with a small press in 1976; this was followed by *Counting* (1978), *Black Tickets* (1979), which won the Sue Kaufman Award for First Fiction from the American Academy and Institute for Arts and Letters, and the novel *Machine Dreams* (1984). Her work has appeared in *Fiction*, *Redbook*, *Iowa Review*, and *Fiction International*. She lives in Cambridge, Massachusetts.

In an interview with *Newsweek* (No. 94, Oct. 22, 1979), Phillips describes writing as "almost a metaphysical process." She goes on to explain by saying that "it's a privilege to have a passion. Real writers serve their material. They allow it to pass through them and have the opportunity to move beyond the daily limitations of being inside themselves. It's like being led by a whisper." Phillips is speaking here of more than Byron's and Camus's idea of creating as living doubly, though, of course, that meaning is also intended; she is saying something about the artist as a vehicle, a mouthpiece, through which the community guarantees, if not its survival, at least a record of its passage through time. Whether it is the collective unconscious or tribal memory, the whisper makes itself felt in the mind of the story-teller, like Shelley's west wind or Auden's intolerable neural itch.

Phillips has an amazing ear for the nuances and idioms of ordinary speech; her strippers, seamstresses, and drug addicts are drawn deftly and convincingly. Many of these characters, who step precariously along the razor's edge of sanity, remain in the reader's mind primarily as voices; others, who struggle to survive poverty or social disadvantage, are remembered for a single detail, such as cracked lipstick or a "pale strand of scalp." Phillips turns the same discerning eye on personal relationships, frustration, domestic violence, and betrayal, reminding one of her acknowledged debt to Faulkner, Welty, and Flannery O'Connor. "I'm interested in what homes consists of," she says. "Because we move around so much, families are forced to be immediate; they must stand on their relationships, rather than on stereotypes or assumptions or a common history."

Phillips's work stems as much from a commitment to process, rather than to theory or traditional forms and ideas, as it does from close observation. "I believe that you are led to discover what things mean and how things are related to each other through the process of doing the work." Her training as a poet has no doubt influenced her stategies as a prose writer. Many of her shortest stories are less than a page in length and even the longer pieces are imbued with a sense of verbal economy. "I became more challenged by the difficulty of writing fiction," she said. "I was really attracted by the subversive look of the paragraph. In a poem you're always having to confront the identity of the writer. In fiction the reader becomes less defended against that identity and more open to the text."

The Stripper

When I was fifteen back in Charleston, my cousin Phoebe taught me to strip. She was older than my mother but she had some body. When I watched her she'd laugh, say That's all right Honey sex is sex. It don't matter if you do it with monkeys. Yeah she said, You're white an dewy an tickin like a time bomb an now's the time to learn. With that long blond hair you can't lose. An don't you paint your face till you have to, every daddy wants his daughter. That's what she said. The older dancers wear makeup an love the floor, touchin themselves. The men get scared an cluster round, smokin like paper on a slow fire. Once in Laramie I was in one of those spotted motels after a show an a man's shadow fell across the window. I could smell him past the shade, hopeless an cracklin like a whip. He scared me, like I had a brother who wasn't right found a bullwhip in the shed. He used to take it out some days and come back with such a look on his face. I don't wanna know what they know. I went into the bathroom an stood in the fluorescent light. Those toilets have a white strip across em that you have to rip off. I left it on an sat down. I brushed my hair an counted. Counted till he walked away kickin gravel in the parkin lot. Now I'm feelin his shadow fall across stages in Denver an Cheyenne. I close my eyes an dance faster, like I used to dance blind an happy in Pop's closet. His suits hangin faceless on the racks with their big woolly arms empty. I play five clubs a week, $150 first place. I dance three sets each against five other girls. We pick jukebox songs while the owner does his gig on the mike. Now Marlene's gonna slip ya into a little darkness Let's get her up there with a big hand. The big hands clap an I walk the bar all shaven an smooth, rhinestoned velvet on my crotch. Don't ever show em a curly hair Phoebe told me, Angels don't have no curly hair. That's what she said. Beggin, they're starin up my white legs. That jukebox is cookin an they feel their fingers in me. Honey you know it ain't fair what you do Oh tell me why love is a lie jus like a ball an chain. Yeah I'm a white leather dream in a cowboy hat, a ranger with fringed breasts. Baby stick em up Baby don't touch Baby I'm a star an you are dyin. Better find a soft blond god to take you down. I got you Baby I got you Let go.

Edgar Allan Poe

Edgar Allan Poe was born in 1809 to itinerant actors in Boston and orphaned before the age of three. He became the ward of a Richmond, Virginia, couple, John and Francis Allan, whose name he adopted. Poe travelled with the Allans to Scotland and England in 1815. His studies at the University of Virginia were terminated as a result of his drinking and carousing, a pattern that would plague his life. A brief military career was followed by dismissal from West Point and various short-lived jobs, including the editorship of the Richmond *Southern Literary Messenger*. Marriage to his thirteen-year-old cousin, Virginia Clemm, ended with her death in 1847, after which he became engaged to a wealthy widow. However, a celebratory binge left him unconscious in a Baltimore street; he died three days later in 1849. A legendary Romantic figure, who is credited with inventing the detective story, Poe won a number of literary prizes and left an impressive body of poetry, fiction, and criticism; however, the fame, mostly posthumous, which came to him for his Gothic horror tales and literary sorties with the supernatural was never far removed from poverty and personal disaster. His stories were collected in *Tales of the Grotesque and Arabesque* (1840) and *Tales by Edgar A. Poe* (1845).

Poe made a major contribution to the development of the short story, both as a writer and as a theorist. What he called *ratiocination* is operative in the detective stories, such as "The Purloined Letter," where the reader is caught up in the various mental processes of C. Auguste Dupin trying to unravel the crime. Poe's horror stories, such as "The Fall of the House of Usher" and "The Cask of Amontillado," achieve their power by objectifying extreme psychological states, as D. H. Lawrence points out in *Studies in Classic American Literature* (1923), so that the unconscious desire to possess, or be possessed, utterly is projected in the images of burying, or being buried, alive.

Poe's reviews of the work of Nathaniel Hawthorne reveal a first-rate critical mind at work, trying to describe, much as Aristotle did for Greek drama in his *Poetics*, the nature of literary composition in fiction. Poe rejects superficial notions of originality and novelty for something that is deeper, involving both the mind that writes and the mind that reads. "But the true originality—true in respect of its purposes—is that which, in bringing out the half-formed, the reluctant, or the unexpressed fancies of mankind, or in exciting the more delicate pulses of the heart's passion, or in giving birth to some universal sentiment or

instinct in embryo, thus combines with the pleasurable effect of apparent novelty, a real egoistic delight. The reader, in the case first supposed, (that of the absolute novelty,) is excited, but embarrassed, disturbed, in some degree even pained at his own want of perception, at his own folly in not having himself hit upon the idea. In the second case, his pleasure is doubled. He is filled with an intrinsic and extrinsic delight. He feels and intensely enjoys the seeming novelty of the thought, enjoys it as really novel, as absolutely original with the writer—and himself. They two, he fancies, have, alone of all men, thought thus. They two have, together, created this thing. Henceforward there is a bond of sympathy between them, a sympathy which irradiates every subsequent page of the book."

Many of Poe's major critical statements originated as reviews of the work of other writers. In a review of Nathaniel Parker Willis, for example, Poe tried to define style, dismissing mere experiment, or what he called "sleight-of-pen trickeries." He considered the work of art a technical challenge, "a difficulty happily overcome," and attributed the success of a work to imaginative genius, rather than to the fanciful scribblings or games of "all the little frisky men, personally considered." In the 1847 review of Hawthorne, Poe simplifies his thoughts by stating that originality in fiction is a matter of *tone*, not just content. He also repeats his famous remarks about the importance of a single, unified effect in the short story, or tale, which have been excerpted for inclusion in the Afterwords.

Perhaps Poe's insistence on thought and design in the creative process was consciously or unconsciously intended not only to help him set himself apart from the ordinary pack of scribblers, but also to distract readers from the deeply disturbing content of much of his work. In a moving letter to James R. Lowell, he acknowledges those elements in his character that proved to be self-destructive: "I have thus rambled and dreamed away whole months and awake, at last, to a sort of mania for composition. Then I scribble all day, and read all night, so long as the disease endures. . . . I live continually in a reverie of the future. I have no faith in human perfectability. I think that human exertion will have no appreciable effect upon humanity. Man is now only more active—not more happy—than he was 6000 years ago. . . . I have been too deeply conscious of the mutability and evanescence of temporal things, to give any continuous effort to anything—to be consistent in anything. My life has been whim—

impulse—passion—a longing for solitude—a scorn of all things present, in an earnest desire for the future." And yet, for all his scepticism and personal misgivings, his work has endured and created for him a lasting legacy.

The Purloined Letter

Nil sapienatiæ odiosius acumine nimio.[1]

—Seneca

At Paris, just after dark one gusty evening in the autumn of 18———, I was enjoying the twofold luxury of meditation and a meerschaum, in company with my friend, C. Auguste Dupin, in his little back library, or book-closet, *au troisième*, No. 33 *Rue Dunôt, Faubourg St. Germain.*[2] For one hour at least we had maintained a profound silence; while each, to any casual observer, might have seemed intently and exclusively occupied with the curling eddies of smoke that oppressed the atmosphere of the chamber. For myself, however, I was mentally discussing certain topics which had formed matter for conversation between us at an earlier period of the evening; I mean the affair of the Rue Morgue, and the mystery attending the murder of Marie Rogêt.[3] looked upon it, therefore, as something of a coincidence, when the door of our apartment was thrown open and admitted our old acquaintance, Monsieur G———, the Prefect of the Parisian police.

We gave him a hearty welcome; for there was nearly half as much of the entertaining as of the contemptible about the man, and we had not seen him for several years. We had been sitting in the dark, and Dupin now arose for the purpose of lighting a lamp, but sat down again, without doing so, upon G.'s saying that he had called to consult us, or rather to ask the opinion of my friend, about some official business which had occasioned a great deal of trouble.

"If it is any point requiring reflection," observed Dupin, as he forbore to enkindle the wick, "we shall examine it to better purpose in the dark."

"That is another of your odd notions," said the Prefect, who had the fashion of calling everything "odd" that was beyond his comprehension, and thus lived amid an absolute legion of "oddities."

"Very true," said Dupin, as he supplied his visitor with a pipe, and rolled toward him a comfortable chair.

"And what is the difficulty now?" I asked. "Nothing more in the assassination way I hope?"

"Oh, no; nothing of that nature. The fact is, the business is *very* simple indeed, and I make no doubt that we can manage it sufficiently well ourselves; but then I thought Dupin would like to hear the details of it because it is so excessively *odd*."

"Simple and odd," said Dupin.

"Why, yes; and not exactly that either. The fact is, we have all been a good deal puzzled because the affair is so simple, and yet baffles us altogether."

"Perhaps it is the very simplicity of the thing which puts you at fault," said my friend.

"What nonsense you *do* talk!" replied the Prefect, laughing heartily.

"Perhaps the mystery is a little *too* plain," said Dupin.

"Oh, good heavens! who ever heard of such an idea?"

"A little too self-evident."

"Ha! ha! ha!—ha! ha! ha!—ho! ho! ho!" roared our visitor, profoundly amused, "oh, Dupin, you will be the death of me yet!"

"And what, after all, *is* the matter on hand?" I asked.

"Why, I will tell you," replied the Prefect, as he gave a long, steady, and contemplative puff, and settled himself in his chair. "I will tell you in a few words; but, before I begin, let me caution you that this is an affair demanding the greatest secrecy, and that I should most probably lose the position I now hold, were it known that I confided it to any one."

"Proceed," said I.

"Or not," said Dupin.

"Well, then; I have received personal information, from a very high quarter, that a certain document of the last importance has been purloined from the royal apartments. The individual who purloined it is known; this beyond a doubt; he was seen to take it. It is known, also, that it still remains in his possession."

"How is this known?" asked Dupin.

"It is clearly inferred," replied the Prefect, "from the nature of the document, and from the non-appearance of certain results which would at once arise from its passing out of the robber's possession—that is to say, from his employing it as he must design in the end to employ it."

"Be a little more explicit," I said.

"Well, I may venture so far as to say that the paper gives its holder a certain power in a certain quarter where such power is immensely valuable." The Prefect was fond of the cant of diplomacy.

"Still I do not quite understand," said Dupin.

"No? Well; the disclosure of the document to a third person, who shall be nameless, would bring in question the honor of a personage of most exalted station; and this fact gives the holder of the document an ascendancy over the illustrious personage whose honor and peace are so jeopardized."

"But this ascendancy," I interposed, "would depend upon the robber's knowledge of the loser's knowledge of the robber. Who would dare—"

"The thief," said G., "is the Minister D——, who dares all things, those unbecoming as well as those becoming a man. The method of the theft was not less ingenious than bold. The document in question—a letter, to be frank—had been received by the personage robbed while in the royal *boudoir*. During its perusal she was suddenly interrupted by the entrance of the other exalted personage from whom especially it was her wish to conceal it. After a hurried and vain endeavor to thrust it in a drawer, she was forced to place it, open as it was, upon a table. The address, however, was uppermost, and, the contents thus unexposed, the letter escaped notice. At this juncture enters the Minister D——. His lynx eye immediately perceives the paper, recognizes the handwriting of the address, observes the confusion of the personage addressed, and fathoms her secret. After some business transactions, hurried through in his ordinary manner, he produces a letter somewhat similar to the one in question, opens it, pretends to read it, and then places it in close juxtaposition to the other. Again he converses, for some fifteen minutes, upon the public affairs. At length, in taking leave, he takes also from the table the letter to which he had no claim. Its rightful owner saw, but, of course, dared not call attention to the act, in the presence of the third personage who stood at her elbow. The minister decamped; leaving his own letter—one of no importance—upon the table."

"Here, then," said Dupin to me, "you have precisely what you demand to make the ascendancy complete—the robber's knowledge of the loser's knowledge of the robber."

"Yes," replied the Prefect; "and the power thus attained has, for some months past, been wielded, for political purposes, to a very dangerous extent. The personage robbed is more thoroughly convinced, every day, of the necessity of reclaiming her letter. But this, of course, cannot be done openly. In fine, driven to despair, she has committed the matter to me."

"Than whom," said Dupin, amid a perfect whirlwind of smoke, "no more sagacious agent could, I suppose, be desired, or even imagined."

"You flatter me," replied the Prefect; "but it is possible that some such opinion may have been entertained."

"It is clear," said I, "as you observe, that the letter is still in the possession of the minister; since it is this possession, and not any employment of the letter, which bestows the power. With the employment the power departs."

"True," said G.; "and upon this conviction I proceeded. My first care was to make thorough search of the minister's hotel;[4] and here my chief embarrassment lay in the necessity of searching without his knowledge. Beyond all things, I have been warned of the danger which would result from giving him reason to suspect our design."

"But," said I, "you are quite *au fait* in these investigations. The Parisian police have done this thing often before."

"Oh, yes; and for this reason I did not despair. The habits of the minister gave me, too, a great advantage. He is frequently absent from home all night. His servants are by no means numerous. They sleep at a distance from their master's apartment, and, being chiefly Neapolitans, are readily made drunk. I have keys, as you know, with which I can open any chamber or cabinet in Paris. For three months a night has not passed, during the greater part of which I have not been engaged, personally, in ransacking the D—— Hotel. My honor is interested, and, to mention a great secret, the reward is enormous. So I did not abandon the search until I had become fully satisfied that the thief is a more astute man than myself. I fancy that I have investigated every nook and corner of the premises in which it is possible that the paper can be concealed."

"But is it not possible," I suggested, "that although the letter may be in possession of the minister, as it unquestionably is, he may have concealed it elsewhere than upon his own premises?"

"This is barely possible," said Dupin. "The present peculiar condition of affairs at court, and especially of those intrigues in which D—— is known to be involved, would render the instant availability of the document—its susceptibility of being produced at a moment's notice—a point of nearly equal importance with its possession."

"Its susceptibility of being produced?" said I.

"That is to say, of being *destroyed*," said Dupin.

"True," I observed; "the paper is clearly then upon the premises. As for its being upon the person of the minister, we may consider that as out of the question."

"Entirely," said the Prefect. "He has been twice waylaid, as if by footpads, and his person rigidly searched under my own inspection."

"You might have spared yourself this trouble," said Dupin. "D——, I presume, is not altogether a fool, and, if not, must have anticipated these waylayings, as a matter of course."

"Not *altogether* a fool," said G., "but then he is a poet, which I take to be only one remove from a fool."

"True," said Dupin, after a long and thoughtful whiff from his meerschaum, "although I have been guilty of certain doggerel myself."

"Suppose you detail," said I, "the particulars of your search."

"Why, the fact is, we took our time, and we searched *everywhere*. I have had long experience in these affairs. I took the entire building, room by room; devoting the nights of a whole week to each. We examined, first, the furniture of each apartment. We opened every possible drawer; and I presume you know that, to a properly trained police-agent, such a thing as a '*secret*' drawer is impossible. Any man is a dolt who permits a '*secret*' drawer to escape him in a search of this kind. The thing is so plain. There is a certain amount of bulk—of space—to be accounted for in every cabinet. Then we have accurate rules. The fiftieth part of a line could not escape us. After the cabinets we took the chairs. The cushions we probed with the fine long needles you have seen me employ. From the tables we removed the tops."

"Why so?"

"Sometimes the top of a table, or other similarly arranged piece of furniture, is removed by the person wishing to conceal an article; then the leg is excavated, the article deposited within the cavity, and the top replaced. The bottoms and tops of bedposts are employed in the same way."

"But could not the cavity be detected by sounding?" I asked.

"By no means, if, when the article is deposited, a sufficient wadding of cotton be placed around it. Besides, in our case, we were obliged to proceed without noise."

"But you could not have removed—you could not have taken to pieces all articles of furniture in which it would have been possible to make a deposit in the manner you mention. A letter may be compressed into a thin spiral roll; not differing much in shape or bulk from a large knitting-needle, and in this form it might be inserted into the rung of a chair, for example. You did not take to pieces all the chairs?"

"Certainly not; but we did better—we examined the rungs of every chair in the hotel, and, indeed, the jointings of every description of furniture, by the aid of a most powerful microscope. Had there been any traces of recent disturbance we should not have failed to detect it instantly. A single grain of gimlet-dust, for example, would have been as obvious as an apple. Any disorder in the gluing—any unusual gaping in the joints—would have sufficed to insure detection."

"I presume you looked to the mirrors, between the boards and the plates, and you probed the beds and the bedclothes, as well as the curtains and carpets."

"That of course; and when we had absolutely completed every particle of furniture in this way, then we examined the house itself. We divided its entire surface into compartments, which we numbered, so that none might be missed; then we scrutinized each individual square inch throughout the premises, including the two houses immediately adjoining, with the microscope, as before."

"The two houses adjoining!" I exclaimed; "you must have had a great deal of trouble."

"We had; but the reward offered is prodigious."

"You included the *grounds* about the houses?"

"All the grounds are paved with brick. They gave us comparatively little trouble. We examined the moss between the bricks, and found it undisturbed."

"You looked among D——'s papers, of course, and into the books of the library?"

"Certainly; we opened every package and parcel; we not only opened every book, but we turned over every leaf in each volume, not contenting ourselves with a mere shake, according to the fashion of some of our police officers. We also measured the thickness of every book-*cover*, with the most accurate admeasurement, and applied to each the most jealous scrutiny of the microscope. Had any of the bindings been recently meddled with, it would have been utterly impossible that the fact should have escaped observation. Some five or six volumes, just from the hands of the binder, we carefully probed, longitudinally, with needles."

"You explored the floors beneath the carpets?"

"Beyond doubt. We removed every carpet, and examined the boards with the microscope."

"And the paper on the walls?"

"Yes."

"You looked into the cellars?"

"We did."

"Then," I said, "you have been making a miscalculation, and the letter is not upon the premises, as you suppose."

"I fear you are right there," said the Prefect. "And now, Dupin, what would you advise me to do?"

"To make a thorough research of the premises."

"That is absolutely needless," replied G——. "I am not more sure that I breathe than I am that the letter is not at the hotel."

"I have no better advice to give you," said Dupin. "You have, of course, an accurate description of the letter?"

"Oh, yes!"—And here the Prefect, producing a memorandum-book, proceeded to read aloud a minute account of the internal, and especially of the external, appearance of the missing document. Soon after finishing the perusal of this description, he took his departure, more entirely depressed in spirits than I had ever known the good gentleman before.

In about a month afterward he paid us another visit, and found us occupied very nearly as before. He took a pipe and a chair and entered into some ordinary conversation. At length I said:

"Well, But G., what of the purloined letter? I presume you have at last made up your mind that there is no such thing as overreaching the Minister?"

"Confound him, say I—yes; I made the re-examination, however, as Dupin suggested—but it was all labor lost, as I knew it would be."

"How much was the reward offered, did you say?" asked Dupin.

"Why, a very great deal—a *very* liberal reward—I don't like to say how much, precisely; but one thing I *will* say, that I wouldn't mind giving my individual check for fifty thousand francs to any one who could obtain me that letter. The fact is, it is becoming of more and more importance every day; and the reward has been lately doubled. If it were trebled, however, I could do no more than I have done."

"Why, yes," said Dupin, drawlingly, between the whiffs of his meerschaum, "I really—think, G., you have not exerted yourself—to the utmost in this matter. You might—do a little more, I think, eh?"

"How?—in what way?"

"Why—puff, puff—you might—puff, puff—employ counsel in the matter, eh?—puff, puff, puff. Do you remember the story they tell of Abernethy?"

"No; hang Abernethy!"

"To be sure! hang him and welcome. But, once upon a time, a certain rich miser conceived the design of sponging upon this Abernethy for a medical opinion. Getting up, for this purpose, an ordinary conversation in a private company, he insinuated his case to the physician, as that of an imaginary individual.

"'We will suppose,' said the miser, 'that his symptoms are such and such; now, doctor, what would *you* have directed him to take?'

"'Take!' said Abernethy, 'why, take *advice*, to be sure.'"

"But," said the Prefect, a little discomposed, "I am *perfectly* willing to take advice, and to pay for it. I would *really* give fifty thousand francs to any one who would aid me in the matter."

"In that case," replied Dupin, opening a drawer, and producing a check-book, "you may as well fill me up a check for the amount mentioned. When you have signed it, I will hand you the letter."

I was astounded. The Prefect appeared absolutely thunderstricken. For some minutes he remained speechless and motionless, looking incredulously at my friend with open mouth, and eyes that seemed starting from their sockets; then apparently recovering himself in some measure, he seized a pen, and after several pauses and vacant stares, finally filled up and signed a check for fifty thousand francs, and handed it across the table to Dupin. The latter examined it carefully and deposited it in his pocket-book; then, unlocking an *escritoire*, took thence a letter and gave it to the prefect. This functionary grasped it in a perfect agony of joy, opened it with a trembling hand, cast a rapid glance at its contents, and then, scrambling and struggling to the door, rushed at length unceremoniously from the room and from the house, without having uttered a syllable since Dupin had requested him to fill up the check.

When he had gone, my friend entered into some explanations.

"The Parisian police," he said, "are exceedingly able in their way. They are persevering, ingenious, cunning, and thoroughly versed in the knowledge which their duties seem chiefly to demand. Thus, when G—— detailed to us his mode of searching the premises at the Hotel D——, I felt entire confidence in his having made a satisfactory investigation—so far as his labors extended."

"So far as his labors extended?" said I.

"Yes," said Dupin. "The measures adopted were not only the best of their kind, but carried out to absolute perfection. Had the letter been deposited within the range of their search, these fellows would, beyond a question, have found it."

I merely laughed—but he seemed quite serious in all that he said.

"The measures, then," he continued, "were good in their kind, and well executed; their defect lay in their being inapplicable to the case and to the man. A certain set of highly ingenious resources are, with the Prefect, a sort of Procrustean bed, to which he forcibly adapts his designs. But he perpetually errs by being too deep or too shallow for the matter in hand; and many a school-boy is a better reasoner than he. I knew one about eight years of age, whose success at guessing in the game of 'even and odd' attracted universal admiration. This game is simple, and is played with marbles. One player holds in his hand a number of these toys, and demands of another whether that number is even or odd. If the guess is right, the guesser wins one; if wrong, he loses one. The boy to whom I allude won all the marbles of the school. Of course he had some principle of guessing; and this lay in mere observation and admeasurements of the astuteness of his opponents. For example, an arrant simpleton is his opponent, and holding up his closed hand, asks, 'Are they even or odd?' Our school-boy replies, 'Odd,' and loses; but upon the second trial he wins, for he then says to himself: 'The simpleton had them even upon the first trial, and his amount of cunning is just sufficient to make him have them odd upon the second; I will therefore guess odd';—he guesses odd, and wins. Now, with a simpleton a degree above the first, he would have reasoned thus: 'This fellow finds that in the first instance I guessed odd, and, in the second, he will propose to himself, upon the first impulse, a simple variation from even to odd, as did the first simpleton; but then a second thought will suggest that this is too simple a variation, and finally he will decide upon putting it even as before. I will therefore guess even';—he guesses even, and wins. Now this mode of reasoning in the school-boy, whom his fellows termed 'lucky,'—what, in its last analysis, is it?"

"It is merely," I said, "an identification of the reasoner's intellect with that of his opponent."

"It is," said Dupin; "and, upon inquiring of the boy by what means he effected the thorough identification in which his success consisted, I received answer as follows; 'When I wish to find out how wise, or how stupid or how good, or how wicked is any one, or what are his thoughts at the moment, I fashion the expression of my face, as accurately as possible, in accordance with the expression of his, and then wait to see what thoughts or sentiments arise in my mind or heart, as if to match or correspond with the expression.'

"This response of the school-boy lies at the bottom of all the spurious profundity which has been attributed to Rochefoucault, to La Bougive, to Machiavelli, and to Campanella."

"And the identification," I said, "of the reasoner's intellect with that of his opponent, depends, if I understand you aright, upon the accuracy with which the opponent's intellect is admeasured."

"For its practical value it depends upon this," replied Dupin; "and the Prefect and his cohort fail so frequently, first, by default of this identification and, secondly, by ill-admeasurement, or rather through non-admeasurement, of the intellect with which they are engaged. They consider only their *own* ideas of ingenuity; and, in searching for any thing hidden, advert only to the modes, in which *they* would have hidden it. They are right in this much—that their own ingenuity is a faithful representative of that of the *mass*; but when the cunning of the individual felon is diverse in character from their own, the felon foils them, of course. This always happens when it is above their own, and very usually when it is below. They have no variation of principle in their investigations; at best, when urged by some unusual emergency—by some extraordinary reward—they extend or exaggerate their old modes of *practice*, without touching their principles. What, for example, in this case of D——, has been done to vary the principle of action? What is all this boring, and probing, and sounding, and scrutinizing with the microscope, and dividing the surface of the building into registered square inches—what is it all but an exaggeration of the *application* of the one principle or set of principles of search, which are based upon the one set of notions regarding human ingenuity, to which the Prefect, in the long routine of his duty, has been accustomed? Do you not see he has taken it for granted that *all* men proceed to conceal a letter, not exactly in a gimlet-hole bored in a chair-leg, but, at least, in *some* out-of-the-way hole or corner suggested by the same tenor of thought which would urge a man to secrete a letter in a gimlet-hole bored in a chair-leg? And do you not see also, that such *recherchés* nooks for concealment are adapted only for ordinary occasions, and would be adopted only by ordinary intellects; for, in all cases of concealment, a disposal of the article concealed—a disposal of it in this *recherché* manner,—is, in the very first instance, presumable and presumed; and thus its discovery depends, not at all upon the acumen, but altogether upon the mere care, patience, and determination of the seekers; and where the case is of importance—or, what amounts to the same thing in the political eyes, when the reward is of magnitude,—the qualities in question have never been known to fail. You will now understand what I meant in suggesting that, had the purloined letter been hidden anywhere within the limits of the Prefect's examination—in other words, had the principle of its concealment been comprehended within the principles of the Prefect—its discovery would have been a matter altogether beyond question. This functionary, however, has been thoroughly mystified; and the remote source of his defeat lies in the supposition that the Minister is a fool, because he has acquired renown as a poet. All fools are poets; this the Prefect *feels*; and he is merely guilty of a *non distributio medii* in thence inferring that all poets are fools."

"But is this really the poet?" I asked. "There are two brothers, I know; and both have attained reputation in letters. The Minister I believe has written learnedly on the Differential Calculus. He is a mathematician, and no poet."

"You are mistaken; I know him well; he is both. As poet *and* mathematician, he would reason well; as mere mathematician, he could not have reasoned at all, and thus would have been at the mercy of the Prefect."

"You surprise me," I said, "by these opinions, which have been contradicted by the voice of the world. You do not mean to set at naught the well-digested idea of centuries. The mathematical reason has long been regarded as *the* reason *par excellence*."

"'*Il y a à parier*,'" replied Dupin, quoting from Chamfort, "'*que toute idée publique, toute convention reçue, est une sottise, car elle a convenu au plus grand nombre*.'⁵ The mathematicians, I grant you, have done their best to promulgate the popular error to which you allude, and which is none the less an error for its promulgation as truth. With an art worthy a better cause, for example, they have insinuated the term 'analysis' into application to algebra. The French are the originators of this particular deception; but if a term is of any importance—if words derive any value from applicability—then 'analysis' conveys 'algebra' about as much as, in Latin, '*ambitus*' implies 'ambition,' '*religio*' 'religion,' or '*homines honesti*' a set of *honorable* men."

"You have a quarrel on hand, I see," said I, "with some of the algebraists of Paris; but proceed."

"I dispute the availability, and thus the value, of that reason which is cultivated in any especial form other than the abstractly logical. I dispute, in particular, the reason educed by mathematical study. The mathematics are the science of form and quantity, mathematical reasoning is merely logic applied to observation upon form and quantity. The great error lies in supposing that even the truths of what is called *pure* algebra are abstract or general truths. And this error is so egregious that I am confounded at the universality with which it has been received. Mathematical axioms are *not* axioms of general truth. What is true of *relation*—of form and quantity—is often grossly false in regard to morals, for example. In this latter science it is very usually *un*true that the aggregated parts are equal to the whole. In chemistry also the axiom fails. In the consideration of motive it fails; for two motives, each of a given value, have not, necessarily, a value when united, equal to the sum of their values apart. There are numerous other mathematical truths which are only truths within the limits of *relation*. But the mathematician argues from his *finite truths*, through habit, as if they were of an absolutely general applicability—as the world indeed imagines them to be. Bryant, in his very learned 'Mythology,' mentions an analogous source of error, when he says that 'although the pagan fables are not believed, yet we forget ourselves continually, and make inferences from them as existing realities.' With the algebraists, however, who are pagans themselves, the 'pagan fables' *are* believed and the inferences are made, not so much through lapse of memory as through an unaccountable addling of the brains. In short, I never yet encountered the mere mathematician who would be trusted out of equal roots, or one who did not clandestinely hold it as a point of his faith that $x + px$ was absolutely and unconditionally equal to q. Say to one of these gentlemen, by way of experiment, if you please, that you believe occasions may occur where $x2 + px$ is not altogether equal to q, and, having made him understand what you mean, get out of his reach as speedily as convenient, for, beyond doubt, he will endeavor to knock you down.

"I mean to say," continued Dupin, while I merely laughed at his last observations, "that if the Minister had been no more than a mathematician, the Prefect would have been under no necessity of giving me this check. I knew him, however, as both mathematician and poet, and my measures were adapted to his capacity, with reference to the circumstances by which he was surrounded. I knew him as a courtier, too, and as a bold *intriguant*. Such a man, I considered, could not fail to be aware of the ordinary policial modes of action. He could not have failed to anticipate—and events have proved that he did not fail to anticipate—the waylayings to which he was subjected. He must have foreseen, I reflected, the secret investigations of his premises. His frequent absences from home at night, which were hailed by the Prefect as certain aids to his success, I regarded only as *ruses*, to afford opportunity for thorough search to the police, and thus the sooner to impress them with the conviction to which G——, in fact, did finally arrive—the conviction that the letter was not upon the premises. I felt, also, that the whole train of thought, which I was at some pains in detailing to you just now, concerning the invariable principle of policial action in searches for articles concealed—I felt that this whole train of thought would necessarily pass through the mind of the minister. It would imperatively lead him to despise all the ordinary *nooks* of concealment. *He* could not, I reflected, be so weak as not to see that the most intricate and remote recess of his hotel would be as open as his commonest closets to the eyes, to the probes, to the gimlets, and to the microscopes of the Prefect. I saw, in fine, that he would be driven, as a matter of course, to *simplicity*, if not deliberately induced to it as a matter of choice. You will remember, perhaps, how desperately the Prefect laughed when I suggested, upon our first interview, that it was just possible this mystery troubled him so much on account of its being so *very* self-evident."

"Yes," said I, "I remember his merriment well. I really thought he would have fallen into convulsions."

"The material world," continued Dupin, "abounds with very strict analogies to the immaterial; and thus some color of truth has been given to the rhetorical dogma, that metaphor, or simile, may be made to strengthen an argument as well as to embellish a description. The principle of the *vis inertiæ*, for example, seems to be identical in physics and metaphysics. It is not more true in the former, that a large body is with more difficulty set in motion than a smaller one, and that its subsequent *momentum* is commensurate with this difficulty, than it is, in the latter, that intellects of the vaster capacity, while more forcible, more constant, and more eventful in their movements than those of inferior grade, are yet the less readily moved, and more embarrassed, and full of hesitation in the first few steps of their progress. Again: have you ever noticed which of the street signs, over the shop doors, are the most attractive of attention?"

"I have never given the matter a thought," I said.

"There is a game of puzzles," he resumed, "which is played upon a map. One party playing requires another to find a given word—the name of town, river, state, or empire—any word, in short, upon the motley and perplexed surface of the chart. A novice in the game generally seeks to embarrass his opponents by giving them the most minutely lettered names; but the adept selects such words as stretch, in large characters, from one end of the chart to the other. These, like the over-largely lettered signs and placards of the street, escape observation by dint of being excessively obvious; and here the physical oversight is precisely analogous with the moral inapprehension by which the intellect suffers to pass unnoticed those considerations which are too obtrusively and too palpably self-evident. But this is a point, it appears, somewhat above or beneath the understanding of the Prefect. He never once thought it probable, or possible, that the minister had deposited the letter immediately beneath the nose of the whole world, by way of best preventing any portion of that world from perceiving it.

"But the more I reflected upon the daring, dashing, and discriminating ingenuity of D——; upon the fact that the document must always have been *at hand*, if he intended to use it to good purpose; and upon the decisive evidence, obtained by the Prefect, that it was not hidden within the limits of the dignitary's ordinary search— the more satisfied I became that, to conceal this letter, the minister had resorted to the comprehensive and sagacious expedient of not attempting to conceal it at all.

"Full of these ideas, I prepared myself with a pair of green spectacles, and called one fine morning, quite by accident, at the Ministerial hotel. I found D—— at home, yawning, lounging, and dawdling, as usual, and pretending to be in the last extremity of *ennui*. He is, perhaps, the most really energetic human being now alive—but that is only when nobody sees him.

"To be even with him, I complained of my weak eyes, and lamented the necessity of the spectacles, under cover of which I cautiously and thoroughly surveyed the whole apartment, while seemingly intent only upon the conversation of my host.

"I paid especial attention to a large writing-table near which he sat, and upon which lay confusedly, some miscellaneous letters and other papers, with one or two musical instruments and a few books. Here, however, after a long and very deliberate scrutiny, I saw nothing to excite particular suspicion.

"At length my eyes, in going the circuit of the room, fell upon a trumpery fili-gree card-rack of pasteboard, that hung dangling by a dirty blue ribbon, from a little brass knob just beneath the middle of the mantelpiece. In this rack, which had three or four compartments, were five or six visiting cards and a solitary letter. This last was much soiled and crumpled. It was torn nearly in two, across the middle—as if a design, in the first instance, to tear it entirely up as worthless, had been altered, or stayed, in the second. It had a large black seal, bearing the D—— cipher *very* conspicuously, and was addressed, in a diminutive female hand, to D——, the minister himself. It was thrust carelessly, and even, as it seemed, contemptuously, into one of the uppermost divisions of the rack.

"No sooner had I glanced at this letter than I concluded it to be that of which I was in search. To be sure, it was, to all appearance, radically different from the one of which the Prefect had read us so minute a description. Here the seal was large and black, with the D—— cipher; there it was small and red, with the ducal arms of the S—— family. Here, the address, to the minister, was diminutive and feminine; there the superscription, to a certain royal personage, was markedly bold and decided; the size alone formed a point of correspondence. But, then, the *radicalness* of these differences, which was excessive; the dirt; the soiled and torn condition of the paper, so inconsistent with the *true* methodical habits of D——, and so suggestive of a design to delude the beholder into an idea of the worthlessness of the document;—these things, together with the hyperobtrusive situation of this document, full in the view of every visitor, and thus exactly in accordance with the conclusions to which I had previously arrived; these things, I say, were strongly corrobative of suspicion, in one who came with the intention to suspect.

"I protracted my visit as long as possible, and, while I maintained a most animated discussion with the minister, upon a topic which I knew well had never failed to interest and excite him, I kept my attention really riveted upon the letter. In this examination, I committed to memory its external appearance and arrangement in the rack; and also fell, at length, upon a discovery which set at rest whatever trivial doubt I might have entertained. In scrutinizing the edges of the paper, I observed them to be more *chafed* than seemed necessary. They presented the *broken* appearance which is manifested when a stiff paper, having been once folded and pressed with a folder, is refolded in a reversed direction, in the same creases or edges which had formed the original fold. This discovery was sufficient. It was clear to me that the letter had been turned, as a glove, inside out, redirected and re-sealed. I bade the minister good-morning, and took my departure at once, leaving a gold snuff-box upon the table.

"The next morning I called for the snuff-box, when we resumed, quite eagerly, the conversation of the preceding day. While thus engaged, however, a loud report, as if of a pistol, was heard immediately beneath the windows of the hotel, and was succeeded by a series of fearful screams, and the shoutings of a terrified mob. D—— rushed to a casement, threw it open, and looked out. In the meantime I stepped to the card-rack, took the letter, put it in my pocket, and replaced it by a *facsimile*, (so far as regards externals) which I had carefully prepared at my lodgings—imitating the D—— cipher, very readily, by means of a seal formed of bread.

"The disturbance in the street had been occasioned by the frantic behavior of a man with a musket. He had fired it among a crowd of women and children. It proved, however, to have been without ball, and the fellow was suffered to go his way as a lunatic or a drunkard. When he had gone, D—— came from the window, whither I had followed him immediately upon securing the object in view. Soon afterward I bade him farewell. The pretended lunatic was a man in my own pay."

"But what purpose had you," I asked, "in replacing the letter by a facsimile? Would it not have been better, at the first visit, to have seized it openly, and departed?"

"D——," replied Dupin, "is a desperate man, and a man of nerve. His hotel, too, is not without attendants devoted to his interests. Had I made the wild attempt you suggest, I might never have left the Ministerial presence alive. The good people of Paris might have heard of me no more. But I had an object apart from these considerations. You know my political prepossessions. In this matter, I act as a partisan of the lady concerned. For eighteen months the Minister has had her in his power. She has now him in hers—since, being unaware that the letter is not in his possession, he will proceed with his exactions as if it was. Thus will he inevitably commit himself, at once, to his political destruction. His downfall, too, will not be more precipitate than awkward. It is all very well to talk about the *facilis descensus Averni*;[6] but in all kinds of climbing, as Catalani said of singing, it is far more easy to get up than to come down. In the present instance I have no sympathy—at least no pity—for him who descends. He is that *monstrum horrendum*, an unprincipled man of genius. I confess, however, that I should like very well to know the precise character of his thoughts, when, being defied by her whom the Prefect terms 'a certain personage,' he is reduced to opening the letter which I left for him in the card-rack."

"How? Did you put any thing particular in it?"

"Why—it did not seem altogether right to leave the interior blank—that would have been insulting. D——, at Vienna once, did me an evil turn, which I told him, quite good-humoredly, that I should remember. So, as I knew he would feel some curiosity in regard to the identity of the person who had outwitted him, I thought it a pity not to give him a clew. He is well acquainted with my MS.,[7] and I just copied into the middle of the blank sheet the words—

"'——Un dessein si funeste,
S'il n'est digne d'Atrée, est digne de Thyeste.'[8]

They are to be found in Crébillon's 'Atrée.' "

1. Nothing is more offensive to the wise than an excess of trickery.
2. On the third floor above the ground in a fashionable district in Paris.
3. These are the subjects of previous detective stories by Poe.
4. "Hotel" in the French sense: a large building; in the case a private house in the city.
5. "The odds are that any public idea or accepted opinion is stupid, because it has suited the majority of people."
6. "The easy descent to Hell" as described by Vergil in *The Aeneid*.
7. MS—handwriting.
8. "A scheme so horrible, / If it is unworthy of Atreus, is worthy of Thyestes." The allusion is to a particularly revolting episode of revenge in Greek mythology.

Katherine Anne Porter

Katherine Anne Porter was born in 1890 in Indian Creek, Texas, and educated in schools in Texas and Louisiana. She ran away from New Orleans to get married at age sixteen; the union did not last. At twenty-one, she took off for Chicago where she did newspaper work and, on assignment, inadvertently found herself in a line-up for movie auditions. She sang Scottish ballads in costume, spent time in a sanatorium, and did more newspaper work in Denver, all the while writing. Towards the end of World War I, she almost died from influenza, like Miranda in *Pale Horse, Pale Rider*; the experience profoundly altered her life: "It simply just divided my life, cut across it like that. So that everything before that was just getting ready, and after that I was in some strange way altered, ready. It took me a long time to go out and live in the world again. I was really 'alienated' in the pure sense. It was, I think, the fact that I really had participated in death, that I knew what death was, and had almost experienced it. I had what the Christians call the 'beatific vision,' and the Greeks called the 'happy day,' the happy vision just before death. Now if you have had that, and survived it, come back from it, you are no longer like other people, and there's no use deceiving yourself that you are. But you see, I did: I made the mistake of thinking I was quite like everybody else, of trying to live like other people. It took me a long time to realize that that simply wasn't true, that I had my own needs and that I had to live like me."

Living "like me" involved taking off to Mexico, ostensibly to study Aztec and Mayan art designs, and becoming involved in the Obrégon Revolution of 1921; it also involved resisting conventional roles for women and harnessing her energies to write. "You're brought up with the notion of feminine chastity and inaccessibility, yet with the curious idea of feminine availability in all spiritual ways, and in giving service to anyone who demands it. And I suppose that's why it has taken me twenty years to write this novel [*Ship of Fools*]; it's been interrupted by just anyone who could jimmy his way into my life." Her first collection of stories, *Flowering Judas*, was published in 1930. A Guggenheim Fellowship took her to Berlin, Basel, and Madrid; her return to the U.S. was marked by numerous awards, periods of teaching and lecturing, and the publication of *Hacienda* (1934), *Noon Wine* (1937), *Pale Horse, Pale Rider* (1939), *The Leaning Tower and Other Stories* (1944), a book of essays called *The Days*

Before (1952), *Ship of Fools* (1962), and *The Collected Essays and Occasional Writings of Katherine Anne Porter* (1970). She died in 1980.

Writing, Porter says, in *The Paris Review* interview, "is an act of faith. But one of the marks of a gift is to have the courage of it." "Art is a vocation as much as anything in this world. For the real artist, it is the most natural thing in the world, not as necessary as air and water, perhaps, but as food and water. But we really do lead almost a monastic life, you know; to follow it you very often have to give up something."

"So, I shall tell the truth," Porter says in "My First Speech," discussing the origin of her characters, "but the result will be fiction. It is a curious long process, roundabout to the last degree, like a slow chemical change, and I believe it holds true as much when one is not recreating one's own life and past but the life-history of another person. I think there are very few living characters in fiction who were not founded on a real living original. . . . I should dare say that none of these characters so living in fiction would have recognized their own portraits, for if the transformation is successful the character becomes something else in its own right, as alive as the person who posed for the portrait."

Porter rejects nihilism and cultivated violence in art just as readily as she rejects the autobiographical: "Human life itself may be almost pure chaos, but the work of the artist—the only thing he's good for—is to take these handfuls of confusion and disparate things, things that seem to be irreconcilable, and put them together in a frame to give them some kind of shape and meaning." However, this does not mean that she thinks art must please or prettify: "artists do not always create a pleasant world, because that is not their business. If they do that, you will be right not to trust them in anything. We must all leave that to people whose affair it is, to smooth our daily existence a little. Great art is hardly ever agreeable; the artist should remind you that, for some, experience is a horror in this world, and that the human imagination also knows horror. He should direct you to points of view you have not examined before, or cause you to comprehend, even if you do not sympathize with predicaments not your own, ways of life, manners of speech, even of dress, above all of the unique human heart, outside of your normal experience. And this can better be done by presentation than by argument. This presentation must be real, with a truth beyond the artist's own prejudices, loves, hates; I mean his personal ones. The outright propagandist sets up in me such a fury of opposition I am not apt to care much whether he has got his facts straight or not."

She was a firm advocate of craftsmanship and more than once described herself as a worker, a carpenter, even a bricklayer: "In the work of art, nothing can be accidental: the sprawling, chaotic sense of that word as we use it in everyday life, where so many things happen to us that we by no means plan, it takes craftsmanship quite often beyond our powers to manage to plan even a short day for ourselves. The craftsmanship of the artist can make what he wishes of anything that excites his imagination. Craftsmanship is a homely, workaday thing. It is a little like making shoes, or weaving cloth. A writer may be inspired occasionally: that's his good luck; but he doesn't learn to write by inspiration: he works at it. In that sense the writer is a worker, a workingman, a workingwoman. Writing is not an elegant pastime, it is a sober and hardworked trade, which gives great joy to the worker. The artist is first a worker. He must roll up his sleeves and get to work like a bricklayer." In a similar letter to Edward Schwartz, she says that one of her works "was written in one single sitting in a great burst of emotional recollection yet with my mind working soberly as a carpenter at his bench, choosing the right pieces and cutting them to shape and scale—this is not duality, not really, but we have many faculties material and immaterial and they work together harmoniously sometimes. . . ."

Porter, in "No Plot, My Dear, No Story," says, "Except in emergencies, when you are trying to manufacture a quick tale and make some easy money, you don't really need a plot." She claims to "love the purity of language . . . the basic pure human speech that exists in every language" but to detest the abuses language has undergone, the jargon of trades, professions, and vested interests. In response to a question about style, however, she says: "I've been called a stylist until I really could tear my hair out. And I simply don't believe in style. The style is you. . . . You do not create a style. You work, and develop yourself; your style is an emanation from your own being."

Flowering Judas

Braggioni sits heaped upon the edge of a straight-backed chair much too small for him, and sings to Laura in a furry, mournful voice. Laura has begun to find reasons for avoiding her own house until the latest possible moment, for Braggioni is there almost every night. No matter how late she is, he will be sitting there with a surly, waiting expression, pulling at his kinky yellow hair, thumbing the strings of his guitar, snarling a tune under his breath. Lupe the Indian maid meets Laura at the door, and says with a flicker of a glance towards the upper room, "He waits."

Laura wishes to lie down, she is tired of her hairpins and the feel of her long tight sleeves, but she says to him, "Have you a new song for me this evening?" If he says yes, she asks him to sing it. If he says no, she remembers his favorite one, and asks him to sing it again. Lupe brings her a cup of chocolate and a plate of rice, and Laura eats at the small table under the lamp, first inviting Braggioni, whose answer is always the same: "I have eaten, and besides, chocolate thickens the voice."

Laura says, "Sing, then," and Braggioni heaves himself into song. He scratches the guitar familiarly as though it were a pet animal, and sings passionately off key, taking the high notes in a prolonged painful squeal. Laura, who haunts the markets listening to the ballad singers, and stops every day to hear the blind boy playing his reed-flute in Sixteenth of September Street, listens to Braggioni with pitiless courtesy, because she dares not smile at his miserable performance. Nobody dares to smile at him. Braggioni is cruel to everyone, with a kind of specialized insolence, but he is so vain of his talents, and so sensitive to slights, it would require a cruelty and vanity greater than his own to lay a finger on the vast cureless wound of his self-esteem. It would require courage, too, for it is dangerous to offend him, and nobody has this courage.

Braggioni loves himself with such tenderness and amplitude and eternal charity that his followers—for he is a leader of men, a skilled revolutionist, and his skin has been punctured in honorable warfare—warm themselves in the reflected glow, and say to each other: "He has a real nobility, a love of humanity raised above mere personal affections." The excess of this self-love has flowed out, inconveniently for her, over Laura, who, with so many others, owes her comfortable situation and her salary to him. When he is in a a very good humor, he tells her, "I am tempted to forgive you for being a *gringa. Gringita!*" and Laura, burning, imagines herself leaning forward suddenly, and with a sound back-handed slap wiping the suety smile from his face. If he notices her eyes at these moments he gives no sign.

She knows what Braggioni would offer her, and she must resist tenaciously without appearing to resist, and if she could avoid it she would not admit even to herself the slow drift of his intention. During these long evenings which have spoiled a long month for her, she sits in her deep chair with an open book on her knees, resting her eyes on the consoling rigidity of the printed page when the sight and sound of Braggioni singing threaten to identify themselves with all her remembered afflictions and to add their weight to her uneasy premonitions of the future. The gluttonous bulk of Braggioni has become a symbol of her many disillusions, for a revolutionist should be lean, animated by heroic faith, a vessel of abstract virtues. This is nonsense, she knows it now and is ashamed of it. Revolution must have leaders, and leadership is a career for energetic men. She is, her comrades tell her, full of romantic error, for what she defines as cynicism in them is merely "a developed sense of reality." She is almost too willing to say, "I am wrong, I suppose I don't really understand the principles," and afterward she makes a secret truce with herself, determined not to surrender her will to such expedient logic. But she cannot help feeling that she has been betrayed irreparably by the disunion between her way of living and her feeling of what life should be, and at times she is almost contented to rest in this sense of grievance as a private store of consolation. Sometimes she wishes to run away, but she stays. Now she longs to fly out of this room, down the narrow stairs, and into the street where the houses lean together like conspirators under a single mottled lamp, and leave Braggioni singing to himself.

Instead she looks at Braggioni, frankly and clearly, like a good child who understands the rules of behavior. Her knees cling together under sound blue serge, and her round white collar is not purposely nun-like. She wears the uniform of an idea, and has renounced vanities. She was born Roman Catholic, and in spite of her fear of being seen by someone who might make a scandal of it, she slips now and again into some crumbling little church, kneels on the chilly stone, and says a Hail Mary on the gold rosary she bought in Tehuantepec. It is no good and she ends by examining the altar with its tinsel flowers and ragged brocades, and feels tender about the battered doll-shape of some male saint whose white, lace-trimmed drawers hang limply around his ankles below the hieratic dignity of his velvet robe. She has encased herself in a set of principles derived from her early training, leaving no detail of gesture or of personal taste untouched, and for this reason she will not wear lace made on machines. This is her private heresy, for in her special group the machine is sacred, and will be the salvation of the workers. She loves fine lace, and there is a tiny edge of fluted cobweb on this collar, which is one of twenty precisely alike, folded in blue tissue paper in the upper drawer of her clothes chest.

Braggioni catches her glance solidly as if he had been waiting for it, leans forward, balancing his paunch between his spread knees, and sings with tremendous emphasis, weighing his words. He has, the song relates, no father and no mother, nor even a friend to console him; lonely as a wave of the sea he comes and goes, lonely as a wave. His mouth opens round and yearns sideways, his balloon cheeks grow oily with the labor of song. He bulges marvelously in his expensive garments. Over his lavender collar, crushed upon a purple necktie, held by a diamond hoop: over his ammunition belt of tooled leather worked in silver, buckled cruelly around his gasping middle: over the tops of his glossy yellow shoes Braggioni swells with ominous ripeness, his mauve silk hose stretched taut, his ankles bound with the stout leather thongs of his shoes.

When he stretches his eyelids at Laura she notes again that his eyes are the true tawny yellow cat's eyes. He is rich, not in money, he tells her, but in power, and this power brings with it the blameless ownership of things, and the right to indulge his love of small luxuries. "I have a taste for the elegant refinements," he said once, flourishing a yellow silk handkerchief before her nose. "Smell that? It is Jockey Club, imported from New York." Nonetheless he is wounded by life. He will say so presently. "It is true everything turns to dust in the hand, to gall on the tongue." He sighs and his leather belt creaks like a saddle girth. "I am disappointed in everything as it comes. Everything." He shakes his head. "You, poor thing, you will be disappointed too. You are born for it. We are more alike than you realize in some things. Wait and see. Some day you will remember what I have told you, you will know that Braggioni was your friend."

Laura feels a slow chill, a purely physical sense of danger, a warning in her blood that violence, mutilation, a shocking death, wait for her with lessening patience. She has translated this fear into something homely, immediate, and sometimes hesitates before crossing the street. "My personal fate is nothing, except as the testimony of a mental attitude," she reminds herself, quoting from some forgotten philosophic primer, and is sensible enough to add, "Anyhow, I shall not be killed by an automobile if I can help it."

"It may be true I am as corrupt, in another way, as Braggioni," she thinks in spite of herself, "as callous, as incomplete," and if this is so, any kind of death seems preferable. Still she sits quietly, she does not run. Where could she go? Uninvited she has promised herself to this place; she can no longer imagine herself as living in another country, and there is no pleasure in remembering her life before she came here.

Precisely what is the nature of this devotion, its true motives, and what are its obligations? Laura cannot say. She spends part of her days in Xochimilco, near by, teaching Indian children to say in English, "The cat is on the mat." When she appears in the classroom they crowd about her with smiles on their wise, inno- cent, clay-colored faces, crying, "Good morning, my titcher!" in immaculate voices, and they make of her desk a fresh garden of flowers every day.

During her leisure she goes to union meetings and listens to busy important voices quarreling over tactics, methods, internal politics. She visits the prisoners of her own political faith in their cells, where they entertain themselves with counting cockroaches, repenting of their indiscretions, composing their memoirs, writing out manifestoes and plans for their comrades who are still walking about free, hands in pockets, sniffing fresh air. Laura brings them food and cigarettes and a little money, and she brings messages disguised in equivocal phrases from the men outside who dare not set foot in the prison for fear of disappearing into the cells kept empty for them. If the prisoners confuse night and day, and complain, "Dear little Laura, time doesn't pass in this infernal hole, and I won't know when it is time to sleep unless I have a reminder," she brings them their favorite narcotics, and says in a tone that does not wound them with pity, "Tonight will really be night for you," and though her Spanish amuses them, they find her comforting, useful. If they lose patience and all faith, and curse the slowness of their friends in coming to their rescue with money and influence, they trust her not to repeat everything, and if she inquires, "Where do you think we can find money, or influence?" they are certain to answer, "Well, there is Braggioni, why doesn't he do something?"

She smuggles letters from headquarters to men hiding from firing squads in back streets in mildewed houses, where they sit in tumbled beds and talk bitterly as if all Mexico were at their heels, when Laura knows positively they might appear at the band concert in the Alameda on Sunday morning, and no one would notice them. But Braggioni says, "Let them sweat a little. The next time they may be careful. It is very restful to have them out of the way for a while." She is not afraid to knock on any door in any street after midnight, and enter in the darkness, and say to one of these men who is really in danger: "They will be looking for you—seriously—tomorrow morning after six. Here is some money from Vicente. Go to Vera Cruz and wait."

She borrows money from the Roumanian agitator to give to his bitter enemy the Polish agitator. The favor of Braggioni is their disputed territory, and Brag- gioni holds the balance nicely, for he can use them both. The Polish agitator talks love to her over café tables, hoping to exploit what he believes is her secret senti- mental preference for him, and he gives her misinformation which he begs her to repeat as the solemn truth to certain persons. The Roumanian is more adroit. He is generous with his money in all good causes, and lies to her with an air of ingen- uous candor, as if he were her good friend and confidant. She never repeats any- thing they may say. Braggioni never asks questions. He has other ways to discover all that he wishes to know about them.

Nobody touches her, but all praise her gray eyes, and the soft, round under lip which promises gayety, yet is always grave, nearly always firmly closed: and they cannot understand why she is in Mexico. She walks back and forth on her errands, with puzzled eyebrows, carrying her little folder of drawings and music and school papers. No dancer dances more beautifully than Laura walks, and she inspires some amusing, unexpected ardors, which cause little gossip, because nothing comes of them. A young captain who had been a soldier in Zapata's army attempted, during a horseback ride near Cuernavaca, to express his desire for her with the noble simplicity befitting a rude folk-hero: but gently, because he was gentle. This gentleness was his defeat, for when he alighted, and removed her foot from the stirrup, and essayed to draw her down into his arms, her horse, ordinarily a tame one, shied fiercely, reared and plunged away. The young hero's horse careered blindly after his stable-mate, and the hero did not return to the hotel until rather late that evening. At breakfast he came to her table in full charro dress, gray buckskin jacket and trousers with strings of silver buttons down the leg, and he was in a humorous, careless mood. "May I sit with you?" and "You are a wonderful rider. I was terrified that you might be thrown and dragged. I should never have forgiven myself. But I cannot admire you enough for your riding!"

"I learned to ride in Arizona," said Laura.

"If you will ride with me again this morning, I promise you a horse that will not shy with you," he said. But Laura remembered that she must return to Mexico City at noon.

Next morning the children made a celebration and spent their playtime writing on the blackboard, "We lov ar ticher," and with tinted chalks they drew wreaths of flowers around the words. The young hero wrote her a letter: "I am a very foolish, wasteful, impulsive man. I should have first said I love you, and then you would not have run away. But you shall see me again." Laura thought, "I must send him a box of colored crayons," but she was trying to forgive herself for having spurred her horse at the wrong moment.

A brown, shock-haired youth came and stood in her patio one night and sang like a lost soul for two hours, but Laura could think of nothing to do about it. The moonlight spread a wash of gauzy silver over the clear spaces of the garden, and the shadows were cobalt blue. The scarlet blossoms of the Judas tree were dull purple, and the names of the colors repeated themselves automatically in her mind, while she watched not the boy, but his shadow, fallen like a dark garment across the fountain rim, trailing in the water. Lupe came silently and whispered expert counsel in her ear: "If you will throw him one little flower, he will sing another song or two and go away." Laura threw the flower, and he sang a last song and went away with the flower tucked in the band of his hat. Lupe said, "He is one of the organizers of the Typographers Union, and before that he sold corridos in the Merced market, and before that, he came from Guanajuato, where I was born. I would not trust any man, but I trust least those from Guanajuato."

She did not tell Laura that he would be back again the next night, and the next, nor that he would follow her at a certain fixed distance around the Merced market, through the Zócolo, up Francisco I. Madero Avenue, and so along the Paseo de la Reforma to Chapultepec Park, and into the Philosopher's Footpath, still with that flower withering in his hat, and an indivisible attention in his eyes.

Now Laura is accustomed to him, it means nothing except that he is nineteen years old and is observing a convention with all propriety, as though it were founded on a law of nature, which in the end it might well prove to be. He is beginning to write poems which he prints on a wooden press, and he leaves them stuck like handbills in her door. She is pleasantly disturbed by the abstract, unhurried watchfulness of his black eyes which will in time turn easily towards another object. She tells herself that throwing the flower was a mistake, for she is twenty-two years old and knows better; but she refuses to regret it, and persuades herself that her negation of all external events as they occur is a sign that she is gradually perfecting herself in the stoicism she strives to cultivate against that disaster she fears, though she cannot name it.

She is not at home in the world. Every day she teaches children who remain strangers to her, though she loves their tender round hands and their charming opportunist savagery. She knocks at unfamiliar doors not knowing whether a friend or a stranger shall answer, and even if a known face emerges from the sour gloom of that unknown interior, still it is the face of a stranger. No matter what this stranger says to her, nor what her message to him, the very cells of her flesh reject knowledge and kinship in one monotonous word. No. No. No. She draws her strength from this one holy talismanic word which does not suffer her to be led into evil. Denying everything, she may walk anywhere in safety, she looks at everything without amazement.

No, repeats this firm unchanging voice of her blood; and she looks at Braggioni without amazement. He is a great man, he wishes to impress this simple girl who covers her great round breasts with thick dark cloth, and who hides long, invaluably beautiful legs under a heavy skirt. She is almost thin except for the incomprehensible fullness of her breasts, like a nursing mother's, and Braggioni, who considers himself a judge of women, speculates again on the puzzle of her notorious virginity, and takes the liberty of speech which she permits without a sign of modesty, indeed, without any sort of sign, which is disconcerting.

"You think you are so cold, *gringita!* Wait and see. You will surprise yourself some day! May I be there to advise you!" He stretches his eyelids at her, and his ill-humored cat's eyes waver in a separate glance for the two points of light marking the opposite ends of a smoothly drawn path between the swollen curve of her breasts. He is not put off by that blue serge, nor by her resolutely fixed gaze. There is all the time in the world. His cheeks are bellying with the wind of song. "O girl with the dark eyes," he sings, and reconsiders. "But yours are not dark. I can change all that. O girl with the green eyes, you have stolen my heart away!" then his mind wanders to the song, and Laura feels the weight of his attention being shifted elsewhere. Singing thus, he seems harmless, he is quite harmless, there is nothing to do but sit patiently and say "No," when the moment comes. She draws a full breath, and her mind wanders also, but not far. She dares not wander too far.

Not for nothing has Braggioni taken pains to be a good revolutionist and a professional lover of humanity. He will never die of it. He has the malice, the cleverness, the wickedness, the sharpness of wit, the hardness of heart, stipulated for loving the world profitably. *He will never die of it.* He will live to see himself kicked out from his feeding trough by other hungry world-saviors. Traditionally he must sing in spite of his life which drives him to bloodshed, he tells Laura, for his father was a Tuscany peasant who drifted to Yucatan and married a Maya woman: a woman of race, an aristocrat. They gave him the love and knowledge of music, thus: and under the rip of his thumbnail, the strings of the instrument complain like exposed nerves.

Once he was called Delgadito by all the girls and married women who ran after him; he was so scrawny all his bones showed under his thin cotton clothing, and he could squeeze his emptiness to the very backbone with his two hands. He was a poet and the revolution was only a dream then; too many women loved him and sapped away his youth, and he could never find enough to eat anywhere, anywhere! Now he is a leader of men, crafty men who whisper in his ear, hungry men who wait for hours outside his office for a word with him, emaciated men with wild faces who waylay him at the street gate with a timid, "Comrade, let me tell you . . ." and they blow the foul breath from their empty stomachs in his face.

He is always sympathetic. He gives them handfuls of small coins from his own pocket, he promises them work, there will be demonstrations, they must join the unions and attend the meetings, above all they must be on the watch for spies. They are closer to him than his own brothers, without them he can do nothing—until tomorrow, comrade!

Until tomorrow. "They are stupid, they are lazy, they are treacherous, they would cut my throat for nothing," he says to Laura. He has good food and abundant drink, he hires an automobile and drives in the Paseo on Sunday morning, and enjoys plenty of sleep in a soft bed beside a wife who dares not disturb him; and he sits pampering his bones in easy billows of fat, singing to Laura, who knows and thinks these things about him. When he was fifteen, he tried to drown himself because he loved a girl, his first love, and she laughed at him. "A thousand women have paid for that," and his tight little mouth turns down at the corners. Now he perfumes his hair with Jockey Club, and confides to Laura: "One woman is really as good as another for me, in the dark. I prefer them all."

His wife organizes unions among the girls in the cigarette factories, and walks in picket lines, and even speaks at meetings in the evening. But she cannot be brought to acknowledge the benefits of true liberty. "I tell her I must have my freedom, net. She does not understand my point of view." Laura has heard this many times. Braggioni scratches the guitar and meditates. "She is an instinctively virtuous woman, pure gold, no doubt of that. If she were not, I should lock her up, and she knows it."

His wife, who works so hard for the good of the factory girls, employs part of her leisure lying on the floor weeping because there are so many women in the world, and only one husband for her, and she never knows where nor when to look for him. He told her: "Unless you can learn to cry when I am not here, I must go away for good." That day he went away and took a room at the Hotel Madrid.

It is this month of separation for the sake of higher principles that has been spoiled not only for Mrs. Braggioni, whose sense of reality is beyond criticism, but for Laura, who feels herself bogged in a nightmare. Tonight Laura envies Mrs.

Braggioni, who is alone, and free to weep as much as she pleases about a concrete wrong. Laura has just come from a visit to the prison, and she is waiting for tomorrow with a bitter anxiety as if tomorrow may not come, but time may be caught immovably in this hour, with herself transfixed, Braggioni singing on forever, and Eugenio's body not yet discovered by the guard.

Braggioni says: "Are you going to sleep?" Almost before she can shake her head, he begins telling her about the May-day disturbances coming on in Morelia, for the Catholics hold a festival in honor of the Blessed Virgin, and the Socialists celebrate their martyrs on that day. "There will be two independent processions, starting from either end of town, and they will march until they meet, and the rest depends . . ." He asks her to oil and load his pistols. Standing up, he unbuckles his ammunition belt, and spreads it laden across her knees. Laura sits with the shells slipping through the cleaning cloth dipped in oil, and he says again he cannot understand why she works so hard for the revolutionary idea unless she loves some man who is in it. "Are you not in love with someone?" "No," says Laura. "And no one is in love with you?" "No." "Then it is your own fault. No woman need go begging. Why, what is the matter with you? The legless beggar woman in the Alameda has a perfectly faithful lover. Did you know that?"

Laura peers down the pistol barrel and says nothing, but a long, slow faintness rises and subsides in her; Braggioni curves his swollen fingers around the throat of the guitar and softly smothers the music out of it, and when she hears him again he seems to have forgotten her, and is speaking in the hypnotic voice he uses when talking in small rooms to a listening, close-gathered crowd. Some day this world, now seemingly so composed and eternal, to the edges of every sea shall be merely a tangle of gaping trenches, of crashing walls and broken bodies. Everything must be torn from its accustomed place where it has rotted for centuries, hurled skyward and distributed, cast down again clean as rain, without separate identity. Nothing shall survive that the stiffened hands of poverty have created for the rich and no one shall be left alive except the elect spirits destined to procreate a new world cleansed of cruelty and injustice, ruled by benevolent anarchy: "Pistols are good, I love them, cannon are even better, but in the end I pin my faith to good dynamite," he concludes, and strokes the pistol lying in her hands. "Once I dreamed of destroying this city, in case it offered resistance to General Ortíz, but it fell into his hands like an overripe pear."

He is made restless by his own words, rises and stands waiting. Laura holds up the belt to him: "Put that on, and go kill somebody in Morelia, and you will be happier," she says softly. The presence of death in the room makes her bold. "Today, I found Eugenio going into a stupor. He refused to allow me to call the prison doctor. He had taken all the tablets I brought him yesterday. He said he took them because he was bored."

"He is a fool, and his death is his own business," says Braggioni, fastening his belt carefully.

"I told him if he had waited only a little while longer, you would have got him set free," says Laura. "He said he did not want to wait."

"He is a fool and we are well rid of him," says Braggioni, reaching for his hat.

He goes away. Laura knows his mood has changed, she will not see him any more for a while. He will send word when he needs her to go on errands into strange streets, to speak to the strange faces that will appear, like clay masks with the power of human speech, to mutter their thanks to Braggioni for his help. Now she is free, and she thinks, I must run while there is time. But she does not go.

Braggioni enters his own house where for a month his wife has spent many hours every night weeping and tangling her hair upon her pillow. She is weeping now, and she weeps more at the sight of him, the cause of all her sorrows. He looks about the room. Nothing is changed, the smells are good and familiar, he is well acquainted with the woman who comes toward him with no reproach except grief on her face. He says to her tenderly: "You are so good, please don't cry any more, you dear good creature." She says, "Are you tired, my angel? Sit here and I will wash your feet." She brings a bowl of water, and kneeling, unlaces his shoes, and when from her knees she raises her sad eyes under her blackened lids, he is sorry for everything, and bursts into tears. "Ah, yes, I am hungry, I am tired, let us eat something together," he says, between sobs. His wife leans her head on his arm and says, "Forgive me!" and this time he is refreshed by the solemn, endless rain of her tears.

Laura takes off her serge dress and puts on a white linen nightgown and goes to bed. She turns her head a little to one side, and lying still, reminds herself that it is time to sleep. Numbers tick in her brain like little clocks, soundless doors close of themselves around her. If you would sleep, you must not remember anything, the children will say tomorrow, good morning, my teacher, the poor prisoners who come every day bringing flowers to their jailor. 1-2-3-4-5—it is monstrous to confuse love with revolution, night with day, life with death—ah, Eugenio!

The tolling of the midnight bell is a signal, but what does it mean? Get up, Laura, and follow me: come out of your sleep, out of your bed, out of this strange house. What are you doing in this house? Without a word, without fear she rose and reached for Eugenio's hand, but he eluded her with a sharp, sly smile and drifted away. This is not all, you shall see—Murderer, he said, follow me, I will show you a new country, but it is far away and we must hurry. No, said Laura, not unless you take my hand, no; and she clung first to the stair rail, and then to the topmost branch of the Judas tree that bent down slowly and set her upon the earth, and then to the rocky ledge of a cliff, and then to the jagged wave of a sea that was not water but a desert of crumbling stone. Where are you taking me, she asked in wonder but without fear. To death, and it is a long way off, and we must hurry, said Eugenio. No, said Laura, not unless you take my hand. Then eat these flowers, poor prisoner, said Eugenio in a voice of pity, take and eat: and from the Judas tree he stripped the warm bleeding flowers, and held them to her lips. She saw that his hand was fleshless, a cluster of small white petrified branches, and his eye sockets were without light, but she ate the flowers greedily for they satisfied both hunger and thirst. Murderer! said Eugenio, and Cannibal! This is my body and my blood. Laura cried No! and at the sound of her own voice, she awoke trembling, and was afraid to sleep again.

V. S. Pritchett

In his introduction to *The Oxford Book of Short Stories* (1981), V. S. Pritchett says: "The novel tends to tell us everything whereas the short story tells us only one thing, and that, intensely." In addition to its economy, the short story is known for its suggestiveness; it resembles "a painting or even a song which we can take in at once, yet brings the recesses and contours of larger experience to the mind." Perhaps his most interesting recent statement about the short story is to be found at the conclusion of that essay:

"For myself, the short story springs from a spontaneously poetic as distinct from a prosaic impulse—yet it is not 'poetical' in the sense of a shuddering sensibility. Because the short story has to be succinct and has to suggest things that have been 'left out,' are, in fact, there all the time, the art calls for a mingling of the skills of the rapid reporter or traveller with an eye for incident and an ear for real speech, the instincts of the poet and ballad-maker, and the sonnet writer's concealed discipline of form. The writer has to cultivate the gift for aphorism and wit. A short story is always a disclosure, often an evocation—as in Lawrence or Faulkner—frequently the celebration of character at bursting point; it approaches the mythical. Above all, more than the novelist who is sustained by his discursive manner, the writer of short stories has to catch our attention at once not only by the novelty of his people and scene but by the distinctiveness of his voice, and to hold us by the ingenuity of his design: for what we ask for is the sense that our now restless lives achieve

shape at times and that our emotions have their architecture. Particularly in the writers of this century we also notice the sense of people as strangers. A modern story comes to an open end. People are left carrying the aftermath of their tale into a new day of which, alarmingly, they can as yet know nothing."

Victor Sawdon Pritchett was born in Ipswich, England, in 1900. He worked as a travelling salesman before becoming a journalist and served as a correspondent during the Spanish Civil War. His collections of stories include *You Make Your Own Life* (1938), *It May Never Happen* (1947), *Collected Stories* (1956), *More Collected Stories* (1983), and *Complete Collected Stories* (1991). He is well known as a writer of travel books and has several critical works to his credit, including *The Living Novel* (1947), *Books in General* (1953), and *The Spanish Temper* (1954).

Pritchett is especially adept at establishing a convincing narrative voice in his stories, as well as pacing his materials. In "The Saint," for example, there is a wonderful moment when the antagonist, Mr. Timberlake, head of the Church of the Last Purification of Toronto, is suspended from a tree over the river, about to sink ignominiously in the unfathomable depths of Error. Pritchett manages to sustain that moment brilliantly for three full paragraphs with allusions to Euclid, Christ walking on the water, Greek statues of Apollo, and John the Baptist's head resting on a platter, each rendered hilarious by the ironic deadpan voice of the postlapsarian narrator.

The Saint

When I was seventeen years old I lost my religious faith. It had been unsteady for some time and then, very suddenly, it went as the result of an incident in a punt on the river outside the town where we lived. My uncle, with whom I was obliged to stay for long periods of my life, had started a small furniture-making business in the town. He was always in difficulties about money, but he was convinced that in some way God would help him. And this happened. An investor arrived who belonged to a sect called the Church of the Last Purification, of Toronto, Canada. Could we imagine, this man asked, a good and omnipotent God allowing His children to be short of money? We had to admit we could not imagine this. The man paid some capital into my uncle's business and we were converted. Our family were the first Purifiers—as they were called—in the town. Soon a congregation of fifty or more were meeting every Sunday in a room at the Corn Exchange.

At once we found ourselves isolated and hated people. Everyone made jokes about us. We had to stand together because we were sometimes dragged into the courts. What the unconverted could not forgive in us was first that we believed in successful prayer and, secondly, that our revelation came from Toronto. The success of our prayers had a simple foundation. We regarded it as "Error"—our name for Evil—to believe the evidence of our senses, and if we had influenza or consumption, or had lost our money or were unemployed, we denied the reality of these things, saying that since God could not have made them they therefore did not exist. It was exhilarating to look at our congregation and to know that what the vulgar would call miracles were performed among us, almost as a matter of routine, every day. Not very big miracles, perhaps; but up in London and out in Toronto, we knew that deafness and blindness, cancer and insanity, the great scourges, were constantly vanishing before the prayers of the more advanced Purifiers.

"What!" said my schoolmaster, an Irishman with eyes like broken glass and a sniff of irritability in the bristles of his nose. "What! Do you have the impudence to tell me that if you fell off the top floor of this building and smashed your head in, you would say you hadn't fallen and were not injured?"

I was a small boy and very afraid of everybody, but not when it was a question of my religion. I was used to the kind of conundrum the Irishman had set. It was use-less to argue, though our religion had already developed an interesting casuistry.

"I *would* say so," I replied with coldness and some vanity. "And my head would not be smashed."

"You would not say so," answered the Irishman. "You would not say so." His eyes sparkled with pure pleasure. "You'd be dead."

The boys laughed, but they looked at me with admiration.

Then, I do not know how or why, I began to see a difficulty. Without warning and as if I had gone into my bedroom at night and had found a gross ape seated in my bed and thereafter following me about with his grunts and his fleas and a look, relentless and ancient, scored on his brown face, I was faced with the problem that prowls at the centre of all religious faith. I was faced by the difficulty of the origin of evil. Evil was an illusion, we were taught. But even illusions have an origin. The Purifiers denied this.

I consulted my uncle. Trade was bad at the time and this made his faith abrupt. He frowned as I spoke.

"When did you brush your coat last?" he said. "You're getting slovenly about your appearance. If you spent more time studying books"—that is to say, the Purification literature—"and less with your hands in your pockets and playing about with boats on the river, you wouldn't be letting Error in."

All dogmas have their jargon; my uncle as a businessman loved the trade terms of the Purification. "Don't let Error in" was a favourite one. The whole point about the Purification, he said, was that it was scientific and therefore exact; in consequence it was sheer weakness to admit discussion. Indeed, betrayal. He unpinched his pince-nez, stirred his tea, and indicated I must submit or change the subject. Preferably the latter. I saw, to my alarm, that my arguments had defeated my uncle. Faith and doubt pulled like strings round my throat.

"You don't mean to say you don't believe that what our Lord said was true?" my aunt asked nervously, following me out of the room. "Your uncle does, dear."

I could not answer. I went out of the house and down the main street to the river, where the punts were stuck like insects in the summery flash of the reach. Life was a dream, I thought; no, a nightmare, for the ape was beside me.

I was still in this state, half sulking and half exalted, when Mr. Hubert Timberlake came to the town. He was one of the important people from the headquarters of our church and he had come to give an address on the Purification at the Corn Exchange. Posters announcing this were everywhere. Mr. Timberlake was to spend Sunday afternoon with us. It was unbelievable that a man so eminent would actually sit in our dining-room, use our knives and forks, and eat our food. Every imperfection in our home and our characters would jump out at him. The Truth had been revealed to man with scientific accuracy—an accuracy we could all test by experiment—and the future course of human development on earth was laid down, finally. And here in Mr. Timberlake was a man who had not merely performed many miracles—even, it was said with proper reserve, having twice raised the dead—but had actually been to Toronto, our headquarters, where this great and revolutionary revelation had first been given.

"This is my nephew," my uncle said, introducing me. "He lives with us. He thinks he thinks, Mr. Timberlake, but I tell him he only thinks he does. Ha, ha." My uncle was a humorous man when he was with the great. "He's always on the river," my uncle continued. "I tell him he's got water on the brain. I've been telling Mr. Timberlake about you, my boy."

A hand as soft as the best quality chamois leather took mine. I saw a wide upright man in a double-breasted navy-blue suit. He had a pink square head with very small ears and one of those torpid, enamelled smiles which were said by our enemies to be too common in our sect.

"Why, isn't that just fine?" said Mr. Timberlake, who, owing to his contacts with Toronto, spoke with an American accent. "What say we tell your uncle it's funny he thinks he's funny."

The eyes of Mr. Timberlake were direct and colourless. He had the look of a retired merchant captain who had become decontaminated from the sea and had reformed and made money. His defence of me had made me his at once. My doubts vanished. Whatever Mr. Timberlake believed must be true, and as I listened to him at lunch, I thought there could be no finer life than his.

"I expect Mr. Timberlake's tired after his address," said my aunt.

"Tired?" exclaimed my uncle, brilliant with indignation. "How can Mr. Timberlake be tired? Don't let Error in!"

For in our faith the merely inconvenient was just as illusory as a great catastrophe would have been, if you wished to be strict, and Mr. Timberlake's presence made us very strict.

I noticed then that, after their broad smiles, Mr. Timberlake's lips had the habit of setting into a long depressed sarcastic curve.

"I guess," he drawled, "I guess the Al-mighty must have been tired sometimes, for it says He relaxed on the seventh day. Say, do you know what I'd like to do this afternoon?" he said, turning to me. "While your uncle and aunt are sleeping off this meal let's you and me go on the river and get water on the brain. I'll show you how to punt."

Mr. Timberlake, I saw to my disappointment, was out to show he understood the young. I saw he was planning a "quiet talk" with me about my problems.

"There are too many people on the river on Sundays," said my uncle uneasily.

"Oh, I like a crowd," said Mr. Timberlake, giving my uncle a tough look. "This is the day of rest, you know." He had had my uncle gobbling up every bit of gossip from the sacred city of Toronto all the morning.

My uncle and aunt were incredulous that a man like Mr. Timberlake should go out among the blazers and gramophones of the river on a Sunday afternoon. In any other member of our church they would have thought this sinful.

"Waal, what say?" said Mr. Timberlake. I could only murmur.

"That's fixed," said Mr. Timberlake. And on came the smile as simple, vivid, and unanswerable as the smile on an advertisement. "Isn't that just fine!"

Mr. Timberlake went upstairs to wash his hands. My uncle was deeply offended and shocked, but he could say nothing. He unpinched his glasses.

"A very wonderful man," he said. "So human," he apologized.

"My boy," my uncle said, "this is going to be an experience for you. Hubert Timberlake was making a thousand a year in the insurance business ten years ago. Then he heard of the Purification. He threw everything up, just like that. He gave up his job and took up the work. It was a struggle, he told me so himself this morning. 'Many's the time,' he said to me this morning, 'when I wondered where my next meal was coming from.' But the way was shown. He came down from Worcester to London and in two years he was making fifteen hundred a year out of his practice."

To heal the sick by prayer according to the tenets of the Church of the Last Purification was Mr. Timberlake's profession.

My uncle lowered his eyes. With his glasses off, the lids were small and uneasy. He lowered his voice too.

"I have told him about your little trouble," my uncle said quietly with emotion. I was burned with shame. My uncle looked up and stuck out his chin confidently.

"He just smiled," my uncle said. "That's all."

Then we waited for Mr. Timberlake to come down.

I put on white flannels and soon I was walking down to the river with Mr. Timberlake. I felt that I was going with him under false pretences; for he would begin explaining to me the origin of evil and I would have to pretend politely that he was converting me when already, at the first sight of him, I had believed. A stone bridge, whose two arches were like an owlish pair of eyes gazing up the reach, was close to the landing-stage. I thought what a pity it was the flannelled men and the sunburned girls there did not know I was getting a ticket for the Mr. Timberlake who had been speaking in the town that very morning. I looked round for him and when I saw him I was a little startled. He was standing at the edge of the water looking at it with an expression of empty incomprehension. Among the white crowds his air of brisk efficiency had dulled. He looked middle-aged, out of place, and insignificant. But the smile switched on when he saw me.

"Ready?" he called. "Fine!"

I had the feeling that inside him there must be a gramophone record going round and round, stopping at that word.

He stepped into the punt and took charge.

"Now I just want you to paddle us over to the far bank," he said, "and then I'll show you how to punt."

Everything Mr. Timberlake said still seemed unreal to me. The fact that he was sitting in a punt, of all commonplace material things, was incredible. That he should propose to pole us up the river was terrifying. Suppose he fell into the river? At once I checked the thought. A leader of our church under the direct guidance of God could not possibly fall into a river.

The stream is wide and deep in this reach, but on the southern bank there is a manageable depth and a hard bottom. Over the clay banks the willows hang, making their basketwork print of sun and shadow on the water, while under the gliding boats lie cloudy, chloride caverns. The hoop-like branches of the trees bend down until their tips touch the water like fingers making musical sounds. Ahead in midstream, on a day sunny as this one was, there is a path of strong light which is hard to look at unless you half close your eyes, and down this path on the crowded Sundays go the launches with their parasols and their pennants; and also the rowboats with their beetle-leg oars, which seem to dig the sunlight out of the water as they rise. Upstream one goes, on and on between the gardens and then between fields kept for grazing. On the afternoon when Mr. Timberlake and I went out to settle the question of the origin of evil, the meadows were packed densely with buttercups.

"Now," said Mr. Timberlake decisively when I had paddled to the other side. "Now I'll take her."

He got over the seat into the well at the stern.

"I'll just get you clear of the trees," I said.

"Give me the pole," said Mr. Timberlake, standing up on the little platform and making a squeak with his boots as he did so. "Thank you, sir. I haven't done this for eighteen years, but I can tell you, brother, in those days I was considered some poler."

He looked round and let the pole slide down through his hands. Then he gave the first difficult push. The punt rocked pleasantly and we moved forward. I sat facing him, paddle in hand, to check any inward drift of the punt.

"How's that, you guys?" said Mr. Timberlake, looking round at our eddies and drawing in the pole. The delightful water swished down it.

"Fine," I said. Deferentially I had caught the word.

He went on to his second and his third strokes, taking too much water on his sleeve, perhaps, and uncertain in his steering, which I corrected, but he was doing well.

"It comes back to me," he said. "How am I doing?"

"Just keep her out from the trees," I said.

"The trees?" he said.

"The willows," I said.

"I'll do it now," he said. "How's that? Not quite enough? Well, how's this?"

"Another one," I said. "The current runs strong this side."

"What? More trees?" he said. He was getting hot.

"We can shoot out past them," I said. "I'll ease us over with the paddle." Mr. Timberlake did not like this suggestion.

"No, don't do that. I can manage it," he said. I did not want to offend one of the leaders of our church, so I put the paddle down; but I felt I ought to have taken him farther along away from the irritation of the trees.

"Of course," I said, "we could go under them. It might be nice."

"I think," said Mr. Timberlake, "that would be a very good idea."

He lunged hard on the pole and took us towards the next archway of willow branches.

"We may have to duck a bit, that's all," I said.

"Oh, I can push the branches up," said Mr. Timberlake.

"It is better to duck," I said.

We were gliding now quickly towards the arch; in fact, I was already under it. "I think I should duck," I said. "Just bend down for this one."

"What makes the trees lean over the water like this?" asked Mr. Timberlake. "Weeping willows—I'll give you a thought there. How Error likes to make us dwell on sorrow. Why not call them *laughing* willows?" discoursed Mr. Timberlake as the branch passed over my head.

"Duck," I said.

"Where? I don't see them," said Mr. Timberlake, turning round.

"No, your head," I said. "The branch," I called.

"Oh, the branch. This one?" said Mr. Timberlake, finding a branch just against his chest, and he put out a hand to lift it. It is not easy to lift a willow branch and Mr. Timberlake was surprised. He stepped back as it gently and firmly leaned against him. He leaned back and pushed from his feet. And he pushed too far. The boat went on. I saw Mr. Timberlake's boots leave the stern as he took an unthoughtful step backwards. He made a last-minute grasp at a stronger and higher branch, and then there he hung a yard above the water, round as a blue damson that is ripe and ready, waiting only for a touch to make it fall. Too late with the paddle and shot ahead by the force of his thrust, I could not save him.

For a full minute I did not believe what I saw; indeed, our religion taught us never to believe what we saw. Unbelieving, I could not move. I gaped. The impossible had happened. Only a miracle, I found myself saying, could save him.

What was most striking was the silence of Mr. Timberlake as he hung from the tree. I was lost between gazing at him and trying to get the punt out of the small branches of the tree. By the time I had got the punt out, there were several yards of water between us, and the soles of his boots were very near the water as the branch bent under his weight. Boats were passing at the time but no one seemed to notice us. I was glad about this. This was a private agony. A double chin had appeared on the face of Mr. Timberlake and his head was squeezed between his shoulders and his hanging arms. I saw him blink and look up at the sky. His eyelids were pale like a chicken's. He was tidy and dignified as he hung there, the hat was not displaced, and the top button of his coat was done up. He had a blue silk handkerchief in his breast pocket. So unperturbed and genteel he seemed that as the tips of his shoes came nearer and nearer to the water, I became alarmed. He could perform what are called miracles. He would be thinking at this moment that only in an erroneous and illusory sense was he hanging from the branch of the tree over six feet of water. He was probably praying one of the closely reasoned prayers of our faith, which were more like conversations with Euclid than appeals to God. The calm of his face suggested this. Was he, I asked myself, within sight of the main road, the town recreation ground, and the landing-stage crowded with people, was he about to re-enact a well-known miracle? I hoped that he was not. I prayed that he was not. I prayed with all my will that Mr. Timberlake would not walk upon the water. It was my prayer and not his that was answered.

I saw the shoes dip, the water rise above his ankles and up his socks. He tried to move his grip now to a yet higher branch—he did not succeed—and in making this effort his coat and waistcoat rose and parted from his trousers. One seam of shirt with its pant-loops and brace-tabs broke like a crack across the middle of Mr. Timberlake. It was like a fatal flaw in a statue, an earthquake crack that made the monumental mortal. The last Greeks must have felt as I felt then, when they saw a crack across the middle of some statue of Apollo. It was at this moment I realized that the final revelation about man and society on earth had come to nobody and that Mr. Timberlake knew nothing at all about the origin of evil.

All this takes long to describe, but it happened in a few seconds as I paddled towards him. I was too late to get his feet on the boat and the only thing to do was to let him sink until his hands were nearer the level of the punt and then to get him to change hand-holds. Then I would paddle him ashore. I did this. Amputated by the water, first a torso, then a bust, then a mere head and shoulders, Mr. Timberlake, I noticed, looked sad and lonely as he sank. He was a declining dogma. As the water lapped his collar—for he hesitated to let go of the branch to hold the punt—I saw a small triangle of deprecation and pathos between his nose and the corners of his mouth. The head resting on the platter of water had the sneer of calamity on it, such as one sees in the pictures of a beheaded saint.

"Hold on to the punt, Mr. Timberlake," I said urgently. "Hold on to the punt."

He did so.

"Push from behind," he directed in a dry business-like voice. They were his first words. I obeyed him. Carefully I paddled him towards the bank. He turned and, with a splash, climbed ashore. There he stood, raising his arms and looking at the water running down his swollen suit and making a puddle at his feet.

"Say," said Mr. Timberlake coldly, "we let some Error in that time."

How much he must have hated our family.

"I am sorry, Mr. Timberlake," I said. "I am most awfully sorry. I should have paddled. It was my fault. I'll get you home at once. Let me wring out your coat and waistcoat. You'll catch your death—"

I stopped. I had nearly blasphemed. I had nearly suggested that Mr. Timberlake had fallen into the water and that to a man of his age this might be dangerous.

Mr. Timberlake corrected me. His voice was impersonal, addressing the laws of human existence rather than myself.

"If God made water it would be ridiculous to suggest He made it capable of harming His creatures. Wouldn't it?"

"Yes," I murmured hypocritically.

"O.K.," said Mr. Timberlake. "Let's go."

"I'll soon get you across," I said.

"No," he said. "I mean let's go on. We're not going to let a little thing like this spoil a beautiful afternoon. Where were we going? You spoke of a pretty landing-place farther on. Let's go there."

"But I must take you home. You can't sit there soaked to the skin. It will spoil your clothes."

"Now, now," said Mr. Timberlake. "Do as I say. Go on."

There was nothing to be done with him. I held the punt into the bank and he stepped in. He sat like a bursting and sodden bolster in front of me while I paddled. We had lost the pole, of course.

For a long time I could hardly look at Mr. Timberlake. He was taking the line that nothing had happened and this put me at a disadvantage. I knew something considerable had happened. That glaze, which so many of the members of our sect had on their faces and persons, their minds and manners, had been washed off. There was no gleam for me from Mr. Timberlake.

"What's the house over there?" he asked. He was making conversation. I had steered into the middle of the river to get him into the strong sun. I saw steam rise from him.

I took courage and studied him. He was a man, I realized, in poor physical condition, unexercised and sedentary. Now the gleam had left him, one saw the veined empurpled skin of the stoutish man with a poor heart. I remember he had said at lunch:

"A young woman I know said: 'Isn't it wonderful? I can walk thirty miles in a day without being in the least tired.' I said: 'I don't see that bodily indulgence is anything a member of the Church of the Last Purification should boast about.'"

Yes, there was something flaccid, passive, and slack about Mr. Timberlake. Bunched in swollen clothes, he refused to take them off. It occurred to me, as he looked with boredom at the water, the passing boats, and the country, that he had not been in the country before. That it was something he had agreed to do but wanted to get over quickly. He was totally uninterested. By his questions—What is that church? Are there any fish in this river? Is that a wireless or a gramophone?—I understood that Mr. Timberlake was formally acknowledging a world he did not live in. It was too interesting, too eventful a world. His spirit, inert and preoccupied, was elsewhere in an eventless and immaterial habitation. He was a dull man, duller than any man I had ever known; but his dullness was a sort of earthly deposit left by a being whose diluted mind was far away in the effervescence of metaphysical matters. There was a slightly pettish look on his face as (to himself, of course) he declared he was not wet and he would not have a heart attack or catch pneumonia.

Mr. Timberlake spoke little. Sometimes he squeezed water out of his sleeve. He shivered a little. He watched his steam. I had planned, when we set out, to go up as far as the lock, but now the thought of another two miles of this responsibility was too much. I pretended I wanted to go only as far as the bend we were approaching, where one of the richest buttercup meadows was. I mentioned this to him. He turned and looked with boredom at the field. Slowly we came to the bank.

We tied up the punt and we landed.

"Fine," said Mr. Timberlake. He stood at the edge of the meadow just as he had stood at the landing-stage—lost, stupefied, uncomprehending.

"Nice to stretch our legs," I said. I led the way into the deep flowers. So dense were the buttercups there was hardly any green. Presently I sat down. Mr. Timberlake looked at me and sat down also. Then I turned to him with a last try at persuasion. Respectability, I was sure, was his trouble.

"No one will see us," I said. "This is out of sight of the river. Take off your coat and trousers and wring them out."

Mr. Timberlake replied firmly: "I am satisfied to remain as I am.

"What is this flower?" he asked, to change the subject.

"Buttercup," I said.

"Of course," he replied.

I could do nothing with him. I lay down full length in the sun; and, observing this and thinking to please me, Mr. Timberlake did the same. He must have supposed that this was what I had come out in the boat to do. It was only human. He had come out with me, I saw, to show me that he was only human.

But as we lay there I saw the steam still rising. I had had enough.

"A bit hot," I said, getting up.

He got up at once.

"Do you want to sit in the shade?" he asked politely.

"No," I said. "Would you like to?"

"No," he said. "I was thinking of you."

"Let's go back," I said. We both stood up and I let him pass in front of me. When I looked at him again, I stopped dead. Mr. Timberlake was no longer a man in a navy-blue suit. He was blue no longer. He was transfigured. He was yellow. He was covered with buttercup pollen, a fine yellow paste of it made by the damp, from head to foot.

"Your suit," I said.

He looked at it. He raised his thin eyebrows a little, but he did not smile or make any comment.

The man is a saint, I thought. As saintly as any of those gold-leaf figures in the churches of Sicily. Golden he sat in the punt; golden he sat for the next hour as I paddled him down the river. Golden and bored. Golden as we landed at the town and as we walked up the street back to my uncle's house. There he refused to change his clothes or to sit by a fire. He kept an eye on the time for his train back to London. By no word did he acknowledge the disasters or the beauties of the world. If they were printed upon him, they were printed upon a husk.

Sixteen years have passed since I dropped Mr. Timberlake in the river and since the sight of his pant-loops destroyed my faith. I have not seen him since, but today I heard that he was dead. He was fifty-seven. His mother, a very old lady with whom he had lived all his life, went into his bedroom when he was getting ready for church and found him lying on the floor in his shirt-sleeves. A stiff collar with the tie half inserted was in one hand. Five minutes before, she told the doctor, she had been speaking to him.

The doctor, who looked at the heavy body lying on the single bed, saw a middle-aged man, wide rather than stout and with an extraordinarily box-like thick-jawed face. He had got fat, my uncle told me, in later years. The heavy liver-coloured cheeks were like the chaps of a hound. Heart disease, it was plain, was the cause of the death of Mr. Timberlake. In death the face was lax, even coarse and degenerate. It was a miracle, the doctor said, that he had lived as long. Any time during the last twenty years the smallest shock might have killed him.

I thought of our afternoon on the river. I thought of him hanging from the tree. I thought of him indifferent and golden in the meadow. I understood why he had made for himself a protective, sedentary blandness, an automatic smile, a collection of phrases. He kept them on like the coat after his ducking. And I understood why—though I had feared it all the time we were on the river—I understood why he did not talk to me about the origin of evil. He was honest. The ape was with us. The ape that merely followed me was already inside Mr. Timberlake eating out his heart.

Leon Rooke

Leon Rooke was born in Roanoke Rapids, North Carolina, in 1934. He spent the war years on his grandparents' farm, where he received as a Christmas present his first book, *Terry and the Pirates*. He worked briefly as a crooner, sports editor, and lightning rod installer until he left home in 1953, trying his hand as a playwright, living in Alaska, San Francisco, New Orleans, and Fanny Gap, Virginia. During this period he was drafted and spent eighteen months in the army. He was writer-in-residence at the University of North Carolina in 1965; in 1969 his wife's academic career took them to Victoria, British Columbia, where they remained for twenty years and became Canadian citizens. Rooke has taught, published widely in literary magazines, edited anthologies, and won numerous awards, including the Canada-Australia Prize. He now lives in Erin Mills, Ontario. Rooke's publications include twelve collections of short stories, *Last One Home Sleeps in the Yellow Bed* (1968), *The Broad Back of the Angel* (1977), *The Love Parlour* (1977), *Cry Evil* (1980), *Death Suite* (1981), *A Bolt of White Cloth* (1984), *The Happiness of Others* (1991), and three novels, *Fat Woman* (1980), *The Magician in Love* (1981), *Shakespeare's Dog* (1982), and *A Good Baby* (1990).

In trying to locate him somewhere between the traditions of the American South and the "Canadian establishment," interviewer Geoff Hancock elicited this response from Rooke (*Canadian Fiction Magazine*, No. 38, 1981): "The only tradition I perceive is that one where we find the writer attempting to write well and knowing from the start the likelihood of failure. An international community of thieves raiding whatever landscape is before them." Rooke is a kind of literary Houdini, who claims that "Good things often happen when a writer paints himself into a corner. . . ever concocting new forms of entrapment. This time, chained and in a box underwater. Next time around, a stronger chain and the water is shark-infested."

Rooke describes fiction as "real life coming at you from another angle. It's for all those people out there who want and need and often are enriched by that 'other' angle." He considers form "a thing apart from structure . . . the overall shape which holds the work. The mould. But a mould that isn't fixed, varying, as it does, with any given work. What it is that makes a good reader, finishing the story, catch his breath. Pure form is like a ship that has had a good passage and has, out on the open sea, come to anchor for the night. You've got where you were going and everything is

perfect. That's why many of the typically traditional stories being written today no longer satisfy. You know the route too well and you know before you get there that you've been there before. Such stories can have form, of course, but it's form manufactured by the thousands, and the magic is absent."

Rooke dismisses mechanical gimmicks, such as unbound pages or "listing 64 descriptions of one inch of the female thigh": "Plot, which was always the least important element for everything except Agatha Christie mysteries and Dime Westerns, takes an unlamented back seat. Language, which a lot of writers try to diguise as something else, tries not to be ashamed of itself. What beguiles me most is a liberated approach to point of view and delineation of character. . . . I'm in a peculiar position. I'm a traditional writer, but at times a more experimental one. Most writers are one or the other. My position isn't fixed, it isn't firm. It's always at the mercy of whatever material I'm dealing with. Some stories demand a traditional form. I don't think traditional form is exhausted or ever can be. Because it always changes. Frequently, the two come together in an amalgamation that is both traditional and experimental. . . . One of the things that keeps me in the traditional camp is that I am unwilling to relinquish character. It's important to me to see characters in fiction as living human beings. I extend this to include even the extremes. In my 'Magi' story I've got several 'spirit' people running around. . . . I believe in them for the purposes of this fiction."

While advocating a flexible use of tradition, Rooke believes that innovation and experiment must serve the needs of the fictional materials being explored, rather than being ends in themselves. "Remember that the death bell tolls for fiction every month that *Chatelaine* makes an appearance. That stuff, their stuff, is not even fiction; they are little blurbs for the crematorium. The writer on automatic pilot. The prevalence of such material has to be fought." He claims that the short story must entertain, but that it is "entertainment, plus": "One of the functions of literature is to change society. To change the way people think. To redress grievances. To mould society, to pace out, confirm, and secure certain desired directions. I'm a stoop-shouldered moralist. . . . There is nothing so stunning as excellence. It absolutely rivets the backbone, it stirs about and resurrects the always-tired soul."

His apprenticeship in fiction made him seek out strong stylists: "Wright Morris, for instance. Stylists, I find, are rarely disappointing. If the style is strong then the content usually is as well." When pushed to define style, Rooke calls it "the unique imprint of the single writer. Style to me is like a woman walking in high heels. The way they know how. And one never exactly the same as another. The way the toes are pointed right, the way the legs shoot up straight, how the head is carried, that's style. Put the woman in high heels and give her a name and put her on the road: that's what the stylist does putting words onto the page."

Rooke claims that the materials of his fiction come largely unbidden. When asked by interviewer Peter O'Brien (*So to Speak*) whether his stories are written "against the 'shoddy evils' of the world," Rooke replied: "I'd say that, to a certain extent, the creation in fiction of any authentic, living character is political. It is political, one, because it forces the reader to recognize that there are people different from (also similar to) himself, and two, what the author is then able to do with that recognition is powerful, is an earth-shaker, really. Civilized people—readers—have an interest in entering other skins. So long as that condition holds, then all is not completely hopeless. That's the trouble with *bad* fiction; it confirms the shoddy, the superficial, the false. It affirms the tacky. Evil by itself, however, gets pretty grim. Joy, fun, honour, mirth, pleasure, love, integrity, all the higher pursuits—they get their run as well."

Biographical Notes

BRIEF BIOGRAPHICAL NOTES on some of the people called to give evidence for or against me:

MARCELINE ABLE (1964–) Material to come.

WANDA LEE CASSLAKE My Dead Friend.
Wanda Casslake came into my life nine years ago when I was thirty-five and branching out and never left it although she quit her own for reasons that remain to be extricated by someone better equipped to deal with biographical history than I am. Natural actor and wonderful human being. A pleasure-loving woman with a generous heart who always made the most of her appearance, on-screen or off, and only wanted everyone to think the worst of her. Bust like a boy's. Married to:

ROBIN HARVEY (1935–) Actor.
On camera, he rarely knew what to do with his hands: one had to take enormous care with angles because his head tended to photograph excessively large. The Floating Wedge, as this is called in the trade. The best a critic could ever think to say of him (*Great Speckled Bird*) was that he knew 'how to undress casually while indifferently smoking a joint.' He could at times surprise us, but he was, for the most part, an awful bore. Robin found little in life about which to be enthusiastic. He was fond of reminiscing over the recent past. If I went out with Robin and Wanda for a night of drinking and relaxation after a gruelling day on the set, Robin's sole delight was in reminiscing over what the three of us had done the previous evening. Actually, he was never sure what we'd done and would remain unsure even after we had told him. Powerfully built, but with a slow, uncomplicated mind.
Canadian. Most of the people in these Notes are. I cite this with some hesitancy, since in my view the information yields little that is vital. Circumstance is irrelevant, origin is not, and accident is the father of mankind. National origin has significance

relative only to transitory phenomena. It was for this reason that the stork, flying through skies belonging to no one, was selected to carry our early burden (trademark, by the way, of our first eight films). Such oddities of persuasion received frequent airings by Wanda and me. Robin Harvey found these musings of no consequence and normally went off to talk and drink with other individuals, some of whom no doubt were only too happy to tell him what he had done the previous evening. Wanda— who made a point of never telling me where she was from or what her family situation had been, just as she would never reveal her age or why she had married Robin or admit that she had ever read a book—Wanda, being the argumentative type, naturally disputed all notions relative to the common brotherhood of living beings exclusive of any vital differences incurred through country of origin, religion etc., foo-fawing for that matter any lofty ideas I might propose.

'Why then', I might ask her, 'do you continue to work? Work without a higher purpose is a pokey thing indeed.'

I do it for the money, came her inevitable reply. *I do it because I enjoy titillating the hicks, and because being denigrated by a society made up of people who are not as honest about themselves as I am affords me considerable masochistic kicks.*

'If I thought that', I would tell her, 'I would fire your can tomorrow. You are a great artist and through your art we are reshaping the planet.'

Oh, Martin, she would say in her fiery yet sad little way, *you are only trying to find an excuse for this terrible thing we do.*

Wanda Casslake took the opposite view on every question I ever raised, from the simplest to the most abstruse, even arguing that her breasts were 'of quite the normal size'—this despite ample proof to the contrary which for years flowed through 16mm projectors every Saturday night at a hundred private cinema clubs and societies around the world. All now confiscated, I should explain. Scheduled for destruction the minute my last appeal is refused. Nothing of her remains in my possession except ten stills shot one sour, forlorn evening a week before her death. But not shot by me. These photographs, incidentally, I have wanted unpublished for the good reason that Wanda's flat chest does not lift them above the obscene. They have no redeeming social value. They are as dirty as they come. Which is why I held on to them. The point I would make about their existence is that filth remains filth until someone with a humanist perspective comes along and transforms it, often through art, into a thing that takes the measure of the beauty and depth of human life.

Police continue to snoop about, paid informers lurking on every corner.

'I want those pictures, Martin,' Robin tells me.

'Oh, shove it,' I tell him. 'Wanda was adamant in maintaining that she owed nothing to you, that her marriage to you was largely accidental, regrettable, barely worth the paper that made it official.'

I'll sue you, he says.

Opportunist, 5' 8", balding, something of a card shark, proponent of the *laid-back* life and for that reason a happy choice for roles opposite Wanda as his every indifferently delivered line and gesture served to symbolize a) the dehumanization of oppressed working classes everywhere; b) twentieth-century man gone soft through luxury; and c) that intelligent women will always give themselves to brutes too dense to value what they are receiving.

Drinks too much. Recently converted to Catholicism.

Her co-star through the twenty-three films comprising the *Night* series.

Less said of him the better.

RITA ISLINGTON (age approximately 42) Education, occupation, marital status, etc. unknown.

A short time ago, fresh on the heels of my incarceration and release on bond, a woman showed up at my door, announced that her name was as listed above, and that she had an interest in buying her sister's photographs, no questions asked— though she hoped my price would not be unreasonable.

'Who was your sister?'

Wanda Lee Casslake.

'I never would have known.' A shrug of her shoulders. 'Who told you I have them?'

I can't say.

'Did Robin send you?'

I suppose you mean her husband. I have never met him.

'How did you find me?'

Through your lawyer.

'Are you acting on behalf of yourself or for others?'

I want only to salvage what remains of my sister's reputation.

'She was a great actress.'

I do not agree.

'Where was Wanda born? What were her parents like? For a long time I've been very interested.'

Such questions are not pertinent to this negotiation.

'Are we negotiating?'

I hope so. I do not like to have my time wasted.

'Have you ever worked in cinema?'

You are prying. Let us talk price.

'What in your view constitutes a reasonable sum?'

I think you will find my offer liberal.

She opened her purse. As it turned out, the sum offered was liberal indeed. My black onyx bowl was soon stacked high with her currency.

'No,' I said.

No?

For the first time she seemed to be about to lose her temper. I sensed, if I may say so, a whiff of danger.

You will not sell them to me?

I sensed, emanating from her, an uncompromising hatred. Her skin had gone white. A moment later she smiled and my suspicions seemed ludicrous. On an impulse I decided to let her have the negatives. *Without charge.* The last is important to the view I have of myself, which is why I have it italicized. I have never made money unfairly off any person and would certainly not do so off Wanda. I did what I could for Wanda. I tried to make her happy, without becoming too involved.

Don't get too close to me, Martin, she would say. *Don't get involved.*

I gave her a job, propped her up when her faith in herself was low. I lent her money and saw to it that her child was taken care of when Robin wouldn't and Wanda herself was in no shape to do so. The material we had to work with professionally was often of dubious quality though I did my best to imbue it with substance. (This is equivocation: the fact is I yearn to burn my bridges and start over.) But I did these things with no intention of acquiring credit for myself. I did them out of the simple belief that we owe loyalty to those we would call our friends, and with full knowledge that had our situations been reversed she would have done as much for me. Wanda was argumentative, she liked to make people believe that she had not a brain in her head; in fact she was an extraordinary woman who repudiated her own vast gifts out of a deep-seated psychosis I could never probe but which the camera often understood.

'Would you care to see the child?' I asked Rita Islington.

I believe not. I do not care for children.

Strange Rita Islington.

I surrendered the negatives to her for no other reason than that she intrigued me. In the years I had known Wanda she had never mentioned having a sister. Yet how frequently do I mention my six brothers?

I trusted her.

She reeked of scent—an exotic perfume almost as permeating as incense. She wore spiked heels made of a lovely soft leather the colour of the sky. Her co-ordinated purse boasted a musical signature. Her hair was fully a yard long, with a high sheen even in my dimly lit reception-room. She refused to take off her glasses, the lenses of which were so curved and dark I never saw her eyes, despite my frequently assumed stance to this or that side of her.

Pardon me. Am I making you nervous? You appear unable to stand still.

Her voice was throaty, mellifluous—as if it liked to recline on a velvet cushion when not in use. Her language was precise, which characteristic heightened an already regal bearing, reminiscent of that developed by Marlene Dietrich while under the baton of Josef von Sternberg. Moreover, having once offered payment of money (there was never any hint that she was prepared to go further), she seemed not at all surprised that I refused it:

Gallantry still lives, n'est-ce pas?—and allowed her ungloved hand to rest in mine longer than form would concede necessary. Nor did she make any objection to my stated intention to retain as my personal property the single set of prints made from those very negatives and which occupied in plain view the walls enclosing us. *Mmmmm,* I recall she said, *I find this affection you have for the small bosom incomprehensible.*

'I was fond of Wanda.'

I noted that she appeared herself to be normally endowed, though her dress was not of a style to call attention to this.

She had visibly lovely legs, and the most beautiful lips I have ever seen.

Since she gave no indication of hurry, I offered her coffee. She declined. She did not drink of the bean, she said. I then offered alcohol, and this also she refused. Though she did say a moment later that she would drink with me if I insisted. By this hour she had arranged herself comfortably on my sofa, and had already, without looking at them, dispatched the negatives to her purse.

'Why should I insist?' I asked rudely. 'I would hardly be likely to compel a total stranger to drink with me.' As a matter of fact, my composure was broken. Prior to her arrival I had been drinking steadily.

Is it true, she wanted to know, *that you were my sister's lover?*

'Never,' I said. 'I am married—or was—and treasure fidelity.'

How odd, she laughed, *for a porn king.*

Such statements intimidated me.

She wore a fur hat, in addition to other finery. I vividly recall this because my estranged wife had only recently lost a similar hat. My impression, before making a proper study, had been that this woman was wearing my wife's property.

'How did you come by your nice hat?'

It was the gift of my first husband.

'You have been married then . . . more than once?'

You are notoriously inquisitive. This, I would guess, is of value to one of your calling.

'It wasn't a calling. It was simply something to do. Easy money. Corn for the butterballs.'

That does not correspond with my sister's image of you.

'A rabid fanatic?'

She rose to go, once more offering her hand. I kissed it. I don't believe I have ever done that before. Even in jest. I opened the door. A drab light spilled in from the hall. I suddenly did not want her to go. I felt like a man about to go over a cliff on a bicycle (*Night Plus Morning*, 1973). I could hear loneliness rushing at me in full stampede.

'Don't go yet. Please.'

Goodbye. You have been most kind.

That remark turned the trick. My spirits lifted. I no longer had any interest in keeping her.

Her ankles disappeared inside the Rolls Corniche Mark II parked at the curb.

ELAINE HIGHTOWER WOLFE (1942–) Female Caucasian, born in Manhattan, matriculated at Wyoming State Christian College for Women (BA) and Colorado University at Boulder (MA in Human Resources). A former waitress, carhop, interior decorator, receptionist, currently part-time media/projects critic for erratically published journals. Emigrated to Canada in 1967, married five years later, no children.

My estranged wife.

Writes from time to time an uninspired, thematic, therapeutic verse which is then set to music and given the occasional performance at well-attended feminist meetings. Does a nice softshoe when drunk (rarely).

The most marvellous of women.

Identifying scars: on her lower abdomen, which I shall not tell you about.

For the period of time with which these Notes are concerned, she was living apart from me, though in the same neighbourhood, until such time as, in our counsellor's phrase, 'we got our priorities sorted out.' The above disclosure has hidden reference to a) the vanity of Elaine Wolfe which drives her to want and need an independent life, and b) the relative insecurity of Elaine Wolfe which drives her to want and need a husband, together with c) outside pressures which insist that she not throw away her life. We are both entrapped and our emotions made banal by the afterburn of love achieved through six years of matrimony.

Eyes: blue.

Chin: erect.

That she is a pretty woman, an intelligent and humorous woman, and a powerfully intense personality is affirmed often enough by

EDWARD HIGHTOWER (1919–) Father of the above

OLIVE HIGHTOWER (–) Mother of the above

GERTRUDE HIGHTOWER MEWS (1896–) Grandmother of the above and sundry relatives and friends (see Notes below). A wealth of additional values has been likewise aggressively advanced, to wit:

Elaine is a fine woman, a tower of strength.

Elaine has only your happiness in mind.

Elaine is selfless to the extreme. There is nothing she wouldn't do for you.

You had better get a hold of yourself or you are going to lose this veritable jewel who is unabashedly still in love with you but is no one's fool, who adores the ground you walk on and has never looked at another man but who cannot forever be treated as a doormat. Moreover, she has charm, a sweet disposition, money of her own, and a character that is positively radiant. You are going to wake up one morning an old man alone if you don't soon come to realize and appreciate that an angel is what you have.

Agreed, and then some.

No sooner had my mystery caller, Rita Islington, departed than did Elaine Wolfe arrive to remind me of these many paragon qualities (not that *she* would; her presence, I am saying, did so), while at the same time hoping to wring out of me the identity of the woman in question, together with that mission which had summoned her to my door.

Who was she? What did she want? Oh, Martin, you're not going to make those films again!

Because we can't stand to make another unhappy we often opt for the quickest cruelty. I immediately took to the telephone, not at that time disconnected, dialling one

PETER MAHONEY (1918–) Noted attorney, city council member, twice unsuccessful candidate for mayor on the NDP ticket, author of the monographs *Divorce in Las Vegas, The Scottish Decree, Totem and Taboo*, etc.

'She is harassing me,' I told this man, and he immediately divined that my reference was to Elaine Wolfe. He asked that I summon her to the phone. I complied and judge that he reminded her of the delicacy of the situation, that he and her parents' lawyers were working diligently to iron out an agreement which he could promise her would in due time be resolved to everyone's satisfaction, including the court's.

But I don't want a divorce, she told him. *I don't even want this separation.*

I was then recalled. *Guard against depression*, he warned. *Don't do anything silly.*

'I'll get twenty years.'

He laughed. *We shall see.*

'If we thought we had some chance of getting Angelia,' I said, 'we could hold on.'

My wife wept. We both wept.

Does it have to be like this? she cried.

'I don't know.'

I forgive you. If that's all that's standing between us. If there is anything to forgive.

We hugged, fondled and continued to weep. 'It helps,' I admitted, 'but you know very well there is no way out. You have your future, not to mention your reputation, to think about.'

I don't care about that! It's my place to stand beside you!

I reminded her that her parents' hearts would be broken, their health thrown in jeopardy, if she took up with me again.

'Already your father has had one mild attack. That comes directly to my door.'

Yes, but Angelia! Unless we're together Angelia will surely be taken away. It's that bitch Marceline's fault! I could wring her neck!

'She's a friend of the court. We can't touch Marcy.'

Oh, Martin, why did you ever have anything to do with her!

We wrung our hands, moaned until our throats hurt, ranted over the injustices done to us by society and friends, searched about helplessly for a ray of sunshine, and finally threw ourselves together on the floor and found brief happiness in that physical union which assuages the bleakest hour.

Oh, love, oh, beauty!

Christ, I love a passionate woman.

Weeping without hope, she then fled.

I was utterly distraught, a crawling wound, too worn out even to endure the long struggle toward bliss via alcohol. In my self-pity I reached for the one kind review my work has ever received, seeking pathetic recompense from

MICHAEL OBLE (–) Semi-reputable freelance art and film critic, Assistant Librarian at the Spadina Street branch of the Toronto Public Library, author of the celebrated article (*en Route*, the in-flight magazine of Air Canada, June 1978, pp. 29, 40, 51), *Pornography with a Message: The Underground Films of Martin D. Wolfe.*

The most recent of the 23 films of M. D. Wolfe opens with a massively detailed, nearly interminable sequence made up of the same repeated, gradually expanding scene. Fade in on a barren plain where a clump of antlike creatures congregates. Viewed by a single hand-held camera at considerable distance, a lone figure appears. Puffs of smoke drift up lazily into an overcast sky. The figure falls. As the smoke wafts away we have superimposed, the camera infinitesimally nearer, an all but exact re-enactment. This time one can faintly hear the pop of gunfire a few seconds after the figure has again collapsed. Superimpose and begin once more, the same scene imperceptibly nearer, the action extending a few frames longer.

Our audience begins to fidget and some to demand a return of their money.

It turns out before long that our victim is a woman; with each rebirth of the scene more and more flesh is exposed. Is Wolfe giving us, then, an elaborate striptease? Those hesitating in the aisles decide to reclaim their seats. This may after all be the show the posters promised.

More smoke and gunfire. We are well into Biographical Nights before it comes to us that what we are perceiving is not what have perceived; and by the time this 90-minute feature drives to its close the original seven-second opening takes all of one hour to recount and has become another narrative indeed. Along the way, the distant, rather pretty gunfire has given way to machine-gun bursts, rocket fire, and in the end to full-scale battlefield explosions which are integrated with the sustained shrieks and howls of ferocious dogs. Overheard fragments of speech become diatribes, though here too there are surprises, for the language is no longer English. The once barren plain has become a mirage in which any environment is possible. Wolfe can even manage to find in it room to continue his obsessions with factory interiors. Figures seen initially in military uniforms, later in priestly robes or in the elegant attire of heads of state, are next seen as beggars, convicts, amputee veterans, and eventually as the working-class representatives without which no Wolfe film is complete. Nothing is secure, Wolfe appears to be telling us. Nothing is to be counted on. Place is totally unreliable. Who we are is the most specious of inventions. Wolfe's few converts will know, however, that whatever else this director may be, he is not a mere illusionist. His scene employs mirage as metaphor but inside that mirage much is hardcore naturalism. Thus when the camera swings away from a tight shot of the face of our old friend Wanda, looking more enigmatic than ever, we are not altogether astonished that the wide lens reveals the familiar over-large, bobbing head of Robin Harvey as he does his sexual labour over her. Blue-collar Harvey this is—hungover, laid-back, no doubt thinking of his wages as he looks indifferently out at us. Clearly his mind is not on Wanda. He sees us, it would seem, and nods a non-committal greeting. The camera withdraws farther. We are inside Wolfe's infamous textile factory. As far as the eye can see, a thousand looms are projected, repeating this act of bestial rape, of intermittent harmony. The factory hums with vicious lust, though the greater horror resides in the machines which roar on in the production of more and more undistributed profit.

Wolfe has moved out from the most distantly objective portrayal of one victim's story into the dark and tangled heart of material in which perpetrator, victim and spectator blindly collaborate. He confronts his audience with the bitter notion that misconceptions which apply to his subject matter apply to our own lives as well. Guilt weighs heavily on us all, he would have us acknowledge, but the eye which finally perceives truth is the one that must make the largest sacrifice. His is the one to educate priests, reform heads of state, dismantle the military, deliver us into good and secure biographical night. A sense of shifting guilt permeates this film, as indeed it does much of the Night series in its entirety. All parties absorb a share—the working classes, for instance, with which Wolfe is most allied, in their need for heroes, even in their need for God. Yet he repudiates the belief that they have a need for someone, *human potentates, to tell them how to run their lives. Better God, he argues, than us. Their virtues are seen as constant and surpass the ill or goodwill of those who would so instruct. Identities shift in his films in order to dramatize a theory of universal brotherhood but once that is seen he wants us to recognize that the main weight of guilt never shifts. It is an incorrigible property of that elusive party so rarely physically present where atrocity prevails. The people who exploit and kill Wanda in this film are indicted but the burden of guilt flows elsewhere. This ultimate source is nameless but one can never doubt that it exists, or that it is plotting new crimes even as this one transpires, or that at all cost it must be tracked down. Wanda, unfortunately, does not suspect. She believes in her heart that this is happening to her because of something she has done. She does not aggressively resist her destruction partly because she views this end as rightful payment for her vanity, for her few moments of pleasure, for wanting something better. It is this twisted nobility of spirit, this forlorn innocence that moves us so and for which she earns our begrudging respect. We leave the theatre with sex-drive diminished, with the lust to revenge her permanently intact.*

But are Wolfe's films high-class porn, or are they art? One is beginning to hear murmurs of support. More than a few have passed up Swedish Hotbox *and* The Devil in Miss Jones *for* Biographical Nights. *Martin Wolfe, we can suppose, does not live in hell; his films, however, remind us that he would be vastly happier if the public his films are aimed at were less content to do so. Despite their intensely sexual nature, his films make deeply religious statements so arduous in their pursuit of change that, left to their own devices, they might in time confound the Pope, foment revolution and topple governments. That they are made in the first place is an expression of the director's optimism and faith.*

Biographical Nights *exposes with startling clarity the design which has persisted through the whole of this man's cinematic career. He radically marries pornography with earnest morality. Base lust is his symbol for greed in all its forms. Pornography is the vessel which transports his devious socio-political message, geared to lure an unsuspecting public into the theatre—and out of it a different person. It is for this unique premise that he might be justifiably attacked. Undoubtedly, his defence would be that while the New Wave gave us masterpieces, it politically affected little. One can almost hear Wolfe laying down the ground rules to his incredible and infinitely patient Wanda: 'The most permanent revolution begins by gathering its harvest from the bottom. We can reform drunks and degenerates, if we can turn a nation of confirmed voyeurs into activists, we can reform anyone. Your hot breath, your boy's chest, and Robin's glazed eyes, will render them susceptible. His aim, I believe, is to crack heads wide open. To this end he disposes of Freud, incorporates Masters and Johnson, and goes Marx one better.'*

OBLE, OBLE, my eternal thanks to Oble. A review I was all but tempted to send to my mother. A few thoughts are wrong but I cannot quibble. When this item first came to our notice my wife and I, with Robin and Wanda, booked a table at Antoine's and held an extended post-mortem. Elaine read it, read it again, cried, and went back to it once more. 'It's so right', she gushed. 'Beautiful, it's beautiful.' Her eyes shone. She wriggled close, unable to touch me often enough. I couldn't eat my escargots or dip my bread in their juices without poking her in the ribs. 'You're wonderful, oh, Wanda isn't Martin wonderful?' The pleasure this man Oble gave her, how I wish he had been at the table. She had never been more radiant, so much the Pike's Peak of Love. It grieved me that I had no more reviews to show her, no trophies to pull from my pockets. I felt wretched, thinking of all the years I had made this fine woman endure public disgrace. And how I, too, needed that praise . . . doubt piled upon doubt, scorn heaped upon scorn, all receding now.

Robin's mouth silently shaped this or that imponderable word. 'I don't get it,' he muttered at last. 'What does this turkey mean? Was I hung over? Why can't he just call it a good skin flick and let it go at that?'

When Wanda read it she howled. She laughed so hard and so long we were obliged to apologize to Antoine and his other guests. 'Oh-oh-oh!' she gasped, 'this is killing me! What a hoax! Oh, Martin, did you have to pay him a lot of money?'

Elaine, wounded for my sake, turned on her in a fury: 'That isn't true, you're a beast to say that.'

'It is true, our pictures are garbage, that's all they are, Martin's not a saint and I'm not Garbo, if the public had any sense we'd all be in jail.'

Elaine burst into tears. She wrenched at the table-cloth, spilt her water, shook violently all over, quite fed up with our companions.

Robin appealed to us all. 'Look, we're here to have a good time, forget our troubles. Let's behave ourselves. I'm confused about that mention of rockets. I never saw any rockets.'

'If they want to call *smut* political and a means for social change,' stormed Wanda, 'that's their business. All the *Nights* pictures are trash! *Dirt! Filth! Slop!* Nothing more!' She was in a rage, bristling, her beautiful eyes steaming with venom.

'You're frightened,' I told her. 'Why? Why does it scare you that the films might be good? That they might be worthwhile?'

'I know who *I* am! I know *what* I am too. I don't need any jerk cinephile to justify my existence!'

Elaine too was primed for war, in no mood to let this coarse assessment slide. She banged the salt shaker on Wanda's salad plate, picked up a fork and raked it over the table like a dagger. 'You were wonderful in that picture!' she shouted. 'You are a fine human being! A wonderful mother! Martin's too modest, I don't suppose he's told you that he gets letters from strangers saying how you have changed their lives!'

'One,' I corrected. 'One letter.'

'Yes! From a man reborn! From a man martyred in Ethiopia because of what the *Night* pictures did to him.'

Wanda reddened. But she did not speak, her thoughts deflected by Ethiopia's unknown dead. I was devising a theory about Wanda. It would destroy her, I sensed, if she ever came to realize that she'd somehow come out of whatever foul, stench-infested, brutalizing place she'd started from and developed into the extraordinary person she now was. If it ever dawned on her that she was out of it now. No one is ever *safely* out of it. There is no green benign place, no happily anointed field, no sanctuary where one may cast off the memory of what once was. No amount of sophisticated cinema talk, none of the high-fashion clothes or expensive restaurants or the nice car and lavish apartment she could now afford could convince her that she had not been murdered once upon a time. These outer trappings were fine, they gave pleasure, but the heart and soul that is murdered once is one that stays murdered forever. It marches on . . .

Look, Martin, I heard one of them say, *he's plotting out our next picture.*

. . . it marches on in our false bones, enjoying good food, good music, physical love, the company of friends, it takes luxuries and comforts as they come, but it will not be deceived. It knows this delicious camouflage can't resurrect what has been permanently destroyed. Wanda would allow no one to tamper with this horrible, abiding vision. That vision must not be altered because to alter it she would have to forgive. And nothing—whether person, place or God—deserved forgiveness of those crimes committed against her, the mundane stench of which she breathed daily. They deserved reminders. The steady vigil of accusation. This was the film I had always wanted to make of Wanda and never had. Eternal victim. Everpresent accuser. Perpetual riddle of human life. A straight narrative, no tricks, no gimmicks, an old-fashioned tale, one that parents could take their children to see.

The ardour of expression at our table had thinned. Elaine was squeezing Wanda's hands across the table, her shoulders routed between two candlesticks. 'One letter,' she was saying. 'But such a letter! Lives made over—that's what art can accomplish!'

Wanda squeezed out a thin laugh.

'What I object to in all this review business,' said Robin, 'is how critics can only talk about directors these days. One mention he gives me, one stinking line! If I hear another word about Russ Meyer or Bertolucci or that crowd I'll throw up.'

'Not here, I hope,' teased Wanda. 'Not tonight.' She smiled at my wife. Eyes gone lazy. Her enigmatic face. 'I apologize. Pay no attention to me. You know I never know what I'm saying.' She lifted the champagne bottle out of its ice-bed and poured our glasses full. 'I didn't know I was part of a revolution. Guerrilla action, is that what it is, Martin? Me, a poor girl off the farm in . . .' She paused, batted her eyelids at me, inserted a thumb briefly in her mouth: 'Look at Martin, he's suddenly all ears. I almost gave away where I was from. You're such a pest, Martin, so boring—as if it matters where I was born or how poor or rich my parents were. For all the years I've known him he's been itching to hear me confess that I was born an orphan, raised in a church home where I was beaten and went unfed, or that if I had a father I was kept out of school and raped and made to sleep under the front porch with dogs.'

'That's Martin to a T,' piped in Elaine as if this remark struck her as a sudden revelation. 'He's got theories about us all. Because I was overly protected in my youth he's convinced that even today I need a nanny in my room and the light on when I sleep. It's only through subterfuge that I ever got to see his films. I had to lie and claim I was shopping or seeing friends.'

I raised my glass in a toast to these two teasers.

'What do *you* think?' Robin asked me, jabbing a finger at Oble's review. 'Do you take this brainy stuff seriously?'

'Yes,' the women chorused. 'Tell us what you think!'

My wife's hand cruised along my thigh as she snuggled her head against me.

The truth is that, between one thing and another, I was close to tears. 'I do think,' I said, 'that except for Elaine, this is the first truly nice thing anyone has said about me since I was twelve years old.'

'Boo!' croaked Robin. 'He's drunk.'

The women regarded me with wonder, smiling tenderly, warmed to see so much sentimentality exposed. 'Oh, God,' mourned Wanda, 'he's going to cry now. He always does on the set.'

'When *I* was twelve,' joked Robin, 'I was looking to reform school as a step up in the world.'

'You still are,' observed Elaine, shushing him. She turned to me. 'What was said to you at twelve? Can you remember?'

'Vividly. My mother came in from work one day and found me sweeping. Into the corner where I had the dust-pan waiting ...'

The women's eyes never left me. They were enjoying this moment, yet at the same time feared the cavalry would charge over the next hill and whisk me to safety before I could reveal my secret.

'He was desperately poor,' said Elaine by way of illumination. 'His mother, alone, had to raise seven children. Martin had no shoes and when his teeth rotted they were extracted by slamming doors. He won't forgive anyone for this. He holds us all responsible.'

'What did your mother say?' asked Wanda.

'She said I was beautiful. That I had a beautiful soul. She told me I had the spirit of an angel.'

Wanda sighed, not masking her disappointment, murmuring, 'Now that's true deprivation'—no doubt recalling her own forced labour as a child and finding my gallantry feeble by comparison. 'To hell with this,' remarked Robin. 'I'm tired of hearing about disadvantaged people.' He excused himself and left the table. My wife contentedly massaged my thigh. I survived the brutal confession. We stuffed ourselves with food and kept the champagne flowing.

It was a fine evening. Our last together with Wanda.

MARY NAPELS (b.d. & description withheld by request)
Helpful neighbour, homemaker and good sport, nicknamed 'Mosie' by her friends: 'Hello, Mosie.'

Hi, Martin, how is my favorite convict this evening?

Contributor of $500 toward my bail. Overweight, but doesn't like to be reminded. Confronts every issue with brutal fact.

You deserved it, Martin. I hate your films. I don't care that they are part of our sexual liberation. I'd rather be uptight with Queen Victoria. I don't care about your good intentions. Your condemnations smack of the celebratory. I recall with a shudder that scene from Peppermint Nights *when you have Göring meditating on his victims like Narcissus bent over his image at the pool. I bathe a long time after viewing your films.*

'Why did you put up money for my bail?'

One feels protective of fools. And you've toned down the vulgarity, you've become more tasteful of late.

Dropped by only yesterday evening, by appointment, and helped me cook a succulent dinner.

Don't worry. I won't jeopardize your chances for getting Wanda's kid returned. I'm perfectly willing to tell the judge you'd make a lovely parent.

For this repast we were joined by

SANDRA OLSON (1939–)

A semi-official visit. Former enemy, now new-found supporter and co-conspirator, a Family Affairs investigator.

How's tricks, gang?

she asked, plopping down beside the crab dish a bottle of Spanish burgundy with a home-made label.

I come with greetings from Angelia Latishia Casslake who pines for her return to the pornographer's bosom. Now, don't weep, Martin, but this altercation with your wife worsened your case.

'There is no altercation. She left because her parents promised her they'd die of a broken heart if she stayed with me.'

We can hardly tell that to the court. Nor can we tell it that her father has threatened your life. We are up the familiar creek, honey bunch.

We weep, all three. One good cry leads to another and soon Sandra is regaling us with vivid reports of her own fanatical and brutal father whose stated mission in life had been the terrorization of all females and the blowing up of all foreign embassies and banks on home soil. To succeed in the latter he was often obliged to be out of town, for which his family gave incessant thanks to their dimly perceived saviour. I held her hand while she told me of the nightly humiliations, and how reprieve came at last when one of his Montreal bombs prematurely exploded. Later on, with Mosie off to her bed, I told Sandra Olson something of my own story.

Martin Martin Martin I feel so sorry for you!

'Oh, I don't know. Other people have survived worse nightmares.'

I should have curled up and died! It's awful, awful!

That my tale was more terrible than her own she conceded, and this, I judge, made her feel better—as it did me—about facing the dawn which by this hour was nearly upon us.

I'm going home now. Try not to worry.

'Oh, you're a joker, Olson, you are.'

I could not sleep. Donning a disguise that would fool no one, least of all myself—slouch hat, upturned trenchcoat, a walking stick to complement an imagined limp—I aimlessly followed footpaths, lanes and alleys in the neighbourhood, gaining forlorn solace in thinking about

MIRANDA PROBST (now in her eighties) My high school French teacher. Children's counsellor and church organist, retired. She befriended me when I was a youth and isolated from my peers.

You were such a nice, awkward, almost backward child. Much too sensitive for your own good. So shy, so honest. I told you I would pass you but you said you deserved to

fail. You must come and see me again before I die. What have you done with your life, dear boy? You must tell me sometime, I know it would make me proud. My friends here will be green with envy over this new shawl.

'POOPS' THOMAS (about my age) Obese boyhood chum, the only person I was ever able to torment without fear of reprisal. Nothing known of his adult life. Where are you, Poops? Have you found happiness?

LEO YSELOVICH (–) My high school history teacher who pushed the cycle theory with such malice and vengeance that I have not abandoned it to this day. Born a Dukhobor, old religious sect exiled (7,000 of them) to Canada from Tsarist Russia in 1898 after years of famine and persecution (*Night of the Tsars*, 1974). He wore the same sweater year after year and seemed always to walk over the same path dogs had taken a moment before. Tall, bespectacled, a chain-smoker. Elderly now and possibly deceased. I like to think he influenced lives more complimentary to him than mine. Hounded out of the public school system at age fifty-six for alleged homosexuality, not heard of since.

RUDOLPH PUCARD (1926–) A servant of the people.

RCMP vice detective. Pucard had but one goal, to 'send smut merchants back where they came from.' Grim, bedevilled little bachelor a shade up from Maigret. Attended perhaps fifty screenings of the *Night* films in search of a psychological edge to be used against their perpetrators. Became, as a result, confused. Grieved deeply over Wanda's suicide.

Wanda: *I like him fine. Have you ever noticed that his right eyelid droops? I like that.*

My arresting officer, January 1978. *We've got the Able girl's statement, sonny-boy. It's a crock of scum but the department wants you and they don't care how.* Refused to testify under oath at the pre-trial hearing that the accused had unlawful carnal knowledge of one Marceline Able, minor, and that he did thereafter with reprehensible greed force her to work for him on the street as a common prostitute.

My lawyer: *Your Honour, I object to the nasty manner in which the prosecuting attorney has dropped this ugly charge.*

Me: *It's all a filthy lie, Your Honour.*

The Judge: *I would advise the honourable defence attorney to restrain his client or I shall have him gagged.*

My lawyer: (whisper): *Shut up, you fool.*

The Judge: *Detective Pucard, to your knowledge was the accused this child's pimp?*

Pucard: *Your Honour, I uncovered no such evidence.*

The Judge: *Hang the evidence. In your line of inquiry did you assume he was so engaged?*

Pucard: *No, Your Honour.*

The Judge: *Well, we've got to stop this vile business somewhere. Objection denied.*

ALBERT ROSEN (1931–1978) Fascist, rabid anti-Semite and lifelong cinema freak.

The only documented case of a man whose character was reformed through film. After seeing the *Night* series, this stranger wrote me, he was committing his life to a war against evil. Shot down outside a mosque in Addis Ababa, Ethiopia, Sunday, 21 March, 1978, by guards of the red terror, while attempting to distribute food and med-icine to the poor. A nail driven into his chest, attached to it a note which named him the people's enemy. One of 148 verified dead, mostly children, shot or hacked to death that day. Another day after so many and so many. His body and theirs littering the streets, removal forbidden. Notes pinned to bodies read: This mother's son put the people's well-being above ideology. (Amnesty International Bulletin.)

—— WOLFE (1936–1936). Born dead. My sister.

SISTER MARY OF ST. DAVID (–1978)

Raped and murdered on this street corner one month ago, criminal party not yet discovered. One Christmas eve three years ago she passed Elaine and me right about here, transporting on her shoulder an undecorated tree.

It is an evil thing that you do, Martin. My prayers go with you.

'Mine with you, Sister.'

SO MANY OTHERS

Nameless and unknown, disfigured in the memory, strangers, friends and shadowy walk-ons. The truck driver for Maple Leaf Foods who on a road past Long Beach, BC, pulled Wanda Lee Casslake too late from her carbon monoxide end to everything.

The motor wasn't running any more. I reached in, turned off the ignition. She toppled over. I don't know how long she'd been dead.

On the front seat a note: *Let Elaine and Martin have Angelia, she'll be happy with them.*

So many more. Over the faces of all these, superimposed, enduring year after year, the innocent, amazed eyes of a boy from nowhere, looking forward through time at me. My own eyes. My own, the same eyes, looking back at him.

'How goes it, old friend?'

My eyes never close. There is nothing you do that I can't see.

'Will you never be satisfied?'

You may have fooled Oble but you shall never fool me. A thousand people have passed before me, Martin, but you are the biggest disappointment of all.

'I'm tired now, old friend. I'm going home.'

You've disgraced me, Martin. People like you have no home.

Dawn. True dawn. A red wash above the city, the air fresh for a change. I tell you much is to be said for living one's life by the sea. The milkman making his rounds. A street cleaner high in the orange cab of his giant machine. Rows of parked cars, the occasional cat or dog. Another night survived.

When I get back to my building I find my wife curled up on the hallway floor. Asleep. The hall isn't heated, a thin coat stretches from her head to her feet. Mouth a little open, her eyes puffy, her hair a mess. Her hands are ice-cold.

'Elaine,' I say. 'Elaine, you have got to stop doing this.'

She awakens in a fright, then sees it is only me. She stretches her arms, yawns noisily, and scrambles to her feet.

You keep moving the key.

'Yes, to keep you out. But you've got to stop camping in the hall.'

I know. This time I think I caught a cold.

She walks in behind me, turns on the lights, and begins immediately to clean up the place.

Sloppy housekeeper. Whoever is looking after you now.

She tires, however. She fluffs up a pillow, sits on the sofa, plops the pillow on her lap.

I've decided. Martin. Hell or high water, I'm not leaving again.

'We've been through all this before.'

I sit down beside her. Her head lolls, or mine does, and her arm falls softly around.

We're so tired, she says.

She sneezes, grabs a tissue and blows her nose. The tissue floats down. We stare in front of us. There is nothing to see but bare wall.

It's our chance of getting Angelia back. If my parents die of shame they'll just have to. I'm staying, Martin.

'I guess so. If you're sure.'

I'm going to bed now.

'I'll join you if I may.'

We do not bother to undress. We drag ourselves to the bed and tumble in. Our backs curve, our knees bend. We are twins, lengths of soft curving flesh harpooned to the mattress by a single throw. To diffuse the light Elaine sweeps hair across her face.

Be quiet, she moans. *Don't say a word.*

I have grit in my eyes; it's this that causes tears.

Five minutes later we irritably sigh, kick like gypsies in a dance. Sob and sink down again. A pillow smothers her.

You're thinking, she accuses. *You've got to stop it, Martin, I can't sleep.*

MARCELINE ABLE

Viper. Liar. Killer of this sleep. Amorphous runner, derelict from the lost lagoon, guide for the lunatic's museum. Freelance jibber-jabber who singlehandedly brought my mogul's empire tumbling down. *He put his hands all over me sir and when I said I wouldn't I wasn't that kind of girl he hit me and threw me down and then he did it to me so help me God I wouldn't lie about a thing like that and it went on for days and days until I was so sore I couldn't move all my pleading with him done no good and finally he was tired of me I guess and he said if I worked for him on he street he'd look after me he said a girl like me pretty and young and kind of classy you know I could make a lot of money on the street and he'd see to it I got a good share I told him I didn't want to but he made me sir he said it was all I was good for. . .*

Discovered by Wanda, loitering on a street corner one day (*Hey, Miss, could you spare a quarter?*) and hired by her for part-time child-minding work.

You can see that she needs help, Martin. She's loony, she's a bit confused, but she isn't dangerous, I'm only doing what you would have done for her in my place, and you know all the trouble I've had getting someone to look after Angelia.

'She's bad news, Wanda.'

No, she isn't. You should have seen me when I was her age. The responsibility will be good for her. You're always preaching compassion, I should think you'd show a little now.

A runaway, as it turned out. Hitch-hiker, acid-dropper, vagrant, groupie, Moon disciple, racist, back-stabber, shop-lifter and compulsive whiner:

Everybody dumps on me!

Hating above all things the square and the phony.

I hate a phony, don't you just hate a square, Martin?

I went without appointment one day to Wanda's place and knew something was wrong the minute I knocked on the door. It was Marcie who finally came. 'Where's Wanda?' I asked and she said *Wanda's shopping, how would I know where Wanda is?* Strange, something about her that wouldn't let me go away. 'What's going on?' I asked, 'where's the kid?' *Oh, the kid*, she said, *the kid, I guess she's around somewhere.* And then giggles leading into hysterical laughter as she backed against the wall and slumped down. Angelia in the kitchen, weeping hopelessly, barricaded inside the cramped cabinet where the garbage was stowed. *Well, she was freaking me, Mister, suppose you just motor on out of here.*

'Wanda, Wanda, you've got to get rid of that nut you hired.'

What harm can she do, be patient, she's only trying to find herself. Charlie Manson's great granddaughter.

He was always coming on to me grabbing and wanting me to ball with him I wouldn't of minded so much except he was always coming on so righteous like you know and know-it-all just like my parents he was always dropping by the place when Wanda was out and I could tell what he was after but I gave him the cold shoulder I wouldn't have nothing to do with him I guess he's got a thing about young girls or something he's kinda uptight about sex you know weird. But me I was just looking after the kid the way I was s'posed to and I did good too which wasn't easy the kid was always wanting something a real attention-grabber if you know the kind I mean well the kid was like that something awful but I was looking after her see and ignoring Martin. It wasn't till later I found out he was in the porno business that nearly blew my mind when I heard that because he'd always seemed so straight to me him and Wanda was real close and at first I thought they had a thing going but I don't know you never can tell people and I was looking out for myself I mean I had my own life to lead right? But then him and Elaine they started ganging up on me they told all sorts of stories on me to Wanda and I could tell the way she was looking at me she had her doubts and then there was that time when she lost her money I know she thought I stole it though she never said nothing about it she was real tight you know wouldn't spend a dime on herself anyway they told Wanda I was really fucking up the kid which really freaked me they said I was mean to the kid I even beat her but that was an outright lie. What's true though is that I was after Wanda to get me a role in one of their pictures I could be a pretty good actress I think if anybody ever gave me the chance I'm very photogenic to tell the truth. I know what they'll tell you they'll say I told them I'd do anything to be in the movie business I'd even do it with a black or a Chink any kinky thing they wanted but that's just a rotten lie like I told you I didn't even know that was the kind of picture Martin makes. So when I told them they could chuck it I wasn't having anything to do with dirt like that well that's when Martin raped me nearly as I recall I'm a little confused now what with it being such a terrible ordeal I went through and when the policeman arrested me for soliciting that's when I told him how come I was in this bad spot which I'm telling you about on my own free will . . .

Deranged, demented, vicious. An idiotic little jerk. Emptyheaded for the most part. Even ordinary at times. Even at times, God help me, amusing:

I was with a Moog Synthesizer man before I come here.

'With who?'

We were really grooving on each other for a week or two, crashing out at this deserted house he knew about, about ten of us. Funny thing was, every morning we'd wake up and nobody could find their shoes. We'd all be walking around dopey-like on the freezing floor asking each other where's my shoes, what happened to my fucking shoes?

'What had happened to them?'

Well then one night I saw him. He had his toesack and he was scooting from bed to bed cramming all the shoes he could find in his bag. And then he went outside in the snow and threw them every which way far as he could, every one of them. Then he came back inside and went to sleep.

'Would he throw away his own?'

No, that's why he was doing it, that was his whole idea. So we'd have to wear his, taking turns, I mean wearing his while trying to find our own. Hiking boots, about size twelve.

'Didn't anyone suspect him?'

Well we were pretty stoned, most of us either coming off a trip or taking off on one. No, he'd sort of stay in his sleeping-bag all day grinning, he really got off on it, seeing us walk around in his shoes. He was trying to make friends is what he said, loaning out his shoes. He said it made him feel real good, like Jesus when he threw bread upon the water and the crumbs turned into swans, that's the funny way he talked.

'Why did you leave him?'

Oh, they practically killed him when they found out he was throwing their shoes out in the snow. And he was kind of a drip you know.

She could be nice, she could lay a faint finger on the heart-strings when she was in a sentimental or depressed mood:

You people, you and Elaine and Wanda and even Angelia sometimes, I know you want to love me, I know you try to. I makes me feel kind of creepy, you want to know the truth, I never felt that way before. I keep asking myself when's the hatchet going to fall.

Mindless. Totally without conscience. Yet we rarely felt her evil was intentional, that it was motivated, that she had any reasons for the way she behaved. One day Elaine and I, talking about her, worked ourselves into a nervous state, and went running over. *Hurry, Martin, she's doing something terrible, I can feel it, can't you?* Horrible scene. Marcie in the bathroom trying to stuff Angelia's head down the commode.

Why did you do it, goddamn you, Marcie, what's wrong with you?
A shrug. I don't know.
I don't know either. It's God, I think.

GOD

God is the proven traitor. I sometimes think his body is the rot in this air. That the battle for our souls was lost, our fate sealed incalculable ages ago. At the very minute we looked and began to fabricate something better than ourselves. That's when we killed God, at the very instant we in our image created Him. Not, as is usually supposed, to explain our origins or sweeten our destiny—but simply to shift the blame elsewhere. We strung the bastard up. That's when we did it and that's why.

It is Elaine, rising petulantly out of sleep, who first hears the banging on our door. *Quick,* she says, *get it before I wake up.* She flops back down, groaning, hand over her ear. I get to the door somehow. My neighbour Mary Napels is there. She glares at me, striding inside.

Have you seen it? Have you seen this vile rag? It's hideous, you'll never be able to adopt Angelia now!

She thrusts a rolled newspaper in my hands. I look stupidly at her and ask her what time it is.

Open it! she shouts. *Let's see you explain your way out of this.* She grabs the tabloid back, yanks the sheets flat, and drums a finger violently on the page. *There! It's disgusting, how could you let them do this?*

DEATH STALKS THE BEACH

the headline reads

AS SMUT QUEEN HAS LAST PARTY

Wanda with her flat chest, in her birthday celebration with Robin, black boxes to obscure genitalia and to hide Robin's eyes, smart lawyer's device for staving off libel suits. My photographs, last gift from Wanda. At last victorious, giving the one performance she always claimed for herself and giving it in *The People's Inquirer.*

Elaine sways barefooted in the doorway: *What is it? What has gone wrong now?*
Mary rushes to her. *It's Martin, he's sold those photos to a scandal sheet.*
Nonsense.

A bottom-of-the-page insert claims my attention: a grim, cloudy photograph captioned HER DEATH CAR. Not Wanda's car, not even a real beach, but a studio blow-up of what a real one is. Through the early morning mist I can just make out the grey curved stem of a woman's neck, the dead face lodged between window and seat, so elegiacally turned. 'Professionally posed,' the parenthesis informs. 'Meanwhile, her long-time director and bosom-chum Martin Wolfe, awaiting trial for the alleged rape of a juvenile, continues his efforts to adopt the queen's small child. Get 'em while young, eh Martin?'

MARTIN DEWITT WOLFE (1934–) Film-maker (now retired).
Night With Wanda, etc.

'I give up, Elaine. I quit.' I pass this new bouquet to my wife, to let her have a whiff. I give her such imaginative gifts, she might say. Human smut skilfully disguised as a gift to all mankind. Thank God for the press, which keeps us abreast of ourselves. Thank God. The last picture show. It's over.

How could you do it, Martin? Mary Napels is weeping at the tombside. Somebody has swiped the last crumb off God's plate.

'I didn't. Somebody else did.'

That woman, Elaine cries. *Rita Islington! Wouldn't that be it, Martin? You gave her the negatives. But why? Why would she do such a thing to her own sister?*

'Why not?' I say. But then I look at the two women, both of them horrified. Weeping and yet ready and able to give solace. I know well that look in my wife's eyes; it is frequently there, frequently inquiring: *Have you lost faith, Martin? Oh, no, Martin, you couldn't!*

I'm sorry, Martin, my neighbour says. *It just seemed too much, the final straw. You know? I had no right to suggest . . .*

She comes over to give me a hug. Elaine comes too and the three of us stand holding on to each other. One more word and we would weep like a fountain.

My wife breaks suddenly away from our triumvirate, shaking her fist at the sky: *Angelia!* she shouts. *How are we going to save her?*

ANGELIA LATISHIA CASSLAKE (1974–) An innocent child.

The star of my next film:

> *The most recent film of M. D. Wolfe opens in a massively detailed, nearly interminable sequence made up of the same repealed, gradually expanding scene. Fade in on a barren plain where a clump of ant-like creatures congregates. As the scene comes closer we notice that these figures are strangely reminiscent of demons on a canvas by Brueghel, gnomes leering from behind haystacks etc. Each time the scene is replayed our vision is improved. For instance, we observe that the item being wagged by each of a crowd of chanting, hydrocephalic idiots is in fact the grotesque and elongated human penis. Another group whom we had originally supposed to be gossipy old women becomes eventually a chorus line of judges, each one of them bewigged. We are ten minutes into the film before it is possible to see that the idiots surround a fire. Bound to a stake in the centre of his blazing pyre is a little girl, no more than four years old. Off to the left is another victim, who looks remarkably like Wanda Casslake. She is being stabbed repeatedly with pitchforks, wielded by two other women, one elegant and austere, the other a mad-eyed juvenile. The Wanda-woman rises again and again, bleeding and struggling over to the fire as if she could give succour to the child at the stake. At last Wanda expires, her death role being amplified stereophonically throughout the theatre. One of the idiots, however, is seen on closer inspection to be a film director—he wears dark glasses and an Italian open-necked shirt; he has a folding director's chair strapped to his shoulders. With him are two women, very impressive types. We soon discover that these three are in fact attempting to rescue the little girl. Pretending to add faggots, they in fact remove the most treacherous. The director loosens the cords which tie her while the women create a diversion—they writhe provocatively around the bodies of the idiots, licking their own lips and cupping their naked breasts as if to offer a drink of milk—he takes the child from the fire and places her piggyback where the director's chair was previously strapped. He adjusts his dark glasses and gives a blast of the whistle round his*

neck to alert his friends that the mission has been accomplished. *Unfortunately, this also alerts the enemy—so that the women and the director have to run like hell, the idiots barking after them while the judges blow tin bugles and stomp their heels. But they make it. All the way across the expanding screen they run, miniature angels seemingly getting nowhere, so tiny the camera's eye barely perceives them. The idiots and the judges abandon the chase and attack each other. In this way is the foe at last vanquished, harmless dots bleeding into the barren plain.*

FADE OUT.

FADE IN: EXTERIOR. FLYING STORK, SWADDLED BABY.

PAN.

CUT TO: DISTANT 'X' ON BARREN PLAIN.

CUT TO: SWOOPING BIRD.

Bob Shaw

Bob Shaw was born in Belfast in 1931. He says his father, a policeman who came from farming stock and who "by the time he was 30 had had one German bullet and two IRA bullets in him," considered writing unhealthy and science fiction "black magic stuff." Shaw attended high school and technical college before taking up employment as a public relations officer for Short Brothers and Harland aircraft manufacturers, as a journalist for *The Belfast-Telegraph*, and as a free-lance writer. Subsequent employment with Vickers Shipbuilding took him to England, where he now lives and writes free-lance in Grappenhall, Warrington, Cheshire. Shaw is the author of more than twenty works of fiction, including such novels as *Night Walk* (1967), *The Ground Zero Man* (1971), *Comic Kaleidescope* (1977), *The Ceres Solution* (1981), and *The Peace Machine* (1985); his collections of short fiction include *Tomorrow Lies in Ambush* (1973) and *A Better Mantrap* (1982).

In Robert Silverberg's *Worlds of Wonder* (1987), Silverberg describes "Light of Other Days" as a "small, quiet, well-nigh perfect short story . . . built around two interlocking cores: a troubled marriage and a technological wonder." Of the technology, he says: "Slow glass, taken by itself, is the sort of notion that comes once or twice at best in a science-fiction writer's lifetime, the sort of thing that stirs his colleagues to lusty applause and bleak bileful envy. Like most brilliant ideas, it's a perfectly obvious one—to anyone with the wit to see it." The story took him only four hours to write, Shaw says in an essay called "The Profession of Science Fiction: XI: Escape to Infinity" (*Foundation*, No. 10, June 1976), but he carried the idea around for years before finding the proper vehicle or "instruments" for it. He considers plot his principal instrument as a science fiction writer. While he understands how some writers might eschew plot and say, "Let's get the distractions out of the way so that you can concentrate on the actual writing, the message, the insight into human affairs, etc.," Shaw has no qualms about his own search for a strong story line. "In my case . . . the best method is to devise a plot which is like a machine which will hold the idea-diamond in a claw under a spotlight and turn it this way and that. The machine has to be intelligent, of course, so that it can (a) select all the good facets and make sure they are given due prominence, and (b) identify all the flaws and do its best to ensure that they become lost in the dazzle and fireworks." He claims that concern for "the successful construction of a plot does not create an incentive to write carelessly"; on the contrary, "the comfort of knowing that everything is tight and sure and solidly made is stimulating and keeps the mind at a high pitch. Another major consideration is that this approach to plotting necessitates intense examination of the story idea and can make you more aware of its ramifications, sometimes to the point where fertile new areas are discovered and opened up."

Shaw considers science fiction "escapist, but in a positive sense . . . because it is an escape to reality." He rejects the mundane world of the so-called realists—which he associates with "mortgages, the TUC, engine wear, national insurance contributions, prostate troubles" and dismisses as "merely local phenomena"—in favour of a transcendental fiction where change is possible and where general truths are revealed. He considers realistic fiction mere arithmetic, whereas science fiction is algebra. However, he insists that he goes to "considerable pains to introduce real people in the situations. Real people (it isn't entirely necessary for them to be human beings) give a story significance. The universe is marvellous only if there's a somebody there to do the marvelling, but in science fiction it is important to strike the right balance between characterisation and exposition. In a story which has a strong idea the human interest stuff can get in the way of what the reader may legitimately regard as the main work in hand. This is why I try to express character in terms of action, and it has something to do with why I write a type of story which Harry Harrison has described as 'plot supported.'

"The general aim of my work," Shaw concludes, "is—if I may be permitted a bit of imagery—to wrench open a door in the grey circumscribing world of the here-and-now and show the technicolour infinities beyond it, which is what science fiction did for me. Incidentally, I regard that as a lofty aim. The kind of stories I particularly enjoy reading, the sort Henry Kuttner did so well, are those which begin in a normal-seeming present and then, very gradually, steer you across an unseen line into strange dimensions. I enjoy writing stories like that, too, because they half-convince me that the wrinkles in the continuum, which I mentioned earlier, are close at hand, that maybe we won't have to wait Stapledonian aeons until the door-knobs open blue eyes and blink at us, or time-travellers step out of glowing circles into our living rooms, or stars shine beneath the last step of the cellar stairs."

Light of Other Days

Leaving the village behind, we followed the heady sweeps of the road up into a land of slow glass.

I had never seen one of the farms before and at first found them slightly eerie—an effect heightened by imagination and circumstance. The car's turbine was pulling smoothly and quietly in the damp air so that we seemed to be carried over the convolutions of the road in a kind of supernatural silence. On our right the mountain sifted down into an incredibly perfect valley of timeless pine, and everywhere stood the great frames of slow glass, drinking light. An occasional flash of afternoon sunlight on their wind bracing created an illusion of movement, but in fact the frames were deserted. The rows of windows had been standing on the hillside for years, staring into the valley, and men only cleaned them in the middle of the night when their human presence would not matter to the thirsty glass.

They were fascinating, but Selina and I didn't mention the windows. I think we hated each other so much we both were reluctant to sully anything new by drawing it into the nexus of our emotions. The holiday, I had begun to realize, was a stupid idea in the first place. I had thought it would cure everything, but, of course, it didn't stop Selina being pregnant and, worse still, it didn't even stop her being angry about being pregnant.

Rationalizing our dismay over her condition, we had circulated the usual statements to the effect that we would have *liked* having children—but later on, at the proper time. Selina's pregnancy had cost us her well-paid job and with it the new house we had been negotiating and which was far beyond the reach of my income from poetry. But the real source of our annoyance was that we were face to face with the realization that people who say they want children later always mean they want children never. Our nerves were thrumming with the knowledge that we, who had thought ourselves so unique, had fallen into the same biological trap as every mindless rutting creature which ever existed.

The road took us along the southern slopes of Ben Cruachan until we began to catch glimpses of the gray Atlantic far ahead. I had just cut our speed to absorb the view better when I noticed the sign spiked to a gatepost. It said: "SLOW GLASS—Quality High, Prices Low—J. R. Hagan." On an impulse I stopped the car on the verge, wincing slightly as tough grasses whipped noisily at the bodywork.

"Why have we stopped?" Selina's neat, smoke-silver head turned in surprise.

"Look at that sign. Let's go up and see what there is. The stuff might be reasonably priced out here."

Selina's voice was pitched high with scorn as she refused, but I was too taken with my idea to listen. I had an illogical conviction that doing something extravagant and crazy would set us right again.

"Come on," I said, "the exercise might do us some good. We've been driving too long anyway."

She shrugged in a way that hurt me and got out of the car. We walked up a path made of irregular, packed clay steps nosed with short lengths of sapling. The path curved through trees which clothed the edge of the hill and at its end we found a low farmhouse. Beyond the little stone building tall frames of slow glass gazed out towards the voice-stilling sight of Cruachan's ponderous descent towards the waters of Loch Linnhe. Most of the panes were perfectly transparent but a few were dark, like panels of polished ebony.

As we approached the house through a neat cobbled yard a tall middle-aged man in ash-colored tweeds arose and waved to us. He had been sitting on the low rubble wall which bounded the yard, smoking a pipe and staring towards the house. At the front window of the cottage a young woman in a tangerine dress stood with a small boy in her arms, but she turned disinterestedly and moved out of sight as we drew near.

"Mr. Hagan?" I guessed.

"Correct. Come to see some glass, have you? Well, you've come to the right place." Hagan spoke crisply, with traces of the pure highland which sounds so much like Irish to the unaccustomed ear. He had one of those calmly dismayed faces one finds on elderly road-menders and philosophers.

"Yes," I said. "We're on holiday. We saw your sign."

Selina, who usually has a natural fluency with strangers, said nothing. She was looking towards the now empty window with what I thought was a slightly puzzled expression.

"Up from London, are you? Well, as I said, you've come to the right place—and at the right time, too. My wife and I don't see many people this early in the season."

I laughed. "Does that mean we might be able to buy a little glass without mortgaging our home?"

"Look at that now," Hagan said, smiling helplessly. "I've thrown away any advantage I might have had in the transaction. Rose, that's my wife, says I never learn. Still, let's sit down and talk it over." He pointed at the rubble wall then glanced doubtfully at Selina's immaculate blue skirt. "Wait till I fetch a rug from the house." Hagan limped quickly into the cottage, closing the door behind him.

"Perhaps it wasn't such a marvelous idea to come up here," I whispered to Selina, "but you might at least be pleasant to the man. I think I can smell a bargain."

"Some hope," she said with deliberate coarseness. "Surely even you must have noticed that ancient dress his wife is wearing? He won't give much away to strangers."

"Was that his wife?"

"Of course that was his wife."

"Well, well," I said, surprised. "Anyway, try to be civil with him. I don't want to be embarrassed."

Selina snorted, but she smiled whitely when Hagan reappeared and I relaxed a little. Strange how a man can love a woman and yet at the same time pray for her to fall under a train.

Hagan spread a tartan blanket on the wall and we sat down, feeling slightly self-conscious at having been translated from our city-oriented lives into a rural tableau. On the distant slate of the Loch, beyond the watchful frames of slow glass, a slow-moving steamer drew a white line towards the south. The boisterous mountain air seemed almost to invade our lungs, giving us more oxygen than we required.

"Some of the glass farmers around here," Hagan began, "give strangers, such as yourselves, a sales talk about how beautiful the autumn is in this part of Argyll. Or it might be the spring, or the winter. I don't do that—any fool knows that a place which doesn't look right in summer never looks right. What do you say?"

I nodded compliantly.

"I want you just to take a good look out towards Mull, Mr. . . ."

"Garland."

". . . Garland. That's what you're buying if you buy my glass, and it never looks better than it does at this minute. The glass is in perfect phase, none of it is less than ten years thick—and a four-foot window will cost you two hundred pounds."

"*Two hundred!*" Selina was shocked. "That's as much as they charge at the Scenedow shop in Bond Street."

Hagan smiled patiently, then looked closely at me to see if I knew enough about slow glass to appreciate what he had been saying. His price had been much higher than I had hoped—but *ten years thick!* The cheap glass one found in places like the Vistaplex and Pane-o-rama stores usually consisted of a quarter of an inch of ordinary glass faced with a veneer of slow glass perhaps only ten or twelve months thick.

"You don't understand, darling," I said, already determined to buy. "This glass will last ten years and it's in phase."

"Doesn't that only mean it keeps time?"

Hagan smiled at her again, realizing he had no further necessity to bother with me. "Only, you say! Pardon me, Mrs. Garland, but you don't seem to appreciate the miracle, the genuine honest-to-goodness miracle, of engineering precision needed to produce a piece of glass in phase. When I say the glass is ten years thick it means it takes light ten years to pass through it. In effect, each one of those panes is ten light-years thick—more than twice the distance to the nearest star— so a variation in actual thickness of only a millionth of an inch would . . ."

He stopped talking for a moment and sat quietly looking towards the house. I turned my head from the view of the Loch and saw the young woman standing at the window again. Hagan's eyes were filled with a kind of greedy reverence which made me feel uncomfortable and at the same time convinced me Selina had been wrong. In my experience husbands never looked at wives that way, at least, not at their own.

The girl remained in view for a few seconds, dress glowing warmly, then moved back into the room. Suddenly I received a distinct, though inexplicable, impression she was blind. My feeling was that Selina and I were perhaps blundering through an emotional interplay as violent as our own.

"I'm sorry," Hagan continued, "I thought Rose was going to call me for something. Now, where was I, Mrs. Garland? Ten light-years compressed into a quarter of an inch means . . ."

I ceased to listen, partly because I was already sold, partly because I had heard the story of slow glass many times before and had never yet understood the principles involved. An acquaintance with scientific training had once tried to be helpful by telling me to visualize a pane of slow glass as a hologram which did not need coherent light from a laser for the reconstitution of its visual information, and in which every photon of ordinary light passed through a spiral tunnel coiled outside the radius of capture of each atom in the glass. This gem of, to me, incomprehensibility not only told me nothing, it convinced me once again that a mind as nontechnical as mine should concern itself less with causes than effects.

The most important effect, in the eyes of the average individual, was that light took a long time to pass through a sheet of slow glass. A new piece was always jet black because nothing has yet come through, but one could stand the glass beside, say, a woodland lake until the scene emerged, perhaps a year later. If the glass was then removed and installed in a dismal city flat, the flat would—for that year—appear to overlook the woodland lake. During the year it wouldn't be merely a very realistic but still picture—the water would ripple in sunlight, silent animals would come to drink, birds would cross the sky, night would follow day, season would follow season. Until one day, a year later, the beauty held in the subatomic pipelines would be exhausted and the familiar gray cityscape would reappear.

Apart from its stupendous novelty value, the commercial success of slow glass was founded on the fact that having a scenedow was the exact emotional equivalent of owning land. The meanest cave dweller could look out on misty parks—and who was to say they weren't his? A man who really owns tailored gardens and estates doesn't spend his time proving his ownership by crawling on his ground, feeling, smelling, tasting it. All he receives from the land are light patterns, and with scenedows those patterns could be taken into coal mines, submarines, prison cells.

On several occasions I have tried to write short pieces about the enchanted crystal but, to me, the theme is so ineffably poetic as to be, paradoxically, beyond the reach of poetry—mine at any rate. Besides, the best songs and verse had already been written, with prescient inspiration, by men who had died long before slow glass was discovered. I had no hope of equaling, for example, Moore with his:

> Oft in the stilly night,
> Ere slumber's chain has bound me,
> Fond Memory brings the light,
> Of other days around me . . .

It took only a few years for slow glass to develop from a scientific curiosity to a sizable industry. And much to the astonishment of we poets—those of us who remain convinced that beauty lives though lilies die—the trappings of that industry were no different from those of any other. There were good scenedows which cost a lot of money, and there were inferior scenedows which cost rather less. The thickness, measured in years, was an important factor in the cost but there was also the question of *actual* thickness, or phase.

Even with the most sophisticated engineering techniques available thickness control was something of a hit-and-miss affair. A coarse discrepancy could mean that a pane intended to be five years thick might be five and a half, so that light which entered in summer emerged in winter; a fine discrepancy could mean that noon sunshine emerged at midnight. These incompatibilities had their peculiar charm—many night workers, for example, liked having their own private time zones—but, in general, it cost more to buy scenedows which kept closely in step with real time.

Selina still looked unconvinced when Hagan had finished speaking. She shook her head almost imperceptibly and I knew he had been using the wrong approach. Quite suddenly the pewter helmet of her hair was disturbed by a cool gust of wind, and huge clean tumbling drops of rain began to spang round us from an almost cloudless sky.

"I'll give you a check now," I said abruptly, and saw Selina's green eyes triangulate angrily on my face. "You can arrange delivery?"

"Aye, delivery's no problem," Hagan said, getting to his feet. "But wouldn't you rather take the glass with you?"

"Well, yes—if you don't mind." I was shamed by his readiness to trust my scrip.

"I'll unclip a pane for you. Wait here. It won't take long to slip it into a carrying frame." Hagan limped down the slope towards the seriate windows, through some of which the view towards Linnhe was sunny, while others were cloudy and a few pure black.

Selina drew the collar of her blouse closed at her throat. "The least he could have done was invite us inside. There can't be so many fools passing through that he can afford to neglect them."

I tried to ignore the insult and concentrated on writing the check. One of the outsize drops broke across my knuckles, splattered the pink paper.

"All right," I said, "let's move in under the eaves till he gets back." You worm, I thought as I felt the whole thing go completely wrong. I just had to be a fool to marry you. A prize fool, a fool's fool—and now that you've trapped part of me inside you I'll never ever, never ever, *never ever* get away.

Feeling my stomach clench itself painfully, I ran behind Selina to the side of the cottage. Beyond the window the neat living room, with its coal fire, was empty but the child's toys were scattered on the floor. Alphabet blocks and a wheelbarrow the exact color of freshly pared carrots. As I stared in, the boy came running from the other room and began kicking the blocks. He didn't notice me. A few moments later the young woman entered the room and lifted him, laughing easily and whole-heartedly as she swung the boy under her arm. She came to the window as she had done earlier. I smiled self-consciously, but neither she nor the child responded.

My forehead prickly icily. *Could they both be blind?* I sidled away.

Selina gave a little scream and I spun towards her.

"*The rug!*" she said. "It's getting soaked."

She ran across the yard in the rain, snatched the reddish square from the dappling wall and ran back, towards the cottage door. Something heaved convulsively in my subconscious.

"Selina," I shouted. "Don't open it!"

But I was too late. She had pushed open the latched wooden door and was standing, hand over mouth, looking into the cottage. I moved close to her and took the rug from her unresisting fingers.

As I was closing the door I let my eyes traverse the cottage's interior. The neat living room in which I had just seen the woman and child was, in reality, a sickening clutter of shabby furniture, old newspapers, cast-off clothing and smeared dishes. It was damp, stinking and utterly deserted. The only object I recognized from my view through the window was the little wheelbarrow, paintless and broken.

I latched the door firmly and ordered myself to forget what I had seen. Some men who live alone are good housekeepers; others just don't know how.

Selina's face was white. "I don't understand. I don't understand it."

"Slow glass works both ways," I said gently. "Light passes out of the house, as well as in."

"You mean . . . ?"

"I don't know. It isn't our business. Now steady up—Hagan's coming back with our glass." The churning in my stomach was beginning to subside.

Hagan came into the yard carrying an oblong, plastic-covered frame. I held the check out to him, but he was staring at Selina's face. He seemed to know immediately that our uncomprehending fingers had rummaged through his soul. Selina avoided his gaze. She was old and ill-looking, and her eyes stared determinedly towards the nearing horizon.

"I'll take the rug from you, Mr. Garland," Hagan finally said. "You shouldn't have troubled yourself over it."

"No trouble. Here's the check."

"Thank you." He was still looking at Selina with a strange kind of supplication. "It's been a pleasure to do business with you."

"The pleasure was mine," I said with equal, senseless formality. I picked up the heavy frame and guided Selina towards the path which led to the road. Just as we reached the head of the now slippery steps Hagan spoke again.

"Mr. Garland!"

"It wasn't my fault," he said steadily. "A hit-and-run driver got them both, down on the Oban road six years ago. My boy was only seven when it happened. I'm entitled to something."

I nodded wordlessly and moved down the path, holding my wife close to me, treasuring the feel of her arms locked around me. At the bend I looked back through the rain and saw Hagan sitting with squared shoulders on the wall where we had first seen him.

He was looking at the house, but I was unable to tell if there was anyone at the window.

☙ Ray Smith

Ray Smith was born in 1941 and raised in Mabou, Cape Breton, and Halifax. He is a graduate of Dalhousie University and has served in the RCAF and worked as a systems analyst. He lives in Montreal and teaches English at Dawson College. He served as writer-in-residence at the University of Alberta in 1986–7. His publications include *Cape Breton Is the Thought Control Centre of Canada* (1969), *Lord Nelson Tavern* (1974), *Century* (1986), a second collection of linked stories, and *A Night at the Opera* (1992).

In an essay on short fiction called "Dinosaur" (*The Narrative Voice*), Smith says: "If we can reconstruct a novel from a fragment it is a dinosaur, extinct, and no damn use to a writer today. It was useful thirty, forty years ago: alive, flexible, adventurous, still growing, still discovering. In a word: healthy." He demands of the fiction writer totally new forms, structures, styles that do not permit the reader to anticipate what comes next. What *comes* next in fiction is more important than what happens next, since, in his view, plot has lost its significance.

"The statement of any sort of plot is: this is a way of seeing the relations between events; or, this kind of relation between events is a significant kind. Men have used all sorts of plots. The Greeks accepted *deus ex machina*; we call it a cheat. Dickens and Shakespeare both used lots of coincidence. Their imitators used coincidence as a crutch and a reaction took place. The twentieth century plot is, in this sense, a massive reaction against the plots of shameless junk like the Horatio Alger books. This sort of shift happens when a fresh writer says, 'Hold it a moment, it may look fine to you and your readers, but my world is not full of long lost brothers, millionaires in disguise and runaway horses bearing terrified virgins. In fact, my world hasn't included a coincidence since last Christmas when two of my gift books contained the word 'Zeugma.' And furthermore, I think it is far more interesting to look at a series of rather subtle, low key events to see if they will lead a character to some significant perception of the world.' "

Even the reaction against linear plot, which favours logical discontinuity, juxtaposition, and collage, has outrun its usefulness, according to Smith, now that it is institutionalized. Similarly, point of view, which was "once a useful tool . . . has become an end in itself, and so a tyranny." He objects to the expectation many readers have of "a single point of view that is right, is the norm, the proper form"; instead, he insists that "the only criterion for judging a how [any technique or, in this instance, point of view] is: does it work? A normal beginning for an artist is: 'I wonder what would happen if. . . .' Right. I wonder what would happen if we said to hell with point of view. Let's try a ten page story with a hundred and twelve points of view. Explode it all over everywhere. Will it work? . . . The reader has to be willing to suspend his expectations, but any reader worth a damn should be ready for this from time to time."

Smith's aim as a contemporary fiction writer is, perhaps, to "begin with a cluster of images, moods, words, people that [take] the shape of a line starting out in front of my eyes toward the right, but curving gracefully to the left and disappearing in the hazy distance." Thus he controls the reader's mind "by arranging and manipulating his expectations. When we read things, it seems to me, we are continually trying to guess what comes next." One of the functions of the writer is to make sure the reader doesn't make too many correct guesses, thus indicating a narrative that is neither lyrical curve nor exciting jagged track, but only a boring straight line.

Smith sees much of his writing as "part of a body of work called 'speculative fiction.' Generally ironic in tone. Aesthetic in approach; which means, I suppose, an indirect approach to the many social and political problems of the world around us. This is in clear contrast to the other rising body of writing which includes things like revolutionary writings, the new journalism, documentary novels and the like, all of which try to grapple directly with the aforementioned soc and pol problems. I should emphasize, or repeat, that spec fic doesn't ignore the world, but approaches it somewhat indirectly. The telling point is that both types have pretty much rejected the whole creaking apparatus of . . . psychological realism."

Elaborating on this kind of fiction, Smith outlines its precedents: "Some big dogs in speculative fiction: Jorge Luis Borges, Vladimir Nabokov. Coming big dog: Kurt Vonnegut, Jr. Prominent younger dogs: Thomas Pynchon, John Barth, Donald Barthelme, Richard Brautigan. Incidentally, from considering these writers, their views, careers, antecedents and whatnot you can see spec fic as a continuing historical alternative, trace its ups and downs, off-shoots, roots and other such aspects as critical enquiry can profitably illuminate."

Cape Breton Is the Thought Control Centre of Canada

A CENTENNIAL PROJECT

Why don't we go away?
   Why?
   Why not?
   Because.
   If we went away things would be different.
   No. Things would be the same. Change starts inside.
   No. Change can start outside.
   Possibly.
   Then, can we go away?
   No. Perhaps. All right. It doesn't matter.

So you believe in Canada and you're worried about American economic domination? But you can't understand international finance? What you do know is that a landlord can give a tenant thirty days to get out, eh? And the tenant can stay longer if he has a lease, but you don't recall having signed a lease with the Americans?

So you're saying to yourself: What can I do? What can I do? I can't influence Bay Street . . . what can I do? . . .'

Well . . . uhhh . . . thought of blowing the Peace Bridge?

The Americans are loath to fight without a divine cause. Assume we provide this by electing an NDP Government, stirring ourselves up with anti-American slogans like: 'Give me liberty or give me death!' or (the most divine of all) passing legislation that is prejudicial to American money.

With their divine cause, the Americans would destroy our Armed Forces in one week. (This makes a fine game; you can play it out on a map.) Canada will have ceased to exist as a free nation. Now: *Think of the fun you'd have in the Resistance!* It's a great subject for daydreaming: Be the first kid on your block to gun down a Yankee Imperialist.

A virgin named, say, Judy, an attractive girl in her early twenties, is so curious about sexual intercourse that, despite certain misgivings, she goes to a party determined to find a man willing to do the deed. She wears an alluring but tasteful dress, has her hair done, and bescents herself with a flattering perfume.

At the party are certain men of her own age whom Judy knows and finds attractive; and certain men of her own age whom she doesn't know and finds attractive. All realize that Judy is a virgin and that she wishes to experience intercourse. Each feels he would like to help her. At the party are other girls, but they do not figure in the story, being all the same as Judy.

The party progresses pleasantly enough. The guests dance and sing and drink enough alcohol to feel light-headed, but not enough to become maudlin, violent, or unconscious. A good time is had by all.

The end of the party nears, and Judy has not yet been offered help. Desperate, she decides to make the proposal herself. In no time at all, the men are seated about her discussing the problem with her. This goes on for several hours until the men pass out and Judy walks home alone. On a dark and lonely street, she is pulled into an alleyway and raped by a stranger who leaves her with her clothes torn, her body sore and bleeding, and her eyes streaming tears.

A week later, her virginity restored in a Venus-wise bath, she goes through the same events. Judy is a happy girl, for she leads a sane, healthy, and well-balanced life.

❖ ❖ ❖

Consider the Poles. They have built a nation which, if not great and powerful, is at least distinct.

Of course, the Poles have their own language, and they have been around for a thousand years. But they have survived despite the attentions paid them by their neighbours, the Russians and the Germans.

Analogies are never perfect, but the Poles do have what we want. Consider the Poles; consider the price they have paid and paid and paid.

❖ ❖ ❖

Wit: Did you hear about the Canadian pacifist who became a Canadian nationalist?
  Self: No; why did he do that?
  Wit: Because he wanted to take advantage of the economical Red, White, and Blue fares.

❖ ❖ ❖

Recently a friend conned me into explaining my interest in compiled fiction, an example of which you are now reading. 'Hey, that's great,' he said. 'That really sounds interesting.'

'I'm interested in it,' I replied, razoring out the distinction.

'But I hope you aren't expecting to sell any of these compilations. The publishers won't touch anything as new as that.'

'Well, that's their business, isn't it? I mean, if they figure it's not for their magazine or it's lousy or something, they reject it. It's a basic condition. If you want to demand they publish your stuff, the best and fastest way is to buy the magazine, fire the editor, and hire a yes-man.'

'I didn't mean. . . .'

'I know what you meant; but, in fact, the technique isn't new at all. I got it from Ezra Pound and he got it from some French poets. Other precedents might be Francis Bacon's essays, the Book of Proverbs . . . the whole Bible. . . .'

'But. . . .'

My friend babbled on. He talks a lot about writing but, so far as I know, doesn't do any.

❖ ❖ ❖

You can't see up through the mist (up through the high timber where the air is clean and good) but you know the dawn is already gleaming on the snow peaks; soon it will reach down here and burn away the mist and then it will be too late. Where the hell is that bloody supply column? You hunch forward between the rock and the tree and peer into the gloom. The armoured-car escort will appear . . . there: when it gets . . . there Mackie and Joe will heave the cocktails and when the flame breaks Campbell will open up with the Bren. . . . Christ, you hope you get some arms out of this because if you don't you'll have to pack it up soon. . . . Christ, it's cold, your joints can't take much more of . . . a growl from down around the bend . . . a diesel growl. . . .

❖ ❖ ❖

Do you love me?

Yes, I love you. You're my wife.

Why did you say, You're my wife?

Uhh. . . .

You said it because you think just because I'm your wife you have to love me when really it has nothing to do with it.

Perhaps. It's more complicated than that.

It's always more complicated. Why can't it be simple? You always say things are too complicated when what you really mean is you don't want to talk to me. Why can't things be simple?

They are. I love you. As simple as that. So simple there's no point talking about it.

Complicated, too, I suppose.

So complicated that to talk about it would always oversimplify it. It's the same with everything.

Then what. . . . Oh! You're impossible to talk to.

You know that isn't true.

Yes.

So. . . .

Then what is important?

Doing.

Doing what?

Heh-heh-heh. . .

Mmmmm. . . .

❖ ❖ ❖

Toronto is a truly despicable city.

❖ ❖ ❖

'. . . like a horse's arse!' Einar finishes. You all laugh because Einar tells a good joke and because you're all damned scared as the car flees through the prairie night. 'And what about the girl from. . . .' Suddenly the night is day . . . silence . . . then the roar . . . someone gasps, 'Did we do that?' You stop the car and stare back down the road at the towering flames . . . another flash . . . its roar . . . and again . . . thousands of barrels of oil. . . . 'Well,' says Einar, 'Now I seen the sun risin' in the west. I guess I can die happy.' Your laughter shakes some sense back into you: you'd better get the hell out of here or you'll maybe die quick. . . .

Two men sit on a park bench. They are just men; perhaps office workers enjoying the sunshine during their noon break. For the sake of convenience, let us call them Bill and George. They are acquainted.

Bill: Nice day.

George: Yes it is. Though the weatherman said we might get rain later.

Bill: Yeah, it looks like it.

George: It's in the air.

This chatter goes on for a while. Presently Bill remembers a bottle of whisky in his pocket.

Bill: Like a sip of rye?

George: Ummerrahhohhehh. . . .

This mumbling goes on until George, quivering through his entire frame, dies.

Bill: What a crazy guy. Bill opens the bottle and takes a drink. He sighs with satisfaction, replaces the bottle in his pocket, takes from another pocket a revolver, and blows his brains out.

A distant whirr and three more flights of geese knife south through the big Manitoba sky. There was a day when you might have shot at the geese. Now you're waiting for something else to come down the wind through the sedge; there it is, the peculiar aroma of Lucky Strike tobacco and a Texas accent quietly cursing the mud. . . .

Well, I suppose we could move to England.

I hate England, you know I hate England. It rained and rained. . . .

Oh hell, it didn't rain that much; that was just overcast and occasional drizzle. Besides we were there in March and April.

Well, it was so dirty, God. I don't mean filth, you know, just . . . grime . . . centuries of grime on everything. . . .

But the pubs, don't forget the pubs.

Sure, I know, but who wants to spend every evening drinking beer?

Yeah, I suppose.

Perhaps we could move to the States.

Be serious.

I was only joking.

❖ ❖ ❖

The Americans believe they answered all first questions in 1776; since then they've just been hammering out the practical details.

❖ ❖ ❖

'Then *boom!*' cries Johnny. 'Boom and the plant got no roof anymore, eh? Haha-ha!' The smoky room fills with laughter. Johnny knows no fear . . . but no nothing else either. When will they ever learn? You'll try again; your fist hits the table. 'A big boom? Fine. Great. So the papers photograph it for the front page, and it's pro-ducing again the next day. But two pounds of plastic at the right place on a few essential machines and this joint won't put out a pound of steel for two years. . . .'

❖ ❖ ❖

Well, then, consider one Pole. Consider Count Z. Count Z. is a Pole: *ergo*, a Polish patriot. He has his fingers into both the Defence and Foreign Affairs pies. Perhaps he is Prime Minister, perhaps an *éminence grise*. At forty he is vigorous, experienced, and intelligent.

From the window of his office, Count Z. gazes down into the bustling streets of Warsaw. Fifteen years of peace have prompted a cultural revival. In the near dis-tance, several lines of new smoke-stacks puff their evidence of Poland's stable and bullish economy. Count Z. shades his eyes; in the far distance, the wind washes over the wheat fields which, in two months time, should become the third bumper crop in three years.

Yet Count Z. is not happy. Of course he is proud to be leading Poland to a new prosperity. But the peasants on his estate have been whispering an old saying: The Pole only buys new clothes so he'll look respectable when he commits suicide. Count Z. sighs and sits down to his work: how can I commit suicide today? (Count Z. has a subtle and self-deprecating sense of humour.)

An aide enters with the Foreign Office reports. Count Z.'s ambassadors in the Balkans say the Germans and the Russians are supplying arms and money to opposing factions in Bulgaria, Hungary, and Rumania (or whatever they were called in Count Z.'s time). The tension is moderate but unstable. Count Z. frowns.

Next the Count looks through an economic estimate sheet. Trade with Ger-many will increase by 12.5 per cent over the next year. This is because of a Polish-German trade agreement of two years ago. Count Z. smiles.

But next is the latest note from St Petersburg. A deadlock has been reached in talks over the disputed ten square miles of Pripet marshland. Resumption of talks is put off indefinitely. Count Z. frowns.

Another aide enters and hands Count Z. a report on Polish defences. He reads it with great interest, although he already knows what it will say: both the eastern and western defence lines are out of date and out of repair. To construct new ones would require half the capital in the country. Financially, given five years, one could be constructed. Diplomatically, however, both must be built at once so as not to risk provoking (or tempting) either the Germans or the Russians. Count Z. sighs. If he were English, he would jerry-build something. But in the holy name of St Stanislaus, how can he insult his Poland with jerry-building?

A visitor is announced: the paunchy, guffawing, monocled Baron Otto von und zu something-dorf, who was instrumental, from the German end, in working out the trade agreement. After four of his own utterly unfunny and incomprehensible jokes, the German says:

'But my dear Count Z., Poland a Defence Line in the East against the Depredations of the savage Cossack Hordes wishes to build, I understand, ja? Your friendly German Cousins—in the spirit which the Trade Agreement possible was made— the Cost of this Defence Line to share would be willing. We Germans, as you well know, *Kultur* love, and we to Civilization a Duty it consider Mankind from the Ravenings of the Bear to protect. . . .'

'Sharing only the cost?'

'Well . . . ho-ho-ho . . . of course, we a few Divisions to garrison . . . Transportation Arrangements . . . Security Measures would want . . . ho-hoho, and to a Slice of Liverwurst yourself help. . . .'

A few minutes after Baron Otto has gone, Prince Igor is announced. Prince Igor is lean and foppish. Only the most delicate efforts prevented his being recalled last year when a prostitute was found beaten to death. He speaks elaborately epigrammatic French, using the occasional Russian phrase to illustrate the quaint wisdom of the peasants.

'*Mon cher* Count Z., I have heard from Petersburg of the unfortunate breakdown in talks. Of course, love shall always exist between the Tsar and his beloved Slavic cousins. . . . The fat Prussian loves war. . . . As a token of his esteem, the magnanimous Tsar wishes his gallant Polish brothers to take immediate and indisputable possession into perpetuity of the invaluable ten square miles of Mother Russia. In addition, our mutual father wishes to build for his valiant Polish children a defence line along the Polish-German (ah, that term, it disgusts me: *c'est une mésalliance*, the union of an eagle and a pig) border. . . . But will you have a sip of vodka? . . . .'

Prince Igor returns to his villa where he finds his aides taking practice shots at the neighbour's cattle. He tells them of his subtle joke: both the pig and the eagle are interchangeable symbols of Germany and Poland.

This subtlety has not been lost on Count Z. He takes a last look at the bustling streets, the puffing smokestacks, and the waving wheat which may or may not get harvested. . . .

In the following weeks, Count Z. more and more frequently plays host to Baron Otto and Prince Igor. As politely as possible, he explains that he prefers Polish sausage to liverwurst; that vodka upsets his digestion. Baron Otto tells jokes which turn like millstones; Prince Igor weaves his *chinoiseries*. They smile till their jaws crack; they drop threatening innuendoes.

Count Z. broods. His wife and his mistress both comment on the pallor of his complexion. He will not be consoled. When he looks into the streets below his office, his eyes imagine a scene filled with arrogant, swaggering Prussians or cruel, drunken Cossacks. Tension is mounting in the Balkans: a Russian uhlan and a German dragoon have fought a duel in Sofia. The salons are hissing with rumour.

Baron Otto and Prince Igor deliver their ultimata on the same day. Accept the liverwurst and not the vodka, accept the vodka and not the liverwurst, or else. Count Z. takes a last glance out the window and sighs. At least they got the harvest in. He rejects the offers. Three weeks later he is cut down while leading a hopeless cavalry charge.

Some time later, Baron Otto and Prince Igor sit down together in what used to be Count Z.'s office. They agree that the treacherous Poles are a blot on humanity, else why did they start a war they were sure to lose (as has been proven)? Baron Otto and Prince Igor agree to divide Poland, using the line where their armies met as a basis for discussions. There will be no arguments over a few square miles here and there, for Poland is a ravaged wasteland. Of course the harvest will be seized to feed the occupying troops: the Poles are pigs, let them root in the ground for acorns if they are hungry. Prince Igor accepts some liverwurst; Baron Otto praises the vodka.

The Balkan situation is smoothed out. The Germans begin building a defence line along the eastern border of their Polish provinces; the Russians begin building a defence line along the western border of their Polish provinces. These lines will take ten years to build (the Polish slave labourers are so lazy). At that time, both the Germans and the Russians will want to test the other's line. They will go to war. The war will rage back and forth across Poland until. . . .

But let the reader construct the rest. Polish history is very simple in this way. The Poles also are simple: they love Poland.

Would you rather be smothered under a pillow of American greenbacks or cut open on a U.S. Marine's bayonet?

Curfew for civilians is long past. You sit hunched by the window listening to the laughing soldiers staggering back to their billets. *Espèce de chameaux*; they cannot take a Molson *bleu*; it is too strong for them. If you were allowed in the *tavernes*, you would show them. . . . 'Allons,' whispers Jean-Paul. Silently, silently you slide the window up and wait as the others slip onto the roof. You follow, letting the window slide down behind you. You must hurry; already the others are onto the next roof, and creeping toward the fourth house along where the CIA is holding Marc prisoner. . . .

❖ ❖ ❖

Visit/ez EXPO 67

❖ ❖ ❖

Uhh . . . I guess I'd better tell you I don't like eggs fried in butter.

But . . . but. . . .

I'm sorry, but it's true.

But . . . ohh, why the hell didn't you tell me before? God, all this time I've been frying your eggs in butter and. . . .

I didn't want to hurt you.

Well, why did you tell me now? Do you want to hurt me now?

No. Of course, you might have decided all by yourself, but if I have any more eggs fried in butter, the cumulative hurt to me (and of course to you) will have been more than the single sharp hurt of telling you. Do you see?

Ohh. . . .

It took a long time to decide when was the right moment. . . .

Yes . . . yes, I see. Yes. It was the right thing to do.

I love you.

Oh! I love you.

During the winter, he was twenty-five; George found his work tending more and more to figure drawing. He was interested and getting good results. So, as artists will do, he set out to explore the subject more fully, spending most of his time drawing and perhaps three days a month painting this and that in a variety of styles just to keep his hand in. During the next three winters, he got together three shows of the figure drawings and each year he got better press and sales. *Canadian Art*, as it was then called, gave the third show a very good review indeed.

On the basis of these successes, George applied for and got a Canada Council grant. He used it to visit the Arctic. When he returned to Toronto, he started twelve paintings, forty-three drawings, and twenty-two prints in silkscreen, lino, and wood. He destroyed each upon completion. At last he gave up trying.

For five months he drank, slept with a variety of women, and read detective novels. A newspaper reviewer came to interview him, and George told him to go to hell.

Finally George prepared a canvas, rectangular with proportions of 2:1. On this canvas he painted the Maple Leaf flag. He hung this painting on the wall of his studio and went back to drawing nudes. Because he had already satisfied himself, at least temporarily, about figures, the drawings were quite bad. But they got him working again, which is the only way to start. After a few weeks, George found a few curiosities and set about exploring these. They led him back to painting, and since that time his work has gotten steadily better, despite the fact that his recent show received confused and confusing reviews, and one critic was angry about something.

'Are you sure it's the right cove?' whispers the man in the trenchcoat.

'Keep shut,' mutters Willard. Willard is being tough, but it's for the stranger's own good; he wouldn't like going ashore to the wrong reception party. Still, he's got a right to be nervous: it's an hour since you cut the *Rachel B*'s engine and no light yet. You peer through the gathering fog. If they don't show in five minutes, you'll have to take the man in the trenchcoat back to the mainland, and that'll mean coming back again and again until you see . . . the light: one long, three short . . . one long, three short. You answer: two long, two short. 'Take her in, Willard,' and the man in the trenchcoat fumbles with his suitcase while Willard dips the muffled oars into the slick black water. . . .

I have had stories rejected by a number of magazines in Canada and the U.S. No American magazine has ever kept a story longer than three weeks, and no Canadian magazine has kept one less than three months.

These stories have averaged ten pages each. That means the Canadian editors were reading just over one page a week; about two words an hour.

Do you realize that most people with the appropriate dictionary can read any language (even limiting it to our own alphabet) faster than two words an hour?

North America is a large island to the west of the continent of Cape Breton. (Pronounced: Caybrittn)

So what if you have to stay at home with the children? Lots of women in France fought in the Resistance; you can do your part too. Take the church supper tonight, for instance. All those National Guardsmen from New Jersey just got homesick; they wanted a home-cooked meal. So Mrs Parsons said to their commandant, 'Why, Colonel, we've always been friendly with your people, living so close to the border. I'm sure the Ladies Auxiliary would love to give your boys a meal. . . .' The commandant didn't object when you were chosen to make the soup, and he still doesn't know you've planned a very special soup in memory of your Bill who was shot down in front of his customs shed the day it all began. . . .

If the Americans would just read their own Constitutional documents instead of memorizing them. . . .

Do you love me?
　　Yes, I love you.
　　Ohhh!
　　What now, hmmm? Come here.
　　Oh. What? Eh? What is it?
　　The . . . the way you said it. . . .
　　Said what?
　　You know, the way you said I love you.
　　What about it?

You know very well—you didn't mean it.

I did so . . . really.

No you didn't. You hardly looked at me and you went right back to reading your book.

I did mean it. You see . . . hell, I hate explaining. . . .

(He explains for half an hour. The burden of his thesis is that married love is different from single-people love. Thus, he loves her twenty-four hours a day, loves her in such a way that it affects his whole life, including the way he pours himself a glass of orange juice in the morning. 'It is a love beyond saying,' he explains, 'I state it in my every action, my every word, my every thought. It is like "presence" or something.' He explains that saying 'I love you' is for single people and that he prefers not to say it except at certain times when he feels for her that simple, heart-throbbing love of single people that comes to him when he watches her hip as she bends over or as she sweeps her hair from her eyes. 'At times like that I say, "I love you."' She says she sees and he says, 'Do you see?' and she repeats, 'Yes, I see.')

I love you.

And I love you. . . . I love you.

(The question now is whether he will make love to her or go back to reading his book. This question has no answer because the scene is an amalgam of scenes, one each week since they got married a few years ago. But before they do, one little exchange remains.)

Well then, if you didn't feel like saying, 'I love you,' why did you say it?

It's better to say it even if it is a technical lie.

What an old funny you are.

Anyway, I love you.

I love you.

See, the way I look at it, your problem is that Joe Yank is the biggest kid on the block. Now I know you're pretty friendly with him—he being your cousin and all—but someday he's going to say, 'Johnny Canuck, my boot is dirty. Lick it.'

Now then, are you going to get down on your hands and knees and lick or are you going to say, 'Suck ice, Joe Yank'? Because if you do say, 'Suck ice,' he's going to kick you in the nuts. And either way, you're going to lick those boots. It just depends on how you want to take it.

Of course, you can always kick him first.

Maybe we could just stay here.

I suppose.

I mean, I like Canada, really. It's not a bad place.

It *is* home.

Perhaps, though, we could go to Montreal for a change.

Could we?

Why not? Drop your school Parisian accent and unify Canada.

Oh!

We'll have to wait till Expo's over, or we'll never get an apartment; we already have friends there. . . . I don't see why not. . . .

I love you!

Me too!

The internal walls of an octagonal room are covered with mirrors. In the room stands a man naked. He is an ordinary-looking man; other people would say so if they could get in to see him. They cannot get in to see him because they do not know where the entrance to the room is or, if they did, how to open it. Likewise the man does not know where the exit is or how to open it. Possibly he would not use it if he could. Likewise back again, possibly those outside would not enter if they could.

In any case, the man is ordinary looking; but at times he thinks himself surpassingly beautiful and at times surpassingly ugly. The man acts out these conflicting feelings, all the while watching himself in the mirrors. With one hand he strokes his beautiful body; with the other (it holds a whip) he lashes his ugly body. The times when he does these things are, it would seem, all times, and they run concurrently.

The situation lends itself to various interpretations. We might consider them; but let us not.

❖ ❖ ❖

For Centennial Year, send President Johnson a gift: an American tourist's ear in a matchbox. Even better, don't bother with the postage.

Gertrude Stein

Gertrude Stein Raffel begins her account of her famous aunt's life with the following limerick:

> There once was a family called Stein,
> There was Ep, there was Gert, there was Ein.
> Ep's sculpture is punk, Gert's poetry bunk,
> And nobody understands Ein.

After dismissing the shades of Epstein and Einstein, she goes on to give an account of her aunt's childhood, in Baltimore, where she was born in 1874, and in Paris, Vienna, and California. Stein went from Oakland and San Francisco to Radcliffe College, so self-conscious about her weight that she hired a boy to box with her daily. Abandoning the idea of medicine, she left for Paris, where she resided with her brother, critic and art historian Leo Stein (*The ABC of Aesthetics*) at 27 rue de Fleurus, which became a sort of gallery and salon. Surrounded by masters and masterpieces, Stein gradually developed the ideas that would shape her writing. According to her niece, Stein—a somewhat unsympathetic and unpredictable gypsy figure the family was not entirely comfortable with—"did for the English language what the French painters [presumably the Cubists and Fauvists] did for French painting." Her publications include *Tender Buttons* (1914), *Things As They Are* (1903), *Three Lives* (1906), *The Making of Americans* (written, 1906–8; published, 1925), *How to Write* (1931), *A Long Gay Book* (1932), *The Autobiography of Alice B. Toklas* (1932), *Lectures in America* (1934), and *Brewsie and Willie* (1945).

One of the most useful compilations of material by and about Stein is *A Primer for the Gradual Understanding of Gertrude Stein*, edited by Robert Bartlett Haas (1971), which includes portions of her major manifestos, including "A Transatlantic Interview" (1946). In this interview, Stein argues against the view that her work is difficult: "After all, my only thought is a complicated simplicity. I like a thing simple, but it must be simple through complication." Some readers might consider her compositions as maddeningly simple.

Of these early years in Paris, she says: "I began to play with words then. I was a little obsessed by words of equal value. Picasso was painting my portrait at that time, and he and I used to talk this thing over endlessly. At this time he had just begun on cubism. And I felt that the thing I got from Cézanne was not the last composition. You had to recognize words had lost their value in the Nineteenth Century, particularly towards the end, they had lost much of their variety, and I felt that I could not go on, that I had to recapture the value of the individual word, find out what it meant and act within it."

In "Composition as Explanation," one of a series of lectures she gave to the literary societies at Oxford and Cambridge in 1926, Stein says: "Each period of living differs from any other period of living not in the way life is but in the way life is conducted and that authentically speaking is composition." The feeling of immersion in a prolonged, or continuous, present influenced her sense of artistic purpose, so that even the verbal portraits she made have the character of multiple beginnings, of language struggling with its grammar and syntax as well as its connotations and denotations, of language reduced to lists, series, and linguistic functions. In "Poetry and Grammar," she says: "Words have to do everything in poetry and prose and some writers write more in articles and prepositions and some say you should write in nouns, and of course one has to think of everything."

In "What Are Masterpieces," Stein suggests that media such as radio, cinema, newspapers, and photography have, in a sense, usurped the content that the artist used to pretend to be rendering; as a result, he or she must now strike out for terrain that has less to do with copy than creation, that, like the crime novel, dispenses with the body (content) in advance and gets on with the real business of detection. Certainly, the reader must function as a detective much of the time in Stein's writing: "The manner and habits of Bible times or Greek or Chinese have nothing to do with us today because of their identity. . . they do not exist by human nature because everybody always knows everything there is to know about human nature, they exist because they came to be as something that is an end in itself and in that respect it is opposed to the business of living which is relation and necessity."

What she is arguing for in writing, of course, is non-referentiality, a dismissal of the conventions of narrative and discursive writing, for a language disembodied, disengaged from conventional expectations and constraints and from preconceptions about its relation to the natural world or human nature. This would most certainly mean eliminating the strategies of narrative and logic; it might also mean eliminating sight and sound in a specific composition, cutting words that stimulate the senses to the exclusion of the intellect, refusing to write *about* anything, but trying, instead, to write *directly*, with the full attention riveted on process, and letting the composition create its own context and meaning and justification.

Portrait of Mable Dodge at the Villa Curonia

The days are wonderful and the nights are wonderful and the life is pleasant.

Bargaining is something and there is not that success. The intention is what if application has that accident results are reappearing. They did not darken. That was not an adulteration.

So much breathing has not the same place when there is that much beginning. So much breathing has not the same place when the ending is lessening. So much breathing has the same place and there must not be so much suggestion. There can be there the habit that there is if there is no need of resting. The absence is not alternative.

Any time is the half of all the noise and there is not that disappointment. There is no distraction. An argument is clear.

Packing is not the same when the place which has all that is not emptied. There came there the hall and this was not the establishment. It had not all the meaning.

Blankets are warmer in the summer and the winter is not lonely. This does not assure the forgetting of the intention when there has been and there is every way to send some. There does not happen to be a dislike for water. This is not heartening.

As the expedition is without the participation of the question there will be nicely all that energy. They can arrange that the little color is not bestowed. They can leave it in regaining that intention. It is mostly repaid. There can be an irrigation. They can have the whole paper and they send it in some package. It is not inundated.

A bottle that has all the time to stand open is not so clearly shown when there is green color there. This is not the only way to change it. A little raw potato and then all that softer does happen to show that there has been enough. It changes the expression.

It is not darker and the present time is the best time to agree. This which has been feeling is what has the appetite and the patience and the time to stay. This is not collaborating.

All the attention is when there is not enough to do. This does not determine a question. The only reason that there is not that pressure is that there is a suggestion. There are many going. A delight is not bent. There had been that little wagon. There is that precision when there has not been an imagination. There has not been that kind abandonment. Nobody is alone. If the spread that is not a piece removed from the bed is likely to be whiter then certainly the sprinkling is not drying. There can be the message where the print is pasted and this does not mean that there is that esteem. There can be the likelihood of all the days not coming later and this will not deepen the collected dim version.

It is a gnarled division that which is not any obstruction and the forgotten swelling is certainly attracting, it is attracting the whiter division, it is not sinking to be growing, it is not darkening to be disappearing, it is not aged to be annoying. There can not be sighing. This is this bliss.

Not to be wrapped and then to forget undertaking, the credit and then the resting of that interval, the pressing of the sounding when there is no trinket is not altering, there can be pleasing classing clothing.

A sap that is that adaptation is the drinking that is not increasing. There can be that lack of quivering. That does not originate every invitation. There is not wedding introduction. There is not all that filling. There is the climate that is not existing there is that plainer. There is the likeliness lying in liking likely likeliness. There is that dispensation. There is the paling that is not reddening, there is the reddening that is not reddening, there is that protection, there is that destruction, there is not the present lessening there is the argument of increasing. There is that that is not that which is that resting. There is not that occupation. There is that particular half of directing that there is that particular whole direction that is not all the measure of any combination. Gliding is not heavily moving. Looking is not vanishing. Laughing is not evaporating. There can be the climax. There can be the same dress. There can be an old dress. There can be the way there is that way there is that which is not that charging what is a regular way of paying. There has been William. All the time is likely. There is the condition. There has been admitting. There is not the print. There is that smiling. There is the season. There is that where there is not that which is where there is what there is which is beguiling. There is a paste.

Abandon a garden and the house is bigger. This is not smiling. This is comfortable. There is the comforting of predilection. An open object is establishing the loss that there was when the vase was not inside the place. It was not wandering.

A plank that was dry was not disturbing the smell of burning and altogether there was the best kind of sitting there could never be all the edging that the largest chair was having. It was not pushed. It moved then. There was not that lifting. There was that which was not any contradiction and there was not the bland fight that did not have that regulation. The contents were not darkening. There was not that hesitation. It was occupied. That was not occupying any exception. Any one had come. There was that distribution.

There was not that velvet spread when there was a pleasant head. The color was paler. The moving regulating is not a distinction. The place is there.

Likely there is not that departure when the whole place that has that texture is so much in the way. It is not there to stay. It does not change that way. A pressure is not later. There is the same. There is not the shame. There is that pleasure.

In burying that game there is not a change of name. There is not perplexing and co-ordination. The toy that is not round has to be found and looking is not straining such relation. There can be that company. It is not wider when the length is not longer and that does make that way of staying away. Every one is exchanging returning. There is not a prediction. The whole day is that way. Any one is resting to say that the time which is not reverberating is acting in partaking.

A walk that is not stepped where the floor is covered is not in the place where the room is entered. The whole one is the same. There is not any stone. There is the wide door that is narrow on the floor. There is all that place.

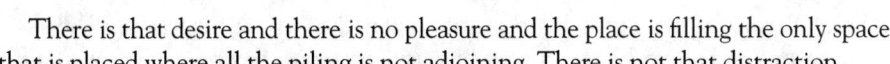

There is that desire and there is no pleasure and the place is filling the only space that is placed where all the piling is not adjoining. There is not that distraction.

Praying has intention and relieving that situation is not solemn. There comes that way.

The time that is the smell of the plain season is not showing the water is running. There is not all that breath. There is the use of the stone and there is the place of the stuff and there is the practice of expending questioning. There is not that differentiation. There is that which is in time. There is the room that is the largest place when there is all that is where there is space. There is not that perturbation. The legs that show are not the certain ones that have been used. All legs are used. There is no action meant.

The particular space is not beguiling. There is that participation. It is not passing any way. It has that to show. It is why there is no exhalation.

There is all there is when there has all there has where there is what there is. That is what is done when there is done what is done and the union is won and the division is the explicit visit. There is not all of any visit.

Lesson One

A dog said that he was going to learn to read. The other dogs said he could learn to bark but he could not learn to read. They did not know that dog, if he said he was going to learn to read, he would learn to read. He might be drowned dead in water but if he said that he was going to learn to read he was going to learn to read.

He never was drowned in water not dead drowned and he never did learn to read. Are there any children like that. One two three. Are there any children like that. Four five six. Are there any children like that. Seven eight nine are there any children like that.

Ten. Yes there are ten children like that and each one of the ten had a dog like that. Ten dogs like that and ten children like that, and the dogs and the children played tit for tat but there was no learning to read in that, not even if they each one of them was fat, fat just like that.

Next to this was a hare and next to the hare was a bird a daily bird. A daily bird is just a third of an ordinary bird, a daily bird being just a third was very likely heard and when he was heard well was it reading he heard, yes he heard them trying to learn to read the ten dogs and the ten children and as he the bird was a daily bird, and a daily bird is a third of a bird, he heard them every day trying to do less than a third of what they heard, so he said said the bird, I will get together ten daily birds and see who learns to read first ten children ten dogs or ten daily birds.

The first dog who tried to learn to read not the one who said he was going to learn to read that one did not need to have ten dogs to learn to read, he was the one dog who had it as a great need to learn to read. But would he learn to read. Who can tell, a bell learns to read, why not a dog, why not, the dog had tears in his eyes why not. A dog. But the first dog who really tried to learn to read he was a Saint Bernard a big dog so big that if he opened his mouth it was just the same as any word and when he said a word it was a big word. Saying a word even a big word is not the same as reading that word. Oh no said the daily bird no indeed it is not, not, not knot.

Just notice that if you say not knot, how do you know if you do not know how to read, which knot has a knot, and which not has not a knot. So you see you have to learn to read. The daily bird knew what was what.

The daily bird was all excited. He had heard a word. It might have been worm the word he heard but it was not. The word he heard was po-ta-toe. Sweet po-ta-toe, a lovely word, a sweet word, that was the word the daily bird heard. And he said hoe, no they mean hoe or ho and he said ha no they mean tea and he said toe oh yes toe, toe is that so. And then he said no it is not so it is potatoe and he smiled and smiled and said oh potatoe sweet potatoe that is so.

Daily birds like sweet potatoes that grow and if he could not read he could hear it said that they would hoe sweet potatoes in that bed.

Bed Bed, of course a bed when all is said is where you sleep, where any little boy or girl is put to sleep in a bed. But a bed when all is said is where they put potatoes to grow, and the daily bird knew that was so. Bed bed when any dog says bed bed, he means a cushion a basket a kennel or straw but when any child says bed he means a bed stead where he can lay himself down without a frown and with a pillow made of down he sleeps sweetly until he wakes up and comes down, down the stairs. Who cares which way down is spelt but it is spelt the same whether it is in the bed or out, remember all the little ten children were stout, but even so they did go in and out. But to the daily bird a bed when all is said is where the seeds are said to be in bed because they plant them so and so the daily bird when he heard po-ta-toe knew that that was a bed and so he said sweet potatoe bed, when all is said so sweet is a sweet potatoe bed and he heard the daily bird heard that word. Potatoe is what he heard and he read well he could not read but he read that they would plant potatoe seed in that bed and so he said oh how he said potatoe sweet oh sweet sweet sweet potatoe bed. And he was so pleased he was not dead, he was not in bed, and so he said, yes so he said, this the daily bird said.

Remember they plant sweet potatoes in the spring and eat them in the fall and that is all over when children are not fat but tall.

Oh dear yes that is all.

Think about spelling without yelling spell oh spell potatoe and know it is so. Potatoe, even if so has no e and potatoe has an e on toe. Potatoe.

So, now sew and so, so is so and sew is not so, you see to know whether sew is so or so is sew how necessary it is so that is to read is so necessary so it is. And read just think of read if red is read, and read is read, you see when all is said, just now read just then read, do you see even if a little boy or a little girl is very well fed if they do not read how can they know whether red is read and read is red. How can they know, oh no how can they know.

Dogs barking is different they bark louder that says so and so and they bark lower and that says and so and they make a little noise and that says so and so but well even if one dog said he would learn to read there was really no need and so well no, he would not learn to read, what did a dog care to know whether know is no, whether sew is so, whether read is red, what indeed did any little dog need to know, but a daily bird well a daily bird does not sing he twitters so, it is always just so, and so if he reads red or sees sew, even sow or even so so, even if it is printed on a shed and the daily bird sits upon the shed, no it is not for him to know the difference between so and sew and sow.

But a little boy and a little girl with or without a curl or a little boy with or without a toy, it would annoy a little boy oh surely it would annoy a little boy not to know that no is know this knot is not that sew is so and a little girl just even without a curl could not allow that if she saw a cow she would not bow because she did not know how to read a cow when she saw it said on paper or on a shed that a cow is red. Think of the little girl with or without a curl who could not allow a cow to be a cow because she did not know how to read a cow. Think, oh think of that little girl now.

And so the daily bird was asleep on the bough and that is how it came to be now just now.

All alone a daily bird, it is a daily bird you can tell it is a daily bird because it is never heard. Daily daily daily bird.

Now the ten children who were stout were beginning to move about, and one said and another said and another said and another said and another said and another and another said and another said and another and another and they all ten said now if we count will we like it better that we see a bird a dog a cow or a hen, and when when they said a hen, they all began to cry and say no not I, I want to see a daily bird, a daily bird and that was all that was heard all the ten little children who were fat, they were just that, and being fat, they were afraid and being afraid they were not layed where they had seen a dog or cow oh dear not now, they would rather than read than weed, so that was what they knew, now remember about knew and new. Just remember, it makes one think of a cat just like that, it makes one think of a dog or a frog it makes one think of a man or a can it makes one think of also ran. Just think of that, a bird can twitter and sing and fly like anything, but a daily bird well a daily bird is a third of a bird, and eating is not everything, there is reading and writing, there is running and walk-ing, there is sitting and hitting, there is barking and talking, there is white and black. Oh dear to read white and black. It looks very funny indeed it does. White And Black. It does look very funny indeed indeed it does.

Robert Stone

Robert Stone was born in Brooklyn in 1937. As has been noted before, his life and fiction have a Conradian air to them. Because his mother was schizophrenic, he spent three years in an orphanage as a child. From 1955 to 1958, he served in the U.S. Navy, in the amphibious force of the Atlantic Fleet and then as a senior enlisted journalist on Operation Deep Freeze in the Antarctica. In 1962, while in California on a writing fellowship, he joined up with Ken Kesey's Merry Pranksters and headed across the U.S. on a bus driven by Neal Cassady, the original for Dean Moriarty in Jack Kerouac's On the Road. He worked as a copyboy and caption writer for New York Daily News, an actor, an advertising copywriter, then as a free-lance writer in California, England, and Vietnam. His first novel, Hall of Mirrors (1968), won the William Faulkner Award and was adapted for the screen as WUSA; his Vietnam novel, Dog Soldiers (1974), won the National Book Award and was adapted for the screen as Who'll Stop the Rain. Travel and research into Central American politics led to the writing of his third novel, A Flag for Sunrise (1981), which was a runner-up for the Pulitzer Prize. He won the American Academy and Institute of Arts and Letters Award and the John Dos Passos Prize for literature, both in 1982. His fourth novel, Children of Light, a scathing look at the film industry, appeared in 1986. Stone has taught at Amherst College, Princeton, Harvard, University of California, and New York University. He lives in Massachusetts. His most recent novel is Outerbridge Reach (1992).

In an article in Harper's Magazine (June 1988), called "The Reason for Stories: Toward a Moral Fiction," Robert Stone takes issue with William Gass over the relationship of morality to art. Where Gass argues that art exists outside morality, or is a morality unto itself, Stone insists that "the laws of both language and art impose choices that are unavoidably moral." "Stories explain the nature of things," he says. "Any fictional work of serious intent argues for the significance of its story. A reader holds the characters in judgment, investing sympathy or withholding it, always alert for recognitions, hoping to see his lonely state reflected across time, space, and circumstance. How then can fiction ever be independent of morality: to be so, it would have to be composed of something other than language. . . . Things are in the saddle, Emerson said, and ride mankind. 'Whirl is king.' Things happen ruthlessly, without mercy; the elemental force of things bears down upon us. From one moment to the next we hardly know what's going on, let alone what it all means. Civilization and its attendant morality are not structures, they're more like notions, and sometimes they can seem very distant notions. They can be blown away in a second. In the worst of times we often look for them in vain. Sometimes the morality to which we publicly subscribe seems so alien to our actual behavior that it seems to emanate from some other sphere. One might call it a fiction, but it's a fiction that we most urgently require. . . . Storytelling is not a luxury to humanity; it's almost as necessary as bread. We cannot imagine ourselves without it because each self is a story. The perception each of us has of his own brief transient passage through things is also a kind of fiction, not because its matter is necessarily untrue, but because we tend to shape it to suit our own needs. We tell ourselves our own stories selectively, in order to keep our sense of self intact. As dreams are to waking life, so fiction is to reality. The brain can't function without clearing its circuits during sleep, nor can we contemplate and analyze our situation without living some of the time in the world of the imagination, sorting and refining the random promiscuity of events."

"The moral imperative of fiction," Stone says, "provides no excuse for smug moralizing, religiosity, or propaganda. On the contrary, it forbids them. Nor does it require that every writer equip his work with some edifying message advertising progress, brotherhood and light. It does not require a writer to be a good man, only a good wizard."

In an interview with Maureen Karagueuzian (Tri-Quarterly, No. 53, 1982), Stone says his writing begins with character: "If I can understand characters, who they are and what they want, then events will proceed from the characters. You know, the axiom, 'Character is fate' is literally true in fiction." He claims to be concerned in his writing with both a sense of place and an awareness of historical forces. "I am interested in people against the background of social forces, but mostly in people. I personally am very interested in what's going on politically; so are some of my characters—at least they're affected by political events, whether they're interested in them or not." Asked how he feels about the short story form versus the novel, Stone says: "I think a short story is very, very difficult to write. In a way, it's harder than a novel. A novel takes years and a story takes weeks or months, at the most. But I think writing a successful short story is very difficult. Stories built out of anecdotes—and usually they are—don't occur to me very often. I like larger pictures and the convolutions and ironies of event—not what a short story is built on. I think the short story is something like a joke; at least it has the structure of a joke—or any sort of anecdote. The curve of its dynamic breaks, just like a pitch. And when it finishes, it has illustrated something. All short stories are the same. It's always: this is how it is. That's the unspoken. And to do that successfully, to make a statement in a relatively short space about how things are is very difficult; and the people who do it well have a great gift."

Helping

One gray November day, Elliot went to Boston for the afternoon. The wet streets seemed cold and lonely. He sensed a broken promise in the city's elegance and verve. Old hopes tormented him like phantom limbs, but he did not drink. He had joined Alcoholics Anonymous fifteen months before.

Christmas came, childless, a festival of regret. His wife went to Mass and cooked a turkey. Sober, Elliot walked in the woods.

In January, blizzards swept down from the Arctic until the weather became too cold for snow. The Shawmut Valley grew quiet and crystalline. In the white silences, Elliot could hear the boards of his house contract and feel a shrinking in his bones. Each dusk, starveling deer came out of the wooded swamp behind the house to graze his orchard for whatever raccoons had uncovered and left behind. At night he lay beside his sleeping wife listening to the baying of dog packs running them down in the deep moon-shadowed snow.

Day in, day out, he was sober. At times it was almost stimulating. But he could not shake off the sensations he had felt in Boston. In his mind's eye he could see dead leaves rattling along brick gutters and savor that day's desperation. The brief outing had undermined him.

Sober, however, he remained, until the day a man named Blankenship came into his office at the state hospital for counseling. Blankenship had red hair, a brutal face, and a sneaking manner. He was a sponger and a petty thief whom Elliot had seen a number of times before.

"I been having this dream," Blankenship announced loudly. His voice was not pleasant. His skin was unwholesome. Every time he got arrested the court sent him to the psychiatrists and the psychiatrists, who spoke little English, sent him to Elliot.

Blankenship had joined the Army after his first burglary but had never served east of the Rhine. After a few months in Wiesbaden, he had been discharged for reasons of unsuitability, but he told everyone he was a veteran of the Vietnam War. He went about in a tiger suit. Elliot had had enough of him.

"Dreams are boring," Elliot told him.

Blankenship was outraged. "Whaddaya mean?" he demanded.

During counseling sessions Elliot usually moved his chair into the middle of the room in order to seem accessible to his clients. Now he stayed securely behind his desk. He did not care to seem accessible to Blankenship. "What I said, Mr. Blankenship. Other people's dreams are boring. Didn't you ever hear that?"

"Boring?" Blankenship frowned. He seemed unable to imagine a meaning for the word.

Elliot picked up a pencil and set its point quivering on his desktop blotter. He gazed into his client's slack-jawed face. The Blankenship family made their way through life as strolling litigants, and young Blankenship's specialty was slipping on ice cubes. Hauled off the pavement, he would hassle the doctors in Emergency for pain pills and hurry to a law clinic. The Blankenships had threatened suit against half the property owners in the southern part of the state. What they could not extort at law they stole. But even the Blankenship family had abandoned Blankenship. His last visit to the hospital had been subsequent to an arrest for lifting a case of hot-dog rolls from Woolworth's. He lived in a Goodwill depository bin in Wyndham.

"Now I suppose you want to tell me your dream? Is that right, Mr. Blankenship?"

Blankenship looked left and right like a dog surrendering eye contact. "Don't you want to hear it?" he asked humbly.

Elliot was unmoved. "Tell me something, Blankenship. Was your dream about Vietnam?"

At the mention of the word "Vietnam," Blankenship customarily broke into a broad smile. Now he looked guilty and guarded. He shrugged. "Ya."

"How come you have dreams about that place, Blankenship? You were never there."

"Whaddaya mean?" Blankenship began to say, but Elliot cut him off.

"You were never there, my man. You never saw the goddam place. You have no business dreaming about it! You'd better cut it out!"

He had raised his voice to the extent that the secretary outside his open door paused at her word processor.

"Lemme alone," Blankenship said fearfully. "Some doctor you are."

"It's all right," Elliot assured him. "I'm not a doctor."

"Everybody's on my case," Blankenship said. His moods were volatile. He began to weep.

Elliot watched the tears roll down Blankenship's chapped, pitted cheeks. He cleared his throat. "Look, fella . . ." he began. He felt at a loss. He felt like telling Blankenship that things were tough all over.

Blankenship sniffed and telescoped his neck and after a moment looked at Elliot. His look was disconcertingly trustful; he was used to being counselled.

"Really, you know, it's ridiculous for you to tell me your problems have to do with Nam. You were never over there. It was me over there, Blankenship. Not you."

Blankenship leaned forward and put his forehead on his knees.

"Your troubles have to do with here and now," Elliot told his client. "Fantasies aren't helpful."

His voice sounded overripe and hypocritical in his own ears. What a dreadful business, he thought. What an awful job this is. Anger was driving him crazy.

Blankenship straightened up and spoke through his tears. "This dream . . ." he said. "I'm scared."

Elliot felt ready to endure a great deal in order not to hear Blankenship's dream.

"I'm not the one you see about that," he said. In the end he knew his duty. He sighed. "O.K. All right. Tell me about it."

"Yeah?" Blankenship asked with leaden sarcasm. "Yeah? You think dreams are friggin' boring!"

"No, no," Elliot said. He offered Blankenship a tissue and Blankenship took one. "That was sort of off the top of my head. I didn't really mean it."

Blankenship fixed his eyes on dreaming distance. "There's a feeling that goes with it. With the dream." Then he shook his head in revulsion and looked at Elliot as though he had only just awakened. "So what do you think? You think it's boring?"

"Of course not," Elliot said. "A physical feeling?"

"Ya. It's like I'm floating in rubber."

He watched Elliot stealthily, aware of quickened attention. Elliot had caught dengue in Vietnam and during his weeks of delirium had felt vaguely as though he were floating in rubber.

"What are you seeing in this dream?"

Blankenship only shook his head. Elliot suffered a brief but intense attack of rage.

"Hey, Blankenship," he said equably, "here I am, man. You can see I'm listening."

"What I saw was black," Blankenship said. He spoke in an odd tremolo. His behavior was quite different from anything Elliot had come to expect from him.

"Black? What was it?"

"Smoke. The sky maybe."

"The sky?" Elliot asked.

"It was all black. I was scared."

In a waking dream of his own, Elliot felt the muscles on his neck distend. He was looking up at a sky that was black, filled with smoke-swollen clouds, lit with fires, damped with blood and rain.

"What were you scared of?" he asked Blankenship.

"I don't know," Blankenship said.

Elliot could not drive the black sky from his inward eye. It was as though Blankenship's dream had infected his own mind.

"You don't know? You don't know what you were scared of?"

Blankenship's posture was rigid. Elliot, who knew the aspect of true fear, recognized it there in front of him.

"The Nam," Blankenship said.

"You're not even old enough," Elliot told him.

Blankenship sat trembling with joined palms between his thighs. His face was flushed and not in the least ennobled by pain. He had trouble with alcohol and drugs. He had trouble with everything.

"So wherever your black sky is, it isn't Vietnam."

Things were so unfair, Elliot thought. It was unfair of Blankenship to appropriate the condition of a Vietnam veteran. The trauma inducing his post-traumatic stress had been nothing more serious than his own birth, a routine procedure. Now, in addition to the poverty, anxiety, and confusion that would always be his life's lot, he had been visited with irony. It was all arbitrary and some people simply got elected. Everyone knew that who had been where Blankenship had not.

"Because, I assure you, Mr. Blankenship, you were never there."

"Whaddaya mean?" Blankenship asked.

When Blankenship was gone, Elliot leafed through his file and saw that the psychiatrists had passed him upstairs without recording a diagnosis. Disproportionately angry, he went out to the secretary's desk.

"Nobody wrote up that last patient," he said. "I'm not supposed to see people without a diagnosis. The shrinks are just passing the buck."

The secretary was a tall, solemn redhead with prominent front teeth and a slight speech disorder. "Dr. Sayyid will have kittens if he hears you call him a shrink, Chas. He's already complained. He hates being called a shrink."

"Then he came to the wrong country," Elliot said. "He can go back to his own."

The woman giggled. "He is the doctor, Chas."

"Hates being called a shrink!" He threw the file on the secretary's table and stormed back toward his office. "That fucking little zip couldn't give you a decent haircut. He's a prescription clerk."

The secretary looked about her guiltily and shook her head. She was used to him.

Elliot succeeded in calming himself down after a while, but the image of black sky remained with him. At first he thought he would be able to simply shrug the whole thing off. After a few minutes, he picked up his phone and dialed Blankenship's probation officer.

"The Vietnam thing is all he has," the probation officer explained. "I guess he picked it up around."

"His descriptions are vivid," Elliot said.

"You mean they sound authentic?"

"I mean he had me going today. He was ringing my bells."

"Good for Blanky. Think he believes it himself?"

"Yes," Elliot said. "He believes it himself now."

Elliot told the probation officer about Blankenship's current arrest, which was for showering illegally at midnight in the Wyndham Regional High School. He asked what Probation knew about Blankenship's present relationship with his family.

"You kiddin'?" the P.O. asked. "They're all locked down. The whole family's inside. The old man's in Bridgewater. Little Donny's in San Quentin or somewhere. Their dog's in the pound."

Elliot had lunch alone in the hospital staff cafeteria. On the far side of the double-glazed windows, the day was darkening as an expected snowstorm gathered. Along Route 7, ancient elms stood frozen against the gray sky. When he had finished his sandwich and coffee, he sat staring out at the winter afternoon. His anger had given way to an insistent anxiety.

On the way back to his office, he stopped at the hospital gift shop for a copy of *Sports Illustrated* and a candy bar. When he was inside again, he closed the door and put his feet up. It was Friday and he had no appointments for the remainder of the day, nothing to do but write a few letters and read the office mail.

Elliot's cubicle in the social-services department was windowless and lined with bookshelves. When he found himself unable to concentrate on the magazine and without any heart for his paperwork, he ran his eye over the row of books beside his chair. There were volumes by Heinrich Muller and Carlos Castaneda, Jones' life of Freud, and *The Golden Bough*. The books aroused a revulsion in Elliot. Their present uselessness repelled him.

Over and over again, detail by detail, he tried to recall his conversation with Blankenship.

"You were never there," he heard himself explaining. He was trying to get the whole incident straightened out after the fact. Something was wrong. Dread crept over him like a paralysis. He ate his candy bar without tasting it. He knew that the craving for sweets was itself a bad sign.

Blankenship had misappropriated someone else's dream and made it his own. It made no difference whether you had been there, after all. The dreams had crossed the ocean. They were in the air.

He took his glasses off and put them on his desk and sat with his arms folded, looking into the well of light from his desk lamp. There seemed to be nothing but whirl inside him. Unwelcome things came and went in his mind's eye. His heart beat faster. He could not control the headlong promiscuity of his thoughts.

It was possible to imagine larval dreams traveling in suspended animation undetectable in a host brain. They could be divided and regenerate like flatworms, hide in seams and bedding, in war stories, laughter, snapshots. They could rot your socks and turn your memory into a black-and-green blister. Green for the hills, black for the sky above. At daybreak they hung themselves up in rows like bats. At dusk they went out to look for dreamers.

Elliot put his jacket on and went into the outer office, where the secretary sat frowning into the measured sound and light of her machine. She must enjoy its sleekness and order, he thought. She was divorced. Four redheaded kids between ten and seventeen lived with her in an unpainted house across from Stop & Shop. Elliot liked her and had come to find her attractive. He managed a smile for her.

"Ethel, I think I'm going to pack it in," he declared. It seemed awkward to be leaving early without a reason.

"Jack wants to talk to you before you go, Chas."

Elliot looked at her blankly.

Then his colleague, Jack Sprague, having heard his voice, called from the adjoining cubicle. "Chas, what about Sunday's games? Shall I call you with the spread?"

"I don't know," Elliot said. "I'll phone you tomorrow."

"This is a big decision for him," Jack Sprague told the secretary. "He might lose twenty-five bucks."

At present, Elliot drew a slightly higher salary than Jack Sprague, although Jack had a Ph.D. and Elliot was simply an M.S.W. Different branches of the state government employed them.

"Twenty-five bucks," said the woman. "If you guys have no better use for twenty-five bucks, give it to me."

"Where are you off to, by the way?" Sprague asked.

Elliot began to answer, but for a moment no reply occurred to him. He shrugged. "I have to get back," he finally stammered. "I promised Grace."

"Was that Blankenship I saw leaving?"

Elliot nodded.

"It's February," Jack said. "How come he's not in Florida?"

"I don't know," Elliot said. He put on his coat and walked to the door. "I'll see you."

"Have a nice weekend," the secretary said. She and Sprague looked at him indulgently as he walked toward the main corridor.

"Are Chas and Grace going out on the town?" she said to Sprague. "What do you think?"

"That would be the day," Sprague said. "Tomorrow he'll come back over here and read all day. He spends every weekend holed up in this goddam office while she does something or other at the church." He shook his head. "Every night he's at A.A. and she's home alone."

Ethel savored her overbite. "Jack," she said teasingly, "are you thinking what I think you're thinking? Shame on you."

"I'm thinking I'm glad I'm not him, that's what I'm thinking. That's as much as I'll say."

"Yeah, well, I don't care," Ethel said. "Two salaries and no kids, that's the way to go, boy."

Elliot went out through the automatic doors of the emergency bay and the cold closed over him. He walked across the hospital parking lot with his eyes on the pavement, his hands thrust deep in his overcoat pockets, skirting patches of shattered ice. There was no wind, but the motionless air stung; the metal frames of his glasses burned his skin. Curlicues of mud-brown ice coated the soiled snowbanks along the street. Although it was still afternoon, the street lights had come on.

The lock on his car door had frozen and he had to breathe on the keyhole to fit the key. When the engine turned over, Jussi Björling's recording of the Handel Largo filled the car interior. He snapped it off at once.

Halted at the first stoplight, he began to feel the want of a destination. The fear and impulse to flight that had got him out of the office faded, and he had no desire to go home. He was troubled by a peculiar impatience that might have been with time itself. It was as though he were waiting for something. The sensation made him feel anxious; it was unfamiliar but not altogether unpleasant. When the light changed he drove on, past the Gulf station and the firehouse and between the greens of Ilford Common. At the far end of the common he swung into the parking lot of the Packard Conway Library and stopped with the engine running. What he was experiencing, he thought, was the principle of possibility.

He turned off the engine and went out again into the cold. Behind the leaded library windows he could see the librarian pouring coffee in her tiny private office. The librarian was a Quaker of socialist principles named Candace Music, who was Elliot's cousin.

The Conway Library was all dark wood and etched mirrors, a Gothic saloon. Years before, out of work and booze-whipped, Elliot had gone to hide there. Because Candace was a classicist's widow and knew some Greek, she was one of the few people in the valley with whom Elliot had cared to speak in those days. Eventually, it had seemed to him that all their conversations tended toward Vietnam, so he had gone less and less often. Elliot was the only Vietnam veteran Candace knew well enough to chat with, and he had come to suspect that he was being probed for the edification of the East Ilford Friends Meeting. At that time he had still pretended to talk easily about his war and had prepared little discourses and picaresque anecdotes to recite on demand. Earnest seekers like Candace had caused him great secret distress.

Candace came out of her office to find him at the checkout desk. He watched her brow furrow with concern as she composed a smile. "Chas, what a surprise. You haven't been in for an age."

"Sure I have, Candace. I went to all the Wednesday films last fall. I work just across the road."

"I know, dear," Candace said. "I always seem to miss you."

A cozy fire burned in the hearth, an antique brass clock ticked along on the marble mantel above it. On a couch near the fireplace an old man sat upright, his mouth open, asleep among half a dozen soiled plastic bags. Two teen-age girls whispered over their homework at a table under the largest window.

"Now that I'm here," he said, laughing, "I can't remember what I came to get."

"Stay and get warm," Candace told him. "Got a minute? Have a cup of coffee."

Elliot had nothing but time, but he quickly realized that he did not want to stay and pass it with Candace. He had no clear idea of why he had come to the library. Standing at the checkout desk, he accepted coffee. She attended him with an air of benign supervision, as though he were a Chinese peasant and she a medical missionary, like her father. Candace was tall and plain, more handsome in her middle sixties than she had ever been.

"Why don't we sit down?"

He allowed her to gentle him into a chair by the fire. They made a threesome with the sleeping old man.

"Have you given up translating, Chas? I hope not."

"Not at all," he said. Together they had once rendered a few fragments of Sophocles into verse. She was good at clever rhymes.

"You come in so rarely, Chas. Ted's books go to waste."

After her husband's death, Candace had donated his books to the Conway, where they reposed in a reading room inscribed to his memory, untouched among foreign-language volumes, local genealogies, and books in large type for the elderly.

"I have a study in the barn," he told Candace. "I work there. When I have time." The lie was absurd, but he felt the need of it.

"And you're working with Vietnam veterans," Candace declared.

"Supposedly," Elliot said. He was growing impatient with her nodding solicitude.

"Actually," he said, "I came in for the new Oxford 'Classical World.' I thought you'd get it for the library and I could have a look before I spent my hard-earned cash."

Candace beamed. "You've come to the right place, Chas, I'm happy to say." He thought she looked disproportionately happy. "I have it."

"Good," Elliot said, standing. "I'll just take it, then. I can't really stay."

Candace took his cup and saucer and stood as he did. When the library telephone rang, she ignored it, reluctant to let him go. "How's Grace?" she asked.

"Fine," Elliot said. "Grace is well."

At the third ring she went to the desk. When her back was turned, he hesitated for a moment and then went outside.

The gray afternoon had softened into night, and it was snowing. The falling snow whirled like a furious mist in the headlight beams on Route 7 and settled implacably on Elliot's cheeks and eyelids. His heart, for no good reason, leaped up in childlike expectation. He had run away from a dream and encountered possibility. He felt in possession of a promise. He began to walk toward the roadside lights.

Only gradually did he begin to understand what had brought him there and what the happy anticipation was that fluttered in his breast. Drinking, he had started his evenings from the Conway Library. He would arrive hung over in the early afternoon to browse and read. When the old pain rolled in with dusk, he would walk down to the Midway Tavern for a remedy. Standing in the snow outside the library, he realized that he had contrived to promise himself a drink.

Ahead, through the storm, he could see the beer signs in the Midway's window warm and welcoming. Snowflakes spun around his head like an excitement.

Outside the Midway's package store, he paused with his hand on the doorknob. There was an old man behind the counter whom Elliot remembered from his drinking days. When he was inside, he realized that the old man neither knew nor cared who he was. The package store was thick with dust; it was on the counter, the shelves, the bottles themselves. The old counterman looked dusty. Elliot bought a bottle of King William Scotch and put it in the inside pocket of his overcoat.

Passing the windows of the Midway Tavern, Elliot could see the ranks of bottles aglow behind the bar. The place was crowded with men leaving the afternoon shifts at the shoe and felt factories. No one turned to note him when he passed inside. There was a single stool vacant at the bar and he took it. His heart beat faster. Bruce Springsteen was on the jukebox.

The bartender was a club fighter from Pittsfield called Jackie G., with whom Elliot had often gossiped. Jackie G. greeted him as though he had been in the previous evening. "Say, babe?"

"How do," Elliot said.

A couple of the men at the bar eyed his shirt and tie. Confronted with the bartender, he felt compelled to explain his presence. "Just thought I'd stop by," he told Jackie G. "Just thought I'd have one. Saw the light. The snow . . ." He chuckled expansively.

"Good move," the bartender said. "Scotch?"

"Double," Elliot said.

When he shoved two dollars forward along the bar, Jackie G. pushed one of the bills back to him. "Happy hour, babe."

"Ah," Elliot said. He watched Jackie pour the double. "Not a moment too soon."

For five minutes or so, Elliot sat in his car in the barn with the engine running and his Handel tape on full volume. He had driven over from East Ilford in a Baroque ecstasy, swinging and swaying and singing along. When the tape ended, he turned off the engine and poured some Scotch into an apple-juice container to store providentially beneath the car seat. Then he took the tape and the Scotch into the house with him. He was lying on the sofa in the dark living room, listening to the Largo, when he heard his wife's car in the driveway. By the time Grace had made her way up the icy back-porch steps, he was able to hide the Scotch and rinse his glass clean in the kitchen sink. The drinking life, he thought, was lived moment by moment.

Soon she was in the tiny cloakroom struggling off with her overcoat. In the process she knocked over a cross-country ski, which stood propped against the cloakroom wall. It had been more than a year since Elliot had used the skis.

She came into the kitchen and sat down at the table to take off her boots. Her lean, freckled face was flushed with the cold, but her eyes looked weary. "I wish you'd put those skis down in the barn," she told him. "You never use them."

"I always like to think," Elliot said, "that I'll start the morning off skiing."

"Well, you never do," she said. "How long have you been home?"

"Practically just walked in," he said. Her pointing out that he no longer skied in the morning enraged him. "I stopped at the Conway Library to get the new Oxford 'Classical World.' Candace ordered it."

Her look grew troubled. She had caught something in his voice. With dread and bitter satisfaction, Elliot watched his wife detect the smell of whiskey.

"Oh God," she said. "I don't believe it."

Let's get it over with, he thought. Let's have the song and dance.

She sat up straight in her chair and looked at him in fear.

"Oh, Chas," she said, "how could you?"

For a moment he was tempted to try to explain it all.

"The fact is," Elliot told his wife, "I hate people who start the day cross-country skiing."

She shook her head in denial and leaned her forehead on her palm and cried.

He looked into the kitchen window and saw his own distorted image. "The fact is I think I'll start tomorrow morning by stringing head-high razor wire across Anderson's trail."

The Andersons were the Elliots' nearest neighbors. Loyall Anderson was a full professor of government at the state university, thirty miles away. Anderson and his wife were blond and both of them were over six feet tall. They had two blond children, who qualified for the gifted class in the local school but attended regular classes in token of the Andersons' opposition to élitism.

"Sure," Elliot said. "Stringing wire's good exercise. It's life-affirming in its own way."

The Andersons started each and every day with a brisk morning glide along a trail that they partly maintained. They skied well and presented a pleasing, wholesome sight. If, in the course of their adventure, they encountered a snowmobile, Darlene Anderson would affect to choke and cough, indicating her displeasure. If the snowmobile approached them from behind and the trail was narrow, the Andersons would decline to let it pass, asserting their statutory right-of-way.

"I don't want to hear your violent fantasies," Grace said.

Elliot was picturing razor wire, the Army kind. He was picturing the decapitated Andersons, their blood and jaunty ski caps bright on the white trail. He was picturing their severed heads, their earnest blue eyes and large white teeth reflecting the virginal morning snow. Although Elliot hated snowmobiles, he hated the Andersons far more.

He looked at his wife and saw that she had stopped crying. Her long, elegant face was rigid and lipless.

"Know what I mean? One string at Mommy and Daddy level for Loyall and Darlene. And a bitty wee string at kiddie level for Skippy and Samantha, those cunning little whizzes."

"Stop it," she said to him.

"Sorry," Elliot told her.

Stiff with shame, he went and took his bottle out of the cabinet into which he had thrust it and poured a drink. He was aware of her eyes on him. As he drank, a fragment from old Music's translation of "Medea" came into his mind. "Old friend, I have to weep. The gods and I went mad together and made things as they are." It was such a waste; eighteen months of struggle thrown away. But there was no way to get the stuff back in the bottle.

"I'm very sorry," he said. "You know I'm very sorry, don't you, Grace?"

The delectable Handel arias spun on in the next room.

"You must stop," she said. "You must make yourself stop before it takes over."

"It's out of my hands," Elliot said. He showed her his empty hands. "It's beyond me."

"You'll lose your job, Chas." She stood at the table and leaned on it, staring wide-eyed at him. Drunk as he was, the panic in her voice frightened him. "You'll end up in jail again."

"One engages," Elliot said, "and then one sees."

"How can you have done it?" she demanded. "You promised me."

"First the promises," Elliot said, "and then the rest."

"Last time was supposed to be the last time," she said.

"Yes," he said, "I remember."

"I can't stand it," she said. "You reduce me to hysterics." She wrung her hands for him to see. "See? Here I am, I'm in hysterics."

"What can I say?" Elliot asked. He went to the bottle and refilled his glass. "Maybe you shouldn't watch."

"You want me to be forbearing, Chas? I'm not going to be."

"The last thing I want," Elliot said, "is an argument."

"I'll give you a fucking argument. You didn't have to drink. All you had to do was come home."

"That must have been the problem," he said.

Then he ducked, alert at the last possible second to the missile that came for him at hairline level. Covering up, he heard the shattering of glass, and a fine rain of crystals enveloped him. She had sailed the sugar bowl at him; it had smashed against the wall above his head and there was sugar and glass in his hair.

"You bastard!" she screamed. "You are undermining me!"

"You ought not to throw things at me," Elliot said. "I don't throw things at you."

He left her frozen into her follow-through and went into the living room to turn the music off. When he returned she was leaning back against the wall, rubbing her right elbow with her left hand. Her eyes were bright. She had picked up one of her boots from the middle of the kitchen floor and stood holding it.

"What the hell do you mean, that must have been the problem?"

He set his glass on the edge of the sink with an unsteady hand and turned to her. "What do I mean? I mean that most of the time I'm putting one foot in front of the other like a good soldier and I'm out of it from the neck up. But there are times when I don't think I will ever be dead enough—or dead long enough—to get the taste of this life off my teeth. That's what I mean!"

She looked at him dry-eyed. "Poor fella," she said.

"What you have to understand, Grace, is that this drink I'm having"—he raised the glass toward her in a gesture of salute—"is the only worthwhile thing I've done in the last year and a half. It's the only thing in my life that means jack shit, the closest thing to satisfaction I've had. Now how can you begrudge me that? It's the best I'm capable of."

"You'll go too far," she said to him. "You'll see."

"What's that, Grace? A threat to walk?" He was grinding his teeth.

"Don't make me laugh. You, walk? You, the friend of the unfortunate?"

"Don't you hit me," she said when she looked at his face. "Don't you dare."

"You, the Christian Queen of Calvary, walk? Why, I don't believe that for a minute."

She ran a hand through her hair and bit her lip. "No, we stay," she said. Anger and distraction made her look young. Her cheeks blazed rosy against the general pallor of her skin. "In my family we stay until the fella dies. That's the tradition. We stay and pour it for them and they die."

He put his drink down and shook his head.

"I thought we'd come through," Grace said. "I was sure."

"No," Elliot said. "Not altogether."

They stood in silence for a minute. Elliot sat down at the oilcloth-covered table. Grace walked around it and poured herself a whiskey.

"You are undermining me, Chas. You are making things impossible for me and I just don't know." She drank and winced. "I'm not going to stay through another drunk. I'm telling you right now. I haven't got it in me. I'll die."

He did not want to look at her. He watched the flakes settle against the glass of the kitchen door. "Do what you feel the need of," he said.

"I just can't take it," she said. Her voice was not scolding but measured and reasonable. "It's February. And I went to court this morning and lost Vopotik."

Once again, he thought, my troubles are going to be obviated by those of the deserving poor. He said, "Which one was that?"

"Don't you remember them? The three-year-old with the broken fingers?"

He shrugged. Grace sipped her whiskey.

"I told you. I said I had a three-year-old with broken fingers, and you said, 'Maybe he owed somebody money.'"

"Yes," he said. "I remember now."

"You ought to see the Vopotiks, Chas. The woman is young and obese. She's so young that for a while I thought I could get to her as a juvenile. The guy is a biker. They believe the kid came from another planet to control their lives. They believe this literally, both of them."

"You shouldn't get involved that way," Elliot said. "You should leave it to the caseworkers."

"They scared their first caseworker all the way to California. They were following me to work."

"You didn't tell me."

"Are you kidding?" she asked. "Of course I didn't." To Elliot's surprise, his wife poured herself a second whiskey. "You know how they address the child? As 'dude.' She says to it, 'Hey, dude.'" Grace shuddered with loathing. "You can't imagine! The woman munching Twinkies. The kid smelling of shit. They're high morning, noon and night, but you can't get anybody for that these days."

"People must really hate it," Elliot said, "when somebody tells them they're not treating their kids right."

"They definitely don't want to hear it," Grace said. "You're right." She sat stirring her drink, frowning into the glass. "The Vopotik child will die, I think."

"Surely not," Elliot said.

"This one I think will die," Grace said. She took a deep breath and puffed out her cheeks and looked at him forlornly. "The situation's extreme. Of course, sometimes you wonder whether it makes any difference. That's the big question, isn't it?"

"I would think," Elliot said, "that would be the one question you didn't ask."

"But you do," she said. "You wonder: Ought they to live at all? To continue the cycle?" She put a hand to her hair and shook her head as if in confusion. "Some of these folks, my God, the poor things cannot put Wednesday on top of Tuesday to save their lives."

"It's a trick," Elliot agreed, "a lot of them can't manage."

"And kids are small, they're handy and underfoot. They make noise. They can't hurt you back."

"I suppose child abuse is something people can do together," Elliot said.

"Some kids are obnoxious. No question about it."

"I wouldn't know," Elliot said.

"Maybe you should stop complaining. Maybe you're better off. Maybe your kids are better off unborn."

"Better off or not," Elliot said, "it looks like they'll stay that way."

"I mean our kids, of course," Grace said. "I'm not blaming you, understand? It's just that here we are with you drunk again and me losing Vopotik, so I thought why not get into the big unaskable questions." She got up and folded her arms and began to pace up and down the kitchen. "Oh," she said when her eye fell upon the bottle, "that's good stuff, Chas. You won't mind if I have another? I'll leave you enough to get loaded on."

Elliot watched her pour. So much pain, he thought; such anger and confusion. He was tired of pain, anger, and confusion; they were what had got him in trouble that very morning.

The liquor seemed to be giving him a perverse lucidity when all he now required was oblivion. His rage, especially, was intact in its salting of alcohol. Its contours were palpable and bleeding at the borders. Booze was good for rage. Booze could keep it burning through the darkest night.

"What happened in court?" he asked his wife.

She was leaning on one arm against the wall, her long, strong body flexed at the hip. Holding her glass, she stared angrily toward the invisible fields outside. "I lost the child," she said.

Elliot thought that a peculiar way of putting it. He said nothing.

"The court convened in an atmosphere of high hilarity. It may be Hate Month around here but it was buddy-buddy over at Ilford Courthouse. The room was full of bikers and bikers' lawyers. A colorful crowd. There was a lot of bonding." She drank and shivered. "They didn't think too well of me. They don't think too well of broads as lawyers. Neither does the judge. The judge has the common touch. He's one of the boys."

"Which judge?" Elliot asked.

"Buckley. A man of about sixty. Know him? Lots of veins on his nose?"

Elliot shrugged.

"I thought I had done my homework," Grace told him. "But suddenly I had nothing but paper. No witnesses. It was Margolis at Valley Hospital who spotted the radiator burns. He called us in the first place. Suddenly he's got to keep his reservation for a campsite in St. John. So Buckley threw his deposition out." She began to chew on a fingernail. "The caseworkers have vanished—one's in L.A., the other's in Nepal. I went in there and got run over. I lost the child."

"It happens all the time," Elliot said. "Doesn't it?"

"This one shouldn't have been lost, Chas. These people aren't simply confused. They're weird. They stink."

"You go messing into anybody's life," Elliot said, "that's what you'll find."

"If the child stays in that house," she said, "he's going to die."

"You did your best," he told his wife. "Forget it."

She pushed the bottle away. She was holding a water glass that was almost a third full of whiskey.

"That's what the commissioner said."

Elliot was thinking of how she must have looked in court to the cherry-faced judge and the bikers and their lawyers. Like the schoolteachers who had tormented their childhoods, earnest and tight-assed, humorless and self-righteous. It was not surprising that things had gone against her.

He walked over to the window and faced his reflection again. "Your optimism always surprises me."

"My optimism? Where I grew up our principal cultural expression was the funeral. Whatever keeps me going, it isn't optimism."

"No?" he asked. "What is it?"

"I forget," she said.

"Maybe it's your religious perspective. Your sense of the divine plan."

She sighed in exasperation. "Look, I don't think I want to fight anymore. I'm sorry I threw the sugar at you. I'm not your keeper. Pick on someone your own size."

"Sometimes," Elliot said, "I try to imagine what it's like to believe that the sky is full of care and concern."

"You want to take everything from me, do you?" She stood leaning against the back of her chair. "That you can't take. It's the only part of my life you can't mess up."

He was thinking that if it had not been for her he might not have survived. There could be no forgiveness for that. "Your life? You've got all this piety strung out between Monadnock and Central America. And look at yourself. Look at your life."

"Yes," she said, "look at it."

"You should have been a nun. You don't know how to live."

"I know that," she said. "That's why I stopped doing counseling. Because I'd rather talk the law than life." She turned to him. "You got everything I had, Chas. What's left I absolutely require."

"I swear I would rather be a drunk," Elliot said, "than force myself to believe such trivial horseshit."

"Well, you're going to have to do it without a straight man," she said, "because this time I'm not going to be here for you. Believe it or not."

"I don't believe it," Elliot said. "Not my Grace."

"You're really good at this," she told him. "You make me feel ashamed of my own name."

"I love your name," he said.

The telephone rang. They let it ring three times, and then Elliot went over and answered it.

"Hey, who's that?" a good-humored voice on the phone demanded.

Elliot recited their phone number.

"Hey, I want to talk to your woman, man. Put her on."

"I'll give her a message," Elliot said.

"You put your woman on, man. Run and get her."

Elliot looked at the receiver. He shook his head. "Mr. Vopotik?"

"Never you fuckin' mind, man. I don't want to talk to you. I want to talk to the skinny bitch."

Elliot hung up.

"Is it him?" she asked.

"I guess so.

They waited for the phone to ring again and it shortly did.

"I'll talk to him," Grace said. But Elliot already had the phone.

"Who are you, asshole?" the voice inquired. "What's your fuckin' name, man?"

"Elliot," Elliot said.

"Hey, don't hang up on me, Elliot. I won't put up with that. I told you go get that skinny bitch, man. You go do it."

There were sounds of festivity in the background on the other end of the line—a stereo and drunken voices.

"Hey," the voice declared. "Hey, don't keep me waiting, man."

"What do you want to say to her?" Elliot asked.

"That's none of your fucking business, fool. Do what I told you."

"My wife is resting," Elliot said. "I'm taking her calls."

He was answered by a shout of rage. He put the phone aside for a moment and finished his glass of whiskey. When he picked it up again the man on the line was screaming at him. "That bitch tried to break up my family, man! She almost got away with it. You know what kind of pain my wife went through?"

"What kind?" Elliot asked.

For a few seconds he heard only the noise of the party. "Hey, you're not drunk, are you, fella?"

"Certainly not," Elliot insisted.

"You tell that skinny bitch she's gonna pay for what she did to my family, man. You tell her she can run but she can't hide. I don't care where you go—California, anywhere—I'll get to you."

"Now that I have you on the phone," Elliot said, "I'd like to ask you a couple of questions. Promise you won't get mad?"

"Stop it!" Grace said to him. She tried to wrench the phone from his grasp, but he clutched it to his chest.

"Do you keep a journal?" Elliot asked the man on the phone. "What's your hat size?"

"Maybe you think I can't get to you," the man said. "But I can get to you, man. I don't care who you are, I'll get to you. The brothers will get to you."

"Well, there's no need to go to California. You know where we live."

"For God's sake," Grace said.

"Fuckin' right," the man on the telephone said. "Fuckin' right I know."

"Come on over," Elliot said.

"How's that?" the man on the phone asked.

"I said come on over. We'll talk about space travel. Comets and stuff. We'll talk astral projection. The moons of Jupiter."

"You're making a mistake, fucker."

"Come on over," Elliot insisted. "Bring your fat wife and your beat-up kid. Don't be embarrassed if your head's a little small."

The telephone was full of music and shouting. Elliot held it away from his ear.

"Good work," Grace said to him when he had replaced the receiver.

"I hope he comes," Elliot said. "I'll pop him."

He went carefully down the cellar stairs, switched on the overhead light, and began searching among the spiderwebbed shadows and fouled fishing line for his shotgun. It took him fifteen minutes to find it and his cleaning case. While he was still downstairs, he heard the telephone ring again and his wife answer it. He came upstairs and spread his shooting gear across the kitchen table. "Was that him?"

She nodded wearily. "He called back to play us the chain saw."

"I've heard that melody before," Elliot said.

He assembled his cleaning rod and swabbed out the shotgun barrel. Grace watched him, a hand to her forehead. "God," she said. "What have I done? I'm so drunk."

"Most of the time," Elliot said, sighting down the barrel, "I'm helpless in the face of human misery. Tonight I'm ready to reach out."

"I'm finished," Grace said. "I'm through, Chas. I mean it."

Elliot rammed three red shells into the shotgun and pumped one forward into the breech with a satisfying report. "Me, I'm ready for some radical problem-solving. I'm going to spray that no-neck Slovak all over the yard."

"He isn't a Slovak," Grace said. She stood in the middle of the kitchen with her eyes closed. Her face was chalk white.

"What do you mean?" Elliot demanded. "Certainly he's a Slovak."

"No he's not," Grace said.

"Fuck him anyway. I don't care what he is. I'll grease his ass."

He took a handful of deer shells from the box and stuffed them in his jacket pockets.

"I'm not going to stay with you, Chas. Do you understand me?"

Elliot walked to the window and peered out at his driveway. "He won't be alone. They travel in packs."

"For God's sake!" Grace cried, and in the next instant bolted for the downstairs bathroom. Elliot went out, turned off the porch light and switched on a spotlight over the barn door. Back inside, he could hear Grace in the toilet being sick. He turned off the light in the kitchen.

He was still standing by the window when she came up behind him. It seemed strange and fateful to be standing in the dark near her, holding the shotgun. He felt ready for anything.

"I can't leave you alone down here drunk with a loaded shotgun," she said. "How can I?"

"Go upstairs," he said.

"If I went upstairs it would mean I didn't care what happened. Do you understand? If I go it means I don't care anymore. Understand?"

"Stop asking me if I understand," Elliot said. "I understand fine."

"I can't think," she said in a sick voice. "Maybe I don't care. I don't know. I'm going upstairs."

"Good," Elliot said.

When she was upstairs, Elliot took his shotgun and the whiskey into the dark living room and sat down in an armchair beside one of the lace-curtained windows. The powerful barn light illuminated the length of his driveway and the whole of the back yard. From the window at which he sat, he commanded a view of several miles in the direction of East Ilford. The two-lane blacktop road that ran there was the only one along which an enemy could pass.

He drank and watched the snow, toying with the safety of his 12-gauge Remington. He felt neither anxious nor angry now but only impatient to be done with whatever the night would bring. Drunkenness and the silent rhythm of the falling snow combined to make him feel outside of time and syntax.

Sitting in the dark room, he found himself confronting Blankenship's dream. He saw the bunkers and wire of some long-lost perimeter. The rank smell of night came back to him, the dread evening and quick dusk, the mysteries of outer darkness: fear, combat, and death. Enervated by liquor, he began to cry. Elliot was sympathetic with other people's tears but ashamed of his own. He thought of his own tears as childish and excremental. He stifled whatever it was that had started them.

Now his whiskey tasted thin as water. Beyond the lightly frosted glass, illuminated snowflakes spun and settled sleepily on weighted pine boughs. He had found a life beyond the war after all, but in it he was still sitting in darkness, armed, enraged, waiting.

His eyes grew heavy as the snow came down. He felt as though he could be drawn up into the storm and he began to imagine that. He imagined his life with all its artifacts and appetites easing up the spout into white oblivion, everything obviated and foreclosed. He thought maybe he could go for that.

When he awakened, his left hand had gone numb against the trigger guard of his shotgun. The living room was full of pale, delicate light. He looked outside and saw that the storm was done with and the sky radiant and cloudless. The sun was still below the horizon.

Slowly Elliot got to his feet. The throbbing poison in his limbs served to remind him of the state of things. He finished the glass of whiskey on the windowsill beside his easy chair. Then he went to the hall closet to get a ski jacket, shouldered his shotgun, and went outside.

There were two cleared acres behind his house; beyond them a trail descended into a hollow of pine forest and frozen swamp. Across the hollow, white pastures stretched to the ridge-line, lambent under the lightening sky. A line of skeletal elms weighted with snow marked the course of frozen Shawmut Brook.

He found a pair of ski goggles in a jacket pocket and put them on and set out toward the tree line, gripping the shotgun, step by careful step in the knee-deep snow. Two raucous crows wheeled high overhead, their cries exploding the morning's silence. When the sun came over the ridge, he stood where he was and took in a deep breath. The risen sun warmed his face and he closed his eyes. It was windless and very cold.

Only after he had stood there for a while did he realize how tired he had become. The weight of the gun taxed him. It seemed infinitely wearying to contemplate another single step in the snow. He opened his eyes and closed them again. With sunup the world had gone blazing blue and white, and even with his tinted goggles its whiteness dazzled him and made his head ache. Behind his eyes, the hypnagogic patterns formed a monsoon-heavy tropical sky. He yawned. More than anything, he wanted to lie down in the soft, pure snow. If he could do that, he was certain he could go to sleep at once.

He stood in the middle of the field and listened to the crows. Fear, anger, and sleep were the three primary conditions of life. He had learned that over there. Once he had thought fear the worst, but he had learned that the worst was anger. Nothing could fix it; neither alcohol nor medicine. It was a worm. It left him no peace. Sleep was the best.

He opened his eyes and pushed on until he came to the brow that overlooked the swamp. Just below, gliding along among the frozen cattails and bare scrub maple, was a man on skis. Elliot stopped to watch the man approach.

The skier's face was concealed by a red-and-blue ski mask. He wore snow goggles, a blue jumpsuit, and a red woolen Norwegian hat. As he came, he leaned into the turns of the trail, moving silently and gracefully along. At the foot of the slope on which Elliot stood, the man looked up, saw him, and slid to a halt. The man stood staring at him for a moment and then began to herringbone up the slope. In no time at all the skier stood no more than ten feet away, removing his goggles, and inside the woolen mask Elliot recognized the clear blue eyes of his neighbor, Professor Loyall Anderson. The shotgun Elliot was carrying seemed to grow heavier. He yawned and shook his head, trying unsuccessfully to clear it. The sight of Anderson's eyes gave him a thrill of revulsion.

"What are you after?" the young professor asked him, nodding toward the shotgun Elliot was cradling.

"Whatever there is," Elliot said.

Anderson took a quick look at the distant pasture behind him and then turned back to Elliot. The mouthhole of the professor's mask filled with teeth. Elliot thought that Anderson's teeth were quite as he had imagined them earlier. "Well, Polonski's cows are locked up," the professor said. "So they at least are safe."

Elliot realized that the professor had made a joke and was smiling. "Yes," he agreed.

Professor Anderson and his wife had been the moving force behind an initiative to outlaw the discharge of firearms within the boundaries of East Ilford Township. The initiative had been defeated, because East Ilford was not that kind of town.

"I think I'll go over by the river," Elliot said. He said it only to have something to say, to fill the silence before Anderson spoke again. He was afraid of what Anderson might say to him and of what might happen.

"You know," Anderson said, "that's all bird sanctuary over there now."

"Sure," Elliot agreed.

Outfitted as he was, the professor attracted Elliot's anger in an elemental manner. The mask made him appear a kind of doll, a kachina figure or a marionette. His eyes and mouth, all on their own, were disagreeable.

Elliot began to wonder if Anderson could smell the whiskey on his breath. He pushed the little red bull's-eye safety button on his gun to Off.

"Seriously," Anderson said, "I'm always having to run hunters out of there. Some people don't understand the word 'posted.'"

"I would never do that," Elliot said. "I would be afraid."

Anderson nodded his head. He seemed to be laughing. "Would you?" he asked Elliot merrily.

In imagination, Elliot rested the tip of his shotgun barrel against Anderson's smiling teeth. If he fired a load of deer shot into them, he thought, they might make a noise like broken china. "Yes," Elliot said. "I wouldn't know who they were or where they'd been. They might resent my being alive. Telling them where they could shoot and where not."

Anderson's teeth remained in place. "That's pretty strange," he said. "I mean, to talk about resenting someone for being alive."

"It's all relative," Elliot said. "They might think, 'Why should he be alive when some brother of mine isn't?' Or they might think, 'Why should he be alive when I'm not?'"

"Oh," Anderson said.

"You see?" Elliot said. Facing Anderson, he took a long step backward. "All relative."

"Yes," Anderson said.

"That's so often true, isn't it?" Elliot asked. "Values are often relative."

"Yes," Anderson said. Elliot was relieved to see that he had stopped smiling.

"I've hardly slept, you know," Elliot told Professor Anderson. "Hardly at all. All night. I've been drinking."

"Oh," Anderson said. He locked his lips in the mouth of the mask. "You should get some rest."

"You're right," Elliot said.

"Well," Anderson said, "got to go now."

Elliot thought he sounded a little thick in the tongue. A little slow in the jaw.

"It's a nice day," Elliot said, wanting now to be agreeable.

"It's great," Anderson said, shuffling on his skis.

"Have a nice day," Elliot said.

"Yes," Anderson said, and pushed off.

Elliot rested the shotgun across his shoulders and watched Anderson withdraw through the frozen swamp. It was in fact a nice day, but Elliot took no comfort in the weather. He missed night and falling snow.

As he walked back toward his house, he realized that now there would be whole days to get through, running before the antic energy of whiskey. The whiskey would drive him until he dropped. He shook his head in regret. "It's a revolution," he said aloud. He imagined himself talking to his wife.

Getting drunk was an insurrection, a revolution—a bad one. There would be outsize bogus emotions. There would be petty moral blackmail and cheap remorse. He had said dreadful things to his wife. He had bullied Anderson with his violence and unhappiness, and Anderson would not forgive him. There would be damn little justice and no mercy.

Nearly to the house, he was startled by the desperate feathered drumming of a pheasant's rush. He froze, and out of instinct brought the gun up in the direction of the sound. When he saw the bird break from its cover and take wing, he tracked it, took a breath and fired once. The bird was a little flash of opulent color against the bright-blue sky. Elliot felt himself flying for a moment. The shot missed.

Lowering the gun, he remembered the deer shells he had loaded. A hit with the concentrated shot would have pulverized the bird, and he was glad he had missed. He wished no harm to any creature. Then he thought of himself wishing no harm to any creature and began to feel fond and sorry for himself. As soon as he grew aware of the emotion he was indulging, he suppressed it. Pissing and moaning, mourning and weeping, that was the nature of the drug.

The shot echoed from the distant hills. Smoke hung in the air. He turned and looked behind him and saw, far away across the pasture, the tiny blue-and-red figure of Professor Anderson motionless against the snow. Then Elliot turned again toward his house and took a few labored steps and looked up to see his wife at the bedroom window. She stood perfectly still, and the morning sun lit her nakedness. He stopped where he was. She had heard the shot and run to the window. What had she thought to see? Burnt rags and blood on the snow. How relieved was she now? How disappointed?

Elliot thought he could feel his wife trembling at the window. She was hugging herself. Her hands clasped her shoulders. Elliot took his snow goggles off and shaded his eyes with his hand. He stood in the field staring.

The length of the gun was between them, he thought. Somehow she had got out in front of it, to the wrong side of the wire. If he looked long enough he would find everything out there. He would find himself down the sight.

How beautiful she is, he thought. The effect was striking. The window was so clear because he had washed it himself, with vinegar. At the best of times he was a difficult, fussy man.

Elliot began to hope for forgiveness. He leaned the shotgun on his forearm and raised his left hand and waved to her. Show a hand, he thought. Please just show a hand.

He was cold, but it had got light. He wanted no more than the gesture. It seemed to him that he could build another day on it. Another day was all you needed. He raised his hand higher and waited.

Audrey Thomas

Audrey Thomas was born in 1935 in Binghamton, New York, and educated at Smith College in the U.S. and St. Andrews University in Scotland. She and her former husband immigrated to Canada in 1958, where he taught in Vancouver, and she completed her M.A. at the University of British Columbia in 1963. They spent two years in Ghana in the mid-sixties. Thomas says she left the United States partly for political reasons (she was a student during the McCarthy hearings and saw what happened to writers who were "on trial" then) and has remained active in Amnesty International, P.E.N., and the Writers' Union of Canada. She lives on Galiano Island, not far from Vancouver, and has taught intermittently at the universities of Victoria, British Columbia, and Concordia. She published her first collection of stories, *Ten Green Bottles*, in 1967. This was followed by several novels, *Mrs. Blood* (1970), *Songs My Mother Taught Me* (1973), *Blown Figures* (1974), *Latakia* (1979), and *Intertidal Life* (1984), two short novels in a single volume, *Munchmeyer and Prospero on the Island* (1971), and several collections of stories: *Ladies & Escorts* (1977), *Real Mothers* (1981), *Two in the Bush and Other Stories* (1981), *Goodbye Harold, Good Luck* (1986), and *Wild Blue Yonder* (1990). An issue of the literary quarterly *Room of One's Own*, (Vol. 10, No. 3 and 4, 1986), is devoted to the work of Thomas and contains critical commentary, a selected bibliography, and an interview.

Some of her more interesting statements about fiction are quoted in an article by Liam Lacey for *The Globe and Mail* (Saturday, Nov. 3, 1990). Writing a short story "is a frame of mind. I'm sure the image isn't original, but I like to compare it to skipping a stone across a pond. Each place it touches the water, it sets off circles of ripples, and those circles overlap with each other. It's all the same stone, though." When asked specifically about technique, Thomas is cagey: "It sounds a bit like something you'd pick up in a sex shop, doesn't it?" However, she is very innovative and conscientious about matters of craft, mocking the idea that "stories write themselves." "I violently disagree with the idea that you don't know what you're doing as a writer. You don't pre-plan every detail, but you're more or less in control. I liken it to taking a puppy for a walk. It's going to go on the walk you decide, although not perhaps the way you planned. Sometimes the puppy stops and drags behind. Sometimes it worries this twig for longer than you'd care to, and that twig turns out to be the central symbol of your story. Sometimes you drag that puppy gasping back home with you and sometimes the puppy dies. But you're still the one determining where the walk goes." In response to one of her creative writing students asking what, basically, she wanted in a story, Thomas replied: "Basically, I'm looking for perfection; it never goes out of style."

Thomas sees herself in the mainstream of twentieth-century short fiction. "Nothing has really changed in the short story. It's always about the human heart. Alice Munro, Flannery O'Connor, Eudora Welty, William Trevor all write from the heart. The other thing is they all write from their neighbourhoods, either physically or spiritually. It's true I don't feel rooted in one place, but most of the places I write about I've lived in, shopped there, that sort of thing. The short story is like a little black dress: it's very versatile. No one should be without one." However, her work is much more verbally playful, and linguistically textured, than that of many of her contemporaries. "I like to use humour in my stories, but I'm not really doing those things with language as jokes. It's about language and its power. It's what T. S. Eliot's Sweeney said: 'I gotta use words when I talk to you.' Words aren't like those little letter puzzles, where you fit the letters L-O-V-E into the puzzle, and they fit right into the same slots. This is where men and women get into trouble, I think—they think they mean the same things by the same words when they really don't. I don't have any answers for this. Chekhov said in one of his letters that the role of the artist was to state the question correctly, and I think that's all I can do."

As these comments about language (and those in her essay "Basmati Rice") suggest, Thomas is interested in prose that maintains open borders with poetry. She acknowledges, in an interview with Allen Twigg (*Strong Voices*), having first learned from Australian novelist Patrick White about breaking sentences and using fragmentation for emphasis. When asked by Twigg about the unconventional quality of her prose, Thomas replies: "Well, the novel is essentially a middle-class form. I know I'm not unique in saying that. The novel has a tradition or received morality behind it. And if you no longer believe in that—or if you believe there isn't any such collective morality in the society in which you live—then the novel is about breaking down all that. And the minute your novel is about breaking down, it's not a novel anymore. It's a book. I write books."

Local Customs

Years from now will he say to himself, "the breasts of that American girl had a bloom on them, like grapes." A combination of sun oil and the blowing sand, of course, but magic then, magic and terrifying to the twelve-year-old boy who was trying to look and not to look, both at the same time. Years from now will he perhaps rub his thumb and two fingers together and smile? As though he had actually touched them instead of merely staring across at her from his usual observation post under the dusty tamarisk tree. She and her friend are talking to the blind man, who lies propped on one elbow, on his suncot, not looking at either girl but somewhere off to one side. This has nothing to do with modesty; the blind man never looks at the people to whom he is talking. The wind and the fifteen yards between them keep Edward from hearing the conversation, but every so often he hears the blind man laugh and say "We Churmans, ha ha ha, we Churmans." His second day on the beach, Edward chased a newspaper which was blowing away in the wind. He brought the runaway pages to a middle-aged man, very tanned, who was sitting under one of the beach umbrellas. The paper was in German but Edward knew that most Germans spoke English. "Is this your paper?" he said, embarrassed by his high, thin, schoolboy voice. The man frowned in his direction.

"*Bitte?*"

"Your paper." Edward thrust it at the man.

"Ah, the newspaper. My wife's newspaper, I am afraid. I am blind."

Edward could just make out the shape of the man's eyes behind the thick dark glasses.

That day at lunch Anna said, "I wonder what's the matter with that man? It looks as though there's something wrong with his legs." Edward's father was reading a book, reaching absently for a forkful of salad from time to time. Edward took after his father; they were both long and thin and had the kind of skin that did not tan. Anna was his father's girlfriend.

"Who?" said Edward's father, not looking up.

"The German man over there, with the wife who is always smiling. She holds onto him—or rather, he holds onto her—wherever they go. She pretty well has to stand him up and sit him down."

"He's blind," Edward said. "He told me so this morning."

"Ah, so." Anna nodded her head at him and smiled. She had big white even teeth and was very pretty. Edward liked her in spite of himself. She was almost always willing to play cards or backgammon with him and she never called him Teddy, the way his mother did. ("Teddy's being so difficult lately," he heard her say, talking on the telephone to one of her friends. And then, "like father, like son.") And he knew Anna had nightmares. The walls between the rooms were thin and he had heard her crying out and moaning in the night. Edward knew a lot about bad dreams.

"His wife is Greek," Edward said, "but they've lived in Germany for years and years. She inherited a house in one of the villages, so they come here in the summer. They also have a house in Munich and a chalet in the Austrian alps."

"You are very good at finding things out," Anna said.

"Not really. He likes to talk."

And it was true—the blind man liked to talk. In English, in German, in bad Greek. From the time they arrived in the morning, his wife driving the white Mercedes, until they left in the late afternoon, the blind man lay on his suncot and talked to anyone who would listen. His wife, in a black bathing suit, her dark hair pulled into a low knot at the back of her neck, made trips across the beach and up to the café-bar for bottles of cold water and glasses of iced coffee. It was hard to tell how old she was, with her smooth brown skin and calm, untroubled face. She seemed to smile at everyone and had a special smile and greeting for Edward ever since he had rescued her newspaper. Twice a day she took her husband's hand and led him into the blue water, where they stood side by side up to their necks, facing the open sea for perhaps ten minutes. Then they turned and walked slowly back to their place under the beach umbrella. She handed him his towel and got him settled and went back for a swim on her own. She was a very strong swimmer and one day Edward had a strange thought. What if she got fed up looking after her husband and simply swam away?

In the last few days the wind has gotten worse. The umbrella man has stopped renting out umbrellas because the wind just knocks them out of their stands. "*Oxi*," he said, "no," shaking his head this morning at Edward, who likes to help with the umbrellas and cots, lining them up very early and then collecting the money from the people who want to rent them. One hundred drachmas for an umbrella, fifty drachmas each for a cot.

"*Kaputt*," the umbrella man says, "*verstehen?*"

"I'm *not German*," Edward insists, but the umbrella man ignores this and always addresses him as though he were. Although Edward knows perfectly well that there were good Germans and bad Germans during the Second World War it upsets him to actually be mistaken for one. Anna said once that she couldn't understand how the Greeks could bear to see a German without wanting to put a bullet through his head.

For three days now the wind has howled all night, rattling the louvred doors and windows in the hotel bedrooms, blowing sand into all the corners. A forest fire is raging in the north. All the young men from the northern villages have been conscripted to fight the fire. Big-bellied water bombers fly back and forth all day. Dmitri, Edward's friend who owns the hotel and café-bar, tells him that some of the islanders are saying it was the tourists who caused the fire but that this isn't true. Last year's fire was started by an old man burning brush in his field and this year's was probably caused by lightning.

"Or maybe the government starts it, who knows?"

Edward does not understand. Dmitri likes him because he collects all the empty bottles from the beach and generally makes himself useful. Dmitri doesn't mind Edward asking him questions.

"Why would the government start a fire?"

"Take people's mind from politics, from troubles."

Edward still doesn't understand. It is a small island; sometimes, in the evenings, you can smell the forests burning in the north. The sunsets are spectacular.

Empty containers for Manhattan Ice-Cream, Tartuffo Gelato Italiano, Coke bottles, Sprite bottles, Pizz lemonade, beer, water bottles, Marlboro packets: during the night the wind sweeps all the rubbish into heaps against the low stone wall which separates the beach from the café and the parking lot in front of the small hotel. By 7:00 A.M. Edward has had his first swim of the day and is sorting through the rubbish. If he finds bits of broken glass, or bottle caps, he places them carefully in a plastic bag.

"You good boy," Dmitri says, "maybe you no go back to England. You stay here with me."

Dmitri isn't married. Everybody thinks, at first, that his sister Fotula is his wife. It is really Fotula who owns the place; property here is passed on to the daughters, not the sons. Dmmi, as his friends and family call him, spent five years working in restaurants in New Jersey and Montreal, living in cheap boarding houses and sending money back so that Fotula could build the thirteen-room hotel. In return she sent him photographs of how the work was coming on. Anna has the pink card which advertises the hotel pasted in her diary:

NEAR BEACH RESTAURANT
PERA AMMOS
IF YOU ENJOY SWIMMING AND PINETREES
SURROUNDING IS NO BETTER PLACE

Dmmi and Fotula wear T-shirts made for them by a satisfied client. PERA AMMOS they say, GOLDEN SANDS BEACH RESORT. On the glass case in front of the bar are a lot of pictures of Dmmi in his T-shirt, with his arm around various pretty girls. He says to Edward, "You think I should make new T-shirt? 'Fotula is no my wife'?" He is a handsome dark-haired man of about forty-five. At least Anna says he is handsome; Edward notices he is getting a fat belly.

The whole family works at one job or another about the place. No matter how early Edward arrives with his sack of bottles, the old granny, the *yia yia*, is already sitting on a straight chair on one side of the door to the kitchen, stuffing tomatoes or green peppers, stringing beans. The old grandpa sits on the other side peeling an enormous pan of potatoes. Dmitri and Fotula's older brother, who is a bit simple, sweeps up and waits on tables. A handsome nephew runs the gift shop and even the umbrella man is some sort of relation. The older brother and his wife, who is the chambermaid, have two naughty children who are alternately kissed and slapped. They hold up the wet sheets for their mother to hang on the line, and fall asleep, in the evenings, on their granny's lap.

Edward is an only child. Since the divorce, his parents never speak to one another except over the telephone, and his grandparents live in distant cities. He has already been a boarder at school for three years.

"You think I should get a wife?" Dmitri says to Edward one day. "Maybe nice English womans?" They are busy setting out chairs and wiping down tables.

Edward smiles but doesn't answer. If he had thought Dmitri was Fotula's husband, Dmitri had thought Anna was Edward's older sister. He had shown them to the same room. Anna had thought this was very funny.

On the beach an Englishman walks by; he is big and boisterous and wears a black T-shirt with CATS printed on one side, two green cat's eyes on the other. "I say," he calls to no one in particular, certainly not to the boy, for Edward has seen this man has no time for children, "crossing the beach in this wind is like crossing the Gobi Desert!" He is a stupid man with a stupid wife and two stupid daughters. The girls parade around in just their bikini bottoms and are dreadful show-offs. Their breasts have just begun to swell. One has nipples the colour of field mushrooms; the other's are dusty pink, like pencil rubbers. They play Frisbee and a game involving two large plastic bats and a tennis ball; they stand at the water's edge each afternoon, squealing and hoping everybody is looking at them, flinging their arms around and missing perfectly easy throws. Edward watches them from the shade of the tamarisk tree. One day they asked him to play and when he shook his head and hurried away they laughed.

"We Churmans," the blind man says, "ha ha ha." He is passing around photographs of his houses.

It is hard to know where to look. Although there is a sign in Greek, English, German and Italian which says NUDITY IS FORBIDDEN, many women are barebreasted. And some of the Greek women are very fat. They look terrible in their two-piece suits, their stomachs spilling over in yellowish rolls. Some have dreadful scars and he doesn't see how they can expose themselves like that, talking away to one another, shouting at their children, passing out food. The little Greek boys fill empty Pizz bottles with sea-water and run along the shore, pouring out the water in long streams, shouting "Pizz, pizz" and laughing.

But the other beach is much worse. On the other beach, the beach where Anna and Edward's father go, everyone is stark naked—man, woman and child. Anna knew about the other beach before they came; she has been to this island once before. On their first day, after the business about the rooms had been sorted out and they had unpacked, Anna said, "Come with me and I will show you the most beautiful beach in the world." She led them up a path along the steep cliffs beyond the bay. They walked for about ten minutes and then she started down towards the water. They followed, slipping and sliding behind her, not always sure where to put their feet, until they came out on a small beach covered in smooth grey pebbles, as though they had stumbled upon a gigantic nest of stone eggs. A hundred yards from shore two men, completely naked, were diving from a large rock. "And now," Anna said, spreading her towel over the smooth, round pebbles, "now we take off our clothes and let the sun shine all over us." She was unbuttoning her skirt as she spoke. Soon she and his father had shed all their clothes, their bodies very pale compared to the few other people lying on the beach or swimming in the blue-green water.

"Come on Teddy," his father said, "it's all right. Anna says we're allowed to swim nude over here. Off with your clothes. You look as though you could do with a bit of sunshine."

Nude. It rhymed with rude. What an ugly word.

Anna stood smiling at him. "It feels so nice; why don't you give it a try?"

"In a minute," he said. He spread out his towel and carefully anchored it at the corners with large grey stones.

Anna and his father lay down side by side, faces to the sun, holding hands.

"Aren't you glad we came?" she asked. She leaned over and kissed his father on the belly. His father's cock stirred and thickened. Edward went quickly to the water's edge, pulled off his shorts and ran into the water. The rocks were slippery here and he fell once or twice but was quickly over his head.

When Anna had stood there smiling at him she was wearing only the necklace of blue beads his father had bought her in Athens. For their "anniversary" he had said. The man in the shop swore they were genuine mummy beads and now Edward, swimming, remembered the Mummy Room at the British Museum and one mummy in particular. The brownish bandages covering the body were covered in turn by a broken net of blue beads. Where did the jeweller in Athens get his? From men who robbed tombs? It seemed strange to him, as he floated on his back in the cool water, the sun so hot against his closed eyes, that Anna would want to wear something like that, something that had been shut up in a tomb for hundreds and hundreds of years, maybe something that had a curse on it.

Edward had been on a school tour of the museum and the guide had told them all about curses connected with the tombs. When they were going through from one hall to another there had been a marble statue of a girl, a goddess maybe, lying on her stomach, asleep. One of the boys pretended to stick his finger up her bum when the guard wasn't looking.

When Edward came out of the water he quickly wrapped himself in his towel and moved away from Anna and his father.

He went one more time to the pebble beach and sat in the shade of the cliff. A French couple came to share the shade and the woman showed him an angry red circle on her arm. "*La méduse,*" she said, "*attention!*" Edward was surprised that anyone would think he was French. Her husband was wearing only the top of his wetsuit and had been spearing fish. When Edward looked puzzled (what was a *méduse?*) he said, "jelay-fish" then turned his back and began talking to his wife in rapid French.

After that Edward said he preferred the sandy beach by the hotel. For a moment he thought his father was angry. Then he shrugged. "It's up to you. We can join you at lunchtime. If you need anything, just put it on the bill." And so their routine was quickly established. Edward stayed on the sandy beach; he helped Dmitri and the umbrella man; he swam; he watched. Sometimes he ate lunch with his father and Anna. Sometimes he helped Dmitri and his brother wait on tables. Lunch was their busiest time, for the buses had arrived from the town by then, and the people in cars and young men riding motor scooters or hanging on behind the driver. The beach filled up and everybody wanted beer or Sprite or Pizz, salad, moussaka, fish and chips, ice-cream and iced coffee. One day

Dmitri asked him to take an order to the family with the English girls and he refused. Dmitri laughed.

"What's the matter? They your girlfriends?"

Edward shook his head, furious. He went back to his room and lay on his bed until lunchtime was almost over. Anna, worried that he'd had too much sun, brought him a big plate of watermelon and played Snap with him until the sun was lower in the sky. His father sat on the adjoining balcony reading a book and when he suggested they all go to the other taverna, about ten minutes away and in the opposite direction to the pebbly beach, Edward, who had always refused before out of loyalty to Dmitri, agreed at once. Anna and his father liked the other taverna better in the evenings. It was lively and cooler and often had local musicians. The evening was pleasant and they stayed late, walking back along the cliffs. A girl had fallen from the path and onto the rocks a few weeks before. She had been drunk and there was no moon. A German girl. Edward thought of her lying there in the darkness, her head split open like a watermelon, and watched very carefully where he put his feet.

And the next day Dmitri offered to show him some card tricks so they were friends again.

"So how you like this ice-land," Dmitri said, shuffling the cards. Edward shook his head, puzzled. "Karpathos, how you like it?"

"Eye-land," Edward corrected him, "this eye-land."

On the beach Greek-American women changed from one language to another in the middle of a sentence. "Okay, *pethi mou*, now you're really going to get it!" Switching the backs of their children's legs with narrow bamboo fishing poles. Edward was learning, slowly, but the air was full of words he didn't understand. He tried to imagine Dmmi learning English in Elizabeth, New Jersey.

One morning when Edward went down to arrange his things in his favourite spot under the tamarisk tree, a young man was there, curled up in a cotton sleeping bag. Edward wasn't sure what to do. He felt that this was his spot, although he knew that it wasn't, not really. He also knew that if he didn't arrange his things now, before he had breakfast, somebody else would come along and claim it. The tree provided shade all day and you didn't have to pay for an umbrella. And the whole beach was there in front of him, like a continuous film. As he stood there, undecided, the young man turned over and opened his eyes.

"Good morning," he said. He was German. "I am taking your place?"

Edward shrugged. "Not really. But I like it here under the tree. I don't tan very well," he confessed.

The young man sat up and the sleeping bag fell back around his waist. He laughed.

"I also. I do not tan very well." He showed Edward his back. "Yesterday I fall asleep in the sun. Now I am all burned up." When he stepped out of the sleeping bag the backs of his legs were bright red.

"You could get sunstroke," Edward said. "You should be careful."

The man nodded. "Yah. I drank some beer and I fall asleep. Very dumb."

"Where were you?"

"On the other beach, mit the rocks."

"Where are you staying?"

"I have a little tent," he said. "I am staying on the beaches mostly. But the wind is too strong and pulls it down, my tent. And the sun is very hot."

"You should stay out of the sun today," Edward said, "or you will get sick." He offered him one side of the shade from the tree.

The man went to shave and wash up in the public washroom and Edward went for his breakfast. Anna and his father were still asleep. The only people in the café were Dmitri and the old granny and grandpa and the couple Anna called "the newly-weds," although the girl didn't wear a wedding ring. She was taking a picture of her boyfriend eating yoghurt and honey. She was always taking pictures of her boyfriend or he of her. "James Hooper," he said to her now, posing, "this is your life."

The young German asked if he could join Edward for breakfast. Edward said yes, but added he had to hurry and help the umbrella man set out the cots and umbrellas. The man nodded and smiled. Edward liked the way he looked right at you.

"*Kalli-mara*," Dmitri said to Edward, "*Tee-kanees?*"

"*Kalla*," Edward replied.

"You speak Greek?" the young man said to Edward.

"A little."

They spent the day together, under the tamarisk tree. The young man's name was Karl. He was tall and thin, with reddish hair and pale blue eyes. He seemed always to be wearing a slight frown but he had a nice smile. He had a degree in psychology, he said, but couldn't get a job, so he was selling potatoes in a shop in Berlin.

"I am very bad. Some ladies come in and they want very cheap potatoes, not much money, and some are wanting very expensive potatoes, high class, and I always forget what lady wants what potatoes. I am not a very good potato-seller."

Edward told him a little about his school and where he lived in Sussex and a little about his father and Anna, although he said "my father and stepmother" which was what she was, really, and it sounded nicer.

"Are you married?" he said.

"Me? I am too shy. Someday maybe."

The German was travelling alone. He was very well organized and had only his small rucksack and tent and cotton sleeping bag. Edward's father and Anna made fun of the Americans with their enormous packs. "Life-support systems," they called them. They would approve of the way this man travelled so lightly.

"I bring only—what you call them—necessaries," he said. "But a book of course. One book. However, even with one book I am not very far." It was a very fat paperback, *Gravity's Rainbow*.

"What's it about?" Edward asked.

"The wars," the young man said.

Edward thought he said "divorce."

"But I am not in the mood for reading. I like to watch. For example," he said, smiling, "you notice how the women lie when they lie on the beach. Always with one leg up, only one, like so," and he bent his right leg into a triangle. "And the mothers, they are always calling so loudly to their children, do this, don't do that. And the young girls are always rubbing each other with oil." He showed Edward a small black notebook in which he wrote down what he saw. Edward told him about the "newly-weds" who were always taking pictures and about all the Greeks from New Jersey.

"Yah. On this island most all the men go away to make money. They send money back. They come back to visit, to die. They fix up the villages."

They were going to a village that night, Edward said, to a festival. They were being picked up by a taxi. He wanted to invite his new friend to come with them but wasn't sure how Anna and his father would feel about that. Dmitri's handsome nephew was supposed to be minding the gift shop but instead was showing off with a friend of his, a young man in a white panama hat, for some Greek-American girls. They had a tape-recorder going full blast.

" 'Beat it'," the young German said, laughing. " 'Beat it'. You like Michael Jackson? You like to dance?"

Edward shrugged. The blind man's wife came across the beach in her black bathing suit. She smiled her special smile.

"And how are you today?" she said.

"Everybody knows you," his new friend said, admiringly. It made Edward feel good to hear him say it.

That evening they arrived early at the mountain village because Anna wanted to be up there when the sun set. Edward had sat in front with the taxi driver, whose name was Adonis. He had a horn that played "My Old Kentucky Home." The air was very cool and they sat on a stone wall, outside the church, waiting for the procession to begin. Anna wore an embroidered shawl over her sundress and looked very beautiful. But Edward's father became impatient when he discovered the procession wouldn't start for some time and suggested they go for a walk. So they walked away from the village, past grape-vines and terraces of olive trees, past a house where two small children were being coached in the dancing by a mama and a proud grandpa. And further along a very new, very black baby goat showed off for them while its mother calmly ate her dinner. Anna and Edward's father walked with their arms around one another; Edward dropped a little behind. The sunset turned the stone terraces, the fields, their faces, the whole sky golden, then rose, then a deep orangey-red. Somewhere a group of musicians were playing the strange, mournful, repetitive music they had heard before at the other taverna on the beach. Edward said it reminded him of bees and his father smiled at him. "That's a very interesting perception."

Walking back to the main village they came upon the musicians entering a house. "They will go from house to house tonight and make up songs to honour the people," Anna said. She had been reading the guidebook. A little further on, through an open doorway, Edward saw a man in a brown suit, humming to himself, select a gaudy tie from an open chest of drawers.

The taverna, which was famous for its home-made sausages, was jammed with people. The proprietor's son, not much older than Edward, was very busy laying plastic tablecloths, bringing baskets of bread, bottles of retsina and beer, plates of the famous sausages. The blind man and his wife were sitting with a large group. When she saw Edward, the blind man's wife, in a full red skirt and red blouse, her hair braided into a crown on top of her head, got up from the table and came across the room. She gave Edward and his father and Anna each a sprig of wild thyme.

"It is the custom here," she said, "on feast days."

"If there were some instrument to measure happiness," Anna said, "I'm sure that mine, tonight, would break it."

"Anna," Edward's father said, "will you do me the honour of marrying me?"

Edward saw his friend, the young German, over in a corner reading his book. They smiled and waved.

"Another new friend?" Edward's father said.

"He has a degree in clinical psychology," Edward said, "but has to sell potatoes in Berlin."

"Isn't he wonderful?" Anna said. "Edward, would you do me the honour of marrying me?"

One morning very early Edward and Karl walked over the cliffs and all the way into the town. Karl showed him how to find the path even when it didn't look as though there was one and how there were small heaps of stone every so often, "little stone men" Karl called them, when the path made a sudden turn, and splashes of red paint. Karl needed to find out when boats were leaving for Crete. He had to be in Athens on a certain day to get his flight back to Berlin. He really wanted to take an old boat that went all the way to Piraeus but nobody knew exactly when it would arrive and nobody knew where he could get a ticket. "Dmmi says it is a very funny boat," Karl told Edward, "but when I say how funny he just laughs." Instead of his usual singlet or khaki shirt Karl was wearing a blue shirt covered in bright flowers. It made him look quite different. "You like it?" Karl said. "I wear it for the very first time."

Edward imagined himself, in a few years, travelling from place to place with his rucksack on his back.

The walk along the cliffs took just over an hour and they watched the sun rise as they walked along. The air smelled of wild thyme and oregano. They passed a field of oats, golden in the morning light.

"So sometimes I am thinking we are in the Bible," Karl said.

In town they had a Nescafé at the port and then visited the bank, the travel agent, the post office, a vegetable shop where they bought round yellow melons and grapes, a shop that sold yoghurt, one that sold nuts and spirits. Everything fit neatly into Karl's rucksack.

Anna had asked Edward to try and match some embroidery silk. They found a shop with hundreds of boxes of silks and cottons, and with the aid of the proprietor, a very old man, they were able to match the sample exactly. The shop had a painted fish on a sign outside the door and it also sold fishing equipment—fishing line and sinkers, fishnet, flippers, masks. Karl, who had a snorkelling outfit, offered to buy one for Edward. That afternoon they took their gear to the pebble beach and went snorkelling in the deep water. Edward was amazed to find that he could see right through the bodies of some of the fish. Sometimes they brushed against his mask; sometimes they brushed against his body or swam between his legs. Karl, who was swimming alongside him, warned him away from a group of what looked like pale purple bubbles. Back on the beach, drying off, he told Edward they were jellyfish. Edward remembered the French woman and her warning about the *méduse*.

Anna came over to where they were sitting and asked to borrow the mask and snorkel. Edward's flippers were too small; Karl's were too big. She stood there, smiling, swinging the mask and talking to the young man. She was a soft brown all over and wore nothing but the blue and silver necklace.

Edward noticed how, when the water ran over the shingle as it flowed back into the sea, it made a hissing sound.

The blind man lies on his suncot and laughs—"Ha ha ha, we Churmans, ha ha ha." Edward, tired of sitting still, wishing Anna were there so he could show her his latest card trick, gets up, picks up his snorkelling equipment and goes down to the water.

Edward sees the octopus first. As the crowd gathers, he keeps repeating it: "I'm the one that found it!" He wishes Anna and his father would come back.

He had been snorkelling for about an hour and as he came in towards the beach he kept his face down in the water until the last minute, until he was almost lying on the sand. That was when a clump of something swam between his mask and the edge of the shore. Whatever it was had brushed against his cheek and he stood up in a panic. It was a small octopus, the tips of its tentacles curling and uncurling, just under the surface of the water. Perhaps it had hurt itself when it collided with his mask. Edward knelt down in the water to have a better look. The young man in the panama hat was walking by. His green-and-white striped swimming trunks were much too tight and now he stood above Edward, smiling.

"What you got?"

Edward didn't like the young man but he was too excited to keep quiet and ignore him.

"It's an octopus! It crashed right into my mask! Do you think it's hurt?"

"*Otopothi*," the young man said, squatting down. "Very nice to eat." He gave it a poke with his finger and the tentacles curled in upon themselves like strange warty fingers, like the tips of young ferns. Its eyes were shut tight. The young man laughed. He wore a large gold cross on a gold chain. His chest, his belly, his legs were covered in whorls of coarse black hair.

"Very nice to eat. I show you." He reached down quickly and picked up the creature. Now the tentacles twisted around the young man's hand. He offered the octopus to Edward.

"You like? I show you how to fix. Dmmi cook it for you." The tentacles curled, uncurled ("*la méduse, attention!*"). Edward put his hands behind his back.

The man in the panama hat laughed, showing glints of gold among his strong white teeth.

"You no like?"

Edward hesitated. A small crowd had gathered. The young man laughed again and called to two of his friends. He said something in Greek and they laughed and came forward. Edward wondered what it would be like to grab the octopus and run with it, drop it in the blind man's lap. Would the blind man's wife stop smiling, then?

The three young men moved out a bit into the water, forming a loose triangle. The man in the hat let the octopus go and they began to play with it, scooting it through the water towards one another, standing up to their knees in water, laughing. Edward stood near but not too near, watching. The octopus was frantic now; it turned an ugly red and squirted its ink at the young men. Their legs were covered in it and this made them laugh even harder. The man in the panama hat called something to two pretty Greek girls and rubbed the black stuff into the skin of his thighs. The girls giggled.

As more and more people joined the crowd Edward called out, "I'm the one that found it! It crashed right into my mask!" But still he stood at the edge of the game, in his flippers, holding the mask and snorkel. He wanted to touch the octopus, to hold it, maybe get somebody to take a photograph. He could see the "newly-weds" in the crowd; the girl, as usual, had her camera on a cord around her wrist. He could see the English girls, who had left off making an elaborate sand castle and stood there, shameless, their little titties sticking out for everybody to see. But the idea of really holding the thing made him feel sick. The way it would twist and turn, curl and uncurl against his hand. It was horrible to think about, horrible to look at, boneless, like a wrinkled purse made of skin. Big ones could kill a man. What if there were big ones out there, under the cliffs where he'd been swimming? The afternoon sun beat down on the back of his neck.

The man in the panama hat was tired of the game. He scooped up the octopus and looked around for Edward.

"You sure you no like? Very nice to eat." (Surprising his father and Anna at dinner that night. "Dmmi cooked something special. I caught it.") He shook his head.

"Okay. Thank you for my supper." The man in the hat began to walk to the far side of the beach, where the rocks were. The crowd broke up. Edward took his flippers off and followed at a distance, walking just at the edge of the water.

When the man got to the rocks he began slapping the octopus against the rocks, very hard. The first blow must have killed it. Slap, slap—it sounded like wet wash against a rock, like wet towels. In the showers at school, sometimes the prefects would slap the younger boys with towels. Slap. Slap. It was horrible, beastly. Why hadn't he swum back out with it and let it go? Edward knew what he was doing; he'd seen the fishermen sometimes) early in the morning, slapping octopus against the rocks and his German friend had explained why they did this.

"We are pounding the veal," he said, "they are pounding the octopus." He had given Edward his address in Berlin. "Maybe someday you will come and see me." Edward wished Karl was there right now. He'd know what to do.

The man in the panama hat walked back along the beach, the dead octopus draped over his arm, the tentacles hanging down, not twisting now, limp, harmless.

One of the pretty Greek girls called to him and he stopped. While Edward watched the young man tore off a tentacle and threw it to the girl. She caught it, ("bravo, bravo" called the man in the panama hat), wound it around her wrist like some horrible bracelet, smiled and went on talking to her friend.

The two stupid English girls had gone up to the café for ice-cream or drinks. Their mother and father were asleep in their suncots farther along the beach. Edward, who was now very familiar with the kitchen of Dmitri and Fotula, thought that the mother's skin was turning the colour of a cockroach. He put on his flippers and glancing around to make sure no one was looking, he quickly stamped the sandcastle into the ground. Served them right. Then he turned and walked backwards, went into the sea. He wet his mask, spit on it, rubbed the spit around. He put the mask on, bit the mouthpiece of the snorkel, turned away from the beach and began to swim. He tried not to think about the dead octopus, about the tentacle torn off and draped over the girl's arm or the possibility of others out there somewhere, waiting.

And that night he has a strange dream. He is on one of the turquoise and cream buses, going into the port. There is a young man on the bus and perhaps an older man who isn't feeling very well. He turns around in his seat and in the seat behind Edward sees a Greek girl holding an octopus in her lap. He thinks, "now I will get to see the colour of its eyes." He suggests to the girl that she tickle it so that its eyes will open. She does this and it looks right at him—its eyes are a bright, bright blue. Then it begins to turn into a baby, quite a pretty round-faced baby, and it smiles. But as it opens its mouth wider Edward can see that as well as having a mouth and lips it has a hole, like a large siphon, at the back of its throat. It is very round, this hole, and fleshy, and the edges are moving slightly in and out.

Edward wakes up to the sound of Anna crying out in the other room.

José Leandro Urbina

José Leandro Urbina was born in Chile in 1949. He studied literature at the University of Chile, but was forced into exile by the 1973 military coup. He fled to Argentina for three years, but a coup d'état in that country set him in motion again and he arrived in Canada in 1977. He continued his studies at Carleton University in Ottawa and became a Canadian citizen. He was one of the founding editors of the publishing company Cordillera. His stories have appeared in magazines and anthologies around the world and he has been the recipient of various arts grants from the Canada Council and the Ontario Arts Council. Urbina's first collection of stories, *Las malas juntas*, was published in Spanish in 1978; the English version, *Lost Causes*, appeared in 1987 in a translation by Urbina's wife, Christina Shantz. Urbina has lived in New York, working as a free-lance writer and film-maker, and, most recently, in Bethesda, Maryland, from where his wife commutes to work in Washington, D.C., and he pursues his doctorate at the Catholic University of the Americas on the relationship between fiction and history in four novels about the discovery of America. In 1992 he published a novel in Spanish, *Cobro revertido* (Collect Call), which was short-listed in the prestigious Planeta competition in Spain.

Urbina's ideas on brevity in fiction are intimately linked with his political experiences in Chile and Argentina. As he says in a statement prepared for this anthology, "Outrageous as it may seem, my notion of brevity in the short story has to do with my understanding and experience of the joke, as a narrative structure and in its social and cultural function.

"The day after the military coup d'état in Chile in 1973 and Allende's death in the presidential palace, there were already jokes circulating in Santiago about the dead President. Most of them didn't perform the function attributed to the joke by Bergson, of shaming people who oppose a flexible social order. Most of them seemed funny to the people who supported the army's violence, and offensive to the supporters of the former President. Some of those jokes were failures because of their stupidity. Some of them, funny in retrospect, were sickening in the circumstances.

"Then the opposition created their own repertory of jokes, and the generals were not amused.

"Later, in Argentina, my contacts with the cruel humour of Buenos Aires and the people's somewhat cynical attitude towards politics after years of military dictatorship led me to use the very short story, similar to the joke in its dual status, to express aspects of the painful Chilean experience without being unbearably sentimental or pitiful.

"As well as their narrative effectiveness, short short stories have the advantage of being easy to circulate and turn into anecdotes. This can broaden the scope of the political story, even though it may strip it of literary values. My short story, 'Our father who art in heaven,' was photocopied and circulated widely during the Pinochet regime, even though the book was semi-available. Many people have told me that they know of a case 'in real life' just like the one in the story I wrote around the theme of the involuntary or innocent traitor and the 'comic' possibilities of the title (may God forgive)."

Our Father Who Art in Heaven

While the sergeant was interrogating his mother and sister, the captain took the child by the hand to the other room.

—Where is your father? he asked.

—He's in heaven, whispered the boy.

—What's that? Is he dead? asked the captain, surprised.

—No, said the child. Every night he comes down from heaven to eat with us.

The captain raised his eyes and discovered the little door in the ceiling.

Portrait of a Lady

In the light of dawn that filtered timidly through the window, she smoothed her dress carefully. One of her fingernails cleaned the others. She moistened her fingertips with saliva and smoothed her eyebrows. As she finished arranging her hair, she heard the jailers coming along the passageway.

In front of the interrogation room, remembering the pain, her legs trembled. Then they put a hood on her and she crossed the threshold. Inside was the same voice as the day before. The same footsteps as the day before came over to her chair, bringing the damp voice right up her ear.

—Where were we yesterday, Miss Jimenez?

—We were saying that you should remember you're dealing with a lady, she said. A blow smashed into her face. She felt her jawbone crack.

—Where were we, Miss Jimenez?

—We were saying that you should remember you're dealing with a lady, she said.

W. D. Valgardson

William Dempsey Valgardson was born of Irish and Icelandic parents in Winnipeg in 1939 and raised in Gimli, an Icelandic fishing community on Lake Winnipeg. He studied at the United College and taught school for several years before completing his M.F.A. at the University of Iowa. He teaches Creative Writing at the University of Victoria. His publications include several collections of short stories—*Bloodflowers* (1973), *God Is Not a Fish Inspector* (1975), *Red Dust* (1978), and *What Can't Be Changed Shouldn't Be Mourned* (1990). He has also published two novels, *Gentle Sinners* (1980), which won the *Books in Canada* First Novel Award and was made into a film, and *The Girl with the Botticelli Face* (1992), as well as a book of poems, *The Gutting Shed* (1976).

Valgardson has said in an interview in 1981 with Alan Twigg (*Strong Voices*) that he feels himself capable of any crime. "I tell my students that there are two journeys every writer must take. The first journey is into the lives of others. But the second journey is the most terrifying. It is the journey into the self. I think what happens with a lot of people is that they turn away. They suddenly become aware of their motivations and they realize some of the things they are capable of. They don't understand that just because they're capable of something they don't have to do it."

When he talks about becoming a writer, Valgardson speaks of his skill with words as a compensation for being small and not having the physical skills valued in his community as a youth. "I was a dreamer and a reader. At some stage I obviously learned that you can fight with words. You can lay people wide open with words! You might have to learn to run like hell after you've said what you said . . . but I think there's a lot of people who become lawyers for that reason. And politicians. And writers." He speaks of the discovery of Al Purdy's *The Cariboo Horses* as an empowering experience, giving him the confidence to write as a Canadian. "For me writing is like an Eskimo carving. The form is in the stone. The trick is for me to find the form. And so it's a case of exploration. I write to discover what I think. I don't think and then write. If you think and then write, you often get propaganda. For instance, I think the worst things any writer can do is impose symbols. That's a dreadful thing, to nail them on. It should be like driftwood. You don't nail the knots on. The water washes and erodes and what's left are those hard knobs. That is the way that symbols should be. They should rise out of the material naturally. Then go back

over your material and see what you've got. Then heighten it. You see connections. Because one's genius is in spots. It's not necessarily coherent all the way through. So you try to make it coherent. It's like painting. You add touches."

In an interview with Geoff Hancock in *Canadian Fiction Magazine*, (No. 32/33, 1979), he claims to write mainly out of "a mood, a feeling, an emotion" and to force his stories through many drafts. "I never work from a plot. I don't know who said a plot is the last refuge of a hack, but I firmly believe it. I'm far more concerned with theme. Every story has to tell at least two stories and if you're capable, if you have the skill, hopefully your story is multi-layered and therefore will continue to have interest for a long time. Writers and readers enjoy the kinds of secrets that lie within a story, in the explorations."

In discussing structure and design, Valgardson favours the unfamiliar and the unexpected: "One critic said he had the feeling that so far into my stories he felt he was on firm ground and then the sand turned and he felt as if he was sliding and he didn't know what happened to him. There is that kind of quality there sometimes." "I think open-ended stories are much more intriguing than closed stories. Certainly, I wouldn't want to opt for one kind or another. It depends on the story itself as to what form it's going to take. The needs of the theme. Myself, I really admire 'The Lady or the Tiger?' and have admired it ever since I was a very small child. It is a story that people want to talk about five minutes after, a day after, a year after they've read it. A lot of stories with severely closed endings cease to be of interest once the endings have been read."

Valgardson claims to have learned from Hemingway to love the simple sentence; and from Jane Austen, complexity of structure. He also singles out Barthelme, Coover, and Europeans such as Ilse Aischinger, author of *The Bound Man*. However, he seems most profoundly influenced by writers of the Deep South, particularly Flannery O'Connor, for both moral vision and the starkness and elemental nature of the human encounters in his stories. Setting is very important in Valgardson's work. However, when accused of exaggerating the harshness of the Canadian scene for dramatic effect, he laughs: "One of the people I know went looking for her husband one day. He was late coming home for supper. He was a farmer. She found him with his tractor fallen over on him in a pool of water. He was pinned beneath the tractor and couldn't move and could just barely hold his head above the surface. She was faced with a dilemma. As long as she held his head up, he wouldn't drown. But if she stayed with him, he was going to die slowly from his injuries. I didn't make that up. That's the way life is. She had to make the best decision she could. Maybe some day, I'll write this in a fiction. But that's

reality. The land is not malevolent. It's just simply there. In the Interlake area of Manitoba, and in Northern Manitoba, it's a very harsh environment. Have your car break down when it's thirty below with wind, as has happened to me, and have suddenly to walk five miles to the closest house, and then say to yourself, 'Valgardson makes up a stark land.' No way. The stark land is just there."

Celebration

While Mabel fried the potatoes, she watched Eric out of the corner of her left eye. He was stretched precariously over a kitchen chair, the sharp points of his shoulder blades pressed against the high wooden back, his spine resting on the edge of the wooden seat. The heavy lids of his eyes were nearly closed but she knew that he was only feigning sleep and that beneath the wrinkled skin and thin lashes, his eyes were constantly shifting, following her every move. The last time she had taken her eyes off him, he had kicked her in the back of the leg.

She saw Eric's hands tense. He started to ease himself toward her.

"I've got a pan of hot grease," she warned. As she spoke, she lifted the pan from the stove.

"Lousy bitch," he replied, just barely moving his lips. "Lousy bitch."

The windows were feathered with frost and, in the corners of the frames, ice had gathered in thick knots. Cold drafts swirled under the door. It was only four o'clock but, already, outside the windows, it was as black as if the sky had been drenched in tar. The darkness had forced its way into the corners of the room and under the furniture. Here, it lay like a silent animal, ready to pounce at the first opportunity. Outside, a blizzard tore at the frozen land.

"We need more wood," she said, rattling the cast-iron pan against the stove to emphasize her point. "We gotta keep up the heat."

There was a space-heater sitting mutely in the middle of the floor. It worked but they had been unable to pay their last year's fuel bill and the deliveryman had cut them off. They had to depend on wood for both cooking and heating.

"Get it yourself," he replied at last.

Mabel seldom spoke. Now, because she had been drinking, she shifted her wide hips and said, with the studied seriousness of someone who has come to a conclusion after long thought, "You're ugly when you're drunk."

Eric snorted. "You're ugly all the time."

On the table, there was an open quart jar. It was a third full of homebrew. Eric's arm, as though it had a life of its own, snaked across the table, picked up the jar and brought it to his mouth. He drank without taking his eyes from Mabel, put the jar back and wiped his mouth with his sleeve. The social worker had said she thought she could get them onto welfare and they were celebrating. Eric had walked five miles to buy the liquor from a pulp cutter. Mabel and he had shared the first half but then, seeing how quickly it was being used up, he had decided to keep the rest for himself.

"Don't be so cheap," she said. She let go of the pan and pushed her red sweater up over her elbows. She had short arms and legs and her clothes were always too long for her. "Gimme a drink."

When he was sober, Eric was generous, letting her have money for mail-order clothes and, when they went into town, buying her french fries and taking her to bingo. When he drank, he was different. He sat and brooded about how little he had, listing a life's accumulation of grievances. It was then that they fought. Mostly, it was kicks and slaps but, sometimes, when she turned on him, they fought with fists and feet, teeth and nails. Once, he had broken her arm with a piece of stovewood and, once, she had cut open his thigh with an axe.

She was short, shorter than he was, with straight dark hair hacked off at the shoulders. Her body was round, with three large rolls of fat between her hips and her large breasts. Eric had found her in the Eddyville beer parlour. They had not married but, despite their differences, had stayed together for ten years.

Mabel turned the potatoes over, checking to see that they were brown and crisp, then skidded the pan to the edge of the stove.

"Feed them kids," Eric said. They both spoiled the children but they were his particular pets. He never denied them anything. He fed them jawbreakers and raspberry drops and potato chips and bought them plastic dolls with pink cheeks. Even when he was drunk, he did no more than brush them out of his way.

"That's what I'm doing."

Incensed by her answering back, he opened his eyes. They were as pale as shallow water in harsh sunlight.

"No-damn-good hotel trash. Lying under a table with your skirt over your head, that's you."

"I ain't been in a hotel for over a year and when I was, I walked out on my own two feet. Nobody had to carry me." She turned her head just enough to watch half his face purse with annoyance.

With a hint of satisfaction, she dumped a portion of the potatoes into a foil pie pan and placed it on the floor beside the couch. The four-year-old's brown arm darted out and dragged the pan into the shadows. Right away, the two-year-old began a broken cry of despair. It started slowly at first with spaces in between each cry but the spaces quickly became shorter. It was as though she was winding up a spring. If it was not stopped, her cry would become an endless wail.

"Josie, you give her some or I'll give you the broom," her mother threatened. There was the shuffling of aluminum on wood. The crying stopped.

Whenever their parents fought, the children hid under the Toronto couch, lying absolutely still, making no sound for hours on end. They were like two small animals hiding in a cave; only their large, dark eyes moved. A stranger might have spent an hour or more in the room and never known they were there.

Mabel dug in the bottom of the woodbox. The box was high, with a lid that folded back. It was large enough to contain two grown people. The top half of her body disappeared over the edge so that all that was visible was the wide expanse of her buttocks in a voluminous blue dress, men's grey wool socks and snow boots, one brown, one black. She heaved herself back up and held three sticks out so that Eric could see them. Her face was bright red from the effort of nearly standing on her head.

"That's all there is. We gotta have more."

His eyes regarded her with the distant blankness they assumed when he dealt with anyone in authority. Deliberately, he picked at his teeth before saying, "Get it yourself."

She filled the stove, then skidded his plate over the pink oilcloth. Although he was hungry, he let it sit.

"You've done nothing all day," she said.

Angered by the truth of her statement, he struck the table with his fist. He accidentally hit the rim of the pan. Potatoes were catapulted across the room.

"See what you made me do," he squawked. He had wanted the potatoes. In his surprise, he pushed his chair backward until it was resting on its rear legs.

Mabel moved her plate out of his reach.

"Pick that up," he ordered, swallowing three times as he thought about his lost supper.

She remained where she was, stuffing her mouth with potatoes.

"Whore! That's all you are."

Emboldened by the liquor, she retorted, "That's all you could get."

He lashed out with his boot but she was too far away. He lost his precarious balance. For a moment, he hung suspended, one leg stuck straight out, one foot on the floor, one hand flung out as though to grab the air and hold him in place. He fell flat on his back. Startled, he lay while his wife finished another mouthful of potatoes. Without changing position, he slowly raised his fist toward the open beams of the ceiling and shook it in silent rage as though to challenge a host of malevolent gods secreted among the rafters.

His eyes travelled across the smoke-darkened ceiling, down the wall, over Mabel's moon-like face and locked on her vigorously chewing mouth.

"I got nothin'," he shouted, "I never had nothin' and what I had, you eat."

The two-year-old, seeing that no-one was looking her way, crept out from under the couch and began to gather slices of fried potato, cramming them into her mouth until her cheeks bulged. She had on a pink sweater, green corduroy overalls and knitted slippers with felt rabbit's ears on the toes. When her mouth and hands could hold no more, she scurried back to the safety of the couch.

Gazing down upon her husband as he lay with his clenched fist raised stiffly toward heaven, Mabel said, without any change of expression, "We gotta have more wood." Her arm curved around her aluminum foil plate, cradling it so carefully that it might have been made of beaten silver.

"Is that all you can think about? Your own comfort?" Eric's face had grown mottled. "I might have injured a vital element," he paused to add weight to his statement, then added, "fatally." He saw in that instant the tragedy of his own death and was overwhelmed by it. To impress upon her what might have been, he let his arms fall to his side and rolled his eyes back into his head. In his raw, red face, they looked like eggs that had been boiled and peeled.

Mabel wasn't impressed. "We gotta have more wood," she repeated.

"You," Eric screeched, his voice thin and high, "have no respect." His upper body popped up as though it was attached to his hips by a suddenly released spring. "No respect."

He was slight, with a long face and hardly any chin. When he got dressed up in his grey suit, he looked distinguished in a minor way like a failed bookkeeper. He had cut pulp and hired out as a shorehand all his life but, because of his drinking, had never been able to hold a job more than six months. It was one of his grievances and it made him sensitive to slights, both imagined and real.

"You don't care what happens to me," he said with the hurt voice of a child. "I might as well be alone."

The thought had not occurred to him before. Normally he lived in the present, accepting it as unchangeable. The future was a mystery, revealed only when it became the present. Now, his idea, falling on fertile soil, sprouted and immediately blossomed. He saw himself unencumbered with Mabel. His face took on a settled look.

"You might as well get going," he said, as if something had been concluded. "You can take your clothes and five dollars."

Mabel looked away. In spite of all their disputes, they had never done two things: laid charges against one another or walked out on one another. The morning after she had hit Eric with an axe, Mabel had sat at his bedside, giving him sips of Pepsi and vodka from a soft-drink bottle.

"I got no place to go," she replied in a quiet, defeated voice.

He paid no attention. "I'll get somebody else. I've made up my mind."

His attention had wandered from her. Groping behind himself, he found the chair, righted it and, lost in thought, lifted himself backward up the rungs until he was seated in his former position. He stared at the ceiling.

"I'll get the wood," Mabel said, her face averted.

Ten feet from the front door, wood was stacked in rows. A narrow, waist-high path had been dug so that they could get to the woodpile and beyond. Normally, it was kept clear but, now, the path was five inches deep in loose snow.

The woodpile was so close that Mabel didn't bother to put on a jacket. Because of the draft on the floor, she was wearing fleece-lined boots. As she stepped outside, blown snow rose as thickly as smoke from damp leaves. She hurried, running to the woodpile, pulling a stick loose, then using it to knock three more pieces free. Before she had the wood stacked in her arms, the layer of heat next to her skin had been swept away. Particles of dry snow struck her skin as sharply as sand. She gave a violent shiver.

She would have stacked more wood in her arms but the wind beat against her, drawing tears from her eyes. Squeezing her head down into her shoulders, keeping her face turned away from the wind, she struggled back. The white layer of frost that covered the wood burned the soft flesh of her bare hands. By the time she reached the door, she was desperate to get inside. She bent to grasp the latch. Lifting it, she pushed. The door did not open. Often, because of ice forming on the frame, the door stuck. She gave it a push with her knee. It still did not budge.

"Eric," she yelled. "The door's stuck." She kicked against the rough boards.

"Open the door, Eric." She thought for a moment that he might not be able to hear her over the wind but she knew immediately that that could not be. However, he did not hold his liquor well and it was possible he had passed out.

She dropped the wood, caught the handle and jerked up. She threw her body against the door but the door did not move.

Pounding with the flat of one hand, she yelled, "Let me in. I'm freezing."

When there was no response, she picked up one of the sticks and began to beat on the door but it was made of birch slabs and did no more than shiver. At first, she held the stick like a bat. When that did not work, she changed her tactics, holding the log like a ram and concentrating her blows on the latch. The metal handle buckled, then broke but the door did not give way. She knew then that Eric had to have set the wooden bar in place. Years before, she had been nervous about his being away at night so he had bolted angle-iron to each side of the frame. With a two-by-four set across the door, nothing short of an axe would be sufficient to break in.

She dropped the log. Her anger and the exertion had combined to stave off the effects of the cold but now, as she stood panting, her entire body began to shake. Snow had sifted into her boots, collecting in a cold band around her ankles. Crouching awkwardly to gain the protection of the snowdrifts, she instinctively made her body as small as possible to preserve her warmth. Her hands were shaking so much that she crossed them tightly over her breasts. For the first time, as she squatted, helpless, she realized that Eric might not let her in and that, if he didn't, she would die. The anger that had sprung up only a short time before was swept away by fear.

Turning to the door, she placed her face against it and called out plaintively, "Eric, please let me in." When there was no reply, she began to plead in a loud, anguished voice, saying *please* over and over again. Fear cleared her mind, dispelling the blurred confusion of the liquor. It was as though her mind had expanded, become a vast plain on which there was no light but over which she could see with perfect clarity.

She needed shelter. Unable to find it where she was, she had to seek it elsewhere. She saw, as plainly as if she was looking at it from an airplane, the stretch of road that led to the next camp. She thought of trying to reach it, then gave up the idea. On the open road, the wind would be unobstructed and would sweep down on her with its full fury. The trip would take her three hours. Dressed the way she was, she wouldn't get past the first mile.

The cabin was long and low. Snow drifts rose nearly to the eaves. The side windows were partially hidden. Shivering so hard that she had a difficult time making her hands obey, she left the protection of the doorway and crawled onto the drift. The bank was steep and she had to dig her bare hands into the snow so that she could pull herself forward. On top of the drift, she rose into a crouching position. She took two steps. The brittle crust gave way beneath her. Her right leg plunged down past the knee and she pitched forward.

The shock of falling and the painful wrench of her knee made her lie still for a full minute before the cold forced her to lift one stiff hand, dig it into the snow and pull herself forward. She reached out with the other hand. Her leg felt as though it had been broken. The ice had made a shallow but painful gash from her ankle to her knee. When her leg came free, her boot remained trapped at the bottom of the hole. She did not try to retrieve it but floundered ahead, half-crawling, half-swimming, muttering, "Oh God. Oh, God." Snow pushed past the neck of her dress and up the sleeves of her sweater.

Lying flat, she pressed her face to the window. Her hair and eyebrows were crusted with snow, the round flesh of her face was white and drawn. She tried to see inside but the glass was so thickly covered with ice that the warmth and light were reduced to no more than an orange glow.

Using her hands like claws, she tapped at the window. There was no answer. She tried to make a fist. Her fingers would not close.

Desperately, she struck at the glass. The window broke.

Pressing her face to the hole, she called, "Eric, let me in."

A shadow obscured the light, then a board covered the hole and she knew that Eric was barring the window with a fishbox lid. She could hear him hammering nails. In a frenzy, she flailed at the glass, cutting her hands. She felt nothing. Blood ran over her fingers and immediately congealed.

She began to cry then. Her tears froze on her face. Defeated, she twisted her heavy body away from the window and began crawling back to the door. Her mind, only a short time before had been clear and immense. Now, it began to contract as it started to close off everything except the instinct for survival.

When she reached the path, she slid down to the bottom of the trail and crouched in the doorway. Blowing snow curled over the lip of the drift and settled on her like confetti. The small, remaining part of her conscious thought would have kept her there, straining helplessly at the heat which was such a short distance away. Instinct made her get up to begin an awkward, relentless pacing.

She walked as far as the woodpile, returned, beating her arms on her body. Because of her wrenched knee and her missing boot, she limped as badly as a cripple. Sometimes, she stumbled and fell but, always, she got up. For a time, she increased her pace until she was nearly running. Occasionally, she stopped and stood helplessly, as though she had forgotten what it was that she was doing. Her eyes became unfocused, staring directly ahead of her. All the time she walked, her body jerked and shook and from her mouth there came a steady, unceasing moan.

The door opened. Light spilled onto the path and great gusts of steam billowed upward. Leaning heavily on the doorframe, engulfed in light and steam, Eric might have been standing at the entrance to hell.

"Had enough?" he called belligerently, his head waving from side to side, his words slurred.

Mabel was at the farthest point of her journey. Turning, she stumbled back along the trail she had ploughed in the snow, her legs rising and falling in the jerky, unco-ordinated movements of a spastic.

"You had . . ." Eric began again but Mabel, her eyes staring as though they had been frozen in their sockets, her face burned white, her hair thick with snow, pushed past him, nearly knocking him down. She staggered clumsily across the room, pieces of caked snow falling from her. In front of the stove, she slipped to her knees.

Eric watched her, then with stiff, exaggerated care, bent and picked up the pieces of wood she had dropped in front of the door. Shutting the door behind him, he closed one eye, sighted the stove like he was going to shoot it and crossed the room, his body teetering this way and that, constantly on the verge of falling. He managed to stuff the wood into the stove.

"You're okay," he said. His speech was slurred, indefinite. "I decided to keep you." He staggered sideways for two steps. "That'll teach you to mind your mouth."

When Mabel did not reply but remained huddled as close to the stove as she could get, he steadied himself by catching hold of the back of a chair and leaned over her. Water streamed down her face and body and gathered in a pool around her. Her eyes were shut; her mouth gaped open. As he hung over her, she slumped to the floor and lay on her right side.

"I'll get you a drink. That's all you need." She made no indication she had heard him. He went to the table and his skinny red hands tipped the jar up, spilling the last of the homebrew into a fish-paste glass. He picked up the glass and held it out to her back. She did not move. His hand turned in a constant, unsteady circle.

Unable to keep the floor from tipping first one way, then the other, he got down on his knees and walked on them to her.

"Have a drink," he said. The liquor slopped over his fingers.

Mabel began to cough. Her cough was shallow and persistent, as though a piece of dry bread had caught in her windpipe.

Eric pushed his face up to hers. Even through his drunkenness, what he saw worried him. He tried to put the glass on the stove and failed. It fell to the floor and rolled away.

He pushed himself to his feet, staggered to the washstand for the basin, then continued to the door.

It was while he was on his knees in the doorway, scraping snow into the wash-basin that she screamed. Her scream, high and unbroken, filled the room. At the same time, she began to twist about as if to escape from pain inflicted upon her by some unseen tormentor.

Eric looked at her uncomprehendingly. Snow blew over him in a twisting funnel. In the brief time he had the door open, twin fingers of snow had formed at each corner of the sill.

He brought the half-filled pan of snow to her, setting it on the floor. Not knowing how to deal with her writhing, he sat back, his legs tucked under him, staring at her with the puzzled, stupid expression of a cat seeing something it is curious about but does not understand. He reached a handful of snow toward her but she cried, "Get away. Get away." She crawled to the far end of the stove.

Unable to stand her screaming and afraid of what he had done, he said, "I'll go for help."

It took him ten minutes to get dressed. He found his flashlight tucked in a rubber boot, tested it, then staggered outside. Negotiating the path was not too difficult. Its narrowness guided him and the high banks gave him support. The cold helped clear his head but the wind, driving full into his face, made him retch. After he had thrown up, he felt more in control of himself but his co-ordination was still so poor that when he fell into the snow, he had to make three attempts to get to his feet. The wind and the darkness confused him.

By the time he reached the highway, he was breathing so hard that he had to rest. The snow had drifted in places until it rose to his crotch. There was no way that a vehicle could get in or out of the access road. For a time, he leaned against a tree trunk, his back to the wind, waiting for someone to come by. There was nothing but the roar of the wind in the frozen trees. His feet started to get cold so he decided to start walking to the next camp. He knew that there was a truck with chains there.

He had stumbled along for half an hour when the snow turned milky, then began to sparkle. He moved onto the shoulder of the road and waved his flashlight in an arc. The pale light divided. A truck pulled up beside him.

He climbed into the cab. When he had caught his breath, he said, "My wife got lost in the storm and got herself frozen. I gotta get her to town."

There was no place to turn around. The road had narrowed to one lane and even this was deep in loose snow. The truck driver was tall and had a long, untidy beard. He peered through the windshield. There was nothing to see but the snow that slanted across the twin beams of light. It was obvious that he was anxious to keep going.

"Bad?" he asked.

Eric nodded.

They started back. Eric walked behind and to one side of the truck, marking the edge of the road with his flashlight. There was hardly any shoulder before a deep ditch began. With snow blanketing everything, it would be easy to put a wheel off the road. If that happened, they would need a tractor to free the truck.

Their progress was slow. Three times, Eric thought he had found the access road. The first two times, he was wrong. The third time, he waded into the snow to identify a tree stump that marked the corner. They left the truck with its lights on and its flashers going.

As they opened the door, they could hear Mabel screaming.

"Leave me alone," she yelled when she saw them. "Don't touch me." Her flesh, thawing, felt as though it had swollen to four times its normal size and as if the skin had been roughly cut from it with a piece of broken glass.

Spreading their arms wide, they herded her into a corner. They pinned her there, one holding her arms, the other her legs, then rolled her in a quilt so that she was completely covered. To keep her from tearing off the quilt, they wound it with sideline. The wind tore at them; the snow blinded them. Mabel was short and heavy. They floundered through the snow. The quilt sagged awkwardly in the middle, frequently slipping out of their mittened hands. They lost their footing time and again. When they finally reached the truck, they were both so winded that they had to lay Mabel on the road and lean against the truck to rest before they could lift her inside.

The ride was a nightmare of noise and motion. Snow engulfed them, blinding them with its whiteness. Wind tore at the truck. They skidded time and again, sometimes ploughing down the road sideways. When that happened, they both sat rigid, holding their breath, waiting for the wheels to catch on a rut and overturn them.

When they reached curves where snow had drifted into banks, the truck driver, not daring to slow down, sped up, racing at the white barriers. When they struck, snow flew up in a solid wall, completely covering the windshield until the wipers cleared it away. At such times, the truck shuddered as though under repeated blows. Once, they did not make it all the way through a drift and Eric plunged into the storm, wrenched a shovel from the side of the truck and attacked the snow in a frenzy.

As soon as the wheels were clear, he threw his shoulder against the tailgate, straining until he felt his body would crack. Slowly, inch by inch, the truck moved ahead. Once the wheels caught, the driver did not dare stop and Eric, with one hand on the box, ran to reach the door. He pulled himself inside and then sagged against the dashboard, sucking in gusts of warm air.

Whenever they were tempted to slow down, Mabel's cries and groans spurred them on.

It took them two hours before the faint glow of streetlights appeared on either side of them. The town itself was lost in the blizzard.

The driver flung the truck recklessly toward the hospital. It swayed, skidded, bounced like it was a duck boat in a choppy sea. Without warning, the hospital loomed out of the snow. The truck driver jammed on the brakes and the truck spun in two complete circles before stopping with its rear wheels on the lower step.

They half-dragged and half-carried Mabel in through the entrance and laid her on the floor in front of the receptionist's desk. Little strangled cries rose from the quilt. The receptionist rang for the doctor, then wheeled in a bed. They heaved Mabel onto it.

The doctor appeared. He was a brisk little man with grey hair cut close to his head to make him look younger. He had been a doctor in Eddyville for twenty years and nothing surprised him any longer.

"What," he said, studying the wet quilt wrapped with rope, "have we here?"

"Mabel," Eric answered. "She froze herself so bad she might die."

"It looks," the doctor replied, "more like she might be smothered." He treated their injuries every time they went on a drunk and he was prepared for anything. He reached into his pocket, took out a pair of curved surgical scissors and cut the rope.

When they pulled the quilt free, he inspected Mabel's face and hands and feet. She lay on her back, twitching and gasping like a beached fish.

"Get her into a room," he said to a nurse who had materialized at the end of the bed.

"How bad is she?" the truck driver asked.

"We'll see tomorrow morning. She'll probably lose some toes and fingers." He scowled at Eric. "If you're going to kill each other, why don't you get it over with?"

The receptionist, an elderly lady with blue-tinged hair, was more sympathetic. "You were lucky to get here," she said.

The truck driver smiled. He was relieved that the trip was over. "And how. Half an hour more of this and nothing will move, not even the snowplows." To Eric, he said, "You got anywhere to stay? You can sleep at my place."

"I'll stay at the hotel," Eric replied. Now that the trip was over, his head ached fiercely and he wanted a drink. A fast beer, then two slow ones would drive the pain away. He felt in his pockets. "Oh, hell," he said, "I forgot my wallet."

"That's okay," the truck driver replied. "My old lady'll give you some supper, then we'll get some sleep. You can have the kids' bed. They can sleep on the couch."

At these last words, Eric gave a sudden start and his eyes widened as if, without warning, a terrible vision had been thrust upon him. He took a step toward the door, then stopped. Snow and darkness beat against the glass. His tongue pressed against the back of his teeth, forming a single word, but he made no sound.

Guy Vanderhaeghe

Guy Vanderhaeghe was born in 1951 in Esterhazy, Saskatchewan. He studied History at the University of Saskatchewan and worked as a teacher, archivist, and researcher before the publication of his first collection of stories, Man Descending (1982), which won the Governor General's Award. His second collection of stories, The Trouble with Heroes, appeared in 1983, followed by a third, Things As They Are? (1992), and two novels: My Present Age (1984) and Homesick (1989). Vanderhaeghe explains in an interview with Allan Twigg (Strong Voices) how his belief that individuals make a psychological descent about age thirty, and must come to terms with the dark side of their nature, grew out of his personal experience of becoming diabetic and beginning to lose his eyesight. His interest in failure, and in characters who are "immoderate" in the conduct of their lives, stems from his belief that "these people are like icebergs. They're useful because they're indicators of things that are going on underneath." Thus his identification with figures such as Samuel Johnson in eighteenth-century England and Soren Kierkegaard in twentieth-century Europe.

"I believe very strongly in print. Arguments in print can be examined again and again and again. Whereas television and radio and cinema primarily leave impressions. They persuade us by impressions rather than by analysis and logic. I often feel I'm in a way like one of those highly specialized, nineteenth-century industrial workers who were destroyed by technological innovation. It seems to me that writers are one of those dying species overwhelmed by technology. Television, records, video and film are the important means of mass communication now. It's not the book. But obviously I believe in the book."

Vanderhaeghe speaks of solitude as important to the creative process. "This whole question of isolation is interesting. I believe you can live almost anywhere as a writer and not be isolated because you can always get your hands on books. The intellectual communion that I have does not necessarily have to be personal. It can go on through books. And I can get a book from anywhere in the world in Saskatoon. And there's an advantage to living in Saskatoon in that it isolates you from all those extracurricular things like literary feuding, literary social life, all those things that sometimes deflect from writing. Think of Faulkner sitting in Oxford, Mississippi and writing some of the great novels of the twentieth century in this little backwoods city that only had a little rinky-dink university. In one sense he was isolated but not isolated in any important way."

In an essay called "Influences," published in Canadian Literature, Vanderhaeghe suggests that bad writing can be as influential as good writing in stimulating the imagination of the young. He remembers the impact in his own life of A History of the World and Boys' Own Annual, two titles in the family's literary arsenal. He realizes, in retrospect, that he was absorbing certain ideas about the ways of fiction, not only in those books that ended with the "cruel joke: To be continued," but also in those where the young hero was "on the point of being pitched overboard to sharks":

"I like to think now that he would have remained forever frozen in that queer limbo of near death if I hadn't assumed the responsibility of rescuing him. Because at some point in my childhood I came to realize that what I was reading was fiction, a structure created by the imagination. If I were daring enough I might collaborate in the making of it. Or as I saw it then: the boy can be saved. So at about the age of seven or eight I set about saving him, manufacturing ploys and desperate acts of desperate courage that would deliver him from implacable fate. In other words, I began an apprenticeship. I was learning to write."

In an interview with Andrew Garrod (Speaking for Myself: Canadian Writers in Interview, 1986), Vanderhaeghe acknowledges a debt to Evelyn Waugh: "One of the things I learned from Waugh is an approach that's almost like a film script: rapid transitions of scene and dialogue with no real apparent direction to it—just lines playing off against each other. The purity of his prose, which is to me a model of clarity." Vanderhaeghe advocates neither a plain style, nor a high style in fiction, but one that is forged from a breadth of reading. "The short story," he says, "has to hit like a hammer stroke. There has to be a revelation that makes the whole story suddenly make some kind of psychological and emotional sense. It has to be immediate." In response to a comment about his skill with dialogue, Vanderhaeghe says: "I think I've always been an extremely good listener, and I'm a bit of a mimic. If I'm around people who have a kind of accent, it doesn't take me long to pick it up. I have an ear of some kind. Secondly, I think I learned something by reading transcripts of interviews. The way people speak often makes no sense whatever; they repeat themselves or do things with their hands to explain what they mean. Dialogue is really a literary convention; the writer does not attempt to reproduce speech but to reproduce the effect of the spoken word."

Going to Russia

"Another of your letters arrived at my house yesterday," the doctor announces. "That makes four now." He says this in a colourless, insipid voice, in the way he says most things.

It is only the significant pause which follows that alerts me I am expected to respond, and distracts my attention from the scene outside his office window. For several minutes I have been watching two children as they tramp stiffly off into the distance. They lead me to think of my daughter, and to wonder if she misses my visits.

Here we are on the outskirts of the city, where the new suburbs dwindle into prairie, and prairie into winter sky. The children, stuffed into bulky snowsuits, totter along, their arms stiffly extended like tiny astronauts foraging on the frozen cinder of a spent star.

Suburban tots often come to explore these splendid spaces. I have navigated them too, in my imagination, warm behind a double pane of glass. I find it strange that this blank sweep of land terrifies some of my fellow inmates and that they feel the need to keep their blinds down night and day. I like it. It makes me think of Russia.

"Yes?" I say finally, a little late, but nevertheless meaning to politely encourage him.

"Mr. Caragan, I thought when we met last Wednesday we agreed there would be no more letters."

The man has me there. But I am an impulsive fellow and that was Wednesday. By Thursday I felt I owed him some kind of explanation as to what had moved me to write the first three letters. "That's true," I admit, "that was the understanding."

"But?"

I shrug.

Dr. Herzl spreads a sheet of paper on his desk. His fingers rub diligently at the fold marks. When he is satisfied everything is shipshape, he begins to read to himself. I note a barely perceptible flicker in his upper lip. When he finishes, he looks up at me sharply. An old tactic I recognize immediately. "This doesn't make much sense to me," he says.

"No?"

"Excuse me," he says, pausing. "I'm not a critic. . . ." The doctor smiles to signal me that this is an offering from his store of inexhaustible wit. "But I find your language rather . . . formal, stilted," he says at last, finding the words he wants. "As if you are under great strain, as if you are trying to keep a lid on your feelings when you write me these letters." He searches the page. "For instance, there's this: 'I answer in writing because my thought will thus be more fully expressed, and more distinctly perceived, like a sound amid silence.' Doesn't that sound a bit unusual to you?"

"There's quotation marks around that."

"Pardon?"

"I didn't write that. There's quotation marks around that."

"Oh." The doctor hesitates. "Who *did* write it then?"

"Mikhail Osipovich Gershenzon."

A doubtful look passes over his face. He suspects me of pulling his leg. Dr. Herzl considers me a great joker, albeit an unbalanced, a lunatic one.

"It's true," I assure him.

"I am not familiar . . . "

"So who is? But then, you don't need to be," I say. "I explained it all in the letter. It's all in there. I used Gershenzon as an example. I was trying to help you see why I write—"

I am interrupted. "Yes, I'm sure. But you understand—fourteen pages in your tiny handwriting—I only skimmed it."

"Of course." I don't know whatever led me to believe he would profit from the story of the Corner-to-Corner Correspondence. Or that anyone else would, for that matter. When I told Janet, who is young, an artist, and believes herself to be in possession of a sensitive soul, about the series of letters exchanged between Gershenzon and Viacheslav Ivanovitch Ivanov while they recuperated in a rest-home in Russia, she said: "I don't get it. What's a corner-to-corner correspondence?"

"It was called that because each of the correspondents was in opposite corners of the same room. That's why it was called the Corner-to-Corner Correspondence," I said, ending my obvious explanation lamely.

"They couldn't talk? What was it, throat cancer?"

"No, as I said before, these guys were poets, philosophers, men of letters. Remember?" I prodded. "It was just that they felt more comfortable, surer of themselves, when writing. They had time to reflect on what they wanted to say, to test their ideas. To compose."

"That's the weirdest thing I ever heard—writing to someone in the same room," she said. "That sort of thing just gets in the way of real feelings. It's a kind of mask to hide who you really are, and what you're all about."

That was her final judgment, and from Janet's considered decisions there is no appeal, as I have learned to my sorrow. Still, I was almost in love, and at that precarious point one imagines it is important to be understood. So at our next planned meeting, two days later, I took along with me a passage I had copied from on of Gershenzon's letters. It was to demonstrate to her the subtleties which are the province of the written word, and, more importantly, to signal her what was going on in my mind.

"You see, honey," I said, trying to explain what Gershenzon meant to me, "he felt out of step with things going on around him. He might have said to old Ivanov: 'Viacheslav, what's the matter with me? I don't feel I belong, I don't feel right. Why is it I don't think what other people think, or feel what other people say they feel?' He could have put it that way. He could have, but he didn't. What he did do was write:

> This is the life I lead by day. But on a deeper level of consciousness I lead a different life. There, an insistent, persistent, hidden voice has been saying for years: No, no, this is not it! Some other kind of will in me turns away in misery and distaste from all of culture, from all that is being said and done around me. It finds all this tedious and vain,

like a struggle of phantoms flailing away in a void; it seems to know another world, to foresee a different life, not yet to be found on earth but which will come and cannot fail to come, for only then will true reality be achieved. To me this voice is the voice of my real self. I live like a foreigner acclimatized in an alien land; the natives like me and I like them, I diligently work for their good, share their sorrows and rejoice in their joys, but at the same time I know that I am a stranger. I secretly long for the fields of my homeland, for its different spring, the smell of its flowers, and the way its women speak. Where is my homeland? I shall never see it, I shall die in foreign parts.

Of course, when I looked up from the page, it was only to discover that Janet had gone to the bathroom to apply her contraceptive foam.

"I hear that you're still refusing to see your wife," says Dr. Herzl, introducing a new topic.

"That's not entirely true. I said I wouldn't see her alone. If she brings our daughter with her, well, that's a different story."

"Why won't you speak to your wife alone?"

"I explain that in my second letter—"

"Why don't you explain it to me now. Face to face, without the pretences of these letters." There is a measure of asperity in the good doctor's voice. From the very beginning I knew he didn't like me. I do not have a confessional nature and he holds that against me.

I stare back stolidly.

"Is it because you're ashamed? Is that whey you won't allow your wife to visit?"

"Yes." There is little harm in agreeing with him. He has made up his mind on this point long ago.

"Ashamed of what? Your affair? Or what you did at the gallery?"

Why not? "Both," I affirm, blithely shouldering a double load, the tawdry fardels of sexual guilt.

"Speaking of the gallery," says Dr. Herzl, "your wife agrees with me. She believes that the depiction of the penis was what triggered the incident there."

"She does, does she?"

"She thinks you felt it was undersized. She says you're prone to read a disproportionate significance into that sort of thing."

This is so like Miriam that I offer no complaint against this preposterous interpretation of my actions. I had my reasons.

Dr. Herzl clears his throat. "How am I to understand your silence?"

"The suggestion is too silly to grace with a comment."

"How did you feel when you did it?"

"Cold."

"I see," says the doctor, letting his fingers wander through the paper on his desk. "Well, I believe we've made some progress. We've begun to talk to one another, at any rate. Now is as good a time to stop as any." He closes my file. Perhaps the fact that it bulges with my correspondence reminds him. "You do see that writing letters is a way of avoiding the problem?" he asks hopefully.

"I want to see my daughter. You tell Miriam to bring Cynthia here."

"I'm sorry," says Dr. Herzl. Mrs. Caragan says that would be impossible."

In my room I lie down on my bed and speculate how Miriam is making out. I know she is not starving. I am on full salary while incapacitated. The teachers' federation knows how to negotiate a collective agreement, and insanity is paid its rich deserts.

As far as the other things go—the neighbours' whispers, the long, woeful faces of acquaintances—the proud prow of Miriam's clipper can cleave those mundane waters. And her real friends, the ones that never liked me, will be intent on keeping her busy, or, as they would prefer, "involved."

For a number of years, I was "involved" too. Miriam demanded it. She was terribly concerned that we didn't trade our ideals for a mortgage, that we didn't become ordinary people. The flight from ordinariness kept me on a pretty strenuous schedule. I'd get home from the high school where I teach something called social studies just in time to grab a cheese sandwich and receive a briefing while the paint dried on my placard. Then we'd all load into a Volkswagen van owned by a troll with a social conscience, a short, hairy guy who made pieces of knotty-pine furniture capacious and sturdy enough to stand up to hard use by the giants I assumed were his clients, and drive off to let our opinions be known.

But about four years ago, when Miriam and I were fighting about Cynthia, and I was drinking even more than I was just before I got tossed in here, I gave up being involved and began my own journey; and there is no way that I'm going to give Miriam the chance to coax me back to Canada, now that I'm safely here, on the borders of Russia.

There's an irony, too, in how my travels began. They commenced at one of Miriam's protest rallies. About a dozen lonely souls were picketing a Liberal Fund-Raising Dinner—the reason why I now fail to recollect. It was the usual dispirited occasion. I was a little drunk and bored. The cars kept pulling up to the front of the hotel and discharging Liberals who slunk tight-lipped through our righteous gauntlet. One particularly incensed woman of our number kept demanding to know whether the Liberals were dining on macaroni and cheese that night. "Are you?" she shrilled in their faces. "Are you eating macaroni and cheese tonight?" The implication being that her own feisty spirit was sustained solely on that starchy, plebeian fuel.

It was all going more or less our way until a large, ruddy, drunk, middle-aged Liberal turned a passionate eye on our assembly. He was very angry. He seemed to have missed the point about the macaroni and cheese. He thought we were objecting to our country. "Hey, you bastards!" he bellowed, while his wife tried to drag him into the lobby, "I love my country! I love Canada!" he yelled, actually striking his chest with his fist. "And if you don't, why don't you get out! *Why don't you go to Russia if you don't like it here?*"

The poor man's obvious sincerity touched me as much as his logic bewildered me. Why did he presume those people had any interest in going to Russia? Didn't he know it was *Sweden* they wanted to get to? Volvos, guiltless sex, Bergman films, functional furniture. Hey, I wanted to shout back, these people would prefer Sweden! And realizing for the first time where my wife and her friends were bound, I admitted I didn't want to go along. I was the one the gentleman was addressing. Although at the time I didn't know my longing was for Russia.

Oh, not the Russia he meant. Not Soviet Russia. But nineteenth-century Russia, the Russia of Dostoevsky's saintly prostitutes and Alyosha; of Tolstoy's Pierre; and Aksionov, the sufferer in "God Sees the Truth but Waits." A country where the characters in books were allowed to ask one another the questions: How must I live to be happy? What is goodness? Why does man suffer? What is to be done?

I had set a timid foot on that Eurasian continent years ago when, as a student in a course on European literature in translation, I had read some of the Russian masters. I returned because I was unhappy and because I sensed that only in Russia does unhappiness find a meaning. Like Aksionov, who suffered in place of the real murderer and thief, I felt a hundred times worse, a hundred times more guilt. I don't suppose I let it show much. I punished Miriam by putting our daughter's framed photograph on the end table, by drinking too much, and by being rude to people she wished desperately to impress.

Still, I was faithful to her in a purely technical sense until I met Janet several months ago. Janet is a young artist who supports herself as a substitute teacher; we met in the staffroom of my high school. At the end of that particular day, a bitterly cold one late in November, I spotted her waiting at the bus stop, looking hypothermic in the kind of tatty old fur coat creative people buy at Salvation Army thrift stores. I offered her a ride. She, in turn, when I had driven her home, offered me coffee.

I think it was the splendour of the drawings and paintings lending life to her old, decaying, high-ceilinged apartment that attracted me to her. Perhaps I felt she could salvage any wreck and breathe life into it, as she had that apartment. *Here*, I thought, gazing at the fire on her walls, *is a Russian soul*.

I asked if I could come back another day to make a purchase. She assured me that I could, that she would be delighted. I returned, bought a drawing. Returned again and carried away a canvas. Simply put, one thing led to another. We became lovers. Regularly, on school-days between three-thirty and four-thirty p.m., she screwed me with clinical detachment. If I close my eyes I can see her hard little jockey-body rocking above me, muscles strained and taut (I could pluck the cords on her neck) as she mutely galloped me hither and thither, while I snorted away under her like old Dobbin.

That it was nothing more than a little equestrian exercise I lacked the courage to see.

Dr. Herzl makes a point of telling me how pleased he is that there have been no more letters since last we met. He sits behind his desk, bathed in pale March sunshine and self-assurance. I am struck by his aseptic smile and unlined face, hardly the face of a man privy to so many sorrows. More than most men, certainly.

Out of the blue he asks: "I think we're ready to talk about the Opening. And Janet. Don't you?"

"We could." I clear my throat and look at my hands. They're very soft. The therapists here have tried to encourage me to take up handicrafts. However, if I cannot make boots like Tolstoy I will do nothing in that line.

"I'm interested to know the reasons why you posed for her. Particularly in light of what subsequently happened, it seems an odd thing for you to do."

"I didn't want to."

"But you did nevertheless."

"Obviously."

"Why?"

"Because she said she needed to sketch from life, and now that she wasn't a student she didn't get the opportunity. She couldn't afford to pay a model."

"So you wanted to help her with her work?"

"Yes." I knew how much it meant to her. Even then I knew what she was: a gifted, intense, ambitious girl, who was also a little bit stupid about things that had nothing to do with her art, and therefore did not concern her.

I can see by the look in the doctor's eyes that he is about to chance something. "Could it have been that modelling was a way of exposing yourself? Exposing yourself without having to fear consequences?"

"No."

He presses his hands together. "Why did you take such violent exception when you learned that the sketches were to be shown?" he asks softly.

"You can't be serious."

"Perfectly. I am perfectly serious. Tell me why."

"Because she didn't tell me," I say. I am unable to keep the anger out of my voice. "I saw it on a poster. 'Janet Markowsky: Studies in the Male Nude'."

"Any other reason?"

Sure. This is a small city. I'm a teacher. Somebody would recognize me. How the hell could I walk into a classroom after very kid in the school had gone down to take a gander at old Caragan's wazoo?"

"You're exaggerating."

"And you don't know kids. Anyway, it was the principle of the thing. Don't you see?" My hands have begun to tremble, I trap them between my knees.

"Were you disturbed that there were drawings of other men?"

"No."

"Are you sure?"

"I went to Janet and I said, 'For God's sake, what are you doing to me? I can't take this right now. Please, take the sketches out of the show.'" It *was* a bad time for me. Cynthia's birthday was coming up and every year she gets older, the more her face haunts me.

"And?"

"She said she was very sorry but this opportunity had suddenly presented itself. A small gallery had an immediate opening because the artist slotted had decided to show in Calgary. Janet said she hadn't time to produce new work. She had to go with the drawings. With what she had. 'Janet,' I said, 'I'm a teacher, put a mustache on me. Anything!'

"'I can't touch them,' she said. 'I could screw them up really badly. You can never tell what you'll do when you start mucking around with things.'"

"I phoned Ms. Markowsky yesterday and I asked her a question," says Herzl severely.

"What question?" I am surprised.

"I asked her if you wanted her to change the penises. It was just a hunch," he says, very much the clever, smug detective. "She said you did. She said you wanted them made bigger."

I put my head in my hands. I should have known it. The little bitch is the type to make sure she gets even. She won't forgive me for ruining her Opening. Herzl, the moron, gave her the clue she needed to do it. Not that I really mind. "I wanted a mustache," I say tiredly.

Herzl is really on a roll now. "Why did you take all your clothes off and walk through the gallery, Mr. Caragan? Did you think you would frighten people with your penis? Do you think it is menacing?"

"Because I'm crazy," I say. "Because I thought Life should imitate Art."

The hospital is silent at night. Nothing like I would have imagined—no dim cries, or the muffled sounds of sleepers dreaming bad dreams. Everyone has sunk into the opaque slumber of the correctly dosed and medicated. Except me. I hide my pills under my tongue and make a magnificent show of swallowing.

I hear the night-duty nurse go by. The moon is so bright tonight, so full and white and gleaming, that I can write my fifth letter to Dr. Herzl without showing a light under my door and risking detection at three o'clock in the morning.

On my shaky plastic desk my books are piled. I have Herzen, Dostoevsky, Gogol, Turgenev, Lermontov, Soloviev, Leontiev, Gorky, Chekhov, Pushkin, Tolstoy and Rozanov to keep me company in exile. Day by day I feel a little of my guilt subside as I share her sentence. Like her father, Cynthia sleeps in an institution.

The people who care for her tell me she doesn't remember me from visit to visit. That is why Miriam never goes to visit the child.

It is pointless, she says. *Cynthia is profoundly retarded, and nothing will ever change that. I refuse to feel guilt.*

But my daughter is four years old now. She is no longer a baby. She must remember me.

And whenever I look into her wise, calm eyes set like stones in their Asiatic folds, I sense the grandeur of Russia, the infinite, colossal steppes sleeping there.

Alice Walker

Alice Walker was born to a family of sharecroppers in Eatonton, Georgia, in 1944. She is the author of numerous books of poems, short stories (see *In Love & Trouble: Stories of Black Women*, 1973, and *You Can't Keep a Good Woman Down*, 1981), non-fiction, and novels, including *The Third Life of Grange Copeland* (1970), *The Color Purple* (1982), which won an American Book Award and the Pulitzer Prize and has been made into a film, and *Possessing the Secret of Joy* (1992). She attended Spelman College in Atlanta for two and a half years, then, as she explains, *fled* to Sarah Lawrence College in 1964, where "I found all that I was looking for at the time—freedom to come and go, to read leisurely, to go my own way, dress my own way, and conduct my personal life as I saw fit." She was deeply involved in the civil rights movement in the 1960s; then, while still committed to her interracial marriage to her Jewish husband, a civil rights lawyer, wrote a letter to *Ms.* magazine, protesting Israel's annexation of the Golan Heights and the resultant suffering of Palestinians for whom this was the only homeland. Walker now lives in northern California.

In her book of essays, *In Search of Our Mothers' Gardens: Womanist Prose* (1983), Alice Walker gives eloquent expression to her primary concerns: the fight for racial equality, women's rights, and social change. The mood of the book is upbeat, although she does not hide the anger that is the legacy of her heritage; she suggests that while white American writers tend to be gloomy and defeatist in their works, black writers "seem always involved in a moral and/or physical struggle, the result of which is expected to be some kind of larger freedom. Perhaps this is because our literary tradition is based on slave narratives, where escape for the body and freedom for the soul went together, or perhaps this is because black people have never felt themselves guilty of global, cosmic sins."

Although black writers Toni Morrison and James Baldwin have written fiction that is as bleak and guilt-ridden as any, Walker does put her finger on a fundamental concern of all writers: "It is, in the end, the saving of lives that we writers are about. . . . We do it because we care." Such a statement is even more poignant in her own case, since she writes elsewhere of her suicide attempts, of having grown up conditioned to think of herself as unlovely and inferior. In her essay "The Black Writer and the Southern Experience," she partially attributes the sense of affirmation in the black writer to "a religion that had been given to pacify him as a slave but which he soon transformed into an antidote against bitterness."

In a convocation address, Walker advised her largely female audience to read recent women's liberation literature. "For you will find, as women have found through the ages, that changing the world requires a lot of free time. Requires a lot of mobility. Requires money, and, as Virginia Woolf put it so well, 'a room of one's own,' preferably with a key and a lock. Which means that women must be prepared to think for themselves, which means, undoubtedly, trouble with boyfriends, lovers, and husbands, which means all kinds of heartache and misery, and times when you will wonder if independence, freedom of thought, or your own work is worth it all."

Walker lost her respect for Faulkner, she says, because of his gradualism and lack of leadership in the struggle for racial equality. But she maintained a high regard for Flannery O'Connor: "That she retained a certain distance (only, however, in her later, mature work) from the inner workings of her black characters seems to me all to her credit, since, by deliberately limiting her treatment of them to cover their observable demeanor and actions, she leaves them free, in the reader's imagination, to inhabit another landscape, another life, than the one she creates for them. This is a kind of grace many writers do not have when dealing with representatives of an oppressed people within a story, and their insistence on knowing everything, on being God, in fact, has burdened us with more stereotypes than we can ever hope to shed."

About her own writing, Walker says: "One thing I try to have in my life and my fiction is an awareness of and openness to mystery, which, to me, is deeper than any politics, race, or geographical location." "I like those of my short stories," she says, "that show the plastic, shaping, almost painting quality of words. In 'Roselily' and 'The Child Who Favors Daughter' the prose is poetry, or, prose and poetry run together to add a new dimension to the language. But the most I would say about where I am trying to go is this: I am trying to arrive at that place where black music already is; to arrive at that unself-conscious sense of collective oneness; that naturalness, that (even when anguished) grace." And in her provocative essay "The Unglamorous but Worthwhile Duties of the Black Revolutionary Artist, or of the Black Writer Who Simply Works and Writes," Walker lists the humble tasks of becoming informed, cherishing the old and the heritage passed down to you, offering guidance for living to those who need it, and, above all, writing, keeping the record.

The Child Who Favored Daughter

> *That my daughter should*
> *fancy herself in love*
> *with any man!*
> *How can this be?*
>
> —Anonymous

She knows he has read the letter. He is sitting on the front porch watching her make the long trek from the school bus down the lane into the front yard. *Father, judge, giver of life.* Shadowy clouds indicating rain hang low on either side of the four o'clock sun and she holds her hand up to her eyes and looks out across the rows of cotton that stretch on one side of her from the mailbox to the house in long green hedges. After an initial shutting off of breath caused by fear, a calm numbness sets in and as she makes her way slowly down the lane she shuffles her feet in the loose red dust and tries to seem unconcerned. But she wonders how he knows about the letter. Her lover has a mother who dotes on the girl he married. It could have been her, preserving the race. Or the young bride herself, brittled to ice to find a letter from her among keepsakes her husband makes no move to destroy. Or—? But that notion does not develop in her mind. She loves him.

> *Fire of earth*
> *Lure of flower smells*
> *The sun*

Down the lane with slow deliberate steps she walks in the direction of the house, toward the heavy silent man on the porch. The heat from the sun is oppressively hot but she does not feel its heat so much as its warmth, for there is a cold spot underneath the hot skin of her back that encloses her heart and reaches chilled arms around the bottom cages of her ribs.

> *Lure of flower smells*
> *The sun*

She stops to gaze intently at a small wild patch of black-eyed Susans and a few stray buttercups. Her fingers caress lightly the frail petals and she stands a moment wondering.

> *The lure of flower smells*
> *The sun*
> *Softly the scent of—*
> *Softly the scent of flowers*
> *And petals*
> *Small, bright last wishes*

2

He is sitting on the porch with his shotgun leaning against the banister within reach. If he cannot frighten her into chastity with his voice he will threaten her with the gun. He settles tensely in the chair and waits. He watches her from the time she steps from the yellow bus. He sees her shade her eyes from the hot sun and look widely over the rows of cotton running up, nearly touching him where he sits. He sees her look, knows its cast through any age and silence, knows she knows he has the letter.

Above him among the rafters in a half-dozen cool pots shielded from the afternoon sun the sound of dirt daubers. And busy wasps building onto their paper houses a dozen or more cells. Late in the summer, just as the babies are getting big enough to fly he will have to light paper torches and burn the paper houses down, singeing the wings of the young wasps before they get a chance to fly or to sting him as he sits in the cool of the evening reading his Bible.

Through eyes half closed he watches her come, her feet ankle deep in the loose red dust. Slowly, to the droning of the enterprising insects overhead, he counts each step, surveys each pause. He sees her looking closely at the bright patch of flowers. She is near enough for him to see clearly the casual slope of her arm that holds the schoolbooks against her hip. The long dark hair curls in bits about her ears and runs in corded plainness down her back. Soon he will be able to see her eyes, perfect black-eyed Susans. Flashing back fragmented bits of himself. Reflecting his mind.

> *Memories of years*
> *Unknowable women—*
> *sisters*
> *spouses*
> *illusions of soul*

When he was a boy he had a sister called "Daughter." She was like honey, tawny, wild, and sweet. She was a generous girl and pretty, and he could not remember a time when he did not love her intensely, with his whole heart. She would give him anything she had, give anybody anything she had. She could not keep money, clothes, health. Nor did she seem to care for the love that came to her too easily. When he begged her not to go out, to stay with him, she laughed at him and went her way, sleeping here, sleeping there. Wherever she was needed, she would say, and laugh. But this could not go on forever; coming back from months with another woman's husband, her own mind seemed to have struck her down. He was struck down, too, and cried many nights on his bed; for she had chosen to give her love to the very man in whose cruel, hot, and lonely fields he, her brother, worked. Not treated as a man, scarcely as well as a poor man treats his beast.

> *Memories of years*
> *Unknowable women—*
> *sisters*
> *spouses*
> *illusions of soul*

When she came back all of her long strong hair was gone, her teeth wobbled in her gums when she ate, and she recognized no one. All day and all night long she would sing and scream and tell them she was on fire. He was still a boy when she began playing up to him in her cunning way, exploiting again his love. And he, tears never showing on his face, would let her bat her lashless eyes at him and stroke his cheeks with her frail, clawlike hands. Tied on the bed as she was she was at the mercy of everyone in the house. They threw her betrayal at her like sharp stones, until they satisfied themselves that she could no longer feel their ostracism or her own pain. Gradually, as it became apparent she was not going to die, they took to flinging her food to her as if she were an animal and at night when she howled at the shadows thrown over her bed by the moon his father rose up and lashed her into silence with his belt.

On a day when she seemed nearly her old self she begged him to let her loose from the bed. He thought that if he set her free she would run away into the woods and never return. His love for her had turned into a dull ache of constant loathing, and he dreamed vague fearful dreams of a cruel revenge on the white lover who had shamed them all. But Daughter, climbing out of bed like a wary animal, knocked him unconscious to the floor and night found her impaled on one of the steel-spike fence posts near the house.

That she had given herself to the lord of his own bondage was what galled him! And that she was cut down so! He could not forgive her the love she gave that knew nothing of master and slave. For though her own wound was a bitter one and in the end fatal, he bore a hurt throughout his life that slowly poisoned him. In a world where innocence and guilt became further complicated by questions of color and race, he felt hesitant and weary of living as though all the world were out to trick him. His only guard against the deception he believed life had in store for him was a knowledge that evil and deception *would come* to him; and a readiness to provide them with a match.

The women in his life faced a sullen barrier of distrust and hateful mockery. He could not seem to help hating even the ones who loved him, and laughed loudest at the ones who cared for him, as if they were fools. His own wife, beaten into a cripple to prevent her from returning the imaginary overtures of the white landlord, killed herself while she was still young enough and strong enough to escape him. But she left a child, a girl, a daughter; a replica of Daughter, his dead sister. A replica in every way.

> Memories of once
> like a mirror reflecting—
> all hope, all loss

His hands are not steady and he makes a clawing motion across the air in front of his face. She is walking, a vivid shape in blue and white, across the yard, underneath the cedar trees. She pauses at the low limb of the big magnolia and seems to contemplate the luminous gloss of the cone-shaped flowers beyond her reach. In the hand away from the gun is the open letter. He holds it tightly by a corner. The palms of his hands are sweating, his throat is dry. He swallows compulsively and rapidly bats his eyes. The slight weight of her foot sends vibrations across the gray boards of the porch. Her eyes flicker over him and rest on the open letter.

Automatically his hand brings the letter upward a little although he finds he cannot yet, facing her strange familiar eyes, speak.

With passive curiosity the girl's eyes turn from the letter to the gun leaning against the banister to his face, which he feels growing blacker and tighter as if it is a mask that, when it is completely hardened, will drop off. Almost casually she sways back against the porch post, looking at him and from time to time looking over his head at the brilliant afternoon sky. Without wanting it his eyes travel heavily down the slight, roundly curved body and rest on her offerings to her lover in the letter. He is a black man but he blushes, the red underneath his skin glowing purple, and the coils of anger around his tongue begin to loosen.

"White man's slut!" he hisses at her through nearly sealed lips and clenched teeth. Her body reacts as if hit by a strong wind and lightly she sways on her slender legs and props herself more firmly against the post. At first she gazes directly into his eyes as if there is nowhere else to look. Soon she drops her head.

She leads the way to the shed behind the house. She is still holding her books loosely against her thigh and he makes his eyes hard as they cover the small light tracks made in the dust. The brown of her skin is full of copper tints and her arms are like long golden fruits that take in and throw back the hues of the sinking sun. Relentlessly he hurries her steps through the sagging door of boards, with hardness he shoves her down into the dirt. She is like a young willow without roots under his hands and as she does not resist he beats her for a long time with a harness from the stable and where the buckles hit there is a welling of blood which comes to be level with the tawny skin then spills over and falls curling into the dust of the floor.

Stumbling weakly toward the house through the shadows of the trees, he tries to look up beseechingly to the stars, but the sky is full of clouds and rain beats down around his ears and drenches him by the time he reaches the back steps. The dogs run excitedly and hungry around the damp reaches of the back porch and although he feeds them not one will stand unmoving beneath his quickscratching fingers. Dully he watches them eat and listens to the high winds in the trees. Shuddering with chill he walks through the house to the front porch and picks up the gun that is getting wet and sits with it across his lap, rocking it back and forth on his knees like a baby.

It is rainsoaked, but he can make out "I love you" written in a firm hand across the blue face of the letter. He hates the very paper of the letter and crumples it in his fist. A wet storm wind lifts it lightly and holds it balled up against the taut silver screen on the side of the porch. He is glad when the wind abandons it and leaves it sodden and limp against the slick wet boards under his feet. He rests his neck heavily on the back of his chair. Words of the letter—her letter to the white devil who has disowned her to marry one of his own kind—are running on a track in his mind. "Jealousy is being nervous about something that has never, and probably won't ever, belong to you." A wet waning moon fills the sky before he nods.

3

No amount of churchgoing changed her ways. Prayers offered nothing to quench her inner thirst. Silent and lovely, but barren of essential hope if not of the ability to love, hers was a world of double images, as if constantly seen through tears. It was Christianity as it invaded her natural wonderings that threw color into high and fast relief, but its hard Southern rudeness fell flat outside her house, its agony of selfishness failed completely to pervade the deep subterranean country of her mind. When asked to abandon her simple way of looking at simple flowers, she could only yearn the more to touch those glowing points of bloom that lived and died away among the foliage over there, rising and fading like certain stars of which she was told, coming and being and going on again, always beyond her reach. Staring often and intently into the ivory hearts of fallen magnolia blossoms she sought the answer to the question that had never really been defined for her, although she was expected to know it, but she only learned from this that it is the fallen flower most earnestly hated, most easily bruised.

> The lure of flowersmells
> The sun

In the morning, finding the world newly washed but the same, he rises from stiff-jointed sleep and wanders through the house looking at old photographs. In a frame of tarnish and gilt, her face forming out of the contours of a peach, the large dead eyes of beautiful Daughter, his first love. For the first time he turns it upside down then makes his way like a still sleeping man, wonderingly, through the house. At the back door he runs his fingers over the long blade of his pocketknife and puts it, with gentleness and resignation, into his pocket. He knows that as one whose ultimate death must conform to an aged code of madness, resignation is a kind of dying. A preparation for the final event. He makes a step in the direction of the shed. His eyes hold the panicked calm of fishes taken out of water, whose bodies but not their eyes beat a frantic maneuver over dry land.

In the shed he finds her already awake and for a long time she lies as she was, her dark eyes reflecting the sky through the open door. When she looks at him it is not with hate, but neither is it passivity he reads in her face. Gone is the silent waiting of yesterday, and except for the blood she is strong looking and the damp black hair trailing loose along the dirt floor excites him and the terror she has felt in the night is nothing to what she reads now in his wide-stretched eyes.

He begs her hoarsely, when it clears for him that she is his daughter, and not Daughter, his first love, if she will deny the letter. Deny the letter; the paper eaten and the ink drunk, the words never wrung from the air. Her mouth curls into Daughter's own hilarity. She says quietly no. No, with simplicity, a shrug, finality. No. Her slow tortured rising is a strong advance and scarcely bothering to look at him, she reflects him silently, pitilessly with her black-pond eyes.

"Going," she says, as if already there, and his heart buckles. He can only strike her with his fist and send her sprawling once more into the dirt. She gazes up at him over her bruises and he sees her blouse, wet and slippery from the rain, has slipped completely off her shoulders and her high young breasts are bare. He gathers their fullness in his fingers and begins a slow twisting. The barking of the dogs creates a frenzy in his ears and he is suddenly burning with unnamable desire. In his agony he draws the girl away from him as one pulling off his own arm and with quick slashes of his knife leaves two bleeding craters the size of grapefruits on her bare bronze chest and flings what he finds in his hands to the yelping dogs.

> *Memories of once*
> *constant and silent*
> *lie a mirror*
> *reflecting*

Today he is slumped in the same chair facing the road. The yellow school bus sends up clouds of red dust on its way. If he stirs it may be to Daughter shuffling lightly along the red dirt road, her dark hair down her back and her eyes looking intently at buttercups and stray black-eyed Susans along the way. If he stirs it may be he will see his own child, a black-eyed Susan from the soil on which she walks. A slight, pretty flower that grows on any ground; and flowers pledge no allegiance to banners of any man. If he stirs he might see the perfection of an ancient dream, his own nightmare; the answer to the question still whispered about, undefined. If he stirs he might feel the energetic whirling of wasps about his head and think of ripe late-summer days and time when scent makes a garden of the air. If he stirs he might wipe the dust from the dirt daubers out of his jellied eyes. If he stirs he might take up the heavy empty shotgun and rock it back and forth on his knees, like a baby.

Eudora Welty

Eudora Welty was born in 1909 in Jackson, Mississippi. After studying at Mississippi State College for Women and the University of Wisconsin and working for various newspapers and radio stations in Mississippi, she began to write fiction in the 1930s, publishing her first collection, A Curtain of Green, in 1941. This was followed by other collections of stories, The Wide Net (1943), The Golden Apples (1949), The Bride of Innisfallen (1955), and Thirteen Stories (1965), and two novels, Delta Wedding (1946) and The Ponder Heart (1956). The Collected Stories of Eudora Welty appeared in 1980. She seems to have begun writing at a very early age, publishing in her mid-twenties, but did not publish in a wide circulation magazine such as The Atlantic Monthly until 1941. She places little importance on the details of her own upbringing (her mother's milk cow or her father's insurance company), but does admit that she was a voracious reader.

Welty is admired for her quiet celebration of the lives of ordinary people and for her ear for the rhythms of colloquial speech. In the preface to her Collected Stories, she admits to a love for all her characters, whatever their sex or race, and considers the author's leap into another skin the most important work of the imagination. Alice Munro describes "The Worn Path" as an almost perfect story; Katherine Anne Porter has praised its dream-like quality, where external act and internal reality merge so powerfully.

Welty's reviews and other non-fiction writings, The Eye of the Story (1977) and Conversations with Eudora Welty (1985), are storehouses of useful and provocative statements about the craft of fiction. One of her critical preoccupations has been with the difficulty of defining, or coming to terms with, structure in fiction: "The first thing we notice about our story is that we can't really see the solid outlines of it—it seems bathed in something of its own. It is wrapped in an atmosphere. This is what makes it shine, perhaps, as well as what initially obscures its plain, real shape." Hemingway, she says, specializes in action that produces a kind of "dazzling light," while Faulkner's stories are "comet-like . . . wildly careening"; D. H. Lawrence, on the other hand, has sometimes no obvious plot or shape at all, yet his stories have a marvellous "cloak of self-luminous air."

Welty insists on the temperamental basis of art: "For the source of the short story is lyrical. And all writers speak from, and speak to, emotions eternally the same in all of us: love, pity, terror do not show favorites or leave any of us out." Consequently, atmosphere, or mystery, replaces plot as the central concern of the story. "So, the first thing we see about a story is its mystery. And in the best stories, we return at last to see mystery again. Every good story has mystery—not the puzzle kind, but the mystery of allurement. As we understand the story better, it is likely that the mystery does not necessarily decrease; rather it simply grows more beautiful."

According to Welty, "Plot is what we see with. What's seen is what we are interested in" (italics added). She defines form as "the residue, the thrown-off shape, of the very act of writing. . . . From the writer's point of view, we might say that form is somehow connected with the process of the story's work—that form is the work. From the reader's point of view, we might say that form is connected with recognition; it is what makes us know, in a story, what we are looking at, what unique thing we are for a length of time contemplating. It does seem that the part of the mind which form speaks to and reaches is memory."

"A narrative line," she says, "is in its deeper sense, of course, the tracing out of a meaning, and the real continuity of a story lies in this probing forward. The real dramatic force of a story depends on the strength of the emotion that has set it going. The emotional value is the measure of the reach of the story."

In her fascinating essay called "Writing and Analyzing a Story," Welty suggests that writing each story poses a new technical problem. All the wrestling a writer indulges in to find the right shape for her fiction, Welty says, does not explain the element of mystery at work in the creative process: "I think it goes to show, all the same, that subject, method, form, style, all wait upon—indeed hang upon—a sort of double thunderclap at the author's ears: the break of the living world upon what is already stirring inside the mind, and the answering impulse that in a moment of high consciousness fuses impact and image and fires them off together. . . . Between the writer and the story he writes, there is the undying third character."

Welty is, like Faulkner and Flannery O'Connor, a regionalist, her stories rooted in the talk and in the social and geographical particulars of the South. Although "touched off by place," she is equally determined to see through the particulars to the essential truth, the universality, of her materials. In speaking of the incident—seeing an old woman crossing a winter landscape—which inspired her to write "A Worn

Path," Welty says: "The sight of her made me write the story. I invented an errand for her, but that only seemed a living part of the figure she was herself . . . her going was the first thing, her persisting in her landscape was the real thing. . . . I brought her up close enough, by imagination, to describe her face, make her present to the eyes, but the full-length figure moving across the winter fields was the indelible one and the image to keep, and the perspective extending into the vanishing distance the true one to hold in mind."

A Worn Path

It was December—a bright frozen day in the early morning. Far out in the country there was an old Negro woman with her head tied in a red rag, coming along a path through the pinewoods. Her name was Phoenix Jackson. She was very old and small and she walked slowly in the dark pine shadows, moving a little from side to side in her steps, with the balanced heaviness and lightness of a pendulum in a grandfather clock. She carried a thin, small cane made from an umbrella, and with this she kept tapping the frozen earth in front of her. This made a grave and persistent noise in the still air, that seemed meditative like the chirping of a solitary little bird.

She wore a dark striped dress reaching down to her shoe tops, and an equally long apron of bleached sugar sacks, with a full pocket: all neat and tidy, but every time she took a step she might have fallen over her shoelaces, which dragged from her unlaced shoes. She looked straight ahead. Her eyes were blue with age. Her skin had a pattern all its own of numberless branching wrinkles and as though a whole little tree stood in the middle of her forehead, but a golden color ran underneath, and the two knobs of her cheeks were illumined by a yellow burning under the dark. Under the red rag her hair came down on her neck in the frailest of ringlets, still black, and with an odor like copper.

Now and then there was a quivering in the thicket. Old Phoenix said, "Out of my way, all you foxes, owls, beetles, jack rabbits, coons and wild animals! . . . Keep out from under these feet, little bobwhites. . . . Keep the big wild hogs out of my path. Don't let none of those come running my direction. I got a long way." Under her small black-freckled hand her cane, limber as a buggy whip, would switch at the brush as if to rouse up any hiding things.

On she went. The woods were deep and still. The sun made the pine needles almost too bright to look at, up where the wind rocked. The cones dropped as light as feathers. Down in the hollow was the mourning dove—it was not too late for him.

The path ran up a hill. "Seem like there is chains about my feet, time I get this far," she said, in the voice of argument old people keep to use with themselves. "Something always take a hold of me on this hill—pleads I should stay."

After she got to the top she turned and gave a full, severe look behind her where she had come. "Up through pines," she said at length. "Now down through oaks."

Her eyes opened their widest, and she started down gently. But before she got to the bottom of the hill a bush caught her dress.

Her fingers were busy and intent, but her skirts were full and long, so that before she could pull them free in one place they were caught in an other. It was not possible to allow the dress to tear. "I in the thorny bush," she said. "Thorns, you doing your appointed work. Never want to let folks pass, no sir. Old eyes thought you was a pretty little *green* bush."

Finally, trembling all over, she stood free, and after a moment dared to stoop for her cane.

"Sun so high!" she cried, leaning back and looking, while the thick tears went over her eyes. "The time getting all gone here."

At the foot of this hill was a place where a log was laid across the creek.

"Now comes the trial," said Phoenix.

Putting her right foot out, she mounted the log and shut her eyes. Lifting her skirt, leveling her cane fiercely before her, like a festival figure in some parade, she began to march across. Then she opened her eyes and she was safe on the other side.

"I wasn't as old as I thought," she said.

But she sat down to rest. She spread her skirts on the bank around her and folded her hands over her knees. Up above her was a tree in a pearly cloud of mistletoe. She did not dare to close her eyes, and when a little boy brought her a plate with a slice of marble-cake on it she spoke to him. "That would be acceptable," she said. But when she went to take it there was just her own hand in the air.

So she left that tree, and had to go through a barbed-wire fence. There she had to creep and crawl, spreading her knees and stretching her fingers like a baby trying to climb the steps. But she talked loudly to herself: she could not let her dress be torn now, so late in the day, and she could not pay for having her arm or her leg sawed off if she got caught fast where she was.

At last she was safe through the fence and risen up out in the clearing.

Big dead trees, like black men with one arm, were standing in the purple stalks of the withered cotton field. There sat a buzzard.

"Who you watching?"

In the furrow she made her way along.

"Glad this not the season for bulls," she said, looking sideways, "and the good Lord made his snakes to curl up and sleep in the winter. A pleasure I don't see no two-headed snake coming around that tree, where it come once. It took a while to get by him, back in the summer."

She passed through the old cotton and went into a field of dead corn. It whispered and shook and was taller than her head. "Through the maze now," she said, for there was no path.

Then there was something tall, black, and skinny there, moving before her.

At first she took it for a man. It could have been a man dancing in the field. But she stood still and listened, and it did not make a sound. It was as silent as a ghost.

"Ghost," she said sharply, "who be you the ghost of? For I have heard of nary death close by."

But there was no answer—only the ragged dancing in the wind.

She shut her eyes, reached out her hand, and touched a sleeve. She found a coat and inside that an emptiness, cold as ice.

"You scarecrow," she said. Her face lighted. "I ought to be shut up for good," she said with laughter. "My senses is gone. I too old. I the oldest people I ever know. Dance, old scarecrow," she said, "while I dancing with you."

She kicked her foot over the furrow, and with mouth drawn down, shook her head once or twice in a little strutting way. Some husks blew down and whirled in streamers about her skirts.

Then she went on, parting her way from side to side with the cane, through the whispering field. At last she came to the end, to a wagon track where the silver grass blew between the red ruts. The quail were walking around like pullets, seeming all dainty and unseen.

"Walk pretty," she said. "This the easy place. This the easy going."

She followed the track, swaying through the quiet bare fields, through the little strings of trees silver in their dead leaves, past cabins silver from weather, with the doors and windows boarded shut, all like old women under a spell sitting there. "I walking in their sleep," she said, nodding her head vigorously.

In a ravine she went where a spring was silently flowing through a hollow log. Old Phoenix bent and drank. "Sweet-gum makes the water sweet," she said, and drank more. "Nobody know who made this well, for it was here when I was born."

The track crossed a swampy part where the moss hung as white as lace from every limb. "Sleep on, alligators, and blow your bubbles." Then the track went into the road.

Deep, deep the road went down between the high green-colored banks. Overhead the live-oaks met, and it was as dark as a cave.

A black dog with a lolling tongue came up out of the weeds by the ditch. She was meditating, and not ready, and when he came at her she only hit him a little with her cane. Over she went in the ditch, like a little puff of milkweed.

Down there, her senses drifted away. A dream visited her, and she reached her hand up, but nothing reached down and gave her a pull. So she lay there and presently went to talking. "Old woman," she said to herself, "that black dog come up out of the weeds to stall you off, and now there he sitting on his fine tail, smiling at you."

A white man finally came along and found her—a hunter, a young man, with his dog on a chain.

"Well, Granny!" he laughed. "What are you doing there?"

"Lying on my back like a June-bug waiting to be turned over, mister," she said, reaching up her hand.

He lifted her up, gave her a swing in the air, and set her down. "Anything broken, Granny?"

"No sir, them old dead weeds is springy enough," said Phoenix, when she had got her breath. "I thank you for your trouble."

"Where do you live, Granny?" he asked, while the two dogs were growling at each other.

"Away back yonder, sir, behind the ridge. You can't even see it from here."

"On your way home?"

"No sir, I going to town."

"Why, that's too far! That's as far as I walk when I come out myself, and I get something for my trouble." He patted the stuffed bag he carried, and there hung down a little closed claw. It was one of the bobwhites, with its beak hooked bitterly to show it was dead. "Now you go on home, Granny!"

"I bound to go to town, mister," said Phoenix. "The time come around."

He gave another laugh, filling the whole landscape. "I know you old colored people! Wouldn't miss going to town to see Santa Claus!"

But something held old Phoenix very still. The deep lines in her face went into a fierce and different radiation. Without warning, she had seen with her own eyes a flashing nickel fall out of the man's pocket onto the ground.

"How old are you, Granny?" he was saying.

"There is no telling, mister," she said, "no telling."

Then she gave a little cry and clapped her hands and said, "Git away from here, dog! Look! Look at that dog!" She laughed as if in admiration. "He ain't scared of nobody. He a big black dog." She whispered, "Sic him!"

"Watch me get rid of that cur," said the man. "Sic him, Pete! Sic him!"

Phoenix heard the dogs fighting, and heard the man running and throwing sticks. She even heard a gunshot. But she was slowly bending forward by that time, further and further forward, the lid stretched down over her eyes, as if she were doing this in her sleep. Her chin was lowered almost to her knees. The yellow palm of her hand came out from the fold of her apron. Her fingers slid down and along the ground under the piece of money with the grace and care they would have in lifting an egg from under a setting hen. Then she slowly straightened up, she stood erect, and the nickel was in her apron pocket. A bird flew by. Her lips moved. "God watching me the whole time. I come to stealing."

The man came back, and his own dog panted about them. "Well, I scared him off that time," he said, and then he laughed and lifted his gun and pointed it at Phoenix.

She stood straight and faced him.

"Doesn't the gun scare you?" he said, still pointing it.

"No, sir, I seen plenty go off closer by, in my day, and for less than what I done," she said, holding utterly still.

He smiled, and shouldered the gun. "Well, Granny," he said, "you must be a hundred years old, and scared of nothing. I'd give you a dime if I had any money with me. But you take my advice and stay home, and nothing will happen to you."

"I bound to go on my way, mister," said Phoenix. She inclined her head in the red rag. Then they went in different directions, but she could hear the gun shooting again and again over the hill.

She walked on. The shadows hung from the oak trees to the road like curtains. Then she smelled wood-smoke, and smelled the river, and she saw a steeple and the cabins on their steep steps. Dozens of little black children whirled around her. There ahead was Natchez shining. Bells were ringing. She walked on.

In the paved city it was Christmas time. There were red and green electric lights strung and crisscrossed everywhere, and all turned on in the daytime. Old

Phoenix would have been lost if she had not distrusted her eyesight and depended on her feet to know where to take her.

She paused quietly on the sidewalk where people were passing by. A lady came along in the crowd, carrying an armful of red-, green-, and silver-wrapped presents; she gave off perfume like the red roses in hot summer, and Phoenix stopped her.

"Please, missy, will you lace up my shoe?" She held up her foot.

"What do you want, Grandma?"

"See my shoe," said Phoenix. "Do all right for out in the country, but wouldn't look right to go in a big building."

"Stand still then, Grandma," said the lady. She put her packages down on the sidewalk beside her and laced and tied both shoes tightly.

"Can't lace 'em with a cane," said Phoenix. "Thank you, missy. I doesn't mind asking a nice lady to tie up my shoe, when I gets out on the street."

Moving slowly and from side to side, she went into the big building, and into a tower of steps, where she walked up and around and around until her feet knew to stop.

She entered a door, and there she saw nailed up on the wall the document that had been stamped with the gold seal and framed in the gold frame, which matched the dream that was hung up in her head.

"Here I be," she said. There was a fixed and ceremonial stiffness over her body.

"A charity case, I suppose," said an attendant who sat at the desk before her.

But Phoenix only looked above her head. There was sweat on her face, the wrinkles in her skin shone like a bright net.

"Speak up, Grandma," the woman said. "What's your name? We must have your history, you know. Have you been here before? What seems to be the trouble with you?"

Old Phoenix only gave a twitch to her face as if a fly were bothering her.

"Are you deaf?" cried the attendant.

But then the nurse came in.

"Oh, that's just old Aunt Phoenix," she said. "She doesn't come for herself—she has a little grandson. She makes these trips just as regular as clockwork. She lives away back off the Old Natchez Trace." She bent down. "Well, Aunt Phoenix, why don't you just take a seat? We won't keep you standing after your long trip." She pointed.

The old woman sat down, bolt upright in the chair.

"Now, how is the boy?" asked the nurse.

Old Phoenix did not speak.

"I said, how is the boy?"

But Phoenix only waited and stared straight ahead, her face very solemn and withdrawn into rigidity.

"Is his throat any better?" asked the nurse. "Aunt Phoenix, don't you hear me? Is your grandson's throat any better since the last time you came for the medicine?"

With her hands on her knees, the old woman waited, silent, erect and motionless, just as if she were in armor.

"You mustn't take up our time this way, Aunt Phoenix," the nurse said. "Tell us quickly about your grandson, and get it over. He isn't dead, is he?"

At last there came a flicker and then a flame of comprehension across her face, and she spoke.

"My grandson. It was my memory had left me. There I sat and forgot why I made my long trip."

"Forgot?" The nurse frowned. "After you came so far?"

Then Phoenix was like an old woman begging a dignified forgiveness for waking up frightened in the night. "I never did go to school, I was too old at the Surrender," she said in a soft voice. "I'm an old woman without an education. It was my memory fail me. My little grandson, he is just the same, and I forgot it in the coming."

"Throat never heals, does it?" said the nurse, speaking in a loud, sure voice to old Phoenix. By now she had a card with something written on it, a little list. "Yes. Swallowed lye. When was it?—January—two, three years ago—"

Phoenix spoke unasked now. "No, missy, he not dead, he just the same. Every little while his throat begin to close up again, and he not able to swallow. He not get his breath. He not able to help himself. So the time come around, and I go on another trip for the soothing medicine."

"All right. The doctor said as long as you came to get it, you could have it," said the nurse. "But it's an obstinate case."

"My little grandson, he sit up there in the house all wrapped up, waiting by himself," Phoenix went on. "We is the only two left in the world. He suffer and it don't seem to put him back at all. He got a sweet look. He going to last. He wear a little patch quilt and peep out holding his mouth open like a little bird. I remembers so plain now. I not going to forget him again, no, the whole enduring time. I could tell him from all the others in creation."

"All right." The nurse was trying to hush her now. She brought her a bottle of medicine. "Charity," she said, making a check mark in a book.

Old Phoenix held the bottle close to her eyes, and then carefully put it into her pocket.

"I thank you," she said.

"It's Christmas time, Grandma," said the attendant. "Could I give you a few pennies out of my purse?"

"Five pennies is a nickel," said Phoenix stiffly.

"Here's a nickel," said the attendant.

Phoenix rose carefully and held out her hand. She received the nickel and then fished the other nickel out of her pocket and laid it beside the new one. She stared at her palm closely, with her head on one side.

Then she gave a tap with her cane on the floor.

"This is what come to me to do," she said. "I going to the store and buy my child a little windmill they sells, made out of paper. He going to find it hard to believe there such a thing in the world. I'll march myself back where he waiting, holding it straight up in this hand."

She lifted her free hand, gave a little nod, turned around, and walked out of the doctor's office. Then her slow step began on the stairs, going down.

Rudy Wiebe

Rudy Wiebe was born in 1934 in Speedwell, Saskatchewan, four years after his parents emigrated from the Soviet Union. He grew up in Coaldale, Alberta, and graduated from the University of Alberta in 1956. His studies took him to Tübingen, Germany, and then to the Mennonite Brethren Bible College in Winnipeg, where he received a B.Th. He received his M.A. from the University of Alberta in 1960 and, after a stint in the U.S., returned to teach there in 1967. Wiebe identifies with the Christian anarchism of the Anabaptists, who, he says, were very advanced in their thinking and determined to supplant social structures that they believed had no divine sanction. Thus his registration as a conscientious objector when he taught in the U.S. during the Vietnam War and his tireless efforts to examine and explain the importance of Canada's aboriginal heritage. His publications include the novels *Peace Shall Destroy Many* (1962), *First and Vital Candle* (1966), *The Blue Mountains of China* (1970), *The Temptations of Big Bear* (1973), *The Scorched-Wood People* (1977), *The Mad Trapper* (1980), and *My Lovely Enemy* (1983); two collections of short stories, *Where Is the Voice Coming From?* (1974) and *The Angel of the Tar Sands and Other Stories* (1982); a play, *Far as the Eye Can See* (1977); as well as *Alberta: A Celebration* and the anthology, *The Story Makers* (1981). He published *Playing Dead, A Contemplation Concerning the Arctic* in 1989.

In his introduction to *The Story Makers*, Wiebe writes: "The impulse to make story needs no defence. Where it arises, who knows. It simply is, like the impulse to sing, to dance, to play games. It would seem, however, that story-making is the uniquely human of these impulses for, though many animals sing, play games, perform intricate and beautiful dances, it still remains to be discovered whether any make stories." He goes on to discuss story as a source of entertainment, of pleasure, that derives from man's need to, and propensity for, naming and shaping his world. He lists five impulses to make story: dreaming how we wish things were; recounting what happened; explaining why things are as they are; instructing ourselves and our children; and making an imitation.

Wiebe is equally interested in the *how* of story-making. The quality of story, he says, "depends rather less on what happens than on how the story is made." This may mean viewing external reality eccentrically or altering the order in which things happen: "This making of a picture is no slavish copying of the actual

life scene; far from it. . . . Life is usually so scattered that meaningful patterns rarely occur. The maker selects and orders the event pattern in such a way that the impression of recognizable life is felt, an impression (not real life itself) that may be more powerful and incisive than if we had actually lived through the event, because the maker is lending his eyes out and we see more deeply with his than we do with our own."

As Wiebe suggests to interviewer Thomas Gerry in 1985 (*So to Speak*), he does not see his interest in formal experimentation as creating a barrier between reader and writer. "No. I would think that my exploration in form is trying to expand and to loosen rather than to set up barriers to protect yourself. In that sense, society, at least the way I experienced it as a kid, used the language actually to keep you ignorant or to restrict what you could know, and to hem in what might have been your natural predilections if you had had a wider, more flexible language in which to embody them." In addition to enlarging our parameters for thought and feeling, fiction can celebrate, even release, the magical—perhaps one should call it the religious—element in experience. "But there are so many things in this world that are magical—we call them magical or strange or incredible—that we have no scientific explanation for. And if we only had scientific explanations for things, what an impoverished world we would have. The whole point of being a novelist, surely, is that you can think beyond the typical hard facts of what life hammers into you at every turn."

Wiebe's novels and short stories often deal with characters pushed to the limits, beyond law, even beyond sanity. "In a short story you deal with people driven to the margin of their existence. This kind of religious fanaticism is something I've had a lot of experience with—not as drastic as that, of course. . . well, almost—people who would shoot people if they denied their way of looking at God. That kind of incredible fanaticism is there in the Bible and there are people who imitate it. I'm talking about something I've experienced. The short story can do that: drive people to the edges of possible behaviour and thought. That's what fiction is for! To show you pictures of that. It's a lot better to encounter it in a story than to have to experience it physically."

Anyone trying to understand his work will want to consider the relation between fiction and history, because so much of Wiebe's work is rooted in historical events and makes use of verifiable fact. He sees the novel, and fiction generally, as "social document, to a certain extent," concerned with historical accuracy— "a political instrument" that explores "individual morality in relation to a community morality of how people do live together." However, he insists, in an interview with Donald Cameron (*Conversations with Canadian Novelists—2*), that while "fiction is one of the greatest ways in which one can express one's hopes and aspirations . . . for what humanity is capable of," a major problem for the writer is how to present the facts: "There are many ways of seeing facts, the facts we believe are history or the facts of actual things we see done." If, as he suggests, the line between history and fiction is impossible to survey, there are countless

stories out there waiting to be given imaginative shape. "What I suppose I'm doing, really, is trying to unbury the story that I see is there, without going to the crutch of inventing any person to help me along.

"In one sense historical novels are not really historical at all," Wiebe concludes, but are "about people struggling with exactly the kinds of things that we struggle with, except for a slight shift in time and place. But that surely is all that fiction ever does anyway. How many human themes are there: love, war, what? You could sum them up on the fingers of two hands. It's how you get at it, how you face the thing, that counts. Consciously building a story is my way of trying to get at those big, big questions."

A Night in Fort Pitt
or (If You Prefer) The Only Perfect Communists in the World

Late one November evening in the thirty-third year of the reign of Queen Victoria, a solitary horseman might have been seen riding along the hills that parallel the North Saskatchewan River. He had been riding west since before daybreak, but now long after sunset the giant sweep of the frozen river suddenly confronted him, forcing him south, or as nearly south as he could surmise from the stars that glittered occasionally, momentarily, between storm clouds. And the wind which had been threatening snow all day now roared, it seemed, with a malignant fury up the cliff down whose steep slope he could not risk his exhausted horse, though he knew that he must somewhere, somehow get across the valley if he was to find shelter at Fort Pitt, the only white settlement along three hundred miles of river between Fort Carlton and Victoria House.

The night before the rider and his small party had endured among bare poplars in the fold of a creek; when they emerged that morning onto the prairie before dawn to continue their journey, they discovered the entire sky brilliant with aurora, torn sheets of light gently glowing and leaping into blaze above them and smouldering away again. The man had stopped his horse, watched, stunned; felt himself shrink as it were into and then grow incandescent in that immense dome of brilliance until sunrise burned it into sheer light, and he became aware that his Indian guide and Métis companion had vanished into the apparently flat earth; leaving nothing but the line of their passing in the hoary grass. The quick winter afternoon was already darkening before he caught up with them in their relentless track. The radiance of aurora still informed him and he told them they had veered too far south; sunset perhaps verified his perception, for after the long day's ride they still had not encountered the river. He refused to accept another night in the open and swung onto his weary mount. His men had already unburdened theirs, preparing to weather the storm they insisted was driving up from the west in a brushy hollow. So they watched him ride west alone, the prairie so open he could inevitably be found if lost, as impatient and as superior with all necessary knowledge as every white man they had ever met, riding into darkness following stars.

And now in stinging snow the stars were lost, though it did not matter since he had found the North Saskatchewan River. Well, it did matter, because he knew that every Hudson's Bay settlement was on the north bank; he must cross over the river or he would miss Pitt, he could ride as far as he had already ridden in a month, another five hundred miles across prairie into the glacial mountains themselves and not encounter a white man. As if at the thought, his horse stopped. No urging could move it so he slid off, straightening his long legs against the ground with a groan. The horse turned its long, squarish head to him, nudged him, breaking the icicles off its nostrils against his buffalo coat and then finding the warmth of his armpit. Perhaps this hammer-headed bay from Fort Carlton could become as good a companion to him as Blackie had been—the storm shifted an instant and he realized they were on a point of cliff. Perhaps a tributary cut its way into the river here as steeply as the main river. Where was he? Even if he got down into the valley, if Fort Pitt was built half a mile back from the river in a bend like Fort Carlton, he would never find it. He sheltered his crusted eyes against the whistling snow that enclosed him: the air seemed as solid as any frozen prairie. He would walk on it easily as dreaming out into the sky. . . .

The cheekstrap of the bridle hit his frozen face when the horse moved. He felt that, his arm slid onto its neck.

> He knew he could not lose this one certain warm body also, his mittens clamped onto its stiff mane and so suddenly he was led forward and down, sideways and down, the incline almost vertical and shifting like relentless sand, but that one body was solidly with him, there, whenever they slipped they slid closer together, their six feet all one and always somehow set certainly into the side of that incline of what might be rock or frozen clay, deadly as ice, but so reliable, so trustworthy he would never let go of this horse, never leap aside even if river ice parted into water as it had when he leaped from Blackie sinking, scrambled to safety while seeing his horse sink into blackness and there was its beautiful head bursting up, its front legs, neck arched, and knees clawing ice with its deadly shod feet, trying to climb up into the bright air by sheer terror, nostrils flaring bloody and the ice smashing now again and again in ringing iron, and he turned away, sprinted for his rifle—he was an English soldier, soldiers can always offer the ultimate mercy of running for their bloody rifles—and he knelt there expert sharpshooter on the white, deceptive ice until the shots hammered back at him tripled from the cliffs and the long water ran flat again and implacably empty; on his knees, crying.

But this hammer-head bay led him so easily down . . . down five hundred feet or a thousand—instinctively he was counting steps, an officer must always carry some facts, even if they are estimated—and they scrambled out between broken boulders (or were they frozen buffalo?) and there was river ice again, certainly, hard as the cliff here and he was still clutching the horse. But with his arms and legs now, completely, and it moved with his frozen face in its mane, he could smell prairie slough hay, hear scrub oaks at Fort Garry scarlet as cardinals in October light, the chant of *Te Deum* prayed by monks in a roofless Irish ruin, and he became aware that the sting of snow had quietened: there was an upthrust darkness moving beside him, a dense blackness and he loosened one hand, reached out: it was most certainly the usual twenty-foot spruce palisade. Never anything in stone like the permanent ruins of Ireland. And a gate in the wooden wall; hanging open. Perhaps the Indians here were all dead, the gates hanging so open.

The bay followed him through that hanging gate like any dog and the storm was so abruptly quiet he felt himself breathing. High peaked roofs, gabled, around a square, he could not distinguish a light or a sound. Perhaps smallpox had discovered them all, Indian and Métis and white alike, as in Fort Carlton. Winter would keep the bodies perfectly, death already blossomed over them like spring flowers. He limped across the open square to avoid what lay at the edge of every shadow, what might move, dreadfully: a door, darkness in the centre building. He seemed to have reached the heart of something, corpses were keening all around him, at the very hoared edges of his fur cap and he wheeled around, listening. But there was only his own small breathing, nothing but the horse snoring, bent low like grass behind him. So he turned back to the door and began to pound on it. Nothing. The plank door would not budge to his fists, its cracks blacker than its wood, and he tilted forward, hands, face clutching the frame, they were all dead, O open up, *o miserere mei* . . . he heard a sound. Inside. Against his face an opening, of light, the skin of a face, a young woman's face. Impossibly beautiful.

Such materializations are possible out of the driving blackness of a prairie blizzard, lantern-light and such sudden woman's beauty as perfect as it is unbelievable? He found himself bending forward slowly, past the worn planks of the doorframe, tilting slowly into her light, his frozen cheek, his still tactile tongue . . . and felt . . . nothing. Those eyes, the black brows and exquisite nose, was it white, that skin in the golden light? Was it believable though impossible?

It is possible that when Lieutenant General, the Right Honourable Sir William Francis Butler, Knight Grand Cross of the Order of the Bath and member of the Privy Council of Ireland died in his bed in Bansha Castle, County Tipperary, on June 7, 1910, died as his daughter then wrote, 'of a recent affection of the heart . . . that was brought to a crisis by a chill', it is possible that on his deathbed thirty-nine and a half years later Sir William could still not decide: was that face he instantly loved at Fort Pitt on the North Saskatchewan River in the North-Western Territories of Canada on November 18, 1870, loved as only the truest Victorian male who believed all his life that Jesus Christ and Napoleon Bonaparte were the greatest men in all of human history could love, a latter day romantic when romanticism was still acceptable in a male if he was also practical and above all heroic, dear god, was a man who championed the innocent and detested the brutalities of war all his life while becoming one of Victoria's most honoured and decorated soldiers, a member of Field Marshal Wolseley's brilliant Officers Ring that fought for the Empire on four continents, and who dreamed for forty years of 'the Great Lone Land' as he called the Canadian prairie and never saw again and idealized every Indian person he lived near for those few months in 1870 and 1871 when they were either dying of smallpox or more or less starving despite their unselfish greedless tradition of sharing everything, which makes Indians, as he wrote then 'the only perfect communists in the world, who, if they would only be as the Africans or the Asiatics it would be all right for them; if they would be our slaves they might live, but as they won't be that, won't toil and delve and hew for us, and will persist in hunting, fishing, and roaming over the beautiful prairie land which the Great Spirit gave them: in a word, since they will be free—we will kill them'; this Butler who on the same journey contemplated the parklands of the Saskatchewan, observed their remarkable similarity to the English downs and found it 'mortifying to an Englishman' that they were, as he so concisely put it, 'totally undeveloped': this Butler was forced over an unseeable landscape by a November blizzard to be confronted by a woman's face, her thick black braids hanging to her hips; wearing a loose nightgown.

The nightgown was probably not thin. More likely it was heavy flannel since any Hudson's Bay fort at the time (they were really nothing of forts but rather clusters of log buildings surrounded by log palisades, all of which could and did, as easily by accident as by design, burn to the ground) was badly heated by cavernous open-hearth fireplaces, doubtless she wore that heavy flannel of solid red or delicate floral design which the Company traded with the Cree and which those people suspended as gift offerings to the Thunderbird on the Centre Tree of their thirst dance lodges in June. And here it would hang as gracefully, draping between braids, shoulders and arms and nipples and hips a slender revelation. And the very handsome, six-foot-two and always brave and presently very hoar-frosted Lieutenant Butler, late of her Majesty's 69th Regiment in India and the Fenian Raids in Quebec across the Canadian border from New York, and most recently renowned as Intelligence Officer of the Colonel Wolseley Red River Expedition against the Métis founder of Manitoba, Louis Riel: frozen or not, Butler must fall instantly in love.

As he stood there, erect and frozen, clamped to the handsawn plank of the doorframe, his faithful pony having discharged its final faithful duty of carrying him to safety and about to collapse in faithful exhaustion behind him, did Lieutenant Butler say, 'Madam, I very nearly gave up hope of ever reaching succour'?

And did she reply as stiffly, 'O sir, our rude abode is but little better than the storm, nevertheless . . .'?

And he, accepting her hesitation: 'Madam, if I may be so importunate . . .'?

And she, accepting his: 'O sir, of course, do come in sir, come in out of the storm'?

And did she turn to send the dark servant woman standing behind her scurrying to the kitchen to revive the fire that was no more than embers in the hearth?

Perhaps that was how Fort Pitt, named after the great Prime Minister but doomed never to be as famous as Pittsburgh, named after his father the Great Commoner, perhaps that was how Fort Pitt offered itself to him. Or did she exclaim out of the lamplight, 'O la sir, what a storm brings you here!' and he, bursting into laughter, reply, 'What you see is mere weather, my fine wench. There will yet be greater storms than this!' Staring so closely down into the luminous whiteness of breasts her nightgown made but small attempt to contain.

Her father, Hudson's Bay Factor John Sinclair, had only a brutal litany of disease and starvation and death to offer him at Fort Pitt. He always kept the palisade gate locked—some damn Indian had tore it loose—every building locked, they were under siege and if thirty-two of sixty people at Fort Carlton was dead including the factor, and half the McDougall missionary family at Victoria dead too, then Pitt had been saved because he wouldn't let one goddamn Indian into the place, trade or no trade, locked them all out, and he had been damn quick in summer when he first heard the smallpox spreading and he got some blood out of a Saulteaux Indian vaccinated at the mission in Prince Albert and used that to vaccinate everybody—well, damn near everybody—in Pitt and he had kept every Cree locked out, every bloody one of them: Butler could barely restrain himself. Use them, use them any way you can, use their very blood . . . but he sat at the kitchen table devouring (with perfect Army manners, of course) the mound of buffalo steak and potatoes Mary (now properly dressed, of course) served him before the pine fire blazing on the hearth—where was the mother, the inevitable Indian, at best Métis, mother? The free traders, muttered Sinclair into his rum, had destroyed the hide and fur trade anyway, what did they care about Indians, just soak the buggers in whisky, steal all they could from them today and to hell with tomorrow, so now even at Pitt, the very heart of buffalo country, the beasts were gone, not enough robes this summer to make three decent bundles and he'd have nothing at all to eat except potatoes if Big Bear, that ugly little bastard that never got sick, hadn't dragged in ten to trade and he'd risked taking them even though half of Big Bear's band was spitting blood, they caught it fighting the Peigans near the border who got it from the American Bloods, hell, they said it was the US Army deliberately infecting the Indians down there to wipe them off the face of the earth because it was costing them damn near a million dollars each to shoot them! The smallpox was sure cheaper, about as cheap as wolfers throwing strychnine all over the prairie, and about as effective. There'd soon be nothing but corpses stinking up the whole goddamn stinking North-West.

Butler looked at him carefully: Sinclair was typical enough, a poor Scot forced to spend his whole life remembering home from the other side of the world, living who knows how in what overwhelming monotony of daily life and endless, endless miserable seasons repeating themselves, too old now for even the occasional Indian woman to rouse him, and suddenly a government official appears out of the night at whom he could momentarily blurt whatever he wanted, an official not on the summer boats but riding an assignment in the dead of a deadly boring winter on orders from the Lieutenant Governor of the Territories—there was one at long last—someone who had been within breathing distance of all those invisible Hudson's Bay lords in London barely seven months before, who had often smelled the 'goddamn heather' and seen the Queen herself who had finally survived her grief for Albert and was now the emerging mother of a world empire: what poor lonely sot of a homesick Scot wouldn't seize such an opportunity to snore every pessimistic worry he had aloud into his grog?

To be starving in Pitt, Sinclair suddenly roared, is like freezing to death in Newcastle! This is buffalo country, one herd moved over these hills for seventeen days and nights in '62, over two million, there was no end of them summer or winter and he'd fed every fort from Rocky Mountain House to Vermilion and The Pas, every goddamn fur dragged out of this country and every bloody ounce of stuff dragged back into it in every bloody York boat—every fuckin' trader had Pitt pemmican in his gut and now Big Bear brings in ten jesus carcasses and he has to burn the hides and boil the fuckin' jesus christ out of the meat! But at least that old bugger knew what he was doing, telling people to leave the fort and scatter in the bush and maybe the winter would be cold enough to kill the white man's disease, though what they would live on, even their dogs and miserable horses so far gone. . . .

Butler saw Mary Sinclair turn like a flame in front of the fire. After a month of half-fried bannock and pemmican—which had all the taste of boiled shoeleather—her baked potatoes were beyond any remembered cream and butter, dear god their very aroma—and she facing solitary winter darkness, a lifetime of that incredible skin drying up in cold and mosquito-and-blackfly heat, such a shape hammered slack by year after year pregnancies. At her bend by the hearth for another rack of buffalo rib he felt his body thaw and stretch completely, his powerful legs, toes flaring so fluidly, a kind of tensile vividness she awoke in his hands hard from cold and clenched reins all day, a touch of, somehow, flesh and resistance needed; despite heavy cotton the length of her leg, her curved thigh, her quick smile past her shoulder, her extraordinary face even when seen sideways or upside-down. Her father snored, fat arms flat on the table: every night such a lullaby and every night lying somewhere innocent, somewhere in this clumsy building, every night she was here naked against cotton and he rolled in his deerskin sack on the frozen prairie, sweetest jesus why is there no comfort in the world ever *together*?

The Métis servant came sluffing down the stairs. The bed for the gentleman was warming with hot stones between buffalo robes, would he go up? It was Mary who spoke, Mary who led him up the narrow stairs through her own shadow to the door, opening it without so much as a glance: she gave him the lantern and was gone, not a gesture of her lithe body even at his stumbled goodnight, and thank you again . . . the hall was empty before he grasped her going. Wind moaned in crevices. Well, doubtless to help the Métis woman hoist her father back into bed again. He stripped quickly, blew out the light. The stones were too hot, the robes total ice; he felt his body slowly shrinking into a huddle. Be I as chaste as ice, as pure as snow, I shall not . . . he sensed a footstep and sat up: she was there, he knew. But it was several seconds before the rustle she made told him she was lifting the heavy cotton nightgown over her head.

Could he say anything when she came in beside him, he the Irishman of endless easy words, when she laughed aloud so gently at all his sweaty underwear? And she peeled it off him, chuckling again at the memory of his goodnight, did he think Pitt was a hotel and she a chambermaid? Hot stones in bed were no better than campfires: you were always roasted on one side and freezing on the other. He may have had a small hesitation,

> The bed . . . is too narrow.
> Wide enough for one is wide enough for two.

And her skin fit completely around him, her head warm as opening lips in the hollow of his neck. If despite twelve years of Her Majesty's army his body still did not know what to do, she doubtless helped him to that too; and perhaps his own skin and various tongues in that black room taught him something of her invisible shape.

Perhaps this happened to William Francis Butler in Fort Pitt in the North-Western Territories of Canada on the night of November 18, 1870. Perhaps, if he was *really* lucky and Mary Sinclair was, thanks to her mother (certainly not her father), one of the world's perfect communists.

There is of course another story; the one Mary Sinclair told forty years later. Before the rebellion, she said, when I was only a young girl, an English officer came to Fort Pitt. He was tall and very good looking and he talked and talked and he could talk so well I thought perhaps I could love him. He told me about his home in Ireland, he came out of the snow and storm one night like someone from a different world and then when his men arrived after him he rode on to Fort Edmonton and I could only think about him. But he came back again, and he asked me to marry him. He asked me to go live with him in the Old Country. There I was, a child of the Saskatchewan, what would I do in another country? Perhaps I cried a little, but I sent him away. And after a while I did not think about him so often.

I sent him away. That is how Mary Sinclair later told it; but not Butler. He wrote a book, and he mentions her only in the same sentence as 'buffalo steaks and potatoes'. For these in Fort Pitt, he writes, 'I had the brightest eyed little lassie, half Cree, half Scotch, in the whole North-West to wait upon me,' and he mentions this 'lassie' not at all on his return journey from Fort Edmonton at the end of December, 1870, when bitter cold and a lack of sled dogs forced him, so he writes, to wait at Fort Pitt for seven days. Did she then also with steak and potatoes wait upon him? Serve him? Such a handsome Victorian soldier wrapped in tall furs on government assignment would perhaps not have remembered that she sent him away, especially not after he discovered in Ottawa a mere four months later that all the 'excellent colonial ministers', as he calls them, had large families and that 'an army officer who married a minister's daughter might perchance be a fit and proper person to introduce the benefits of civilization to the Cree and Blackfeet Indians on the western prairies, but if he elected to remain in single cussedness in Canada he was pretty certain to find himself a black sheep among the ministerial flock of aspirants for place.' Premier John A. Macdonald's only daughter Mary was handicapped beyond any possible marriage, and the most beautiful girl on the prairies could certainly not have helped Butler be an 'aspirant for place' in lumber Ottawa so, despite letters as excellent as excellent colonial ministers could make them for his excellent service, the tall officer returned to the heart of the Empire still a lieutenant, still without a permanent government appointment, still without a steady war in which to achieve the fortune that could purchase his promotion; he could not know that soon the kingdoms of hot Africa would provide him with a quarter of a century of men he could, with his enormous organizational efficiency, help to kill. In Fort Pitt on the Saskatchewan in November and December, 1870, during cold so severe no Englishman could imagine it, a beautiful young woman 'waited upon me', as he said; sent him away, as she said.

Or is a fourth story possible? Did they dream together, narrow bed or not? Did they see those enormous herds of buffalo that once flowed along the rivers there, such a streaming of life never again seen anywhere on the surface of the earth or even in the depths of the sea? And in the darkness did they see the long, hesitant parade of the Cree chiefs approaching Treaty Number Six that ordered them thereby to cede, release, surrender, and yield up all that land forever, and behind them the one chief who would not, the chief Big Bear as the whites called him, but perhaps better translated 'Too Much' or 'More Than Enough Bear' who would ask them all how could one person give away forever what they had all forever had, who had more than enough of everything except the power to persuade his people of his defiant vision until Fort Pitt was burning, was becoming a great pillar of smoke bent over the river and the empty hills and all that flour and rancid treaty pork they had never wanted, had abhorred as soon as ever they saw it, surrounded them, rained on them, dripped black and stinking out of the very air they were forced to breathe?

> She knows that darkness alone can offer what he longs to accept. Smell and touch and the tongue in the ear, yes, taste itself, yes, yes—but not sight. Eyes for him are impossible.

The fire locked inside each palisade log, the factor's house, the spruce walls close about their narrow bed springs into light, fire lifts Fort Pitt, transforms it into air and its place, here, on this earth, is lost to any memory, the valley and the hills changed as they are already eternally changed beyond the going of the animals and some day the Hutterite farmers will break through the bristly poplars, domesticate them into wheat fields and a plough furrow along the bank of the still relentless river one day reveals a shard of blue willow china; its delicate pastoral a century's confirmation of her waiting upon him, of her serving him?

> Behind the double darkness of his clenched eyes he sees again the length of his rifle barrel and the black hair whorled behind Blackie's straining ear: the blood explodes exactly there! They had to cross today, the daily plan is irrevocable, iron shoes or not on thin ice or no ice they must cross, and his groans, his endlessly contained and most irregular, totally unplanned, tears.

They may have dreamed something together. Possibly they dreamed the scarlet riders of the police he would recommend the Canadian government establish to force English law upon the western plains, the police whose thin implacable lines would weave the red shroud of the old Queen's authority over every child of the Saskatchewan until Inspector Francis Jeffrey Dickens, the great novelist's third son who aspired to his appointment by patronage, not by excellent merit of excellent colonial service, would at Fort Pitt become the most infamous officer in the history of the world-famous force. Force indeed.

Or they dreamed again the gaunt Cree dying, scraping their pustulated legs and arms and breasts and infants' faces along the gates, the doorframes, the windows of the locked fort to force the white man's disease back upon him, to somehow smear him with his own putrefaction. And perhaps they also dreamed Big Bear walking so emaciated among his people, his magnificent voice persuading them they must scatter to the woods and the animals, that only on the solitary land would they be given the strength to destroy this invisible, this incomprehensible evil that rotted them, his words and his great scarred face proof of his lifelong power over the white man's diseases, his name certain and forever More Than Enough Bear for everything except the white man's words on the white man's paper, words that would one day endlessly whisper to him behind the thick, sweating walls of Stony Mountain Penitentiary.

Was it Big Bear who helped her say to him then: go away.

Only she could dream that. It is impossible for Lieutenant William Francis Butler to dream such a hopeless dream; even in a narrow bed in Fort Pitt, even in Mary Sinclair's warm and beautiful arms.

Ethel Wilson

Ethel Wilson was born in Port Elizabeth, South Africa, in 1888, daughter of a Methodist missionary. Her mother died when she was two and she went to live in England with her father, who died only seven years later. At age ten she immigrated to Vancouver to live with her grandmother, but completed her secondary education at a boarding school back in England. She attended Normal School in Vancouver and became an elementary schoolteacher. She married Wallace Wilson, a physician, in 1921. Her first short story, "I Just Love Dogs," appeared in 1937 in *The New Statesman* and *The Nation*, but she did not publish a book until 1947, when she was in her fifties and her novel *Hetty Dorval* appeared. This was followed by *The Innocent Traveller* (1949), a series of interconnected sketches; *Swamp Angel* (1954), a novel; *Equations of Love* (1952), two novellas; *Love and Salt Water* (1956), a novel; and *Mrs. Golightly and Other Stories* (1961). She died in 1980.

Wilson was not very forthcoming on the craft of writing, though she did make some comments that are useful for a study of her fiction. For example, she considered character and plot "a kind of chicken and the egg, depending on the writer," a statement not unlike Henry James's view that character is a manifestation of plot and plot a working out of character. Wilson goes on, in an article called "The Bridge or the Stokehold: Views of the Novelist's Art" (*Canadian Literature*, 5, 1960), to discuss the origins of fictional characters, citing Conrad and Proust and then explaining the genesis of one of her own characters in a fragmentary remark overhead by chance—"formed other connections . . ."—that grew into the novella *Lilly's Story*.

Wilson clearly advocated cultivating the powers of observing and listening. She also knew a good deal about perspective, how changing lights of perspective could radically alter our ways of viewing characters in fiction: "Speaking still of people in a book, there comes the influence of light, which may change everything. There was, lately, a freighter which, surprisingly, came to anchor very close to shore and just below our study windows. It caused me intense and daily pleasure. On a grey evening, the ship was a lovely ghost. On a fine morning the freighter was dazzling white where the sunshine fell and the silver gulls flew over. The light faded, and the ship became a dirty tub. The ship was the same ship; the light was different; its effect was perhaps false. Upon us all, light falls, and we seem to the beholder to change; and upon the impending work of the novelist, light falls, and changes a scene and the people in a room."

In her essay "Cat among the Falcons" (*Canadian Literature*, 2, 1959), Wilson describes writing as "looney" and claims that "The Gift is imponderable and unpredictable, and there is no satisfactory substitute." She recommends, as training for "the highly personal art and act of writing," a good basic education in writing skills to be followed by extensive but informal reading: "I cannot avoid the conviction that a writer who can already handle his tools and write is thereafter self-taught by writing (how the view opens out), and thus a literature is made." She praises "the explosion of personality in truly original writing" that sometimes happens when a writer is in excellent form: "There is a moment, I think, within a novelist of any originality, whatever his country or his scope, when some sort of synthesis takes place over which he has only partial control. There is an incandescence, and from it meaning emerges, words appear, they take shape in their order, a fusion occurs."

Wilson considered the short story "slippery—hard to catch and hold in the hand." "I have written a few short stories, and observe with respect and some pleasure the opportunity for economy of expression, for the recognition of line and contour, and the open opportunity for inference. The short story is a strong, delicate and tricky art, almost done with mirrors." She placed equal importance on structure, stating that the short story is "enormously dependent within its small compass on structure. If structure is faulty a short story may be all at sea, as a well intentioned ship whose rudder is faulty is all at sea. The ship and the rudder will probably not arrive at their desired destinations."

From Flores

Up at Flores Island, Captain Findlay Crabbe readied his fishboat the *Effie Cee* for the journey home and set out in good spirits while the weather was fair. But even by the time he saw the red shirt flapping like mad from the rocky point just north of the Indian's place the wind had freshened. Nevertheless Fin Crabbe told the big man at the wheel to turn into shore because there must be some trouble there and that Indian family was pretty isolated. As the man at the wheel turned the nose of the boat towards the shore, the skipper listened to the radio. The weather report was good, and so he went out on the small deck well satisfied and stood there with his hands on his hips, looking at the shore where the red flag was.

The third man on the fishboat was just a young fellow. Up at Flores Island he had come down to the float with his gear all stowed in a duffel bag and asked the skipper to take him down to Port Alberni. He was an anxious kid, tall, dark, and thin-faced. He said he'd pay money for the ride and he spoke of bad news which with a young man sounds like parents or a girl and with an older young man sounds like a wife or children or a girl. Fin Crabbe said shortly that the boy could come, although the little *Effie Cee* was not geared for passengers. He didn't need to pay.

Captain Crabbe was small. He had come as an undersized boy to the west coast of Vancouver Island and there he had stayed. He had been fairish and was now bald. His eyes were sad like a little bloodhound's eyes and pink under, but he was not sad. He was a contented man and rejoiced always to be joined again with his wife and his gangling son and daughter. Mrs Crabbe's name was Effie but she was called Mrs Crabbe or Mom and her name had come to be used only for the *Effie Cee* which was by this time more Effie than Mrs Crabbe was. 'I'm taking home an Indian basket for Mrs Crabbe,' the skipper might say. 'Mrs Crabbe sure is an authority on Indian baskets.' Fin Crabbe was his name up and down the coast but at home he was the Captain or Pop, and so Mrs Crabbe would say, 'The Captain plans to be home for Christmas. The Captain's a great family man. I said to him "Pop, if you're not home for Christmas, I'll . . ."' Thus they daily elevated each other in esteem and loved each other with simple mutual gratification. In bed no names were needed by Mrs Crabbe and the Captain. (When they shall be dead, as they will be, what will avail this happy self-satisfaction. But now they are not dead, and the Captain's wife as often before awaits the Captain who is on his way down the coast from Flores Island, coming home for Christmas.)

Fin Crabbe had planned for some time to reach Port Alberni early in Christmas week and that suited Ed, the big crewman, too. Ed was not a family man although he had a wife somewhere; but what strong upspringing black curly hair he had and what gambling eyes. He was powerful, not to be governed, and a heller when he drank. He was quick to laugh, quick to hit out, quick to take a girl, quick to leave her, a difficult wilful volatile enjoying man of poor judgement, but he got along all right with little Fin Crabbe. He did not want to spend Christmas in Flores Island when there was so much doing in Alberni and Port Alberni.

Captain Crabbe's family lived in Alberni proper, which to the dweller in a city seems like a fairly raw small town at the end of a long arm through the forest to nowhere, and to the dweller up the coast or in the Queen Charlottes seems like a small city with every comfort, every luxury, motor cars speeding in and out by the long road that leads through the forest to the fine Island Highway, lighted streets, plumbing, beer parlours, a hospital, churches, schools, lumber mills, wharves. It lives for and on trees and salt water. Behind it is a huge hinterland of giant forests. Before it lies the long tortuous salt-water arm of the open sea.

Captain Crabbe, as the bow of the *Effie Cee* turned towards the pine-clad but desolate and rocky shore, cutting across the tricky undulations of the ocean, again gave his habitual look at the sky, north and west. The sky was overclouded but so it usually is in these parts at this time of year. Since these rocky shores are not protected as are the rocky shores of the British Columbia mainland by the long stretches of sweet liveable gulf islands and by the high barrier of mountainous Vancouver Island itself, the west coast of the island lies naked to the Pacific Ocean, which rolls in all the way from Asia and breaks upon the reefs and rocks and hard sands, and the continuous brewing of weather up in an air cauldron in the north seethes and spills over and rushes out of the Gulf of Alaska, often moderating before it reaches lower latitudes; but sometimes it roars down and attacks like all hell. The fishboat and tugboat men know this weather well and govern themselves accordingly. Next morning, perhaps the ocean smiles like a dissolute angel. The fishboat and tugboat men know that, too, and are not deceived. So that although Fin Crabbe knew all this as well as he knew his own thumb, he did not hesitate to turn the *Effie Cee* towards the shore when he saw the red shirt flapping at the end of the rock point but he had no intention of stopping there nor of spending any time at all unless his judgement warranted it, for on this trip his mind was closely set to home.

The turning aside of the fishboat in her journey irked the young passenger very much. Since the weather report on the radio was fairly good and anyway he was used to poor weather, he felt no concern about that. But here was delay and how much of it. He did not know how often he had read the letter, which he again took out of his pocket, not looking at big Ed nor at little Captain Crabbe but frowning at the letter and at some memory. He was possessed entirely, usurped, by impatience for contact, by letter, by wire or—best of all—by speech and sight and touch with the writer of this letter. Now that he had started on the journey towards her, now that he had started, now that he was on his way, his confusion seemed to clear. He read again in the letter: 'Dear Jason I am very unhappy I don't know I should tell you I've thought and thought before I wrote you and then what kind of a letter because I could say awful things and say you must come to Vancouver right away and marry me or believe me I could just cry and cry or I could write and say plain to you O Jason do I beseech you think if we couldn't get married right away. I could say I love you and I do.'

The young man folded the letter again. He looked with distaste at the red flag that signified an Indian's trouble and his own delay and his mind ran backwards again. The letter had found him at last and only two days ago. He had left the camp and had crossed to Flores and there an old man with a beard had told him that Fin Crabbe was all set to go to Alberni the next morning, and he had enquired for Captain Crabbe. As he had walked up and down the float pushing time forward, sometimes a violence of joy rose in him and surprised him. This was succeeded by a real fear that something would happen to prevent the fishboat from leaving, would prevent them reaching Alberni very soon, while all the time Josie did not even know whether he had received the letter. Many feelings were induced in him by what Josie had written, and now he thought ceaselessly about her to whom, only three days before, he had barely given a thought. He unfolded the letter again.

'I gess I don't know too much about love like in the pictures but I do love you Jason and I wouldnt ever ever be a person who would throw this up at you. I don't sleep very good and some nights I threton to myself to kill myself and tho I am awful scared of that maybe that would be better and easiest for us all and the next night I say no. Lots of girls go through with this but what do they do with the Baby and no real home for it and then I am bafled again and the time is going.'

Jason, looking out to the ocean but not seeing it, was aware of a different Josie. If a person had told me, he thought, that I'd want to get married and that I'd be crazy for this baby I'd say they were crazy, I'd say they were nuts, and impatience against delay surged over him again. The boat neared the mouth of the bay.

'One thing I do know I couldnt go back to the prairies with the Baby,' (no, that's right, you couldn't go back) 'so where would the Baby and me go. Mother would let me feel it every day even if she didnt mean to tho she would take us but Father no never. Then I think its the best thing for the Baby I should drown myself its quite easy in Vancouver its not like the prairies I do mean that.'

The skipper was talking back and forth to the crewman at the wheel and the *Effie Cee* slowed down. There were beams of sunshine that came and went.

'I cant believe its me and I do pitty any poor girl but not begging you Jason because you must decide for yourself. Some people would pay no attention to this letter but I kind of feel youre not like some people but O please Jason get me a word soon and then I can know what. Josie.'

From the pages arose the helpless and lonely anguish of little Josie and this anguish entered and consumed him too and it was all part of one storm of anxiety and anger that she was alone and she so quiet, and not her fault (he said), and impatience rose within him to reach a place where he could say to her Don't you worry kid, I'm coming! He thought with surprise Maybe I'm a real bad guy and I never knew it, maybe we're all bad and we don't know it. He read once more: 'I am bafled again and the time is going . . . I do love you Jason.' He put his head in his hands with dumb anger that she should be driven to this, but as soon as he reached a telephone in Alberni everything would be all right. As he suddenly looked up he thought he would go mad at this turning off course for any sick guy, or any kid who'd been crazy enough to break an arm. In his frustration and impatience there was an infusion of being a hero and rushing to save someone. Some hero, he said very sourly to himself, some hero.

The *Effie Cee* slowed to a stop and a black volley of cormorants, disturbed, flew away in a dark line. There was an Indian and an Indian woman and a little boy in a rowboat almost alongside the fishboat. The little boy was half lying down in an uncomfortable way and two rough sticks were tied to his leg. Three smaller children stood solemnly on the rocky shore looking at the two boats. Then they turned to play in a clumsy ceremonial fashion among the barnacled rocks. They did not laugh as they played.

Jason put the letter in his pocket and stood up. The rowboat jiggled on the water and Captain Crabbe was bending down and talking to the Indian. He listened and talked and explained. The Indian's voice was slow and muffled, but not much talk was needed. Anyone could see. 'Okay,' said the skipper and then he straightened himself and turned to look at Ed and Jason as much as to say . . . and Jason said, 'Better I got into the rowboat and helped him lift the kid up,' and the skipper said 'Okay.'

All this time the woman did not say anything. She kept her hands wrapped in her stuff dress and looked away or at the child. Jason slipped over the side and the rowboat at once became overcrowded, which made it difficult for him and the Indian to lift the child up carefully without hurting him and without separating the boats. The Indian child made no sound and no expression appeared on his face so no one knew how much pain he suffered or whether he suffered at all. His eyes were brown and without meaning like the dusky opaque eyes of a fawn. The Indian spoke to his wife and she reached out her hands and held on to the fishboat so that the two craft would not be parted. Jason and the father succeeded in slipping their arms—'This way,' said Jason, 'see? do it this way'—under the child and raised him gradually up to where Ed and the skipper were kneeling. Everyone leaned too much to one side of the rowboat and Jason tried to steady it so that they would not fall with the child into the sea. All this time the woman had not spoken but had accepted whatever other people did as if she had no rights in the matter. When the child was safely on board, Jason sprang onto the deck and at once, at once, the *Effie Cee* turned and tore away with a white bone of spume in her mouth and a white wake of foam behind, leaving the Indians in the rowboat and the children on the shore looking after her.

'Best lay him on the floor, he'd maybe roll off of the bunk,' said Fin Crabbe when they had lifted the child inside. 'Mustn't let you get cold, Sonny,' he said, and took down a coat that swung from a hook. The child regarded him in silence and with fear in his heart. One two another white man taking him to some place he did not know.

'Make supper Ed, and I'll take the wheel,' said the skipper. The boat went faster ahead, rising and plunging as there was now a small sea running.

What'd I better do, thought Fin Crabbe and did not consult the crewman who hadn't much judgement. There were good reasons for going on through and trying to make Alberni late in the night or in early morning. That would surprise Mrs Crabbe and she would be pleased, and the young fella seemed desperate to get to Alberni on account of this bad news; but here was this boy he'd taken aboard and the sooner they got him into hospital the better. I think it's his hip (he thought), I could turn back to Tofino but it'd be dark then and would he be any better off landing him in the dark and likely no doctor. Anyway I can make Ucluelet easy and spend the night. I don't like to take no chances but all in all I think we'll go on. And they went on.

Evening came and black night. It was winter cold outside and Jason crowded into the wheelhouse and looked out at the dark. The coming of night brought him nearer the telephone, so near he could all but touch it, but he could not touch it.

The *Effie Cee* could not make much speed now and ploughed slowly for hours never ending, it seemed to Jason, through water that had become stormy and in the dark she followed a sideways course so that she could cut a little across the waves that were now high and deep. Ed had the wheel and Captain Crabbe stood beside him. The storm increased. The boat's nose plunged into the waves and rose with the waves and the water streamed over. There was a wallowing, a sideways wallowing. The little fishboat became a world of noise and motion, a plunging, a rising, a plunging again. Jason wedged the child against the base of the bunk. The child cried out, and vomited with seasickness and fear. 'Now now,' said Jason, patting him. 'Try the radio again,' said Captain Crabbe.

Jason fiddled with the radio. 'Can't seem to get anything,' he said.

'Let me,' said the skipper.

'Bust,' he said.

But now the storm rapidly accelerated and the waves, innocent and savage as tigers, leaped at the *Effie Cee* and the oncoming rollers struck broadside and continuously. The little boy made sounds like an animal and Jason, in whom for the first time fear of what might come had struck down all elation and expectation, took the child's hand and held it. The little plunging boat was now the whole world and fate to Jason and to Fin Crabbe and to the Indian boy but not to Ed who had no fear. Perhaps because he had no love he had no fear. Standing over the wheel and peering into the dark, he seemed like a great black bull and it was to Jason as though he filled the cabin.

Ed turned the boat's nose towards shore to get away from the broadside of the waves. Fin Crabbe shouted at him to be heard above the storm. The boat had been shipping water and Jason, crouching beside the shaking child in a wash of water heard the words 'Ucluelet' and 'lighthouse' and 'rocks' but Ed would not listen. The skipper went on shouting at him and then he seized the wheel. He pushed the big man with all his strength, turning the wheel to starboard. Jason and the Indian child saw the big man and the little man fighting in the small space, in the din of the ocean, the howl of the wind, for possession of the wheel. As quick as a cat Ed drew off and hit the older man a great blow. Fin Crabbe crumpled and fell. He lay in the wash of water at Ed's feet and Ed had his way, so the fishboat drove inshore, hurled by the waves onto the reefs, or onto the hard sand, or onto the place that Ed knew that he knew, whichever the dark should disclose, but not to the open sea. Captain Crabbe tried to raise himself and Jason crawled over towards him.

The skipper could not stand in the pitching boat. He looked up at Ed who was his executioner, the avenger of all that he had ever done, driving on against death for sure.

The thought of the abandonment of Josie (for now a belief was formed terribly in him that she was to be abandoned) pierced Jason through and through and then in the immediate danger the thought of Josie was no longer real but fled away on the wind and water, and there was nothing but fear. Without knowing what he did, he seized and held the child. Never could a man feel greater despair than Jason in the walnut shell of a reeling boat soon to be cracked between land and water. Ed, bent over the wheel, knowing everything, knowing just where they were, but not knowing, looked only forward into the blackness and drove on. The sea poured into the boat and at the same minute the lights went out and they were no longer together. Then the *Effie Cee* rose on a great wave, was hurled upwards and downwards, struck the barnacled reef, and split, and the following seas washed over.

A few days later the newspapers stated that in the recent storm on the west coast of Vancouver Island the fishboat *Effie Cee* was missing with two men aboard. These men were Findlay Crabbe aged fifty-six and Edward Morgan aged thirty-five, both of Alberni. Planes were continuing the search.

A day or two afterwards the newspapers stated that it was thought that there might have been a third man aboard the *Effie Cee*. He was identified as Jason Black aged twenty-two, employed as a logger up the coast near Flores Island.

On the second morning after the wreck of the *Effie Cee* the skies were a cold blue and the ocean lay sparkling and lazy beneath the sun. Up the Alberni Canal the sea and air were chilly and brilliant but still. Mrs Crabbe spent the day waiting on the wharf in the cold sunshine. She stood or walked or sat, accompanied by two friends or by the gangling son and daughter, and next day it was the same, and the next. People said to her, 'But he didn't set a day? When did he *say* he'd be back?'

'He never said what day,' she said. 'The Captain couldn't ever say what day. He just said the beginning of the week, maybe Monday was what he said.' She said 'he said, he said, he said' because it seemed to establish him as living. People had to stop asking because they could not bear to speak to Mrs Crabbe standing and waiting on the busy wharf, paying the exorbitant price of love. They wished she would not wait there because it made them uncomfortable and unhappy to see her.

Because Josie did not read the papers, she did not know that Jason was dead. Days had passed and continued to pass. Distraught, alone, deprived of hope and faith (two sovereign remedies) and without the consolation of love, she took secretly and with terror what she deemed to be the appropriate path.

The Indian, who had fully trusted the man who took his son away, heard nothing more. He waited until steady fine weather came and then took his family in his small boat to Tofino. From there he made his way to Alberni. Here he walked slowly up and down the docks and at last asked someone where the hospital was; but at the hospital no one seemed to know anything about his only son.

Virginia Woolf

Virginia Stephen was born in 1882 in London, where she was educated in the library of her father, Sir Leslie Stephen, a well-known scholar and editor of the *Dictionary of National Biography*. She married Leonard Woolf, a journalist and political philosopher, in 1912. The couple settled in fashionable Bloomsbury, where they started The Hogarth Press, which published Katherine Mansfield, E. M. Forster, T. S. Eliot, and a number of Virginia's own works, including the stories in *Monday and Tuesday* (1921) and the following novels: *Jacob's Room* (1922), *Mrs. Dalloway* (1925), *To the Lighthouse* (1927), and *The Waves* (1931). Woolf's physical and emotional condition was fragile at the best of times and compounded, it is now believed, by possible abuse as a child and by being unfairly denied the formal education allowed her half brothers. Her non-fiction writings, particularly *A Room of One's Own* (1929) and *Three Guineas* (1938), provide a moving record of her intellectual courage and her struggles on behalf of women's rights. Fearing another severe mental breakdown, she took her own life by drowning in 1941.

The Common Reader (1925; second series, 1932) contains many of her reviews and pronouncements on the art of fiction, including the famous manifesto of psychological realism, "Modern Fiction," in which she makes her case against the realistic novels of H. G. Wells, Arnold Bennett, and John Galsworthy, whose works, she felt, ignored "the dark places of psychology" and were obsessed with surfaces, with action, manners, and materiality: "Look within and life, it seems, is very far from being 'like this.' Examine for a moment an ordinary mind on an ordinary day. The mind receives a myriad of impressions—trivial, fantastic, evanescent, or engraved with the sharpness of steel. From all sides they come, an incessant shower of innumerable atoms; and as they fall, as they shape themselves into the life of Monday or Tuesday, the accent falls differently from of old; the moment of importance came not here but there; so that, if a writer were a free man and not a slave, if he could write what he chose, not what he must, if he could base his work upon his own feeling and not upon convention, there would be no plot, no comedy, no tragedy, no love interest or catastrophe in the accepted style, and perhaps not a single button sewn on as the Bond Street tailors would have it. Life is not a series of gig lamps symmetrically arranged; life is a luminous halo, a semi-transparent envelope surrounding us from the beginning of consciousness to the end. Is it not the task of the novelist to convey this varying, this unknown and uncircumscribed spirit, whatever aberration or complexity it may display, with as little mixture of the alien and external as possible? We are not pleading merely for courage and sincerity; we are suggesting that the proper stuff of fiction is a little other than custom would have us believe it."

As she suggests in *Books and Portraits*, "We are by this time alive to the fact that inconclusive stories are legitimate; that is to say, though they leave us feeling melancholy and perhaps uncertain, yet somehow they provide a resting-point for the mind—a solid object casting its shade of reflection and speculation. The fragments of which it is composed may have the air of having come together by chance."

Woolf's letters and diaries record her efforts to "grope and experiment" with new forms, for a work with "no scaffolding; scarcely a brick to be seen; all crepuscular, but the heart, the passion, humour, everything as bright as fire in the mist." She rejected traditional notions of character, arguing that "characters are to be merely views: personality must be avoided at all costs. I'm sure my Conrad adventure taught me this. Directly you specify hair, age, etc. something frivolous, or irrelevant, gets into the book." Part of her plan was to "dig out beautiful caves behind my characters: I think that gives exactly what I want; humanity, humour, depth. The idea is that the caves shall connect and each comes to daylight at the present moment." Subterranean imagery abounds in the diaries, not only caves, but also the image of the fiction writing "tunnelling," "deep in the richest strata," boring down to the deep wells (not the H. G. Wells!) of feeling.

To achieve her desired effects, what has come to be called stream of consciousness, Woolf needed to rework the medium of prose fiction. She dispensed, to a large extent, with dialogue and conventional action. "I can make up situations, but I cannot make up plots," she said. "That is: if I pass a lame girl I can, without knowing I do it, instantly make up a scene. . . . This is the germ of such fictitious gifts as I have." To render the inner life of these situations, she had "to break up, dig deep, make prose move—yes I swear—as prose has never moved before; from the chuckle, the babble, to the rhapsody." The greatest book in the world, she said, "would be one that was made entirely solely and with integrity of one's thoughts. Suppose one could catch them before they became 'works of art'? Catch them hot and sudden as they rise in the mind—walking up Asheham hill for instance. Of course one cannot; for the process of language is slow and deluding. One must stop to find a word. Then, there is the form of the sentence, soliciting one to fill it."

In a letter to Vita Sackville-West, Woolf tries to define style: "As for the *mot juste*, you are quite wrong. Style is a very simple matter; it is all rhythm. Once you get that, you can't use the wrong words. But on the other hand here am I sitting after half the morning, crammed with ideas, and visions, and so on, and can't dislodge them, for lack of the right rhythm. Now this is very profound, what rhythm is, and goes far deeper than words. A sight, an emotion, creates this wave in the mind, long before it makes words to fit it; and in writing (such is my present belief) one has to recapture this, and set this working (which has nothing apparently to do with words) and then, as it breaks and tumbles in the mind, it makes words to fit it: But no doubt I shall think differently next year." Woolf related her method to painting and music, talking about the text as a canvas, or score, and writing as a process of composition and layering: "I should like to write four lines at a time, describing the same feeling, as a musician does; because it always seems to me that things are going on at so many different levels simultaneously."

Moments of Being: 'Slater's Pins Have No Points'

'Slater's pins have no points—don't you always find that?' said Miss Craye, turning round as the rose fell out of Fanny Wilmot's dress, and Fanny stooped with her ears full of the music, to look for the pin on the door.

The words gave her an extraordinary shock, as Miss Craye struck the last chord of the Bach fugue. Did Miss Craye actually go to Slater's and buy pins then, Fanny Wilmot asked herself, transfixed for a moment? Did she stand at the counter waiting like anybody else, and was she given a bill with coppers wrapped in it, and did she slip them into her purse and then, an hour later, stand by her dressing table and take out the pins? What need had she of pins? For she was not so much dressed as cased, like a beetle compactly in its sheath, blue in winter, green in summer. What need had she of pins—Julia Craye—who lived, it seemed, in the cool, glassy world of Bach fugues, playing to herself what she liked and only consenting to take one or two pupils at the Archer Street College of Music (so the Principal, Miss Kingston said) as a special favour to herself, who had 'the greatest admiration for her in every way'. Miss Craye was left badly off, Miss Kingston was afraid, at her brother's death. Oh, they used to have such lovely things, when they lived at Salisbury and her brother Julius was, of course, a very well-known man: a famous archaeologist. It was a great privilege to with them, Miss Kingston said ('My family had always known them—they were regular Salisbury people,' Miss Kingston said), but a little frightening for a child; one had to be careful not to slam the door or bounce into the room unexpectedly. Miss Kingston, who gave little character sketches like this on the first day of term while she received cheques and wrote out receipts for them, smiled here. Yes, she had been rather a tomboy; she had bounced in and set all those green Roman glasses and things jumping in their case. The Crayes were none of them married. The Crayes were not used to children. They kept cats. The cats, one used to feel, knew as much about the Roman urns and things as anybody.

'Far more than I did!' said Miss Kingston brightly, writing her name across the stamp, in her dashing, cheerful, full-bodied hand, for she had always been practical.

Perhaps then, Fanny Wilmot thought, looking for the pin, Miss Craye said that about 'Slater's pins having no points', at a venture. None of the Crayes had ever married. She knew nothing about pins—nothing whatever. But she wanted to break the spell that had fallen on the house; to break the pane of glass which sep-arated them from other people. When Polly Kingston, that merry little girl, had slammed the door and made the Roman vases jump, Julius, seeing that no harm was done (that would be his first instinct) looked, for the case was stood in the window, at Polly skipping home across the fields; looked with the look his sister often had, that lingering, desiring look.

'Stars, sun, moon,' it seemed to say, 'the daisy in the grass, fires, frost on the window pane, my heart goes out to you. But,' it always seemed to add, 'you break, you pass, you go.' And simultaneously it covered the intensity of both these states of mind with 'I can't reach you—I can't get at you,' spoken wistfully, frustratedly. And the stars faded, and the child went.

That was the kind of spell, that was the glassy surface that Miss Craye wanted to break by showing, when she had played Bach beautifully as a reward to a favourite pupil (Fanny Wilmot knew that she was Miss Craye's favourite pupil) that she too felt as other people felt about pins. Slater's pins had no points.

Yes, the 'famous archaeologist' had looked like that, too. 'The famous archae-ologist'—as she said that endorsing cheques, ascertaining the day of the month, speaking so brightly and frankly, there was in Miss Kingston's voice an indescrib-able tone which hinted at something odd, something queer, in Julius Craye. It was the very same thing that was odd perhaps in Julia too. One could have sworn, thought Fanny Wilmot, as she looked for the pin, that at parties, meetings (Miss Kingston's father was a clergyman) she had picked up some piece of gossip, or it might only have been a smile, or a tone when his name was mentioned, which had given her 'a feeling' about Julius Craye. Needless to say, she had never spoken about it to anybody. Probably she scarcely knew what she meant by it. But when-ever she spoke of Julius, or heard him mentioned, that was the first thought that came to mind: there was something odd about Julius Craye.

It was so that Julia looked too, as she sat half turned on the music stool, smil-ing. It's on the field, it's on the pane, it's in the sky—beauty; and I can't get at it; I can't have it—I, she seemed to add, with that little clutch of the hand which was so characteristic, who adore it so passionately, would give the whole world to pos-sess it! And she picked up the carnation which had fallen on the floor, while Fanny searched for the pin. She crushed it, Fanny felt, voluptuously in her smooth, veined hands stuck about with water-coloured rings set in pearls. The pressure of her fingers seemed to increase all that was most brilliant in the flower; to set it off; to make it more frilled, fresh, immaculate. What was odd in her, and perhaps in her brother too, was that this crush and grasp of the fingers was combined with a perpetual frustration. So it was even now with the carnation. She had her hands on it; she pressed it; but she did not possess it, enjoy it, not altogether.

None of the Crayes had married, Fanny Wilmot remembered. She had in mind how one evening when the lesson had lasted longer than usual and it was dark,

Julia Craye had said, 'It's the use of men, surely, to protect us,' smiling at her that same odd smile, as she stood fastening her cloak, which made her, like the flower, conscious to her finger tips of youth and brilliance, but, like the flower too, Fanny suspected, inhibited.

'Oh, but I don't want protection,' Fanny had laughed, and when Julia Craye, fixing on her that extraordinary look, had said she was not so sure of that, Fanny positively blushed under the admiration in her eyes.

It was the only use of men, she had said. Was it for that reason then, Fanny wondered, with her eyes on the floor, that she had never married? After all, she had not lived all her life in Salisbury. 'Much the nicest part of London,' she had said once, (but I'm speaking of fifteen or twenty years ago) is Kensington. One was in the Gardens in ten minutes—it was like the heart of the country. One could dine out in one's slippers without catching cold. 'Kensington—it was like a village then, you know,' she had said.

Here she had broken off, to denounce acridly, the draughts in the Tubes.

'It was the use of men,' she had said, with a queer, wry acerbity. Did that throw any light on the problem why she had not married? One could imagine every sort of scene in her youth, when with her good, blue eyes, her straight, firm nose, her piano playing, her rose flowering with chaste passion in the bosom of her muslin dress, she had attracted first the young men to whom such things, and the china tea-cups and the silver candlesticks, and the inlaid tables (for the Crayes had such nice things) were wonderful; young men not sufficiently distinguished; young men of the Cathedral town with ambitions. She had attracted them first, and then her brother's friends from Oxford or Cambridge. They would come down in the summer, row her up the river, continue the argument about Browning by letter, and arrange perhaps on the rare occasions when she stayed in London to show her—Kensington Gardens?

'Much the nicest part of London—Kensington. I'm speaking of fifteen or twenty years ago,' she had said once. 'One was in the Gardens in ten minutes—in the heart of the country.' One could make that yield what one liked, Fanny Wilmot thought, single out for instance, Mr Sherman, the painter, an old friend of hers; make him call for her by appointment one sunny day in June; take her to have tea under the trees. (They had met, too, at those parties to which one tripped in slippers without fear of catching cold.) The aunt or other elderly relative was to wait there while they looked at the Serpentine. They looked at the Serpentine. He may have rowed her across. The compared it with the Avon. She would have considered the comparison very seriously, for views of rivers were important to her. She sat hunched a little, a little angular, though she was graceful then, steering. At the critical moment, for he had determined that he must speak now—it was his only chance of getting her alone—he was speaking with his head turned at an absurd angle, in his great nervousness, over his shoulder—at that very moment she interrupted fiercely. He would have them into the Bridge, she cried. It was a moment of horror, of disillusionment, of revelation for both of them. I can't have it, I can't possess it, she thought. He could not see why she had come then. With a great splash of his oar he pulled the boat round. Merely to snub him? He rowed her back and said good-bye to her.

The setting of that scene could be varied as one chose, Fanny Wilmot reflected. (Where had that pin fallen?) It might be Ravenna—or Edinburgh, where she had kept house for her brother. The scene could be changed and the young man and the exact manner of it all; but one thing was constant—her refusal and her frown and her anger with herself afterwards and her argument, and her relief—yes, certainly her immense relief. The very next day perhaps she would get up at six, put on her cloak, and walk all the way from Kensington to the river. She was so thankful that she had not sacrificed her right to go and look at things when they are at their best—before people are up, that is to say. She could have her breakfast in bed if she liked. She had not sacrificed her independence.

Yes, Fanny Wilmot smiled, Julia had not endangered her habits. They remained safe, and her habits would have suffered if she had married. 'They're ogres,' she had said one evening, half laughing, when another pupil, a girl lately married, suddenly bethinking her that she would miss her husband, had rushed off in haste.

'They're ogres,' she had said, laughing grimly. An ogre would have interfered perhaps with breakfast in bed; with walks at dawn down to the river. What would have happened (but one could hardly conceive this) had she had children? She took astonishing precautions against chills, fatigue, rich food, the wrong food, draughts, heated rooms, journeys in the Tube, for she could never determine which of these it was exactly that brought on those terrible headaches that gave her life the semblance of a battlefield. She was always engaged in outwitting the enemy, until it seemed as if the pursuit had its interest; could she have beaten the enemy finally she would have found life a little dull. As it was, the tug-of-war was perpetual—on one side the nightingale or the view which she loved with passion—yes, for views and birds she felt nothing less than passion; on the other, the damp path or the horrid long drag up a steep hill which would certainly make her good for nothing next day and bring on one of her headaches. When, therefore, from time to time, she managed her forces adroitly and brought off a visit to Hampton Court the week the crocuses (those glossy bright flowers were her favourites) were at their best, it was a victory. It was something that lasted; something that mattered for ever. She strung the afternoon on the necklace of memorable days, which was not too long for her to be able to recall this one or that one; this view, that city; to finger it, to feel it, to savour, sighing, the quality that made it unique.

'It was so beautiful last Friday,' she said, 'that I determined I must go there.' So she had gone off to Waterloo on her great undertaking—to visit Hampton Court— alone. Naturally, but perhaps foolishly, one pitied her for the thing she never asked pity for (indeed she was reticent habitually, speaking of her health only as a warrior might speak of his foe)—one pitied her for always doing everything alone. Her brother was dead. Her sister was asthmatic. She found the climate of Edinburgh good for her. It was too bleak for Julia. Perhaps too she found the associations painful, for her brother, the famous archaeologist, had died there; and she had loved her brother. She lived in a little house off the Brompton Road entirely alone.

Fanny Wilmot saw the pin on the carpet; she picked it up. She looked at Miss Craye. Was Miss Craye so lonely? No, Miss Craye was steadily, blissfully, if only for a moment, a happy woman. Fanny had surprised her in a moment of ecstasy. She sat there, half turned away from the piano, with her hands clasped in her lap holding the carnation upright, while behind her was the sharp square of the window, uncurtained, purple in the evening, intensely purple after the brilliant electric lights which burnt unshaded in the bare music room. Julia Craye sitting hunched and compact holding her flower seemed to emerge out of the London night, seemed to fling it like a cloak behind her. It seemed in its bareness and intensity the effluence of her spirit, something she had made which surrounded her, which was her. Fanny stared.

All seemed transparent for a moment to the gaze of Fanny Wilmot, as if looking through Miss Craye, she saw the very fountain of her being spurt up in pure, silver drops. She saw back and back into the past behind her. She saw the green Roman vases stood in their case; heard the choristers playing cricket; saw Julia quietly descend the curving steps on to the lawn; saw her pour out tea beneath the cedar tree; softly enclose the old man's hand in hers; saw her going round and about the corridors of that ancient Cathedral dwelling place with towels in her hand to mark them; lamenting as she went the pettiness of daily life; and slowly ageing, and putting away clothes when summer came, because at her age they were too bright to wear; and tending her father's sickness; and cleaving her way ever more definitely as her will stiffened towards her solitary goal; travelling frugally; counting the cost and measuring out of her tight shut purse the sum needed for this journey, or for that old mirror; obstinately adhering whatever people might say in choosing her pleasures for herself. She saw Julia—

She saw Julia open her arms; saw her blaze; saw her kindle. Out of the night she burnt like a dead white star. Julia kissed her. Julia possessed her.

'Slater's pins have no points,' Miss Craye said, laughing queerly and relaxing her arms, as Fanny Wilmot pinned the flower to her breast with trembling fingers.

The Fascination of the Pool

It may have been very deep—certainly one could not see to the bottom of it. Round the edge was so thick a fringe of rushes that their reflections made a darkness like the darkness of very deep water. However in the middle was something white. The big farm a mile off was to be sold and some zealous person, or it may have been a joke on the part of a boy, had stuck one of the posters advertising the sale, with farm horses, agricultural implements, and young heifers, on a tree stump by the side of the pool. The centre of the water reflected the white placard and when the wind blew the centre of the pool seemed to flow and ripple like a piece of washing. One could trace the big red letters in which Romford Mill was printed in the water. A tinge of red was in the green that rippled from bank to bank.

But if one sat down among the rushes and watched the pool—pools have some curious fascination, one knows not what—the red and black letters and the white paper seemed to lie very thinly on the surface, while beneath went on some profound under-water life like the brooding, the ruminating of a mind. Many, many people must have come there alone, from time to time, from age to age, dropping their thoughts into the water, asking it some question, as one did oneself this summer evening. Perhaps that was the reason of its fascination—that it held in its waters all kinds of fancies, complaints, confidences, not printed or spoken aloud, but in a liquid state, floating one on top of another, almost disembodied. A fish would swim through them, be cut in two by the blade of a reed; or the moon would annihilate them with its great white plate. The charm of the pool was that thoughts had been left there by people who had gone away and without their bodies their thoughts wandered in and out freely, friendly and communicative, in the common pool.

Among all these liquid thoughts some seemed to stick together and to form recognizable people—just for a moment. And one saw a whiskered red face formed in the pool leaning low over it, drinking it. I came here in 1851 after the heat of the Great Exhibition. I saw the Queen open it. And the voice chuckled liquidly, easily, as if he had thrown off his elastic side boots and put his top hat on the edge of the pool. Lord, how hot it was! and now all gone, all crumbled, of course, the thoughts seemed to say, swaying among the reeds. But I was a lover, another thought began, sliding over the other silently and orderly as fish not impeding each other. A girl; we used to come down from the farm (the placard of its sale was reflected on the top of the water) that summer, 1662. The soldiers never saw us from the road. It was very hot. We lay here. She was lying hidden in the rushes with her lover, laughing into the pool and slipping into it, thoughts of eternal love, of fiery kisses and despair. And I was very happy, said another thought glancing briskly over the girl's despair (for she had drowned herself). I used to fish here. We never caught the giant carp but we saw him once—the day Nelson fought at Trafalgar. We saw him under the willow—my word! what a great brute he was! They say he was never caught. Alas, alas sighed a voice, slipping over the boy's voice. So sad a voice must come from the very bottom of the pool. It raised itself under the others as a spoon lifts all the things in a bowl of water. This was the voice we all wished to listen to. All the voices slipped gently away to the side of the pool to listen to the voices which so sad it seemed—it must surely know the reason of all this. For they all wished to know.

One drew closer to the pool and parted the reeds so that one could see deeper, through the reflections, through the faces, through the voices to the bottom. But there under the man who had been to the Exhibition; and the girl who had drowned herself and the boy who had seen the fish; and the voice which cried alas alas! yet there was always something else. There was always another face, another voice. One thought came and covered another. For though there are moments when a spoon seems about to lift all of us, and our thoughts and long-ings and questions and confessions and disillusions into the light of day, somehow the spoon always slips beneath and we flow back again over the edge into the pool. And once more the whole of its centre is covered over with the reflection of the placard which advertises the sale of Romford Mill Farm. That perhaps is why one loves to sit and look into pools.

 Afterwords

Writings on the Art of Fiction and the Act of Critical Reading

As I said in the Introduction, writers are not always the most accurate and reliable guides to their own work. Flannery O'Connor admitted to an audience that "your asking me to talk about story-writing is just like asking a fish to lecture on swimming." And yet, she went on to write and talk brilliantly and movingly about the craft of story-writing. While her comments are often not as flashy and self-assured—or so full of fashionable jargon—as the essays of her critics, O'Connor's common-sense ideas about writing and reading stories are well worth considering. Although she was conscious of the need for critical terminology, she preferred to keep the discussion as simple as possible.

In "Writing Short Stories," the essay included in this anthology, she says that describing a story in terms of plot, character, and theme is "like trying to describe the expression on a face by saying where the eyes, nose, and mouth are." Instead of theme, she proposes talking about a story's *meaning,* which is less easily extractable and which is likely to emerge only from a consideration of the story in its entirety; she also draws attention to the importance of *idiom,* or local speech patterns, suggesting that idiom "characterizes a society" and that "our history lives in our talk." In her view, a storywriter is more in need of a good ear than a dictionary or thesaurus.

I have deliberately chosen statements about the craft of fiction that are, for the most part, quite general and can be used in thinking about any of the stories included here. Most writers don't want to talk about what they are trying to do in a specific story, especially in terms that will limit the story to a single interpretation or interfere with the pleasure and excitement of a reader's first encounter with the text. However, they can be very insightful when talking generally about the aims and techniques of fiction. If you read Clark Blaise's comments about how to begin or end a story, you will not be able to ignore the telling and subtle ways in which a writer reaches out to grab you by the wrist, or by the throat. Of course, you don't have to take Blaise's word as gospel, especially when Chekhov advises that only the middle of a story is important, that beginnings and endings should be chucked.

The point of considering these diverse statements on short fiction is that they will help you develop your own critical approaches and your own working vocabulary. If you take the time to read through the controversial statements, most of which are written in an engaging, conversational style, and through the mélange of brief quotations in the Notes on the Authors, you will have treated yourself to a painless but instructive crash course in how to read and how to begin to talk about—perhaps even how to write—the short story.

MARGARET ATWOOD

From *An End to Audience?*

I believe that poetry is the heart of the language, the activity through which language is renewed and kept alive. I believe that fiction writing is the guardian of the moral and ethical sense of the community. Especially now that organized religion is scattered and in disarray, and politicians have, Lord knows, lost their credibility, fiction is one of the few forms left through which we may examine our society not in its particular but in its typical aspects; through which we can see ourselves and the ways in which we behave towards each other, through which we can see others and judge them and ourselves.

Writing is a craft, true, and discussions of the position of colons and the rhyming of *plastic* and *spastic* have some place in it. You cannot be a concert pianist without having first learned the scales, you cannot throw a porcelain vase without having put in a good number of hours at the wheel. But writing is also a vocation. By *vocation* I mean a lifetime pursuit to which you feel called. There is a big difference between a doctor who goes into medicine because he wants to cure people and one who goes into it because that's where he thinks the money is. They may both be able to fix your broken leg, technically just as well; but there is a difference.

Under the right conditions, the first may turn into Norman Bethune. The second never will. If you want to be a writer, you should go into the largest library you can find and stand there contemplating the books that have been written. Then you should ask yourself, "Do I really have anything to add?" If you have the arrogance or the humility to say yes, you will know you have the vocation.

Writing is also a profession, and, at its best, an honorable one. It has been made honorable by those who have already been members of it. Whether you like it or not, every time you set pen to paper you're staring at the same blank space that confronted Milton, Melville, Emily Brontë, Dostoevsky and George Eliot, George Orwell and William Faulkner and Virginia Woolf and William Carlos Williams, not to mention the latest hero, Gabriel García Márquez. Imitation is not emulation; nobody expects you to write the books of these writers over again. But unless you're trying to do as well, unless you're trying to do as well as you can, you are not worthy of the profession. There's a certain amount of cynicism among writers, just as there is among doctors. But if all doctors were hacking off legs with septic instruments in barber shops and losing sponges inside people's lungs because they're drunk during the operation, we would not think of medicine as an honorable profession but as a game played for money by charlatans and quacks, and doctors would still quite rightly be known as leeches.

Writing can also be an art, and one of the reasons that so many writers dodge this on television talk shows is that art is hard to define or describe. Money is easier to talk about, so we talk about money. Nevertheless, art happens. It happens when you have the craft and the vocation and are waiting for something else, something extra, or maybe not waiting; in any case it happens. It's the extra rabbit coming out of the hat, the one you didn't put there. It's Odysseus standing by the blood-filled trench, except that the blood is his own. It is bringing the dead to life and giving voices to those who lack them so that they may speak for themselves. It is not "expressing yourself." It is opening yourself, discarding your *self*, so that the language and the world may be evoked through you. *Evocation* is quite different from *expression*. Because we are so fixated on the latter, we forget that writing also does the former. Maybe the writer expresses; but evocation, calling up, is what writing does for the reader. Writing is also a kind of sooth-saying, a truth-telling. It is a naming of the world, a reverse incarnation: the flesh becoming word. It's also a witnessing. *Come with me*, the writer is saying to the reader. *There is a story I have to tell you, there is something you need to know.* The writer is both an eye-witness and I-witness, the one to whom personal experience happens and the one who makes experience personal for others. The writer *bears witness*. Bearing witness is not the same as self-expression.

There's something compulsive about the act of writing. All writers play Ancient Mariner at times to the reader's Wedding Guest, hoping that they are holding the reader with their glittering eye, at least long enough so he'll turn the next page. The tale the Mariner tells is partly about himself, true, but it's partly about the universe and partly about something the Wedding Guest needs to know; or at least, that's what the story tells us.

Jacob, so one of the stories goes, wrestled with an angel all night, neither prevailing against the other; and he would not let go until the angel blessed him. *What is your name?* said the angel, unable to give the blessing until the name was spoken. When the angel gave the blessing, it was not for Jacob alone but for his people. There is not a writer alive who would fail to interpret this story as a parable of his own relationship with his art. The encounter with language is a struggle in which each side is equally active, for what writer has not felt the language taking him over at times, blocking him at others? We all hope for the blessing; we all hope finally to be able to speak our name. And, we hope that if we receive the blessing it will not be for ourselves alone.

JOHN BERGER

Lost Off Cape Wrath

(First appeared in *Three-penny Review*, Winter, 1988, as "The Credible Word")

Today the discredit of words is very great. Most of the time the media transmit lies. In the face of an intolerable world, words appear to be able to change very little. State power has become congenitally deaf, which is why—but the editorialists forget it—terrorists are reduced to bombs and hijacking.

The power of reason to overthrow tyranny was in fact an illusion. Likewise, to believe that the pen is mightier than the sword is today a sign of relative privilege. Words are systematically used to confuse.

Yet it is to words that we confess our confusion and our impotence, our anger and our visions. With words we still name our losses and our endurance. We do this because we have no other recourse, but also because man is incurably open to words, and slowly they form his judgment. This judgment, which those with power habitually fear, is formed slowly like a riverbed, by currents of words. But words make such currents only when they are credible.

I once had a dream. In the dreamt country a decree had been passed which was binding and which everybody accepted: according to this decree every word, either spoken or thought, had to be cashed for what it signified. It was as if the language and its economy had returned to the gold standard, so that every coin or bill was exchangeable for its equivalent in gold. If you thought *tree* in that country, the tree had to appear and be there. In thinking *tree*, tree became present. In thinking *morning*, morning was. It was not, as in the first chapter of Genesis, a process of naming and so simultaneously creating; it was a question of speaking with *what* words meant. The words, according to the new decree, could not be left free-standing: they were porters of what they signified. All this applied not only to nouns but also to verbs, adverbs, etc. When you thought *dig*, the act of digging was enacted. If you added the adverb *sadly*, sadness came and was as unmistakable as salt on the lips.

For a long time in the dreamt country everybody respected the decree. As a result there was great clarity. There was also a certain cumbersomeness, because space was becoming too restricted for everything thought and said to be placed within it. There was no confusion as before, but there was overcrowding. Tentatively people began to test what would happen if certain words weren't cashed. Could clarity be preserved more economically? And it was at this moment that the people made an unexpected discovery. As a result of the decree having been in effect for so long, everything which existed had become eloquent with all the words, thoughts, phrases which had ever been cashed for it. People found themselves in a *speaking* universe, in which words were no longer necessary.

A word-spinner's utopian dream! Yet buried within it is perhaps a clue about how writing becomes credible (when it does) and about the clarity of words.

One does not look *through* writing onto reality—as through a clean or dirty windowpane. Words are never transparent. They create their own space, the space of experience, not that of existence. Clarity of the written word has little to do with style as such. A baroque text can be clear; a simple one can be dim. Clarity, in my view, is a gift of the way the space created by words in a given text is arranged.

The task of arranging this space is not unlike that of furnishing and arranging a home. The aim is similar: to accommodate with ease what belongs there and to welcome those who enter. There are hospitable and inhospitable writings. Hospitality and clarity go together. Yet what does accommodate mean here? It means allowing each event recounted its own proper space. By event I mean what would become present if the word were cashed. In semiological jargon: the signified. The space required is not of course physical. A scarf may demand more space than a cloud. Everything depends upon the particular experience being recounted.

Lived events are ambiguous because no experience comes alone, and so a single event entails many others. A lived event—from the point of view of the purist—keeps bad company, is promiscuous. This is perhaps where the principal difference between science and art begins.

Let us take an extremely simple example of ambiguity in the practice of narration. *The ship sailed out of the port.* An adventure or a farewell? From the quayside the mood is passive; from the stern of the ship it is active. The ensuing words will remove certain ambiguities and, at the same time, will entail other, new ones. *He looked toward the horizon.* An act of will, an act of habit? *The screeching gulls reminded him of his father, lost off Cape Wrath.*

Each event, each object, needs to be allowed the space of its ambiguities, and each subsequent one needs to acknowledge the ambiguities it has eliminated.

The father's death "acknowledges" the ship's sailing away. The suggestion that the father was a sailor or a fisherman "acknowledges" the son's looking at the horizon. An unspoken dialogue is taking place between the events. The problem of narration is not, as is often believed, the problem of "finding the words," but that of choosing and placing events, of allowing or instigating this wordless dialogue.

The complexity of choices involved, when they concern a whole text, would defeat the most sophisticated computer, because it could never be adequately programmed. The writer, programmed by his experience of life and of the inarticulate, accommodates intuitively, rarely by calculation. He becomes his own writing's instinct for self-preservation: an instinct applied to keeping open the space for reciprocal ambiguities without end.

The moment the writer's attention is diverted by considerations of style, rhetoric, or verbal glory, his words, instead of containing, will merely evoke. The moment he simply repeats facts instead of imagining the experience of them, his writing will be reduced to a document. The credibility of words involves a strange dialectic. It is the writer's openness to the ambiguity and uncertainty of any experience (even the experience of determination and certainty) which gives clarity, and thus a kind of certitude, to his writing. He has to abjure words so that, abandoned, they join the "object," the narrated event, which then becomes eloquent with them. The country in my dream was, in fact, literature.

Authenticity in literature does not come from the writer's personal honesty. Authenticity comes from a single faithfulness: that to the ambiguity of experience. Its energy is to be found in how one event leads to another.

The writer should be informed to the maximum about what he is writing. In the modern world, in which thousands of people are dying every hour as a consequence of politics, no writing anywhere can begin to be credible unless it is informed by political awareness and principles. Writers who have neither produce utopian trash. The unpardonable perversity of our *fin de siècle* is that of its innocence.

If a writer is not driven by a desire for the most demanding verbal precision, the true ambiguity of events escapes him. The amorphous does not require accommodation; it simply fills the room (or book) like a gas. He can abjure words only when he has asked too much of them. And at that moment the ambivalent eloquence of the event saves him.

Recently a new book of mine came out in Britain. I received the first copy from the publisher. It was so badly designed, so grubbily laid out, and so carelessly produced that the sight of it, instead of affording a small pleasure, was sad and discouraging—as dirty clothes can sometimes be. My son, Jacob, was with me and we decided to burn it.

We dropped the book into the wood stove which was heating the kitchen. Outside it was snowing. A few minutes later, far from discouraged, we were watching it burn. The lines of print, the black words, turned white, whiter than the paper. Then an entire page became uniformly incandescent, and radiant with energy. The pages burning were like ideal pages being written.

Clark Blaise

To Begin, to Begin

> *Endings are elusive, middles*
> *are nowhere to be found, but*
> *worst of all is to begin, to begin, to begin.*
>
> – Donald Barthelme

The most interesting thing about a story is not its climax or dénouement—both dated terms—nor even its style and characterization. It is its beginning, its first paragraph, often its first sentence. More decisions are made on the basis of the first few sentences of a story than on any other part, and it would seem to me after having read thousands of stories, and beginning hundreds of my own (completing, I should add, only about fifty), that something more than luck accounts for the occasional success of the operation. What I propose is theoretical, yet rooted in the practice of writing and of reading-as-a-writer; good stories *can* start unpromisingly, and well-begun stories can obviously degenerate, but the observation generally holds: the story seeks its beginning, the story many times is its beginning, amplified.

The first sentence of a story is an act of faith—or astonishing bravado. A story screams for attention, as it must, for it breaks a silence. It removes the reader from the everyday (no such imperative attaches to the novel, for which the reader makes his own preparations). It is an act of perfect rhythmic balance, the single crisp gesture, the drop of the baton that gathers a hundred disparate forces into a single note. The first paragraph is a microcosm of the whole, but in a way that only the whole can reveal. If the story begins one sentence too soon, or a sentence too late, the balance is lost, the energy diffused.

It is in the first line that the story reveals its kinship to poetry. Not that the line is necessarily "beautiful," merely that it can exist utterly alone, and that its force draws a series of sentences behind it. The line doesn't have to "grab" or "hook" but it should be striking. Good examples I'll offer further on, but consider first some bad ones:

> *Catelli plunged the dagger deeper in her breast, the dark blood oozed like cherry syrup.* . . .

> *The President's procession would pass under the window at 12:03, and Slattery would be ready.* . . .

Such sentences can be wearying; they strike a note too heavily, too prematurely. They "start" where they should be ending. The advantages wrested will quickly dissipate. On the other hand, the "casual" opening can be just as damaging:

> *When I saw Bob in the cafeteria he asked me to a party at his house that evening and since I wasn't doing much anyway I said sure, I wouldn't mind. Bob's kind of an ass, but his old man's loaded and there's always a lot of grass around* . . . .

Or *in medias res*:

> *"Linda, toast is ready! Linda, are you awake?"*

Now what's wrong with these sentences? The tone is right. The action is promising. They're real, they communicate. Yet no experienced reader would go past them. The last two start too early, (what the critics might call imitative fallacy) and the real story is still imprisoned somewhere in the body.

Lesson One: as in poetry, a good first sentence of prose implies its opposite. If I describe a sunny morning in May (the buds, the wet-winged flies, the warm sun and cool breeze), I am also implying the perishing quality of a morning in May, and a good sensuous description of May sets up the possibility of a May disaster. It is the singular quality of that experience that counts. May follows from the sludge of April and leads to the drone of summer, and in a careful story the action will be mindful of May; it must be. May is unstable, treacherous, beguiling, seductive, and whatever experience follows from a first sentence will be, in essence, a story about the May-ness of human affairs.

What is it, for example, in this sentence from Hugh Hood's story "Falling from Us, Vanishings" that hints so strongly at disappointment:

> *Brandishing a cornucopia of daffodils, flowers for Gloria, in his right hand, Arthur Merlin crossed the dusky oak-panelled foyer of his apartment building and came into the welcoming sunlit avenue.*

The name Merlin? The flourish of the opening clause, associations of the name Gloria? Here is a lover doomed to loneliness, yet a lover who seeks it, despite appearances. Nowhere, however, is it stated. Yet no one, I trust, would miss it.

Such openings are everywhere, at least in authors I admire.

> *The girl stood with her back to the bar, slightly in everyone's way.*
> (Frank Tuohy)

The thick ticking of the tin clock stopped. Mendel, dozing, awoke in fright.
(Bernard Malamud)

I owe the discovery of Ughar to the conjunction of a mirror and an encyclopedia.
(Jorge Luis Borges)

*For a little while when Walter Henderson was nine years old, he thought falling dead
was the very zenith of romance, and so did a number of his friends.* (Richard Yates)

Our group is against the war. But the war goes on. (Donald Barthelme)

The principal dish at dinner had been croquettes made of turnip greens.
(Thomas Mann)

*The sky had been overcast since early morning; it was a still day, not hot, but
tedious, as it usually is when the weather is gray and dull, when clouds have been
hanging over the fields for a long time, and you wait for the rain that does not come.*
(Anton Chekhov)

I wanted terribly to own a dovecote when I was a child. (Isaac Babel—and I
didn't even know what a dovecote was when I started reading.)

At least two or three times a day a story strikes me in the same way, and I read it
through. By then I don't care if the climax and dénouement are elegantly
turned—chances are they will be—I'm reading it because the first paragraph gave
me confidence in the power and vision of the author.

Lesson Two: art wishes to begin, even more than end. Fashionable criticism—
much of it very intelligent—has emphasized the so-called "apocalyptic impulse,"
the desire of fiction to bring the house down. I can understand the interest in
endings—it's easier to explain why things end than how they began, for one
thing. For another, the ending is a contrivance—artistic and believable, yet in
many ways predictable; the beginning, however, is always a mystery. Criticism
likes contrivances, and has little to say of mysteries. My own experience, as a
writer and especially as a "working" reader is closer to genesis than apocalypse,
and I cherish openings more than endings. My memory of any given story is likely
to be its first few lines.

Lesson Three: art wishes to begin *again*. The impulse is not only to finish, it is
to capture. In the stories I admire, there is a sense of a continuum disrupted, then
re-established, and both the disruption and reordering are part of the *beginning* of
a story. The first paragraph tells us, in effect, that "this is how things have always
been," or at least, how they have been until the arrival of the story. It may summarize, as Faulkner does in "That Evening Sun":

> *Monday is no different from any other weekday in Jefferson now. The streets are
> paved now, and the telephone and electric companies are cutting down more and
> more of the shade trees. . . .*

or it may envelop a life in a single sentence, as Bernard Malamud's often do:

> *Manischevitz, a tailor, in his fifty-first year suffered many reverses and indignities.*

Whereupon Malamud embellishes the history, a few sentences more of indignities, aches, curses, until the fateful word that occurs in almost all stories, the simple terrifying adverb:

Then.

Then, which means to the reader: "I am ready." The moment of change is at hand, the story shifts gears and for the first time, *plot* intrudes on poetry. In Malamud's story, a Negro angel suddenly ("then") appears in the tailor's living room, reading a newspaper.

> *Suddenly there appeared. . .*
> *Then one morning. . .*
> *Then one evening she wasn't home to greet him. . .*

Or, in the chilling construction of Flannery O'Connor:

> *. . . there appeared at her door three young men . . . they walked single file, the middle one bent to the side carrying a black pig-shaped valise. . . .*

A pig-shaped valise! This is the apocalypse, if the reader needs one; whatever the plot may reveal a few pages later is really redundant. The mysterious part of the story—that which *is* poetic yet sets it (why not?) above poetry—is over. The rest of the story will be an attempt to draw out the inferences of that earlier upheaval. What is often meant by "climax" in the conventional short story is merely the moment that the *character* realizes the true, the devastating, meaning of "then". He will try to ignore it, he will try to start again (in my story "Eyes" the character thinks he can escape the voyeurs—himself, essentially—by moving to a rougher part of town); he can't of course.

Young readers, especially young readers who want to write, should forget what they're taught of "themes" and all the rest. Stories aren't written that way. Stories are delicate interplays of action and description; "character" is that force which tries to maintain balance between the two. "Action" I equate with danger, fear, apocalypse, life itself; "description" with quiescence, peace, death itself. And the purest part of a story, I think, is from its beginning to its "then." "Then" is the moment of the slightest tremor, the moment when the author is satisfied that all the forces are deployed, the unruffled surface perfectly cast, and the insertion, gross or delicate, can now take place. It is the cracking of the perfect, smug egg of possibility.

On Ending Stories

Stories begin mysteriously, but end deliberately. A writer can't really *will* a story to open, but in the act of writing, the appropriate ending (event, tone, revelation, effect) will probably suggest itself. Most endings arise in the act of writing (a few stories "arrive" so fully formed that the ending is as mysterious as the opening; the writer is rarely so fortunate), and they all share a single purpose: to give a final emphasis to a particular aspect of the story. Literally, it's the writer's last word on the subject: he'd better choose those words carefully. The opening anticipates the conflict. The ending immortalizes the resolution.

There are only two kinds of endings: those that lead you back into the story, and those that lead you—gently, or violently—away. I associate the first kind of ending with de Maupassant and Chekhov, and with modernists who adapted those stories for their own purposes—Hemingway, Joyce, James. Of authors who lead away from the story, who wish to emphasize the artifice of the story, or wish to address the reader directly, I associate dozens of our contemporaries. Impatience with art is as old as faith in art; the choice of ending is the battlefield for those particular feelings.

You are aware of stories that end with a let-down. "That's it? It's over?" you ask yourself. There's a Hemingway story (there are many Hemingway stories like it) that ends, "Bill selected a sandwich from the lunch basket and walked over to have a look at the rods." That's an ending? Norman Levine can fade out in the same way. It's subversive, of course, a subversion of the expected neatness of closure, the gathering up of narrative and thematic threads, the welling-up of music, the frozen gesture that summarizes *the whole meaning of the story*. . . .We realize that the short story initially paid its debts to theatre, or to fable; audiences expected a big pay-off at the end. When it didn't happen, it was revolution, it was art. Chekhov subverted the expectation dramatically: his vision of a static, purposeless society required the destruction of climax and resolution; the lack of an expected ending makes us feel the lack of resolution, vitality, movement. It preserves tension. You can read that last paragraph, then go back in a circular fashion to the first sentence, and *it almost makes sense*. Joyce adapted the Russian vision to the Irish reality, seeing in that paralysis and indecision an opening to unconscious inhibitions. The so-called "epiphanies" that end his stories are merely the revelation of the subconscious exerting mastery over the blighted, conscious lives. Joyce's stories end when the buried life is suddenly manifest. In their separate way, James and Hemingway and a number of other modernists and their followers have done the same: sunk the ending deep in the story's texture, forced the reader to dig up the whole story in order to resolve its tensions. The author is not overtly helping the reader: the story *is* its ending.

I think of these endings as the most disturbing. They hit a glancing blow at the reader, but generally ignore him. By approximating the most casual of voices, they manage (in the hands of masters) to sound most urgent. By ignoring us, they speak to us directly. What remains unresolved and undisclosed becomes inviting and forbidding. They offer us no way out of their bland circularity; thus, they linger with us. For me, they are the saddest stories. (Certainly a mastery of that kind of openness, and that kind of "dropped" ending, accounts for the remarkable power of the American author Ray Carver—a very contemporary Hemingway-like voice.)

Endings that lead us away from the story can do so gently or abruptly. The most traditional kind of ending is the one that serves as a prose equivalent to the theatrical last scene, the rising of music and receding of the camera, as lights go out, one-by-one, and characters fade off together in a figurative sunset. Such endings announce a faith in continuity, order, harmony—no matter what particular horrors may have been investigated in the story. They are sophisticated and traditional ways of updating the old "happily ever after" ending so familiar from the fables. Even if the endings are thematically "sad," they are formally (or cosmically) "happy"; they lead us away from the specific exemplum (the story) to a generalized harmony. They are religious in form, if not content.

How can you detect such an ending? Well, they *sound* like endings. From Eudora Welty we get, "Outside the redbirds were flying and criss-crossing, the sun was in all the bottles on the prisoned trees, and the young peach was shining in the middle of them with the bursting light of spring. . . ." From Margaret Laurence's first collection, "The sea spray was bitter and salt, but to them it was warm, too. They watched on the sand their exaggerated shadows, one squat and bulbous, the other bone-slight and clumsily elongated, pigeon and crane. The shadows walked with hands entwined like children who walk through the dark."

Again, from Laurence's second volume of stories, "It seemed to me now that in some unconscious and totally unrecognised way, Piquette might have been the only one, after all, who had heard the crying of the loons."

Such endings strike me as reassuring, reconciling. A writer with a disturbing, alienated vision probably would not employ such an ending (and, indeed, individual authors hold a number of endings in their repertory; as I said earlier, it all depends on the desired effect from any particular story). These endings, however, are "safe," and they grow out of essentially recollective experiences; they are mellow, and they are the kinds of endings that self-conscious writers have instinctively subverted.

There are other endings to be discussed: they are violent, or playful; metafictional or accusatory. In some stories, I think of the image of a trap-door—Cheever does this well—in which the last paragraph is so *utterly* at odds with the material that has come before that an entirely new, last-minute interpretation is forced onto the whole story. (Why not? Anything that works is legitimate.) Cheever himself seems particularly fond of the ending to "The Country Husband" (he even mentions it in the foreword to his *Collected Stories*). It goes like this:

> "Here, pussy, here, poor pussy!" But the cat gives her a skeptical look and stumbles away in its skirts. The last to come is Jupiter. He prances through the tomato vines, holding in his generous mouth the remains of an evening slipper. Then it is dark; it is a night where kings in golden suits ride elephants over the mountains.

A rhetorical flourish, then—the opposite of the stoical close of Hemingway and friends. An impulsive reaching out; the tension between the dreamer and the fouled dreamland is always present in Cheever (it has its terse side, too; the ending of "O Youth and Beauty!" reads, "The pistol went off and Louise got him in mid-air. She shot him dead.") Cheever's endings never slide off the page, and if they close with the music welling up, it's a full symphonic number.

I must confess to my own fondness for this kind of close—as though the full possibility of the story did not occur to the author (or to me, since I often use it) until the last minute. . . . I have used variants of this ending, choosing to close the nightmare of a Cincinnati school-day with questions about the promised land, and rounding off the tale of generational conflict, sexual discovery, disillusionment (all that stuff that won't let go of me) with a deliberately skewered vision taken from a different time and place, emphasizing the titanic force of connectedness, on the one occasion it had indisputably happened. (As Hemingway said in a different close, "it was a good thing to have in reserve." And as he said in another one, one that also won't let me go, "Seems like when they get started they don't leave a guy nothing.")

There are other endings; the interrogative, ending with an accusing question that throws the whole story up in the air, but aiming it for the reader's heart. There are Judgemental endings, such as Flannery O'Connor's: "The tide of darkness seemed to sweep him back to her, postponing from moment to moment his entry into the world of guilt and sorrow."

All I would leave a good reader with is the injunction to look at endings as urgent, final communications. They are the cords we have bitten (sometimes only raggedly chewed) in the act of giving birth.

Raymond Carver

On Writing

Back in the mid-1960s, I found I was having trouble concentrating my attention on long narrative fiction. For a time I experienced difficulty in trying to read it as well as in attempting to write it. My attention span had gone out on me; I no longer had the patience to try to write novels. It's an involved story, too tedious to talk about here. But I know it has much to do now with why I write poems and short stories. Get in, get out. Don't linger. Go on. It could be that I lost any great ambitions at about the same time, in my late twenties. If I did, I think it was good it happened. Ambition and a little luck are good things for a writer to have going for him. Too much ambition and bad luck, or no luck at all can be killing. There has to be talent.

Some writers have a bunch of talent; I don't know any writers who are without it. But a unique and exact way of looking at things, and finding the right context for expressing that way of looking, that's something else. *The World According to Garp* is, of course, the marvelous world according to John Irving. There is another world according to Flannery O'Connor, and others according to William Faulkner and Ernest Hemingway. There are worlds according to Cheever, Updike, Singer, Stanley Elkin, Ann Beattie, Cynthia Ozick, Donald Barthelme, Mary Robison, William Kittredge, Barry Hannah, Ursula K. Le Guin. Every great or even every very good writer makes the world over according to his own specifications.

It's akin to style, what I'm talking about, but it isn't style alone. It is the writer's particular and unmistakable signature on everything he writes. It is his world and no other. This is one of the things that distinguishes one writer from another. Not talent. There's plenty of that around. But a writer who has some special way of looking at things and who gives artistic expression to that way of looking: that writer may be around for a time.

Isak Dinesen said that she wrote a little every day, without hope and without despair. Someday I'll put that on a three-by-five card and tape it to the wall beside my desk. I have some three-by-five cards on the wall now. "Fundamental accuracy of statement is the ONE sole morality of writing." Ezra Pound. It is not everything by ANY means, but if a writer has "fundamental accuracy of statement" going for him, he's at least on the right track.

I have a three-by-five up there with this fragment of a sentence from a story by Chekhov: " . . . and suddenly everything became clear to him." I find these words filled with wonder and possibility. I love their simple clarity, and the hint of revelation that's implied. There is mystery, too. What has been unclear before? Why is it just now becoming clear? What's happened? Most of all—what now? There are consequences as a result of such sudden awakenings. I feel a sharp sense of relief—and anticipation.

I overheard the writer Geoffrey Woolf say "No cheap tricks" to a group of writing students. That should go on a three-by-five card. I'd amend it a little to "No tricks." Period. I hate tricks. At the first sign of a trick or a gimmick in a piece of fiction, a cheap trick or even an elaborate trick, I tend to look for cover. Tricks are ultimately boring and I get bored easily, which may go along with my not having much of an attention span. But extremely clever chi-chi writing, or just plain tomfoolery writing, puts me to sleep. Writers don't need tricks or gimmicks or even necessarily need to be the smartest fellows on the block. At the risk of appearing foolish, a writer sometimes needs to be able to just stand and gape at this or that thing—a sunset or an old shoe—in absolute and simple amazement.

Some months back, in the *New York Times Book Review*, John Barth said that ten years ago most of the students in his fiction writing seminar were interested in "formal innovation," and this no longer seems to be the case. He's a little worried that writers are going to start writing mom and pop novels in the 1980s. He worries that experimentation may be on the way out, along with liberalism. I get a little nervous if I find myself within earshot of somber discussions about "formal innovation" in fiction writing. Too often "experimentation" is a license to be careless, silly or imitative in the writing. Even worse, a license to try to brutalize or alienate the reader. Too often such writing gives us no news of the world, or else describes a desert landscape and that's all—a few dunes and lizards here and there, but no people; a place unihabited by anything recognizably human, a place of interest only to a few scientific specialists.

It should be noted that real experiment in fiction is original, hard-earned and cause for rejoicing. But someone else's way of looking at things—Barthelme's, for instance—should not be chased after by other writers. It won't work. There is only one Barthelme, and for another writer to try to appropriate Barthelme's peculiar sensibility or *mise en scène* under the rubric of innovation is for that writer to mess around with chaos and disaster and, worse, self-deception. The real experimenters have to Make It New, as Pound urged, and in the process have to find things out for themselves. But if writers haven't taken leave of their senses, they also want to stay in touch with us, they want to carry news from their world to ours.

It's possible, in a poem or a short story, to write about commonplace things and objects using commonplace but precise language, and to endow those things—a chair, a window curtain, a fork, a stone, a woman's earring—with immense, even startling power. It is possible to write a line of seemingly innocuous dialogue and have it send a chill along the reader's spine—the source of artistic delight, as Nabokov would have it. That's the kind of writing that most interests me. I hate sloppy or haphazard writing whether it flies under the banner of experimentation or else is just clumsily rendered realism. In Isaac Babel's wonderful short story, "Guy de Maupassant," the narrator has this to say about the writing of fiction: "No iron can pierce the heart with such force as a period put just at the right place." This too ought to go on a three-by-five.

Evan Connell said once that he knew he was finished with a short story when he found himself going through it and taking out commas and then going through the story again and putting commas back in the same places. I like that way of working on something. I respect that kind of care for what is being done. That's all we have, finally, the words, and they had better be the right ones, with the punctuation in the right places so that they can best say what they are meant to say. If the words are heavy with the writer's own unbridled emotions, or if they are imprecise and inaccurate for some other reason—if the words are in any way blurred—the reader's eyes will slide right over them and nothing will be achieved. The reader's own artistic sense will simply not be engaged. Henry James called this sort of hapless writing "weak specification."

I have friends who've told me they had to hurry a book because they needed the money, their editor or their wife was leaning on them or leaving them—something, some apology for the writing not being very good. "It would have been better if I'd taken the time." I was dumbfounded when I heard a novelist friend say this. I still am, if I think about it, which I don't. It's none of my business. But if the writing can't be made as good as it is within us to make it, then why do it? In the end, the satisfaction of having done our best, and the proof of that labor, is the one thing we can take into the grave. I wanted to say to my friend, for heaven's sake go do something else. There have to be easier and maybe more honest ways to try and earn a living. Or else just do it to the best of your abilities, your talents, and then don't justify or make excuses. Don't complain, don't explain.

In an essay called, simply enough, "Writing Short Stories," Flannery O'Connor talks about writing as an act of discovery. O'Connor says she most often did not know where she was going when she sat down to work on a short story. She says she doubts that many writers know where they are going when they begin something. She uses "Good Country People" as an example of how she put together a short story whose ending she could not even guess at until she was nearly there:

> When I started writing that story, I didn't know there was going to be a Ph.D.
> with a wooden leg in it. I merely found myself one morning writing a description
> of two women I knew something about, and before I realized it, I had equipped
> one of them with a daughter with a wooden leg. I brought in the Bible salesman,

but I had no idea what I was going to do with him. I didn't know he was going to steal that wooden leg until ten or twelve lines before he did it, but when I found out that this was what was going to happen, I realized it was inevitable.

When I read this some years ago it came as a shock that she, or anyone for that matter, wrote stories in this fashion. I thought this was my uncomfortable secret, and I was a little uneasy with it. For sure I thought this way of working on a short story somehow revealed my own shortcomings. I remember being tremendously heartened by reading what she had to say on the subject.

I once sat down to write what turned out to be a pretty good story, though only the first sentence of the story had offered itself to me when I began it. For several days I'd been going around with this sentence in my head. "He was running the vacuum cleaner when the telephone rang." I knew a story was there and that it wanted telling. I felt it in my bones, that a story belonged with that beginning, if I could just have the time to write it. I found the time, an entire day—twelve, fifteen hours even—if I wanted to make use of it. I did, and I sat down in the morning and wrote the first sentence, and other sentences promptly began to attach themselves. I made the story just as I'd make a poem; one line and then the next, and the next. Pretty soon I could see a story, and I knew it was my story, the one I'd been wanting to write.

I like it when there is some feeling of threat or sense of menace in short stories. I think a little menace is fine to have in a story. For one thing it's good for the circulation. There has to be tension, a sense that something is imminent, that certain things are in relentless motion, or else, most often, there simply won't be a story. What creates tension in a piece of fiction is partly the way the concrete words are linked together to make up the visible action of the story. But it's also the things that are left out, that are implied, the landscape just under the smooth (but sometimes broken and unsettled) surface of things.

V. S. Pritchett's definition of a short story is "something glimpsed from the corner of the eye, in passing." Notice the "glimpse" part of this. First the glimpse. Then the glimpse given life, turned into something that illuminates the moment and may, if we're lucky—that word again—have even further-ranging consequences and meaning. The short story writer's task is to invest the glimpse with all that is in his power. He'll bring his intelligence and literary skill to bear (his talent), his sense of proportion and sense of the fitness of things: of how things out there really are and how he sees those things—like no one else sees them. And this is done through the use of clear and specific language, language used so as to bring to life the details that will light up the story for the reader. For the details to be concrete and convey meaning, the language must be accurate and precisely given. The words can be so precise they may even sound flat, but they can still carry; if used right, they can hit all the notes.

ANTON CHEKHOV

The Matter of Technique in Short-Story Writing

You underscore trifles in your writings, and yet you are not a subjective writer by nature; it is an acquired trait in you. To give up this acquired subjectivity is as easy as to take a drink. One needs only to be more honest, to throw oneself overboard everywhere, not to obtrude oneself into the hero of one's own novel, to renounce oneself for at least a half hour. You have a story in which a young wedded couple kiss all through dinner, grieve without cause, weep oceans of tears. Not a single sensible word; nothing but *sentimentality*. And you did not write for the reader. You wrote because *you* like that sort of chatter. But suppose you were to describe the dinner, how they ate, what they ate, what the cook was like, how insipid your hero is, how content with his lazy happiness, how insipid your heroine is, how funny is her love for this napkin-bound, sated, overfed goose,—we all like to see happy, contented people, that is true,—but to describe them, what they said and how many times they kissed is not enough—you need something else: to free yourself from the personal expression that a placid honey-happiness produces upon everybody. . . . Subjectivity is a terrible thing. It is bad in this alone, that it reveals the author's hands and feet. I'll bet that all priests' daughters and clerks' wives who read your works are in love with you, and if you were a German you would get free beer in all the Bierhalle where the German women serve. If it were not for this subjectivity you would be the best of artists. You know how to laugh, sting and ridicule, you possess a rounded style, you have experienced much, have seen so much,—alas! The material is all wasted. . . .

> From a letter to Alexander P. Chekhov, April 1883. Reprinted here from *Letters on the Short Story, the Drama, and Other Literary Topics by Anton Chekhov*, ed. Louis S. Friedland, trans. Constance Garnett (New York: Minton, Balch and Co., 1924), pp. 69–70.

In my opinion a true description of Nature should be very brief and have a character of relevance. Commonplaces such as, "the setting sun bathing in the waves of the darkening sea, poured its purple gold, etc."—"the swallows flying over the surface of the water twittered merrily,"—such commonplaces one ought to abandon. In descriptions of Nature one ought to seize upon the little particulars, grouping them in such a way that, in reading, when you shut your eyes, you get a picture.

For instance, you will get the full effect of a moonlight night if you write that on the mill-dam a little glowing star-point flashed from the neck of a broken bottle, and the round, black shadow of a dog, or a wolf, emerged and ran, etc. Nature becomes animated if you are not squeamish about employing comparisons of her phenomena with ordinary human activities, etc.

In the sphere of psychology, details are also the thing. God preserve us from commonplaces. Best of all is it to avoid depicting the hero's state of mind; you ought to try to make it clear from the hero's actions. It is not necessary to portray many characters. The centre of gravity should be in two persons: him and her. . . .

I write this to you as a reader having a definite taste. Also, in order that you, when writing, may not feel alone. To be alone in work is a hard thing. Better poor criticism than none at all. Is it not so?

From a letter to Alexander P. Chekhov, May 10, 1886. Reprinted here from *Letters*, pp. 70–71.

Oh, you of little faith,—you are interested to know what flaws I found in your "Mignon." Before I point them out I warn you that they have a technical rather than a critico-literary interest. Only a writer can appreciate them, but a reader not at all. Here they are. . . . I think that you, an author scrupulous and untrusting, afraid that your characters will not stand out clearly enough, are too much given to thoroughly detailed description. The result is an overwrought "motleyness" of effect that impairs the general impression.

In order to show how powerfully music can affect one at times, but distrustful of the reader's ability to understand you readily, you zealously set forth the psychology of your Feodrik; the psychology is successful, but then the interval between two such moments as "amari, morire" and the pistol-shot, is dragged out unduly, and the reader, before he reaches the suicide-scene, has had time to recover from the pain of "amari, morire." But you must give the reader no chance to recover: he must always be kept in suspense. These remarks would not apply if "Mignon" were a novel. Long, detailed works have their own peculiar aims, which require a most careful execution regardless of the total impression. But in short stories it is better to say not enough than to say too much, because,— because—I don't know why! . . . .

From a letter to I. L. Shcheglov, January 22, 1888. Reprinted here from *Letters*, p. 106.

. . . You write that the hero of my "Party" is a character worth developing. Good Lord! I am not a senseless brute, you know; I understand that. I understand that I cut the throats of my characters and spoil them, and that I waste good material. . . . On my conscience, I would gladly have spent six months over the "Party"; I like taking things easy, and see no attraction in publishing in white-hot haste. I would willingly, with pleasure, with feeling, in a leisurely way, describe the *whole* of my hero, describe his state of mind while his wife was in labor, his trial, the unpleasant feeling he has after he is acquitted; I would describe the midwife and the doctors having tea in the middle of the night, I would describe the rain. . . . It would give me nothing but pleasure, because I like to take pains and dawdle. But what am I to do? I begin a story on September 10th with the thought that I must finish it by October 5th at the latest; if I don't I shall fail the editor and be left without money. I let myself go at the beginning and write with an easy mind; but by the time I get to the middle I begin to grow timid and to fear that my story will be too long; I have to remember that the *Sieverny Viestnik* has not much money, and that I am one of their expensive contributors. This is why the beginning of my stories is always very promising and looks as though I were starting on a novel, the middle is huddled and timid, and the end is, as in a short sketch, like fireworks. And so in planning a story one is bound to think first about its framework: from a crowd of leading or subordinate characters one selects one person only—wife or husband; one puts him on the canvas and paints him alone, making him prominent, while the others one scatters over the canvas like small coin, and the result is something like the vault of heaven: one big moon and a number of very small stars around it. But the moon is not a success, because it can only be understood if the stars too are intelligible, and the stars are not worked out. And so what I produce is not literature, but something like the patching of Trishka's coat. What am I to do? I don't know, I don't know. I must trust to time which heals all things.

Speaking on my conscience again, I have not yet begun my literary work, though I have received a literary prize. Subjects for five stories and two novels are languishing in my head. One of the novels was thought of long ago, and some of the characters have grown old without managing to get themselves written. In my head there is a whole army of people asking to be let out and waiting for the words of command. All that I have written so far is rubbish in comparison with what I should like to write and should write with rapture. It is all the same to me whether I write "The Party" or "Lights," or a vaudeville or a letter to a friend—it is all dull, spiritless, mechanical, and I get annoyed with critics who attach any importance to "Lights," for instance. I fancy that I deceive them with my work just as I deceive many people with my face, which looks serious or overcheerful. I don't like being successful; the subjects which sit in my head are annoyed, jealous of what has already been written. I am vexed that the rubbish has been done and the good things lie about in the lumber-room like old books. Of course, in thus lamenting I rather exaggerate, and much of what I say is only my fancy, but there is something of the truth in it, a good big part of it. What do I call good? The images which seem best to me, which I love and jealously guard lest I spend and spoil them for the sake of some "Party" written against time. . . . If my love is mistaken, I am wrong, but then it may not be mistaken! I am either a fool and a conceited fellow or I really am an organism capable of being a good writer. All that I now write displeases and bores me, but what sits in my head interests, excites, and moves me—from which I conclude that everybody does the wrong thing and I alone know the secret of doing the right one. Most likely all writers think that. But the devil himself would break his neck at these problems. . . .

From a letter to A. S. Souvorin, October 27, 1888. Reprinted here from *Letters*, pp. 11-13.

You abuse me for objectivity, calling it indifference to good and evil, lack of ideals and ideas, and so on. You would have me, when I describe horse-thieves, say: "Stealing horses is an evil." But that has been known for ages without my saying so. Let the jury judge them; it's my job simply to show what sort of people they are. I write: you are dealing with horse-thieves, so let me tell you that they are not beggars but well-fed people, that they are people of a special cult, and that horse-stealing is not simply theft but a passion. Of course it would be pleasant to combine art with a sermon, but for me personally it is extremely difficult and almost impossible, owing to the conditions of technique. You see, to depict horse-thieves in seven hundred lines I must all the time speak and think in their tone and feel in their spirit, otherwise, if I introduce subjectivity, the image becomes blurred and the story will not be as compact as all short stories ought to be. When I write, I reckon entirely upon the reader to add for himself the subjective elements that are lacking in the story.

> From a letter to A. S. Souvorin, April 1, 1890. Reprinted here from *Letters*, p. 64.

I read your story with great pleasure. Your hand is acquiring firmness, and your style is improving. I like the whole story, except the ending, which appears to me to lack force. . . . But this is a matter of taste and not so important. If one is to talk about flaws one should not confine oneself to details. You have a defect and a very serious one. In my opinion it is this: you do not polish your things, and hence they seem frequently to be florid and overloaded. Your works lack the compactness that makes short things alive. There is skill in your stories; there is talent, literary sense, but very slight art. You put your characters together in the right way, but not plastically. You are either too lazy or you do not wish to slough off at one stroke all that is useless. To make a face from marble means to remove from the slab everything that is not the face. Do I make myself clear? Do you understand? There are two or three awkward expressions which I underlined.

> From a letter to E. M. Sh——, November 17, 1895. Reprinted here from *Letters*, pp. 82–83.

. . . More advice: when reading the proofs, cross out a host of concrete nouns and other words. You have so many such nouns that the reader's mind finds it a task to concentrate on them, and he soon grows tired. You understand it at once when I say, "The man sat on the grass;" you understand it because it is clear and makes no demands on the attention. On the other hand, it is not easily understood, and it is difficult for the mind, if I write, "A tall, narrow-chested, middle-sized man, with a red beard, sat on the green grass, already trampled by pedestrians, sat silently, shyly, and timidly looked about him." That is not immediately grasped by the mind, whereas good writing should be grasped at once,—in a second. . . .

> From a letter to Maxim Gorky, September 3, 1899. Reprinted here from *Letters*, p. 88.

Joseph Conrad

The Creative Process

1. A Romantic Realist

I have not sought for special imaginative freedom or a larger play of fancy in my choice of characters and subjects. The nature of the knowledge, suggestions or hints used in my imaginative work has depended directly on the conditions of my active life. It depended more on contacts, and very slight contacts at that, than on actual experience; because my life as a matter of fact was far from being adventurous in itself. Even now when I look back on it with a certain regret (who would not regret his youth?) and positive affection, its colouring wears the sober hue of hard work and exacting calls of duty, things which in themselves are not much charged with a feeling of romance. If these things appeal strongly to me even in retrospect it is, I suppose, because the romantic feeling of reality was in me an inborn faculty. This in itself may be a curse but when disciplined by a sense of personal responsibility and a recognition of the hard facts of existence shared with the rest of mankind becomes but a point of view from which the very shadows of life appear endowed with an internal glow. And such romanticism is not a sin. It is none the worse for the knowledge of truth. It only tries to make the best of it, hard as it may be; and in this hardness discovers a certain aspect of beauty.

I am speaking here of romanticism in relation to life, not of romanticism in relation to imaginative literature, which, in its early days, was associated simply with medieval subjects sought for in a remote past. My subjects are not medieval and I have a natural right to them because my past is very much my own. If their course lie out of the beaten path of organized social life, it is, perhaps, because I myself did in a short break away from it early in obedience to an impulse which must have been very genuine since it has sustained me through all the dangers of disillusion. But that origin of my literary work was very far from giving a larger scope to my imagination. On the contrary, the mere fact of dealing with matters outside the general run of everyday experience laid me under the obligation of a more scrupulous fidelity to the truth of my own sensations. The problem was to make unfamiliar things credible. To do that I had to create for them, to reproduce for them, to envelop them in their proper atmosphere of actuality. This was the hardest task of all and the most important, in view of that conscientious rendering of truth in thought and fact which has always been my aim.

Preface to Within the Tides (1915)

2. IMAGINED LIFE CLEARER THAN REALITY

What is it that Novalis says? 'It is certain my conviction gains infinitely the moment another soul will believe in it.' And what is a novel if not a conviction of our fellow-men's existence strong enough to take upon itself a form of imagined life clearer than reality and whose accumulated verisimilitude of selected episodes puts to shame the pride of documentary history?

A Personal Record (1912), Chapter 1

3. CHERISHING UNDYING HOPE

It must not be supposed that I claim for the artist in fiction the freedom of moral Nihilism. I would require from him many acts of faith of which the first would be the cherishing of an undying hope; and hope, it will not be contested, implies all the piety of effort and renunciation. It is the God-sent form of trust in the magic force and inspiration belonging to the life of this earth. We are inclined to forget that the way of excellence is in intellectual, as distinguished from emotional, humility. What one feels so hopelessly barren in declared pessimism is just its arrogance. It seems as if the discovery made by many men at various times that there is much evil in the world were a source of proud and unholy joy unto some of the modern writers. That frame of mind is not the proper one in which to approach seriously the art of fiction. It gives an author—goodness only knows why—an elated sense of his own superiority. And there is nothing more danger-ous than such an elation to that absolute loyalty towards his feelings and sensa-tions an author should keep hold of in his most exalted moments of creation.

To be hopeful in an artistic sense it is not necessary to think that the world is good. It is enough to believe that there is no impossibility of its being made so.

'Books' (1905); reprinted in *Notes on Life and Letters* (1921)

4. RESCUE WORK

Action in its essence, the creative art of a writer of fiction may be compared to rescue work carried out in darkness against cross gusts of wind swaying the action of a great multitude. It is rescue work, this snatching of vanishing phrases of tur-bulence, disguised in fair words, out of the native obscurity into a light where the struggling forms may be seen, seized upon, endowed with the only possible form of permanence in this world of relative values—the permanence of memory. And the multitude feels it obscurely too; since the demand of the individual to the artist is, in effect, the cry 'Take me out of myself!' meaning really, out of my per-ishable activity into the light of imperishable consciousness.

'Henry James, An Appreciation' (1905); reprinted in *Notes on Life and Letters* (1921)

5. THE NOVELIST'S MOST PRECIOUS POSSESSION

Liberty of the imagination should be the most precious possession of a novelist. To try voluntarily to discover the fettering dogmas of some romantic, realistic, or naturalistic creed in the free work of its own inspiration, is a trick worthy of human perverseness which, after inventing an absurdity, endeavours to find for it a pedigree of distinguished ancestors. It is a weakness of inferior minds when it is not the cunning device of those who, uncertain of their talent, would seek to add lustre to it by the authority of a school. Such, for instance, are those who have proclaimed Stendhal for a prophet of Naturalism. But Stendhal himself would have accepted no limitation of his freedom. Stendhal's mind was of the first order. His spirit above must be raging with a peculiarly Stendhalesque scorn and indignation. For the truth is that more than one kind of intellectual cowardice hides behind the literary formulas. And Stendhal was pre-eminently courageous. He wrote his two great novels, which so few people have read, in a spirit of fearless liberty.

'Books' (1905); reprinted in *Notes on Life and Letters* (1921)

6. ART AND TEMPERAMENT

My own impression is that what he really meant was that my manner of telling, perfectly devoid of familiarity as between author and reader, aimed essentially at the intimacy of a personal communication, without any thought for other effects. As a matter of fact, the thought for effects is there all the same (often at the cost of mere directness of narrative), and can be directed in my unconventional grouping and perspective, which are purely temperamental and wherein all my 'art' consists.

Letter to Richard Curle (14 July 1913), *Life and Letters* (1927) ed. G. Jean-Aubry

7. THE CRAFT OF WRITING

You do not leave enough to the imagination. I do not mean as to facts—the facts cannot be too explicitly stated; I am alluding simply to the phrasing. True, a man who knows so much (without taking into account the manner in which his knowledge was acquired) may well spare himself the trouble of meditating over the words, only that words, groups of words, words standing alone, are symbols of life, have the power in their sound or their aspect to present the very thing you wish to hold up before the mental vision of your readers. The things 'as they are' exist in words; therefore words should be handled with care lest the picture, the image of truth abiding in facts, should become distorted—or blurred.

These are the considerations for a mere craftsman—you may say; and you may also conceivably say that I have nothing else to trouble my head about. However the *whole* of the truth lies in the presentation; therefore the expression should be studied in the interest of veracity. This is the only morality of *art* apart from *subject*.

I have travelled a good way from my original remark—not enough left to the imagination in the phrasing. I beg leave to illustrate my meaning from extracts. . . . 'When the whole horror of his position forced itself with an agony

of apprehension upon his frightened mind, Pa'Tua for a space lost his reason.' . . .
In this sentence the reader is borne down by the full expression. The words: *with
an agony of apprehension* completely destroy the effect—therefore interfere with
the truth of the statement. The word *frightened* is fatal. It seems as if it had been
written without any thought at all. It takes away all sense of reality—for if you
read the sentence *in its place on the page* you will see that the word *'frightened'* (or
indeed any word of that sort) is inadequate to express the true state of that man's
mind. No word is adequate. The imagination of the reader should be left free to
arouse his feeling.

. . . 'When the whole horror of his position forced itself upon his mind, Pa'Tua
for a space lost his reason . . . ' This is truth; this it is which, thus stated, carries
conviction because it is a *picture* of a mental state. And look how finely it goes on
with a perfectly legitimate effect . . . 'He screamed aloud, and the hollow of the
rocks took up his cries' . . . It is magnificent! It is suggestive. It is truth effectively
stated. But 'and hurled them back to him mockingly' is nothing at all. It is a
phrase anybody can write to fit any sort of situation; it is the sort of thing I write
twenty times a day and (with the fear of overtaking fate behind me) spend half
my nights in taking out of my work—upon which depends the daily bread of the
house (literally—from day to day); not to mention (I dare hardly think of it) the
future of my child, of those nearest and dearest to me, between whom and the
bleakest want there is only my pen—as long as life lasts. And I can sell all I
write—as much as I can.

This is said to make it manifest that I practise the faith which I take the liberty
to preach. . . .

Letter to Sir Hugh Clifford (9 October 1899), Life and Letters (1927)

8. To Make You See

. . . it is only through an unremitting never-discouraged care for the shape and
ring of sentences that an approach can be made to plasticity, to colour, and that
the light of magic suggestiveness may be brought to play for an evanescent instant
over the commonplace surface of words: of the old, old words, worn thin, defaced
by ages of careless usage.

The sincere endeavour to accomplish that creative task, to go as far on that road
as his strength will carry him, to go undeterred by faltering, weariness, or reproach,
is the only valid justification for the worker in prose. And if his conscience is clear,
his answer to those who, in the fullness of a wisdom which looks for immediate
profit, demand specifically to be edified, consoled, amused; who demand to be
promptly improved, or encouraged, or frightened, or shocked, or charmed, must run
thus: My task which I am trying to achieve is, by the power of the written word to
make you hear, to make you feel—it is, before all, to make you *see*. That—and no
more, and it is everything. If I succeed, you shall find there according to your
deserts: encouragement, consolation, fear, charm—all you demand—and, perhaps,
also that glimpse of truth for which you have forgotten to ask.

Preface to The Nigger of the Narcissus (1897)

Mavis Gallant

What Is Style?

I do not reread my own work unless I have to; I fancy no writer does. The reason why, probably, is that during the making of the story every line has been read and rewritten and read again to the point of glut. I am unable to "see" the style of the two stories presented here, and would not recognize its characteristics if they were pointed out to me. Once too close, the stories are already too distant. If I read a passage aloud, I am conscious of a prose rhythm easy for me to follow, that must be near to the way I think and speak. It seems to be my only link with a finished work.

The manner of writing, the thread spun out of the story itself, may with time have grown instinctive. I know that the thread must hold from beginning to end, and that I would like it to be invisible. Rereading "Baum, Gabriel" and "His Mother," all I can relate is that they are about loss and bewilderment, that I cannot imagine the people described living with any degree of willingness anywhere but in a city—in spite of Gabriel's imaginings about country life—and that a café as a home more congenial than home appears in both. The atmosphere, particularized, is of a fading world, though such a thing was far from my mind when the stories were written. It may be that the Europe of the nineteen-seventies already secreted the first dangerous sign of nostalgia, like a pervasive mist: I cannot say. And it is not what I have been asked to discuss.

Leaving aside the one analysis closed to me, of my own writing, let me say what style is *not*: it is not a last-minute addition to prose, a charming and universal slipcover, a coat of paint used to mask the failings of a structure. Style is inseparable from structure, part of the conformation of whatever the author has to say. What he says—this is what fiction is about—is that something is taking place and that nothing lasts. Against the sustained tick of a watch, fiction takes the measure of a life, a season, a look exchanged, the turning point, desire as brief as a dream, the grief and terror that after childhood we cease to express. The life, the look, the grief are without permanence. The watch continues to tick where the story stops.

A loose, a wavering, a slipshod, an affected, a false way of transmitting even a fragment of this leaves the reader suspicious: What is this too elaborate or too simple language hiding? What is the author trying to disguise? Probably he doesn't know. He has shown the works of the watch instead of its message. He may be untalented, just as he may be a gifted author who for some deeply private reason (doubt, panic, the pressures of a life unsuited to writing) has taken to rearranging the works in increasingly meaningless patterns. All this is to say that content, meaning, intention and form must make up a whole, and must above all have a reason to be.

There are rules of style. By applying them doggedly any literate, ambitious and determined person should be able to write like Somerset Maugham. Maugham was conscious of his limitations and deserves appreciation on that account: "I knew that

I had no lyrical quality, I had a small vocabulary . . . I had little gift for metaphors; the original striking simile seldom occurred to me. Poetic flights and the great imaginative sweep were beyond my powers." He decided, sensibly, to write "as well as my natural defects allowed" and to aim at "lucidity, simplicity and euphony." The chance that some other indispensable quality had been overlooked must have been blanketed by a lifetime of celebrity. Now, of course, first principles are there to be heeded or, at the least, considered with care; but no guided tour of literature, no commitment to the right formula or to good taste (which is changeable anyway) can provide, let alone supplant, the inborn vitality and tension of living prose.

Like every other form of art, literature is no more and nothing less than a matter of life and death. The only question worth asking about a story—or a poem, or a piece of sculpture, or a new concert hall—is, "Is it dead or alive?" If a work of the imagination needs to be coaxed into life, it is better scrapped and forgotten. Working to rule, trying to make a barely breathing work of fiction simpler and more lucid and more euphonious merely injects into the desperate author's voice a tone of suppressed hysteria, the result of what E. M. Forster called "confusing order with orders." And then, how reliable are the rules? Listen to Pablo Picasso's rejection of a fellow-artist: "He looks up at the sky and says, 'Ah, the sky is blue,' and he paints a blue sky. Then he takes another look and says, 'The sky is mauve, too,' and he adds some mauve. The next time he looks he notices a trace of pink, and he adds a little pink." It sounds a proper mess, but Picasso was talking about Pierre Bonnard. As soon as we learn the name, the blues, mauves and pinks acquire a meaning, a reason to be. Picasso was right, but only in theory. In the end, everything depends on the artist himself.

Style in writing, as in painting is the author's thumbprint, his mark. I do not mean that it establishes him as finer or greater than other writers, though that can happen too. I am thinking now of prose style as a writer's armorial bearings, his name and address. In a privately printed and libellous pamphlet, Colette's first husband, Willy, who had fraudulently signed her early novels, tried to prove she had gone on to plagiarize and plunder different things he had written. As evidence he offered random sentences from work he was supposed to have influenced or inspired. Nothing, from his point of view, could have been more self-defeating. Colette's manner, robust and personal, seems to leap from the page. Willy believed he had taught Colette "everything," and it may have been true—"everything," that is, except her instinct for language, her talent for perceiving the movement of life and a faculty for describing it. He was bound to have influenced her writing; it couldn't be helped. But by the time he chose to print a broadside on the subject, his influence had been absorbed, transmuted and—most humbling for the teacher—had left no visible trace.

There is no such thing as a writer who has escaped being influenced. I have never heard a professional writer of any quality or standing talk about "pure" style, or say he would not read this or that for fear of corrupting or affecting his own; but I have heard it from would-be writers and amateurs. Corruption—if that is the word—sets in from the moment a child learns to speak and to hear language used and misused. A young person who does not read, and read widely, will never write anything—at least, nothing of interest. From time to time, in France, a novel is published purporting to come from a shepherd whose only influence has been the baaing of lambs on some God-forsaken slope of the Pyrenees. His artless and untampered-with mode of expression arouses the hope that there will be many more like him, but as a rule he is never heard from again. For "influences" I would be inclined to substitute "acquisitions." What they consist of, and amount to, are affected by taste and environment, preferences and upbringing (even, and sometimes particularly, when the latter has been rejected), instinctive selection. The beginning writer has to choose, tear to pieces, spit out, chew up and assimilate as naturally as a young animal—as naturally and as ruthlessly. Style cannot be copied, except by the untalented. It is, finally, the distillation of a lifetime of reading and listening, of selection and rejection. But if it is not a true voice, it is nothing.

Nadine Gordimer

The Flash of Fireflies

Why is it that while the death of the novel is good for post-mortem at least once a year, the short story lives on unmolested? It cannot be because—to borrow their own jargon—literary critics regard it as merely a minor art form. Most of them, if pressed, would express the view that it is a highly specialized and skilful form, closer to poetry, etc. But they would have to be pressed; otherwise they wouldn't bother to discuss it at all. When Chekhov crops up, it is as a playwright, and Katherine Mansfield is a period personality from the Lady Chatterley set. Yet no one suggests that we are practicing a dead art form. And, like a child suffering from healthy neglect, the short story survives.

"To say that no one now much likes novels is to exaggerate very little. The large public which used to find pleasure in prose fictions prefer movies, television, journalism, and books of 'fact,'" Gore Vidal wrote recently (*Encounter*, December, 1967). If the cinema and television have taken over so much of the novel's territory, just as photography forced painting into wastelands which may or may not be made to bloom, hasn't the short story been overrun, too? This symposium is shoptalk and it would seem unnecessary for us to go over the old definitions of where and how the short story differs from the novel, but the answer to the question must lie somewhere here. Both novel and story use the same material: human experience. Both have the same aim: to communicate it. Both use the same medium: the written word. There is a general and recurrent dissatisfaction with the novel as a means of netting ultimate reality—another term for the quality of human life—and inevitably there is even a tendency to blame the tools; words have become hopelessly blunted by overuse, dinned to death by admen, and, above all, debased by political creeds that have twisted and changed their meaning. Various ways out have been sought. In England, a return to classicism in technique and a turning to the exoticism of sexual aberration and physical and mental abnormality as an extension of human experience and therefore of subject matter; in Germany and America, a splendid abandon in making a virtue of the vice of the novel's inherent clumsiness by stuffing it not with nineteenth-century horsehair narrative but twentieth-century anecdotal-analytical plastic foam; in France, the "laboratory novel" struggling to get away from the anthropocentric curse of the form and the illusion of depth of the psychological novel, and landing up very much where Virginia Woolf was, years ago, staring at the mark on the wall. Burroughs has invented the reader-participation novel. For the diseased word, George Steiner has even suggested silence.

If the short story is alive while the novel is dead, the reason must lie in approach and method. The short story, as a form and as a *kind of creative vision*, must be better equipped to attempt the capture of ultimate reality at a time when (whichever way you choose to see it) we are drawing nearer to the mystery of life or are losing ourselves in a bellowing wilderness of mirrors, as the nature of that reality becomes more fully understood or more bewilderingly concealed by the discoveries of science and the proliferation of communication media outside the printed word.

Certainly the short story always has been more flexible and open to experiment than the novel. Short-story writers always have been the subject at the same time to both a stricter technical discipline and a wider freedom than the novelist. Short-story writers have known—and solved by nature of their choice of form—what novelists seem to have discovered in despair only now: the strongest convention of the novel, prolonged coherence of tone, to which even the most experimental of novels must confirm unless it is to fall apart, is false to the nature of whatever can be grasped of human reality. How shall I put it? Each of us has a thousand lives and a novel gives a character only one. *For the sake of the form.* The novelist may juggle about with chronology and throw narrative overboard; all the time his characters have the reader by the hand, there is a consistency of relationship throughout the experience that cannot and does not convey the quality of human life, where contact is more like the flash of fireflies, in and out, now here, now there, in darkness. Short-story writers see by the light of the flash; theirs is the art of the only thing one can be sure of—the present moment. Ideally, they have learned to do without explanation of what went before, and what happens beyond this point. How the characters will appear, think, behave, comprehend, tomorrow or at any other time in their lives, is irrelevant. A discrete moment of truth is aimed at—not *the* moment of truth, because the short story doesn't deal in cumulatives.

The problem of how best to take hold of ultimate reality, from the technical and stylistic point of view, is one that the short-story writer is accustomed to solving specifically in relation to an area—event, mental state, mood, appearance—which is heightenedly manifest in a single situation. Take fantasy for an example. Writers are becoming more and more aware of the waviness of the line that separates fantasy from the so-called rational in human perception. It is recognized that fantasy is no more than a shift in angle; to put it another way, the rational is simply another, the most obvious, kind of fantasy. Writers turn to the less obvious fantasy as a wider lens on ultimate reality. But this fantasy is something that changes, merges, emerges, disappears as a pattern does viewed through the bottom of a glass. It is true for the moment when one looks down through the glass; but the same vision does not transform everything one sees, consistently throughout one's whole consciousness. Fantasy in the hands of short-story writers is so much more success-ful than when in the hands of novelists because it is necessary for it to hold good only for the brief illumination of the situation it dominates. In the series of devel-oping situations of the novel the sustainment of the tone of fantasy becomes a high-pitched ringing in the reader's ears. How many fantasy novels achieve what they set out to do: convey the shift and change, to and fro, beneath, above, and around the world of appearances? The short story recognizes that full comprehen-sion of a particular kind in the reader, like full apprehension of a particular kind in the writer, is something of limited duration. The short story is a fragmented and restless form, a matter of hit or miss, and it is perhaps for this reason that it suits modern consciousness—which seems best expressed as flashes of fearful insight alternating with near-hypnotic states of indifference.

These are technical and stylistic considerations. Marxist criticism sees the sur-vival of an art form in relation to social change. What about the socio-political implications of the short story's survival? George Lukács has said that the novel is a bourgeois art form whose enjoyment presupposes leisure and privacy. It implies the living room, the armchair, the table lamp, just as epic implies the illiterates round the tribal story-teller, and Shakespeare implies the two audiences—that of the people and that of the court—of a feudal age. From this point of view the novel marks the apogee of an exclusive, individualist culture; the nearest it ever got to a popular art form (in the sense of bringing people together in direct partic-ipation in an intellectually stimulating experience) was the nineteenth-century custom of reading novels aloud to the family. Here again it would seem that the short story shares the same disadvantages as the novel. It is an art form solitary in communication; yet another sign of the increasing loneliness and isolation of the individual in a competitive society. You cannot enjoy the experience of a short story unless you have certain minimum conditions of privacy in which to read it; and these conditions are those of middle-class life. But of course, a short story, by reason of its length and its *completeness*, totally contained in the brief time you give to it, depends less than the novel upon the classic conditions of middle-class life, and perhaps corresponds to the breakup of that life which is taking place. In that case, although the story may outlive the novel, it may become obsolete when the period of disintegration is replaced by new social forms and the art forms that express them. One doesn't have to embrace the dreariness of conventional "social realism" in literature to grant this. That our age is threshing about desperately for a way out of individual human isolation, and that our present art forms are not adequate to it, it is obvious to see in all the tatty dressing-up games, from McLuhan's theories to pop art, in which we seek a substitute for them.

JOHN HAWKES

From *An Interview*
20 *March* 1964

For many critics, your books show, if not the direct influence of, then affinities with, European works—perhaps more so than do most American novels. This connection may be a tie to a kind of internationalism noticed in the 'twenties, 'thirties, and 'forties, but less common now. Do you think American writers can learn anything from European writers, or is that period over?

Your word "affinities" seems to me more to the point than "influences." Certainly it's true that in many ways my own fiction appears to be more European than American. But the fact is that I've never been influenced by European writing. The similarities between my work and European work—those qualities I may have in common with, say, Kafka and Robbe-Grillet and Günter Grass—come about purely because of some kind of imaginative underworld that must be shared by Americans and Europeans alike. I don't think writers actually learn from each other. But obviously we tend to appreciate in European writers what we sometimes fail to recognize in our own writers—that absolute need to create from the imagination a totally new and necessary fictional landscape or visionary world.

You mentioned Céline earlier this morning.

Yes, Céline is an extraordinary writer, and his *Journey to the End of the Night* is a great novel. His comic appetite for invented calamities suggests the same truth we find in the comic brutalities of the early Spanish picaresque writers, which is where I locate the beginnings of the kind of fiction that interests me most.

Let's turn to the older writers in the United States. For example, James, Hemingway, Fitzgerald, or Faulkner. Do any of these writers seem particularly significant to you at the present time—do they seem more or less significant than they did in the past?

As a writer I'm concerned with innovation in the novel, and obviously I'm committed to nightmare, violence, meaningful distortion, to the whole panorama of dislocation and desolation in human experience. But as a man—as reader and teacher—I think of myself as conventional. I remember that after Faulkner's death, which followed so closely on the death of Hemingway, there was a kind of journalistic polling of critics and reviewers in an effort to assess our position and re-assess our writers in terms of influence and reputation. I think that at the time there was a general inclination to unseat the accepted great contemporary writers in America, to relegate Faulkner, Hemingway, and Fitzgerald to history, and instead to acclaim, say, Norman Mailer and James Baldwin. And we've also seen at least one recent effort to debunk the achievement and pertinency of Henry James. I myself deplore these efforts and judgments. James gave us all the beauties, delicacies, psychic complications of a kind of bestial sensibility; Fitzgerald's handling of dream and nightmare seems to me full of rare light and novelistic skill; Faulkner produced a kind of soaring arc of language and always gave us the enormous pleasure of confronting the impossible at the very moment it was turning into the probable. I think of all these achievements as the constants of great fictional ability. I think these writers will always survive shifts in literary taste and changing conditions in the country, and will always in a sense remain unequaled. Incidentally, after my reading last night a man asked me if there was anything of Faulkner or Faulkner's influence in my work. He was thinking of the passage from *Second Skin*, and I answered that I didn't see much Faulkner in that book. But as a matter of fact, while I was reading from *The Lime Twig* last night, I became quite conscious again of echoes of a Faulknerian use of inner consciousness and expanded prose rhythms. The echoes are undeniable, I think— Faulkner is still the American writer I most admire—though at this point I ought to insist again that in general my world is my own, and that my language, attitudes and conceptions are unique.

Such a view, then, would link you to the experimental writers of the avant-garde. As you know, the "avant-garde" was a rather popular concept about twenty years ago, but seems to be less so now. Do you have any views on the writer as experimenter?

Of course I think of myself as an experimental writer. But it's unfortunate that the term "experimental" has been used so often by reviewers as a pejorative label intended to dismiss as eccentric or private or excessively difficult the work in question. My own fiction is not merely eccentric or private and is not nearly so difficult as it has been made out to be. I should think that every writer, no matter what kind of fiction writer he may be or may aspire to be, writes in order to create the future. Every fiction of any value has about it something new. At any rate, the function of the true innovator or specifically experimental writer is to keep prose alive and constantly to test in the sharpest way possible the range of our human sympathies and constantly to destroy mere surface morality. What else were we trying to get at?

The concept of the avant-garde.

America has never had what we think of as the avant-garde. Gertrude Stein, Djuna Barnes, whose novel *Nightwood* I admire enormously, Henry Miller—no doubt these are experimental writers. But I don't think we've ever had in this country anything like the literary community of the French Surrealists or the present day French anti-novelists. And I'm not sure such a community would be desirable. On the other hand, in the past few years we've probably heard more than ever before about an existing avant-garde in America—we've witnessed the initial community of Beat writers, we're witnessing now what we might call the secondary community of Beat writers, recently many of us have defended *The Tropic of Cancer*. But I confess I find no danger, no true sense of threat, no possibility of sharp artistic upheaval in this essentially topical and jargonistic rebellion. Henry Miller's view of experience is better than most, Edward Dahlberg is a remarkably gifted writer who has still not received full recognition, I for one appreciate Norman Mailer's pugilistic stance. But none of this has much to do with the novel, and so far Beat activity in general seems to have resulted in sentimentality or dead language. My own concept of "avant-garde" has to do with something constant which we find running through prose fiction from Quevedo, the Spanish picaresque writer, and Thomas Nashe at the beginnings of the English novel, down through Lautréamont, Céline, Nathanael West, Flannery O'Connor, James Purdy, Joseph Heller, myself. This constant is a quality of coldness, detachment, ruthless determination to face up to the enormities of ugliness and potential failure within ourselves and in the world around us, and to bring to this exposure a savage or saving comic spirit and the saving beauties of language. The need is to maintain the truth of the fractured picture; to expose, ridicule, attack, but always to create and to throw into new light our potential for violence and absurdity as well as for graceful action. I don't like soft, loose prose or fiction which tries to cope too directly with life itself or is based indulgently on personal experience. On the other hand, we ought to respect resistance to commonplace authority wherever we find it, and this attitude at least is evident in the Beat world. But I suppose I regret so much attention being spent on the essentially flatulent products of a popular cult. A writer who truly and greatly sustains us is Nabokov.

I think many Beat writers have a kind of popularity. Whom do you think of as your audience, and what sort are you looking for?

The question of audience makes me uncomfortable. I write out of isolation, and struggle only with the problems of the work itself. I've never been able to look for an audience. And yet after a number of years spent in relative obscurity, I'm pleased that my books are gaining readers. I think that works of the imagination are particularly important now to younger readers, and I think it's clear that my fiction is being studied in colleges and universities. Apparently it's being read even by New York high school students. But at any rate I care about reaching all readers who are interested in the necessity and limitless possibilities of prose fiction, and I think there must be a good many of them. I'm trying to write about large issues of human torments and aspirations, and I'm convinced that considerable numbers of people in this country must have imaginative needs quite similar to mine.

One kind of reader is the critic. At its best, do you find any particular kind of criticism helpful—criticism appearing in larger circulation magazines or in smaller magazines? Does criticism mean anything at all to you as a writer?

I think the critic's function is mainly in terms of the reader. The critic makes the work more accessible, meaningful, and hence essential to the reader. I happen not to share the contempt for literary or academic criticism which appears to be current now. The critical efforts of the magazine *Critique*, for instance, which devoted one of its special issues to John Barth's novels and mine, are enormously helpful and gratifying. Generally I think I've benefited from criticism, though over the years what I've gained specifically from the critical judgment of a friend like Albert Guerard is almost too great to mention. I won't pretend not to be affected by newspaper reviews—but despite some of the silences and some of the more imperceptive or hostile responses, I have the impression that reviewers and readers alike in America are becoming increasingly receptive to original work. Certainly I've fared far better in America than in England where in one of the few sympathetic notices of my work to appear in that country I was described as a "deadly hawk moth."

What do you think of the Sunday New York Times *book review section?*

The problem is so old I'm tempted to call it one of our dead horses. But I don't read the *New York Times* book review section (or any other book review section for that matter), and I could be very wrong. I think the scene is changing momentarily— perhaps the *New York Times* book section will become serious one of these days and give the lie to us all. It would be a welcome irony. It may sound paradoxical, but if they ever gave my own work the attention it deserves I'd be deeply moved.

An aspect of your work that I have always appreciated, which I think many other critics have not, is the comic element. You have referred several times to comic writing—would you like to say something more about what you regard as the importance of comedy in your work?

I'm grateful to you for viewing my fiction as comic. Men like Guerard have written about the wit and black humor in my novels, but I think you're right that reviewers in general have concentrated on the grotesque and nightmarish qualities of my work, have made me out to be a somber writer dealing only with pain, perversion, and despair. Comedy puts all this into a very different perspective, I think. Of course I don't mean to apologize for the disturbing nature of my fiction by calling it comic, and certainly don't mean to minimize the terror with which this writing confronts the reader—my aim has always been the opposite, never to let the reader (or myself) off the hook, so to speak, never to let him think that the picture is any less black than it is or that there is any easy way out of the nightmare of human existence. But though I'd be the first to admit to sadistic impulses in the creative process, I must say that my writing is not mere indulgence in violence or derangement, is hardly intended simply to shock. As I say, comedy, which is often closely related to poetic uses of language, is what makes the difference for me. I think that the comic method functions in several ways: on the one hand it serves to create sympathy, compassion, and on the other it's a means for judging human failings as severely as possible; it's a way of exposing evil (one of the pure words I mean to preserve) and of persuading the reader that even he may not be exempt from evil; and of course comic distortion tells us that anything is possible and hence expands the limits of our imaginations. Comic vision always suggests futurity, I think, always suggests a certain hope in the limitless energies of life itself. In *Second Skin* I tried consciously to write a novel that couldn't be mistaken for anything but a comic novel. I wanted to expose clearly what I thought was central to my fictional efforts but had been generally overlooked in *The Cannibal*, *The Lime Twig*, *The Beetle Leg*. Obviously Faulkner was one of the greatest of all comic writers—Nabokov is a living example of comic genius.

Do you have any comments on Flannery O'Connor as a comic writer?

For pure, devastating, comic brilliance and originality she stands quite alone in America—except perhaps for Nathanael West. Both of these writers maintain incredible distance in their work, both explode the reality around us into meaningful new patterns, both treat disability and inadequacy and hypocrisy with brutal humor, both of them deal fiercely with paradox and use deceptively simple language in such a way as to achieve fantastic verbal surprise and remarkable poetic expression. No doubt Flannery O'Connor is a more ruthless writer than West. But in an essay of mine called "Flannery O'Connor's Devil," which appeared in *The Sewanee Review*, I tried to suggest some of these similarities and also mentioned that I first read West and Flannery O'Connor at the same time and from that moment on felt a sustaining involvement with both of them. About six years ago I visited Flannery O'Connor in Milledgeville, Georgia, and have been writing to her since then. She's an extraordinary woman with what I like to think of as a demonic sensibility. I've been trying to persuade Flannery O'Connor that as a writer she's on the devil's side. Her answer is that my idea of the devil corresponds to her idea of God. I must admit that I resist this equation. Certainly in her two great short stories, "A Good Man Is Hard to Find," and "The Life You Save May Be Your Own," as well as in her brilliant first novel, *Wise Blood*, it's the unwavering accuracy and diabolism of her satiric impulse that impresses me most. At any rate, her imaginative authority, her absolute originality of voice and language, her unflinching, unsparing treatment of the reader as well as her materials—all of this suggests the importance of her fictional gifts. I do think that Nathanael West is the only other American writer whose fictional spirit is comparable to hers.

To continue, perhaps with your opinions on contemporary American authors, would you comment on Carson McCullers? What do you think is her place in the literature of our time?

I admire her compassion and the fine warm mordant tones and slow cadences of her writing. It seems to me that Carson McCullers deals more directly and consistently with the materials of childhood fantasy than perhaps any other American writer, which might help to account for her power. It's as if she's telling stories about legendary children to other children who have already died. But the differences between Carson McCuller's humor and Flannery O'Connor's black wit, which is like a steel trap snapping shut on the reader's mind, make me aware again of the loss involved in grouping writers together under such terms as "Gothic." I'm sure we could go on at length about Saul Bellow and Bernard Malamud, but obviously these are two of our most important comic novelists. I think that *Henderson the Rain King*, which seems to have flowered enormously and wonderfully out of his perfect short novel *Seize the Day*, is Bellow's finest work. Malamud is one of the purest creators I know of.

There are some personal questions here about how you write and you may answer them or not as you like. The first is, do you outline your novels before you start writing?

I've never outlined a novel before starting to write it—at the outset I've never been aware of the story I was trying to handle except in the most general terms. The beginnings of my novels have always been mere flickerings in the imagination, though in each case the flickerings have been generated, clearly enough, by a kind of emotional ferment that had been in process for some time. I began *The Cannibal* after reading a brief notice in *Time* magazine about an actual cannibal discovered in Bremen, Germany (where I had been, coincidentally, during the war); I started *The Lime Twig* when I read a newspaper account of legalized gambling in England. My other novels were begun similarly with mere germs of ideas, and not with substantial narrative materials or even with particular characters. In each case what appealed to me was a landscape or world, and in each case I began with something immediately and intensely visual—a room, a few figures, an object, something prompted by the initial idea and then literally seen, like the visual images that come to us just before sleep. However, here I ought to stress that my fiction has nothing to do with automatic writing. Despite these vague originations and the dream-like quality of some of these envisioned worlds, my own writing process involves a constant effort to shape and control my materials as well as an effort to liberate fictional energy. *The Beetle Leg* and *The Lime Twig*, for instance, underwent extensive revision. I spent four years revising *The Lime Twig* which, as you know, is a short book. And I must say that once a first draft is finished I certainly do resort to outlines, sometimes to elaborate charts and diagrams. I suppose this writing method involves considerable waste motion. But since I'm compelled to work with poetic impulses there seems to be no alternative.

Would you say something about your working conditions?

Like most people, I've written under a variety of conditions. I wrote my first novel in a writing class when I returned to college after the war; I wrote a short novel in the cab of a pick-up truck in Montana; I've written at night after work and in the early mornings before going to work; the first draft of *The Lime Twig* was written during my first academic summer after I began teaching; *Second Skin* was written last year on a kind of paradise island in the West Indies. In his book *Enemies of Promise*, Cyril Connolly said that one of the greatest obstacles to the young writer was the "perambulator in the hall." But I was married at a fairly early age and have always felt that the conditions of ordinary life, no matter how difficult they might prove to be, were the most desirable conditions for writing. My prose might be radical, but my habits are quite ordinary. On the other hand, I admit that I did have mixed feelings when a Guggenheim fellowship and several grants allowed me to take a year off from teaching at Brown—it was difficult to face the prospect of a year of ideal writing conditions without a certain amount of anxiety, especially since I had always resisted the notion of making special allowances for writers. However, I confess that now after those arcadian months in the West Indies—I worked on *Second Skin* every morning and spent the afternoon in the water washing away the filth of creative effort—I feel very differently about complete freedom and ideal writing conditions. *Second Skin* couldn't have taken the form it did without the time and locale made possible by the grants. I'm reminded that a few years ago Irving Howe gave a lecture at Brown in which he said that if Raskolnikhov tried to commit his murder today he'd receive a special delivery letter announcing that he'd been awarded a Guggenheim fellowship. It's an amusing and accurate comment on our own special artistic state of affairs and the risks existing today for the subsidized artist and subsidized culture. Subsidy seems absurdly contrary to the integrity of the writer's necessary anti-social stance. But personally I think Foundation gifts are worth the risks involved. My own grants were unexpected boons which I look back on with nothing but considerable gratitude. I think that writers—and especially younger writers—should receive as much help and encouragement as possible.

To a certain extent you anticipated a few moments ago my next question, but I'll ask it, anyhow. To what degree are you worried about structure in your novels? Do you generally think of your novels in terms of a formal structure of the narrator, or do you discover structure as you write?

My novels are not highly plotted, but certainly they're elaborately structured. I began to write fiction on the assumption that the true enemies of the novel were plot, character, setting, and theme, and having once abandoned these familiar ways of thinking about fiction, totality of vision or structure was really all that remained. And structure—verbal and psychological coherence—is still my largest concern as a writer. Related or corresponding event, recurring image and recurring action, these constitute the essential substance or meaningful density of my writing. However, as I suggested before, this kind of structure can't be planned in advance but can only be discovered in the writing process itself. The success of the effort depends on the degree and quality of consciousness that can be brought to bear on fully liberated materials of the unconscious. I'm trying to hold in balance poetic and novelistic methods in order to make the novel a more valid and pleasurable experience. Of course it's obvious that from *The Cannibal* to *Second Skin* I've moved from nearly pure vision to a kind of work that appears to resemble much more closely the conventional novel. In a sense there was no other direction to take, but in part this shift came about, I think, from an increasing need to parody the conventional novel. As far as the first-person narrator goes, I've worked my way slowly toward that method by a series of semi-conscious impulses and sheer accidents. *The Cannibal* was written in the third person, but in revision I found myself (perversely or not) wishing to project myself into the fiction and to become identified with its most criminal and, in a conventional sense, least sympathetic spokesman, the neo-Nazi leader of the hallucinated uprising. I simply went through the manuscript and changed the pronouns from third to first person, so that the neo-Nazi Zizendorf became the teller of those absurd and violent events. The result was interesting, I think, not because *The Cannibal* became a genuine example of first-person fiction, but because its "narrator" naturally possessed an unusual omniscience, while the authorial consciousness was given specific definition, definition in terms of humor and "black" intelligence. When I finished *The Beetle Leg* (a third-person novel), I added a prologue spoken in the first person by a rather foolish and sadistic sheriff, and this was my first effort to render an actual human voice. Similarly, Hencher's first-person prologue in *The Lime Twig* (also a third-person novel) was an afterthought, but his was a fully created voice that dramatized a character conceived in a certain depth. This prologue led me directly to *Second Skin* which, as you know, is narrated throughout in the first person by Skipper who, as I say, had his basis in Hencher.

On the matter of structure would you comment on the relationship of Sidney Slyter to the main action of The Lime Twig?

As soon as he read the manuscript of *The Lime Twig*, James Laughlin, the publisher of New Directions (who, by the way, has been a sustaining friend since I began to write), suggested that this novel might be more accessible if it had some kind of gloss or reader's guide. I believe that he even suggested the idea of a newspaper sportswriter as an appropriate kind of "chorus" to comment on the action of the novel. I don't know how I arrived at the sportswriter's name (I may have been trying to echo comically the common English term "blighter"), but at any rate that's how Sidney Slyter came into being, with his snake-like character embodied in the ugly sibilance of his name which was also related, of course, to Sybilline, the dark temptress in the novel. To me it's interesting that Sidney Slyter's column was in effect another afterthought, since actually his sleazy character and cheap column afforded me perhaps the best opportunity for dramatizing the evil inherent in the world of *The Lime Twig*. Slyter's curiosity, his callow optimism, his lower middle class English ego, his tasteless rhetoric, his vaguely obscene excitement in the presence of violence—all this makes him one of the most degrading and perversely appealing figures in the novel. I would say that in reporting the criminal actions of the novel, Slyter carries degradation to its final end. I've been told that he's an authentic type, which pleases me since I've never known such a man and have only a passing interest in horse racing sheets. Perhaps Sidney Slyter is some indication of why *The Lime Twig* was overlooked or ridiculed in England.

What is the relationship between William Hencher and Michael Banks? Is Hencher some sort of prologue for Michael Banks? One of the most shocking parts of the book is to find Hencher killed so early.

I thought his death was amusing. But given my need to parody the novel form, in this case to parody the soporific plot of the thriller, Hencher's death seems to me an appropriate violation of fictional expectation or fictional "rules." However, *The Lime Twig* begins and ends with Hencher; his early violent death is analogous, I think, to all that follows; and to me he reappears as Cowles (the murdered fat man) and as the constable. I meant the pseudo-mystery of his death to pervade the novel. On the thriller level, Hencher is literally a member of Larry's underworld gang, is an instrument of Michael's fatality. Like Michael Banks, Hencher—because of his need for love—is killed by the race horse; if we understand Michael's own story then we understand Hencher's death. But of course you're right that Hencher's introduction serves as a prologue to all the episodes of the novel in which Michael's fantasies become real. Michael and Margaret Banks were conceived as representing England's anonymous post-war youth (the borrowing of the hero's name from the Mary Poppins series has obvious significance), while I saw post-war England itself as the spiritless, degraded landscape of the modern world, in this case dominated by the destructive fatality of the gambling syndicate. But it seemed to me that the drab reality of contemporary England was a direct product of the war, and that Michael and Margaret were in a sense the innocent spawn of the war. However, since Michael and Margaret were mere children during the war, incapable even of recalling the bombing of London, the problem became one of dramatizing the past, of relating wartime England to post-war England, of providing a kind of historical consciousness for characters who had none of their own. Hencher served this function. He became the carrier of Michael and Margaret's past as well as of their future; I thought of him as the seedbed of their pathetic lives. To me Hencher is a thoroughly sympathetic character, though some readers would probably consider him (wrongly, I think) to be merely crippled, perverse, distasteful. My own feeling is that Hencher's innocence, like Michael and Margaret's, can only suffer destruction by ruthless victimizers in a time of impoverishment. But paradoxically, in *The Lime Twig* as in my other novels, even the victimizers have "their dreams of shocking purity," to quote Albert Guerard.

Does teaching creative writing at Brown influence your own work in any way? Have you noticed any changes?

I think not. It may be that teaching has made clearer to me the possibilities for disrupting conventional forms of fiction, and no doubt I've benefited considerably from the imaginative exchange that occurs between teacher and student. There's a reassuring immediacy in students' needs and abilities. But it seems to me that the pleasures of teaching have to do with other people's writing and discoveries, rather than with your own. As you know, writing students are infinitely capable; the very variety of their work demands an appreciation from the teacher which forces him away from his own personal bias, and this, I think, is one of the most important aspects of academic life for the writer. There's a special value in a student's own work, and in his resistance as well as his enthusiastic response to the teacher.

This anticipates, then, the next question, which is whether as a teacher you discern any trends among students as writers or whether you find all kinds and don't see any general patterns among them.

I've always tried not to generalize about students. Ten years ago the most exciting students were as unpredictable as they seem to me today. The trends and patterns that do appear to be developing among student writers strike me as superficial. As far as the undergraduate sexual revolution is concerned, I don't find it evident in student writing. That is, I've known unusually gifted and mature younger writers throughout my years of teaching.

Are there any younger writers whom you think undervalued?

It seems to me that Grace Paley has not received the recognition she deserves. Three very different but promising first novels, *This Passing Night* by Clive Miller, *Seven Days of Mourning* by L. S. Simckes, and *Run River* by Joan Didion should have received more appreciation, I feel. On the other hand, William Melvin Kelley, who began to write in a class of mine at Harvard, wrote a first novel, *A Different Drummer*, which received an award from the National Institute of Arts and Letters—obviously a hopeful indication that early encouragement is perhaps more prevalent now than it used to be. And Susan Sontag's first novel, *The Benefactor*, has received appropriate attention, though I must say I disagree with those reviews that described the prose in this book as an easy imitation of French style. Susan Sontag's writing is often pure, controlled, disturbing in the best sense, and highly pleasurable. Her novel assumes a genuinely significant attitude toward sexual experience, her use of a first-person male narrator reveals an extraordinary kind of imaginative knowledge.

We are back almost to where we came in with internationalism and French influence.

I would still say that internationalism rather than influence is the point. Malamud and Nabokov are international writers, but their work really doesn't raise the question of influence. I think that a younger writer like Susan Sontag is promising precisely because of those moments in her novel where she's turning philosophical abstraction into concretely rendered life and is overcoming mere influence through her own imaginative pressures.

Would you want to say a few words about what you think is the ideal relationship between the writer and the university where he teaches?

It pleases me that Flannery O'Connor wrote her first novel in the writing program at Iowa and that so many writers, including for instance Malamud, Nabokov, and Susan Sontag, either are or have been teachers. I suppose the university world is a good one for the writer because it provides him with a literal experience in which he's both involved and detached in terms of life materials and intellectual and artistic effort. I think the writer, like other faculty members, should teach with commitment and offer what he can to the life around him; I think the university should encourage the writer's work with time off. There's no question any more about the place of the writer or artist within the university; the only question concerns the extent to which the university is equipped to foster artistic activity. Personally—and despite what I said earlier—I wouldn't give up teaching entirely even if I could.

I don't know quite how to phrase this, but it seems that in your work one of the things that is unique, in comparison with other modern writers, is the setting of your novels in an alien situation, one which you personally have never experienced as far as the actual milieu is concerned. You have never been in England, for instance, and the setting of The Beetle Leg *and the others is far from literal. Is there any particular reason for this? Do you feel you are getting at important matters more effectively than you would have out of your own, more immediate world?*

I take literally rather than figuratively the cliché about breaking new ground. Or I take literally the idea that the imagination should always uncover new worlds for us—hence my "mythic" England, Germany, Italy, American west, tropical island, and so on. I want to write about worlds that are fresh to me. But in his preface to *The Secret Agent*, Conrad speaks of the sights and sounds of London crowding in on him and inhibiting his imagination. And this danger of familiarity is something I've tried almost unthinkingly to avoid. As I've said, my writing depends on absolute detachment, and the unfamiliar or invented landscape helps me to achieve and maintain this detachment. Such a landscape provides an initial and helpful challenge. I don't want to write autobiographical fiction, though I admire Agee's *A Death in the Family* or the ways in which Conrad or Ford Madox Ford transform elements of personal experience and elements of subjective life into fiction. I want to try to create a world, not represent it. And of course I believe that the creation ought to be more significant than the representation.

We can have a last question. In The Lime Twig *you killed off Michael Banks and Margaret, the gang survive, at the end the detectives do not accomplish much. Despite what you've said about comedy, this novel doesn't appear to be very hopeful. Would you care to comment on this problem?*

For me the blackest fictions liberate the truest novelistic sympathy. When Michael is killed the whole world collapses with him, and comically—that is, the race track is littered with the bodies of the fallen jockeys and horses. And at the moment of Margaret's death, Larry, the head of the gang, is speaking comically about his hopes of journeying to a new world full of lime trees. (It's a journey which he won't be able to take of course, since his gigantic plan has failed.) But at any rate Michael has destroyed the "golden bowl" of earthly pleasure and destructive dream and has atoned for his betrayal of Margaret. This ending along with the novel's general pairing off of sensual and destructive experiences to me suggests a kind of hope. The fictional rhythm itself is in a way hopeful. But I admit I'm reluctant to argue too strongly for the necessity of hope.

What about the detectives? Are they anything more than comic?

The detectives represent law and order, or the baffled and banal mind at large. Specifically, and along with Sidney Slyter, they may be seen as images of the absurd and lonely author himself. Even the author is not exempt from judgment in my fiction. But at least the detectives, in trying to learn what the reader has presumably learned already (and it's clear, I think, that these obtuse men from Scotland Yard will never solve the "crime"), are attempting to complete the cycle of mysterious experience. At least they, like ourselves, will go on hunting for clues.

NATHANIEL HAWTHORNE

Notes on the Craft of Fiction

His [the author's] writings, to do them justice, are not altogether destitute of fancy and originality; they might have won him greater reputation but for an inveterate love of allegory, which is apt to invest his plots and characters with the aspect of scenery and people in the clouds, and to steal away the human warmth out of his conceptions. His fictions are sometimes historical, sometimes of the present day, and sometimes, so far as can be discovered, have little or no reference either to time or space. In any case, he generally contents himself with a very slight embroidery of outward manners,—the faintest possible counterfeit of real life,—and endeavors to create an interest by some less obvious peculiarity of the subject. Occasionally a breath of Nature, a raindrop of pathos and tenderness, or a gleam of humor, will find its way into the midst of his fantastic imagery, and make us feel as if, after all, we were yet within the limits of our native earth. . . .

> From the author's introduction to "Rappaccini's Daughter," originally published in the *Democratic Review*, December 1844.

The author of *Twice-Told Tales* has a claim to one distinction which, as none of his literary brethren will care about disputing it with him, he need not be afraid to mention. He was, for a good many years, the obscurest man of letters in America.

These stories were published in magazines and annuals extending over a period of ten or twelve years, and comprising the whole of the writer's young manhood, without making (so far as he has ever been aware) the slightest impression on the public. . . .

After a long while the first collected volume of the "Tales" was published. By this time, if the Author had ever been greatly tormented by literary ambition (which he does not remember or believe to have been the case), it must have perished, beyond resuscitation, in the dearth of nutriment. This was fortunate; for the success of the volume was not such as would have gratified a craving desire for notoriety. . . .

As he glances over these long-forgotten pages, and considers his way of life while composing them, the Author can very clearly discern why all this was so. After so many sober years, he would have reason to be ashamed if he could not criticise his own work as fairly as another man's; and, though it is little his business, and perhaps still less his interest, he can hardly resist a temptation to achieve something of the sort. If writers were allowed to do so, and would perform the task with perfect sincerity and unreserve, their opinions of their own productions would often be more valuable and instructive than the works themselves.

At all events, there can be no harm in the Author's remarking that he rather wonders how the *Twice-Told Tales* should have gained what vogue they did than that it was so little and so gradual. They have the pale tint of flowers that blossomed in too retired a shade—the coolness of a meditative habit, which diffuses itself through the feeling and observation of every sketch. Instead of passion there is sentiment, and, even in what purport to be pictures of actual life, we have allegory, not always so warmly dressed in its habiliments of flesh and blood as to be taken into the reader's mind without a shiver. Whether from lack of power, or an unconquerable reserve, the Author's touches have often an effect of tameness; the merriest man can hardly contrive to laugh at his broadest humor; the tenderest woman, one would suppose, will hardly shed warm tears at his deepest pathos. The book, if you would see anything in it, requires to be read in the clear, brown, twilight atmosphere in which it was written; if opened in the sunshine, it is apt to look exceedingly like a volume of blank pages.

With the foregoing characteristics, proper to the production of a person in retirement (which happened to be the Author's category at the time), the book is devoid of others that we should quite as naturally look for. The sketches are not, it is hardly necessary to say, profound; but it is rather more remarkable that they so seldom, if ever, show any design on the writer's part to make them so. They have none of the abstruseness of idea, or obscurity of expression, which mark the written communications of a solitary mind with itself. They never need translation. It is, in fact, the style of a man of society. Every sentence, so far as it embodies thought or sensibility, may be understood and felt by anybody who will give himself the trouble to read it, and will take up the book in a proper mood.

This statement of apparently opposite peculiarities leads us to a perception of what the sketches truly are. They are not the talk of the secluded man with his own mind and heart (had it been so, they could hardly have failed to be more deeply and permanently valuable), but his attempts, and very imperfectly successful ones, to open an intercourse with the world. . . .

From the author's preface to the 1851 edition of *Twice-Told Tales*. Reprinted here from *Works*, I, 13–17.

HENRY JAMES

On the Genesis of "The Real Thing"

In pursuance of my plan of writing some very short tales—things of from 7,000 to 10,000 words, the easiest length to "place," I began yesterday the little story that was suggested to me some time ago by an incident related to me by George du Maurier—the lady and gentleman who called upon him with a word from Frith, an oldish, faded, ruined pair—he an officer in the army—who unable to turn a penny in any other way, were trying to find employment as models. I was struck with the pathos, the oddity, and typicalness of the situation—the little tragedy of good-looking gentlefolk, who had been all their life stupid and well-dressed, living, on a fixed income, at country-houses, watering places, and clubs, like so many others of their class in England, and were now utterly unable to *do* anything, had no clever-ness, no art nor craft to make use of as a *gagne-pain*—could only show themselves, clumsily, for the fine, clean, well-groomed animals that they were, only hope to make a little money by—in this manner—just simply *being*. I thought I saw a sub-ject for very brief treatment in this *donnée*—and I think I do still; but to do any-thing worth while with it I must (as always, great Heavens!) be very clear as to what is in it and what I wish to get out of it. I tried a beginning yesterday, but I instantly became conscious that I must straighten out the little idea. It must be an idea—it can't be a "story" in the vulgar sense of the word. It must be a picture; it must illustrate something. God knows that's enough—if the thing *does* illustrate. To make little anecdotes of this kind real *morceaux de vie* is a plan quite inspiring enough. *Voyons un peu*, therefore, what one can put into this one—I mean how much of life. One must put a little action—not a stupid, mechanical, arbitrary action, but something that is of the real essence of the subject. I thought of repre-senting the husband as jealous of the wife—that is, jealous of the artist employing her, from the moment that, in point of fact, she begins to sit. But this is vulgar and obvious—worth nothing. What I wish to represent is the baffled, ineffectual, incompetent character of their attempt, and how it illustrates once again the ever-lasting English amateurishness—the way superficial, untrained, unprofessional effort goes to the wall when confronted with trained, competitive, intelligent, *qualified* art—in whatever line it may be a question of. It is out of *that* element that my little action and movement must come; and now I begin to see just how—as one always *does*—Glory be to the Highest—when one begins to look at a thing hard and straight and seriously—to fix it—as I am so sadly lax and desultory about doing. What subjects I should find—for *everything*—if I could only achieve this more as a habit! Let my contrast and complication here come from the opposi-tion—to my melancholy Major and his wife—of a couple of little vulgar profes-sional people who know, with the consequent bewilderment, vagueness, depression of the former—their failure to understand how such people can be better than *they*—their failure, disappointment, disappearance—going forth into the vague again. *Il y a bien quelque chose à tirer de ça.* They have no pictorial sense. They are only clean and stiff and stupid. The others are dirty, even—the melancholy Major and his wife remark on it, wondering. The artist is beginning a big illustrated book, a new edition of a famous novel—say *Tom Jones*: and he is willing to try to work them in—for he takes an interest in their predicament, and feels—skeptically, but, with his flexible artistic sympathy—the appeal of their type. He is willing to give them a trial. Make it out that *he* himself is on trial—he is young and "rising," but he has still his golden spurs to win. He can't afford, *en somme*, to make many mistakes. He has regular work in drawing every week for a serial novel in an illustrated paper; but the great project—that of a big house—of issuing an illustrated Fielding promises him a big lift. He has been intrusted with (say) *Joseph Andrews*, experimentally; he will have to do this brilliantly in order to have the engagement for the rest confirmed. He has already two models in his service—the "complication" must come from *them*. One is a common, clever, London girl, of the smallest origin and without conventional beauty, but of aptitude, of perceptions—knowing thoroughly *how*. She says "lydy" and "plice" but she has the pictorial sense; and can look like anything he wants her to look like. She poses, in short, in perfection. So does her colleague, a professional Italian, a little fellow—ill dressed, smelling of garlic, but admirably serviceable, quite universal. They must be contrasted, confronted, *juxtaposed* with the others; whom they take for people who *pay*, themselves, till they learn the truth when they are overwhelmed with derisive amazement. The denouncement simply that the melancholy Major and his wife won't do—they're not "in it." Their surprise—their helpless, proud assent—without other prospects: yet at the same time *their* degree of more silent amazement at the success of the two inferior people—who are so much less nice-looking than themselves. Frankly, however, is this contrast enough of a story, by itself? It seems to me Yes—for it's an IDEA—and how the deuce should I get *more* into 7,000 words? It must be simply fifty pp. of my manuscript. The little tale of *The Servant* (*Brooksmith*) which I did the other day for *Black and White* and which I thought of at the same time as this, proved a very tight squeeze into the same tiny number of words, and I probably shall find that there is much more to be done with this than the compass will admit of. Make it tremendously succinct—with a very short pulse or rhythm—and the closest selection of detail—in other words *summarize* intensely and keep down the lateral development. It *should* be a little gem of bright, quick, vivid form. I shall get every grain of "action" that the space admits of if I make something, for the artist, hang in the balance—depend on the way he does this particular work. It's when he finds that he shall lose his great opportunity if he keeps on with them, that he has to tell the gentlemanly couple, that, frankly, they won't serve his turn—and make them wander forth into the cold world again. I must keep them the age I've made them—fifty and forty—because it's more touching, but I must bring up the age of the two real models to almost the same thing. That increases the incomprehensibility (to the amateurs) of their usefulness. Picture the immanence, in the latter, of the idle, provided-for, country-house habit—the blankness of their *manière d'être*. But in how tremendously few words I must do it. This is a lesson—a *magnificent* lesson—if I'm to do a good many. Something as admirably compact and *selected* as Maupassant.

FRANZ KAFKA

Fact or Fiction: You Be the Judge
Translated by Martin Greenberg

11 February. While I read the proofs of 'The Judgment', I'll write down all the relationships which have become clear to me in the story as far as I now remember them. This is necessary because the story came out of me like a real birth, covered with filth and slime, and only I have the hand that can reach to the body itself and the strength of desire to do so:

The friend is the link between father and son, he is their strongest common bond. Sitting alone at his window, Georg rummages voluptuously in this consciousness of what they have in common, believes he has his father within him, and would be at peace with everything if it were not for a fleeting, sad thoughtfulness. In the course of the story the father, with the strengthened position that the other, lesser things they share in common give him—love, devotion to the mother, loyalty to her memory, the clientele that he (the father) had been the first to acquire for the business—uses the common bond of the friend to set himself up as Georg's antagonist. Georg is left with nothing; the bride, who lives in the story only in relation to the friend, that is, to what father and son have in common, is easily driven away by the father since no marriage has yet taken place, and so she cannot penetrate the circle of blood relationship that is drawn around father and son. What they have in common is built up entirely around the father, Georg can feel it only as something foreign, something that has become independent, that he has never given enough protection, that is exposed to Russian revolutions, and only because he himself has lost everything except his awareness of the father does the judgement, which closes off his father from him completely, have so strong an effect on him.

Georg has the same number of letters as Franz. In Bendemann, 'mann' is a strengthening of 'Bende' to provide for all the as yet unforeseen possibilities in the story. But Bende has exactly the same number of letters as Kafka, and the vowel *e* occurs in the same places as does the vowel *a* in Kafka.

Frieda has as many letters as F. and the same initial, Brandenfeld has the same initial as B., and in the word 'Feld' a certain connexion in meaning, as well. Perhaps even the thought of Berlin was not without influence and the recollection of the Mark Brandenburg perhaps had some influence.

12 February. In describing the friend I kept thinking of Steuer. Now when I happened to meet him about three months after I had written the story, he told me that he had become engaged about three months ago.

After I read the story at Weltsch's yesterday, old Mr Weltsch went out and, when he returned after a short time, praised especially the graphic descriptions in the story. With his arm extended he said, 'I see this father before me,' all the time looking directly at the empty chair in which he had been sitting while I was reading.

My sister said, 'It is our house.' I was astonished at how mistaken she was in the setting and said, 'In that case, then, Father would have to be living in the toilet.'

MARGARET LAURENCE

On "The Loons"

This story was first published in *The Atlantic Advocate*, in 1966. The roots of it go back a very long way into my childhood. The ways in which memories and "created" events intertwine in this story probably illustrate a few things about the nature of fiction. When I was about eleven or twelve, I got to know a young Métis girl who was several years younger than I. The Matron of the Neepawa Hospital was a close friend of our family, and the Métis child was in her care because the girl had tuberculosis of the bone in one leg. When the girl was well enough to walk (first with a cast, then with an awkward leg brace), she used to visit our house often. She was, not surprisingly, very shy and withdrawn, and I was puzzled by her at the time. Only many years later did I realize how unhappy she must have been. I learned something about her when we were both grown up—she did indeed marry an English-Canadian, and the marriage turned out badly. I never heard anything more. She became the basis of the character of Piquette Tonnerre.

The character of Vanessa is based on myself as a child, and the MacLeod family is based on my own childhood family, but here is where the process of fiction becomes interesting. When I knew the Métis girl, my father had died several years previously. He was in fact a lawyer, not a doctor. We did indeed have a cottage at Clear Lake, Riding Mountain, and this is the very beloved place I am describing in the fictional Diamond Lake, Galloping Mountain. The loons used to be there, nesting on the shore, when I was a child, and we used to hear their eerie unforgetable cry. The loons did move away when the cottages increased in number and more and more people came in. All these things somehow wove themselves into the story. Other things surfaced, part of the mental baggage which one carries inside one's head always. When I was young, fires in winter among the collection of destitute shacks at the foot of the hill, in the valley below town, were tragically common. Years later, when I lived in Vancouver, I used to read in the newspapers about fires destroying the flimsy shanties of native peoples. All these various things combined in my mind with a sense of outrage at the treatment of Indian and Métis people in this country throughout our history. History for me, as with social issues, is personalized—these events happen to real people; people with names, families and places of belonging. The loons seemed to symbolize in some way the despair, the uprootedness, the loss of the land that many Indians and Métis must feel. And so, by some mysterious process which I don't claim to understand, the story gradually grew in my mind until it found its own shape and form.

I never knew a family exactly like the Tonnerre family, but the fictional family first appeared in my writing in *The Stone Angel*. Next came the writing of the short story, "The Loons." Something about that fire, and the terrible and unnecessary waste of lives, must have almost obsessed me, for that event came into my fiction twice more after the short story—a relatively brief reference in my novel *The Fire-Dwellers*, and a long scene and many other references in my novel *The Diviners*.

Although certain details are taken from one's own life, and from memories of places and people, I think that the fiction comes to have its own special reality. In fact, the fictional town of Manawaka often seems as real to me as my own town of Neepawa, and its people seem very real in my mind. Of course, the odd thing about fiction is that even when the characters are based to some extent on actual people, they cease to be those people and become themselves. Ultimately, Vanessa is herself and not me at all, just as Piquette is herself.

And the process of fiction remains, thank God, mysterious.

URSULA K. LE GUIN

The Hand That Rocks the Cradle Writes the Book

(An abbreviated version of "The Fisherwoman's Daughter" from *Dancing at the Edge of the World*)

" 'So of course,' wrote Betty Flanders, pressing her heels rather deeper in the sand, 'there was nothing for it but to leave.' "

That is the first sentence of Virginia Woolf's *Jacob's Room*. It is a woman writing. Sitting on the sand by the sea, writing. It's only Betty Flanders, and she's only writing a letter. But first sentences are doors to worlds. This world of Jacob's room, so strangely empty at the end of the book when the mother stands in it, holding out a pair of her son's old shoes and saying, "What am I to do with these?"—this is a world in which the first thing one sees is a woman, a mother of children, writing.

On the shore, by the sea, outdoors, is that where women write? Not at a desk, in a writing room? Where does a woman write, what does she look like writing, what is my image, your image, of a woman writing? I asked my friends: "A woman writing: what do you see?" There would be a pause, then the eyes would light up, seeing. Some sent me to paintings, Fragonard, Cassatt, but mostly these turned out to be paintings of a woman reading or with a letter, not actually writing or reading the letter but looking up from it with unfocused eyes: Will he never never return? Did I remember to turn off the pot roast? . . . Another friend responded crisply, "A woman writing is taking dictation." And another said, "She's sitting at the kitchen table, and the kids are yelling." And that last is the image I shall pursue.

Here is a woman who had several children and was a successful novelist, writing a letter to her husband about 150 years ago, or maybe last night: "If I am to write, I must have a room to myself, which shall be *my* room. All last winter I felt the need of some place where I could go and be quiet. I could not [write in the dining room] for there was all the setting of tables and clearing up of tables and dressing and washing of children, and everything else going on, and . . . I never felt comfortable there, though I tried hard. Then if I came into the parlor where you were, I felt as if I were interrupting you, and you know you sometimes thought so too." Fourteen years and several more children later, that woman wrote *Uncle Tom's Cabin*—most of it at the kitchen table.

A room of one's own—yes. One may ask why Mr. Harriet Beecher Stowe got a room to himself to write in, while the woman who wrote the most morally effective American novel of the 19th century got the kitchen table. But then one may also ask why she accepted the kitchen table. Any self-respecting man would have sat there for five minutes and then stalked out, shouting, "Nobody can work in this madhouse, call me when dinner's ready!" But Harriet, a self-respecting woman, went on getting dinner, with the kids all underfoot *and* writing her novels. The first question, to be asked with awe, is surely, How? But then, Why? *Why* are women such patsies?

The quick feminist-fix answer is that they are victims and/or accomplices of the patriarchy, which is true but doesn't really get us anywhere new. Let us go to another woman novelist for help.

Margaret Oliphant, the author of *Hester, Kirsteen, Miss Marjoribanks* and a fascinating autobiography, belonged to the generation just after Stowe's. She was a successful writer very young, married, had three kids, went on writing, was left a widow with heavy debts and the three kids plus her brother's three kids to bring up, did so, went on writing.

"The writing ran through everything. But then it was also subordinate to everything, to be pushed aside for any little necessity. I had no table even to myself much less a room to work in, but sat at the corner of the family table with my writing-book, with everything going on as if I had been making a shirt instead of writing a book. . . . My mother sat always at needlework of some kind, and talked to whoever might be present, and I took my share in the conversation, going on all the same with my story, the little groups of imaginary persons, these other talks, evolving themselves, quite undisturbed."

How's that for an image: the group of imaginary people talking in the imaginary room in the real room among the real people talking, and all of it going on perfectly quiet and unconfused. . . . But it's shocking. She can't be a real writer. Real writers writhe on solitary sofas in cork-lined rooms, agonizing after *le mot juste*—don't they?

Oliphant's autobiography gives us a glimpse of why a novelist might not merely endure writing in the kitchen or the parlor amid the children and the housework, but might endure it willingly. She seems to feel that she profited, that her writing profited, from the difficult, obscure, chancy connection between the art work and the emotional/manual/managerial complex of skills and tasks called housework, and that to sever that connection would put the writing itself at risk, would make it, in her word, unnatural.

The received wisdom of course is just the opposite: that any attempt to combine art work with housework and family responsibility is impossible, unnatural. And the punishment for unnatural acts, among the critics and keepers of the Canon of English Literature, is death.

What is the ethical basis of this judgment and sentence upon the housewife-artist? It is a very noble and austere one, with religion at its foundation: it is the idea that the artist must sacrifice himself to his art. (I use the pronoun advisedly.) His responsibility is to his work alone. This heroic stance has been taken as the norm—as natural to the artist—and artists, both men and women, who do not assume it have tended to feel a little shabby and second-rate.

Not, however, Virginia Woolf. She observed factually that the artist needs a little income and a room to work in, but did not speak of heroism. Indeed, she said, "I doubt that a writer can be a hero. I doubt that a hero can be a writer." And when I see a writer assume the full heroic posture, I incline to agree. Here, for example, is Joseph Conrad:

"For twenty months I wrestled with the Lord for my creation . . . mind and will and conscience engaged to the full, hour after hour, day after day . . . a lonely struggle in a great isolation from the world. I suppose I slept and ate the food put before me and talked connectedly on suitable occasions, but I was never aware of the even flow of daily life, made easy and noiseless for me by a silent, watchful, tireless affection."

A woman who boasted that her conscience had been engaged to the full in such a wrestling match would be called to account by both women and men; and women are now calling men to account. What "put food" before him? What made daily life so noiseless? What in fact was this "tireless affection" which sounds to me like an old Ford in a junkyard but is apparently intended as a delicate gesture toward a woman whose conscience was engaged to the full, hour after hour, day after day, for 20 months, in seeing to it that Joseph Conrad could wrestle with the Lord in a very relatively "great isolation," well housed, clothed, bathed and fed?

Every artist needs some kind of moral support or sense of solidarity, for there *is* a heroic aspect to the practice of art; it is lonely, risky, merciless work. The artist with the least access to social or esthetic solidarity or approbation has been the artist-housewife. A person who undertakes responsibility both to her art and to her dependent children has undertaken a full-time double job that can be simply, practically, destroyingly impossible. But that isn't how the problem is posed—as a recognition of immense practical difficulty. If it were, practical solutions would be proposed, beginning with child care. Instead the issue is stated, even now, as a moral one, a matter of ought and ought not. The poet Alicia Ostriker puts it neatly: "That women should have babies rather than books is the considered opinion of Western civilization. That women should have books rather than babies is a variation on that theme." Hence the approbation accorded Austen, the Brontës, Dickinson and Plath, who though she made the mistake of having two children compensated for it by putting her head in the oven. The misogynist Canon of Literature can include these women because they can be perceived as incomplete women, as female men.

Still, I have to grit my teeth to criticize the either-books-or-babies doctrine, because it has given real, true comfort to women who could not or chose not to marry and have children, and saw themselves as "having" books instead. But though the comfort may be real, I think the doctrine false. It's just the flip side of the theory that books come from the scrotum. This final reduction of the notion of sublimation is endorsed by our chief macho dodo writer, who has announced that "the one thing a writer needs to have is *balls*." But he doesn't carry the theory of penile authorship to the extent of saying that if you "get" a kid you can't "get" a book and so fathers can't write. The analogy collapsed into identity, the you-can't-create-if-you-procreate myth, is applied to women only.

I've found I have to stop now and say clearly what I'm not saying. I'm not saying a writer *ought* to have children. I'm not saying a parent ought to be a writer, I'm not saying any woman ought to write books or have kids. Being a mother is one of the things a woman can do—like being a writer. It's a privilege. It's not an obligation or a destiny. I'm talking about mothers who write because it is almost a taboo topic—because women have been told that they *ought not* to try to be both a mother and a writer because both the kids and the books will pay—because it can't be done—because it's unnatural.

This refusal to allow both creation and procreation to women is cruelly wasteful: not only has it impoverished our literature by banning the housewives, but it has caused unbearable personal pain and self-mutilation: Woolf, obeying the wise doctors who said she must not bear a child; Plath, who put glasses of milk by her kids' beds and then put her head in the oven.

A sacrifice, not of somebody else but of oneself, is demanded of women artists. I am proposing that this ban on a woman artist's full sexuality is harmful not only to the woman but to the art.

There is less censure now, and more support for a woman who wants both to bring up a family and work as an artist. But it's a small degree of improvement. The difficulty of trying to be responsible, hour after hour, day after day, for maybe 20 years, for the well-being of children and the excellence of books, is immense: it involves an endless expense of energy and an impossible weighing of competing priorities. And we don't know much about the process, because writers who are mothers haven't talked much about their motherhood—for fear of boasting? for fear of being trapped in the Mom trap, discounted?—nor have they talked much about their writing as in any way connected with their parenthood, since the heroic myth demands that the two functions be considered utterly opposed and mutually destructive.

But we heard a hint of something else from Oliphant; and here is the painter Käthe Kollwitz:

"I am gradually approaching the period in my life when work comes first. When both the boys were away for Easter, I hardly did anything but work. Worked, slept, ate, and went for short walks. But above all I worked.

"And yet I wonder whether the 'blessing' isn't missing from such work. No longer diverted by other emotions, I work the way a cow grazes."

That is marvellous—"I work the way a cow grazes." That is the best description of the "professional" at work I know.

"Perhaps in reality I accomplish a little more," Kollwitz continues. "The hands work and work, and the head imagines it's producing God knows what, and yet, formerly, when my working time was so wretchedly limited, I was more productive, because I was more sensual; I lived as a human being must live, passionately interested in everything. . . . Potency, potency is diminishing."

This *potency* felt by a woman is a potency that has been denied by women as well as men, and not just women eager to collude with misogyny.

Back in the 1970's one prominent feminist scholar wrote that Jane Austen was able to write because she had created around her "a child-free space." Germ-free I knew, odor-free I knew, but child-free? And Austen? who wrote in the parlor, and was a central figure to a lot of nieces and nephews? But I tried to accept this, because although my experience didn't fit it, I was, like many women, used to feeling that my experience was faulty, not right—that it was *wrong*. So I was probably wrong to keep on writing in what was then a fully child-filled space. However, feminist thinking evolved rapidly to a far more complex and realistic position, and I, stumbling along behind, have been enabled by it to think a little for myself.

The greatest enabler for me was always, is always, Virginia Woolf. And I quote now from the first draft of her paper "Professions for Women" where she gives her great image of a woman writing:

"I figure her really in an attitude of contemplation, like a fisherwoman, sitting on the bank of a lake with her fishing rod held over its water. Yes that is how I see her. She was not thinking; she was not reasoning; she was not constructing a plot; she was letting her imagination down into the depths of her consciousness while she sat above holding on by a thin but quite necessary thread of reason."

Now I interrupt to ask you to add one small element to this scene. Let us imagine that a bit farther up the bank of the lake sits a child, the fisherwoman's daughter. She's about 5 and she's making people out of sticks and mud and telling stories with them. She's been told to be very quiet please while Mama fishes, and she really is very quiet except when she forgets and sings or asks questions; and she watches in fascinated silence when the following dramatic events take place. There sits our woman writing, our fisherwoman, when "suddenly there is a violent jerk; she feels the line race through her fingers.

"The imagination has rushed away; it has taken to the depths; it has sunk heaven knows where—into the dark pool of extraordinary experience. The reason has to cry 'Stop!' the novelist has to pull on the line and haul the imagination to the surface. The imagination comes to the top in a state of fury.

"Good heavens she cries—how dare you interfere with me—how dare you pull me out with your wretched little fishing line? And I—that is, the reason—have to reply, 'My dear you were going altogether too far. Men would be shocked.' Calm yourself I say, as she sits panting on the bank—panting with rage and disappointment. We have only got to wait 50 years or so. In 50 years I shall be able to use all this very queer knowledge that you are ready to bring me. But not now. You see I go on, trying to calm her, I cannot make use of what you tell me—about women's bodies for instance—their passions—and so on, because the conventions are still very strong. If I were to overcome the conventions I should need the courage of a hero, and I am not a hero.

"I doubt that a writer can be a hero. I doubt that a hero can be a writer. . . .

"Very well, says the imagination, dressing herself up again in her petticoat and skirts, we will wait. We will wait another 50 years. But it seems to me a pity."

It seems to me a pity. It seems to me a pity that more than 50 years have passed and the conventions, though utterly different, still exist to protect men from being shocked, still admit only male experience of women's bodies, passions and existence. It seems to me a pity that so many women, including myself, have accepted this denial of their own experience and narrowed their perception to fit it, writing as if their sexuality were limited to copulation, as if they knew nothing about pregnancy, birth, nursing, mothering, puberty, menstruation, menopause, except what men are willing to hear, nothing except what men are willing to hear about housework, childwork, lifework, war, peace, living and dying as experienced in the female body and mind and imagination. "Writing the body," as Woolf asked, is only the beginning. We have to rewrite the world.

White writing, the French feminist Hélène Cixous calls it, writing in milk, in mother's milk. I like that image, because, even among feminists, the woman writer has been more often considered in her sexuality as a lover than in her sexuality as pregnant-bearing-nursing-caring-for-children. Mother still tends to get disappeared. And in losing the artist-mother we lose where there's a lot to gain. Alicia Ostriker thinks so. "The advantage of motherhood for a woman artist," she says—have you ever heard anyone say that before? the *advantage* of motherhood for an artist?—"The advantage of motherhood for a woman artist is that it puts her in immediate and inescapable contact with the sources of life, death, beauty, growth, corruption. . . . If the woman artist has been trained to believe that the activities of motherhood are trivial, tangential to the main issues of life, irrelevant to the great themes of literature, she should untrain herself. The training is misogynist, it protects and perpetuates systems of thought and feeling which prefer violence and death to love and birth, and it is a lie."

Here is a passage from a novel where what Woolf, Ms. Cixous and Ms. Ostriker asked for is happening, however casually and unpretentiously. In Margaret Drabble's *Millstone*, Rosamund, a young scholar and freelance writer, has a baby about 8 months old, Octavia. They share a flat with a friend, Lydia, who's writing a novel. Rosamund is working away on a book review when she hears "small happy noises" coming from Lydia's room and goes to investigate.

"The sight that met my eyes when I opened the door was enough to make anyone quake. [Octavia] had her back to the door and was sitting in the middle of the floor surrounded by a sea of torn, strewed, chewed paper. I stood there transfixed, watching the neat small back of her head and her thin stalk-like neck and flowery curls: suddenly she gave a great screech of delight and ripped another sheet of paper. 'Octavia,' I said in horror, and she started guiltily, and looked round at me with a charming deprecating smile: her mouth, I could see, was wedged full of wads of Lydia's new novel. . . .

"The damage was not, in fact, as great as it appeared at first sight to be, for babies, though persistent, are not thorough: but at first sight it was frightful. . . . In a way it was clearly the most awful thing for which I had ever been responsible, but as I watched Octavia crawl around the sitting room looking for more work to do, I almost wanted to laugh. . . . It really was a terrible thing . . . and yet in comparison with Octavia being so sweet and so alive it did not seem so very terrible."

I have seen Margaret Drabble's work dismissed with the usual list of patronizing adjectives reserved for women who write as women, not imitation men. Let us not let her be disappeared. Her work is deeper than its bright surface. What is she talking about in this funny passage? Why does the girl-baby eat not her mother's manuscript but another woman's manuscript? Couldn't she at least have eaten a manuscript by a man?—no, no, that's not the point. The point, or part of it, is that babies eat manuscripts. They really do. The poem not written because the baby cried, the novel put aside because of a pregnancy, and so on. Babies eat books. But they spit out wads of them that can be taped back together; and they are only babies for a couple of years, while writers live for decades; and it is terrible, but not very terrible. And that's part of the point too—that the supreme value of art depends on other equally supreme values. But that subverts the hierarchy of values; "men would be shocked. . . . "

In Ms. Drabble's comedy of morals the absence of the hero-artist is a strong ethical statement. Nobody lives in a great isolation, nobody sacrifices human claims, nobody even scolds the baby. Nobody is going to put their head, or anybody else's head, into an oven: not the mother, not the writer, not the daughter—these three and one who, being women, do not separate creation and destruction into *I create/You are destroyed*, or vice versa. Who are responsible, take responsibility, for both the baby and the book.

The books-or-babies myth is not only a misogynist hang-up, it can be a feminist one. And it is feminism that has empowered me to criticize not only my society and myself but—for a moment now—feminism itself. Some of the women I respect most, writing for publications that I depend on for my sense of women's solidarity and hope, continue to declare that it is "virtually impossible for a heterosexual woman to be a feminist," as if heterosexuality were heterosexism; and that social marginality, such as that of lesbian, childless, black or native American women, "appears to be necessary" to form the feminist. Applying these judgments to myself, and believing that as a woman writing at this point I have to be a feminist to be worth beans, I find myself, once again, excluded—disappeared.

The rationale of the exclusionists, as I understand it, is that the material privilege and social approbation our society grants the heterosexual wife, and particularly the mother, prevent her solidarity with less privileged women and insulate her from the kind of anger and the kind of ideas that lead to feminist action. There is truth in this; maybe it's true for a lot of women; I can oppose it only with my experience, which is that feminism has been a life-saving *necessity* to women trapped in the wife/mother "role." What do the privilege and approbation accorded the housewife-mother by our society in fact consist of? Being the object of infinite advertising? Being charged by psychologists with total answerability for children's mental well-being, and by our Government with total answerability for children's welfare, while being regularly equated with apple pie by sentimental warmongers? As a social "role," motherhood, for any woman I know, simply means that she does everything everybody else does plus bringing up the kids.

To push mothers back into "private life," a mythological space invented by the patriarchy, on the theory that their acceptance of the "role" of mother invalidates them for public, political, artistic responsibility, is to play Old Nobodaddy's game, by his rules, on his side.

In *Writing Beyond the Ending*, Rachel Blau DuPlessis shows how women novelists write about the woman artist; they make her an ethical force, an activist trying "to change the life in which she is also immersed." To have and bring up kids is to be about as immersed in life as one can be, but it does not always follow that one drowns. A lot of us can swim.

Here, again, I'm likely to be told that I'm supporting the Superwoman syndrome, saying that a woman *should* have kids, write books, be politically active and make perfect sushi. I am not saying that. We're all asked to be Superwoman; I'm not asking it, our society does that. All I can tell you is that I believe it's a lot easier to write books while bringing up kids than to bring up kids while working nine to five plus housekeeping. But that is what our society, while sentimentalizing over Mom and the Family, demands of most women—unless it refuses them any work at all and dumps them onto welfare and says, Bring up your kids on food stamps, Mom, we might want them for the Army. Talk about superwomen, those are the superwomen. Those are the mothers up against the wall. Those are the marginal women, without either privacy or publicity; and it's because of them more than anyone else that the woman artist has a responsibility to "try to change the life in which she is also immersed."

And now I come back round to the bank of that lake, where the fisherwoman sits, our woman writer, who had to bring her imagination up short because it was getting too deeply immersed.

The imagination dries herself off, still swearing under her breath, and buttons up her blouse, and comes to sit beside the little girl, the fisherwoman's daughter. "Do you like books?" she says, and the child says: "Oh, yes. When I was a baby I used to eat them, but now I can read. I can read all of Beatrix Potter by myself and when I grow up I'm going to write books, like Mama."

"Are you going to wait till your children grow up?"

"Oh, I don't think so," says the child. "I'll just go ahead and do it."

"Then will you do as Harriet and Margaret and so many Harriets and Margarets have done and are still doing, and hassle through the prime of your life trying to do two full-time jobs that are incompatible with each other in practice, however enriching their interplay may be both to the life and the art?"

"I don't know," says the little girl. "Do I have to?"

"Yes," says the imagination, "if you aren't rich and you want kids."

"I might want one or two," says reason's child. "But why do women have two jobs where men only have one? It isn't reasonable, is it?"

"Don't ask me!" snaps the imagination. "I could think up a dozen better arrangements before breakfast! But who listens to me?"

The child sighs and watches her mother fishing. The fisherwoman, having forgotten that her line is no longer baited with the imagination, isn't catching anything, but she's enjoying the peaceful hour; and when the child speaks again she speaks softly: "Tell me, Auntie. What is the one thing a writer has to have?"

"I'll tell you," says the imagination. "The one thing a writer has to have is not balls. Nor is it even, speaking strictly on the evidence, a room of her own, though that is an amazing help, as is the good will and cooperation of the opposite sex, or at least the local, in-house representative of it. But she doesn't have to have that. The one thing a writer has to have is a pencil and some paper. That's enough, so long as she knows that she and she alone is in charge of that pencil, and responsible, she and she alone, for what it writes on the paper. In other words, that she's free. Not wholly free. Never wholly free. Maybe very partially. Maybe only in this one act, this sitting for a snatched moment being a woman writing, fishing the mind's lake. But in this, responsible; in this, autonomous; in this, free."

"Auntie," says the little girl, "can I go fishing with you now?"

CLAUDE LÉVI-STRAUSS

A Writing Lesson

Translated by John Russell

I wanted somehow to arrive at a figure, however approximate, for the total of the Nambikwara population. In 1915 Rondon had put it at twenty thousand, which was probably too high. But at that time the nomadic bands were of several hundred people apiece, and all the indications I had collected along the line pointed to a rapid decline. Thirty years ago, for instance, the known fraction of the Sabané group comprised more than a thousand individuals; when that same group visited the telegraph station of Campos Novos in 1928 it consisted of one hundred and twenty-seven men, plus their women and children. In November 1929, moreover, an influenza epidemic broke out when the group was camping at the point known as Espirro. The disease turned into a form of pulmonary oedema, and three hundred Indians died of it within forty-eight hours. The whole group disintegrated, leaving the sick and dying to fend for themselves. Of the thousand Sabané who had once been known of, only nineteen men and their families were still alive in 1938. This decline is due not only to the epidemic, but also to the fact that some years ago the Sabané were in a state of war with some of their easterly neighbours.

But a large group installed not far from Tres Buritis was wiped out by influenza in 1927: of the six or seven survivors, only three were still alive in 1938. The Tarundé group, once one of the largest, numbered twelve men, with their families, in 1936: three years later these twelve were reduced to four.

What was the position at the time of my arrival? Probably a bare two thousand Indians were scattered about the territory. I could not hope to make a systematic count, because certain groups were always hostile, and because, during the nomadic season, all the bands were continually on the move. But I tried to persuade my friends at Utiarity to take me to their village at a time when a rendezvous had been arranged with other allied or related bands. Thus I hoped to estimate the present size of a gathering of this sort and to compare it with the reunions that had been scrutinized in earlier years. I promised to bring them presents, and effect some exchanges, but the leader of the band remained hesitant: he was not sure of his guests, and if my companions and I were to disappear in the region where no white men had penetrated since the incident of the seven telegraph-workers in 1925, then the precarious peace which existed there would be compromised for a long time to come.

In the end he agreed, on condition that we cut down the size of our party, and took only four oxen to carry our presents. Even so, he said, we should have to forswear the usual tracks, because our beasts would never get through the dense vegetation which abounded in the lower reaches of each valley. We should have to go by the plateau, improvising our route as we went along.

This was a very dangerous expedition, but it now seems to me largely grotesque. We had hardly left Juruena when my Brazilian colleague remarked to me on the absence of the Nambikwara women and children: only the men were with us, each armed with bow and arrows. All the literature of travel indicated this as a sign that an attack was imminent. Our feelings were mixed, therefore, as we went forward, verifying from time to time the position of our Smith and Wesson revolvers ('*Cemite Vechetone*' was our men's name for them) and our rifles. These fears proved misplaced: towards the half-way point of the day's march we caught up with the remainder of the band, whom their provident chief had sent on ahead of us, the day before, knowing that our mules would make much better time than the women, laden as these were with their baskets and encumbered with little children.

Soon after this, however, the Indians got lost. The new itinerary was not as straightforward as they had supposed. Towards evening we had to come to a halt in the bush. We had been promised that there would be game thereabouts and the Indians, counting on our rifles, had brought no food with them. We, for our part, had brought only emergency rations which could not be shared out all round. A troop of deer which had been nibbling away at the edge of a spring fled at our approach. The next morning everybody was in a thoroughly bad humour: ostensibly, this took for its object the leader of the band, whom they considered to be responsible for the venture which he and I had devised between us. Instead of going off to hunt or collect wild food on their own account, they decided to spend the day lying in the shade, leaving it to their leader to find the solution to their problem. He went off, accompanied by one of his wives: towards evening we saw them coming back with their baskets heavy-laden with grasshoppers that they had spent the entire day in collecting. Grasshopper pie is not one of their favourite dishes, but the entire party fell on it, none the less, with relish. Good humour broke out on all sides, and on the next morning we got under way again.

And, at last, we got to the rendezvous. This was a sandy terrace above a water-course, bordered with trees between which the Indians had laid out some little gardens. Incoming groups arrived at intervals during the day and by the evening there were seventy-five people in all: seventeen families, grouped under thirteen crude shelters hardly more solid than those which served in camp. I was told that when the rains began the whole company would take refuge in five round huts built for several months' wear. Many of the natives seemed never to have seen a white man, and their more than dubious welcome combined with their leader's extreme nervousness seemed to suggest that he had forced their hand, somewhat, in the whole matter. Neither we nor the Indians felt at all at our ease and, as there were no trees, we had to lie, like the Nambikwaras, on the bare ground. No one slept: we kept, all night long, a polite watch upon one another.

It would have been rash to prolong the adventure, and I suggested to the leader that we should get down to our exchanges without further delay. It was then that there occurred an extraordinary incident which forces me to go back a little in time. That the Nambikwara could not write goes without saying. But they were also unable to draw, except for a few dots and zigzags on their calabashes. I distributed pencils and paper among them, none the less, as I had done with the Caduveo. At first they made no use of them. Then, one day, I saw that they were all busy drawing wavy horizontal lines on the paper. What were they trying to do? I could only conclude that they were writing—or, more exactly, that they were trying to do as I did with my pencils. As I had never tried to amuse them with drawings, they could not conceive of any other use for this implement. With most of them, that was as far as they got: but their leader saw further into the problem. Doubtless he was the only one among them to have understood what writing was for. So he asked me for one of my notepads; and when we were working together he did not give me his answers in words, but traced a wavy line or two on the paper and gave it to me, as if I could read what he had to say. He himself was all but deceived by his own play-acting. Each time he drew a line he would examine it with great care, as if its meaning must suddenly leap to the eye; and every time a look of disappointment came over his face. But he would never give up trying, and there was an unspoken agreement between us that his scribblings had a meaning that I did my best to decipher; his own verbal commentary was so prompt in coming that I had no need to ask him to explain what he had written.

And now, no sooner was everyone assembled than he drew forth from a basket a piece of paper covered with scribbled lines and pretended to read from it. With a show of hesitation he looked up and down his 'list' for the objects to be given in exchange for his people's presents. So-and-so was to receive a machete in return for his bow and arrows, and another a string of beads in return for his necklaces—and so on for two solid hours. What was he hoping for? To deceive himself, perhaps: but, even more, to amaze his companions and persuade them that *his* intermediacy was responsible for the exchanges. He had allied himself with the white man, as equal with equal, and could now share in his secrets. We were in a hurry to get away, since there would obviously be a moment of real danger at which all the marvels I had brought would have been handed over. . . . So I did not go further into the matter and we set off on the return journey, still guided by the Indians.

There had been something intensely irritating about our abortive meeting, and about the mystifications of which I had just been the unknowing instrument. Added to that, my mule was suffering from aphtha, and its mouth was causing it pain, so that by turns it hurried impatiently forward and stopped dead in its tracks. We got into a quarrel with one another and, quite suddenly, without realizing how it happened, I found myself alone, and lost, in the middle of the bush.

What was I to do? What people do in books: fire a shot in the air to let my companions know what had happened. I dismounted and did so. No reply. I fired again, and as there seemed to be an answer I fired a third shot. This scared my mule, who went off at a trot and pulled up some distance away.

I put weapons and photographic equipment neatly at the foot of a tree, memorized its position, and ran off to recapture my mule, who seemed quite peaceably disposed. He let me get right up to him and then, just as I reached for the reins, he made off at full speed. This happened more than once until in despair I jumped at him and threw both my arms round his tail. This unusual proceeding took him by surprise, and he decided to give in. Back in the saddle, I made as if to collect my belongings, only to find that we had twisted and turned so often that I had no idea where they were.

Demoralized by this episode, I decided to rejoin our troop. Neither my mule nor I knew where they had gone. Sometimes I would head him in a direction that he refused to take; sometimes I would let him lead, only to find that he was simply turning in a circle. The sun was going down, I was no longer armed, and I expected at every moment to be the target of a volley of arrows. I was not, admittedly, the first white man to penetrate that hostile zone. But none of my predecessors had come back alive and, quite apart from myself, my mule was a tempting prey for people who rarely have anything very much to get their teeth into. These dark thoughts passed, one by one, through my mind as I waited for the sun to go down, thinking that since I at least had some matches with me I could start a bush-fire. Just as I was about to strike the first match I heard voices: two of the Nambikwara had turned back, the moment my absence was noticed, and had been following me all afternoon. For them to recover my equipment was child's play and, at nightfall, they led me to the camp where our whole troop was waiting for me.

Still tormented by this absurd incident, I slept badly. To while away the hours I went back, in my mind, to the scene of the previous morning. So the Nambikwara had learnt what it meant to write! But not at all, as one might have supposed, as the result of a laborious apprenticeship. The symbol had been borrowed, but the reality remained quite foreign to them. Even the borrowing had had a sociological, rather than an intellectual object: for it was not a question of knowing specific things, or understanding them, or keeping them in mind, but merely of enhancing the prestige and authority of one individual—or one function—at the expense of the rest of the party. A native, still in the period of the stone age, had realized that even if he could not himself understand the great instrument of understanding he could at least make it serve other ends. For thousands of years, after all, and still today in a great part of the world, writing has existed as an institution in societies in which the vast majority of people are quite unable to write. The villages where I stayed in the Chittagong hills in Pakistan are populated by illiterates; yet each village has a scribe who fulfils his function for the benefit both of individual citizens and of the village as a whole. They all know what writing is and, if need be, can write: but they do it from outside as if it were a mediator, foreign to themselves, with whom they communicate by an oral process. But the scribe is rarely a functionary or an employee of the group as a whole; his knowledge is a source of power—so much so, in fact, that the functions of scribe and usurer are often united in the same human being. This is not merely because the usurer needs to be able to read and write to carry on his trade, but because he has thus a twofold empire over his fellows.

Writing is a strange thing. It would seem as if its appearance could not have failed to wreak profound changes in the living conditions of our race, and that these transformations must have been above all intellectual in character. Once men know how to write, they are enormously more able to keep in being a large body of knowledge. Writing might, that is to say, be regarded as a form of artificial memory, whose development should be accompanied by a deeper knowledge of the past and, therefore, by a greater ability to organize the present and the future. Of all the criteria by which people habitually distinguish civilization from barbarism, this should be the one most worth retaining: that certain peoples write and others do not. The first group can accumulate a body of knowledge that helps it to move ever faster towards the goal that it has assigned to itself; the second is confined within limits that the memory of individuals can never hope to extend, and it must remain the prisoner of a history worked out from day to day, with neither a clear knowledge of its own origins nor a consecutive idea of what its future should be.

Yet nothing of what we know of writing, or of its role in evolution, can be said to justify this conception. One of the most creative phases in human history took place with the onset of the neolithic era: agriculture and the domestication of animals are only two of the developments which may be traced to this period. It must have had behind it thousands of years during which small societies of human beings were noting, experimenting, and passing on to one another the fruits of their knowledge. The very success of this immense enterprise bears witness to the rigour and the continuity of its preparation, at a time when writing was quite unknown. If writing first made its appearance between the fourth and third millennium before our era, we must see it not, in any degree, as a conditioning factor in the neolithic revolution, but rather as an already-distant and doubtless indirect result of that revolution. With what great innovation can it be linked? Where technique is concerned, architecture alone can be called into question. Yet the architecture of the Egyptians or the Sumerians was no better than the work of certain American Indians who, at the time

America was discovered, were ignorant of writing. Conversely, between the invention of writing and the birth of modern science, the western world has lived through some five thousand years, during which time the sum of its knowledge has rather gone up and down than known a steady increase. It has often been remarked that there was no great difference between the life of a Greek or Roman citizen and that of a member of the well-to-do European classes in the eighteenth century. In the neolithic age, humanity made immense strides forward without any help from writing; and writing did not save the civilizations of the western world from long periods of stagnation. Doubtless the scientific expansion of the nineteenth and twentieth centuries could hardly have occurred, had writing not existed. But this condition, however necessary, cannot in itself explain that expansion.

If we want to correlate the appearance of writing with certain other characteristics of civilization, we must look elsewhere. The one phenomenon which has invariably accompanied it is the formation of cities and empires: the integration into a political system, that is to say, of a considerable number of individuals, and the distribution of those individuals into a hierarchy of castes and classes. Such is, at any rate, the type of development which we find, from Egypt right across to China, at the moment when writing makes its débuts; it seems to favour rather the exploitation than the enlightenment of mankind. This exploitation made it possible to assemble workpeople by the thousand and set them tasks that taxed them to the limits of their strength: to this, surely, we must attribute the beginnings of architecture as we know it. If my hypothesis is correct, the primary function of writing, as a means of communication, is to facilitate the enslavement of other human beings. The use of writing for disinterested ends, and with a view to satisfactions of the mind in the fields either of science or the arts, is a secondary result of its invention—and may even be no more than a way of reinforcing, justifying, or dissimulating its primary function.

There are, however, exceptions to this rule. Ancient Africa included empires in which several hundred thousand subjects acknowledged a single rule; in pre-Colombian America, the Inca empire numbered several million subjects. But, alike in Africa and in America, these ventures were notably unstable: we know, for instance, that the Inca empire was established in the twelfth century or thereabouts. Pizarro's soldiers would never have conquered it so easily if it had not already, three centuries later, been largely decomposed. And, from the little we know of the ancient history of Africa, we can divine an analogous situation: massive political groups seem to have appeared and disappeared within the space of not many decades. It may be, therefore, that these instances confirm, instead of refuting, our hypothesis. Writing may not have sufficed to consolidate human knowledge, but it may well have been indispensable to the establishment of an enduring dominion. To bring the matter nearer to our own time: the European-wide movement towards compulsory education in the nineteenth century went hand in hand with the extension of military service and the systematization of the proletariat. The struggle against illiteracy is indistinguishable, at times, from the increased powers exerted over the individual citizen by the central authority. For it is only when everyone can read that Authority can decree that 'ignorance of the law is no defence'.

All this moved rapidly from the national to the international level, thanks to the mutual complicity which sprang up between new-born states—confronted as these were with the problems that had been our own, a century or two ago—and an international society of peoples long privileged. These latter recognize that their stability may well be endangered by nations whose knowledge of the written word has not, as yet, empowered them to think in formulae which can be modified at will. Such nations are not yet ready to be 'edified'; and when they are first given the freedom of the library shelves they are perilously vulnerable to the ever more deliberately misleading effects of the printed word. Doubtless the die is already cast, in that respect. But in my Nambikwara village people were not so easily taken in. Shortly after my visit the leader lost the confidence of most of his people. Those who moved away from him, after he had tried to play the civilized man, must have had a confused understanding of the fact that writing, on this its first appearance in their midst, had allied itself with falsehood; and so they had taken refuge, deeper in the bush, to win themselves a respite. And yet I could not but admire the genius of their leader, for he had divined in a flash that writing could redouble his hold upon the others and, in so doing, he had got, as it were, to the bottom of an institution which he did not as yet know how to work. The episode also drew my attention to a further aspect of Nambikwara life: the political relations between individuals and groups. This I was shortly to be able to scrutinize more directly.

We were still at Utiarity when an epidemic of purulent ophthalmia broke out among the natives. This infection, gonococchic in origin, soon spread to every one of them. Apart from being terribly painful, it led to what threatened to be permanent blindness. For several days the entire band was paralysed. They treated their eyes with water, in which a certain kind of bark had been soaked: this they introduced into the eye with the help of leaves rolled into the shape of a funnel. The disease spread to my own group. My wife was the first to catch it. She had taken part in all our previous expeditions and had taken her full share in the study of material culture: but now she was so seriously ill that I had to send her back home. Most of our bearers went sick, and so did my Brazilian associate. Before long it was out of the question to go any farther. I ordered the main body of our party to rest, left our doctor behind to do what he could for them, and myself pushed on with two men and a few animals to the station of Campos Novos, near which a number of Indian bands had been reported. There I spent a fortnight in semi-idleness, picking the barely ripe fruit of an orchard which had 'gone back to Nature': guavas whose bitter taste and stony texture belied the promise of their scent; *caju*, vivid in colour as any parakeet, with a flesh that concealed within its spongy cells an astringent, delicately flavoured juice. And when the larder was empty we had only to get up at dawn and make our way to a thicket, a few hundred yards from the camp, where wood-pigeons would turn up, sharp on time every day, and offer themselves as our prey. At Campos Novos, too, I met two bands which had arrived from the north, drawn by the rumour of the presents I had brought with me.

These two bands were as ill disposed towards one another as they were towards me. From the outset, my gifts were not so much solicited as exacted. During the first few days only one of the bands was in evidence, together with a native from the Utiarity group who had gone on ahead of me. Did he show too much interest in a young woman who belonged to our hosts' group? I believe he did. Relations were bad, almost from the start, between the strangers and their visitor, and he dropped into the habit of coming over to my camp in search of a more cordial welcome. He also shared my meals. This fact was taken note of: and one day when he was out hunting I was visited by a delegation of four Indians. There was a distinct menace in the tone of voice in which they urged me to put poison into his food. They would bring me all that I needed: four little tubes bound together with cotton and filled with grey powder. I was very much put out: yet, as an outright refusal would turn the whole band against me, I felt it best to go carefully, in view of their maleficent intentions. So I decided to know less of their language than I really did. Faced with my look of total incomprehension, the Indians repeated to me over and over again that my guest was *kakoré*, very wicked, and that I should get rid of him as soon as possible. Eventually they made off, with every sign of discontentment. I warned my guest of what had occurred, and he at once took to his heels; not till months later, when I revisited the region, did I see him again.

Luckily the second band arrived on the following day, giving the Indians a new target for their hostility. The meeting took place at my camp, which was both neutral ground and the terminal point of their respective journeyings. I had, therefore, a front seat in the stalls. The men of each party came up on their own; a lengthy conversation followed between their respective leaders, consisting mainly of monologues, in alternation, on a plaintive, nasal note that I did not remember having encountered before. 'We are very angry!' one group kept on whining. 'You are our enemies!' To which the others replied: 'We are not at all angry! We are your brothers! Friends! We can understand each other!' and so on. Once this exchange of protests and provocations was over, a common camp was set up, close to my own. After some dancing and singing, during which each group played down its own contribution and glorified that of its adversaries—'The Tamaindé sang so well! And we sing so badly!'—quarrelling began again, and before long tempers began to run high. The night had hardly begun when the noise of argument-cum-singing set up a tremendous row, the significance of which was lost upon me. Threatening gestures could be seen, and once or twice men actually came to blows and had to be separated. The menaces consisted, in every case, of gestures relating in some way to the sexual organs. A Nambikwara shows hostility by taking his penis in both hands and pointing it towards his adversary. This is the prelude to an attack on the adversary in question, with a view to wrenching off the tuft of *buriti* straw that hangs down from the front of his belt, just above his private parts. These parts are 'hidden by the straw' and the point of fighting is to get the other man's straw away from him. This is an entirely symbolic action, for the masculine *cache-sexe* is so fragile, and in any case so insubstantial, that it serves neither to protect nor, in any true sense, to dissimulate the parts in question. Another mark of victory is to wrest your opponent's bow and arrows from him and put them down some distance away. At all such times the Indians take on attitudes of extreme intensity, as if in a state of violent contained rage. Eventually these individual quarrels end up in a general pitched battle. But on this occasion they died down at dawn. Still in the same state of evident exasperation, and with the roughest of gestures, the adversaries began to scrutinize one another closely, fingering an ear-ring here and a cotton bracelet or feathered ornament there, and muttering rapidly throughout: 'Give . . . give . . . give . . . look at that . . . how pretty!' to which the owner would reply: 'No, no . . . it's ugly, old, worn-out. . . .'

This reconciliatory inspection marks the end of the conflict. It introduces, as between the two groups, another kind of relationship: that of the commercial exchange. The material culture of the Nambikwara may be of the rudest, but each band's manufactures are, none the less, highly prized in the outer world. Those in the east are short of pottery and seed-beads. Those in the north consider that their southerly neighbours make particularly beautiful necklaces. The meeting of two groups, once established upon a pacific level, will therefore engender a whole series of reciprocal gifts: the battlefield turns into a market-place.

But the exchanges go forward almost imperceptibly: the morning after the quarrelling everyone went about his normal occupations, and objects or products changed hands without either donor or recipient making any outward allusion to what was going forward. Balls of thread and raw cotton; lumps of wax or resin; urucu paste; shells, earrings, bracelets, and necklaces; tobacco and seed-beads; feathers and strips of bamboo that could be made into arrowheads; bunches of palm-fibres and porcupine-quills; complete pots and potsherds; calabashes. This mysterious traffic went on until the day was half over, when the two groups separated and went off, each on his own way.

The Nambikwara leave everything, on such occasions, to the generosity of their 'opposite number'. Totally foreign to them is the notion that anyone could set a price on any object, discuss that price, haggle over it, insist on getting it, or 'chalk it up' as a debt. I once offered an Indian a forest-knife in return for his having carried a message to a nearby group. When he came back I did not immediately give him the knife, because I assumed that he would come and ask for it. But nothing of the kind: and the next day I couldn't find him anywhere. His friends told me that he had gone away in a rage, and I never saw him again. I had to entrust the present to another Indian. This being so, it is not surprising that when the exchanges are over one side or the other is often discontented with the result; and that, as weeks and then months go by, and he counts up, over and over again, the presents he received, and compares them with those he has given, he becomes more and more bitter. Often this bitterness turns to aggression. Many a war has broken out for no other reason. There are other causes, of course: a murder, or a rape to be either brought off or avenged. It does not seem as if a band feels itself bound to take collective reprisals for an injury done to any one of its members. But such is the animosity which reigns between groups that often every advantage is taken of pretexts of this kind, especially if the group in question feels itself in a strong position. The case is then presented by a warrior, who set out his grievances in the same tone and in much the style of the encounter-ritual: 'Hallo there! Come here! Now look here—I'm very angry! Really very angry indeed! Arrows! Big arrows!'

Specially dressed for the occasion—tufts of *buriti* straw striped with red, jaguar-skin helmets—the men assemble behind their leader and dance. A divinatory rite must be observed: the chief, or the sorcerer, if one exists, hides an arrow in a corner of the bush. The next day the men search for the arrow and, if it is stained with blood, war is declared: if not, they call it all off. Many expeditions that begin in this way come to an end after a few miles' march. The war party loses all its enthusiasm and excitement and turns back towards home. But sometimes the venture is pressed to its conclusion, and blood is shed. The Nambikwara attack at dawn, after having first scattered to create the conditions of an ambush. The signal to attack passes from man to man by means of the whistle that each carries round his neck. This whistle, made up of two tubes of bamboo tied together with cotton, makes a noise like that of the cricket and, doubtless for that reason, bears the same name. The war-arrows are those used in peace-time for hunting the bigger game, but their points are cut to a saw-edge. Arrows poisoned with curare, though common in hunting, are never used in battle, because anyone wounded by one of them would get it out before the poison had had time to get into his veins.

ALISTAIR MACLEOD

'At the Moment': Notes on Fiction

I am interested 'at the moment' in getting words down on the page that convey what it is like to be living a certain kind of life in a certain place and at a certain time in history. I believe that the writer should tell the truth about what he (or of course she) knows in a creative manner that is not necessarily 'holding a mirror up to life.' I do feel that fictional characters can often be as 'true' (or more 'true') than actual characters if their author creates them well enough. I like to think that writing is an act of communication and, as such, the writer should strive to be clear rather than coy. Being clear, to my mind, is not the same as being simplistic. I also believe that 'art' begins in the emotional part of the author which means that the writer should 'care' or 'feel' deeply about his subject. If a writer has no sympathy for his characters or the human condition he will have difficulty arousing an emotional response in the reader. 'No tears in the writer—no tears in the reader,' is a quotation I remember from somewhere. This is, of course, not the same as going on emotional binges. crying on the page, etc. and I realize that 'strong feeling' is not art. However I believe that it often leads to the best art. There is a danger in over-intellectualizing emotion and/or intuition as Keats pointed out.

I think that if an author believes in the value of what he has to say through his work, he must be very persistent and strong in that belief and he must be 'willing to stand the rain.' There is a danger/temptation to be too much influenced by critical trends or the statements of those who worship at the altars of different religions—especially if they are considered the high priests of their time. It is good to remember that Henry James once dismissed the Dorset writer as 'poor little Thomas Hardy' and that Virginia Woolf said that the writings of Joyce reminded her of a young undergraduate scratching his pimples.

Some months before his death I was talking to George Ryga. 'Nearly all of the good literature,' he said, 'comes from all of the bad places.' I think of this statement more often now than I thought I would at the time. I think of it when reading *Wuthering Heights* or *The Mayor of Casterbridge* or *The Sound and the Fury* (rising out of that most maligned state of Mississippi) and I think of it when reading the work and criticism associated with the brilliantly determined David Adams Richards. I do not necessarily think of 'bad places,' but I do think of a kind of literature that rises out of the people and goes back to them. This is why undergraduates far removed from such books by space and time still sit on the edges of their chairs when they read them. This is the power and wonder of 'story.' It may well be that human nature does not change and that such books were written not for trends but 'for the record.' It is good to remember this as a reader and even more so as a writer. Good writing which is done with love and care and which 'is about something' will last a long, long time. And though sometimes in danger of being temporarily 'swamped' will, in the words of the late Stan Rogers, 'rise again.' I do believe.

ALICE MUNRO

What Is Real?

Whenever people get an opportunity to ask me questions about my writing, I can be sure that some of the questions asked will be these:

"Do you write about real people?"

"Did those things really happen?"

"When you write about a small town are you really writing about Wingham?" (Wingham is the small town in Ontario where I was born and grew up, and it has often been assumed, by people who should know better, that I have simply "fictionalized" this place in my work. Indeed, the local newspaper has taken me to task for making it the "butt of a soured and cruel introspection.")

The usual thing, for writers, is to regard these either as very naive questions, asked by people who really don't understand the difference between autobiography and fiction, who can't recognize the device of the first-person narrator, or else as catch-you-out questions posed by journalists who hope to stir up exactly the sort of dreary (and to outsiders, slightly comic) indignation voiced by my hometown paper. Writers answer such questions patiently or crossly according to temperament and the mood they're in. They say, no, you must understand my characters are composites; no, those things didn't happen the way I wrote about them; no, of course not, that isn't Wingham (or whatever other place it may be that has had the queer unsought-after distinction of hatching a writer). Or the writer may, riskily, ask the questioners what is real, anyway? None of this seems to be very satisfactory. People go on asking these same questions because the subject really does interest and bewilder them. It would seem to be quite true that they don't know what fiction is.

And how could they know, when what it is, is changing all the time, and we differ among ourselves, and we don't really try to explain because it is too difficult?

What I would like to do here is what I can't do in two or three sentences at the end of a reading. I won't try to explain what fiction is, and what short stories are (assuming, which we can't, that there is any fixed thing that it is and they are), but what short stories are to me, and how I write them, and how I use things that are "real." I will start by explaining how I read stories written by other people. For one thing, I can start reading them anywhere; from beginning to end, from end to beginning, from any point in between in either direction. So obviously I don't take up a story and follow it as if it were a road, taking me somewhere, with views and neat diversions along the way. I go into it, and move back and forth and settle here and there, stay in it for a while. It's more like a house. Everybody knows what a house does, how it encloses space and makes connections between one enclosed space and another and presents what is outside in a new way. This is the nearest I can come to explaining what a story does for me, and what I want my stories to do for other people.

So when I write a story I want to make a certain kind of structure, and I know the feeling I want to get from being inside that structure. This is the hard part of the explanation, where I have to use a word like "feeling," which is not very precise, because if I attempt to be more intellectually respectable I will have to be dishonest. "Feeling" will have to do.

There is no blueprint for the structure. It's not a question of, "I'll make this kind of house because if I do it right it will have this effect." I've got to make, I've got to build up, a house, a story, to fit around the indescribable "feeling" that is like the soul of the story, and which I must insist upon in a dogged, embarrassed way, as being no more definable than that. And I don't know where it comes from. It seems to be already there, and some unlikely clue, such as a shop window or a bit of conversation, makes me aware of it. Then I start accumulating the material and putting it together. Some of the material I may have lying around already, in memories and observations, and some I invent, and some I have to go diligently looking for (factual details), while some is dumped in my lap (anecdotes, bits of speech). I see how this material might go together to make the shape I need, and I try it. I keep trying and seeing where I went wrong and trying again.

I suppose this is the place where I should talk about technical problems and how I solve them. The main reason I can't is that I'm never sure I do solve anything. Even when I say that I see where I went wrong, I'm being misleading. I never figure out how I'm going to change things, I never say to myself, "That page is heavy going, that paragraph's clumsy, I need some dialogue and shorter sentences." I feel a part that's wrong, like a soggy weight; then I pay attention to the story, as if it were really happening somewhere, not just in my head, and in its own way, not mine. As a result, the sentences may indeed get shorter, there may be more dialogue, and so on. But though I've tried to pay attention to the story, I may not have got it right; those shorter sentences may be an evasion, a mistake. Every final draft, every published story, is still only an attempt, an approach, to the story.

I did promise to talk about using reality. "Why, if Jubilee isn't Wingham, has it got Shuter Street in it?" people want to know. Why have I described somebody's real ceramic elephant sitting on the mantelpiece? I could say I get momentum from doing things like this. The fictional room, town, world, needs a bit of starter dough from the real world. It's a device to help the writer—at least it helps me— but it arouses a certain baulked fury in the people who really do live on Shuter Street and the lady who owns the ceramic elephant. "Why do you put in something true and then go on and tell lies?" they say, and anybody who has been on the receiving end of this kind of thing knows how they feel.

"I do it for the sake of my art and to make this structure which encloses the soul of my story, that I've been telling you about," says the writer. "That is more important than anything."

Not to everybody, it isn't.

So I can see there might be a case, once you've written the story and got the momentum, for going back and changing the elephant to a camel (though there's always a chance the lady might complain that you made a nasty camel out of a beautiful elephant), and changing Shuter Street to Blank Street. But what about the big chunks of reality, without which your story can't exist? In the story *Royal Beatings*, I use a big chunk of reality: the story of the butcher, and of the young men who may have been egged on to "get" him. This is a story out of an old newspaper; it really did happen in a town I know. There is no legal difficulty about using it because it has been printed in a newspaper, and besides, the people who figure in it are all long dead. But there is a difficulty about offending people in that town who would feel that use of this story is a deliberate exposure, taunt and insult. Other people who have no connection with the real happening would say, "Why write about anything so hideous?" And lest you think that such an objection could only be raised by simple folk who read nothing but Harlequin Romances, let me tell you that one of the questions most frequently asked at universities is, "Why do you write about things that are so depressing?" People can accept almost any amount of ugliness if it is contained in a familiar formula, as it is on television, but when they come closer to their own place, their own lives, they are much offended by a lack of editing.

There are ways I can defend myself against such objections. I can say, "I do it in the interests of historical reality. That is what the old days were really like." Or, "I do it to show the dark side of human nature, the beast let loose, the evil we can run up against in communities and families." In certain countries I could say, "I do it to show how bad things were under the old system when there were prosperous butchers and young fellows hanging around livery stables and nobody thought about building a new society." But the fact is, the minute I say *to show* I am telling a lie. I don't do it to show anything. I put this story at the heart of my story because I need it there and it belongs there. It is the black room at the centre of the house with all other rooms leading to and away from it. That is all. A strange defence. Who told me to write this story? Who feels any need of it before it is written? I do. I do, so that I might grab off this piece of horrid reality and install it where I see fit, even if Hat Nettleton and his friends were still around to make me sorry.

The answer seems to be as confusing as ever. Lots of true answers are. Yes and no. Yes, I use bits of what is real, in the sense of being really there and really happening, in the world, as most people see it, and I transform it into something that is really there and really happening, in my story. No, I am not concerned with using what is real to make any sort of record or prove any sort of point, and I am not concerned with any methods of selection but my own, which I can't fully explain. This is quite presumptuous, and if writers are not allowed to be so—and quite often, in many places, they are not—I see no point in the writing of fiction.

FLANNERY O'CONNOR

Writing Short Stories

I have heard people say that the short story was one of the most difficult literary forms, and I've always tried to decide why people feel this way about what seems to me to be one of the most natural and fundamental ways of human expression.[1] After all, you begin to hear and tell stories when you're a child, and there doesn't seem to be anything very complicated about it. I suspect that most of you have been telling stories all your lives, and yet here you sit—come to find out how to do it.

Then last week, after I had written down some of these serene thoughts to use here today, my calm was shattered when I was sent seven of your manuscripts to read.

After this experience, I found myself ready to admit, if not that the short story is one of the most difficult literary forms, at least that it is more difficult for some than for others.

I still suspect that most people start out with some kind of ability to tell a story but that it gets lost along the way. Of course, the ability to create life with words is essentially a gift. If you have it in the first place, you can develop it; if you don't have it, you might as well forget it.

But I have found that the people who don't have it are frequently the ones hell-bent on writing stories. I'm sure anyway that they are the ones who write the books and the magazine articles on how-to-write-short-stories. I have a friend who is taking a correspondence course in this subject, and she has passed a few of the chapter headings on to me—such as, "The Story Formula for Writers," "How to Create Characters," "Let's Plot!" This form of corruption is costing her twenty-seven dollars.

I feel that discussing story-writing in terms of plot, character, and theme is like trying to describe the expression on a face by saying where the eyes, nose, and mouth are. I've heard students say, "I'm very good with plot, but I can't do a thing with character," or, "I have this theme but I don't have a plot for it," and once I heard one say, "I've got the story but I don't have any technique."

Technique is a word they all trot out. I talked to a writers' club once, and during the question time, one good soul said, "Will you give me the technique for the frame-within-a-frame short story?" I had to admit I was so ignorant I didn't even know what that was, but she assured me there was such a thing because she had entered a contest to write one and the prize was fifty dollars.

But setting aside the people who have no talent for it, there are others who do have the talent but who flounder around because they don't really know what a story is.

I suppose that obvious things are the hardest to define. Everybody thinks he knows what a story is. But if you ask a beginning student to write a story, you're liable to get almost anything—a reminiscence, an episode, an opinion, an anecdote, anything under the sun but a story. A story is a complete dramatic action—and in good stories, the characters are shown through the action and the action is controlled through the characters, and the result of this is meaning that derives from the whole presented experience. I myself prefer to say that a story is a dramatic event that involves a person because he is a person, and a particular person—that is, because he shares in the general human condition and in some specific human situation. A story always involves, in a dramatic way, the mystery of personality. I lent some stories to a country lady who lives down the road from me, and when she returned them, she said, "Well, them stories just gone and shown you how some folks *would* do," and I thought to myself that that was right; when you write stories, you have to be content to start exactly there—showing how some specific folks *will* do, *will* do in spite of everything.

Now this is a very humble level to have to begin on, and most people who think they want to write stories are not willing to start there. They want to write about problems, not people; or about abstract issues, not concrete situations. They have an idea, or a feeling, or an overflowing ego, or they want to Be A Writer, or they want to give their wisdom to the world in a simple-enough way for the world to be able to absorb it. In any case, they don't have a story and they wouldn't be willing to write it if they did; and in the absence of a story, they set out to find a theory or a formula or a technique.

Now none of this is to say that when you write a story, you are supposed to forget or give up any moral position that you hold. Your beliefs will be the light by which you see, but they will not be what you see and they will not be a substitute for seeing. For the writer of fiction, everything has its testing point in the eye, and the eye is an organ that eventually involves the whole personality, and as much of the world as can be got into it. It involves judgment. Judgment is something that begins in the act of vision, and when it does not, or when it becomes separated from vision, then a confusion exists in the mind which transfers itself to the story.

Fiction operates through the senses, and I think one reason that people find it so difficult to write stories is that they forget how much time and patience is required to convince through the senses. No reader who doesn't actually experience, who isn't made to feel, the story is going to believe anything the fiction writer merely tells him. The first and most obvious characteristic of fiction is that it deals with reality through what can be seen, heard, smelt, tasted, and touched.

Now this is something that can't be learned only in the head; it has to be learned in the habits. It has to become a way that you habitually look at things. The fiction writer has to realize that he can't create compassion with compassion, or emotion with emotion, or thought with thought. He has to provide all these things with a body; he has to create a world with weight and extension.

I have found that the stories of beginning writers usually bristle with emotion, but *whose* emotion is often very hard to determine. Dialogue frequently proceeds without the assistance of any characters that you can actually see, and uncontained thought leaks out of every corner of the story. The reason is usually that the student is wholly interested in his thoughts and his emotions and not in his dramatic action, and that he is too lazy or highfalutin to descend to the concrete where fiction operates. He thinks that judgment exists in one place and sense-impression in another. But for the fiction writer, judgment begins in the details he sees and how he sees them.

Fiction writers who are not concerned with these concrete details are guilty of what Henry James called "weak specification." The eye will glide over their words while the attention goes to sleep. Ford Madox Ford taught that you couldn't have a man appear long enough to sell a newspaper in a story unless you put him there with enough detail to make the reader see him.

I have a friend who is taking acting classes in New York from a Russian lady who is supposed to be very good at teaching actors. My friend wrote me that the first month they didn't speak a line, they only learned to see. Now learning to see is the basis for learning all the arts except music. I know a good many fiction writers who paint, not because they're any good at painting, but because it helps their writing. It forces them to look at things. Fiction writing is very seldom a matter of saying things; it is a matter of showing things.

However, to say that fiction proceeds by the use of detail does not mean the simple, mechanical piling-up of detail. Detail has to be controlled by some overall purpose, and every detail has to be put to work for you. Art is selective. What is there is essential and creates movement.

Now all this requires time. A good short story should not have less meaning than a novel, nor should its action be less complete. Nothing essential to the main experience can be left out of a short story. All the action has to be satisfactorily accounted for in terms of motivation, and there has to be a beginning, a middle, and an end, though not necessarily in that order. I think many people decide that they want to write short stories because they're short, and by short, they mean short in every way. They think that a short story is an incomplete action in which a very little is shown and a great deal suggested, and they think you suggest something by leaving it out. It's very hard to disabuse a student of this notion, because he thinks that when he leaves something out, he's being subtle; and when you tell him that he has to put something in before anything can be there, he thinks you're an insensitive idiot.

Perhaps the central question to be considered in any discussion of the short story is what do we mean by short. Being short does not mean being slight. A short story should be long in depth and should give us an experience of meaning. I have an aunt who thinks that nothing happens in a story unless somebody gets married or shot at the end of it. I wrote a story about a tramp who marries an old woman's idiot daughter in order to acquire the old woman's automobile. After the marriage, he takes the daughter off on a wedding trip in the automobile and abandons her in an eating place and drives on by himself. Now that is a complete story. There is nothing more relating to the mystery of that man's personality that could be shown through that particular dramatization. But I've never been able to convince my aunt that it's a complete story. She wants to know what happened to the idiot daughter after that.

Not long ago that story was adapted for a television play, and the adapter, knowing his business, had the tramp have a change of heart and go back and pick up the idiot daughter and the two of them ride away, grinning madly. My aunt believes that the story is complete at last, but I have other sentiments about it— which are not suitable for public utterance. When you write a story, you only have to write one story, but there will always be people who will refuse to read the story you have written.

And this naturally brings up the awful question of what kind of a reader you are writing for when you write fiction. Perhaps we each think we have a personal solution for this problem. For my own part, I have a very high opinion of the art of fiction and a very low opinion of what is called the "average" reader. I tell myself that I can't escape him, that this is the personality I am supposed to keep awake, but that at the same time, I am also supposed to provide the intelligent reader with the deeper experience that he looks for in fiction. Now actually, both of these readers are just aspects of the writer's own personality, and in the last analysis, the only reader he can know anything about is himself. We all write at our own level of understanding, but it is the peculiar characteristic of fiction that its literal surface can be made to yield entertainment on an obvious physical plane to one sort of reader while the selfsame surface can be made to yield meaning to the person equipped to experience it there.

Meaning is what keeps the short story from being short. I prefer to talk about the meaning in a story rather than the theme of a story. People talk about the theme of a story as if the theme were like the string that a sack of chicken feed is tied with. They think that if you can pick out the theme, the way you pick the right thread in the chicken-feed sack, you can rip the story open and feed the chickens. But this is not the way meaning works in fiction.

When you can state the theme of a story, when you can separate it from the story itself, then you can be sure the story is not a very good one. The meaning of a story has to be embodied in it, has to be made concrete in it. A story is a way to say something that can't be said any other way, and it takes every word in the story to say what the meaning is. You tell a story because a statement would be inadequate. When anybody asks what a story is about, the only proper thing is to tell him to read the story. The meaning of fiction is not abstract meaning but experienced meaning, and the purpose of making statements about the meaning of a story is only to help you to experience that meaning more fully.

Fiction is an art that calls for the strictest attention to the real—whether the writer is writing a naturalistic story or a fantasy. I mean that we always begin with what is or with what has an eminent possibility of truth about it. Even when one writes a fantasy, reality is the proper basis of it. A thing is fantastic because it is so real, so real that it is fantastic. Graham Greene has said that he can't write, "I stood over a bottomless pit," because that couldn't be true, or "Running down the stairs I jumped into a taxi," because that couldn't be true either. But Elizabeth Bowen can write about one of her characters that "she snatched at her hair as if she heard something in it," because that is eminently possible.

I would even go so far as to say that the person writing a fantasy has to be even more strictly attentive to the concrete detail than someone writing in a naturalistic vein—because the greater the story's strain on the credulity, the more convincing the properties in it have to be.

A good example of this is a story called "The Metamorphosis" by Franz Kafka. This is a story about a man who wakes up one morning to find that he has turned into a cockroach overnight, while not discarding his human nature. The rest of the story concerns his life and feelings and eventual death as an insect with human nature, and this situation is accepted by the reader because the concrete detail of the story is absolutely convincing. The fact is that this story describes the dual nature of man in such a realistic fashion that it is almost unbearable. The truth is not distorted here, but rather, a certain distortion is used to get at the truth. If we admit, as we must, that appearance is not the same thing as reality, then we must give the artist the liberty to make certain rearrangements of nature if these will lead to greater depths of vision. The artist himself always has to remember that what he is rearranging *is* nature, and that he has to know it and be able to describe it accurately in order to have the authority to rearrange it at all.

The peculiar problem of the short-story writer is how to make the action he describes reveal as much of the mystery of existence as possible. He has only a short space to do it in and he can't do it by statement. He has to do it by showing, not by saying, and by showing the concrete—so that his problem is really how to make the concrete work double time for him.

In good fiction, certain of the details will tend to accumulate meaning from the action of the story itself, and when this happens they become symbolic in the way they work. I once wrote a story called "Good Country People," in which a lady Ph.D. has her wooden leg stolen by a Bible salesman whom she has tried to seduce. Now I'll admit that, paraphrased in this way, the situation is simply a low joke. The average reader is pleased to observe anybody's wooden leg being stolen.

But without ceasing to appeal to him and without making any statements of high intention, this story does manage to operate at another level of experience, by letting the wooden leg accumulate meaning. Early in the story, we're presented with the fact that the Ph.D. is spiritually as well as physically crippled. She believes in nothing but her own belief in nothing, and we perceive that there is a wooden part of her soul that corresponds to her wooden leg. Now of course this is never stated. The fiction writer states as little as possible. The reader makes this connection from things he is shown. He may not even know that he makes the connection, but the connection is there nevertheless and it has its effect on him. As the story goes on, the wooden leg continues to accumulate meaning. The reader learns how the girl feels about her leg, how her mother feels about it, and how the country woman on the place feels about it; and finally, by the time the Bible salesman comes along, the leg has accumulated so much meaning that it is, as the saying goes, loaded. And when the Bible salesman steals it, the reader real-izes that he has taken away part of the girl's personality and has revealed her deeper affliction to her for the first time.

If you want to say that the wooden leg is a symbol, you can say that. But it is a wooden leg first, and as a wooden leg it is absolutely necessary to the story. It has its place on the literal level of the story, but it operates in depth as well as on the surface. It increases the story in every direction, and this is essentially the way a story escapes being short.

Now a little might be said about the way in which this happens. I wouldn't want you to think that in that story I sat down and said, "I am now going to write a story about a Ph.D. with a wooden leg, using the wooden leg as a symbol for another kind of affliction." I doubt myself if many writers know what they are going to do when they start out. When I started writing that story, I didn't know there was going to be a Ph.D. with a wooden leg in it. I merely found myself one morning writing a description of two women that I knew something about, and before I realized it, I had equipped one of them with a daughter with a wooden leg. As the story progressed, I brought in the Bible salesman, but I had no idea what I was going to do with him. I didn't know he was going to steal that wooden leg until ten or twelve lines before he did it, but when I found out that this was what was going to happen, I realized that it was inevitable. This is a story that produces a shock for the reader, and I think one reason for this is that it produced a shock for the writer.

Now despite the fact that this story came about in this seemingly mindless fashion, it is a story that almost no rewriting was done on. It is a story that was under control throughout the writing of it, and it might be asked how this kind of control comes about, since it is not entirely conscious.

I think the answer to this is what Maritain calls "the habit of art." It is a fact that fiction writing is something in which the whole personality takes part—the conscious as well as the unconscious mind. Art is the habit of the artist; and habits have to be rooted deep in the whole personality. They have to be cultivated like any other habit, over a long period of time, by experience; and teaching any kind of writing is largely a matter of helping the student develop the habit of art. I think this is more than just a discipline, although it is that; I think it is a way of looking at the created world and of using the senses so as to make them find as much meaning as possible in things.

Now I am not so naïve as to suppose that most people come to writers' conferences in order to hear what kind of vision is necessary to write stories that will become a permanent part of our literature. Even if you do wish to hear this, your greatest concerns are immediately practical. You want to know how you can actually write a good story, and further, how you can tell when you've done it; and so you want to know what the form of a short story is, as if the form were something that existed outside of each story and could be applied or imposed on the material. Of course, the more you write, the more you will realize that the form is organic, that it is something that grows out of the material, that the form of each story is unique. A story that is any good can't be reduced, it can only be expanded. A story is good when you continue to see more and more in it, and when it continues to escape you. In fiction two and two is always more than four.

The only way, I think, to learn to write short stories is to write them, and then to try to discover what you have done. The time to think of technique is when you've actually got the story in front of you. The teacher can help the student by looking at his individual work and trying to help him decide if he has written a complete story, one in which the action fully illuminates the meaning.

Perhaps the most profitable thing I can do is to tell you about some of the general observations I made about these seven stories I read of yours. All of these observations will not fit any one of the stories exactly, but they are points nevertheless that it won't hurt anyone interested in writing to think about.

The first thing that any professional writer is conscious of in reading anything is, naturally, the use of language. Now the use of language in these stories was such that, with one exception, it would be difficult to distinguish one story from another. While I can recall running into several clichés, I can't remember one image or one metaphor from the seven stories. I don't mean there weren't images in them; I just mean that there weren't any that were effective enough to take away with you.

In connection with this, I made another observation that startled me considerably. With the exception of one story, there was practically no use made of the local idiom. Now this is a Southern Writers' Conference. All the addresses on these stories were from Georgia or Tennessee, yet there was no distinctive sense of Southern life in them. A few place-names were dropped, Savannah or Atlanta or Jacksonville, but these could just as easily have been changed to Pittsburgh or Passaic without calling for any other alteration in the story. The characters spoke as if they had never heard any kind of language except what came out of a television set. This indicates that something is way out of focus.

There are two qualities that make fiction. One is the sense of mystery and the other is the sense of manners. You get the manners from the texture of existence that surrounds you. The great advantage of being a Southern writer is that we don't have to go anywhere to look for manners; bad or good, we've got them in abundance. We in the South live in a society that is rich in contradiction, rich in irony, rich in contrast, and particularly rich in its speech. And yet here are six stories by Southerners in which almost no use is made of the gifts of the region.

Of course the reason for this may be that you have seen these gifts abused so often that you have become self-conscious about using them. There is nothing worse than the writer who doesn't *use* the gifts of the region, but wallows in them. Everything becomes so Southern that it's sickening, so local that it is unintelligible, so literally reproduced that it conveys nothing. The general gets lost in the particular instead of being shown through it.

However, when the life that actually surrounds us is totally ignored, when our patterns of speech are absolutely overlooked, then something is out of kilter. The writer should then ask himself if he is not reaching out for a kind of life that is artificial to him.

An idiom characterizes a society, and when you ignore the idiom, you are very likely ignoring the whole social fabric that could make a meaningful character. You can't cut characters off from their society and say much about them as individuals. You can't say anything meaningful about the mystery of a personality unless you put that personality in a believable and significant social context. And the best way to do this is through the character's own language. When the old lady in one of Andrew Lytle's stories says contemptuously that she has a mule that is older than Birmingham, we get in that one sentence a sense of a society and its history. A great deal of the Southern writer's work is done for him before he begins, because our history lives in our talk. In one of Eudora Welty's stories a character says, "Where I come from, we use fox for yard dogs and owls for chickens, but we sing true." Now there is a whole book in that one sentence; and when the people of your section can talk like that, and you ignore it, you're just not taking advantage of what's yours. The sound of our talk is too definite to be discarded with impunity, and if the writer tries to get rid of it, he is liable to destroy the better part of his creative power.

Another thing I observed about these stories is that most of them don't go very far inside a character, don't reveal very much of the character. I don't mean that they don't enter the character's mind, but they simply don't show that he has a personality. Again this goes back partly to speech. These characters have no distinctive speech to reveal themselves with; and sometimes they have no really distinctive features. You feel in the end that no personality is revealed because no personality is there. In most good stories it is the character's personality that creates the action of the story. In most of these stories, I feel that the writer has thought of some action and then scrounged up a character to perform it. You will usually be more successful if you start the other way around. If you start with a real personality, a real character, then something is bound to happen; and you don't have to know what before you begin. In fact it may be better if you don't know what before you begin. You ought to be able to discover something from your stories. If you don't, probably nobody else will.

1. In another mood on another occasion Flannery O'Connor began as follows: "I have very little to say about short-story writing. It's one thing to write short stories and another thing to talk about writing them, and I hope you realize that your asking me to talk about story-writing is just like asking a fish to lecture on swimming. The more stories I write, the more mysterious I find the process and the less I find myself capable of analyzing it. Before I started writing stories, I suppose I could have given you a pretty good lecture on the subject, but nothing produces silence like experience, and at this point I have very little to say about how stories are written."

FRANK O'CONNOR

On Writing the Short Story
(From an interview with Anthony Whittier)

Why do you prefer the short story for your medium?

Because it's the nearest thing I know to lyric poetry—I wrote lyric poetry for a long time, then discovered that God had not intended me to be a lyric poet, and the nearest thing to that is the short story. A novel actually requires far more logic and far more knowledge of circumstances, whereas a short story can have the sort of detachment from circumstances that lyric poetry has.

Faulkner has said, "Maybe every novelist wants to write poetry first, finds he can't, and then tries the short story, which is the most demanding form after poetry. And, failing at that, only then does he take up novel writing." What do you think about this?

I'd love to console myself, it's that neat—it sounds absolutely perfect except that it implies, as from a short-story writer, that the novel is just an easy sort of thing that you slide gently into, whereas, in fact, my own experience with the novel is that it was always too difficult for me to do. At least to do a novel like *Pride and Prejudice* requires something more than to be a failed B.A. or a failed poet or a failed short-story writer, or a failed anything else. Creating in the novel a sense of continuing life is the thing. We don't have that problem in the short story, where you merely suggest continuing life. In the novel, you have to create it, and that explains one of my quarrels with modern novels. Even a novel like *As I Lay Dying*, which I admire enormously, is not a novel at all, it's a short story. To me a novel is something that's built around the character of time, the nature of time, and the effects that time has on events and characters. When I see a novel that's supposed to take place in twenty-four hours, I just wonder why the man padded out the short story.

Yeats said, "O'Connor is doing for Ireland what Chekhov did for Russia." What do you think of Chekhov?

Oh, naturally I admire Chekhov extravagantly, I think every short-story writer does. He's inimitable, a person to read and admire and worship—but never, never, never to imitate. He's got all the most extraordinary technical devices, and the moment you start imitating him without those technical devices, you fall into a sort of rambling narrative, as I think even a good story writer like Katherine Mansfield did. She sees that Chekhov apparently constructs a story without episodic interest, so she decides that if she constructs a story without episodic interest it will be equally good. It isn't. What she forgets is that Chekhov had a long career as a journalist, as a writer for comic magazines, writing squibs, writing vaudevilles, and he had learned the art very, very early of maintaining interest, of creating a bony structure. It's only concealed in the later work. They think they can do without that bony structure, but they're all wrong. . . .

What about working habits? How do you start a story?

"Get black on white" used to be Maupassant's advice—that's what I always do. I don't give a hoot what the writing's like, I write any sort of rubbish which will cover the main outlines of the story, then I can begin to see it. When I write, when I draft a story, I never think of writing nice sentences about, "It was a nice August evening when Elizabeth Jane Moriarty was coming down the road." I just write roughly what happened, and then I'm able to see what the construction looks like. It's the design of the story which to me is most important, the thing that tells you there's a bad gap in the narrative here and you really ought to fill that up in some way or another. I'm always looking at the design of a story, not the treatment. Yesterday I was finishing off a piece about my friend A. E. Coppard, the greatest of all the English storytellers, who died about a fortnight ago. I was describing the way Coppard must have written these stories, going around with a notebook, recording what the lighting looked like, what that house looked like, and all the time using metaphor to suggest it to himself. "The road looked like a mad serpent going up the hill," or something of the kind, and "She said so-and-so, and the man in the pub said something else." After he had written them all out, he must have got the outline of his story, and he'd start working in all the details. Now, I could never do that at all. I've got to see what these people did, first of all, and *then* I start thinking of whether it was a nice August evening or a spring evening. I have to wait for the theme before I can do anything.

Do you rewrite?

Endlessly, endlessly, endlessly. And keep on rewriting, and after it's published, and then after it's published in book form, I usually rewrite it again. I've rewritten versions of most of my early stories and one of these days, God help, I'll publish these as well.

Do you keep notes as a source of supply for future stories?

Just notes of themes. If somebody tells me a good story, I'll write it down in my four lines; that is the secret of the theme. If you make the subject of a story twelve or fourteen lines, that's a treatment. You've already committed yourself to the sort of character, the sort of surroundings, and the moment you've committed yourself, the story is already written. It has ceased to be fluid, you can't design it any longer, you can't model it. So I always confine myself to my four lines. If it won't go into four, that means you haven't reduced it to its ultimate simplicity, reduced it to the fable. . . .

TILLIE OLSEN

From *Silences*

And, if in addition to the infinite capacity, to the daily responsibilities, there are children?

Balzac, you remember, described creation in terms of motherhood. Yes, in intelligent passionate motherhood there are similarities, and in more than the toil and patience. The calling upon total capacities; the reliving and new using of the past; the comprehensions; the fascination, absorption, intensity. All almost certain death to creation—(so far).

Not because the capacities to create no longer exist, or the need (though for a while, as in any fullness of life, the need may be obscured), but because the circumstances for sustained creation have been almost impossible. The need cannot be first. It can have at best, only part self, part time. (Unless someone else does the nurturing. Read Dorothy Fisher's "Babushka Farnham" in *Fables for Parents*.) More than in any other human relationship, overwhelmingly more, motherhood means being instantly interruptable, responsive, responsible. Children need one *now* (and remember, in our society, the family must often try to be the center for love and health the outside world is not). The very fact that these are real needs, that one feels them as one's own (love, not duty); *that there is no one else responsible for these needs*, gives them primacy. It is distraction, not meditation, that becomes habitual; interruption, not continuity; spasmodic, not constant toil. The rest has been said here. Work interrupted, deferred, relinquished, makes blockage—at best, lesser accomplishment. Unused capacities atrophy, cease to be.

When H. H. Richardson, who wrote the Australian classic *Ultima Thule*, was asked why she—whose children, like all her people, were so profoundly written—did not herself have children, she answered: "There are enough women to do the childbearing and childrearing. I know of none who can write my books." I remember thinking rebelliously, yes, and I know of none who can bear and rear my children either. But literary history is on her side. Almost no mothers—as almost no part-time, part-self persons—have created enduring literature . . . so far.

If I talk now quickly of my own silences—almost presumptuous after what has been told here—it is that the individual experience may add.

In the twenty years I bore and reared my children, usually had to work on a paid job as well, the simplest circumstances for creation did not exist. Nevertheless writing, the hope of it, was "the air I breathed, so long as I shall breathe at all." In that hope, there was conscious storing, snatched reading, beginnings of writing, and always "the secret rootlets of reconnaissance."

When the youngest of our four was in school, the beginnings struggled toward endings. This was a time, in Kafka's words, "like a squirrel in a cage: bliss of movement, desperation about constriction, craziness of endurance."

Bliss of movement. A full extended family life; the world of my job (transcriber in a dairy-equipment company); and the writing, which I was somehow able to carry around within me through work, through home. Time on the bus, even when I had to stand, was enough; the stolen moments at work, enough; the deep night hours for as long as I could stay awake, after the kids were in bed, after the household tasks were done, sometimes during. It is no accident that the first work I considered publishable began: "I stand here ironing, and what you asked me moves tormented back and forth with the iron."

In such snatches of time I wrote what I did in those years, but there came a time when this triple life was no longer possible. The fifteen hours of daily realities became too much distraction for the writing. I lost craziness of endurance. What might have been, I don't know; but I applied for, and was given, eight months' writing time. There was still full family life, all the household responsibilities, but I did not have to hold an eight-hour job. I had continuity, three full days, sometimes more—and it was in those months I made the mysterious turn and became a writing writer.

Then had to return to the world of work, someone else's work, nine hours, five days a week.

This was the time of festering and congestion. For a few months I was able to shield the writing with which I was so full, against the demands of jobs on which I had to be competent, through the joys and responsibilities and trials of family. For a few months. Always roused by the writing, always denied. "I could not go to write it down. It convulsed and died in me. I will pay."

My work died. What demanded to be written, did not. It seethed, bubbled, clamored, peopled me. At last moved into the hours meant for sleeping. I worked now full time on temporary jobs, a Kelly, a Western Agency girl (girl!), wandering from office to office, always hoping to manage two, three writing months ahead. Eventually there was time.

I had said: always roused by the writing, always denied. Now, like a woman made frigid, I had to learn response, to trust this possibility for fruition that had not been before. Any interruption dazed and silenced me. It took a long while of surrendering to what I was trying to write, of invoking Henry James's "passion, piety, patience," before I was able to re-establish work.

When again I had to leave the writing, I lost consciousness. A time of anesthesia. There was still an automatic noting that did not stop, but it was as if writing had never been. No fever, no congestion, no festering. I ceased being peopled, slept well and dreamlessly, took a "permanent" job. The few pieces that had been published seemed to have vanished like the not-yet-written. I wrote someone, unsent: "So long they fed each other—my life, the writing—;—the writing or hope of it, my life—; but now they begin to destroy." I knew, but did not feel the destruction.

As for myself, who did not publish a book until I was fifty, I who raised children without household help or the help of the "technological sublime" (the atom bomb was in manufacture before the first automatic washing machine); who worked outside the house on everyday jobs as well (as nearly half of all women do now, though a woman with a paid job, except as a maid or prostitute, is still rarest of any in literature); who could not kill the essential angel (there was no one else to do her work); would not—if I could—have killed the caring part of the Woolf angel, as distant from the world of literature most of my life as literature is distant (in content too) from my world:

The years when I should have been writing, my hands and being were at other (inescapable) tasks. Now, lightened as they are, when I must do those tasks into which most of my life went, like the old mother, grandmother in my *Tell Me a Riddle* who could not make herself touch a baby, I pay a psychic cost: "the sweat beads, the long shudder begins." The habits of a lifetime when everything else had to come before writing are not easily broken, even when circumstances now often make it possible for writing to be first; habits of years—response to others, distractibility, responsibility for daily matters—stay with you, mark you, become you. The cost of "discontinuity" (that pattern still imposed on women) is such a weight of things unsaid, an accumulation of material so great, that everything starts up something else in me; what should take weeks, takes me sometimes months to write; what should take months, takes years.

I speak of myself to bring here the sense of those others to whom this is in the process of happening (unnecessarily happening, for it need not, must not continue to be) and to remind us of those (I so nearly was one) who never come to writing at all.

We must not speak of women writers in our century (as we cannot speak of women in any area of recognized human achievement) without speaking also of the invisible, the as-innately-capable: the born to the wrong circumstances—diminished, excluded, foundered, silenced.

We who write are survivors, "*only's*."[1] *One-out-of-twelve.*

1. For myself, "survivor" contains its other meaning: one who must bear witness for those who foundered, try to tell how and why it was that they, also worthy of life, did not survive. And pass on ways of surviving; and tell our chancy luck, our special circumstances.
"*Only's*" is an expression out of the 1950s Civil Rights time: the young Ralph Abernathy reporting to his Birmingham Church congregation on his trip up north for support:

> I go to Seattle and they tell me, "Brother, you got to meet so and so,
> why he's the only Negro Federal Circuit Judge in the Northwest"; I
> go to Chicago and they tell me, "Brother, you've got to meet so and

so, why he's the only full black professor of Sociology there is"; I go
to Albany and they tell me, "Brother, you *got* to meet so and so, why
he's the only black senator in the state legislature . . ." [long dramatic
pause] . . . WE DON'T WANT NO ONLY'S.

Only's are used to rebuke ("to be models"); to imply the unrealistic, "see, it can be done,
all you need is capacity and will." Accepting a situation of "only's" means: "let inequality
of circumstance continue to prevail."

EDGAR ALLAN POE

On the Aim and Technique of the Short Story

The tale proper, in our opinion, affords unquestionably the fairest field for the
exercise of the loftiest talent, which can be afforded by the wide domains of mere
prose. Were we bidden to say how the highest genius could be most advantageously employed for the best display of its own powers, we should answer, without hesitation—in the composition of a rhymed poem, not to exceed in length
what might be perused in an hour. Within this limit alone can the highest order
of true poetry exist. We need only here say, upon this topic, that, in almost all
classes of composition, the unity of effect or impression is a point of the greatest
importance. It is clear, moreover, that this unity cannot be thoroughly preserved
in productions whose perusal cannot be completed at one sitting. We may continue the reading of a prose composition, from the very nature of prose itself,
much longer than we can persevere, to any good purpose, in the perusal of a
poem. This latter, if truly fulfilling the demands of the poetic sentiment, induces
an exaltation of the soul which cannot be long sustained. All high excitements
are necessarily transient. Thus a long poem is a paradox. And, without unity of
impression, the deepest effects cannot be brought about. Epics were the offspring
of an imperfect sense of Art, and their reign is no more. A poem *too* brief may
produce a vivid, but never an intense or enduring impression. Without a certain
continuity of effort—without a certain duration or repetition of purpose—the
soul is never deeply moved. There must be the dropping of the water upon the
rock. De Béranger has wrought brilliant things—pungent and spirit-stirring—but,
like all immassive bodies, they lack *momentum*, and thus fail to satisfy the Poetic
Sentiment. They sparkle and excite, but, from want of continuity, fail deeply to
impress. Extreme brevity will degenerate into epigrammatism; but the sin of
extreme length is even more unpardonable. *In medio tutissimus ibis.*

Were we called upon, however, to designate that class of composition which,
next to such a poem as we have suggested, should best fulfil the demands of high
genius—should offer it the most advantageous field of exertion—we should unhesitatingly speak of the prose tale, as Mr. Hawthorne has here exemplified it. We
allude to the short prose narrative, requiring from a half-hour to one or two hours in

its perusal. The ordinary novel is objectionable, from its length, for reasons already stated in substance. As it cannot be read at one sitting, it deprives itself, of course, of the immense force derivable from *totality*. Worldly interests intervening during the pauses of perusal, modify, annul, or counteract, in a greater or less degree, the impressions of the book. But simple cessation in reading, would, of itself, be sufficient to destroy the true unity. In the brief tale, however, the author is enabled to carry out the fulness of his intention, be it what it may. During the hour of perusal the soul of the reader is at the writer's control. There are no external or extrinsic influences—resulting from weariness or interruption.

A skilful literary artist has constructed a tale. If wise, he has not fashioned his thoughts to accommodate his incidents; but having conceived, with deliberate care, a certain unique or single *effect* to be wrought out, he then invents such incidents— he then combines such events as may best aid him in establishing this preconceived effect. If his very initial sentence tend not to the outbringing of this effect, then he has failed in his first step. In the whole composition there should be no word written, of which the tendency, direct or indirect, is not to the one pre-established design. And by such means, with such care and skill, a picture is at length painted which leaves in the mind of him who contemplates it with a kindred art, a sense of the fullest satisfaction. The idea of the tale has been presented unblemished, because undisturbed; and this is an end unattainable by the novel. Undue brevity is just as exceptionable here as in the poem; but undue length is yet more to be avoided.

We have said that the tale has a point of superiority even over the poem. In fact, while the *rhythm* of this latter is an essential aid in the development of the poet's highest idea—the idea of the Beautiful—the artificialities of this rhythm are an inseparable bar to the development of all points of thought or expression which have their basis in *Truth*. But Truth is often, and in very great degree, the aim of the tale. Some of the finest tales are tales of ratiocination. Thus the field of this species of composition, if not in so elevated a region on the mountain of Mind, is a table-land of far vaster extent than the domain of the mere poem. Its products are never so rich, but infinitely more numerous, and more appreciable by the mass of mankind. The writer of the prose tale, in short, may bring to his theme a vast variety of modes or inflections of thought and expression—(the ratiocinative, for example, the sarcastic, or the humorous) which are not only antagonistical to the nature of the poem, but absolutely forbidden by one of its most peculiar and indispensable adjuncts; we allude, of course, to rhythm. It may be added here, *par parenthèse*, that the author who aims at the purely beautiful in a prose tale is laboring at great disadvantage. For Beauty can be better treated in the poem. Not so with terror, or passion, or horror, or a multitude of other such points. And here it will be seen how full of prejudice are the usual animadversions against those *tales of effect*, many fine examples of which were found in the earlier numbers of "Blackwood's." The impressions produced were wrought in a legitimate sphere of action, and constituted a legitimate although sometimes an exaggerated interest. They were relished by every man of genius: although there were found many men of genius who condemned them without just ground. The true critic will but demand that the design intended be accomplished, to the fullest extent, by the means most advantageously applicable.

We have very few American tales of real merit—we may say, indeed, none, with the exception of "The Tales of a Traveller" of Washington Irving, and these "Twice-Told Tales" of Mr. Hawthorne. Some of the pieces of Mr. John Neal abound in vigor and originality; but in general, his compositions of this class are excessively diffuse, extravagant, and indicative of an imperfect sentiment of Art. Articles at random are, now and then, met with in our periodicals which might be advantageously compared with the best effusions of the British Magazines; but, upon the whole, we are far behind our progenitors in this department of literature.

Of Mr. Hawthorne's Tales we would say, emphatically, that they belong to the highest region of Art—an Art subservient to genius of a very lofty order. We had supposed, with good reason for so supposing, that he had been thrust into this present position by one of the impudent *cliques* which beset our literature, and whose pretensions it is our full purpose to expose at the earliest opportunity; but we have been most agreeably mistaken. We know of few compositions which the critic can more honestly commend than these "Twice-Told Tales." As Americans, we feel proud of the book.

Mr. Hawthorne's distinctive trait is invention, creation, imagination, originality—a trait which, in the literature of fiction, is positively worth all the rest. But the nature of originality, so far as regards its manifestation in letters, is but imperfectly understood. The inventive or original mind as frequently displays itself in novelty of *tone* as in novelty of matter. Mr. Hawthorne is original at *all* points.

It would be a matter of some difficulty to designate the best of these tales; we repeat that, without exception, they are beautiful. "Wakefield" is remarkable for the skill with which an old idea—a well-known incident—is worked up or discussed. A man of whims conceives the purpose of quitting his wife and residing *incognito*, for twenty years, in her immediate neighborhood. Something of this kind actually happened in London. The force of Mr. Hawthorne's tale lies in the analysis of the motives which must or might have impelled the husband to such folly, in the first instance, with the possible causes of his perseverance. Upon this thesis a sketch of singular power has been constructed.

"The Wedding Knell" is full of the boldest imagination—an imagination fully controlled by taste. The most captious critic could find no flaw in this production.

"The Minister's Black Veil" is a masterly composition of which the sole defect is that to the rabble its exquisite skill will be *caviare*. The *obvious* meaning of this article will be found to smother its insinuated one. The *moral* put into the mouth of the dying minister will be supposed to convey the *true* import of the narrative; and that a crime of dark dye, (having reference to the "young lady") has been committed, is a point which only minds congenial with that of the author will perceive.

"Mr. Higginbotham's Catastrophe" is vividly original and managed most dexterously.

"Dr. Heidegger's Experiment" is exceedingly well imagined, and executed with surpassing ability. The artist breathes in every line of it.

"The White Old Maid" is objectionable, even more than "The Minister's Black Veil," on the score of its mysticism. Even with the thoughtful and analytic, there will be much trouble in penetrating its entire import.

"The Hollow of the Three Hills" we would quote in full, had we space;—not as evincing higher talent than any of the other pieces, but as affording an excellent example of the author's peculiar ability. The subject is commonplace. A witch subjects the Distant and the Past to the view of a mourner. It has been the fashion to describe, in such cases, a mirror in which the images of the absent appear; or a cloud of smoke is made to arise, and thence the figures are gradually unfolded. Mr. Hawthorne has wonderfully heightened his effect by making the ear, in place of the eye, the medium by which the fantasy in conveyed. The head of the mourner is enveloped in the cloak of the witch, and within its magic folds there arise sounds which have an all-sufficient intelligence. Throughout this article also, the artist is conspicuous—not more in positive than in negative merits. Not only is all done that should be done, but (what perhaps is an end with more difficulty attained) there is nothing done which should not be. Every word *tells*, and there is not a word which does not tell. . . .

In the way of objection we have scarcely a word to say of these tales. There is, perhaps, a somewhat too general or prevalent *tone*—a tone of melancholy and mysticism. The subjects are insufficiently varied. There is not so much of *versatility* evinced as we might well be warranted in expecting from the high powers of Mr. Hawthorne. But beyond these trivial exceptions we have really none to make. The style is purity itself. Force abounds. High imagination gleams from every page. Mr. Hawthorne is a man of the truest genius. We only regret that the limits of our Magazine will not permit us to pay him that full tribute of commendation, which, under other circumstances, we should be so eager to pay.

From a review, originally published in *Graham's Magazine*, May 1842, of Nathaniel Hawthorne's *Twice-Told Tales*. Reprinted from *The Complete Works of Edgar Allan Poe* (1902), Vol. XI, 106–113.

. . . Nothing is more clear than that every plot, worth the name, must be elaborated to its *dénouement* before anything be attempted with the pen. It is only with the *dénouement* constantly in view that we can give a plot its indispensable air of consequence, or causation, by making the incidents, and especially the tone at all points, tend to the development of the intention.

There is a radical error, I think, in the usual mode of constructing a story. Either history affords a thesis—or one is suggested by an incident of the day—or, at best, the author sets himself to work, in the combination of striking events to form merely the basis of his narrative—designing, generally, to fill in with description, dialogue, or authorial comment, whatever crevices of fact, or action, may, from page to page, render themselves apparent.

I prefer commencing with the consideration of an *effect*. Keeping originality *always* in view—or he is false to himself who ventures to dispense with so obvious and so easily attainable a source of interest—I say to myself, in the first place, "Of the innumerable effects, or impressions, of which the heart, the intellect, or (more generally) the soul is susceptible, what one shall I, on the present occasion, select?" Having chosen a novel, first, and secondly a vivid effect, I consider whether it can be best wrought by incident or tone—whether by ordinary incidents and peculiar tone, or the converse, or by peculiarity both of incident and tone—afterward looking about me (or rather within) for such combinations of event, or tone, as shall best aid me in the construction of the effect. . . .

> From "The Philosphy of Composition," originally published in *Graham's Magazine*, April 1846. Reprinted here from *Works*, XIV, 193–194.

In the preface to my sketches of New York Literati, while speaking of the broad distinction between the seeming public and real private opinion respecting our authors, I thus alluded to Nathaniel Hawthorne:

"For example, Mr. Hawthorne, the author of 'Twice-Told Tales,' is scarcely recognized by the press or by the public, and when noticed at all, is noticed merely to be damned by faint praise. Now, my opinion of him is, that although his walk is limited and he is fairly to be charged with mannerism, treating all subjects in a similar tone of dreamy *innuendo*, yet in this walk he evinces extraordinary genius, having no rival either in America or elsewhere; and this opinion I have never heard gainsaid by any one literary person in the country. That this opinion, however, is a spoken and not a written one, is referable to the facts, first, that Mr. Hawthorne is a poor man, and, secondly, that he *is not* an ubiquitous quack."

The reputation of the author of "Twice-Told Tales" has been confined, indeed, until very lately, to literary society; and I have not been wrong, perhaps, in citing him as *the* example, *par excellence*, in this country, of the privately-admired and publicly-unappreciated man of genius. . . .

Beyond doubt, this inappreciation of him on the part of the public arose chiefly from the two causes to which I have referred—from the facts that he is neither a man of wealth nor a quack;—but these are insufficient to account for the whole effect. No small portion of it is attributable to the very marked idiosyncrasy of Mr. Hawthorne himself. In one sense, and in great measure, to be peculiar is to be original, and than the true originality there is no higher literary virtue. This true or commendable originality, however, implies not the uniform, but the continuous peculiarity—a peculiarity springing from ever-active vigor of fancy— better still if from ever-present force of imagination, giving its own hue, its own character to everything it touches, and, especially, *self impelled to touch everything*.

It is often said, inconsiderately, that very original writers always fail in popularity—that such and such persons are too original to be comprehended by the mass. "Too peculiar," should be the prase, "too idiosyncratic." It is, in fact, the excitable, undisciplined and childlike popular mind which most keenly feels the original. . . .

The fact is, that if Mr. Hawthorne were really original, he could not fail of making himself felt by the public. But the fact is, he is *not* original in any sense. Those who speak of him as original, mean nothing more than that he differs in his manner or tone, and in his choice of subjects, from any author of their acquaintance—their acquaintance not extending to the German Tieck, whose manner, in *some* of his works, is absolutely identical with that *habitual* to Hawthorne. But it is clear that the element of the literary originality is novelty. The element of its appreciation by the reader is the reader's sense of the new. Whatever gives him a new and insomuch a pleasurable emotion, he considers original, and whoever frequently gives him such emotion, he considers an original writer. In a word, it is by the sum total of these emotions that he decides upon the writer's claim to originality. I may observe here, however, that there is clearly a point at which even novelty itself would cease to produce the legitimate originality, if we judge this originality, as we should, by the effect designed: this point is that at which *novelty becomes nothing novel*; and here the artist, *to preserve his originality*, will subside into the commonplace.....

These points properly understood, it will be seen that the critic (unacquainted with Tieck) who reads a single tale or essay by Hawthorne, may be justified in thinking him original; but the tone, or manner, or choice of subject, which induces in this critic the sense of the new, will—if not in a second tale, at least in a third and all subsequent ones—not only fail of inducing it, but bring about an exactly antagonistic impression. In concluding a volume, and more especially in concluding all the volumes of the author, the critic will abandon his first design of calling him "original," and content himself with styling him "peculiar."

With the vague opinion that to be original is to be unpopular, I could, indeed, agree, were I to adopt an understanding of originality which, to my surprise, I have known adopted by many who have a right to be called critical. They have limited, in a love for mere words, the literary to the metaphysical originality. They regard as original in letters, only such combinations of thought, of incident, and so forth, as are, in fact, absolutely novel. It is clear, however, not only that it is the novelty of *effect* alone which is worth consideration, but that this effect is *best* wrought, for the end of all fictitious composition, pleasure, by shunning rather than by seeking the absolute novelty of combination. Originality, thus understood, tasks and startles the intellect, and so brings into undue action the faculties to which, in the lighter literature, we least appeal. And thus understood, it cannot fail to prove unpopular with the masses, who, seeking in this literature amusement, are positively offended by instruction. But the true originality—true in respect of its purposes—is that which, in bringing out the half-formed, the reluctant, or the unexpressed fancies of mankind, or in exciting the more delicate pulses of the heart's passion, or in giving birth to some universal sentiment or instinct in embryo, thus combines with the pleasurable effect of *apparent* novelty, a real egoistic delight. The reader, in the case first supposed, (that of the absolute novelty,) is excited, but embarrassed, disturbed, in some degree even pained at his own want of perception, at his own folly in not having himself hit upon the idea. In the second case, his pleasure is doubled. He is filled with an intrinsic and extrinsic delight. He feels and intensely enjoys the seeming novelty of the thought, enjoys it as really novel, as absolutely original with the writer—*and himself.* They two, he fancies, have, alone of all men, thought thus. They two have, together, created this thing. Henceforward there is a bond of sympathy between them, a sympathy which irradiates every subsequent page of the book.

There is a species of writing which, with some difficulty, may be admitted as a lower degree of what I have called the true original. In its perusal, we say to ourselves, not "how original this is!" nor "here is an idea which I and the author have alone entertained," but "here is a charmingly obvious fancy," or sometimes even, "here is a thought which I am not sure has ever occurred to myself, but which, of course, has occurred to all the rest of the world." This kind of composition (which still appertains to a high order) is usually designated as "the natural." It has little external resemblance, but strong internal affinity to the true original, if, indeed, as I have suggested, it is not of this latter an inferior degree. It is best exemplified, among English writers, in Addison, Irving and *Hawthorne*. The "ease" which is so often spoken of as its distinguishing feature, it has been the fashion to regard as ease in appearance alone, as a point of really difficult attainment. This idea, however, must be received with some reservation. The natural style is difficult only to those who should never intermeddle with it—to the unnatural. It is but the result of writing with the understanding, or with the instinct, that the *tone*, in composition, should be that which, at any given point or upon any given topic, would be the tone of the great mass of humanity. The author who, after the manner of the North Americans, is merely at *all* times *quiet*, is, of course, upon *most* occasions, merely silly or stupid, and has no more right to be thought "easy" or "natural" than has a cockney exquisite or the sleeping beauty in the wax-works.

The "peculiarity" or sameness, or monotone of Hawthorne, would, in its mere character of "peculiarity," and without reference to what *is* the peculiarity, suffice to deprive him of all chance of popular appreciation. But as his failure to be appreciated, we can, *of course*, no longer wonder, when we find him monotonous at decidedly the worst of all possible points—at that point which, having the least concern with Nature, is the farthest removed from the popular intellect, from the popular sentiment and from the popular taste. I allude to the strain of allegory which completely overwhelms the greater number of his subjects, and which in some measure interferes with the direct conduct of absolutely all.

In defence of allegory, (however, or for whatever object, employed,) there is scarcely one respectable word to be said. Its best appeals are made to the fancy—that is to say, to our sense of adaptation, not of matters proper, but of matters improper for the purpose, of the real with the unreal; having never more of intelligible connection than has something with nothing, never half so much of effective affinity as has the substance for the shadow. The deepest emotion aroused within us by the happiest allegory, *as* allegory, is a very, very imperfectly satisfied sense of the writer's ingenuity in overcoming a difficulty we should have preferred his not having attempted to overcome. The fallacy of the idea that allegory, in any of its moods, can be made to enforce a truth—that metaphor, for example, may illustrate as well as embellish an argument—could be promptly demonstrated: the converse of the supposed fact might be shown, indeed, with very little trouble—but these are topics foreign to my present purpose. One thing is clear, that if allegory ever establishes a fact, it is by dint of overturning a fiction. Where the suggested meaning runs though the obvious one in a *very* profound under-current so as never to interfere with the upper one without our own volition, so as never to show itself unless *called* to the surface, there only, for the proper uses of fictitious narrative, is it available at all. Under the best circumstances, it must always interfere with that unity of effect which to the artist, is worth all the allegory in the world. Its vital injury, however, is rendered to the most vitally important point in fiction—that of earnestness or verisimilitude. . . .

The obvious causes, however, which have prevented Mr. Hawthorne's *popularity*, do not suffice to condemn him in the eyes of the few who belong properly to books, and to whom books, perhaps, do not quite so properly belong. These few estimate an author, not as do the public, altogether by what he does, but in great measure—indeed, even in the greatest measure—by what he evinces a capability of doing. In this view, Hawthorne stands among literary people in America much in the same light as did Coleridge in England. The few, also, through a certain warping of the taste, which long pondering upon books as books merely never fails to induce, are not in condition to view the errors of a scholar as errors altogether. At any time these gentlemen are prone to think the public not right rather than an educated author wrong. But the simple truth is that the writer who aims at impressing the people is *always* wrong when he fails in forcing that people to receive the impression. How far Mr. Hawthorne has addressed the people at all, is, of course, not a question for me to decide. His books afford strong internal evidence of having been written to himself and his particular friends alone. . . .

He is peculiar and *not* original—unless in those detailed fancies and detached thoughts which his want of general originality will deprive of the appreciation due to them, in preventing them forever reaching the *public* eye. He is infinitely too fond of allegory, and can never hope for popularity so long as he persists in it. This he will not do, for allegory is at war with the whole tone of his nature, which disports itself never so well as when escaping from the mysticism of his Goodman Browns and White Old Maids into the hearty, genial, but still Indian-summer sunshine of his Wakefields and Little Annie's Rambles. Indeed *his* spirit of "metaphor run-mad" is clearly imbibed from the phalanx and phalanstery atmosphere in which he has been so long struggling for breath. He has not half the material for the exclusiveness of authorship that he possesses for its universality. He has the purest style, the finest taste, the most available scholarship, the most delicate humor, the most touching pathos, the most radiant imagination, the most consummate ingenuity; and with these varied good qualities he has done *well* as a mystic. But is there any one of these qualities which should prevent his doing doubly as well in a career of honest, upright, sensible, prehensible and comprehensible things? Let him mend his pen, get a bottle of visible ink, come out from the Old Manse, cut Mr. Alcott, hang (if possible) the editor of "The Dial," and throw out of the window to the pigs all his odd numbers of "The North American Review."

From "Tale Writing—Nathaniel Hawthorne," originally published in *Godey's Magazine and Lady's Book*, November 1847. This article was a revision and expansion of Poe's earlier review (1842) of Hawthorne's *Twice-Told Tales*. Reprinted here from *Works*, XIII, 141–150, 154–155.

Katherine Anne Porter

Three Statements about Writing

1939: The Situation in American Writing

Answers to Seven Questions

1. Are you conscious, in your own writing, of the existence of a "usable past"? Is this mostly American? What figures would you designate as elements in it? Would you say, for example, that Henry James's work is more relevant to the present and future of American writing than Walt Whitman's?

All my past is "usable," in the sense that my material consists of memory, legend, personal experience, and acquired knowledge. They combine in a constant process of re-creation. I am quite unable to separate the influences of literature or the history of literary figures from influences of background, upbringing, ancestry; or to say just what is American and what is not. On one level of experience and a very important one, I could write an autobiography based on my reading until I was twenty-five.

Henry James and Walt Whitman are relevant to the past and present of American literature or of any other literature. They are world figures, they are both artists, it is better not to mortgage the future by excluding either. Be certain that if the present forces and influences bury either of them, the future will dig him up again. The James-minded and the Whitman-minded people have both the right to their own kind of nourishment.

For myself I choose James, holding as I do with the conscious, disciplined artist, the serious expert against the expansive, indiscriminately "cosmic" sort. James, I believe, was the better workman, the more advanced craftsman, a better thinker, a man with a heavier load to carry than Whitman. His feelings are deeper and more complex than Whitman's; he had more confusing choices to make, he faced and labored over harder problems. I am always thrown off by arm-waving and shouting, I am never convinced by breast-beating or huge shapeless statements of generalized emotion. In particular, I think the influence of Whitman on certain American writers has been disastrous, for he encourages them in the vices of self-love (often disguised as love of humanity, or the working classes, or God), the assumption of prophetic powers, of romantic superiority to the limitations of craftsmanship, inflated feeling and slovenly expression.

Neither James nor Whitman is more relevant to the present and future of American literature than, say, Hawthorne or Melville, Stephen Crane or Emily Dickinson; or for that matter, any other first-rank poet or novelist or critic of any time or country. James or Whitman? The young writer will only confuse himself, neglect the natural sources of his education as artist, cramp the growth of his sympathies, by lining up in such a scrimmage. American literature belongs to the great body of world literature, it should be varied and free to flow into what channels the future shall open; all attempts to limit and exclude at this early day would be stupid, and I sincerely hope, futile. If a young artist must choose a master to admire and emulate, that choice should be made according to his own needs from the widest possible field and after a varied experience of study. By then perhaps he shall have seen the folly of choosing a master. One suggestion: artists are not political candidates; and art is not an arena for gladiatorial contests.

2. Do you think of yourself as writing for a definite audience? If so, how would you describe this audience? Would you say that the audience for serious American writing has grown or contracted in the last ten years?

In the beginning I was not writing for any audience, but spent a great while secretly and with great absorption trying to master a craft, to find a medium; my respect for this medium and the masters of it—no two of them alike—is very great. My search was all for the clearest and most arresting way to tell the things I wished to tell. I still do not write for any definite audience, though perhaps I have in mind a kind of composite reader.

It appears to me that the audience for serious American writing has grown in the past ten years. This opinion is based on my own observation of an extended reputation, a widening sphere of influence, an increasing number of readers, among poets, novelists, and critics of our first rank.

It is true that I place great value on certain kinds of perceptive criticism but neither praise nor blame affects my actual work, for I am under a compulsion to write as I do; when I am working I forget who approved and who dispraised, and why. The worker in an art is dyed in his own color, it is useless to ask him to change his faults or his virtues; he must, rather more literally than most men, work out his own salvation. No novelist or poet could possibly ask himself, while working: "What will a certain critic think of this? Will this be acceptable to my publisher? Will this do for a certain magazine? Will my family and friends approve of this?" Imagine what that would lead to. . . . And how much worse, if he must be thinking, "What will my political cell or block think of this? Am I hewing to the party line? Do I stand to lose my job, or head, on this?" This is really the road by which the artist perishes.

3. Do you place much value on the criticism your work has received? Would you agree that the corruption of the literary supplements by advertising in the case of the newspapers—and political pressures—in the case of the liberal weeklies—has made serious literary criticism an isolated cult?

As to criticism being an isolated cult, for the causes you suggest or any other, serious literary criticism was never a crowded field; it cannot be produced by a formula or in bulk any more than can good poetry or fiction. It is not, any more than it ever was, the impassioned concern of a huge public. Proportionately to number, both of readers and publishers, there are as many good critics who have a normal audience as ever. We are discussing the art of literature and the art of criticism, and this has nothing to do with the vast industry of copious publishing, and hasty reviewing, under pressure from the advertising departments, or political pressure. It is a pernicious system: but I surmise the same kind of threat to freedom in a recently organized group of revolutionary artists who are out to fight and suppress if they can, all "reactionary" artists—that is, all artists who do not subscribe to their particular political faith.

4. Have you found it possible to make a living by writing the sort of thing you want to, and without the aid of such crutches as teaching and editorial work? Do you think there is any place in our present economic system for literature as a profession?

No, there has not been a living in it, so far. The history of literature, musical composition, painting shows there has never been a living in art, except by flukes of fortune; by weight of long, cumulative reputation, or generosity of a patron; a prize, a subsidy, a commission of some kind; or (in the American style) anonymous and shamefaced hackwork; in the English style, a tradition of hackwork, openly acknowledged if deplored. The grand old English hack is a melancholy spectacle perhaps, but a figure not without dignity. He is a man who sticks by his trade, does the best he can with it on its own terms, and abides by the consequences of his choice, with a kind of confidence in his way of life that has some merit, certainly.

Literature as a profession? It is a profession, and the professional literary man is on his own as any other professional man is.

If you mean, is there any place in our present economic system for the practice of literature as a source of steady income and economic security, I should say, no. There never has been, in any system, any guarantee of economic security for the artist, unless he took a job and worked under orders as other men do for a steady living. In the arts, you simply cannot secure your bread and your freedom of action too. You cannot be a hostile critic of society and expect society to feed you regularly. The artist of the present day is demanding (I think childishly) that he be given, free, a great many irreconcilable rights and privileges. He wants as a right freedoms which the great spirits of all time have had to fight and often to die for. If he wants freedom, let him fight and die for it too, if he must, and not expect it to be handed to him on a silver plate.

5. Do you find, in retrospect, that your writing reveals any allegiance to any group, class, organization, region, religion, or system of thought, or do you conceive of it as mainly the expression of yourself as an individual?

I find my writing reveals all sorts of sympathies and interests which I had not formulated exactly to myself; "the expression of myself as an individual" has never been my aim. My whole attempt has been to discover and understand human motives, human feelings, to make a distillation of what human relations and experiences my mind has been able to absorb. I have never known an uninteresting human being, and I have never known two alike; there are broad classifications and deep similarities, but I am interested in the thumbprint. I am passionately involved with these individuals who populate all these enormous migrations, calamities; who fight wars and furnish life for the future; these beings without which, one by one, all the "broad movements of history" could never take place. One by one—as they were born.

6. How would you describe the political tendency of American writing as a whole since 1930? How do you feel about it yourself? Are you sympathetic to the current tendency toward what may be called "literary nationalism"—a renewed emphasis, largely uncritical, on the specifically "American" elements in our culture?

Political tendency since 1930 has been to the last degree a confused, struggling, drowning-man-and-straw-hat sort of thing, stampede of panicked crowd, each man trying to save himself—one at a time trying to work out his horrible confusions. How do I feel about it? I suffer from it, and I try to work my way out to some firm ground of personal belief, as the others do. I have times of terror and doubt and indecision, I am confused in all the uproar of shouting maddened voices and the flourishing of death-giving weapons. . . . I should like to save myself, but I have no assurance that I can, for if the victory goes as it threatens, I am not on that side.[1] The third clause of this question I find biased. Let me not be led away by your phrase "largely uncritical" in regard to the "emphasis on specifically American" elements in our culture. If we become completely uncritical and nationalistic, it will be the most European state of mind we could have. I hope we may not. I hope we shall have balance enough to see ourselves plainly, and choose what we shall keep and what discard according to our own needs; not be rushed into fanatic self-love and self-praise as a defensive measure against assaults from abroad. I think the "specifically American" things might not be the worst things for us to cultivate, since this is America, and we are Americans, and our history is not altogether disgraceful. The parent stock is European, but this climate has its own way with transplantations, and I see no cause for grievance in that.

7. Have you considered the question of your attitude toward the possible entry of the United States into the next world war? What do you think the responsibilities of writers in general are when and if war comes?

I am a pacifist. I should like to say now, while there is still time and place to speak, without inviting immediate disaster (for I love life), to my mind the responsibility of the artist toward society is the plain and simple responsibility of any other human being, for I refuse to separate the artist from the human race: his prime responsibility "when and if war comes" is not to go mad. Madness takes many subtle forms, it is the old deceiver. I would say, don't be betrayed into all the old outdated mistakes. If you are promised something new and blissful at the mere price of present violence under a new master, first examine these terms carefully.

New ideas call for new methods, the old flaying, drawing, and quartering for the love of God and the King will not do. If the method is the same, trust yourself, the idea is old, too. If you are required to kill someone today, on the promise of a political leader that someone else shall live in peace tomorrow, believe me, you are not only a double murderer, you are a suicide, too.

1940: INTRODUCTION TO *FLOWERING JUDAS*

It is just ten years since this collection of short stories first appeared. They are literally first fruits, for they were written and published in order of their present arrangement in this volume, which contains the first story I ever finished. Looking at them again, it is possible still to say that I do not repent of them; if they were not yet written, I should have to write them still. They were done with intention and in firm faith, though I had no plan for their future and no notion of what their meaning might be to such readers as they would find. To any speculations from interested sources as to why there were not more of them, I can answer simply and truthfully that I was not one of those who could flourish in the conditions of the past two decades. They are fragments of a much larger plan which I am still engaged in carrying out, and they are what I was then able to achieve in the way of order and form and statement in a period of grotesque dislocations in a whole society when the world was heaving in the sickness of a millennial change. They were first published by what seems still merely a lucky accident, and their survival through this crowded and slowly darkening decade is the sort of fate no one, least of all myself, could be expected to predict or even to hope for.

We none of us flourished in those times, artists or not, for art, like the human life of which it is the truest voice, thrives best by daylight in a green and growing world. For myself, and I was not alone, all the conscious and recollected years of my life have been lived to this day under the heavy threat of world catastrophe, and most of the energies of my mind and spirit have been spent in the effort to grasp the meaning of those threats, to trace them to their sources and to understand the logic of this majestic and terrible failure of the life of man in the Western world. In the face of such shape and weight of present misfortune, the voice of the individual artist may seem perhaps of no more consequence than the whirring of a cricket in the grass; but the arts do live continuously, and they live literally by faith; their names and their shapes and their uses and their basic meanings survive unchanged in all that matters through times of interruption, diminishment, neglect; they outlive governments and creeds and the societies, even the very civilizations that produced them. They cannot be destroyed altogether because they represent the substance of faith and the only reality. They are what we find again when the ruins are cleared away. And even the smallest and most incomplete offering at this time can be a proud act in defense of that faith.

1942: TRANSPLANTED WRITERS

One of the most disquieting by-products of the world disorders of the past few years has been the displacement of the most influential writers. The ablest German authors and journalists, for example, are no longer in Berlin and Leipzig, but in London and New York. The most articulate of the Spanish intelligentsia are not in Madrid but in Mexico City and Buenos Aires. This paradoxical situation must have far-reaching consequences, not only for the intellectuals themselves but for Germany, England and the United States, Spain, Mexico, and the Argentine. What, in your opinion, may these consequences be, immediate and remote, desirable and unfortunate?

The deepest harm in forced flight lies in the incurable wound to human pride and self-respect, the complete dislocation of the spiritual center of gravity. To be beaten and driven out of one's own place is the gravest disaster that can occur to a human being, for in such an act he finds his very humanity denied, his person dismissed with contempt, and this is a shock very few natures can bear and recover any measure of equilibrium.

Artists and writers, I think, do not suffer more than other people under such treatment, but they are apt to be more aware of the causes of their sufferings, they are better able to perceive what is happening, not only to them, but to all their fellow beings. I would not attempt to prophesy what the consequences of all this world displacement by violence of so many people might be; but I can only hope they will have learned something by it, and will leave in the grave of Europe their old quarrels and the old prejudices that have brought this catastrophe upon all of us. We have here enough of those things to fight without that added weight.

Americans are not going anywhere, and I am glad of it. Here we stay, for good or ill, for life or death; and my hope is that all those articulate intelligences who have been driven here will consent to stand with us, and help us put an end to this stampede of human beings driven like sheep over one frontier after another; I hope they will make an effort to understand what this place means in terms of the final battlefield. For the present, they must live here or nowhere, and they must share the responsibility for helping to make this a place where man can live as man and not as victim, pawn, a lower order of animal driven out to die beside the road or to survive in stealth and cunning.

The force at work in the world now is the oldest evil with a new name and new mechanisms and more complicated strategies; if the intelligent do not help to clarify the issues, maintain at least internal order, understand themselves and help others to understand the nature of what is happening, they hardly deserve the name. I agree with Mr. E. M. Forster that there are only two possibilities for any real order: in art and in religion. All political history is a vile mess, varying only in degrees of vileness from one epoch to another, and only the work of saints and artists gives us any reason to believe that the human race is worth belonging to.

Let these scattered, uprooted men remember this, and remember that their one function is to labor at preserving the humanities and the dignity of the human spirit. Otherwise they are lost and we are lost with them and whether they stay here or go yonder will not much matter.

1. At the time this was written it was clear enough that I was opposed to every form of authoritarian, totalitarian government or religion, under whatever name in whatever country. I still am.

V. S. PRITCHETT

Short Stories

For a long time the short story was the poor relation of the novel. It was the chapter left over, the anecdote to be tossed off in a spare moment. Even in the hands of genius, like those of Maupassant and Chekhov, the short story was thought to be the *pis aller* of writers who would have written novels if they had only known how, for Chekhov wasted two or three years trying and Maupassant is a failure as a novelist. We now think differently: the originating genius of Poe in America, of these French and Russian writers and (very late) of Kipling in Britain, has turned out to be decisive and, in this century, writers have had the excitement of a new, intensely individual prose art at their disposal. It is a hybrid. It owes much to the quickness, the objectivity and cutting of the cinema; it owes much to the poet on the one hand and the newspaper reporter on the other; something also to the dramatic compression of the theatre, and everything to the restlessness, the alert nerve, the scientific eye and the short breath of contemporary life. It is the art of the short expectation of life. It fulfills Poe's demand that works of art should be short and immediate in effect. It succeeds on condition that it gets off on the right foot and bears in mind what is said to be the motto of the Bank of England: never explain, never apologize.

If the short story is natural to our age, it makes one crucial requirement which many young writers who attempt this form fatally lack. Maxim Gorki, who inherited a natural power of storytelling from his grandmother, makes it clear in his autobiography that without personality—possibly without the right grandmother—the storyteller is sunk. He describes how his grandmother kept the simple Russian sailors on a ship captivated by her tales. One was about a goblin who ran a splinter in his paw and screamed out, "I can't bear it, little mice, it hurts so much." And, says Gorki, "She lifted her own foot in her hands and rocked comically, screwing up her face as if she actually felt the pain."

The good storyteller knows that, orally or writing, he is putting on a personal, individual act. A novelist can dispense with that. Trollope had almost no personality; quite a number of excellent modern novelists have an average personality common to them all. The novelist is able, for long periods, to rely on the cumulative weight and diffusion of his material. Not so the storyteller. A miniaturist like

Colette, as delicate as a cat, a dramatist of nervous alarm and the inner precipice like Elizabeth Bowen, a reporter like Hemingway, intrepid travellers into the tropics of character like Eudora Welty and Carson McCullers owe the indispensable shock they give to the reader to their personality.

Moralists used to condemn even the greatest novels as dangerous, drugging daydreams. There was something in this argument. Their length, their inclusiveness, their shapelessness—despite all the efforts of Henry James and Flaubert—were bemusing. The story, on the other hand, wakes the reader up. Not only that; it answers the primitive craving for art, the wit, paradox and beauty of shape, the longing to see a dramatic pattern and significance in our experience, the desire for the electric shock. The modern reader is longing for a revival of the tale which the novel, in its complexity and sophistication, has so thoroughly repressed in the brief two hundred and fifty years of its life. But in stressing the "art" of the short story, I do not mean to convey something precious or nicely removed from life. Chekhov's stories form a passionate, indignant yet scientific record of Russian life in his time. Maupassant has described the Normandy peasant forever. All conscience spreads entangled from Conrad's tale of the Captain who hides the refugee in his cabin; all the fatality attending the rebel and the soldier is in Frank O'Connor's tale of the Irishmen playing cards with their British prisoners, while they wait orders to execute them. These stories are not missing chapters or scenarios for novels. Expanded, they would "explain," "apologize" and fail to pierce.

The modern nervous system is keyed up. The very collapse of standards, conventions and values, which has so bewildered the impersonal novelist, has been the making of the story writer who can catch any piece of life as it flies and make his personal performance out of it.

IAN REID

Problems of Definition
(From *The Short Story*)

CRITICAL NEGLECT

Over the last 150 years the short story has come to figure conspicuously in the literature of several countries. Appearing in diverse periodicals as well as in books, it is probably the most widely read of all modern genres, and not only light-weight entertainers but also many distinguished fiction-writers during this period have found it congenial. Yet even now it seldom receives serious critical attention commensurate with that importance. Not until the OED Supplement of 1933 did the term 'short story' itself, designating a particular kind of literary product, gain formal admittance into the vocabulary of English readers. Theoretical discussion of the form had begun nearly a century before that tardy christening with some essays by Edgar Allan Poe, but was slow to develop and is still in an immature state. It seems to be impeded especially by problems connected with the popularity of the short-story genre.

Slightness and slickness, for instance, while not invariably resulting from brevity, do often infect the short story when it is adapting itself to market requirements. Magazine publication expanded hugely during the nineteenth century, tending to encourage stereotypes, mannerisms, gimmickry and the like. Consequently critics are sometimes reluctant to take the short story seriously as a substantial genre in its own right. Bernard Bergonzi, for one, thinks that 'the modern short-story writer is bound to see the world in a certain way' because the form he is using has an insidiously reductive effect: it is disposed 'to filter down experience to the prime elements of defeat and alienation.' More satirically, Howard Nemerov applies these belittling strictures:

> Short stories amount for the most part to parlor tricks, party favors with built-in snappers, gadgets for inducing recognitions and reversals: a small pump serves to build up the pressure, a tiny trigger releases it, there follows a puff and a flash as freedom and necessity combine; finally a celluloid doll drops from the muzzle and descends by parachute to the floor. These things happen, but they happen to no-one in particular.

There are indeed many magazine stories that one could justly dismiss in such terms, and it may well be true that even the acme of short fiction hardly matches the greatest novels in depicting the complex and wide-ranging nature of much human experience. Complexity and breadth, however, are not always the most central or interesting features of our lives. Only a naive reader would confuse significance with bulk. The lyric is by no means less potent and meaningful, inherently, than a discursive poem, and the short story can move us by an intensity which the novel is unable to sustain.

Small-scale prose fiction deserves much more careful criticism, theoretical and practical, than it has usually had. It gets elbowed out of curricula at the universities and elsewhere by its heftier relatives, novel, poetry and drama; and of the countless academic journals very few regularly give space to essays on this neglected genre. Good books about the novel are legion; good books about the short story are extremely scarce. Most of those in English were written on the side by practitioners such as H. E. Bates, Frank O'Connor and Sean O'Faolain. Germany has produced numerous scholarly studies of short fiction, but these are frequently impaired by a finicky taxonomic purism which would set the *Novelle* in contradistinction to the *Kurzgeschichte*, each regarded as a discrete type, whereas in English usage 'short story' is an inclusive concept. The Russian school of formalist criticism, flourishing in the 1920s, generated sound work on theoretical aspects of the short story (notably essays by Boris Eichenbaum and Victor Shklovsky) and of its ancestor the *Märchen* (Vladimir Propp's classic account of 'The Morphology of the Folktale'), but permutations in the genre during the last half-century have outdated some of their findings. Those formalist investigations have recently been extended somewhat by the analytical 'narratology' of French structuralists such as Tzvetan Todorov and Claude Bremond, who however have not yet attended closely to any compositional principles which might be said to set the short story apart from the novel.

PROTEAN VARIETY

If on the one hand their popularity has tempted short stories towards the reductive formulae of merchandise, on the other hand it has sometimes encouraged protean variety. The tale-telling impulse is too irrepressibly fecund to be confined within any single narrative pattern. Therefore the history of the modern short story embraces diverse tendencies, some of which have stretched, shrunk or otherwise altered previous conceptions of the nature of the genre. Ideas once proposed as definitive about the proper structure and subject material of the short story have needed revising to meet the facts of literary evolution. For example, nineteenth-century critics frequently insisted on the need for a firmly developed plot design in any 'true' short story; this was part of their effort to make the form respectable in terms of current taste, to lift it beyond its lowly origins. Some modern writers have undermined that principle of neat plot-making, both by bringing their fictions back in contact with various prototypical modes and by moving away from narrative techniques used in the novel towards the methods both of poetry (in their language, which is often more figurative and rhythmic than was usual in nineteenth-century prose) and of drama (in their tendency to keep the narrator's voice out and rely on direct presentation of character and situation).

While it may be a sign of vigour, this variegated development is not conducive to establishing a precise descriptive vocabulary which would satisfy all critics. Yet if perfect consensus is lacking, adequate working definitions are nevertheless possible and helpful provided one recognizes that they must refer to predominant norms rather than all-inclusive categories, to evolving features rather than fixities and definites. At risk of eroding completely any idea of an essential generic type, a quasi-Platonic form of the short story, we need to be empirically mindful of changes undergone by short prose fiction before and since its widespread acceptance in the Romantic period as a field of serious literary activity. If the New Testament parable, medieval French *fabliau*, seventeenth-century Chinese *p'ing-hua*, nineteenth-century American tall tale or recent experimental prose poem are to be regarded as outside the pale, they should still provide reference points for us in delimiting the territory of the short story proper. Accordingly the following chapters will examine some 'primitive' and proximate varieties of fiction, and look into the possibility that there may be certain formal properties which distinguish *the* short story ('Short-story', as Brander Matthews and others wanted to call it) from stories that just happen to be short.

WHEN IS A STORY NOT A STORY?

The simple term 'story' itself needs some preliminary attention. How strictly should one interpret it? Does it imply at least some plot, some sequence of narrated actions, or can a 'story' be purely descriptive in a static way?

E. M. Forster once represented himself as saying, in 'a sort of drooping regretful voice, "Yes—oh dear yes—the novel tells a story".' And the short story, we might think, can hardly justify its name if, on a smaller scale, it does not do likewise. Herbert Gold, contributing to an 'International Symposium on the Short Story' in the *Kenyon Review* (XXX, 4, 1968), asserts that 'the story-teller must have a story to tell, not merely some sweet prose to take out for a walk'. That seems reasonable as far as it goes. There remains, however, the fundamental question: what does 'story' mean? Few critics deign to examine such a rudimentary concept. We all know (it is ordinarily supposed) what a story is: a recital of events. But what constitutes an event? How many events go to make up a minimal story? Need they all be logically related to one another? Gerald Prince pursues these questions in his recent study *A Grammar of Stories*, using transformational principles derived from linguistics to account for the nature of tacit rules operating in various kinds of narrative. An event, he remarks, is a structural unit that can be summarized by a sentence of the simple kind which, in linguistic parlance, is the transform of less than two discrete elementary strings. Thus, 'Adam said that it was all Eve's fault' records a single event, whereas 'Adam blamed Eve, who had initially encouraged him to eat the apple' records two events, being derived from the transforms of two discrete elementary strings. At any rate, neither of these examples is a story in the proper sense. No story exists, says Prince, until three or more events are conjoined, with at least two of them occurring at different times and being causally linked. Other theorists have made similar observations: Claude Bremond, for instance, calls the requisite group of three events or stages of development *une séquence élémentaire*. 'Eve took a bite of the apple and then Adam did so too': that does not amount to even a skeletal story. But this does: 'Eve took a bite of the apple and then, at her urging, Adam did so too, as a result of which they became crazy and bit each other.' Temporal movement and logical linkage are just enough to make it a story, though no doubt insufficient to make it an interesting one.

We might ask in passing why a three-phase action is generally accepted as basic. Prince and others say nothing to explain this; it is adduced axiomatically, since it probably lies (though they do not admit as much) outside the scope of their strictly objective method, in the field of affective aesthetics. There may well be a connection here with Aristotle's sage remark, in the seventh chapter of his *Poetics*, that a plot must have beginning, middle and end in order to be a whole. And the same aesthetic pattern is evinced in that incremental trebling of actions which recurs in so many durably appealing tales. Our sense of shapeliness would not be satisfied if the poor woodcutter had only two magic wishes, or if four billy goats gruff crossed the troll's bridge, or if Goldilocks found five plates of porridge in the bears' cottage. (Indeed, in the latter story, there are not only three items in each bearish set but three sets too: only after the intruder has tried food, chairs and beds is it timely for the owners to return.) That there are seven dwarfs in Snow White's tale, that the valiant tailor kills seven flies with one blow—these and other numerical formulae are of a different sort, since they do not produce a structure of incremental narration. And besides, the point is not that a tripartite sequence is invariable in simple stories, just that its frequency seems to support the idea that a deep-rooted aesthetic preference is behind it.

We might also ask how important, or narrow, are the principles of temporal ordering and causal connectivity on which Prince insists. He is not alone in that insistence; most generalizations about the nature of narrative are to the same effect and beg the same question. Arthur C. Danto, in his *Analytical Philosophy of History* (Cambridge, 1965), proposes that 'narratives are forms of explanation' (p. 233); accordingly, 'to tell a story is to exclude *some* happenings. . . . Stories, to be stories, must leave things out' (pp. 11–12). But how much can be left out? For Danto, 'explanation' means a delineated pattern of causation, and he expects this to involve a temporal process, a change of situation. Must every story be rationally coherent in those ways? Help with the problem could perhaps have been expected from the contemporary linguists who pursue under such various banners as discourse analysis or *Textgrammatik* or *translinguistique* the aim of distinguishing between a succession of sentences which are intelligibly connected and a succession of sentences which are randomly jumbled. But actually this kind of linguistic inquiry proves too inflexible to be applied usefully to literary narrative, which sometimes allows events to become unbonded while still retaining the reader's interest in the 'story'. Fiction can be as disjunctive, yet as emotionally compelling, as a weird dream; and not to let 'story' cover such cases would be to make the generic category more constricted than some modern story-tellers wish it to be. At a time when the border-lines of definition are in practice shifting outwards, an inclusive theoretical view has to be taken. To begin with, at least, let us regard almost any piece of brief fictional prose as a short story provided that, while it may lack a coherently sequential plot, it retains some clear formal relation to plotted stories. It may for instance present a surrealistic counterpart to any cause-and-effect organization of material, as in Sylvia Plath's 'Johnny Panic and the Bible of Dreams', Jan Gerhard Toonder's 'The Spider', or Franz Kafka's 'Ein Landarzt'. Or it may leave the reader to elicit a plot from disconnected data; Robert Coover's 'The Babysitter' offers a variety of alternative developments from the initial situation, each of these being a more or less credible fulfilment of fantasies in the minds of the characters. There is no defined story of an orthodox sort in 'The Babysitter', no single arrangement of happenings in whose actuality the author solicits our conventional belief. But psychological action is certainly there, and we may select a story from the available possibilities if we wish. More subversive still, yet parodically relevant to the tradition of plotted stories, is Jorge Luis Borges' 'El jardin de los senderos que se bifurcan' (The Garden of Forking Paths), which collapses normal distinctions between the veracious and the invented and which itself splits into several incompatible plot-paths so as to undermine the premise of causality on which narrative has usually depended. We can call these 'anti-stories' *if* we like, but that is implicitly to concede that they need to be seen in relation to the mainstream. Seemingly adversative developments often come to be absorbed within a generic tradition.

Having extended the concept 'short story' in certain respects, let us now venture some delimiting comments. For while narrowly prescriptive definitions will not do, since it is already clear that this genre has no monotypic purity, it would be useless to go to the latitudinarian extreme of including in it every kind of brief prose fiction. For instance, as Alfred G. Engstrom observes, 'legends of demons, saints, gods and the like and tales of outright wizardry' seldom have a claim to be considered short stories. They do not focus, as a rule, on human affairs and at any rate are not primarily intended as fictions. Thus we can discard the sort of thing recounted by Yeats in *The Celtic Twilight*, a scrapbook of local superstitions and spooky gossip, or material such as that collected by Martin Buber in *Tales of the Hasidim*, consisting largely of legendary anecdotes. But it is important to emphasize that what disqualifies such pieces is not the subject matter in itself, because that can give rise to admissible stories like Flaubert's 'La Légende de Saint Julien L'Hospitalier' which are shaped with artistry so as to convey a fully human dimension. The point is that unless there is something more than a fragmentary or an episodic structure, something more than a pious or a credulous tone, the potential interest of character in action will hardly be realized. This does not contradict the previous point that some apparently disjointed narratives may qualify as short stories. In particular instances it is usually easy to recognize sub-literary material by its lack of either formal poise or psychological cogency. *Exempla* about tediously saintly figures, snippets of legend about marvels and eerie occurrences: such things differ quite patently from those tales that are imaginatively cohesive even when fantastic and elliptical, or from tales that explore a mental and moral dimension by evoking the preternatural, as in Hawthorne's 'Young Goodman Brown' with its symbols of devilry and witchcraft.

How long is short?

With the kind of reservation just noted, one can say that in current usage 'short story' is generally applied to almost any kind of fictitious prose narrative briefer than a novel. This, however, needs further refining. What range of sizes does the term cover? How much contraction or protraction is allowable? Presumably the lower limit comes down in theory to a mere sentence, of the sort exemplified earlier, though in practice it is hard to imagine how anything under a page or two can offer more than a skinny outline of happenings (as with Hemingway's stringently abbreviated piece 'A Short Story') or a diminutive gesture towards some narrative possibilities (as with Fielding Dawson's 'Thunder Road'). The upper limit is less clear, and its demarcation will depend partly on whether author, reader or middleman is made the primary point of reference. Poe said that a 'tale' (which for the moment can be taken as a synonym; this and related designations will be discussed in later chapters) is capable of being perused at one sitting. The trouble with that idea, as William Saroyan once remarked, is that some people can sit for longer than others. Shifting the pragmatic focus, one may choose to let the matter of length be decided not by the reader's span of concentration so much as by editorial exigencies; Henry James mentions the 'hard-and-fast rule' among contemporary magazines of keeping inside the range of between six and eight thousand words. But of course such rules vary from time to time and magazine to magazine, so that a single piece of writing may fall within the bounds according to one editor yet be out of bounds according to another; generic lines need to be less arbitrarily drawn. An alternative possibility is to accept as short stories whatever an author wishes to nominate—or allows to be nominated—as such. Somerset Maugham notes in the preface to his *Complete Short Stories* that the smallest item there comes to about 1,600 words in all, the longest to about 20,000, and that is approximately the median range—though some authors would include briefer and longer work: in Frank Sargeson's *Collected Stories* a few pieces are less than 500 words, while one runs to about 32,000.

None of these alternatives seems wholly adequate. There is, however, no need to choose between them, because at any rate it would be unsatisfactory to make a word-count the sole criterion. Genre is not arithmetically defined. Aristotle could say that a tragic plot must have 'a certain magnitude', yet he made no attempt to measure that magnitude precisely; and while it can be said incontrovertibly that a short story must have a certain brevity, confining it within specific dimensions is futile. But if structural considerations, tectonic elements, are more important, they must nevertheless bear a relation to sheer size. That Sargeson story of 32,000 words, for instance, approaches in scale some other works of his which have been announced and accepted as 'novels'. What length can a short story reach without becoming a short novel? Is there indeed an intermediate category, as the increasingly frequent use in English criticism of the Italian word *novella* appears to suggest? This brings us up against another obstacle: the lack of a precise trans-lingual vocabulary for comparative purposes.

TRANSLATING TERMS

Generic definition becomes considerably more awkward once we extend the inquiry beyond literature and criticism in English. There is no exact equivalent to 'short story' in the usage of other European languages, only a cluster of like terms, most of which are confusingly cognate with the English word 'novel'. This difficulty needs clarifying historically. (The following paragraph is indebted to Gerald Gillespie's review of the terminological problem in *Neophilologus* for 1967.)

'Novel', from the sixteenth to the eighteenth centuries, had a meaning which, like the French *nouvelle*, stemmed from Italian *novella* and Spanish *novela*; it was applied, usually in the plural, to tales or short stories of the type contained in such works as Boccaccio's *Decameron*, the *Heptaméron* of Marguerite de Navarre, Cervantes' *Novelas Ejemplares* or Pettie's *Petite Pallace*. It referred to a fictitious prose narrative with characters or actions representing everyday life (sometimes in the past but more often in the present—hence 'new', a matter of novelty, a *novella*); and as such it stood in contrast to the traditional 'romance', which was less realistic and longer. As late as 1774 'novel' was still being regarded as a narrative of small compass: Chesterfield in his *Letters* described it as 'a kind of abbreviation of a Romance'. Only in the nineteenth century, when the old romance had declined further as a genre, did the concept of the novel expand to fill the space available.

By then the word 'novel' had lost its original associations. But on the Continent its cognates, especially the German *Novelle*, continued to be linked in many writers' minds with the Renaissance *novella* despite an increasing disparity in size between much of their work and that small-scale prototype. In Boccaccio's hands the *novella* was very succinct, seldom extending to more than about ten pages. This was one of the ways in which it opposed the medieval romance, a diffuse form. But it did normally delineate a completed span of action (such as the full course of love intrigue), and hence nineteenth-century writers could claim to be working within a tradition that stemmed from the *Decameron* even when their own narratives stretched to 150 pages. The process of expansion was in fact already under way in the *Novelas Ejemplares* (1613) of Cervantes, perhaps as important a progenitor as Boccaccio himself. A few critics, however, look sceptically at the idea of a tradition reaching from those earlier figures down into modern literature, and argue that the Italian term *novella* should not be applied to post-Renaissance forms; with works like Kleist's 'Michael Kohlhaas' or Mérimée's 'Carmen' or Conrad's 'The Secret Sharer' or Lawrence's 'The Virgin and the Gipsy' we no longer have (these rigorists point out) the kind of economy, narrative frame, light tone, and so forth, that Boccaccio established. But that view is too fastidious. Every literary genre continually alters its shape, and due weight should be given to the fact that many writers did see themselves as belonging to a certain tradition.

In France a distinction between *nouvelle* and *conte* was available but not consistently observed. In 1664 La Fontaine entitled a collection of his verse tales (some of them derived from Boccaccio) *Nouvelles*; but a second series of the same works, issued the next year, was called *Contes et Nouvelles*. Even in the Romantic period these two terms were sometimes indiscriminately used, by de Musset and Nodier for instance, but around the mid-nineteenth century a distinction began to emerge: as Albert J. George observes in his study *Short Fiction in France, 1800–1850*, 'the word *conte* was assuming a meaning that differentiated it from *nouvelle*, the former accepted as more concentrated, with one major episode, the latter more complex and consisting of several scenes' (p. 234). *Conte*, like the English 'tale', implied a narrative manner reminiscent of oral delivery, and frequently contained an element of fantasy; a *nouvelle*, on the other hand, 'included a series of incidents for the analysis and development of character or motive' (George, p. 9), and—after Mérimée— tended towards an objective tone. But confusion remained; later in the century, works of this latter sort were often labelled *contes*, by Maupassant for instance.

In Germany, over that same period, classification was taken more seriously. Exactly what constituted a true *Novelle* was not a matter of complete agreement, but no-one doubted that it was a distinct and important genre. Various structural theories had their day, with Ludwig Tieck asserting that the action of a *Novelle* must have a 'curious, striking turning-point' (*sonderbaren, auffallenden Wendepunkt*), Paul Heyse that it must have a quintessential silhouette, others that it must have a linear development, still others that it should follow a concentric path, and so forth. One fairly consistent tendency, however, among *Novelle* practitioners was to extend their compositions substantially. Consequently, when some German writers in recent times started to produce much more compressed stories, a different word had to be coined to distinguish these: *Kurzgeschichte*. This directly translates the English 'short story'—but its usage is narrowly confined to stories of a few pages only, whereas 'short story' is normally more flexible. Moreover, such had been the prestige of the *Novelle* that the *Kurzgeschichte* came to be regarded by some as an essentially inferior form: 'an illegitimate child of the *Novelle*', in Johannes Klein's words (*ein illegitimes Kind der Novelle*). But even those German critics who do view the *Kurzgeschichte* without such prejudice have usually regarded it as something to be set in firm contradistinction to the *Novelle*. Thus Ruth J. Kilchenmann declares that the *Kurzgeschichte* presents 'a fragment of extracted experience' (*ein Stück herausgerissenes Leben*) while the *Novelle* is 'constructed around a crisis' (*auf einen Höhepunkt zu konstruiert*); that the plot of the *Kurzgeschichte* consists of 'netlike interweaving' (*netzhafte Verflechtung*) while that of the *Novelle* follows a 'rising and sharply falling curve' (*aufsteigende und scharf abfallende Kurve*); and that, in general, 'the compact, causally and logically built up form of the *Novelle* is in distinct contrast with the often desultorily, often arabesquely extended or concentrated and elliptical configuration of the *Kurzgeschichte*' (*Die dichte, kausal und logisch aufgebaute Form der Novelle hebt sich deutlich ab von der oft sprunghaften, oft arabeskenhaft erweiterten oder gerafften und aussparenden Gestaltung der Kurzgeschichte*). This impressionistic scheme is attractive in its tidiness. Unfortunately short fiction, even in Germany, is too perversely untidy to conform to any such contrast.

What all this terminological flux indicates is a simple principle of literary evolution which was previously exemplified by the linked histories of the words 'novel' and 'romance'. As described by the Russian formalist Jurij Tynjanov half a century ago, this principle is based on the recognition that at any given time literature as a whole consists of a complex system of interrelated variable elements, including generic concepts. These concepts change as their context in the system changes. Thus, as we have seen, the scope of the 'novel' in eighteenth-century English literature became altered in direct proportion to a corresponding shift in the scope of the 'romance'. And similarly, 'short story' and novella are relative, even symbiotic, categories, sharing space as components in a total literary system which from time to time undergoes mutations:

> The size of a thing, the quantity of verbal material, is not an indifferent feature; we cannot, however, define the genre of a work if it is isolated from the system . . . The study of isolated genres outside the features characteristic of the genre system with which they are related is impossible.

We shall need to return to the question whether the field of the short story is contiguous with that of the novel, or should be separated from it by an intermediate field. But these fields exist temporally as well as spatially, and in order to clarify our terms further we must now trace in broader outline the antecedents and emergence of what is usually meant by the 'modern short story'.

JEAN-PAUL SARTRE

Reading As Directed Creation

(From the essay "Why Write?" in *What Is Literature?* by Jean-Paul Sartre)

One of the chief motives of artistic creation is certainly the need or feeling that we are essential in relationship to the world. If I fix on canvas or in writing a certain aspect of the fields or the sea or a look on someone's face which I have disclosed, I am conscious of having produced them by condensing relationships, by introducing order where there was none, by imposing the unity of mind on the diversity of things. That is, I feel myself essential in relation to my creation. But this time it is the created object which escapes me; I cannot reveal and produce at the same time. The creation becomes inessential in relation to the creative activity. First of all, even if it appears finished to others, the created object always seems to us in a state of suspension; we can always change this line, that shade, that word. Thus, it never forces itself. A novice painter asked his teacher, 'When should I consider my painting finished?' And the teacher answered, 'When you can look at it in amazement and say to yourself '*I*'m the one who did *that!*'

Thus, it is not true that one writes for oneself. That would be the worst blow. In projecting one's emotions on paper, one barely manages to give them a languid extension. The creative act is only an incomplete and abstract moment in the production of a work. If the author existed alone he would be able to write as much as he liked; the work as object would never see the light of day and he would either have to put down his pen or despair. But the operation of writing implies that of reading as its dialectical correlative and these two connected acts necessitate two distinct agents. It is the joint effort of author and reader which brings upon the scene that concrete and imaginary object which is the work of the mind. There is no art except for and by others.

Reading seems, in fact, to be the synthesis of perception and creation. It posits the essentiality of both the subject and the object. The object is essential because it is strictly transcendent, because it imposes its own structures, and because one must wait for it and observe it; but the subject is also essential because it is required not only to disclose the object (that is, to make it possible for there to be an object), but also so that this object might exist absolutely (that is, to produce it). In a word, the reader is conscious of disclosing in creating, of creating by disclosing. In reality, it is not necessary to believe that reading is a mechanical operation and that signs make an impression upon him as light does on a photographic plate. If he is inattentive, the object will never 'catch' with him (in the sense in which we say that fire 'catches' or 'doesn't catch'). He will draw some phrases out of the shadow, but they will seem to have appeared at random. If he is at his best, he will project beyond the words a synthetic form, each phrase of which will be no more than a partial function: the 'theme', the 'subject', or the 'meaning'. Thus, from the very beginning, the meaning is no longer contained in the words, since it is he, on the contrary, who allows the significance of each of them to be understood; and the literary object, though realized through language, is never given *in* language. On the contrary, it is by nature a silence and an opponent of the word. . . . In, short, reading is directed creation.

But on the other hand, the words are there like traps to arouse our feelings and to reflect them towards us. Each word is a path of transcendence; it shapes our feelings, names them, attributes them to an imaginary personage who takes it upon himself to live them for us and who has no other substance than these borrowed passions; he confers objects, perspectives, and a horizon upon them.

❖ ❖ ❖

Since the creation can find its fulfillment only in reading, since the artist must entrust to another the job of carrying out what he has begun, since it is only through the consciousness of the reader that he can regard himself as essential to his work, all literary work is an appeal. To write is to make an appeal to the reader that he lead into objective existence the revelation which I have undertaken by means of language. . . . The writer appeals to the reader's freedom to collaborate in the production of his work. . . . The reader renders himself credulous; he descends into credulity which, though it ends by enclosing him like a dream, is at every moment conscious of being free.

❖ ❖ ❖

Thus, reading is a pact of generosity between author and reader. Each one trusts the other as much as he demands of himself. For this confidence is itself generosity. Nothing can force the author to believe that his reader will use his freedom; nothing can force the reader to believe that the author has used his. Both of them make a free decision. There is established a dialectical going-and-coming; when I read, I make demands; if my demands are met, what I am then reading provokes me to demand more of the author, which means to demand of the author that he demand more of me. And, vice versa, the author's demand is that I carry my demands to the highest pitch. Thus, my freedom, by revealing itself, reveals the freedom of the other.

❖ ❖ ❖

However bad and hopeless the humanity which it paints may be, the work must have an air of generosity. Not, of course, that this generosity is to be expressed by means of edifying discourses and virtuous characters; it must not even be premeditated, and it is quite true that fine sentiments do not make fine books. But it must be the very warp and woof of the book, the stuff out of which the people and things are cut; whatever the subject, a sort of essential lightness must appear everywhere and remind us that the work is never a natural datum, but an *exigence* and a *gift*. . . . The result of which is that there is no 'gloomy literature', since, however dark may be the colours in which one paints the world, one paints it only so that free men may feel their freedom as they face it.

❖ ❖ ❖

One does not write for slaves. The art of prose is bound up with the only regime in which prose has meaning, democracy. When one is threatened, the other is too. And it is not enough to defend them with the pen. A day comes when the pen is forced to stop, and the writer must then take up arms. Thus, however you might have professed, literature throws you into battle. Writing is a certain way of wanting freedom; once you have begun, you are committed, willy-nilly.

GERTRUDE STEIN

From *A Transatlantic Interview*, 1946

Sherwood Anderson wrote, "For me the work of Gertrude Stein consists in a rebuilding, an entire new recasting of life, in the city of words." Is this an adequate summation of what you are trying to do?

It is and it isn't. The thing was not so simple as all that. In the beginning you must remember that I have always been from my babyhood a liberal reader of all English literature. In San Francisco they had a Mechanics Library. As it happened, it had an uncommonly good collection for an ordinary town, and they had a really marvellously complete Seventeenth and Eighteenth Century English Literature collection, and the early Nineteenth Century. And when I was a youngster I used to spend days and days reading things there, and that was my early contact. And then when I became a scientist and became a psychologist, I was only being a scientist for a while, but I did not really care for science. I then went to England and read Elizabethan plays extensively which were very rich in word value.

Everything I have done has been influenced by Flaubert and Cézanne, and this gave me a new feeling about composition. Up to that time composition had consisted of a central idea, to which everything else was an accompaniment and separate but was not an end in itself, and Cézanne conceived the idea that in composition one thing was as important as another thing. Each part is as important as the whole, and that impressed me enormously, and it impressed me so much that I began to write *Three Lives* under this influence and this idea of composition and I was more interested in composition at that moment, this background of word-system, which had come to me from this reading that I had done. I was obsessed by this idea of composition, and the Negro story ("Melanctha" in *Three Lives*) was a quintessence of it.

You see I tried to convey the idea of each part of a composition being as important as the whole. It was the first time in any language that anyone had used that idea of composition in literature. Henry James had a slight inkling of it and was in some senses a forerunner, while in my case I made it stay on the page quite composed. You see he made it sort of like an atmosphere, and it was not solely the realism of the characters but the realism of the composition which was the important thing, the realism of the composition of my thoughts.

After all, to me one human being is as important as another human being, and you might say that the landscape has the same values, a blade of grass has the same value as a tree. Because the realism of the people who did realism before was a realism of trying to make people real. I was not interested in making the people real but in the essence or, as a painter would call it, value. One cannot live without the other. This was an entirely new idea and had been done a little by the Russians but had not been conceived as a reality until I came along, but I got it largely from Cézanne. Flaubert was there as a theme. He, too, had a little of the feeling about this thing, but they none of them conceived it as an entity, no more than any painter had done other than Cézanne. They all fell down on it, because the supremacy of one interest overcame them, while the Cézanne thing I put into words came in the *Three Lives* and was followed by the *Making of Americans*.

In the *Making of Americans* I began the same thing. In trying to make a history of the world my idea here was to write the life of every individual who could possibly live on the earth. I hoped to realize that ambition. My intention was to cover every possible variety of human type in it. I made endless diagrams of every human being, watching people from windows and so on until I could put down every type of human being that could be on the earth. I wanted each one to have the same value. I was not at all interested in the little or big men but to realize absolutely every variety of human experience that it was possible to have, every type, every style and nuance. I have always had this obsession, and that is why I enjoy talking to every GI. I must know every possible nuance.

Conception of this has to be based on a real feeling for every human being. The surprises of it are endless. Still there are the endless surprises, the combination that you don't expect, the relation of men to character that you do not expect. It never ends. All the time in it you see what I am singling out is that one thing has the same value as another. There are of course people who are more important than others in that they have more importance in the world, but this is not essential, and it ceases to be. I have no sense of difference in this respect, because every human being comprises the combination form. Just as everybody has the vote, including the women, I think children should, because as soon as a child is conscious of itself, then it has to me an existence and has a stake in what happens. Everybody who has that stake has that quality of interest, and in the *Making of Americans* that is what I tried to show.

In writing the *Three Lives* I was not particularly conscious of the question of style. The style which everybody shouted about surprised me. I was only interested in these other things. In the beginning gradually I became more conscious of the way you did this thing and I became gradually more conscious of it and at that time particularly of a need for evenness. At this time I threw away punctuation. My real objection to it was that it threw away this balance that I was trying to get, this evenness of everybody having a vote, and that is the reason I am impatient with punctuation. Finally I got obsessed with these enormously long sentences and long paragraphs. All that was an effort to get this evenness, and this went on until it sort of exhausted itself.

On the *Making of Americans* I had written about one thousand pages, and I finished the thing with a sort of rhapsody at the end. Then I started in to write *Matisse, Picasso, and Gertrude Stein.* You will see in each one of these stories that they began in the character of *Making of Americans*, and then in about the middle of it words began to be for the first time more important than the sentence structure or the paragraphs. Something happened. I mean I felt a need. I had thought this thing out and felt a need of breaking it down and forcing it into little pieces. I felt that I had lost contact with the words in building up these Beethovian passages. I had lost that idea gained in my youth from the Seventeenth Century writers, and the little rhymes that used to run through my head from Shakespeare, who was always a passion, got lost from the overall pattern. I recognized and I recognize (if you look at the *Long Gay Book*) this something else I knew would guide that.

I began to play with words then. I was a little obsessed by words of equal value. Picasso was painting my portrait at that time, and he and I used to talk this thing over endlessly. At this time he had just begun on cubism. And I felt that the thing I got from Cézanne was not the last composition. You had to recognize words had lost their value in the Nineteenth Century, particularly towards the end, they had lost much of their variety, and I felt that I could not go on, that I had to recapture the value of the individual word, find out what it meant and act within it.

Also the fact that as an American my mind was fresher towards language than the average English mind, as we had more or less renewed the word structure in our language. All through that middle period the interest was with that largely, ending up with *Tender Buttons.* In this I think that there are some of the best uses of words that there are. The movement is simple and holds by little words. I had at the same time a new interest in portraiture. I began then to want to make a more complete picture of each word, and that is when the portrait business started. I wait until each word can intimate some part of each little mannerism. In each one of them I was not satisfied until the whole thing formed, and it is very difficult to put it down, to explain, in words.

While during that middle period I had these two things that were working back to the compositional idea, the idea of portraiture and the idea of the recreation of the word. I took individual words and thought about them until I got their weight and volume complete and put them next to another word, and at this same time I found out very soon that there is no such thing as putting them together without sense. It is impossible to put them together without sense. I made innumerable efforts to make words write without sense and found it impossible. Any human being putting down words had to make sense out of them.

All these things interested me very strongly through the middle years from about after the *Making of Americans* until 1911, leading up to *Tender Buttons*, which was the apex of that. That was the culmination. Then came the war, and through the war I was travelling a great deal.

After the war the form of the thing, the question of the play form, began to interest me very much. I did very little work during the war. As soon as the war was over I settled down and wrote the whole of the *Geography and Plays*. That turned into very strong interest in play form, and then I began to be slowly impressed by the idea of narration.

After all, human beings are interested in two things. They are interested in the reality and interested in telling about it. I had struggled up to that time with the creation of reality, and then I became interested in how you could tell this thing in a way that anybody could understand and at the same time keep true to your values, and the thing bothered me a great deal at that time. I did quite a few plays and portraits, and that ended roughly with the *Four Saints*, 1932. Most of the things that are in the *Useful Knowledge*, including a book of poetry which was not printed, were constant effort, and after that I was beginning the narration consisting in plays at first, ending with the *Four Saints*.

After the *Four Saints* the portrait narration began, and I went back to the form of narration, and at that time I had a certain reputation, no success, but a certain reputation, and I was asked to write a biography, and I said "No." And then as a joke I began to write the *Autobiography of Alice Toklas*, and at that moment I had made a rather interesting discovery. A young French poet had begun to write, and I was asked to translate his poems, and there I made a rather startling discovery that other people's words are quite different from one's own, and that they can not be the result of your internal troubles as a writer. They have a totally different sense than when they are your own words. This solved for me the problem of Shakespeare's sonnets, which are so unlike any of his other work. These may have been his own idea, undoubtedly they were, but the words have none of the violence that exists in any of the poems, in any of the plays. They have a roughness and violence in their juxtaposition which the sonnets do not have, and this brought me to a great deal of illumination of narrative, because most narrative is based not about your opinions but upon someone else's.

Therefore narrative has a different concept than poetry or even exposition, because, you see, the narrative in itself is not what is in your mind but what is in somebody else's. Plays use it less, and so I did a tour de force with the *Autobiography of Alice Toklas*, and when I sent the first half to the agent, they sent back a telegram to see which one of us had written it! But still I had done what I saw, what you do in translation or in a narrative. I had recreated the point of view of somebody else. Therefore the words ran with a certain smoothness. Shakespeare never expressed any feelings of his own in those sonnets. They have too much smoothness. He did not feel "This is my emotion, I will write it down." If it is your own feeling, one's words have a fullness and violence.

Then I became more and more interested in the subject of narration, and my work since this, the bulk of my work since then, has been largely narration, and I had done children's stories. I think *Paris, France* and *Wars I Have Seen* are the most successful of this. I thought I had done it in *Everybody's Autobiography*. I worked very hard on that and was often very exhausted, but it is often confused and not clarified. But in *Wars I Have Seen* and in *Paris, France*, to my feeling, I have done it more completely.

I have done the narration, because in narration your great problem is the problem of time in telling a story of anybody. And that is why newspaper people never become writers, because they have a false sense of time. They have to consider not the time in which to write but the time in which the newspaper is coming out. Three senses of time to struggle with, the time the event took place, the time they are writing, and the time it has to come out. Their sense of time can not be but false. Hemingway, on account of his newspaper training, has a false sense of time. One will sooner or later get this falsity of time, and that is why newspapers cannot be read later out of their published time.

I found out that in the essence of narration is this problem of time. You have as a person writing, and all the really great narration has it, you have to denude yourself of time so that writing time does not exist. If time exists, your writing is ephemeral. You can have a historical time, but for you the time does not exist, and if you are writing about the present, the time element must cease to exist. I did it unconsciously in the *Autobiography of Alice Toklas*, but I did it consciously in *Everybody's Autobiography* and in the last thing *Wars I Have Seen*. In it I described something momentous happening under my eyes and I was able to do it without a great sense of time. There should not be a sense of time, but an existence suspended in time. That is really where I am at the present moment, I am still largely meditating about this sense of time.

Words hold an interest that you never lose, but usually at one moment one is more preoccupied with one thing than another, the parts mould into the whole. The narrative phase began in the middle thirties and has continued to the present time. Anderson was interested in the phase I was going through at the moment that he knew me. The thing that worried him the most was the narrative, and like other writers of that period he had not freed himself from the Nineteenth Century influence. He was sort of a cutout of the old into the new design. This is well illustrated in a little book he wrote about farmers.

Will you give an account of the results of your experimentation with writing since your lecture tour in the United States?

This has already been covered. There is one thing that impressed me a good many years ago. The characters in the novels of the Nineteenth Century lived a queer kind of way. That is to say people lived and died by these characters. They took a violent interest in them: the Dickens characters, the George Eliot characters, the Meredith characters. They were more real to the average human being than the people they knew. They were far more real, and they would discuss them and feel for them like people they knew. At the end of the Nineteenth Century that died out. Meredith was the last to produce characters who people felt were alive. In the characters of Henry James this is really very little true, the characters do not live very much. The ensemble lives, but nobody gets excited about the characters.

You see there really has been no real novel writing in that sense in the Twentieth Century. The most creative writings were western stories and detective stories, but these were not enough. The hero was usually a dead man in the beginning of the book, and the rest of it is largely a question of a system, one man's way of doing a thing or Scotland Yard's way. The individual that made the Nineteenth Century live practically does not live in the Twentieth Century, where the individual does not stick out enough for the people reading about him. Take Sherwood Anderson, Hemingway, Fitzgerald, in all these it is the title and the form of the book that you remember rather than the characters in the book. That is the reason that the novel has not been a successful form of the Twentieth Century. Proust did it the best, but he made an old-fashioned thing of it. You take the average novel that is written in America today. No character sticks out, and no women's club gets all het up and excited about the character in the latest novel they read, or very little, surely.

You realize how they did in the Nineteenth Century. People really worried about and felt for these characters. Now, you see, even the cinema doesn't do it for them. A few actors or actresses do, but not the characters they portray. As long as the novel has existed, the characters were dominant. Can you imagine any one today weeping over a character? They get excited about the book but not the character.

This has interested me very much. I think that is the reason why the novel as a form has not been successful in the Twentieth Century. That is why biographies have been more successful than novels. This is due in part to this enormous publicity business. The Duchess of Windsor was a more real person to the public and while the divorce was going on was a more actual person than anyone could create. In the Nineteenth Century no one was played up like that, like the Lindbergh kidnapping really roused people's feelings. Then Eleanor Roosevelt is an actuality more than any character in the Twentieth Century novel ever achieved.

To my mind the novel form has not been a successful affair in the Twentieth Century. There has been nothing that you can honestly call a novel. There has not been one in the Twentieth Century with the possible exception of Proust. That makes the novel scheme quite out of the question. One falls back on the thing like I did in *Ida*, where you try to handle a more or less satirical picture within the individual. No individual that you can conceive can hold their own beside life. There has been so much in recent years. Napoleon was, you might say, an ogre in his time. The common people did not know all the everyday things, did not know him intimately, there was not this enormous publicity. People now know the details of important people's daily life unlike they did in the Nineteenth Century. Then the novel supplied imagination where now you have it in publicity, and this changed the whole cast of the novel. So the novel is not a living form, and people try to get out of the difficulty by essay and short story form, and that is a feeble form at best.

The only serious effort that has been made is the detective story, and in a kind of a way Wallace is the only novelist of the Twentieth Century. He failed in the same way. He created an atmosphere of crime and did not have characters that people worried about. You cannot say that there is a novel of the Twentieth Century. I mean a more or less creative writer has never written anything that could in any reasonable sense of the word be called a novel. I have created a lot of characters, but that is another story.

❖ ❖ ❖

Will you trace for me something of the nature of the development of your acceptance?

I became fairly early in the game a writer's writer. Sherwood Anderson and people like that scattered all over the country were interested, and it gave them something to think about—Bromfield, Hemingway, Anderson, Wendell Wilcox—and it disseminated between one and another. When I was at a dinner party at Beverly Hills in Hollywood, there were a great many of the big vedettes of the cinema. After the dinner all those people were seated in front of me, and I did not know what it was all about or what they wanted, and finally one blurted out, "What we want to know is how do you get so much publicity?" So I told them, "By having such a small audience. Begin with a small audience. If that small audience really believes, they make a big noise, and a big audience does not make a noise at all."

What is your attitude toward lecturing?

Picasso and I were talking the other day. I always said I never minded living in France. I write with my eyes, not with my ears or mouth. I hate lecturing because you begin to hear yourself talk, because sooner or later you hear your voice, and you do not hear what you say. You just hear what they hear you say. As a matter of fact, as a writer I write entirely with my eyes. The words as seen by my eyes are the important words, and the ears and mouth do not count. I said to Picasso, "When you were a kid you never looked at things." He seemed to swallow the things he saw but he never looked, and I said, "In recent years you have been looking, you see too much, it is a mistake for you." He said, "You are quite right." A writer should write with eyes, and a painter paint with his ears. You should always paint knowledge which you have acquired, not by looking but by swallowing. I have always noticed that in portraits of really great writers the mouth is always firmly closed.

What about your relationship with Richard Wright?

Richard Wright I first encountered through his writings on my work. I was impressed by the quality of his writings. I think in the first place he has a great mastery of the English language, and I think, to my mind, he has succeeded in doing the most creative work that has been done in many a year. His *Black Boy* is a very masterly novel, and every time he writes there is a form. He dominates his language. He holds it. *Uncle Tom's Children* has a piece of consummate description in the first of the story. I do not think there has been anything done like it since I wrote *Three Lives*. There has not been anything so good in the English language since. The others are merely followers. Richard Wright is not a follower. He does admire my writing thoroughly. He did a criticism of *Wars I Have Seen*. I saw it in a newspaper and was astounded by the quality of the writing and asked who he was and was given some of his books. He writes very wonderful letters. His meditations on the American scene are the most interesting I have heard from anybody. I think he is a very, very interesting person.

In Esquire, *July 1945, Sinclair Lewis wrote: " . . . When the exhibitionist deliberately makes his rites as confusing as possible, he is permitted to go on only because so many people are afraid to blurt out, 'I don't know what it means.' For that same reason, Gertrude Stein, the Mother Superior of all that shoddy magic, is still extensively admired even though she is also extensively unread."*

The best answer to that is what Picasso said, a perfectly good answer. In the first place this is my answer. The facts of the case are that all these people, including myself, are people with a considerably large endowment, and most of us spent thirty years of our life in being made fun of and laughed at and criticized and having no existence and being without a cent of income. The work needs concentration, and one is often exhausted by it. No one would do this merely for exhibitionism; there is too much bitterness. Picasso said, "You see, the situation is very simple. Anybody that creates a new thing has to make it ugly. The effort of creation is so great, that trying to get away from the other things, the contemporary insistence, is so great that the effort to break it gives the appearance of ugliness. Your followers can make it pretty, so generally followers are accepted before the master. The master has the stain of ugliness. The followers who make it pretty are accepted. The people then go back to the original. They see the beauty and bring it back to the original."

Sinclair Lewis would never accept, for instance, that the GI is an entirely different creature from the Sammy of the last war. It would never occur to him to enter into things. He follows the journalistic form and is a newspaperman with a gift for writing books. I have been accused of repetition, but that is not so, and Sinclair Lewis is talking as they talked thirty years ago. The young man and the GI of today would never come to talk to me if I was an exhibitionist or a repetitionist, because time would have killed that. These do not last through time. The point is that the repetition is in Lewis; it is not in me. Lewis is saying what they said thirty years ago about *Tender Buttons*. Anderson also was protesting against it. You see the thing I mean is very well stated in *Composition*. I do not consider that any creative artist is anything but contemporary. Only he is sensitive to what is contemporary long before the average human being is. He puts down what is contemporary, and it is exactly that. Sooner or later people realize it.

I remember one day in the rue Raspail I was walking with Picasso. There came down the street a camouflaged truck, and he stood absolutely still and stared at it and said, "That is what you and I have been doing for years. What is the matter with these people?" He had known fifteen years before they knew that it was contemporary. Picasso said that no one is capable of understanding you who is not capable of doing the same work himself.

Why have you not explained more generally what you are attempting to do?

You explain it to anyone who asks, but if the asking desire is not there, the explanation is useless. You can explain when there is contact, and that person who has made contact can explain to others. It is in *Wars I Have Seen* and *Everybody's Autobiography*. But the thing you have to remember is that it is what these people like, and what Sinclair Lewis cannot understand is that it lives and is ageless.

He is the perfect example of the false sense of time of the newspaper world. He lives in the past and present and not the future. They have no time other than false time. He makes *Main Street* as if time were the main thing, which it isn't. He does not see that *Main Street* is made up of clear accounts of things. He was always dominated by an artificial time when he wrote *Main Street*. After all, the average human being is selfish and as such is interesting, everybody is, and he gives a little character to it. All right, but that is a cliché. He did not create actual human beings at any time. That is what makes it newspaper. Sinclair Lewis is the typical newspaperman who writes novels as a newspaperman, and everything he says is newspaper. The difference between a thinker and a newspaperman is that a thinker enters right into things; a newspaperman is superficial.

When I was in America one day there were three young newspapermen and a photographer, and they had just come out of college and took themselves very seriously, but eventually we got talking about things in general. The only one of the four of them who understood my writing was the photographer. He said, "I don't have to remember what you say. I am not involved with the mechanics of remembering it, and so I can understand it. They are too busy trying to remember what you say."

Why did you answer questionnaires like those in Little Review *and* transition *cryptically, with a chip on your shoulder?*

That does not interest me; it is like the Gallup Poll. After all, my only thought is a complicated simplicity. I like a thing simple, but it must be simple through complication. Everything must come into your scheme; otherwise you cannot achieve real simplicity. A great deal of this I owe to a great teacher, William James. He said, "Never reject anything. Nothing has been proved. If you reject anything, that is the beginning of the end as an intellectual." He was my big influence when I was at college. He was a man who always said, "Complicate your life as much as you please, it has got to simplify."

Nothing can be the same thing to the other person. Nobody can enter into anybody else's mind; so why try? One can only enter into it in a superficial way. You have slight contacts with other people's minds, but you cannot enter into them.

Then why did you publish manuscripts that were really written only for yourself?

There is the eternal vanity of the mind. One wants to see one's children in the world and have them admired like any fond parent, and it is a bitter blow to have them refused or mocked. It is just as bitter for me to have a thing refused as for any little writer with his first manuscript. Anything you create you want to exist, and its means of existence is in being printed.

Audrey Thomas

Basmati Rice: An Essay about Words

My study is on the second floor of our house and faces East. I like that and I get up early to write, perhaps not simply because I enjoy the sunrise (especially in winter, when all has been so black, and then gradually light, like hope, returns) but out of some atavistic hope that my thoughts, too, will rise with the sun and illumine the blank pages in front of me.

We live in a corner house and my study is right above a busy street. People whom I cannot see often pass beneath my window and throw up snatches of conversation before moving out of earshot. And I hear footsteps, light, heavy, singly or in groups, and the sound of buggy wheels or grocery carts. Now, I can see the sidewalk on the other side of the street, see people hurrying along or dawdling, the young woman from the St. James Daycare a block away, out for a walk with her little charges who all seem to march (or skip or run) to a different drummer, a father with his baby tucked inside his ski jacket, a blind man, a woman with her arms full of grocery bags. I cannot hear their footsteps nor anything they might be saying and sometimes a wonderful thing happens where someone will pass beneath my window, and say something while someone is walking by on the other side of the street, and so I get the wonderful absurdity of seeing the old lady in the red coat who lives at the Senior Citizen Lodge at 16th and Macdonald (I know because she asked me to take her picture, waving her hand-made Union Jack, the day the Queen came down 16th Avenue) going by on one side and hearing a gruff teenage male voice saying, "so I said to him nobody talks like that to me and . . ." The movie I watch has the wrong soundtrack!

I am interested in such absurdities, in the word *absurd* itself, from the Latin for inharmonious, foolish. L. *ab*, from, *surdus*, deaf, inaudible, harsh (used metaphorically here, deaf to reason, hence irrational). I am interested in the fact that I spend a lot of my days at a desk, or table, and that the desk or table needs always to face a window. This is not just so I will have something to look at when "illumination" comes slowly (or not at all) but because, in what is essentially an inside occupation (and a very lonely one at that, I can't even stand to have a radio on when I'm working) I am able to feel even a little bit connected with the outside. I often see myself like a diver in one of those old-fashioned diving bells, both in and apart from everything in the universe around me. There is a little piece of brown paper taped to the window frame. I got it from a bread wrapper several years ago when I was spending a winter in Montreal. It says

> PAIN
> FRAIS DU JOUR

in blue letters and underneath

> BREAD
> BAKED FRESH DAILY

Some days, if I'm wrestling with a piece or a passage that seems especially difficult I fold the paper so that it reads:

> PAIN
> BAKED FRESH DAILY

and for some perverse reason that cheers me up. That the French word for bread and the English word for misery of one kind or another *look* alike is another of those absurdities that interest me. There is no real connection, as there is, say, with the English *blessed* and the French *blesser*, to wound—it's just chance. But my mind, when in a certain state of heightened awareness (which I might point out, can just as easily be brought on by laughter as by tears), makes that kind of connection easily.

Here's another. It was early November when I began thinking about this essay, and the tree outside my window was almost bare of leaves. The weather was turning cold and a cold rain was falling. "Autumn leaves" I wrote on my pad, "autumn leaves." Over and over. And then suddenly "WINTER enters." Again, no real linguistic connection, but writing the phrase over and over gave me a new way of looking at the leaves.

I love words. I love the way they suddenly surprise you; I love the way *everyone*, high or low, uses them to paint pictures—that is to say metaphorically. In the past week a phrase, not new, but surely not much in vogue of recent years, has been said in my hearing, or I've read it in the paper, no less than five times: so and so is "between a rock and a hard place." Once in a line-up at the main post office downtown, once spoken by a friend, and in three different newspaper articles. Where does this phrase come from? I can't find it in Bartlett's, at least not under "rock," or "place," or "hard." Why is it suddenly being said? It is certainly a most poetic (and uncomfortable) image. I wouldn't want to be there, nor would you. Somebody says, of somebody else, "I've got him eating out of my hand," probably unaware of the root of the word "manipulate." When I was a child I heard constant warnings about kids who were "too big for their britches" or "too big for their boots" and we were all, without exception, potential big-eared little pitchers. And yet it seemed to me that all the adults I knew—parents, relatives, teachers, corrected me if I played around with words myself—or with grammar or sentence structure. It was as though all the metaphorical language in the world had already been invented and I wasn't there on the day that it happened. Once I started reading poetry I realized that poets seemed to have a certain freedom that ordinary, hard-working decent folks didn't (or didn't allow themselves) to have. They invented and re-invented language all the time. (Prose that got too metaphorical was considered suspect unless it were in the Sunday Sermon or spoken by Roosevelt or Churchill.) That was when I decided I would become a poet, and probably why. My poems were terrible—a lot of them were very "Christian" in a romantic way, full of Crusaders, lepers, infidels, and angels—and some of them, I regret to say, won prizes. But I do remember the day we were asked to write limericks (Grade 4? Grade 5?) and I came up with this in about five minutes:

> There was once a fellow named Farrell
> Whose life was in terrible peril
> He fell in with some rogues
> Who stole all but his brogues
> And had to slink home in a barrel.

(I don't know where I got "brogues" from or how I knew what it meant; it certainly wasn't a word used in our family.)

I wrote dozens of limericks after that first one. I knew it wasn't Real Poetry but I also suspected the other stuff, the stuff my teachers and my mother and various judges liked wasn't Real Poetry either. Nevertheless, for all my desire to write poetry, what I was always better at was prose. Who knows why one writer works better in one genre than another? What I'd really like to be is "ambidextrous," like Michael Ondaatje or Margaret Atwood, but I'm not. It's always prose for me. (Why do most of us see poetry as "higher"? Because it seems more of a distillate of the creative unconscious than prose? Perfume as opposed to cologne? I once had a poet in a graduate prose class in Montreal. He needed one more course to get his degree and had chosen mine. We were all working on stories and one night he said to me, in much despair, "I've never written 'he said' and 'she said' before." Of course he wasn't a *narrative* poet: not for him *Beowulf* or *The Idylls of the King*, or, closer to home, *The Titanic*, or *Brébeuf and His Brethren*.) I still sometimes have the awful feeling that I failed because I failed to write poetry, even while I know that prose can be just as exciting or dense, "packed," innovative as any poem. It probably has something to do with the fact that we write our notes, our memos, our letters, in prose, we speak in prose to one another, even when we speak metaphorically: "Lay off me, will you?", "I'm really blue today," "What's for dinner, honey?", "You're driving me up the wall."

Sometimes a sentence or a phrase gives me the idea for an entire story (once, even, for the very last line of a novel I didn't write for another three years, when I overheard a man in a pay phone say to whomever was on the other end: "Get rid of it." That's all I heard him say and then he hung up). This summer my daughter and I were in Greece. We witnessed a very bizarre incident involving a young English boy, an octopus, and a man in a panama hat. I knew that that in itself could provide the central image for a new story but then, a few days later, I heard a French woman on another beach say "La méduse; il faut prener garde," and suddenly, because of this incident with the octopus, I saw not the jelly fish to which she had been referring but the great snaky tentacles of an octopus and *then* I saw that what I really wanted to write about was all that sexuality that was there on the beach, in that heat, under the intense blue sky: the bare-breasted European woman, the young Greek men showing off to their girlfriends and whoever else would watch. All the bodies. The story is seen through the eyes of a 12-year-old English boy, very properly brought up, for whom the octopus becomes the symbol of everything most feared and most desired, "the nightmare spread out upon the rock." Later on, on quite a different island, a Greek man said two things that have become incorporated into the octopus story. He said, when we were listening to some very sad Greek music, "There are no happy men in Greece, only happy childrens." He also asked, "you like this ice-land" and since the temperature was over 80° we stared at him. He meant "island" but it took us a while to figure that out. Now, in my story, the young boy hears words and phrases he doesn't completely understand ("la méduse; il faut prener garde" "you like this ice-land?") and this just adds to his general sense of unease.

Another recent story was inspired by a newspaper clipping about a man who had been charged with common assault for massaging the feet of strange women. I began to do some foot research and discovered something I must have learned in my university zoology course, that the number of bones in the human foot is the same as the number of letters in the alphabet. And so the story begins: "There are twenty-six bones in the foot; that is the alphabet of the foot" and goes on to tell a story which is a complete fabrication except for the fact that both men (the "real" man and the man in my story) get arrested, charged and fined.

Another story, which is the title story of the collection I'm presently working on, came as a message written on a mirror in the George Dawson Inn in Dawson Creek. The message was not intended for me but showed up on the mirror in the bathroom after my daughter had taken a very hot shower. It said, "Good-bye Harold, Good Luck" and whoever had written it must have counted on the fact that Harold would take a shower. (And the maid had obviously not gone over the mirror with *Windex*.) We had a lot of fun trying to figure out who Harold was and whether the message was written in anger or love. In the story, "they" (a mother who is contemplating a divorce and her child) do meet up with Harold, but of course he doesn't know that they have seen the message (and they're not absolutely sure he has).

I cut things out of newspapers, often really horrible things and I'm never sure why.

MURDERER SET WIFE ADRIFT ON RAFT

TIGER BITES TRAINER TO DEATH
(Horrified Wife Looks On)

DOLPHINS NUDGE BOYS BODY TO SHORE

That last one really haunts me, not just the image, but that word "nudge." The dolphins with their blunt "noses," gently nudging the dead boy towards the shore. That one will probably end up in a story.

PLAN YOUR PLOT

(This one was in the gardening column of the *Province*) and one from the *Vancouver Courier* recently prompted a note to a friend.

POUND WARNS PETS

I cut it out, and wrote underneath, "You're an old bitch gone in the teeth."

And so it goes. And so it goes. And so it goes on and on. I read Rev. Skeat, I read Fowler's *Modern English Usage*, given to me by an ex-boyfriend who wrote, as a greeting, the definition of *oxymoron*, which just about summed up our relationship! I have the *Shorter Oxford Dictionary* but long to have the real one, all those volumes as full of goodies as good Christmas puddings. I have the Bible, the Book of Common Prayer, Shakespeare and *Partridge's Origins*. I have Collins' phrase books in several languages ("that man is following me everywhere"). I have maps and rocks and shells and bits of coral from various places to which I have travelled. I scan the personal columns, the names of ships in port. And I have my eyes and ears.

I am a dilettante (related to the Italian for "delight"). I never learn any language properly but love to dabble in them. I have studied, at one time or another, Latin, Anglo-Saxon, Middle English, Old Norse, French, Italian and, most recently Greek. I spent a winter in Athens a few years ago and saw, every day, little green vans scurrying around the city with ΜΕΤΑΦΟΡΗ posted on a card in the front windshield. "Metaphors." When I enquired I discovered that these vans are for hire and they *transfer* goods from one section of the city to another. Now I long to write an essay called "A Metaphor Is Not a Truck."

Last year I took two terms of sign language at night school. I was amused by the fact that in ASL (American Sign Language) the sign for "woman" has to do with the tying of bonnet strings and the sign for man with the tipping of a hat. These are charming archaisms, like "horsepower" in English. (I am also interested in mirrors, mirror images, going into and through mirrors, so signing, which one does to someone facing you, is fascinating—and very difficult. I often came home with an aching hand.) I would like to take more sign language; I would like to become, as an African man once said to me, about English, "absolutely fluid in that language."

Words words words. Sometimes it all gets on top of me and I feel like the monster made out of words in *The Faerie Queene*. I can't leave them alone; I am obsessed. I move through the city watching for signs with letters missing ("Beef live with onions" advertises a cheap café near Granville and Broadway, "ELF SERVE" says a gas station out on Hastings) and I am always on the lookout for messages within words: can you see the harm in pharmacy, the dent in accident, the over in lover? In short, I play.

There is a phenomenon, most commonly observed in photography but also talked about by people who make stained glass. It is called "halation" and it refers to the spreading of light beyond its proper boundary. (With stained glass it happens when two colours are next to one another.) I think words can do that too, or perhaps I should say that I would like to think that there is no "proper boundary" for words. Let them spill over from one language to another, let them leap out at us like kittens at play. "Wit," said Mark Van Doren, "is the only wall between us and the dark." If a writer, if an artist of *any* sort, stops approaching his materials with wit, with laughter, then he is lost. The other day I was making a curry and listening to some old Beatles' songs on the radio. John or Paul was yelling, "Can't Buy Me Love" and I was thinking about Basmati rice. Suddenly I realized "Basmati rice" had the same number of syllables as "Can't Buy Me Love," so every time John or Paul or whoever got to the chorus I yelled out "Basmati Rice!" and did a little soft shoe shuffle while I stirred the curry sauce. (Everybody had a good time.)

ALICE WALKER

From *An Interview with Claudia Tate*

Are black women writers more concerned with dramatizing intimate male-female encounters than social confrontations with white society?

I can't think of any twentieth-century black woman writer who is first and foremost interested in what white folks think. I exempt Phillis Wheatley and all the nineteenth-century black women writers who *did* have that problem. Twentieth-century black women writers all seem to be much more interested in the black community, in intimate relationships, with the white world as a *backdrop*, which is certainly the appropriate perspective, in my view. We black women writers know very clearly that our survival depends on trust. We will not have or cannot have anything until we examine what we do to and with each other. There just has not been enough examination or enough application of findings to real problems in our day-to-day living. Black women continue to talk about intimate relationships so that we can recognize what is happening when we see it, then maybe there will be some change in behavior on the part of men and women.

When you see *For Colored Girls Who Have Considered Suicide When the Rainbow Is Enuf*, for example, and you see what the behavior looks like on stage and you recognize it, you are recognizing it as behavior you've seen in the real world and you can judge the consequences of it. This recognition has to become very ordinary for all black people. We must be able to see what is happening, recognize such behavior and *make a judgment*. Judgment is crucial because judgment is lacking in black people these days.

Let's see if I can explain what I mean by that. There was a time when behavior was judged much more strictly than it is now. If you were walking down the street and some black man felt he was perfectly right to accost you and say sneaky, nasty little things to you, there was a time when the community rose up and said, "That's wrong! You can't do that. This is Miss so-and-so's child." There was a time when the community looked at this kind of behavior with the eyes of judgment. But today black people see, without judgment. They think that to be nonjudgmental is progress. But in fact, it isn't when your non-judgment means that people suffer. And they do because there is no one saying with the whole authority of the community that what you are doing is hurting us as a community.

Do you think that black women are capitalizing on an antagonistic press, as Ishmael Reed said not too long ago?

I read somewhere that Reed said he had sold only eight thousand copies of his last book, and he was upset. He felt that if he had been a black lesbian poet he would have sold many more. But I have bought nearly all of Reed's books, and I did not buy them because he is a black lesbian poet. I bought them because he is writing about the black community, presumably from inside it. Since I *am* the black community, I represent his audience. And it is this audience that is ultimately important.

In any case, I think anybody can *only write*. Writing or not writing is not dependent on what the market is—whether your work is going to sell or not. If it were, there is not a black woman who would write. And that includes Phillis Wheatley. Think of *her* antagonistic market! I mean if you really thought about the market, you would probably just take a job canning fish. Even the most successful black women writers don't make a lot of money, compared to what white male and female writers earn just routinely. We live in a society that is racist and white. That is one problem. Another is, we don't have a large black readership; I mean, black people, generally speaking, don't read. That is our *main* problem. Instead of attacking each other, we could try to address that problem by doing whatever we can to see that more black works get out into the world—which, for example, Reed does with his publishing company—and by stimulating an interest in literature among black people. Black women writers seem to be trying to do just that, and that's really commendable.

This brings to mind Ntozake Shange's book, *Nappy Edges*, which I just read and liked a lot. It has a wonderful introduction where she refers to a speech she made at Howard. She talked about how black people should try to relate to their writers and permit them the same kind of individuality they permit their jazz musicians. It's beautifully written, and funny, and I'm sure the audience loved what she was saying. Black women instinctively feel a need to connect with their reading audience, to be direct, to build a readership for us all, but more than that, to build *independence*. None of us will survive except in very distorted ways if we have to depend on white publishers and white readers forever. And white critics. If Reed only sold a few thousand copies of his book, he might look at who *controls* publishing first, and then he might look at who is buying his stuff or not buying it, in order to determine whether there is some serious breakdown in communication between him and his potential readers. Although I have all of his early books, it gets harder to lay out money for books that speak of black women as barracudas. As black women become more aware of sexism—when, in fact, they are as sensitive to sexism as they are now to racism, *and they will become so*—then a lot of black male writers are going to be in serious trouble. You notice we do not buy books by William Styron in droves, either.

In any case, to blame black women for one's low sales is just depressing to think about, considering the sad state of our general affairs. Skylab is falling; the nukes are leaking; we're running out of oil and gas; there's a recession. People don't have jobs. Most writers I know, white and black, live with an enormous amount of anxiety over just getting by. That black male writers, no less than black men generally, think that when they don't get something they want, it is because of black women, and not because of the capitalist system that is destroying us all, is almost too much irony to bear. Capitalist society. Racist capitalist society. Racist, sexist and colorist capitalist society which doesn't give a damn about art except art that can be hoarded or sold for big bucks. It doesn't care about art that is crucial to our community because it doesn't care about our community—which is perhaps its only consistency.

If the black community fails to support its own writers, it will never have the knowledge of itself that will make it great. And for foolish, frivolous and totally misinformed reasons—going directly back to its profound laziness about the written message as opposed to one that's sung—it will continue to blunder along, throwing away this one and that one, and never hearing or using what is being said. That is basically what happened with Zora Neale Hurston. The time has to come when the majority of black people, not just two or three, will want their own novels and poems, will want their own folk tales, will want their own folk songs, will want their own whatever. There is so much that is ours that we've lost, and we don't even know we're missing it: ancient Egypt, ancient Ethiopia, Eatonville, Florida! And yet there's no general sense that the spirit can be amputated, that a part of the soul can be cut off because of ignorance of its past development. But I know one thing: when we really respect ourselves, our own minds, our own thoughts, our own words, when we really love ourselves, we won't have any problem whatsoever selling and buying books or anything else.

Look what happens with Jews and books. Jews make Jewish books bestsellers. Whatever is written by and about them they cherish and keep it going. When we feel *we* are worth money, when we feel that *we* are worth time, when we feel that *we* are worth love, we'll do it. But until we do, we won't. And that's that! This whole number about depending on white people for publicity and for this and that and so forth. . . . All I can say is I hope it will soon be over. I am tired of it.

By and large black women writers support themselves, they support each other and support a sense of community much more so than any other group I've ever come in contact with, except for the civil rights era when people tended to be collective. That was true of them, and it is true of us. And I like that.

What is your responsibility to your audience?

I'm always happy to have an audience. It's very nice because otherwise it would be very lonely and futile if I wrote and had no audience. But on the other hand, although *I'm willing* to think about the audience before I write, usually I don't. I try, first of all, to know what I feel and what I think and then to write that. And if there's an audience, well, fine, but if not, I don't worry about it.

Had I ever written a story with all white characters? Well, of course I have. Years ago I wrote a wonderful story which I must find, if it's not packed in a trunk somewhere back in Brooklyn. It's a good story, and I know I'll publish it one day. But at the time I wrote it, nobody would buy it because it was a very chilling view of white people, of these particular white people I had written what I saw. I had written what I thought. I had written what I felt, but this was a view that was totally unacceptable to everyone. Nobody wanted this particular view.

So what I do generally is write, and if there's an audience, there is one, but if there isn't one, I just pack it up and wait.

Have people asked you whether Meridian *is autobiographical?*

Oh yes. I don't think people really understand that a book like *Meridian* is autobiographical only in the sense of projection. Meridian is entirely better than I am, for one thing. She is an exemplary person; she is an exemplary, *flawed* revolutionary because it seems to me that the revolutionary worth following is one who is flawed. When I was talking about the flaw before I didn't mean that it made these people less worthy of following. It made them more worthy of following.

My life has been, since I became an adult, much more middle-class than Meridian's. Although what happens often when I write is that I try to make models for myself. I project other ways of seeing. Writing to me is not about audience actually. It's about living. It's about expanding myself as much as I can and seeing myself in as many roles and situations as possible. Let me put it this way. If I could live as a tree, as a river, as the moon, as the sun, as a star, as the earth, as a rock, I would. Writing permits me to be more than I am. Writing permits me to experience life as any number of strange creations.

Are you drawn toward the folk hero/heroine as the focal point of your work?

I am drawn to working-class characters as I am to working-class people in general. I have a basic antagonism toward the system of capitalism. Since I'm only interested in changing it, I'm not interested in writing about people who already fit into it. And the working-class can never fit comfortably into a capitalist society.

I think my whole program as a writer is to deal with history just so I know where I am. It was necessary for me to write a story like *The Third Life of Grange Copeland*, which starts in the twenties and has passages that go back even further, so I could, later on, get to *Meridian*, to *In Love and Trouble* and then on to *The Color Purple*. I can't move through time in any other way, since I have strong feelings about history and the need to bring it along. One of the scary things is how much of the past, especially our past, gets forgotten.

You've often written that some of your stories were also your mother's stories:

> Yet so many of the stories that I write, that we all write, are our mothers' stories. Only recently did I fully realize this; that through years of listening to my mother's stories of her life, I have absorbed not only the stories themselves, but something of the manner in which she spoke, something of the urgency that involves the knowledge that her stories—like her life—must be recorded. . . .She had handed down respect for possibilities—and the will to grasp them. . . .Guided by my heritage of love and beauty and a respect for strength—in search of my mother's garden, I found my own.
>
> —*"In Search of Our Mothers' Gardens,"*
> Ms., May 1974, p. 70

Yes, some of the stories in *In Love and Trouble* came out of my mother's stories, for instance, "Strong Horse Tea." She often talked about how poor people, "in the olden days," had to make up home remedies for sick people. She used to crack me up with the story about my brother who stuttered and how he was stuttering and stuttering and they couldn't figure out what to do about it. So finally someone told her to hit him in the mouth with a cow's melt. As far as I can figure out, it's something like a spleen. Anyway, it's something raw and wet and bloody, and you get a grip on it and just hit the stutterer in the mouth with it. That would make anyone stop stuttering or stop talking altogether. But anyway, she did that; she hit him in the mouth with the cow's melt and he stopped stuttering.

Anyway, my mother would ramble on and tell about how she would make tea out of the cow's hoof when one of us felt ill. Years later when I was living in Mississippi, when I wrote most of those stories, her world was all around me.

People tend to think that life really does progress for everyone eventually, that people progress, but actually only *some* people progress. The rest of the people don't. There's always somebody using "strong horse tea" in the world; this day, this minute, there's some poor woman making strong horse tea for a child because she's too poor to get a doctor. Now that may not be the case in California; it may not even be in Georgia or Mississippi; it might be in India. But somewhere it is current. This is what I started to understand while I was in Mississippi. So I made up the story about the woman who tried to save her baby because the doctor wouldn't come. You know that the baby died and most of the people around the mother, the white people especially, could not even comprehend that she suffered, that she suffered as any mother would suffer.

"The Revenge of Hannah Kemhuff" in *In Love and Trouble* is also based on one of my mother's stories about a time during the Depression when she went to a local commissary to get food and was refused. I carried the germ for that story of hers with me for years and years, just waiting for an opportunity to use it where it would do the most good.

I wrote "The Child Who Favored Daughter" [*In Love and Trouble*] in 1966, after my first summer in Mississippi. I wrote it out of trying to understand how a black father would feel about a daughter who fell in love with a white man. Now, this was very apropos because I had just come out of a long engagement with a young man who was white, and my father never accepted him. I did not take his nonacceptance lightly. I knew I needed to understand the depth of his antagonism. After all, I was twenty or so, and couldn't quite understand his feelings since history is taught in the slapdash fashion that it is taught. I needed to comprehend what was going on with him and what would go on with any black man of his generation brought up in the South, having children in the South, whose child fell in love with someone who is "the enemy."

I had been writing the story for, oh I guess, almost six months and I took it with me to Mississippi. Ironically, it was over that story, in a sense, that I met the man I did, in fact, marry. We met in the movement in Mississippi, and I was dragging around this notebook, saying "I'm a writer." Most people think when you say you're a writer, and especially when you're twenty, that you can't be serious. Well, I read the story to him and he was convinced.

"To Hell with Dying" [*In Love and Trouble*] was the first story I wrote and it was also my first published story. I wrote that story when I was still at Sarah Lawrence. It is my most autobiographical story. But again, the way autobiography works for a writer is different from what you'd think of as being autobiographical. It's autobiographical though, in fact, none of it happened. The *love* happened.

The story is created out of a longing. There was this man I really loved, not in the romantic sense, but I loved, cared about him, and he died while I was away at school. I didn't have any money to go home for the funeral. So the story was my tribute. It was what I could give. Referring to your question about audience, this story really wasn't about having an audience at all. All the audience I gave a damn about was dead. *He* was the audience. I would have been happy if he had known this was what I was thinking about when I couldn't go to his funeral.

Eudora Welty

The Reading and Writing of Short Stories

Experience teaches us that when we are in the act of writing we are alone and on our own, in a kind of absolute state of Do Not Disturb. And experience tells us further that each story is a specific thing, never a general thing—never. The words in the story we are writing now might as well never have been used before. They all shine; they are never smudged. Stories are *new* things, stories make words new; that is one of their illusions and part of their beauty. And of course the great stories of the world are the ones that seem new to their readers on and on, always new because they keep their power of revealing something.

But although all stories in the throes of being written seem new and although good stories are new and persist, there will always be some characteristics and some functions about them as old as time, as human nature itself, to keep them more or less alike, at least of a family; and there may be other things, undiscovered yet, in the language, in technique, in the world's body of knowledge, to change them out of our present recognition. Critics, historians, and scholars deal with these affairs—and keep good track of them—while for us, the practitioners, the writing of stories seems to simmer down—between stories—into some generalities that are worth talking about. . . .

How do we write a story? Our own way. Beyond that, I think it is hard to assign a process to it.

The mind in writing a story is in the throes of imagination, and it is not in the calculations of analysis. There is a Great Divide in the workings of the mind, shedding its energy in two directions: it creates in imagination, and it tears down in analysis. The two ways of working have a great way of worrying the life out of each other. But why can't they both go their ways in peace?

Let's not, to begin with, deny the powers and achievements of good criticism. That would be smug, ignorant, and blind. Story criticism can seem blind itself, when it is ingrown and tedious; on the other hand, it can see things in large wholes and in subtle relationships we should be only stupid not to investigate. It can illuminate even though, in the face of all its achievements, its business is not: to tell *how*. There is the Great Divide.

I feel like saying as a friend, to beginning writers, Don't be unduly worried by the analyses of stories you may see in some textbooks or critical articles. They are brilliant, no doubt useful to their own ends, but should not be alarming, for in a practical sense they just do not bear in a practical way on writing. To use my own case, that being the only one I can rightly speak of, I have been baffled by analysis and criticism of some of my stories. When I see them analyzed—most usually, "reduced to elements"—sometimes I think, "This is none of me." Not that I am too proud to like being reduced, especially; but that I could not remember *starting* with those elements—with anything that I could so label. The fact that a story will reduce to elements, can be analyzed, does not necessarily mean it started with them—certainly not consciously. A story can start with a bird song.

Criticism, or more strictly, analysis, is an impossible way to learn how the story was written. Analysis is a one-way process, and is only good after the event. In the newsreel pictures when the dive is shown in reverse, a swimmer can come back out of the water; the splash is swallowed up, he rises in the air and is safe and dry back on the diving board. But in truth you can't come by way of analysis back to the starting point of inspiration; that's against some law of the universe, it might almost seem. I myself lack a scientific upbringing; I hear the arrow of time exists, and I feel quite certain, by every instinct, so does the arrow of creation.

. . . A story is not the same thing when it ends that it was when it began. Something happens—the writing of it. It *becomes*. And as a story becomes, I believe we as readers understand by becoming too—by enjoying.

Let's look at some short stories as writers of stories ourselves and people who like them; let's see a little how they are disposed, watch them in their motions, and enjoy them.

Luckily, we shall have none of the problems of *not* enjoying them. Putting a story in its place—we shall escape that. Putting a story in its place when its place has become the important thing means absolutely not giving over to the story. It also means taking oneself with proper seriousness, keeping close watch not to make a fool of oneself, and watching limbs, lest one go out on a few. Enjoying them, we can go out on many a limb. Yet there is really a tougher requirement for enjoying: flexibility and openness of the mind—of the pores, possibly. For heaven forbid we should feel disgrace in seeking understanding by way of pleasure.

We would be sure of this, I believe, if we asked ourselves, How would we wish a story of our own to be understood? By way of delight—by its being purely read, for the first fresh impact and the wonder attached; isn't this the honest answer? It seems to me too that almost the first hope we ever had, when we gave someone a story all fresh and new, was that the story would *read* new. And that's how we should read.

What bliss! Think how often this is denied us. That's why we think of child-hood books so lovingly. But hasn't every writer the rightful wish to have his story so read? And isn't this wish implicit in the story itself? By reading secondhand-edly, or obediently as taught, or by approaching a story without an open mind, we wrong its very first attribute—its uniqueness, with its sister attribute of freshness. We are getting to be old, jaded readers—instructed, advised readers, victims of summaries and textbooks; and if we write stories as victims of this attitude our-selves, what will happen to us? While we read and while we write, let's forget what we're being forever told and find the fresh world again—of enjoyment and pleasure and the story unspoiled, delighted in or hated for its own sake.

By enjoying, I don't mean to be *easy* on a story. Not all melted, the way William Saroyan at times requests readers to be. I mean only not to bother the story—not interrupt and interpret it on the side as if the conscience were at stake. To see it clear and itself, we must see it objectively.

After all, the constellations, patterns, we are used to seeing in the sky are purely subjective; it is because our combining things, our heroes, existed in the world almost as soon as we did that we were able long ago to see Perseus up there, and not a random scattering of little lights. Let's look at a particular story and see it solitary out in space, not part of some trend. It doesn't matter a bit for the moment who wrote it or when, or what magazine or book it appeared in or got rejected from, or how much or how little money the author got for it or whether he had an agent, or that he received letters in the mail when it was printed, saying, "It is found that your story does not reduce to the elements of a story." We're seeing this story as a little world in space, just as we can isolate one star in the sky by a concentrated vision.

The first thing we notice about our story is that we can't really see the solid outlines of it—it seems bathed in something of its own. It is wrapped in an atmos-phere. This is what makes it shine, perhaps, as well as what initially obscures its plain, real shape.

We are bearing in mind that the atmosphere in a story may be its chief glory— and for another thing, that it may be giving us an impression altogether contrary to what lies under it. The brightness may be the result of whizzing in a circle. Some action stories fling off the brightest clouds of obscuring and dazzling light, like ours here. Our penetrating look brings us the suspicion finally that this busy object is quite dark within, for all its clouds of speed, those primary colours of red and yellow and blue. It looks like one of Ernest Hemingway's stories, and it is.

Now a story behaves, it goes through motions—that's part of it. Some stories leave a train of light behind them, meteorlike, so that much later than they strike our eye we may see their meaning like an after-effect. These wildly careening sto-ries are in many ways among the most interesting of all—the kind of story some-times called apocalyptic. I think of Faulkner's stories as being not meteors but comets; in a way still beyond their extravagance and unexpectedness and disre-gard of the steadier laws of time and space, Faulkner's stories are cometlike in that they do have a wonderful course of their own: they reappear, in their own time they reiterate their meaning, and by reiteration show a whole further story over and beyond their single significance.

If we have thought of Hemingway's stories, then, as being bare and solid as billiard balls, so scrupulously cleaned of adjectives, of every unneeded word as they are, of being plain throughout as a verb in itself is plain, we may come to think twice about it. The atmosphere that cloaks D. H. Lawrence's stories is of sensation, which is a pure but thick cover, a cloak of self-luminous air, but the atmosphere that surrounds Hemingway's stories is just as thick and to some readers less illuminating. Action can be inscrutable, more than sensation can be. It can be just as voluptuous, too, just as vaporous, and much more desperately concealing.

So the first thing we see about a story is its mystery. And in the best stories, we return at the last to see mystery again. Every good story has mystery—not the puzzle kind, but the mystery of allurement. As we understand the story better, it is likely that the mystery does not necessarily decrease; rather it simply grows more beautiful.

Now, of what is this story composed, the one we're sighting? What is the plot, in other words?

E. M. Forster in his book on the novel makes the acute distinction between plot and narrative thread. A story is a "narrative of events arranged in their time-sequence. A plot is also a narrative of events, the emphasis falling on causality." With a plot, instead of keeping on asking, What next? we ask, Why? . . .

As we all have observed, plot can throw its weight in any of several ways, varying in their complexity, flexibility, and interest: onto the narrative, or situation; onto the character; onto the interplay of characters; and onto some higher aspects of character, emotional states, and so on, which is where the rules leave off, if they've come with us this far, and the uncharted country begins. . . .

The plot of a short story in many instances is quite openly a projection of character. In a highly specialized instance, but a good example, the whole series of ghostly events in *The Turn of the Screw* may obviously be taken as a vision—a set of hallucinations of the governess who tells us the story. The story is a manufactured evidence against the leading character, in effect.

Not always does plot project character, even primarily. William Sansom, a young English writer, might be mentioned as one new writer who pays his highest respect to pure idea. Virginia Woolf too was at least as interested in a beam of light as she was in a tantrum.

In outward semblance, many stories have plots in common—which is of no more account than that many people have blue eyes. Plots are, indeed, what we see with. What's seen is what we're interested in. . . .

When plot, whatever it does or however it goes, becomes the outward manifestation of the very germ of the story, then it is purest—then the narrative thread is least objectionable, then it is not in the way. When it is identifiable in every motion and progression of its own with the motions and progression of simple revelation, then it is at its highest use. Plot can be made so beautifully to reveal character, reveal atmosphere and the breathing of it, reveal the secrets of hidden, inner (that is, "real") life, that its very unfolding is a joy. It is a subtle satisfaction—that comes from where? Probably it comes from a deep-seated perception we all carry in us of the beauty of organization—of that less strictly definable thing, of form.

Where does form come from—how do you "get it"? My guess is that form is evolved. It is the residue, the thrown-off shape, of the very act of writing, as I look at it. It is the work, its manifestation in addition to the characters, the plot, the sensory impressions—is the result of these, which comes to more than their mathematical total. It is these plus something more. This something more springs from the whole. It pertains to the essence of the story. From the writer's point of view, we might say that form is connected with the process of the story's work—that form *is* the work. From the reader's point of view, we might say that form is connected with recognition; it is what makes us know, in a story, what we are looking at, what unique thing we are for a length of time intensely contemplating. It does seem that the part of the mind which form speaks to and reaches is the memory.

In stories today, form, however acutely and definitely it may be felt, does not necessarily imply a formal structure. It is not accounted for by structure, rather. A story with a "pattern," an exact kind of design, may lack a more compelling overall quality which we call form. Edgar Allan Poe and other writers whose ultimate aim depended on pattern, on a perfect and dovetailing structure (note the relation to puzzles and to detection and mystery here), might have felt real horror at a story by D. H. Lawrence first of all because of the unmitigated shapelessness of Lawrence's narrative. Lawrence's world of action and conversation is as far from the frozen perfection, the marblelike situations, of Poe as we can imagine; Lawrence's story world is a shambles—a world just let go, like a sketchy housekeeper's un-straightened-up room. More things are important than this dust! Lawrence would say, and he would be as right as the crier of that cry always is.

And what about his characters? Are they real, recognizable, neat men and women? Would you know them if you saw them? Not even, I think, if they began to speak on the street as they speak in the stories, in the very words—they would only appear as deranged people. For the truth seems to be that Lawrence's characters don't really speak their words—not conversationally, not to one another; they are *not* speaking on the street, but are playing like fountains or radiating like the moon or storming like the sea, or their silence is the silence of wicked rocks. It is borne home to us that Lawrence is writing of our human relationships on earth in terms of eternity, and these terms set Lawrence's form.

The author himself appears in authorship in phases like the moon, and sometimes blesses us and sometimes smites us while we stand there under him. But we see that his plots and his characters are alike sacrificed to something; there is something which Lawrence considers as transcending them both. Others besides him have thought that something does. But Lawrence alone, that I have knowledge of now, thinks the transcending thing is found direct through the senses. It is the world of the senses that Lawrence writes in, works in, thinks in, takes as his medium—and if that is strange to us, isn't the loss ours? Through this world he will send his story. It is the plot too; it is his story's reason for being, with sex the channel the senses most deeply, mysteriously, run through, cutting down through layers and centuries and country after country of hypocrisy. . . .

We all use the everyday world in our stories, and some of us feel inclined or even bound to give it at least a cursory glance and treatment, but Lawrence does not care. He feels no responsibility there at all. He does not care if the mechanics and props of everyday life suffer in his stories from distortion unto absurdity, if his narrative thins and frays away into silliness. Those things aren't what he's concerned with. His plots might remind you of some kind of tropical birds—that are awkward in structure and really impossible-looking when they're on the ground, and then when they take wing and fly, a miracle happens. All that clumsiness and outrageousness is gone; the bird's body becomes astonishingly functional, and iridescent in flight. . . .

A story's major emphasis may fall on the things that make it up—on character, on plot, on its physical or moral world, in sensory or symbolic form. And perhaps the way this emphasis is let fall may determine the value of the story; may determine not how well it is written, but the worth of its being written.

Of course fashion and the habits of understanding stories at given periods in history may play their parts unconsciously or wilfully. But mainly, I venture to think, the way emphasis falls, the value of a story, is the thing nearest dependent upon the individual and personal factor involved, the writer behind the writing.

The fine story writers seems to be in a sense obstructionists. As if they hold back their own best interests. It's a strange illusion. For if we look to the source of the deepest pleasure we receive from a writer, how surprising it seems that this very source is the quondam obstruction. The fact is, in seeking our source of pleasure we have entered another world again. We are speaking of beauty.

And beauty is not a blatant or promiscuous or obvious quality; indeed at her finest she is somehow associated with obstruction—with reticence of a number of kinds. . . . Time after time Lawrence refuses to get his story told, to let his characters talk in any natural way; the story is held up forever, and through so delaying and through such refusal on the author's part, we enter the magical world of pure sense, of evocation—the shortest cut known through the woods.

Could it be that one who carps at difficulties in a writer ("Why didn't he write it like this? Why didn't he write another story?"), at infringements of the rules and lack of performance of duty, fails to take note of beauty? And fails to see straight off that beauty springs from deviation, from desire not to comply but to act inevitably, as long as truth is in sight, whatever that inevitability may mean?

Where does beauty come from, in the short story? Beauty comes from form, from development of idea, from after-effect. It often comes from carefulness, lack of confusion, elimination of waste—and yes, those are the rules. But that can be on occasion a cold kind of beauty, when there are warm kinds. And beware of tidiness. Sometimes spontaneity is the most sparkling kind of beauty—Katherine Mansfield had it. It is a fortuitous circumstance attending the birth of some stories, like a fairy godmother that has—this time—accepted the standing invitation and come smiling in.

Beauty may be missed or forgotten sometimes by the analyzers because it is not a means, not a way of getting the story along, or furthering a thing in the world. For beauty is a result—as form is a result. It *comes*. We are lucky when beauty comes, for often we try, but then when the virtues of our story are counted, beauty is standing behind the door. I think it may be wrong to try for beauty; we should try for other things, and then hope.

Intensity and beauty are qualities that will come out of man's imagination and out of his passion—which use sensitivity for their finding and focusing power. (This can't beg the question quite so hopelessly as assigning the best stories to genius.) It seems to be true that for practical purposes, in writing a story, beauty is in greatest accord with sensitivity.

The two things that cannot be imitated, beauty and sensitivity, are or may be kin to each other. But there is only one of them we can strive for. Sensitivity in ourselves. It is our technique. In the end, our technique is sensitivity, and beauty may be our reward.

A short-story writer can try anything. He has tried anything—but presumably not everything. Variety is, has been, and no doubt will remain endless in possibilities, because the power and stirring of the mind never rests. It is what this power will try that will most pertinently define the short story. Not rules, not aesthetics, not problems and their solution. It is not rules as long as there is imagination; not aesthetics as long as there is passion; not success as long as there is intensity behind the effort that calls forth and communicates, that will try and try again.

And at the other end of the stories is the reader. There is no use really to fear "the reader." The surly old bugaboo who wants his money's worth out of a magazine—yes, he is there (or I suspect it is a she, still wanting her money's worth and having yet to be convinced she's got it); but there is another reader too, perhaps with more at stake.

Inescapably, this reader exists—the same as ourselves; the reader who is also a user of imagination and thought. This reader picks up a story, maybe our new story, and behold, sees it fresh, and meets it with a storehouse of hope and interest.

And, reader and writer, we can wish each other well. Don't we after all want the same thing? A story of beauty and passion and truth.

Virginia Woolf

Women and Fiction

The title of this article can be read in two ways: it may allude to women and the fiction that they write, or to women and the fiction that is written about them. The ambiguity is intentional, for in dealing with women as writers, as much elasticity as possible is desirable; it is necessary to leave oneself room to deal with other things besides their work, so much has that work been influenced by conditions that have nothing whatever to do with art.

The most superficial inquiry into women's writing instantly raises a host of questions. Why, we ask at once, was there no continuous writing done by women before the eighteenth century? Why did they then write almost as habitually as men, and in the course of that writing produce, one after another, some of the classics of English fiction? And why did their art then, and why to some extent does their art still, take the form of fiction?

A little thought will show us that we are asking questions to which we shall get, as answer, only further fiction. The answer lies at present locked in old diaries, stuffed away in old drawers, half-obliterated in the memories of the aged. It is to be found in the lives of the obscure—in those almost unlit corridors of history where the figures of generations of women are so dimly, so fitfully perceived. For very little is known about women. The history of England is the history of the male line, not of the female. Of our fathers we know always some fact, some distinction. They were soldiers or they were sailors; they filled that office or they made that law. But of our mothers, our grandmothers, our great-grandmothers, what remains? Nothing but a tradition. One was beautiful; one was red-haired; one was kissed by a Queen. We know nothing of them except their names and the dates of their marriages and the number of children they bore.

Thus, if we wish to know why at any particular time women did this or that, why they wrote nothing, why on the other hand they wrote masterpieces, it is extremely difficult to tell. Anyone who should seek among those old papers, who should turn history wrong side out and so construct a faithful picture of the daily life of the ordinary women in Shakespeare's time, in Milton's time, in Johnson's time, would not only write a book of astonishing interest, but would furnish the critic with a weapon which he now lacks. The extraordinary woman depends on the ordinary woman. It is only when we know what were the conditions of the average woman's life—the number of her children, whether she had money of her own, if she had a room to herself, whether she had help in bringing up her family, if she had servants, whether part of the housework was her task—it is only when we can measure the way of life and the experience of life made possible to the ordinary woman that we can account for the success or failure of the extraordinary woman as a writer.

Strange spaces of silence seem to separate one period of activity from another. There was Sappho and a little group of women all writing poetry on a Greek island six hundred years before the birth of Christ. They fall silent. Then about the year 1000 we find a certain court lady, the Lady Murasaki, writing a very long and beautiful novel in Japan. But in England in the sixteenth century, when the dramatists and poets were most active, the women were dumb. Elizabethan literature is exclusively masculine. Then, at the end of the eighteenth century and in the beginning of the nineteenth, we find women again writing—this time in England—with extraordinary frequency and success.

Law and custom were of course largely responsible for these strange intermissions of silence and speech. When a woman was liable, as she was in the fifteenth century, to be beaten and flung about the room if she did not marry the man of her parents' choice, the spiritual atmosphere was not favourable to the production of works of art. When she was married without her own consent to a man who thereupon became her lord and master, 'so far at least as law and custom could make him', as she was in the time of the Stuarts, it is likely she had little time for writing, and less encouragement. The immense effect of environment and suggestion upon the mind, we in our psychoanalytical age are beginning to realize. Again, with memoirs and letters to help us, we are beginning to understand how abnormal is the effort needed to produce a work of art, and what shelter and what support the mind of the artist requires. Of those facts the lives and letters of men like Keats and Carlyle and Flaubert assure us.

Thus it is clear that the extraordinary outburst of fiction in the beginning of the nineteenth century in England was heralded by innumerable slight changes in law and customs and manners. And women of the nineteenth century had some leisure; they had some education. It was no longer the exception for women of the middle and upper classes to choose their own husbands. And it is significant that of the four great women novelists—Jane Austen, Emily Brontë, Charlotte Brontë, and George Eliot—not one had a child, and two were unmarried.

Yet, though it is clear that the ban upon writing had been removed, there was still, it would seem, considerable pressure upon women to write novels. No four women can have been more unlike in genius and character than these four. Jane Austen can have had nothing in common with Gorge Eliot; George Eliot was the direct opposite of Emily Brontë. Yet all were trained for the same profession; all, when they wrote, wrote novels.

Fiction was, as fiction still is, the easiest thing for a woman to write. Nor is it difficult to find the reason. A novel is the least concentrated form of art. A novel can be taken up or put down more easily than a play or a poem. George Eliot left her work to nurse her father. Charlotte Brontë put down her pen to pick the eyes out of the potatoes. And living as she did in the common sitting-room, surrounded by people, a woman was trained to use her mind in observation and upon the analysis of character. She was trained to be a novelist and not to be a poet.

Even in the nineteenth century, a woman lived almost solely in her home and her emotions. And those nineteenth-century novels, remarkable as they were, were profoundly influenced by the fact that the women who wrote them were excluded by their sex from certain kinds of experience. That experience has a great influence upon fiction is indisputable. The best part of Conrad's novels, for instance, would be destroyed if it had been impossible for him to be a sailor. Take away all that Tolstoi knew of war as a soldier, of life and society as a rich young man whose education admitted him to all sorts of experience, and *War and Peace* would be incredibly impoverished.

Yet *Pride and Prejudice*, *Wuthering Heights*, *Villette*, and *Middlemarch* were written by women from whom was forcibly withheld all experience save that which could be met with in a middle-class drawing-room. No first-hand experience of war or seafaring or politics or business was possible for them. Even their emotional life was strictly regulated by law and custom. When George Eliot ventured to live with Mr Lewes without being his wife, public opinion was scandalized. Under its pressure she withdrew into a suburban seclusion which, inevitably, had the worst possible effects upon her work. She wrote that unless people asked of their own accord to come and see her, she never invited them. At the same time, on the other side of Europe, Tolstoi was living a free life as a soldier, with men and women of all classes, for which nobody censured him and from which his novels drew much of their astonishing breadth and vigour.

But the novels of women were not affected only by the necessarily narrow range of the writer's experience. They showed, at least in the nineteenth century, another characteristic which may be traced to the writer's sex. In *Middlemarch* and in *Jane Eyre* we are conscious not merely of the writer's character, as we are conscious of the character of Charles Dickens, but we are conscious of a woman's presence—of someone resenting the treatment of her sex and pleading for its rights. This brings into women's writing an element which is entirely absent from a man's, unless indeed, he happens to be a working-man, a Negro, or one who for some other reason is conscious of disability. It introduces a distortion and is frequently the cause of weakness. The desire to plead some personal cause or to make a character the mouthpiece of some personal discontent or grievance always has a distressing effect, as if the spot at which the reader's attention is directed were suddenly two-fold instead of single.

The genius of Jane Austen and Emily Brontë is never more convincing than in their power to ignore such claims and solicitations and to hold on their way unperturbed by scorn or censure. But it needed a very serene or a very powerful mind to resist the temptation to anger. The ridicule, the censure, the assurance of inferiority in one form or another which were lavished upon women who practised an art, provoked such reactions naturally enough. One sees the effect in Charlotte Brontë's indignation, in George Eliot's resignation. Again and again one finds it in the work of the lesser women writers—in their choice of a subject, in their unnatural self-assertiveness, in their unnatural docility. Moreover, insincerity leaks in almost unconsciously. They adopt a view in deference to authority. The vision becomes too masculine or it becomes too feminine; it loses its perfect integrity and, with that, its most essential quality as a work of art.

The great change that has crept into women's writing is, it would seem, a change of attitude. The woman writer is no longer bitter. She is no longer angry. She is no longer pleading and protesting as she writes. We are approaching, if we have not yet reached, the time when her writing will have little or no foreign influence to disturb it. She will be able to concentrate upon her vision without distraction from outside. The aloofness that was once within the reach of genius and originality is only now coming within reach of ordinary women. Therefore the average novel by a woman is far more genuine and far more interesting today than it was a hundred or even fifty years ago.

But it is still true that before a woman can write exactly as she wishes to write, she has many difficulties to face. To begin with, there is the technical difficulty—so simple, apparently; in reality, so baffling—that the very form of the sentence does not fit her. It is a sentence made by men; it is too loose, too heavy, too pompous for a woman's use. Yet in a novel, which covers so wide a stretch of ground, an ordinary and usual type of sentence has to be found to carry the reader on easily and naturally from one end of the book to the other. And this a woman must make for herself, altering and adapting the current sentence until she writes one that takes the natural shape of her thought without crushing or distorting it.

But that, after all, is only a means to an end, and the end is still to be reached only when a woman has the courage to surmount opposition and the determination to be true to herself. For a novel, after all, is a statement about a thousand different objects—human, natural, divine; it is an attempt to relate them to each other. In every novel of merit these different elements are held in place by the force of the writer's vision. But they have another order also, which is the order imposed upon them by convention. And as men are the arbiters of that convention, as they have established an order of values in life, so too, since fiction is largely based on life, these values prevail there also to a very great extent.

It is probable, however, that both in life and in art the values of a woman are not the values of a man. Thus, when a woman comes to write a novel, she will find that she is perpetually wishing to alter the established values—to make serious what appears insignificant to a man, and trivial what is to him important. And for that, of course, she will be criticized; for the critic of the opposite sex will be genuinely puzzled and surprised by an attempt to alter the current scale of values, and will see in it not merely a difference of view, but a view that is weak, or trivial, or sentimental, because it differs from his own.

But here, too, women are coming to be more independent of opinion. They are beginning to respect their own sense of values. And for this reason the subject matter of their novels begins to show certain changes. They are less interested, it would seem, in themselves; on the other hand, they are more interested in other women. In the early nineteenth century, women's novels were largely autobiographical. One of the motives that led them to write was the desire to expose their own suffering, to plead their own cause. Now that this desire is no longer so urgent, women are beginning to explore their own sex, to write of women as women have never been written of before; for of course, until very lately, women in literature were the creation of men.

Here again there are difficulties to overcome, for, if one may generalize, not only do women submit less readily to observation than men, but their lives are far less tested and examined by the ordinary processes of life. Often nothing tangible remains of a woman's day. The food that has been cooked is eaten; the children that have been nursed have gone out into the world. Where does the accent fall? It is difficult to say. Her life has an anonymous character which is baffling and puzzling in the extreme. For the first time, this dark country is beginning to be explored in fiction; and at the same moment a woman has also to record the changes in women's minds and habits which the opening of the professions has introduced. She has to observe how their lives are ceasing to run underground;

she has to discover what new colours and shadows are showing in them now that they are exposed to the outer world.

If, then, one should try to sum up the character of women's fiction at the present moment, one would say that it is courageous; it is sincere; it keeps closely to what women feel. It is not bitter. It does not insist upon its femininity. But at the same time, a woman's book is not written as a man would write it. These qualities are much commoner than they were, and they give even to second- and third-rate work the value of truth and the interest of sincerity.

But in addition to these good qualities, there are two that call for a word more of discussion. The change which has turned the English woman from a nondescript influence, fluctuating and vague, to a voter, a wage-earner, a responsible citizen, has given her both in her life and in her art a turn towards the impersonal. Her relations now are not only emotional; they are intellectual, they are political. The old system which condemned her to squint askance at things through the eyes or through the interests of husband or brother, has given place to the direct and practical interests of one who must act for herself, and not merely influence the acts of others. Hence her attention is being directed away from the personal centre which engaged it exclusively in the past to the impersonal, and her novels naturally become more critical of society, and less analytical of individual lives.

We may expect that the office of gadfly to the state, which has been so far a male prerogative, will now be discharged by women also. Their novels will deal with social evils and remedies. Their men and women will not be observed wholly in relation to each other emotionally, but as they cohere and clash in groups and classes and races. That is one change of some importance. But there is another more interesting to those who prefer the butterfly to the gadfly—that is to say, the artist to the reformer. The greater impersonality of women's lives will encourage the poetic spirit, and it is in poetry that women's fiction is still weakest. It will lead them to be less absorbed in facts and no longer content to record with astonishing acuteness the minute details which fall under their own observation. They will look beyond the personal and political relationships to the wider questions which the poet tries to solve—of our destiny and the meaning of life.

The basis of the poetic attitude is of course largely founded upon material things. It depends upon leisure, and a little money, and the chance which money and leisure give to observe impersonally and dispassionately. With money and leisure at their service, women will naturally occupy themselves more than has hitherto been possible with the craft of letters. They will make a fuller and a more subtle use of the instrument of writing. Their technique will become bolder and richer.

In the past, the virtue of women's writing often lay in its divine spontaneity, like that of the blackbird's song or the thrush's. It was untaught; it was from the heart. But it was also, and much more often, chattering and garrulous—mere talk spilt over paper and left to dry in pools and blots. In future, granted time and books and a little space in the house for herself, literature will become for women, as for men, an art to be studied. Women's gift will be trained and strengthened.

The novel will cease to be the dumping-ground for the personal emotions. It will become, more than at present, a work of art like any other, and its resources and its limitations will be explored.

From this it is a short step to the practice of the sophisticated arts, hitherto so little practised by women—to the writing of essays and criticism, of history and biography. And that, too, if we are considering the novel, will be of advantage; for besides improving the quality of the novel itself, it will draw off the aliens who have been attracted to fiction by its accessibility while their hearts lay elsewhere. Thus will the novel be rid of those excrescences of history and fact which, in our time, have made it so shapeless.

So, if we may prophesy, women in time to come will write fewer novels, but better novels; and not novels only, but poetry and criticism and history. But in this, to be sure, one is looking ahead to that golden, that perhaps fabulous, age when women will have what has so long been denied them—leisure, and money, and a room to themselves.

 # Glossary

This glossary is not a bible or rule of law. It's a very subjective attempt to provide working definitions for words that come up over and over again in the discussion of short fiction. Every good teacher or student of literature will have his or her own definitions of plot, character, setting, and a host of other useful, and at times frustratingly vague, terms. The authors themselves often don't agree on the meaning and usefulness of critical terms. Flannery O'Connor said that describing a story in terms of plot, character, and setting is "like trying to describe the expression on a face by saying where the eyes, nose, and mouth are"; and John Hawkes goes even further by suggesting that plot, character, setting, and theme are the enemies of fiction.

A glossary is a point of departure. Consider these definitions as tentative probes, as starting-places for developing your own critical vocabulary, and remember Ralph Waldo Emerson's remark about consistency being "the hobgoblin of little minds." Much of the excitement of studying literature lies in the perpetual struggle with terminology and the gradual development of very personal insights and analytical skills.

If you want an even broader understanding of literary terminology than these brief capsule comments can provide, check out M. H. Abrams's *A Glossary of Literary Terms* and consider skimming all the notes on the authors in *The Art of Short Fiction*. In the notes you'll find a lively debate under way; actually, *crossfire* and *counterattack* might better describe the exchange, since authors can become quite heated and opinionated when it comes to discussing the craft. A similar excursion through the statements on the art of fiction and the act of critical reading is contained in the Afterwords, where Alice Munro talks about what is "real" in fiction and Mavis Gallant tackles the notion of "style," will prove equally useful and entertaining.

Action is what happens in a story, what the characters do or have done to them. Action may be distinguished from **plot** by not invoking causality or chronology and by not necessarily suggesting a unified sequence of events. Action may refer to external, physical events or internal, psychological events in the narrative. Action usually involves **conflict** and leads to some sort of **closure** or resolution, a change of behaviour or a change of heart, perhaps in the nature of that moment of illumination that Joyce called an **epiphany**. See also **plot** and pp. 158, 828.

Allegory is often taken to refer primarily to stories such as *Pilgrim's Progress*, in which the characters represent abstractions such as Faith, Truth, and Hope and the journey itself represents life. To some extent, literature is constantly edging towards the allegorical, since language is a symbolic medium and any verbal figure may be construed to represent both object and idea. So, too, all stories may be said to be representative, in an obvious way, of life as we know it.

However, although all literature leans in the direction of the symbolic and the allegorical, allegory, properly speaking, requires all, or most, of the key elements in a story to bear a one-to-one relationship with a parallel structure outside the narrative. To say, for example, that a story about an unfortunate butcher in Toronto is an allegory of the Life and Crucifixion of Christ would, normally, entail identifying a close adherence to the biblical parallels; similarly, to call a story about the moral collapse of a professor of English in Edmonton an allegory of the Fall of Man would be rather meaningless unless we could identify in the text clear parallels to God, Eve, the serpent, and the Garden of Eden. See p. 848.

Antagonist, the character in a story who acts as a foil for, or stands in opposition to, the **protagonist**, or **hero**. The **conflict** between these characters constitutes the **action**, or **plot**. In modern stories, the antagonist is often simply a projection of some facet of the hero's character.

Atmosphere. Like **mood**, atmosphere may refer to the feeling that envelops all or part of a story, making it seem entirely, or by degrees, brooding, sinister, giddy, sad, or hilarious. However, atmosphere seems to be less a product of the laying on of descriptive detail (for example, Poe's dark, gloomy manors, cellars, and dungeons, with their sense of confinement and claustrophobia; or Alistair MacLeod's lonely, isolated, and elemental backdrops against which a small human drama is acted out) than the product of something less easily described. Eudora Welty's observations on this score are fascinating: "The first thing we notice about our story is that we can't really see the solid outlines of it—it seems wrapped in an atmosphere. This is what makes it shine, perhaps, as well as what initially obscures its plain, real shape."

See also **mood** and **tone** as well as Welty in the notes and Afterwords and p. 887.

Character. A character is a figure, consisting possibly of a name or title and a set of qualities, who plays a part in a fictional narrative. The part may be major or minor, depending on how much time is devoted to each character by the author. All fictional characters are fabrications, however close they might appear to be to figures in real life; thus they are all one- or, at best, two-dimensional. A flat character is one of limited complexity, who has been given only a few of what we think of as human qualities. A rounded character, given enough qualities to appear more complex, gives us a greater illusion of reality. The limits of the short story often necessitate giving all but the central character limited complexity.

Many writers suggest that plot is inextricably rooted in character. Henry James considered character to be the manifestation of plot; and plot, the expression of character.

Characters are created by way of a linguistic short-hand, which allows the observant and verbally gifted writer to find just the right word, the telling gesture, the significant detail, and the appropriate action to convince us to suspend our disbelief. A realist writer may concentrate most of his or her energy on physical details, including speech, gesture, clothing, and external action; a psychological realist will pay more attention to rendering the inner life of the mind and emotions, letting ideas and plot—even sentences—fragment and roll on in what has come to be called the **stream of consciousness**.

There is no shortage of kinds of characterization. Archetypal criticism tends to focus on fictional characters as types, such as the typical figures of romance literature: hero, heroine, villain, monster, sage, guide, and so on. The characters in allegorical fiction may be little more than ciphers, representing such ideas or philosophical positions as good and evil. A contemporary writer of fiction may exploit several kinds of characterization in a single work.

Character relations may be a useful term for discussing the patterning in a story, the way in which each character is associated with a different idea or value. By closely attending to the character relations in a story, along with the image-clusters, you may be able to make certain assumptions about the meaning that emerges as you read.

See note and Afterwords on James, Laurence, Munro, Flannery O'Connor, Welty, and others and pp. 95, 103, 120–21, 243, 290, 321, 388, 397, 478, 500, 513, 550, 619, 752, 777–78, 823, 828, 834.

Climax is the dramatic high point in a story, or the turning point in the action. The climax is usually followed by the **dénouement**, or untying (unravelling) of the **plot**, where debts are paid, conflicts are resolved, or knowledge is achieved. Many writers of short stories reject the notion of climax, conflict, and resolution, arguing that the short story, like the poem, requires more subtle organization and less mechanical expectations. Virginia Woolf, for example, insisted that "inconclusive stories are legitimate" and that stories should be open-ended. See also **closure** and **dénouement**.

Closure is a term used to refer to the wrapping up or resolution of conflicts and complications in a story. Stories that are too neatly tied up, with a clichéd or surprise ending, quickly fall out of favour with a sophisticated reading public, who are prepared to accept that art might well reflect the complexities of life, where death is not always a "neat" ending; in fact, it can be very messy for those left to pick up the pieces and, more so, for those who don't recognize it as an ending at all.

The convention of the open-ended story seems firmly entrenched in, if not actually the bone marrow of, the short story. Clark Blaise's brilliant essay (pp. 769–72) on the many conventions of ending a story should be read in its entirety. See also **climax** and **dénouement**, as well as Pritchett, Woolf, Gordimer, and Frank O'Connor in the notes and Afterwords; also, Ian Reid's essay "Problems of Definition."

Concreteness and specificity in fiction are illusions achieved through a piling up of sensory detail, words and phrases that call up in the mind images and sounds and tastes and smells and textures from the empirical world. Since words are **symbols**, not trees, carburetors, or lipstick containers, the way they are used is crucial to creating the illusion of reality. For many years, the realist writer has insisted that his task is to *show*, not tell—not to speak of a character's suffering, but to set the character in motion and let the reader intuit the pain from what is said and done by the character. This kind of fiction favours narratives driven by descriptive detail directed at the senses and frowns upon so-called authorial intrusion.

More recently, however, Wayne Booth has argued in *The Rhetoric of Fiction* that telling is also *showing*. He suggests that we must not forget the fictional nature of fiction, that art is, first of all, not reality but artifice, *a thing made*, with its own rules and its own claim to existence in a world of things. Booth reminds us that authors can do, and have always done, exactly what they want in the game that is fiction, pretending to be all-knowing God, enjoying the role of puppeteer and commentator, stopping the narrative to make pronouncements about life and art, or accepting the limits of an ill-informed and self-deluded narrator who may be as unpleasant as she is unreliable.

However, it remains true that varying degrees of concreteness contribute to both authenticity of voice and the sense of playfulness that make us either suspend our desbelief or simply exult in pleasures of artistic sleight-of-hand. See pp. 776–77, 783.

Conflict is basic to both drama and fiction and refers to the internal tension or external opposition faced by the central character. The conflict may be set off by a memory, event, or situation in the life of the central character. While most stories contain some element of conflict or complication, contemporary short fiction may not resolve its conflict at all, or at least not in the manner of the plot-driven story.

Dénouement refers, in French, to the untying of a knot. In drama and fiction, the term usually refers to that moment of truth in a story when the action has reached its peak, or climax, and the conflict is about to be resolved.

Dialogue is the term commonly used to describe what characters in fiction say to each other. Dialogue in fiction can be straightforward or, like the dialogue in drama (in say, Pinter or Chekhov), quite subtle and ironic, with as much left unsaid or implied. Beginning readers and writers of fiction often feel that a text doesn't look right unless it's peppered with bits of dialogue, but a serious writer will use dialogue sparingly or not at all. Hemingway's "Hills like White Elephants" is notable for being an exception to this rule, though the story, which uses dialogue exclusively, is masterfully spare and transparent.

Convincing dialogue is not easy to create. A writer may benefit from a good ear, but imitating ordinary speech is not enough to produce convincing and efficient dialogue. As Guy Vanderhaeghe suggests, "Dialogue is really a literary convention; the writer does not attempt to reproduce speech but to reproduce the *effect* of the spoken word" (italics added).

Diction refers, simply, to word choice. A fiction writer may choose a limited range of diction, restricting himself or herself to words used in ordinary conversation, or take advantage of a wider choice of words. Often word choice is dictated by the impression a writer wants to give of his or her characters, particularly the narrator. An educated narrator may be characterized by an abundance of ornate words and sophisticated phrases, which simpler, more humble characters would regard as pretentious (they'd probably say *highfalutin*). Obviously, different levels of diction will be quite common in stories where there are several narrators and where dialogue is extensive.

Conrad insisted that fiction was composed of "words, nothing but words" and claimed that the right word was a lever with which an author could move the world. You might want to consult Owen Barfield's *Poetic Diction* or Winnifred Nowottny's *The Language Poets Use*. See also **character**, **imagery** and **style**, and Conrad in notes and Afterwords and pp. 774, 782–83.

Dramatic irony occurs when the reader is aware of a discrepancy between a character's understanding of his or her situation and the real nature of that situation in the story.

Epiphany is a term that was first brought into critical usage by James Joyce. It refers to the sudden moment of illumination in a story, during which the central character sees herself or her situation in a new light. Of course, not all stories move towards an epiphany; in stories or novels with a naive narrator, the reader may come to an understanding of the nature of event and motivation that is beyond the ken of the narrator.

Episodic narration is the term applied to stories whose forward movement has less to do with character development than with the pleasure of inventing new and surprising episodes or incidents. These episodes may be entertaining, may even illustrate a **theme**, but they seldom advance our understanding of character.

Exposition is a term used to describe those passages in a story that present information considered essential to an understanding of the narrative, such as background information about a character or about preceding events. If this background information is presented in a dramatic form, rather than simply narrated, it's usually called a **flashback**. While the term *expository prose* is usually applied to non-fiction writing whose purpose is largely the transmission of information, exposition is often the place where a writer's greatest skill is evident and where, because the task of filling in details may seem more pedestrian, the greatest potential for failure resides. In such passages, the inexperienced author may be easily distracted by his or her own cleverness and abundant vocabulary.

Fantastical writing is as old as literature itself, encompassing the perception that there is more to life and human experience than is revealed by the world of the senses, or what is called empirical reality. Along with **science fiction**, fantastical writing has experienced a rebirth in this century, perhaps in recognition of the fact that reason and objective science have narrowed our range of experience without being able to spare us the horrors of war, hunger, social unrest, and spiritual malaise.

Writers such as Kafka, Cortázar, García Márquez, and Borges have been in the forefront of fantasy writing, stripping away such limiting conventions as credibility, coincidence, and consistency, allowing ghosts and mortals to intermingle and the most unlikely transformations and events to occur. See pp. 31, 484, 788, 831.

Figurative language is the term used to describe language when it moves, for meaning or effect, beyond standard, or literal, usage. Some common figures of speech, (also known as *tropes*, or turns, which give the word new or extended meaning) are simile (describing one thing in terms of another: "He has an appetite like a blast furnace"), metaphor (a direct linking of different items without the use of *like* or *as*: "He is a pig"), personification, pun, hyperbole, paradox, and oxymoron. The figurative element in fiction may include syntax, with cuts and inversions that distort or alter meaning, or extend even to the overall structure of the story, where hyperbole (or exaggeration) may produce the tall tale or where the metaphorical impulse is so pervasive that the story slides into allegory.

First-person narratives are told by a character who refers to himself or herself as I and may be the central character or a mere observer in the story. It's a very intimate and engaging **point of view** from which to tell a story, but has definite limitations, since the first-person narrator can only speculate, unless told, on what is going on in heads other than his own or in situations where he is not present.

Flashback is the fictional technique of breaking the narrative flow of a story in order to inject, or insert, material from the past that is relevant to our understanding of character or situation. As a technique it's very telling, in both senses of the word, since flashback has to be employed subtly to avoid seeming clichéd and since it must be introduced at just the right moment, when something new is needed to advance the narrative and to sustain the interest of the reader.

Form is not an easy word to define, as it is often used in such a way as to make it indistinguishable from shape, **structure**, design, and all other words that have to do with the organization and patterning of elements in a story.

When Sherwood Anderson distinguished form from **plot** (in *A Story Teller's Story*, pp. 351–62), he was speaking of a subtler way of writing that would make the story less dependent on physical action or clever story ideas and more on other seeming intangibles: "For such men as myself you must understand there is always a great difficulty about telling the tale after the scent has been picked up. The tales that continually came to me in the way indicated above could not of course become tales until I had clothed them. Having, from a conversation overhead or in some other way, got the tone of a tale, I was like a woman has has just become impregnated. Something was growing inside me. At night when I lay in my bed I could feel the heels of the tale kicking against the walls of my body." Anderson, like the Romantic poets before him, is advocating organic form, the notion that every idea or situation (like the seed of a flower or tree) has its own inherent form, if the writer will take the time to discover it. He wanted his *words*—the clothing of the tale—to have the same subtlety and conjuring power as the brush-strokes of a master painter.

While not all short story writers think of form in quite this way, most would agree that it is opposed to easy writing, or writing to a formula (as in the Harlequin romance, which often employs stock characters and interchangeable plots and settings). Eudora Welty calls form "the residue, the thrown-off shape, of the very act of writing." See also **structure** and the notes and Afterwords for Welty and Flannery O'Connor. See pp. 95–96, 130, 141, 158, 274, 290, 345, 389, 619, 728, 787, 889.

Frame story refers to a story that contains a story, or a story told within another fictional setting. A famous example is Conrad's *Heart of Darkness*, where Marlow's story of his fateful trip into the African jungle is told in the context of an "innocent" outing with his cronies on the Thames River near London.

Gothic elements in fiction are not unrelated to **myth**, but tend to focus on the working out of extreme, nightmare situations. Gothic fiction may concern itself with primal fears, such as rape and castration, or primal taboos such as incest. Whereas classic gothic tales in the nineteenth century may have required remote settings replete with darkness and decay, neo-gothic stories tend to locate the powers of darkness in the quotidian world of the motel, bus station, dentist's office, or bathroom.

Hero and **heroine** are antiquated terms derived mainly from the criticism of Classical drama and epic poetry, for the **protagonist** or central character of a work of literature. These terms seem particularly inappropriate for describing the protagonists or anti-heroes of short fiction, whose situations are so often humble and domestic. See p. 566.

Idiom usually refers to patterns of speech that are coloured by situation and locale, as in the phrase "local idiom." Flannery O'Connor is a strong advocate of using regional idiom, not to excess, where everyone in the story is wallowing in dialect, but as a means of placing and individualizing characters. She insists that "our history lives in our talk" and that "the sound of our talk is too definite to be discarded with impunity, and if the writer tries to get rid of it, he is liable to destroy the better part of his creative power."

Idiom cannot be entirely distinguished from—and is no substitute for—those other idiosyncrasies of speech and thought that go to make a character unique. See Flannery O'Connor in Afterwords (pp. 833–34).

Imagery. When Conrad used the word *image*, he was referring to things, events, and people called up before the senses, usually the reader's inner eye. In the sentence "The fat man drove to town in a blue station wagon" several images (or mental pictures) are immediately obvious. First, you have the overall image containing everything that is in the sentence. However, you also have an image of a man, an image of an action (driving), and an image of an object (the station wagon). Less obvious, but still significant, you have images imbedded in the adjectives: an image of rotundity in the word *fat* and an image of colour in the word *blue*.

An image is a word or group of words that calls up before the senses enough detail to make a reader feel that something concrete has been represented. Abstract words, such as *love*, *beauty*, and *truth*, are somewhat unreliable in fiction, as they call up nothing specific to the senses. The word *famine*, for example, is abstract and would not normally (except with the advent of television, when gaunt faces and bloated bellies are so common a sight) call up a concrete representation. However, in this line by Samuel Johnson—"Stern famine guards the solitary coast"—you can see how the idea assumes a quality (sternness), a place or habitation (the coast), and an activity (guarding), thereby assuming an impression of concreteness.

Patterns of imagery are repositories of meaning in a story. Sometimes, a group of images (those associated, say, with animals or machines) will cluster around a certain character. Along with character relations, image clusters help give a story shape and resonance. When an image recurs frequently, it may take on sufficient weight to become symbolic. See p. 410.

Interior monologue describes the convention of having a character reveal his thoughts directly to the reader, giving us the impression that we are engaged in psychic eavesdropping. Of course, the thoughts revealed to us are much more coherent on the page than we know them to be when we examine our own mental processes. Still, in the best interior monologues, the author will try to convey some sense of the internal chaos—fragmentation, illogic, discontinuity, et cetera—that are characteristic of the so-called **stream of consciousness**. See note on Virginia Woolf.

Limited omniscience is the most common, and perhaps the most flexible, narrative **point of view** from which to tell a story, because it usually involves complete knowledge about one character and the ability to speak directly about everything else that is happening in a story. In other words, it has some of the intimacy and immediacy of **first-person narration** and much of the flexibility of **omniscient narration**.

Magic realism is a term that has crossed over from painting (think of René Magritte, Max Ernst, André Rousseau, and Alex Colville) to literature, and refers to a tendency to ransack the unconscious for images and to highlight certain aspects of the so-called real world in order to render them, once again, unusual. Like the **fantastical writer**, the magic realist may suspend the laws of nature, juxtapose objects unrelated in "reality," and draw them with such concreteness and specificity that they seem "more real than the real."

Gabriel García Márquez is often described as a magic realist, although he claims that nothing happens in his books that does not have its base in reality. His stories are imbued with a strange light, the half light between sleep and waking, where unexpected things happen and unexplainable states of mind prevail. *La vida es sueño*, the Spanish say—life is a dream. The magic realist's fictional world is certainly a world of dreams, in which a ghost, an out-of-body experience, or a sentient tree will be described with excruciating attention to detail.

See also **fantastical writing**, **metafiction**, and the notes on Borges, Coover, Cortázar, Hawkes, and García Márquez.

Metafiction is a term that describes a type of fiction in which the techiques or conventions of writing have themselves become the subject of fiction. Wallace Stevens once insisted that all poems are about poetry; the same might be said in connection with short stories. And yet, as John Barth has suggested, "All fiction about fiction is, in fact, fiction about life." This paradox underlies literature of all ages. And some of the famous early practitioners of the novel—Cervantes in *Don Quixote*, Henry Fielding in *Tom Jones* and *Joseph Andrews*, and Thomas Sterne in *Tristram Shandy*, to take three familiar examples—enjoyed and exploited their own awareness of artifice and the act of writing. Self-reflexive fiction has become more common in this century, perhaps as an extreme reaction against the dominance of the realistic mode.

As Joe David Bellamy explains in the Introduction to *Superfiction*, "These fictions all dramatize the sweeping perception that art and language help *create* reality rather than serving as inert vehicles through which a self-evidently recognizable external reality is made manifest—a major ideological split between the new fiction and the old. Language, these writers are saying, *helps to constitute our reality*. Imagination (making things up) is a major form of perception, not a mere literary luxury but an absolutely necessary means of getting from one moment to the next."

See John Barth's "Life Story," Donald Barthelme's "Sentence," Italo Calvino's "Meosis," Amy Hempel's "The Harvest," and Ray Smith's "Cape Breton Is the Thought Control Centre of Canada" as quite distinct examples of the metafictional impulse. See pp. 31, 41, 189–90, 773, 790.

Mood is the prevailing or overriding feeling of a story (melancholy, anger, humour, terror, ecstasy, delight). Mood is determined not only by the nature of the **conflict** and the manner of its resolution, but also by the rendering of **setting** or locale, and the **tone** of the narration. Mood is often established in the first few lines of a story, by the way the narrator selects his or her words. Starting a story with a clichéd description of place or weather ("it was a dark and stormy night") may no longer be sophisticated enough to establish mood; however, a few key words or phrases that indicate all is not as it seems to be on the raincoast or in the seemingly ordered affairs of Hallie Crane ("After the Season") or in the artsy world of Ray Thompson in "Food People," will quickly establish expectations of disaster, or a comic reversal of fortune.

A good example of how a mood of hilarity is quickly built up by a series of carefully planted small details can be found in the first paragraph of V. S. Pritchett's "The Saint." See also **atmosphere** and **tone**.

Myth is a means of organizing or making sense of the world, which draws on unconscious **symbols** known as archetypes that reveal to us the nature of reality. In its earliest forms, myth employed the figures of gods and heroes, working out their psychodramas on a grand scale. While these dramas have been largely domesticated in the realistic novel or story, substituting so-called ordinary humans in the most humble of circumstances, fiction continues, at one level, to be mythic, or mythopeic, since it endeavours to reveal through the use of symbols and symbolic action what is unknown, or only partially known, to the conscious mind.

Naturalism was a nineteenth-century movement that had its roots in the philosophical writings of Thomas Malthus, Charles Darwin, and Thomas Huxley. The naturalistic writer tried to present an objective, dispassionate but largely "realistic" portrait of ordinary life with a good deal of emphasis placed on detailing the relationship between character, destiny, and natural environment. Naturalist writers, such as Emile Zola, Stephen Crane, and Theodore Dreiser, were quite varied in their approaches, but most rendered a world where human behaviour was determined by nature and heredity.

Since naturalism was allied to science, it's not surprising that its methods of rendering "reality" might reasonably be expected to resemble those of the laboratory, particularly dissection, cataloguing, documentation, and analysis. Heavy emphasis was placed on the physiological and sociological, as opposed to the spiritual or imaginative, dimensions of human behaviour. Characters in thrall to their glands or to social forces beyond their control can be found in twentieth-century works by Thomas Hardy, James Joyce, William Faulkner, Frederick Phillip Grove, Eugene O'Neill, and Arthur Miller.

Omniscient narration, also known as third-person narration, assumes the god-like stance of knowing everything and having access to the minds and histories of all characters in a story.

Parable is the term used to describe a simple story that points up a moral or a religious lesson, such as those contained in the biblical accounts of the Prodigal Son and the Good Samaritan. Two of the earliest literary critics, Horace and Aristotle, concurred in the view that the chief aims of literature were to teach and delight; much subsequent critical debate has turned around the relative weight to be given each of these functions. A story that is blatantly "preachy" will quickly alienate a sophisticated reader; however, stories that are all dance, that seem to lack a moral centre, may prove to be equally limited and euphemeral.

Persona refers to the mask a poet or fiction writer puts on to tell a story. Akutagawa, in his story "In a Grove," employs a series of masks or personae, each of which adds to, and qualifies, our sense of what has transpired.

Plot is the series of actions, or events, that make up a story. These events are likely to be causally linked: A causes B; B leads to C; C produces D, and so on.

Plot is most often linked to **character**, some element inside or in the external circumstances of the character that drives him or her to act in a certain way. E. M. Forster suggests that curiosity and logic are central to plot. In *Aspects of the Novel*, he describes *story* as the "chopped-off length of the tapeworm of time" and distinguishes it from plot. Story, he says, is "the narrative of events in their time-sequence," whereas plot is "the narrative of events, with emphasis falling on causality. 'The king died and then the queen died' is a story. 'The king died and then the queen died of grief' is a plot."

Most writers and critics of short fiction are aware of the advantages and pitfalls of plot-driven writing. John Hawkes called plot one of the enemies of fiction. Sherwood Anderson rejected it in favour of **form**: "There was a notion that ran through all story-telling in America, that stories must be built about a plot and that absurd Anglo-Saxon notion that they must point a moral, uplift the people, make better citizens, etc. The magazines were filled with these plot stories and most of the plays on our stage were plot plays. 'The Poison Plot,' I called it in conversation with my friends as the plot notion did seem to me to poison all story-telling. What was wanted I thought was form, not plot, an altogether more elusive and difficult thing to come at."

See notes and Afterwords for Woolf (I can make up situations, but I cannot make up plots), Blaise (plot is the revelation of inevitability), Faulkner (the story makes its own plot), Flannery O'Connor, and others. See pp. 20, 95, 103, 130, 243, 464, 600, 641, 648, 702, 752, 843, 858, 888.

Point of view is the vantage point, or angle of vision, from which events in a story are told. The most common way of narrating a story is from the **omniscient**, or third-person, point of view, where the narrator knows everything and can dip in and out of the lives and minds of all the characters. Sometimes, the author will favour, or restrict himself or herself to complete knowledge of a single character, exercising what is called limited omniscience. While the omniscient, or third-person, narrator has greater freedom of movement in a story by virtue knowing everything, many authors prefer the immediacy of **first-person narration**, telling the story from the point of view of a single character, who may be the **protagonist** or a mere observer of events. First-person narration is often more intense, because of the sense of total possession of one character's mind and the potential for piling on huge amounts of psychological detail; but this point of view imposes limits on what can be known by the narrator and, consequently, told to the reader about other characters. First-person narrative is, therefore, an ideal vehicle for irony, since the blind spots or limited vision of the narrator can be used for comic or ironic purposes. Such first-person narrators are often referred to as naive, or unreliable, narrators.

Although not as often as in the novel, the short story may also employ more than one narrator or more than a single point of view. Akutagawa's "In a Grove," cast in the manner of a detective story, is a polyphonic narrative, here containing numerous accounts of a murder, including that of the victim. See pp. 69, 648.

Protagonist refers to the **hero** or central character, whose problem or **conflict** constitutes the **action** or **plot** of the story.

Realism is a literary tendency that emerged in the eighteenth century with the journalistic fictions of Daniel Defoe, who claimed to be giving his reader the true-to-life stories of a one-time prostitute named Moll Flanders and a shipwrecked Robinson Crusoe. The history of fiction may be seen as a struggle between the realistic-reportorial impulse and the romantic-idealistic impulse, with the former gaining ascendance far into the twentieth century as fiction became the voice or sounding-board for a growing middle class. Technically, realism aims for accuracy of representation, rejecting coincidence and focussing instead on the probable and the believable. The realist writer, who purports to offer a slice of life, or to hold a mirror up to nature, usually focusses his attention on the unexceptional character engaged in his or her unadventurous, even humdrum, existence, living amidst failure, unfulfilled dreams, and rare moments of transcendence in food, sex, or television.

Joseph Conrad, Henry James, and Virginia Woolf were part of the reaction against literary realism, which they felt was too exterior and ignored the "hidden stream" of life. In its place, they offered what has come to be known as psychological realism, an attempt to offer a verbal approximation of the workings of the human mind, with its non-linear unfolding of events, its juxtaposition and counterpoint of images, and its more intensely poetic use of language. Joyce's *Dubliners* is often considered a triumph of the realistic mode, precisely because it manages to fuse external reality and the internal world of dreams. See pp. 41, 46, 53, 95, 130, 148, 171, 224, 299–300, 345–46, 432, 457, 465, 484, 551, 641, 824–27.

Rhythm seems, at first, to be a term more relevant to poetry or music. However, prose also has rhythms that, though closer to the undulations of ordinary speech or conversation than to the measurable progressions of metrical verse, are nonetheless there to be enjoyed by the trained ear. The gap between poetry and prose seems less significant in the short story, where brevity and economy of expression are so important and where lyrical intensity is more often the rule than the exception.

Rhythm, or pacing, in fiction may refer not only to the shape and flow of individual sentences, but also to the patterning of ideas and events in the story, the way in which information is introduced, characters are developed, and events unfolded. You might want to consult E. K. Brown's *The Rhythm of the Novel*. See also **style** and **structure** as well as comments by Nadine Gordimer and Frank O'Connor in the Afterwords..

Science fiction encompasses that area of **fantastical writing** committed to exploring and exploiting the fiction possibilities of science and tecnhology. An early practitioner such as

Jonathan Swift found much to parody in scientific institutions of his time and in the uses of technology to manipulate and oppress rather than liberate mankind. In addition to his biting satires of the abuse of science (attempts to breed hairless sheep, for example), Swift imagined in *Gulliver's Travels* a flying island that is not too far removed from the blimps, helicopters, and space stations so familiar to the *Star Wars* art and actuality of our time.

Jules Verne, H. G. Wells, and a host of more recent writers such as Bob Shaw and Ursula K. Le Guin have found scientific and technological speculation a fertile ground for critiquing our world and imagining different social and political models. Not surprisingly, the environmental crisis facing us has quickly challenged both the nuclear threat and Cold War power struggles for the attention of the writer of science fiction. See **metafiction** and **fantastical writing**.

Setting usually refers to the element of place in narrative fiction, the physical background or geographical location of the **action** in a story. If you think of an author setting the stage for his character, you will have a better idea of how the illusion of place is created, not by huge back-drops with intricately painted details, but rather by focussing attention on a few concrete particulars that are representative of the larger picture.

Weather, landscapes, and urban interiors (such as homes, apartments, factories, and stores) are all typical materials for the creation of setting. However, the props, or furnishings, of these rooms are even more useful than generic references to sea or mountain or clouds, and reveal a good deal about taste, social class, beliefs, and shared cultural values. See pp. 61, 243, 331, 457, 464, 513, 550, 702, 833.

Stream of consciousness is a narrative technique that tries to create a verbal equivalent for human thought processes, emphasizing the fragmented, discontinuous (non-linear and non-logical) nature of consciousness. In the hands of Joyce, Virginia Woolf, and a host of other authors, stream of consciousness shifted the focus of fiction from the world of action and manners to the inner life and became an important technique in the repertory of psychological realism. See also **realism** and the note on Virginia Woolf.

Structure in a short story refers to the building blocks, the way in which the elements are arranged, or put together to make a more meaningful whole. French critics employ a useful term, *progression d'effets*, which translates literally as the progression of effects. Instead of being presented chronologically in the order of its happening, plot may be fragmented and discontinuous in the interests of heightening theme or more obviously reflecting the way the mind perceives and processes experience, moving backwards and forwards in time.

The term *structure* may be applied equally to the larger building blocks of fiction (such as **characters**, linear or non-linear **plot**, descriptive passages, pacing, **point of view**) and to the smaller linguistic elements (**diction**, **imagery**, metaphor, and **symbol**). However, sooner or later you end up saying that structure consists of everything in a story, which renders the term less than useful.

Many critics use the terms *structure* and *form* interchangeably, but it may be more useful to reserve the word *form* for the less mechanical elements shaping a work of fiction. Structure is a term borrowed from other arts, such as sculpture and architecture, which might lead you to think of it as the skeleton, or framework, of a story, form being the story's final fleshed-out shape or body. An interesting metaphor, but one that tends to link structure too exclusively with action or plot. See also **form**. See pp. 41, 189, 291, 326, 345, 728, 745, 795, 836.

Style is one of the most interesting and difficult terms used in literary discussions. M. H. Abrams describes style as a "characteristic manner of expression . . . *how* a speaker or writer says whatever he says." He draws attention to **diction**, figurative language, **rhythm**, sentence structure, and rhetorical devices. I like this definition, as it suggests that the foundations of prose—indeed, all writing—are grounded in the way in which sentences are put together, in the very choice and deployment of words.

According to Annie Dillard in *Living by Fiction*, when you start to look closely at sentences, you begin to notice that some writers, such as Hemingway, are especially fond of a plain, journalistic style, with short, punchy declarative sentences or possibly loose, disjointed sentences that run on to inordinate lengths. Another writer, such as Faulkner, may employ a high style, using ornate or poetic prose with lots of figurative language, possibly formal **syntax**, and elevated **diction**. See pp. 95, 103, 243, 257, 277, 321, 364, 500, 600, 619–20, 753, 772, 784–86, 888, 895.

Consider Mavis Gallant's definition: style "is not a last-minute addition to prose, a charming and universal slip-cover, a coat of paint used to mask the failings of a structure. Style is inseparable from structure, part of the conformation of whatever the author has to say. . . . Style in writing, as in painting, is the author's thumbprint, his mark. I do not mean that it establishes him as finer or greater than other writers, though that can happen too. I am thinking now of prose style as a writer's armorial bearings, his name and address. . . . Style cannot be copied, except by the untalented. It is, finally, the distillation of a lifetime of reading and listening, of selection and rejection. But if the voice is not true, it is nothing."

See Gallant in notes and Afterwords. Have a look, too, at the liberties taken with sentence structure in the first page of Julio Cortázar's "Bestiary."

Symbol is created in a story when an image (a person, event, or object) begins to assume, by repetition or increased function, a more than local, or literal, significance, and comes to stand for more than itself. For example, a figure in a black coat might acquire symbolic value in a story by virtue of the nature and frequency of his or her appearances. It may not be accurate to say (except in the case of allegory) that the black coat equals death, but only that the image has acquired symbolic value to the point that its occurrence in the story brings to mind thoughts of death or mortal danger.

Authors quite often resent symbolic interpretations of their work, because they feel that such interpretations are usually oversimplified, reducing what may be a complex and multi-faceted work to a mechanical formula. The best stories, so it seems, are those in which the symbolism emerges naturally from the materials, from character and situation, rather than appearing stuck on like cake decorations.

It should be remembered, however, that language itself is a symbol system, using words or groups of words to represent objects, persons, feelings, and ideas. Thus, all literature is, by nature, symbolic. See pp. 702, 831.

Theme is often used to refer to the overriding subject or idea of a story. However, most fiction writers object to the term because it suggests that a complicated verbal structure, full of nuance and suggestion, can be reduced to a single sentence or a mere word. If a writer wanted to make a simple statement about love or death or computer maintenance, he or she would not write a story. The writer wants a reader to become immersed in the *how*—the technique, the words, the shaping principles—of the story, from which will emerge respect, understanding, and a deeper sense of what the author intends. See pp. 550, 830.

Tone is a musical term, often used to describe the author's attitude towards the characters and events in a story, sometimes eliciting such qualifiers as *whimsical, ironic, sarcastic,* or *satirical.* If you strip the music away from a song, you are left only with words and how they are spoken, the tone of voice, the little asides and descriptive details that give away important information. We can usually detect something, by listening closely to the narrator's voice, in his or her tone, that might betray the real motive for telling the story.

Tone may be revealed in a variety of ways, in the choice of **diction** (using, say, the word *contemplative* rather than the word *thoughtful* to describe a character), **imagery** (referring to a character in animal terms, as feline or simian), and in character relations (the particular groupings of characters, such as in a story). See also **mood** and **atmosphere**.

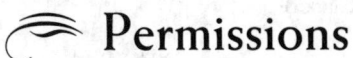